W9-BBZ-418

Hippocrene
Practical Dictionaries

English–Deutsch
German–Englisch

Stephen Jones BA

HIPPOCRENE BOOKS, New York

First Hippocrene Edition, 1983

© Laurence Urdang Associates, 1982

Glossary of Menu Terms and special American
usage entries © Hippocrene Books, 1983

ISBN 0-88254-902-2 (h.c.)
ISBN 0-88254-813-1 (pbk)

Printed in the United States of America

Abbreviations/Abkürzungen

acc accusative, Akkusativ
adj adjective, Adjektiv
adv adverb, Adverb
anat anatomy, Anatomie
arch architecture, Architektur
art article, Artikel
astrol astrology, Astrologie
astron astronomy, Astronomie
biol biology, Biologie
bot botany, Botanik
chem chemistry, Chemie
coll colloquial,
   umgangssprachlich
comm commerce, Kommerz
dat dative, Dativ
derog derogatory, geringschätzig
elec electricity, Elektrizität
f feminine, Femininum
fig figurative, figürlich
gen genitive, Genetiv
geog geography, Erdkunde
gramm grammar, Grammatik
impol impolite, unhöflich
interj interjection, Ausruf
Jur Jura, Rechtswesen, law
Komm Kommerz, commerce
m masculine, Maskulinum
math mathematics, Mathematik
mech mechanics, machine,
   Mechanik
med medicine, Medizin

mil military, militärisch
mot motoring, Kraftfahrzeuge
n noun, Hauptwort, Substantiv
naut nautical, Schiffahrt
neut neuter, Neutrum
phone telephone, Telefon
phot photography, Photographie
pl plural, Plural
pol politics, Politik
poss possessive, possessiv
prep preposition, Präposition
pron pronoun, Pronomen,
   Fürwort
psychol psychology, Psychologie
rail railways, Eisenbahn
rel religion, Religion
Schiff Schiffahrt, nautical
sing singular, Singular, Einzahl
tech technical, Technik
Telef Telefon, telephone
TV television, Fernsehen
umg. umgangssprachlich,
   colloquial
univ university, Universität
unz. unzählbar, mass noun
US American, Amerikanisch
v verb, Verbum, Zeitwort
V vide (see, siehe)
Wissensch Naturwissenschaft,
   science
zool zoology, Zoologie

German pronunciation

a bald [balt]
a: sagen ['za:gən]
e Telefon [tele'fo:n]
e: nehmen ['ne:mən]
ε Geld [gεlt]
ε: Bär [bε:r]
i Idee [i'de:]
i: bieten ['bi:tən]
ɔ Holz [hɔlts]
o Rosette [ro'zεtə]
o: Mohn [mo:n]
u bunt [bunt]
u: Schnur [ʃnu:r]
y fünf [fynf]
y: kühl [ky:l]
ə Butter ['butər]
œ böse ['bœzə]
œ: Möbel ['mœbəl]
ai bei [bai]
au Haus [haus]
ɔy Freund [frɔynt]
ã Chance ['ʃã:sə]
ɛ̃ Terrain [tɛ'rɛ̃:]
ɔ̃ Champignon ['ʃampinjɔ̃]

b Bad [ba:t]
d Dank [daŋk]
f Frau [frau]
g gut [gu:t]
h halb [halp]
j ja [ja:]
k Kind [kint]
l Lied [li:t]
m Mensch [mɛnʃ]
n neu [nɔy]
p Person [pεr'zo:n]
r Rad [ra:t]
s falls [fals]
t Gerät [gə'rε:t]
v Wein [vain]
z Reise ['raizə]
ç ich [iç]
x Buch [bu:x]
ʃ Schuh [ʃu:]
ʒ Garage [ga'ra:ʒə]
ŋ lang [laŋ]

The sign ' precedes a syllable having primary stress.

Aussprache auf Englisch

a hat [hat]
e bell [bel]
i big [big]
o dot [dot]
ʌ bun [bʌn]
u book [buk]
ə alone [əˈloun]
a: card [ka:d]
ə: word [wə:d]
i: team [ti:m]
o: torn [to:n]
u: spoon [spu:n]
ai die [dai]
ei ray [rei]
oi toy [toi]
au how [hau]
ou road [roud]
eə lair [leə]
iə fear [fiə]
uə poor [puə]

b back [bak]
d dull [dʌl]
f find [faind]
g gaze [geiz]
h hop [hop]
j yell [jel]
k cat [kat]
l life [laif]
m mouse [maus]
n night [nait]
p pick [pik]
r rose [rouz]
s sit [sit]
t toe [tou]
v vest [vest]
w week [wi:k]
z zoo [zu:]
ɵ think [ɵiŋk]
ð those [ðouz]
ʃ shoe [ʃu:]
ʒ treasure [ˈtreʒə]
tʃ chalk [tʃo:k]
dʒ jump [dʒʌmp]
ŋ sing [siŋ]

Das Zeichen ' steht vor einer Silbe mit Hauptbetonung.
Das Zeichen , steht vor einer Silbe mit Nebenbetonung.

Guide to the dictionary

English irregular plural forms are shown at the headword and in the text. The following categories of plurals forms are considered regular:

cat	cats
glass	glasses
fly	flies
half	halves
wife	wives

German plurals are shown for most words (for example, **Gemälde**) but not for many compounds (for example, **Wandgemälde**). The label *pl -* indicates that the plural does not vary.

Where no gender is shown for a German noun, it may be masculine or feminine, for example **Abgeordnete(r)**. Adjectival nouns are shown by **-(r)** or **-(s)**, the final letter being used according to the article, for example: **der Abgeordnete, ein Abgeordneter, die Abgeordnete, eine Abgeordnete, Abgeordnete** (*pl*).

Under a German headword, a sub-entry may be shown preceded by a dash. The full form may be obtained by adding the sub-entry to the nearest preceding full word, less that part after the vertical strokes, if any. Thus, **außerhalb** is shown as follows:

außer‖dem *adv* besides. **-halb** *adv*, *prep* outside.

Irregular verbs listed in the verb tables are marked with an asterisk in the body of the dictionary.

Many English adverbs are not shown in the dictionary if they are regularly formed, that is, by the addition of -(*al*)*ly* to the adjective.

Leitfaden für das Wörterbuch

Englische unregelmäßige Plurale sind bei dem Stichwort und im Text gezeigt. Die folgenden Kategorien von Pluralformen sind als regelmäßig anzusehen:

cat	cats
glass	glasses
fly	flies
half	halves
wife	wives

Deutsche Plurale sind für die meisten Wörter angeführt (z.B. **Gemälde**), aber nicht für viele zusammengesetzte Wörter (z.B. **Wandgemälde**). Das Zeichen *pl* - deutet an, daß der Plural mit dem Singular identisch ist.

Wo kein Geschlecht für ein deutsches Hauptwort angegeben ist, kann es sowohl männlich als auch weiblich sein, z.B. **Abgeordnete(r)**. Hauptworte, die aus Adjektiven gebildet sind, sind folgendermaßen gekennzeichnet -(**r**) oder -(**s**), wobei der letzte Buchstabe von dem Artikel abhängt, z.B. **der Abgeordnete, ein Abgeordneter, die Abgeordnete, eine Abgeordnete, Abgeordnete** (*pl*).

Hinter einem deutschen Stichwort, findet man öfter eine weitere Eintragung hinter einem Strich. Das komplette Wort erhält man durch Hinzufügen dieses Wortes an das vorherige Wort ohne den Teil hinter die Vertikalen, wenn nötig. So ist z.B. **außerhalb** wie folgt gezeigt:

außer‖dem *adv* besides. **-halb** *adv*, *prep* outside.

Unregelmäßige Verben, die in der separaten Liste aufgeführt sind, sind mit einem Sternchen (*) bei den Stichwörtern angezeigt.

Viele englische Adverbien sind in dem Wörterbuch nicht aufgeführt, wenn sie aus den Adjektiven regelmäßig durch die Nachsilbe -(*al*)*ly* gebildet sind.

German irregular verbs

Infinitive	Preterite	Past Participle
backen	backte (buk)	gebacken
bedingen	bedang (bedingte)	bedungen
befehlen	befahl	befohlen
beginnen	begann	begonnen
beißen	biß	gebissen
bergen	barg	geborgen
bersten	barst	geborsten
bewegen	bewog	bewogen
biegen	bog	gebogen
bieten	bot	geboten
binden	band	gebunden
bitten	bat	gebeten
blasen	blies	geblasen
bleiben	blieb	geblieben
bleichen	blich	geblichen
braten	briet	gebraten
brauchen	brauchte	gebraucht (brauchen)
brechen	brach	gebrochen
brennen	brannte	gebrannt
bringen	brachte	gebracht
denken	dachte	gedacht
dreschen	drosch	gedroschen
dringen	drang	gedrungen
dürfen	durfte	gedurft
empfehlen	empfahl	empfohlen
erkiesen	erkor	erkoren
erlöschen	erlosch	erloschen
erschrecken	erschrak	erschrocken
essen	aß	gegessen
fahren	fuhr	gefahren
fallen	fiel	gefallen
fangen	fing	gefangen
fechten	focht	gefochten
finden	fand	gefunden
flechten	flocht	geflochten
fliegen	flog	geflogen

Infinitive	Preterite	Past Participle
fliehen	floh	geflohen
fließen	floß	geflossen
fressen	fraß	gefressen
frieren	fror	gefroren
gären	gor	gegoren
gebären	gebar	geboren
geben	gab	gegeben
gedeihen	gedieh	gediehen
gehen	ging	gegangen
gelingen	gelang	gelungen
gelten	galt	gegolten
genesen	genas	genesen
genießen	genoß	genossen
geschehen	geschah	geschehen
gewinnen	gewann	gewonnen
gießen	goß	gegossen
gleichen	glich	geglichen
gleiten	glitt	geglitten
glimmen	glomm	geglommen
graben	grub	gegraben
greifen	griff	gegriffen
haben	hatte	gehabt
halten	hielt	gehalten
hängen	hing	gehangen
hauen	haute (hieb)	gehauen
heben	hob	gehoben
heißen	hieß	geheißen
helfen	half	geholfen
kennen	kannte	gekannt
klimmen	klomm	geklommen
klingen	klang	geklungen
kneifen	kniff	gekniffen
kommen	kam	gekommen
können	konnte	gekonnt
kriechen	kroch	gekrochen
laden	lud	geladen
lassen	ließ	gelassen (lassen)
laufen	lief	gelaufen

Infinitive	Preterite	Past Participle
leiden	litt	gelitten
leihen	lieh	geliehen
lesen	las	gelesen
liegen	lag	gelegen
lügen	log	gelogen
mahlen	mahlte	gemahlen
meiden	mied	gemieden
melken	melkte (molk)	gemolken (gemelkt)
messen	maß	gemessen
mißlingen	mißlang	mißlungen
mögen	mochte	gemocht
müssen	mußte	gemußt
nehmen	nahm	genommen
nennen	nannte	genannt
pfeifen	pfiff	gepfiffen
preisen	pries	gepriesen
quellen	quoll	gequollen
raten	riet	geraten
reiben	rieb	gerieben
reißen	riß	gerissen
reiten	ritt	geritten
rennen	rannte	gerannt
riechen	roch	gerochen
ringen	rang	gerungen
rinnen	rann	geronnen
rufen	rief	gerufen
salzen	salzte	gesalzen (gesalzt)
saufen	soff	gesoffen
saugen	sog	gesogen
schaffen	schuf	geschaffen
schallen	schallte (scholl)	geschallt
scheiden	schied	geschieden
scheinen	schien	geschienen
sheißen	schiß	geschissen
schelten	schalt	gescholten
scheren	schor	geschoren
schieben	schob	geschoben
scheißen	schoß	geschossen
schinden	schund	geschunden

Infinitive	Preterite	Past Participle
schlafen	schlief	geschlafen
schlagen	schlug	geschlagen
schleichen	schlich	geschlichen
schleifen	schliff	geschliffen
schleißen	schliß	geschlissen
schließen	schloß	geschlossen
schlingen	schlang	geschlungen
schmeißen	schmiß	geschmissen
schmelzen	schmolz	geschmolzen
schnauben	schnob	geschnoben
schneiden	schnitt	geschnitten
schreiben	schrieb	geschrieben
schreien	schrie	geschrie(e)n
schreiten	schritt	geschritten
schweigen	schwieg	geschwiegen
schwellen	schwoll	geschwollen
schwimmen	schwamm	geschwommen
schwinden	schwand	geschwunden
schwingen	schwang	geschwungen
schwören	schwor	geschworen
sehen	sah	gesehen
sein	war	gewesen
senden	sandte	gesandt
sieden	sott	gesotten
singen	sang	gesungen
sinken	sank	gesunken
sinnen	sann	gesonnen
sitzen	saß	gesessen
sollen	sollte	gesollt (sollen)
spalten	spaltete	gespalten (gespaltet)
speien	spie	gespie(e)n
spinnen	spann	gesponnen
sprechen	sprach	gesprochen
sprießen	sproß	gesprossen
springen	sprang	gesprungen
stechen	stach	gestochen
stecken	steckte (stak)	gesteckt
stehen	stand	gestanden
stehlen	stahl	gestohlen

Infinitive	Preterite	Past Participle
steigen	stieg	gestiegen
sterben	starb	gestorben
stieben	stob	gestoben
stinken	stank	gestunken
stoßen	stieß	gestoßen
streichen	strich	gestrichen
streiten	stritt	gestritten
tragen	trug	getragen
treffen	traf	getroffen
treiben	trieb	getrieben
treten	trat	getreten
triefen	triefte (troff)	getrieft
trinken	trank	getrunken
trügen	trog	getrogen
tun	tat	getan
verderben	verdarb	verdorben
verdrießen	verdroß	verdrossen
vergessen	vergaß	vergessen
verlieren	verlor	verloren
verschleißen	verschliß	verschlissen
verzeihen	verzieh	verziehen
wachsen	wuchs	gewachsen
wägen	wog (wägte)	gewogen (gewägt)
waschen	wusch	gewaschen
weben	wob	gewoben
weichen	wich	gewichen
weisen	wies	gewiesen
wenden	wandte	gewandt
werben	warb	geworben
werden	wurde	geworden (worden)
werfen	warf	geworfen
wiegen	wog	gewogen
winden	wand	gewunden
wissen	wußte	gewußt
wollen	wollte	gewollt (wollen)
wringen	wrang	gewrungen
zeihen	zieh	geziehen
ziehen	zog	gezogen
zwingen	zwang	gezwungen

Unregelmäßige Verben

Infinitive	Präteritum	Partizip Perfekt
abide	abode	abode
arise	arose	arisen
awake	awoke	awoke
be	was	been
bear	bore	borne *or* born
beat	beat	beaten
become	became	become
begin	began	begun
bend	bent	bent
bet	bet	bet
beware		
bid	bid	bidden *or* bid
bind	bound	bound
bite	bit	bitten
bleed	bled	bled
blow	blew	blown
break	broke	broken
breed	bred	bred
bring	brought	brought
build	built	built
burn	burnt *or* burned	burnt *or* burned
burst	burst	burst
buy	bought	bought
can	could	
cast	cast	cast
catch	caught	caught
choose	chose	chosen
cling	clung	clung
come	came	come
cost	cost	cost
creep	crept	crept
cut	cut	cut
deal	dealt	dealt
dig	dug	dug
do	did	done
draw	drew	drawn
dream	dreamed *or* dreamt	dreamed *or* dreamt

Infinitive	Präteritum	Partizip Perfekt
drink	drank	drunk
drive	drove	driven
dwell	dwelt	dwelt
eat	ate	eaten
fall	fell	fallen
feed	fed	fed
feel	felt	felt
fight	fought	fought
find	found	found
flee	fled	fled
fling	flung	flung
fly	flew	flown
forbid	forbade	forbidden
forget	forgot	forgotten
forgive	forgave	forgiven
forsake	forsook	forsaken
freeze	froze	frozen
get	got	got
give	gave	given
go	went	gone
grind	ground	ground
grow	grew	grown
hang	hung *or* hanged	hung *or* hanged
have	had	had
hear	heard	heard
hide	hid	hidden
hit	hit	hit
hold	held	held
hurt	hurt	hurt
keep	kept	kept
kneel	knelt	knelt
knit	knitted *or* knit	knitted *or* knit
know	knew	known
lay	laid	laid
lead	led	led
lean	leant *or* leaned	leant *or* leaned
leap	leapt *or* leaped	leapt *or* leaped
learn	learnt *or* learned	learnt *or* learned
leave	left	left

Infinitive	Präteritum	Partizip Perfekt
lend	lent	lent
let	let	let
lie	lay	lain
light	lit *or* lighted	lit *or* lighted
lose	lost	lost
make	made	made
may	might	
mean	meant	meant
meet	met	met
mow	mowed	mown
must		
ought		
pay	paid	paid
put	put	put
quit	quitted *or* quit	quitted *or* quit
read	read	read
rid	rid	rid
ride	rode	ridden
ring	rang	rung
rise	rose	risen
run	ran	run
saw	sawed	sawn *or* sawed
say	said	said
see	saw	seen
seek	sought	sought
sell	sold	sold
send	sent	sent
set	set	set
sew	sewed	sewn *or* sewed
shake	shook	shaken
shear	sheared	sheared *or* shorn
shed	shed	shed
shine	shone	shone
shoe	shod	shod
shoot	shot	shot
show	showed	shown
shrink	shrank	shrunk
shut	shut	shut
sing	sang	sung

Infinitive	Präteritum	Partizip Perfekt
sink	sank	sunk
sit	sat	sat
sleep	slept	slept
slide	slid	slid
sling	slung	slung
slink	slunk	slunk
slit	slit	slit
smell	smelt *or* smelled	smelt *or* smelled
sow	sowed	sown *or* sowed
speak	spoke	spoken
speed	sped *or* speeded	sped *or* speeded
spell	spelt *or* spelled	spelt *or* spelled
spend	spent	spent
spill	spilt *or* spilled	spilt *or* spilled
spin	spun	spun
spit	spat	spat
split	split	split
spread	spread	spread
spring	sprang	sprung
stand	stood	stood
steal	stole	stolen
stick	stuck	stuck
sting	stung	stung
stink	stank *or* stunk	stunk
stride	strode	stridden
strike	struck	struck
string	strung	strung
strive	strove	striven
swear	swore	sworn
sweep	swept	swept
swell	swelled	swollen *or* swelled
swim	swam	swum
swing	swung	swung
take	took	taken
teach	taught	taught
tear	tore	torn
tell	told	told
think	thought	thought

Infinitive	Preterite	Past Participle
throw	threw	thrown
thrust	thrust	thrust
tread	trod	trodden
wake	woke	woken
wear	wore	worn
weave	wove	woven
weep	wept	wept
win	won	won
wind	wound	wound
wring	wrung	wrung
write	wrote	written

Glossary of menu terms

There is lots to eat in German-speaking countries: five meals a day are about standard, and there's plenty of scope for snacks — especially nice when traveling with children. **Frühstück** (breakfast) is usually light, perhaps coffee or chocolate and bread; **Zweites Frühstück** (second breakfast) is more serious and will probably feature food that seems like a U.S.-style light lunch. But in the middle of the day comes **Mittagessen** (lunch) which is usually the main meal of the day. In late afternoon, there is **Kaffee mit Kuchen** (coffee and cake and a lot more), and finally **Abendbrot** (supper).

German cuisine is based on the foods the countries produce. Expect to eat simple, hearty food quite fresh from the farm. In Austria, the influence of Hungarian cooking provides some diversion, and in German Switzerland, the French and Italian neighbors have left a pleasing mark. Game is often featured; it is certainly worth trying.

There are many designations in German for establishments which serve food. In large towns, most common is **Restaurant** (the German word is **Gaststätte**); in the country, you will find **Gasthaus** or **Gasthof**. A **Bierstube** or **Weinstube** will serve some food as well as beer or wine, rather like an English pub. Restaurants usually offer full meals, but the menu may not be broken into courses or types of food (appetizers, first courses, meat dishes, fish, etc.). Most restaurants offer one or more **Gedeck** (fixed-priced meal), usually including soup, entrée with one or more vegetable, and a light dessert, no substitutions or additions permitted. These meals are often excellent values. Be sure to tell the waiter that you are having the set meal before you order.

Hotel dining rooms generally offer good **Kaffee mit Kuchen,** but if you are away from your hotel, try a **Café** or **Konditorei.** These places are also good for a light breakfast or a snack at almost any time.

By law, German eating places must list all charges, including service, on the menu in the price of each item. It is still customary, however, to leave a small tip, perhaps 5%, on the table.

Vorspeisen (Hors d'Oeuvre)

Beefsteak Tartar raw ground beef served with raw egg and onion
Bismarckhering pickled herring with onion and spices
Eiersalat egg salad
Froschschenkel frogs' legs
Gänseleber goose liver
Käsebrot open-faced cheese sandwich
Kaviar caviar
Lachsbrot open-faced salmon sandwich
Lachsalm slices of smoked salmon
Ochsenzungesalat salad of sliced tongue
Rollmops bits of smoked herring with mustard, onion, and pickle
Westfälischer Schinken raw cured ham from Westphalia

Würste (Sausages)

Blutwurst blood sausage
Bratwurst grilled pork sausage (spiced)
Knackwurst (or **Knockwurst**) sausage of pork or beef, rather like our hot dog
Leberwurst liver sausage
Wienerwurst Vienna sausage, on the order of small hot dogs
Weisswurst white veal sausage flavored with herbs (a specialty of Munich)

Eierspeisen (Egg Dishes)

Omelette omelette, served plain (**natur**) or with various stuffings (**gefüllt**), e.g.:
mit Champignons with mushrooms;
mit Fines Herbes with herbs, as parsley, tarragon, chives; **mit Geflügelleber**

with chicken livers; **mit Schinken** with ham; **Spanisches** with tomato and onion sauce
Pfannkuchen a sort of egg pancake, also served plain (**natur**) or stuffed (**gefüllt**): **mit Käse** with cheese; **mit Schinken** with ham; **mit Speck** with bacon
Pochierte Eier poached eggs
Rührei scrambled eggs
Spiegeleier (or **Setzeier**) fried eggs
Weichgekochte Eier soft-cooked eggs
Wachsweiche Eier medium-cooked eggs

Fischgerichte (Seafood)

Aal eel
Austern oysters
Dorsch codfish
Forellen trout
Hecht pike
Heilbutt halibut
Hummer lobster
Jacobsmuscheln scallops, coquilles
Krabben shrimp; for the larger shrimp, Germans usually use the Italian word **scampi**
Schellfisch haddock
Seezunge sole; prepared in many different ways in Germany: fried, baked, in various sauces, etc.

Suppen (Soups)

Bauernsuppe "peasant soup": mixed vegetable soup
Biersuppe soup of beer with spices
Bohnensuppe bean soup
Brühe broth: **Fleischbrühe**, meat broth; **Geflügelbrühe**, chicken broth; **Fischbrühe**, fish broth
Champignonrahmsuppe cream of mushroom soup
Kartoffelsuppe potato soup
Leberknödelsuppe dumplings of chopped liver, onion, and spices, in broth
Linsensuppe lentil soup
Nudelsuppe mit Huhn chicken noodle soup
Tomatensuppe tomato soup
Zwiebelsuppe onion soup

Hauptgerichte (Main meat Dishes

Bauernschmaus "the peasant's delight": platter of bacon, sausages, sauerkraut, mashed potatoes, and dumplings
Burgunderschinken ham cooked in wine sauce with vegetables
Cordon Bleu slices of veal with ham and cheese dipped in batter and fried
Deutsches Beefsteak fried ground beef, with onion rings and potatoes (Note: the term "steak" on German menus often denotes what an American would call Salisbury steak, or hamburger; for something more like the American idea of steak, see **Lendensteak**)
Eisbein pickled ham hocks with sauerkraut and mashed potatoes
Filet Goulasch "Beef Stroganoff": strips of beef cooked in sour cream with onions and mushrooms
Frikadellen fried meat balls
Gulyas (Austria) goulash; spicy stew
Hackrahmsteak ground meat patty in browned cream gravy
Hammelkeule roast leg of lamb
Hammelkotelette lamb chop, grilled
Hasenpfeffer stew of pieces of hare, marinated in wine and spices, then cooked in the marinade with onions and mushrooms
Kalbsbrust Gefüllte mit Geflügelleber breast of veal, rolled and stuffed with chicken livers, ham, etc.
Kalbshirn mit Rührei calf brains with scrambled eggs
Kalbskotelette veal chop, grilled
Kalbsleber mit Zwiebeln calf liver with onions
Kalbsmilch sweetbreads
Kalbsschnitzel veal cutlet; see also **Wienerschnitzel**
Königsberger Klops large meat balls served in a sour cream sauce with capers
Lendensteak tenderloin steak (usually offered with a variety of sauces; if you prefer plain, ask for **"natur"**)
Pfeffersteak steak coated with ground

peppercorns and grilled
Rehbraten roast venison; **Rehrücken** saddle of venison
Rostbraten roast beef (Germany); minute steak (Austria)
Roulades thin slices of veal rolled and stuffed with a variety of stuffings and garnishes
Sauerbraten roast beef marinated with wine and spices and vinegar, then pot-roasted with vegetables
Schmorbraten pot roast
Schnitzel usually a thin-sliced pan-fried veal cutlet; but sometimes pork **(Schweineschnitzel)** or other meat; prepared in a number of different ways, associated with different areas, as **Holstein-erschnitzel** (topped with a fried egg), **Schwäbischeschnitzel** (with sour cream sauce), and, the most famous, **Wiener-schnitzel** (breaded, with a lemon slice and various other garnishes)
Schweinefüsse pigs' feet
Schweinekotelette pork chop: **natur** (plain) or with a variety of sauces
Schweinslendchen pork tenderloin
Ungarischer Gulasch chunks of meat cooked with paprika, onions, and other vegetables
Wiener Rostbraten beef loin fried in butter with onions

Geflügel und Wild (Fowl and Game)

Backhuhn or **Brathuhn** fried chicken
Damwildkeule roast leg of venison
Fasan im Topf pheasant roasted in casserole
Förstertopf mit Pilzen casserole of venison with mushrooms
Frikassee vom Huhn fricasséed chicken
Gansbraten roast goose
Geflügelleber chicken livers
Geflügelragout chicken stew
Kapaun capon
Puterbraten roast turkey
Rebhuhn partridge
Rehbraten roast venison

Rehrücken saddle of venison
Supreme vom Masthuhn boned breast of chicken
Wiener Backhuhn chicken Vienna style: breaded and deep fried with parsley.
Wildschweinbraten roast of wild boar

Gemüse und Beilagen (Vegetables and Side dishes)

Apfelrotkohl or **-kraut** red cabbage cooked with apples
Artischockenhertzen artichoke hearts
Aubergine eggplant
Beete beets
Blumenkohl cauliflower
Dicke Bohnen broad beans (fava)
Erbsen peas
Grüne Bohnen green beans
Gurkensalat cucumber salad
Karotten carrots
Kartoffeln potatoes, the most common accompaniment to the meat dish in Germany; some of the more common ways they are listed on the menu: **Bratkartoffeln** potatoes boiled, sliced and pan-fried; **Gebackene Kartoffeln** baked potatoes; **Herzoginkartoffeln** "dutchess" potatoes: mashed, shaped and browned in oven; **Kartoffelknödel** potato dumplings; **Kartoffelpuffer** potato pancakes; **Pommes Frites** French-fried potatoes; **Würfelkartoffeln** fried diced potatoes
Kartoffelsalat German potato salad, served either hot **(heiss)**, sautéed onions and bacon poured over sliced boiled potatoes with vinegar dressing; or cold **(kalt)**, with vinegar dressing poured over sliced potatoes and chopped onions
Kohl cabbage
Krautsalat coleslaw
Lattich lettuce
Möhren carrots
Nudeln noodles
Obstsalat fruit salad
Pilzen mushrooms
Rosenkohl Brussel sprouts

Salatplatte salad; may indicate anything from a simple green salad to more elaborate affairs including vegetables, meats, and a variety of dressings

Spätzle short thick noodles often served with meat dishes; preparation varies from area to area

Spinat spinach

Steckrübe turnips

Succini zucchini

Zwiebeln onions

Süssspeisen (Desserts)

Apfelstrudel mixture of apples and spices rolled in very thin pastry and baked

Apfelsinen oranges

Arme Ritter a sort of French toast; bread dipped in batter and fried

Auflauf souffle; the German version may be heavier than the French

Eierschaum whipped custard of egg yolks and sugar, flavored with wine, similar to Italian zabaione

Eis or **Eiskrem** ice cream; may be served in a bowl (**Eisbecher**) with various syrups or fruit toppings; in German Switzerland, **Glace**

Eistorte ice cream cake

Englischer Kuchen pound cake

Erdbeeren strawberries

Haselnussrahm hazelnut cream

Himbeeren raspberries

Käsetorte cheesecake

Königskuchen "King's cake": rum-flavored layer cake with almonds, currants, and raisins

Mohrenkopf "Moor's head": dome-shaped cake filled with custard or whipped cream and topped with chocolate

Pfirsichen peaches

Schokoladencremetorte chocolate layer cake filled with a rich chocolate cream

Getränke (Beverages)

Apfelsinesaft orange juice

Bier beer; **Oktoberbier** is the dark beer enjoyed at the *Oktoberfest*

Himbeersaft raspberry juice; very popular with children

Kaffee coffee; in Austria often served **mit Schlag** or in Germany, **mit Schlagsahne** (whipped cream)

Kirsch brandy distilled from cherries

Kümmel caraway-seed-flavored liqueur

Milch milk

Mineralwasser mineral water

Schnapps brandy

Schokolade chocolate, usually served hot

Tee tea

Wasser water; **Eiswasser** ice water

English–Deutsch

A

a, an [ə, ən] *art* ein *m*, eine *f*, ein *neut.*
once a year einmal im Jahr. *50 kilometres
an hour* 50 Kilometer pro Stunde.
aback [ə'bak] *adv* **taken aback** verblüfft,
überrascht.
abandon [ə'bandən] *v* (*leave*) verlassen;
(*give up*) aufgeben. *n* **with abandon**
ungezwungen. **abandoned** *adj* verfallen.
abashed [ə'baʃt] *adj* verlegen.
abate [ə'beit] *v* abnehmen.
abattoir ['abətwaɪ] *n* Schlachthaus *neut.*
abbey ['abi] *n* Abtei *f.* **abbess** *n* Äbtissin *f.*
abbot *n* Abt *m.*
abbreviate [ə'briːvieit] *v* (ab)kürzen.
abbreviation *n* Abkürzung *f.*
abdicate ['abdikeit] *v* abdanken. **abdication** *n* Abdankung *f.*
abdomen ['abdəmən] *n* Bauch *m,*
Unterleib *m.* **abdominal** *adj* Leib-,
abdominal.
abduct [əb'dʌkt] *v* entführen. **abduction** *n*
Entführung *f.*
aberration [abə'reiʃən] *n* Abweichung *f;*
(*optics, astron*) Aberration *f.* **mental aberration** Geistesverirrung *f.*
abet [ə'bet] *v* begünstigen, Vorschub leisten (+*dat*).
abeyance [ə'beiəns] *n* **in abeyance** in der
Schwebe.
abhor [əb'hoɪ] *v* hassen, verabscheuen.
abhorrence *n* Abscheu (vor) *m.* **abhorrent**
adj abscheulich.
*abide [ə'baid] *v* bleiben, verweilen; (*tolerate*) ausstehen. **abide by** festhalten an.
ability [ə'biləti] *n* Fähigkeit *f;* (*skill*) Geschicklichkeit *f.* **to the best of one's ability**
nach besten Kräften.
abject [,abdʒekt] *adj* (*wretched*) elend;
(*contemptible*) verächtlich, gemein.

ablaze [ə'bleiz] *adj, adv* brennend, in
Flammen. **set ablaze** entflammen.
able ['eibl] *adj* fähig; (*talented*) geschickt,
begabt. **be able** können, fähig sein; (*be in
a position to*) in der Lage sein. **ably** *adv*
geschickt.
abnormal [ab'noɪml] *adj* anormal,
abnorm; (*unusual*) ungewöhnlich; (*mal-
formed*) mißgestaltet. **abnormality** *n*
Abnormität *f;* Mißbildung *f.*
aboard [ə'boɪd] *adj, adv* (*ship*) an Bord.
go aboard an Bord gehen, einsteigen.
abode [ə'boud] *V* abide. *n* Wohnsitz *m.*
abolish [ə'boliʃ] *v* abschaffen, beseitigen.
abominable [ə'hominəbl] *adj* scheußlich.
abominate *v* verabscheuen. **abomination**
n Abscheu *m.*
aborigine [abə'ridʒini] *n* Ureinwohner *m.*
aboriginal *adj* Ur-, ursprünglich.
abortion [ə'boɪʃən] *n* (*miscarriage*)
Fehlgeburt *f;* (*termination of pregnancy*)
Abtreibung *f.* **abortive** *adj* mißlungen.
abound [ə'baund] *v* im Überfluß vorhanden sein. **abound in** reich sein an.
about [ə'baut] *adv* (*approximately*)
ungefähr, etwa; (*nearby*) in der Nähe.
prep (*concerning*) über; (*around*) um ...
herum. **be about to do something** eben
etwas tun wollen. **walk about** hin- und
herlaufen.
above [ə'bʌv] *prep* über. *adv* oben. **above-
mentioned** oben erwähnt, obig. **above
board** offen, ehrlich.
abrasion [ə'breiʒən] *n* Abschleifen *neut,*
Abrieb *m;* (*wound*) Abschürfung *f.* **abra-
sive** *adj* abschleifend.
abreast [ə'brest] *adv* **keep abreast of**
Schritt halten mit.
abridge [ə'bridʒ] *v* (ab)kürzen. **abridge-
ment** *n* Abkürzung *f.*
abroad [ə'broɪd] *adv* (*go*) ins Ausland;
(*be*) im Ausland.

abrupt [ə'brʌpt] *adj* (*sudden*) plötzlich; (*brusque*) kurz, unhöflich.

abscess ['abses] *n* Abszeß *m*.

abscond [əb'skɒnd] *v* flüchten.

absent ['absənt] *adj* abwesend. **absent-minded** geistesabwesend. **absentee** *n* Abwesende(r). **absence** *n* Abwesenheit *f*; (*lack*) Mangel *m*.

absolute ['absəluɪt] *adj* völlig, vollkommen, absolut; (*unconditional*) bedingungslos; (*pure*) rein. **absolutely** *adv* völlig; (*interj*) gewiß! **absolutism** n Absolutismus *m*.

absolve [əb'zɒlv] *v* entbinden, freisprechen.

absorb [əb'zɔɪb] *v* aufsaugen, absorbieren. **absorbed in thought** in Gedanken vertieft. **absorbent** *adj* absorbierend. **absorbent cotton** Watte *f*. **absorbing** *adj* fesselnd.

abstain [əb'stein] *v* (*voting*) seine Stimme enthalten. **abstain from** verzichten auf. **abstinence** *n* Enthaltsamkeit *f*.

abstemious [əb'stiːmiəs] *adj* mäßig, enthaltsam.

abstract ['abstrakt] *adj* abstrakt, theoretisch. **abstraction** *n* Abstraktion *f*.

absurd [əb'sɔɪd] *adj* unsinnig, lächerlich. **absurdity** *n* Unsinn *m*.

abundance [ə'bʌndəns] *n* Überfluß *m*, Reichtum *m*. **abundant** *adj* reichlich. **abundant in** reich an.

abuse [ə'bjuːz; *v* ə'bjuːs] *v* mißbrauchen; (*insult*) beleidigen. *n* Mißbrauch *m*; Beschimpfung *f*. **abusive** *adj* beleidigend.

abyss [ə'bis] *n* Abgrund *m*. **abysmal** *adj* abgrundtief; (*fig*) grenzenlos.

academy [ə'kadəmi] *n* Akademie *f*; (*private school*) Internat *m*. **academic** *adj* akademisch.

accede [ak'siːd] *v* (*agree*) zustimmen (+ *dat*), (*join*) beitreten (+ *dat*); (*throne*) besteigen.

accelerate [ək'seləreit] *v* (*mot*) gasgeben; (*make quicker*) beschleunigen; (*go faster*) schneller werden. **acceleration** *n* Beschleunigung *f*. **accelerator** *n* Gaspedal *neut*.

accent ['aksənt] *n* Akzent *m*. **accentuate** *v* betonen.

accept [ək'sept] *v* akzeptieren, annehmen; (*agree*) zusagen (+ *dat*). **acceptable** *adj* annehmbar. **acceptance** *n* Annahme *f*.

access ['akses] *n* Zutritt *m*, Zugang *m*. **accessible** *adj* erreichbar.

accessory [ək'sesəri] *n* (*mot*) Zubehörteil *m*; (*law*) Mitschuldige(r).

accident ['aksidənt] *n* (*mishap*) Unfall *m*; (*chance*) Zufall *m*. **accidental** *adj* zufällig.

acclaim [ə'kleim] *v* zujubeln (+ *dat*). *n* (*also* **acclamation**) Beifall *m*, Lob *neut*.

acclimatize [ə'klaimətaiz] *v* angewöhnen, akklimatisieren.

accolade ['akəleid] *n* Auszeichnung *f*.

accommodate [ə'kɒmədeit] *n* (*put up*) unterbringen; (*help*) aushelfen. **accommodating** *adj* hilfreich. **accommodation** *n* Unterkunft *f*.

accompany [ə'kʌmpəni] *v* begleiten. **accompaniment** *n* Begleitung *f*. **accompanist** *n* Begleiter(in).

accomplice [ə'kʌmplis] *n* Mittäter *m*.

accomplish [ə'kʌmpliʃ] *v* vollbringen, vollenden. **accomplished** *adj* gebildet, gewandt. **accomplishment** *n* Durchführung, Vollendung *f*.

accord [ə'kɔɪd] *v* übereinstimmen. *n* Übereinstimmung *f*, Einklang *m*. **of one's own accord** freiwillig. **in accordance with** gemäß (+ *dat*): *in accordance with the rules* den Regeln gemäß. **accordingly** *adv* dementsprechend, deswegen. **according to** laut (+ *gen*).

accordion [ə'kɔɪdiən] *n* Akkordeon *neut*.

accost [ə'kost] *v* ansprechen.

account [ə'kaunt] *n* (*bill*) Rechnung *f*; (*bank, etc*) Konto *neut*; (*report*) Bericht *m*. **accounts** *pl n* Bücher *pl*. **current account** Scheckkonto *neut*. **savings account** Sparkonto *neut*. **on account** auf Konto. **on account of** wegen (+ *gen*), auf Grund (+ *gen*). **on no account** auf keinen Fall. **take into account** berücksichtigen. *v* **account for** erklären. **accountable** *adj* verantwortlich. **accountant** *n* Buchhalter *m*.

accrue [ə'kruɪ] *v* auflaufen.

accumulate [ə'kjuːmjuleit] *v* anhäufen, sich häufen. **accumulation** *n* Anhäufung *f*.

accurate ['akjurət] *adj* genau, exakt; (*correct*) richtig. **accuracy** *n* Genauigkeit *f*.

accuse [ə'kjuːz] *v* anklagen. **the accused** der/die Angeklagte(r). **accusation** *n* Anklage *f*. **accusative** *n* Akkusativ *m*.

accustom [ə'kʌstəm] *v* **become accustomed to** sich gewöhnen an. **accustomed** *adj* gewöhnlich, üblich.

ace [eis] *n* (*cards*) As *neut*. *adj* (*coll*) erstklassig.

ache [eik] *n* Schmerz *m*. *v* schmerzen, weh tun.

achieve [ə'tʃiːv] *v* durchführen, vollbringen; (*reach*) erlangen. **achievement** *n* Vollendung *f*. (*success*) Erfolg *m*.

acid ['asid] *n* Säure *f*. *adj* sauer.

acknowledge [ək'nolidʒ] *n* anerkennen; (*admit*) zugeben. **acknowledge receipt** Empfang bestätigen. **acknowledgment** *n* Anerkennung *f*.

acne ['akni] *n* Pickel *m*, Akne *f*.

acorn ['eikɔːn] *n* Eichel *f*.

acoustic [ə'kuːstik] *adj* akustisch. **acoustics** *pl n* Akustik *f sing*.

acquaint [ə'kweint] *v* bekannt machen. **be acquainted with** kennen (+*acc*). **get acquainted with** kennenlernen (+*acc*). **acquaintance** *n* Bekannte(r).

acquiesce [akwi'es] *v* sich fügen. **acquiescence** *n* Ergebung *f*. **acquiescent** *adj* fügsam.

acquire [ə'kwaiə] *v* erwerben, bekommen. **acquisition** *n* Erwerb *m*. **acquisitive** hab süchtig, gierig.

acquit [ə'kwit] *v* (*law*) freisprechen. **acquittal** *n* Freisprechung *f*.

acrid ['akrid] *adj* scharf, beißend.

acrimony ['akriməni] *n* Bitterkeit *f*. **acrimonious** *adj* bitter, beißend.

acrobat ['akrəbat] *n* Akrobat *m*. **acrobatic** *adj* akrobatisch. **acrobatics** *pl n* Akrobatik *f sing*.

across [ə'kros] *adv* hinüber, herüber. *prep* (quer) über (+*acc*). jenseits (+*gen*), auf der anderen Seite.

act [akt] *v* handeln, tun; (*behave*) sich verhalten; (*theatre*) (eine Rolle) spielen. **act on** wirken auf. *n* Handlung, Tat *f*; (*law*) Gesetz *neut*; (*theatre*) Aufzug *m*. **acting** *adj* amtierend; *n* (*theatre*) Spielen *neut*. **actor** *n* Schauspieler *m*. **actress** *n* Schauspielerin *f*.

action ['akʃən] *n* Handlung *f*; (*deed*) Tat *f*; (*effect*) Wirkung *f*; (*law*) Klage *f*, (*battle*) Gefecht *neut*.

active ['aktiv] *adj* tätig, aktiv. **activate** *v* aktivieren. **activist** *n* Aktivist *m*. **activity** *n* Tätigkeit *f*. **activities** *n* Unternehmungen *pl*.

actual ['aktʃuəl] *adj* wirklich, eigentlich. tatsächlich **actually** *adv* wirklich, tatsächlich. *interj* eigentlich.

actuate ['aktjueit] *v* in Gang bringen.

acupuncture ['akjupʌŋktʃə] *n* Akupunktur *f*.

acute [ə'kjuːt] *adj* scharf, heftig; (*angle*) spitz; (*person*) scharfsinnig; (*med*) akut.

adamant ['adəmənt] *adj* unnachgiebig.

Adam's apple [adəm'zapl] *n* Adamsapfel *m*.

adapt [ə'dapt] *v* anpassen; verändern. **adapted to** geeignet für. **adaptable** *adj* anpassungsfähig. **adaptation** *n* (*theatre*) Bearbeitung *f*. **adaptor** *n* (*for plug*) Zwischenstecker *m*.

add [ad] *v* (*figures*) addieren; (*word, sentence*) hinzufügen. **add up** addieren. **addition** *n* (*math*) Addition *f*; (*something added*) Zugabe *f*, Zutat *m*. **in addition** außerdem. **in addition to** zusätzlich zu. **additional** *adj* zusätzlich, weiter. **additive** *n* Zusatz *m*.

addendum [ə'dendəm] *n* Zusatz *m*.

adder ['adə] *n* (*snake*) Natter *m*.

addict ['adikt; *v* ə'dikt] *n* Süchtige(r); (*coll*) Fanatiker *m*. **drug addict** Rauschgiftsüchtige(r). **addicted** süchtig. **addiction** *n* Sucht *f*.

address [ə'dres] *v* (*letter*) addressieren; (*person*) anreden. *n* Adresse *f*, Anschrift *f*; (*speech*) Anrede *f*. **address book** Adreßbuch *neut*. **addressee** *n* Empfänger *m*.

adenoids ['adənɔidz] *pl n* Polypen *pl*.

adept [ə'dept] *adj* geschickt, erfahren.

adequate ['adikwət] *adj* (*quantity*) ausreichend, genügend; (*quality*) annehmbar.

adhere [əd'hiə] *v* **adhere to** haften *or* kleben an (+*dat*); (*belief, etc.*) festhalten an (+*dat*). **adhesive** *adj* klebrig, haftend. **adhesive tape** Klebeband *neut*. **adherent** *n* Anhänger *m*.

adjacent [ə'dʒeisənt] *adj* angrenzend.

adjective ['adʒiktiv] *n* Adjektiv *neut*, Eigenschaftswort *neut*.

adjoin [ə'dʒɔin] *v* angrenzen (an). **adjoining** *adj* angrenzend, anliegend.

adjourn [ə'dʒɜːn] *v* vertagen. **adjournment** *n* Vertagung *f*.

adjudicate [ə'dʒuːdikeit] *v* Recht sprechen, entscheiden. **adjudicator** *n* Schiedsrichter *m*.

adjust [ə'dʒʌst] *v* anpassen; berichtigen; (*tech*) einstellen. **adjust to** sich anpassen an. **adjustable** *adj* einstellbar. **adjustment** *n* Anpassung, Einstellung *f*.

ad-lib ['ad'lib] *adv* frei. *v* improvisieren.

administer [əd'ministə] v verwalten.
administer justice Recht sprechen.
administration n Verwaltung f. **administrative** adj Verwaltungs-. **administrator** n Verwalter m.

admiral ['admərəl] n Admiral m.

admire [əd'maiə] v bewundern, hochschätzen. **admirable** adj bewundernswert. **admiration** n Bewunderung f.

admission [əd'miʃən] n Eintritt m; (acknowledgment) Zugeständnis neut.

admit [əd'mit] v (let in) hereinlassen, zulassen; (concede) zugeben. **admittance** n Zutritt, Eintritt m. **no admittance** Zutritt verboten.

adolescence [adə'lesns] Jugend f. **adolescent** adj jugendlich. n Jugendliche(r).

adopt [ə'dopt] v (child) adoptieren; (idea) annehmen, übernehmen. **adoption** n Adoption f; Übernahme f.

adore [ə'doɪ] v lieben; (rel) verehren. **adorable** adj entzückend. **adoration** n Verehrung f.

adorn [ə'doɪn] v schmücken. **adornment** n Schmuck m.

adrenaline [ə'drenəlin] n Adrenalin neut.

adrift [ə'drift] adj, adv (naut) treibend; (fig) hilflos.

adroit [ə'droit] adj gewandt, geschickt.

adulation [adju'leiʃən] n Lobhudelei f.

adult ['adʌlt] n Erwachsene(r). adj erwachsen; (animal, plant) ausgewachsen.

adulterate [ə'dʌltəreit] v verfälschen. **adulteration** n Verfälschung f.

adultery [ə'dʌltəri] n Ehebruch m. **adulterer** n Ehebrecher(in).

advance [əd'vains] v vorwärts gehen, vorrücken; (make progress) Fortschritte machen; (cash) vorschießen; (cause) fördern; (tech) vorstellen. n Vorrücken neut, Fortschritt m; Vorschuß m. **in advance** im voraus. **advancement** n Beförderung f.

advantage [əd'vaintidʒ] n Vorteil m. **take advantage of** ausnutzen (+acc). **advantageous** adj vorteilhaft.

advent ['advənt] n Ankunft f; (rel) Advent m.

adventure [əd'ventʃə] n Abenteuer m. **adventurer** n Abenteurer m. **adventurous** adj gewagt.

adverb ['advəɪb] n Adverb neut, Umstandswort neut.

adversary ['advəsəri] n Gegner m.

adverse ['advəɪs] adj widrig, ungünstig. **adversity** n Mißgeschick neut, Not f.

advertise ['advətaiz] v anzeigen. **advertisement** n Anzeige f. **advertising** n Reklame, Werbung f.

advise [əd'vaiz] v (be)raten, empfehlen; (comm) benachrichtigen. **advisable** adj ratsam. **adviser** n Berater m. **advice** n Rat m, Ratschlag m; (comm) Avis neut.

advocate ['advəkeit] v befürworten.

aerial ['eəriəl] n Antenne f. adj Luft-.

aerodynamics [eərədai'namiks] n Aerodynamik f.

aeronautics [eərə'noitiks] n Aeronautik f, Flugwesen neut.

aeroplane ['eərəplein] n Flugzeug neut.

aerosol ['eərəsol] n Sprühdose f, Spray neut.

aesthetic [iɪs'θetik] adj ästhetisch.

affair [ə'feə] n Angelegenheit f, Sache f; (love affair) (Liebes) Affäre f.

affect[1] [ə'fekt] v (influence) (ein)wirken auf, beeinflüssen. **affected** adj (moved) bewegt.

affect[2] [ə'fekt] v (pretend) vorgeben. **affectation** n Affektation f. **affected** adj geziert.

affection [ə'fekʃən] n Zuneigung f, Liebe f. **affectionate** adj liebevoll.

affiliated [ə'filieitid] adj angeschlossen. **affiliated company** Tochtergesellschaft f. **affiliation** n Verbindung f, Mitgliedschaft f.

affinity [ə'finəti] n Zuneigung f; (chem) Affinität f.

affirm [ə'fəɪm] v behaupten. **affirmation** n Behauptung f. **affirmative** adj bestätigend.

affix [ə'fiks] v befestigen, ankleben (an).

afflict [ə'flikt] v betrüben. **affliction** n Leiden neut.

affluent ['afluənt] adj wohlhabend, reich. **affluence** n Wohlstand m.

afford [ə'foɪd] v sich leisten (können); (allow) gewähren.

affront [ə'frʌnt] v beleidigen. n Beleidigung f.

afloat [ə'flout] adj, adv schwimmend; (boat) auf dem Meere.

afoot [ə'fut] adv im Gang.

aforesaid [ə'foɪsed] adj vorher erwähnt.

afraid [ə'freid] adj ängstlich, erschrocken, bange. **be afraid of** Angst haben vor. **be afraid to** sich scheuen. I am afraid I must ... ich muß leider ...

afresh [ə'freʃ] *adv* von neuem, noch einmal.

Africa ['afrikə] *n* Afrika *neut.* **African** *n* Afrikaner(in). *adj* afrikanisch.

aft [aːft] *adj* Achter-. *adv* achtern.

after ['aːftə] *conj* nachdem. *prep* nach, hinter. *adv* später, nachher. *adj* (*naut*) Achter-. **after all** schließlich. **shortly after** kurz danach.

after-effect *n* Nachwirkung *f.*

afterlife ['aːftəlaif] *n* Leben nach dem Tode *neut.*

aftermath ['aːftəmaθ] *n* Auswirkung *f.*

afternoon [ˌaːftə'nuːn] *n* Nachmittag *m.* **good afternoon!** guten Tag!

aftershave ['aːftəʃeiv] *n* Rasierwasser *neut.*

after-taste *n* Nachgeschmack *m.*

afterthought ['aːftəθɔit] *n* nachträglicher Einfall *m.*

afterwards ['aːftəwədz] *adv* nachher, später, danach.

again [ə'gen] *adv* wieder, noch einmal, nochmals; (*moreover*) ferner. **again and again** immer wieder.

against [ə'genst] *prep* gegen. **as against** im Vergleich zu.

age [eidʒ] *n* (*person*) Alter *neut;* (*era*) Zeitalter *neut.* **age group** Altersgruppe *f.* **at the age of** ... im Alter von .... **of age** volljährig. **old age** (hohes) Alter *neut.* *v* alt werden. **aged** *adj* (*elderly*) betagt. *aged five years* fünf Jahre alt. **under age** minderjährig.

agency ['eidʒənsi] *n* Agentur *f.*

agenda [ə'dʒendə] *n* Tagesordnung *f.*

agent ['eidʒənt] *n* Agent *m*, Vermittler *m;* (*chem*) Wirkstoff *m.*

aggravate ['agrəveit] *v* verschlimmern, (*coll*) ärgern. **aggravation** *n* Verschlimmerung *f;* Ärger *m.*

aggregate ['agrigət] *adj* gesamt, ganz. *n* Summe *f.*

aggression [ə'greʃən] *n* Angriff *m*, Aggression *f.* **aggressive** *adj* aggresiv. **aggressor** *n* Angreifer *m.*

aghast [ə'gaɪst] *adj* entsetzt.

agile ['adʒail] *adj* agil, flink. **agility** *n* Flinkheit *f.*

agitate ['adʒiteit] *v* schütteln. **agitated** *adj* beunruhigt. **agitation** *n* Beunruhigung *f.*

agnostic [ag'nostik] *n* Agnostiker *m.* **agnosticism** *n* Agnostizismus *m.*

ago [ə'gou] *adv* vor: *a year ago* vor einem Jahr. *a moment ago* soeben. *a long time ago* schon lange her. *a short time ago* vor kurzem.

agog [ə'gog] *adj* gespannt.

agony ['agəni] *n* Qual *f*, Agonie *f.* **agonize over** sich quälen über.

agree [ə'grii] *v* (*concur*) übereinstimmen, einverstanden sein; (*date, etc.*) vereinbaren; (*consent*) zustimmen; (*be in agreement*) einig sein. *eggs do not agree with me* ich kann Eier nicht vertragen. **agreed!** einverstanden! **agreeable** *adj* angenehm. **agreement** *n* Übereinstimmung *f* (*written*) Abkommen *neut.*

agriculture ['agrikʌltʃə] *n* Landwirtschaft *f.* **agricultural** *adj* landwirtschaftlich.

aground [ə'graund] *adv* **run aground** stranden.

ahead [ə'hed] *adv* vorwärts. **straight ahead** gerade aus. **go ahead** fortfahren.

aid [eid] *n* Hilfe *f.* *v* helfen (+*dat*).

aim [eim] *v* (*gun*) richten; (*intend*) zielen. *n* Ziel *neut.* **aimless** *adj* ziellos.

air [eə] *n* Luft *f;* (*appearance*) Aussehen *neut;* (*music*) Lied *neut.* *v* (*laundry*) trocknen; (*views*) bekanntmachen. **go by air** fliegen. **airy** *adj* luftig.

airbed ['eəbed] *n* Luftmatratze *f.*

airborne ['eəbɔin] *adj* in der Luft; Luft-.

air-conditioned *adj* klimatisiert. **air-conditioning** *n* Klimaanlage *f.*

air-cooled *adj* (*mech*) luftgekühlt.

aircraft ['eəkraːft] *n* Flugzeug *neut.*

airfield ['eəfiːld] *n* Flugplatz *m.*

air force *n* Luftwaffe *f.*

air lift *n* Luftbrücke *f.*

airline ['eəlain] *n* Luftverkehrsgesellschaft *f.* **airline passenger** Fluggast *m.*

airmail ['eəmeil] *n* Luftpost *f.* **by airmail** mit Luftpost.

airport ['eəpɔit] *n* Flughafen *m.*

air-raid *n* Luftangriff *m.*

air steward *n* Steward *m.* **air stewardess** *n* Stewardeß *f.*

airtight ['eətait] *adj* luftdicht.

aisle [ail] *n* Gang *m.*

ajar [ə'dʒaɪ] *adj* halboffen.

akin [ə'kin] *adj* **akin to** ähnlich (+*dat*).

alabaster ['aləbaɪstə] *n* Alabaster *m.*

à la carte [alaɪ'kaɪt] *adv* nach der Speisekarte, à la carte.

alarm [ə'laɪm] *n* Alarm *m;* (*unrest*) Beunruhigung *f.* *v* beunruhigen. **alarm clock** Wecker *m.*

6

alas [ə'las] *interj* leider! o weh!
albatross ['albətrɔs] *n* Albatros *m.*
albino [al'biːnou] *n* Albino *m.*
album ['albəm] *n* Album *neut.*
alchemy ['alkəmi] *m* Alchimie *f.* **alchemist** *n* Alchimist *m.*
alcohol ['alkəhɔl] *n* Alkohol *m.* **alcoholic** *adj* alkoholisch. *n* Alkoholiker *m.* **alcoholism** *n* Alkoholismus *m.* **non-alcoholic** *adj* alkoholfrei.
alcove ['alkouv] *n* Nische *f.*
alderman ['ɔːldəmən] *n* Ratsherr *m.*
ale [eil] *m* Bier *neut.*
alert [ə'ləːt] *adj* wachsam, munter. *v* warnen. **on the alert** auf der Hut.
algebra ['aldʒibrə] *n* Algebra *f.*
alias ['eiliəs] *adv* sonst . . . genannt, alias. *n* Deckname *m.*
alibi ['alibai] *n* Alibi *neut.*
alien ['eiliən] *n* Fremde(r), Ausländer *m. adj* fremd. **alienate** *v* entfremden. **alienation** *n* Entfremdung *f.*
alight¹ [ə'lait] *v* (*from bus*) aussteigen.
alight² [ə'lait] *adj, adv* brennend, in Flammen. **set alight** entflammen.
align [ə'lain] *v* ausrichten. **alignment** *n* Ausrichtung *f.*
alike [ə'laik] *adj, adv* gleich.
alimentary canal [ali'mentəri] *m* Nährungskanal *m.*
alimony ['aliməni] *n* Unterhalt *m,* Alimente *pl.*
alive [ə'laiv] *adj* lebend, am Leben. **alive with** wimmelnd von.
alkali ['alkəlai] *n* Alkali *neut.* **alkaline** *adj* alkalisch.
all [ɔːl] *adj* alle, sämtliche *pl. pron* alles, das Ganze. *adv* ganz. **all over** vorbei. **all gone** alle, weg. **above all** vor allem. **all at once** auf einmal. **at all** überhaupt. **all day** den ganzen Tag. **all right** in Ordnung, okay.
allay [ə'lei] *v* beruhigen.
allege [ə'ledʒ] *v* angeben, behaupten. **alleged** *adj* angeblich. **allegation** *n* Behauptung *f.*
allegiance [ə'liːdʒəns] *n* Treue *f.*
allegory ['aligəri] *n* Allegorie *f.* **allegorical** *adj* allegorisch.
allergy ['alədʒi] *n* Allergie *f.* **allergic** *adj* allergisch (gegen).
alleviate [ə'liːvieit] *v* erleichtern.
alley ['ali] *n* Gasse *f.* **bowling alley** Kegelbahn *f.*

alliance [ə'laiəns] *n* (*pol*) Bündnis *neut.* **form an alliance** ein Bündnis schließen.
allied ['alaid] *adj* verbündet, alliiert.
alligator ['aligeitə] *n* Alligator *m.*
alliteration [əlitə'reiʃən] *n* Alliteration *f.* **alliterative** *adj* alliterierend.
allocate ['aləkeit] *v* zuteilen.
allot [ə'lɔt] *v* (*distribute*) zuteilen; (*assign*) bestimmen. **allotment** *n* Zuteilung *f*; (*garden patch*) Schrebergarten *m.*
allow [ə'lau] *v* erlauben, gestatten. **allow for** berücksichtigen. *will you allow me* (*to*)? darf ich? **allowance** *n* Erlaubnis *f*; (*money*) Rente *f.*
alloy ['alɔi; *v* ə'lɔi] *n* Legierung *f. v* legieren.
allude [ə'luːd] *v* **allude to** anspielen auf (+ *acc*). **allusion** *n* Anspielung *f.*
allure [ə'ljuə] *n* Reiz *m. v* verlocken. **alluring** *adj* verlockend.
ally ['alai; *v* ə'lai] *n* Verbündete(r); (*pol*) Alliierte(r). *v* **ally oneself with** sich verbünden mit. **the Allies** die Alliierten.
almanac ['ɔːlmənak] *n* Jahrbuch *neut,* Almanach *m.*
almighty [ɔːl'maiti] *adj* allmächtig; (*coll*) gewaltig. **the Almighty** der Allmächtige.
almond ['aːmənd] *n* Mandel *f.*
almost ['ɔːlmoust] *adv* fast, beinahe.
alms [aːmz] *pl n* Almosen *neut sing.*
aloft [ə'lɔft] *adv* (*be*) oben; (*go*) nach oben.
alone [ə'loun] *adj, adv* allein. **leave alone** bleiben lassen. *leave me alone!* laß mich in Ruhe!
along [ə'lɔŋ] *prep* entlang (+ *acc*): *along the coast* die Küste entlang. *adv* vorwärts, weiter; mit: *come along* mitkommen. **along with** zusammen mit. **get along with someone** mit jemandem gut auskommen. **alongside** *prep* neben (+ *acc or dat*); (*ship*) längseits (+ *gen*).
aloof [ə'luːf] *adj* zurückhaltend.
aloud [ə'laud] *adv* laut. **read aloud** vorlesen.
alphabet ['alfəbit] *n* Alphabet *neut.* **alphabetical** *adj* alphabetisch.
Alps [alps] *pl n* Alpen *pl.* **alpine** *adj* Alpen-.
already [ɔːl'redi] *adv* schon, bereits.
Alsatian [al'seiʃən] *n* (*dog*) Schäferhund *m. adj* elsässisch.
also ['ɔːlsou] *adv* auch, ebenfalls; (*moreover*) ferner.

altar ['ɔːltə] *n* Altar *m*.

alter ['ɔːltə] *v* (*modify*) (ab-, ver)ändern; (*become changed*) sich (ver)ändern. **alteration** *n* (Ab-, Ver)Änderung *f*; (*building*) Umbau *m*.

alternate [ɔːl'tɜːnət; *v* 'ɔːltəneit] *adj* abwechselnd. *v* abwechseln.

alternative [ɔːl'tɜːnətiv] *adj* ander. *n* Alternative *f*. *there is no alternative* es gibt keine andere Möglichkeit.

although [ɔːl'ðou] *conj* obwohl, obgleich, wenn auch.

altitude ['altitjuːd] *m* Höhe *f*.

alto ['altou] *n* Alt *m*, Altstimme *f*.

altogether [ɔːltə'geðə] *adv* insgesamt, im ganzen; völlig.

altruistic [altru'istik] *adj* altruistisch.

aluminium [alju'miniəm] *n* Aluminium *neut*.

always ['ɔːlweiz] *adv* immer, stets; schon immer.

am [am] *V* be.

amalgamate [ə'malgəmeit] *v* (*tech*) amalgamieren; (*fig*) vereinigen.

amass [ə'mas] *v* aufhäufen.

amateur ['amətə] *n* Amateur *m*. *adj* Amateur-.

amaze [ə'meiz] *v* erstaunen, verblüffen. **amazed at** erstaunt über. **amazement** *n* Erstaunen *neut*. **amazing** *adj* erstaunlich; (*coll*) sagenhaft.

ambassador [am'basədə] *n* Botschafter *m*.

amber ['ambə] *n* Bernstein *m*. *adj* bernsteinfarb, gelb.

ambidextrous [ambi'dekstrəs] *adj* beidhändig.

ambiguous [am'bigjuəs] *adj* zweideutig; unklar.

ambition [am'biʃən] *n* Ehrgeiz *m*, Ambition *f*. **ambitious** *adj* ehrgeizig, ambitiös.

ambivalence [am'bivələns] *n* Ambivalenz *f*. **ambivalent** *adj* ambivalent.

amble ['ambl] *v* schlendern.

ambulance ['ambjuləns] *n* Krankenwagen *m*.

ambush ['ambuʃ] *n* Hinterhalt *m*. *v* aus dem Hinterhalt überfallen.

ameliorate [ə'miːliəreit] *v* (*make better*) verbessern; (*get better*) besser werden. **amelioration** *n* Verbesserung *f*.

amenable [ə'miːnəbl] *adj* zugänglich; (*accountable*) verantwortlich.

amend [ə'mend] *v* (ab)ändern; ergänzen, richtigstellen. **make amends for**

wiedergutmachen. **amendment** *n* (*to a motion*) Ergänzung *f*.

amenities [ə'miːnətiz] *pl n* Vorzüge *pl*, moderne Einrichtungen *pl*.

America [ə'merikə] *n* Amerika *neut*. **American** *n* Amerikaner(in); *adj* amerikanisch.

amethyst ['aməθist] *n* Amethyst *m*.

amiable ['eimiəbl] *adj* freundlich, liebenswürdig.

amicable ['amikəbl] *adj* freundschaftlich, friedlich.

amid [ə'mid] *prep* mitten unter (+*dat*).

amiss [ə'mis] *adj* verkehrt, nicht richtig. **take amiss** übelnehmen.

ammonia [ə'mouniə] *n* Ammoniak *neut*.

ammunition [amju'niʃən] *n* Munition *f*.

amnesia [am'niːziə] *n* Gedächtnisverlust *m*.

amnesty ['amnəsti] *n* Amnestie *f*.

amoeba [ə'miːbə] *n* Amöbe *f*.

among [ə'mʌŋ] *prep* unter, zwischen (+*dat*); bei (+*dat*). **among other things** unter anderem. **among ourselves/yourselves/themselves** miteinander, untereinander.

amoral [ei'morəl] *adj* amoralisch.

amorous ['amərəs] *adj* verliebt; liebevoll.

amorphous [ə'mɔːfəs] *adj* (*chem*) amorph; formlos.

amount [ə'maunt] *n* (*of money*) Betrag *m*, Summe *f*; (*quantity*) Menge *f*. **amount to** betragen. *it amounts to the same* es läuft auf das gleiche hinaus.

ampere ['ampeə] *n* Ampere *neut*.

amphibian [am'fibiən] *n* Amphibie *f*. **amphibious** *adj* amphibisch; (*vehicle*) Amphibien-.

amphitheatre ['amfiθiətə] *n* Amphitheater *neut*; (*lecture room*) Hörsaal *m*.

ample ['ampl] *adj* ausreichend, reichlich.

amplify ['amplifai] *v* verstärken. **amplification** *n* Verstärkung *f*. **amplifier** *n* Verstärker *m*.

amputate ['ampjuteit] *v* amputieren. **amputation** *n* Amputation *f*.

amuse [ə'mjuːz] *v* belustigen, amüsieren; (*entertain*) unterhalten. **be amused by** or **about** lustig finden. **amusing** *adj* lustig, unterhaltend. **amusement** *n* Unterhaltung *f*.

anachronism [ə'nakrənizəm] *n* Anachronismus *m*. **anachronistic** *adj* anachronistisch.

anaemia [əˈniːmiə] n Anämie, Blutarmut f. **anaemic** adj anämisch, blutarm.
anaesthetic [anəsˈθetik] n Betäubungsmittel neut. **under anaesthetic** unter Narkose. **anaesthetize** v betäuben.
anagram [ˈanəgram] n Anagramm neut.
analogy [əˈnalədʒi] n Ähnlichkeit f, Analogie f. **analogous** adj analog, ähnlich.
analysis [ənˈaləsis] n Analyse f. **analyse** v analysieren. **analytical** adj analytisch.
anarchy [ˈanəki] n Anarchie f. **anarchist** n Anarchist m.
anathema [əˈnaθəmə] n (rel) Kirchenbann m. **that is anathema to me** das ist mir ein Greuel.
anatomy [əˈnatəmi] n Anatomie f. **anatomical** adj anatomisch.
ancestor [ˈansestə] n Vorfahr m, Ahn m.
anchor [ˈaŋkə] n Anker m. v befestigen. **ride at anchor** vor Anker liegen. **weigh anchor** den Anker lichten.
anchovy [ˈantʃəvi] n Anschovis f.
ancient [ˈeinʃənt] adj alt, uralt; aus alter Zeit, antik.
ancillary [anˈsiləri] adj zusätzlich, Hilfs-.
and [and] conj und.
anecdote [ˈanikdout] n Anekdote f.
anemone [əˈnemeni] n Anemone f.
anew [əˈnjuː] adv von neuem, wieder.
angel [ˈeindʒəl] n Engel m. **angelic** adj engelhaft.
angelica [anˈdʒelikə] n Angelika f.
anger [ˈaŋgə] n Zorn m, Ärger m. v ärgern. **in anger** im Zorn. **angry** adj ärgerlich, zornig. **be angry** sich ärgern, böse sein.
angina [anˈdʒainə] n Angina f.
angle[1] [ˈaŋgl] n Winkel m, Ecke f; (coll) Gesichtspunkt m. **be at an angle to** einen Winkel bilden mit.
angle[2] [ˈaŋgl] v angeln (nach). **angler** n Angler m. **angling** n Angeln neut.
anguish [ˈaŋgwiʃ] n Qual f.
angular [ˈaŋgjulə] adj winkelig, eckig.
animal [ˈaniməl] n Tier neut. adj tierisch, animalisch. **animal fat** Tierfett neut. **animal kingdom** Tierreich neut.
animate [ˈanimeit] v beleben; begeistern. **animated** adj lebhaft. **animated cartoon** Zeichentrickfilm m.
animosity [aniˈmosəti] n Feindseligkeit f.
aniseed [ˈanisiːd] n Anis m.
anisette [ˌaniˈzet] n Anisett m.
ankle [ˈaŋkl] n (Fuß)Knöchel m.
annals [ˈanlz] pl n Annalen pl.

annex [əˈneks; n ˈaneks] n (to building) Anbau m. v (country) annektieren. **annexation** n Annexion f.
annihilate [əˈnaiəleit] v vernichten. **annihilation** n Vernichtung f.
anniversary [ˌaniˈvɔːsəri] n Jahrestag m. **wedding anniversary** Hochzeitstag m.
annotate [ˈanəteit] v kommentieren. **annotation** n Anmerkung f.
announce [əˈnauns] v ankündigen, ansagen, anzeigen. **announcement** n Ankündigung f, Ansage f; (radio) Durchsage f. **announcer** n (radio) Ansager m.
annoy [əˈnoi] v belästigen, ärgern. **be annoyed at** or **with** sich ärgern über (+acc). **annoyance** n Belästigung f.
annual [ˈanjuəl] adj jährlich; Jahres-. n (book) Jahrbuch neut; (plant) einjährige Pflanze f.
annul [əˈnʌl] v annullieren. **annulment** n Annullierung f.
anode [ˈanoud] n Anode f.
anomaly [əˈnoməli] n Anomalie f.
anonymous [əˈnoniməs] adj anonym, ungenannt.
anorak [ˈanərak] n Anorak m.
another [əˈnʌðə] pron, adj (a different) ein anderer; (an additional) noch ein. **one another** einander, sich.
answer [ˈainsə] n Antwort f; (solution) Lösung f. v antworten, erwidern. **answer back** unverschämt antworten. **answer for** verantwortlich sein für. **answerable** adj verantwortlich.
ant [ant] n Ameise f.
antagonize [anˈtagənaiz] v reizen, entfremden. **antagonist** n Gegner m, Feind m. **antagonistic** adj feindselig.
antecedent [antiˈsiːdənt] adj früher.
antelope [ˈantəloup] n Antilope f.
antenatal [antiˈneitl] adj vor der Geburt. **antenatal care** Schwangerschaftsvorsorge f.
antenna [anˈtenə] m (insect) Fühler m; (radio) Antenne f.
anthem [ˈanθəm] n Hymne f. **national anthem** Nationalhymne f.
anthology [anˈθolədʒi] n Anthologie f.
anthropology [anθrəˈpolədʒi] n Anthropologie f. **anthropological** adj anthropologisch.
anti-aircraft [antiˈeəkraːft] adj Fliegerabwehr-. **anti-aircraft gun** Fliegerabwehrkanone f.

antibiotic [antibai'otik] *n* Antibiotikum *neut. adj* antibiotisch.
antibody ['anti,bodi] *n* Antikörper *m*.
anticipate [an'tisipeit] *v* (*expect*) erwarten; (*foresee*) voraussehen. **anticipation** *n* Erwartung *f*. **in anticipation of** in Erwartung (+*gen*).
anticlimax [anti'klaimaks] *n* Enttäuschung *f*.
anticlockwise [anti'klokwaiz] *adj, adv* dem Uhrzeigersinn entgegen.
antics ['antiks] *pl n* Possen *pl*.
anticyclone [anti'saikloun] *n* Hochdruckgebiet *neut*.
antidote ['antidout] *n* Gegenmittel (gegen) *neut*.
antifreeze ['antifriz] *n* Frostschutzmittel *neut*.
antipathy [an'tipəθi] *n* Antipathie *f*, Abneigung *f*.
antique [an'tiːk] *adj* antik, altertümlich. *n* Antiquität *f*. **antiquated** *adj* veraltet. **antiquity** *n* Altertum *neut*.
anti-Semitic [antisə'mitik] *adj* antisemitisch.
antiseptic [anti'septik] *n* Antiseptikum *neut. adj* antiseptisch.
antisocial [anti'souʃəl] *adj* gesellschaftsfeindlich; (*person*) unfreundlich.
antithesis [an'tiθəsis] *n* Gegensatz *m*.
antler ['antlə] *n* Geweihsprosse *f*.
antonym ['antənim] *n* Antonym *neut*.
anus ['einəs] *n* After *m*.
anvil ['anvil] *n* Amboß *m*.
anxious ['aŋkʃəs] *adj* (*worried*) beunruhigt, besorgt; (*desirous*) begierig (nach). **be anxious to do something** gespannt sein, etwas zu tun. **anxiety** *n* Angst *f*, Besorgnis *f*.
any ['eni] *pron* irgendein, welche. *adv* etwas. **any faster** schneller, etwas schneller. **any more?** noch mehr? **do you want any?** wollen sie welche? **I haven't any money** ich habe kein Geld. **I can't do it any longer** ich kann es nicht mehr machen. **anybody** *pron* (irgend) jemand; (*everybody*) jeder. **anyhow** *adv* jedenfalls. **anyone** *pron see* **anybody**. **anything** *pron* (irgend) etwas; (*everything*) alles. **anytime** *adv* jederzeit. **anyway** *adv* jedenfalls, sowieso. **anywhere** *adv* irgendwo(hin); (*everywhere*) überall.
apart [ə'paːt] *adv* auseinander, getrennt. **apart from** abgesehen von.

apartheid [ə'paːteit] *n* Apartheid *f*.
apartment [ə'paːtmənt] *n* Wohnung *f*.
apathy ['apəθi] *n* Apathie *f*. **apathetic** *adj* apathisch.
ape [eip] *n* Affe *m*. *v* nachäffen.
aperitive [ə'perətiv] *n* Aperitif *m*.
aperture ['apətjuə] *n* Öffnung *f*; (*phot*) Blende *f*.
apex ['eipeks] *n* Spitze *f*.
aphid ['eifid] *n* Blattlaus *f*.
aphrodisiac [afrə'diziak] *n* Aphrodisiakum *neut*.
apiece [ə'piːs] *adv* (*per person*) pro Person; (*for each article*) pro Stück.
apology [ə'polədʒi] *n* Entschuldigung *f*. **apologetic** *adj* entschuldigend. **apologize** sich entschuldigen.
apoplexy ['apəpleksi] *n* Schlaganfall *m*.
apostle [ə'posl] *n* Apostel *m*.
apostrophe [ə'postrəfi] *n* Apostroph *m*, Auslassungszeichen *neut*.
appal [ə'poːl] *v* entsetzen. **appalling** *adj* entsetzlich.
apparatus [apə'reitəs] *n* Apparat *m*, Gerät *neut*.
apparent [ə'parənt] *adj* (*obvious*) offenbar; (*seeming*) scheinbar. **apparently** allem Anschein nach.
apparition [apə'riʃən] *n* Erscheinung *f*, Geist *m*.
appeal [ə'piːl] *n* Appell *m*, dringende Bitte *f*; (*charm*) Anziehungskraft *f*; (*law*) Berufung *f*. *v* **appeal against** (*law*) Berufung einlegen gegen. **appeal for** dringend bitten um. **appeal to** (*turn to*) appellieren, sich wenden an; (*please*) gefallen (+*dat*). **appealing** *adj* reizvoll.
appear [ə'piə] *v* (*seem*) scheinen; (*become visible, present itself*) erscheinen; (*crop up*) auftauchen. **appearance** *n* Erscheinen *neut*; (*look*) Anschein *m*.
appease [ə'piːz] *v* beruhigen; (*hunger*) stillen. **appeasement** *n* Beruhigung *f*.
appendix [ə'pendiks] *n* (*in book*) Anhang *m*; (*anat*) Blinddarm *m*. **appendicitis** *n* Blinddarmentzündung *f*.
appetite ['apitait] *n* Appetit *m*. **appetizer** *n* Appetitshappen *m*. **appetizing** *adj* appetitlich.
applaud [ə'ploːd] *v* Beifall klatschen (+*dat*), applaudieren (+*dat*); (*fig*) loben.
apple ['apl] *n* Apfel *m*. **apple juice** Apfelsaft *m*. **apple tree** Apfelbaum *m*. **apple sauce** Apfelmus *neut*.

appliance [ə'plaiəns] *n* Gerät *neut.*
applicable ['aplikəbl] *adj* zutreffend.
applicant ['aplikənt] *n* Kandidat *m.*
apply [ə'plai] *v* anwenden; (*be valid*)
gelten. **apply for** (*job*) sich bewerben um.
apply to sich wenden an. **apply oneself to**
sich bemühen um. **application** *n*
Anwendung *f;* (*job*) Bewerbung *f.* **applied**
adj angewandt.
appoint [ə'point] *v* anstellen, ernennen.
appointed *adj* vereinbart. **well appointed**
gut ausgestattet. **appointment** *n* Anstellung *f;* (*meeting*) Verabredung *f.*
apportion [ə'poɪʃən] *v* zuteilen.
appraisal [ə'preizl] *n* Schätzung *f.*
appreciable [ə'priːʃəbl] *adj* merkbar.
appreciate [ə'priːʃieit] *v* schätzen; (*understand*) verstehen; (*be grateful for*)
dankbar sein für; (*increase in value*) im
Wert steigen. **appreciation** *n* (*gratitude*)
Anerkennung *f;* (*in value*) Wertzuwachs
m. **appreciative** *adj* anerkennend.
apprehend [apri'hend] *v* (*understand*)
begreifen; (*seize*) verhaften. **apprehensive**
adj angstvoll.
apprentice [ə'prentis] *n* Lehrling *m.*
apprenticeship *n* Lehre *f.*
approach [ə'proutʃ] *v* (*come near*) sich
nähern; (*a place*) nähern; (*someone*) sich
wenden an. *n* Herankommen *neut;* (*attitude*) Einstellung *f;* (*access*) Zugang *m.*
approachable *adj* zugänglich.
appropriate [ə'proupriət; *v* ə'prouprieit]
adj geeignet (+ *dat*). *v* sich aneignen.
approve [ə'pruːv] *v* (*agree*) zustimmen;
(*pass, endorse*) billigen, genehmigen.
approve of billigen. **approved** *adj*
bewährt. **approval** *n* Billigung *f,*
Genehmigung *f.* **on approval** auf Probe.
approximate [ə'proksimət] *adj* ungefähr.
approximately *adv* ungefähr, etwa.
apricot ['eiprikot] *n* Aprikose *f.*
April ['eiprəl] *n* April *m.*
apron ['eiprən] *n* Schürze *f.*
apt [apt] *adj* (*remark*) passend. **apt at geschickt in. be apt to do something** geneigt
sein, etwas zu tun. **aptitude** *n* (*gift*)
Begabung *f.*
aqualung ['akwəlʌŋ] *n* Unterwasser-
atmungsgerät *neut.*
aquarium [ə'kweəriəm] *n* Aquarium *neut.*
Aquarius [ə'kweəriəs] *n* Wassermann *m.*
aquatic [ə'kwatik] *n* Wasser-.
aqueduct ['akwidʌkt] *n* Aquädukt *m.*
Arab ['arəb] *n* Araber *m. adj or* **Arabian,**

Arabic arabisch. **Arabic** *n* arabische
Sprache *f.*
arable ['arəbl] *adj* **arable land** Ackerland
neut.
arbitrary ['aɪbitrəri] *adj* willkürlich.
arbitrate ['aɪbitreit] *v* entscheiden. **arbitration** *n* Schiedspruch *m.* **arbitrator** *n*
Schiedsrichter *m.*
arc [aɪk] *n* Bogen *m.*
arcade [aɪ'keid] *n* Arkade *f.*
arch [aɪtʃ] *n* (*architecture*) Bogen *m. v*
(sich) wölben. *adj* Erz-. **archway** *n*
Bogengang *m.*
archaeology [aɪki'olədʒi] *n* Archäologie *f.*
archaeological *adj* archäologisch. **archaeologist** *n* Archäologe *m.*
archaic [aɪ'keiik] *adj* altertümlich.
archbishop [aɪtʃ'biʃəp] *n* Erzbischof *m.*
archduke [aɪtʃ'djuɪk] *n* Erzherzog *m.*
archer ['aɪtʃə] *n* Bogenschütze *m.* **archery**
n Bogenschießen *neut.*
archetype ['aɪkitaip] *n* Vorbild *neut;*
(*psychol*) Archetyp *m.*
archipelago [aɪki'peləgou] *n* Archipel *m.*
architect ['aɪkitekt] *n* Architekt *m.* **architecture** *n* Architektur *f.*
archives ['aɪkaivz] *pl n* Archiv *neut sing.*
ardent ['aɪdənt] *adj* eifrig, begeistert.
ardour ['aɪdə] *n* Eifer *m.*
arduous ['aɪdjuəs] *adj* mühsam,
anstrengend.
are [aɪ] *V* be.
area ['eəriə] *n* (*measurement*) Fläche *f;*
(*region*) Gebiet *neut.* Zone *f.*
arena [ə'riːnə] *n* Arena *neut.*
argue ['aɪgjuː] *v* streiten; (*case*) diskutier-
en; (*maintain*) behaupten. **argument** *n*
Streit *m;* (*reasoning*) Argument *neut.*
argumentative *adj* streitlustig.
arid ['arid] *adj* trocken, dürr.
Aries ['eəriz] *n* Widder *m.*
***arise** [ə'raiz] *v* (*come into being*) ent-
stehen; (*get up*) aufstehen.
arisen [ə'rizn] *V* arise.
aristocracy [ari'stokrəsi] *n* Adel *m,* Aris-
tokratie *f.* **aristocrat** *n* Aristokrat *m.* **aristocratic** *adj* aristokratisch.
arithmetic [ə'riθmətik] *n* Arithmetik *f.*
arithmetical *adj* arithmetisch.
arm[1] [aɪm] *n* Arm *m.* (*of chair*)
Seitenlehne *f.* **arm in arm** Arm in Arm.
with open arms mit offenen Armen.
arm[2] [aɪm] *n* (*weapon*) Waffe *f. v*
bewaffnen. **arms race** Wettrüsten *neut.*

coat of arms Wappen *neut.* armed forces
Streitkräfte *pl.*

armament ['aɪməmənt] *n* Kriegsausrüstung *f.*

armchair ['aɪmtʃeə] *n* Sessel, Lehnstuhl *m.*

armistice ['aɪmistis] *n* Waffenstillstand *m.*

armour ['aɪmə] *n* (*suit of*) Rüstung *f;* (*of ship, tank*) Panzerung *f.* armoured *adj* gepanzert.

armpit ['aɪmpit] *n* Achselhöhle *f.*

army ['aɪmi] *n* Armee *f,* Heer *neut.* join the army zum Militär gehen.

aroma [ə'roumə] *n* Aroma *neut,* Duft *m.*

arose [ə'rouz] *V* arise.

around [ə'raund] *adv* ringsherum, rundherum; auf allen Seiten; (*nearby*) in der Nähe. *prep* um ... herum, rings um; (*approximately*) ungefähr. look around (for) sich umsehen (nach). turn around sich umdrehen.

arouse [ə'rauz] *v* wecken; (*suspicion*) erregen.

arrange [ə'reindʒ] *v* (*put in order*) anordnen; (*meeting*) verabreden; (*holidays*) festsetzen. (*see to it*) arrangieren, einrichten; (*music*) bearbeiten. arrangement *n* Anordnung *f;* (*agreement*) Vereinbarung *f;* (*music*) Bearbeitung *f.* make arrangements Vorbereitungen treffen.

array [ə'rei] *n* Aufstellung *f.*

arrears [ə'riəz] *pl n* Rückstände *pl.* in arrears im Rückstand *m*

arrest [ə'rest] *v* (*thief*) verhaften; (*halt*) anhalten; *n* Verhaftung *f.* under arrest in Haft, verhaftet. arresting *adj* fesselnd.

arrive [ə'raiv] *v* ankommen; (*fig*) gelangen. arrival *n* Ankunft *f.* late arrival Spätankömmling *m.*

arrogance ['arəgəns] *n* Hochmut *m.* arrogant *adj* hochmütig, eingebildet.

arrow ['arou] *n* Pfeil *m.*

arse [aɪs] *n* (*vulgar*) Arsch *m.*

arsenal ['aɪsənl] *n* Arsenal *neut.*

arsenic ['aɪsnik] *n* Arsenik *neut.*

arson ['aɪsn] *n* Brandstiftung *f.* arsonist *n* Brandstifter *m.*

art [aɪt] *n* Kunst *f.* arts *pl* Geisteswissenschaften *pl.* arts and crafts Kunstgewerbe *neut sing.* art gallery Kunstgalerie *f.* art school Kunstschule *f.* work of art Kunstwerk *neut.*

artefact ['aɪtifakt] *n* Artefakt *neut.*

artery ['aɪtəri] *n* Arterie *f.*

arthritis [aɪ'θraitis] *n* Arthritis *f.*

artichoke ['aɪtitʃouk] *n* Artischocke *f.*

article ['aɪtikl] *n* Artikel *m;* (*newspaper*) Zeitungsartikel *m,* Bericht *m.* article of clothing Bekleidungstück *neut.*

articulate [aɪ'tikjulət] *adj.* to be articulate sich gut ausdrücken.

articulated lorry [aɪtikjuleitid] *n* Sattelschlepper *m.*

artifice ['aɪtifis] *n* Trick *m.*

artificial [aɪti'fiʃəl] *adj* (*manmade*) künstlich, Kunst-; (*affected*) affektiert. artificial respiration künstliche Atmung *f.*

artillery [aɪ'tiləri] *n* Artillerie *f.*

artisan [aɪti'zan] *n* Handwerker *m.*

artist ['aɪtist] *n* Künstler *m;* (*painter*) Maler *m.* artiste *n* Artist(in). artistic *adj* künstlerisch.

as [az] *conj, prep* (*while*) als, während; (*in the way that*) wie, sowie; (*since*) da, weil; (*in role of*) als. as ... as (eben)so ... wie. as far as soweit. as if als ob. as long as solange. as soon as sobald. as it were sozusagen. as well auch.

asbestos [az'bestos] *n* Asbest *m.*

ascend [ə'send] *v* aufsteigen. ascendant *adj* vorherrschend. ascent *n* Aufstieg *m.* Ascension *n* Himmelfahrt *f.*

ascertain [asə'tein] *v* feststellen.

ascetic [ə'setik] *adj* askethisch. *n* Asket *m.*

ash[1] [aʃ] *n* (*cinder*) Asche *f.* ashtray *n* Aschenbecher *neut.*

ash[2] [aʃ] *n* (*tree*) Esche *f.*

ashamed [ə'feimd] *adj* be ashamed sich schämen.

ashore [ə'ʃɔɪ] *adv* am Ufer. go ashore an Land gehen.

Ash Wednesday *n* Aschermittwoch *m.*

Asia ['eiʃə] *n* Asien *neut.* Asian *n* Asiat *m; adj* asiatisch.

aside [ə'said] *adv* beiseite. aside from außer. step aside zur Seite treten. turn aside from sich wegwenden von.

ask [aɪsk] *v* (*to question*) fragen; (*request*) bitten. ask a question eine Frage stellen.

askew [ə'skjuɪ] *adv* verschoben, schief.

asleep [ə'sliɪp] *adj, adv* be asleep schlafen. fall asleep einschlafen.

asparagus [ə'sparəgəs] *n* Spargel *m.*

aspect ['aspekt] *n* (*appearance*) Aussehen *neut;* (*of a problem*) Aspekt *m.*

asphalt ['asfalt] *n* Asphalt *m.*

asphyxiate [əs'fiksieit] *v* ersticken. asphyxiation *n* Erstickung *f.*

aspic ['aspik] n Aspik m.
aspire [ə'spaiə] v **aspire to** streben nach.
aspiring adj hochstrebend.
aspirin ['aspərin] n Aspirin neut.
ass [as] n Esel m.
assail [ə'seil] v angreifen. **assailant** n Angreifer m.
assassin [ə'sasin] n Attentäter m, Mörder m. **assassinate** v ermorden. **assassination** n Ermordung f.
assault [ə'soɪlt] v angreifen, überfallen.. n Angriff m. **indecent assault** Sittlichkeitsverbrechen neut.
assemble [ə'sembl] v (congregate) sich versammeln; (put together) montieren, zusammenbauen; (bring together) versammeln. **assembly** n (people) Versammlung f; (tech) Montage f. **assembly hall** Aula f. **assembly line** Fließband.
assent [ə'sent] v zustimmen (+ dat). n Zustimmung f.
assert [ə'soɪt] v (insist on) bestehen auf; (declare) erklären. **assertion** n Behauptung f. **(self-)assertive** adj selbstsicher.
assess [ə'ses] v (for tax) bewerten; (estimate) schätzen. **assessment** n Bewertung f.
asset ['aset] n Vorteil m. **assets** pl Vermögen neut sing.
assiduous [ə'sidjuəs] adj fleißig.
assign [ə'sain] v zuteilen, bestimmen. **assignment** n Aufgabe f.
assimilate [ə'simileit] v aufnehmen. **assimilation** n Aufnahme f.
assist [ə'sist] v helfen (+ dat). **assistance** n Hilfe f. **assistant** n Helfer m. **sales assistant** n Verkäufer m.
associate [ə'sousieit; n ə'sousiət] v verbinden. n Kollege m, Mitarbeiter m; (comm) Partner m. **association** n (club) Verein m, Verband m; (link) Verbindung f.
assorted [ə'soɪtid] adj verschiedenartig,. gemischt. **assortment** n Sortiment neut.
assume [ə'sjuɪm] v (suppose) annehmen; (take over) übernehmen.
assure [ə'ʃuə] v (convince) versichern (+ dat), versprechen; (ensure) sicherstellen. **assurance** n (assertion) Versicherung f; (confidence) Selbstsicherheit f. **life assurance** Lebensversicherung f.
asterisk ['astərisk] n Sternchen neut.
asthma ['asmə] n Asthma neut.
astonish [ə'stoniʃ] v erstaunen, verblüffen.

be astonished (at) erstaunt sein (über), sich wundern (über). **astonishing** adj erstaunlich. **astonishment** n Erstaunen neut.
astound [ə'staund] v bestürzen, erstaunen.
astray [ə'strei] adv **go astray** in die Irre gehen. **lead astray** vom rechten Weg abführen.
astride [ə'straid] adv rittlings. prep rittlings auf (+ dat).
astringent [ə'strindʒənt] adj zusammenziehend.
astrology [ə'strolədʒi] n Astrologie f. **astrologer** n Astrologe m. **astrological** adj astrologisch.
astronaut ['astrənoɪt] n Astronaut m.
astronomy [ə'stronəmi] n Astronomie f. **astronomer** n Astronom m. **astronomical** adj astronomisch.
astute [ə'stjuɪt] adj scharfsinnig.
asunder [ə'sʌndə] adv auseinander.
asylum [ə'sailəm] n Asyl neut. **lunatic asylum** Irrenanstalt f. **political asylum** politisches Asyl neut.
at [at] prep (place) in, zu, bei, an, auf; (time) um, zu, in; (age, speed) mit; (price) zu. **at school** in der Schule. **at four o'clock** um vier Uhr. **at my house** bei mir. **at home** zuhause. **at (age) 65** mit 65. **at Christmas** zu Weihnachten. **at peace** in Frieden.
ate [et] V eat.
atheist ['eiθiist] n Atheist m.
Athens ['aθinz] n Athen neut.
athlete ['aθliɪt] n Athlet m. **athletic** adj athletisch. **athletics** n (Leicht)Athletik f.
Atlantic [ət'lantik] n Atlantik m.
atlas ['atləs] n Atlas m.
atmosphere ['atməsfiə] n Atmosphäre f. **atmospheric** adj atmosphärisch, Luft-.
atom ['atəm] n Atom neut. **atomic** adj Atom-. **atomic bomb** Atombombe f. **atomic power** Atomkraft f. **atomic reactor** Atomreaktor m.
atone [ə'toun] v **atone for** büßen, wiedergutmachen. **atonement** n Buße f.
atrocious [ə'trouʃəs] adj grausam, brutal; (coll) scheußlich. **atrocity** n Greueltat f.
attach [ə'tatʃ] v (affix) befestigen, anhängen; (connect) anschließen; (to a letter) beifügen. **be attached to** mögen, lieb haben. **attach oneself to** sich anschließen an. **attachment** n (liking) Anhänglichkeit f; (fixture) Anschluß m.

attaché [ə'taʃei] n Attaché. **attaché case** Aktentasche f.

attack [ə'tak] v angreifen; (criticize) tadeln, kritisieren. n Angriff m. **heart attack** Herzanfall m.

attain [ə'tein] v erreichen, gelangen zu. **attainable** adj erreichbar.

attempt [ə'tempt] v versuchen, wagen. n Versuch m.

attend [ə'tend] v (school) besuchen; (meeting) beiwohnen (+dat); (lecture) hören. **attend to** sich kümmern um. **attendance** n Anwesenheit f. **good attendance** gute Teilnahme f. **attendant** n Wächter(in).

attention [ə'tenʃən] n Aufmerksamkeit f; (care) Pflege f; (machine) Wartung f. **pay attention to** aufpassen auf. **stand at attention** Haltung annehmen.

attic ['atik] n Dachkammer f.

attire [ə'taiə] n Kleidung f. v kleiden.

attitude ['atitjuid] n Einstellung f, Verhalten neut.

attorney [ə'təini] n (lawyer) Rechtsanwalt m. **power of attorney** Vollmacht f.

attract [ə'trakt] v anziehen; (attention) erregen. **attraction** n Anziehung f; (charm) Reiz m, Anziehungskraft f. **attractive** adj attraktiv.

attribute [ə'tribjuit; n 'atribjuit] v zuschreiben (+dat). n Eigenschaft f. **attributable** adj zuzuschreiben (+dat).

attrition [ə'triʃən] n Abnutzung f. **war of attrition** Zermürbungskrieg m.

aubergine ['ouhəʒiin] n Aubergine f.

auburn ['oibən] adj kastanienbraun.

auction ['oikʃən] n Auktion f, Versteigerung f. v versteigern. **auctioneer** n Versteigerer m.

audacious [oi'deiʃəs] adj kühn. **audacity** n (boldness) Wagemut m; (cheek) Frechheit f.

audible ['oidəbl] adj hörbar.

audience ['oidjəns] n (people) Publikum neut, Zuhörer pl; (interview) Audienz f.

audiovisual [oidiou'viʒuəl] adj audiovisuell.

audit ['oidit] v (Rechnungen) prüfen. n Rechnungsprüfung f. **auditor** n Rechnungsprüfer m.

audition [oi'diʃən] n (theatre) Sprech-, Hörprobe f. v eine Hörprobe abnehmen.

auditorium [oidi'toiriəm] n Hörsaal m

augment [oig'ment] v vermehren; (grow) zunehmen.

August ['oigəst] n August m.

aunt [aint] n Tante f.

au pair [ou 'peə] n Au-pair-Mädchen neut.

aura ['oirə] n Aura f; (med) Vorgefühl neut.

auspicious [oi'spiʃəs] adj günstig.

austere [oi'stiə] adj (person) streng; (surroundings) nüchtern. **austerity** n Strenge f.

Australia [o'streiljə] n Australien neut. **Australian** n Australier(in); adj australisch.

Austria ['ostriə] n Österreich neut. **Austrian** n Österreicher(in); adj österreichisch.

authentic [oi'θentik] adj echt, authentisch. **authenticity** n Echtheit f.

author ['oiθə] n (writer) Schriftsteller m, Autor m; (of a particular item) Verfasser m.

authority [oi'θorəti] n Autorität f; (expert) Fachmann m. **on good authority** aus guter Quelle. **the authorities** die Behörden pl. **authoritarian** adj autoritär.

authorize ['oiθəraiz] v genehmigen, bevollmächtigen. **authorization** n Genehmigung f.

autobiography [oitoubai'ogrəfi] n Autobiographie f.

autocratic [oitou'kratik] adj autokratisch.

autograph ['oitəgraif] n Autogramm neut. v unterschreiben.

automatic [oitə'matik] adj automatisch, selbsttätig. **automatic transmission** Automatik f.

automobile ['oitəməbiil] n Wagen m, Auto neut.

autonomous [oi'tonəmos] adj autonom, unabhängig. **autonomy** n Autonomie f.

autopsy ['otopsi] n Autopsie f.

autumn ['oitəm] n Herbst m. **autumnal** adj herbstlich, Herbst-.

auxiliary [oig'ziljəri] adj Hilfs-, Zusatz-, zusätzlich. n Hilfskraft f.

avail [ə'veil] n **to no avail** nutzlos. v **avail oneself of** Gebrauch machen von, sich bedienen (+gen).

available [ə'veiləbl] adj (obtainable) erhältlich; (usable) verfügbar. **be available** zur Verfügung stehen. **availability** n Erhältlichkeit f.

avalanche ['avəlainʃ] n Lawine f.

avant-garde [avã'gaid] adj avantgardistisch. n Avantgarde f.

avarice ['avəris] n Geiz m. avaricious adj geizig.

avenge [ə'vendʒ] v rächen. avenge oneself on sich rächen an.

avenue ['avinjuː] n Allee f.

average ['avəridʒ] n Durchschnitt m. adj durchschnittlich, Durchschnitts-. on average im Durchschnitt.

averse [ə'vəːs] adj abgeneigt. aversion n Abneigung f.

avert [ə'vəːt] v (gaze) abwenden; (danger) verhindern.

aviary ['eiviəri] n Vogelhaus neut.

aviation [eivi'eiʃən] n Luftfahrt f. aviator n Flieger m.

avid ['avid] adj gierig (auf). avidity n Begierde f.

avocado [avə'kaːdou] n Avocado(birne) f.

avoid [ə'void] v vermeiden; (person) aus dem Wege gehen (+ dat). avoidable adj vermeidbar.

await [ə'weit] v erwarten.

*awake [ə'weik] v (wake up) aufwachen; (rouse) wecken; (arouse) erwecken. be awake wach sein. wide awake munter. awaken v erwecken.

award [ə'woːd] v verleihen. n Preis m.

aware [ə'weə] adj bewußt (+ gen). awareness n Bewußtsein neut.

away [ə'wei] adv weg, fort. adj (absent) abwesend. she is away sie ist verreist.

awe [oː] n Ehrfurcht f. awesome adj (impressive) imponierend; (frightening) erschreckend.

awful ['oːful] adj furchtbar.

awhile [ə'wail] adv eine Weile, eine Zeitlang.

awkward ['oːkwəd] adj (clumsy) ungeschickt, linkisch; (embarrassing) peinlich; (contrary) widerspenstig.

awning ['oːniŋ] n Markise f.

awoke [ə'wouk] V awake.

awoken [ə'woukn] V awake.

axe or US ax [aks] n Axt f.

axiom ['aksiəm] n Axiom neut.

axis ['aksis] n Achse f.

axle ['aksl] n Achse f.

B

babble ['babl] v plappern; (water) plätschern.

baboon [bə'buːn] n Pavian m.

baby ['beibi] n Baby neut, Säugling m. baby carriage Kinderwagen m. babyish adj kindisch. babysit v babysitten. babysitter n Babysitter m.

bachelor ['batʃələ] n Junggeselle m.

back [bak] n (anat) Rücken m; (rear) Rückseite f; (football) Verteidiger m. adj hinter, Hinter-. adv zurück. v (bet on) wetten auf; (support) unterstützen; (reverse) rückwärts fahren. back out v sich zurückziehen.

backache ['bakeik] n Rückenschmerz m.

backbone ['bakboun] n Rückgrat neut, Wirbelsäule f.

backdate [ˌbak'deit] v zurückdatieren.

backer ['bakə] n Förderer m.

backfire [ˌbak'faiə] v (car) fehlzünden; (plan) fehlschlagen.

background ['bakgraund] n Hintergrund m.

backhand ['bakhand] n (sport) Rückhandschlag m.

backlash ['baklaʃ] n (politische) Reaktion f.

backlog ['baklog] n Rückstand m.

backside ['baksaid] n Hinterteil neut, Hintern m.

backstage ['baksteidʒ] adj, adv hinter den Kulissen.

backstroke ['bakstrouk] n Rückenschwimmen neut.

backward ['bakwəd] adj zurückgeblieben.

backwards ['bakwədz] adv zurück, rückwärts.

backwater ['bakwoːtə] n Stauwasser neut.

backyard [bak'jaːd] n Hinterhof m.

bacon ['beikən] n (Schinken)Speck m.

bacteria [bak'tiəriə] pl n Bakterien pl.

bad [bad] adj schlecht, schlimm; (naughty) böse; (food) faul, verfault. bad-tempered mißgelaunt.

bade [bad] V bid.

badge [badʒ] n Abzeichen neut.

badger ['badʒə] n Dachs m. v plagen.

badminton ['badmintən] n Federballspiel neut.

baffle ['bafl] v verblüffen.

bag [bag] n Beutel m, Sack m; (paper) Tüte f; (handbag) Tasche f. baggage n Gepäck neut. baggy adj bauschig. bagpipes pl n Dudelsack m sing.

bail¹ [beil] *n* (*security*) Kaution *f*. *v* gegen Kaution freilassen.

bail² *or* **bale** [bail] *v* **bail out** (*boat*) ausschöpfen; (*from aeroplane*) abspringen; (*help*) aushelfen.

bailiff ['beilif] *n* Gerichtsvollzieher *m*.

bait [beit] *n* Köder *m*. *v* ködern; (*tease*) quälen.

bake [beik] *v* backen. **baker** *n* Bäcker *m*. **bakery** Bäckerei *f*.

balance ['baləns] *n* Gleichgewicht *neut*; (*scales*) Waage *f*; (*of account*) Saldo *m*; (*amount left*) Rest *m*. *v* ausgleichen. **balance sheet** Bilanz *f*.

balcony ['balkəni] *n* Balkon *m*.

bald [boild] *adj* kahl.

bale¹ [beil] *n* Ballen *m*.

bale² [beil] *V* **bail²**.

ball¹ [boil] *n* (*sport*) Ball *m*; (*sphere*) Kugel *f*.

ball² [boil] *n* (*dance*) Ball *m*.

ballad ['baləd] *n* Ballade *f*.

ballast ['baləst] *n* Ballast *neut*.

ball bearing *n* Kugellager *neut*.

ballet ['balei] *n* Ballett *neut*. **ballet dancer** Ballettänzer(in).

ballistic [bə'listik] *adj* ballistisch.

balloon [bə'luːn] *n* Ballon *m*; (*toy*) Luftballon *m*.

ballot ['balət] *n* Abstimmung *f*.

ball-point pen *n* Kugelschreiber *m*.

ballroom ['boilrum] *n* Tanzsaal *m*.

balmy ['baimi] *adj* sanft, lindernd.

bamboo [bam'buː] *n* Bambus *m*.

ban [ban] *v* verbieten. *n* Verbot *neut*.

banal [bə'naːl] *adj* banal.

banana [bə'naːnə] *n* Banane *f*.

band¹ [band] *n* Gruppe *f*; (*music*) Band *f*, Kapelle *f*; (*criminals*) Bande *f*. *v* **band together** sich vereinen.

band² [band] *n* (*strip*) Band *neut*, Binde *f*.

bandage ['bandidʒ] *n* Bandage *f*, Binde *f*. *v* bandagieren.

bandit ['bandit] *n* Bandit *m*.

bandy ['bandi] *adj* krummbeinig. *v* **bandy words** streiten.

bang [baŋ] *n* Knall *m*. *v* (*sound*) knallen; (*strike*) schlagen; (*door*) zuknallen.

bangle ['baŋgl] *n* (Arm)Spange *f*.

banish ['baniʃ] *v* verbannen.

banister ['banistə] *n* Treppengeländer *neut*.

banjo ['bandʒou] *n* Banjo *neut*.

bank¹ [baŋk] *n* (*river*) Ufer *neut*; (*sand*) Bank *f*.

bank² [baŋk] *n* (*comm*) Bank *f*. *v* (*money*) auf die Bank bringen. **bank on** sich verlassen auf. **bank account** *n* Bankkonto *neut*. **banker** *n* Bankier *m*. **banker's card** Scheckkarte *f*. **bank holiday** *n* Feiertag *m*. **banknote** *n* Banknote *f*.

bankrupt ['baŋkrʌpt] *adj* bankrott. *n* Bankrotteur *m*. **go bankrupt** Bankrott machen. **bankruptcy** Bankrott *m*.

banner ['banə] *n* Banner *neut*.

banquet ['baŋkwit] *n* Bankett *neut*.

banter ['bantə] *v* necken. *n* Neckerei *f*.

baptism ['baptizəm] *n* Taufe *f*. **baptize** *v* taufen.

bar [baɪ] *n* (*drink*) Bar *f*; (*rod*) Stange *f*, Barre *f*; (*chocolate*) Tafel *f*. *v* (*door*) verriegeln; (*ban*) verbieten.

barbarian [baɪ'beəriən] *n* Barbar *m*. **barbaric** *adj* barbarisch.

barbecue ['baɪbikjuɪ] *n* Barbecue *neut*. *v* am Spieß braten.

barbed wire [baɪbd] *n* Stacheldraht *m*.

barber ['baɪbə] *n* Barbier *m*, Friseur *m*.

barbiturate [baɪ'bitjurət] *n* Barbitursäure *f*.

bare [beə] *adj* nackt; (*trees*) kahl; (*empty*) leer; (*mere*) bloß. *v* entblößen. **barefoot** *adj* harfuß. **bare-headed** *adj* mit bloßem Kopf. **barely** *adv* kaum.

bargain ['baɪgin] *n* (*good buy*) Gelegenheitskauf *m*. (*deal*) Geschäft *neut*. *v* feilschen. **collective bargaining** *pl*. **into the bargain** obendrein.

barge [baɪdʒ] *n* Lastkahn *m*. *v* **barge in** hereinstürzen.

baritone ['baritoun] *n* Bariton *m*.

bark¹ [baɪk] *v* (*dog*) bellen. *n* Bellen *neut*.

bark² [baɪk] *n* (*tree*) Rinde *f*.

barley ['baɪli] *n* (*crop*) Gerste *f*; (*in soup*) Graupen *pl*.

barmaid ['baɪmeid] *n* Barmädchen *neut*.

barman ['baɪman] *n* Barmann *m*.

barn [baɪn] *n* Scheune *f*.

barometer [bə'romitə] *n* Barometer *neut*.

baron ['barən] *n* Baron *m*.

baronet ['barənit] *n* Baronet *m*.

baroque [bə'rok] *adj* barock.

barracks ['barəks] *n* Kaserne *f*.

barrage ['baraɪʒ] *n* (*dam*) Damm *m*; (*mil*) Sperrfeuer *neut*; (*of questions*) Flut *f*.

barrel ['barəl] *n* Faß *neut*.

barren ['barən] *adj* unfruchtbar; (*desolate*) wüst.

barricade [bari'keid] *n* Barrikade *f. v* verbarrikadieren.
barrier ['bariə] *n* Schranke *f.*
barrister ['baristə] *n* Rechtsanwalt *m.*
barrow ['barou] *n* Schubkarren *m.*
bartender ['baitendə] *n* Barmann *m.*
barter ['baitə] *n* Tauschhandel *m. v* tauschen; (*haggle*) feilschen.
base¹ [beis] *n* (*bottom*) Fuß *m,* Boden *m;* (*basis*) Basis *f;* (*mil*) Stützpunkt *m;* (*chem*) Base *f. v* gründen. **be based on** basieren auf (+*dat*).
base² [beis] *adj* (*vile*) gemein.
baseball ['beisboil] *n* Baseball *m.*
basement ['beismənt] *n* Kellergeschoß *neut.*
bash [baʃ] *v* (heftig) schlagen. **have a bash!** versuch's mal!
bashful ['baʃful] *adj* schüchtern.
basic ['beisik] *adj* grundsätzlich, Grund-. **basically** *adv* im Grunde.
basil ['bazl] *n* Basilienkraut *neut.*
basin ['beisin] *n* (*washbasin, river basin*) Becken *neut;* (*dish*) Schale *f.*
basis ['beisis] *n* Basis *f,* Grundlage *f.*
bask [bask] *v* sich sonnen.
basket ['baiskit] *n* Korb *m.* **basketball** *n* Basketball *m.*
bass¹ [beis] *n* (*music*) Baß *m.* **bass guitar** Baßgitarre *f.* **double bass** Kontrabaß *m.*
bass² [bas] *n* Seebarsch *m.*
bassoon [bə'suin] *n* Fagott *neut.*
bastard ['baistəd] *n* Bastard *m;* (*derog*) Schweinehund *m.*
baste [beist] *v* (*meat*) mit Fett begießen.
bastion ['bastjən] *n* Bollwerk *neut.*
bat¹ [bat] *n* (*sport*) Schlagholz *neut. v* **without batting an eyelid** ohne mit der Wimper zu zucken.
bat² [bat] *n* (*zool*) Fledermaus *f.*
batch [batʃ] *n* Stoß *m.*
bath [baiθ] *n* Bad *neut. v* baden. **have or take a bath** ein Bad nehmen. **bathroom** *n* Badezimmer *neut.* **bathtub** *n* Badewanne *f.* **baths** *pl n* Schwimmbad *neut sing.*
baton ['batn] *n* (*music*) Taktstock *m.*
battalion [bə'taljən] *n* Bataillon *neut.*
batter¹ ['batə] *v* (*strike*) verprügeln.
batter² ['batə] *n* (*cookery*) Schlagteig *m.*
battery ['batəri] *n* Batterie *f.*
battle ['batl] *n* Schlacht *f;* (*fig*) Kampf *m. v* kämpfen. **battlefield** *n* Schlachtfeld *neut.* **battleship** Schlachtschiff *neut.*
bawl [boil] *v* brüllen, heulen.
bay¹ [bei] *n* (*coast*) Bai *f,* Bucht *f.*

bay² [bei] *n* **keep at bay** abwehren.
bay³ [bei] *n* (*tree*) Lorbeer *m.* **bay leaf** Lorbeerblatt *neut.*
bayonet ['beiənit] *n* Bajonett *neut. v* bajonettieren.
bay window *n* Erkerfenster *neut.*
bazaar [bə'zai] *n* Basar *m.*
*be** [bii] *v* sein; (*be situated*) liegen, stehen. *v aux* (*in passive*) werden. **There is/are** es gibt. *the book is on the table* das Buch liegt auf dem Tisch. *I want to be an engineer* ich will Ingenieur werden. *how much is that car?* wieviel kostet der Wagen
beach [biitʃ] *n* Strand *m. v* (*boat*) auf den Strand setzen.
beacon ['biikən] *n* Leuchtfeuer *neut.*
bead [biid] *n* Perle *f.*
beak [biik] *n* Schnabel *m.*
beaker ['biikə] *n* Becher *m.*
beam [biim] *n* (*wood*) Balken *m;* (*light*) Strahl *m. v* strahlen.
bean [biin] *n* Bohne *f.*
*bear¹** [beə] *v* (*carry, yield*) tragen, (*tolerate*) ertragen, leiden; (*child*) gebären. **bring pressure to bear on** Druck ausüben auf. **bear right** sich nach rechts halten.
bear² [beə] *n* (*zool*) Bär *m.*
beard [biəd] *n* Bart *m.*
bearing ['beəriŋ] *n* (*posture*) Haltung *f;* (*relation*) Beziehung *f;* (*tech*) Lager *neut.* **bearings** *pl n* Orientierung *f sing.*
beast [biist] *n* Tier *neut;* (*cattle*) Vieh *neut;* (*person*) Bestie *f.* **beastly** *adj* (*coll*) scheußlich.
*beat** [biit] *v* schlagen. *n* (*stroke*) Schlag *m;* (*music*) Rhythmus *m;* (*policeman's*) Revier *neut.*
beaten ['biitn] *V* beat.
beautiful ['bjuitəful] *adj* schön. **beautifully** *adv* ausgezeichnet. **beauty** *n* Schönheit *f.*
beaver ['biivə] *n* Biber *m.*
became [bi'keim] *V* become.
because [bi'koz] *conj* weil. **because of** wegen (+*gen*).
*become** [bi'kʌm] *v* werden. **becoming** *adj* passend.
bed [bed] *v* Bett *neut;* (*garden*) Beet *neut.* **river bed** Flußbett *neut.* **seabed** *n* Meeresboden *m.* **bedclothes** *pl n* Bettwäsche *f sing.* **bedridden** *adj* bettlägerig. **bedroom** *n* Schlafzimmer *neut.* **bedsitter** *n* Einzimmerwohnung *f.* **bedspread** *n* Bettdecke *f.* **bedtime** *n* Schlafenzeit *f.*

bee [biː] n Biene f.
beech [biːtʃ] n Buche f.
beef [biːf] n Rindfleisch neut.
beehive ['biːhaiv] n Bienenstock m.
been [biːn] V be.
beer [biə] n Bier neut.
beetle ['biːtl] n Käfer m.
beetroot ['biːtruːt] n. rote Bete f.
before [bi'foː] conj bevor, ehe; prep vor;
adv (time) zuvor, früher; (ahead) voran.
beforehand adv im voraus.
befriend [bi'frend] v befreunden.
beg [beg] v (for money) betteln; (beseech)
bitten. beggar n Bettler m.
began [bi'gan] V begin.
*begin [bi'gin] v beginnen, anfangen.
beginner n Anfänger m. beginning n
Anfang m, Beginn m.
begrudge [bi'grʌdʒ] v mißgönnen.
begun [bi'gʌn] V begin.
behalf [bi'haːf] n on behalf of im Namen
von. on my behalf um meinetwillen.
behave [bi'heiv] v sich verhalten, sich
betragen; (behave well) sich gut
benehmen. behave yourself! benimm
dich! behaviour n Benehmen neut,
Verhalten neut.
behind [hi'haind] prep hinter. adv (in the
rear) hinten; (back) zurück; (behind
schedule) im Rückstand. n (coll)
Hinterteil neut. behindhand adv im
Rückstand.
*behold [bi'hould] v sehen, betrachten.
beholder m Betrachter m.
beige [beiʒ] adj beige.
being ['biːiŋ] n (existence) (Da)Sein neut;
(creature) Wesen neut, Geschöpf neut.
for the time being einstweilen. come into
being entstehen. human being Mensch m.
belated [bi'leitid] adj verspätet.
belch [beltʃ] v rülpsen; (fumes) ausspeien.
n Rülpsen neut.
belfry ['belfri] n Glockenturm m.
Belgium ['beldʒəm] n Belgien neut. Belgian n Belgier(in). adj belgisch.
belief [bi'liːf] n Glaube m; (conviction)
Überzeugung f. believe v glauben
(+ dat). believe in glauben an (+ acc).
believable adj glaublich. believer n
Gläubige(r).
bell [bel] n Glocke f; (on door) Klingel m.
belligerent [bi'lidʒərənt] adj (country)
kriegführend; (person) aggressiv.
bellow ['belou] v brüllen. n Gebrüll neut.

bellows ['belouz] n Blasebalg m.
belly ['beli] n Bauch m.
belong [bi'loŋ] v gehören (+ dat); (be a
member) angehören (+ dat). belongings
pl n Eigentum neut sing; Sachen pl.
beloved [bi'lʌvid] adj geliebt. n
Geliebte(r).
below [bi'lou] prep unter. adv unten.
belt [belt] n Gürtel m. v (coll) verprügeln.
belt up! halt die Klappe!
bemused [bi'mjuːzd] adj verwirrt.
bench [bentʃ] n Bank f; (work table)
Arbeitstisch m.
*bend [bend] v biegen; (be bent) sich
beugen. n Kurve f.
beneath [bi'niːθ] prep unter.
benefactor ['benəfaktə] n Wohltäter m.
benefactress n Wohltäterin f.
beneficent [bi'nefisənt] adj wohltätig.
beneficial [benə'fiʃəl] adj vorteilhaft, nützlich.
benefit ['benəfit] n Nutzen m, Gewinn m.
v nützen. benefit from Nutzen ziehen
aus.
benevolence [bi'nevələns] n Wohltätigkeit f. benevolent adj wohltätig.
benign [bi'nain] adj gütig; (tumour) gutartig.
bent [bent] V bend. adj krumm,
verbogen; (dishonest) unehrlich. be bent
on versessen sein auf (+ acc).
bequeath [bi'kwiːð] v vermachen.
beret ['berei] n Baskenmütze f.
berry ['beri] n Beere f.
berserk [bə'səːk] adj go berserk wild werden, toben.
berth [bəːθ] n (mooring) Liegeplatz m;
(bunk) Koje f. give a wide berth to einen
weiten Bogen machen um (+ acc).
beside [bi'said] prep neben. be beside
oneself with außer sich sein vor (+ dat).
besides prep außer. adv außerdem.
besiege [bi'siːdʒ] v belagern.
best [best] adj best. adv am besten,
bestens. n das Beste. do one's best sein
Bestes tun. at best höchstens. best man
Trauzeuge m.
bestial ['bestjəl] adj bestialisch.
bestow [bi'stou] v bestow upon schenken
(+ dat).
bestseller [best'selə] n Bestseller m.
bet [bet] v wetten. n Wette f.
betray [bi'trei] v verraten. betrayal n Verrat m.

better ['betə] adj, adv besser. n das Bessere. v verbessern. **get the better of** übertreffen. **better oneself** sich verbessern.
between [bi'twiin] prep zwischen. adv dazwischen. **between you and me** unter uns.
beverage ['bevəridʒ] n Getränk neut.
*__beware__ [bi'weə] v sich hüten vor (+ dat). **beware of the dog** Vorsicht
Vorsicht–bissiger Hund!
bewilder [bi'wildə] v verwirren, verblüffen.
beyond [bi'jond] prep uber ... hinaus, jenseits (+ gen); mehr als. adv jenseits, darüber hinaus. **beyond compare** unvergleichlich. **he is beyond help** ihm ist nicht mehr zu helfen.
bias ['baiəs] n Neigung f. **biased** adj voreingenommen.
bib [bib] n Latz m.
Bible ['baibl] n Bibel f.
bibliography [bibli'ogrəfi] n Bibliographie f.
biceps ['baiseps] n Bizeps m.
bicker ['bikə] v zanken.
bicycle ['baisikl] n Fahrrad neut.
*__bid__ [bid] v (offer) bieten; (cards) reizen. n (offer) Angebot neut; (attempt) Versuch m. **bid someone welcome** jemanden willkommen heißen. **bidder** n Bieter m.
bidden ['bidn] V bid.
bidet ['biidei] n Bidet neut.
biennial [bai'eniəl] adj zweijährig.
big [big] adj groß. **big-headed** adj eingebildet. **big-hearted** adj großherzig.
bigamy ['bigəmi] n Bigamie f.
bigot ['bigət] n Frömmler m. **bigotted** adj bigott. **bigotry** n Bigotterie f.
bikini [bi'kiini] n Bikini m.
bilateral [bai'latərəl] adj bilateral.
bilingual [bai'liŋgwəl] adj zweisprachig.
bill¹ [bil] n (in restaurant) Rechnung f; Banknote f; (comm) Wechsel m; (pol) Gesetzentwurf m; (poster) Plakat neut. v fakturieren. **billboard** n Plakattafel f.
bill² [bil] n (beak) Schnabel m.
billiards ['biljədz] n Billard neut.
billion ['biljən] n Billion f; (US) Milliarde f.
bin [bin] n Kiste f; (dustbin) Mülleimer m.
binary ['bainəri] adj binär.
*__bind__ [baind] v (tie) binden; (oblige)

verpflichten. **binding** adj bindend. n (book) Einband m.
binoculars [bi'nokjuləz] pl n Feldstecher m.
biography [bai'ogrəfi] n Biographie f. **biographer** n Biograph m. **biographical** adj biographisch.
biology [bai'olədʒi] n Biologie f. **biological** adj biologisch. **biologist** n Biologe m.
birch [bəitʃ] n Birke f; (rod) Birkenrute f.
bird [bəid] n Vogel m.
birth [bəiθ] n Geburt f. **date of birth** Geburtsdatum neut. **birth certificate** Geburtsurkunde f. **birth control** Geburtenregelung f. **birthday** Geburtstag m. **birthmark** Muttermal neut.
biscuit ['biskit] n Biskuit m, Keks m.
bisexual [bai'sekʃuəl] adj bisexuell.
bishop ['biʃəp] n Bischof m.
bison ['baisən] n Bison m.
bit¹ [bit] V bite. n (morsel) Bißchen, Stückchen neut: **a bit of bread** ein Stückchen Brot. **a bit frightened** ein bißchen ängstlich.
bit² [bit] n (harness) Gebiß neut; (drill) Bohreisen neut.
bitch [bitʃ] n Hündin f; (woman) Weibsstück neut.
*__bite__ [bait] v beißen. n (mouthful) Bissen m; (wound) Biß m. **bite to eat** Imbiß m.
bitten ['bitn] V bite.
bitter ['bitə] v bitter; (weather) scharf. **to the bitter end** bis zum bitteren Ende. **bitterness** n Bitterkeit f.
bizarre [bi'zai] adj bizarr, seltsam.
black ['blak] adj schwarz. n (colour) Schwarz neut; (person) Schwarze(r).
blackberry ['blakbəri] n Brombeere f.
blackbird ['blakbəid] n Amsel f.
blackboard ['blakbəid] n Wandtafel f.
blackcurrant [,blak'kʌrənt] n schwarze Johannisbeere f.
blacken ['blakn] v schwarz machen.
black eye n blaues Auge neut.
blackhead ['blakhed] n Mitesser m.
blackleg ['blakleg] n Streikbrecher m.
blackmail ['blakmeil] n Erpressung f. **blackmailer** n Erpresser m.
black market n schwarzer Markt m. **black marketeer** Schwarzhändler m.
black out v (darken) verdunkeln; (faint) ohnmächtig werden. **black-out** n Verdunkelung f; Ohnmachtsanfall m; (elec) Stromausfall m.

black pudding n Blutwurst f.
blacksmith ['blaksmiθ] n Schmied m.
bladder ['bladə] n Blase f.
blade [bleid] n (razor, knife) Klinge f;
(grass) Halm m; (tech) Blatt neut;
(propellor) Flügel m.
blame [bleim] v tadeln, die Schuld geben
(+ dat). n Schuld f, Tadel m. I am to
blame for this ich bin daran schuld.
blameless adj untadelig.
blancmange [bləˈmonʒ] n Pudding m.
bland [bland] adj sanft, mild.
blank [blaŋk] adj leer, unausgefüllt. n
(form) Formular neut; (cartridge)
Platzpatrone f. **blank cheque** Blankoscheck m.
blanket ['blaŋkit] n Decke f. adj Gesamt-,
allgemein.
blare [bleə] v schmettern. n Schmettern
neut.
blaspheme [blasˈfiːm] v lästern. **blasphemy**
n Gotteslästerung f.
blast [blaɪst] n Explosion f; (of wind)
(heftiger) Windstoß m. v sprengen.
blatant ['bleitənt] adj offenkundig.
blaze [bleiz] n Brand m, Feuer neut. v
lodern.
blazer ['bleizə] n Blazer m.
bleach [bliːtʃ] v bleichen. n Bleichmittel
neut.
bleak [bliːk] adj kahl; (fig) trostlos.
bleat [bliːt] v (sheep) blöken; (goat) meckern. n Blöken neut, Meckern neut.
bled [bled] V **bleed.**
*****bleed** [bliːd] v bluten; (brakes, radiators)
entlüften. **bleeding** adj blutend.
blemish ['blemiʃ] n Makel m.
blend [blend] v mischen. n Mischung f.
bless [bles] v segnen. **blessing** n Segen m.
blew [bluː] V **blow**[1].
blind [blaind] adj blind; (corner) unüber-
sichtlich. n (window) Rouleau neut. v
blenden; (fig) verblenden. **blind alley**
Sackgasse f. **blindfold** v die Augen
verbinden (+ dat). adv mit verbundenen
Augen.
blink [bliŋk] v blinzeln.
bliss [blis] n Wonne f. **blissful** glückselig.
blister ['blistə] n Blase f.
blizzard ['blizəd] n Schneesturm m.
blob [blob] n Tropfen m.
bloc [blok] n Block m.
block [blok] n (wood) Klotz m; (stone)
Block m; (US) Häuserblock m; (in pipe)
Verstopfung f; (barrier) Sperre f. v

blockieren; verstopfen. **writing block**
Schreibblock m. **blockade** n Blockade f.
blockage n Verstopfung f.
bloke [blouk] n Kerl m.
blond [blond] adj blond. **blonde** n
Blondine f.
blood [blʌd] n Blut neut. **in cold blood**
kaltblütig. **blood clot** Blutgerinnsel neut.
blood pressure Blutdruck m. **blood test**
Blutuntersuchung f. **bloodthirsty** adj
blutdurstig. **blood transfusion** Blutübertragung f. **blood vessel** Blutgefäß neut.
bloody adj blutig; (coll) verdammt.
bloom [bluːm] v blühen. n Blüte f.
blossom ['blosəm] n Blüte f. v blühen.
blot [blot] n Fleck m; (of ink) Tintenklecks m. v (make dirty) beschmieren.
blot out auslöschen.
blotch [blotʃ] n Fleck m; Klecks m.
blotting paper n Löschpapier neut.
blouse [blauz] n Bluse f.
*****blow**[1] [blou] v blasen; (of wind) wehen;
(fuse) durchbrennen. **blow over**
vorbeigehen. **blow up** (explode) sprengen.
blow the horn (mot) hupen. **blow one's
nose** sich die Nase putzen.
blow[2] [blou] n Schlag m; (misfortune)
Unglück neut.
blowlamp ['bloulamp] n Lötlampe f.
blown [bloun] V **blow**[1].
blowout ['blouaut] n (mot) geplatzter
Reifen m, Reifenpanne f.
blubber ['blʌbə] n Walfischspeck m.
blue [bluː] adj blau; (depressed)
niedergeschlagen. n Blau neut. **bluebell** n
Glockenblume f. **blueberry** n Heidelber-
ee f. **bluebottle** n Schmeißfliege f. **the
blues** Blues m sing.
bluff [blʌf] v bluffen. n Bluff m.
blunder ['blʌndə] n (dummer) Fehler m,
Schnitzer m. v (stumble) stolpern; (make
mistake) einen Schnitzer machen.
blunt [blʌnt] adj stumpf. v stumpf
machen; (enthusiasm) abstumpfen.
blur [bləː] v verwischen, verschmieren.
blurred adj verschwommen.
blush [blʌʃ] v erröten. n Erröten neut.
boar [boː] n Eber m. **wild boar**
Wildschwein m.
board [boːd] n (wooden) Brett neut;
(comm) Aufsichtsrat m. v (train) einsteigen in (+ acc). **board and lodging**
Unterkunft und Verpflegung f. **boarding
house** Pension f. **boarding school**
Internat neut.

boast [boust] v prahlen, angeben. n Prahlerei f. **boaster** n Prahler m.

boat [bout] n Boot neut. **in the same boat** in der gleichen Lage.

bob [bob] v sich auf- und abbewegen; (hair) kurz schneiden.

bobbin ['bobin] n Spule f.

bobsleigh ['bobslei] n Bobsleigh m.

bodice ['bodis] n Mieder neut.

body ['bodi] n Körper, Leib m; (corpse) Leiche f; (of people) Gruppe f; (car) Karosserie f. **bodily** adj körperlich.

bog [bog] n Sumpf m. v **get bogged down** steckenbleiben. **boggy** adj sumpfig.

bogus ['bougəs] adj falsch, unecht.

bohemian [bə'hiːmiən] adj (fig) zigeunerhaft, ungebunden. n (fig) Bohemien m.

boil¹ [boil] v kochen. **boiler** n Kessel m. **boiling** adj kochend.

boil² [boil] n (sore) Furunkel m.

boisterous ['boistərəs] adj ungestüm, laut.

bold [bould] adj kühn, tapfer; (cheeky) frech. **boldness** n Kühnheit f.

bolster ['boulstə] n Kissen neut. **bolster up** (fig) unterstützen.

bolt [boult] n (door) Riegel m; (screw) Bolzen m; (lightning) Blitzstrahl m; (cloth) Rolle f. v (door) verriegeln; (attach with bolts) anbolzen; (food) hinunterschlingen; (dash) (hastig) fliehen.

bomb [bom] n Bombe f. v bombardieren. **go down a bomb** einen Bombenerfolg haben. **bombard** v bombardieren. **bombardment** n Beschießung f. **bomber** n (aeroplane) Bombenflugzeug neut. **bombing** n Bombenangriff m.

bond [bond] n (tie) Bindung f; (comm) Schuldschein m.

bone [boun] n Knochen m, Bein neut; (fish) Gräte f. v (meat) die Knochen entfernen aus; (fish) entgräten.

bonfire ['bonfaiə] n Gartenfeuer neut.

bonnet ['bonit] n Haube f; (mot) Motorhaube f.

bonus ['bounəs] n Bonus m.

bony ['bouni] adj knochig.

book [buk] n Buch neut; (notebook) Heft neut. v (record) buchen; (reserve) reservieren. **bookcase** n Bücherschrank m. **booking office** Fahrkartenschalter m. **bookkeeping** n Buchhaltung f. **bookmaker** n Buchmacher m. **bookshop** n Buchhandlung f.

boom [buːm] n (sound) Dröhnen neut; (econ) Konjunktur f; (naut) Baum m. v dröhnen.

boost [buːst] v Auftrieb geben (+dat), (tech) verstärken. n Auftrieb m.

boot [buːt] n Stiefel m; (mot) Kofferraum m.

booth [buːð] n Bude f. **telephone booth** Telephonzelle f.

booze [buːz] (coll) v saufen. n alkoholisches Getränk neut. **boozer** n Säufer m.

border ['boːdə] n (of country) Grenze f; (edge) Rand m. v grenzen. **borderline** n Grenze f. **borderline case** Grenzfall m.

bore¹ [boː] V bear¹.

bore² [boː] v (drill) bohren; (a hole) ausbohren; (cylinder) ausschleifen. n Kaliber neut.

bore³ [boː] v (weary) langweilen. n langweiliger Mensch m. **be bored** sich langweilen. **boredom** n Langeweile f. **boring** adj langweilig.

born [boːn] adj geboren. she was born blind sie ist von der Geburt blind.

borne [boːn] V bear¹.

borough ['bʌrə] n Stadtbezirk m.

borrow ['borou] v borgen, entleihen. **borrower** n Entleiher m.

bosom ['buzəm] n Busen m. **bosom friend** Busenfreund m.

boss [bos] n Boß, Chef m. v **boss around** herumkommandieren. **bossy** adj herrisch.

botany ['botəni] n Botanik f. **botanical** adj botanisch. **botanical gardens** botanischer Garten m. **botanist** n Botaniker m.

both [bouθ] adj, pron beide(s). **both** (of the) dogs beide Hunde. **both ... and** sowohl ... als or wie auch.

bother ['boðə] v (disturb) belästigen, stören; (take trouble) sich Mühe geben. n Belästigung f. **bothersome** adj lästig.

bottle ['botl] n Flasche f. v in Flaschen füllen. **bottled** adj in Flaschen, Flaschen-. **bottleneck** n (fig) Engpaß m. **bottle opener** n Flaschenöffner m.

bottom ['botəm] n Boden m; (coll: anat) Hintern m. adj **bottom gear** erster Gang m.

bough [bau] n Ast m.

boulder ['bouldə] n Felsbrocken m.

bounce [bauns] v (of ball) hochspringen; (of cheque) platzen. **bounce around** herumhüpfen. **bouncer** n (coll) Rausschmeißer m.

bought [bɔːt] V buy.
bound¹ [baund] V bind.
bound² [baund] n (leap) Sprung m, Satz m. v springen.
bound³ [baund] n (limit) Grenze f. **out of bounds** betreten verboten!
bound⁴ [baund] adj **bound for** unterwegs nach. **outward/homeward bound** auf der Ausreise/Heimreise.
bound⁵ [baund] adj (obliged) verpflichtet. He is bound to win er wird bestimmt gewinnen.
boundary ['baundəri] n Grenze f.
bouquet [buːkei] n (flowers) Blumenstrauß m; (of wine) Blume f.
bourgeois ['buəʒwaː] adj bourgeois. n Bourgeois m. **bourgeoisie** n Bourgeoisie f.
bout [baut] n (of illness) Anfall m; (fight) Kampf m.
bow¹ [bau] v (lower head) sich verbeugen. n Verbeugung f.
bow² [bou] n (music, archery) Bogen m; (ribbon) Schleife f.
bow³ [bau] n (naut) Bug m.
bowels ['bauəlz] pl n Darm m sing; Eingeweide pl. **open or move one's bowels** sich entleeren.
bowl¹ [boul] n (basin) Schüssel f, Schale f.
bowl² [boul] v (ball) werfen. n Holzkugel f. **bowls** n Kegelspiel neut. **play bowls** kegeln.
box¹ [bɔks] n (container) Schachtel f, Kasten m; (theatre) Loge f; (court) Stand m.
box² [bɔks] v (sport) boxen. **box someone's ears** jemanden ohrfeigen. **boxer** n Boxer m. **boxing** n Boxen neut.
Boxing Day n zweiter Weihnachtsfeiertag m.
box office n (theatre) Kasse f.
boy [bɔi] n Junge m, Knabe m. **boyfriend** n Freund m. **boyhood** n Jugend f. **boyish** n knabenhaft.
boycott ['bɔikɔt] n Boykott m. v boykottieren.
bra [braː] n Büstenhalter m, BH m.
brace [breis] n Paar neut; (tech) Stütze f. v stützen. **braces** pl n Hosenträger pl.
bracelet ['breislit] n Armband neut.
bracing ['breisiŋ] adj erfrischend.
bracken ['brakən] n Farnkraut neut.
bracket ['brakit] n (parenthesis) Klammer f; (support) Träger m.

brag [brag] v prahlen, angeben. **braggart** n Prahler m.
braille [breil] n Brailleschrift f.
brain [brein] n Gehirn neut; Verstand m; Intelligenz f. **brainwashing** n Gehirnwäsche f. **brainwave** n Geistesblitz m. **brainy** adj klug.
braise [breiz] v schmoren.
brake [breik] n Bremse f. v bremsen. **brake pedal** Bremspedal neut.
bramble ['brambl] n (bush) Brombeerstrauch m; (berry) Brombeere f.
bran [bran] n (Weizen)Kleie f.
branch [braːntʃ] n Zweig m; (of bank) Zweigstelle f; (department) Abteilung f. v **branch off** abzweigen.
brand [brand] n (of goods) Marke f; (cattle) Brandzeichen neut. v (mark) brandmarken. **brand-new** adj nagelneu.
brand name Markenname m.
brandish ['brandiʃ] v schwingen.
brandy ['brandi] n Weinbrand m.
brass [braːs] n Messing neut; (music) Blasinstrumente pl. adj Messing-.
brassiere ['brasiə] n Büstenhalter m.
brave [breiv] adj mutig, tapfer. v trotzen. **bravery** n Mut m, Tapferkeit f.
brawl [brɔːl] n Rauferei f. v raufen.
brawn [brɔːn] n Muskelkraft f; (cookery) Sülze f.
brazen ['breizn] adj (fig) unverschämt.
breach [briːtʃ] n Bruch m; (mil) Bresche f. v durchbrechen; (law) übertreten. **breach of contract** Vertragsbruch m. **breach of the peace** Friedensbruch m.
bread [bred] n Brot neut. v (cookery) panieren. **bread and butter** Butterbrot neut. **breadwinner** n Brotverdiener m.
breadth [bredθ] n Breite f, Weite f.
***break** [breik] v brechen; (coll) kaputt machen; (law) übertreten; (promise) nicht halten; (day) anbrechen. n Bruch m; (gap) Lücke f; (rest) Pause f; (opportunity) Chance f. **break away** sich losreißen. **break down** (mot) eine Panne haben; (person) zusammenbrechen. **break in** (burgle) einbrechen; (animal) abrichten. **break out** ausbrechen. **break up** zerbrechen; (school) in die Ferien gehen.
breakable ['breikəbl] adj zerbrechlich.
breakage ['breikidʒ] n Bruchschaden m.
breakdown ['breikdaun] n (mot) Panne f. **nervous breakdown** Nervenzusammenbruch m.

breakfast ['brekfəst] *n* Frühstück *neut*. *v* frühstücken.

breakthrough ['breikθruː] *n* Durchbruch *m*.

breast [brest] *n* Brust *f*, Busen *m*. **breastbone** *n* Brustbein *neut*. **breast-stroke** *n* Brustschwimmen *neut*.

breath [breθ] *n* Atem *m*. **out of breath** außer Atem.

breathe [briːð] *v* atmen. **breathe in** einatmen. **breathe out** ausatmen.

bred [bred] *V* breed.

***breed** [briːd] *v* (*increase*) sich vermehren; (*animals*) züchten; (*fig*) erzeugen. *n* (*of dog*) Rasse *f*. **breeding** *n* Zucht *f*; (*education*) Erziehung *f*.

breeze [briːz] *n* Brise *f*.

brew [bruː] *v* brauen. *n* Bräu *neut*. **brewery** *n* Brauerei *f*.

bribe [braib] *v* bestechen. *n* Bestechungsgeld *neut*. **bribery** *n* Bestechung *f*.

brick [brik] *n* Ziegelstein *m*. **bricklayer** *n* Maurer *m*.

bride [braid] *n* Braut *f*. **bridal** *adj* bräutlich, hochzeitlich. **bridegroom** *n* Bräutigam *m*. **bridesmaid** *n* Brautjungfer *f*.

bridge¹ [bridʒ] *n* Brücke *f*; (*violin*) Steg *m*. *v* überbrücken.

bridge² [bridʒ] *n* (*card game*) Bridge *neut*.

bridle ['braidl] *n* Zaum *m*.

brief [briːf] *adj* kurz. *v* instruieren. **briefcase** *n* Aktentasche *f*. **briefing** *n* Anweisung *f*. **briefly** *adv* kurz. **briefs** *pl n* Slip *m sing*.

brigade [bri'geid] *n* Brigade *f*. **brigadier** *n* Brigadegeneral *m*.

bright [brait] *adj* hell, leuchtend; (*clever*) klug. **brighten** *v* aufheitern. **brightness** *n* Glanz *m* (*tech*) Beleuchtungsstärke *f*.

brilliance ['briljəns] *n* Glanz *m*, Brillanz *f*. **brilliant** *adj* glänzend, brillant; (*clever*) scharfsinnig.

brim [brim] *n* Rand *m*; (*hat*) Krempe *f*.

brine [brain] *n* Salzwasser *neut*. **in brine** eingepökelt, Salz-.

***bring** [briŋ] *v* bringen. **bring about** veranlassen. **bring along** mitbringen. **bring down** herunterbringen; (*prices*) herabsetzen. **bring up** (*child*) erziehen; (*vomit*) erbrechen.

brink [briŋk] *n* Rand *m*.

briquette [bri'ket] *n* Brikett *f*.

brisk [brisk] *adj* schnell, lebhaft.

bristle ['brisl] *n* Borste *f*.

Britain ['britn] *n* (*Great Britain*) Großbritannien *neut*. **British** *adj* britisch. **the British** die Briten. **Briton** Brite *m*, Britin *f*.

brittle ['britl] *adj* spröde.

broad [broːd] *adj* breit. **broadly** *adv* im allgemeinen.

broadcast ['broːdkaist] *v* übertragen. *n* Sendung *f*. **broadcasting** *n* Rundfunk *m*. **broadcasting corporation** *n* Rundfunkgesellschaft *f*.

brochure ['brouʃuə] *n* Broschüre *f*.

broke [brouk] *V* break. *adj* (*coll*) pleite.

broken ['broukn] *V* break.

broker ['broukə] *n* Makler *m*.

bronchitis [broŋ'kaitis] *n* Bronchitis *f*.

bronze [bronz] *n* Bronze *f*. *adj* aus Bronze, Bronze-; (*colour*) bronzefarben.

brooch [broutʃ] *n* Brosche *f*.

brood [bruːd] *n* Brut *f*. *v* brüten. **broody** *adj* brütig.

brook [bruk] *n* Bach *m*.

broom [bruːm] *n* Besen *m*; (*bot*) Ginster *m*. **broomstick** *n* Besenstiehl *m*.

broth [broθ] *n* Brühe *f*.

brothel ['broθl] *n* Bordell *neut*.

brother ['brʌðə] *n* Bruder *m*. **Smith Bros.** Gebrüder Smith. **brothers and sisters** Geschwister *pl*. **brotherhood** *n* Bruderschaft *f*. **brother-in-law** *n* Schwager *m*. **brotherly** *adj* brüderlich.

brought [broːt] *V* bring.

brow [brau] *n* (*forehead*) Stirn *f*; (*eyebrow*) Augenbraue *f*; (*of hill*) Bergkuppe *f*.

brown [braun] *adj* braun. *n* Braun *neut*. *v* bräunen.

browse [brauz] *v* weiden; (*in book*) durchblättern.

bruise [bruːz] *n* blaue Flecke *f*, Quetschung *f*. *v* quetschen.

brunette [bru'net] *adj* brünett. *n* Brünette *f*.

brush [brʌʃ] *n* Bürste *f*; (*paintbrush*) Pinsel *m*; (*undergrowth*) Unterholz *neut*. *v* bürsten. **brush past** vorbeistreichen.

brusque [brusk] *adj* brüsk.

Brussels ['brʌsəlz] *n* Brüssel *neut*. **Brussels sprouts** Rosenkohl *m*.

brute [bruːt] *n* Tier *neut*; (*person*) brutaler Mensch *m*. **brutal** *adj* brutal. **brutality** *n* Brutalität *f*.

bubble ['bʌbl] *n* Blase *f*. *v* sprudeln. **bubbly** *adj* sprudelnd.

buck¹ [bʌk] n Bock m; (US coll) Dollar m.

buck² [bʌk] v bocken. **buck up** (hurry) sich beeilen; (cheer up) munter werden.

bucket ['bʌkit] n Eimer m. **bucketful** n Eimervoll m.

buckle ['bʌkl] n Schnalle f. v anschnallen.

bud [bʌd] n Knospe f. v knospen. **nip in the bud** im Keim ersticken. **budding** adj angehend.

buddy ['bʌdi] n (coll) Kumpel m.

budge [bʌdʒ] v (sich) bewegen.

budgerigar ['bʌdʒərigaː] n Wellensittich m.

budget ['bʌdʒit] n Budget neut. v budgetieren.

buffalo ['bʌfəlou] n Büffel m; (bison) Bison m.

buffer ['bʌfə] n Puffer m.

buffet¹ ['bʌfit] n (blow) Schlag m. v stoßen.

buffet² ['bufei] n (meal) Büffett neut.

bug [bʌg] n Wanze f. v (coll) ärgern.

bugle ['bjuːgl] n Signalhorn neut.

***build** [bild] v bauen. n Körperbau m. **build up** aufbauen. **builder** n Baumeister m. **building** n Gebäude neut, Haus neut. **built-in** adj eingebaut.

built [bilt] V build.

bulb [bʌlb] n (flower) Zwiebel f; (lamp) Glühbirne f. **bulbous** adj zwiebelförmig.

Bulgaria [bʌl'georiə] n Bulgarien neut. **Bulgarian** adj bulgarisch. n Bulgare m. Bulgarin f.

bulge [bʌldʒ] v anschwellen. n Schwellung f. Ausbauchung f.

bulk [bʌlk] n Masse f; (greater part) Hauptteil m. **bulky** adj umfangreich.

bull [bul] n (cattle) Stier m; (animal) Bulle f; (coll: nonsense) Quatsch m. **bulldog** n Bulldogge m. **bulldozer** n Bulldozer m. **bullfight** n Stierkampf m.

bullet ['bulit] n (Gewehr)Kugel f.

bulletin ['bulətin] n Bulletin neut.

bullion ['buliən] n Gold-, Silberbarren pl.

bully ['buli] v einschüchtern. n Tyrann m.

bum [bʌm] n (tramp) Bummler m, Landstreicher m.

bump [bʌmp] v stoßen (gegen). n Stoß m; (on the head) Beule f. **bumper** n (of car) Stoßstange f. adj **bumper crop** Rekordernte f.

bun [bʌn] n (hair) Haarknoten m; (cake) Kuchen m; (bread roll) Brötchen neut.

bunch [bʌntʃ] n Bündel neut. **bunch of** flowers Blumenstrauß m. **bunch of grapes** Weintraube f. **bunch of keys** Schlüsselbund m.

bundle ['bʌndl] n Bündel neut. v zusammenbündeln.

bungalow ['bʌngəlou] n Bungalow m.

bungle ['bʌngl] v verpfuschen. **bungler** n Pfuscher.

bunion ['bʌnjən] n entzündeter Fußballen m.

bunk [bʌnk] n Koje f.

bunker ['bʌnkə] n Bunker m; (golf) Sandgrube f.

buoy [boi] n Boje f.

burden ['bəːdn] n Last f. v belasten.

bureau ['bjuərou] n Büro neut; (desk) Schreibtisch m.

bureaucracy [bju'rokrəsi] n Bürokratie f. **bureaucrat** n Bürokrat m. **bureaucratic** adj bürokratisch.

burglar ['bəːglə] n Einbrecher m. **burglary** n Einbruchsdiebstahl m.

burial ['beriəl] n Beerdigung f, Begräbnis neut.

***burn** [bəːn] v brennen; (set alight) verbrennen. n Brandwunde f. **burn oneself** (or one's fingers) sich (die) Finger verbrennen.

burnt [bəːnt] V burn. adj (food) angebrannt.

burrow ['bʌrou] n (of rabbit) Bau m. v graben.

***burst** [bəːst] v platzen. n (of shooting) Feuerstoß m; (of speed) Spurt m. **burst out laughing/crying** in Lachen/Tränen ausbrechen. **burst tyre** geplatzter Reifen m.

bury ['beri] v begraben; (one's hands, face) vergraben.

bus [bʌs] n Bus m, Autobus m. **bus driver** Busfahrer m. **bus conductor** Busschaffner m. **bus stop** Bushaltestelle f.

bush [buʃ] n Busch m. **bushy** adj buschig.

business ['biznis] n Geschäft neut. that's none of your business das geht dich nichts an. **businessman** n Geschäftsmann m. **businesswoman** n Geschäftsfrau f.

bust¹ [bʌst] n (breasts) Busen m; (sculpture) Büste f.

bust² [bʌst] (coll) adj (bankrupt) pleite; (broken) kaputt. v zerbrechen, kaputt machen

bustle ['bʌsl] n Aufregung f. v **bustle about** herumsausen.

busy ['bizi] n (*occupied*) beschäftigt; (*hardworking*) fleißig; (*telephone*) besetzt. v busy oneself with sich beschäftigen mit.

but [bʌt] conj aber. prep außer. adv (*merely*) nur. **not only ... but also** nicht nur ... sondern auch. **nothing but** nichts als. **but for** ohne.

butane ['bjuːtein] n Butan neut.

butcher [butʃə] n Fleischer m, Metzger m. **butcher's shop** Metzgerei f, Fleischerei f.

butler ['bʌtlə] n Butler m.

butt¹ [bʌt] n (*thick end*) dickes Ende neut; (*of cigarette*) Stummel m.

butt² [bʌt] n (*of jokes*) Zielscheibe f.

butt³ [bʌt] v (*with the head*) mit dem Kopf stoßen. n Kopfstoß.

butter ['bʌtə] n Butter f. v mit Butter bestreichen.

buttercup ['bʌtəkʌp] n Butterblume f.

butterfly ['bʌtəflai] n Schmetterling m.

buttocks ['bʌtəks] pl n Gesäß neut sing.

button ['bʌtn] n Knopf m. v (zu)knöpfen.

buttonhole n Knopfloch neut.

buttress ['bʌtris] n Strebepfeiler m.

*buy [bai] v kaufen. **buy in** einkaufen. **buyer** n Käufer(in).

buzz [bʌz] v summen. n Summen neut. **buzzer** n Summer m.

by [bai] prep (*close to*) bei, neben; (*via*) über; (*past*) an ... vorbei; (*before*) bis; (*written by*) von. adv vorbei. **by day** bei tage. **by bus** mit dem Bus. **by that** (*mean, understand*) damit. **by and by** nach und nach. **by-election** Nachwahl f. **bypass** n Umgehungstraße f. **by-product** n Nebenprodukt neut. **bystander** n Zuschauer m.

C

cab [kab] n (*taxi*) Taxi neut; (*horse-drawn*) Droschke f; (*in truck*) Fahrerhaus neut.

cabaret ['kabərei] n Kabarett neut.

cabbage ['kabidʒ] n Kohl m, Kraut neut.

cabin ['kabin] n Hütte f; (*naut*) Kabine f.

cabinet ['kabinit] n Schrank m; (*pol*) Kabinett neut. **cabinet-maker** n Möbeltischler m.

cable ['keibl] n (*elec, telegram*) Kabel neut; (*rope*) Tau neut, Seil neut. **cable address** Telegrammanschrift f. **cable railway** Drahtseilbahn f.

cackle ['kakl] v gackern. n Gegacker neut.

cactus ['kaktəs] n Kaktus m.

caddie ['kadi] n Golfjunge m.

cadence ['keidəns] n (*music*) Kadenz f. **cadenza** n Kadenz f.

cadet [kə'det] n Kadett m.

café ['kafei] n Café neut.

cafeteria [kafə'tiəriə] n Selbstbedienungsrestaurant neut.

caffeine ['kafiːn] n Koffein neut.

cage [keidʒ] n Käfig m. v in einen Käfig sperren.

cake [keik] n Kuchen m; (*soap*) Tafel f. v **be caked with mud** vor Schmutz starren.

calamine ['kaləmain] n Galmei m.

calamity [kə'laməti] n Unheil neut, Katastrophe f.

calcium ['kalsiəm] n Kalzium neut.

calculate ['kalkjuleit] v kalkulieren, berechnen. **calculating** adj berechnend. **calculation** n Berechnung f. **calculator** n (*mech*) Rechner m.

calendar ['kaləndə] n Kalender m.

calf¹ [kaːf] n (*young cow*) Kalb neut. **calfskin** n Kalbleder neut.

calf² [kaːf] n (*anat*) Wade f. **calf muscle** Wadenmuskel m.

calibre ['kalibə] n Kaliber neut.

call [koːl] v rufen; anrufen; (*a doctor*) holen; (*regard as*) halten für. n Ruf m; (*phone*) Anruf m; (*demand*) Aufforderung f. **call for** verlangen. **call off** (*cancel*) absagen. **callbox** n Telefonzelle f. **caller** n (*visitor*) Besucher m; (*phone*) Anrufer m. **calling** n Berufung f. **call-up** n Einberufung f.

callous ['kaləs] adj gefühllos, herzlos.

calm [kaːm] adj ruhig. n Ruhe, Stille f; (*naut*) Windstille f. v or **calm down** (sich) or beruhigen.

calorie ['kaləri] n Kalorie f.

came [keim] V come.

camel ['kaməl] n Kamel neut. **camelhair** n Kamelhaar neut.

camera ['kamərə] n Kamera f, Fotoapparat m. **cameraman** n Kameramann m.

camouflage ['kaməflaːʒ] n Tarnung f; (*zool*) Schutzfärbung f. v tarnen.

camp [kamp] n Lager neut. v lagern; (*go camping*) campen, zelten. **camp bed** n Feldbett neut. **camper** n Camper m. **camping** n Camping neut. **camp site** n Campingplatz m.

campaign [kam'pein] n (mil, pol) Feldzug m; Kampagne f. v **campaign for** (fig) werben um, kämpfen für.

campus ['kampəs] n Universitätsgelände neut.

camshaft ['kamʃaɪft] n Nockenwelle f.

*can¹ [kan] v (be able) können; (be allowed, may) dürfen.

can² [kan] n (tin) Dose f, Büchse f. v konservieren.

Canada ['kanədə] n Kanada neut. **Canadian** adj kanadisch; n Kanadier(in).

canal [kə'nal] n Kanal m.

canary [kə'neəri] n Kanarienvogel m.

cancel ['kansəl] v (meeting) absagen, (arrangement) aufheben; (stamp) entwerten; (cross out) durchstreichen. **cancellation** n Absage f; Aufhebung f.

cancer ['kansə] n (med) Krebs m. **Cancer** (astrol) Krebs m. **breast cancer** Brustenkrebs m. **lung cancer** Lungenkrebs m.

candid ['kandid] adj offen, ehrlich.

candidate ['kandidət] n Kandidat m.

candle ['kandl] n Kerze f. **candle light** n Kerzenlicht neut, **candlestick** Leuchter m.

candour ['kandə] n Offenheit f; Ehrlichkeit f.

candy ['kandi] n Kandiszucker m; (US: sweet) Bonbon neut.

cane [kein] n (walking stick) Spazierstock m. **sugar cane** Zuckerrohr m. **cane sugar** Rohrzucker m.

canine ['keinain] adj Hunde-, Hunds-. **canine tooth** Eckzahn m.

canister ['kanistə] n Kanister m.

cannabis ['kanəbis] n Haschisch neut.

cannibal ['kanibəl] n Kannibale m.

cannon ['kanən] n Kanone f.

canoe [kə'nuː] n Kanu neut. v Kanu fahren.

canon ['kanən] n Domherr m; (rule) Kanon m.

can opener n Büchsenöffner m.

canopy ['kanəpi] n Baldachin m.

canteen [kan'tiːn] n (restaurant) Kantine f.

canter ['kantə] n Handgalopp m. v Handgalopp reiten.

canton ['kantən] n Kanton m.

canvas ['kanvəs] n Segeltuch neut; (artist's) Leinwand f.

canvass ['kanvəs] v werben.

canyon ['kanjən] n Cañon m, Schlucht f.

cap [kap] n (hat) Kappe f, Mütze f; (lid) Kappe f. v (fig) übertreffen.

capable ['keipəbl] adj (able to do something) fähig (zu); (skilled) begabt. **capability** n Fähigkeit f.

capacity [kə'pasəti] n (volume) Inhalt m; (of ship) Laderaum m; (talent) Talent m. **in the capacity of** als. **filled to capacity** voll (besetzt).

cape¹ [keip] n (cloak) Cape neut, Umhang m.

cape² [keip] n (geog) Kap neut

caper¹ ['keipə] n Kapriole f. v kapriolen.

caper² ['keipə] n (cookery) Kaper f.

capital ['kapitl] n (city) Hauptstadt f; (comm) Kapital neut. adj (main) Haupt-; (comm) Kapital-; (splendid) großartig. **capitalism** n Kapitalismus m. **capitalist** n Kapitalist m. adj kapitalistisch. **capital punishment** Todesstrafe n.

capitulate [kə'pitjuleit] v kapitulieren (vor).

capricious [kə'priʃəs] adj launenhaft. **Capricorn** ['kaprikoːn] n Steinbock m.

capsize [kap'saiz] v kentern.

capsule ['kapsjuːl] n Kapsel f.

captain ['kaptin] n (mil) Hauptmann m; (naut) Kapitän m; (sport) Mannschaftsführer m. v (sport) führen.

caption ['kapʃən] n (picture) Erklärung f; (heading) Überschrift f.

captive ['kaptiv] n Gefangene(r). adj gefangen. **captivity** n Gefangenschaft f. **captor** n Fänger m.

capture ['kaptʃə] v gefangennehmen; (animal) einfangen. n Gefangennahme f.

car [kaɪ] n (mot) Wagen m, Auto neut; (rail) Wagen m. **by car** mit dem Auto.

caramel ['karəmel] n Karamel m.

carat ['karət] n Karat neut.

caravan ['karəvan] n (mot) Wohnwagen m; (oriental) Karawane f.

caraway ['karəwei] n Kümmel m.

carbohydrate [kaɪbə'haidreit] n Kohlehydrat neut.

carbon ['kaɪbən] n Kohlenstoff m. **carbon copy** Durchschlag m. **carbon dioxide** Kohlendioxid neut; (in drinks) Kohlensäure f. **carbon paper** Kohlepapier neut.

carburettor ['kaɪbjuretə] **carburetor** n Vergaser m.

carcass ['kaɪkəs] n Kadaver m.

card [kaɪd] n Karte f. **cardboard** n Pappe f. **cardboard box** Pappschachtel f. **card**

game Kartenspiel *neut.* **card index** Kartei *f.*

cardiac ['kaɪdiak] *adj* Herz-.

cardigan ['kaɪdigən] *n* Wolljacke *f.*

cardinal ['kaɪdənl] *n* Kardinal *m. adj* grundsätzlich.

care [keə] *n* (*carefulness*) Sorgfalt *f*; (*looking after*) Pflege *f*; (*worry*) Sorge *f.* **take care** sich hüten; achtgeben. **take care of** (*look after*) pflegen; (*see to*) erledigen. *v* **care about** sich kümmern um. **care for** (*look after*) pflegen; (*see to*) sorgen für; (*like*) mögen. **carefree** *adj* sorgenfrei. **careful** *adj* sorgfältig; (*cautious*) vorsichtig. **carefulness** *n* Sorgfalt *f*; Vorsicht *f.* **careless** *adj* unachtsam, nachlässig. **carelessness** *n* Nachlässigkeit *f.*

career [kə'riə] *n* Laufbahn *f*, Karriere *f.*

caress [kə'res] *v* liebkosen. *n* Liebkosung *f*; Kuß *m.*

cargo ['kaɪgou] *n* Fracht *f.* **cargo plane** Transportflugzeug *neut.* **cargo ship** Frachtschiff *neut.*

caricature ['karikətjuə] *n* Karikatur *f. v* karikieren.

carnal ['kaɪnl] *adj* fleischlich.

carnation [kaɪ'neiʃən] *n* Nelke *f.*

carnival ['kaɪnivəl] *n* Karneval *m*, Fasching *m.*

carnivorous [kaɪ'nivərəs] *adj* fleischfressend.

carol ['karəl] *n* Weihnachtslied *neut.*

carpenter ['kaɪpəntə] *n* Zimmermann *m*, Tischler *m.* **carpentry** *n* Zimmerhandwerk *neut.*

carpet ['kaɪpit] *n* Teppich *m. v* mit einem Teppich belegen.

carriage ['karidʒ] *n* (*rail*) (Eisenbahn) Wagen *m*; (*transport*) Transport *f*; (*posture*) Haltung *f.* **carriageway** Fahrbahn *f.*

carrier ['kariə] *n* Träger *m*; (*med*) Keimträger *m*; (*comm*) Spediteur *m.* **carrier bag** Tragebeutel *m.*

carrot ['karət] *n* Mohrrübe *f*, Möhre *f.*

carry ['kari] *v* tragen; (*transport*) befördern. **carry out** ausführen. **carry cot** Tragbettchen *neut.*

cart [kaɪt] *n* Karren *m.*

cartilage ['kaɪtəlidʒ] *n* Knorpel *m.*

cartography [kaɪ'togrəfi] *n* Kartographie *f.*

carton ['kaɪtən] *n* Karton *m.*

cartoon [kaɪ'tuɪn] *n* Karikatur *f*; (*film*) Trickfilm *m.* **cartoonist** *n* Karikaturenzeichner *m.*

cartridge ['kaɪtridʒ] *n* Patrone *f.* **cartridge paper** Zeichenpapier *neut.*

carve [kaɪv] *v* (*in wood*) schnitzen; (*in stone*) meißeln; (*meat*) vorschneiden. **carving** *n* Schnitzerei *f.*

cascade [kas'keid] *n* Kaskade *f.*

case[1] [keis] *n* (*affair, instance*) Fall *m*; (*law*) Sache *f.* **in case** falls. **in case of** im Falle (+ *gen*). **in any case** auf jeden Fall.

case[2] [keis] *n* (*suitcase*) Koffer *m*; (*for cigarettes, camera*) Etui *neut*; (*tech*) Gehäuse *neut.*

cash [kaʃ] *n* Bargeld *neut. v* einlösen. **cash on delivery** per Nachnahme. **pay cash** bar zahlen. **cash desk** Kasse *f.*

cashier [ka'ʃiə] *n* Kassierer(in).

cashmere [kaʃ'miə] *n* Kaschmir *m.*

casing ['keisiŋ] *n* Gehäuse *neut.*

casino [kə'siɪnou] *n* Kasino *neut.*

casket ['kaɪskit] *n* Kästchen *neut*; (*coffin*) Sarg *m.*

casserole ['kasəroul] *n* (*vessel*) Kasserolle *f*; (*meal*) Schmorbraten *m. v* schmoren.

cassette [kə'set] *n* Kassette *f.* **cassette recorder** Kassettenrecorder *m.*

cassock ['kasək] *n* Soutane *f.*

*cast [kaɪst] *v* werfen; (*metal*) gießen; (*theatre*) besetzen. *n* (*theatre*) Besetzung *f.*

caste [kaɪst] *n* Kaste *f.*

castle ['kaɪsl] *n* Burg *f*, Schloß *neut*; (*chess*) Turm *m. v* (*chess*) rochieren.

castor oil ['kaɪstə] *n* Möbelrolle *f.*

castrate [kə'streit] *v* kastrieren. **castration** *n* Kastration *f.*

casual ['kaʒuəl] *adj* beiläufig; (*careless*) nachlässig; (*informal*) leger. **casual labour** Gelegenheitsarbeit *f.*

casualty ['kaʒuəlti] *n* Verletzte(r). **casualties** *pl n* (*mil*) Ausfälle *pl.* **casualty department** Unfallstation *f.*

cat [kat] *n* Katze *f.* **tom cat** Kater *m.*

catalogue ['katəlog] *n* Katalog *m.*

catalyst ['katəlist] *n* Katalysator *m.*

catamaran [katəmə'ran] *n* Katamaran *neut.*

catapult ['katəpʌlt] *n* Katapult *neut.*

cataract ['katərakt] *n* (*med*) grauer Star *m*; Wasserfall *m.*

catarrh [kə'taɪ] *n* Katarrh *m.*

catastrophe [kə'tastrəfi] *n* Katastrophe *f.* **catastrophic** *adj* katastrophal.

*catch [katʃ] *v* fangen; (*bus, train*) nehmen, erreichen; (*surprise*) ertappen; (*illness*) sich zuziehen. *n* Fang *m*.

category ['katəgəri] *n* Katagorie *f*. **categorical** *adj* kategorisch.

cater ['keitə] *v* **cater for** versorgen. **catering** *n* Bewirtung *f*.

caterpillar ['katəpilə] *n* Raupe *f*. **caterpillar track** Gleiskette *f*.

cathedral [kə'θiːdrəl] *n* Dom *m*, Kathedrale *f*.

cathode ['kaθoud] *n* Kathode *f*.

catholic ['kaθəlik] *adj* (*rel*) katholisch; universal. *n* Katholik(in). **Roman Catholic** römisch-katholisch.

catkin ['katkin] *n* Kätzchen *neut*.

cattle ['katl] *pl n* Vieh *neut sing*, Rindvieh *neut sing*. **cattle shed** Viehstall *m*.

catty ['kati] *adj* (*coll*) gehässig.

caught [kɔːt] *V* catch.

cauliflower ['koliflauə] *n* Blumenkohl *m*.

cause [cɔːz] *n* Ursache *f*, (*reason*) Grund *m*; (*interests*) Sache *f*. *v* verursachen, veranlassen.

causeway ['kɔːzwei] *n* Damm *m*.

caustic ['kɔːstik] *adj* ätzend; (*fig*) beißend.

caution ['kɔːʃən] *n* Vorsicht *f*. *v* warnen (vor). **cautious** *adj* vorsichtig.

cavalry ['kavəlri] *n* Kavallerie *f*.

cave [keiv] *n* Höhle *f*. *v* **cave in** einstürzen. **cavern** *n* Höhle *f*.

caviar ['kaviaː] *n* Kaviar *m*.

cavity ['kavəti] *n* Hohlraum *m*; (*in tooth*) Loch *neut*.

cease [siːs] *v* aufhören; (*fire*) einstellen. **ceasefire** *n* Feuereinstellung *f*. **ceaseless** *adj* unaufhörlich.

cedar ['siːdə] *n* Zeder *f*.

ceiling ['siːliŋ] *n* Decke *f*; (*fig*) Höchstgrenze *f*.

celebrate ['seləbreit] *v* feiern. **celebrated** *adj* berühmt. **celebration** *n* Feier *f*. **celebrity** *n* Berühmtheit *f*.

celery ['seləri] *n* Sellerie *m* or *f*.

celestial [sə'lestiəl] *adj* himmlisch.

celibacy ['selibəsi] *n* Zölibat *neut* or *m*, Ehelosigkeit *f*. **celibate** *adj* ehelos.

cell [sel] *n* Zelle *f*.

cellar ['selə] *n* Keller *m*.

cello ['tʃelou] *n* Cello *neut*.

cellophane ['seləfein] *n* Zellophan *neut*.

cellular ['seljulə] *adj* zellular.

cement [sə'ment] *n* Zement *m*. *v* zementieren; (*fig*) binden.

cemetery ['semətri] *n* Friedhof *m*.

cenotaph ['senətaːf] *n* Ehrenmal *m*.

censor ['sensə] *n* Zensor *m*. *v* zensieren. **censorship** *n* Zensur *f*.

censure ['senʃə] *n* Tadel *m*. *v* tadeln.

census ['sensəs] *n* Volkszählung *f*.

cent [sent] *n* Cent *m*. **per cent** Prozent *neut*.

centenary [sen'tiːnəri] *n* Hundertjahrfeier *f*.

centigrade ['sentigreid] *adv* Celsius.

centimetre ['sentimiːtə] *n* Zentimeter *neut*.

centipede ['sentipiːd] *n* Tausendfuß *m*.

centre ['sentə] *n* Zentrum *neut*, Mittelpunkt *m*. *adj* Zentral-. *v* **centre around** sich drehen um. **centre on** sich konzentrieren auf. **centre forward** (*sport*) Mittelstürmer *m*. **centre half** Mittelläufer *m*. **centre of gravity** Schwerpunkt *m*. **centrepiece** *n* Tafelaufsatz *m*. **central** *adj* zentral, Zentral-. **Central America** Mittelamerika *neut*. **central heating** Zentralheizung *f*. **central station** Hauptbahnhof *m*.

centrifugal [sen'trifjugəl] *adj* zentrifugal. **centrifugal force** Zentrifugalkraft *f*.

century ['sentʃuri] *n* Jahrhundert *neut*.

ceramic [sə'ramik] *adj* keramisch. **ceramics** *n* Keramik *f*.

cereal ['siəriəl] *n* Getreide *neut*. **breakfast cereal** Getreideflocken *pl*.

ceremony ['serəməni] *n* Zeremonie *f*. **ceremonial** *adj* zeremoniell. **ceremonious** *adj* zeremoniös.

certain ['sɔːtn] *adj* bestimmt, gewiß; (*sure*) sicher. **for certain** bestimmt. **certainly** *adv* sicherlich, gewiß. **certainty** *n* Sicherheit *f*.

certificate [sə'tifikət] *n* Bescheinigung *f*. **certification** *n* Bescheinigung *f*. **certify** *v* bestätigen.

cervix ['sɔːviks] *n* (*anat*) Gebärmutterhals *m*.

cesspool ['sespuːl] *n* Senkgrube *f*.

chafe [tʃeif] *v* reiben.

chaffinch ['tʃafintʃ] *n* Buchfink *m*.

chain [tʃein] *n* Kette *f*. *v* anketten. **chain reaction** Kettenreaktion *f*. **chain smoker** Kettenraucher *m*. **chainstore** *n* Kettenladen *m*.

chair [tʃeə] *n* Stuhl *m*; (*armchair*) Sessel *m*; (*at meeting*) Vorsitz *m*. *v* (*meeting*) den Vorsitz führen. **chairlift** *n* Sesselbahn *f*. **chairman** Vorsitzende(r).

chalet

chalet ['ʃaleɪ] *n* Chalet *neut.*
chalk [tʃɔːk] *n* Kreide *f.* *v* mit Kreide schreiben.
challenge ['tʃalɪndʒ] *n* Aufforderung *f*; (*objection*) Einwand *m.* *v* auffordern; (*question*) bestreiten. **challenger** *n* Herausforderer *m.*
chamber ['tʃeɪmbə] *n* Kammer *f.* **chamber music** Kammermusik *f.* **chamber pot** Nachttopf *m.*
chameleon [kəmiːlɪən] *n* Chamäleon *neut.*
chamois ['ʃamwaɪ] *n* Gemse *f*; (*leather*) Sämischleder *neut.*
champagne [ʃam'peɪn] *n* Champagner *m.*
champion ['tʃampɪən] *n* (*sport*) Meister *m,* Sieger *m*; (*defender*) Verfechter *m.* *v* (*cause*) verfechten. **championship** *n* Meisterschaft *f.*
chance [tʃaɪns] *n* Zufall *m*; (*opportunity*) Gelegenheit *f*; (*possibility*) Chance *f,* Möglichkeit *f.* *v* riskieren. **by chance** zufällig. **stand a chance** Chancen haben. **take a chance** sein Glück versuchen. **no chance!** keine Spur!
chancellor [tʃaɪnsələ] *n* Kanzler *m.*
chandelier [ʃandə'lɪə] *n* Kronleuchter *m.*
change [tʃeɪndʒ] *v* (*modify*) (ab-, ver)ändern; (*exchange*) (aus)tauschen; (*become changed*) sich (ver)ändern; (*trains*) umsteigen; (*clothes*) sich umziehen; (*money*) wechseln. **change gear** schalten. **change into** (sich) verwandeln in. **change over to** übergehen zu. *n* (Ab-, Ver)Änderung *f*; (Ver)Wandlung *f*; (*small change*) Kleingeld *neut.* **change of life** Wechseljahre *pl.* **for a change** zur Abwechselung. **changeable** *adj* veränderlich. **changeless** *adj* unveränderlich.
channel ['tʃanl] *n* Kanal *m*; (*fig*) Weg *m.* *v* lenken. **through official channels** durch die Instanzen. **English Channel** der Ärmelkanal.
chant [tʃaɪnt] *v* intonieren. *n* Gesang *m.*
chaos ['keɪos] *n* Chaos *neut*; (*mess*) Durcheinander *neut.*
chap[1] [tʃap] *v* (*skin*) rissig machen; (*become chapped*) aufspringen.
chap[2] [tʃap] *n* (*coll*) Kerl *m.*
chapel ['tʃapəl] *n* Kapelle *f.*
chaperon ['ʃapəroʊn] *n* Anstandsdame *f.* *v* begleiten.
chaplain ['tʃaplɪn] *n* Kaplan *m.*
chapter ['tʃaptə] *n* Kapitel *neut*; (*branch*) Ortsgruppe *f.*

char[1] [tʃaɪ] *v* (*burn*) verkohlen.
char[2] [tʃaɪ] *n* (*cleaning lady*) Putzfrau *f.*
character ['karəktə] *n* Charakter *m*; (*personality*) Persönlichkeit *f*; (*theatre*) Person *f*; (*reputation*) Ruf *m*; (*letter*) Buchstabe *m.* **characteristic** *n* Kennzeichen *neut*; *adj* charakteristisch. **characterize** *v* charakterisieren.
charcoal ['tʃaɪkoʊl] *n* Holzkohle *f*; (*for drawing*) Reißkohle *f.*
charge [tʃaɪdʒ] *n* (*cost*) Preis *m*; (*of firearm*) Ladung *f*; (*mil*) Angriff *m*; (*law*) Anklage *f*; (*elec*) Ladung *f.* *v* (*firearm, battery*) laden; (*price*) verlangen; (*attack*) angreifen. **be in charge of** verantwortlich sein für. **bring a charge against** anklagen.
chariot ['tʃarɪət] *n* Streitwagen *m.*
charity ['tʃarəti] *n* Nächstenliebe *f,* Wohltätigkeit *f*; (*organization*) Wohlfahrtseinrichtung *f.* **charitable** *adj* wohltätig *f.*
charm [tʃaɪm] *n* (*personal*) Scharm *m,* Reiz *m*; (*magic word*) Zauberwort *neut*; (*trinket*) Amulett *neut.* *v* entzücken. **charming** entzückend, scharmant.
chart [tʃaɪt] *n* (*naut*) Seekarte *f*; Diagramm *neut.*
charter ['tʃaɪtə] *n* Verfassungsurkunde *f*; (*naut, aero*) Charter *m.* *v* chartern. *adj* Charter-.
chase [tʃeɪs] *v* verfolgen, jagen. *n* Verfolgung *f,* Jagd *f.*
chasm ['kazəm] *n* Abgrund *m.*
chassis ['ʃasi] *n* Fahrgestell *neut.*
chaste [tʃeɪst] *adj* keusch. **chastity** *n* Keuschheit *f.*
chastise [tʃas'taɪz] *v* strafen.
chat [tʃat] *n* plaudern, sich unterhalten. *n* Plauderei *f.*
chatter ['tʃatə] *v* schnattern; (*teeth*) klappern. *n* Geschnatter *neut*; Klappern *neut.*
chauffeur ['ʃoʊfə] *n* Chauffeur *m.*
chauvinism ['ʃoʊvɪnɪzəm] *n* Chauvinismus *m.* **chauvinist** *n* Chauvinist *m.*
cheap [tʃiːp] *adj* billig, preiswert; (*base*) gemein.
cheat [tʃiːt] *v* betrügen. *n* Betrüger *m,* Schwindler *m.*
check [tʃek] *v* (*inspect*) prüfen, kontrollieren; (*hinder*) (ver)hindern; (*look up*) nachsehen; (*tick*) abhaken. **check in** sich anmelden. **check out** (*hotel*) abreisen. *n* Kontrolle *f*; (*bill*) Rechnung *f*; (*check*) Scheck *m*; (*chess*) Schach *m*; (*pattern*) Karo *neut.* **checklist** *n* Kontrolliste *f.*

checkmate n Schachmatt neut. **check-point** Kontrollpunkt m. **check-up** n (med) ärztliche Untersuchung f.

cheek [tʃiːk] n (anat) Wange f, Backe f; (impudence) Frechheit f. **cheeky** adj frech.

cheer [tʃiə] v jubeln; (applaud) zujubeln (+dat); (encourage) aufmuntern. **cheer up** aufmuntern. n Beifallsruf m, Hurra neut. **cheers!** interj prost! **cheerful** adj fröhlich. **cheerio!** interj tschüs!

cheese [tʃiːz] n Käse f. **cheesecake** n Käsekuchen m; **cheesecloth** n Musselin m.

cheetah ['tʃiːtə] n Gepard m.

chef [ʃef] n Küchenchef m.

chemical ['kemikl] adj chemisch. **chemicals** pl n Chemikalien pl.

chemist ['kemist] n Chemiker m; (dispensing chemist) Apotheker m. **chemist's shop** Apotheke f.

chemistry ['kemistri] n Chemie f.

cheque [tʃek] n Scheck m. **chequebook** n Scheckbuch neut, **cheque card** Deckkarte f.

cherish ['tʃeriʃ] v (feeling) hegen; (person) lieb haben.

cherry ['tʃeri] n Kirsche f; (tree) Kirschbaum m.

chess [tʃes] n Schach neut. **chessboard** n Schachbrett neut. **chessman** n Schachfigur f.

chest [tʃest] n (anat) Brust f; (container) Kiste f; (trunk) Truhe f. **that's a weight off my chest** da fällt mir ein Stein vom Herzen.

chestnut ['tʃesnʌt] n (sweet chestnut) (Eß)Kastanie f; (horse chestnut) (Roß)Kastanie f; (tree) Kastanienbaum m; (brown horse) Braune(r) m.

chew [tʃuː] v kauen. **chewing gum** Kaugummi m.

chick [tʃik] n Küken neut. **chicken** n Huhn neut; (for eating) Hähnchen neut. adj (coll) feige. **chicken soup** Hühnerbrühe f.

chicory ['tʃikəri] n Zichorie f; (salad plant) Chicorée f.

chief [tʃiːf] n (pl -s) Chef m, Leiter m; (of tribe) Häuptling m. adj Haupt-, erster. **chieftain** m Häuptling m.

chilblain ['tʃilblein] n Frostbeule f.

child [tʃaild] n (pl -ren) Kind neut. **with child** schwanger. **childbirth** n Entbindung

f. **childhood** n Kindheit f. **childish** adj kindisch. **childlike** adj kindlich.

Chile ['tʃili] n Chile neut. **Chilean** adj chilenisch. n Chilene m, Chilenin f.

chill [tʃil] n Kältegefühl neut; (fever) Schüttelfrost m. **chilled** adj (drink) gekühlt. **chilly** adj fröstelnd.

chilli ['tʃili] n Cayennepfeffer m.

chime [tʃaim] v (bell) läuten. n Geläut neut.

chimney ['tʃimni] n Schornstein m. **chimney sweep** Schornsteinfeger m.

chimpanzee [tʃimpən'ziː] n Schimpanse m.

chin [tʃin] n Kinn neut.

china ['tʃainə] n Porzellan neut. adj Porzellan-. **china clay** Kaolin neut.

China ['tʃainə] n China neut. **Chinese** adj chinesisch; n Chinese m, Chinesin f.

chink¹ [tʃiŋk] n (fissure) Ritze f, Spalt m.

chink² [tʃiŋk] v (sound) klirren. n Klirren neut.

chip [tʃip] n Splitter m, chips pl Pommes frites pl; (crisps) Chips pl. **chipped** adj (china) angestoßen.

chiropodist [ki'ropədist] n Fußpfleger(in). **chiropody** n Fußpflege f.

chirp [tʃəːp] v zirpen. n Gezirp neut. **chirpy** adj munter.

chisel ['tʃizl] n Meißel m. v meißeln.

chivalrous [ʃivəlrəs] adj ritterlich. **chivalry** n Ritterlichkeit f.

chives [tʃaivz] pl n Schnittlauch m sing.

chlorine ['klɔːriːn] n Chlor neut. **chlorinate** v chlorieren.

chlorophyll ['klɔrəfil] n Chlorophyll neut.

chocolate ['tʃokələt] n Schokolade f. adj (colour) schokoladenbraun.

choice [tʃois] n Wahl f; (selection) Auswahl f. adj auserlesen.

choir ['kwaiə] n Chor m. **choirboy** Chorknabe m.

choke [tʃouk] v ersticken, würgen; (throttle) erwürgen. n (mot) Starterklappe f.

cholera ['kolərə] n Cholera f.

cholesterol [kə'lestərol] n Cholesterin neut.

__*__**choose** [tʃuːz] v wählen; (select) auswählen; (prefer) vorziehen. **choosy** adj wählerisch.

chop¹ [tʃop] v (food) zerhacken; (wood) spalten. n Kotelett neut.

chop² [tʃop] v **chop and change** schwanken, wechseln.

chopsticks ['tʃopstiks] *pl n* Eßstäbchen *pl.*

chord [kɔːd] *n (music)* Akkord *m.*

chore [tʃɔː] *n* lästige Pflicht *f.*

choreographer [kori'ogrəfə] *n* Choreograph *m.* **choreography** *n* Choreographie *f.*

chorus ['kɔːrəs] *n* Chor *m*; *(of song)* Refrain *m.*

chose [tʃouz] *V* **choose**.

chosen ['tʃouzn] *V* **choose**.

Christ [kraist] *n* Christus *m.*

christen ['krisn] *v* taufen. **christening** *n* Taufe *f.*

Christian ['kristʃən] *adj* christlich. *n* Christ *m,* Christin *f.* **Christian name** Vorname *m.* **Christianity** *n* Christentum *neut.*

Christmas ['krisməs] *n* Weihnachten *pl.* **Christmas card** Weihnachtskarte *f.* **Christmas present** Weihnachtsgeschenk *neut.* **Christmas tree** Weihnachtsbaum *m.*

chrome [kroum] *n (plating)* Verchromung *f. adj (yellow)* chromgelb. **chrome-plated** *adj* verchromt.

chromium ['kroumiəm] *n* Chrom *neut.*

chronic ['kronik] *adj (med)* chronisch.

chronicle ['kronikl] *n* Chronik *f.*

chronological [kronə'lodʒikəl] *adj* chronologisch.

chrysalis ['krisəlis] *n* Puppe *f.*

chrysanthemum [kri'sanθəməm] *n* Chrysantheme *f.*

chubby ['tʃʌbi] *adj* pausbäckig.

chuck [tʃʌk] *v (coll)* werfen.

chuckle ['tʃʌkl] *v* glucksen, kichern. *n* Kichern *neut.*

chunk [tʃʌŋk] *n* Klumpen *m,* Stück *neut.*

church [tʃɜːtʃ] *n* Kirche *f.* **church-goer** *n* Kirchgänger *m.* **churchyard** *n* Kirchhof *m.*

churn [tʃɜːn] *n (butter)* Butterfaß *neut*; *(milk)* Milchkanne *f. v (fig)* aufwühlen.

chute [ʃuːt] *n* Rutsche *f.*

cider ['saidə] *n* Apfelwein *m.*

cigar [si'gaː] *n* Zigarre *f.*

cigarette [sigə'ret] *n* Zigarette *f.* **cigarette end** Zigarettenstümmel *m.* **cigarette lighter** *n* Feuerzeug *neut.*

cinder ['sində] *n* Zinder *m.*

cine camera ['sini] *n* Filmkamera *f.*

cinema ['sinəmə] *n* Kino *neut.*

cinnamon ['sinəmən] *n* Zimt *m.*

circle ['sɜːkl] *n* Kreis *m*; *(theatre)* Rang *m. v* umkreisen. **circular** *adj* kreisförmig, rund. **circulate** *v* zirkulieren, umlaufen; *(send round)* in Umlauf setzen. **circulation** *n* Umlauf *m*; *(blood)* Kreislauf *m.*

circuit ['sɜːkit] *n* Umlauf *m*; *(elec)* Stromkreis *m.*

circumcise ['sɜːkəmsaiz] *n* beschneiden. **circumcision** *n* Beschneidung *f.*

circumference [sɜː'kʌmfərəns] *n* Umfang *m.*

circumscribe ['sɜːkəmskraib] *v* umschreiben.

circumstance ['sɜːkəmstans] *n* Umstand *m.* **under the circumstances** unter diesen Umständen. **under no circumstances** auf keinen Fall.

circus ['sɜːkəs] *n* Zirkus *m.*

cistern ['sistən] *n* Zisterne *f.*

cite [sait] *v* zitieren.

citizen ['sitizn] *n* Bürger(in); *(of country)* Staatsangehörige(r). **citizenship** *n* Staatsangehörigkeit *f.*

citrus ['sitrəs] *adj* **citrus fruit** Zitrusfrucht *f.*

city ['siti] *n* Stadt *f.*

civic ['sivik] *n* städtisch.

civil ['sivl] *adj (polite)* höflich, freundlich; *(not military)* Zivil-. **civility** *n* Höflichkeit *f.* **civil engineer** Bauingenieur *m.* **civil rights** Bürgerrechte *pl.*

civilian [sə'viljən] *adj* Zivil-. *n* Zivilist *m.*

civilization [,sivilai'zeiʃən] *n* Zivilisation *f.* **civilize** *v* zivilisieren. **civilized** *adj* zivilisiert.

clad [klad] *adj* bekleidet; *(tech)* umkleidet.

claim [kleim] *v* verlangen, Anspruch erheben auf. *n* Anspruch *m*; *(right)* Anrecht *neut.* **claimant** *n* Antragsteller *m.*

clairvoyant [kleə'voiənt] *n* Hellseher(in).

clam [klam] *n* Muschel *f.*

clamber ['klambə] *v* klettern.

clammy ['klami] *adj* feucht, klebrig.

clamour ['klamə] *n* Geschrei *neut. v* **clamour for** rufen nach.

clamp [klamp] *n* Klammer *f,* Krampe *f. v* verklammern. **clamp down on** unterdrücken.

clan [klan] *n* Sippe *f.*

clandestine [klan'destin] *adj* heimlich.

clang [klaŋ] *n* Schall *m,* Klirren *neut. v* schallen, klirren.

clank [klaŋk] *n* Gerassel *neut*; Klappern *neut. v* rasseln, klappern.

clap [klap] v (applaud) klatschen, Beifall spenden (+dat); (hit) schlagen, klapsen. n (tap) Klaps m. **clapper** n (bell) Klöppel m. **clapping** n Klatschen neut.

claret ['klarət] n Rotwein m, Bordeaux m.

clarify ['klarəfai] v klären. **clarification** n Klärung f.

clarinet [klarə'net] n Klarinette f. **clarinettist** n Klarinettist m.

clash [klaʃ] v kollidieren, zusammenprallen; (argue) sich streiten; (colours) nicht zusammenpassen. n Knall m; (conflict) Konflikt m.

clasp [klaːsp] v umklammern; n Haspe f, Klammer f.

class [klaːs] n Klasse f; (lesson) Stunde f. v klassieren. **class-conscious** adj klassenbewußt. **classroom** n Klassenzimmer f. **classy** adj (coll) klasse, erstklassig.

classic ['klasik] adj klassisch. **classics** pl n die alten Sprachen pl. **classical** adj klassisch. **classicism** n Klassik f.

classify ['klasifai] v klassifizieren. **classification** n Klassifizierung f.

clatter ['klatəl v klappern. n Klappern neut.

clause [kloːz] n (in document) Klausel f.

claustrophobia [kloːstrə'foubiə] n Platzangst f.

claw [kloː] n Kralle f, Klaue f. v zerkratzen.

clay [klei] n Lehm m, Ton m.

clean [kliːn] adj rein, sauber; (paper) weiß. adv ganz. v reinigen, putzen, saubermachen. **clean up** aufräumen. **come clean** gestehen. **cleaner** n (woman) Putzfrau f. **cleaning** n Reinigen neut. **cleanness** n Sauberkeit f. **cleanly** adj reinlich. **clean-shaven** adj glattrasiert.

cleanse [klenz] v reinigen.

clear [kliə] adj klar; (sound, meaning) deutlich, klar; (road, way) frei; (glass) durchsichtig. v räumen; (table) abräumen; (road) freimachen; (forest) roden; (authorize) freigeben. **clearance** n Räumung f; (authorization) Freigabe f; (tech) Spielraum m. **clearcut** adj (fig) eindeutig. **clearing** n Lichtung f. **clearly** adv offensichtlich.

clef [klef] n Notenschlüssel m.

clench [klentʃ] v (fist) zusammenballen.

clergy ['kləːdʒi] n Klerus m. **clergyman** n Geistliche(r) m; Kleriker m.

clerical ['klerikəl] adj geistlich. **clerical work** Büroarbeit f.

clerk [klaːk] n Büroangestellte(r); (sales clerk) Verkäufer(in).

clever ['klevə] adj klug, gescheit; (crafty) raffiniert. **cleverness** n Klugheit f.

cliché ['kliːʃei] n Klischee neut.

click [klik] n Klicken neut. v klicken.

client ['klaiənt] n Kunde m, Kundin f. **clientele** n Kundschaft f.

cliff [klif] n Klippe f.

climate ['klaimət] n Klima neut.

climax ['klaimaks] n Höhepunkt m.

climb [klaim] v klettern; (ascend) steigen; (mountain) besteigen. n Aufstieg m. **climb up** hinaufklettern auf. **climb down** hinabsteigen. **climber** n (mountaineer) Bergsteiger m. **climbing** n (mountaineering) Bergsteigen neut.

***cling** [kliŋ] v sich klammern (an); (fig) hängen (an).

clinic ['klinik] n Klinik f. **clinical** adj klinisch.

clink [kliŋk] n Klirren neut. v klirren.

clip[1] [klip] v (hair) schneiden; (dog) stutzen; (ticket) knipsen. **clipping** n (newspaper) Zeitungsausschnitt m.

clip[2] [klip] n (fastener) Klammer f, Klemme f. v **clip together** zusammenklammern.

clitoris ['klitəris] n Kitzler m, Klitoris f.

cloak [klouk] n Umhang m. **cloakroom** n Garderobe f; (WC) Toilette f.

clock [klok] n Uhr f. **clockwise** adj, adv im Uhrzeigersinn. **clockwork** n Uhrwerk neut.

clog [klog] n Holzschuh m. v verstopfen.

cloister ['kloistə] n Kreuzgang m.

close[1] [klouz] v zumachen, schließen. n Ende neut; Schluß m. **close down** eingehen. **closed** adj (shop) geschlossen; (road) gesperrt.

close[2] [klous] adj nahe; (intimate) vertraut; (careful) genau; (weather) schwül. adv knapp. **close to** in der Nähe (+gen or von). **close together** dicht zusammen. **that was close!** das war knapp! **closely** adv genau, gründlich. **close-up** n Nahaufnahme f.

closet ['klozit] n Schrank m.

clot [klot] n Klümpchen neut; (of blood) Blutgerinnsel neut. v gerinnen.

cloth [kloθ] n (material) Stoff m, Tuch neut; (for wiping) Lappen m.

clothe [klouð] v (be)kleiden. **clothes** pl n Kleider pl. **clothes brush** Kleiderbürste f.

clothes line Wäscheleine *f.* clothes peg Wäscheklammer *f.* clothing *n* Kleidung *f.*
cloud [klaud] *n* Wolke *f.* cloud over sich bewölken.
clove¹ [klouv] *n* (*spice*) Gewürznelke *f.*
clove² [klouv] *n* clove of garlic Knoblauchzehe *f.*
clover ['klouvə] *n* Klee *m.*
clown [klaun] *n* Clown *m.*
club [klʌb] *n* (*association*) Klub *m,* Verein *m*; (*weapon*) Keule *f*; (*golf*) Golfschläger *m.* clubfoot *n* Klumpfuß *m.*
clue [kluː] *n* Spur *f,* Anhaltspunkt *m. I haven't a clue* ich habe keine Ahnung *f.*
clump [klʌmp] *n* Klumpen *neut*; (*of bushes*) Gebüsch *neut.*
clumsy ['klʌmzi] *adj* unbeholfen, linkisch.
clung [klʌŋ] *V* cling.
cluster ['klʌstə] *n* Traube *f. v* cluster around schwärmen um.
clutch [klʌtʃ] *n* (*fester*) Griff *m*; (*mot*) Kupplung *f. v* sich festklammern an. clutch at greifen nach.
clutter ['klʌtə] *n* Unordnung *f,* Durcheinander *neut. v* vollstopfen.
coach [koutʃ] *n* Kutsche *f*; (*rail*) Wagen *m*; (*sport*) Trainer *m. v* eintrainieren.
coagulate [kou'agjuleit] *v* gerinnen.
coal [koul] *n* Kohle *f.* coal-mine Kohlenbergwerk *neut.*
coalition [kouə'liʃən] *n* (*pol*) Koalition *f.*
coarse [kɔːs] *adj* grob; (*vulgar*) ordinär.
coast [koust] *n* Küste *f.* coastal *adj* Küsten-. coastline *n* Küstenlinie *f.*
coat [kout] *n* Mantel *m*; (*of animal*) Fell *neut,* Pelz *m*; (*of paint*) Anstrich *m. v* bestreichen. coated *adj* überzogen. coathanger *n* Kleiderbügel *m.* coating *n* Überzug *m.*
coax [kouks] *v* beschwatzen.
cobbler ['koblə] *n* Schuster *m.*
cobra ['koubrə] *n* Kobra *neut.*
cobweb ['kobweb] *n* Spinngewebe *neut.*
cocaine [kə'kein] *n* Kokain *neut.*
cock¹ [kok] *n* (*male chicken*) Hahn *m*; (*male bird*) (Vogel)Männchen *neut.*
cock² [kok] *v* (*gun*) spannen; (*ears*) spitzen.
cockle ['kokl] *n* (*shellfish*) Herzmuschel *f.*
cockpit ['kokpit] *n* Kanzel *f,* Kabine *f.*
cockroach ['kokroutʃ] *n* Küchenschabe *f.*
cocktail ['kokteil] *n* Cocktail *neut.*
cocoa ['koukou] *n* Kakao *m.*
coconut ['koukənʌt] *n* Kokosnuß *m.*
cocoon [kə'kuːn] *n* Kokon *m,* Puppe *f.*

cod [kod] *n* Kabeljau *m.*
code [koud] *n* Kode *m.*
codeine ['koudiːn] *n* Kodein *neut.*
coeducation [kouedju'keiʃən] *n* Gemeinschaftserziehung *f.*
coerce [kou'əːs] *v* zwingen. coercion *n* Zwang *m.*
coexist [kouig'zist] *v* koexistieren. coexistence *n* Koexistenz *f.*
coffee ['kofi] *n* Kaffee *m.* coffee bar Café *neut.*
coffin ['kofin] *n* Sarg *m.*
cog [kog] *n* Radzahn *neut.* cogwheel Zahnrad *neut.*
cognac ['konjak] *n* Kognak *m.*
cohabit [kou'habit] *v* (*ehelich*) zusammenwohnen.
coherent [kou'hiərənt] *adj* zusammenhängend.
coil [koil] *n* Rolle *f*; *v* aufwickeln.
coin [koin] *n* Münze *f. v* prägen. coinbox *n* (*phone*) Münzfernsprecher *m.*
coincide [kouin'said] *v* zusammenfallen; (*agree*) übereinstimmen. coincidence *n* Zufall *m.* coincidental zufällig.
colander ['koləndə] *n* Durchschlag *m.*
cold [kould] *adj* kalt. *I am/feel cold* mir ist kalt. *n* Kälte *f*; (*med*) Erkältung *f.* catch cold sich erkälten. in cold blood kaltblütig. coldly *adv* (*fig*) gefühllos, unfreundlich. cold store Kühlhaus *neut.*
coleslaw ['koulslɔː] *n* Krautsalat *m.*
colic ['kolik] *n* Kolik *f.*
collaborate [kə'labəreit] *v* zusammenarbeiten. collaboration *n* zusammenarbeit *f.* collaborator *n* Mitarbeiter *m*; (*in war*) Kollaborateur *m.*
collapse [kə'laps] *v* einstürzen; (*person*) zusammenbrechen. *n* Einsturz *m*; (*fig, med*) Zusammenbruch *m.* collapsible *adj* zusammenklappbar.
collar ['kolə] *n* Kragen *m*; (*for dog*) Halsband *m.* collarbone *n* Schlüsselbein *neut.*
colleague ['koliːg] *n* Kollege *m,* Kollegin *f.*
collect [kə'lekt] *v* sammeln; (*fetch*) abholen; (*taxes*) eignehmen; (*come together*) zusammenkommen. collect call (*phone*) R-Gespräch *neut.* collected *adj* (*calm*) gefaßt. collection *n* Sammlung *f*; (*rel*) Kollekte *f*; (*mail*) Leerung *f.* collective *adj* kollektiv. collective bargaining Tarifverhandlungen *pl.* collector *n* Sammler *m*; (*of taxes*) Einnehmer *m.*

college ['kolidʒ] n Hochschule f; (at Oxford, etc.) College neut. **technical college** Realschule f.

collide [kə'laid] v kollidieren, zusammenprallen.

colloquial [kə'loukwiəl] adj umgangsprachlich.

Cologne [kə'loun] n Köln neut. **eau de Cologne** Kölnischwasser neut.

colon ['koulon] n (anat) Dickdarm m; (gram) Doppelpunkt m.

colonel ['kəɪnl] n Oberst m.

colony ['koləni] n Kolonie f. **colonial** adj Kolonial-. **colonialism** Kolonialismus m. **colonize** v kolonisieren.

colossal [kə'losəl] adj kolossal, riesig.

colour ['kʌlə] n Farbe f; (fig) Ton m, Charakter m. **colours** pl Fahne f sing. v färben (also fig), kolorieren. **colour bar** Rassenschranke f. **colour-blind** adj farbenblind. **coloured** adj farbig. **coloured man/woman** Farbige(r). **colour film** Farbfilm m. **colourful** adj farbig, bunt. **colour television** Farbfernsehen neut.

colt [koult] n Fohlen neut.

column ['koləm] n Säule f; (in newspaper) Spalte f; (mil) Kolonne f. **columnist** n Kolumnist m.

coma ['koumə] n Koma f.

comb [koum] n Kamm m. v kämmen; (fig) durchkämmen.

combat ['kombat] v bekämpfen. n Kampf m, Gefecht neut.

combine [kəm'bain; n 'kombain] v vereinigen, verbinden; (come together) sich vereinigen. n Konzern m. **combine harvester** Mähdrescher m.

combustion [kəm'bʌstʃən] n Verbrennung f. **combustible** adj brennbar.

*come [kʌm] v kommen. **come about** geschehen. **come across** stoßen auf. **come back** zurückkommen. **come from** herkommen von stammen aus. **come near** sich nähern. **come on** weiterkommen; (make progress) fortschreiten. **come on!** los!; weiter! **come out** herauskommen. **come through** durchkommen. **come to** (arrive at) ankommen an, gelangen an; (amount to) sich belaufen auf; (regain consciousness) zu sich kommen. **comeback** n Comeback neut.

comedy ['komədi] n Komödie f. **comedian** n Komiker m.

comet ['komit] n Komet m.

comfort ['kʌmfət] n Bequemlichkeit f, Komfort m; (solace) Trost m. v trösten. **comfortable** adj bequem; (room, etc.) komfortabel.

comic ['komik] adj komisch, lustig; (theatre) Komödien-. n (person) Komiker m; (paper) Comic neut. **comical** adj komisch.

comma ['komə] n Komma neut.

command [kə'maind] n (order) Befehl m; (mil) Oberbefehl m; (mastery) Beherrschung f. v (instruct) befehlen; (be in charge of) kommandieren. **commander** n Befehlshaber m; (mil) Kommandant m. **commandment** n Gebot neut. **commando** n Kommando neut.

commemorate [kə'meməreit] v gedenken (+gen), feiern. **commemoration** n Gedächtnisfeier f.

commence [kə'mens] v beginnen, anfangen. **commencement** n Beginn m, Anfang m.

commend [kə'mend] v (praise) loben; (entrust) anvertrauen. **commendable** adj lobenswert.

comment ['koment] n (remark) Bemerkung f; (annotation) Anmerkung f. v kommentieren, Bemerkungen machen. **commentary** n Reportage f. **commentator** n Kommentator m.

commerce ['koməɪs] n Handel m, Kommerz m. **commercial** adj kommerziell, geschäftlich, Handels-. **commercialize** v kommerzialisieren.

commiserate [kə'mizəreit] v commiserate with bemitleiden.

commission [kə'miʃən] n Auftrag m; (committee) Kommission f; (fee) Provision f; (mil) Offizierspatent neut. v (person) beauftragen; (thing) bestellen. **commissioner** n Bevollmächtigte(r).

commit [kə'mit] v (offence) begehen. **commit oneself** sich verpflichten. **commitment** n Verpflichtung f.

committee [kə'miti] n Ausschuß m, Kommission f.

commodity [kə'modəti] n Ware f. **commodities** pl Grundstoffe pl.

common ['komən] adj gemein, gemeinsam; (abundant) weit verbreitet; (vulgar) gemein, ordinär. **Common Market** Gemeinsamer Markt m. **commonplace** adj alltäglich. **commonsense** n gesunder Menschenverstand m.

commotion [kə'mouʃən] *n* Erregung *f*, Aufruhr *m*.
commune ['komjuːn] *n* Kommune *f*, Gemeinschaft *f*.
communicate [kə'mjuːnikeit] *v* mitteilen; (*illness*) übertragen. **communicative** *adj* gesprächig. **communication** *n* Kommunikation *f*; (*message*) Mitteilung *f*. **communications** *pl n* Verkehrswege *pl*.
communism ['komjunizəm] *n* Kommunismus *m*. **communist** *adj* kommunistisch. *n* Kommunist(in).
community [kə'mjuːnəti] *n* Gemeinschaft *f*.
commute [kə'mjuːt] *v* (*travel*) pendeln; (*a sentence*) herabsetzen. **commuter** *n* Pendler *m*.
compact¹ [kəm'pakt] *adj* kompakt, dicht.
compact² ['kompakt] *n* (*agreement*) Vertrag *m*, Pakt *m*.
companion [kəm'panjən] *n* Begleiter(in); Genosse *m*, Genossin *f*. **companionable** *adj* gesellig. **companionship** *n* Gesellschaft *f*.
company ['kʌmpəni] *n* Gesellschaft *f*; (*firm*) Gesellschaft *f*, Firma *f*; (*theatre*) Truppe *f*; (*mil*) Kompanie *f*.
compare [kəm'peə] *v* vergleichen; (*match up to*) sich vergleichen lassen. **comparable** *adj* vergleichbar. **comparative** *adj* relativ; (*gram*) steigernd. **comparatively** *adv* verhältnismäßig. **comparison** *n* Vergleich *m*. **in comparison with** im Vergleich zu.
compartment [kəm'paːtmənt] *n* Abteilung *f*.
compass ['kʌmpəs] *n* Kompaß *m*. **pair of compasses** Zirkel *m*.
compassion [kəm'paʃən] *n* Mitleid *neut*. **compassionate** *adj* mitleidig.
compatible [kəm'patəbl] *adj* vereinbar.
compel [kəm'pel] *v* zwingen.
compensate ['kompənseit] *v* (*money*) entschädigen; (*balance out*) ausgleichen. **compensation** *n* Entschädigung *f*; Ausgleich *m*.
compete [kəm'piːt] *v* konkurrieren, sich bewerben; (*take part*) teilnehmen. **competition** *n* Wettbewerb *m*; (*comm*) Konkurrenz *f*. **competitive** *adj* konkurrenzfähig. **competitor** *n* (*sport*) Teilnehmer(in); (*comm*) Konkurrent(in).
compile [kəm'pail] *v* kompilieren.
complacent [kəm'pleisnt] *adj* selbstzufrieden.

complain [kəm'plein] *v* klagen. **complain about/to** sich beschweren über/bei. **complaint** *n* Klage *f*, Beschwerde *f*.
complement ['kompləmənt] *n* Ergänzung *f*. *v* ergänzen; (*go together*) zusammenpassen. **complementary** *adj* komplementär.
complete [kəm'pliːt] *v* vollenden, vervollständigen; (*form*) ausfüllen. *adj* vollständig, vollendet. **completely** *adv* völlig, vollständig, ganz und gar. **completion** *n* Vollendung *f*.
complex ['kompleks] *adj* kompliziert. *n* (*psychol*) Komplex *m*.
complexion [kəm'plekʃən] *n* Teint *m*.
complicate ['komplikeit] *v* verwickeln, komplizieren. **complicated** *adj* kompliziert. **complication** *n* Komplikation *f*, Schwierigkeit *f*.
compliment ['kompləmənt] *n* Kompliment *neut*. *v* komplimentieren. **complimentary** *adj* höflich, artig. **complimentary ticket** Freikarte *f*.
comply [kəm'plai] *v* sich fügen. **comply with** (*rules*) sich halten an; (*request*) erfüllen.
component [kəm'pounənt] *n* Bestandteil *m*.
compose [kəm'pouz] *v* komponieren. **composed** *adj* gefaßt. **be composed of** bestehen aus. **composer** *n* Komponist *m*. **composite** *adj* zusammengesetzt. **composition** *n* Komposition *f*; (*piece of music*) (Musik)Stück *neut*.
compost ['kompost] *n* Kompost *m*.
composure [kəm'pouʒə] *n* Gefaßtheit *f*.
compound ['kompaund] *n* Zusammensetzung *f*; (*chem*) Verbindung *f*; *adj* zusammengesetzt, gemischt.
comprehend [kompri'hend] *v* verstehen, begreifen. **comprehensible** *adj* verständlich. **comprehension** *n* Verständnis *n*.
comprehensive [kompri'hensiv] *adj* umfassend. **comprehensive school** *n* Gesamtschule *f*.
compress [kəm'pres; *n* 'kompres] *v* verdichten, zusammendrücken. *n* (*med*) Kompresse *f*. **compressed** *adj* zusammengedrückt. **compressed air** Preßluft *f*. **compression** *n* Verdichtung *f*. **compressor** *n* Verdichter *m*.
comprise [kəm'praiz] *v* bestehen aus.
compromise ['komprəmaiz] *n* Kompromiß *m or neut*. *v* einen Kompromiß schließen; (*expose*) kompromittieren.

compulsion [kəm'pʌlʃən] n Zwang m.
compulsive adj Zwangs-. compulsory adj
Zwangs-.
compunction [kəm'pʌŋkʃən] n Gewissens-
sbisse pl, Reue f.
computer [kəm'pjuːtə] n Computer m.
comrade ['komrid] n Genosse m, Genossin f; Kamerad(in). comradeship n
Kameradschaft f.
concave [kon'keiv] adj konkav, Hohl-.
conceal [kən'siːl] v verbergen, verstecken;
(fact, etc.) verschweigen.
concede [kən'siːd] v zugeben, einräumen;
(right) bewilligen.
conceit [kən'siːt] n Einbildung f, Eitelkeit
f. conceited adj eingebildet.
conceive [kən'siːv] v (plan) erdenken;
(child) empfangen; (thoughts) fassen.
conceive of sich vorstellen (+acc). conceivable adj denkbar, vorstellbar.
concentrate ['konsəntreit] v konzentrier-
en. concentrate on sich konzentrieren
auf. concentrated adj konzentriert. concentration n Konzentration f.
concentric [kən'sentrik] adj konzentrisch.
concept ['konsept] n Begriff m, Idee f.
conception n Vorstellung f; (of child)
Empfängnis f.
concern [kən'səːn] v betreffen, angehen;
(worry) beunruhigen. n (worry) Besorgnis
f, Sorge f; (interest) Interesse neut;
(comm) Betrieb m. concern oneself with
sich befassen mit. as far as I am concerned von mir aus. that's not your concern! das geht Sie nichts an! concerning
adj betreffend.
concert ['konsət] n Konzert neut.
concerted [kən'səːtid] adj konzertiert.
concerto [kən'tʃəːtou] n Konzert neut.
concession [kən'seʃən] n Konzession f.
concessionnaire n Konzessionär m.
conciliate [kən'silieit] v versöhnen. concil-
iation n Versöhnung f. conciliatory adj
versöhnlich.
concise [kən'sais] adj kurz, knapp.
conclude [kən'kluːd] v schließen. conclude
that den Schluß ziehen, daß. conclusive
adj (evidence) schlüssig.
concoct [kən'kokt] v zusammenbrauen.
concrete ['konkriːt] adj konkret; (made of
concrete) Beton-. n Beton m.
concussion [kən'kʌʃən] n (med) Gehirner-
schütterung f.
condemn [kən'dem] v verurteilen. condemnation n Verurteilung f.

condense [kən'dens] v kondensieren. condensation n Kondensation f. condensed
milk Kondensmilch f.
condescend [kondi'send] v sich herablassen. condescending adj herablassend.
condescension n Herablassung f.
condition [kən'diʃən] n (state) Zustand
m; (requirement) Bedingung f, Voraussetzung f. conditions pl Umstände pl. on
condition that unter der Bedingung, daß.
out of condition (sport) in schlechter
Form. conditional adj bedingt.
condolence [kən'douləns] n Beileid neut.
condom ['kondom] n Kondom neut.
condone [kən'doun] v verzeihen.
conducive [kən'djuːsiv] adj förderlich.
conduct [kən'dʌkt; n 'kondʌkt]] v führen;
(orchestra) dirigieren; (elec) leiten. conduct oneself sich verhalten. n Führung f;
(behaviour) Verhalten neut.
conductor [kən'dʌktə] n (music) Dirigent
m; (bus) Schaffner(in).
cone [koun] n (shape) Kegel m; (ice
cream) Waffeltüte f; (bot) Zapfen m.
confectioner [kən'fekʃənə] n
Süßwarenhändler m. confectionery n
Süßwaren pl.
confederation [kənˌfedə'reiʃən] n Bund
m.
confer [kən'fəː] v (bestow) verleihen; (discuss) konferieren. conference n Konferenz f.
confess [kən'fes] v bekennen, gestehen;
(rel) beichten. confession n Geständnis
neut; (rel) Beichte f. confessional n
Beichtstuhl m.
confetti [kən'feti] n Konfetti pl.
confide [kən'faid] v anvertrauen. confide
in vertrauen (+dat). confidence n Vertrauen neut; (in oneself) Selbstvertrauen
neut. confident adj zuversichtlich; selbstsicher. confidential adj vertraulich.
confine [kən'fain] v (limit) beschränken;
(lock up) einsperren. confinement n (in
prison) Haft f; (childbirth) Niederkunft f.
confirm [kən'fəːm] v bestätigen; (rel)
konfirmieren. confirmation n Bestätigung
f; Konfirmation f.
confiscate ['konfiskeit] v beschlagnahmen.
confiscation n Beschlagnahme f.
conflict ['konflikt, v kon'flikt] n Konflikt
m, Streit m. v widerstreiten (+dat). conflict of interests Interessenkonflikt m.
conflicting adj widerstreitend.

conform [kən'fɔːm] v (*tally*) übereinstimmen (mit); (*to rules*) sich fügen (+ *dat*). **conformist** n Konformist.

confound [kən'faund] v (*surprise*) erstaunen; (*mix up*) verwechseln. **confound it!** verdammt!

confront [kən'frʌnt] v konfrontieren; (*enemy*) entgegentreten (+ *dat*). **confrontation** n Konfrontation f.

confuse [kən'fjuːz] v (*mix up*) verwechseln (mit); (*perplex*) verwirren. **confused** adj (*person*) verwirrt; (*situation*) verworren. **confusion** n Verwirrung f.

congeal [kən'dʒiːl] v gerinnen.

congenial [kən'dʒiːniəl] adj freundlich, gemütlich.

congenital [kən'dʒenitl] adj angeboren.

congested [kən'dʒestid] adj überfüllt. **congestion** n Stauung f; (*traffic*) Verkehrsstauung f.

conglomeration [kənˌglɔmə'reiʃən] n Anhäufung f, Konglomerat neut.

congratulate [kən'gratjuleit] v beglückwünschen. **congratulations** pl n Glückwünsche pl.

congregate ['kɔŋgrigeit] v sich versammeln. **congregation** n Versammlung f.

congress ['kɔŋgres] n Kongreß m. **congressman/woman** Abgeordnete(r).

conifer ['kɔnifə] n Nadelbaum m. **coniferous** adj Nadel-.

conjecture [kən'dʒektʃə] n Vermutung f.

conjugal ['kɔndʒugəl] adj ehelich.

conjugate ['kɔndʒugeit] v (*gramm*) konjugieren.

conjunction [kən'dʒʌŋkʃən] n Vereinigung f; (*gramm, astrol*) Konjunktion f.

conjunctivitis [kənˌdʒʌŋkti'vaitis] n Bindehautentzündung f.

conjure ['kʌndʒə] v **conjure up** heraufbeschwören. **conjurer** n Zauberkünstler m. **conjuring trick** Zauberkunststück neut.

connect [kə'nekt] v verbinden; (*phone, etc*.) anschließen. **connection** n Verbindung f; (*phone, rail*) Anschluß m. **in connection with** im Zusammenhang mit.

connoisseur [kɔnə'səː] n Kenner m.

connotation [kɔnə'teiʃən] n Nebenbedeutung f.

conquer ['kɔŋkə] v erobern, besiegen; (*fig*) überwinden, beherrschen. **conqueror** n Eroberer m. **conquest** n Eroberung f.

conscience ['kɔnʃəns] n Gewissen neut.

conscientious [kɔnʃi'enʃəs] adj pflichtbewußt.

conscious ['kɔnʃəs] adj bewußt. **consciousness** n Bewußtsein neut.

conscript ['kɔnskript] v einziehen. n Wehrpflichtige(r). **conscription** n Wehrpflicht f.

consecrate ['kɔnsikreit] v weihen.

consecutive [kən'sekjutiv] adj aufeinanderfolgend.

consensus [kən'sensəs] n Übereinstimmung f.

consent [kən'sent] v zustimmen (+ *dat*). n Zustimmung f.

consequence ['kɔnsikwəns] n Folge f, Konsequenz f. **of no consequence** unbedeutend. **consequently** adv folglich.

conserve [kən'səːv] v erhalten; (*energy*) sparen. **conservation** n Schutz m, Erhaltung f. **conservative** adj konservativ; n Konservative(r). **conservatory** n Treibhaus neut; (*music*) Musikhochschule f.

consider [kən'sidə] n (*think about*) überlegen; (*regard as*) halten für. **considerate** adj rücksichtsvoll. **consideration** n (*thought*) Überlegung f; (*thoughtfulness*) Rücksicht f. **considering** prep in Anbetracht (+ *gen*).

consign [kən'sain] v versenden. **consignee** n Empfänger m. **consignment** n Sendung f. **consignor** n Absender m.

consist [kən'sist] v **consist of** bestehen aus. **consistency** n (*of substance*) Dichte f. **consistent** adj konsequent. **consistent with** vereinbar mit.

console [kən'soul] v trösten. **consolation** n Trost m. **consolation prize** Trostpreis m.

consolidate [kən'solideit] v stärken; (*comm*) konsolidieren. **consolidation** n Stärkung f.

consommé [kən'sɔmei] n Fleischbrühe f.

consonant ['kɔnsənənt] n Konsonant m.

conspicuous [kən'spikjuəs] adj (*visible*) sichtbar; (*striking*) auffallend.

conspire [kən'spaiə] v sich verschwören. **conspiracy** n Verschwörung f. **conspirator** n Verschwörer m.

constable ['kʌnstəbl] n Polizist m.

constant ['kɔnstənt] adj beständig, konstant; (*continual*) dauernd. **constantly** adv ständig.

constellation [konstə'leifən] *n* Sternbild *neut.*

constipation [konsti'peifən] *n* (Darm)Verstopfung *f.*

constituency [kən'stitjuənsi] *n* Wahlkreis *m.* **constituent** *n* Wähler *m.*

constitute ['konstitjuːt] *v* bilden, darstellen. **constitution** *n* (*pol*) Grundgesetz *m,* Verfassung *f;* (*of person*) Konstitution *f.*

constrain [kən'strein] *v* zwingen. **constraint** *n* Zwang *m,* Druck *m.*

constrict [kən'strikt] *v* zusammendrücken, einengen.

construct [kən'strʌkt] *v* bauen, konstruieren; (*argument*) aufstellen. **construction** *n* Bau *m,* Konstruktion *f.* **constructive** *adj* konstruktiv.

consul ['konsəl] *n* Konsul *m.* **consulate** *n* Konsulat *neut.*

consult [kən'sʌlt] *v* zu Rate ziehen, konsultieren; (*book*) nachsehen in. **consultant** *n* Berater *m.* **consultation** *n* Konsultation *f.* **consulting room** Sprechzimmer *neut.*

consume [kən'sjuːm] *v* verzehren; (*money, time*) verbrauchen. **consumer** *n* Verbraucher *m.*

contact ['kontakt] *n* Verbindung *f,* Kontakt *m. v* sich in Verbindung setzen mit. **be in contact with** in Verbindung stehen mit.

contagious [kən'teidʒəs] *adj* ansteckend.

contain [kən'tein] *v* enthalten; (*feelings*) beherrschen. **contain oneself** sich beherrschen. **container** *n* Behälter *m;* (*for goods transport*) Container *m.* **container ship** Containerschiff *m.*

contaminate [kən'taməneit] *v* verseuchen. **contamination** *n* Verseuchung *f.*

contemplate ['kontəmpleit] *v* (*observe*) nachdenklich betrachten; (*think about*) nachdenken über; (*doing something*) vorhaben. **contemplation** *n* Betrachtung *f;* Nachdenken *neut.*

contemporary [kən'tempərəri] *adj* zeitgenössisch; (*modern*) modern. *n* Zeitgenosse *m.*

contempt [kən'tempt] *n* Verachtung *f.* **contemptible** *adj* verächtlich. **contemptuous** *adj* voller Verachtung *f.*

contend [kən'tend] *v* kämpfen; (*assert*) behaupten.

content[1] ['kontent] *n* Inhalt *m.* **contents** *pl* Inhalt *m sing.* **table of contents** Inhaltsverzeichnis *neut.*

content[2] [kən'tent] *adj* zufrieden. **contentment** *n* Zufriedenheit *f.*

contention [kən'tenfən] *n* Streit *m;* (*assertion*) Behauptung *f.*

contest ['kontest; *v* kən'test] *n* Wettkampf *m. v* bestreiten. **contestant** *n* Bewerber(in).

context ['kontekst] *n* Zusammenhang *m.*

continent ['kontinənt] *n* Festland *neut,* Kontinent *m.* **continental** *adj* Kontinental-.

contingency [kən'tindʒənsi] *n* Eventualität *f.*

continue [kən'tinjuː] *v* fortfahren, weitermachen; (*something*) fortsetzen; (*go further*) weitergehen. **continual** *adj* wiederholt. **continually** *adv* immer wieder. **continuation** *n* Fortsetzung *f.* **continuous** *adj* beständig.

contort [kən'toːt] *v* verdrehen. **contortion** *n* Verdrehung *f.* **contortionist** *n* Schlangenmensch *m.*

contour ['kontuə] *n* Umrißlinie *f.*

contraband ['kontrəbænd] *n* Schmuggelware *f.*

contraception [kontrə'sepfən] *n* Empfängnisverhütung *f.* **contraceptive** *adj* empfängnisverhütend. *n* empfängnisverhütendes Mittel *neut.*

contract ['kontrakt; *v* kən'trakt] *n* Vertrag *m. v* (*become smaller*) sich zusammenziehen; (*illness*) sich zuziehen. **contraction** *n* Zusammenziehung *f.* **contractor** *n* (*building*) Bauunternehmer *m.*

contradict [kontrə'dikt] *v* widersprechen. **contradiction** *n* Widerspruch *m.* **contradictory** *adj* sich widersprechend.

contralto [kən'traltou] *n* (*voice*) Alt *m;* (*singer*) Altistin *f.*

contraption [kən'trapfən] *n* komisches Ding *neut.*

contrary [kən'treəri; (*opposite*) 'kontrəri] *adj* (*person*) widerspenstig; (*opposite*) entgegengesetzt. *n* Gegenteil *m,* **on the contrary** im Gegenteil.

contrast [kən'traist; *n* 'kontraist] *v* (*compare*) vergleichen. **contrast with** kontrastieren mit. *n* Kontrast *m.* **in contrast to** im Gegensatz zu.

contravene [kontrə'viːn] *v* verstoßen gegen. **contravention** *n* Verstoß *m.*

contribute [kən'tribjut] *v* beitragen; (*money*) spenden. **contribution** *n* Beitrag *m.* **contributor** *n* Beitragende(r); (*to newspaper, etc.*) Mitarbeiter *m.*

contrive [kən'traiv] v (plan) ausdenken. I contrived to meet him es gelang mir, ihn zu treffen.

control [kən'troul] v (curb) zügeln; (machine) steuern. n Leitung f. **controls** pl n Steuerung f. **under/out of control** unter/außer Kontrolle.

controversial [kɒntrə'vəːʃəl] adj umstritten. **controversy** n Streitfrage f, Kontroverse f.

convalesce [kɒnvə'les] v genesen, gesund werden. **convalescence** n Genesungszeit f.

convection [kən'vekʃən] n Konvektion f.

convenience [kən'viːnjəns] n Bequemlichkeit f; (advantage) Vorteil m. **public convenience** Bedürfnisanstalt f. **convenient** adj (suitable) passend; (time) gelegen; (advantageous) vorteilhaft.

convent ['kɒnvənt] n Kloster neut; (school) Klosterschule f.

convention [kən'venʃən] n (meeting) Tagung f; (agreement) Konvention f; (custom) Brauch m, Konvention f. **conventional** adj konventionell.

converge [kən'vəːdʒ] v konvergieren.

converse [kən'vəːs] v sich unterhalten, sprechen. **conversation** n Unterhaltung f, Gespräch neut.

convert [kən'vəːt; n 'kɒnvəːt] v umwandeln; (rel) bekehren. n Bekehrte(r). **conversion** n Umwandlung f; (rel) Bekehrung f.

convertible [kən'vəːtəbl] adj um-, verwandelbar. n (mot) Kabrio(lett) neut.

convex ['kɒnveks] adj konvex.

convey [kən'vei] v (goods) befördern; (news) übermitteln. **conveyance** n (law) Übertragung f; (vehicle) Fahrzeug neut.

convict [kən'vikt; n •'kɒnvikt] v verurteilen. n Verurteilte(r). **conviction** n (belief) Überzeugung f; (law) Verurteilung f.

convince [kən'vins] v überzeugen. **convincing** adj überzeugend.

convivial [kən'viviəl] adj fröhlich, heiter.

convoy ['kɒnvoi] n (mil) Konvoi m.

convulsion [kən'vʌlʃən] n Zuckung f.

cook [kuk] v kochen; (a meal) zubereiten. n Koch m, Köchin f. **cooker** n Herd m. **cookery** n Küche f. **cookery book** Kochbuch neut. **cooking** n Küche f.

cool [kuːl] adj kühl. v abkühlen. **cooled** adj gekühlt. **coolness** n Kühle f.

coop [kuːp] n Hühnerkäfig m. v **coop up** einsperren.

cooperate [kou'opəreit] v zusammenarbeiten. **cooperation** n Zusammenarbeit f, Kooperation f. **cooperative** adj (helpful) hilfsbereit; kooperativ. n Genossenschaft f, Kooperative f.

coordinate [kou'ɔːdineit] v koordinieren. n (math) Koordinate f. **coordination** n Koordinierung f.

cope [koup] v **cope with** fertigwerden mit.

copious ['koupiəs] adj reichlich.

copper[1] ['kɒpə] n (metal) Kupfer neut. adj kupfern; (colour) kupferfarben.

copper[2] ['kɒpə] n (coll) Polyp m.

copulate ['kɒpjuleit] v sich paaren. **copulation** n Paarung f.

copy ['kɒpi] n Kopie f; (book) Exemplar neut; (newspaper) Nummer f. v kopieren. **copyright** n Copyright neut.

coral ['kɒrəl] n Koralle f.

cord [kɔːd] n Schnur f.

cordial ['kɔːdiəl] adj herzlich.

cordon ['kɔːdn] n Absperrkette f. v **cordon off** absperren.

corduroy ['kɔːdəroi] n Kord m.

core [kɔː] n (apple) Kernhaus neut. v entkernen. **to the core** durch und durch.

cork [kɔːk] n (material) Kork m; (for bottle) Korken m, Pfropfen m. adj korken. **corkscrew** n Korkenzieher m.

corn[1] [kɔːn] n Korn neut, Getreide neut; (maize) Mais m; (wheat) Weizen m.

corn[2] [kɔːn] n (on foot) Hühnerauge neut.

corner ['kɔːnə] n Ecke f, Winkel m; (mot) Kurve f; (sport) Eckball m. v in die Enge treiben.

cornet ['kɔːnit] n (music) Kornett neut; (ice cream) Eistüte f.

coronary ['kɒrənəri] adj koronar. **coronary thrombosis** Koronarthrombose f.

coronation [kɒrə'neiʃən] n Krönung f.

coroner ['kɒrənə] n Leichenbeschauer m.

corporal[1] ['kɔːpərəl] adj körperlich. **corporal punishment** Prügelstrafe f.

corporal[2] ['kɔːpərəl] n (mil) Obergefreite(r) m.

corporation [ˌkɔːpə'reiʃən] n Körperschaft f; (city authorities) Gemeinderat m.

corps [kɔː] n Korps neut.

corpse [kɔːps] n Leiche f.

correct [kə'rekt] adj richtig; (proper) korrekt. v korrigieren. **correction** n Korrektur f.

correlation [korə'leiʃən] n Wechselbeziehung f.

correspond [korə'spond] v entsprechen (+dat); (write) korrespondieren. **correspondence** n Entsprechung f; Korrespondenz f. **corresponding** adj entsprechend.

corridor ['koridoɪ] n Gang m.

corrode [kə'roud] v zerfressen; (become corroded) rosten. **corrosion** n Korrosion f.

corrupt [kə'rʌpt] v bestechen. adj bestechlich, korrupt. **corruption** n Bestechung f, Korruption f.

corset ['koɪset] n Korsett neut.

cosmetic [koz'metik] adj kosmetisch. **cosmetic surgery** chirurgische Kosmetik f. **cosmetics** pl n Schönheitsmittel pl.

cosmic ['kozmik] adj kosmisch.

cosmopolitan [kozmə'politən] adj kosmopolitisch.

***cost** [kost] v kosten. n Preis m, Kosten pl. **costs** Unkosten pl. **cost of living** Lebenshaltungskosten pl.

costume ['kostjuɪm] n Kostüm neut.

cosy ['kouzi] adj gemütlich.

cot [kot] n Kinderbett neut.

cottage ['kotidʒ] n Hütte f, Häuschen neut. **cottage cheese** Huttenkäse m.

cotton ['kotn] n Baumwolle f. adj Baumwoll-. **cotton wool** Watte f.

couch [kautʃ] n Couch f.

cough [kof] n Husten m. v husten.

could [kud] V can.

council ['kaunsəl] n Rat m. **councillor** m Rat m.

counsel ['kaunsəl] v beraten. n Rat m.

count[1] [kaunt] v zählen; (be valid) gelten. n (number) (Gesamt)Zahl f. **count on** rechnen mit.

count[2] [kaunt] n (noble) Graf m.

counter[1] ['kauntə] n (shop) Ladentisch m, Theke f; (bank) Schalter m; (game) Spielmarke f.

counter[2] ['kauntə] adv entgegen. adj entgegengesetzt. v entgegnen.

counteract [kauntə'rakt] v entgegenwirken (+dat).

counterattack ['kauntərə,tak] n Gegenangriff m.

counter-clockwise adj, adv dem Uhrzeigersinn entgegen.

counterfeit ['kauntəfit] adj gefälscht. v fälschen.

counterfoil ['kauntə,foil] n Kontrollabschnitt m.

counterpart ['kauntə,paɪt] n Gegenstück neut.

countess ['kauntis] n Gräfin f.

country ['kʌntri] n Land neut; (homeland) Heimat f; (pol) Land neut, Staat m. adj Land-. **in the country** auf dem Lande. **country house** Landhaus neut. **countryman** n Landmann m. **fellow countryman** Landsmann m. **countryside** Landschaft f.

county ['kaunti] n Grafschaft f.

coup [kuɪ] n Coup m, (pol) Staatsstreich m. **coup de grâce** Gnadenstoß m.

couple ['kʌpl] n Paar neut; (married couple) Ehepaar neut. **a couple of** ein paar.

coupon ['kuɪpon] n Coupon m, Gutschein m.

courage ['kʌridʒ] n Mut m, Tapferkeit f. **courageous** adj mutig, tapfer.

courier ['kuriə] n Kurier m; (tour guide) Reiseleiter(in).

course [koɪs] n Lauf m; (study) Kurs(us) m; (meal) Dahn f; (direction) Richtung f. v laufen. **of course** natürlich, selbstverständlich. **in the course of** im Laufe (+gen).

court [koɪt] n (royal) Hof m; (law) Gericht neut. v (lover) werben um. **court martial** Kriegsgericht neut. **court-martial** v vor ein Kriegsgericht stellen. **courtroom** n Gerichtssaal m. **courtyard** n Hof m.

courtesy ['kəɪtəsi] n Höflichkeit f. **courteous** adj höflich.

cousin ['kʌzn] n Cousin m, Vetter m; Kusine f, Base f.

cove [kouv] n Bucht f.

cover ['kʌvə] v (be)decken; (extend over) sich erstrecken über; (include) einschließen. n (lid) Deckel m; (of book) (Schutz)Umschlag m. **covering** n (Be)Deckung f.

cow [kau] n Kuh f. v einschüchtern. **cowshed** n Kuhstall m.

coward ['kauəd] n Feigling m. **cowardice** n Feigheit f. **cowardly** adj feige.

cower ['kauə] v kauern.

coy [koi] adj spröde.

crab [krab] n Krebs m.

crack [krak] n (slit) Spalt m, Riß m; (sound) Krach m. v krachen; (break) brechen; (nut) knacken; (egg) aufschlagen; (joke) reißen. **crack up** (coll) zusammenbrechen. **cracker** n (firework)

Knallfrosch m; (Christmas) Knallbonbon m; (biscuit) Keks m.

crackle ['krakl] v knistern. n Knistern neut.

cradle ['kreidl] n Wiege f. v wiegen.

craft [kraːft] n (trade) Handwerk neut, Gewerbe neut; (skill) Kunstfertigkeit f; (ship) Schiff neut. **craftsman** n Handwerker m, Künstler m. **crafty** adj schlau, listig.

cram [kram] v hineinstopfen; (study) pauken.

cramp [kramp] n (med) Krampf m; (clamp) Krampe f. v hemmen.

cranberry ['kranbəri] n Preiselbeere f.

crane [krein] n Kran m; (bird) Kranich m.

crank [kraŋk] n Kurbel f; (odd person) Kauz m. v ankurbeln. **crankshaft** n Kurbelwelle f.

crap [krap] n (vulgar) Scheiße f.

crash [kraʃ] n (sound) Krach m, (mot) Zusammenstoß m; (aero) Absturz m. v stürzen (gegen); (sound) krachen. **crash helmet** Sturzhelm m.

crate [kreit] n Kiste f.

crater ['kreitə] n Krater m.

cravat [krə'vat] n Halstuch neut, Krawatte f.

crave [kreiv] v erbitten. **crave for** sehnen nach. **craving** n Sehnsucht f.

crawl [kroːl] v kriechen. n Kriechen neut; (swimming) Kraulstil m.

crayfish ['kreifiʃ] n Flußkrebs m.

crayon ['kreiən] n Farbstift m.

craze [kreiz] n (coll) Manie f. **crazy** adj verrückt.

creak [kriːk] v knarren. n Knarren neut.

cream [kriːm] n Sahne f, Rahm m; (skin) Creme f. **cream-coloured** adj cremefarben. **creamy** adj sahnig.

crease [kriːs] n Falte f, Kniff m. v falten.

create [kri'eit] v erschaffen; (cause) verursachen. **creation** n Schöpfung f; (product) Werk neut. **creative** adj schöpferisch. **creator** n Schöpfer m. **creature** n Lebewesen neut, Geschöpf neut.

credentials [kri'denʃəlz] pl n (identity papers) Ausweispapiere pl.

credible ['kredəbl] adj glaubhaft, glaubwürdig.

credit ['kredit] n (comm) Guthaben neut, Kredit m. v Glauben schenken (+ dat). **on credit** auf Kredit. **take the credit for**

sich als Verdienst anrechnen. **creditable** adj rühmlich. **credit card** Kreditkarte f.

creditor n Gläubiger m.

credulous ['kredjuləs] adj leichtgläubig.

creed [kriːd] n Bekenntnis neut, Kredo neut.

*****creep** [kriːp] v kriechen, schleichen. n Kriechen neut.

cremate [kri'meit] v einäschern. **cremation** n Einäscherung f. **crematorium** n Krematorium neut.

crept [krept] V **creep.**

crescent ['kresnt] n Mondsichel f.

cress [kres] n Kresse f.

crest [krest] n (of mountain) Bergkamm m; (of wave) Wellenkamm m; (coat of arms) Wappen neut.

crevice ['krevis] n Spalte f, Sprung m.

crew [kruː] n Besatzung f, Mannschaft f.

crib [krib] n Kinderbett neut.

cricket[1] ['krikit] n (insect) Grille f.

cricket[2] ['krikit] n Kricket neut.

crime [kraim] n Verbrechen neut. **criminal** adj verbrecherisch, kriminell. n Verbrecher(in).

crimson ['krimzn] n Karmesinrot neut.

cringe [krindʒ] v sich ducken.

crinkle ['kriŋkl] v kraus machen. n Kräuselung f. **crinkly** adj kraus.

cripple ['kripl] n Krüppel m. v lähmen.

crisis ['kraisis] n (pl -ses) Krise f.

crisp [krisp] adj knusprig. **crisps** pl n Chips pl. **crispy** adj knusprig.

criterion [krai'tiəriən] n (pl -a) Kriterium neut.

critic ['kritik] n Kritiker m. **critical** adj kritisch. **criticism** n Kritik f. **criticize** v kritisieren.

croak [krouk] v (person, crow) krächzen; (frog) quaken. n Krächzen neut; Quaken neut.

crochet ['krouʃei] v häkeln. **crochet hook** Häkelnadel f. **crochet work** Häkelarbeit f.

crockery ['krokəri] n Geschirr neut.

crocodile ['krokədail] n Krokodil neut.

crocus ['kroukəs] n Krokus m.

crook [kruk] n (shepherd's) Hirtenstab m; (villain) Gauner m. **crooked** adj gekrümmt; (dishonest) krumm.

crop [krop] n (harvest) Ernte f; (whip) Reitpeitsche f. v (cut) stutzen. **crop up** auftauchen.

croquet ['kroukei] n Krocket neut.

cross [kros] *n* Kreuz *neut*; (*crossbreed*) Kreuzung *f*. *adj* Quer-; (*annoyed*) böse, ärgerlich. *v* kreuzen, überqueren. **cross over** hinübergehen. **cross one's mind** einfallen (+*dat*). **crossbow** *n* Armbrust *f*. **crossbreed** *n* Kreuzung *f*. **cross-country** *adj* Gelände-. **cross-examination** *n* Kreuzverhör *m*. **cross-eyed** *adj* schielend. **crossing** *n* Kreuzung *f*; (*rail*) Bahnübergang *m*; (*border*) Überfahrt *f*. **cross-legged** *adj* mit überschlagenen Beinen. **cross-reference** *n* Kreuzverweisung *f*. **crossroads** *n* Straßenkreuzung *f*; (*fig*) Scheideweg *m*. **cross-section** *n* Querschnitt *m*. **crosswind** *n* Seitenwind *m*. **crossword** *n* Kreuzworträtsel *neut*.

crotchet ['krotʃit] *n* (*music*) Viertelnote *f*.

crouch [krautʃ] *v* sich ducken.

crow [krou] *n* Krähe *f*. *v* krähen. **crow's feet** Krähenfüße *pl*. **crow's nest** (*naut*) Mastkorb *m*.

crowd [kraud] *n* Menge. *v* **crowd around** sich drängen um. **crowded** *adj* gedrängt.

crown [kraun] *n* Krone *f*. *v* krönen.

crucial ['kruːʃəl] *adj* kritisch, entscheidend.

crucifixion [ˌkruːsi'fikʃən] *n* Kreuzigung *f*. **crucify** *v* kreuzigen.

crude [kruːd] *adj* roh; (*person*) grob. **crude oil** Rohöl *neut*. **crudeness** *n* Roheit *f*.

cruel ['kruːəl] *adj* grausam. **cruelty** *n* Grausamkeit *f*.

cruise [kruːz] *v* (*boat*) kreuzen; (*aircraft*) fliegen. *n* Kreuzfahrt *f*. **cruiser** *n* (*naut*) Kreuzer *m*.

crumb [krʌm] *n* Krume *f*; (*coll*) Brocken *m*.

crumble ['krʌmbl] *v* zerkrümeln. **crumbly** *adj* krümelig.

crumple ['krʌmpl] *v* zerknittern.

crunch [krʌntʃ] *v* knirschen. *n* Knirschen *neut*. **crunchy** *adj* knusprig.

crusade [kruː'seid] *n* Kreuzzug *m*. **crusader** *n* Kreuzfahrer *m*.

crush [krʌʃ] *v* zerdrücken; unterdrücken. *n* Gedränge *neut*. **crushing** *adj* Überwältigend.

crust [krʌst] *n* Kruste *f*.

crustacean [krʌ'steiʃən] *n* Krustentier *neut*.

crutch [krʌtʃ] *n* Krücke *f*.

cry [krai] *v* (*shout*) schreien, (*weep*) weinen. *n* Schrei *m*, Ruf *m*. **cry out** auf-

schreien. **a far cry from** ein weiter Weg von.

crypt [kript] *n* Krypta *f*.

crystal ['kristl] *n* Kristall *m*.

cub [kʌb] *n* Junge(s) *neut*; (*fox, wolf*) Welpe *m*; (*scout*) Wölfling *m*.

cube [kjuːb] *n* Würfel *m*; (*math*) Kubikzahl *f*. **cubic** *adj* würfelförmig. **cubic centimetre** Kubikzentimeter *neut*. **cubic capacity** (*mot*) Hubraum *m*.

cubicle ['kjuːbikl] *n* Kabine *f*.

cuckoo ['kukuː] *n* Kuckuck *m*.

cucumber [kju'kʌmbə] *n* Gurke *f*.

cuddle ['kʌdl] *v* herzen, liebkosen.

cue[1] [kjuː] *n* (*theatre*) Stichwort *neut*.

cue[2] [kjuː] *n* (*billiards*) Billardstock *m*.

cuff[1] [kʌf] *n* (*shirt*) Manschette *f*; (*trousers*) AUfschlag *m*. **cufflink** *n* Manschettenknopf *m*.

cuff[2] [kʌf] *n* Ohrfeige *f*, Klaps *m*. *v* klapsen.

culinary ['kʌlinəri] *adj* kulinarisch, Küchen-.

culminate ['kʌlmɪˌneit] *v* kulminieren. **culmination** *n* Höhepunkt *m*.

culprit ['kʌlprit] *n* Täter *m*.

cult [kʌlt] *n* Kult *m*.

cultivate ['kʌltiˌveit] *v* bebauen, kultivieren; (*fig*) pflegen. **cultivation** *n* Kultur *f*.

culture ['kʌltʃə] *n* Kultur *f*. **cultural** *adj* kulturell.

cumbersome ['kʌmbəsəm] *adj* sperrig, schwer zu handhaben.

cunning ['kʌniŋ] *adj* schlau, listig. *n* List *f*.

cup [kʌp] *n* Tasse *f*; (*trophy*) Pokal *m*. **cup final** Pokalendspiel *neut*. **cup tie** Pokalspiel *neut*.

cupboard ['kʌbəd] *n* Schrank *m*.

curate ['kjuərət] *n* Unterpfarrer *m*.

curator [kjuə'reitə] *n* Konservator *m*.

curb [kəːb] *v* zügeln. *n* Zaum *m*; (*kerb*) Bordstein *m*.

curdle ['kəːdl] *v* gerinnen.

cure [kjuə] *v* (*illness*) heilen; (*smoke*) räuchern; (*salt*) einsalzen. *n* Heilmittel *neut*.

curfew ['kəːfjuː] *n* Ausgehverbot *m*.

curious ['kjuəriəs] *adj* (*inquisitive*) neugierig; (*odd*) seltsam. **curiosity** *n* Neugier *f*.

curl [kəːl] *n* Locke *f*, Kräuselung *f*. *v* (*sich*) kräuseln. **curly** *adj* lockig, kraus.

currant ['kʌrənt] *n* Korinthe *f*.

currency ['kʌrənsi] n (money) Währung f.
current ['kʌrənt] adj (present) gegenwärtig; (common) gebräuchlich, üblich. n
Strom m. current account Scheckkonto
neut. current events Zeitgeschehen neut.
currently adv zur Zeit.
curry ['kʌri] n Curry neut. curry powder
Curry(pulver) neut. curry sauce Cur-
rysoße f.
curse [kəːs] v verfluchen; (swear) fluchen.
n Fluch m.
curt [kəːt] adj knapp, barsch.
curtail [kəːˈteil] v abkürzen. curtailment n
Abkürzung f; Einschränkung f.
curtain ['kəːtn] n Gardine f; (theatre)
Vorhang m.
curtsy ['kəːtsi] n Knicks m. v knicksen.
curve [kəːv] n Kurve f. v sich biegen.
curved adj bogenförmig, gekrümmt.
cushion ['kuʃən] n Kissen neut. v polstern.
custard ['kʌstəd] n Vanillesoße f.
custody ['kʌstədi] n Aufsicht f; (arrest)
Haft f.
custom ['kʌstəm] n (habit) Gewohnheit f;
(tradition) Brauch m. (customers) Kundschaft f. customary adj gewöhnlich. customer n Kunde m, Kundin f. customs n
Zoll m. customs duty Zoll m. customs
official Zollbeamte(r) m.
*cut [kʌt] n Schnitt m; (wound)
Schnittwunde f; (in wages) Kürzung f;
(coll: share) Anteil m. v schneiden;
(prices) herabsetzen; (wages) kürzen. cut
off (phone) trennen.
cute [kjuːt] adj (coll) niedlich.
cuticle ['kjuːtikl] n Oberhaut f; (on nail)
Nagelhaut f.
cutlery ['kʌtləri] n Besteck neut.
cutlet ['kʌtlit] n Kotelett neut.
cycle ['saikl] n Zyklus m; (bicycle) Fahrrad neut. v radfahren. cycling n Radsport
m. cyclist n Radfahrer(in).
cyclone ['saikloun] n Zyklon m.
cylinder ['silində] n Zylinder m. cylinder
block Motorblock m. cylinder capacity
Hubraum m. cylinder head Zylinderkopf
m.
cymbals ['simbəlz] pl n Becken neut sing.
cynic ['sinik] n Zyniker(in). cynical adj
zynisch. cynicism Zynismus m.
cypress ['saiprəs] n Zypresse f.
Cyprus ['saiprəs] n Zypern neut. Cypriot
n Zypriot(in). adj zypriotisch.
cyst [sist] n Zyste f.

Czechoslovakia [ˌtʃekəsləˈvakiə] n die
Tschechoslowakei f. Czechoslovakian n
Tschechoslowake m, Tschechoslowakin
f. adj tschechoslowakisch.

D

dab [dab] v betupfen. n Tupfen m.
dabble ['dabl] v plätschern. he dabbles in
art er beschäftigt sich nebenbei mit
Kunst. dabbler n Dilettant m.
dad [dad] n Vati m, Papa m.
daffodil ['dafədil] n Narzisse f.
daft [daːft] adj (coll) blöd(e), doof.
dagger ['dagə] n Dolch m.
daily ['deili] adj, adv täglich. daily paper
Tageszeitung f.
dainty ['deinti] adj (person) niedlich;
(food) lecker.
dairy ['deəri] n Molkerei f. dairy produce
Milchprodukte pl.
daisy ['deizi] n Gänseblümchen neut.
dam [dam] n Damm m. v eindämmen.
damage ['damidʒ] v beschädigen;
verletzen. n Schaden m. damages pl n
(compensation) Schadenersatz m sing.
damn [dam] v verdammen. interj
verdammt!
damp [damp] adj feucht. n Feuchtigkeit f.
dampen v befeuchten.
damson ['damzən] n Pflaume f.
dance [daːns] n Tanz m. v tanzen. dancer
n Tänzer(in). dance hall Tanzsaal m.
dancing n Tanz m; Tanzen neut.
dandelion ['dandiˌlaiən] n Löwenzahn m.
dandruff ['dandrəf] n Schuppen pl.
Dane [dein] n Däne m, Dänin f. Danish
adj dänisch.
danger ['deindʒə] n Gefahr f. in (or out
of) danger in/außer Gefahr. dangerous
adj gefährlich.
dangle ['daŋgl] v baumeln; baumeln lassen.
dare [deə] v wagen, riskieren; (challenge)
herausfordern. daring adj wagemutig;
(risky) gewagt; n Mut m.
dark [daːk] adj finster; (esp colour)
dunkel. n Dunkelheit f. in the dark im
Dunkeln; (fig) nicht im Bilde. darken v
(sich) verdunkeln. darkness n Dunkelheit

f. Finsternis *f.* **darkroom** *n* Dunkelkammer *f.*

darling ['dɑːlɪŋ] *n* Liebling *m. adj* lieb.

darn [dɑːn] *v* stopfen. **darning** *n* Stopfen *neut.*

dart [dɑːt] *v* schießen, sausen; *n* Pfeil *m.* **darts** *pl n* (*game*) (Pfeilwerfen) *neut sing.*

dash [daʃ] *v* (*smash*) zerschlagen; (*rush*) stürzen. *n* (*punctuation*) Gedankenstrich *m*; (*rush*) Stürzen *neut*; (*addition*) Schuß *m.* **dashboard** *n* Armaturenbrett *neut.* **dashing** *adj* schneidig.

data ['deitə] *pl n* Daten *pl.* **data processing** Datenverarbeitung *f.*

date[1] [deit] *n* Datum *neut*; (*appointed day*) Termin *m*; (*with someone*) Verabredung *f. v* (*letter*) datieren. **dated** *adj* altmodisch.

date[2] [deit] *n* (*fruit*) Dattel *f.*

dative ['deitiv] *n* Dativ *m.*

daughter ['dɔːtə] *n* Tochter *f.* **daughter-in-law** *n* Schwiegertochter *f.*

daunt [dɔːnt] *v* entmutigen.

dawdle ['dɔːdl] *v* trödeln.

dawn [dɔːn] *n* Tagesanbruch *m*; (Morgen)Dämmerung *f*; (*fig*) Anfang *m. v* dämmern (*also fig*).

day [dei] *n* Tag *m.* **daylight** Tageslicht *neut.*

daze [deiz] *v* betäuben. **dazed** *adj* benommen.

dazzle ['dazl] *v* blenden.

dead [ded] *adj* tot. **dead man/woman** Tote(r). **the dead** die Toten *pl.* **deaden** *v* dämpfen. **dead certain** todsicher. **dead end** Sackgasse *f*; (*fig*) totes Geleise *neut.* **deadline** *n* Termin *m.*

deaf [def] *adj* taub. **deaf aid** Hörgerät *neut.* **deaf mute** Taubstumme(r). **deafen** *v* taub machen.

*** deal** [diːl] *n* Geschäft *neut. v* handeln; (*cards*) austeilen. **deal with** (*attend to*) sich befassen mit; (*resolve*) erledigen. **a great/good deal of** viel. **dealer** *n* Händler *m*; (*cards*) Kartengeber *m.* **dealings** *pl n* Beziehungen *pl.*

dealt [delt] *V* deal.

dean [diːn] *n* Dekan *m.*

dear [diə] *adj* (*beloved*) lieb; (*expensive*) teuer. (*in letters*) Dear Mr. Smith Lieber Herr Smith, Sehr geehrter Herr Smith. *n* Liebling *m.* **dearly** *adv* herzlich.

death [deθ] *n* Tod *m*; (*case of death*) Todesfall *m.* **deathbed** *n* Sterbebett *neut.* **death penalty** Todesstrafe *f.*

debase [diˈbeis] *v* entwerten.

debate [diˈbeit] *n* Debatte *f. v* debattieren, diskutieren.

debit ['debit] *n* Soll *neut*; Lastscrift *f. v* belasten.

debris ['deibriː] *n* Schutt *m*, Trümmer *pl.*

debt [det] *n* Schuld *f.* **in debt** verschuldet. **debtor** *n* Schuldner *m.*

decade ['dekeid] *n* Jahrzehnt *neut*

decadence ['dekədəns] *n* Dekadenz *f.* **decadent** *adj* dekadent.

decanter [diˈkantə] *n* Karaffe *f.*

decapitate [diˈkapiˌteit] *v* enthaupten. **decapitation** *n* Enthauptung *f.*

decay [diˈkei] *v* verfallen. *n* Verfall *m.* **tooth decay** Karies *f.*

deceased [diˈsiːst] *adj* verstorben. **the deceased** der/die Verstorbene.

deceit [diˈsiːt] *n* Täuschung, Betrug *m.* **deceitful** *adj* betrügerisch.

deceive [diˈsiːv] *v* täuschen.

December [diˈsembə] *n* Dezember *m.*

decent ['diːsənt] *adj* (*respectable*) anständig; (*kind*) freundlich. **decency** *n* Anstand *m.*

deceptive [diˈseptiv] *adj* täuschend.

decibel ['desiˌbel] *n* Dezibel *neut.*

decide [diˈsaid] *v* entscheiden; (*make up one's mind*) sich entscheiden. **decided** *adj* entschieden. **decision** *n* Entscheidung *f*; (*of committee*) Beschluß *m.* **make a decision** eine Entscheidung treffen. **decisive** *adj* entscheidend.

deciduous [diˈsidjuəs] *adj* (*trees*) Laub-.

decimal ['desiməl] *adj* Dezimal-.

decipher [diˈsaifə] *v* entziffern.

deck [dek] *n* Deck *neut*; (*of cards*) Pack *neut.* **deckchair** *n* Liegestuhl *m.*

declare [diˈkleə] *v* erklären. **declaration** *n* Erklärung *f.*

decline [diˈklain] *v* ablehnen; (*gram*) deklinieren.

decompose [ˌdiːkəmˈpouz] *v* zerfallen.

decor ['deikɔː] *n* Ausstattung *f.*

decorate ['dekəˌreit] *v* schmücken; (*room*) tapezieren; (*mil*) auszeichnen. **decoration** *n* Verzierung *f*; (*of room*) Dekoration *f*; (*mil*) Orden *m.*

decoy ['diːkɔi] *n* Lockvogel *m.*

decrease [diˈkriːs] *v* (*make less*) vermindern; (*become less*) abnehmen. *n* Abnahme *f.*

decree [diˈkriː] *n* Erlaß *m.*

decrepit [di'krepit] adj hinfällig.
dedicate ['dedi,keit] v widmen; (rel)
weihen. dedication n (book) Widmung f;
(to duty, etc.) Hingabe f; (rel)
Einweihung f.
deduce [di'djuɪs] v schließen (aus).
deduct [di'dʌkt] v abziehen. deduction n
Abzug m.
deed [diːd] n Tat f; (document) Urkunde
f.
deep [diːp] adj tief. deep freeze Tiefkühl-
schrank m. deep-frozen adj tiefgekühlt,
Tiefkühl-.
deer [diə] n Hirsch m.
deface [di'feis] v entstellen.
default [di'foɪlt] n Unterlassung f. v (with
payments) in Verzug kommen.
defeat [di'fiɪt] v schlagen, besiegen. n
Niederlage f.
defect ['diɪfekt; v di'fekt] n Fehler m,
Defekt m. v (pol) überlaufen. defective
adj fehlerhaft, defektiv.
defence [di'fens] n Verteidigung f.
defenceless adj schutzlos.
defend [di'fend] v verteidigen. defendant n
Angeklagte(r). defender n Verteidiger m.
defensive adj defensiv, Verteidigungs-.
defer [di'fəɪ] v (postpone) verschieben.
defer to (yield to) nachgeben (+dat).
deferment n Verschiebung f.
defiance [di'faiəns] n Trotz m. defiant adj
trotzig, unnachgiebig.
deficiency [di'fiʃənsi] n Unzulänglichkeit
f, Mangel m. deficient adj (defective)
defektiv, mangelhaft; (inadequate) unzulänglich.
deficit ['defisit] n Defizit neut, Fehlbetrag
m.
define [di'fain] v definieren, genau
erklären. (well) defined adj deutlich. definite adj klar, deutlich. definitely adv
bestimmt. definition n Erklärung f, Definition f; (phot) Schärfe f.
deflate [di'fleit] v die Luft ablassen aus.
deflation (pol) Deflation f.
deform [di'foɪm] v deformieren, entstellen. deformed adj deformiert, verformt.
deformity n Mißbildung f.
defraud [di'froɪd] v betrügen.
defrost [diɪ'frost] v abtauen.
deft [deft] adj flink.
defunct [di'fʌŋkt] adj verstorben; (fig)
nicht mehr bestehend.
defy [di'fai] v (resist) trotzen; (challenge)
herausfordern.

degenerate [di'dʒenəˌreit; adj di'dʒenərit]
v degenerieren. adj degeneriert.
degrade [di'greid] v erniedrigen, entehren.
degradation n Erniedrigung f. degrading
adj erniedrigend.
degree [di'griɪ] n Grad m. to a high
degree in hohem Maße.
dehydrate [diɪ'haidreit] v trocknen. dehy-
drated adj getrocknet, Trocken-.
deign [dein] v sich herablassen.
dejected [di'dʒektid] adj niedergeschlagen.
delay [di'lei] v (postpone) aufschieben. n
Verzögerung f, Aufschub m. be delayed
(train, etc.) Verspätung haben. without
delay unverzüglich.
delegate ['deləgeit; 'deləgit] v delegieren.
n Delegierte(r). delegation m Delegation
f.
delete [di'liɪt] v tilgen, streichen.
deliberate [di'libərət; v di'libəreit] adj
(intentional) absichtlich. v nachdenken.
deliberately adv absichtlich. deliberation
n Überlegung f.
delicate ['delikət] adj (fragile) zart; (fine)
fein; (situation) heikel. delicacy n
Zartheit f; (food) Delikatesse f.
delicious [di'liʃəs] adj köstlich.
delight [di'lait] n Freude f, Vergnügen
neut. v erfreuen. delighted adj erfreut,
entzückt. delightful adj entzückend.
delinquency [di'liŋkwənsi] n Straffäl-
ligkeit f. delinquent adj delinquent. n
Delinquent m.
delirious [di'liriəs] adj in Delirium. delirium n Delirium neut, Fieberwahn m.
deliver [di'livə] v (goods) (aus)liefern;
(rescue) befreien; (a woman in childbirth)
entbinden. deliverance n Befreiung f.
delivery n (Aus)Lieferung f; Entbindung
f.
delta ['deltə] n Delta neut.
delude [di'luɪd] v täuschen. delusion n
Täuschung f.
deluge ['deljuɪdʒ] n Flut f.
delve [delv] v delve into erforschen.
demand [di'maɪnd] v verlangen. n
Verlangen neut; (for a commodity, etc.)
Nachfrage f. on demand auf Verlangen.
demanding adj anspruchsvoll.
demented [di'mentid] adj wahnsinnig.
democracy [di'mokrəsi] n Demokratie f.
democrat n Demokrat m. democratic adj
demokratisch.

demolish [di'moliʃ] v abbrechen. **demolition** n Abbruch m.
demon ['diːmən] n Teufel m.
demonstrate ['demənˌstreit] v demonstrieren. **demonstration** n Demonstration f.
demoralize [di'morəˌlaiz] v demoralisieren. **demoralization** n Demoralisation f.
demure [di'mjuə] adj bescheiden.
den [den] n Höhle f; (room) Bude f.
denial [di'naiəl] n Leugnung f.
denim ['denim] adj Denim-. **denims** pl n Jeans pl.
Denmark ['denmɑːk] n Dänemark neut.
denomination [diˌnomi'neiʃən] n (rel) Bekenntnis neut; (of banknote) Nennwert m. **denominator** n Nenner m. **common denominator** gemeinsamer Nenner m.
denote [di'nout] v bezeichnen.
denounce [di'nauns] v brandmarken.
dense [dens] adj dicht, dick. **density** n Dichte f.
dent [dent] n Beule f. v einbeulen.
dental ['dentl] adj Zahn-.
dentist ['dentist] n Zahnarzt m. **dentistry** n Zahnheilkunde f.
denture ['dentʃə] n (künstliches) Gebiß neut.
denude [di'njuːd] v entblößen.
denunciation [dinʌnsi'eiʃən] n Denunziation f.
deny [di'nai] v leugnen; (responsibility) ablehnen; (allegation) dementieren. **deny oneself** sich versagen.
deodorant [diː'oudərənt] n Desodorans neut.
depart [di'pɑːt] v abfahren; (fig) abweichen. **departure** n (person) Weggehen neut; (train) Abfahrt f; (aeroplane) Abflug m.
department [di'pɑːtmənt] n Abteilung f; (pol) Ministerium neut. **department store** Warenhaus neut.
depend [di'pend] v depend on abhängen von; (rely on) sich verlassen auf. **it (all) depends** es kommt darauf an. **dependable** adj zuverlässig. **dependant** n Familienangehörige(r). **dependent** adj abhängig (+von).
depict [di'pikt] v schildern.
deplete [di'pliːt] v erschöpfen. **depletion** n Erschöpfung f.
deplore [di'ploː] v bedauern. **deplorable** adj bedauernswert.

deport [di'poːt] v deportieren. **deport oneself** sich verhalten. **deportation** n Deportation f. **deportment** n Haltung f.
depose [di'pouz] v absetzen.
deposit [di'pozit] v deponieren. n (surety) Kaution f; (down payment) Anzahlung f; (sediment) Niederschlag m. **deposit account** Sparkonto neut.
depot ['depou] n Depot neut.
depraved [di'preivd] adj lasterhaft, verworfen.
depreciate [di'priːʃiˌeit] v an Wert verlieren. **depreciation** n Wertminderung f.
depress [di'pres] v niederdrucken, deprimieren. **depressed** adj deprimiert. **depressing** adj deprimierend. **depression** n Depression f.
deprive [di'praiv] v berauben.
depth [depθ] n Tiefe f. **in depth** gründlich.
deputy ['depjuti] n Stellvertreter m. adj stellvertretend.
derail [di'reil] v entgleisen. **derailment** n Entgleisen neut.
derelict ['derilikt] adj (building) baufällig.
deride [di'raid] v verspotten. **derision** n Spott m. **derisory** adj spöttisch.
derive [di'raiv] v ableiten; (originate) stammen; (gain) gewinnen. **derivation** n Herkunft f.
derogatory [di'rogətəri] adj geringschätzig.
descend [di'send] v hinabsteigen; (from train) aussteigen. **be descended from** abstammen von. **descendant** n Nachkomme m. **descent** n Abstieg m; Abstammung f.
describe [di'skraib] v beschreiben. **description** n Beschreibung f.
desert¹ ['dezət] n Wüste f.
desert² [di'zəːt] n (something deserved) Verdienst neut. **deserts** pl Lohn m sing.
desert³ [di'zəːt] v verlassen; (mil) desertieren. **deserter** n Deserteur m. **desertion** n Verlassen neut; (mil) Desertion f.
deserve [di'zəːv] v verdienen.
design [di'zain] n Entwurf m; (drawing) Zeichnung f; (pattern) Muster neut. v entwerfen, planen.
designate ['deziɡˌneit] v bezeichnen. **designation** n Bezeichnung f.
desire [di'zaiə] v wünschen, begehren; (ask for) wollen. n Wunsch m; (sexual) Begierde f. **desirous of** begierig nach.

desk [desk] n Schreibtisch m.
desolate ['desəlɪt] v wüst, öde; (person) trostlos.
despair [di'speə] v verzweifeln. n Verzweiflung f.
desperate ['despərət] adj verzweifelt; (situation) hoffnungslos.
despicable [di'spikəbl] adj verächtlich.
despise [di'spaiz] v verachten.
despite [di'spait] prep trotz (+gen).
despondent [di'spondənt] adj mutlos.
despot ['despot] n Gewaltherrscher m, Despot m. **despotism** n Despotismus m.
dessert [di'zəit] n Nachtisch m. **dessert spoon** Dessertlöffel m.
destiny ['destəni] n Schicksal neut. **destined** adj ausersehen, bestimmt. **destination** n (post) Bestimmungsort m; (travel) Reiseziel neut.
destitute ['destitjuit] adj notleidend, bedürftig.
destroy [di'stroi] v zerstören, vernichten. **destroyer** n Zerstörer m. **destruction** n Zerstörung f. **destructive** adj zerstörerisch.
detach [di'tatʃ] v losmachen, abtrennen. **detached** adj (house) Einzel-; (fig) objektiv. **detachment** n Objektivität f; (mil) Abteilung f.
detail ['diiteil] n Einzelheit f, Detail neut. **further details** Näheres neut; nähere Angaben pl. v detaillieren **detailed** adj eingehend.
detain [di'tein] v aufhalten; (arrest) verhaften.
detect [di'tekt] v entdecken. **detection** n Aufdeckung f. **detective** n Detektiv m. **detective story** Kriminalroman m.
détente [dei'tãint] n Entspannung f.
detention [di'tenʃən] n (law) Haft m; (school) Nachsitzen neut.
deter [di'təi] v abschrecken.
detergent [di'təidʒənt] n Reinigungsmittel neut.
deteriorate [di'tiəriə,reit] v sich verschlechtern. **deterioration** n Verschlechterung f.
determine [di'təimin] v bestimmen; (decide) sich entschließen. **determined** adj entschlossen. **determination** n Entschlossenheit f.
detest [di'test] v hassen, verabscheuen. **detestable** adj abscheulich.
detonate ['detə,neit] v detonieren.
detour ['diituə] n Umweg m.

detract [di'trakt] v **detract from** beeinträchtigen.
detriment ['detrimənt] n Schaden m, Nachteil m. **detrimental (to)** adj schädlich (für).
devalue [dir'valjui] v abwerten. **devaluation** n Abwertung f.
devastate ['devə,steit] v verwüsten. **devastating** adj vernichtend. **devastation** n Verwüstung f.
develop [di'veləp] v (sich) entwickeln. **developer** n Entwickler m. **developing** n Entwicklungs-. **development** n Entwicklung f.
deviate ['diivi,əit] v abweichen. **deviation** n Abweichung f.
device [di'vais] n Gerät neut, Vorrichtung f; (trick) Trick m.
devil ['devl] n Teufel m. **talk of the devil** den Teufel an die Wand malen. **devilish** adj teuflisch.
devious ['diiviəs] adj weitschweifig; (dishonest) krumm, unaufrichtig.
devise [di'vaiz] v ausdenken, erfinden.
devoid [di'void] adj **devoid of** ohne, frei von.
devolution [,diivə'luiʃən] n Dezentralisation f.
devote [di'vout] v widmen, hingeben. **devoted** adj ergeben. **be devoted to someone** sehr an jemandem hängen. **devotee** n Anhänger(in). **devotion** n Ergebenheit f.
devour [di'vauə] v verschlingen.
devout [di'vaut] adj fromm, andächtig.
dew [djui] n Tau m.
dexterous ['dekstrəs] adj gewandt, flink. **dexterity** n Gewandtheit f.
diabetes [,diaə'biitiiz] n Zuckerkrankheit f. **diabetic** adj zuckerkrank. n Diabetiker m.
diagnose [,diaəg'nouz] v diagnostizieren, erkennen. **diagnosis** n Diagnose f. **diagnostic** adj diagnostisch.
diagonal [dai'agənəl] adj diagonal. n Diagonale f.
diagram ['daiə,gram] n Diagramm neut, Schaubild neut.
dial ['daiəl] n (phone) Wählscheibe f. v wählen. **dialling tone** Amtszeichen neut.
dialect ['diaəlekt] n Dialekt m.
dialogue ['daiəlog] n Dialog m.
diameter [dai'amitə] n Durchmesser m.
diamond ['daiəmənd]n Diamant m; (cards) Karo neut; (sport) Spielfeld neut. adj diamanten.

diaper ['daɪəpə] *n* Windel *f.*
diaphragm ['daɪəˌfram] *n* (*anat*) Zwerchfell *neut*; (*contraceptive*) (Okklusiv)Pessar *neut.*
diarrhoea [ˌdaɪə'rɪə] *n* Durchfall *m.*
diary ['daɪərɪ] *n* Tagebuch *neut.*
dice [daɪs] *pl n* Würfel *pl. v* (*cookery*) in Würfel schneiden.
dictate [dɪk'teɪt] *n* diktieren. **dictating machine** Diktiergerät *neut.* **dictation** *n* Diktat *neut.* **dictator** *n* Diktator *m.* **dictatorial** *adj* diktatorisch. **dictatorship** *n.*
dictionary ['dɪkʃənərɪ] *n* Wörterbuch *neut.*
did [dɪd] *V* do.
die [daɪ] *v* sterben. **die away** schwächer werden. **die out** aussterben.
diesel ['diːzəl] *adj* Diesel-. **diesel engine** Dieselmotor *m.*
diet ['daɪət] *n* Kost *f*, Nahrung *f*; (*for weight loss*) Abmagerungskur *f*; (*for convalescence, etc.*) Diät *f*, Schonkost *f. v* eine Abmagerungskur machen.
differ ['dɪfə] *v* sich unterscheiden; (*think differently*) anderer Meinung sein. **difference** *n* Unterschied *m.* **different** *adj* verschieden, unterschiedlich; (*another*) anderer. **differential** *adj* unterschiedlich. *n* (*mot*) Differentialgetriebe *neut.*
difficult ['dɪfɪkəlt] *adj* schwer, schwierig. **difficulty** *n* Schwierigkeit *f.*
*dig [dɪg] *v* graben. **dig up** ausgraben.
digest [daɪ'dʒest; *n* 'daɪdʒest] *v* verdauen. *n* Auslese *f.* **digestible** *adj* verdaulich. **digestion** *n* Verdauung *f.*
digit ['dɪdʒɪt] *n* (*figure*) Ziffer *f*; (*finger*) Finger *m*; (*toe*) Zehe *f.*
dignified ['dɪgnɪˌfaɪd] *adj* würdevoll.
dignity ['dɪgnətɪ] *n* Würde *f.*
digress [daɪ'gres] *v* abschweifen. **digression** *n* Abschweifung *f.*
digs [dɪgz] *pl n* (*coll*) Bude *f sing.*
dilapidated [dɪ'lapɪˌdeɪtɪd] *adj* baufällig.
dilate [daɪ'leɪt] *v* (sich) weiten.
dilemma [dɪ'lemə] *n* Dilemma *neut.* **be in a dilemma** in der Klemme sitzen.
diligence ['dɪlɪdʒəns] *n* Fleiß *m.* **diligent** *adj* fleißig, gewissenhaft.
dilute [daɪ'luːt] *v* (*with water*) verwässern; verdünnen. *adj* (*also* **diluted**) verwässert.
dim [dɪm] *adj* trübe; (*light, vision*) schwach; (*coll: stupid*) dumm. *v* verdunkeln.
dimension [dɪ'menʃən] *n* Dimension *f.* **dimensions** *pl* Ausmaße *pl.*

diminish [dɪ'mɪnɪʃ] *v* (sich) vermindern. **diminishing** *adj* abnehmend.
diminutive [dɪ'mɪnjutɪv] *adj* winzig.
dimple ['dɪmpl] *n* Grübchen *neut.*
din [dɪn] *n* Lärm *m*, Getöse *neut.*
dine [daɪn] *v* speisen, essen. **diner** *n* (*person*) Tischgast *m*; (*rail*) Speisewagen *m*; (*restaurant*) Speiselokal *neut.* **dining car** Speisewagen *m.* **dining room** Eßzimmer *neut.* **dining table** Eßtisch *n.*
dinghy ['dɪŋgɪ] *n* Dingi *neut*, Beiboot *neut.* **rubber dinghy** Schlauchboot *neut.*
dingy ['dɪndʒɪ] *adj* trübe.
dinner ['dɪnə] *n* Abendessen *neut*; (*at midday*) Mittagessen *neut*; (*public*) Festessen *neut.* **dinner jacket** Smoking *m.* **dinner party** Diner *neut.*
dinosaur ['daɪnəˌsɔɪ] *n* Dinosaurier *m.*
dip [dɪp] *v* (ein)tauchen; (*slope down*) sich senken. **dip one's lights** (*mot*) abblenden. *n* Senkung *f*; (*bathe*) Bad *neut.* **dip switch** Abblendschalter *m.*
diploma [dɪ'ploumə] *n* Diplom *neut.*
diplomacy [dɪ'plouməsɪ] *n* Diplomatie *f.* **diplomat** *n* Diplomat *m.* **diplomatic** *adj* diplomatisch.
dipstick ['dɪpstɪk] *n* (*mot*) Ölmeßstab *m.*
dire [daɪə] *adj* schrecklich; (*urgent*) dringend.
direct [dɪ'rekt] *adj* direkt. *v* dirigieren, leiten; (*aim*) richten; (*give directions*) den Weg zeigen (+ *dat*); (*order*) anweisen. **direction** *n* Richtung *f*; Leitung *f*; **directions** *pl* (*for use*) Gebrauchsanweisung *f sing*; (*instructions*) Anweisungen *pl.* **directly** *adv* (*immediately*) unmittelbar; (*straight towards*) direkt, gerade. **director** *n* Direktor *m*, Leiter *m*; (*theatre, film*) Regisseur *m.* **directory** *n* Telefonbuch *neut.*
dirt [dəɪt] *n* Schmutz *m*, Dreck *m.* **dirt cheap** spottbillig. **dirty** *adj* schmutzig, dreckig.
disability [dɪsə'bɪlətɪ] *n* Körperbehinderung *f.* **disability pension** Invalidenrente *f.*
disadvantage [ˌdɪsəd'vaɪntɪdʒ] *n* Nachteil *m.* **disadvantageous** *adj* ungünstig, unvorteilhaft.
disagree [ˌdɪsə'griɪ] *v* nicht übereinstimmen; (*argue*) sich streiten. **disagreeable** *adj* unangenehm. **disagreement** *n* Meinungsverschiedenheit *f.*

disappear [ˌdisə'piə] v verschwinden. **disappearance** n Verschwinden neut.

disappoint [ˌdisə'point] v enttäuschen. **disappointed** adj enttäuscht. **disappointing** adj enttäuschend. **disappointment** n Enttäuschung f.

disapprove [ˌdisə'pruːv] v **disapprove of** mißbilligen. **disapproval** n Mißbilligung f.

disarm [dis'aɪm] v entwaffnen; (pol) abrüsten. **disarmament** n Abrüstung f. **disarming** adj entwaffnend.

disaster [di'zaɪstə] n Katastrophe f, Unglück neut. **disastrous** adj katastrophal.

disband [dis'band] v (sich) auflösen.

disc or US **disk** [disk] n Scheibe f; (record) Schallplatte f.

discard [dis'kaɪd] v ablegen.

disc brake n Scheibenbremse f. **disc jockey** Disk-Jockey m.

discern [di'səɪn] v (perceive) wahrnehmen; (differentiate) unterscheiden. **discernible** adj wahrnehmbar. **discerning** adj einsichtig.

discharge [dis'tʃaɪdʒ] v (dismiss) entlassen; (gun) abschießen; (duty) erfüllen; (ship) entladen; (of wound) eitern. n (med) Ausfluß m.

disciple [di'saipl] n Jünger m.

discipline ['disiplin] n Disziplin f. v disziplinieren; (train) schulen.

disclaim [dis'kleim] v ablehnen. **disclaimer** n Dementi neut.

disclose [dis'klouz] v enthüllen. **disclosure** n Bekanntmachung f.

discolour [dis'kʌlə] v (sich) verfärben. **discoloration** n Verfärbung f.

discomfort [dis'kʌmfət] n Unbehagen neut.

disconcert [diskən'səɪt] v aus der Fassung bringen.

disconnect [diskə'nekt] v trennen; (elec) abschalten.

disconsolate [dis'konsələt] adj trostlos.

discontinue [diskən'tinjuɪ] v aufhören; (something) einstellen.

discord ['diskoɪd] n (disagreement) Zwietracht f; (music) Diskordanz f. **discordant** adj diskordant.

discotheque ['diskətek] n Diskothek f.

discount ['diskaunt] v (ignore) außer Acht lassen. n Rabatt m.

discourage [dis'kʌridʒ] v entmutigen;

(dissuade) abraten. **discouraging** adj entmutigend.

discover [dis'kʌvə] v entdecken. **discoverer** n Entdecker m. **discovery** n Entdeckung f.

discredit [dis'kredit] v in Verruf bringen.

discreet [di'skriːt] adj diskret, verschwiegen.

discrepancy [di'skrepənsi] n Widerspruch m, Diskrepanz f.

discretion [di'skreʃən] n Diskretion f, Takt m. **at your discretion** nach Ihrem Gutdünken.

discriminate [di'skrimiˌneit] v unterscheiden. **discriminate** (against) diskriminieren. **discriminating** adj anspruchsvoll. **discrimination** n (racial, etc.) Diskriminierung f.

discus ['diskəs] n Diskus m.

discuss [di'skʌs] v besprechen, diskutieren; (in writing) behandeln. **discussion** n Besprechung f, Diskussion f.

disease [di'ziːz] n Krankheit f. **diseased** adj krank.

disembark [disim'baɪk] v an Land gehen.

disengage [disin'geidʒ] v sich losmachen. **disengage the clutch** auskuppeln.

disfigure [dis'figə] v entstellen. **disfigurement** n Entstellung f.

disgrace [dis'greis] n Schande f. v Schande bringen über. **disgraceful** adj schändlich.

disgruntled [dis'grʌntld] adj mürrisch.

disguise [dis'gaiz] v verkleiden; (voice) verstellen. n Verkleidung f. **in disguise** verkleidet.

disgust [dis'gʌst] n Ekel m (vor). v anekeln. **disgusting** adj ekelhaft, widerlich.

dish [diʃ] n Schüssel f, Schale f; (meal) Gericht neut. **dishes** pl Geschirr neut sing. **wash the dishes** abspülen. **dishcloth** n (for drying) Geschirrtuch neut; (for mopping) Lappen m.

dishearten [dis'haɪtn] v entmutigen.

dishevelled [di'ʃevəld] adj in Unordnung; (hair) zerzaust.

dishonest [dis'onist] adj unehrlich, unaufrichtig. **dishonesty** n Unehrlichkeit f. **dishonour** n Unehre f, Schande f. v schänden. **dishonourable** adj unehrenhaft.

dishwasher ['diʃˌwoʃə] n Geschirrspülmaschine f.

disillusion [disi'lu:ʒən] v ernüchtern, desillusionieren. **be disillusioned about** die Illusion verloren haben über.

disinfect [disin'fekt] v desinfizieren. **disinfectant** n Desinfektionsmittel neut.

disinherit [disin'herit] v enterben.

disintegrate [dis'inti,greit] v (sich) auflösen, (sich) zersetzen. **disintegration** n Auflösung f.

disinterested [dis'intristid] adj unparteiisch.

disjointed [dis'dʒointid] adj unzusammenhängend.

disk V **disc.**

dislike [dis'laik] v nicht mögen. n Abneigung f (gegen).

dislocate ['dislə,keit] v verrenken. **dislocation** n Verrenkung f.

dislodge [dis'lodʒ] v verschieben.

disloyal [dis'loiəl] adj untreu. **disloyalty** n Untreue f.

dismal ['dizməl] adj trübe, niederdrückend.

dismantle [dis'mantl] v abmontieren.

dismay [dis'mei] v bestürzen. n Bestürzung f, Angst f.

dismiss [dis'mis] v wegschicken; (employee) entlassen; (idea) ablehnen. **dismissal** n Entlassung f.

dismount [dis'maunt] v absteigen.

disobey [disə'bei] v nicht gehorchen (+dat). **disobedience** n Ungehorsam m. **disobedient** adj ungehorsam.

disorder [dis'oidə] n Unordnung f; (med) Störung f.

disorganized [dis'oigənaizd] adj unordentlich.

disown [dis'oun] v ableugnen; (child) verstoßen.

disparage [dis'paridʒ] v herabsetzen. **disparaging** v geringschätzig.

disparity [dis'pariti] n Unterschied m.

dispassionate [dis'paʃənit] adj unparteiisch.

dispatch [dis'patʃ] v absenden; (person) entsenden. n Versand m, Abfertigung f; (report) Meldung f.

dispel [dis'pel] v vertreiben.

dispense [dis'pens] v ausgeben. **dispense with** verzichten auf. **dispenser** n Verteiler m. **dispensing chemist** Apotheker(in).

disperse [dis'spəis] v zerstreuen.

displace [dis'pleis] v versetzen; (replace) ersetzen; (water) verdrängen. **displacement** n (naut) Wasserverdrängung f.

display [di'splei] v zeigen; (goods, etc.) auslegen. n (goods) Auslage f; (feelings) Zurschaustellung f; (parade) Entfaltung f.

displease [dis'pli:z] v mißfallen (+dat). **displeased** adj ärgerlich. **displeasure** n Mißfallen neut.

dispose [di'spouz] v **dispose of** (get rid of) beseitigen, wegwerfen; (have at disposal) verfügen uber. **disposed** adj geneigt. **disposable** adj zum Wegwerfen, Einweg-. **disposal** n Beseitigung f. **have at one's disposal** zur Verfügung haben. **be at someone's disposal** jemandem zur Verfügung stehen. **disposition** n Natur f, Art f.

disproportion [disprə'poiʃən] n Mißverhältnis neut. **disproportionate** adj unverhältnismäßig.

disprove [dis'pruːv] v widerlegen.

dispute [di'spjuːt] v (contest) bestreiten; (argue) disputieren. n Streit m. **trade dispute** Arbeitsstreitigkeit f.

disqualify [dis'kwoli,fai] v disqualifizieren, ausschließen. **disqualification** n Disqualifikation f.

disregard [disrə'gaid] v nicht beachten.

disrepute [disrə'pjuːt] n Verruf m. **bring into disrepute** in Verruf bringen. **disreputable** adj (notorious) verrufen.

disrespect [disrə'spekt] n Respektlosigkeit f. **disrespectful** adj respektlos.

disrupt [dis'rʌpt] v stören, unterbrechen. **disruption** n Störung f.

dissatisfied [di'satis,faid] adj unzufrieden.

dissect [di'sekt] v sezieren.

dissent [di'sent] n abweichende Meinung f. v anderer Meinung sein.

dissident ['disidənt] n Dissident m.

dissimilar [di'similə] v unähnlich.

dissociate [di'sousieit] v **dissociate oneself from** sich lossagen von.

dissolve [di'zolv] v (sich) auflösen; (meeting) aufheben.

dissuade [di'sweid] v abraten (+dat).

distance ['distəns] n Ferne f, Entfernung f; (gap) Abstand m. **in the distance** in der Ferne. **keep one's distance** Abstand halten. **distant** adj fern, entfernt.

distaste [dis'teist] n Abneigung f. **distasteful** adj unangenehm.

distended [di'stendid] adj ausgedehnt.

distil [di'stil] v destillieren. **distillery** n Brennerei f.

distinct [di'stiŋkt] *adj (different)* verschieden; *(clear)* deutlich, ausgeprägt. **distinction** *n (difference)* Unterschied *m*; *(merit)* Würde *f*. **of distinction** von Rang. **gain a distinction** sich auszeichnen. **distinctive** *adj* kennzeichnend.

distinguish [di'stiŋgwiʃ] *v* unterscheiden; *(perceive)* erkennen. **distinguish oneself** sich auszeichnen. **distinguishable** *adj* erkennbar. **distinguished** *adj* hervorragend.

distort [di'stɔːt] *v* verdrehen; *(truth)* entstellen. **distortion** *n* Verdrehung *f*.

distract [di'strakt] *v* ablenken. **distracted** *adj* verwirrt, außer sich. **distraction** *n* Ablenkung *f*; *(amusement)* Unterhaltung *f*; *(madness)* Wahnsinn *m*.

distraught [di'strɔːt] *adj* verwirrt, bestürzt.

distress [di'stres] *n* Not *f*; *(suffering)* Leid *neut*, Qual *f*. *v* betrüben, quälen. **distress signal** Notsignal *m*.

distribute [di'stribjut] *v* verteilen. **distribution** *n* Verteilung *f*. **distributor** *n* Verteiler *m*.

district ['distrikt] *n* Gebiet *neut*, Gegend *f*; *(of town)* Viertel *neut*; *(administrative)* Bezirk *m*. *adj* Bezirks-. **district attorney** Staatsanwalt *m*.

distrust [dis'trʌst] *v* mißtrauen (+ *dat*). *n* Mißtrauen *neut*.

disturb [di'stɜːb] *v* stören; *(worry)* beunruhigen. **disturbance** *n* Störung *f*. **disturbances** *pl (pol)* Unruhen *pl*. **disturbing** *adj* beunruhigend.

disused [dis'juːzd] *adj* außer Gebrauch.

ditch [ditʃ] *n* Wassergraben *m*. *v (coll)* im Stich lassen.

ditto ['ditou] *adv* ebenfalls, dito. **ditto mark** Wiederholungszeichen *neut*.

divan [di'van] *n* Divan *m*, Sofa *neut*.

dive [daiv] *v* tauchen; *(from board)* einen Kopfsprung machen; *(aero)* stürzen. *n* Tauchen *neut*; Kopfsprung *m*; *(aero)* Sturzflug *m*. **diver** *n* Taucher *m*.

diverge [dai'vɜːdʒ] *v* auseinandergehen.

diverse [dai'vɜːs] *adj* verschieden.

divert [dai'vɜːt] *v* ableiten; *(traffic)* umleiten. **diversion** *n* Ablenkung *f*; *(mot)* Umleitung *f*. **diversity** *n* Verschiedenheit *f*.

divide [di'vaid] *v* (sich) teilen.

dividend ['dividend] *n* Dividende *f*.

divine [di'vain] *adj* göttlich. *v* erraten.

division [di'viʒən] *n* Teilung *f*; *(math, mil)* Division *f*; *(comm)* Abteilung *f*.

divorce [di'vɔːs] *n* (Ehe)Scheidung *f*. *v* scheiden. **divorced** *adj* geschieden. **get divorced** sich scheiden lassen. **divorcee** *n* Geschiedene(r).

divulge [dai'vʌldʒ] *v* preisgeben.

dizzy ['dizi] *adj* schwindlig. **dizziness** *n* Schwindel *m*.

*do [duː] *v* tun, machen. **that will do!** *(that's enough)* das genügt! **that won't do** *(that's no good)* das geht nicht! **How do you do?** Guten Tag! *I could do with the money* ich könnte das Geld gut gebrauchen. **do away with** abschaffen. **do in** *(coll)* umbringen. **do up** *(coll)* überholen. **do without** verzichten auf.

docile ['dousail] *adj* fügsam.

dock¹ [dok] *n* Dock *neut*. **docks** *pl* Hafenanlagen *pl*. *v (ship)* docken.

dock² [dok] *n (law)* **in the dock** auf der Anklagebank *f*.

dock³ [dok] *v (cut)* stutzen; *(pay)* kürzen.

doctor ['doktə] *n (of medicine)* Arzt *m*, Ärztin *f*; *(as title)* Doktor *m*.

doctrine ['doktrin] *n* Lehre *f*.

document ['dokjumənt] *n* Urkunde *f*, Dokument *neut*. **documents** *pl* Papiere *pl*. *v* urkundlich belegen. **documentary** *adj* urkundlich. *n* Lehrfilm *neut*.

dodge [dodʒ] *v* beiseitespringen; *(avoid)* ausweichen. *n* Kniff *m*.

dog [dog] *n* Hund *m*. **dog-eared** *adj* mit Eselsohren. **dogged** *adj* hartnäckig. **dog kennel** Hundehütte *f*.

dogma ['dogmə] *n* Dogma *neut*. **dogmatic** *adj* dogmatisch.

do-it-yourself [,duːitjɔː'self] *adj* zum Selbermachen; Bastler-.

dole [doul] *n* Stempelgeld *neut*. **go on the dole** stempeln gehen. *v* **dole out** verteilen.

doll [dol] *n* Puppe *f*.

dollar ['dolə] *n* Dollar *m*.

dolphin ['dolfin] *n* Delphin *m*.

domain [də'mein] *n* Bereich *neut*.

dome [doum] *n* Kuppel *f*.

domestic [də'mestik] *adj* häuslich, Haus-; *(national)* inländisch, Innen-. **domestic animal** Haustier *neut*. **domesticate** *v (tame)* zähmen.

dominate ['domi,neit] *v* beherrschen. **dominant** *adj* (vor)herrschend; *(music, biol)* dominant. **domination** *n* Herrschaft *f*.

domineering [domi'niəriŋ] *adj* herrisch.

dominion [dəˈminjən] *n* Herrschaft *f*; (*country*) Dominion *neut.*

domino [ˈdominou] *n* Dominostein *m.* **dominoes** *pl* Dominospiel *neut sing.*

don [don] *v* (*clothes*) anziehen; (*hat*) aufsetzen.

donate [dəˈneit] *v* stiften, spenden. **donation** *n* Spende *f*, Stiftung *f.* **donor** *n* Spender *m.*

done [dʌn] *V* **do.**

donkey [ˈdoŋki] *n* Esel *m.*

doom [duːm] *n* Verhängnis *neut.* **doomed** *adj* verloren.

door [doː] *n* Tür *f.* **out of doors** draußen. **doorbell** Türklingel *f.* **doorhandle** *n* Türgriff *m.* **doorway** *n* Türöffnung *f*; Torweg *m.*

dope [doup] *n* (*coll*) Rauschgift *neut.* *v* (*sport*) dopen.

dormant [ˈdoːmənt] *adj* schlafend.

dormitory [ˈdoːmitəri] *n* Schlafsaal *m.* (*US: student house*) Wohnheim *m.*

dormouse [ˈdoːmaus] *n* Haselmaus *f.*

dose [dous] *n* Dosis *f.* *v* dosieren.

dot [dot] *n* Punkt *m.*

dote [dout] *v* **dote on** vernarrt sein in.

dotted [ˈdotid] *adj* übersät (mit). **dotted line** punktierte Linie *f.*

double [ˈdʌbl] *adj* doppelt, Doppel-. *adv* doppelt, zweimal. *n* das Doppelte; (*film*) Double *neut.* **doubles** *n* (*sport*) Doppelspiel *neut.* *v* verdoppeln; (*fold*) falten. **double-barrelled** *adj* doppelläufig. **double-bass** Kontrabaß *m.* **double-cross** *v* betrügen. **double-decker** Doppeldecker *m.* **double meaning** Zweideutigkeit *f.*

doubt [daut] *n* Zweifel *m.* *v* bezweifeln. **doubt whether** zweifeln, ob. **doubtful** *adj* zweifelhaft. **doubtless** *adv* ohne Zweifel, zweifellos.

dough [dou] *n* Teig *m.* **doughnut** *n* Krapfen *m.*

dove [dʌv] *n* Taube *f.*

dowdy [ˈdaudi] *adj* schäbig, schlampig.

down¹ [daun] *adv* hinab, herab; hinunter, herunter; unten. *I went down the road* ich ging die Straße hinunter. **up and down** auf und ab.

down² [daun] *n* (*feathers*) Daunen *pl.*

downcast [ˈdaunˌkaːst] *adj* niedergeschlagen.

downfall [ˈdaunˌfoːl] *n* Sturz *m.*

downhearted [ˌdaunˈhaːtid] *adj* mutlos.

downhill [ˌdaunˈhil] *adv* bergab.

downpour [ˈdaunˌpoː] *n* Wolkenbruch *m.*

downright [ˈdaunˌrait] *adv* völlig, höchst.

downstairs [ˌdaunˈsteəz] *adv* unten. *she came downstairs* sie kam nach unten.

downstream [ˌdaunˈstriːm] *adv* stromabwärts.

downtrodden [ˈdaunˌtrodn] *adj* unterworfen.

downward [ˈdaunwəd] *adj* Abwärts-, sinkend.

downwards [ˈdaunwədz] *adv* abwärts.

dowry [ˈdauəri] *n* Mitgift *f.*

doze [douz] *v* dösen. *n* Schläfchen *neut.*

dozen [ˈdʌzn] *n* Dutzend *neut.*

drab [drab] *adj* eintönig, farblos.

draft [draːft] *n* (*plan*) Konzept *neut*, Entwurf *m*; (*comm*) Tratte *f*; (*mil*) Aushebung *f.* *v* entwerfen; (*mil*) ausheben.

drag [drag] *v* schleppen, schleifen. *n* **drag on** sich in die Länge ziehen.

dragon [ˈdragən] *n* Drache *m.* **dragonfly** *n* Libelle *f.*

drain [drein] *n* Abfluß *m*; (*fig*) Belastung *f.* *v* ablassen; (*water*) ableiten; (*fig*) erschöpfen. **drainage** *n* Entwässerung *f.* **drainpipe** *n* Abflußrohr *neut.*

drama [ˈdraːmə] *n* Drama *neut.* **dramatic** *adj* dramatisch. **dramatize** *v* dramatisieren.

drank [draŋk] *V* **drink.**

drape [dreip] *v* drapieren. *n* (*curtain*) Vorhang *m.* **draper** *n* Tuchhändler *m.*

drastic [ˈdrastik] *adj* drastisch.

draught *or US* **draft** [draːft] *n* Zug *m*; (*naut*) Tiefgang *m.* **draughts** *n* Damespiel *neut.* **draught beer** Bier vom Faß. **draughtsman** *n* Zeichner *m.* **draughty** *adj* zugig.

*****draw** [droː] *v* ziehen; (*curtain*) zuziehen; (*picture*) zeichnen; (*money*) abheben; (*public*) anziehen; (*water*) schöpfen; (*sport*) unentschieden spielen. *n* (*lottery*) Ziehung *f*; (*sport*) Unentschieden *neut.* **draw near** sich nähern. **draw up** (*document*) ausstellen. **drawback** *n* Nachteil *m.* **drawbridge** *n* Zugbrücke *f.* **drawer** *n* Schublade *f.* **drawing** *n* Zeichnung *f.* **drawing pin** *n* Heftzwecke *f.* **drawing room** Salon *m.*

drawl [droːl] *v* schleppend sprechen.

drawn [droːn] *V* **draw.**

dread [dred] *n* Furcht *f*, Angst *f.* *v* Angst haben vor. **dreadful** *adj* furchtbar.

*dream [driːm] *n* Traum *m. v* träumen.
dreamer *n* Träumer *n* **dreamy** *adj*
träumerisch.
dreamt [dremt] *V* dream.
dreary ['driəri] *adj* trübe, düster.
dredge [dredʒ] *v* (*river*) ausbaggern.
dredger *n* Bagger *m.*
dregs [dregz] *pl n* Bodensatz *m sing*; (*fig*)
Abschaum *m sing.*
drench [drentʃ] *v* durchnässen.
dress [dres] *v* (sich) anziehen; (*wound*)
verbinden. *n* (*clothes*) Kleidung *f*; (*woman's*) Kleid *neut.* **dress designer**
Modezeichner *m.* **dresser** *n* (*furniture*)
Küchenschrank *m.* **dressing** n (*salad*)
Soße *f*; (*med*) Verband *m.* **dressing gown**
Morgenrock *m.* **dressing room** (*theatre*)
Garderobe *f.* **dressing table** Toiletten-
tisch *m.* **dressmaking** *n* Damenschneide-
rei *f.* **dress suit** Gesellschaftsanzug *m.*
drew [druː] *V* draw.
dribble ['dribl] *v* tröpfeln; (*football*) drib-
beln. *n* Tröpfeln *neut.*
drier ['draiə] *n* Trockner *m.*
drift [drift] *v* treiben; (*coll*) sich treiben
lassen. *n* (*snow*) Verwehung *f*; (*tendency*)
Tendenz *f.* **drifter** *n* (*person*) Vagabund
m.
drill [dril] *n* Bohrmaschine *f*; (*training*)
Drill *m. v* (*holes*) bohren; (*train*) trainier-
en, drillen.
*drink [driŋk] *v* trinken; (*animal, coll*)
saufen. *n* Getränk *neut*; (*cocktail, etc.*)
Drink *m.* **drinker** *n* Trinker *m* (*coll*)
Säufer *m.*
drip [drip] *v* tropfen, triefen. *n* Tropfen *m*
drip-dry *adj* bügelfrei. **dripping** *adj*
triefend. *n* Schmalz *neut.*
*drive [draiv] *v* treiben; (*vehicle*) fahren.
n Fahrt *f*; (*tech*) Antrieb *m*; (*mil*)
Kampagne *f.* **drive mad** verrückt
machen. **drive-in** (**cinema**) Autokino
neut.
drivel ['drivl] *v* sabbern, geifern. *n*
Quatsch *m.*
driver ['draivə] *n* Fahrer *m*, Chauffeur *m.*
driver's license Führerschein *m.*
driving ['draiviŋ] *adj* Treib-; (*mot*) Fahr-;
(*rain*) heftig. *n* Fahren *neut.* **driving lessons** Fahrunterricht *m.* **driving licence**
Führerschein *m.* **driving school** Fahr-
schule *f.* **driving test** Fahrprüfung *f.*
drizzle ['drizl] *n* Sprühregen *m. v* nieseln.
drone [droun] *v* summen. *n* Drohne *f.*

droop [druːp] *v* (schlaff) herunterhängen;
(*flower*) welken.
drop [drop] *n* (*of water*) Tropfen *m*; (*fall*)
Fall, Sturz *m. v* (*fall*) fallen; (*let fall*)
fallen lassen; (*passenger*) absetzen;
(*bomb*) abwerfen. **drop in** vorbeikommen.
drop off (**to sleep**) einschlafen. **drop-out** *n*
Dropout *m.*
drought [draut] *n* Dürre *f.*
drove [drouv] *V* drive.
drown [draun] *v* ertrinken. **drown out**
ubertönen.
drowsy ['drauzi] *adj* schläfrig.
drudge [drʌdʒ] *n* Packesel *m.* **drudgery** *n*
Plackerei *f.*
drug [drʌg] *n* (*medicinal*) Droge *f*; (*narcotic*) Rauschgift *neut. v* betäuben. **drug
addict** Rauschgiftsüchtige(r).
drum [drʌm] *n* Trommel *f. v* trommeln.
drummer *n* Trommler *m.* **drumstick** *n*
Trommelstock *m.*
drunk [drʌŋk] *V* drink. *adj* betrunken;
(*coll*) besoffen. *n* Betrunkene(r). **get
drunk** sich betrinken; (*coll*) besoffen werden. **drunken** *adj* betrunken. **drunkard** *n*
Trinker *m*; (*coll*) Säufer *m.* **drunkenness** *n*
Betrunkenheit *f.*
dry [drai] *adj* trocken; (*wine*) herb. *v*
trocknen. **dry up** austrocknen; (*dishes*)
abtrocknen. **dry-clean** chemisch reinigen.
dry cleaner chemische Reinigung *f.* **dry
dock** Trockendock *neut.* **dry land** fester
Boden *m.*
dual ['djuəl] *adj* doppelt. **dual-purpose** *adj*
Mehrzweck-.
dubbed ['dʌbd] *adj* (*film*) synchronisiert.
dubious ['djuːbiəs] *adj* zweifelhaft, dubi-
ös.
duchess ['dʌtʃis] *n* Herzogin *f.*
duck[1] [dʌk] *n* Ente *f.*
duck[2] [dʌk] *v* sich ducken; (*under water*)
untertauchen.
duct [dʌkt] *n* Kanal *m.*
dud [dʌd] *adj* wertlos. *n* Niete *f*, Versager
m.
due [djuː] *adj* (*suitable*) gebührend; (*payment*) fällig. *the train is due at 7 o'clock*
der Zug soll (planmäßig) um 7 Uhr
ankommen. *adv* **due east** genau nach
Osten. **due to** infolge (+*gen*). **in due
course** zur rechten Zeit. *I am due to* ich
muß.
duel ['djuəl] *n* Duell *neut.*
duet [dju'et] *n* Duett *neut.*

dug [dʌg] V **dig**.
duke [djuːk] n Herzog m.
dull [dʌl] adj (colour) matt, düster; (pain) dumpf; (boring) langweilig, uninteressant; (stupid) dumm. **dullness** n Düsterkeit f, Trübe f. v abstumpfen.
duly ['djuːli] adv gebührend, ordnungsgemäß.
dumb [dʌm] adj stumm; (coll: stupid) doof. **deaf and dumb** taubstumm. **dumbfound** v verblüffen.
dummy ['dʌmi] n (baby's) Schnuller m; (tailor's) Schneiderpuppe f; (imitation) Attrappe f.
dump [dʌmp] n Müllhaufen m, Müllkippe f. v abladen.
dumpling ['dʌmpliŋ] n Knödel m, Kloß m.
dunce [dʌns] n Dummkopf m.
dune [djuːn] n Düne f.
dung [dʌŋ] n Mist m.
dungeon ['dʌndʒən] n Kerker m.
duplicate ['djuːplikət; v 'djuːplikeit] n Duplikat neut. v verdoppeln; (make copies) vervielfältigen, kopieren. adj doppelt. **duplication** n Verdoppelung f. **duplicator** n Vervielfältigungsmaschine f.
durable ['djuərəbl] adj dauerhaft.
duration [dju'reiʃən] n Dauer f.
during ['djuəriŋ] prep während (+gen).
dusk [dʌsk] n (Abend)Dämmerung f. **dusky** adj düster.
dust [dʌst] n Staub m. v abstauben. **dustbin** n Mülleimer m. **dustcart** Müllwagen m. **duster** n Staubtuch neut. **dustman** n Müllabfuhrmann m. **dusty** adj staubig.
duty ['djuːti] n Pflicht f; (task) Aufgabe f; (tax) Zoll m, Abgabe f. **off/on duty** außer/im Dienst. **duty-free** adj zollfrei. **dutiful** adj pflichtbewußt.
Dutch [dʌtʃ] adj holländisch. **Dutchman** n Holländer m. **Dutchwoman** n Holländerin f.
duvet ['duːvei] n Federbett neut.
dwarf [dwɔːf] n Zwerg m. adj zwergenhaft.
***dwell** [dwel] n wohnen. **dwell on** bleiben bei. **dwelling** n Wohnung f.
dwelt [dwelt] V **dwell**.
dwindle ['dwindl] v abnehmen.
dye [dai] n Farbstoff m. v färben.
dyke [daik] n Deich m, Damm m.
dynamic [dai'namik] adj dynamisch. **dynamics** n Dynamik f.

dynamite ['dainə,mait] n Dynamit neut.
dynamo ['dainə,mou] n Dynamo n.
dynasty ['dinəsti] n Dynastie f.
dysentery ['disəntri] n Ruhr f.
dyslexia [dis'leksiə] n Legasthenie f, Wortblindheit f.
dyspepsia [dis'pepsiə] n Verdauungsstörung f.

E

each [iːtʃ] adj, pron jeder, jede, jedes. adv je. **each other** einander, sich.
eager ['iːgə] adj eifrig. **eagerness** Eifer m.
eagle ['iːgl] n Adler m.
ear[1] [iə] n (anat) Ohr neut; (hearing) Gehör neut. **earache** n Ohrenschmerzen pl. **eardrum** n Trommelfell neut. **earlobe** n Ohrläppchen neut. **earring** n Ohrring m. **earshot** n **within/out of earshot** in/außer Hörweite.
ear[2] [iə] n (of corn) Ähre f.
earl [əːl] n Graf m.
early ['əːli] adj, adv früh; (soon) bald.
earn [əːn] v verdienen. **earnings** pl n Einkommen neut sing.
earnest ['əːnist] adj ernsthaft. n **in earnest** im Ernst.
earth [əːθ] n Erde f. v (elec) erden. **earthly** adj irdisch. **earthenware** n Steingut neut. **earthquake** n Erdbeben neut. **earthworm** n Regenwurm m.
earwig ['iəwig] n Ohrwurm m.
ease [iːz] n Leichtigkeit f; (comfort) Behagen neut. v erleichtern. **at ease** behaglich. **with ease** ohne Mühe.
easel ['iːzl] n Staffelei f.
east [iːst] n Osten m. adj also **easterly** östlich, Ost-. adv also **eastwards** nach Osten; ostwärts. **eastern** adj östlich; orientalisch.
Easter ['iːstə] n Ostern neut.
easy ['iːzi] adj leicht. **easily** adv leicht, mühelos; (by far) bei weitem. **easy-going** adj ungezwungen.
***eat** [iːt] v essen; (of animals) fressen.
eaten ['iːtn] V **eat**.
eavesdrop ['iːvzdrop] v lauschen.
ebb [eb] n Ebbe f; (fig) Tiefstand m. v verebben.

ebony ['ebəni] *n* Ebenholz *neut.*
eccentric [ik'sentrik] *adj* exzentrisch. *n* Sonderling *m.*
ecclesiastical [ikliːziːˈastikl] *adj* kirchlich.
echo ['ekou] *n* Echo *neut. v* widerhallen.
eclipse [iˈklips] *n* Finsternis *f. v* verfinstern; (*fig*) in den Schatten stellen.
ecology [iˈkolədʒi] *n* Ökologie *f.* **ecological** *adj* ökologisch.
economy [iˈkonəmi] *n* Wirtschaft *f*; (*thrift*) Sparsamkeit *f.* **economic** *adj* ökonomisch, wirtschaftlich, Wirtschafts-. **economical** *adj* sparsam, wirtschaftlich. **economics** *n* Volkswirtschaft *f.* **economist** *n* Volkswirtschaftler *m.* **economize** *v* sparen (an).
ecstasy ['ekstəsi] *n* Ekstase *f.* **ecstatic** *adj* ekstatisch.
eczema ['eksimə] *n* Ekzem *neut.*
edge [edʒ] *n* Rand *m.* **on edge** nervös.
edible ['edəbl] *adj* eßbar.
edit ['edit] *v* redigieren. **edition** *n* Ausgabe *f.* **editor** *n* Redakteur *m.*
editorial [ˌediˈtoːriəl] *adj* Redaktions-. *n* Leitartikel *m.*
educate ['edjuˌkeit] *n* erziehen, ausbilden. **education** *n* Bildung *f*, Erziehung *f*; (*system*) Schulwesen *neut.* **educational** *adj* pädagogisch.
eel [iːl] *n* Aal *m.*
eerie ['iəri] *adj* unheimlich.
effect [iˈfekt] *n* Wirkung *f*; (*impression*) Eindruck *m.* **have an effect on** wirken auf. **in effect** in Wirklichkeit. **effective** *adj* wirksam. **effectiveness** *n* Wirksamkeit *f.*
effeminate [iˈfeminət] *adj* weibisch.
effervesce [efəˈves] *v* sprudeln. **effervescent** *adj* sprudelnd.
efficiency [iˈfiʃənsi] *n* Leistungsfähigkeit *f.* **efficient** *adj* (*person*) tüchtig; (*effective*) wirksam; (*machine*) leistungsfähig.
effigy ['efidʒi] *n* Abbild *neut.*
effort ['efət] *n* Anstrengung *f*, Mühe *f.* **make an effort** sich anstrengen. **make every effort** sich alle Mühe geben. **effortless** *adj* mühelos.
egg [eg] *n* Ei *neut. v* **egg on** reizen. **boiled egg** gekochtes Ei *neut.* **fried egg** Spiegelei *neut.* **scrambled egg** Rührei *neut.* **egg cup** Eierbecher *m.* **eggshell** *n* Eierschale *f.*
ego ['iːgou] *pron* Ich *neut.* **egoism** *n* Egoismus *m.* **egoist** *n* Egoist *m.*
Egypt ['iːdʒipt] *n* Ägypten *neut.* **Egyptian** *adj* ägyptisch; *n* Ägypter(in).

eiderdown ['aidədaun] *n* Federbett *neut.*
eight [eit] *adj* acht. *n* Acht *f.* **eighth** *adj* acht; *n* Achtel *neut.*
eighteen [eiˈtiːn] *adj* achtzehn. **eighteenth** *adj* achtzehnt.
eighty ['eiti] *adj* achtzig. **eightieth** *adj* achtzigst.
either ['aiðə] *pron* einer (eine, eines) von beiden. **on either side** auf beiden Seiten. **either ... or ...** entweder ... oder ....
ejaculate [iˈdʒakjuleit] *v* (*utter*) ausstoßen; ejakulieren.
eject [iˈdʒekt] *v* ausstoßen.
eke [iːk] *v* **eke out** (*add to*) ergänzen.
elaborate [iˈlabərət; *v* iˈlabəreit] *adj* ausführlich, genau ausgearbeitet. *v* **elaborate on** eingehend erörtern. **elaboration** *n* Ausarbeitung *f.*
elapse [iˈlaps] *v* vergehen.
elastic [iˈlastik] *adj* elastisch. **elastic band** Gummiband *neut.*
elated [iˈleitid] *adj* begeistert, froh.
elbow ['elbou] *n* Ellbogen *m.*
elder¹ ['eldə] *adj* älter. *n* Ältere(r).
elder² ['eldə] *n* (*tree*) Holunder *m.*
elderly ['eldəli] *adj* älter.
eldest ['eldist] *adj* ältest. *n* Älteste(r).
elect [iˈlekt] *v* wählen. **election** *n* Wahl *f.* **elector** *n* Wähler *m.* **electorate** *n* Wählerschaft *f.*
electric [əˈlektrik] *adj also* **electrical** elektrisch. **electrical engineering** Elektrotechnik *f.* **electric blanket** Heizdecke *f.* **electric chair** elektrischer Stuhl *m.* **electric cooker** Elektroherd *neut.* **electrician** *n* Elektriker *m.* **electricity** *n* Strom *m*, Elektrizität *f.*
electrify [əˈlektrifai] *v* elektrifizieren. **electrifying** *adj* (*fig*) elektrisierend.
electronic [eləkˈtronik] *n* elektronisch. **electronics** *n* Elektronik *f sing.*
elegant ['eligənt] *adj* elegant.
element ['eləmənt] *n* Element *neut.* **elementary** *adj* elementar.
elephant ['elifənt] *n* Elefant *m.*
elevate ['eliveit] *v* heben; (*promote*) erheben. **elevation** *n* Hochheben *neut*; (*promotion*) Erhebung *f.* **elevator** *n* Aufzug *m.*
eleven [iˈlevn] *adj* elf. **eleventh** *adj* elft.
eligible ['elidʒəbl] *adj* wählbar. **be eligible** in Frage kommen. **be eligible for** berechtigt sein zu. **eligibility** *n* Eignung *f.*

eliminate [i'limineit] n beseitigen; (sport) ausscheiden. elimination n Beseitigung f; Ausscheidung f.

élite [ei'liːt] n Elite f.

ellipse [i'lips] n Ellipse f. elliptical adj elliptisch.

elm [elm] n Ulme f.

elocution [elə'kjuːʃən] n Sprechkunde f.

elope [i'loup] v entlaufen. elopement n Entlaufen neut.

eloquent ['eləkwənt] adj (person) redegewandt. eloquence n Redegewandtheit f.

else [els] adv sonst. anyone else? sonst noch jemand? someone else jemand anders. nothing else nichts weiter. elsewhere adv anderswo, woanders.

elucidate [i'luːsideit] v aufklären. elucidation n Aufklärung f.

elude [i'luːd] v entgehen (dat).

emaciated [i'meisieitid] adj abgemagert.

emanate ['eməneit] v ausströmen (aus); (fig) herstammen (von).

emancipate [i'mansipeit] v befreien, emanzipieren. emancipated adj emanzipiert. emancipation n Befreiung f.

embalm [im'baːm] v einbalsamieren.

embankment [im'baŋkmənt] n Damm m; (road) Uferstraße f.

embargo [im'baːgou] n Handelssperre f.

embark [im'baːk] v sich einschiffen (nach); (fig) sich einlassen (in).

embarrass [im'barəs] v in Verlegenheit bringen. be embarrassed verlegen sein. embarrassment n Verlegenheit f.

embassy ['embəsi] n Botschaft f.

embellish [im'beliʃ] v verzieren.

embers 'embəz] pl n Glut f sing.

embezzle [im'bezl] v unterschlagen. embezzlement n Unterschlagung f.

embitter [im'bitə] v verbittern.

emblem ['embləm] n Sinnbild neut.

embody [im'bodi] v verkörpern. embodiment n Verkörperung f.

embossed [im'bost] adj erhaben.

embrace [im'breis] v umarmen; (include) umfassen. n Umarmung f.

embroider [im'broidə] v (be)sticken; (story) ausschmücken. embroidery n Stickerei f.

embryo ['embriou] n Embryo m.

emerald ['emərəld] n Smaragd m. emerald green smaragdgrun.

emerge [i'məːdʒ] v (from water) auftauchen; (appear) hervorkommen. emergence n Auftauchen neut.

emergency [i'məːdʒənsi] n Notfall m. adj Not-. emergency exit Notausgang m.

emigrate ['emigreit] v auswandern. emigration n Auswanderung f. emigrant n Auswanderer m.

eminent ['eminənt] adj hervorragend, erhaben. eminence n Erhöhung f.

emit [i'mit] v von sich geben. emission n Ausstrahlung f.

emotion [i'mouʃən] n Gefühl neut. emotional adj Gefühls-; (excitable) erregbar; (full of feeling) gefühlvoll.

empathy ['empəθi] n Einfühlung f.

emperor ['empərə] n Kaiser m.

emphasis ['emfəsis] n (pl -ses) Nachdruck m. emphasize v betonen, unterstreiken. emphatic adj nachdrücklich.

empire ['empaiə] n Reich neut.

empirical [im'pirikəl] adj empirisch.

employ [im'ploi] v (use) verwenden; (appoint) anstellen. be employed beschäftigt or tätig sein. employee n Angestellte(r); (as opposed to employer) Arbeitnehmer m. employer n Arbeitgeber m. employment n Arbeit f, Beschäftigung f.

empower [im'pauə] v ermächtigen.

empress ['empris] n Kaiserin f.

empty ['empti] adj leer. v leeren. emptiness n Leere f.

emulate ['emjuleit] v nacheifern (dat).

emulsion [i'mʌlʃən] n Emulsion f. emulsify v emulgieren.

enable [i'neibl] v ermöglichen.

enact [i'nakt] v verordnen; (law) erlassen.

enamel [i'naməl] n Emaille f; (teeth) Zahnschmelz m. v emaillieren.

enamour [i'namə] v be enamoured of verliebt sein in.

encase [in'keis] v umschließen.

enchant [in'tʃaɪnt] v entzücken. enchanting adj entzückend. enchantment n Zauber m, Entzücken neut.

encircle [in'səːkl] v umringen.

enclose [in'klouz] v einschließen; (in letter) beifügen. enclosed adj (in letter) beigefügt. enclosure n Einzäunung f; (in letter) Anlage f.

encore ['oŋkoː] interj noch einmal! n Zugabe f.

encounter [in'kauntə] v treffen; (difficulties) stoßen auf. n Begegnung f; (mil) Gefecht neut.

encourage [in'kʌridʒ] v ermutigen; (promote) fördern. encouragement n Ermutigung f.

encroach [in'krout∫] v eindringen (in). **encroachment** n Eingriff m.

encyclopedia [insaiklə'piːdiə] n Enzyklopädie f.

end [end] n Ende neut; (finish) Schluß m; (purpose) Zweck m. v beend(ig)en; (come to an end) zu Ende gehen. **ending** n Ende neut. **endless** adj unendlich.

endanger [in'deindʒə] v gefährden.

endeavour [in'devə] v sich anstrengen, versuchen. n Versuch m, Bestrebung f.

endemic [en'demik] adj endemisch.

endive ['endiv] n Endivie f.

endorse [in'dɔis] v indossieren; (approve of) billigen. **endorsement** n Vermerk m; Billigung f.

endow [in'dau] v stiften. **endowed with** begabt mit. **endowment** n Ausstattung f, Stiftung f.

endure [in'djuə] v ertragen. **enduring** adj beständig.

enemy ['enəmi] n Feind m. adj Feind-.

energy ['enədʒi] n Energie f. **energetic** adj energisch.

enforce [in'fɔis] v durchsetzen. **enforcement** n Durchsetzung f.

engage [in'geidʒ] v (employ) anstellen; (tech) einschalten; (enemy) angreifen. **engaged** adj (to be married) verlobt; (occupied) besetzt. **get engaged** sich verloben. **engagement** n (to marry) Verlobung f; (appointment) Verabredung f.

engine ['endʒin] n Motor m; (rail) Lokomotive f. **engine driver** Lokomotivführer m.

engineer [endʒi'niə] n Ingenieur m. v (fig) organisieren. **engineering** n Technik f.

England ['iŋglənd] n England neut.

English ['iŋgli∫] adj englisch. (the) **English (language)** (das) Englisch(e), die englische Sprache. *I am English* ich bin Engländer(in). **English Channel** Ärmelkanal m. **Englishman** n Engländer m. **Englishwoman** n Engländerin f.

engrave [in'greiv] v gravieren. **engraving** n Stich m.

engrossed [in'groust] adj vertieft.

engulf [in'gʌlf] v (overcome) überwältigen.

enhance [in'hains] v verstärken.

enigma [i'nigmə] n Rätsel neut. **enigmatic** adj rätselhaft.

enjoy [in'dʒoi] v genießen, Freude haben an. **enjoy oneself** sich (gut) unterhalten.

enjoyment n Freude f. **enjoy yourself!** viel spaß/Vergnügen!

enlarge [in'laidʒ] v (sich) vergrößern. **enlargement** n Vergrößerung f.

enlighten [in'laitn] v aufklären. **enlightened** adj aufgeklärt. **enlightenment** n Aufklärung f.

enlist [in'list] v (help) in Anspruch nehmen; (in army) sich melden.

enmity ['enməti] n Feindseligkeit f.

enormous [i'nɔiməs] adj riesig, ungeheuer.

enough [i'nʌf] adv genug. **be enough** genügen. **have enough of something** (be tired of) etwas satt haben.

enquire [in'kwaiə] adv sich erkundigen, fragen. **enquiry** n Nachfrage f.

enrage [in'reidʒ] v wütend machen. **enraged** adj wütend.

enrich [in'rit∫] v bereichern.

enrol [in'roul] v einschreiben; (in club) als Mitglied aufnehmen; (oneself) beitreten (dat). **enrolment** n Aufnahme f.

ensign ['ensain] n (naut) (Schiffs)Flagge f.

enslave [in'sleiv] n versklaven.

ensue [in'sjui] v (darauf) folgen. **ensuing** adj darauffolgend.

ensure [in'∫uə] v gewährleisten, sichern.

entail [in'teil] v mit sich bringen.

entangle [in'taŋgl] v verstricken. **entangled** adj verstrickt.

enter ['entə] v (go in) eintreten; (a room) hineintreten in; (in book) einschreiben; (sport) sich anmelden.

enterprise ['entəpraiz] n (concern) Unternehmen neut; (initiative) Initiative f. **private enterprise** freie Wirtschaft f. **enterprising** adj unternehmungslustig.

entertain [entə'tein] v (amuse) unterhalten; (feelings) hegen; (as guests) gastlich bewirten. **entertaining** adj unterhaltsam. **entertainment** n Unterhaltung f.

enthral [in'θroil] v entzücken. **enthralling** adj entzückend.

enthusiasm [in'θuizi‚azəm] n Begeisterung f. **Enthusiasmus** m. **enthusiastic** adj begeistert, enthusiastisch.

entice [in'tais] v verlocken. **enticement** n Anreiz m. **enticing** adj verlockend.

entire [in'taiə] adj ganz. **entirely** adv ganz, völlig, durchaus. **entirety** n Gesamtheit f.

entitle [in'taitl] v berechtigen (zu).

entity ['entəti] n Wesen neut.

entrails ['entreilz] *pl n* Eingeweide *pl.*
entrance[1] ['entrəns] *n* (*going in, fee*) Eintritt *m*; (*way in*) Eingang *m.*
entrance[2] [in'traıns] *v* entzücken.
entrant ['entrənt] *n* (*sport*) Teilnehmer(in); (*for exam*) Kandidat *m.*
entreat [in'triːt] *v* ernstlich bitten. **entreaty** *n* Bitte *f.*
entrenched [in'trentʃt] *v* **become entrenched** sich festsetzen.
entrepreneur [,ɔntrəprə'nəː] *n* Unternehmer *m.*
entrust [in'trʌst] *v* (*thing*) anvertrauen (*dat*); (*person*) betrauen (mit).
entry ['entri] *n* Eintritt *m*; (*into country*) Einreise *f*; (*comm*) Posten *m*; (*theatre*) Auftritt *m.* **no entry** Eintritt verboten.
entwine [in'twain] *v* umwinden.
enunciate [i'nʌnsiˌeit] *v* aussagen; (*state*) ausdrücken.
envelop [in'veləp] *v* einwickeln; (*fig*) umhüllen.
envelope ['envəˌloup] *n* Umschlag *m.*
enviable ['enviəbl] *adj* beneidenswert.
envious ['enviəs] *adj* neidisch (*of* auf). **be envious of** beneiden.
environment [in'vaiərənmənt] *n* Umgebung *f.* **the environment** Umwelt *f.* **environmental** *adj* Umwelt-.
envisage [in'vizidʒ] *v* sich vorstellen.
envoy ['envoi] *n* Bote *m.*
envy ['envi] *v* beneiden. *n* Neid *m.*
enzyme ['enzaim] *n* Enzym *neut.*
epaulet ['epəlet] *n* Epaulette *f.*
ephemeral [i'femərəl] *adj* vergänglich.
epic ['epik] *adj* (*poetry*) episch; heldenhaft. *n* Heldengedicht *neut.*
epicure ['epikjuə] *n* Feinschmecker *m.*
epidemic [epi'demik] *n* Epidemie *f. adj* epidemisch.
epilepsy ['epilepsi] *n* Epilepsie *f.* **epileptic** *adj* epileptisch; *n* Epileptiker(in).
epilogue ['epilog] *n* Epilog *m.*
Epiphany [i'pifəni] *n* Epiphanias *neut.*
episcopal [i'piskəpəl] *adj* bischöflich.
episode ['episoud] *n* Episode *f.*
epitaph ['epiˌtaːf] *n* Grabschrift *f.*
epitome [i'pitəmi] *n* Inbegriff *m.*
epoch ['iːpok] *n* Epoche *f.*
equable ['ekwəbl] *adj* (*person*) gelassen.
equal ['iːkwəl] *adj* gleich (+ *dat*). **be equal to** gleichen (+ *dat*); (*be able*) gewachsen sein (+ *dat*). **equal in size** von gleicher Größe. *n* Gleichgestellte(r). *v* gleichen (+ *dat*). **gleich sein** (+ *dat*). **equality** *n*

Gleichheit *f*; (*pol*) Gleichberechtigung *f.*
equalize *v* gleichmachen. **equally** *adv* ebenso, in gleichem Maße.
equanimity [ekwə'niməti] *n* Gleichmut *m.*
equate [i'kweit] *v* gleichstellen. **equation** *n* Gleichung *f.*
equator [i'kweitə] *n* Äquator *m.* **equatorial** *adj* äquatorial.
equestrian [i'kwestriən] *adj* Reit-, Reiter-.
equilateral [,iːkwi'latərəl] *adj* gleichseitig.
equilibrium [,iːkwi'libriəm] *n* Gleichgewicht *neut.*
equinox ['ekwinoks] *n* Tagundnachtgleiche *f.*
equip [i'kwip] *v* ausrüsten, ausstatten. **equipment** *n* Ausrüstung *f*, Einrichtung *f.*
equity ['ekwəti] *n* Billigkeit *f*; (*law*) Billigkeitsrecht *f.*
equivalent [i'kwivələnt] *adj* gleichwertig. **be equivalent to** gleichkommen (*dat*). *n* Gegenstück *neut.*
era ['iərə] *n* Epoche *f*, Ära *f.*
eradicate [i'radiˌkeit] *v* ausrotten. **eradication** *n* Ausrottung *f.*
erase [i'reiz] *v* ausradieren, tilgen. **eraser** *n* Radiergummi *m.*
erect [i'rekt] *v* errichten. *adj* aufrecht. **erection** *n* Errichtung *f*; (*anat*) Erektion *f.*
ermine ['əːmin] *n* Hermelin *m.*
erode [i'roud] *v* zerfressen. **erosion** *n* Zerfressung *f.*
erotic [i'rotik] *adj* erotisch. **eroticism** *n* Erotik *f.*
err [əː] *v* sich irren.
errand ['erənd] *n* (Boten)Gang *m.*
erratic [i'ratik] *adj* unberechenbar.
error ['erə] *n* Fehler *m*, Irrtum *m*; (*of compass*) Abweichung *f*; (*oversight*) Versehen *neut.* **erroneous** *adj* irrtümlich.
erudite ['eruːdait] *adj* gelehrt.
erupt [i'rupt] *v* (*volcano*) ausbrechen. **eruption** *n* Ausbruch *m*; (*skin*) Hautausschlag *m.*
escalate ['eskəˌleit] *v* (*a war*) steigern, eskalieren. **escalation** *n* Eskalation *f.* **escalator** *n* Rolltreppe *f.*
escalope ['eskəˌlop] *n* Schnitzel *neut.*
escape [is'keip] *v* entkommen (+ *dat*); (*fig*) entgehen (+ *dat*). *n* Flucht *f*; (*of liq uid*) Ausfluß *m.* **have a narrow escape** mit knapper Not entkommen.
escort [i'skoːt; *n* 'eskoːt] *v* begleiten. *n* (*mil*) Eskorte *f.*

esoteric [esə'terik] *adj* esoterisch.
especial [i'speʃəl] *adj* besonder, speziell.
especially *adv* besonders.
espionage ['espiə,naːʒ] *n* Spionage *f.*
esplanade [,esplə'neid] *n* Esplanade *f.*
essay ['esei] *n* (*school*) Aufsatz *m*; (*literary*) Essay *m.*
essence ['esns] *n* Wesen *neut*; (*extract*) Essenz *f.*
essential [i'senʃəl] *adj* wesentlich; (*indispensable*) untentbehrlich, unbedingt notwendig. **essentially** *adv* im wesentlichen.
establish [i'stabliʃ] *v* einrichten, aufstellen; (*a fact*) feststellen; (*found*) gründen. **establishment** *n* Gründung *f*; (*comm*) Unternehmen *neut.*
estate [i'steit] *n* (*of deceased*) Nachlaß *m*; (*of noble*) Landsitz *m.* **housing estate** Siedlung *f.* **real estate** Immobilien *pl.* **estate agent** Grundstücksmakler *m.* **estate car** Kombiwagen *m.*
esteem [i'stiːm] *n* Achtung *f. v* hochschätzen.
estimate ['esti,meit; *n* 'estimət] *v* schätzen (auf). *n* (Ab)Schätzung. **estimation** *n* Ansicht (*opinion*) *f.*
estuary ['estjuəri] *n* (Fluß)Mündung *f.*
eternal [i'təːnl] *adj* ewig. **eternity** *n* Ewigkeit *f.*
ether ['iːθə] *n* Äther *m.* **ethereal** *adj* ätherisch.
ethical ['eθikl] *adj* ethisch, sittlich. **ethics** *n* Ethik *f.*
ethnic ['eθnik] *adj* ethnisch, Volks-.
etiquette ['eti,ket] *n* Etikette *f.*
etymology [,eti'molədʒi] *n* Etymologie *f.*
Eucharist ['juːkərist] *n* heilige Messe *f.*
eunuch ['juːnək] *n* Eunuch *m*, Verschnittene(r) *m.*
euphemism ['juːfə,mizəm] *n* Euphemismus *m.* **euphemistic** *adj* beschönigend.
euphoria [ju'foːriə] *n* Wohlbefinden *neut*, Euphorie *f.*
Europe ['juərəp] *n* Europa *neut.* **European** *adj* europäisch; *n* Europäer(in). **European Economic Community (EEC)** Europäische Wirtschaftsgemeinschaft (EWG) *f.* **European Community** Europäische Gemeinschaften (EG) *pl.*
euthanasia [juːθə'neiziə] *n* Euthanasie *f*, Gnadentod *m.*
evacuate [i'vakju,eit] *v* (*depart*) aussiedeln; (*empty*) entleeren; (*people*) evakuieren. **evacuation** *n* Evakuierung *f.*

evade [i'veid] *v* ausweichen, entgehen (+ *dat*); (*tax*) hinterziehen.
evaluate [i'valju,eit] *v* abschätzen. **evaluation** *n* Abschätzung *f.*
evangelical [,iːvan'dʒelikəl] *adj* evangelisch. **evangelism** *n* Evangelismus *m.* **evangelist** *n* Evangelist *m.*
evaporate [i'vapə,reit] *v* verdampfen. **evaporated milk** Kondensmilch *f.* **evaporation** *n* Verdampfung *f.*
evasion [i'veiʒən] *n* Ausweichen *neut.* **tax evasion** Steuerhinterziehung *f.* **evasive** *adj* ausweichend. **evasive action** Ausweichmanöver *neut.*
eve [iːv] *n* Vorabend *m.* **Christmas Eve** Heiliger Abend *m.* **New Year's Eve** Sylvesterabend *m.*
even ['iːvən] *adj* eben, gerade. *adv* sogar. *even bigger* noch größer. **even more** noch mehr. **not even** nicht einmal. **even if** wenn auch. **even-handed** *adj* unparteiisch.
evening ['iːvniŋ] *n* Abend *m.* **in the evening** abends, am Abend. **this evening** heute abend. **evening dress** Gesellschaftsanzug *m.* **evening meal** Abendessen *neut.*
event [i'vent] *n* Ereignis *neut*; (*sport*) Disziplin *f.* **in the event of** im Falle (+ *gen*). **eventful** *adj* ereignisvoll.
ever ['evə] *adv* je(mals); (*always*) immer. *have you ever been to Berlin?* sind Sie schon einmal in Berlin gewesen? **ever so** sehr. **for ever** für immer. **evergreen** *adj* immergrün. **everlasting** *adj* ewig.
every ['evri] *adj* jede; alle *pl.* **every day** jeden Tag. **every one** jeder einzelne. **every other day** jeden zweiten Tag. **every so often** hin und wieder. **everybody/everyone** *pron* jeder. **everything** *pron* alles. **everywhere** *adv* überall.
evict [i'vikt] *v* exmittieren. **eviction** *n* Exmission *f.*
evidence ['evidəns] *v* Zeugnis *neut*; Beweis *m.* **give evidence** Zeugnis ablegen. *v* beweisen.
evil ['iːvl] *adj* übel, böse. *n* Übel *neut*, Böse *neut.*
evoke [i'vouk] *v* hervorrufen.
evolve [i'volv] *v* (sich) entwickeln. **evolution** *n* Entwicklung *f*; (*biol*) Evolution *f.*
ewe [juː] *n* Mutterschaf *neut.*
exacerbate [ig'zasə,beit] *v* verschlimmern.

exact [ig'zakt] *adj* genau, exakt. *v* verlangen; (*payment*) eintreiben. **exacting** *adj* anspruchsvoll. **exactly** *adv* genau.

exaggerate [ig'zadʒəˌreit] *v* übertreiben. **exaggerated** *adj* übertrieben. **exaggeration** *n* Übertreibung *f*.

exalt [ig'zolt] *v* erheben; (*praise*) preisen. **exaltation** *n* (*joy*) Wonne *f*. **exalted** *adj* erhaben; (*excited*) aufgeregt.

examine [ig'zamin] *v* untersuchen, prüfen; (*law*) verhören. **examination** *n* Prüfung *f*; (*inspection*) Untersuchung *f*. **medical examination** ärztliche Untersuchung *f*.

example [ig'zaimpl] *n* Beispiel *neut*. **for example** zum Beispiel. **set an example** ein Beispiel geben.

exasperate [ig'zaispəˌreit] *v* zum Verzweifeln bringen. **exasperation** *n* Verzweiflung *f*.

excavate ['ekskəˌveit] *v* ausgraben. **excavation** *n* Ausgrabung *f*. **excavator** *n* (*mech*) Bagger *m*.

exceed [ik'siid] *v* überschreiten. **exceedingly** *adv* höchst.

excel [ik'sel] *v* sich auszeichnen. **excellence** *n* Vorzüglichkeit *f*. **Excellency** *n* Exzellenz *f*. **excellent** *adj* ausgezeichnet, vorzüglich.

except [ik'sept] *prep* außer. **except for** abgesehen von. *v* ausschließen. **exception** *n* Ausnahme *f*. **take exception to** übelnehmen.

excerpt ['eksəɪpt] *n* Auszug *m*.

excess [ik'ses] *n* Übermaß *neut*, Überfluß *m* (an). *adj* Über-. **excess fare** Zuschlag *m*. **excessive** *adj* übermäßig.

exchange [iks'tʃeindʒ] *v* (aus-, um)tauschen; (*money*) wechseln. *n* Austausch *m*; (*phone*) Zentrale *f*. **foreign exchange** Devisen *pl*. **exchange rate** Wechselkurs *m*.

exchequer [iks'tʃekə] *n* Schatzamt *neut*.

excise ['eksaiz] *v* (*cut out*) herausschneiden. **excise duty** indirekter Steuer *m*.

excite [ik'sait] *v* erregen, aufregen. **get excited** sich aufregen. **excitement** *n* Aufregung *f*.

exclaim [ik'skleim] *v* ausrufen. **exclamation** *n* Ausruf *m*. **exclamation mark** Ausrufungszeichen *neut*.

exclude [ik'skluid] *v* ausschließen. **exclusive** *adj* ausschließlich; (*fashionable*) exklusiv. **exclusive of** *also* **excluding** ausschließlich. **exclusion** *n* Ausschluß *m*.

excommunicate [ekskə'mjuɪniˌkeit] *v* exkommunizieren. **excommunication** *n* Exkommunikation *f*.

excrement ['ekskrəmənt] *n* Exkrement *neut*, Kot *m*.

excrete [ik'skriit] *v* ausscheiden. **excretion** *n* Ausscheidung *f*.

excruciating [ik'skruɪʃieitiŋ] *adj* peinigend.

excursion [ik'skəɪʃən] *n* Ausflug *m*.

excuse [ik'skjuɪz] *n* Ausrede *f*. *v* entschuldigen, verzeihen. **excuse me!** Verzeihung!

execute ['eksiˌkjuɪt] *v* (*carry out*) ausführen; (*person*) hinrichten. **execution** *n* Ausführung *f*; Hinrichtung *f*. **executioner** *n* Henker *m*. **executor** *n* Testamentvollstrecker *m*.

executive [ig'zekjutiv] *adj* vollziehend. *n* (*comm*) Geschäftsführer *m*.

exemplify [ig'zempliˌfai] *v* als Beispiel dienen für.

exempt [ig'zempt] *v* befreien (von). *adj* **exempt from** frei von.

exercise ['eksəˌsaiz] *n* Übung *f*; (*of duty*) Ausübung *f*. *v* üben; (*wield*) ausüben. **physical exercise** Leibesübung *f*. **exercise book** Schulheft *neut*.

exert [ig'zəɪt] *v* ausüben. **exert oneself** sich anstrengen. **exertion** *n* Anstrengung *f*.

exhale [eks'heil] *v* ausatmen.

exhaust [ig'zoɪst] *v* erschöpfen. **exhausted** *adj* erschöpft. **exhausting** *adj* anstrengend. **exhaustion** *n* Erschöpfung *f*. *n* **exhaust (gases)** Abgase *pl*. **exhaust pipe** Auspuffrohr *neut*.

exhibit [ig'zibit] *v* zeigen; (*goods*) ausstellen. **exhibition** *n* Ausstellung *f*. **exhibitor** *n* Aussteller *m*.

exhilarate [ig'ziləˌreit] *v* erheitern. **exhilarated** *adj* angeregt, heiter. **exhilarating** erheiternd. **exhilaration** *n* Erheiterung *f*.

exile ['eksail] *n* Verbannung *f*; (*person*) Verbannte(r). *v* verbannen.

exist [ig'zist] *v* existieren, sein. **existence** *n* Dasein *neut*, Existenz *f*. **existing** bestehend.

exit ['egzit] *n* Ausgang. *v* abtreten.

exodus ['eksədəs] *n* Auswanderung *f*; (*coll*) allgemeiner Ausbruch *m*.

exonerate [ig'zonəˌreit] *v* freisprechen (von).

exorbitant [ig'zɔɪbitənt] *adj* übermäßig.
exorcize ['eksɔɪsaiz] *v* austreiben.
exotic [ig'zotik] *adj* exotisch, fremdartig.
expand [ik'spand] *v* (sich) ausdehnen;
(*develop*) entwickeln, erweitern. **expanse**
n Weite *f*, weite Fläche *f*. **expansion** *n*
Ausdehnung *f*; (*of firm*) Erweiterung *f*;
(*pol*) Expansion *f*.
expatriate [eks'peitrieit; *n* eks'peitriət] *vv*
ausbürgern. *n* im Ausland Lebende(r).
expect [ik'spekt] *v* erwarten; (*support*)
annehmen. *She is expecting* sie ist in
anderen Umständen. **expectation** *n*
Erwartung *f*.
expedient [ik'spiːdiənt] *adj* zweckdienlich.
n Notbehelf *m*.
expedition [ˌekspi'diʃən] *n* Expedition *f*.
expel [ik'spel] *v* ausstoßen; (*from school*)
ausschließen.
expenditure [ik'spenditʃə] *n* Ausgabe *f*.
expense [ik'spens] *n* (Geld)Ausgabe *f*.
expenses *pl* Unkosten *pl*. *at my expense*
auf meine Kosten. **at the expense of** zum
Schaden von. **expensive** *adj* teuer, kostspielig.
experience [ik'spiəriəns] *n* Erfahrung *f*;
(*event*) Erlebnis *neut*. *v* erfahren, erleben.
experienced *adj* erfahren.
experiment [ik'sperimənt] *m* Experiment
neut, Probe *f*. *v* experimentieren. **experi-
mental** *adj* Experimental-.
expert ['ekspəɪt] *n* Fachmann *m*,
Sachkundige(r). *adj* geschickt, gewandt.
expertise *n* Sachkenntnis *f*.
expire [ik'spaiə] *v* (*breathe out*) ausatmen;
(*lapse*) verfallen; (*die*) sterben. **expiry** *n*
expiration Ablauf *m*.
explain [ik'splein] *v* erklären. **explanation**
n Erklärung *f*. **explanatory** *adj* erklärend.
be self-explanatory sich von selbst verstehen.
explicit [ik'splisit] *adj* deutlich, ausdrücklich.
explode [ik'sploud] *v* explodieren. **explosion** *n* Explosion *f*.
exploit[1] ['eksploit] *n* Heldentat *f*,
Abenteuer *m*.
exploit[2] [ik'sploit] *v* ausbeuten. **exploitation** *n* Ausbeutung *f*.
explore [ik'sploɪ] *v* erforschen. **explorer** *n*
(Er)Forscher *m*. **exploration** *n* Erfor-
schung *f*. **exploratory** *adj* forschend, For-
schungs-.
exponent [ik'spounənt] *n* (*person*)
Verfechter *m*.

export [ik'spoɪt; *n* 'ekspoɪt] *v* exportieren.
n Export *m*. **exportation** *n* Ausfuhr *f*.
exporter *n* Exporteur *m*. **export trade** *n*
Exporthandel *m*.
expose [ik'spouz] *v* aussetzen; (*phot*)
belichten; (*impostor*) aufdecken. **exposed**
adj (*unprotected*) ungeschützt. **be
exposed to** ausgesetzt sein (+*dat*). **exposure** *n* (*phot*) Belichtung *f* (*med*)
Unterkühlung *f*.
express [ik'spres] *v* ausdrücken. *adj* Eil-,
Schnell-. **express letter** Eilbrief *m*.
express train D-zug *m*. **expression** *n*
Ausdruck *m*. **expressionism** *n* Expres-
sionismus *m*. **expressionless** *adj* aus-
druckslos. **expressive** *adj* ausdrucksvoll.
expressly *adv* ausdrücklich.
expulsion [ik'spʌlʃən] *n* Ausweisung *f*.
exquisite ['ekswizit] *adj* ausgezeichnet;
(*pain*) heftig.
extend [ik'stend] *v* ausdehnen; (*develop*)
erweitern; (*hand*) ausstrecken; (*cover
area*) sich erstrecken. **extension** *n*
Erweiterung *f*; (*comm*) Verlängerung *f*;
(*phone*) Nebenanschluß; (*building*)
Anbau *m*. **extensive** *adj* ausgedehnt.
extent *n* Umfang *m*. **to a certain extent**
bis zu einem gewissen Grade.
exterior [ik'stiəriə] *adj* äußer, Außen-. *n*
das Äußere; (*appearance*) äußeres
Ansehen *neut*.
exterminate [ik'stəɪmiˌneit] *v* ausrotten.
extermination *n* Ausrottung *f*.
external [ik'stəɪnl] *adj* äußer, äußerlich,
Außen-.
extinct [ik'stiŋkt] *adj* ausgestorben; (*volcano*) ausgebrannt. **become extinct** aussterben. **extinction** *n* Aussterben *neut*.
extinguish [ik'stiŋwiʃ] *v* (aus)löschen.
(**fire**) **extinguisher** Feuerlöscher *m*.
extort [ik'stoɪt] *v* erpressen. **extortion** *n*
Erpressung *f*. **extortionate** *adj* erpresserisch. **extortionate price** Wucherpreis *m*.
extra ['ekstrə] *adj* zusätzlich, Extra-. *adv*
besonders. **extras** *pl n* (*expenses*) Sonder-
ausgaben *pl*; (*accessories*)
Sonderzubehörteile *pl*.
extract [ik'strakt; *n* 'ekstrakt] *v* ausziehen; (*tooth*) ziehen; (*numerals*) gewinnen. *n* Auszug *m*. **extraction** *n* Ausziehen
neut; (*tooth, minerals*) Extraktion *f*.
extradite ['ekstrədait] *v* ausliefern. **extradition** *n* Auslieferung *f*.

extramural [ˌekstrə'mjuərəl] *adj* außerplanmäßig.
extraordinary [ik'strɔːdənəri] *adj* außerordentlich, seltsam.
extravagant [ik'strævəgənt] *adj* verschwenderisch; (*exaggerated*) übertrieben.
extreme [ik'striːm] *adj* höchst, letzt; (*fig*) extrem; *n* Extrem *m*, äußerste Grenze *f*.
extremism *n* Extremismus *m*. **extremist** *n* Extremist *m*.
extricate ['ekstriˌkeit] *v* herauswickeln.
extrovert ['ekstrəvɔːt] *adj* (*psychol*) extravertiert. *n* Extravertierte(r).
exuberance [ig'zjuːbərəns] *n* Übermut *m*. **exuberant** *adj* übermütig.
exude [ig'zjuːd] *v* ausschlagen; ausstrahlen.
exultation [ˌegzʌl'teiʃən] *n* Jubel *m*.
eye [ai] *n* Auge *neut*; (*of needle*) Öse *f*. *v* anschauen.
eyeball ['aibɔːl] *n* Augapfel *m*.
eyebrow ['aibrau] *n* Augenbraue *f*.
eye-catching ['aikatʃiŋ] *adj* auffallend.
eyelash ['ailaʃ] *n* Wimper *f*.
eyelid ['ailid] *n* Augenlid *neut*.
eye shadow *n* Lidschatten *m*.
eyesight ['aisait] *n* Sehkraft *f*.
eyewitness ['aiˌwitnis] *n* Augenzeuge *m*.

F

fable ['feibl] *n* Fabel *f*.
fabric ['fabrik] *n* Stoff *m*, Gewebe *neut*. **fabricate** *v* herstellen; (*fig*) erfinden.
fabulous ['fabjuləs] *adj* fabelhaft, sagenhaft.
façade [fə'saːd] *n* Fassade *f*.
face [feis] *n* Gesicht *neut*; (*of clock*) Zifferblatt *neut*; (*surface*) Oberfläche *f*; (*cheek*) Stirn *f*. **pull faces** Fratzen schneiden. *v* gegenüberstehen; (*fig*) entgegentreten; (*of house, etc.*) liegen nach.
facet ['fasit] *n* Facette *f*; (*fig*) Aspekt *m*.
facetious [fə'siːʃəs] *adj* scherzhaft.
facial ['feiʃəl] *adj* Gesichts-.
facile ['fasail] *adj* (*easy*) leicht; (*superficial*) oberflächlich. **facilitate** *v* erleichtern.
facility *n* Leichtigkeit *f*. **facilities** *pl n* Einrichtungen *pl*.

facing ['feisiŋ] *prep* gegenüber. *n* Verkleidung *f*.
facsimile [fak'siməli] *n* Faksimile *neut*.
fact [fakt] *n* Tatsache *f*; (*reality*) Wirklichkeit *f*. **in fact** in der Tat, tatsächlich.
faction ['fakʃən] *n* Faktion *f*.
factor ['faktə] *n* Faktor *m*; (*comm*) Agent *m*.
factory ['faktəri] *n* Fabrik *f*. **factory worker** Fabrikarbeiter(in).
fad [fad] *n* Mode *f*.
fade [feid] *v* verschießen, verblassen; (*flower*) verwelken; (*sound*) schwinden. **faded** *adj* verschossen.
fag [fag] *n* (*coll: tiresome job*) Plackerei *f*. **fagged** *adj* erschöpft.
fail [feil] *v* fehlschlagen, scheitern; (*to do something*) unterlassen; (*in exam*) durchfallen; (*let down*) im Stich lassen. *n* **without fail** unbedingt.
faint [feint] *adj* (*colour*) blaß; (*sound*) leise; (*memory*) schwach. *v* ohnmächtig werden. *n* Ohnmacht *f*.
fair[1] [feə] *adj* (*hair*) hell, blond; (*beautiful*) schön; (*just*) gerecht, fair. **fair chance** aussichtsreiche Chance *f*. **play fair** fair spielen. **fair and square** offen und ehrlich. **fairly** *adv* (*quite*) ziemlich.
fair[2] [feə] *n* Messe *f*; (*funfair*) Jahrmarkt *m*. **fairground** Messegelände *neut*; Rummelplatz *m*.
fairy ['feəri] *n* Fee *f*. *adj* feenhaft, Feen-. **fairy tale** Märchen *neut*.
faith [feiθ] *n* Vertrauen *neut*; (*belief*) Glaube *m*. **faithful** *adj* treu; (*accurate*) getreu. **yours faithfully** hochachtungsvoll.
fake [feik] *v* fälschen. *n* Fälschung *f*; (*person*) Schwindler. *adj* vorgetäuscht.
falcon ['fɔːlkən] *n* Falke *m*.
***fall** [fɔːl] *n* Sturz *m*, Fall *m*; (*fig*) Untergang *m*. *v* fallen; (*prices*) abnehmen; (*curtain*) niedergehen; (*fortress*) genommen werden. **fall asleep** einschlafen. **fall back** sich zurückziehen. **fall down** (*person*) hinfallen; (*building*) einstürzen. **fall in love with** sich verlieben in. **fall into** geraten in. **fall out with** zanken mit. **fall through** durchfallen.
fallacy ['faləsi] *n* Trugschluß *m*.
fallen ['fɔːlən] *V* fall.
fallible ['faləbl] *adj* fehlbar.
fall-out ['fɔːlaut] *n* Niederschlag *m*.
fallow ['falou] *adj* fahl.

false [fɔːls] *adj* falsch; (*person*) untreu; (*thing*) gefälscht. **false alarm** blinder Alarm *m*. **false start** Fehlstart *m*. **falsehood** *n* Lüge *f*. **falsify** fälschen.

falter [ˈfɔːltə] *v* stolpern; (*hesitate*) zögern; (*courage*) versagen.

fame [feim] *n* Ruhm *m*, Berühmtheit *f*.

familiar [fəˈmiljə] *adj* bekannt; (*informal*) ungezwungen. **familiarity** *n* Vertrautheit *f*.

family [ˈfaməli] *n* Familie *f*; (*bot*, *zool*) Gattung *f*. *adj* Familien-.

famine [ˈfamin] *n* Hungersnot *f*.

famished [ˈfamiʃt] *n* **be famished** großen Hunger haben.

famous [ˈfeiməs] *adj* berühmt. **famously** *adv* (*coll*) glänzend.

fan[1] [fan] *n* (*hand*) Fächer *m*; (*mot*, *elec*) Ventilator *m*. **fan belt** *n* Keilriemen *m*.

fan[2] [fan] *n* (*admirer*) Fan *m*.

fanatic [fəˈnatik] *n* Fanatiker(in). **fanatical** *adj* fanatisch.

fancy [ˈfansi] *n* Neigung *f* (zu); (*fantasy*) Phantasie *f*. **take a fancy to** eingenommen sein für. *v* gern haben *adj* schick. **fancy dress** Maskenkostüm *m*.

fanfare [ˈfanfeə] *n* Fanfare *f*.

fang [faŋ] *n* Fangzahn *m*; (*of snake*) Giftzahn *m*.

fantastic [fanˈtastik] *adj* phantastisch; (*coll*) sagenhaft, toll.

fantasy [ˈfantəsi] *n* Phantasie *f*.

far [faː] *adj* fern, entfernt. *adv* fern, weit. **as far as** bis (nach). **by far** bei weitem. **far and near** nahe und fern. **far better** viel besser. **far off** weit weg. **on the far side** auf der anderen Seite.

farce [faːs] *n* Posse *f*; (*fig*) Farce *f*.

fare [feə] *n* Fahrpreis *m*; (*food*) Kost *f*. *v* ergehen.

farewell [feəˈwel] *interj* lebe wohl! *n* Lebewohl *neut*. *adj* Abschieds-. **bid farewell to** Abschied nehmen von.

far-fetched [ˌfaːˈfetʃt] *adj* weit hergeholt.

farm [faːm] *n* Bauernhof *m*. **dairy farm** Meierei *f*. **poultry farm** Geflügelfarm *f*. *v* Landwirtschaft betreiben; (*land*) bebauen. **farm out** (*work*) weitergeben. **farmer** *n* Landwirt *m*, Bauer *m*. **farmhouse** *n* Bauernhaus *neut*. **farming** *n* Landwirtschaft *f*. **farmworker** Landarbeiter(in).

far-sighted [ˌfaːˈsaitid] *adj* weitsichtig.

fart [faːt] *n* (*vulgar*) Furz *m*. *v* furzen.

farther [ˈfaːðə] *adj*, *adv* weiter, ferner.

farthest [ˈfaːðist] *adj* fernst, weitest. *adv* am weitesten.

fascinate [ˈfasiˌneit] *v* faszinieren. **fascinating** *adj* fesselnd. faszinierend. **fascination** *n* Bezauberung *f*, Faszination *f*.

fascism [ˈfaʃizəm] *n* Faschismus *m*. **fascist** *adj* faschistisch. *n* Faschist *m*.

fashion [ˈfaʃən] *n* Mode *f*; (*manner*) Art (und Weise) *f*. **in fashion** modisch. **out of fashion** unmodisch. *v* bilden, gestalten. **fashionable** *adj* modisch. **fashion show** Modeschau *f*.

fast[1] [faːst] *adj*, *adv* (*quick*) schnell, rasch; (*firm*) fest; (*colour*) echt. *my watch is fast* meine Uhr geht vor.

fast[2] [faːst] *v* fasten. *n* Fasten *neut*.

fasten [ˈfaːsn] *v* befestigen, festbinden; (*door*) verriegeln. **fastener** *n* Verschluß *m*.

fastidious [faˈstidiəs] *adj* wählerisch, anspruchsvoll.

fat [fat] *adj* (*person*) dick, fett; (*greasy*) fett, fettig. *n* Fett *neut*.

fatal [ˈfeitl] *adj* tödlich. **fatalistic** *adj* fatalistisch. **fatality** *n* Todesfall *m*.

fate [feit] *n* Schicksal *neut*. **fateful** *adj* verhängnisvoll.

father [ˈfaːðə] *n* Vater *m*. *v* zeugen. **Father Christmas** der Weihnachtsmann. **father-in-law** *n* Schwiegervater *m*. **fatherland** *n* Vaterland *neut*.

fathom [ˈfaðəm] *n* Faden *m*. *v* sondieren; (*fig*) eindringen in.

fatigue [fəˈtiːg] *n* Ermüdung *f*. *v* ermüden. **fatiguing** *adj* mühsam, ermüdend.

fatuous [ˈfatjuəs] *adj* albern.

fault [fɔːlt] *n* Fehler *m*; (*tech*) Störung *f*; (*blame*) Schuld *f*. *It's my fault* es ist meine Schuld. *Whose fault is this?* wer ist daran schuld? **at fault** im Unrecht. **find fault (with)** tadeln.

fauna [ˈfɔːnə] *n* Fauna *f*.

favour [ˈfeivə] *n* Gunst *f*; (*kindness*) Gefallen *m*. **in favour of** zugunsten von (*or +gen*). **be in favour of** einverstanden sein mit. **in his favour** zu seinen Gunsten. **find favour with** Gunst finden bei. *Do me a favour and . . .* Tun sie nur den Gefallen und . . . . **favourable** *adj* günstig. **favourite** *adj* Lieblings-; *n* Liebling *m*; (*sport*) Favorit *m*.

fawn [fɔːn] *n* Rehkalb *neut*. *adj* rehfarbig.

fear [fiə] *n* Furcht *f*, Angst *f*. **fears** *pl n* Befürchtungen *pl*. *v* sich fürchten (vor), Angst haben (vor). **fearful** *adj* (*person*) ängstlich; (*thing*) furchtbar. **fearless** *adj* furchtlos. **fearsome** *adj* schrecklich.

feasible ['fiːzəbl] *adj* möglich. **feasibility** *n* Möglichkeit *f*.

feast [fiːst] *n* Fest *neut*; (*meal*) Festessen *neut*. *v* sich ergötzen (von).

feat [fiːt] *n* Kunststück *neut*.

feather ['feðə] *n* Feder *f*. **featherweight** *n* Federgewicht *neut*.

feature ['fiːtʃə] *n* (*of face*) Gesichtszug *m*; (*characteristic*) Eigenschaft *f*, Kennzeichen *neut*; (*newspaper*) Feature *neut*. *v* darstellen. **feature film** Spielfilm *m*.

February ['februəri] *n* Februar *m*.

fed [fed] *V* feed.

federal ['fedərəl] *adj* Bundes-; (*Swiss*) eidgenössisch. **Federal Republic of Germany** Bundesrepublik Deutschland. **federalism** *n* Föderalismus *m*, **federalist** *n* Föderalist *m*. **federation** *n* Bundesstaat *m*; (*organization*) Verband *m*.

fee [fiː] *n* Gebühr *f*. **school fees** Schulgeld *neut sing*.

feeble ['fiːbl] *adj* schwach, kraftlos. **feeble-minded** *adj* schwachsinnig. **feebleness** *n* Schwachheit *f*.

*feed [fiːd] *v* essen; (*of animals*) fressen; (*cattle*) füttern; (*person*) zu essen geben; (*tech*) zuführen. *n* Futter *neut*; (*tech*) Zufuhr *f*. **be fed up with** (*coll*) satt haben, die Nase voll haben. **feedback** *n* Rückkopplung; (*fig*) Rückwirkung. **feeding** *n* Nahrung *f*; (*animals*) Fütterung *f*.

*feel [fiːl] *v* (*sich*) fühlen; (*detect, sense*) empfinden; (*pulse*) betasten. *I feel cold* mir is kalt. *I feel better* es geht mir besser. *It feels hard* es fühlt sich hart an. *I don't feel like working* ich habe keine Lust zur Arbeit. *n* (*atmosphere*) Stimmung *f*. **feeler** *n* Fühler *m*. **feeling** *n* Gefühl *neut*. **hurt someone's feelings** jemanden verletzen.

feet [fiːt] *V* foot.

feign [fein] *v* simulieren.

feline ['fiːlain] *adj* Katzen-.

fell¹ [fel] *V* fall.

fell² [fel] *v* (*tree*) fällen.

fellow ['felou] *n* Genosse *m*, Genossin *f*; (*coll*) Kerl *m*. **fellow-countryman** *n* Landsmann *m*. **fellow men** Mitmenschen *pl*. **fellowship** *n* Kameradschaft *f*, Gesellschaft *f*.

felony ['feləni] *n* Schwerverbrechen *neut*. **felon** *n* Schwerverbrecher *m*.

felt¹ [felt] *V* feel.

felt² [felt] *n* Filz *m*.

female ['fiːmeil] *adj* weiblich. *n* Weib *neut*; (*of animals*) Weibchen *neut*.

feminine ['feminin] *adj* weiblich. *n* (*gramm*) Femininum *neut*. **femininity** *n* Weiblichkeit *f*.

feminism ['feminizəm] *n* Frauenrechtlertum *neut*. **feminist** *n* Frauenrechtler(in), Feminist(in).

fence [fens] *n* Zaun *m*. *v* (*sport*) fechten. **fence in** *or* **off** einzäunen.

fend [fend] *v* **fend off** abwehren. **fend for oneself** sich allein durchschlagen.

fender ['fendə] *n* (*US*) Kotflugel *m*. (*fireguard*) Kaminvorsetzer *m*;\

fennel ['fenl] *n* Fenchel *m*.

ferment [fə'ment; *n* 'fɔːment] *v* gären (lassen). *n* (*fig*) Unruhe *f*. **fermentation** *n* Gärung *f*.

fern [fəːn] *n* Farn *m*.

ferocious [fə'rouʃəs] *adj* wild, grausam; (*dog*) bissig. **ferocity** *n* Wildheit *f*.

ferret ['ferit] *n* Frettchen *neut*. *v* **ferret out** ausforschen. **ferret about** herumsuchen.

ferry ['feri] *n* Fähre *f*. *v* übersetzen.

fertile ['fəːtail] *adj* fruchtbar. **fertility** *n* Fruchtbarkeit *f*. **fertilization** *n* Befruchtung *f*; (*of land*) Düngung *f*. **fertilize** *v* befruchten; (*land*) düngen. **fertilizer** *n* Düngemittel *neut*.

fervent ['fəːvənt] *adj* glühend, eifrig.

fester ['festə] *v* verfaulen; (*wound*) eitern.

festival ['festəvəl] *n* Fest *neut*.

festive ['festiv] *adj* festlich. **festivity** *n* Fröhlichkeit *f*.

fetch [fetʃ] *v* holen; (*collect*) abholen; (*price*) erzielen. **fetching** *adj* reizend.

fête [feit] *n* Gartenfest *neut*.

fetid ['fiːtid] *adj* übelriechend.

fetish ['fetiʃ] *n* Fetisch *m*.

fetter ['fetə] *v* fesseln. **fetters** *pl n* Fessel *f* sing.

feud [fjuːd] *n* Fehde *f*. *v* sich befehden.

feudal ['fjuːdl] *adj* feudal, Lehns-. **feudalism** *n* Feudalismus *m*.

fever ['fiːvə] *n* Fieber *neut*. **feverish** *adj* fiebrig; (*activity*) fieberhaft.

few [fjuː] *adj, pron* wenige. **a few** einige, ein paar.

fiancé [fi'ɔnsei] *n* Verlobte(r) *m*. **fiancée** *n* Verlobte *f*.

fiasco [fi'askou] *n* Fiasko *neut*, Mißerfolg *m*.

fib [fib] *n* Flunkerei *f*. *v* flunkern. **fibber** *n* Flunkerer *m*.

fibre ['faibə] *n* Faser *f*. **fibreglass** *n* Glasfiber *f*.

fickle ['fikl] *adj* unbeständig. **fickleness** *n* Unbeständigkeit *f*.

fiction ['fikʃən] *n* Erdichtung *f*; (*as genre*) Erzählungsliteratur *f*. **work of fiction** Roman *m*. **fictitious** *adj* fiktiv. **fictitious character** erfundene Person *f*.

fiddle ['fidl] *v* tändeln, spielen. *n* Schwindel *m*; (*violin*) Fiedel *f*. **fiddler** *n* (*violinist*) Fiedler *m*.

fidelity [fi'deləti] *n* Treue *f*.

fidget ['fidʒit] *v* zappeln. **fidgety** *adj* zappelig.

field [fiːld] *n* Feld *neut*; (*mining*) Flöz *neut*; (*fig: sphere*) Bereich *m*. **field glasses** Feldstecker *m*. **fieldwork** *n* Feldforschung *f*.

fiend [fiind] *n* Teufel *m*; (*evil person*) Unhold *m*. **fiendish** *adj* teuflisch.

fierce [fiəs] *adj* wild, grausam. **fierceness** *n* Wildheit *f*.

fiery ['faiəri] *adj* feurig.

fifteen [fif'tiin] *adj* fünfzehn. **fifteenth** *adj* fünfzehnt.

fifth [fifθ] *adj* fünft. *n* Fünftel *neut*.

fifty ['fifti] *adj* fünfzig. **fiftieth** *adj* fünfzigst. **fifty-fifty** *adv* halb und halb.

fig [fig] *n* Feige *f*; (*tree*) Feigenbaum *m*.

***fight** [fait] *v* kämpfen; (*fig*) bekämpfen. **have a fight** sich streiten. *n* Kampf *m*; (*quarrel*) Streit *m*; (*brawl*) Schlägerei *f*.

figment ['figmənt] *n* Erzeugnis der Phantasie *neut*.

figure ['figə] *n* (*number*) Ziffer *f*; (*of person*) Figur *f*; (*diagram*) Zeichnung *f*, Diagramm *neut*. **figure of speech** Redewendung *f*. *v* (*appear*) auftreten; (*coll: reckon*) meinen. **figure out** ausrechnen.

filament ['filəmənt] *n* (*elec*) Glühfaden *m*.

file¹ [fail] *n* (*documents*) Akte *f*; (*folder*) Mappe *f*; (*row*) Reihe *f*. *v* (*letters*) ablegen; (*suit*) vorlegen; (*mil*) defilieren. **filing cabinet** Aktenschrank *m*. **filing clerk** Registrator *m*.

file² [fail] *n* (*tool*) Feile *f*. *v* feilen.

filial ['filiəl] *adj* Kindes-.

fill [fil] *v* (an)füllen; (*with objects*) vollstopfen; (*tooth*) plombieren; (*hole*) zustopfen; (*become full*) sich füllen. **fill up** auffüllen; (*mot*) auftanken.

fillet ['filit] *n* Filet *neut*.

film [film] *n* Film *m*. *v* filmen. **make a film** einen Film drehen.

filter ['filtə] *n* Filter *m or neut*. *v* filtrieren. **filter-tip** *n* Filtermundstück *neut*.

filth [filθ] *n* Dreck *m*, Schmutz *m*. **filthy** *adj* dreckig, schmutzig; (*indecent*) unflätig; (*weather*) scheußlich.

fin [fin] *n* Flosse *f*.

final ['fainl] *adj* letzt, End-; (*definitive*) endgültig. *n* (*sport*) Endspiel *neut*. **finals** *pl n* (*exams*) Abschlußprüfung *f sing*. **finale** *n* Finale *neut*. **finalist** *n* Endspielteilnehmer(in). **finalize** *v* abschließen. **finally** *adv* schließlich, zum Schluß.

finance [fai'nans] *n* Finanzwesen *neut*. *v* finanzieren. **finances** *pl n* Finanzen *pl*. **financial** *adj* finanziell, Finanz-.

finch [fintʃ] *n* Fink *m*.

***find** [faind] *v* finden. **find guilty** für schuldig erklären. **find oneself** sich befinden. **find out** herausfinden; (*a person*) ertappen. *n* Fund *m*. **findings** *pl n* Beschluß *m sing*.

fine¹ [fain] *adj* fein; (*weather*) schön; (*splendid*) gut, herrlich; (*hair*) dünn; (*point*) spitz; (*clothes*) elegant.

fine² [fain] *n* Geldstrafe *f*. *v* mit einer Geldstrafe belegen.

finesse [fi'nes] *n* Feinheit *f*; (*cards*) Schneiden *neut*.

finger ['fingə] *n* Finger *m*. *v* betasten. **fingernail** *n* Fingernagel *m*. **fingerprint** *n* Fingerabdruck *m*.

finish ['finiʃ] *v* aufhören, zu Ende gehen; beenden; (*complete*) vollenden; (*food*) aufessen; (*drink*) auftrinken. *n* Ende *neut*; Schluß *m*. **finished** *adj* fertig.

finite ['fainait] *adj* endlich.

Finland ['finlənd] *n* Finnland *neut*. **Finn** *n* Finne *m*, Finnin *f*. **Finnish** *adj* finnisch.

fir [fəi] *n* Tannenbaum *m*.

fire [faiə] *n* Feuer *neut*; Brand *m*. **catch fire** Feuer fangen. **set fire to** in Brand stecken. *v* (*a gun*) abfeuern; (*with a gun*) schießen; (*mot*) zünden.

fire alarm *n* Feueralarm *m*; (*device*) Feuermelder *m*.

firearms ['faiərɑimz] *pl n* Schußwaffen *pl*.

fire brigade *n* Feuerwehr *f*.

fire drill *n* Feueralarmübung *f*.

fire engine *n* Feuerwehrauto *neut*.

fire escape *n* Nottreppe *f*.

fleeting

fire extinguisher n Feuerlöscher m.
fire-guard n Kaminvorsetzer m.
fireman ['faiəmən] n Feuerwehrmann m.
fireplace ['faiə‚pleis] n Kamin m.
fireproof ['faiə‚pruːf] adj feuerfest.
fireside ['faiə‚said] n Kamin m. adj häuslich.
fire station n Feuerwache f.
firewood ['faiə‚wud] n Brennholz m.
firework ['faiə‚wəːk] n Feuerwerkskörper
m. **fireworks** pl n Feuerwerk neut sing.
firing squad n Exekutionskommando
neut.
firm[1] [fəːm] adj fest, hart; (resolute)
entschlossen. **firm friends** enge Freunde
pl.
firm[2] [fəːm] n Firma f.
first [fəːst] adj erst. **first name** Vorname
m. adv or **firstly** erstens, zuerst, zunächst.
at first zuerst. **come first** (sport) gewinnen. **first aid** erste Hilfe. **first-class** adj
erstklassig.
fiscal ['fiskəl] adj fiskalisch. **fiscal year**
Finanzjahr neut.
fish [fiʃ] n Fisch m; v fischen; (in river)
angeln. **fishbone** n Gräte f. **fisherman** n
Fischer. **fishhook** n Angelhaken m.
fishing n Fischen neut, Angeln neut,
fishing boat Fischerboot neut. **fishing rod**
Angelrute f. **fishmonger** n Fischhändler
m. **fishy** n (coll. suspicious) verdächtig.
fission ['fiʃən] n Spaltung f.
fissure ['fiʃə] n Spalt m.
fist [fist] n Faust m.
fit[1] [fit] adj (suitable) geeignet, angemessen; (healthy) gesund; (sport) fit, in guter
Form. n (clothes) Sitz m. v (clothes)
sitzen; (insert) einsetzen. **fit in** sich
einfügen. **fit into** sich hineinpassen in.
fitness n Gesundheit f; (sport) Fitneß f.
fitter n (mech) Monteur m. **fitting** adj
passend. **fittings** pl n Zubehör neut sing.
fit[2] [fit] n (med) Anfall m.
five [faiv] adj fünf.
fix [fiks] v befestigen (an); (arrange)
bestimmen; (eyes) richten (auf); (repair)
reparieren. n (coll) Klemme f; (drugs)
Fix m.
fizz [fiz] v zischen, sprudeln. **fizzy** adj
sprudelnd, sprudel-.
flabbergast ['flabəgaist] v verblüffen.
flabby ['flabi] adj schlaff.
flag[1] [flag] n Fahne f; (naut) Flagge f. **flag
down** stoppen.

flag[2] [flag] v (wane) nachlassen.
flagrant ['fleigrənt] adj offenkundig.
flair [fleə] n natürliche Begabung f, feine
Nase f.
flake [fleik] n (snow, cereals) Flocke f;
(thin piece) Schuppe f. v **flake off** sich
abschuppen.
flamboyant [flam‚boiənt] adj auffallend.
flame [fleim] n Flamme f. **burst into
flames** in Flammen aufgehen. **old flame**
alte Flamme f.
flamingo [flə'miŋgou] n Flamingo m.
flan [flan] n Torte f.
flank [flaŋk] n Flanke f. v flankieren.
flannel ['flanl] n (material) Flanell m;
(facecloth) Waschlappen m.
flap [flap] n Klappe f; (of skin, etc.) Lappen m. v flattern.
flare [fleə] v flackern; (dress) sich baus-
chen. **flare up** aufflackern. n (naut) Licht-
signal neut; (of dress) Ausbauchung f.
flash [flaʃ] Blitz m; (phot) Blitzlicht neut.
news flash Kurznachricht f. v aufblitzen·
(fig) sich blitzartig bewegen. **flashback** n
Rückblende f. **flashbulb** n Blitzlicht-
lampe f. **flasher** n (mot) Blinker m.
flashlight n Taschenlampe f. **flashy** adj
auffällig.
flask [flaːsk] n Flasche f; (laboratory)
Glaskolben m. **vacuum flask** Warm-
flasche f.
flat[1] [flat] adj platt, flach; (level) eben;
(refusal) glatt. **fall flat** ein glatter Versager sein.
flat[2] [flat] n Wohnung f.
flatter ['flatə] v schmeicheln. **flattering** adj
schmeichelnd. **flattery** n Schmeichelei f.
flatulence ['flatjuləns] n Blähsucht f.
flaunt [floint] v paradieren mit, prunken
mit.
flautist ['floːtist] n Flötist(in).
flavour ['fleivə] n Geschmack m. v
würzen. **flavouring** n Würze f.
flaw [floː] n (crack) Sprung m; (defect)
Makel m. **flawless** adj tadellos.
flax [flaks] n Flachs m.
flea [fliː] n Floh m.
fleck [flek] n Flecken neut. v tüpfeln.
fled [fled] V flee.
*flee [fliː] v fliehen.
fleece [fliːs] n Vlies neut. v (coll) rupfen.
fleecy adj flockig.
fleet [fliːt] n Flotte f.
fleeting ['fliːtiŋ] adj flüchtig.

Flemish ['flemiʃ] *adj* flämisch.
flesh [fleʃ] *n* Fleisch *neut*. **flesh-coloured** *adj* fleischfarben. **fleshly** *adj* fleischlich. **fleshy** *adj* fleischig.
flew [fluː] *V* **fly¹**.
flex [fleks] *n* Schnur *f*. *v* biegen; (*muscles*) zusammenziehen. **flexibility** *n* Biegsamkeit *f*. **flexible** *adj* biegsam, flexibel.
flick [flik] *v* schnellen, schnippen. *n* Schnippchen *neut*.
flicker ['flikə] *v* flackern. *n* Flackern *neut*.
flight¹ [flait] *n* (*flying*) Flug *m*. **flight of stairs** Treppe *f*. **flighty** *adj* launisch.
flight² [flait] *n* (*fleeing*) Flucht *f*.
flimsy ['flimzi] *adj* dünn, schwach.
flinch [flintʃ] *v* zurückschrecken (vor).
***fling** [fliŋ] *v* schleudern, werfen. **fling away** wegwerfen. **fling open** aufreißen.
flint [flint] *n* Feuerstein *m*.
flip [flip] *v* klapsen, schnellen. *n* Klaps *m*.
flippant ['flipənt] *adj* leichtfertig, keck.
flirt [fləːt] *v* flirten. **flirtatious** *adj* kokett.
flit [flit] *v* flitzen.
float [flout] *v* schwimmen, treiben; (*boat*) flott sein. *n* (*angling*) Kokschwimmer *m*. **floating** *adj* schwimmend.
flock [flok] *n* (*sheep*) Herde *f*; (*birds*) Flug *m*. *v* sich scharen.
flog [flog] *v* peitschen, prügeln. **flogging** *adj* Prügelstrafe *f*.
flood [flʌd] *n* Flut *f*. *v* fluten.
floor [floː] *n* (Fuß)Boden *m*; (*storey*) Stock *m*. *v* (*coll*) verblüfen.
flop [flop] *v* plumpsen; (*fail*) versagen. *n* (*failure*) Niete *f*, Versager *m*.
flora ['floːrə] *m* Flora *f*. **floral** *adj* Blumen-.
florist ['florist] *n* Blümenhändler *m*.
flounder ['flaundə] *v* herumplatschen, stolpern.
flour ['flauə] *n* Mehl *neut*. **flour mill** *n* Mühle *f*. **floury** *adj* mehlig.
flourish ['flʌriʃ] *v* (*thrive*) gedeihen. *n* Schnörkel *m*.
flout [flaut] *v* verspotten.
flow [flou] *v* fließen, strömen. *n* Fluß *m*; (*fig*) Strom *m*.
flower ['flauə] *n* (*plant*) Blume *f*; (*bloom*) Blüte *f*. *v* blüten. **flowerbed** *n* Blumenbeet *neut*. **flowerpot** *n* Blumentopf *m*. **flower-seller** *n* Blumenverkäufer(in). **flowery** *adj* blumenreich.
flown [floun] *V* **fly¹**.

flu [fluː] *n* Grippe *f*.
fluctuate ['flʌktjuˌeit] *v* schwanken. **fluctuation** *n* Schwankung *f*.
flue [fluː] *n* Abzugsrohr *neut*.
fluent ['fluənt] *adj* fließend.
fluff [flʌf] *n* Flaum *m*, Federflocke *f*. *v* (*coll*) verpfuschen. **fluffy** *adj* flaumig, flockig.
fluid ['fluid] *n* Flüssigkeit *f*. *adj* flüssig.
fluke [fluːk] *n* (*coll*) Dusel *m*.
flung [flʌŋ] *V* **fling**.
fluorescent [fluə'resnt] *adj* fluoreszierend. **fluorescent light** Leuchtstofflampe *f*.
fluoride ['fluəraid] *n* Fluorid *neut*.
flush¹ [flʌʃ] *v* (*blush*) erröten; (*WC*) spülen. **flush out** ausspülen. *n* Erröten *neut*. **flushed** *adj* erregt.
flush² [flʌʃ] *adj* (*level*) glatt. **be flush** (*coll*) bei Kasse sein.
fluster ['flʌstə] *v* nervös machen, verwirren. **in a fluster** ganz verwirrt.
flute [fluːt] *n* Flöte *f*. **flute-player** *n* Flötenspieler(in).
flutter ['flʌtə] *v* flattern. *n* Flattern *neut*.
flux [flʌks] *n* Fluß *m*; (*tech*) Schmelzmittel *neut*. **in flux** im Fluß.
***fly¹** [flai] *v* fliegen; (*time*) entfliehen; (*flee*) fliehen; (*goods*) im Flugzeug befördern. *n* (*in trousers*) Hosenschlitz *m*. **flyer** *n* (*aero*) Flieger *m*. **flying** *adj* fliegend. **flying visit** Stippvisite *f*. **flyover** *n* Überführung *f*. **flywheel** *n* Schwungrad *neut*.
fly² [flai] *n* (*insect*) Fliege *f*.
foal [foul] *n* Fohlen *neut*.
foam [foum] *n* Schaum *m*. *v* schäumen. **foam rubber** Schaumgummi *m*. **foaming** *adj* schäumend.
focal ['foukəl] *adj* fokal. **focal point** Brennpunkt *m*.
fodder ['fodə] *n* Futter *neut*.
foe [fou] *n* Feind *m*.
fog [fog] *n* Nebel *m*. **foggy** *adj* neblig. **foghorn** *n* Nebelhorn *m*. **foglamp** *n* Nebelscheinwerfer *m*.
foible ['foibl] *n* Schwäche *f*.
foil¹ [foil] *v* vereiteln, verhindern.
foil² [foil] *n* (*metal*) Folie *f*.
foist [foist] *v* **foist something on someone** jemandem etwas andrehen.
fold¹ [fould] *v* (sich) falten; (*paper*) knifen; (*arms*) kreuzen; (*business*) eingehen. *n* Falte *f*; Kniff *m*. **folder** *n* (*for papers*) Mappe *f*.

fold² [fould] *n* (*for sheep*) Pferch *m*.
foliage ['fouliidʒ] *n* Laub *neut*.
folk [fouk] *n* Leute *pl*. **folks** *pl n* (*relations*) Verwandte *pl*. **folk-dance** *n* Volkstanz *m*. **folklore** *n* Folklore *f*. **folk-song** *n* Volkslied *neut*.
follow ['folou] *v* folgen (+ *dat*); (*instructions*) sich halten an; (*profession*) ausüben. **as follows** folgendermaßen. **follow from** sich ergeben aus. **follow up** verfolgen.
folly ['foli] *n* Narrheit *f*.
fond [fond] *adj* zärtlich; (*hopes*) kühn. **be fond of** gern *or* lieb haben. **fondness** *n* Vorliebe *f*.
fondle ['fondl] *v* streicheln.
font [font] *n* Taufbecken *m*.
food [fuːd] *n* Lebensmittel *pl*. Essen *neut*. **food and drink** Essen und Trinken *neut*. **foodstuff** *n* Nahrungsmittel *pl*.
fool [fuːl] *n* Narr *m*, Närrin *f*, Tor *m*. *v* zum Narren halten; betrügen. **fool around** herumalbern. **foolish** *adj* albern, dumm. **foolishness** *n* Torheit *f*.
foot [fut] *n* (*pl* **feet**) Fuß *m*; (*of bed, page*) Fußende *neut*. on foot. zu Fuß. **football** *n* (*game*) Fußballspiel *neut*; (*ball*) Fußball *m*. **foothills** *pl n* Vorgebirge *neut sing*. **foothold** *n* Halt *m*. **gain a foothold** Fuß fassen. **footnote** *n* Anmerkung *f*. **footpath** *n* Fußweg *m*. **footprint** *n* (Fuß)Spur *f*. **footstep** *n* Schritt *m*. **footwear** *n* Schuhzeug *neut*.
for [foɪ] *prep* für. *conj* denn. **leave for London** nach London abreisen. **for fun** aus Spaß. **for joy** vor Freude. **stay for three weeks** drei Wochen bleiben. **what for?** wozu?
forage ['foridʒ] *n* Furage *f*. *v* furagieren.
forbade [foɪˈbad] *V* **forbid**.
*****forbear** [foɪˈbeə] *v* sich enthalten (+ *gen*).
*****forbid** [foɪˈbid] *v* verbieten. **forbidden** *adj* verboten. **forbidding** *adj* bedrohlich.
forbidden [foɪˈbidn] *V* **forbid**.
force [foɪs] *n* Kraft *f*; (*violence*) Gewalt *f*. *v* (*compel*) zwingen; (*a door*) aufbrechen. **by force** gewaltsam. **in force** (*current*) in Kraft. **armed forces** Streitkräfte *pl*. **police force** Polizei *f*. **forced** *adj* gekünstelt. **forceful** *adj* eindringlich. **forcible** *adj* gewaltsam. **forcibly** *adv* zwangsweise.
forceps ['foɪseps] *pl n* Zange *f sing*.
ford [foɪd] *n* Furt *f*. *v* durchwaten.

fore [foɪ] *adj* Vorder-. **come to the fore** hervortreten.
forearm ['foɪraɪm] *n* Unterarm *m*.
forebear ['foɪbə] *n* Vorfahr *m*.
foreboding [foɪˈboudiŋ] *n* Vorahnung *f*.
*****forecast** ['foɪkaɪst] *v* voraussagen. *n* Voraussage *f*. **weather forecast** Wettervorhersage *f*.
forecourt ['foɪkoɪt] *n* Vorhof *m*.
forefather ['foɪfaɪðə] *n* Vorfahr *m*.
forefinger ['foɪfiŋgə] *n* Zeigefinger *m*.
forefront ['foɪfrʌnt] *n* **in the forefront** im Vordergrund.
foreground ['foɪgraund] *n* Vordergrund *m*.
forehand ['foɪhand] *n* (*sport*) Vorhandschlag *m*.
forehead ['forid] *n* Stirn *f*.
foreign ['forən] *adj* fremd, ausländisch, Auslands-. **foreign body** Fremdkörper *m*. **foreign language** Fremdsprache *f*. **foreign minister** Außenminister *m*. **foreign policy** Außenpolitik *f*. **foreigner** *n* Fremde(r), Ausländer(in).
foreleg ['foɪleg] *n* Vorderbein *neut*.
foreman ['foɪmən] *n* Vorarbeiter *m*, Aufseher *m*; (*jury*) Sprecher *m*.
foremost ['foɪmoust] *adj* vorderst. **first and foremost** zu allererst.
forename ['foɪneim] *n* Vorname *m*.
forensic [fəˈrensik] *adj* forensich.
forerunner ['foɪrʌnə] *n* Vorgänger *m*.
*****foresee** [foɪˈsiː] *v* voraussagen.
foresight ['foɪsait] *n* Vorsorge *f*.
foreskin ['foɪskin] *n* Vorhaut *m*.
forest ['forist] *n* Forst *m*, Wald *m*. **forest fire** Waldbrand *m*.
forestall [foɪˈstoɪl] *v* zuvorkommen (+ *dat*).
foretaste ['foɪteist] *n* Vorgeschmack *m*.
*****foretell** [foɪˈtel] *v* vorhersagen.
forethought ['foɪθoɪt] *n* Vorbedacht *m*.
forever [foɪˈevə] *adv* immer, ständig.
foreword ['foɪwoɪd] *n* Vorwort *neut*.
forfeit ['foɪfit] *v* verwirken. *n* Verwirkung *f*. *adj* verwirkt.
forgave [fəˈgeiv] *V* **forgive**.
forge [foɪdʒ] *v* (*metal*) schmieden; (*plan*) ersinnen; (*document*) fälschen. *n* Schmiede *f*. **forgery** *n* Fälschung *f*.
*****forget** [fəˈget] *v* vergessen. **forgetful** *adj* vergeßlich.
*****forgive** [fəˈgiv] *v* verzeihen, vergeben. **forgiveness** *n* Verzeihung *f*. **forgiving** *adj* versöhnlich.

forgiven [fə'gɪvn] V **forgive**.
***forgo** [foɪ'gou] v verzichten auf.
forgot [fə'gɒt] V **forget**.
forgotten [fə'gɒtn] V **forget**.
fork [fɔɪk] n Gabel f; (in road) Gabelung f. v **fork out** (coll: pay) blechen.
forlorn [fə'lɔɪn] adj verlassen, hilflos.
form [fɔɪm] n Gestalt f, Form f; (to fill out) Formular neut. **on form** in Form. v bilden.
formal ['fɔɪməl] adj formell.
format ['fɔɪmat] n Format neut.
formation [fɔɪ'meɪʃən] n Bildung f; (geol, mil) Formation f.
former ['fɔɪmə] adj vorig; (one-time) ehemalig; (of two) jene(r). **formerly** adv früher.
formidable ['fɔɪmɪdəbl] adj furchtbar.
formula ['fɔɪmjulə] n (pl -ae) Formel f; (med) Rezept neut. **formulate** v formulieren. **formulation** n Formulierung f.
***forsake** [fə'seɪk] v (person) verlassen.
forsaken [fə'seɪkn] V **forsake**.
forsook [fə'suk] V **forsake**.
fort [fɔɪt] n Festung f.
forte ['fɔɪteɪ] adv (music) laut. n Stärke f.
forth [fɔɪθ] adv (place) hervor; (time) fort. **and so forth** und so weiter or fort. **back and forth** hin und her.
fortify ['fɔɪtɪˌfaɪ] v (mil) befestigen; (heart-en) ermutigen; (food) anreichern. **fortification** n Befestigung f; (fortress) Festung f.
fortitude ['fɔɪtɪˌtjuɪd] n Mut m.
fortnight ['fɔɪtnaɪt] n vierzehn Tage. **fortnightly** adj vierzehntägig. adv alle vierzehn Tage.
fortress ['fɔɪtrɪs] n Festung f.
fortuitous [fɔɪ'tjuɪɪtəs] adj zufällig.
fortune ['fɔɪtʃən] n Glück neut; (fate) Schicksal neut; (wealth) Vermögen neut. **fortunate** adj glücklich. **fortunately** adv glücklicherweise.
forty ['fɔɪtɪ] adj vierzig.
forum ['fɔɪrəm] n Forum neut.
forward ['fɔɪwəd] adj vorder, Vorder-; (impudent) vorlaut. adv vorwärts. v (goods) spedieren; (letter) nachschicken. n (sport) Stürmer m.
fossil ['fɒsl] n Fossil neut.
foster ['fɒstə] v pflegen; (feelings) Legen. adj Pflege-.
fought [fɔɪt] V **fight**.
foul [faul] adj (dirty) schmutzig; (disgust-

ing) widerlich; (weather) schlecht. v verschmutzen. n (sport) Regelverstoß m.
found¹ [faund] V **find**.
found² [faund] v gründen. **be founded on** beruhen auf. **foundation** n (of building) Grundmauer f; (of institute, firm, etc.) Gründung f; (basis) Grundlage f; (insti-tute) Stiftung f. **founder** n Gründer m.
foundry ['faundrɪ] n Gießerei f.
fountain ['fauntɪn] n Springbrunnen m. **fountain pen** Füllfeder f.
four [fɔɪ] adj vier. **fourth** adj viert; n Viertel neut.
fourteen [fɔɪ'tiɪn] adj vierzehn.
fowl [faul] n Haushuhn neut.
fox [fɒks] n Fuchs m. v (coll) täuschen.
foyer ['fɔɪeɪ] n Foyer neut.
fraction ['frakʃən] n Bruchteil m; (math) Bruch m.
fracture ['fraktʃə] n (med) Knochenbruch m. v zerbrechen.
fragile ['fradʒaɪl] adj zerbrechlich.
fragment ['fragmənt] n Bruchstück neut, Brocken m.
fragrance ['freɪgrəns] n Duft m, Aroma neut. **fragrant** adj duftig, wohlriechend.
frail [freɪl] adj schwach, gebrechlich. **frail-ty** n Schwäche f.
frame [freɪm] n Rahmen m. v einrahmen. **spectacle frame** Brillengestell neut.
France [frɑɪns] n Frankreich neut.
franchise ['frantʃaɪz] n (pol) Wahlrecht neut; (comm) Konzession f.
frank [fraŋk] adj offen, freimütig. **frankly** adv frei, offen. **frankness** n Freimut m.
frantic ['frantɪk] adj wild, rasend.
fraternal [frə'təɪnl] adj brüderlich.
fraud [frɔɪd] n Betrug m, Unterschlagung f; (person) Schwindler(in). **fraudulent** adj betrügerisch.
fraught [frɔɪt] adj voll. **fraught with dan-ger** gefahrvoll.
fray¹ [freɪ] v (sich) ausfransen.
fray² [freɪ] n Rauferei f.
freak [friɪk] n (of nature) Mißbildung f; (event, storm) Ausnahmeerscheinung f. adj anormal.
freckle ['frekl] n Sommersprosse f.
free [friɪ] adj frei; kostenlos. v befreien, freimachen. **free and easy** ungezwungen. **free speech** Redefreiheit f. **free will** freier Wille m. **freedom** n Freiheit f. **freely** adv reichlich.
freelance ['friɪlaɪns] n freier Schriftsteller m. adj freiberuflich tätig.

freemason ['friːmeisn] n Freimaurer n.
*freeze [friːz] v (water) frieren; (food) tiefkühlen. **freeze to death** erfrieren. I'm freezing ich friere. n (comm) Stopp m. **freezer** n Tiefkühltruhe f. **freezing point** Gefrierpunkt m.
freight [freit] n Fracht f; (freight costs) Frachtgebühr f.
French [frentʃ] adj französisch. **Frenchman** n Franzose m. **Frenchwoman** n Französin f. **French horn** Waldhorn neut.
french fries n pl Pommes frites pl.
frenzy ['frenzi] n Raserei f.
frequency ['friːkwənsi] n Frequenz f. **frequent** adj häufig, frequent; v häufig besuchen. **frequently** adv öfters, häufig.
fresco ['freskou] n Fresko neut.
fresh [freʃ] adj frisch; (water) süß; (air) erfrischend; (cheeky) frech. **fresh water** Süßwasser neut. **freshen** v auffrischen. **freshness** n Frische f.
fret [fret] v sich Sorgen machen.
friar ['fraiə] n Mönch m.
friction ['frikʃən] n Reibung f.
Friday ['fraidei] n Freitag m. **Good Friday** Karfreitag m.
fridge [fridʒ] n Kühlschrank m.
fried [fraid] adj gebraten. **fried egg** Spiegelei neut. **fried potatoes** Bratkartoffeln.
friend [frend] n Freund(in). **make friends with** sich befreunden mit. **friendly** adj freundlich, freundschaftlich. **friendship** n Freundschaft f.
frieze [friːz] n Fries m.
frigate ['frigit] n Fregatte f.
fright [frait] n Schreck m. **frighten** v erschrecken. **frightening** adj erschreckend. **frightened** adj erschrocken. **be frightened of** Angst haben vor. **frightful** adj schrecklich.
frigid ['fridʒid] adj frigid. **frigidity** n Frigidität f.
frill [fril] n Rüsche, Krause f. **frilly** adj gekräuselt.
fringe [frindʒ] n Franse f; (edge) Randzone f; (hair) Pony neut. **fringe benefits** Nebenbezüge pl.
frisk [frisk] v herumhüpfen; (search) absuchen. **frisky** adj munter, lebhaft.
fritter ['fritə] v **fritter away** verzetteln.
frivolity [fri'voliti] n Leichtfertigkeit f. **frivolous** adj (person) leichtfertig; (worthless) nichtig.

frizz [friz] v (sich) kräuseln. **frizzy** adj kraus.
fro [frou] adv **to and fro** auf und ab, hin und her.
frock [frok] n Kleid neut.
frog [frog] n Frosch m.
frolic ['frolik] n Spaß m, Posse f. **frolicsome** adj lustig, ausgelassen.
from [from] prep von; (place) aus, von; (to judge from) nach. **Where are you from?** wo kommen Sie her?
front [frʌnt] n Vorderseite f, vorderer Teil m; (mil, pol) Front f; (fa,cade) Fassade f. adj Vor-, Vorder-. **front door** Haustür f. **front room** Vorderzimmer neut. **in front of** vor.
frontier ['frʌntiə] n Grenze f.
frost [frost] n Frost m. v (cookery) glasieren. **frostbite** n Erfrieren neut; (wound) Frostbeule f. **frostbitten** adj erfroren. **frosty** adj frostig.
froth [froθ] n Schaum m. **frothy** adj schäumig.
frown [fraun] n Stirnrunzeln neut. v die Stirn runzeln. **frown on** mißbilligen.
froze [frouz] V **freeze**.
frozen ['frouzn] V **freeze**. adj gefroren; (comm) eingefroren; (food) tiefgekühlt. **frozen over** zugefroren.
frugal ['fruːgəl] adj sparsam.
fruit [fruːt] n Obst neut, Früchte pl; (result, yield) Frucht f. **fruitful** adj fruchtbar. **fruition** n Erfüllung f. **fruitless** adj fruchtlos. **fruit machine** Spielautomat neut. **fruit salad** Obstsalat m. **fruit tree** Obstbaum m. **fruity** adj würzig.
frustrate [frʌ'streit] v vereiteln, frustrieren. **frustrated** adj vereitelt, frustriert. **frustration** n Vereitelung f, Frustration f.
fry [frai] v (in der Pfanne) braten. **frying-pan** n Bratpfanne f.
fuchsia ['fjuːʃə] n Fuchsia f.
fudge [fʌdʒ] n Karamelle f.
fuel ['fjuəl] n Brennstoff; (for engines) Treibstoff m; (mot) Benzin neut. v tanken. **fuel gauge** Treibstoffmesser m. **fuel oil** Brennöl neut.
fugitive ['fjuːdʒitiv] adj flüchtig. n Flüchtling m.
fulcrum ['fulkrəm] n Drehpunkt m.
fulfil [ful'fil] v erfüllen. **fulfilment** n Erfüllung f; (satisfaction) Befriedigung f.
full [ful] adj voll; (after meal) satt. adv direkt, gerade. **pay in full** voll bezahlen. **write out in full** ausschreiben. **full-grown**

adj ausgewachsen. **full moon** Vollmond *m*. **fullness** *n* Fülle *f*. **full stop** Punkt *m*. **full-time** *adj* ganztägig. **fully** *adv* voll, völlig.

fumble ['fʌmbl] *v* umhertasten. **fumble with** herumfummeln an.

fume [fjuːm] *v* dampfen; (*coll*) wütend sein. *n* Dunst *m*, Dampf *m*. **fumigate** *v* ausräuchern.

fun [fʌn] *n* Spaß *m*. **it's fun** es macht Spaß. **for fun** aus Spaß. **in fun** zum Scherz. **have fun** sich amüsieren. **have fun!** viel Spaß/vergnügen! **make fun of** sich lustig machen über.

function ['fʌŋkʃən] *n* Funktion *f*; (*task*) Aufgabe *f*; (*gathering*) Veranstaltung *f*. *v* (*tech*) funktionieren; tätig sein. **functional** *adj* funktionell, zweckmäßig. **functionary** *n* Beamte(r).

fund [fʌnd] *n* Fonds *m*; (*fig*) Vorrat *m*. *v* fundieren.

fundamental [fʌndə'mentl] *adj* grundlegend, grundsätzlich.

funeral ['fjuːnərəl] *n* Begräbnis *neut*.

fungus ['fʌŋgəs] *n* (*pl* -i) Pilz *m*.

funnel ['fʌnl] *n* Trichter *m*; (*ship*) Schornstein *m*.

funny ['fʌni] *adj* (*amusing*) komisch, lustig, spaßhaft; (*strange*) komisch, seltsam. **funny-bone** *n* Musikantenknochen *m*.

fur [fəː] *n* Pelz *m*; (*on tongue*) Belag *m*; (*in boiler*) Kesselstein *m*. **fur coat** Pelzmantel *m*. **furry** *adj* pelzartig, Pelz-; belegt.

furious ['fjuəriəs] *adj* wütend.

furnace ['fəːnis] *n* (Brenn)Ofen *m*.

furnish ['fəːniʃ] *v* (*a room*) möblieren; (*supply*) versehen, ausstatten. **furnishings** *pl n* Möbel *pl*.

furniture ['fəːnitʃə] *n* Möbel *pl*.

furrow ['fʌrou] *n* Furche *f*.

further ['fəːðə] *adj, adv* weiter. **until further notice** bis auf weiteres. *v* fördern. **furthermore** *adv* ferner, überdies. **furthest** *adj* weitest; *adv* am weitesten.

furtive ['fəːtiv] *adj* (*person*) hinterlistig; (*action*) verstohlen.

fury ['fjuəri] *n* Wut *f*.

fuse [fjuːz] *n* (*elec*) Sicherung *f*; (*explosives*) Zünder *m*. *v* (*join, melt*) (ver)schmelzen; (*elec*) sichern; (*elec: blow a fuse*) durchbrennen. **fuse box** Sicherungskasten *m*.

fuselage ['fjuːzəlaːʒ] *n* Rumpf *m*.

fusion ['fjuːʒən] *n* Verschmelzung *f*.

fuss [fʌs] *n* Getue, Theater *neut*. **make a fuss** viel Wesens machen (um). **fussy** *adj* kleinlich.

futile ['fjuːtail] *adj* zwecklos, wertlos. **futility** *n* Zwecklosigkeit *f*.

future ['fjuːtʃə] *n* Zukunft *f*. *adj* künftig. **in future** in Zukunft. **futures** *pl n* (*comm*) Termingeschäfte *pl*. **futuristic** *adj* futuristisch.

fuzz [fʌz] *n* Fussel *f*. **fuzzy** *adj* (*hair*) kraus; (*vision*) verschwommen.

G

gabble ['gabl] *v* schwätzen.

gable ['geibl] *n* Giebel *m*. **gabled** *adj* gegiebelt.

gadget ['gadʒit] *n* Apparat *m*, Gerät *neut*.

gag¹ [gag] *v* knebeln. *n* Knebel *m*.

gag² [gag] (*coll: joke*) *n* Witz *m*. *v* einen Witz reißen.

gaiety ['geiəti] *n* Heiterkeit *f*.

gain [gein] *n* Gewinn *m*. *v* gewinnen; (*of clock*) vorgehen. **gain on** einholen. **gains** *pl n* (*comm*) Profit *m*.

gait [geit] *n* Gang *m*.

gala ['gaːlə] *n* Festlichkeit *f*.

galaxy ['galəksi] *n* Sternsystem *neut*; (*ours*) Milchstraße *f*.

gale [geil] *n* heftiger Wind *m*, Sturmwind *m*.

gallant ['galənt] *adj* tapfer; (*courteous*) ritterlich. **gallantry** *n* Tapferkeit *f*; Ritterlichkeit *f*.

gall bladder [goːl] *n* Gallenblase *f*.

galleon ['galiən] *n* Galeone *f*.

gallery ['galəri] *n* Galerie *f*.

galley ['gali] *n* Galeere *f*; (*kitchen*) Schiffsküche *f*.

gallon ['galən] *n* Gallone *f*.

gallop ['galəp] *n* Galopp *m*. *v* galoppieren.

gallows ['galouz] *n* Galgen *m*.

gallstone ['goːlstoun] *n* Gallenstein *m*.

galore [gə'loː] *adv* in Hülle and Fülle.

galvanize ['galvənaiz] *v* galvanisieren, verzinken; (*fig: stimulate*) anspornen (zu).

gamble ['gambl] *v* um Geld spielen. **gamble on** wetten auf. **gamble with** aufs Spiel

sctzcn. **gambler** n Spieler m. **gambling** n Spielen (um Geld) neut. n Wagnis neut.
game [geim] n Spiel neut; (hunting) Wild neut. **give the game away** den Plan verraten. adj (leg) lahm. **be game for** bereit sein zu. **gamekeeper** n Wildhüter m.
gammon ['gamən] n (geräucherter) Schinken m.
gang [gaŋ] n (criminals) Bande f; (workers) Kolonne f. v **gang up** sich zusammenrotten. **gangster** n Gangster m.
gangrene ['gaŋgriːn] n Brand m.
gangway ['gaŋwei] n (theatre) Gang m; (naut) Laufplanke f.
gaol [dʒeil] V jail.
gap [gap] n Lücke f.
gape [geip] v klaffen; (person) gähnen.
garage ['garaidʒ] n Garage f; (mot: workshop) Autowerkstatt f. v in eine Garage einstellen or unterbringen.
garbage ['gaːbidʒ] n Müll m. **garbage can** Mülkasten m.
garble ['gaːbl] v verstümmeln.
garden ['gaːdn] n Garten m. v im Garten arbeiten. **gardening** n Gartenbau m. **garden party** Gartenfest neut.
gargle ['gaːgl] v gurgeln. n Mundwasser neut.
gargoyle ['gaːgoil] n (arch) Wasserspeier m.
garland ['gaːlənd] n Girlande f, Blumengewinde neut. v bekränzen.
garlic ['gaːlik] n Knoblauch m.
garment ['gaːmənt] n Kleidungsstück neut.
garnish ['gaːniʃ] v (cookery) garnieren. n Garnierung f.
garrison ['garisn] n Garnison f. v (town) besetzen; (troops) in Garnison legen.
garter ['gaːtə] n Strumpfband neut.
gas [gas] n Gas neut; (US: petrol) Benzin neut. **step on the gas** Gas geben. v (poison) vergasen; (slang: chatter) schwätzen. **gasbag** n (coll) Windbeutel m.
gas cooker Gasherd m. **gas fire** Gasheizung f.
gash [gaʃ] v aufschneiden. n klaffende Wunde f.
gasket ['gaskit] n Dichtung f.
gas main n Gasleitung f.
gas meter n Gasmesser m.
gasoline ['gasəliːn] n (US) Benzin neut.
gasp [gaːsp] v keuchen. n Keuchen neut.
gas station n Tankstelle f.
gastric ['gastrik] adj gastrisch, Magen-.

gate [geit] n Tor neut.
gâteau ['gatou] n Torte f.
gateway ['geitwei] n Torweg m.
gather ['gaðə] v sammeln; (people) (sich) versammeln; (flowers, etc.) lesen; (dress) raffen; (deduce) schließen (aus). **gathering** n Versammlung f.
gaudy ['goːdi] adj (colours) grell, bunt.
gauge [geidʒ] v abmessen; (judge) schätzen. n Normalmaß neut; (rail) Spurweite f. **pressure gauge** Druckmesser m.
gaunt [goːnt] adj mager.
gauze [goːz] n Gaze f.
gave [geiv] V give.
gay [gei] adj (colours) bunt; (person) heiter, lustig; (slang: homosexual) warm.
gaze [geiz] v starren (auf). n (starrer) Blick neut.
gazelle [gə'zel] n Gazelle f.
gazetteer [gazə'tiə] n Namensverzeichnis neut.
gear [giə] n (mot) Gang m; (gear wheel) Zahnrad neut; (equipment) Gerät neut, Ausrüstung f. **in gear** eingeschaltet. **change gear** (up or down) Gang herauf or herab setzen. **gearbox** n Getriebe(gehäuse) neut.
geese [giːs] V goose.
gelatine ['dʒelətiːn] n Gelatine f; (explosive) Sprenggelatine f.
gelignite ['dʒelignait] n Gelatinedynamit neut.
gem [dʒem] n Edelstein m, Gemme f.
Gemini ['dʒemini] n Zwillinge pl.
gender ['dʒendə] n Geschlecht neut; (gramm) Genus neut.
gene [dʒiːn] n Gen neut, Erbeinheit f.
genealogy [dʒiːni,alədʒi] n Genealogie f. **genealogist** n Genealoge m.
general ['dʒenərəl] adj allgemein. n General m. **in general** im Allgemeinen. **General Assembly** n Generalversammlung f. **general election** allgemeine Wahlen pl.
generate ['dʒenəreit] v erzeugen, verursachen. **generator** n Generator m, Stromerzeuger m. **generation** n Generation f, Zeitalter m; (production) Erzeugung f.
generic [dʒi'nerik] adj allgemein, generell.
generous ['dʒenərəs] adj großzügig, freigebig. **generosity** n Großzügigkeit f.
genetic [dʒi'netik] adj genetisch, Entstehungs-. **genetics** n Genetik f.

Geneva [dʒi'niːvə] n Genf neut. **Lake Geneva** der Genfer See m.
genial ['dʒiːniəl] adj freundlich, herzlich. **geniality** n Freundlichkeit f.
genital ['dʒenitl] adj Geschlechts-. **genitals** pl n Geschlechtsteile pl.
genitive ['dʒenitiv] n Genitiv m.
genius ['dʒiːnjəs] n Genie neut; (talent) Begabung f.
genocide ['dʒenəsaid] n Völkermord m.
genteel [dʒen'tiːl] adj wohlerzogen, vornehm.
gentle ['dʒentl] adj sanft, mild. **gentleman** n Herr m. **gentleness** n Mildheit f.
gentry ['dʒentri] n Landadel m.
gents [dʒents] n (sign) Herren pl.
genuine ['dʒenjuin] adj echt, wahr. **genuineness** n Wahrheit f, Echtheit f.
genus ['dʒiːnəs] n Gattung f, Sorte f.
geography [dʒi'ogrəfi] n Erdkunde f, Geographie f. **geographical** adj geographisch. **geographer** n Geograph(in).
geology [dʒi'olədʒi] n Geologie f. **geologist** n Geologe m.
geometry [dʒi'omətri] n Geometrie f. **geometric** adj geometrisch.
geranium [dʒə'reiniəm] n Geranie f.
geriatric [dʒeri'atrik] adj geriatrisch. **geriatrics** n Geriatrie f.
germ [dʒəːm] n Keim m, Bakterie f.
German measles n Röteln pl.
Germany ['dʒəːməni] n Deutschland neut. **German** adj deutsch; n Deutsche(r); (language) Deutsch neut. **Federal Republic of Germany** n Bundesrepublik Deutschland (BRD) f; **German Democratic Republic** n Deutsche Demokratische Republik (DDR) f.
germinate ['dʒəːmineit] v Keimen. **germination** n Keimen neut.
gesticulate [dʒe'stikjuˌleit] v wilde Gesten machen.
gesture ['dʒestʃə] n Geste f. v eine Geste machen.
*get [get] v (obtain) bekommen, erhalten; (become) werden. **get hold of** bekommen. **get in** einsteigen. **get married** sich verheiraten. **get off** aussteigen. **get ready** vorbereiten.
geyser ['giːzə] n Geiser m.
ghastly ['gaːstli] adj schrecklich, furchtbar.
gherkin ['gəːkin] n Essiggurke f.
ghetto ['getou] n Getto neut.

ghost [goust] n Gespenst neut, Geist m. **ghostly** adj gespenstisch.
giant ['dʒaiənt] n Riese m. adj riesenhaft.
gibberish ['dʒibəriʃ] n Quatsch m.
gibe [dʒaib] v spotten (über). n Spott m.
giblets ['dʒiblits] pl n Hühnerklein neut.
giddy ['gidi] adj schwind(e)lig. **giddiness** n Schwindel m.
gift [gift] n Geschenk neut; (talent) Begabung f. **gifted** adj begabt.
gigantic [dʒai'gantik] adj riesenhaft, gigantisch.
giggle ['gigl] v kichern. n Gekicher neut.
gill [gil] n (fish) Kieme f.
gilt [gilt] adj vergoldet. n Vergoldung f.
gimmick ['gimik] n Trick m.
gin [dʒin] n Gin m, Wacholderschnapps m.
ginger ['dʒindʒə] n Ingwer m. **gingerbread** n Pfefferkuchen m. **ginger-haired** adj rothaarig.
gingerly ['dʒindʒəli] adv vorsichtig.
gipsy ['dʒipsi] n Zigeuner(in). adj Zigeuner.
giraffe [dʒi'raːf] n Giraffe f.
*gird [gəːd] v umgürten, umlegen.
girder ['gəːdə] n Träger m, Tragbalken m.
girdle ['gəːdl] n Gurt m. v umgürten.
girl [gəːl] n Mädchen neut. **girl friend** Freundin f. **girlhood** n Mädchenjahre pl. **girlish** adj mädchenhaft.
girt [gəːt] V gird.
girth [gəːθ] n Umfang m; (horse) Gurt m.
gist [dʒist] n Wesentliche neut, Hauptpunkt m.
*give [giv] v geben; (gift) schenken (hand over) überreichen. n Elastizität f. **give away** (betray) verraten. **give back** zurückgeben. **give in** nachgeben. **give up** aufgeben.
given ['givn] V give. adj (an)gegeben.
glacier ['glasiə] n Gletscher m.
glad [glad] adj froh, fröhlich, glücklich. **gladness** n Fröhlichkeit, Glücklichkeit f.
glamour [glamə] n bezaubernde Schönheit f. **glamorous** adj bezaubernd.
glance [glaːns] v (fluchtig) blicken, einen Blick werfen. n flüchtiger Blick m.
gland [gland] n Drüse f. **glandular** adj drüsig, Drüsen-. **glandular fever** n Drüsenfieber m.
glare [gleə] v grell leuchten; (stare) starren. **glare at** anstarren. n blendendes Licht neut.

glass [glɑːs] n Glas neut. **glasses** pl Brille f sing. **glassfibre** n Glaswolle f.

glaze [gleiz] n Glasur f. v verglasen; (windows) mit Glasscheiben versehen. **glazier** n Glaser m.

gleam [gliːm] n Schimmer m. v schimmern.

glean [gliːn] v (nach)lesen.

glee [gliː] n Fröhlichkeit f. **gleeful** adj fröhlich.

glib [glib] adj zungenfertig.

glide [glaid] v gleiten. **glider** n Segelflugzeug neut.

glimmer ['glimə] n Schimmer m. v schimmern.

glimpse [glimps] n flüchtiger Blick. v erspähen.

glint [glint] n Glitzern neut. v glitzern.

glisten ['glisn] n Glanz m. v glänzen.

glitter ['glitə] n Funkeln neut. v funkeln.

gloat [glout] v sich hämisch freuen über. **gloating** n Schadenfreude f.

globe [gloub] n (Erd)Kugel f. **global** adj global. **globular** adj kugelförmig.

gloom [gluːm] n Düsternis f, Dunkelheit f; (mood) Trübsinn m. **gloomy** adj düster.

glory ['glɔːri] n Ruhm m, Ehre f. v sich freuen. **glorify** v verherrlichen. **glorious** adj glorreich, herrlich.

gloss [glɔs] n Glanz m. v polieren. **gloss paint** Ölfarbe f. **gloss over** vertuschen.

glossary ['glɔsəri] n Glossar neut, (spezielles) Wortverzeichnis neut.

glove [glʌv] n Handschuh m. **fit like a glove** passen wie angegossen.

glow [glou] n Glühen neut. v glühen.

glucose ['gluːkous] n Traubenzucker m.

glue [gluː] n Klebstoff neut. v kleben.

glum [glʌm] adj mürrisch.

glut [glʌt] n Überfluß m; (comm) Überangebot neut. v sättigen.

glutton ['glʌtən] n Vielfraß m. **gluttonous** adj gefräßig. **gluttony** n Gefräßigkeit f.

gnarled [nɑːld] adj knorrig.

gnash [naʃ] v knirschen.

gnat [nat] n Mücke f.

gnaw [nɔː] v nagen an (+ dat).

gnome [noum] n Zwerg m, Gnom m.

*__go__ [gou] v gehen; (travel) fahren, reisen; (machine) funktionieren, in Betrieb sein; (time) vergehen; (coll: become) werden. **go ahead** fortfahren. **go away** weggehen; (travel) verreisen. **go down** hinuntergehen; (price) fallen. **go out**

hinausgehen; (fire) erlöschen. **go up** hinaufgehen; (prices) steigen. **have a go at** einen Versuch machen mit. **it's no go!** es geht nicht!

goad [goud] n Stachelstock m. v antreiben.

goal [goul] n Ziel neut; (sport) Tor m. **goalkeeper** n Torwart m.

goat [gout] n Ziege f.

gobble ['gobl] v **gobble (down)** (food) hinunterschlingen. **gobble up** verschlingen.

goblin ['goblin] n Kobold m.

god [god] n Gott m. **thank God!** Gott sei dank! **godchild** n Patenkind neut. **goddaughter** n Patentochter f. **goddess** n Göttin f. **godfather** n Pate m. **godmother** n Patin f. **godsend** n Glücksfall m. **godson** n Patensohn m.

goggles ['goglz] pl n Schutzbrille f sing.

gold [gould] n Gold neut. **golden** adj golden. **goldfish** n Goldfisch m. **gold leaf** n Blattgold neut. **gold mine** Goldgrube f. **gold-plated** adj vergoldet. **goldsmith** n goldschmied.

golf [golf] n Golf(spiel) neut. **golfclub** n Golfschläger m. **golf course** Golfplatz m. **golfer** n Golfspieler m.

gondola ['gondələ] n Gondel f.

gone [gon] V **go**.

gong [gon] n Gong m.

gonorrhoea [gonə'riə] n (med) Gonorrhöe f.

good [gud] adj gut; (pleasant) angenehm; (child) brav. n Gute neut, Wohl neut. **good afternoon** guten Tag. **goodbye** interj auf Wiedersehen. **good evening** guten Abend. **good for nothing** nichts Wert. **good-for-nothing** n Taugenichts m. **good-looking** adj gut aussehend. **good morning** guten Morgen. **good night** gute Nacht. **do (someone) good** (jemanden) wohltun. **it's no good** es nützt nichts. **goodness** n Güte f. **goods** pl n Güter pl.

Good Friday n Karfreitag m.

goose [guːs] n (pl geese) Gans f.

gooseberry ['guzbəri] n Stachelbeere f. **play gooseberry** Anstandswauwau spielen.

gore [gɔː] n Blut neut. v aufspießen.

gorge [gɔːdʒ] n (geog) Schlucht f. v **gorge oneself** (coll) sich vollessen.

gorgeous ['gɔːdʒəs] adj wunderschön, prachtvoll.

gorilla [gəˈrilə] n Gorilla m.
gorse [gɔːs] n Stechginster m.
gory [ˈgɔːri] adj blutig.
gospel [ˈgɒspəl] n Evangelium neut.
gossip [ˈgɒsip] n Geschwätz neut; (person) Klatschbase f. v schwätzen.
got [gɒt] V get.
Gothic [ˈgɒθik] adj gotisch.
gotten [ˈgɒtn] V get.
gouge [gaudʒ] v aushöhlen. n Hohleisen neut.
goulash [ˈguːlaʃ] n Gulasch neut.
gourd [guəd] n Kürbis m.
gourmet [ˈguəmei] n Feinschmecker m.
gout [gaut] n Gicht f. **gouty** gichtkrank, gichtisch.
govern [ˈgʌvən] v (country) regieren; (determine) bestimmen; (tech) regeln. **governess** n Gouvernante f. **government** n Regierung f. **governmental** adj Regierungs-. **governor** n Gouverneur m.
gown [gaun] n Kleid neut.
grab [grab] v ergreifen, (an)packen. n (plötzlicher) Griff m.
grace [greis] n Gnade f, Güte f; (prayer) Tischgebet neut. 14 days' grace 14 Tage Aufschub. **Your Grace** Eure Hoheit. **graceful** adj anmutig. **gracious** adj angenehm, gnädig.
grade [greid] n Grad m, Stufe f; (comm) Qualität f; (US) (Schul)Klasse f; (slope) Gefälle neut. v sortieren, einordnen.
gradient [ˈgreidiənt] n Gefälle neut.
gradual [ˈgradjuəl] adj stufenweise, allmählich.
graduate [ˈgradjuət; v ˈgradjueit] n Graduierte(r); (high school) Absolvent(in). v abstufen; (university) promovieren. **graduation** n. Promovierung f; (high school) Absolvieren neut.
graffiti [grəˈfiːtiː] pl n Graffiti neut sing.
graft[1] [graːft] n (bot) Pfropfreis neut; (med) Transplantat neut. v pfropfen; transplantieren.
graft[2] [graːft] n Korruption f.
grain [grein] n Getreide neut, Korn neut; (sand, etc.) Körnchen neut; (wood) n Maserung f. **grainy** adj körnig.
gram [gram] n Gramm neut.
grammar [ˈgramə] n Grammatik f. **grammatical** adj grammatisch. **grammar school** Gymnasium neut.
gramophone [ˈgraməfoun] n Platten-

spieler m. **gramophone record** (Schall)Platte f.
granary [ˈgranəri] n Kornkammer f.
grand [grand] adj groß, großartig. **grand piano** Flügel m. **grandeur** n Erhabenheit f.
grand-dad n also **grandpa** (coll) Opa m.
grand-daughter n Enkelin f.
grandfather [ˈgranˌfaːðə] n Großvater m.
grandma [ˈgranmaɪ] n also **granny** (coll) Oma f.
grandmother [ˈgranˌmʌðə] n Großmutter f.
grandparents [ˈgranˌpeərənts] pl n Großeltern pl.
grandson [ˈgransʌn] n Enkel m.
grandstand [ˈgranstand] n Haupttribüne f.
grand total n Gesamtbetrag m.
granite [ˈgranit] n Granit m.
grant [graːnt] v gewähren; (admit) zugestehen. n (student) Stipendium neut; (subsidy) Subvention f, Zuschuß m.
granule [ˈgranjuːl] n Körnchen neut. **granular** adj körnig, granuliert.
grape [greip] n (Wein)Traube f. **grapevine** n Rebstock m.
grapefruit [ˈgreipfruːt] n Grapefruit neut, Pampelmuse f.
graph [graf] n graphische Darstellung f, Schaubild neut.
grapple [ˈgrapl] v sich auseinandersetzen (mit), ringen (mit).
grasp [graːsp] v greifen, packen; (understand) begreifen. n Griff m. **grasping** adj habgierig.
grass [graːs] n Gras neut; (lawn) Rasen m. v (coll) pfeifen.
grate[1] [greit] n (Feuer)Rost m, Gitter neut.
grate[2] [greit] v (cookery) reiben; (teeth) knirschen. **grate on one's nerves** auf die Nerven gehen.
grateful [ˈgreitful] adj dankbar.
gratify [ˈgratiˌfai] v befriedigen. **gratification** n Befriedigung f. **gratitude** n Dankbarkeit f.
gratuity [grəˈtjuːti] n Trinkgeld neut.
grave[1] [greiv] n Grab neut. **gravedigger** n Totengräber m. **gravestone** n Grabstein m. **graveyard** n Friedhof f.
grave[2] [greiv] adj ernsthaft, schwerwiegend.
gravel [ˈgravəl] n Kies m. **gravelpit** n Kiesgrube f.

75

gravity ['grævəti] n Schwerkraft f; (seriousness) Ernsthaftigkeit f, Ernst m.
gravy ['greivi] n (Braten)Soße f.
graze¹ [greiz] n (med) Abschürfung f. v abschürfen; (touch) leicht berühren.
graze² [greiz] v (animal) (ab)weiden. **grazing** n Weide f.
grease [griːs] n Fett neut, Schmalz neut; (tech, mot) Schmiere f. v schmieren.
great [greit] adj groß; (important) bedeutend; (coll) großartig, toll. **greatly** adv in hohem Maße. **great-grandparents** pl n Urgroßeltern pl. **greatness** n Größe f.
Great Britain n Großbritannien neut.
Greece [griːs] n Griechenland neut. **Greek** adj griechisch; n Grieche m, Griechin f.
greed [griːd] n Gier f (nach). **greedy** adj gierig.
green [griːn] adj grün. n Grün neut. **greenfly** n grüne Blattlaus f. **greengage** n Reineclaude f. **greengrocer's** n Obst- und Gemüseladen m. **greenhouse** n Treibhaus neut. **greens** pl n (cookery) Grünzeug neut.
Greenland ['griːnlənd] n Grönland neut. **Greenlander** n Grönlander m.
greet [griːt] v grüßen, begrüßen, **greeting** n Gruß m, Begrüßung f.
gregarious [gri'geəriəs] adj gesellig.
grenade [grə'neid] n Granate f.
grew [gruː] V grow.
grey [grei] adj grau; (gloomy) trübe. n Grau neut. **greyhound** n Windhund m.
grid [grid] n Gitter neut; (network) Netz neut.
grief [griːf] n Trauer f. **grievance** n Beschwerde f. **grieve** v trauern.
grill [gril] v grillen; (question) einem strengen Verhör unterziehen. n Bratrost m, Grill m.
grille [gril] n Gitter neut.
grim [grim] adj (person) grimmig, verbissen, (prospect) schlimm, hoffnungslos.
grimace [gri'meis] n Grimasse f. v Grimassen schneiden.
grime [graim] n Schmutz m, Ruß m.
grin [grin] n Lächeln neut, Grinsen neut. v lächeln, grinsen.
*grind [graind] v mahlen; (knife) schleifen; (teeth) knirschen. n (coll) Plackerei f. **grinder** n (coffee, etc.) Mühle f.
grip [grip] v (an)packen, festhalten. n Griff m.

gripe [graip] v zwicken. n Kolik f; Bauchschmerzen pl.
grisly ['grizli] adj gräßlich.
gristle ['grisl] n Knorpel m. **gristly** adj knorpelig.
grit [grit] n Splitt m; (coll) Mut m, Entschlossenheit f. **grit one's teeth** die Zähne zusammenbeißen.
groan [groun] n Stöhnen neut. v stöhnen.
grocer ['grousə] n Lebensmittelhändler m. **grocer's shop** Lebensmittelgeschäft neut. **groceries** pl n Lebensmittel pl.
groin [groin] n (anat) Leistengegend f.
groom [gruːm] n (of bride) Bräutigam m; (for horse) (Pferde)Knecht m. v pflegen. **well groomed** gepflegt.
groove [gruːv] n Rinne f, Furche f.
grope [group] v tasten (nach). **gropingly** adv tastend, vorsichtig.
gross [grous] adj grob; (comm) Brutto-; (fat) dick. n Gros neut. **Gross National Product (GNP)** Bruttosozialprodukt neut. **gross weight** Bruttogewicht n.
grotesque [grə'tesk] adj grotesk.
grotto ['grotou] n Grotte f.
ground¹ [graund] V grind.
ground² [graund] n Boden m, Erde f. v (aero) still legen. **ground floor** Erdgeschoß neut. **grounds** pl (of house) Anlagen pl; (coffee) Bodensatz m; (reason) Grund m.
group [gruːp] n Gruppe f. v gruppieren.
grouse¹ [graus] n Birkhuhn neut.
grouse² [graus] v (coll: grumble) meckern. n Beschwerde f.
grove [grouv] n Hain m.
grovel ['grovl] v kriechen (vor). **grovelling** adj kriecherisch.
*grow [grou] v wachsen; (become) werden; (plants) züchten. **grow better** sich bessern. **grow old** alt werden. **grow out of** (clothes) herauswachsen aus; (habit) entwachsen (+dat); (arise from) entstehen aus. **grow up** heranwachsen. **grower** n Züchter. **growing** adj wachsend. **growth** n Wachstum neut; (increase) Zunahme f; (med) Gewächs neut.
grown [groun] V grow. adj erwachsen. **grown-up** n Erwachsene(r).
grub [grʌb] n Made f; (slang: food) Futter neut. **grubby** adj schmutzig, dreckig.
grudge [grʌdʒ] v mißgönnen. n Mißgunst f.

gruelling ['grʊəlɪŋ] *adj* mörderisch.
gruesome ['gruːsəm] *adj* grausam.
gruff [grʌf] *adj* barsch.
grumble ['grʌmbl] *v* schimpfen, murren. *n* Murren *neut.*
grumpy ['grʌmpi] *adj* mürrisch.
grunt [grʌnt] *n* Grunzen *neut. v* grunzen.
guarantee [garən'tiː] *n* Garantie *f*, Gewährleistung *f. v* garantieren, gewährleisten. **guarantor** *n* Gewährsmann *m.*
guard [gaɪd] *n* Wächter *m*, Wache *f. v* (be)schützen, bewachen. **guard against** sich hüten vor. **on one's guard** auf der Hut. **guard of honour** Ehrenwache *f.*
guerrilla [gə'rilə] *n* Guerillakämpfer *m.* **guerilla warfare** Guerillakrieg *m.*
guess [ges] *n* Schätzung *f*, Vermutung *f. v* schätzen, vermuten. **guesswork** *n* Mutmaßung *f.*
guest [gest] *n* Gast *m.* **guest house** Pension *f.* **guestroom** Fremdenzimmer *neut.*
guide [gaɪd] *n* Führer *m*; (*book*) Handbuch *neut. v* führen, leiten. **guide book** Reiseführer *m.*
guild [gild] *n* Gilde *f*, Vereinigung *f.*
guillotine ['gilətiːn] *n* Guillotine *f*; (*for paper*) Papierschneidemaschine *f. v* guillotinieren.
guilt [gilt] *n* Schuld *f*; (*feeling of*) Schuldgefühl *neut.* **guilty** *adj* schuldig. **guilty conscience** schlechtes Gewissen *neut.* **find guilty** für schuldig erklären.
guinea pig ['gini] *n* Guinee *f.* **guinea pig** Meerschweinchen *neut*; (*fig: in experiment*) Versuchskaninchen *neut.*
guitar [gi'taɪ] *n* Gitarre *f.* **guitar player** Gitarrenspieler(in).
gulf [gʌlf] *n* Golf *m.*
gull [gʌl] *n* Möwe *f.*
gullet ['gʌlit] *n* Schlund *m.*
gullible ['gʌləbl] *adj* naiv, leichtgläubig. **gullibility** *n* Leichtgläubigkeit *f.*
gully ['gʌli] *n* Rinne *f.*
gulp [gʌlp] *v* hinunterschlucken. *n* Schluck *m.*
gum[1] [gʌm] *n* (*glue*) Klebstoff *m*; (*from tree*) Gummi *neut*; (*sweet*) Gummibonbon *neut.* **chewing gum** Kaugummi *neut. v* kleben.
gum[2] [gʌm] *n* (*in mouth*) Zahnfleisch *neut.*
gun [gʌn] *n* Gewehr *neut*; (*hand gun*) Pistole *f*; (*large*) Kanone *f.* **stick to one's guns** nicht nachgeben. *v* **gun down** erschießen.
gurgle ['gəɪgl] *n* Gurgeln *neut. v* gurgeln.

gush [gʌʃ] *v* hervorquellen, entströmen. *n* Strom *m*, Guß *m.* **gushing** *adj* überschwenglich.
gust [gʌst] *n* Bö *neut. v* blasen.
gusto ['gʌstou] *n* Schwung *m.* **with gusto** eifrig.
gut [gʌt] *n* Darm *m.* **guts** *pl* Eingeweide *pl*; (*coll*) Mut *m.*
gutter ['gʌtə] *n* (*roof*) Dachrinne; (*street*) Gosse *f.* **gutter press** Schmutzpresse *f.*
guy[1] [gai] (*coll*) *n* Kerl *m.*
guy[2] [gai] *n* Halteseil *neut.* **guy-rope** *n* Spannschnur *f.*
gymnasium [dʒim'neiziəm] *n* Turnhalle *f.* **gymnast** *n* Turner(in). **gymnastic** *adj* gymnastisch. **gymnastics** *n* Gymnastik *f.*
gynaecology [gainə'kolədʒi] *n* Frauenheilkunde *f*, Gynäkologie *f.* **gynaecologist** *n* Frauenarzt *m*, Gynäkologe *m.* **gynaecological** *adj* gynäkologisch.
gypsum ['dʒipsəm] *n* Gips *m.*
gyrate [ˌdʒai'reit] *v* wirbeln.
gyroscope ['dʒairəˌskoup] *n* Giroskop *neut.*

H

haberdasher ['habədaʃə] *n* Kurzwarenhändler *m.* **haberdashery** *n* Kurzwaren *pl.*
habit ['habit] *n* Gewohnheit *f.* **be in the habit of** gewöhnt sein. **habitual** *adj* gewohnt, üblich.
habitable ['habitəbl] *adj* bewohnbar. **habitat** *n* Heimat *f.* **habitation** *n* Wohnung *f.* **unfit for human habitation** für Wohnzwecke ungeeignet.
hack[1] [hak] *v* (zer)hacken. **hacksaw** *n* Metallsäge *f.*
hack[2] [hak] *n* (*horse*) Mietpferd *neut*, Gaul *m*; (*writer*) Lohnschreiber *m.*
hackneyed ['haknid] *adj* abgedroschen, banal.
had [had] *V* **have.**
haddock ['hadək] *n* Schellfisch *m.*
haemorrhage ['heməridʒ] *n* Blutung *f*, Blutsturz *m. v* bluten.
haemorrhoids ['heməroidz] *pl n* Hämorrhoiden *pl.*

77   **handmade**

haggard ['hagəd] *adj* hager, verstört.
haggle ['hagl] *v* feilschen.
Hague [heig] *n* Den Haag *m*.
hail¹ [heil] *n* Hagel *m*. *v* hageln. **hailstone** *n* Hagelkorn *neut*. **hailstorm** *n* Hagelschauer *m*.
hail² [heil] *v* (*greet*) begrüßen; (*call up*) zurufen. **hail from** herkommen von.
hair [heə] *n* (*single*) Haar *neut*; (*person's*) Haar *neut*, Haare *pl*. **hairy** *adj* behaart, haarig.
hairbrush ['heəbrʌʃ] *n* Haarbürste *f*.
haircut ['heəkʌt] *n* Haarschnitt *m*. **have a haircut** sich die Haare schneiden lassen.
hair-do *n* Frisur *f*.
hairdresser ['heə,dresə] *n* Friseur *m*, Friseuse *f*.
hair-dryer ['heə,draiə] *n* Haartrockner *m*.
hair-net *n* Haarnetz *neut*.
hairpin ['heəpin] *n* Haarnadel *f*.
hair-raising ['heə,reiziŋ] *adj* aufregend.
hake [heik] *n* Seehecht *m*.
half [haːf] *n* Hälfte *f*. *adj* halb. *adv* halb, zur Hälfte; (*almost*) beinahe. **at half price** zum halben Preis.
half-and-half *adv* halb-und-halb.
half-back ['haːfbak] *n* Läufer *m*.
half-baked [,haːf'beikt] *adj* (*idea*) halbfertig, nicht durchgedacht.
half-breed ['haːfbriːd] *n* Mischling *m*.
half-brother ['haːf'brʌðə] *n* Halbbruder *m*.
half-hearted [,haːf'haːtid] *adj* gleichgültig, lustlos.
half-hour [,haːf'auə] *n* halbe Stunde *f*. **half-hourly** *adv* jede halbe Stunde.
half-mast [,haːf'maːst] *n* **at half-mast** halbmast.
half-sister ['haːfsistə] *n* Halbschwester *f*.
half-term [,haːf'təːm] *n* Semesterhalbzeit *f*.
half-time [,haːf'taim] *n* Halbzeit *f*.
halfway [,haːf'wei] *adv* in der Mitte, halbwegs.
halfwit ['haːfwit] *n* Schwachkopf *m*. **half-witted** *adj* dumm, blöd.
halibut ['halibət] *n* Heilbutt *m*.
hall [hoːl] *n* Halle *f*, Saal *m*; (*entrance*) Diele *f*, Flur *m*. **hall of residence** Studentenheim *neut*. **hall porter** Hotelportier *m*.
hallmark ['hoːlmaːk] *n* Feingehaltsstempel *m*; (*characteristic*) Kennzeichen *neut*.
hallowed ['haloud] *adj* verehrt.
Hallowe'en [halou'iːn] *n* Abend vor Allerheiligen *m*.

hallucinate [hə'luːsineit] *v* halluzinieren. **hallucination** *n* Halluzination *f*.
halo ['heilou] *n* Glorienschein *m*.
halt [hoːlt] *n* Halt *m*, Pause *f*; (*railway*) Haltestelle *f*. *v* Pause machen; (*put a stop to*) halten lassen.
halter ['hoːltə] *n* Halfter *f*.
halve [haːv] *v* halbieren; (*reduce*) auf die Hälfte reduzieren.
ham [ham] *n* Schinken *m*. **(radio) ham** Radio-amateur *m*.
hamburger ['hambəːgə] *n* Frikadelle *f*.
hamlet ['hamlit] *n* Dörfchen *neut*.
hammer ['hamə] *n* Hammer *m*. *v* hämmern. **hammer and tongs** (*coll*) mit aller Kraft.
hammock ['hamək] *n* Hängematte *f*.
hamper¹ ['hampə] *v* behindern, hemmen.
hamper² ['hampə] *n* Packkorb *m*, Eßkorb *m*.
hamster ['hamstə] *n* Hamster *m*.
hamstring ['hamstriŋ] *n* Knieflechse *f*. *v* (*coll*) lähmen.
hand [hand] *n* Hand *f*; (*of clock*) Zeiger *m*. *v* (*give*) geben. **at** *or* **to hand** zur Hand. **hand in** einreichen. **hand out** austeilen. **hand over** übergeben. **in hand** im Gange. **on the one hand ... on the other hand ...** einerseits ... anderseits ....
handbag ['handbag] *n* Handtasche *f*.
handbook ['handbuk] *n* Handbuch *neut*; (*travel*) Reiseführer *m*.
handbrake ['handbreik] *n* Handbremse *f*.
handcream ['handkriːm] *n* Handcreme *f*.
handcuff ['handkʌf] *v* Handschellen anlegen (+ *dat*). **handcuffs** *pl n* Handschellen *pl*.
handful ['handful] *n* Handvoll *f*.
handicap ['handikap] *n* Behinderung *f*; (*sport*) Handikap *neut*. *v* (*horse*) extra belasten; (*person*) hemmen. **handicapped** *adj* (*med, etc.*) behindert.
handicraft ['handikraːft] *n* Handwerk *neut*.
handiwork ['handiwəːk] *n* Handarbeit *f*.
handkerchief ['haŋkətʃif] *n* Taschentuch *neut*.
handle ['handl] *n* Griff *m*; (*door*) (Tür)Klinke *f*. *v* anfassen, handhaben; (*deal with*) behandeln, sich befassen mit. **handlebar** *n* Lenkstange *f*. **handling** *n* Behandlung *f*.
handmade [,hand'meid] *adj* mit der Hand gemacht.

hand-out ['handaut] *n* Almosen *neut*; (*leaflet*) Prospekt *m*, Werbezettel *m*.
hand-pick [hand'pik] *v* (sorgfältig) auswählen.
handrail ['handreil] *n* Geländer *neut*.
handshake ['handʃeik] *n* Händedruck *m*.
handsome ['hansəm] *adj* schön, stattlich.
handstand ['hand,stand] *n* Handstand *m*.
hand-towel *n* Handtuch *neut*.
handwriting ['hand,raitiŋ] *n* (Hand)Schrift *f*.
handy ['handi] *adj* greifbar, zur Hand; (*adroit*) geschickt, gewandt.
*hang [haŋ] *v* hängen; (*person*) erhängen. *n* (*of a dress*) Sitz *m*. **to get the hang of** beherrschen, begreifen. **hang on** (*phone*) am Apparat bleiben. **hang up** (*phone*) auflegen; (*picture, coat*) aufhängen.
hangar ['haŋə] *n* Flugzeughalle *f*.
hanger ['haŋə] *n* (*for clothes*) Kleiderbügel *m*.
hangover ['haŋouvə] *n* (*coll*) Kater *m*.
hanker ['haŋkə] *v* sich sehnen (nach). **hankering** *n* Verlangen *neut*.
haphazard [,hap'hazəd] *adj* zufällig.
happen ['hapən] *v* geschehen, vorkommen. **happen upon** finden. **happen along** erscheinen. **happening** *n* Ereignis *neut*.
happy ['hapi:] *adj* glücklich, zufrieden. **happy-go-lucky** *adj* sorglos. **happiness** *n* Glück *neut*, Glückseligkeit *f*.
harass ['harəs] *v* quälen, aufreiben.
harbour ['haːbə] *n* Hafen *m*. *v* (*protect*) beherbergen.
hard [haːd] *adj* hart; (*difficult*) schwer, schwierig; (*callous*) gefühllos. **hard-boiled** *adj* hartgekocht; (*coll*) hartnäckig. **hard-pressed** *adj* in schwerer Bedrängnis. **hard up** (*coll*) schlecht bei Kasse. **hard-of-hearing** *adj* schwerhörig.
harden ['haːdn] *v* härten, hart machen; (*become hard*) hart werden.
hardly ['haːdli] *adj* kaum. **hardly ever** fast nie.
hardware ['haːdweə] *n* Eisenwaren *pl*; (*computers*) Hardware *f*.
hardy ['haːdi] *adj* kräftig, abgehärtet; (*plant*) winterfest.
hare [heə] *n* Hase *m*.
haricot ['harikou] *n* weiße Bohne *f*.
hark [haːk] *v* horchen. *interj* hör mal!
harm [haːm] *v* schaden (+ *dat*), verletzen. *n* Schaden *m*, Leid *neut*. **harmful** *adj* schädlich. **harmfulness** *n* Schädlichkeit *f*.

harmless *adj* harmlos. **harmlessness** *n* Harmlosigkeit *f*.
harmonic [haɪ'monik] *adj* harmonisch.
harmonica [haɪ'monikə] *n* Mundharmonika *f*.
harmonious [haɪ'mouniəs] *adj* harmonisch, wohlklingend.
harmonize ['haɪmənaiz] *v* harmonisieren. **harmonization** *n* Harmonisierung *f*.
harmony ['haɪməni] *n* Harmonie *f*; (*agreement*) Einklang *m*, Übereinstimmung *f*.
harness ['haɪnis] *n* (Pferde)Geschirr *neut*. *v* spannen; (*fig*) nutzbar machen.
harp [haɪp] *n* Harfe *f*. *v* **harp on** (*coll*) dauernd reden von.
harpoon [haɪ'puɪn] *n* Harpune *f*. *v* harpunieren.
harpsichord ['haɪpsi,koɪd] *n* Cembalo *neut*.
harrowing ['harouiŋ] *adj* qualvoll, schrecklich.
harsh [haɪʃ] *adj* hart; (*voice*) rauh; (*strict*) streng. **harshness** *n* Strenge *f*, Härte *f*.
harvest ['haɪvist] *n* Ernte *f*. (*time*) Erntezeit *f*. *v* ernten, einbringen. **harvester** *n* (*mech*) Mähdrescher *f*. **Harvest Festival** Erntedankfest *neut*.
hash [haʃ] *n* Haschee *neut*. **make a hash of** (*coll*) verpfuschen.
hashish ['haʃiːʃ] *n* Haschisch *neut*.
haste [heist] *n* Eile *f*. **make haste** sich beeilen. **hasten** *v* sich beeilen; beschleunigen. **hasty** *adj* eilig; (*rushed*) übereilt. **hastiness** Voreiligkeit *f*.
hat [hat] *n* Hut *m*. **eat one's hat** einen Besen fressen. **keep under one's hat** für sich halten.
hatch¹ [hatʃ] *v* ausbrüten. **hatch a plot** ein Komplott schmieden.
hatch² [hatʃ] *n* (*naut*) Luke *f*; (*serving*) Servierfenster *neut*.
hatchet ['hatʃit] *n* Beil *neut*. **bury the hatchet** das Kriegsbeil begraben.
hate [heit] *v* hassen, verabscheuen. *n* *also* **hatred** Haß *m*, Abscheu *m*. **hateful** *adj* hassenswert.
haughty ['hoiti] *adj* hochmütig. **haughtiness** *n* Hochmut *m*.
haul [hoil] *v* ziehen, schleppen. *n* (*coll: booty*) Fang *m*. **haulage** *n* Transport *m*, Spedition *f*. **haulier** *n* Transportunternehmer *m*, Spediteur *m*.
haunch [hoɪntʃ] *n* Hüfte *f*; (*of animal*) Keule *f*, Lende *f*.

haunt [hɔːnt] *v* (*ghost*) spuken in. **haunted** *adj* gespenstig.
*have [hav] *v* haben. *I have to go* ich muß gehen. *I will have it repaired* ich werde es reparieren lassen. *I have got a car* ich habe ein Auto. *he's had it* es ist aus mit ihm. **be had** (*be cheated*) reingelegt sein. **have a tooth out** sich einen Zahn ziehen lassen. **have it out with** sich auseinandersetzen mit.
haven ['heivn] *n* Hafen *m*; (*fig*) Asyl *neut*.
havoc ['havək] *n* Verheerung *f*. **play havoc with** verheeren.
hawk [hɔːk] *n* Habicht *m*, Falke *m*.
hawthorn ['hɔːθɔːn] *n* Hagedorn *m*.
hay [hei] *n* Heu *neut*. **make hay** Heu machen, heuen. **hay fever** Heuschnupfen *m*. **haystack** *n* Heuschober *m*.
haywire ['heiwaiə] *adj* (*coll*) kaputt. **go haywire** kaputtgehen.
hazard ['hazəd] *n* (*danger*) Gefahr *f*; (*risk*) Risiko *neut*; (*chance*) Zufall *m*; (*golf*) Hindernis *neut*. *v* aufs Spiel setzen, wagen. **hazardous** *adj* gefährlich, riskant.
haze [heiz] *n* Dunst *m*, leichter Nebel *m*; (*fig*) Verschwommenheit *f*. **hazy** *adj* dunstig; verschwommen.
hazel ['heizl] *n* Haselstrauch *m*. *adj* (*colour*) nußbraun. **hazelnut** *n* Haselnuß *f*.
he [hiː] *pron* er.
head [hed] *n* Kopf *m*; (*leader*) Leiter *m*; (*top*) Spitze *f*. *v* leiten, führen. **head for** zugehen nach. **head off** umlenken. **per head** pro Kopf. **by a head** um eine Kopflänge *f*.
headache ['hedeik] *n* Kopfweh *neut*, Kopfschmerzen *pl*.
headfirst [,hed'fəːst] *adj* kopfüber.
heading ['hediŋ] *n* Titel *m*. Überschrift *f*.
headlamp ['hedlamp] *n* Scheinwerfer *m*.
headland ['hedlənd] *n* Landzunge *f*, Landspitze *f*.
headline ['hedlain] *n* Schlagzeile *f*.
headlong ['hedlɔŋ] *adv* kopfüber; ungestüm, blindlings.
headmaster [,hed'maːstə] *n* (Schul)Direktor *n*. **headmistress** *n* Direktorin *f*, Vorsteherin *f*.
head office *n* Hauptsitz *m*.
headphones ['hedfəunz] *pl n* Kopfhörer *m sing*.
headquarters [,hed'kwɔːtəz] *n* (*mil*) Hauptquartier *neut*; (*comm*) Hauptsitz *m*.
headrest ['hedrest] *n* Kopfstütze *f*.

headscarf ['hedskaːf] *n* Kopftuch *neut*.
headstrong ['hedstrɔŋ] *adj* eigensinnig.
head waiter *n* Ober(kellner) *m*.
headway ['hedwei] *n* Fortschritte *pl*. **make headway** vorankommen, Fortschritte machen.
heal [hiːl] *v* heilen. **healer** *n* Heiler *m*. **healing** *n* Heilung *f*. *adj* heilend, heilsam.
health [helθ] *n* Gesundheit *f*. **your health!** zum Wohl! **health insurance** Krankenversicherung *f*. **health resort** Kurort *m*. **healthy** *adj* gesund.
heap [hiːp] *n* Haufe(n) *m*. *v* häufen. *heaps better* (*coll*) viel besser. **heap up** anhäufen.
*hear [hiə] *v* hören; (*listen*) zuhören. **hearing** *n* Gehör *neut*; (*law*) Verhör *neut*. **hearing aid** Horgerät *neut*. **hearsay** *n* Hörensagen *neut*. **preliminary hearing** Voruntersuchung *f*.
heard [həːd] *V* hear.
hearse [həːs] *n* Leichenwagen *m*.
heart [haːt] *n* Herz *neut*. **change of heart** Gesinnungswechsel *m*.
heart attack *n* Herzanfall *m*.
heartbeat ['haːtbiːt] *n* Herzschlag *m*.
heart-breaking ['haːtbreikiŋ] *adj* herzzerbrechend. **heart-broken** *adj* untröstlich.
heartburn ['haːtbəːn] *n* Sodbrennen *neut*.
heart failure *n* Herzschlag *m*.
heartfelt ['haːtfelt] *adj* tiefempfunden.
hearth [haːθ] *n* Kamin *m*.
hearty ['haːti] *adj* herzlich. **heartily** adv herzlich, von Herzen.
heat [hiːt] *n* Hitze *f*, Wärme *f*; (*sport*) Vorlauf *m*. **in the heat of passion** (*law*) im Affekt. *v* hitzen. **heated** *adj* (*fig*) erregt. **heating** *n* Heizung *f*. **heatproof** *adj* hitzebeständig. **heat-stroke** *n* Hitzschlag *m*. **heatwave** *n* Hitzewelle *f*.
heath [hiːθ] *n* Heide *f*.
heathen ['hiːðn] *n* Heide *m*. *adj* heidnisch, unzivilisiert.
heather ['heðə] *n* Heidekraut *neut*.
heave [hiːv] *v* hieven; hochheben; (*sigh*) ausstoßen; (*anchor*) lichten. *n* Heben *neut*.
heaven ['hevn] *n* Himmel *m*. **go to heaven** in den Himmel kommen. **to move heaven and earth** (*fig*) Himmel und Erde in Bewegung setzen. **for heaven's sake** um Himmels Willen. **heavenly** *adj* himmlisch. **heavenly body** Himmelskörper *m*.

heavy ['hevi] adj schwer, schwerwiegend; (mood) träge; (book) langweilig. **heaviness** n Schwere f; (mood) Schwerfälligkeit f. **heavy-duty** adj Hochleistungs-. **heavyweight** n (sport) Schwergewichtler m.

Hebrew ['hiːbruː] n Hebräer m. adj hebräisch.

heckle ['hekl] v durch Fragen belästigen. **heckler** n Zwischenrufer m.

hectare ['hektaː] n Hektar neut.

hectic ['hektik] adj hektisch.

hedge [hedʒ] n Hecke f, Heckenzaun m. **hedgerow** n Hecke f.

hedgehog ['hedʒhog] n Igel m.

heed [hiːd] v achtgeben auf. n Beachtung. **heedful** adj achtsam. **heedless** adj achtlos.

heel [hiːl] n Ferse f; (of shoe) Absatz m. v (shoes) mit Absätzen versehen. **take to one's heels** die Beine in die Hand nehmen. **down-at-heel** (fig) schäbig. **well-heeled** adj wohlhabend.

hefty ['hefti] adj kräftig.

heifer ['hefə] n Färse f.

height [hait] n Höhe f; (person) Größe f; (fig) Höhepunkt m. **heighten** v verstärken.

heir [eə] n Erbe m. **heiress** n Erbin f. **heirloom** n Erbstück neut.

held [held] V **hold**[1]

helicopter ['helikoptə] n Hubschrauber m.

hell [hel] n Hölle f. interj zum Teufel! **to hell with** zum Teufel mit. **hellish** adj höllisch.

hello [hə'lou] interj Guten Tag; (on telephone) hallo!

helm [helm] n Steuer neut, Ruder neut. **helmsman** n Steuermann m.

helmet ['helmit] n Helm m.

help [help] v helfen (+ dat). n Hilfe f. **I can't help it** ich kann nichts dafür, ich kann nicht anders. **help yourself** bedienen Sie Sich! **helper** n Helfer(in). **helpful** adj hilfreich. **helping** n Portion f. **helpless** adj hilflos.

hem [hem] n Saum m. v säumen. **hem in** einengen.

hemisphere ['hemiˌsfiə] n Halbkugel f, Hemisphäre f.

hemp [hemp] n Hanf m.

hen [hen] n Huhn neut.

hence [hens] adv von hier; (therefore) deshalb, daher. **a week hence** in einer Woche. **henceforth** fortan, von jetzt an.

henna ['henə] n Henna f.

henpecked ['henpekt] adj **henpecked husband** Pantoffelheld m.

her [həː] pron (acc) sie; (dat) ihr. poss adj ihr.

herald ['herəld] n Herold m. v (fig) einleiten. **heraldic** adj heraldisch, Wappen-. **heraldry** n Heraldik f, Wappenkunde f.

herb [həːb] n Kraut n. **herbal** adj Kräuter-. **herbalist** n Kräuterkenner(in).

herd [həːd] n Herde f. v hüten, zusammentreiben.

here [hiə] adv hier; (to here) hierher. **hereafter** adv in Zukunft. **herewith** adv hiermit.

hereditary [hi'redətəri] adj erblich. **heredity** n Vererbung f, Erblichkeit f.

heresy ['herəsi] n Ketzerei f. **heretic** n Ketzer(in). **heretical** adj Ketzerisch.

heritage ['heritidʒ] n Erbe neut, Erbgut neut.

hermit ['həːmit] n Eremit m. **hermitage** n Klause f.

hernia ['həːniə] n Bruch m.

hero ['hiərou] n Held m. **heroine** n Heldin f. **heroic** adj heroisch, heldenmutig. **heroism** n Heldentum neut.

heron ['herən] n Reiher m.

herring ['heriŋ] n Hering m. **herringbone** n (pattern) Fischgrätenmuster neut. **pickled herring** Rollmops m.

hers [həːz] poss pron ihrer m, ihre f, ihres neut. **herself** pron (reflexive) sich; selbst. **by herself** allein.

hesitate ['heziteit] v zögern. **hesitant** adj zögernd. **hesitation** n Zögern neut, Bedenken neut.

heterosexual [hetərə'sekʃuəl] adj heterosexuell.

*****hew** [hjuː] v hauen.

hewn [hjuːn] V **hew**.

hexagon ['heksəgən] n Sechseck neut.

heyday ['heidei] n Höhepunkt m, Blütezeit f.

hiatus [hai'eitəs] n Lücke f.

hibernate ['haibəneit] v Winterschlafhalten. **hibernation** n Winterschlaf m.

hiccup ['hikʌp] n Schluckauf m, Schlucken m. v den Schluckauf haben.

hid [hid] V **hide**[1].

hidden ['hidn] V **hide¹**.

*hide¹ [haid] v (conceal) verstecken, verbergen; (keep secret) verheimlichen.

hide² [haid] n (skin) Fell neut, Haut f.

hideous ['hidiəs] adj abscheulich, schrecklich.

hiding¹ ['haidiŋ] n Versteck neut. **be in hiding** sich versteckt halten.

hiding² ['haidiŋ] n (thrashing) Prügel neut.

hierarchy ['haiəraːki] n Hierarchie f, Rangordnung f. **hierarchical** adj hierarchisch.

high [hai] adj hoch; (wind) stark.

highbrow ['haibrau] adj intellektuell. n Intellektuelle(r).

hi-fi ['haifai] adj hi-fi. n Hi-Fi.

high frequency n Hochfrequenz f.

high jump n Hochsprung m.

highland ['hailənd] n Bergland neut.

highlight ['hailait] n Höhepunkt m.

highly ['haili] adv höchst, in hohem Grad, stark. **highly strung** überempfindlich.

highness ['hainis] n Höhe f. **Your Highness** Eure Hoheit.

highpitched [,hai'pitʃt] adj hoch.

high point n Höhepunkt m.

high-rise building n Hochhaus neut.

high-spirited adj lebhaft, temperamentvoll.

high street n Hauptstraße f.

high tide n Hochwasser neut.

highway ['haiwei] n Landstraße f.

hijack ['haidʒak] v (aeroplane) entführen. n Entführung f. **hijacker** n Entführer m, Hijacker m.

hike [haik] v wandern. n Wanderung f. **hiker** n Wanderer m.

hilarious [hi'leəriəs] adj lustig. **hilarity** n Lustigkeit f.

hill [hil] n Hügel m, Berg m. **hillside** n Hang m. **hilltop** n Bergspitze f.

him [him] pron (acc) ihn; (dat) ihm. **himself** pron (reflexive) sich; selbst. **by himself** allein.

hind [haind] adj hinter, Hinter-. **hindsight** n **with hindsight** im Rückblick.

hinder ['hində] v (ver)hindern. **hindrance** n Hindernis neut, Hinderung f.

Hindu [hin'duː] n Hindu m. adj Hindu-.

hinge [hindʒ] n Scharnier neut, Gelenk neut. **to hinge on** abhängen (von).

hint [hint] n Wink m. v andeuten.

hip [hip] n Hütte f. **hip-bone** n Hüftbein neut. **hip-joint** n Hüftgelenk neut.

hippopotamus [hipə'potəməs] n Nilpferd neut.

hire [haiə] v (ver)mieten; (staff) anstellen. n Miete f. **hire-car** n Mietwagen m. **hire purchase** Ratenkauf m. **hire-purchase agreement** Teilzahlungsvertrag m.

his [hiz] poss adj sein. poss pron seiner m, seine f, seines neut.

hiss [his] v zischen. n Zischen neut.

history ['histəri] n Geschichte f. **history book** Geschichtsbuch neut. **historian** n Historiker(in). **historic** adj historisch. **historical** adj historisch, geschichtlich.

*hit [hit] v schlagen, stoßen. n Schlag m, Stoß m; (record) Schlager m. **make a hit** (fig) Erfolg haben. **hard hit** schwer getroffen. **hit upon** zufällig finden.

hitch [hitʃ] v befestigen; (horse) anspannen. n (problem) Haken m. **hitchhike** v per Anhalter fahren.

hitherto [,hiðə'tuː] adv bisher.

hive [haiv] n Bienenkorb m. v **hive off** abzweigen.

hoard [hoːd] n Schatz m, Hort m. v sammeln, hamstern.

hoarding ['hoːdiŋ] n Reklamewand f.

hoarse [hoːs] adj rauh, heiser.

hoax [houks] n Falschmeldung f. v zum Besten haben.

hobble ['hobl] v hinken, hoppeln; (horse) fesseln.

hobby ['hobi] n Hobby neut. **hobby horse** n Steckenpferd neut.

hock¹ [hok] n (joint) Sprunggelenk neut.

hock² [hok] n (wine) Rheinwein m.

hockey ['hoki] n Hockey neut.

hoe [hou] n Hacke f. v hacken.

hog [hog] n (Schlacht)Schwein neut; (coll) Vielfraß m. **go the whole hog** aufs Ganze gehen.

hoist [hoist] v hochziehen. n Aufzug m, Kran m.

*hold¹ [hould] v halten; (contain) enthalten. n Halt m, Griff m; (fig) Einfluß m. **hold back** zurückhalten. **hold down** (job) behalten. **hold up** (delay) aufhalten; (rob) überfallen. **hold-up** n (traffic) Stockung f; (robbery) Überfall m.

hold² [hould] n (naut) Frachtraum m, Schiffsraum m.

holder ['houldə] n (owner) Inhaber m.

holding ['houldiŋ] n (land) Grundbesitz m, Guthaben neut. **holding company** Dachgesellschaft f.

hole [houl] n Loch neut.
holiday ['holədi] n Feiertag m, Ruhetag m. **holidays** pl Ferien pl, Urlaub m sing. **go on holiday** verreisen, in die Ferien gehen, auf Urlaub gehen. **holidaymaker** n Feriengast m, Urlauber(in).
Holland ['holənd] n Holland neut, die Niederlände pl.
hollow ['holou] n Höhle f, Loch neut. adj hohl, leer. v (aus)höhlen. **hollowness** n Hohlheit f, Leerheit f.
holly ['holi] n Steckpalme f.
holster ['houlstə] n Pistolenhalfter f.
holy ['houli] adj heilig.
homage ['homidʒ] n Huldigung f. **do or pay homage** huldigen.
home [houm] n Heim neut, Haus neut, Zuhause neut; (institution) Heim neut. **at home** zu Hause. **at home with** vertraut mit. **make yourself at home** mach dich bequem. **go home** nach Hause gehen. **hammer home** (nail) fest einschlagen. adj häuslich; (national) inner, Innen-. **home affairs** innere Angelegenheiten pl. **home market** Binnenmarkt m. **homecoming** n Heimkehr f. **homeland** n Heimat f, Vaterland neut. **homeless** adj obdachlos. **homely** adj heimisch, gemütlich. **be homesick** Heimweh haben. **homesickness** n Heimweh neut. **homeward** adj Heim-; adv heimwärts. **homework** n Hausaufgaben pl.
homicide ['homisaid] n Mord m; (person) Mörder m.
homogeneous [homə'dʒiːniəs] adj gleichartig, homogen.
homosexual [homə'sekʃuəl] adj homosexuell. n Homosexuelle(r). **homosexuality** n Homosexualität f.
honest ['onist] adj ehrlich, aufrecht. **honesty** n Ehrlichkeit f, Aufrichtigkeit f.
honey ['hʌni] n Honig m; (darling) Liebling m, Schatz m. **honey-bee** n Honigbiene f. **honeycomb** n Honigwabe f. **honeymoon** n Hochzeitsreise f.
honeysuckle ['hʌnisʌkl] n Geißblatt neut.
honour ['onə] n Ehre f; (reputation) guter Ruf m. **honours** pl Auszeichnungen pl. v (ver)ehren; (cheque) einlösen. **honourable** adj ehrenvoll; (in titles) ehrenwert.
hood [hud] n Kapuze f; (US: on car) Motorhaube f; (coll) Gangster m. **hoodwink** v täuschen.
hoof [huːf] n Huf m.

hook [huk] n Haken m. v haken **hook up** (coll) anschließen.
hooligan ['huːligən] n Rowdy m. **hooliganism** n Rowdytum neut.
hoop [huːp] n Reif(en) m.
hoot [huːt] v hupen. n Hupen neut.
hop¹ [hop] v hüpfen. n Sprung m.
hop² [hop] n (bot) Hopfen m.
hope [houp] v hoffen (auf). n Hoffnung f. **hopeful** adj hoffnungsvoll; (promising) vielversprechend. **hopefully** adv hoffentlich. **hopeless** adj hoffnungslos. **hopelessness** n Hoffnungslosigkeit f.
horde [hoːd] n Horde f.
horizon [hə'raizn] n Horizont m. **horizontal** adj waagerecht, horizontal.
hormone ['hoːmoun] n Hormon neut.
horn [hoːn] n Horn neut; (mot) Hupe f. **horned** adj gehörnt. **hornrimmed spectacles** Hornbrille f. **horny** adj (hands) schwielig.
hornet ['hoːnit] n Hornisse f.
horoscope ['horəskoup] n Horoskop neut.
horrible ['horibl] adj schrecklich, fürchterlich.
horrid ['horid] adj scheußlich, abscheulich.
horrify ['horifai] v erschrecken, entsetzen. **horrifying** adj entsetzlich.
horror ['horə] n Entsetzen neut, Grausen neut. **horror-stricken** adj von Grausen gepackt.
hors d'oeuvre [oː'dəːvr] n Vorspeise f.
horse [hoːs] n Pferd neut, Roß neut. **on horseback** zu Pferd. **horse chestnut** Roßkastanie f. **horseman** n Reiter m. **horsepower (hp)** Pferdestärke (PS) f. **horse race** n Pferderennen neut. **horseradish** n Meerrettich m.
horticulture ['hoːtikʌltʃə] n Gartenbau m.
hose [houz] n (stockings) Strümpfe pl; (tech, mot) Schlauch m; (in garden) Gartenschlauch m.
hosiery ['houziəri] pl n Strumpfwaren pl.
hospitable [ho'spitəbl] adj gastfreundlich.
hospital ['hospitl] n Krankenhaus neut, Klinik f.
hospitality [hospi'taliti] n Gastfreundschaft f.
host¹ [houst] n Gastgeber m, Wirt m.
host² [houst] n (large number) Masse f, Menge f.
hostage ['hostidʒ] n Geisel m, f.
hostel ['hostəl] n Herberge f. **student hostel** Studentenheim neut. **youth hostel**

Jugendherberge *f*. **hostelry** *n* Wirtshaus *neut*.

hostess ['houstis] *n* Gastgeberin *f*, Wirtin *f*; (*air hostess*) Stewardeß *f*.

hostile ['hostail] *adj* feindlich, feindselig (gegen). **hostility** *n* Feindseligkeit *f*, Feindschaft *f*.

hot [hot] *adj* heiß; (*food*, *drink*) warm. **hotdog** *n* (heißes) Würstchen. **hot meal** warme Mahlzeit. **hot-water bottle** Wärmflasche *f*.

hotel [hou'tel] *n* Hotel *neut*, Gasthof *m*. **hotel register** *n* Fremdenbuch *neut*. **hotelier** *n* Hotelier *m*.

hound [haund] *n* Jagdhund *m*. *v* jagen, verfolgen.

hour ['auə] *n* Stunde *f*. **after hours** nach Geschäftsschluß. **for hours** stundenlang. **hourglass** *n* Sanduhr *f*. **hourly** *adj*, *adv* stündlich. **hourly wage** Stundenlohn *m*.

house [haus; *v* hauz] *n* Haus *neut*; (*theatre*) Publikum *neut*. **House of Commons** Unterhaus *neut*. **House of Lords** Oberhaus *neut*. **House of Representatives** Abgeordnetenhaus *neut*. *v* unterbringen.

houseboat ['hausbout] *n* Hausboot *neut*.

household ['haushould] *n* Haushalt *m*.

housekeeper ['haus,kiːpə] *n* Haushälterin *f*. **housekeeping** *n* Haushaltung *f*. **housekeeping money** Haushaltsgeld *neut*.

housemaid ['hausmeid] *n* Dienstmädchen *neut*. **housemaid's knee** (*med*) Kniescheibenentzündung *f*.

house-warming ['hauswoːmiŋ] *n* Einzugsfest *neut*.

housewife ['hauswaif] *n* Hausfrau *f*.

housework ['hauswəːk] *n* Hausarbeit *f*.

housing ['hauziŋ] *n* Unterbringung *f*, Wohnung *f*; (*tech*) Gehäuse *neut*. **housing estate** Siedlung *f*.

hovel ['hovəl] *n* Schuppen *m*.

hover ['hovə] *v* schweben. **hovercraft** *n* Luftkissenfahrzeug *neut*.

how [hau] *adv* wie. **how do you do?** guten Tag. **how are you?** wie geht es Ihnen? **how much** *or* **how many** wieviel. **however** *adv* aber, jedoch; (*in whatever way*) wie auch immer.

howl [haul] *v* heulen. *n* Heulen *neut*.

hub [hʌb] *n* Nabe *f*; (*fig*) Mittelpunkt *m*. **hub cap** Radkappe *f*.

huddle ['hʌdl] *v* sich zusammendrängen. **huddled** *adj* kauernd.

hue [hjuː] *n* Farbe *f*, Färbung *f*.

huff [hʌf] *n* **in a huff** gekränkt, beleidigt.

hug [hʌg] *v* umarmen. *n* Umarmung *f*.

huge [hjuːdʒ] *adj* riesig, riesengroß.

hulk [hʌlk] *n* (*naut*) Hulk *m*.

hull [hʌl] *n* (*naut*) Rumpf *m*; (*of seed*, *etc*.) Hülse *f*, Schale *f*. *v* enthülsen.

hum [hʌm] *v* summen, brummen. *n* Summen *neut*, Brummen *neut*.

human ['hjuːmən] *adj* menschlich. **human being** Mensch *m*. **human nature** Menschheit *f*, menschliche Natur *f*. **humane** *adj* human. **humanist** *n* Humanist(in). **humanitarian** *adj* menschenfreundlich. **humanity** *n* Menschheit *f*.

humble ['hʌmbl] *adj* demütig, bescheiden; (*lowly*) niedrig. **humiliate** *v* demütigen. **humiliating** *adj* demütigend. **humility** *n* Demut *f*, Bescheidenheit *f*.

humdrum ['hʌmdrʌm] *adj* langweilig, alltäglich.

humid ['hjuːmid] *adj* feucht. **humidity** *n* Feuchtigkeit *f*.

humour ['hjuːmə] *n* Humor *m*; (*mood*) Stimmung *f*, Laune *f*. *v* (*person*) nachgeben (+ *dat*). **sense of humour** Humor *m*. **humorous** *adj* lustig, humorvoll.

hump [hʌmp] *n* Buckel *m*. *v* (*coll*: *carry*) schleppen. **humpback** *n* Bucklige(r). **humpbacked** *adj* bucklig.

hunch [hʌntʃ] *n* (*coll*) Vorahnung *f*.

hundred ['hʌndrəd] *adj* hundert. *n* Hundert *neut*. **hundredth** *adj* hundertst; *n* Hundertstel *neut*. **hundredweight** Zentner *m*.

hung [hʌŋ] *V* hang.

Hungary ['hʌŋgəri] *n* Ungarn *neut*. **Hungarian** *adj* ungarisch; *n* Ungar(in).

hunger ['hʌŋgə] *n* Hunger *m*. *v* hungern. **hunger for** sehnen nach. **hungry** *adj* hungrig. **be hungry** Hunger haben.

hunt [hʌnt] *n* Jagd *f*, Jagen *neut*; (*for person*) Verfolgung *f*. *v* jagen; verfolgen. **hunter** *n* Jäger *m*, (*horse*) Jagdpferd *neut*. **hunting** *n* Jagd *f*.

hurdle ['həːdl] *n* Hürde *f*; (*fig*) Hindernis *neut*.

hurl [həːl] *v* werfen.

hurricane ['hʌrikən] *n* Orkan *m*. **hurricane lamp** Sturmlaterne *f*.

hurry ['hʌri] *v* eilen, sich beeilen; (*something*) beschleunigen. *n* Eile *f*, Hast *f*. **hurry up** mach schnell! **hurried** *adj* eilig, übereilt.

*hurt [hɔit] v (*injure*) verletzen; (*ache*) schmerzen, weh tun; (*offend*) kränken, verletzen. n Verletzung f; Schmerzen neut. **hurtful** adj schädlich.
hurtle ['hɔitl] v stürzen, sausen.
husband ['hʌzbənd] n (Ehe)Mann m. v (*resources*) sparsam umgehen mit. **husbandry** n Landwirtschaft f.
hush [hʌʃ] n Stille f, Ruhe f. v beruhigen.
husk [hʌsk] n Hülse f. v enthülsen.
husky ['hʌski] adj (*voice*) rauh, heiser.
hussar [hə'zai] n Husar m.
hustle ['hʌsl] v drängen. **hustle and bustle** Gedränge neut.
hut [hʌt] n Hütte f.
hutch [hʌtʃ] n Stall m.
hyacinth ['haiəsinθ] n Hyazinthe f.
hybrid ['haibrid] n Kreuzung f, Mischling m. adj Misch-.
hydraulic [hai'drɔilik] adj hydraulisch.
hydrocarbon [ˌhaidrou'kaibən] n Kohlenwasserstoff m.
hydro-electric [ˌhaidroui'lektrik] adj hydroelektrisch.
hydrogen ['haidrədʒən] n Wasserstoff m. **hydrogen bomb** Wasserstoffbombe f. **hydrogen peroxide** Wasserstoffsuperoxyd neut.
hyena [hai'iinə] n Hyäne f.
hygiene ['haidʒiin] n Hygiene f, Gesundheitspflege f. **hygienic** adj hygienisch.
hymn [him] n Kirchenlied neut, Hymne f. **hymnbook** n Gesangbuch neut.
hypersensitive [haipə'sensətiv] adj überempfindlich.
hyphen ['haifən] n Bindestrich m.
hypnosis [hip'nousis] n Hypnose f. **hypnotic** adj hypnotisch. **hypnotist** n Hypnotiseur m. **hypnotize** v hypnotisieren.
hypochondria [haipə'kondriə] n Hypochondrie f. **hypochondriac** adj hypochondrisch. n Hypochonder m.
hypocrisy [hi'pokrəsi] n Heuchelei f. **hypocrite** n Heuchler(in). **hypocritical** adj heuchlerisch.
hypodermic [haipə'dɔimik] adj subkutan. **hypodermic syringe** Spritze f.
hypothesis [hai'poθəsis] n (pl -ses) Hypothese f. **hypothetical** adj hypothetisch.
hysterectomy [histə'rektəmi] n Hysterektomie f.

hysteria [his'tiəriə] n Hysterie f. **hysterical** adj hysterisch; (*coll: funny*) zum Schreien komisch.

I

I [ai] pron ich.
ice [ais] n Eis neut. v (*cookery*) mit Zuckerguß überziehen. **icing** n Zuckerguß m. **ice age** n Eiszeit f. **iceberg** n Eisberg m. **icebox** n Kühlschrank m. **ice cream** n Eis neut. **ice cube** n Eiswürfel m. **icy** adj eisig.
Iceland ['aislənd] n Island neut. **Icelandic** adj isländisch. **Icelander** n Isländer(in).
icicle ['aisikl] n Eiszapfen m.
icon ['aikon] n Ikone f.
idea [ai'diə] n Idee f; (*concept*) Begriff m. *I've no idea* ich habe keine Ahnung.
ideal [ai'diəl] n Ideal neut. adj ideal. **idealism** n Idealismus neut. **idealist** n Idealist m. **idealistic** adj idealistisch. **ideally** adv idealerweise.
identical [ai'dentikəl] adj identisch.
identify [ai'dentifai] v identifizieren; (*recognize*) erkennen. **identification** n Identifizierung f; (*pass*) Ausweis m.
identity [ai'dentiti] n Identität f. **identity card** Personalausweis m. **identity papers** Ausweispapiere pl.
ideology [aidi'olədʒi] n Ideologie f. **ideological** adj ideologisch. **ideologist** n Ideologe m, Ideologin f.
idiom ['idiəm] n Mundart f, Idiom neut. **idiomatic** adj idiomatisch.
idiosyncrasy [ˌidiə'siŋkrəsi] n Eigenart f. **idiosyncratic** adj eigenartig.
idiot ['idiət] n (*coll*) Idiot m, Dummkopf m; (*med*) Blödsinnige(r). **idiocy** n Blödsinn m.
idle ['aidl] adj (*person*) faul, untätig; (*words, etc.*) eitel, unnütz. **idleness** n Faulheit f. **idler** n Faulenzer m.
idol ['aidl] n Idol neut. **idolize** v vergöttern.
idyllic [i'dilik] adj idyllisch.
if [if] conj wenn, falls; (*whether*) ob. **even if** selbst wenn. **if only** wenn ... nur. **if not** falls nicht. **if so** in dem Fall.
ignite [ig'nait] v (ent)zünden.

ignition [ig'niʃən] n Zündung f. **ignition key** Zündschlüssel m.

ignorant ['ignərənt] adj unwissend; (uneducated) ungebildet. **be ignorant of** nicht wissen or kennen. **ignorance** n Unkenntnis f.

ignore [ig'noi] v ignorieren, unbeachtet lassen.

ill [il] adj (sick) krank; (bad) schlimm, böse. **fall ill** krank werden. **ill-at-ease** adj unbehaglich. **ill-bred** schlecht erzogen. **ill-disposed** adj bösartig. **ill-fated** adj unselig. **ill-natured** adj boshaft. **illness** n Krankheit f. **ill-treat** v mißhandeln.

illegal [i'liigəl] adj illegal, gesetzwidrig. **illegality** n Ungesetzlichkeit f.

illegible [i'ledʒəbl] adj unleserlich. **illegibility** n Unleserlichkeit f.

illegitimate [,ili'dʒitimit] adj (child) unehelich; (unlawful) ungesetzlich. **illicit** [i'lisit] adj unzulässig, gesetzwidrig.

illiterate [i'litərit] adj analphabetisch, ungebildet. n Analphabet(in).

illogical [i'lodʒikəl] adj unlogisch.

illuminate [i'luimi,neit] v erleuchten. **illuminated** adj beleuchtet. **illumination** n Beleuchtung f.

illusion [i'luiʒən] n Illusion f. **illusory** adj illusorisch.

illustrate ['ilə,streit] v (book) illustrieren; (idea) erklären. **illustration** n Illustration f, Bild n.

illustrious [i'lʌstriəs] adj berühmt.

image ['imidʒ] n Bild neut. (idea) Vorstellung f; (public) Image neut. **imagery** n Symbolik f.

imagine [i'madʒin] v sich vorstellen or denken. **imaginable** adj denkbar. **imaginary** adj eingebildet, Schein-. **imagination** n Phantasie f. **imaginative** adj phantasiereich.

imbalance [im'baləns] n Unausgeglichenheit f.

imbecile ['imbə,siil] n Schwachsinnige(r) adj schwachsinnig.

imitate ['imi,teit] v nachahmen, imitieren. **imitation** n Nachahmung f; adj künstlich, Kunst-.

immaculate [i'makjulit] adj makellos.

immaterial [,imə'tiəriəl] adj belanglos.

immature [,imə'tjuə] adj unreif, unentwickelt. **immaturity** n Unreife f.

immediate [i'miidiət] adj unmittelbar, direkt. **immediately** adv sofort.

immense [i'mens] adj riesig, ungeheuer.

immerse [i'məis] v versenken, tauchen. **immersion** n Versunkenheit f, Immersion f. **immersion heater** Tauchsieder m.

immigrate ['imi,greit] v einwandern. **immigrant** n Einwanderer m, Einwanderin f. **immigration** n Einwanderung f.

imminent ['iminənt] adj drohend.

immobile [i'moubail] adj bewegungslos, unbeweglich. **immobility** n Unbeweglichkeit f. **immobilize** v unbeweglich machen.

immodest [i'modist] adj schamlos.

immoral [i'morəl] adj unsittlich, unmoralisch. **immorality** n Sittenlosigkeit f.

immortal [i'moitl] adj unsterblich, ewig. **immortality** n Unsterblichkeit f.

immovable [i'muivəbl] adj unbeweglich.

immune [i'mjuin] adj immun (gegen). **immunity** n Immunität f. **immunization** n Impfung f.

imp [imp] v Kobold m.

impact ['impakt] n Anprall m, Stoß m; (effect) Wirking f, Einfluß m.

impair [im'peə] v beeinträchtigen. **impairment** n Beeinträchtigung f.

impart [im'pait] v geben, erteilen.

impartial [im'paiʃəl] adj unparteiisch. **impartiality** n Unparteilichkeit f.

impassable [im'paisəbl] adj ungangbar, unpassierbar.

impasse [am'pais] n Sackgasse f.

impassive [im'pasiv] adj ungeruhrt.

impatient [im'peiʃənt] adj ungeduldig. **impatience** n Ungeduld f.

impeach [im'piitʃ] v anklagen. **impeachment** n Anklage f.

impeccable [im'pekəbl] adj tadellos. **impeccability** n Tadellosigkeit f.

impede [im'piid] v (be)hindern. **impediment** n Verhinderung f. **speech impediment** Sprachfehler m.

impel [im'pel] v (an)treiben. **impelled** adj gezwungen.

impending [im'pendiŋ] adj bevorstehend, drohend.

imperative [im'perətiv] adj dringend notwendig. n (gramm) Imperativ m.

imperfect [im'pəifikt] adj unvollkommen, fehlerhaft. **imperfection** n (blemish) Fehler m.

imperial [im'piəriəl] adj kaiserlich. **imperialism** n Imperialismus m. **imperialist** adj imperialistisch.

imperil [im'perəl] v gefährden.
impermanent [im'pəːmənənt] adj unbeständig.
impersonal [im'pəːsənl] adj unpersönlich. **impersonality** n Unpersönlichkeit f.
impersonate [im'pəːsə‚neit] v sich ausgeben als.
impertinent [im'pəːtinənt] adj frech, unverschämt. **impertinence** n Frechheit f, Unverschämtheit f.
impervious [im'pəːviəs] adj undurchdringlich.
impetuous [im'petjuəs] adj ungestüm, impulsiv. **impetuosity** n Ungestüm neut.
impetus ['impətəs] n Antrieb m, Schwung m.
impinge [im'pindʒ] v eingreifen (in), stoßen (an).
implement ['implimənt; v 'impliment] n Werkzeug neut, Gerät neut. v durchführen.
implicate ['implikeit] v hineinziehen. **implication** n Bedeutung f, Konsequenz f.
implicit [im'plisit] adj (tacit) unausgesprochen; (unquestioning) absolut. **implicitly** adv unbedingt.
implore [im'ploː] v dringend bitten. **imploring** adj flehentlich.
imply [im'plai] v bedeuten.
impolite [impə'lait] adj unhöflich. **impoliteness** n Unhöflichkeit f.
import [im'poːt] v einführen, importieren. n Einfuhr f, Import m. **importer** n Importeur m, Einfuhrhändler m. **imports** pl n Importwaren pl.
importance [im'poːtəns] n Wichtigkeit f, Bedeutung f. **important** adj wichtig.
impose [im'pouz] v auferlegen. **impose upon** mißbrauchen. **imposing** adj imponierend. **imposition** n Auferlegung f; (unreasonable demand) Zumutung f.
impossible [im'posəbl] adj unmöglich. **impossibility** n Unmöglichkeit f.
impostor [im'postə] n Betrüger(in).
impotent ['impətənt] adj impotent. **impotence** n Impotenz f.
impound [im'paund] v beschlagnahmen.
impoverish [im'povəriʃ] v arm machen. **impoverished** adj verarmt.
impregnate ['impreg‚neit] v befruchten, schwanger machen; (fabric, wood, etc.) imprägnieren. **impregnable** adj uneinnehmbar.
impress [im'pres] v beeindrucken. **impres-**

sion n Eindruck m; (book) Auflage f. **impressionism** n (painting) Impressionismus m.
imprint [im'print; n 'imprint] v aufdrücken (auf); (fig) einprägen in. n Stempel m; (fig) Eindruck m.
imprison [im'prizn] v einsperren. **imprisonment** n Haft f, Gefangenschaft f.
improbable [im'probəbl] adj unwahrscheinlich. **improbability** n Unwahrscheinlichkeit f.
impromptu [im'promptjuː] adj improvisiert.
improper [im'propə] adj unpassend, unsittlich.
improve [im'pruːv] v verbessern; (become better) sich verbessern, besser werden. **improvement** n Verbesserung f.
improvise ['imprə‚vaiz] v improvisieren. **improvisation** n Improvisierung f.
impudent ['impjudənt] adj frech, unverschämt. **impudence** n Unverschämtheit f.
impulse ['impʌls] n Antrieb m, Drang m. **impulsive** adj impulsiv.
impure [im'pjuə] adj unrein. **impurity** n Unreinheit f; (extraneous substance) fremde Bestandteile pl.
in [in] prep (place) in, an auf; (time) in, während. (into) in ... hinein or herein. **in the street** auf der Straße. **in the evening** abends. **in bad weather** bei schlechtem Wetter. **in three days' time** nach drei Tagen. **in that** insofern als. **be in** (at home) zu Hause sein.
inability [‚inə'biləti] n Unfähigkeit f. **inability to pay** Zahlungsunfähigkeit f.
inaccessible [‚inak'sesəbl] adj unzugänglich, unerreichbar. **inaccessibility** n Unzugänglichkeit f.
inaccurate [in'akjurit] adj ungenau; (incorrect) falsch. **inaccuracy** n Ungenauigkeit f; Fehler m.
inactive [in'aktiv] adj untätig. **inactivity** n Untätigkeit f.
inadequate [in'adikwit] adj ungenügend, mangelhaft. **inadequacy** n Unzulänglichkeit f, Mangelhaftigkeit f.
inadvertent [‚inəd'vəːtənt] adj unabsichtlich, versehentlich.
inane [in'ein] adj leer, albern.
inanimate [in'animit] adj leblos.
inarticulate [‚inɑː'tikjulit] adj undeutlich. **be inarticulate** sich nicht gut ausdrücken können.

inasmuch [ˌinəz'mʌtʃ] *conj* **inasmuch as** da.

inaudible [in'ɔidəbl] *adj* unhörbar.

inaugurate [i'nɔigjuˌreit] *v* (feierlich) eröffnen. **inauguration** *n* (feierliche) Eröffnung *f*. **inaugural** *adj* Einführungs-.

inborn [ˌin'bɔin] *adj* angeboren.

incapable [in'keipəbl] *adj* unfähig. **incapacity** *n* Unfähigkeit *f*.

incendiary [in'sendiəri] *adj* Brand-. **incendiary bomb** Brandbombe *f*.

incense[1] ['insens] *n* Weihrauch *m*.

incense[2] [in'sens] *v* wütend machen.

incentive [in'sentiv] *n* Ansporn *m*; (*bonus*) Leistungsanreiz *m*.

incessant [in'sesənt] *adj* ständig, unaufhörlich.

incest ['insest] *n* Blutschande *f*. **incestuous** *adj* blutschänderisch.

inch [intʃ] *n* Zoll *m*.

incident ['insidənt] *n* Vorfall *m*, Ereignis *neut*.

incinerator [in'sinəˌreitə] *n* Verbrennungsofen *m*. **incinerate** *v* verbrennen. **incineration** *n* Verbrennung *f*.

incite [in'sait] *v* anregen. **incitement** *n* Anregung *f*, Aufreizung *f*.

incline [in'klain] *v* neigen; (*slope*) abfallen. **inclination** *n* Neigung *f*. **inclined** *adj* geneigt.

include [in'kluid] *v* einschließen. **included** *adj* (*in price*) inbegriffen. **inclusive** *adj* einschließlich. **inclusive of** *also* **including** einschließlich. **inclusion** *n* Einbeziehung *f*.

incognito [ˌinkog'niitou] *adv* inkognito.

incoherent [ˌinkə'hiərənt] *adj* inkonsequent; (*speech*) unklar.

income ['inkʌm] *n* Einkommen *neut*, Einkünfte *pl*. **income tax** Einkommensteuer *f*. **income tax return** Einkommensteuererklärung *f*.

incompatible [inkəm'patəbl] *adj* unvereinbar. **incompatibility** *n* Unvereinbarkeit *f*.

incompetent [in'kompitənt] *adj* unfähig. **incompetence** *n* Unfähigkeit *f*.

incomplete [ˌinkəm'pliit] *adj* unvollständig.

incomprehensible [inˌkompri'hensəbl] *adj* unbegreiflich.

inconceivable [inkən'siivəbl] *adj* unfaßbar. **inconceivability** *n* Unfaßbarkeit *f*.

inconclusive [inkən'kluisiv] *adj* ohne Beweiskraft.

incongruous [in'kongruəs] *adj* unangemessen.

inconsiderate [ˌinkən'sidərit] *adj* rücksichtslos, besinnungslos.

inconsistent [ˌinkən'sistənt] *adj* inkonsequent; (*person*) unbeständig. **inconsistency** *n* Widerspruch *m*.

inconspicuous [inkən'spikjuəs] *adj* unauffällig.

incontinence [in'kontinəns] *n* (*med*) Inkontinenz *f*.

inconvenient [inkən'viinjənt] *adj* ungelegen. **inconvenience** *n* Ungelegenheit *f*. *v* stören, lästig sein (+*dat*).

incorporate [in'kɔipəˌreit] *v* (*combine*) vereinigen; (*comm*) inkorporieren; (*contain, include*) enthalten. **Incorporation** *n* (*comm*) Gründung *f*.

incorrect [inkə'rekt] *adj* unrichtig; (*inexact*) ungenau.

increase [in'kriis] *v* zunehmen; (*in number*) sich vermehren; (*prices*) steigen. *n* Vermehrung *f*, Zunahme *f*; Steigerung *f*; (*wages*) Lohnerhöhung *f*. **increasingly** *adv* immer mehr.

incredible [in'kredəbl] *adj* unglaublich. **incredibility** *n* Unglaublichkeit *f*. **incredibly** *adv* unglaublicherweise; (*coll: extremely*) unglaublich.

incredulous [in'kredjuləs] *adj* skeptisch, ungläubig. **incredulity** *n* Skepsis *f*.

increment ['inkrəmənt] *n* Zunahme *f*.

incriminate [in'krimineit] *v* beschuldigen. **incrimination** *n* Beschuldigung *f*.

incubate ['inkjuˌbeit] *v* ausbrüten. **incubation** *n* Ausbrütung *f*. **incubator** *n* (*for babies*) Brutkasten *m*.

incur [in'kəi] *v* sich zuziehen. **incur debts** Schulden machen. **incur losses** Verluste erleiden.

incurable [in'kjuərəbl] *adj* unheilbar.

indebted [in'detid] *adj* verschuldet.

indecent [in'diisnt] *adj* unanständig. **indecency** *n* Unanständigkeit *f*.

indeed [in'diid] *adv* tatsächlich, wirklich.

indefinite [in'definit] *adj* unbestimmt. **indefinitely** *adv* auf unbestimmte Zeit.

indelible [in'deləbl] *adj* unauslöschlich; (*ink*) wasserfest.

indemnify [in'demnifai] *v* entschädigen. **indemnity** *n* Entschädigung *f*.

indent [in'dent] v (*type*) einrücken. **indentation** n Einrückung f.

independence [indi'pendəns] n Unabhängigkeit f, Selbstständigkeit f.

independent adj unabhängig, selbstständig; (*pol*) parteilos; n (*pol*) Unabhängige(r).

indescribable [indi'skraibəbl] adj unbeschreiblich.

indestructible [indi'strʌktəbl] adj unzerstörbar.

index ['indeks] n (*in book*) Register neut; (*file*) Kartei f; (*cost of living*) Index m. **index finger** Zeigefinger m.

India ['indjə] n Indien neut. **Indian** adj indisch; (*American*) indianisch; n Inder(in); (*American*) Indianer(in). **Indian ink** chinesische Tusche f. **Indian summer** Nachsommer m.

indicate ['indikeit] v anzeigen; (*hint*) andeuten. **indication** n Anzeichen neut; (*idea*) Andeutung f; (*information*) Angabe; (*med*) Indikation f. **indicative** adj anzeigend. **indicator** n (*sign*) Zeichen neut; (*mot*) Richtungsanzeiger m, Blinker m.

indict [in'dait] v anklagen (wegen). **indictment** n Anklageschrift f.

indifferent [in'difrənt] adj gleichgültig; (*poor quality*) mittelmäßig. **indifference** n Gleichgültigkeit f; Mittelmäßigkeit f.

indigenous [in'didʒinəs] adj einheimisch.

indigestion [indi'dʒestʃən] n Verdauungsstörung f. **indigestible** adj unverdaulich.

indignant [in'dignənt] adj empört. **indignation** n Empörung f.

indignity [in'dignəti] n Demütigung f.

indirect [indi'rekt] adj indirekt.

indiscreet [indi'skriːt] adj indiskret, taktlos. **indiscretion** n Vertrauensbruch m, Indiskretion f.

indiscriminate [indi'skriminit] adj rücksichtslos. **indiscriminately** adv ohne Unterschied.

indispensable [indi'spensəbl] adj unerläßlich, unentbehrlich. **indispensability** n Unerläßlichkeit f, Unentbehrlichkeit f.

indisposed [indi'spouzd] adj indisponiert, unpäßlich.

indisputable [indi'spjuːtəbl] adj unbestreitbar.

indistinct [indi'stiŋkt] adj unklar.

individual [indi'vidjuəl] n Individuum neut, Person f. adj einzeln, persönlich, individuell. **individualist** n Individualist(in). **individuality** n Individualität f, Eigenart f. **individually** adv einzeln.

indoctrinate [in'doktri,neit] v unterweisen. **indoctrination** n Unterweisung f.

indolent ['indələnt] adj lässig. **indolence** n Lässigkeit f.

indoor ['indoɪ] adj Haus-, Zimmer-. **indoor swimming pool** Hallenbad neut. **indoors** adv im Haus; (*go*) ins Haus.

induce [in'djuɪs] v (*cause*) verursachen; (*persuade*) überreden. **inducement** n Anreiz m.

indulge [in'dʌldʒ] v (*a person*) nachgeben (+ *dat*); (*oneself*) verwöhnen. **indulgence** n Nachsicht f; Verwöhnung f. **indulgent** adj nachsichtig.

industry ['indəstri] n Industrie f. **industrial** adj industriell. **industrialist** n Industrielle(r). **industrious** adj fleißig.

inebriated [i'niːbrieitid] adj betrunken.

inedible [in'edibl] adj nicht eßbar.

inefficient [ini'fiʃnt] adj unfähig; (*thing*) unwirksam. **inefficiency** n Leistungsunfähigkeit f.

inept [i'nept] adj albern. **ineptitude** n Albernheit f.

inequality [ini'kwoləti] n Ungleichheit f.

inert [i'nəɪt] adj inaktiv; (*person*) schlaff. **inertia** n Trägheit f.

inevitable [in'evitəbl] adj unvermeidlich. **inevitability** n Unvermeidlichkeit f.

inexpensive [inik'spensiv] adj billig, preiswert.

inexperienced [inik'spiəriənst] adj unerfahren.

infallible [in'faləbl] adj unfehlbar. **infallibility** n Unfehlbarkeit f.

infamous ['infəməs] adj schändlich. **infamy** n Schande f.

infancy ['infənsi] n frühe Kindheit f. **be still in its infancy** noch in den Kinderschuhen stecken. **infant** (*baby*) Säugling m; (*small child*) Kleinkind neut. **infantile** adj kindisch.

infantry ['infəntri] n Infanterie f. **infantryman** n Infanterist m.

infatuated [in'fatjueitid] adj vernarrt (in). **infatuation** n Vernarrtheit f.

infect [in'fekt] v infizieren, anstecken. **infection** n Infizierung f, Ansteckung f. **infectious** adj ansteckend.

infer [in'fəɪ] v folgern. **inference** n (conclusion) Schlußfolgerung f.

inferior [in'fiəɾiə] adj minderwertig. **inferiority** n Minderwertigkeit f. **inferiority complex** Minderwertigkeitskomplex m.

infernal [in'fəɪnl] adj höllisch; (coll) verdammt. **inferno** n Inferno neut.

infertile [in'fəɪtail] adj unfruchtbar. **infertility** n Unfruchtbarkeit f.

infest [in'fest] v heimsuchen, plagen. **infestation** n Plage f.

infidelity [,infi'deliti] n Untreue f.

infiltrate [in'filˌtreit] v einsickern in; (pol) unterwandern. **infiltration** n Einsickern neut; Unterwanderung f. **infiltrator** n Unterwanderer m.

infinite ['infinit] adj unendlich. **infinity** n Unendlichkeit f. **infinitesimal** adj winzig.

infinitive [in'finitiv] n (gramm) Infinitiv m, Nennform f.

infirm [in'fəɪm] adj schwach. **infirmary** n Krankenhaus neut. **infirmity** n Krankheit f.

inflame [in'fleim] v entzünden; (fig) erregen. **inflamed** (med) entzündet. **inflammable** adj brennbar. **inflammation** n Entzündung f. **inflammatory** adj (fig) aufrührerisch.

inflate [in'fleit] v aufblasen; (price) übermäßig steigern. **inflatable** adj aufblasbar. **inflated** adj aufgebläht; (fig) aufgeblasen; (price) überhöht. **inflation** n Aufgeblasenheit; (comm) Inflation f. **inflationary** adj inflationistisch.

inflection [in'flekʃən] n Biegung f; (of voice) Modulation f.

inflict [in'flikt] v (blow) versetzen; (pain) zufügen; (burden) aufbürden. **infliction** n Zufügung f; (burden) Last f.

influence ['influəns] n Einfluß m; (power) Macht f. v beeinflussen, Einfluß ausüben auf. **influential** adj einflußreich.

influenza [,influ'enzə] n Grippe f.

influx ['inflʌks] n Zustrom m.

inform [in'foɪm] v benachrichtigen, unterrichten. **inform against** anzeigen.

informal [in'foɪml] adj informell. **informality** n Ungezwungenheit f.

information [,infə'meiʃən] n Auskunft f, Information f, Nachricht f; (data) Angaben pl. **information bureau** Auskunftsbüro neut. **informative** adj lehrreich. **informed** adj informiert. **informer** n Angeber(in).

infra-red [,infrə'red] adj infrarot.

infringe [in'frindʒ] v verstoßen gegen; (rights) verletzen. **infringement** n Verletzung f.

infuriate [in'fjuəriˌeit] v wütend machen. **infuriated** adj wütend.

ingenious [in'dʒiɪnjəs] adj (person) erfinderisch; (device) raffiniert. **ingenuity** n Erfindungsgabe f.

ingot ['iŋgət] n Barren m.

ingrained [in'greind] adj tief eingewurzelt.

ingredient [in'griɪdjənt] n Zutat f.

inhabit [in'habit] v bewohnen. **inhabitable** adj bewohnbar. **inhabitant** n Einwohner(in).

inhale [in'heil] v einatmen. **inhalation** n Einatmung f.

inherent [in'hiərənt] adj angeboren.

inherit [in'herit] v erben. **inheritance** n Erbe neut. **inherited** adj ererbt. **inheritor** n Erbe m, Erbin f.

inhibit [in'hibit] v hemmen; (prevent) hindern. **inhibition** n Hemmung f.

inhospitable [inhə'spitəbl] adj ungastlich.

inhuman [in'hjuɪmən] adj unmenschlich. **inhumanity** n Unmenschlichkeit f.

iniquitous [i'nikwətəs] adj (unjust) ungerecht; (sinful) frevelhaft. **iniquity** n Ungerechtigkeit f, (sin) Sünde f.

initial [i'niʃl] adj anfänglich, Anfangs-. n Anfangsbuchstabe m. **initials** pl n Monogramm neut. **initially** adv am Anfang.

initiate [i'niʃiˌeit] v einführen (in); (start) beginnen. n Eingeweihte(r). **initiation** n Einweihung f.

initiative [i'niʃiətiv] n Initiative f. **take the initiative** die Initiative ergreifen. **initiator** n Anstifter m.

inject [in'dʒekt] v einspritzen. **injection** n give/have an injection eine Spritze geben/bekommen.

injure ['indʒə] v verletzen. **injured party** Geschädigte(r). **injurious** adj schädlich. **injury** n Verletzung f, Wunde f.

injustice [in'dʒʌstis] n Unrecht neut, Ungerechtigkeit f.

ink [iŋk] n Tinte f, Tusche f. **inkblot** n Tintenklecks m. **inkwell** n Tintenfaß neut.

inkling ['iŋkliŋ] n Ahnung f.

inland ['inlənd] adj Binnen-. **Inland Revenue** Steuerbehörde f.

in-laws ['inˌlɔːs] pl n angeheiratete Verwandte pl. **daughter-in-law** Schwiegertochter f. **father-in-law**

Schwiegervater *m.* **mother-in-law** Schwiegermutter *f.* **son-in-law** Schwiegersohn *m.*

***inlay** ['inlei] *v* einlegen. *n* eingelegte Arbeit *f*; *(dentistry)* Plombe *f.*

inlet ['inlet] *n* Meeresarm *m.*

inmate ['inmeit] *n* Insasse *m,* Insassin *f.*

inn [in] *n* Gasthof *m,* Wirtshaus *neut.* **innkeeper** *n* Gastwirt(in).

innate [,i'neit] *adj* angeboren. **innately** *adv* von Natur.

inner ['inə] *adj* inner, Innen-. **innermost** *adj* innerst.

innocent ['inəsnt] *adj* unschuldig, schuldlos. **innocence** *n* Unschuld *f,* Schuldlosigkeit *f.*

innocuous [i'nokjuəs] *adj* harmlos, unschädlich.

innovation [inə'veiʃən] *n* Neuerung *f.* **innovator** *n* Neuerer *m.*

innuendo [,inju'endou] *n* Stichelei *f.*

innumerable [i'njuːmərəbl] *adj* zahllos, unzählig.

inoculate [i'nokju,leit] *v* (ein)impfen. **inoculation** *n* Impfung *f.*

inorganic [,inoː'ganik] *adj* unorganisch.

input ['input] *n* Eingabe *f,* Input *m.*

inquest ['inkwest] *n* gerichtliche Untersuchung *f.*

inquire [in'kwaiə] *v* sich erkundigen (nach). **inquiry** *n* Anfrage *f*; *(examination)* Untersuchung *f,* Prüfung *f.* **inquiry office** Auskunftsbüro *neut.*

inquisition [,inkwi'ziʃən] *n* Untersuchung *f*; *(rel)* Ketzergericht *neut.*

inquisitive [in'kwizətiv] *adj* neugierig.

insane [in'sein] *adj* geisteskrank; *(coll)* verrückt. **insanity** *n* Geisteskrankheit *f.*

insatiable [in'seiʃəbl] *adj* unersättlich. **insatiability** *n* Unersättlichkeit *f.*

inscribe [in'skraib] *v* (auf)schreiben. **inscription** *n* Beschriftung *f*; *(in book)* Widmung *f.*

insect ['insekt] *n* Insekt *neut.* **insecticide** *n* Insektizid *neut.*

insecure [,insi'kjuə] *adj* unsicher. **insecurity** *n* Unsicherheit *f.*

inseminate [in'semineit] *v* befruchten. **insemination** *n* Befruchtung *f.*

insensible [in'sensəbl] *adj* gefühllos; *(unconscious)* bewußtlos.

insensitive [in'sensətiv] *adj* unempfindlich. **insensitivity** *n* Unempfindlichkeit *f.*

inseparable [in'sepərəbl] *adj* untrennbar.

insert [in'səːt; *n* 'insəːt] *v* einfügen, einsetzen. *n* Beilage *f.* **insertion** *n* Einsatz *m.*

inshore [,in'ʃoː] *adj* Küsten-. *adv* zur Küste hin.

inside [,in'said] *adj* inner, Innen-. *adv (be)* drinnen; *(go)* nach innen. *prep* in, innerhalb; *(into)* in ... hinein. *n* Innenseite *f,* Innere *neut.* **insides** *(intestines)* Eingeweide *pl.*

insidious [in'sidiəs] *adj* heimtückisch.

insight ['insait] *n* Einblick *m*; *(understanding)* Verständnis *neut.*

insignificant [,insig'nifikənt] *adj* unbedeutend, unwichtig. **insignificance** *n* Bedeutungslosigkeit *f.*

insincere [,insin'siə] *adj* unaufrichtig. **insincerity** *n* Unaufrichtigkeit *f.*

insinuate [in'sinjueit] *v* zu verstehen geben, andeuten. **insinuation** *n* Andeutung *f.*

insipid [in'sipid] *adj* fade.

insist [in'sist] *v* bestehen (auf). **insistence** *n* Bestehen *neut.* **insistent** *adj* beharrlich.

insolent ['insələnt] *adj* unverschämt, frech. **insolence** *n* Unverschämtheit *f,* Frechheit *f.*

insoluble [in'soljubl] *adj* unauflöslich; *(problem)* unlösbar.

insolvent [in'solvənt] *adj* zahlungsunfähig.

insomnia [in'somniə] *n* Schlaflosigkeit *f.*

inspect [in'spekt] *v* untersuchen, besichtigen. **inspection** *n* Untersuchung *f,* Besichtigung *f.* **inspector** *n* Inspektor *m.*

inspire [in'spaiə] *v* inspirieren, begeistern; *(give rise to)* anregen. **inspiration** *n* Inspiration *f,* Anregung *f.* **inspiring** *adj* anregend.

instability [,instə'biləti] *n* Unbeständigkeit *f.*

install [in'stoːl] *v* einsetzen, einrichten. **installation** *n* Einrichtung *f.*

instalment [in'stoːlmənt] *n* Rate *f.* **instalment plan** Teilzahlungssystem *neut.*

instance ['instəns] *n (case)* Fall *f*; *(example)* Beispiel *neut.* **for instance** zum Beispiel (z.B.).

instant ['instənt] *n* Augenblick *m. adj* sofortig. **instant coffee** Pulverkaffee *m.* **instantaneous** *adj* augenblicklich. **instantly** *adv* sofort.

instead [in'sted] *adv* statt dessen. **instead of** (an)statt (+*gen*).

instep ['instep] *n* Rist *m*, Spann *m*.
instigate ['instigeit] *v* anstiften. **instigation** *n* Anstiftung *f*. **instigator** *n* Anstifter(in).
instil [in'stil] *v* (*teach*) beibringen (+ *dat*).
instinct ['instiŋkt] *n* (Natur)Trieb *m*, Instinkt *m*. **instinctive** *adj* instinktiv; (*automatic*) unwillkürlich.
institute ['institjuːt] *n* Institut *neut*. *v* einführen; (*found*) gründen. **institution** *n* Institut *neut*; (*home*) Anstalt *f*; (*foundation*) Stiftung *f*.
instruct [in'strʌkt] *v* unterweisen; (*teach*) unterrichten. **instruction** *n* Vorschrift *f*; (*teaching*) Unterrichtung *f*. **instructive** *adj* lehrreich. **instructor** *n* Lehrer(in). **instructions for use** Gebrauchsanweisung *f*.
instrument ['instrəmənt] *n* Instrument *neut*; (*tool*) Werkzeug *neut*; (*means*) Mittel *neut*. **instrumental** *adj* (*helpful*) förderlich. **be instrumental in** durchsetzen.
insubordinate [ˌinsə'boːdənət] *adj* widersetzlich. **insubordination** *n* Widersetzlichkeit *f*.
insufficient [ˌinsə'tiʃənt] *adj* unzureichend. **insufficiency** *n* Unzulänglichkeit *f*.
insular ['insjulə] *adj* insular. **insularity** *n* Beschränktheit *f*.
insulate ['insjuleit] *v* isolieren. **insulation** *n* Isolierung *f*. **insulating tape** Isolierband *neut*.
insulin ['insjulin] *n* Insulin *neut*.
insult [in'sʌlt; *n* 'insʌlt] *v* beleidigen, beschimpfen. *n* Beleidigung *f*. **insulting** *adj* beleidigend.
insure [in'ʃuə] *v* versichern. **insurance** *n* Versicherung *f*. **insurance broker** Versicherungsmakler *m*. **insurance policy** Versicherungspolice *f*. **insurance premium** Versicherungsprämie *f*.
insurmountable [ˌinsə'mauntəbl] *adj* unüberwindlich.
insurrection [ˌinsə'rekʃən] *n* Aufstand *m*.
intact [in'takt] *adj* unberührt.
intake ['inteik] *n* Aufnahme *f*, Einlaß *m*.
intangible [in'tandʒəbl] *adj* unfaßbar.
integral ['intigrəl] *adj* wesentlich; (*math*) Integral-.
integrate ['intigreit] *v* integrieren; (*people*) eingliedern. **integration** *n* Integration *f*; Eingliederung *f*. **integrity** *n* Integrität *f*; (*completeness*) Vollständigkeit *f*.
intellect ['intilekt] *n* Intellekt *m*. **intellectual** *adj* intellektuell; *n* Intellektuelle(r).

intelligent [in'telidʒənt] *adj* intelligent.
intelligence *n* Intelligenz *f*; (*information*) Information *f*; (*secret service*) Geheimdienst *m*.
intelligible [in'telidʒəbl] *adj* verständlich, klar.
intend [in'tend] *v* beabsichtigen, die Absicht haben.
intense [in'tens] *adj* stark, intensiv; (*colour*) tief; (*person*) ernsthaft. **intensely** *adv* (*highly*) äußerst. **intensify** *v* verstärken. **intensity** *n* Stärke *f*. **intensive** *adj* intensiv.
intent¹ [in'tent] *n* Absicht *f*, Vorsatz *m*. **to all intents and purposes** im Grunde.
intent² [in'tent] *adj* intent **on** versessen auf.
intention [in'tenʃən] *n* Absicht *f*; (*plan*) Vorhaben *neut*; (*aim*) Ziel *neut*; (*meaning*) Sinn *m*. **intentional** *adj* absichtlich.
inter [in'təː] *v* beerdigen. **interment** *n* Beerdigung *f*.
interact [ˌintər'akt] *v* aufeinander wirken. **interaction** *n* Wechselwirkung *f*.
intercede [ˌintə'siːd] *v* sich verwenden (bei). **intercession** *n* Fürsprache *f*.
intercept [ˌintə'sept] *v* abfangen. **interception** *n* Abfangen *neut*.
interchange [ˌintə'tʃaindʒ] *n* Austausch *m*; (*roads*) (Autobahn) Kreuz/Dreieck *neut*. *v* austauschen.
intercom [ˌintə,kom] *n* Sprechanlage *f*.
intercourse ['intəkoːs] *n* Verkehr *m*, Umgang *m*. **sexual intercourse** Geschlechtsverkehr *m*.
interest ['intrist] *n* Interesse *neut*; (*comm*) Zinsen *pl*; (*advantage*) Vorteil *m*. **interested** *adj* interessiert; (*biased*) beteiligt.
interfere [ˌintə'fiə] *v* (*person*) sich einmischen; (*adversely affect*) stören. **interference** *n* Einmischung *f*; Störung *f*. **interfering** *adj* lästig, störend.
interim [in'tərim] *n* Zwischenzeit *f*. *adj* vorläufig.
interior [in'tiəriə] *n* Innere *neut*. *adj* inner, Binnen-.
interjection [ˌintə'dʒekʃən] *n* Ausruf *m*; (*gramm*) Interjektion *f*.
interlock [ˌintə'lok] *v* ineinandergreifen. **interlocking** *adj* verzahnt.
interlude ['intəluːd] *n* (*interval*) Pause *f*.
intermediate [ˌintə'miːdiət] *adj* Zwischen-.
intermediary *n* Vermittler *m*.
interminable [in'təːminəbl] *adj* endlos.

intermission [,intə'miʃən] *n* Pause *f.* Unterbrechung *f.* **without intermission** pausenlos.

intermittent [,intə'mitənt] *adj* stoßweise, periodisch.

intern [in'tɜɪn] *v* internieren. *n* Assistentenarzt *m.* **internment** *n* Internierung *f.*

internal [in'tɜɪnl] *adj* inner; (*domestic*) Innen-, Inlands-; (*within organization*) intern.

international [,intə'naʃənl] *adj* international.

interpose [,intə'pouz] *v* dazwischenstellen. **interposition** *n* Zwischenstellung *f.*

interpret [in'tɜɪprit] *v* dolmetschen; (*explain*) auslegen; (*theatre, music*) interpretieren. **interpreter** *n* Dolmetscher(in); Interpret(in). **interpretation** *n* Dolmetschen *neut*; Auslegung *f*; Interpretation *f.*

interrogate [in'terəgeit] *v* verhören. **interrogation** *n* Verhör *neut.* **interrogator** *n* Fragesteller *m.*

interrogative [,intə'rogətiv] *adj* fragend; (*gramm*) Frage-. *n* (*gramm*) Interrogativ *m.*

interrupt [,intə'rʌpt] *v* unterbrechen. **interruption** *n* Unterbrechung *f.*

intersect [,intə'sekt] *v* schneiden. **intersection** *n* Kreuzungspunkt *m*; (*mot*) Kreuzung *f.*

intersperse [,intə'spɜɪs] *v* verstreuen.

interval ['intəvəl] *n* Zwischenraum *m*; (*break*) Pause *f*; (*timespan*) Abstand *m*; (*music*) Tonabstand *m.*

intervene [,intə'viɪn] *v* (*interfere*) eingreifen; (*come between*) dazwischentreten. **intervention** *n* Intervention *f*, Eingreifen *neut.*

interview ['intəvjuɪ] *n* Interview *neut. v* interviewen. **interviewee** *n* Interviewte(r). **interviewer** *n* Interviewer *m.*

intestine [in'testin] *n* Darm *m.* **intestines** *pl* Eingeweide *pl.* **intestinal** *adj* Darm-.

intimate¹ ['intimət] *adj* vertraut. **intimacy** *n* Vertrautheit *f.*

intimate² ['intimeit] *v* andeuten. **intimation** *n* Andeutung *f*, Wink *m.*

intimidate [in'timideit] *v* einschüchtern. **intimidation** *n* Einschüchterung *f.*

into ['intu] *prep* in (+ *acc*) hinein/herein. **be into** (*coll*) sich interessieren für. **get into** (*difficulties, etc.*) geraten in. **look into** (*investigate*) untersuchen.

intolerable [in'tolərəbl] *adj* unerträglich.

intolerant [in'tolərənt] *adj* intolerant. **intolerance** *n* Intoleranz *f.*

intonation [,intə'neiʃən] *n* Intonation *f.* **intone** *v* intonieren.

intoxicate [in'toksikeit] *v* berauschen. **intoxicated** *adj* berauscht; (*drunk*) betrunken. **intoxication** *n* Rausch *m.*

intransitive [in'transitiv] *adj* (*gramm*) intransitiv.

intravenous [,intrə'viɪnəs] *adj* intravenös.

intrepid [in'trepid] *adj* unerschrocken.

intricate ['intriket] *adj* kompliziert. **intricacy** *n* Kompliziertheit *f.*

intrigue ['intriɪg; *v* in'triɪg] *n* Intrige *f. v* faszinieren; (*plot*) intrigieren. **intriguing** *adj* faszinierend.

intrinsic [in'trinsik] *adj* wesentlich.

introduce [,intrə'djuɪs] *v* einführen; (*person*) vorstellen. **introduction** *n* Einführung *f*; (*in book*) Einleitung *f*, Vorwort *neut*; Vorstellung *f.* **introductory** *adj* einleitend. **letter of introduction** Empfehlungsbrief *m.*

introspective [,intrə'spektiv] *adj* selbstprüfend. **introspection** *n* Selbstprüfung *f.*

introvert ['intrə,vɜɪt] *n* introvertierter Mensch *m.* **introverted** *adj* introvertiert.

intrude [in'truɪd] *v* hineindrängen; (*interfere*) sich einmischen. **intruder** *n* Eindringling *m.* **intrusion** *n* Eindrängen *neut*; Einmischung *f.* **intrusive** *adj* zudringlich; (*nuisance*) lästig.

intuition [,intjuɪ'iʃən] *n* Intuition *f.* **intuitive** *adj* intuitiv.

inundate ['inʌndeit] *v* überschwemmen. **inundation** *n* Überschwemmung *f*; Flut *f.*

invade [in'veid] *v* überfallen. **invader** *n* Eindringling *m.* **invasion** *n* Einfall *m*, Invasion *f.*

invalid¹ ['invəlid] *n* Kranke(r), Invalide *m.* **invalid²** [in'valid] *adj* ungültig. **invalidate** *v* fürungültig erklären. **invalidation** *n* Ungültigkeitserklärung *f.* **invalidity** *n* Ungültigkeit *f.*

invaluable [in'valjuəbl] *adj* unschätzbar.

invariable [in'veəriəbl] *adj* konstant, unveränderlich. **invariably** *adv* ausnahmslos.

invective [in'vektiv] *n* Beschimpfung *f.*

invent [in'vent] *v* erfinden. **invention** *n* Erfindung *f.* **inventor** *n* Erfinder(in).

inventory ['invəntri] *n* Inventar *neut.* Bestandsverzeichnis *neut*; (*stocktaking*) Bestandsaufnahme *f.*

invert [in'vɔːt] v umkehren. **inversion** n Umkehrung f.

invertebrate [in'vɔːtibrət] adj wirbellos. n wirbelloses Tier neut.

invest [in'vest] v investieren, anlegen. **investment** n Investition f, Anlage f. **investor** n Kapitalanleger m.

investigate [in'vestigeit] v untersuchen. **investigation** n Untersuchung f. **investigator** n Prüfer(in).

invigorating [in'vigəreitiŋ] adj stärkend.

invincible [in'vinsəbl] adj unüberwindlich. **invincibility** n Unüberwindlichkeit f.

invisible [in'vizəbl] adj unsichtbar. **invisibility** n Unsichtbarkeit f.

invite [in'vait] v einladen. **invitation** n Einladung f. **inviting** adj verlockend.

invoice ['invois] n Rechnung f. v in Rechnung stellen.

invoke [in'vouk] v anrufen. **invocation** n Anrufung f.

involuntary [in'vɔləntəri] adj unwillkürlich; (unintentional) unabsichtlich.

involve [in'vɔlv] v (entail) mit sich bringen; (draw into) hineinziehen. **involved** adj verwickelt. **involvement** n Verwicklung f; Rolle f.

inward ['inwəd] adj inner. adv also **inwards** nach innen. **inwardly** adv im Innern.

iodine ['aiədiːn] n Jod neut.

ion ['aiən] n Ion neut.

irate [ai'reit] adj wütend.

Ireland ['aiələnd] n Irland neut. **Irish** adj irisch. **Irishman/woman** n Irländer(in), Ire m, Irin f.

iris ['aiəris] n (eye) Iris f; (flower) Schwertlilie f.

irk [əːk] v ärgern. **irksome** adj ärgerlich.

iron ['aiən] n Eisen neut; (ironing) Bügeleisen neut. adj eisern. v bügeln. **Iron Curtain** Eiserner Vorhang m. **ironing board** n Bügelbrett neut. **ironmonger** n Eisenwarenhändler m.

irony ['aiərəni] n Ironie f. **ironic** adj ironisch.

irrational [i'raʃənl] adj unlogisch; (unreasonable) unvernünftig. **irrationality** n Unvernunft f.

irredeemable [iri'diːməbl] adj untilgbar; (beyond improvement) unverbesserlich.

irregular [i'regjulə] adj unregelmäßig. **irregularity** n Unregelmäßigkeit f.

irrelevant [i'reləvənt] adj belanglos. **irrelevance** n Belanglosigkeit f.

irreparable [i'repərəbl] adj nicht wiedergutzumachen.

irresistible [iri'zistəbl] adj unwiderstehlich.

irrespective [iri'spektiv] adj abgesehen (von), ohne Rücksicht (auf).

irresponsible [iri'spɔnsəbl] adj unverantwortlich, verantwortungslos. **irresponsibility** n Unverantwortlichkeit f, Verantwortungslosigkeit f.

irrevocable [i'revəkəbl] adj unwiderruflich.

irrigate ['irigeit] v bewässern. **irrigation** n Bewässerung f.

irritate ['iriteit] v reizen. **irritable** adj reizbar. **irritant** n Reizmittel neut. **irritation** n Reizung f.

Islam ['izlaim] n Islam m. **Islamic** adj islamisch.

island ['ailənd] n Insel f. **islander** n Inselbewohner(in).

isolate ['aisəleit] v isolieren. **isolated** adj abgesondert; (lonely) einsam. **isolated case** Einzelfall m. **isolation** n Isolierung f; Einsamkeit f. **isolationism** n Isolationismus m.

issue ['iʃuː] n Frage f; (newspaper) Ausgabe f; (offspring) Nachkommenschaft f. v ausgeben; (orders) erteilen.

isthmus ['isməs] n Landenge f.

it [it] pron (nom, acc) es; (dat) ihm.

italic [i'talik] adj kursiv. **italics** pl n Kursivschrift f sing. **in italics** kursiv gedruckt.

Italy ['itəli] n Italien neut. **Italian** adj italienisch; n Italiener(in).

itch [itʃ] v jucken. n Jucken neut.

item ['aitəm] n Gegenstand m; (on agenda) Punkt m; (in newspaper) Artikel m. **itemize** v verzeichnen.

itinerary [ai'tinərəri] n Reiseplan m.

its [its] poss adj sein, ihr. **itself** pron sich; selbst. **by itself** von selbst.

ivory ['aivəri] n Elfenbein neut.

ivy ['aivi] n Efeu m.

J

jab [dʒab] n Stoß m, Stich m; (coll: injection) Spritze f. v Stechen.

jack [dʒak] n (mot) (Wagen)Heber m; (cards) Bube m. v **jack up** aufbocken.

jackal ['dʒakɔɪl] n Schakal m.

jackdaw ['dʒakdɔɪ] n Dohle f.

jacket ['dʒakit] n Jacke f; (book) (Schutz)Umschlag m.

jack-knife ['dʒaknaif] n Klappmesser neut.

jackpot ['dʒakpot] n Jackpot m.

jade [dʒeid] n Nephrit m, Jade m.

jaded ['dʒeidid] adj erschöpft, abgemattet.

jagged ['dʒagid] adj zackig.

jaguar ['dʒagjuə] n Jaguar m.

jail [dʒeil] n Gefängnis neut. v ins Gefängnis werfen, einsperren. **jailer** n (Gefängnis)Wärter m.

jam[1] [dʒam] v einklemmen, verstopfen. **jam on the brakes** heftig auf die Bremse treten. **jam-packed** adj vollgestopft. n Engpaß m, Klemme f. **traffic jam** (Verkehrs)Stockung f.

jam[2] [dʒam] n Marmelade f.

janitor ['dʒanitə] n Hauswart m, Pförtner m.

January ['dʒanjuəri] n Januar m.

Japan [dʒə'pan] n Japan neut. **Japanese** adj japanisch; n Japaner(in).

jar[1] [dʒaɪ] n Glass neut.

jar[2] [dʒaɪ] v kreischen. **jar on one's nerves** einem auf die Nerven gehen. **jarring** adj mißtönend.

jargon ['dʒaɪgən] n Jargon m, Kauderwelsch neut.

jasmine ['dʒazmin] n Jasmin m.

jaundice ['dʒɔɪndis] n Gelbsucht f. **jaundiced** adj gelbsüchtig; (fig) neidisch, voreingenommen.

jaunt [dʒɔɪnt] n Ausflug m. v einen Ausflug machen. **jaunty** adj lebhaft, flott.

javelin ['dʒavəlin] n Speer m.

jaw [dʒɔɪ] n Kiefer m. **jawbone** n Kinnbacken m.

jazz [dʒaz] n Jazz m. **jazz band** Jazzkapelle f.

jealous ['dʒeləs] adj eifersüchtig. **jealousy** n Eifersucht f.

jeans [dʒiɪns] pl n Jeans pl.

jeep [dʒiɪp] n Jeep m.

jeer [dʒiə] v spotten. **jeer at** verspotten. **jeering** adj höhnisch.

jelly ['dʒeli] n Gelee neut. **jellyfish** n Qualle f.

jeopardize ['dʒepədaiz] v gefährden. **jeopardy** n Gefahr f.

jerk [dʒɔɪk] v stoßen, rücken. n Ruck m, Stoß m. **jerkily** adv stoßweise.

jersey ['dʒɔɪzi] n Pullover m; (fabric) Jersey m.

Jerusalem [dʒə'ruɪsələm] n Jerusalem neut.

jest [dʒest] n Scherz m. v scherzen. **jesting** adj scherzhaft. **jestingly** adv in Spaß.

jet [dʒet] n (liquid) Strahl m; (tech) Düse f; (aero) Düsenflugzeug neut. **jet-black** adj rabenschwarz. **jet engine** Düsenmotor m. **jet-propelled** adj mit Düsenantrieb.

jettison ['dʒetisn] v abwerfen; (discard) wegwerfen.

jetty ['dʒeti] n Landungssteg m, Mole f.

Jew [dʒuɪ] n Jude m, Judin f. **Jewish** adj jüdisch.

jewel ['dʒuɪəl] n Edelstein m, Juwel neut; (fig) Perle f. **jeweller** n Juwelier m. **jewellery** n Schmuck m.

jig [dʒig] n Gigue f. v eine Gigue tanzen.

jigsaw ['dʒigsɔɪ] n Puzzlespiel neut, Geduldspiel neut.

jilt [dʒilt] v sitzenlassen.

jingle ['dʒiŋgl] n (sound) Geklingel neut; (radio, etc.) Werbelied neut. v klingeln.

jinx [dʒiŋks] n Unheil neut. v verhexen.

job [dʒob] n Arbeit f; (post) Stelle f; (task) Aufgabe f. **jobless** adj arbeitslos.

jockey ['dʒoki] n Jockei m.

jocular ['dʒokjulə] adj scherzhaft.

jodhpurs ['dʒodpəz] pl n Reithose f.

jog [dʒog] v stoßen; (run) trotten. n Stoß m. **jog trot** n Trott m.

join [dʒoin] v verbinden, vereinigen; (club, etc.) beitreten (+dat). (come together) zusammenkommen. n Verbindungsstelle f; (seam) Naht f. **join in** mitmachen. **joiner** n. Tischler m. **joinery** n Tischlerarbeit f.

joint [dʒoint] n (anat) Gelenk neut; Verbindung f; (cookery) Braten m; (slang: place) Lokal neut. adj Gesamt-. **jointed** adj gegliedert. **jointly** adv gemeinsam.

joist [dʒoist] n Querbalken m, Träger m.

joke [dʒouk] n Witz m, Scherz m. v scherzen. n Spaßvogel m; (cards) Joker m. **jokingly** adv im Spaß.

jolly ['dʒoli] adj lustig. **jolliness** n Lustigkeit f.

jolt [dʒoult] *n* Stoß *m. v* stoßen.
jostle ['dʒosl] *v* anstoßen. *n* Stoß *m.*
jot [dʒot] *n* Jota *neut. v* **jot down** notieren.
journal ['dʒəɪnl] *n* Zeitschrift *f; (diary)* Tagebuch *neut.* **journalism** *n* Zeitungswesen *neut.* **journalist** *n* Journalist(in).
journey ['dʒəɪni] *n* Reise *f. v* (ver)reisen.
jovial ['dʒouviəl] *adj* lustig, jovial. **joviality** *n* Lustigkeit *f.*
joy [dʒoi] *n* Freude *f,* Wonne *f.* **joyful** *adj* erfreut. **joyfulness** *n* Fröhlichkeit *f.*
jubilant ['dʒuːbilənt] *adj* jubelnd, frohlockend. **jubilation** *n* Jubel *m,* Frohlocken *neut.*
jubilee ['dʒuːbiliː] *n* Jubiläum *neut; (celebration)* Jubelfest *neut.*
Judaism ['dʒuːdeiˌizəm] *n* Judentum *neut.*
judge [dʒʌdʒ] *n (law)* Richter; *(expert)* Kenner *m. v* beurteilen; *(value)* (ein)schätzen. **judgment** *n* Beurteilung *f; (law)* Urteil *neut.*
judicial [dʒuːˈdiʃəl] *adj* gerichtlich. **judiciary** *n* Gerichtswesen *neut.*
judicious [dʒuːˈdiʃəs] *adj* wohlüberlegt; *(reasonable)* vernünftig.
judo ['dʒuːdou] *n* Judo *neut.*
jug [dʒʌg] *n* Krug *m,* Kanne *f.*
juggernaut ['dʒʌgənoɪt] *n* Moloch *m; (mot)* Fernlastwagen *m.*
juggle ['dʒʌgl] *v* jonglieren. **juggler** *n* Jongleur *m.*
jugular ['dʒʌgjulə] *n* Drosselader *f.*
juice [dʒuːs] *n* Saft *m.* **juicy** *adj* saftig.
jukebox ['dʒuːkbɒks] *n* Jukebox *f.*
July [dʒuˈlai] *n* Juli *m.*
jumble ['dʒʌmbl] *n* Durcheinander *neut. v* durcheinander bringen. **jumble sale** Basar *m,* Ramschverkauf *m.*
jump [dʒʌmp] *n* Sprung *m. v* springen; *(be startled)* zusammenzucken. **jump at the chance** die Gelegenheit ergreifen. **jumpy** *adj* nervös.
jumper ['dʒʌmpə] *n* Pullover *m.*
junction ['dʒʌŋkʃən] *n (road)* Kreuzung *f; (rail)* Knotenpunkt *m.*
juncture ['dʒʌŋkʃə] *n* Augenblick *m.* **at this juncture** an dieser Stelle.
June [dʒuːn] *n* Juni *m.*
jungle ['dʒʌŋgl] *n* Dschungel *m.*
junior ['dʒuːnjə] *adj* junior, jünger. **junior school** Grundschule *f.*
juniper ['dʒuːnipə] *n* Wacholder *m.*
junk¹ [dʒʌŋk] *n* Trödel *m.* **junk shop** Trödelladen *m.*

junk² [dʒʌŋk] *n (naut)* Dschunke *f.*
junta ['dʒʌntə] *n* Junta *f.*
Jupiter ['dʒuːpitə] *n* Jupiter *m.*
jurisdiction [dʒuərisˈdikʃən] *n* Gerichtsbarkeit *f.*
jury ['dʒuəri] *n* die Geschworene *pl; (quiz, etc.)* Jury *f.* **trial by jury** Schwurgerichtsverhandlung *f.* **juror** *n* Geschworene(r).
just [dʒʌst] *adv (recently)* gerade, eben; *(only)* nur; *(exactly)* genau. **just about** so ungefähr. **just as good** ebenso gut. **just a little** ein ganz klein wenig. *adj* gerecht. **justly** *adv* mit Recht, gerecht.
justice ['dʒʌstis] *n* Gerechtigkeit *f; (judge)* Richter *m.* **Justice of the Peace** Friedensrichter *m.*
justify ['dʒʌstifai] *v* rechtfertigen. **justification** *n* Rechtfertigung *f.* **justifiable** *adj* berechtigt.
jut [dʒʌt] *v* **jut out** hervorragen.
jute [dʒuːt] *n* Jute *f.*
juvenile ['dʒuːvənail] *adj* jugendlich. **juvenile court** Jugendgericht *neut.* **juvenile delinquent** jugendlicher Straftäter *m.* **juvenile delinquency** Jugendkriminalität *f.*
juxtapose [ˌdʒʌkstəˈpouz] *v* nebeneinanderstellen.

K

kaleidoscope [kəˈlaidəskoup] *n* Kaleidoskop *neut.*
kangaroo [kæŋgəˈruː] *n* Känguruh *neut.*
karate [kəˈraːti] *n* Karate *neut.*
kebab [kiˈbab] *n* Kebab *m.*
keel [kiːl] *n* Kiel *m.*
keen [kiːn] *adj (sharp)* scharf; *(hearing)* fein; *(enthusiastic)* eifrig. **keenness** *n* Eifer *f.*
+keep [kiːp] *v* halten, behalten; haben; *(remain)* bleiben; *(preserve, store)* aufbewahren; *(of food)* sich halten; *(support)* versorgen. **keep away** fernhalten. **keep fit** sich gesund erhalten. **keep in mind** im Gedächtnis behalten. **keep on** fortfahren. **keep out!** Eintritt verboten! **keep up with** Schritt halten mit. **keeper** *n* Wächter *m; (animals)* Züchter *m.* **be in keeping with** passen zu. **keepsake** *n* Andenken *neut.*

keg [keg] *n* Faß *neut*.
kennel ['kenl] *n* Hundehütte *f*.
kept [kept] *V* keep.
kerb [kɔːb] *n* Straßenkante *f*.
kernel ['kɔːnl] *n* Kern *m*.
kerosene ['kerəsiːn] *n* Petroleum *neut*.
ketchup ['ketʃəp] *n* Ketchup *m*.
kettle ['ketl] *n* Kessel *m*. **kettledrum** *n* Pauke *f*. **a pretty kettle of fish** eine schöne Bescherung. **a different kettle of fish** was ganz anderes.
key [kiː] *n* Schlüssel *m*; (*piano, typewriter*) Taste *f*; (*music*) Tonart *f*. **keyboard** *n* Tastatur *f*. **keyring** *n* Schlüsselring *m*.
khaki ['kaːki] *adj* khaki.
kick [kik] *v* mit dem Fuß treten *or* stoßen. *n* Fußtritt *m*; (*football*) Schuß *m*; (*fig*) Schwung *m*. **kick-off** *n* Anstoß *m*. **kick off** anstoßen.
kid¹ [kid] *n* (*goat*) Zicklein *neut*; (*leather*) Ziegenleder *neut*; (*child*) Kind *neut*.
kid² [kid] *v* (*coll*) auf den Arm nehmen.
kidnap ['kidnap] *v* entführen. **kidnapper** *n* Entführer *m*, Kidnapper *m*.
kidney ['kidni] *n* Niere *f*. **kidney bean** weiße Bohne *f*. **kidney stone** Nierenstein *m*.
kill [kil] *v* töten, umbringen; (*animals*) schlachten. **kill oneself laughing** sich totlachen. **killer** *n* Mörder *m*. **killing** *n* Tötung *f*. *adj* tötend.
kiln [kiln] *n* Brennofen *m*.
kilo ['kiːlou] *n* Kilo *neut*.
kilogram ['kiləgram] *n* Kilogramm *neut*.
kilometre ['kiləmiːtə] *n* Kilometer *m*.
kin [kin] *n* Verwandte *pl*. **next of kin** nächste(r) Verwandte(r).
kind¹ [kaind] *adj* freundlich, gütig. **kindly** *adj* gütig. **kindness** *n* Güte *f*.
kind² [kaind] *n* Sorte *f*, Art *f*; (*species*) Gattung *f*. **all kinds of** allerlei. **in kind** in Waren.
kindergarten ['kindəgaːtn] *n* Kindergarten *m*, Krippe *f*.
kindle ['kindl] *v* entzünden.
kindred ['kindrid] *n* Verwandschaft *f*.
kinetic [kin'etik] *adj* kinetisch. **kinetics** *n* Kinetik *f*.
king [kiŋ] *n* König *m*. **kingdom** *n* Königreich *neut*. **animal kingdom** Tierreich *neut*.
kink [kiŋk] *n* Knick *m*. *v* knicken.
kiosk ['kiːɔsk] *n* Kiosk *m*. **telephone kiosk** Telephonzelle *f*.

kipper ['kipə] *n* Bückling *m*, Räucherhering *m*.
kiss [kis] *n* Kuß *m*, Küßchen *neut*. *v* küssen. **kiss goodbye** einen Abschiedskuß geben (+*dat*).
kit [kit] *n* Ausrüstung *f*; (*mil*) Gepäck *neut*.
kitchen ['kitʃin] *n* Küche *f*. **kitchenette** *n* Kochnische *f*.
kite [kait] *n* Drachen *m*; (*bird*) Gabelweihe *f*.
kitten ['kitn] *n* Kätzchen *neut*.
kitty ['kiti] *n* Kasse *f*.
kleptomaniac [kleptə'meiniak] *n* Kleptomane *m*.
knack [nak] *n* Kniff *m*, Trick *m*. **get the knack of** den Dreh heraushaben (+*gen*).
knapsack ['napsak] *n* Rucksack *m*.
knave [neiv] *n* Schurke *m*; (*cards*) Bube *m*.
knead [niːd] *v* kneten.
knee [niː] *n* Knie *neut*. **kneecap** *n* Knieschiebe *f*.
***kneel** [niːl] *v* knien.
knelt [nelt] *V* kneel.
knew [njuː] *V* know.
knickers ['nikəz] *pl n* Schlüpfer *m sing*; Höschen *neut sing*.
knife [naif] *n* Messer *neut*. *v* (er)stechen.
knight [nait] *n* Ritter *m*; (*chess*) Springer *m*. **knighthood** Rittertum *neut*. **knightly** *adj* ritterlich.
***knit** [nit] *v* stricken; (*brow*) rünzein. **knitted** *adj* Strick-. **knitting** *n* Strickzeug *neut*. **knitting needle** Stricknadel *f*. **knitwear** *n* Strickwaren *pl*.
knob [nob] *n* Knopf *m*, Griff *m*. **knobbly** ['nobli] *adj* knorrig.
knock [nok] *v* (*strike*) schlagen; (*on door*) klopfen; (*criticize*) heruntermachen. *n* Schlag *m*; Klopfen *neut*. **knock off** (*coll: steal*) klauen; (*work*) Feierabend machen. **knock out** k.o. schlagen.
knot [not] *n* Knoten *m*; (*in wood*) Ast *m*. *v* knoten.
***know** [nou] *v* wissen; (*be acquainted with*) kennen; (*know how to*) können; (*understand*) verstehen. **know-all** Besserwisser *m*. **know-how** *n* Knowhow *neut*. **knowing** *adj* geschickt; (*sly*) schlau. **knowingly** *adv* absichtlich. **be in the know** Bescheid wissen. **known** *adj* bekannt.
knowledge ['nolidʒ] *n* Kenntnis *f*. **knowledgeable** *adj* kenntnisreich.

known [noun] V know.
knuckle ['nʌkl] n Fingerknöchel m.
knuckle down eifrig herangehen. **knuckle under** nachgeben.

L

label ['leibl] n Zettel m; (sticky) Klebezettel neut; (luggage) Anhängezettel neut. v mit einem Zettel versehen; (fig) bezeichnen.
laboratory [lə'borətəri] n Labor neut. **laboratory assistant** Laborant(in).
labour ['leibə] n Arbeit; (work force) Arbeitskräfte pl, (birth) Wehen pl. v (schwer) arbeiten, sich anstrengen. **laboured** adj schwerfällig; (style) mühsam. **labourer** n (ungelernter) Arbeiter m.
laburnum [lə'bəːnəm] n Goldregen m
labyrinth ['labərinθ] n Labyrinth neut.
lace [leis] n Spitze f; (shoe) Schnur f. v schnüren. **lacy** adj Spitzen-.
lacerate ['lasəreit] v zerreißen. **laceration** n Zerreißung f.
lack [lak] v mangeln (an). n Mangel m. **be lacking** fehlen.
lackadaisical [lakə'deizikəl] adj schlapp.
lacquer ['lakə] n Lack m. v lackieren.
lad [lad] n Junge m, Bursche m.
ladder ['ladə] n Leiter f; (stocking) Laufmasche f. **ladder-resistant** adj maschenfest.
laden ['leidn] adj beladen.
ladle ['leidl] n Schöpflöffel m. v ausschöpfen.
lady ['leidi] n Dame f. **Ladies** n (sign) Damen pl. **ladies' man** Frauenheld m.
ladybird Marienkäfer m. **lady-in-waiting** n Hofdame f. **ladylike** adj damenhaft.
lag¹ [lag] v **lag behind** zurückbleiben. n Zeitabstand m.
lag² [lag] v (cover) verkleiden.
lager ['laːgə] n Lagerbier neut.
lagoon [lə'guːn] n Lagune f.
laid [leid] V lay¹.
lain [lein] V lie².
lair [leə] n Lager neut.
laity ['leiəti] n Laienstand m.
lake [leik] n (Binnen)See m
lamb [lam] n Lamm neut; (meat) Lammfleisch neut.

lame [leim] adj lahm, hinkend; (excuse) schwach. v lahm machen. **lameness** n Lahmheit f; Schwäche f.
lament [lə'ment] v (weh)klagen; (regret) bedauern. n Klagelied neut. **lamentable** adj beklagenswert; bedauerlich. **lamentation** n Jammer m.
laminate ['lamineit] v schichten. **laminated** adj beschichtet.
lamp [lamp] n Lampe f; (street) Laterne f. **lamplight** n Lampenlicht neut. **lamppost** n Laternenpfahl m. **lampshade** n Lampenschirm m.
lance [laːns] n Lanze f. v (med) mit einer Lanzette eröffnen, aufstechen. **lance corporal** n Hauptgefreite(r) m.
land [land] n Land neut. v an Land gehen; (aircraft) landen; (goods) abladen. **landing** n Landung f; (stairs) Treppenabsatz m. **landing craft** Landungsboot neut. **landing stage** Landesteg m.
landlady ['landleidi] n Wirtin f.
landlord ['landloːd] n (Gast-)Wirt m.
landmark ['landmaːk] n Wahrzeichen neut; (milestone) Markstein m.
landowner ['landounə] n Grundbesitzer m.
landscape ['landskeip] n Landschaft f. **landscape gardener** Kunstgärtner m. **landscape gardening** Kunstgärtnerei f. **landscape painter** Landschaftsmaler(in)
landslide ['landslaid] n Erdrutsch m. adj (pol) überwältigend.
lane [lein] n (country) (Feld)Weg m, Pfad m; (town) Gasse f; (mot) Spur f. (sport) Rennbahn f.
language ['laŋgwidʒ] n Sprache f; (style) Stil m, Redeweise f. **bad language** Schimpfworte pl. **foreign language** Fremdsprache f.
languish ['laŋgwiʃ] v schmachten.
lanky ['laŋki] adj schlaksig.
lantern ['lantən] n Laterne f.
lap¹ [lap] n (anat) Schoß m; (circuit) Runde f.
lap² [lap] v (drink) auflecken.
lapel [lə'pel] n Revers m or neut.
lapse [laps] n Versehen neut; (mistake) Irrtum m; (time) Zeitspanne f. v (time) vergehen; (from faith) abfallen.
larceny ['laːsəni] n Diebstahl m.
larch [laːtʃ] n Lärche f.

lard [laɪd] *n* Schmalz *neut*. *v* spicken. **larding needle** Sticknadel *f*.

larder ['laɪdə] *n* Speisekammer *f*.

large [laɪdʒ] *adj* groß; (*considerable*) beträchtlich. **at large** auf freiem Fuß *m*. **large as life** in Lebensgröße. **large-scale** *adj* Groß-. **largesse** *n* Freigiebigkeit *f*. **largely** *adv* weitgehend. **largeness** *n* Größe *f*.

lark¹ [laɪk] *n* (*bird*) Lerche *f*.

lark² [laɪk] *n* Spaß *m*. *v* **lark about** Possen treiben.

larva ['laɪvə] *n* Larve *f*. **larval** *adj* Larven-.

larynx ['larɪŋks] *n* Kehlkopf *m*. **laryngitis** *n* Kehlkopfentzündung *f*.

laser ['leɪzə] *n* Laser *m*. **laser beam** Laserstrahl *m*.

lash [laʃ] *v* (*whip*) peitschen; (*tie*) festbinden. *n* Peitschenschnur *f*; (*eyelash*) Wimper *f*. **lash out** ausschlagen.

lass [las] *n* Mädchen *neut*, Mädel *neut*.

lassitude ['lasɪtjuɪd] *n* Mattigkeit *f*.

lasso [la'suɪ] *n* Lasso *m*. *v* mit einem Lasso fangen.

last [laɪst] *adj* letzt. **at last** endlich, schließlich. **last but not least** nicht zuletzt. *last year* im vorigen Jahr. *adv also* **lastly** zuletzt. *v* (*time*) dauern; (*supply*) ausreichen; (*be preserved*) (gut) halten. **lasting** *adj* anhaltend, dauernd.

latch [latʃ] *n* Klinke *f*. *v* einklinken. **latch onto** (*understand*) spitzkriegen.

late [leɪt] *adj* spät; (*tardy*) verspätet; (*deceased*) selig; (*former*) ehemalig. **be late** Verspätung haben. **lately** *adv* neuerdings. **lateness** *n* Verspätung *f*. **later** *adj* später. **latest** *adj* spätest; (*newest*) neuest. **at the latest** spätestens.

latent ['leɪtənt] *adj* latent.

lateral ['latərəl] *adj* seitlich. **laterally** *adv* seitwärts.

lathe [leɪð] *n* Drehbank *f*.

lather ['laɪðə] *n* Seifenschaum *m*. *v* schäumen; (*beat*) verprügeln.

Latin ['latɪn] *adj* lateinisch. *n* Latein *neut*.

Latin America *n* Lateinamerika *neut*. **Latin-American** *adj* lateinamerikanisch.

latitude ['latɪtjuɪd] *n* Breite *f*; (*fig*) Spielraum *m*. **latitudinal** *adj* Breiten-.

latrine [lə'triɪn] *n* Klosett *neut*, Latrine *f*.

latter ['latə] *adj* letzt. **latterly** *adv* neuerdings.

lattice ['latɪs] *n* Gitter *neut*; (*pattern*) Gitterwerk *neut*.

laugh [laɪf] *v* lachen. **laugh at** sich lustig machen über. **laugh off** mit einem Scherz abtun. **laughable** *adj* lächerlich. *n* Lachen *neut*. **laughter** *n* Gelächter *neut*.

launch [loɪntʃ] *n* (*boat*) Barkasse *f*; (*of boat*) Stapellauf *m*; (*of rocket*) Abschuß *m*; (*start*) Start *m*. *v* (*boat*) vom Stapel lassen; (*fig*) in Gang setzen.

launder ['loɪndə] *v* waschen. **launderette** *n* Waschsalon *m*. **laundry** *n* Wäscherei *f*; (*washing*) Wäsche *f*.

laurel ['lorəl] *n* Lorbeer *m*.

lava ['laɪvə] *n* Lava *f*.

lavatory ['lavətəri] *n* Klosett *neut*, Toilette *f*.

lavender ['lavɪndə] *n* Lavendel *m*. *adj* (*colour*) lavendelfarben.

lavish ['lavɪʃ] *adj* verschwenderisch. **lavishness** *n* Verschwendung *f*.

law [loɪ] *n* (*single law*) Gesetz *neut*; (*system*) Recht *neut*; (*study*) Jura *pl*. **law-abiding** *adj* friedlich. **lawcourt** *n* Gerichtshof *m*. **lawful** *adj* rechtmäßig, gesetzlich. **lawless** *adj* gesetzwidrig. **lawsuit** *n* Prozeß *m*. **lawyer** *n* Rechtsanwalt *m*.

lawn [loɪn] *n* Rasen *m*; (*fabric*) Batist *m*. **lawnmower** *n* Rasenmäher *m*. **lawn tennis** Tennis *neut*.

lax [laks] *adj* locker.

laxative ['laksətɪv] *n* Abführmittel *neut*.

***lay¹** [leɪ] *v* legen; (*put down*) setzen, stellen; (*table*) decken. **lay down** hinlegen; (*law*) vorschreiben. **lay off** (*dismiss*) entlassen.

lay² [leɪ] *adj* Laien-. **layman** *n* Laie *m*.

lay-by ['leɪbaɪ] *n* Parkstreifen *m*.

layer ['leɪə] *n* Schicht *f*.

lazy ['leɪzi] *adj* faul. **laze** *v* faulenzen. **laziness** *n* Faulheit *f*. **lazybones** *n* Faulpelz *m*.

***lead¹** [liɪd] *v* leiten, führen. **leader** *n* Führer *m*, Leiter *m*; (*in newspaper*) Leitartikel *m*. **leadership** *n* Führerschaft *f*. **leading** *adj* führend, Haupt-. *n* (*dog's*) Leine *f*; (*theatre*) Hauptrolle *f*; (*cable*) Schnur *f*; (*hint*) Hinweis *m*.

lead² [led] *n* Blei *neut*; (*in pencil*) Bleistiftmine *f*.

leaf [liɪf] *n* Blatt *neut*. **leaflet** *n* (*pamphlet*) Prospekt *m*. *v* **leaf through** durchblättern. **leafy** *adj* belaubt.

league [liɪg] *n* (*association*) Bund *neut*; (*sport*) Liga *f*.

leak [liɪk] *n* Leck *neut*; (*pol*) Durchsickern *neut*. *v* lecken; durchsickern. **leakage** *n* Lecken *neut*. **leaky** *adj* leck.

*lean¹ [liːn] v (sich) lehnen. **lean on** sich stützen auf; (rely on) sich verlassen auf. **leaning** n Neigung f.

lean² [liːn] adj mager.

leant [lent] V **lean¹**

*leap [liːp] v hüpfen, springen. n Sprung m. **look before you leap** erst wägen, dann wagen. **by leaps and bounds** sprunghaft. **leap frog** Bockspringen neut. **leapyear** n Schaltjahr neut.

leapt [lept] V **leap**.

*learn [ləːn] v lernen; (find out) erfahren. **learned** adj gelehrt. **learner** n Anfänger m; (driver) Fahrschüler(in). **learning** n Wissen neut.

learnt [ləːnt] V **learn**.

lease [liːs] n Mietvertrag m, Pachtvertrag m. v (ver)mieten, pachten. **leaseholder** n Pächter(in).

leash [liːʃ] n Leine f.

least [liːst] adj (smallest) kleinst; (slightest) geringst. **at least** mindestens. **not in the least** nicht im geringsten.

leather [ˈleðə] n Leder neut. adj ledern. **leathery** adj lederartig.

*leave¹ [liːv] v verlassen, lassen; (go away) (ab-, ver)reisen, weggehen. **leave off** aufhören. **leave out** ·auslassen. **left-luggage office** Gepäckaufbewahrung f.

leave² [liːv] n (permission) Erlaubnis f; (holiday) Urlaub m. **take one's leave of** Abschied nehmen von.

lecherous [ˈletʃərəs] adj wollustig. **lechery** n Wollust f.

lectern [ˈlektən] n Lesepult neut.

lecture [ˈlektʃə] n Vortrag m, Vorlesung f. v einen Vortrag halten. **lecturer** n Dozent m. **lecture hall** Hörsaal m.

led [led] V **lead¹**.

ledge [ledʒ] n Sims m or neut.

ledger [ˈledʒə] n Hauptbuch neut.

lee [liː] n (naut) Leeseite f.

leech [liːtʃ] n Blutegel m.

leek [liːk] n Porree m.

leer [liə] n anzügliches Grinsen. v anzüglich grinsen.

leeway [ˈliːwei] n Abtrift f; (fig) Spielraum m.

left¹ [left] V **leave¹**.

left² [left] adj link. adv (nach) links, **on the left** links. **left-handed** adj linkshändig. **left-wing** adj Links-.

leg [leg] n Bein neut; (cookery) Keule f; (sport) Lauf m. **be on one's last legs** auf

dem letzten Loch pfeifen. **leggy** adj langbeinig.

legacy [ˈlegəsi] n Legat neut.

legal [ˈliːgəl] adj gesetzlich, rechtlich. **legality** n Gesetzlichkeit f. **legalize** v legalisieren.

legend [ˈledʒənd] n Sage f, Legende f. **legendary** adj sagenhaft, legendär.

legible [ˈledʒəbl] adj leserlich. **legibility** n Leserlichkeit f.

legion [ˈliːdʒən] n Legion f. **legionary** n Legionär m.

legislate [ˈledʒisleit] v Gesetze geben. **legislation** n Gesetzgebung f. **legislative** adj gesetzgebend. **legislator** n Gesetzgeber m.

legitimate [ləˈdʒitimət] adj rechtmäßig; (child) ehelich; (justified) berechtigt. **legitimacy** n Rechtmäßigkeit; Ehelichkeit f.

leisure [ˈleʒə] n Freizeit f. **leisurely** adv ohne Hast.

lemon [ˈlemən] n Zitrone f. adj zitronengelb. **lemonade** n Zitronenlimonade f. **lemon squeezer** Zitronenpresse f.

*lend [lend] v (ver)leihen. **lend a hand** helfen. **lending library** Leihbibliothek f.

length [leŋθ] n Länge f; (of cloth) Stück neut; (time) Dauer f. **at length** (in detail) ausführlich; (at last) schließlich. **lengthen** v (sich) verlängern. **lengthways** adv längs. **lengthy** adj übermäßig lang.

lenient [ˈliːniənt] adj nachsichtig (gegenüber). **leniency** Nachsicht f.

lens [lenz] n Linse f; (photographic) Objektiv neut.

lent [lent] V **lend**.

Lent [lent] n Fastenzeit f.

lentil [ˈlentil] n Linse f.

Leo [ˈliːou] n Löwe m. **leonine** adj Löwen-.

leopard [ˈlepəd] n Leopard m.

leper [ˈlepə] n Leprakranke(r). **leprosy** n Lepra f.

lesbian [ˈlezbiən] adj lesbisch. n Lesbierin f.

less [les] adv weniger. adj geringer. prep minus. **lessen** v (sich) vermindern. **lesser** adj kleiner, geringer.

lesson [ˈlesn] n (in school) Stunde f; (warning) Warnung f. **lessons** pl Unterricht m sing.

lest [lest] conj damit ... nicht.

let

*let [let] *v* lassen; (*rooms, etc.*) vermieten.
let's go gehen wir. **let alone** (*not annoy*)
in Ruhe lassen; (*much less*) geschweige
denn **let down** enttäuschen, im Stich
lassen. **let go** gehen lassen. **let go of** loslassen. **let up** (*coll*) nachlassen.
lethal ['liːθəl] *adj* tödlich.
lethargy ['leθədʒi] *n* Lethargie *f*. **lethargic**
adj lethargisch.
letter ['letə] *n* Brief *m*; (*of alphabet*)
Buchstabe *m*. **letter box** Briefkasten *m*.
lettuce ['letis] *n* Kopfsalat *m*.
leukaemia [luːˈkiːmiə] *n* Leukämie *f*.
level ['levl] *adj* gerade, eben; (*equal*)
gleich. **level crossing** Bahnübergang *m*.
level-headed *adj* nüchtern. **draw level
with** einholen. *v* ebnen; (*make equal*)
gleichmachen. *n* Ebene *f*, Niveau *neut*.
lever ['liːvə] *n* Hebel *m*.
levy ['levi] *n* Abgabe *f*. *v* erheben.
lewd [luːd] *adj* lüstern. **lewdness** *n* Lüs-
ternheit *f*.
liable ['laiəbl] *adj* (*responsible*) verantwortlich. **be liable to** neigen zu. **liability** *n*
Verantwortlichkeit. **limited liability**
(*comm*) mit beschränkter Haftung. **be
liable for** haften für. **liable to prosecution**
strafbar.
liaison [liːˈeizon] *n* Verbindung *f*; (*love
affair*) (Liebes)Verhältnis *neut*.
liar ['laiə] *n* Lügner(in).
libel ['laibəl] *n* Verleumdung *f*. *v* (*schriftlich*) verleumden. **libellous** *adj*
verleumderisch.
liberal ['libərəl] *adj* liberal; (*generous*)
großzügig. *n* Liberale(r). **liberalize** *v*
liberalisieren.
liberate ['libəreit] *v* befreien. **liberation** *n*
Befreiung *f*. **liberator** *n* Befreier *m*.
liberty ['libəti] *n* Freiheit *f*. **at liberty** frei.
Libra ['liːbrə] *n* Waage *f*.
library ['laibrəri] *n* Bibliothek *f*, Bücherei
f. **librarian** *n* Bibliothekar(in).
libretto [liˈbretou] *n* Libretto *neut*,
Textbuch *neut*.
lice [lais] *V* **louse**.
licence ['laisəns] *n* Genehmigung *f*,
Lizenz *f*. **driving licence** Führerschein *m*.
marriage licence Eheerlaubnis *f*. **license** *v*
genehmigen. **licensed** *adj* konzessioniert.
lichen ['laikən] *n* Flechte *f*.
lick [lik] *v* lecken; (*coll: defeat*) besiegen;
(*flames*) züngeln. *n* Lecken *neut*.
lid [lid] *n* Deckel *m*; (*eyelid*) Lid *neut*.

lie¹ [lai] *n* Lüge. *v* lügen.
*lie² [lai] *v* liegen. **lie down** sich hinlegen.
lie in (*coll*) sich ausschlafen.
lieutenant [ləfˈtenənt] *n* Leutnant *m*.
life [laif] *n* Leben *neut*. **lifebelt** *n* Rettungs-
gürtel *m*. **lifeboat** *n* Rettungsboot *neut*.
lifeguard *n* Bademeister *m*. **life insurance**
Lebensversicherung *f*. **life jacket**
Schwimmweste *f*. **lifeless** *adj* leblos. **life-
like** *adj* naturgetreu. **lifesize** *adj* lebens-
groß. **lifetime** *n* Lebenszeit *f*.
lift [lift] *n* Aufzug *m*, Fahrstuhl *m*. *v*
(auf)heben. **give a lift to** (im Auto)
mitnehmen.
*light¹ [lait] *n* Licht *neut*; (*lamp*) Lampe
f. **a light** (*for cigarette*) Feuer *neut*. *v*
anzünden.
light² [lait] *adj* leicht; (*colour*) hell.
lighten¹ ['laitn] *v* (*reduce weight*) erleichtern, leichter machen.
lighten² ['laitn] *v* (*brighten*) sich erhellen,
heller werden.
lighter ['laitə] *n* (*cigarette*) Feuerzeug
neut.
lighthouse ['laithaus] *n* Leuchtturm *m*.
lighting ['laitiŋ] *n* Beleuchtung *f*.
lightning ['laitniŋ] *n* Blitz *m*. **lightning
conductor** Blitzableiter *m*. **flash of lightning** Blitzschlag *m*.
light ['laitweit]**weight** *adj* leicht. *n*
Leichtgewichtler *m*.
light-year ['laitjiə] *n* Lichtjahr *neut*.
like¹ [laik] *adj* gleich (+*dat*), ähnlich
(+*dat*). *prep* wie. **what's it like?** wie ist
es? **like-minded** *adj* gleichgesinnt. **likewise** *adv* gleichfalls.
like² [laik] *v* gern haben; mögen. *do you
like it?* gefällt es Ihnen? (*food*) schmeckt
es (Ihnen)? **likeable** *adj* liebenswürdig.
liking *n* Zuneigung *f*; (*taste*) Geschmack
m.
likely ['laikli] *adj* wahrscheinlich. **likeli-
hood** *n* Wahrscheinlichkeit *f*.
lilac ['lailək] *n* (*colour*) Lila *neut*. *adj*
lilafarben.
lily ['lili] *n* Lilie *f*.
limb [lim] *n* Glied *neut*. **limbs** *pl*
Gliedmaßen *pl*.
limbo ['limbou] *n* (*rel*) Vorhölle *f*. **in limbo** (*fig*) in der Schwebe, in Vergessenheit.
lime¹ [laim] *n* (*mineral*) Kalk *neut*.
lime² [laim] *n* (*tree*) Linde *f*, Lindenbaum
m; (*fruit*) Limonelle *f*.

locate

limit ['limit] n Grenze f, Schranke f. v begrenzen, beschränken. **limited** adj beschränkt; (comm) mit beschränkter Haftung.
limousine ['liməˌziːn] n Limousine f.
limp¹ [limp] v hinken. n Hinken neut.
limp² [limp] adj schlaff.
line [lain] n Linie f, Strich m; (row) Reihe f; (of print) Zeile f; (washing) Leine f; (wrinkle) Falte f. v linieren; (coat, etc.) füttern. **lineage** n Abstammung f. **linear** adj Linear-.
linen ['linin] n Leinen neut. **bed linen** Wäsche f.
liner ['lainə] n (ship) Linienschiff neut, Überseedampfer m.
linesman ['lainzman] n Linienrichter m.
linger ['liŋgə] v verweilen. **lingering** adj (illness) schleichend.
lingerie ['læʒəriː] n (Damen)Unterwäsche f.
linguist ['liŋgwist] n Linguist(in). **linguistic** adj linguistisch. **linguistics** n Linguistik f.
lining ['lainiŋ] n Futter neut, Fütterung f.
link [liŋk] n (of chain) Glied neut; (connection) Verbindung f. v verbinden. **link arms** sich einhaken (bei).
linoleum [li'nouiləm] n Linoleum neut.
linseed ['linˌsiːd] n Leinsamen m. **linseed oil** Leinöl neut.
lint [lint] n Zupfleinen neut.
lion ['laiən] n Löwe m. **lioness** n Löwin f. **lion's share** Löwenanteil m.
lip [lip] n Lippe f; (edge) Rand m; (coll: impudence) Frechheit f. **lip service** Lippendienst m. **lipstick** n Lippenstift m.
liqueur [li'kjuə] n Likör m.
liquid ['likwid] n Flüssigkeit f. adj flüssig. **liquidate** v (comm) liquidieren. **liquidation** n Liquidierung f. **liquidator** n Liquidator m. **liquidity** n Flüssigkeit f.
liquor ['likə] n alkoholisches Getränk neut.
liquorice ['likəris] n Lakritze f.
lisp [lisp] n Lispeln neut. v lispeln.
list¹ [list] n Liste f, Verzeichnis neut. v verzeichnen.
list² [list] n (naut) Schlagseite f. v Schlagseite haben.
listen ['lisn] v hören auf, zuhören (+dat). **listener** n Zuhörer m. **listening device** Abhörgerät neut.
listless ['listlis] adj lustlos.
lit [lit] V light¹.

litany ['litəni] n Litanei f.
literacy ['litərəsi] n die Fähigkeit, lesen und schreiben zu können f. **literate** adj gelehrt. **be literate** lesen und schreiben können.
literal ['litərəl] adj buchstäblich.
literary ['litərəri] adj literarisch.
literature ['litrətʃə] n Literatur f.
lithe [laið] adj geschmeidig.
litigation [liti'geiʃən] n Prozeß m.
litre ['liːtə] n Liter neut.
litter ['litə] n (rubbish) Abfall m; (stretcher) Tragbahre f; (animals) Wurf m. **litter bin** Abfallkorb m.
little ['litl] adj klein. adv wenig. **a little** ein bißchen, ein wenig.
liturgy ['litədʒi] n Liturgie f.
live¹ [liv] v leben; (reside) wohnen.
live² [laiv] adj (alive) lebendig; (radio, etc.) live; (electricity) stromführend. **live broadcast** Livesendung f.
livelihood ['laivlihud] n Lebensunterhalt m.
lively ['laivli] adj lebhaft. **liveliness** n Lebhaftigkeit f.
liver ['livə] n Leber f.
livestock ['laivstok] n Vieh neut.
livid ['livid] adj (coll: angry) wütend.
living ['liviŋ] adj lebendig, am Leben. n Lebensunterhalt m. **make a living** sein Brot verdienen. **living room** Wohnzimmer neut.
lizard ['lizəd] n Eidechse f.
load [loud] n Last f, Belastung f. v (be)laden.
loaf¹ [louf] n Laib m, Brot neut.
loaf² [louf] v **loaf around** faulenzen. **loafer** n Bummler m, Faulenzer m.
loan [loun] n Anleihe f; (credit) Darlehen neut. v leihen.
loathe [louð] v hassen, nicht ausstehen können. **loathing** n Abscheu m. **loathsome** adj abscheulich.
lob [lob] v (sport) lobben. n Lob m.
lobby ['lobi] n Vorhalle f; (pol) Interessengruppe f.
lobe [loub] n Lappen m.
lobster ['lobstə] n Hummer m.
local ['loukəl] adj örtlich, Orts-. n Ortsbewohner m. **local government** Gemeindeverwaltung f. **locality** n Ort m. **localize** v lokalisieren.
locate [lə'keit] v ausfindig machen. **location** n Standort m.

lock¹ [lok] n Schloß neut; (canal) Schleuse f. v verschließen. **lock in** einsperren. **lock out** aussperren. **lock up** verschließen.

lock² [lok] n (of hair) Locke f.

locker ['lokə] n Schließfach neut.

locket ['lokit] n Medaillon neut.

locomotive [,loukə'moutiv] n Lokomotive f.

locust ['loukəst] n Heuschrecke f.

lodge [lodʒ] v (a person) unterbringen; (complaint) einreichen. n (hunting) Jagdhütte f. **lodger** n Untermieter m.

lodgings pl Wohnung f sing, Zimmer neut sing.

loft [loft] n (Dach)Boden m. **lofty** adj hoch.

log [log] n Klotz m; (naut) Log neut. v (naut) loggen, ins Logbuch eintragen.

logarithm ['logəriðəm] n Logarithmus m.

loggerheads ['logəhedz] pl n **be at loggerheads with** in den Haaren liegen mit.

logic ['lodʒik] n Logik f. **logical** adj logisch.

loins [loins] pl n Lenden pl. **loincloth** n Lendentuch neut.

loiter ['loitə] v schlendern. **loiterer** n Schlenderer m.

lollipop ['loli,pop] n Lutscher m.

London ['lʌndən] n London neut.

lonely ['lounli] adj einsam. **loneliness** n Einsamkeit f.

long¹ [loŋ] adj lang.

long² [loŋ] v sich sehnen (nach).

long-distance adj Fern-.

longevity [lon'dʒevəti] n Langlebigkeit f.

longing ['loŋiŋ] n Sehnsucht f.

longitude ['londʒitjuːd] n Länge f. **longitudinal** adj Längen-.

long-playing record n Langspielplatte f.

long-term adj langfristig.

long-winded adj langatmig.

loo [luː] n (coll) Klo neut.

look [luk] n (glance) Blick m; (appearance) Aussehen neut; (expression) Miene f. v schauen, blicken, gucken (auf); (appear) aussehen. **look after** aufpassen auf; (care for) sorgen für. **look for** suchen. **look forward to** sich freuen auf. **look into** untersuchen. **look out!** paß auf!

loom¹ [luːm] v **loom up** aufragen.

loom² [luːm] n Webstuhl m, Webmaschine f.

loop [luːp] n Schleife f, Schlinge f. v eine Schleife machen.

loophole ['luːphoul] n Lücke f.

loose [luːs] adj schlaff, locker; (free) los.

loosen v lösen, lockern. **loose change** Kleingeld neut. **loose translation** freie Übersetzung f.

loot [luːt] n Beute f. v plündern. **looter** n Plünderer m. **looting** n Plünderung f.

lop [lop] v **lop off** abhacken.

lopsided [,lop'saidid] adj schief.

lord [loːd] n Herr m; (noble) Edelmann m. **House of Lords** Oberhaus neut.

lorry ['lori] n Lastkraftwagen (Lkw) m.

***lose** [luːz] v verlieren; (clock) nachgehen. **lose one's way** sich verlieren. **loser** n Verlierer(in). **loss** n Verlust m; (decrease) Abnahme f. **dead loss** (coll) Niete f, Versager m.

lost [lost] V lose.

lot [lot] n Los neut; (fate) Schicksal neut; (land) Bauplatz m. **draw lots** Lose ziehen. **a lot of** viel, eine Menge.

lotion ['louʃən] n Lotion f.

lottery ['lotəri] n Lotterie f.

lotus ['loutəs] n Lotos m.

loud [laud] adj laut; (colour) schreiend. **loudmouth** n Maulheld m. **loudness** n Lautstärke f. **loudspeaker** n Lautsprecher m.

lounge [laundʒ] n Wohnzimmer neut; (hotel) Foyer neut. v faulenzen.

louse [laus] n (pl lice) Laus f. **lousy** adj (slang) saumäßig.

love [lʌv] n Liebe f; (person) Liebling m; (sport) null. v lieben. **love doing something** etwas gern tun. **love affair** Liebesaffäre f. **loveless** adj lieblos. **love letter** Liebesbrief m. **loveliness** n Schönheit f. **lovely** adj lieblich, schön. **lover** n Liebhaber(in), Geliebte(r). **lovesick** adj liebeskrank. **loving** adj liebevoll.

low [lou] adj niedrig; (deep) tief; (sad) niedergeschlagen; (base) ordinär. **lowly** adj bescheiden. **low tide** Niedrigwasser neut.

lower ['louə] v senken, niederlassen; (fig) erniedrigen.

loyal ['loiəl] adj treu. **loyalty** n Treue f.

lozenge ['lozindʒ] n Pastille f.

lubricate ['luːbrikeit] v schmieren, ölen. **lubricant** n Schmiermittel neut. **lubrication** n Schmierung f.

lucid ['luːsid] adj deutlich, klar.

luck [lʌk] n (happiness, fortune) Glück neut; (fate) Schicksal neut; (chance) Zufall m. **luckily** adv glücklicherweise. **lucky** adj glücklich.

lucrative ['luːkrətiv] *adj* gewinnbringend.
ludicrous ['luːdikrəs] *adj* lächerlich.
lug [lʌg] *v* (*carry, drag*) schleppen.
luggage ['lʌgidʒ] *n* Gepäck *neut*. **luggage rack** Gepäcknetz *neut*.
lukewarm ['luːkwoːm] *adj* lauwarm.
lull [lʌl] *n* (*pause*) Pause *f*; (*calm*) Stille *f*.
lullaby ['lʌləˌbai] *n* Wiegenlied *neut*.
lumbago [lʌmˈbeigou] *n* Hexenschuß *m*, Lumbago *f*.
lumber¹ ['lʌmbə] *n* (*timber*) Bauholz *neut*; (*junk*) Plunder *m*. **lumber room** Rumpelkammer *f*.
lumber² ['lʌmbə] *v* schwerfällig gehen.
luminous ['luːminəs] *adj* leuchtend.
lump [lʌmp] *n* Klumpen *m*, Beule *f*. **lump sugar** Würfelzucker *m*. **lump sum** Pauschalsumme *f*. *v* **lump together** zusammenfassen. **lumpy** *adj* klumpig.
lunar ['luːnə] *adj* Mond-.
lunatic ['luːnətik] *n* Wahnsinnige(r). **lunacy** *n* Wahnsinn *m*.
lunch [lʌntʃ] *n* Mittagessen *neut*. *v* zu Mittag essen. **lunchtime** Mittagspause *f*.
lung [lʌŋ] *n* Lunge *f*. **lung cancer** Lungenkrebs *m*.
lunge [lʌndʒ] *v* losstürzen (auf).
lurch¹ [ləːtʃ] *v* taumeln.
lurch² [ləːtʃ] *n* **leave in the lurch** im Stich lassen.
lure [luə] *v* (an)locken. *n* Köder *m*.
lurid ['luərid] *adj* grell.
lurk [ləːk] *v* lauern.
luscious ['lʌʃəs] *adj* köstlich, lecker.
lush [lʌʃ] *adj* saftig.
lust [lʌst] *n* Wollust *f*, Begierde *f*. *v* **lust after** begehren. **lustful** *adj* lüstern.
lustre ['lʌstə] *n* Glanz *m*. **lustrous** *adj* strahlend.
lute [luːt] *n* Laute *f*.
Luxembourg ['lʌksəmˌbəːg] *n* Luxemburg *neut*.
luxury ['lʌkʃəri] *n* Luxus *m*; (*article*) Luxusartikel *m*. **luxuriant** *adj* üppig. **luxurious** *adj* luxuriös.
lynch [lintʃ] *v* lynchen.
lynx [links] *n* Luchs *m*.
lyrical ['lirikəl] *adj* lyrisch.
lyrics ['liriks] *pl n* Lyrik *f sing*, Text *m sing*.

M

mac [mak] *n* Regenmantel *m*.
macabre [məˈkaːbr] *adj* grausig.
macaroni [makəˈrouni] *n* Makkaroni *pl*.
mace¹ [meis] *n* Amtsstab *m*.
mace² [meis] *n* (*cookery*) Muskatblüte *f*.
machine [məˈʃiːn] *n* Maschine *f*. *v* maschinell herstellen. **machine gun** Maschinengewehr *neut*. **machinery** *n* Maschinerie *f*. **machine tool** Werkzeugmaschine *f*. **machinist** *n* Maschinenarbeiter(in).
mackerel ['makrəl] *n* Makrele *f*.
mackintosh ['makinˌtoʃ] *n* Regenmantel *m*.
mad [mad] *adj* wahnsinnig, verrückt; (*angry*) wütend. **madhouse** *n* Irrenhaus *neut*. **madly** *adv* wie verrückt. **madman** *n* Verrückte(r) *m*. **madness** *n* Wahnsinn *m*.
madam ['madəm] *n* gnädige Frau *f*.
made [meid] *V* make.
magazine [ˌmagəˈziːn] *n* (*publication*) Zeitschrift *f*, Illustrierte *f*; (*also warehouse, rifle*) Magazin *neut*.
maggot ['magət] *n* Made *f*. **maggoty** *adj* madig.
magic ['madʒik] *n* Zauberei *f*. *adj also* **magical** Zauber-, zauberhaft. **magician** *n* Zauberer *m*; (*entertainer*) Zauberkünstler *m*.
magistrate ['madʒistreit] *n* Friedensrichter *m*.
magnanimous [magˈnaniməs] *adj* großmütig. **magnanimity** *n* Großmut *f*.
magnate ['magneit] *n* Magnat *m*.
magnet ['magnət] *n* Magnet *m*. **magnetic** *adj* magnetisch. **magnetism** *n* Magnetismus *m*; (*fig*) Anziehungskraft *f*. **magnetize** *v* magnetisieren.
magnificent [magˈnifisnt] *adj* prächtig. **magnificence** *n* Pracht *f*.
magnify ['magnifai] *v* vergrößern. **magnifying glass** Lupe *f*. **magnification** *n* Vergrößerung *f*.
magnitude ['magnitjuːd] *n* Größe *f*, Ausmaß *neut*.
magnolia [magˈnouliə] *n* Magnolie *f*.
magpie ['magpai] *n* Elster *f*.
mahogany [məˈhogəni] *n* (*wood*) Mahagoni *neut*. *adj* Mahagoni-.
maid [meid] *n* Mädchen *neut*; (*servant*)

Dienstmädchen *neut.* **old maid** alte Jungfer *f.*
maiden ['meidən] *n* Mädchen *neut.* **maiden name** Mädchenname *m.* **maiden speech** Jungfernrede *f.*
mail [meil] *n* Post *f.* *v* schicken, absenden. **mailbox** Briefkasten *m.* **mail-order company** Versandhaus *neut.* **mailboat** *n* Paketboot *neut.*
maim [meim] *v* lähmen.
main [mein] *adj* Haupt-, hauptsächlich. **mains** *pl n* (*gas, water*) Hauptleitung *f;* (*elec*) Netz *neut sing.* **mainstay** *n* (*fig*) Hauptstütze *f.* **main street** Hauptstraße *f.*
maintain [mein'tein] *v* erhalten; behaupten. **maintenance** *n* Erhaltung *f;* (*tech, mot*) Wartung *f.*
maisonette [meizə'net] *n* Wohnung *f.*
maize [meiz] *n* Mais *m.*
majesty ['madʒəsti] *n* Majestät *f.* **His/Her/Your Majesty** Seine/Ihre/Eure Majestät. **majestic** *adj* majestätisch.
major ['meidʒə] *n* (*mil*) Major *m;* (*music*) Dur *neut. adj* (*significant*) bedeutend; (*greater*) größer. **majority** *n* Mehrheit *f;* (*law*) Mündigkeit *f.*
*****make** [meik] *v* machen; (*produce*) herstellen; (*force*) zwingen; (*build*) bauen; (*reach*) erreichen. *n* (*brand*) Marke *f;* (*type*) Art *f.* **make good** (*succeed*) Erfolg haben. **make out** vergeben. **makeshift** *adj* Behelfs-. **make-up** *n* Schminke *f.*
maladjusted [malə'dʒʌstid] *adj* verhaltensgestört.
malaria [mə'leəriə] *n* Malaria *f.*
male [meil] *n* Mann *m;* (*animals*) Männchen *neut. adj* männlich. **male nurse** Krankenpfleger *m.*
malevolent [mə'levələnt] *adj* mißgünstig. **malevolence** *n* Mißgunst *f.*
malfunction [mal'fʌŋkʃən] *n* Funktionstörung *f.*
malice ['malis] *n* Böswilligkeit. **malicious** *adj* böswillig.
malignant [mə'lignənt] *adj* böswillig; (*med*) bösartig.
malinger [mə'liŋgə] *v* sich krank stellen, simulieren.
mallet ['malit] *n* Schlegel *m.*
malnutrition [malnju'triʃən] *n* Unterernährung *f.*
malt [moilt] *n* Malz *neut.*
Malta ['moiltə] *n* Malta *neut.* **Maltese** *n* Malteser(in) *adj* maltesisch.

maltreat [mal'triit] *v* mißhandeln, schlecht behandeln. **maltreatment** *n* schlechte Behandlung *f.*
mammal ['maməl] *n* Säugetier *neut.*
mammoth ['maməθ] *n* Mammut *neut. adj* riesig.
man [man] *n* (*pl* **men**) Mann *m;* (*human*) Mensch *m. v* bemannen. **manliness** *n* Mannhaftigkeit *f.* **manly** *adj* mannhaft. **manslaughter** *n* Totschlag *m.*
manage ['manidʒ] *v* (*control*) leiten, führen; (*cope*) zurechtkommen, auskommen. **management** *n* Geschäftsleitung *f,* Direktion *f.* **manager** *n* Leiter *m,* Manager *m.*
mandarin ['mandərin] *n* Mandarin *m;* (*fruit*) Mandarine *f.*
mandate ['mandeit] *n* Mandat *neut.* **mandatory** *adj* verbindlich.
mandolin ['mandəlin] *n* Mandoline *f.*
mane [mein] *n* Mähne *f.*
maneuver [mə'nuːvə] *n* (*US*) Manöver *neut. v* manövrieren.
mange [meindʒ] *n* Räude *f.*
mangle¹ ['maŋgl] *n* (Wäsche)Mangel *f. v* mangeln.
mangle² ['maŋgl] *v* (*disfigure*) verstümmeln.
manhandle [man'handl] *v* grob behandeln, mißhandeln.
mania ['meiniə] *n* Manie *f.* **maniac** *n* Wahnsinnige(r). **manic** *adj* manisch.
manicure ['manikjuə] *n* Maniküre *f. v* maniküren. **manicurist** *n* Maniküre *f.*
manifest ['manifest] *adj* offenbar. *v* erscheinen. **manifestation** *n* Offenbarung *f;* (*symptom*) Anzeichen *neut.*
manifesto [mani'festou] *n* Manifest *neut.*
manifold ['manifould] *adj* mannigfaltig.
manipulate [mə'nipjuleit] *v* manipulieren. **manipulation** *n* Manipulation *f.*
mankind [,man'kaind] *n* Menschheit *f.*
man-made [,man'meid] *adj* künstlich.
manner ['manə] *n* (*way*) Art *f,* Weise *f;* (*behaviour*) Manier *f,* Benehmen *neut.* **mannered** *adj* manieriert. **mannerism** *n* Manierismus *m.*
manoeuvre [mə'nuːvə] *n* Manöver *neut. v* manövrieren.
manor ['manə] *n* Herrensitz *m,* Herrenhaus *neut.*
manpower ['man,pauə] *n* Arbeitskräfte *pl.*
mansion ['manʃən] *n* (herrschaftliches) Wohnhaus *neut.*

mantelpiece ['mantlpiːs] n Kaminsims m or neut.

manual ['manjuəl] adj manuell, Hand-. n Handbuch neut.

manufacture [manju'faktʃə] v herstellen, erzeugen. n Herstellung f, Erzeugung f. **manufacturer** n Hersteller m, Fabrikant m.

manure [mə'njuə] n Dünger m, Mist m. v düngen.

manuscript ['manjuskript] n Manuskript neut. adj handschriftlich.

many ['meni] adj viele. **how many?** wieviele? **many times** oft. **a good many** ziemlich viele.

map [map] n (Land)Karte f; (of town) Stadtplan m. v eine karte machen von.

maple ['meipl] n Ahorn m.

mar [maɪ] v verderben, beeinträchtigen.

marathon ['marəθən] n Marathonlauf m. adj Marathon-.

marble ['maːbl] n Marmor m; (toy) Marmel f.

march [maɪtʃ] n Marsch m. v marschieren. **march past** vorbeimarschieren an.

March [maɪtʃ] n März m.

marchioness [,maɪʃə'nes] n Marquise f.

mare [meə] n Stute f.

margarine [,maɪdʒə'riːn] n Margarine f.

margin ['maɪdʒin] n Rand m; (limit) Grenze f; (profit) Gewinnspanne f. **marginal** adj Rand-; (slight) geringfügig.

marguerite [,maɪgə'riːt] n Gänseblümchen neut.

marigold ['marigould] n Ringelblume f.

marijuana [mari'waɪnə] n Marihuana neut.

marina [mə'riːnə] n Yachthafen m.

marinade [,mari'neid] v marinieren. n Marinade f.

marine [mə'riːn] adj See-, Meeres-. n (shipping) Marine f; (mil) Marineinfanterist m. **mariner** n Matrose m.

marital ['maritl] adj ehelich.

maritime ['maritaim] adj See-, Schiffahrts-.

marjoram ['maɪdʒərəm] n Majoran m.

mark[1] [maɪk] n Marke f, Zeichen neut; (school) Note f; (stain) Fleck m; (distinguishing feature) Kennzeichen neut. v bezeichnen; (note) notieren, vermerken. **marked** adj markant, ausgeprägt. **markedly** adv ausgesprochen.

mark[2] [maɪk] n (currency) Mark f.

market ['maɪkit] n Markt m. v auf den Markt bringen. **marketing** n Marketing neut. **market place** Marktplatz m. **market research** Marktforschung f.

marmalade ['maɪməleid] n Orangenmarmelade f.

maroon[1] [mə'ruːn] adj (colour) rotbraun.

maroon[2] [mə'ruːn] v (naut) aussetzen.

marquee [maɪ'kiː] n großes Zelt neut.

marquess ['maɪkwis] n Marquis m.

marriage ['maridʒ] n Heirat f, Ehe f; (wedding) Hochzeit f; (ceremony) Trauung f. **marriage certificate** Trauschein m.

marrow ['marou] n (of bone) Mark neut; (vegetable) Eierkürbis m. **marrowbone** n Markknochen m.

marry ['mari] v heiraten; (get married) sich verheiraten mit. **married couple** Ehepaar neut.

Mars [maɪz] n Mars m. **Martian** adj Mars-; n Marsbewohner m.

marsh [maɪʃ] n Sumpf m. **marshy** adj sumpfig.

marshal ['maɪʃəl] n Marschall m. v einordnen; (troops) aufstellen.

martial ['maɪʃəl] adj militärisch, Kriegs-.

martin ['maɪtin] n Mauerschwalbe f.

martyr ['maɪtə] n Märtyrer(in). **martyrdom** n Martyrium neut.

marvel ['maɪvəl] n Wunder neut. v staunen (über). **marvellous** adj wunderbar.

marzipan [maɪzi'pan] n Marzipan neut.

mascara [ma'skaɪrə] n Wimperntusche f.

mascot ['maskət] n Maskottchen neut.

masculine ['maskjulin] adj männlich; (manly) mannhaft; (of woman) männisch. n (gramm) Maskulinum m. **masculinity** n Männlichkeit f, Mannhaftigkeit f.

mash [maʃ] v zerquetschen. **mashed potatoes** Kartoffelpüree neut.

mask [maɪsk] n Maske f. v maskieren.

masochist ['masəkist] n Masochist m. **masochism** n Masochismus m.

mason ['meisn] n Maurer m. **masonic** adj Freimaurer-. **masonry** n Mauerwerk neut.

masquerade [maskə'reid] n Maskerade f. v sich ausgeben (als).

mass[1] [mas] n Masse f. v sich ansammeln. adj Massen-. **the masses** die breite Masse. **mass meeting** Massenversammlung f. **mass-produce** v serienmäßig herstellen. **mass production** Massenherstellung f.

mass² [mas] *n* (*rel*) Messe *f*.
massacre ['masəkə] *n* Massaker *neut*, Blutbad *neut*. *v* massakrieren.
massage ['masɑːʒ] *n* Massage *f*. *v* massieren. **masseur** *n* Masseur *m*. **masseuse** *n* Masseuse *f*.
massive ['masiv] *adj* massiv.
mast [mɑːst] *n* Mast *m*.
mastectomy [ma'stektəmi] *n* Brustamputation *f*.
master ['mɑːstə] *n* Herr *m*; (*school*) Lehrer *m*; (*artist*) Meister *m*. *v* meistern. **masterful** *adj* meisterhaft. **masterpiece** *n* Meisterwerk *neut*. **mastery** *n* Beherrschung *f*.
masturbate ['mɑːstəbeit] *v* onanieren. **masturbation** *n* Onanie *f*.
mat [mat] *n* Matte *f*; (*beer*) Untersetzer *m*. **matted** *adj* mattiert.
match¹ [matʃ] *n* Streichholz *neut*.
match² [matʃ] *n* (*equal*) Gleiche(r); (*sport*) Spiel *neut*. *v* anpassen. **meet one's match** seinen Meister finden. **matchless** *adj* unvergleichlich.
mate [meit] *n* (*friend*) Kamarad(in); (*chess*) (Schach)Matt *neut*; (*animal*) Männchen *neut*, Weibchen *neut*; (*naut*) Schiffsoffizier *m*. *v* sich paaren; (*chess*) matt setzen.
material [mə'tiəriəl] *n* Stoff *m*. *adj* materiell; (*important*) wesentlich. **materials** *pl* Werkstoffe *pl*. **materialist** *n* Materialist *m*. **materialistic** *adj* materialistisch.
maternal [mə'təːnl] *adj* mütterlich; mütterlicherseits. **maternal grandfather** Großvater. **maternity** *n* Mutterschaft *f*. **maternity dress** Umstandskleid *neut*. **maternity home** Entbindungsheim *neut*.
mathematics [maθə'matiks] *n* Mathmatik *f*. **mathematical** *adj* mathematisch. **mathematician** *n* Mathematiker *m*.
matinee ['matinei] *n* Matinee *f*.
matins ['matinz] *n* Frühgottesdienst *m*.
matrimony ['matriməni] *n* Ehestand *m*, Ehe *f*. **matrimonial** *adj* ehelich, Ehe-.
matrix ['meitriks] *n* Matrix *f*.
matron ['meitrən] *n* (*school*) Hausmutter *f*; (*nurse*) Oberin *f*.
matter ['matə] *n* Stoff *m*, Materie *f*; (*affair*) Sache *f*; (*pus*) Eiter *m*. *v* von Bedeutung sein. **what's the matter?** was ist los? **it doesn't matter** es macht nichts. **matter-of-fact** *adj* sachlich.
mattress ['matris] *n* Matratze *f*.

mature [mə'tjuə] *adj* reif. *v* reifen. **maturity** *n* Reife *f*.
maudlin ['mɔːdlin] *adj* weinerlich.
maul [mɔːl] *v* zerreißen.
mausoleum [mɔːsə'liəm] *n* Mausoleum *neut*, Grabmal *neut*.
mauve [mouv] *adj* malvenfarben.
maxim ['maksim] *n* Grundsatz *m*.
maximum ['maksiməm] *n* Maximum *neut*. *adj* Höchst-, Maximal-.
*may [mei] *v* mögen, können. **may I?** darf ich? **maybe** *adv* vielleicht.
May [mei] *n* Mai *m*. **mayday** (*SOS*) Maydaysignal *neut*.
mayonnaise [ˌmeiə'neiz] *n* Mayonnaise *f*.
mayor [meə] *n* Bürgermeister *m*. **mayoress** *n* Bürgermeisterin *f*.
maze [meiz] *n* Labyrinth *neut*, Irrgarten *m*.
me [miː] *pron* (*acc*) mich; (*dat*) mir.
meadow ['medou] *n* Wiese *f*.
meagre ['miːgə] *adj* mager, dürr.
meal¹ [miːl] *n* Mahlzeit *f*, Essen *neut*.
meal² [miːl] *n* (*flour*) Mehl *neut*.
*mean¹ [miːn] *v* (*word, etc.*) bedeuten; (*person*) meinen; (*intend*) vorhaben, beabsichtigen.
mean² [miːn] *adj* (*slight*) gering; (*base*) gemein; (*tight-fisted*) geizig. **meanness** *n* Gemeinheit *f*.
mean³ [miːn] *n* Durchschnitt *m*. *adj* mittler, Durchschnitts-.
meander [mi'andə] *v* sich winden. *n* Windung *f*.
meaning ['miːniŋ] *n* (*significance*) Bedeutung *f*; (*sense*) Sinn *m*. **meaningful** *adj* bedeutsam. **meaningless** *adj* sinnlos.
means [miːnz] *n* Mittel *neut*. **by means of** durch, mittels. **by no means** auf keinen Fall. **by all means** selbstverständlich.
meant [ment] *V* **mean¹**.
meanwhile ['miːnwail] *adv* mittlerweile.
measles ['miːzlz] *n* Masern *pl*. **German measles** Röteln *pl*.
measure ['meʒə] *v* messen. *n* Maß *neut*. **measurement** *n* Messung *f*, Maß *neut*.
meat [miːt] *n* Fleisch *neut*. **meatball** *n* Fleischklößchen. **meaty** *adj* fleischig.
mechanic [mi'kanik] *n* Mechaniker *m*. **mechanical** *adj* mechanisch. **mechanics** *n* Mechanik *f*. **mechanism** *n* Mechanismus *m*. **mechanize** *v* mechanisieren.
medal ['medl] *n* Medaille *f*, Orden *m*. **medallion** *n* Schaumünze *f*.

meddle ['medl] v sich (ein)mischen (in).
meddlesome adj zudringlich.
media ['miːdiə] pl n Medien pl. **mass media** Massenmedien pl.
mediate ['miːdieit] v vermitteln. **mediation** n Vermittlung f. **mediator** n Vermittler m.
medical ['medikəl] adj medizinisch, ärztlich. **medical certificate** Krankenschein m. **medical student** Medizinstudent m. **medicament** n Arzneimittel neut. **medicinal** adj heilkräftig. **medicine** n Arznei f, Arzneimittel neut; (science) Medizin f.
medieval [medi'iːvəl] adj mittelalterlich.
mediocre [miːdi'oukə] adj mittelmäßig. **mediocrity** n Mittelmäßigkeit f.
meditate ['mediteit] v meditieren; (reflect) nachdenken (über). **meditation** n (rel) Meditation f; Nachdenken neut.
Mediterranean [meditə'reiniən] n Mittelmeer neut. adj Mittelmeer-.
medium ['miːdiəm] adj mittler, Mittel-. n Mitte f; (spiritualist) Medium neut. **medium-sized** adj mittelgroß.
medley ['medli] n Gemisch neut; (music) Potpourri neut.
meek [miːk] adj mild, sanft. **meekness** n Milde f, Sanftmut f
*meet [miːt] v treffen, begegnen (+dat); (by appointment) sich treffen (mit); (requirements) erfüllen; (call for) abholen. **meeting** n Treffen neut; (session) Versammlung f, Sitzung f.
megaphone ['megəfoun] n Megaphon neut.
melancholy ['melənkəli] n Melancholie f, Trübsinn m. **melancholic** adj melancholisch.
mellow ['melou] adj reif; (person) freundlich, heiter.
melodrama ['melədraːmə] n Melodrama neut. **melodramatic** adj melodramatisch.
melody ['melədi] n Melodie f. **melodious** adj wohlklingend.
melon ['melən] n Melone f.
melt [melt] v schmelzen. **melt away** zergehen. **melting point** Schmelzpunkt m.
member ['membə] n Mitglied m. **membership** n Mitgliedschaft f.
membrane ['membrein] n Membrane f.
memento [mə'mentou] n Andenken neut.
memo ['memou] n (note) Notiz f; (message) Mitteilung f.
memoirs ['memwaːz] pl n Memoiren pl.

memorable ['memərəbl] adj denkwürdig.
memorandum [memə'randəm] n (note) Notiz f; (message) Mitteilung f.
memorial [mi'moːriəl] n Denkmal neut. adj **memorial service** Gedenkgottesdienst m.
memory ['meməri] n (power of) Gedächtnis neut; (of something) Erinnerung f. **memorize** v auswendig lernen.
men [men] V **man**.
menace ['menis] n Drohung f. v bedrohen. **menacing** adj drohend.
menagerie [mi'nadʒəri] n Menagerie f.
mend [mend] v reparieren; (clothes) flicken; (socks, etc.) stopfen. n ausgebesserte Stelle f. **on the mend** (coll) auf dem Wege der Besserung.
menial ['miːniəl] adj niedrig.
menopause ['menəpoɪz] n Wechseljahre pl, Menopause f.
menstrual ['menstruəl] adj Menstruations-. **menstruate** v die Regel haben, menstruieren. **menstruation** n Menstruation f, Monatsblutung f.
mental ['mentl] adj geistig, Geistes-; (slang) verrückt. **mental deficiency** Schwachsinn m. **mental hospital** Nervenheilanstalt f. **mental illness** Geisteskrankheit f. **mentality** n Mentalität f, Gesinnung f. **mentally ill** geisteskrank.
menthol ['menθəl] n Menthol neut.
mention ['menʃən] v erwähnen. n Erwähnung f. **don't mention it!** bitte sehr!
menu ['menjuː] n Speisekarte f, Menü neut.
mercantile ['məːkən,tail] adj kaufmännisch, Handels-.
mercenary ['məːsinəri] adj gewinnsüchtig, geldgierig. n Söldner m.
merchandise ['məːtʃəndaiz] n Waren pl, Handelsgüter pl. v verkaufen.
merchant ['məːtʃənt] n Kaufmann m; (wholesaler) Großhändler m. **merchant navy** Handelsflotte f.
mercury ['məːkjuri] n Quecksilber neut. **Mercury** n Merkur m.
mercy ['məːsi] n Erbarmen neut, Gnade f. **merciful** adj barmherzig. **merciless** adj erbarmungslos.
mere [miə] adj bloß, rein.
merge [məːdʒ] v verschmelzen; (comm) fusionieren. **merger** n Fusion f.
meridian [mə'ridiən] n Meridian m.

meringue [mə'raŋ] *n* Meringe *f*, Baiser *neut*.

merit ['merit] *n* Verdienst *neut*; (*value*) Wert *m*. *v* verdienen.

mermaid ['mɔːmeid] *n* Seejungfrau *f*.

merry ['meri] *adj* lustig, fröhlich. **make merry** feiern. **merry-go-round** *n* Karussell *neut*. **merriment** *n* Lustigkeit *f*.

mesh [meʃ] *n* Masche *f*. *v* ineinandergreifen. **meshed** *adj* maschig.

mesmerize ['mezmɔraiz] *n* hypnotisieren; (*fig*) faszinieren.

mess [mes] *n* Durcheinander *neut*, Unordnung *f*; (*mil*) Messe *f*. *v* beschmutzen. **mess about** herumpfuschen. **mess up** verderben, verpfuschen. **messy** *adj* unordentlich.

message ['mesidʒ] *n* Mitteilung *f*; (*news*) Nachricht *f*. **messenger** *n* Bote *m*.

met [met] *V* meet.

metabolism [mi'tabɔlizm] *n* Stoffwechsel *m*. **metabolic** *adj* metabolisch.

metal ['metl] *n* Metall *neut*. **metallic** *adj* metallisch. **metallurgy** *n* Metallurgie *f*.

metamorphosis [metɔ'mɔːfɔsis] *n* Metamorphose *f*, Verwandlung *f*. **metamorphose** *v* verwandeln.

metaphor ['metɔfɔ] *n* Metapher *f*. **metaphorical** *adj* metaphorisch.

metaphysics [,metɔ'fiziks] *n* Metaphysik *f*. **metaphysical** *adj* metaphysisch.

meteor ['miːtiɔ] *n* Meteor *m*. **meteoric** *adj* meteorartig, plötzlich.

meteorology [,miːtiɔ'rolɔdʒi] *n* Meteorologie *f*, Wetterkunde *f*. **meteorological** *adj* meteorologisch, Wetter-.

meter ['miːtɔ] *n* Messer *m*. **gas meter** Gasuhr *f*. **parking meter** Parkuhr *f*.

methane ['miːθein] *n* Methan *neut*.

method ['meθɔd] *n* Methode *f*; (*procedure*) Verfahren *neut*. **methodical** *adj* methodisch.

methylated spirits ['meθileitid] *n* Brennspiritus *m*.

meticulous [mi'tikjulɔs] *adj* übergenau, peinlich genau.

metre ['miːtɔ] *n* Meter *m or neut*. **metric** *adj* metrisch.

metronome ['metrɔnoum] *n* Metronom *neut*, Taktmesser *m*.

metropolis [mɔ'tropɔlis] *n* Metropole *f*, Hauptstadt *f*.

mice [mais] *V* mouse.

microbe ['maikroub] *n* Mikrobe *f*.

microfilm ['maikrɔ,film] *n* Mikrofilm *m*.

microphone ['maikrɔfoun] *n* Mikrophon *neut*.

microscope ['maikrɔskoup] *n* Mikroskop *neut*. **microscopic** *adj* mikroscopisch; (*tiny*) verschwindend klein.

mid [mid] *adj* mittler, Mittel-. **in mid air** mitten in der Luft. **midday** *n* Mittag *m*.

middle ['midl] *n* Mitte *f*. *adj* mittler, Mittel-. **middle-aged** *adj* im mittleren Alter. **middle-class** *adj* bürgerlich, bourgeois. **middle classes** Mittelstand *m*.

Middle Ages *pl n* Mittelalter *neut*.

Middle East *n* Naher Osten *m*.

midge [midʒ] *n* Mücke *f*.

midget ['midʒit] *n* Zwerg *m*.

midnight ['midnait] *n* Mitternacht *f*.

midsummer ['mid,sʌmɔ] *n* Hochsommer *m*.

midst [midst] *n* Mitte *f*. **in the midst of** mitten unter (+ *dat*).

midwife ['midwaif] *n* Hebamme *f*. **midwifery** *n* Geburtshilfe *f*.

might[1] [mait] *V* may.

might[2] [mait] *n* Macht *f*; (*force*) Gewalt *f*.

mighty ['maiti] *adj* mächtig. *adv* sehr.

migraine ['miːgrein] *n* Migräne *f*.

migrate [mai'greit] *v* abwandern. **migrant** *adj* Wander-; *n* Umsiedler *m*. **migration** *n* Wanderung *f*.

mike [maik] *n* (*coll*) Mikrophon *neut*.

mild [maild] *adj* mild, sanft. **to put it mildly** gelinde gesagt. **mildness** *n* Sanftheit *f*.

mildew ['mildjuː] *n* Mehltau *m*, Moder *m*.

mile [mail] *n* Meile *f*. **mileage** *n* Meilenzahl *f*. **milestone** *n* (*fig*) Markstein *m*.

militant ['militɔnt] *adj* militant, kämpferisch. *n* (*pol*) Radikale(r).

military ['militɔri] *adj* militärisch, Militär-, Kriegs-.

milk [milk] *n* Milch *f*. *v* melken. **milk tooth** *n* Milchzahn *m*. **milky** *adj* milchig. **Milky Way** Milchstraße *f*.

mill [mil] *n* Mühle *f*; (*works*) Fabrik *f*. *v* mahlen. **run-of-the-mill** *adj* mittelmäßig. **miller** *n* Müller *m*.

millennium [mi'leniɔm] *n* Jahrtausend *neut*.

milligram ['mili,gram] *n* Milligramm *neut*.

millilitre ['mili,liːtɔ] *n* Milliliter *neut*.

millimetre ['mili,miːtɔ] *n* Millimeter *neut*.

millinery ['milinɔri] *n* Müte *pl*.

million ['miljən] *n* Million *f*. **millionaire** *n* Millionär *n*. **millionairess** *n* Millionärin *f*.

milometer [mai'lomitə] *n* Meilenzähler *m*, Kilometerzähler *m*.

mime [maim] *n* (*actor*) Mime *m*. *v* mimen.

mimic ['mimik] *v* nachäffen. **mimicry** *n* Nachäffung *f*.

mince [mins] *v* zerhacken. *n* (*mincemeat*) Hackfleisch *neut*. **mincer** *n* Fleischwolf *m*. **mince about** geziert gehen. **mincing** *adj* geziert, affektiert. **not mince one's words** kein Blatt vor den Mund nehmen.

mind [maind] *n* Geist *m*, Verstand *m*; (*opinion*) Meinung *f*. *v* etwas dagegen haben; (*look after*) aufpassen auf. **frame of mind** Gesinnung *f*, Stimmung *f*. **make up one's mind** sich entschließen. **mind out!** paß auf! Achtung! **Never mind!** macht nichts! *I don't mind* ist mir egal.

mine[1] [main] *poss pron* meiner *m*, meine *f*, meines *neut*; der, die, das meine *or* meinige. **a friend of mine** ein Freund von mir. **it's mine** es gehört mir.

mine[2] [main] *n* (*coal, etc.*) Bergwerk *neut*; (*mil*) Mine *f*. *v* minieren. **miner** *n* Bergarbeiter *m*. **minefield** *n* Minenfeld. **mining** *n* Bergbau *m*. **minesweeper** *n* Minensuchboot *neut*.

mineral ['minərəl] *n* Mineral *neut*. *adj* mineralisch. **mineral water** Mineralwasser *neut*.

mingle ['miŋgl] *v* (sich) vermischen.

miniature ['minitʃə] *n* Miniatur *f*. *adj* Klein-.

minimum ['miniməm] *n* Minimum *neut*. **minimal** *adj* Mindest-, Minimal-.

minister ['ministə] *n* (*pol*) Minister *m*; (*rel*) Pfarrer *m*. **ministry** *n* (*pol*) Ministerium *neut*.

mink [miŋk] *n* Nerz *m*.

minor ['mainə] *adj* kleiner, geringer; (*trivial*) geringfügig. *n* (*under age*) Minderjährige(r), (*music*) Moll *neut*. **minority** *n* Minderheit *f*; (*under age*) Minderjährigkeit *f*.

minstrel ['minstrəl] *n* Minnesänger *m*.

mint[1] [mint] *n* (*cookery*) Minze *f*.

mint[2] [mint] *n* (*money*) Münzanstalt *f*. *v* münzen.

minuet [minju'et] *n* Menuett *neut*.

minus ['mainəs] *prep* weniger, minus. *it's minus 20 degrees* wir haben 20 Grad Kälte.

minute[1] ['minit] *n* Minute *f*. **just a minute!** Moment mal!

minute[2] [mai'njuːt] *adj* winzig.

miracle ['mirəkl] *n* Wunder *neut*, Wundertat *f*. **miraculous** *adj* wunderbar. **miraculously** *adv* durch ein Wunder.

mirage ['miraːʒ] *n* Luftspiegelung *f*.

mirror ['mirə] *n* Spiegel *m*. *v* widerspiegeln.

mirth [məːθ] *n* Fröhlichkeit *f*, Lustigkeit *f*.

misadventure [misəd'ventʃə] *n* Unfall *m*, Unglück *neut*.

misanthropist [miz'anθrəpist] *n* Menschenfeind *m*. **misanthropic** *adj* menschenfeindlich.

misapprehension [misapri'henʃən] *n* Mißverständnis *neut*.

misbehave [misbi'heiv] *v* sich schlecht benehmen. **misbehaviour** *n* schlechtes Benehmen *neut*.

miscalculate [mis'kalkjuleit] *v* sich verrechnen.

miscarriage [mis'karidʒ] *n* Fehlgeburt *f*. **miscarriage of justice** Fehlspruch *m*, Rechtsbeugung *f*. **miscarry** *v* eine Fehlgeburt haben; (*go wrong*) mißlingen.

miscellaneous [misə'leiniəs] *adj* vermischt. *n* Verschiedenes *neut*. **miscellany** *n* Gemisch *neut*.

mischance [mis'tʃains] *n* Unfall *m*.

mischief ['mistʃif] *n* Unfug *m*. **mischievous** *adj* schelmisch, durchtrieben. **mischief-maker** *n* Störenfried *m*.

misconception [miskən'sepʃən] *n* Mißverständnis *neut*.

misconduct [mis'kondʌkt] *n* schlechtes Benehmen *neut*.

misconstrue [miskən'struː] *v* mißdeuten.

misdeed [mis'diːd] *n* Untat *f*, Verbrechen *neut*.

misdemeanour [misdi'miːnə] *n* Vergehen *neut*.

miser ['maizə] *n* Geizhals *m*. **miserly** *adj* geizig. **miserliness** *n* Geiz *m*.

miserable ['mizərəbl] *adj* (*unhappy*) unglücklich; (*wretched*) elend.

misery ['mizəri] *n* Elend *neut*, Not *f*.

misfire [mis'faiə] *v* versagen; (*mot*) fehlzünden. *n* Versager *m*; Fehlzündung *f*.

misfit ['misfit] *n* Einzelgänger *m*.

misfortune [mis'fɔːtʃən] *n* Unglück *neut*.

misgiving [mis'giviŋ] *n* Zweifel *m*.

misguided [mis'gaidid] *adj* (*erroneous*) irrig.

mishap ['mishap] *n* Unglück *neut.*

***mishear** [mis'hiǝ] *v* sich verhören.

misinterpret [misin'tǝːprit] *v* mißdeuten.

***mislay** [mis'lei] *v* verlegen.

***mislead** [mis'liːd] *v* irreführen. **misleading** *adj* irreführend.

misnomer [mis'noumǝ] *n* falsche Bezeichnung *f.*

misplace [mis'pleis] *v* verlegen. **misplaced** *adj* (*inappropriate*) unangebracht.

misprint ['misprint] *n* Druckfehler *m.*

miss[1] [mis] *v* (*shot*) verfehlen; (*train, opportunity*) verpassen, versäumen; (*absent friend*) vermissen. *n* Fehlschuß *m.* **missing** *adj* fehlend; (*person*) vermißt.

miss[2] [mis] *n* (*title*) Fräulein *neut.*

missile ['misail] *n* Rakete *f,* Geschoß *neut.* **guided missile** Fernlenkrakete *f.*

mission ['miʃǝn] *n* Mission *f;* (*task*) Auftrag *m;* (*pol*) Gesandschaft *f.* **missionary** *n* Missionar(in).

mist [mist] *n* (feuchter) Dunst *m,* Nebel *m.*

***mistake** [mi'steik] *n* Fehler *m,* Irrtum *m.* *v* verwechseln. **be mistaken** im Irrtum sein.

mister ['mistǝ] *n* Herr *m.*

mistletoe ['misltou] *n* Mistel *f.*

mistress ['mistris] *n* (*lover*) Mätresse *f;* (*school*) Lehrerin *f;* (*of house or animal*) Herrin *f.*

mistrust [mis'trʌst] *v* mißtrauen. *n* Mißtrauen *neut,* Argwohn *m.* **mistrustful** *adj* mißtrauisch.

***misunderstand** [misʌndǝ'stand] *v* mißverstehen. **misunderstanding** *n* Mißverständnis *neut.*

misuse [mis'juːs; *v* mis'juːz] *v* mißbrauchen. *n* Mißbrauch *m.*

mitigate ['mitigeit] *v* mildern. **mitigating circumstances** strafmildernde Umstände *pl.*

mitre ['maitǝ] *n* Bischofsmütze *f.*

mitten ['mitn] *n* Fausthandschuh *m.*

mix [miks] *v* (ver)mischen. *n* Mischung *f.* **mix up** verwechseln. **mixer** *n* Mixer *m.* **mixture** *n* Mischung *f;* (*med*) Mixtur *f.*

moan [moun] *n* Stöhnen *neut. v* stöhnen.

mob [mob] *n* Pöbel *m,* Gesindel *neut.*

mobile ['moubail] *adj* beweglich; (*motorized*) motorisiert. *n* Mobile *neut.* **mobility** *n* Beweglichkeit *f.* **mobilization** *n* Mobilisierung *f.* **mobilize** *v* mobilisieren.

moccasin ['mokǝsin] *n* Mokassin *m.*

mock [mok] *v* verhöhnen, verspotten. *adj* Schein-. **mock trial** Scheinprozeß *m.* **mockery** *n* Verhöhnung *f.* (*travesty*) Zerrbild *neut.* **mocking** *adj* spöttisch.

mode [moud] *n* Weise *f,* Methode *f.*

model ['modl] *n* Modell *neut;* (*pattern*) Muster *neut,* Vorbild *neut;* (*fashion*) Mannequin *neut. adj* vorbildlich, musterhaft. *v* modellieren; (*clothes*) vorführen.

moderate ['modǝrǝt; *v* 'modǝreit] *adj* gemäßigt, mäßig. *v* mäßigen. **moderation** *n* Mäßigung *f.* **in moderation** mit Maß.

modern ['modǝn] *adj* modern. **modernity** *n* Modernität *f.* **modernize** *v* modernisieren. **modernization** *n* Modernisierung *f.*

modest ['modist] *adj* bescheiden; (*reasonable*) vernünftig. **modesty** *n* Bescheidenheit *f.*

modify ['modifai] *v* abändern, modifizieren. **modification** *n* Abänderung *f,* Modifikation *f.*

modulate ['modjuleit] *v* modulieren.

mohair ['mouheǝ] *n* Mohair *m.*

moist [moist] *adj* feucht. **moisture** *n* Feuchtigkeit *f.*

molar ['moulǝ] *n* Backenzahn *m.*

molasses [mǝ'lasiz] *n* Melasse *f.*

mold (*US*) *V* **mould.**

mole[1] [moul] *n* (*birthmark*) Muttermal *neut,* Leberfleck *m.*

mole[2] [moul] *n* (*zool*) Maulwurf *m.*

molecule ['molikjuːl] *n* Molekül *neut.* **molecular** *adj* molekular.

molest [mǝ'lest] *v* belästigen.

mollusc ['molǝsk] *n* Weichtier *neut.*

molt (*US*) *V* **moult.**

molten ['moultǝn] *adj* geschmolzen, flüssig.

moment ['moumǝnt] *n* Moment *m,* Augenblick *m.* **momentary** *adj* momentan, augenblicklich.

monarch ['monǝk] *n* Monarch(in). **monarchy** *n* Monarchie *f.*

monastery ['monǝstǝri] *n* Kloster *neut.* **monastic** *adj* kloster-.

Monday ['mʌndi] *n* Montag *m.*

money ['mʌni] *n* Geld *neut.* **money box** Sparbüchse *f.* **money order** Zahlungsanweisung *f.* **monetary** *adj* Währungs-.

mongolism ['moŋgǝlizm] *n* Mongolismus *m.*

mould

mongrel ['mʌŋgrəl] n Mischling m, Kreuzung f.
monitor ['monitə] n (TV) Monitor m. v überwachen, kontrollieren.
monk [mʌŋk] n Mönch m. **monkish** adj mönchisch.
monkey ['mʌŋki] n Affe m. v **monkey around** herumalbern.
monogamy [mə'nogəmi] n Monogamie f. **monogamous** adj monogam.
monogram ['monəgram] n Monogramm neut.
monologue ['monəlog] n Monolog m.
monopolize [mə'nopəlaiz] v monopolisieren. **monopoly** n Monopol neut.
monosyllable ['monəsiləbl] n einsilbiges Wort neut.
monotonous [mə'notənəs] adj monoton. **monotony** n Monotonie f.
monsoon [mon'suːn] n Monsun m.
monster ['monstə] n Ungeheuer neut; (malformation) Mißbildung f. **monstrous** adj ungeheuer.
month [mʌnθ] n Monat m. **monthly** adj monatlich; n (magazine) Monatsschrift f.
monument ['monjument] n Denkmal neut. **monumental** adj kolossal.
mood [muːd] n Laune f, Stimmung f. **be in a good/bad mood** guter/schlechter Laune sein. **moody** adj launisch.
moon [muːn] n Mond m. **full moon** Vollmond m. **moonlight** n Mondschein m.
moor¹ [muə] n Heide f, Moor neut.
moor² [muə] v (boat) vertäuen. **mooring** n Liegeplatz m.
mop [mop] n Mop m. v aufwischen.
mope [moup] v traurig sein, (coll) Trübsal blasen.
moped ['mouped] n Moped neut.
moral ['morəl] adj moralisch. n (of story) Lehre f. **morals** pl Moral f sing, Sitten pl. **morale** n Morale f. **morality** n Sittlichkeit f. **moral** n Sitten pl.
morbid ['moːbid] adj (fig) schauerlich.
more [moː] adj mehr; (in number) weitere, mehr. adv mehr, weiter. **more rapid** schneller. **more and more** immer mehr. **more or less** mehr oder weniger. **once more** noch einmal. **moreover** adv überdies, ferner hin.
morgue [moːg] n Leichenhaus neut.
morning ['moːniŋ] n Morgen m, Vormittag m. **in the mornings** morgens. **this morning** heute früh.

moron ['moːron] n Schwachsinnige(r). **moronic** adj schwachsinnig.
morose [mə'rous] adj mürrisch.
morphine ['moːfiːn] n Morphium neut.
morse code [mois] n Morsealphabet neut.
morsel ['moisəl] n Bissen m, Stückchen neut.
mortal ['moitl] adj sterblich; (wound) tödlich. **mortality** n Sterblichkeit f.
mortar ['moitə] n (for bricks) Mörtel m; (mil) Granatwerfer m.
mortgage ['moigidʒ] n Hypothek f.
mortify ['moitifai] v demütigen. **mortification** n Demütigung f.
mortuary ['moitʃuəri] n Leichenhaus neut.
mosaic [mə'zeiik] n Mosaik neut.
mosque [mosk] n Moschee f.
mosquito [mə'skiitou] n Moskito m.
moss [mos] n Moos neut. **mossy** adj bemoost.
most [moust] adj die meisten. adv äußerst, höchst; am meisten. n das Meiste. **most people** die meisten Leute, **at most** höchstens. **mostly** adv meistens, größtenteils.
motel [mou'tel] n Motel neut.
moth [moθ] n Motte f. **mothball** n Mottenkugel f.
mother ['mʌðə] n Mutter f. v bemuttern. **on one's mother's side** mütterlicherseits. **mother country** Mutterland neut. **motherhood** n Mutterschaft f. **mother-in-law** Schwiegermutter f. **motherless** adj mutterlos. **motherly** adj mütterlich. **mother-of-pearl** n Perlmutt neut.
motion ['mouʃən] n Bewegung f; (pol) Antrag m. v zuwinken. **set in motion** in Gang setzen.
motivate ['moutiveit] v motivieren. **motivation** n Motivierung f.
motif [mou'tiːf] n Motiv m.
motive ['moutiv] n Beweggrund m.
motor ['moutə] n Motor m. **motor accident** Autounfall m. **motorcar** n Wagen m, Auto neut. **motor cycle** n Mottorrad neut. **motorist** n Autofahrer m.
mottled ['motld] adj gefleckt.
motto ['motou] n Motto neut.
mould¹ [mould] or US **mold** n (tech) Form f; (type) Art f. v bilden, formen; (tech) gießen.
mould² [mould] or US **mold** n (mildew) Schimmel m. **mouldy** adj schimmelig.

moult 112

moult [moult] *or US* **molt** *v* sich mausern.
mound [maund] *n* (Erd)Hügel *m*.
mount[1] [maunt] *v* (*horse*) besteigen. *n* (*frame*) Gestell *neut*; (*horse*) Reittier *neut*.
mount[2] [maunt] *n* Berg *m*, Hügel *m*.
mountain ['mauntən] *n* Berg *m*. **mountaineer** *n* Bergsteiger *m*.
mourn [mɔːn] *v* trauern (um). **mourning** *n* Trauer *f*. **go into mourning** Trauer anlegen.
mouse [maus] *n* (*pl* **mice**) Maus *f*. **mousetrap** *n* Mausefalle *f*.
mousse [muːs] *n* Kremeis *neut*.
moustache [mə'staːʃ] *or US* **mustache** *n* Schnurrbart *m*.
mouth [mauθ] *n* Mund *m*; (*opening*) Öffnung *f*; (*river*) Mündung *f*; (*animal*) Maul *neut*. **mouthful** *n* Mundvoll *m*. **mouthpiece** *n* Mundstück *neut*. **mouthwash** *n* Mundwasser *neut*.
move [muːv] *v* (sich) bewegen; (*emotionally*) rühren; (*house*) umziehen. **movable** *adj* beweglich. **movement** *n* Bewegung *f*. **moving** *adj* rührend. **moving staircase** Rolltreppe *f*.
movie ['muːvi] *n* Film *m*. **go to the movies** ins Kino gehen.
*****mow** [mou] *v* mähen. **mower** *n* (Rasen)Mäher *m*.
mown [moun] *V* **mow**.
Mr ['mistə] *n* Herr *m*.
Mrs ['misiz] *n* Frau *f*.
much [mʌtʃ] *adj, adv* viel. **how much?** wieviel?
muck [mʌk] *n* (*dung*) Mist *m*; (*dirt*) Dreck *m*. **mucky** *adj* schmutzig, dreckig.
mucus ['mjuːkəs] *n* Schleim *m*.
mud [mʌd] *n* Schlamm *m*. **muddy** *adj* schlammig. **mudguard** *n* Kotflügel *m*. **mudslinger** *n* Verleumder(in).
muddle ['mʌdl] *n* Durcheinander *neut*, Wirrwarr *m*. *v* **muddle through** sich durchwursteln. **muddled** *adj* konfus.
muff [mʌf] *n* Muff *m*.
muffle ['mʌfl] *v* (*noise*) dämpfen. **muffler** *n* Schal *m*; (*mot*) Schalldämpfer *m*.
mug [mʌg] *n* Krug *m*, Becher *m*. *v* (*rob*) überfallen. **muggy** *adj* (*weather*) schwül.
mulberry ['mʌlbəri] *n* Maulbeere *f*.
mule [mjuːl] *n* Maulesel *m*. **mulish** *adj* störrisch.
multicoloured [ˌmʌlti'kʌləd] *adj* bunt, vielfarbig.

multiple ['mʌltipl] *adj* mehrfach, vielfach.
multiply ['mʌltiplai] *v* (sich) vermehren; (*math*) multiplizieren. **multiplication** *v* Vermehrung; (*math*) Multiplikation *f*. **multiplicity** *n* Vielfalt *f*.
multiracial [ˌmʌlti'reiʃəl] *adj* gemischtrassig.
multitude ['mʌltitjuːd] *n* Menge *f*. **multitudinous** *adj* zahlreich.
mumble ['mʌmbl] *v* murmeln. *n* Gemurmel *neut*.
mummy[1] ['mʌmi] *n* (*embalmed*) Mumie *f*.
mummy[2] ['mʌmi] *n* (*coll*) Mutti *f*.
mumps [mʌmps] *n* Ziegenpeter *m*.
munch [mʌntʃ] *v* schmetzend kauen.
mundane [mʌn'dein] *adj* alltäglich, banal.
municipal [mju'nisipəl] *adj* städtisch, Stadt-. **municipality** *n* Stadt *f*, Stadtbezirk *m*.
mural ['mjuərəl] *n* Wandgemälde *neut*.
murder ['məːdə] *n* Mord *m*, Ermordung *f*. *v* (er)morden. **murderer** *n* Mörder *m*. **murderous** *adj* mörderisch, tödlich.
murmur ['məːmə] *v* murmeln. *n* Murmeln *neut*.
muscle ['mʌsl] *n* Muskel *m*. **muscular** *adj* (*person*) muskulös.
muse [mjuːz] *n* Muse *f*. *v* (nach)denken.
museum [mju'ziəm] *n* Museum *neut*.
mushroom ['mʌʃrum] *n* Pilz *m*, Champignon *m*. *v* (*coll*) sich ausbreiten.
music ['mjuːzik] *n* Musik *f*. **musical** *adj* musikalisch. **musician** *n* Musiker *m*. **music stand** Notenständer *m*.
musk [mʌsk] *n* Moschus *m*.
musket ['mʌskit] *n* Flinte *f*, Muskete *f*. **musketeer** *n* Musketier *m*.
Muslim ['mʌzlim] *n* Mohammedaner(in). *adj* mohammedanisch.
muslin ['mʌzlin] *n* Musselin *m*.
mussel ['mʌsl] *n* Muschel *f*.
*****must**[1] [mʌst] *v* müssen.
must[2] [mʌst] *n* Most *m*. **musty** *adj* muffig, schimmelig.
mustard ['mʌstəd] *n* Senf *m*.
muster ['mʌstə] *v* antreten lassen. **muster one's courage** sich zusammennehmen. **pass muster** Zustimmung finden.
mutation [mjur'teiʃən] *n* Veränderung *f*; (*biol*) Mutation *f*.
mute [mjuːt] *adj* stumm. *n* Stumme(r); (*music*) Sordine *f*.
mutilate ['mjuːtileit] *v* verstümmeln. **mutilation** *n* Verstümmelung *f*.

nectar

mutiny ['mjuːtini] *n* Meuterei *f.* *v* meutern. **mutineer** *n* Meuterer *m.* **mutinous** *adj* meuterisch.
mutter ['mʌtə] *v* murmeln.
mutton ['mʌtn] *n* Hammelfleisch *neut.*
mutual ['mjuːtʃuəl] *adj* gegenseitig.
muzzle ['mʌzl] *n* Maul *neut;* *(protection)* Maulkorb *m.*
my [mai] *poss adj* mein, meine, mein. **myself** *pron* mich (selbst). **by myself** allein.
mystery ['mistəri] *n* Rätsel *neut,* Geheimnis *neut.* **mysterious** *adj* geheimnisvoll, mysteriös. **mystic** *n* Mystiker(in). *adj* mystisch. **mysticism** *n* Mystizismus *m.* **mystify** *v* täuschen, verblüffen.
myth [miθ] *n* Mythos *m.* **mythical** *adj* mythisch. **mythological** *adj* mythologisch. **mythology** *n* Mythologie *f.*

N

nag [nag] *v* herumnörgeln an. *n* Gaul *m.*
nail [neil] *n* Nagel *m.* *v* (an)nageln. **nail down** zunageln. **nailbrush** *n* Nagelbürste *f.* **nail-file** *n* Nagelfeile *f.* **nail polish** Nagellack *m.* **nail scissors** Nagelschere *f sing.*
naïve [naiˈiːv] *adj* naiv. **naïveté** *n* Naivität *f.*
naked ['neikid] *adj* nackt. **nakedness** *n* Nacktheit *f.*
name [neim] *n* Name *m;* *(reputation)* Ruf *m.* **by name** namentlich. **by the name of** namens. *what's your name?* wie heißen Sie? *v* nennen; *(mention)* erwähnen. **namely** *adv* nämlich.
nanny ['nani] *n* Kindermädchen *neut.*
nap [nap] *n* Nickerchen *neut.*
napkin ['napkin] *n* *(table)* Serviette *f.*
nappy ['napi] *n* Windel *f.*
narcotic [naːˈkotic] *n* Narkotikum *neut.* *adj* narkotisch.
narrate [nəˈreit] *v* erzählen. **narration** *n also* **narrative** Erzählung *f.* **narrative** *adj* Erzählungs-. **narrator** *n* Erzähler(in).
narrow ['narou] *adj* eng, schmal; *(fig)* beschränkt. *v* sich verengen. **narrowly** *adv* *(just)* mit Mühe. **narrow-minded** *adj* engstirnig.

nasal ['neizəl] *adj* Nasen-; *(voice)* nasal.
nasturtium [nəˈstəːʃəm] *n* Kapuzinerkresse *f.*
nasty ['naːsti] *adj* ekelhaft, widerlich; *(serious)* ernst, schlimm; *(person)* gemein, böse.
nation ['neiʃən] *n* Nation *f,* Volk *neut.* **national** *adj* national, Volks-. **nationalism** *n* Nationalismus *m.* **nationality** *n* Staatsangehörigkeit *f.* **nationalization** *n* Verstaatlichung *f.* **nationalize** *v* verstaatlichen. **national anthem** Nationalhymne *f.* **National Insurance** Sozialversicherung *f.*
native ['neitiv] *adj* eingeboren. *n* Eingeborene(r).
nativity [nəˈtivəti] *n* Geburt *f.* **nativity play** Krippenspiel *neut.*
natural ['natʃərəl] *adj* natürlich, Natur-. **natural resources** Naturschätze *pl.* **naturalist** *n* Naturforscher *m.* **naturalize** *v* einbürgern.
nature ['neitʃə] *n* Natur *f.*
naughty ['noːti] *adj* unartig, ungezogen. **naughtiness** *n* Ungezogenheit *f.*
nausea ['noːziə] *n* Übelkeit *f,* Brechreiz *m;* *(seasickness)* Seekrankheit *f.* **nauseating** *adj* widerlich.
nautical ['noːtikəl] *adj* nautisch, Schiffs-. **nautical mile** Seemeile *f.*
naval ['neivəl] *adj* Flotten-, See-. **naval battle** Seeschlacht *f.*
navel ['neivəl] *n* Nabel *m.*
navigate ['navigeit] *v* navigieren. **navigable** *adj* schiffbar. **navigation** *n* Navigation *f.* **navigator** *n* Navigator *m.*
navy ['neivi] *n* Flotte *f,* Kriegsmarine *f.* **navy-blue** *adj* marineblau.
near [niə] *adj* nahe. *adv* nahe, in der Nähe. *prep* in der Nähe (von *or* +gen). nahe an. **nearby** *adv* in der Nähe; *adj* nahe gelegen. **nearly** *adv* fast, beinahe.
neat [niːt] *adj* ordentlich; *(alcohol)* rein, unverdünnt. **neatness** *n* Ordentlichkeit *f.*
necessary ['nesisəri] *adj* nötig, erforderlich. **necessarily** *adv* notwendigerweise. **necessitate** *v* erfordern. **necessity** *n* Notwendigkeit *f.* **necessities** *pl* Bedarfsartikel *pl.*
neck [nek] *n* Hals *m.* **neckerchief** *n* Halstuch *neut.* **necklace** *n* Halskette *f.* **necktie** *n* Krawatte *f.*
nectar ['nektə] *n* Nektar *m.*

née [nei] *adj* geborene.
need [niːd] *v* Bedürfnis *neut*, Bedarf *m*; (*necessity*) Notwendigkeit *f*. **if need arise** im Notfall. **needful** *adj* nötig. **neediness** Armut *f*. **needless** *adj* unnötig. **needy** *adj* arm.
needle [niːdl] *n* Nadel *f*; (*indicator*) Zeiger *m*. *v* (*coll*) reizen. **needlework** *n* Handarbeit *f*.
negate [niˈgeit] *v* annullieren, verneinen. **negation** *n* Annullierung *f*, Verneinung *f*. **negative** *adj* negativ; (*answer*) ablehnend. *n* (*phot*) Negativ *neut*.
neglect [niˈglekt] *v* vernachlässigen. *n* Vernachlässigung *f*.
negligée [ˈnegliʒei] *n* Negligé *neut*.
negligence [ˈneglidʒəns] *n* Nachlässigkeit *f*. **negligent** *adj* nachlässig. **negligible** *adj* geringfügig.
negotiate [niˈgouʃieit] *v* verhandeln. **negotiation** *n* Verhandlung *f*. **negotiator** Vermittler *m*.
Negro [ˈniːgrou] *n* Neger *m*. *adj* Neger-. **Negress** *n* Negerin *f*.
neigh [nei] *v* wiehern. *n* Wiehern *neut*.
neighbour [ˈneibə] *n* Nachbar(in). **neighbourhood** *n* Nachbarschaft *f*. **neighbourly** *adj* freundlich.
neither [ˈnaiðə] *adj, pron* kein (von beiden). **neither ... nor ...** weder ... noch ....
neon [ˈniːon] *n* Neon *neut*.
nephew [ˈnefjuː] *n* Neffe *m*.
nepotism [ˈnepətizəm] *n* Vetternwirtschaft *f*.
nerve [nəːv] *n* Nerv *m*; (*cheek*) Frechheit *f*. **nerves** *pl* Nervosität *f sing*. **nervous** *adj* Nerven-; (*on edge*) nervös. **nervousness** *n* Nervosität *f*. **nervy** *adj* nervös. **nerve-racking** *adj* nervenaufreibend.
nest [nest] *n* Nest *neut*. *v* nisten.
nestle [ˈnesl] *v* sich anschmiegen.
net¹ [net] *n* Netz *neut*; (*fabric*) Tüll *m*. *v* fangen.
net² [net] *adj* (*comm*) netto, Netto-. **net amount** Nettobetrag *m*. **net price** Nettopreis *m*. **net profit** Reingewinn *m*.
Netherlands [ˈneðələndz] *pl n* Niederlände *pl*.
nettle [ˈnetl] *n* Nessel *f*. *v* ärgern. **nettle rash** Nesselausschlag *m*. **grasp the nettle** die Schwierigkeit anpacken.
neurosis [njuˈrousis] *n* Neurose *f*. **neurotic** *adj* neurotisch; *n* Neurotiker(in).

neuter [ˈnjuːtə] *adj* (*gramm*) sächlich. *n* Neutrum *neut*. *v* (*male*) kastrieren; (*female*) sterilisieren.
neutral [ˈnjuːtrəl] *adj* neutral. *n* (*mot*) Leerlauf *m*. **neutrality** *n* Neutralität *f*. **neutralize** *v* neutralisieren.
never [ˈnevə] *adv* nie, niemals. **never-ending** *adj* endlos. **never-failing** *adj* unfehlbar. **nevermore** *adv* nimmermehr. **nevertheless** *adv* nichtsdestoweniger.
new [njuː] *adj* neu; (*strange*) unbekannt. **newborn** *adj* neugeboren. **newcomer** *n* Neuankömmling *m*. **new-fangled** *adj* neumodisch. **newish** *adj* ziemlich neu. **newly** *adv* neulich. **newly-wed** *adj* jungvermählt. **newness** *n* Neuheit *f*. **news** *pl n* Nachrichten *pl*. **newspaper** *n* Zeitung *f*. **newsagent** Zeitungshändler *m*. **news flash** Kurznachricht *f*. **newsstand** *n* Zeitungskiosk *m* **newsworthy** *adj* aktuell.
newt [njuːt] *n* Wassermolch *m*.
New Testament *n* Neujahr *neut*. **New Year's Day** Neujahr *neut*. **New Year's Eve** Sylvester *neut*.
next [nekst] *adj* nächst, nächstfolgend; *adv* gleich daran, nächstens. *prep* neben, bei. **next door** nebenan.
nib [nib] *n* (Füllfeder)Spitze *f*.
nibble [ˈnibl] *v* nagen, knabbern (an). *n* Nagen *neut*, Knabbern *neut*; (*morsel*) Happen *m*.
nice [nais] *adj* nett; (*kind*) freundlich. **nicely** *adv* nett. **nicety** *n* Feinheit *f*.
niche [nitʃ] *n* Nische *f*.
nick [nik] *v* einkerben; (*coll: catch*) erwischen. *n* Kerbe *f*; (*coll*) Gefängnis *neut*; Polizeiwache *f*.
nickel [ˈnikl] *n* Nickel *neut*; (*US*) Fünfcentstück *neut*. *adj* Nickel-. **nickel-plated** *adj* vernickelt.
nickname [ˈnikneim] *n* Spitzname *m*.
nicotine [ˈnikətiːn] *n* Nikotin *neut*.
niece [niːs] *n* Nichte *f*.
niggle [ˈnigl] *v* trödeln.
night [nait] *n* Nacht *f*; (*evening*) Abend *m*. **all night** die ganze Nacht. **goodnight** gute Nacht. **nightclub** *n* Nachtlokal *neut*. **nightdress** *n* Nachthemd *neut*. **nightly** *adj* nächtlich. **nightmare** *n* Alptraum *m*. **nighttime** *n* Nacht *f*.
nightingale [ˈnaitiŋgeil] *n* Nachtigall *f*.
nil [nil] *n* Null *f*.
nimble [ˈnimbl] *adj* flink. **nimbleness** *n* Gewandtheit *f*.

nine [nain] *adj* neun. *n* Neun *f*. **ninth** *adj* neunt; *n* Neuntel *neut*.
nineteen [nain'tiːn] *adj* neunzehn. *n* Neunzehn *f*. **nineteenth** *adj* neunzehnt.
ninety ['nainti] *adj* neunzig. *n* Neunzig *f*. **ninetieth** *adj* neunzigst.
nip [nip] *v* kneifen, zwicken. **nip in the bud** im Keim ersticken.
nipple ['nipl] *n* Brustwarze *f*; (*baby's bottle*) Lutscher *m*; (*tech*) Nippel *m*.
nit [nit] *n* Niß *f*, Nisse *f*.
nitrogen ['naitrədʒən] *n* Stickstoff *m*.
no [nou] *adv* nein. *adj* kein. **on no account** auf keinen Fall. **in no way** keineswegs. **no more** nicht mehr. **no smoking** Rauchen verboten. **no-smoking compartment** Nichtraucher *m*.
noble ['noubl] *adj* edel, adlig. **nobility** *n* Adel *m*, Adelsstand *m*. **nobleman** *n* Edelmann *m*.
nobody ['noubodi] *pron* niemand, keiner.
nocturnal [nok'təːnəl] *adj* nächtlich, Nacht-.
nod [nod] *v* nicken. *n* Nicken *neut*. **nod off** einschlafen.
noise [noiz] *n* Lärm *m*, Geräusch *neut*. **noiseless** *adj* geräuschlos. **noisy** *adj* laut.
nomad ['noumad] *n* Nomade *m*, Nomadin *f*. **nomadic** *adj* nomadisch.
nominal ['nominl] *adj* nominell, Nenn-.
nominate ['nomineit] *v* ernennen. **nomination** *n* Ernennung *f*.
nominative ['nominətiv] *n* (*gramm*) Nominativ *m*.
nonchalant ['nonʃələnt] *adj* unbekümmert. **nonchalance** *n* Gleichgültigkeit *f*.
nondescript ['nondiskript] *adj* nichtssagend.
none [nʌn] *pron* kein; (*person*) niemand. *adv* keineswegs.
nonentity [non'entəti] *n* Unding *neut*; (*coll: person*) Null *f*.
nonetheless [ˌnʌnðə'les] *adv* nichtsdestoweniger.
nonsense ['nonsəns] *n* Unsinn *m*. *interj* Unsinn! Quatsch! **nonsensical** *adj* sinnlos. **stand no nonsense** sich nichts gefallen lassen.
non-smoker [non'smoukə] *n* Nichtraucher(in). **non-smoking compartment** Nichtraucher(abteil) *m*.
non-stop [non'stop] *adj* pausenlos; (*train*) durchgehend.
noodles ['nuːdlz] *pl n* Nudeln *pl*.

noon [nuːn] *n* Mittag *m*. **at noon** zu Mittag.
no-one ['nouwʌn] *pron* keiner, niemand.
noose [nuːs] *n* Schlinge *f*.
nor [noː] *adj* noch. **nor do I** ich auch nicht.
norm [noːm] *n* Norm *f*. **normal** *adj* normal. **normality** *n* Normalität *f*. **normalize** *v* normalisieren. **normally** *adv* normalerweise.
north [noːθ] *n* Norden *m*. *adj* *also* **northerly, northern** nördlich, Nord-. *adv* *also* **northwards** nach Norden, nordwärts. **North America** Nordamerika *neut*. **north-east** *n* Nordosten *m*. **North Pole** Nordpol *m*. **north-west** *n* Nordwesten *m*.
Norway ['noːwei] *n* Norwegen *neut*. **Norwegian** *adj* norwegisch; *n* Norweger(in).
nose [nouz] *n* Nase *f*. **nosy** *adj* (*coll*) neugierig.
nostalgia [no'staldʒə] *n* Nostalgie *f*. **nostalgic** *adj* wehmütig.
nostril ['nostrəl] *n* Nasenloch *neut*.
not [not] *adv* nicht. **not a** kein. **is it not?** *or* **isn't it?** nicht wahr?
notch [notʃ] *n* Kerbe *f*. *v* einkerben.
note [nout] *n* Vermerk *m*, Notiz *f*; (*letter*) Zettel *m*; (*music*) Note *f*; (*money*) Schein *m*; (*importance*) Bedeutung *f*. *v* merken. **take notes** Notizen machen.
nothing ['nʌθiŋ] *pron* nichts. *n* Nichts *neut*. **nothing but** nichts als.
notice ['noutis] *n* Notiz *f*; (*law*) Kündigung *f*. *v* bemerken. **period of notice** Kündigungsfrist *f*. **take notice (of)** achtgeben (auf). **give notice** kündigen. **until further notice** bis auf weiteres. **noticeable** *adj* bemerkenswert. **noticeboard** *n* Anschlagtafel *f*.
notify ['noutifai] *v* melden, benachrichtigen. **notification** *n* Meldung *f*; Benachrichtigung *f*.
notion ['nouʃən] *n* Begriff *m*. **have no notion** keine Ahnung haben.
notorious [nou'toːriəs] *adj* notorisch.
notwithstanding [notwiθ'standiŋ] *prep* trotz (+*gen*).
nougat ['nuːgaː] *n* Nugat *m*.
nought [noːt] *n* Null *f*. **come/bring to nought** zunichte kommen/bringen.
noun [naun] *n* Hauptwort *neut*.
nourish ['nʌriʃ] *v* (er)nähren. **nourishing** *adj* nahrhaft. **nourishment** *n* Ernährung *f*.

novel

novel ['nɔvəl] *adj* neu, neuartig. *n* Roman *m.* **novelist** *n* Romanschriftsteller(in). **novelty** *n* Neuheit *f.*
November [nə'vembə] *n* November *m.*
novice ['nɔvis] *n* Anfänger(in); (*rel*) Novize *m, f.*
now [nau] *adv* jetzt, nun; (*straightaway*) sofort. **now and again** ab und zu, hin und wieder. **nowadays** *adv* heutzutage.
nowhere ['nouweə] *adv* nirgends, nirgendwo. **from nowhere** aus dem Nichts.
noxious ['nokʃəs] *adj* schädlich.
nozzle ['nozl] *n* Schnauze *f,* Ausguß *m.*
nuance ['njuːɑ̃s] *n* Nuance *f,* Schattierung *f.*
nuclear ['njuːklɪə] *adj* Kern-. **nuclear energy** Atomkraft *f.* **nuclear reactor** Kernreaktor *m.*
nucleus ['njuːklɪəs] *n* Kern *m.*
nude ['njuːd] *adj* nackt. **nudist** *n* Nudist(in). **nudity** *n* Nacktheit *f.*
nudge [nʌdʒ] *n* Rippenstoß *m. v* leicht anstoßen.
nugget ['nʌgit] *n* Goldklumpen *m.*
nuisance ['njuːsns] *n* Ärgernis *neut.*
null [nʌl] *adj* nichtig, ungültig. **null and void** null und nichtig.
numb [nʌm] *adj* starr, erstarrt. *v* taub machen.
number ['nʌmbə] *n* Nummer *f;* (*amount*) Anzahl *f;* (*figure*) Ziffer *f. v* numerieren. **number-plate** *n* Nummernschild *neut.* **numeral** *n* Ziffer *f.* **numerous** *adj* zahlreich.
nun [nʌn] *n* Nonne *f.*
nurse [nəːs] *n* Krankenschwester *f,* Krankenpfleger(in). *v* pflegen; (*feed baby*) stillen. **nursemaid** *n* Kindermädchen *neut.* **nursing** *n* Krankenpflege *f.* **nursing home** Privatklinik *f.*
nursery ['nəːsəri] *n* (*in house*) Kinderzimmer *neut;* (*institution*) Krippe *f,* Kindertagesstätte *f;* (*bot*) Gärtnerei *f.* **nurseryman** *n* Pflanzenzüchter *m.* **nursery rhyme** *n* Kinderlied *neut,* Kinderreim *m.* **nursery school** *n* Kindergarten *m.*
nurture ['nəːtʃə] *v* erziehen.
nut [nʌt] *n* Nuß *f;* (*for bolt*) Mutter *f.* **nutcracker** Nußknacker *m.* **nuts** *adj* (*coll*) verrückt. **nutmeg** *n* Muskatnuß *f.*
nutrient ['njuːtrɪənt] *n* Nährstoff *m. adj* nährend. **nutrition** *n* Ernährung *f.* **nutritious** *adj* nahrhaft.

nuzzle ['nʌzl] *v* sich schmiegen (an).
nylon ['nailon] *n* Nylon *neut.* **nylons** *pl* Strümpfe *pl.*
nymph [nimf] *n* Nymphe *f.*

O

oak [ouk] *n* Eiche *f.* (*wood*) Eichenholz *neut.* **oaken** *adj* eichen.
oar [oɪ] *n* Ruder *neut,* Riemen *m.* **oarsman** *n* Ruderer *m.*
oasis [ou'eisis] *n* (*pl* -ses) Oase *f.*
oath [ouθ] *n* Eid *m;* (*swear word*) Fluch *m.*
oats [outs] *pl n* Hafer *m sing.* **oatmeal** *n* Hafermehl *neut.*
obedient [ə'biːdiənt] *adj* gehorsam. **obedience** *n* Gehorsam *m.*
obese [ə'biːs] *adj* fettleibig. **obesity** *n* Fettleibigkeit *f.*
obey [ə'bei] *v* gehorchen (+ *dat*); (*an order*) befolgen.
obituary [ə'bitjuəri] *n* Todesanzeige *f.*
object ['obʒikt; *v* əb'ʒekt] *n* Gegenstand *m;* (*aim*) Ziel *neut;* (*gramm*) Objekt *neut.* *money is no object* Geld spielt keine Rolle. **objective** *adj* objektiv. *v* einwenden (gegen). **objection** *n* Einwand *m,* Einspruch *m.* **objectionable** *adj* unangenehm.
oblige [ə'blaidʒ] *v* (*coerce*) zwingen. **be obliged to do something** etwas tun müssen. **much obliged!** besten Dank! **obligation** *n* Verpflichtung *f.* **obligatory** *adj* verbindlich.
oblique [ə'bliːk] *adj* schräg.
obliterate [ə'blitəreit] *v* auslöschen, tilgen. **obliteration** *n* Auslöschung *f,* Vertilgung *f.*
oblivion [ə'bliviən] *n* Vergessenheit *f.* **oblivious (to)** *adj* blind (gegen).
oblong ['oblon] *n* Rechteck *neut. adj* rechtickig.
obnoxious [əb'nokʃəs] *adj* gehässig.
oboe ['oubou] *n* Oboe *f.* **oboist** *n* Oboist(in).
obscene [əb'siːn] *adj* obszön. **obscenity** *n* Obszönität *f,* Unzüchtigkeit *f.*
obscure [əb'skjuə] *adj* (*dark*) dunkel, düster; (*meaning, etc.*) obskur, udeutlich.

obscurity n Dunkelheit f; Undeutlichkeit f.

observe [əb'zəɪv] v beobachten; (remark) bemerken. observer n Beobachter m. observation n Beobachtung f; Bemerkung f.

obsess [əb'ses] v quälen, heimsuchen. obsessed adj besessen. obsession n Besessenheit f.

obsolescent [obsə'lesnt] adj veraltend. obsolescence n Veralten neut.

obsolete ['obsəliːt] adj überholt, veraltet.

obstacle ['obstəkl] n Hindernis neut.

obstetrics [ob'stetriks] n Geburtshilfe f. obstetrician n Geburtshelfer(in).

obstinate ['obstinət] adj hartnäckig. obstinacy n Hartnäckigkeit f.

obstruct [əb'strʌkt] v versperren, blockieren; (hinder) hemmen. obstruction n Versperrung f; Hemmung f; (obstacle) Hindernis neut.

obtain [əb'tein] v erhalten, bekommen. obtainable adj erhältlich.

obtrusive [əb'truːsiv] adj aufdringlich.

obtuse [əb'tjuːs] adj stumpf.

obvious ['obviəs] adj offensichtlich.

occasion [ə'keiʒən] n Gelegenheit f; (possibility) Möglichkeit f; (cause) Anlaß m. occasional adj gelegentlich.

occult ['okʌlt] adj okkult. the occult okkulte Wissenschaften pl.

occupy ['okjupai] v (person) beschäftigen; (house) bewohnen; (mil) besetzen. occupied adj (phone booth, etc.) besetzt. occupant n Bewohner(in). occupation n Beschäftigung f; (profession) Beruf m; (mil) Besatzung f. occupational adj beruflich.

occur [ə'kəɪ] v vorkommen. it occurs to me es fällt mir ein. occurrence n Ereignis neut.

ocean ['ouʃən] n Ozean m, Meer neut. oceanic adj ozeanisch. ocean-going adj Hochsee-.

ochre ['oukə] adj ockerfarbig.

octagon ['oktəgən] n Achteck neut. octagonal adj achteckig.

octave ['oktiv] n Oktave f.

October [ok'toubə] n Oktober m.

octopus ['oktəpəs] n Tintenfisch m.

oculist ['okjulist] n Augenarzt m.

odd [od] adj (strange) seltsam; (numbers) ungerade. oddity n Seltsamkeit f. oddly (enough) seltsamerweise. oddments pl n Reste pl. oddness n Seltsamkeit f. odds pl n (Gewinn)Chancen pl. at odds with uneins mit. odds and ends Krimskrams m.

ode [oud] n Ode f.

odious ['oudiəs] adj verhaßt.

odour ['oudə] n Geruch m. odourless adj geruchlos.

oesophagus [iː'sofəgəs] n Speiseröhre f.

of [ov] prep von or gen.

off [of] prep fort, weg. adv weg, entfernt; ab. adj (food) verdorben, nicht mehr frisch. go off weggehen; (food) verderben. take off (clothes) ausziehen; (holiday) frei nehmen. switch off ausschalten. off and on ab und zu. off duty dienstfrei.

offal ['ofəl] n Innereien pl.

offend [ə'fend] v kränken, beleidigen. offender n Missetäter(in). offence n Vergehen neut, Verstoß m. take offence (at) Anstoß nehmen (an). offensive adj widerwärtig; n (mil) Angriff m.

offer ['ofə] v (an)bieten. n Angebot neut. offering n (gift) Spende f.

offhand [of'hand] adj lässig.

office ['ofis] n Büro neut; (official position or department) Amt neut. officer n (mil) Offizier. take office das Amt antreten. office staff Büropersonal neut.

official [ə'fiʃəl] n Beamte(r). adj amtlich; (report, function) offiziell. officially adj offiziell.

officious [ə'fiʃəs] adj aufdringlich.

offing ['ofiŋ] n in the offing in Sicht, drohend.

off-licence ['oflaisns] n Wein- und Spirituosenhandlung f.

off-peak [of'piːk] adj außerhalb der Hauptverkehrszeit.

off-putting ['of,putiŋ] adj abstoßend.

off-season [of'siːzn] n stille Saison f.

offset [of'set; n 'ofset] v ausgleichen. n (printing) offsetdruck m.

offshore ['ofʃɔɪ] adj Küsten-. adv von der Küste entfernt, auf dem Meere.

offside [of'said] adj abseits.

offspring ['ofspriŋ] n Nachkommenschaft f.

offstage ['ofsteidʒ] adv hinter den Kulissen.

often ['ofn] adv oft, häufig.

ogre ['ougə] n Ungeheuer neut, Riese m.

oil [oil] n Öl m; (petroleum) Erdöl neut. v ölen. oilfield Ölfeld neut. oil-paint n

Ölfarbe *f.* **oil-painting** *n* Ölgemalde *neut.*
oily *adj* fettig.
ointment ['ointmənt] *n* Salbe *f.*
old [ould] *adj* alt. **grow old** alt werden.
five years old fünf Jahre alt. **old age** Alter
neut. **old-fashioned** *adj* altmodisch.
olive ['oliv] *n* Olive *f.* **olive-green** *adj* oliv-
grün. **olive branch** *n* Ölzweig *m.* **olive oil**
Olivenöl *neut.* **olive tree** Ölbaum *m.*
Olympics [ə'limpiks] *pl* *n* Olympische
Spiele *pl.* Olympiade *f.*
omelette ['omlit] *n* Omelett *neut.*
omen ['oumən] *n* Vorzeichen *neut.* **omi-
nous** *adj* verhängnisvoll, drohend.
omit [ou'mit] *v* auslassen; (*to do something*) unterlassen. **omission** *n* Unterlassung *f.*
omnipotent [om'nipətənt] *adj* allmächtig.
omnipotence *n* Allmacht *f.*
on [on] *prep* (*position*) an, auf; (*concerning*) über. *adv* (*forward*) fort, weiter. **have
on** über. bei sich haben. **on fire** in Brand.
on foot zu Fuß. **on time** pünktlich. **put
on** (*clothes*) anziehen; (*manner*) affektier-
en. **switch on** einschalten.
once [wʌns] *adv, conj* einmal. **at once**
sofort. **once and for all** ein für allemal.
all at once auf einmal, plötzlich.
one [wʌn] *adj* ein, eine, ein. *n* Eins *f.* *pron*
man. **oneself** *pron* sich (selbst). **by oneself** allein. **one-piece** *adj* einteilig. **one-
way street** Einbahnstraße *f.*
onion ['ʌnjən] *n* Zwiebel *f.*
onlooker ['onlukə] *n* Zuschauer(in).
only ['ounli] *adj* einzig. *adv* nur; (*with
times*) erst. *conj* jedoch. **only just** gerade.
not only ... but also ... nicht nur ...
sondern auch ... .
onset ['onset] *n* Anfang *m.*
onslaught ['onslɔit] *n* Angriff *m.*
onus ['ounəs] *n* Last *f.* Verpflichtung *f.*
onward ['onwəd] *adv* vorwärts, weiter.
ooze [uiz] *v* (aus)sickern.
opal ['oupəl] *n* Opal *m.*
opaque [ə'paik] *adj* undurchsichtig.
open ['oupən] *v* öffnen, aufmachen;
(*book*) aufschlagen; (*event, shop*)
eröffnen; (*begin*) anfangen. *adj* offen,
auf. **open-air** *adj* Freiluft-. **in the open air**
im Freien. **with open arms** herzlich.
open-handed *adj* freigiebig. **opening** *n*
Öffnung *f.* (*shop*) Eröffnung *f.* **open-
minded** *adj* aufgeschlossen.
opera ['opərə] *n* Oper *f.* **opera house** Oper

f. Opernhaus *neut.* **opera singer** Opern-
sänger(in). **operatic** *adj* Opern-.
operate ['opəreit] *v* funktionieren, laufen;
(*med, tech, comm*) operieren. **operation** *n*
Arbeitslauf *m,* Betrieb *m;* Operation *f.*
operative *adj* tätig, wirksam; *n* Arbeiter
m.
ophthalmic [of'θalmik] *adj* Augen-. **ophthalmologist** *n* Augenarzt *m.* **ophthalmol-
ogy** *n* Ophthalmologie *f.*
opinion [ə'pinjən] *n* Meinung *f,* Ansicht *f.*
in my opinion meines Erachtens. **opinion
poll** Meinungsumfrage *f.*
opium ['oupiəm] *n* Opium *neut.*
opponent [ə'pounənt] *n* Gegner(in).
opportune [opə'tjuin] *adj* rechtzeitig.
opportunist *n* Opportunist(in).
opportunity [opə'tjuinəti] *n* Gelegenheit
f; (*possibility*) Möglichkeit *f.* **take the
opportunity** die Gelegenheit ergreifen.
oppose [ə'pouz] *v* bekämpfen, sich widersetzen (+*dat*). **opposed** *adj* feindlich
(gegen). **as opposed to** im Vergleich zu.
opposing *adj* (*ideas*) widerstreitend.
opposition *n* Widerstand *m;* (*pol*) Opposition *f.*
opposite ['opəzit] *adj* gegenüberliegend. *n*
Gegenteil *neut.*
oppress [ə'pres] *v* unterdrücken. **oppres-
sion** *n* Unterdrückung *f.* **oppressive** *adj*
bedrückend; (*weather*) schwül.
opt [opt] *v* sich entscheiden (für).
optical ['optikl] *adj* optisch. **optician** *n*
Optiker *m.* **optics** *n* Optik *f.*
optimism ['optimizəm] *n* Optimismus *m.*
optimist *n* Optimist(in). **optimistic** *adj*
optimistisch.
optimum ['optiməm] *n* Optimum *neut.* *adj*
optimal.
option ['opʃən] *n* Wahl *f;* (*comm*) Option
f. **have no option (but to)** keine andere
Möglichkeit haben (, als zu). **optional** *adj*
wahlfrei.
opulent ['opjulənt] *adj* opulent, üppig.
opulence *n* Opulenz *f,* Üppigkeit *f.*
or [oi] *conj* oder. **or else** sonst.
oracle ['orəkl] *n* Orakel *neut.*
oral ['oirəl] *adj* mündlich; (*med*) oral. *n*
mündliche Prüfung *f.*
orange ['orindʒ] *n* Apfelsine *f,* Orange *f.*
adj orange.
orator ['orətə] *n* Redner *m.* **oration** *n*
Rede *f.* **oratory** *n* Redekunst *f.*
orbit ['oibit] *n* Umlaufbahn *f.* *v*
umkreisen.

orchard ['ɔɪtʃəd] n Obstgarten m.
orchestra ['ɔɪkəstrə] n Orchester neut.
orchestral adj Orchester-, orchestral.
orchid ['ɔɪkid] n Orchidee f.
ordain [ɔɪ'dein] v ordinieren, weihen;
(decree) anordnen.
ordeal [ɔɪ'diːl] n schwere Prüfung f.
order ['ɔɪdə] n Ordnung f; (series)
Reihenfolge f; (comm) Bestellung f, Auftrag m; (command) Befehl m; (rel) Orden
m. v (comm) bestellen; (command)
befehlen. **put in order** ordnen. **in order to**
... um ... zu ... .
orderly ['ɔɪdəli] adj ordentlich. n (med)
Sanitäter m.
ordinal ['ɔɪdinl] adj Ordinal-.
ordinary ['ɔɪdənəri] adj gewöhnlich, normal. **out-of-the-ordinary** außerordentlich.
ordinarily adv normalerweise.
ore [ɔɪ] n Erz neut.
oregano [ori'gɑːnou] n Origanum neut.
organ ['ɔɪgən] n Organ neut; (music)
Orgel f. **organist** n Organist(in).
organic [ɔɪ'ganik] adj organisch.
organism ['ɔɪgənizəm] n Organismus m.
organize ['ɔɪgənaiz] v organisieren. **organization** n Organisation f; (association)
Verband m. **organizer** n Organisator m.
orgasm ['ɔɪgazəm] n Orgasmus m.
orgy ['ɔɪdʒi] n Orgie f.
orient ['ɔɪriənt] v orientieren. **the Orient**
Morgenland neut, Orient m. **oriental** adj
orientalisch; n Orientale m, Orientalin f.
orientate ['ɔɪriənteit] v orientieren. **orientation** n Orientierung f.
origin ['ɔɪridʒin] n Ursprung f; Herkunft
f, Entstehung f. **original** adj ursprünglich; (unusual) originell; n Original
neut. **originality** n Originalität f. **originate**
v entstehen.
ornament ['ɔɪnəmənt] n Ornament neut. v
verzieren, schmücken. **ornamental** adj
ornamental.
ornate [ɔɪ'neit] adj reich verziert.
ornithology [ɔɪni'θɔlədʒi] n Ornithologie
f, Vogelkunde f. **ornithologist** n Ornitho-
loge m, Ornithologin f.
orphan ['ɔɪfən] n Waise f, Waisenkind
neut. v verwaisen. **orphanage** n
Waisenhaus neut.
orthodox ['ɔɪθədoks] adj orthodox.
orthopaedic [ɔɪθəˈpiːdik] adj
orthopädisch. **orthopaedics** n Orthopädie
f.

oscillate ['ɔsileit] v oszillieren, schwingen.
oscillation n Schwingung f.
ostensible [o'stensəbl] adj scheinbar.
ostentatious [osten'teiʃəs] adj
großtuerisch. **ostentation** n Prahlerei f.
osteopath ['ostiəpaθ] n Osteopath(in).
ostracize ['ostrəsaiz] v verbannen.
ostrich ['ostritʃ] n Strauß m.
other ['ʌðə] adj, pron ander. **other than**
anders als. **each other** einander. **somebody or other** irgend jemand. **one after
the other** einer/eine/eins nach dem/der
andern.
otherwise ['ʌðəwaiz] adv sonst.
otter ['otə] n Otter m.
***ought** [ɔːt] v sollen. **you ought to do it**
Sie sollten es tun.
ounce [auns] n Unze f.
our [auə] adj unser. **Our Father**
Vaterunser neut. **ours** poss pron unsere.
ourselves uns (selbst).
oust [aust] v vertreiben.
out [aut] adv aus, hinaus, heraus;
(outside) draußen. **come out** herauskommen; (book, etc.) erscheinen. **go out**
hinausgehen. **out of the question** ausgeschlossen. **out-of-date** adj veraltet.
outboard ['autbɔɪd] adj Außenbord-. n
Außenbordmotor m.
outbreak ['autbreik] n Ausbruch m.
outbuilding ['autbildiŋ] n Nebengebäude
neut.
outburst ['autbəɪst] n Ausbruch m.
outcast ['autkaɪst] n Ausgestoßene(r).
outcome ['autkʌm] n Ergebnis neut.
outcry ['autkrai] n Aufschrei m.
***outdo** [aut'duː] v übertreffen.
outdoor ['autdɔɪ] adj Außen-. **outdoor
swimming pool** Freibad neut. **outdoors**
adv draußen.
outer ['autə] adj äußer, Außen-. **outer
garments** Oberkleidung f. **outer space**
Weltraum m.
outfit ['autfit] n Ausstattung f; (coll:
team) Mannschaft f. **outfitter** n (Herren)Ausstatter m.
outgoing ['autgouiŋ] adj (pol) abtretend;
(friendly) gesellig.
***outgrow** [aut'grou] v hinauswachsen
über; (clothes) herauswachsen aus.
outhouse ['authaus] n Anbau m,
Nebengebäude neut.
outing ['autiŋ] n Ausflug m.
outlandish [aut'landiʃ] adj seltsam,
grotesk.

outlaw ['autlɔɪ] n Vogelfreie(r). v ächten.

outlay ['autlei] n Auslage f, Ausgabe f.

outlet ['autlit] n Auslaß m.

outline ['autlain] n Umriß m. v umreißen.

outlive [aut'liv] v überleben.

outlook ['autluk] n Aussicht f; (attitude) Auffassung f.

outlying ['autlaiiŋ] adj entlegen.

outnumber [aut'nʌmbə] v (zahlenmäßig) überlegen sein (+ dat).

outpatient ['autpeiʃənt] n ambulanter Patient m.

outpost ['autpoust] n Vorposten m.

output ['autput] n Leistung f, Output m.

outrage ['autreidʒ] n Schande f. **outraged** adj beleidigt, schockiert. **outrageous** adj frevelhaft.

outright ['autrait; adv aut'rait] adj, adv ganz, völlig; (immediately) sogleich, auf der Stelle.

outside [aut'said; adj 'autsaid] n Äußere neut, Außenseite f. adj äußer, Außen-. prep außerhalb (+ gen). adv (go) hinaus; (be) draußen. **outsider** n Außenseiter(in).

outsize [aut'saiz] adj übergroß. n Übergröße f.

outskirts ['autskɔɪts] pl n Umgebung f sing, Staatrand m sing.

outspoken [aut'spoukən] adj freimütig.

outstanding [aut'standiŋ] adj hervorragend; (not settled) unerledigt.

outstrip [aut'strip] v überholen.

outward ['autwəd] adj äußer. adv also **outwards** nach Außen. **outward-bound** adj auf der Ausreise. **outwardly** adv äußerlich.

outweigh [aut'wei] v überwiegen.

outwit [aut'wit] v überlisten.

oval ['ouvəl] n Oval neut. adj oval.

ovary ['ouvəri] n Eierstock m.

ovation [ou'veiʃən] n Ovation f, Beifallssturm m.

oven ['ʌvn] n (cookery) Backofen m; (industrial, etc.) Ofen m.

over ['ouvə] adv über, hinüber, herüber; (finished) zu Ende; (during) während; (too much) allzu. prep über; (more than) mehr als. **over and over again** immer wieder. **over there** drüben. **all over England** in ganz England. **it's all over** es ist aus.

overall ['ouvərɔɪl] adj gesamt. adv insgesamt. n also **overalls** pl Overall m, Schutzanzug m.

overbalance [ouvə'baləns] v umkippen.

overbearing [ouvə'beəriŋ] adj anmaßend, arrogant.

overboard ['ouvəbɔɪd] adv über Bord.

overcast [ouvə'kaɪst] adj bedeckt, bewölkt.

overcharge [ouvə'tʃaɪdʒ] v zuviel verlangen von.

overcoat ['ouvəkout] n Mantel m.

*****overcome** [ouvə'kʌm] v überwinden. adj (with emotion) tief bewegt.

overcrowded [ouvə'kraudid] adj überfüllt.

*****overdo** [ouvə'duɪ] v übertreiben. **overdo it** zu weit gehen. **overdone** adj (cookery) übergar.

overdose ['ouvədous] n Überdosis f.

*****overdraw** [ouvə'drɔɪ] v überziehen. **overdraft** n (Konto)Überziehung f.

overdrive ['ouvədraiv] n Schongang m.

overdue [ouvə'djuɪ] adj überfällig; (train) verspätet.

overestimate [ouvə'estimeit] v überschätzen.

overexpose [ouvəik'spouz] v (phot) überbelichten.

overfill [ouvə'fil] v überfüllen.

overflow [ouvə'flou; n 'ouvəflou] v überlaufen. n Überlauf m.

overgrown [ouvə'groun] adj überwachsen.

*****overhang** [ouvə'haŋ; n 'ouvəhaŋ] v überhängen. n Überhang m.

overhaul [ouvə'hɔɪl] v überholen. n Überholung f.

overhead [ouvə'hed] adj obenliegend. **overheads** pl n allgemeine Unkosten pl.

*****overhear** [ouvə'hiə] v (zufällig) hören.

overheat [ouvə'hiɪt] v überheizen; (mot) heißlaufen.

overjoyed [ouvə'dʒoid] adj entzückt, außer sich vor Freude.

overland [ouvə'land] adj Überland-.

overlap [ouvə'lap; n 'ouvəlap] v sich überschneiden (mit). n Überscheiden neut, Übergreifen neut.

*****overlay** [ouvə'lei; n 'ouvəlei] v bedecken, belegen. n Auflage f, Bedeckung f.

overleaf [ouvə'liɪf] adv umseitig, umstehend.

overload [ouvə'loud; n 'ouvəloud] v überbelasten. n Überbelastung f.

overlook [ouvə'luk] v (room, etc.) überblicken; (let pass) nicht beachten.

overnight [ouvə'nait] adv über Nacht. **stay overnight** übernachten. adj Nacht-. **overnight case** Handkoffer m.

pair

overpower [ouvə'pauə] v überwältigen.
overrate [ouvə'reit] v überschätzen.
overrule [ouvə'ruːl] v zurückweisen; (person) überstimmen.
*overrun [ouvə'rʌn] v überschwemmen, überlaufen.
overseas [ouvə'siːz] adv in Übersee. adj überseeisch, Übersee-.
overseer [ouvə'siə] n Vorarbeiter m.
overshadow [ouvə'ʃadou] v überschatten.
*overshoot [ouvə'ʃuːt] v hinausschießen über.
oversight ['ouvəsait] n Versehen neut.
*oversleep [ouvə'sliːp] v sich verschlafen.
overspill ['ouvəspil] n Überschuß m.
overt [ou'vəːt] adj offenkundig.
*overtake [ouvə'teik] v überholen.
*overthrow [ouvə'θrou; n 'ouvəθrou] v (um)stürzen. n Umsturz m.
overtime ['ouvətaim] n Überstunden pl. **work overtime** Überstunden machen.
overtone ['ouvətoun] n Nuance f.
overture ['ouvətjuə] n (music) Ouvertüre f.
overturn [ouvə'təːn] v umkippen.
overweight [ouvə'weit] adj (zu) dick, fettleibig.
overwhelm [ouvə'welm] v überwältigen. **overwhelming** adj überwältigend.
overwork [ouvə'wəːk] v (sich) überanstrengen.
overwrought [ouvə'rɔːt] adj nervös, überreizt.
ovulate ['ovjuleit] v ovulieren. **ovulation** n Ovulation f. **ovum** n Ei neut, Eizelle f.
owe [ou] v schulden; (have debts) Schulden haben. **owing** adj zu zahlen. **owing to** infolge or wegen (+gen).
owl [aul] n Eule f.
own [oun] adj eigen. v besitzen; (admit) zugeben. **own up** gestehen. **owner** n Inhaber(in). **ownership** n Besitz m.
ox [oks] n (pl **oxen**) Ochse m, Rind neut.
oxtail Ochsenschwanz m.
oxygen ['oksidʒən] n Sauerstoff m.
oyster ['oistə] n Auster f.

P

pace [peis] n (step) Schritt m; (speed) Geschwindigkeit f, Tempo neut. v schreiten. **keep pace with** Schritt halten mit. **pacemaker** n Schrittmacher m.
Pacific [pə'sifik] n Pazifik m.
pacify ['pasifai] v befrieden. **pacifier** n (for baby) Schnuller m. **pacifism** n Pazifismus m. **pacifist** n Pazifist(in).
pack [pak] n Pack m, Packung f; (cards) Spiel neut; (dogs) Meute f. v einpacken; (stuff) vollstopfen. **package** n Paket neut. **packaging** n Verpackung f. **packet** n Packung f, Päckchen neut. **packhorse** n Lastpferd neut.
pact [pakt] n Pakt m, Vertrag m.
pad¹ [pad] n Polster neut; (paper) Block m; (sport) Schützer m; (ink) Stempelkissen neut. **padding** n Polsterung f.
pad² [pad] v trotten.
paddle¹ ['padl] n Paddel neut. v paddeln. **paddle-steamer** n Raddampfer m.
paddle² ['padl] v (wade) planschen, herumpaddeln.
paddock ['padək] n Pferdekoppel f; (on racecourse) Sattelplatz m.
paddyfield ['padifiːld] n Reisfeld neut.
padlock ['padlok] n Vorhängeschloß neut. v (mit einem Vorhängeschloß) verschließen.
paediatric [piːdi'atrik] adj pädiatrisch. **paediatrician** n Kinderarzt m, Kinderärztin f. **paediatrics** n Kinderheilkunde f.
pagan ['peigən] adj heidnisch. n Heide m, Heldin f.
page¹ [peidʒ] n (book) Seite f.
page² [peidʒ] n (boy) Page m
pageant ['padʒənt] n Festzug m. **pageantry** n Prunk m.
paid [peid] V **pay**.
pail [peil] n Eimer m.
pain [pein] n Schmerz m, Schmerzen pl; (suffering) Leid neut. v peinigen. **take pains** sich Mühe geben. **on pain of** bei Strafe von. **painful** adj schmerzhaft. **painkiller** n schmerzstillendes Mittel neut. **painless** adj schmerzlos. **painstaking** adj sorgfältig.
paint [peint] n Farbe f, Lack m. v anstreichen; (pictures) malen. **paintbrush** n Pinsel m. **painted** adj bemalt. **painter** n Maler(in). **painting** n Gemälde neut.
pair [peə] n Paar neut; (animals) Pärchen neut; (married couple) Ehepaar neut. v **pair off** paarweise anordnen. **a pair of trousers** eine Hose.

pal [pal] *n* (*coll*) Kamerad *m*, Kumpel *m*.
palace ['palǝs] *n* Palast *m*.
palate ['palit] *n* (Vorder)Gaumen *m*; (*taste*) Geschmack *m*. **palatable** *adj* schmackhaft.
pale [peil] *adj* blaß, bleich. *v* blaßwerden. **pale ale** helles Bier *neut*. **paleness** *n* Blässe *f*.
palette ['palit] *n* Palette *f*.
pall¹ [poil] *v* (*become boring*) jeden Reiz verlieren.
pall² [poil] *n* (*for coffin*) Leichentuch *neut*; (*fig*) Hülle *f*. **pall-bearer** *n* Sargträger *m*.
palm¹ [paim] *n* (*of hand*) Handfläche *f*. **palmist** *n* Handwahrsager(in). **palmistry** *n* Handlesekunst *f*.
palm² [paim] *n* (*tree*) Palme *f*.
palpitate ['palpiteit] *v* (*heart*) unregelmäßigschlagen; (*tremble*) beben, zittern.
pamper ['pampǝ] *v* verwöhnen.
pamphlet ['pamflit] *n* Broschüre *f*.
pan [pan] *n* Pfanne *f*.
pancreas ['paŋkriǝs] *n* Bauchspeicheldrüse *f*.
panda ['pandǝ] *n* Panda *m*.
pander ['pandǝ] *v* nachgeben (+*dat*).
pane [pein] *n* (Fenster)Scheibe *f*.
panel ['panl] *n* Tafel *f*; (*door*) Füllung *f*; (*dress*) Einsatzstück *m*; (*instrument*) Armaturenbrett *neut*. *v* täfeln. **panelling** *n* Täfelung *f*.
pang [paŋ] *n* (*of remorse*) Gewissensbisse *pl*.
panic ['panik] *n* Panik *f*. *v* hinreißen (zu). **panic-stricken** *adj* von panischer Angst erfüllt. **panicky** *adj* uberängstlich.
pannier ['paniǝ] *n* (Trag)Korb *m*; (*motorcycle*) Satteltasche *f*.
panorama [,panǝ'raɪmǝ] *n* Panorama *neut*, Rundblick *m*. **panoramic** *adj* panoramisch.
pansy ['panzi] *n* Stiefmütterchen *neut*.
pant [pant] *v* keuchen, schnaufen.
panther ['panθǝ] *n* Panther *m*.
panties ['pantiz] *pl n* (*coll*) Schlüpfer *m sing*, Höschen *neut sing*.
pantomime ['pantǝmaim] *n* Pantomime *f*.
pantry ['pantri] *n* Speiseschrank *m*.
pants [pants] *pl n* (*trousers*) Hose *f sing*; (*underpants*) Unterhose *f sing*. **pantyhose** Strumpfhose *f*.
papal ['peipl] *adj* päpstlich.
paper ['peipǝ] *n* Papier *neut*; (*newspaper*) Zeitung *f*; (*scientific*) Abhandlung *f*. *v* (a

room) tapezieren. **paperback** *n* Taschenbuch *neut*. **paper bag** Tüte *f*. **paperclip** *n* Büroklammer *f*. **paper-thin** *adj* hauchdünn. **paperweight** *n* Briefbeschwerer *m*. **paperwork** *n* Büroarbeit *f*.
paprika ['paprikǝ] *n* Paprika *m*.
par [paɪ] *n* Nennwert *m*, (*golf*) Par *neut*. **on a par with** gleich (+*dat*).
parable ['parǝbl] *n* Parabel *f*.
parachute ['parǝʃuɪt] *n* Fallschirm *m*. *v* mit dem Fallschirm abspringen.
parade [pǝ'reid] *n* Parade *f*. *v* (*march past*) vorbeimarschieren. **parade ground** Paradeplatz *m*.
paradise ['parǝdais] *n* Paradies *neut*.
paradox ['parǝdoks] *n* Paradox *neut*. **paradoxical** *adj* paradox.
paraffin ['parǝfin] *n* Paraffin *neut*.
paragraph ['parǝgraɪf] *n* Absatz *m*.
parallel ['parǝlel] *n* Parallele *f*. *adj* parallel. *v* entsprechen (+*dat*).
paralyse ['parǝlaiz] *v* paralysieren. **paralysed** *adj* gelähmt. **paralysis** *n* (*pl* -ses) Lähmung *f*, Paralyse *f*. **paralytic** *adj* paralytisch; (*coll*) besoffen.
paramilitary [,parǝ'militǝri] *adj* paramilitärisch.
paramount ['parǝmaunt] *adj* äußerst wichtig, überragend.
paranoia [,parǝ'noiǝ] *n* Paranoia *f*. **paranoid** *adj* paranoid.
parapet ['parǝpit] *n* Brüstung *f*.
paraphernalia [,parǝfǝ'neiliǝ] *n* Zubehör *neut*.
paraphrase ['parǝfreiz] *n* Umschreibung *f*, Paraphrase *f*. *v* umschreiben.
paraplegia [parǝ'pliɪdʒǝ] *n* Paraplegie *f*. **paraplegic** *adj* paraplegisch.
parasite ['parǝsait] *n* Parasit *m*, Schmarotzer *m*. **parasitic** *adj* parasitisch.
parasol ['parǝsol] *n* Sonnenschirm *m*.
paratrooper ['parǝ,truɪpǝ] *n* Fallschirmjäger *m*.
parcel ['paɪsǝl] *n* Paket *neut*, Päckchen *neut*; (*of land*) Parzelle *f*. **parcel post** Paketpost *f*. **parcels office** Gepäckabfertigung *f*. *v* **parcel out** austeilen.
parch [paɪtʃ] *v* dörren. **parched** *adj* ausgetrocknet; (*coll*) sehr durstig.
parchment ['paɪtʃmǝnt] *n* Pergament *neut*.
pardon ['paɪdn] *n* Verzeihung *f*. *v* verzeihen (+*dat*); (*law*) begnadigen. **I beg your pardon** *or* **pardon me** Verzeihung! **pardonable** *adj* verzeihlich.

pare [peə] v schälen; (*prices, costs, etc.*) herabsetzen, beschneiden.

parent ['peərənt] n Vater m, Mutter f. **parents** pl Eltern pl. **parentage** n Abkunft f. **parental** adj elterlich.

parenthesis [pə'renθəsis] n (pl -ses) Parenthese f.

parish ['pariʃ] n (Kirchen)gemeinde f. adj Gemeinde-.

parity ['pariti] n Parität f.

park [paik] n Park m. v (*mot*) parken. **car park** Parkplatz m. **no parking** Parken verboten. **parking place** or **lot** Parkplatz m. **parking light** Standlicht neut. **parking meter** Parkuhr f.

parliament ['pailəmənt] n Parlament neut. **member of parliament** Abgeordnete(r), Parlamentarier m. **parliamentary** adj parlamentarisch, Parlaments-.

parlour ['pailə] n Wohnzimmer neut. **ice-cream parlour** Eisdiele f.

parochial [pə'roukiəl] adj Gemeinde-; (*fig*) engstirnig.

parody ['parədi] n Parodie f. v parodieren.

parole [pə'roul] n Bewährung f. **release on parole** auf Bewährung entlassen.

paroxysm ['parəksizəm] n Anfall m.

parrot ['parət] n Papagei m.

parsley ['paisli] n Petersilie f.

parsnip ['paisnip] n Pastinake f.

parson ['paisn] n Pfarrer m. **parsonage** n Pfarrhaus neut.

part [pait] n Teil m; (*theatre*) Rolle f. adj Teil-. v trennen; (*people*) sich trennen; (*hair*) scheiteln. **for my part** meinerseits. **in part** teilweise. **take part (in)** teilnehmen (an).

***partake** [paiteik] v **partake of** (*eat*) zu sich nehmen.

partial ['paiʃəl] adj Teil-; (*biased*) eingenommen. **be partial to** (*coll*) eine Vorliebe haben für. **partially** adv teilweise.

participate [par'tisipeit] v teilnehmen (an). **participant** n Teilnehmer(in). **participation** n Teilnahme f.

participle ['paitisipl] n Partizip neut.

particle ['paitikl] n Teilchen neut.

particular [pə'tikjulə] adj besonder, speziell, (*fussy*) wählerisch. **particulars** pl n Einzelheiten pl. **particularly** adv besonders.

parting ['paitiŋ] n Abschied neut; (*hair*) Scheitel m.

partisan [paiti'zan] n Anhänger m.

partition [pai'tiʃən] n Aufteilung f, Trennung f; (*wall, etc.*) Scheidewand f.

partly ['paitli] adv zum Teil, teils.

partner ['paitnə] n Partner(in). **partnership** n Partnerschaft f.

partridge ['paitridʒ] n Rebhuhn neut.

party ['paiti] n (*pol, law*) Partei f; (*social gathering*) Party f. **be a party to** beteiligt sein an.

pass [pais] v (*go past*) vorbeigehen(an); (*go beyond*) überschreiten, übertreffen; (*exam*) bestehen; (*of time*) vergehen; (*time*) vertreiben; (*hand*) überreichen; (*approve*) billigen; (*sport*) zuspielen. n (*travel document*) Zeitkarte f. **pass away** sterben. **pass off (as)** ausgeben (als). **pass out** (*coll*) ohmächtig werden. **pass up** verzichten auf.

passage ['pasidʒ] n Durchfahrt f, Reise f; (*in book*) Stelle f; (*corridor*) Gang m; (*of time*) Verlauf m.

passenger ['pasindʒə] n Fahrgast m, Reisende(r); (*aeroplane*) Fluggast m.

passion ['paʃən] n Leidenschaft f; (*anger*) Zorn m; (*rel*) Passion f. **passionate** adj leidenschaftlich.

passive ['pasiv] adj passiv. **passivity** n Passivität f.

Passover ['paisouvə] n Passahfest neut.

passport ['paispoit] n (Reise)Paß m.

password ['paiswoid] n Kennwort neut.

past [paist] n Vergangenheit f. adj vergangen. prep nach, über; (*in front of*) an ... vorbei. **ten past six** zehn (Minuten) nach sechs. **half past six** halb sieben. **in the past** früher.

pasta ['pastə] n Teigwaren pl.

paste [peist] n Paste f; (*glue*) Klebstoff m. v kleben.

pastel ['pastəl] adj **pastel colour** Pastellfarbe f.

pasteurize ['pastʃəraiz] v pasteurisieren.

pastime ['paistaim] n Zeitvertreib m.

pastor ['paistə] n Pfarrer m, Pastor m. **pastoral** adj (*poetry*) Hirten-; (*rel*) pastoral.

pastry ['peistri] n Teig m; (*cake*) Tortengebäck neut.

pasture ['paistʃə] n Weide f, Grasland neut.

pasty[1] ['peisti] adj teigig; (*complexion*) bleich.

pasty[2] ['pasti] n Pastete f.

pat [pæt] *n* (leichter) Schlag *m*. *v* klopfen, patschen. **pat on the back** (*v*) beglückwünschen.

patch [pætʃ] *n* Flicken *m*, Lappen *m*; (*on eye*) Augenbinde *f*. *v* flicken. **patchwork** *n* Flickwerk *neut*. **patchy** *adj* ungleichmäßig.

pâté ['pɑtei] *n* Pastete *f*.

patent ['peitənt] *n* Patent *neut*. *adj* patentiert, Patent-; (*obvious*) offenkundig. *v* patentieren.

paternal [pə'təːnl] *adj* väterlich. **paternal grandfather** Großvater väterlicherseits. **paternity** *n* Vaterschaft *f*.

path [pɑːθ] *n* Weg *m*, Pfad *m*. **pathway** *n* Weg *m*, Bahn *f*.

pathetic [pə'θetik] *adj* (*moving*) rührend; (*pitiable*) kläglich.

pathology [pə'θolədʒi] *n* Pathologie *f*. **pathological** *adj* pathologisch. **pathologist** *n* Pathologe *m*, Pathologin *f*.

patience ['peiʃəns] *n* Geduld *f*. **patient** *adj* geduldig, duldsam. *n* Patient(in).

patio ['pætiou] *n* Patio *m*.

patriarchal ['peitriɑːkəl] *adj* patriarchalisch.

patriot ['pætriət] *n* Patriot(in). **patriotic** *adj* patriotisch. **patriotism** *n* Patriotismus *m*.

patrol [pə'troul] *n* Patrouille *f*. *v* durchstreifen. **patrol car** Streifenwagen *m*. **patrolman** *n* Streifenpolizist *m*.

patron ['peitrən] *n* Patron *m*, Gönner *m*. **patronage** *n* Gönnerschaft *f*. **patronize** *v* (*theatre, restaurant*) besuchen; (*person*) gönnerhaft behandeln. **patronizing** *adj* gönnerhaft.

patter¹ ['pætə] *n* (*rain*) Prasseln *neut*. *v* prasseln.

patter² ['pætə] *n* (*speech*) Geplapper *neut*, Rotwelsch *neut*. *v* plappern.

pattern ['pætən] *n* Muster *neut*.

paunch [pɔːntʃ] *n* Wanst *m*. **paunchy** *adj* dickbäuchig.

pauper ['pɔːpə] *n* Arme(r).

pause [pɔːz] *n* Pause *f*. *v* anhalten, zögern.

pave [peiv] *v* pflastern. **pave the way** den Weg bahnen. **pavement** *n* Bürgersteig *m*.

pavilion [pə'viljən] *n* Pavillon *m*.

paw [pɔː] *n* Pfote *f*, Tatze *f*. *v* (*ground*) stampfen auf.

pawn¹ [pɔːn] *n* (*chess*) Bauer *m*.

pawn² [pɔːn] *v* verpfänden. **pawnbroker** *n* Pfandleiher *m*.

*pay [pei] *n* Lohn *m*, Gehalt *neut*. *v* zahlen; (*bill*) bezahlen; (*be worthwhile*) sich lohnen; (*visit, compliment*) machen. **pay attention** achtgeben (auf). **pay homage** huldigen (+ *dat*). **pay for** bezahlen. **payable** *adj* fällig. **payday** *n* Zahltag *m*. **paying guest** zahlender Gast *m*. **payload** *n* Nutzlast *f*. **payment** *n* (Be)Zahlung *f*; (*cheque*) Einlösung *f*.

pea [piː] *n* Erbse *f*.

peace [piːs] *n* Frieden *m*; (*quiet*) Ruhe *f*. **make one's peace with** sich aussöhnen mit. **leave in peace** in Ruhe lassen. **peace of mind** Seelenruhe *f*. **peace treaty** Friedensvertrag *m*. **peaceable** *adj* friedlich. **peaceful** *adj* ruhig.

peach [piːtʃ] *n* Pfirsich *m*.

peacock ['piːkok] *n* Pfau *m*.

peak [piːk] *n* Spitze *f*, Gipfel *m*. *adj* Höchst-, Spitzen-. **peaked** *adj* spitz.

peal [piːl] *v* (*bells*) läuten. *n* Geläute *neut*. **peal of thunder** Donnerschlag *m*.

peanut ['piːnʌt] *n* Erdnuß *f*.

pear [peə] *n* Birne *f*. **pear-shaped** *adj* birnenförmig.

pearl [pəːl] *n* Perle *f*. *adj* Perlen-.

peasant ['peznt] *n* Bauer *m*. *adj* bäuerlich.

peat [piːt] *n* Torf *m*.

pebble ['pebl] *n* Kieselstein *m*.

peck [pek] *v* picken, hacken. *n* Picken *neut*; (*kiss*) (flüchtiger) Kuß *m*. **peckish** *adj* (*coll*) hungrig.

peculiar [pi'kjuːliə] *adj* (*strange*) seltsam. **peculiar to** eigentümlich (+ *dat*). **peculiarity** *n* Eigentümlichkeit *f*.

pedal ['pedl] *n* Pedal *neut*, Fußhebel *m*. *v* (*a bicycle*) fahren.

pedantic [pi'dantik] *adj* pedantisch.

peddle ['pedl] *v* hausieren. **peddler** *n* Hausierer *m*.

pedestal ['pedistl] *n* Sockel *m*. **put on a pedestal** vergöttern.

pedestrian [pi'destriən] *n* Fußgänger(in). *adj* Fußgänger-; (*humdrum*) langweilig, banal. **pedestrian crossing** Fußgängerüberweg *m*. **pedestrian precinct** Fußgängerzone *f*.

pedigree ['pedigriː] *n* Stammbaum *m*.

pedlar ['pedlə] *n* Hausierer *m*.

peel [piːl] *n* Schale *f*. *v* schälen. **peeler** *n* Schäler *m*.

peep [piːp] *v* gucken, verstohlen blicken. *n* verstohlener Blick *m*. **peephole** *n* Guckloch *neut*.

125

peer¹ [piə] v (look) spähen, gucken.
peer² [piə] n (equal) Ebenbürtige(r); (noble) Peer m. **peerage** n Peerwürde f. **peerless** adj unvergleichlich.
peevish ['pi:vɪʃ] adj verdrießlich.
peg [peg] n Pflock m; (coathook) Haken m; (clothes) Klammer f. v anpflöcken; (prices) festlegen. **off the peg** von der Stange.
pejorative [pə'dʒɔrətiv] adj herabsetzend.
pelican ['pelikən] n Pelikan m.
pellet ['pelit] n Kügelchen neut; (shot) Schrotkorn neut.
pelmet ['pelmit] n Falbel f.
pelt¹ [pelt] v (throw) bewerfen.
pelt² [pelt] n (skin) Fell neut, Pelz m.
pelvis ['pelvis] n (anat) Becken neut.
pen¹ [pen] n (writing) (Schreib)Feder f, Federhalter m.
pen² [pen] n (animals) Pferch m, Hürde f. v einpferchen.
penal ['pi:nl] adj Straf-. **penalize** v bestrafen. **penalty** n (gesetzliche) Strafe f. **penalty kick** Elfmeterstoß m.
penance ['penəns] n Buße f.
pencil ['pensl] n Bleistift m. v **pencil in** (a date) vorläufig festsetzen. **pencil-sharpener** n Bleistiftspitzer m.
pendant ['pendənt] n Anhänger m.
pending ['pendiŋ] adj (noch) unentschieden. prep bis.
pendulum ['pendjuləm] n Pendel neut.
penetrate ['penitreit] v durchdringen, eindringen (in). **penetrating** adj durchdringend. **penetration** n Durchdringen neut.
penguin ['peŋgwin] n Pinguin m.
penicillin [peni'silin] n Penizillin neut.
peninsula [pə'ninsjulə] n Halbinsel f. **peninsular** adj Halbinsel-.
penis ['pi:nis] n Penis m.
penitent ['penitənt] adj bußfertig. n Büßer(in). **penitence** n Buße f.
penknife ['nennaif] n Taschenmesser neut.
pen-name n Pseudonym neut.
pennant ['penənt] n Wimpel m.
penny ['peni] n Penny m. Pfennig m. **penniless** adj mittellos.
pension ['penʃən] n Rente f. **pensioner** n Rentner(in).
pensive ['pensiv] adj gedankenvoll.
pent [pent] adj **pent up** (feelings) angestaut, zurückgehalten.
pentagon ['pentəgən] n Fünfeck neut.

Pentagon (US) Pentagon neut. **pentagonal** adj fünfeckig.
penthouse ['penthaus] n Dachwohnung f.
penultimate [pi'nʌltimit] adj vorletzt.
people ['pi:pl] pl n Leute pl, Menschen pl; sing (nation) Volk neut.
pepper ['pepə] n Pfeffer m. **peppercorn** n Pfefferkorn neut. **peppermint** n Pfefferminze f. **peppery** adj pfefferig, scharf.
per [pəː] prep pro. **per capita** pro Kopf.
perceive [pə'siːv] v wahrnehmen; (understand) begreifen. **perceptible** adj spürbar. **perception** n Wahrnehmung f. **perceptive** adj (person) scharfsinnig.
per cent adv, n Prozent neut. **sixty per cent** sechzig Prozent. **percentage** n Prozentsatz m.
perch [pəːtʃ] n Sitzstange f; (fish) Barsch m. v sitzen.
percolate ['pəːkəleit] v durchsickern. **percolator** n Kaffeemaschine f.
percussion [pə'kʌʃən] n (music) Schlaginstrumente pl.
perennial [pə'reniəl] adj beständig; (plant) perennierend. n perennierende Pflanze f.
perfect ['pəːfikt; v pə'fekt] adj vollkommen, vollendet, perfekt. v vervollkommnen. **perfection** n Vollkommenheit f. **perfectionist** n Perfektionist(in). **perfectly** adv (coll) ganz, völlig.
perforate ['pəːfəreit] v perforieren. **perforation** n Perforation f.
perform [pə'fɔːm] v machen, ausführen; (music, play) aufführen, spielen. n (work, output) Leistung f; (music, theatre) Aufführung f. **performer** n Artist(in).
perfume ['pəːfjuːm] n (fragrance) Duft m; (woman's) Parfüm neut. v parfümieren.
perhaps [pə'haps] adv vielleicht.
peril ['peril] n Gefahr f. **perilous** adj gefährlich.
perimeter [pə'rimitə] n Umkreis ; (outer area) Peripherie f.
period ['piəriəd] n Periode f, Frist f; (lesson) Stunde f; (menstrual) Regel f, Periode f; (full stop) Punkt m. **periodic** adj periodisch. **periodical** n Zeitschrift f. **periodically** adv periodisch, von Zeit zu Zeit.
peripheral [pə'rifərəl] adj peripherisch, Rand-. **periphery** n Peripherie f.
periscope ['periskoup] n Periskop neut.
perish ['periʃ] v umkommen, sterben;

(*materials*) verwelken. **perishable** *adj* leicht verderblich.

perjure ['pɜːdʒə] *v* **perjure oneself** meineidig werden. **perjurer** *n* Meineidige(r). **perjury** *n* Meineid *m*.

perk[1] [pɜːk] *v* **perk up** munter werden. **perky** *adj* munter.

perk[2] [pɜːk] *n* (*coll: of job*) Vorteil *m*, Vergünstigung *f*.

perm [pɜːm] *n* Dauerwelle *f*.

permanent ['pɜːmənənt] *adj* dauernd, ständig, permanent. **permanence** *n* Permanenz *f*, Ständigkeit *f*.

permeate ['pɜːmieit] *v* durchdringen. **permeable** *adj* durchlässig.

permit [pə'mit; *n* 'pɜːmit] *v* erlauben, gestatten; (*officially*) zulassen, genehmigen. *n* Genehmigung *f*; (*certificate*) Zulassungsschein *m*. **permissible** *adj* zulässig. **permission** *n* Erlaubnis *f*, Genehmigung *f*. **permissive** *adj* freizügig.

permutation [pɜːmju'teiʃən] *n* Permutation *f*.

pernicious [pə'niʃəs] *adj* bösartig.

perpendicular [ˌpɜːpen'dikjulə] *adj* senkrecht. *n* Senkrechte *f*.

perpetrate ['pɜːpitreit] *v* begehen. **perpetration** *n* Begehung *f*. **perpetrator** *n* Täter *m*.

perpetual [pə'petʃuəl] *adj* beständig, ewig. **perpetuate** [pə'petʃueit] *v* verewigen, fortsetzen.

perplex [pə'pleks] *v* verwirren, verblüffen. **perplexed** *adj* perplex, verwirrt.

persecute ['pɜːsikjuːt] *v* verfolgen. **persecution** *n* Verfolgung *f*. **persecutor** *n* Verfolger(in).

persevere [ˌpɜːsi'viə] *v* beharren, nicht aufgeben. **perseverance** *n* Beharrlichkeit *f*. **persevering** *adj* beharrlich.

persist [pə'sist] *v* (*person*) beharren (bei); (*thing*) fortdauern. **persistence** *n* Beharren *neut*, Hartnäckigkeit *f*. **persistent** *adj* (*person*) hartnäckig; (*questions, etc.*) anhaltend.

person ['pɜːsn] *n* Person *f*. **personal** *adj* persönlich. **personal matter** Privatsache *f*. **personality** *n* Personalität *f*; (*personage*) Persönlichkeit *f*.

personnel [pɜːsə'nel] *n* Personal *neut*, Belegschaft *f*. **personnel department** Personalabteilung *f*. **personnel manager** Personalchef *m*.

perspective [pə'spektiv] *n* Perspektive *f*.

perspire [pə'spaiə] *v* schwitzen, transpirieren. **perspiration** *n* Schweiß *m*.

persuade [pə'sweid] *v* überreden; (*convince*) überzeugen. **persuasion** *n* Überredung *f*; Überzeugung *f*. **persuasive** *adj* überredend; überzeugend.

pert [pɜːt] *adj* keck.

pertain [pə'tein] *v* betreffen. **pertaining to** betreffend. **pertinacious** *adj* hartnäckig. **pertinent** *adj* angemessen.

perturb [pə'tɜːb] *v* beunruhigen.

peruse [pə'ruːz] *v* durchlesen.

pervade [pə'veid] *v* erfüllen, durchdringen. **pervasive** *adj* durchdringend.

perverse [pə'vɜːs] *adj* pervers, widernatürlich. **perversion** *n* Perversion *f*, Verdrehung *f*. **perversion of justice** Rechtsbeugung *f*. **pervert** *v* verdrehen. *n* perverser Mensch *m*.

pest [pest] *n* Schädling *m*; (*coll: person*) lästiger Mensch *m*. **pesticide** *n* Pestizid *neut*.

pester ['pestə] *v* quälen, plagen.

pet [pet] *n* Haustier *neut*; (*darling*) Schätzchen *neut*. *adj* Lieblings-. *v* liebkosen. **pet name** Kosename *m*.

petal ['petl] *n* Blumenblatt *neut*.

petition [pə'tiʃən] *n* Bittschrift *f*.

petrify ['petrifai] *v* versteinern. **petrified** *adj* (*coll*) starr, bestürzt.

petrol ['petrəl] *n* Benzin *neut*. **petrol station** Tankstelle *f*. **petroleum** *n* Erdöl *neut*.

petticoat ['petikout] *n* Unterrock *m*.

petty ['peti] *adj* (*unimportant*) unbedeutend; (*mean*) kleinlich. **petty cash** Kleinkasse *f*.

petulant ['petjulənt] *adj* verdrießlich.

pew [pjuː] *n* Kirchensitz *m*.

pewter ['pjuːtə] *n* Hartzinn *neut*.

phantom ['fantəm] *n* Phantom *neut*, Gespenst *neut*. *adj* Schein-.

pharmacy ['faːməsi] *n* Apotheke *f*. **pharmacist** *n* Apotheker(in).

pharynx ['farinks] *n* Schlundkopf *m*.

phase [feiz] *n* (*tech*) Phase *f*; (*stage*) Stadium *neut*, Etappe *f*.

pheasant ['feznt] *n* Fasan *m*.

phenomenon [fə'nomənən] *n* (*pl* -a) Phänomen *neut*. **phenomenal** *adj* phänomenal.

phial ['faiəl] *n* Ampulle *f*.

philanthropy [fi'lanθrəpi] *n* Philanthropie *f*. **philanthropic** *adj* philanthropisch, menschenfreundlich. **philanthropist** *n* Philanthrop, Menschenfreund *m*.

philately [fi'lætəli] n Briefmarkensammeln neut. philatelist n Briefmarkensammler(in).

philosophy [fi'losəfi] n Philosophie f. philosopher n Philosoph m. philosophical adj philosophisch.

phlegm [flem] n Schleim m, Phlegma neut. phlegmatic adj phlegmatisch.

phobia ['foubiə] n Phobie f.

phone [foun] n (coll) Fernsprecher m. v anrufen. phone booth or box Telefonzelle f.

phonetic [fə'netik] adj phonetisch. phonetics n Phonetik f.

phoney ['founi] adj (coll) falsch, fingiert. n Schwindler m.

phosphate ['fosfeit] n Phosphat neut.

phosphorescence [fosfə'resəns] n Phosphoreszenz f. phosphorescent adj phosphoreszierend.

phosphorus ['fosfərəs] n Phosphor m.

photo ['foutou] n Foto neut.

photocopy ['foutoukopi] n Fotokopie f. v fotokopieren.

photogenic [foutou'dʒenik] adj fotogen.

photograph ['foutəgraːf] n Lichtbild neut, Foto neut. v aufnehmen, fotografieren. photographer n Fotograf m. photographic adj fotografisch. photography n Fotografie f.

phrase [freiz] n (expression) Ausdruck m, Redewendung f; (music) Phrase f. v fassen.

physical ['fizikəl] adj physisch, körperlich. physical education Leibeserziehung f.

physician [fi'ziʃən] n Arzt m, Ärztin f.

physics ['fiziks] n Physik f. physicist n Physiker m.

physiology [fizi'olədʒi] n Physiologie f. physiological adj physiologisch.

physiotherapy [fiziou'θerəpi] n Physiotherapie f.

physique [fi'ziːk] n Körperbau m.

piano [pi'anou] n Klavier neut. pianist n Klavierspieler(in).

pick[1] [pik] v (choose) auswählen, (fruit) pflücken; (lock) knacken. n pick of the bunch (coll) das Beste (von allen).

pick[2] [pik] or pickaxe n Spitzhacke f.

picket ['pikit] n Pfahl m; (strike) Streikposten m. v (factory, etc.) Streikposten aufstellen vor.

pickle ['pikl] n Pökel m. v einpökeln. pickled adj gepökelt; (coll: drunk) blau. pickles pl n Eingepökeltes neut sing.

picnic ['piknik] n Picknick neut.

pictorial [pik'tɔːriəl] adj Bilder-.

picture ['piktʃə] n Bild neut; (painting) Gemälde neut; (film) Film m. v (imagine) sich vorstellen. pictures pl Kino neut sing. picture book Bilderbuch neut. picture postcard Ansichtskarte f.

picturesque [piktʃə'resk] adj pittoresk.

pidgin ['pidʒən] n Mischsprache f.

pie [pai] n (meat) Pastete f; (fruit) Torte f.

piece [piːs] n Stück neut; (part) Teil m; (paper) Blatt neut. piece of advice Ratschlag m. fall to pieces in Stücke gehen, zerfallen. go to pieces zusammenbrechen. v piece together zusammenstellen. piecemeal adv stückweise. piecework n Akkordarbeit f.

pier [piə] n Pier m, Kai m.

pierce [piəs] v durchbohren, durchstechen. piercing adj durchdringend.

piety ['paiəti] n Frömmigkeit f.

pig [pig] n Schwein neut, pig-headed adj störrisch. piglet n Schweinchen neut. pigskin n Schweinsleder neut. pigsty n Schweinestall m. pigtail n Zopf m.

pigment ['pigmənt] n Pigment neut, Farbstoff m. pigmentation n Pigmentation f.

pike [paik] n (fish) Hecht m; (weapon) Pike f, Spieß m.

pilchard ['piltʃəd] n Sardine f.

pile[1] [pail] n (heap) Haufen m, Stapel m. v (an)häufen, stapeln. pile-up n (mot) (Massen)Karambolage f.

pile[2] [pail] n (post) Pfahl m, Joch neut.

pile[3] [pail] n (of carpet) Flor m.

piles [pailz] pl n Hämorrhoiden pl.

pilfer ['pilfə] v klauen. pilferage n Dieberei f.

pilgrim ['pilgrim] n Pilger(in). pilgrimage n Pilgerfahrt f, Wallfahrt f.

pill [pil] n Pille f, Tablette f. the pill (contraceptive) die Pille.

pillage ['pilidʒ] v (aus)plündern. n Plünderung f.

pillar ['pilə] n Pfeiler m, Säule f. pillarbox n Briefkasten m.

pillion ['piljən] n Soziussitz m. ride pillion auf dem Sozius fahren.

pillow ['pilou] n Kopfkissen neut. pillow case n Kissenbezug m.

pilot ['pailət] n Pilot m. v steuern, lenken. pilot light Zündflamme f.

pimento [pi'mentou] n Piment m or neut.

pimp [pimp] n Zuhälter m.

pimple ['pimpl] n Pustel f, Pickel m. **pimply** adj pickelig.

pin [pin] n Stecknadel f. v befestigen. **pin down** festnageln. **pincushion** n Nadelkissen neut.

pinafore ['pinəfoɪ] n Schürze f. **pinafore dress** Kleiderrock m.

pincers ['pinsəz] pl n Zange f sing; (crab's) Krebsschere f sing.

pinch [pintʃ] v zwicken, kneifen; (coll) klauen. n Kneifen neut, Zwicken neut; (salt, etc.) Prise f.

pine[1] [pain] n Kiefer f, Pinie f. **pine cone** n Kiefernzapfen m.

pine[2] [pain] v sich sehnen (nach). **pine away** verschmachten.

pineapple ['painapl] n Ananas f.

ping-pong ['piŋpoŋ] n (coll) Tischtennis neut.

pinion ['pinjən] n (tech) Ritzel m. v fesseln.

pink [piŋk] adj rosa, blaßrot. n (flower) Nelke f. v (mot) klopfen. **in the pink** kerngesund.

pinnacle ['pinəkl] n Spitzturm m; (fig) Gipfel m.

pinpoint ['pinpoint] v ins Auge fassen, hervorheben.

pint [paint] n Pinte f.

pioneer [,paiə'niə] n Pionier m, Bahnbrecher m. v den Weg bahnen für. **pioneering** adj bahnbrechend.

pious ['paiəs] adj fromm.

pip[1] [pip] n (fruit) (Obst)Kern m.

pip[2] [pip] n (sound) Ton m; (mil) Stern m; (on card) Auge neut; (on dice) Punkt m.

pipe [paip] n Rohr neut, Röhre f; (tobacco, music) Pfeife f; (sound) Pfeifen neut. v (liquid) durch Röhren leiten; (play pipes, etc.) pfeifen; (cookery) spritzen. **pipedream** n Luftschloß neut. **pipeline** n Rohrleitung f.

piquant ['piɪkənt] adj pikant.

pique [piɪk] n Groll m.

pirate ['paiərət] n Seeräuber m. **piracy** n Seeräuberei f.

pirouette [piru'et] n Pirouette f. v pirouettieren.

Pisces ['paisiɪz] n Fische pl.

piss [pis] v (vulgar) pissen. n Pisse f.

pistachio [pi'staɪʃiou] n Pistazie f.

pistol ['pistl] n Pistole f.

piston ['pistən] n Kolben m.

pit [pit] n Grube f; (mining) Zeche f, Bergwerk neut. **pitted** adj vernarbt; (corroded) zerfressen.

pitch[1] [pitʃ] v werfen; (tent) aufschlagen. n Wurf m; (sport) Feld neut; (music) Tonhöhe f; (level) Grad m. **pitcher** n Werfer m; (jug) Krug m. **pitchfork** n Mistgabel f.

pitch[2] [pitʃ] n (tar) Pech neut.

pitfall ['pitfoɪl] n Fallgrube f, Falle f.

pith [piθ] n Mark neut. **pithy** adj markig.

pittance ['pitəns] n Hungerlohn m.

pituitary [pi'tjuitəri] n Hirnanhangdrüse f, Hypophyse f.

pity ['piti] n Mitleid neut. v bemitleiden. it's a pity es ist schade, es ist ein Jammer m.

pivot ['pivət] n Drehpunkt m. v sich drehen.

placard ['plakaɪd] n Plakat neut.

placate [plə'keit] v beschwichtigen.

place [pleis] n Platz m; (town, locality) Ort m; (spot) Stelle f. **go places** (coll) es weit bringen. **out-of-place** adj (remark) unangebracht. **placename** n Ortsname m. **place of interest** Sehenswürdigkeit f. **take place** stattfinden. v stellen, legen, setzen; (identify) identifizieren, erkennen.

placenta [plə'sentə] n Plazenta f.

placid ['plasid] adj ruhig, gelassen.

plagiarize ['pleidʒəraiz] v plagiieren. **plagiarism** n Plagiat m.

plague [pleig] n Seuche f, Pest f. v plagen, quälen.

plaice [pleis] n Scholle f.

plain [plein] adj einfach, schlicht; (obvious) klar; (not pretty) unansehnlich. adv einfach. n Ebene f. **plainly** adv offensichtlich. **speak plainly** offen reden.

plaintiff ['pleintif] n Kläger(in).

plaintive ['pleintiv] adj traurig, wehmütig.

plait [plat] n Zopf m, Flechte f. v flechten.

plan [plan] n Plan m; (drawing) Entwurf m, Zeichnung f. v planen; (intend) vorhaben. **according to plan** planmäßig.

plane[1] [plein] adj flach, eben. n Ebene f; (aeroplane) Flugzeug neut.

plane[2] [plein] n (tool) Hobel m. v (ab)hobeln.

planet ['planit] n Planet m.

plank [plaŋk] n Planke f, Diele f.

plankton ['plaŋktən] n Plankton neut.

planning ['plæniŋ] *n* Planung *f.*
plant [plɑːnt] *n* Pflanze *f*; (*factory*) Betrieb *m*, Fabrik *f. v* pflanzen. **plantation** *n* Pflanzung *f.*
plaque [plɑːk] *n* Gedenktafel *f.*
plasma ['plæzmə] *n* Plasma *neut.*
plaster ['plɑːstə] *n* (*med*) Pflaster *neut*; (*of Paris*) Gips *m. v* bepflastern. **adhesive plaster** Heftpflaster *neut.* **plaster cast** Gipsabdruck *m*; (*med*) Gipsverband *m.*
plastic ['plæstik] *n* Kunststoff *m. adj* Kunststoff-.
plate [pleit] *n* (*for food*) Teller *m*; (*tech*) Platte *f*, Scheibe *f. v* (*metal*) plattieren. **gold-plated** *adj* vergoldet.
plateau ['plætou] *n* Hochebene *f*, Plateau *neut.*
platform ['plætfɔːm] *n* (*rail*) Bahnsteig *m*; (*speaker's*) Tribune *f*, (*fig*: *pol*) Parteiprogramm *neut.*
platinum ['plætinəm] *n* Platin *neut.*
platonic [plə'tonik] *adj* platonisch.
platoon [plə'tuːn] *n* (*mil*) Zug *m.*
plausible ['plɔːzəbl] *adj* glaubhaft.
play [plei] *n* Spiel *neut*; (*theatre*) Schauspiel *neut*, Stück *neut*; (*tech*) Spielraum *m. v* spielen. **play safe** kein Risiko eingehen. **playboy** *n* Playboy *m.* **player** *n* Spieler(in); (*actor*) Schauspieler(in). **playful** *adj* scherzhaft. **playground** *n* Spielplatz *m*; (*school*) Schulhof *m.* **playing card** Spielkarte *f.* **playing field** Sportplatz *m.* **playmate** *n* Spielkamerad(in). **plaything** *n* Spielzeug *neut.* **playwright** *n* Dramatiker *m.*
plea [pliː] *n* dringende Bitte *f*; (*law*) Plädoyer *neut.*
plead [pliːd] *v* (*law*) plädieren. **plead for** flehen um.
please [pliːz] *v* gefallen (+ *dat*), Freude machen (+ *dat*). *adv* bitte! **pleasant** angenehm; (*person*) freundlich, nett. **pleased** *adj* zufrieden. **pleasing** *adj* angenehm. **pleasurable** *adj* vergnüglich. **pleasure** *n* Vergnügen *neut.*
pleat [pliːt] *n* Falte *f. v* in Falten legen.
plebiscite ['plebisait] *n* Volksabstimmung *f*, Plebiszit *neut.*
pledge [pledʒ] *n* Pfand *neut*; (*promise*) Versprechen *neut. v* versprechen.
plenty ['plenti] *n* Fülle *f*, Reichtum *m.* **plenty of** eine Menge, viel.
pleurisy ['pluərisi] *n* Rippenfellentzündung *f.*

pliable ['plaiəbl] *adj* biegsam. **pliability** *n* Biegsamkeit *f.*
pliers ['plaiəz] *pl n* Zange *f sing.*
plight [plait] *n* Notlage *f.*
plimsoll ['plimsəl] *n* Turnschuh *m.*
plod [plod] *v* sich hinschleppen, schwerfällig gehen.
plonk[1] [ploŋk] *v* **plonk down** hinschmeißen.
plonk[2] [ploŋk] *n* (*coll*) billiger Wein.
plot[1] [plot] *n* Komplott *neut*; (*in novel*) Handlung *f. v* sich verschwören; (*on map*) einzeichnen. **plotter** *n* Verschwörer(in).
plot[2] [plot] *n* (*land*) Parzelle *f*, Grundstück *neut.*
plough [plau] *n* Pflug *m*; (*astron*) Großer Bär *m. v* (um)pflügen. **ploughman** *n* Pflüger *m.*
pluck [plʌk] *v* pflücken; (*poultry*) rupfen; (*music*) zupfen. *n* (*courage*) Mut *m.* **plucky** *adj* mutig. **pluck up courage** Mut fassen
plug [plʌg] *n* (*elec*) Stecker *m*; (*stopper*) Stöpsel *m. v* verstopfen; (*coll*) befürworten. **plug in** anschließen, einstecken.
plum [plʌm] *n* Pflaume *f*, Zwetschge *f.*
plumage ['pluːmidʒ] *n* Gefieder *neut.*
plumb [plʌm] *n* Senkblei *neut. adj* senkrecht. *v* (*sound*) sondieren. **plumber** *n* Klempner *m.* **plumbing** *n* Klempnerarbeit *f*; (*pipes*) Rohrleitungen *pl f.*
plume [pluːm] *n* Feder *f*; (*of smoke*) Streifen *m.*
plummet ['plʌmit] *v* abstürzen.
plump[1] [plʌmp] *adj* (*fat*) rundlich, mollig. **plumpness** *n* Rundlichkeit *f.*
plump[2] [plʌmp] *v* (*fall*) plumpsen. **plump for** sich entscheiden für.
plunder ['plʌndə] *v* plündern. *n* (*spoils*) Beute *f.*
plunge [plʌndʒ] *v* tauchen; (*fall*) stürzen. *n* Sturz *m.*
pluperfect [pluː'pəfikt] *n* (*gramm*) Vorvergangenheit *f.*
plural ['pluərəl] *adj* Plural-. *n* Plural *m*, Mehrzahl *f.*
plus [plʌs] *prep* plus. *adj* Plus-. *n* Plus *neut.*
plush [plʌʃ] *adj* (*fig*) luxuriös.
Pluto ['pluːtou] *n* Pluto *m.*
ply[1] [plai] *v* (*trade*) ausüben; (*travel*) verkehren.

ply² [plai] *n* (*of yarn*) Strähne *f*. **plywood** *n* Sperrholz *neut*.

pneumatic [nju'mætik] *adj* pneumatisch. **pneumatic tyre** *n* Luftreifen *m*. **pneumatic drill** Preßluftbohrer *m*.

pneumonia [nju'mouniə] *n* Lungenentzündung *f*.

poach¹ [poutʃ] *v* (*cookery*) pochieren. **poached egg** verlorenes Ei *neut*.

poach² [poutʃ] *v* wildern. **poacher** *n* Wilddieb *m*.

pocket ['pokit] *n* Tasche *f*. *adj* Taschen-. *v* in die Tasche stecken, einstecken. **to be in pocket** gut bei Kasse sein. **pocketknife** *n* Taschenmesser *neut*. **pocket-money** Taschengeld *neut*.

pod [pod] *n* Schote *f*.

podgy ['podʒi] *adj* (*coll*) mollig, dick.

poem ['pouim] *n* Gedicht *neut*. **poet** *n* Dichter *m*. **poetess** *n* Dichterin *f*. **poetic** *adj* poetisch, dichterisch. **poetry** *n* Dichtkunst *f*; (*poems*) Gedichte *f*.

poignant ['poinjənt] *adj* schmerzlich; (*wit*) scharf; (*grief*) bitter.

point [point] *n* (*tip*) Spitze *f*; (*place, spot*) Punkt *m*; (*in time*) Zeitpunkt *m*; (*main thing*) Hauptsache *f*. **be on the point of doing** eben tun wollen. **point of view** Standpunkt *m*. **points** *pl n* (*rail*) Weichen *pl*. **that's the point!** das is es ja! **there's no point in** es hat keinen Zweck, zu. *v* spitzen; (*indicate*) (mit dem Finger) zeigen. **point out** hinweisen auf. **pointed** *adj* zugespitzt; (*remark*) treffend, beißend. **pointless** *adj* sinnlos.

poise [poiz] *n* Haltung *f*; (*calmness*) Gelassenheit *f*.

poison ['poizən] *n* Gift *neut*. *v* vergiften. **poisoner** *n* Giftmörder(in). **poisonous** *adj* giftig.

poke [pouk] *n* Stoß *m*, Puff *m*. *v* stoßen; (*fire*) schüren.

poker¹ ['poukə] *n* (*for fire*) Feuerhaken *m*.

poker² ['poukə] *n* (*gambling*) Poker(spiel) *neut*.

Poland ['poulənd] *n* Polen *neut*. **Pole** *n* Pole *m*, Polin *f*. **Polish** *adj* polnisch.

polar ['poulə] *adj* polar. **polar bear** Eisbär *m*.

pole¹ [poul] *n* (*geog*) Pol *m*. **pole star** *n* Polarstern *m*.

pole² [poul] *n* Pfosten *m*, Pfahl *m*; (*telegraph, etc.*) Stange *f*. **pole-vault** *n* Stabhochsprung *m*.

police [pə'liːs] *n* Polizei *f*. *n* (polizeilich) überwachen. *adj* polizeilich, Polizei-. **police force** Polizei *f*. **policeman** *n* Polizist *m*, Schutzmann *m*. **police station** Polizeiwache *f*, Polizeirevier *neut*.

policy¹ ['poləsi] *n* Politik *f*; (*personal*) Methode *f*.

policy² ['poləsi] *n* (*insurance*) Police *f*.

polio ['pouliou] *n* Kinderlähmung *f*.

polish ['poliʃ] *n* Politur *f*; (*floors, furniture*) Bohnerwachs *neut*; (*shoes*) Schuhcreme *f*. *v* polieren; (*furniture*) bohnern; (*shoes*) wichsen. **polished** *adj* poliert; (*fig*) fein, elegant. **polisher** *n* Polierer *m*.

polite [pə'lait] *adj* höflich. **politeness** *n* Höflichkeit *f*.

politics ['politiks] *n* Politik *f*. **political** *adj* politisch. **politician** *n* Politiker *m*.

polka ['polkə] *n* Polka *f*.

poll [poul] *n* (*voting*) Abstimmung *f*; (*opinion poll*) Meinungsumfrage *f*.

pollen ['polən] *n* Pollen *m*, Blütenstaub *m*. **pollinate** *v* befruchten.

pollute [pə'luːt] *v* verschmutzen, verunreinigen. **pollution** *n* (*environmental*) Umweltverschmutzung *f*.

polo ['poulou] *n* Polo *neut*. **polo-neck** *n* Rollkragen *m*.

polygamy [pə'ligəmi] *n* Polygamie *f*. **polygamous** *adj* polygam.

polygon ['poligən] *n* Polygon *neut*.

polytechnic [ˌpoli'teknik] *n* Polytechnikum *neut*.

polythene ['poliθiːn] *n* Polyäthylen *neut*. *adj* **polythene bag** Plastiktüte *f*.

pomegranate ['pomigranit] *n* Granatapfel *m*.

pomp [pomp] *n* Prunk *m*, Pracht *f*. **pomposity** *n* Bombast *m*. **pompous** *adj* bombastisch.

pond [pond] *n* Teich *m*.

ponder ['pondə] *v* nachdenken (über). **ponderous** *adj* schwer; (*movement*) schwerfällig.

pony ['pouni] *n* Pony *neut*, Pferdchen *neut*. **pony-tail** Pferdeschwanz *m*.

poodle ['puːdl] *n* Pudel *m*.

poof [puʃ] *n* (*derog*) Schwule(r) *m*.

pool¹ [puːl] *n* (*pond*) Teich *m*; (*blood, etc.*) Lache *f*; (*swimming*) (Schwimm)Bad *neut*.

pool² [puːl] *n* (*game*) Pool *m*; (*fund*) Kasse *f*. *v* (*resources*) vereinigen. **football pools** Fußballtoto *m*.

131 postulate

poor [puə] *adj* arm, bedürftig; *(earth)* dürr; *(bad)* schlecht. **the poor** die Armen *pl*. **poorly** *adj (coll)* krank, unwohl.
pop¹ [pop] *n* Knall *m*, Puff *m*; *(drink)* Limonade *f*. *v* knallen; *(burst)* platzen. **pop in** schnell vorbeikommen. **pop up** *(appear)* auftauchen.
pop² [pop] *adj* **pop music** Popmusik *f*. **pop song** Schlager *m*.
pope [poup] *n* Papst *m*.
poplar ['poplə] *n* Pappel *f*.
poppy ['popi] *n* Mohn *m*
popular ['popjulə] *adj* populär; *(well-liked)* beliebt; *(of the people)* Volks-. **popularity** *n* Popularität *f*.
population [,popju'leiʃən] *n* Bevölkerung *f*. **populate** *v* bevölkern. **populous** *adj* volkreich.
porcelain ['poıslin] *n* Porzellan *neut. adj* Porzellan-.
porch [poıtʃ] *n* Vorhalle *neut*.
porcupine ['poıkjupain] *n* Stachelschwein *neut*.
pore¹ [poı] *n* Pore *f*.
pore² [poı] *v* **pore over** eifrig studieren, brüten über.
pork [poık] *n* Schweinefleisch *neut*. **pork butcher** Schweineschlächter *m*. **pork chop** Schweinskotelett *neut*. **roast pork** Schweinebraten *m*.
pornography [poı'nogrəfi] *n* Pornographie *f*. **pornographic** *adj* pornographisch; *(film, book)* Porno-.
porous ['poırəs] *adj* porös.
porpoise ['poıpəs] *n* Tümmler *m*.
porridge ['poridʒ] *n* Haferflockenbrei *m*. **porridge oats** Haferflocken *pl*.
port¹ [poıt] *n (harbour)* Hafen *m*; *(town)* Hafenstadt *f*.
port² [poıt] *n (naut)* Backbord *neut. adj* Backbord-.
port³ [poıt] *n (wine)* Portwein *m*.
portly ['poıtli] *adj* wohlbeleibt.
portable ['poıtəbl] *adj* tragbar. **portable radio** Kofferradio *neut*.
portent ['poıtent] *n* Omen *neut*, Vorzeichen *f*. **portentous** *adj* ominös.
porter ['poıtə] *n (rail, etc.)* Gepäckträger *m*.
portfolio [poıt'fouliou] *n* Mappe *f*; *(pol)* Portefeuille *neut*. **minister without portfolio** Minister ohne Geschäftsbereich *m*.
porthole ['poıthoul] *n* Luke *f*.
portion ['poıʃən] *n (food)* Portion *f*; *(share)* (An)Teil *m*.

portrait ['poıtrət] *n* Porträt *neut*. **portray** *v* malen; *(fig)* schildern. **portrayal** *n* Porträt *neut*, Schilderung *f*.
Portugal ['poıtʃugəl] *n* Portugal *neut*. **Portuguese** *adj* portugiesisch; *n* Portugiese *m*, Portugiesin *f*.
pose [pouz] *n* Pose *f*. *v* sitzen, posieren; *(problem)* stellen. **pose as** sich ausgeben als. **poseur** *n* Poseur *m*.
posh [poʃ] *adj* vornehm.
position [pə'ziʃən] *n* Position *f*, Stellung *f*; *(situation)* Lage *f*; *(attitude)* Standpunkt *m*; *(standing)* Rang *m*. *v* stellen.
positive ['pozətiv] *adj* positiv.
possess [pə'zes] *v* besitzen. **possessed** *adj* besessen. **possession** *n* Besitz *m*. **take possession of** in Besitz nehmen. **possessive** *adj (person)* besitzgierig. **possessor** *n* Inhaber(in).
possible ['posəbl] *adj* möglich; *(imaginable)* eventuell. **possibility** *n* Möglichkeit *f*. **possibly** *adv* möglicherweise.
post¹ [poust] *n (pole)* Pfahl *m*, Pfosten *m*. **deaf as a post** stocktaub.
post² [poust] *n (mil)* Posten *m*; *(job)* Stelle *f*. *v* aufstellen.
post³ [poust] *n (mail)* Post *f*. **by post** per Post. **postage stamp** Briefmarke *f*. **postcard** *n* Postkarte *f*. **postman** *n* Briefträger *m*. **post office** Postamt *neut*. *v* zur Post bringen; *(send)* (mit der Post) schicken. **keep someone posted** jemanden auf dem laufenden halten. **postage** *n* Porto *neut*, Postgebühr *f*. **postal** *adj* Post-.
poste restante [poust'testãt] *adv* postlagernd.
poster ['poustə] *n* Plakat *neut*.
posterior [po'stiəriə] *adj* später, hinter. *n* Hintern *m*.
posterity [po'sterəti] *n* Nachwelt *f*.
postgraduate [poust'gradjuit] *n* Doktorand(in).
post-haste *adv* schnellstens.
posthumous ['postjuməs] *adj* postum.
post-mortem [poust'moıtəm] *n* Autopsie *f*.
post-natal [pous'neitl] *adj* postnatal.
postpone [pous'poun] *v* verschieben. **postponement** *n* Verschiebung *f*.
postscript ['poussskript] *n* Postskriptum *neut*.
postulate ['postjuleit] *v* voraussetzen, annehmen.

posture ['postʃə] *n* (Körper)Haltung *f.*
post-war *adj* Nachkriegs-.
pot [pot] *n* Topf *m*; (*tea, coffee*) Kanne *f.*
v (*coll*) schießen. **go to pot** vor die
Hunde gehen. **pot-bellied** *adj*
dickbauchig.
potassium [pə'tasjəm] *n* Kalium *neut.*
potato [pə'teitou] *n* Kartoffel *f.* **boiled
potatoes** Salzkartoffeln *pl.* **chipped** *or*
french-fried potatoes Pommes frites *pl.*
roast *or* **fried potatoes** Bratkartoffeln *pl.*
potent ['poutənt] *adj* stark; (*sexually*)
potent. **potency** *n* Stärke *f*; Potenz *f.*
potential [pə'tenʃəl] *adj* möglich, potential. *n* Potential *neut.*
pothole ['pothoul] *n* Höhle *f.*
potion ['pouʃən] *n* Arzneitrank *m.* **love
potion** Liebestrank *m.*
potluck [pot'lʌk] *n* **take potluck with** (*coll*)
probieren, es riskieren mit/bei.
potted ['potid] *adj* (*meat*) eingemacht;
(*plant*) Topf-; (*version*) gekürzt.
potter ['potə] *v* **potter around**
herumhantieren, herumbasteln.
pottery ['potəri] *n* Töpferwaren *pl*, Steingut *neut.*
potty ['poti] *n* Töpfchen *neut.*
pouch [pautʃ] *n* Beutel *m.*
poultice ['poultis] *n* Breiumschlag *m.*
poultry ['poultri] *n* Geflügel *neut.*
pounce [pauns] *v* springen, sich stürzen.
n Sprung *m*, Satz *m.*
pound[1] [paund] *v* zerstampfen; (*hit*) hämmern, klopfen.
pound[2] [paund] *n* (*currency, weight*)
Pfund *neut.*
pour [poɪ] *v* gießen. **pour out** (*a liquid*)
ausgießen; (*drink*) einschenken; (*come
out*) herausströmen.
pout [paut] *v* schmollen, maulen.
poverty ['povəti] *n* Armut *f.* **poverty-
stricken** *adj* verarmt.
powder ['paudə] *n* Pulver *neut*; (*face*)
Puder *m. v* (*face*) pudern. **powder room**
Damentoilette *f.* **powdery** *adj* pulverig.
power ['pauə] *n* Macht *f*; (*tech*) Kraft *f*;
(*elec*) Strom *m. v* betreiben, antreiben.
great power (*pol*) Großmacht *f.* **powerful**
adj mächtig. **powerless** *adj* machtlos.
power station Kraftwerk *neut.*
practicable ['praktikəbl] *adj*
durchführbar.
practical ['praktikəl] *adj* praktisch.
practice ['praktis] *n* Praxis *f*; (*exercise*)

Übung *f*; (*custom*) Brauch *m*; (*procedure*)
Verfahren *neut. v see* **practise.**
practise ['praktis] *v* üben; (*profession*)
ausüben; (*med, law*) praktizieren. **practised** *adj* geübt.
practitioner [prak'tiʃənə] *n* Praktiker *m.*
medical practitioner praktischer Arzt *m.*
pragmatic [prag'matik] *adj* pragmatisch.
pragmatism *n* Pragmatismus *m.* **pragmatist** *n* Pragmatiker *m.*
Prague [praɪg] *n* Prag *neut.*
prairie ['preəri] *n* Prärie *f.*
praise [preiz] *v* loben. *v* Lob *neut.* **praise-
worthy** *adj* lobenswert.
pram [pram] *n* Kinderwagen *m.*
prance [prains] *v* tänzeln.
prank [praŋk] *n* Streich *m*, Possen *m.*
prattle ['pratl] *v* plappern, schwatzen. *n*
Geplapper *neut*, Geschwätz *neut.*
prawn [proɪn] *n* Garnele *f.*
pray [prei] *v* beten; (*ask*) bitten. **prayer** *n*
Gebet *neut.* **prayerbook** Gebetbuch *neut.*
preach [priːtʃ] *v* predigen. **preacher** *n*
Prediger(in). **preaching** *n* Lehre *f.*
precarious [pri'keəriəs] *adj* unsicher,
gefährlich.
precaution [pri'koɪʃən] *n* Vorkehrung *f.*
precautionary *adj* vorbeugend.
precede [pri'siːd] *v* vorhergehen. **precedence** *n* Vorrang *m.* **precedent** *n*
Präzedenzfall *m.* **order of precedence**
Rangordnung *f.* **preceding** *adj*
vorhergehend.
precinct ['priːsiŋkt] *n* Bezirk *m.* **precincts**
pl Umgebung *f.*
precious ['preʃəs] *adj* kostbar, wertvoll;
(*jewels*) edel. *adv* (*coll*) äußerst.
precipice ['presipis] *n* Abgrund *m.*
precipitate [pri'sipiteit] *v* (*bring about*)
herbeiführen; (*chem*) fällen. **precipitation**
n (*haste*) Hast *f*; (*chem*) Fällung *f*; (*rain,
etc.*) Niederschlag *m.*
précis ['preisi] *n* Zusammenfassung *f. v*
zusammenfassen.
precise [pri'sais] *adj* präzis, genau. **precisely** *adv* genau. **precision** *n* Genauigkeit
f; (*tech*) Präzision *f.*
preclude [pri'kluɪd] *v* ausschließen; (*prevent*) vorbeugen.
precocious [pri'kouʃəs] *adj* frühreif. **pre-
cociousness** *n* Frühreife *f.*
preconceive [ˌpriːkən'siːv] *v* vorher ausdenken. **preconception** *n* Vorurteil *neut.*
precondition [ˌpriːkən'diʃən] *n* Voraussetzung *f.*

press

precursor [,prii'kɔɪsə] *n* Vorläufer(in).
precursory *adj* vorausgehend.
predatory ['predətəri] *adj* räuberisch.
predator *n* Raubtier *neut*.
predecessor ['priidisesə] *n* Vorgänger(in).
predestine [pri'destin] *v* prädestinieren.
predestination *n* Vorbestimmung *f*,
Prädestination *f*.
predicament [pri'dikəmənt] *n* schwierige
Lage *f*.
predicate ['predikət] *n* (*gramm*) Prädikat
neut. *v* aussagen.
predict [pri'dikt] *v* voraussagen. predict-
able *adj* voraussagbar. prediction *n*
Voraussage *f*.
predominate [pri'domineit] *v* vorwiegen.
predominance *n* Vorherrschaft *f*. predominant *adj* vorwiegend.
pre-eminent [prii'eminənt] *adj* hervorragend. pre-eminence *n* Überlegenheit *f*.
preen [priin] *v* (sich) putzen.
prefabricate [prii'fabrikeit] *v* vorfabrizier-
en. prefabricated *adj* Fertig-.
preface ['prehs] *n* Vorwort *neut*. *v*
einleiten.
prefect ['priifekt] *n* (*pol*) Präfekt *m*;
(*school*) Aufsichtsschüler(in).
prefer [pri'fəɪ] *v* vorziehen, lieber haben.
preferable *adj* vorzuziehen. preferably
adv am besten. preference *n* Vorzug *m*.
preferential *adj* bevorzugt.
prefix ['priifiks] *n* Präfix *neut*, Vorsilbe *f*.
pregnant ['pregnənt] *adj* schwanger; (*animals*) trächtig; (*fig*) bedeutend, viel-
sagend. pregnancy *n* Schwangerschaft *f*.
prehistoric [,prithi'storik] *adj* vorgeschich-
tlich. prehistory *n* Vorgeschichte *f*.
prejudice ['predʒədis] *n* Vorurteil *neut*. *v*
beeinträchtigen; (*person*) beeinflussen.
prejudiced *adj* voreingenommen. prejudi-
cial *adj* nachteilig, schädlich.
preliminary [pri'liminəri] *adj* vorläufig,
Vor-.
prelude ['preljuid] *n* Vorspiel *neut*,
Präludium *neut*.
premarital [prii'maritl] *adj* vorehelich.
premature [premə'tʃuə] *adj* frühzeitig.
premature birth Frühgeburt *f*. prematuri-
ty *n* Frühzeitigkeit *f*.
premeditate [prii'mediteit] *v* vorher
überlegen. premeditated *adj* (*crime*) vorsätzlich. premeditation *n* Vorbedacht *m*.
premier ['premiə] *adj* erst. *n*
Premierminister *m*.

premiere ['premieə] *n* Erstaufführung *f*,
Premiere *f*.
premise ['premis] *n* Voraussetzung *f*,
Prämisse *f*.
premises ['premisis] *pl n* Gelände *neut*
sing. business premises Büro *neut*, Ges-
chäftsräume *pl*. on the premises im
Hause.
premium ['priimiəm] *n* Prämie *f*.
premonition [,premə'niʃən] *n* Vorahnung
f.
prenatal [prii'neitl] *adj* prenatal, vor der
Geburt.
preoccupied [prii'okjupaid] *adj* vertieft
(in).
prepare [pri'peə] *v* vorbereiten; (*food*)
zubereiten; (*produce*) herstellen. prepare
for sich vorbereiten auf. preparation *n*
Vorbereitung *f*; (*med*) Präparat *neut*;
(*homework*) Hausaufgaben *pl*. preparato-
ry *adj* vorbereitend. prepared *adj* bereit.
preposition [,prepə'ziʃən] *n* Präposition *f*.
preposterous [pri'postərəs] *adj* absurd,
lächerlich.
prerogative [pri'rogətiv] *n* Vorrecht *neut*.
prescribe [pri'skraib] *v* vorschreiben,
anordnen; (*med*) verordnen. prescription
n Verordnung *f*.
present[1] ['preznt] *adj* (*time*) gegenwärtig;
(*people*) anwesend; (*things*) vorhanden. *n*
Gegenwart *f*. at the present time im
Moment, zur Zeit. be present at
Beiwohnen (+ *dat*) gleich. presently *adv*
gleich. presence *n* (*people*) Anwesenheit *f*,
Beisein *neut*; (*things*) Vorhandensein
neut. presence of mind Geistesgegenwart
f.
present[2] ['preznt; *v* pri'zent] *n* Geschenk
neut. *v* vorlegen; (*gift*) schenken; (*person*)
vorstellen; (*play*) vorführen. presentation
n Vorlegung *f*; Schenkung *f*; Übergabe *f*;
Vorführung *f*.
preserve [pri'zəɪv] *v* bewahren; (*food*)
einmachen. *n* Konserve *f*.
preside [pri'zaid] *v* den Vorsitz führen.
preside over (*meeting*) leiten.
president ['prezidənt] *n* Präsident *m*;
(*comm*) Generaldirektor *m*. presidency *n*
(*pol*) Präsidentschaft *f*; (*meeting*) Vorsitz
m. presidential *adj* Präsidenten-.
press [pres] *v* drücken; (*iron*) bügeln. *n*
Presse *f*. press conference Pressekonfer-
enz *f*. press stud Druckknopf *m*. press-up
n Liegestütz *m*. pressing *adj* dringend.

pressure ['preʃə] n Druck m. **pressure cooker** Schnellkochtopf m. **pressure gauge** Druckmesser m. **pressure group** Interessengruppe f. **pressurize** (*aircraft*) auf Normaldruck halten; (*person*) unter Druck setzen.

prestige [pre'stiːʒ] n Prestige neut. **prestigious** adj Prestige-.

presume [pri'zjuːm] v annehmen; (*dare to*) sich erlauben. **presumably** adv vermutlich. **presumption** n Vermutung f; (*cheek*) Unverschämtheit f. **presumptuous** adj unverschämt.

pretend [pri'tend] v vorgeben. **pretend to** so tun, als ob; (*claim*) Anspruch erheben (auf). **pretence** n Vorwand m, Anschein m. **under false pretences** unter Vorspiegelung falscher Tatsachen. **pretentious** adj anmaßend. **pretentiousness** n Anmaßung f.

pretext ['priːtekst] n Vorwand m, Ausrede f.

pretty ['priti] adj hübsch, niedlich. adv (*coll*) ziemlich. **prettify** v hübsch machen. **prettiness** n Schönheit f.

prevail [pri'veil] v (*win*) siegen (über); (*be prevalent*) vorwiegen, vorherrschen. **prevailing** adj vorherrschend; (*opinion*) allgemein. **prevalence** n Herrschen neut. **prevalent** adj (vor)herrschend.

prevent [pri'vent] v verhindern, verhüten. **prevention** n Verhütung f. **preventive** adj vorbeugend. **preventive measure** Vorsichtsmaßnahme f.

preview ['priːvjuː] n Vorschau f, Probeaufführung f.

previous ['priːviəs] adj vorhergehend, früher. **previously** adv vorher.

prey [prei] n Opfer neut. v **prey on** erbeuten.

price [prais] n Preis m, Kosten pl. v den Preis festsetzen für; (*evaluate*) bewerten. **priceless** adj unschätzbar. **price-tag** n Preiszettel m.

prick [prik] n Stich m. v stechen.

prickle ['prikl] n Stachel m, Dorn m. v prickeln, kribbeln. **prickly** adj stachelig; (*person*) reizbar, übellaunig.

pride [praid] n Stolz m; (*arrogance*) Hochmut m; (*lions*) Rudel neut. v **pride oneself on** stolz sein auf.

priest [priːst] n Priester m. **priestess** n Priesterin f. **priesthood** n Priesterschaft f. **priestly** adj priesterlich.

prim [prim] adj steif, affektiert. **primness** n Steifheit f.

primary ['praiməri] adj erst, ursprünglich; (*main*) primär, Haupt-; (*basic*) grundlegend. **primary school** Grundschule f. **primarily** adv hauptsächlich.

primate ['praimət] n (*biol*) Primat m.

prime [praim] adj erst; (*main*) Haupt-; (*number*) unteilbar; (*best*) erstklassig. **prime minister** Premierminister(in). n Blüte f. v (*gun*) laden; (*paint*) grundieren; (*fig*) vorbereiten. **primer** n (*paint*) Grundierfarbe f; (*book*) Elementarbuch neut. **priming** n Vorbereitung f.

primeval [prai'miːvəl] adj urzeitlich.

primitive ['primitiv] adj (*early*) urzeitlich, Ur-; (*crude, unrefined*) primitiv. **primitiveness** n Primitivität f.

primrose ['primrouz] n Primel f.

prince [prins] n (*ruler*) Fürst m; (*king's son*) Prinz m. **princely** adj fürstlich. **princess** n Fürstin f, Prinzessin f. **principality** n Fürstentum neut.

principal ['prinsəpəl] adj erst, Haupt-. n Vorsteher(in); (*comm*) Kapital neut. **principally** adv hauptsächlich.

principle ['prinsəpəl] n Prinzip neut, Grundsatz m; (*basis*) Grundlage f. **principled** adj mit hohen Grundsätzen.

print [print] v drucken. **printed matter** Drucksache f. **printer** n Drucker m. **printing** n Druck m. **printing press** Druckerei f. n Druck m; (*of photograph*) Abzug m, Kopie f.

prior ['praiə] adj früher. adv **prior to** vor.

priority n Priorität f; (*precedence*) Vorrang m.

prise [praiz] v **prise open** aufbrechen.

prism ['prizm] n Prisma neut.

prison ['prizn] n Gefängnis neut. **prisoner** n Gefangene(r), Häftling m.

private ['praivət] adj privat; (*personal*) persönlich. n gemeiner Soldat m. **privacy** n Privatleben neut, Ruhe f.

privet ['privət] n Liguster m.

privilege ['privəlidʒ] n Privilegium neut, Sonderrecht neut; (*honour*) Ehre f. **privileged** adj bevorrechtet. **be privileged to** die Ehre haben, zu.

privy ['privi] n Abort m. adj **be privy to** eingeweiht sein in. **privy council** Geheimer Rat m.

prize [praiz] n Preis m; (*lottery*) Los neut. adj Preis-. v hochschätzen.

probable ['prɔbəbl] *adj* wahrscheinlich. **probability** *n* Wahrscheinlichkeit *f*.

probation [prə'beiʃən] *n* Probezeit *f*; *(law)* bedingte Freilassung *f*. **probationary** *adj* Probe-.

probe [proub] *n (tech)* Sonde *f*; *(enquiry)* Untersuchung *f*. *v* **probe into** eindringen in, erforschen.

problem ['problǝm] *n* Problem *neut*. **problematical** *adj* problematisch.

proceed [prǝ'siːd] *v* weitergehen; *(continue)* fortfahren; *(begin)* beginnen. **procedure** *n* Vorgehen *neut*. **proceedings** *pl n* *(law)* Verfahren *neut sing*. **proceeds** *pl n* Erlös *m sing*, Ertrag *m sing*.

process ['prouses] *v* bearbeiten, verarbeiten. *n* Verfahren *neut*, Prozeß *m*. **processing** *n* Verarbeitung *f*.

procession [prǝ'seʃǝn] *n* Prozession *f*, Zug *m*.

proclaim [prǝ'kleim] *v* proklamieren, verkünden. **proclamation** *n* Proklamation *f*.

procreate ['proukriːeit] *v* erzeugen. **procreation** *n* Zeugung *f*.

procure [prǝ'kjuǝ] *v* beschaffen, besorgen.

prod [prod] *v* stechen, stoßen; *(coll: induce)* anspornen (zu). *n* Stich *m*, Stoß *m*.

prodigy ['prodidʒi] *n* Wunder *neut*; *(child)* Wunderkind *neut*. **prodigious** *adj* riesig, erstaunlich.

produce [prǝ'djuːs; *n* 'prodjuːs] *v (goods)* erzeugen, herstellen; *(submit)* vorlegen; *(cause, call forth)* hervorrufen; *(theatre)* aufführen; *(films)* herausbringen. *n* Erzeugnis *neut*, Produkte *pl*. **producer** *n* Hersteller; *(theatre, film)* Regisseur *m*.

product *n* Produkt *neut*, Erzeugnis *neut*; *(result)* Ergebnis *neut*. **production** *n* Herstellung *f*, Produktion *f*; *(theatre)* Aufführung *f*; *(film)* Regie *f*. **production line** Fließband *neut*. **productive** *adj* fruchtbar, leistungsfähig. **productivity** *n* Leistungsfähigkeit *f*, Produktivität *f*.

profane [prǝ'fein] *adj* profan. **profanity** *n* Fluchen *neut*.

profess [prǝ'fes] *v* erklären. **profession** *n* *(occupation)* Beruf *m*; *(assertion)* Beteuerung *f*. **professional** *adj* Berufs-, beruflich; *(education)* fachlich, Fach-.

professor [prǝ'fesǝ] *n* Professor(in). **professorship** *n* Lehrstuhl *m*.

proficient [prǝ'fiʃǝnt] *adj* erfahren. **proficiency** *n* Erfahrenheit *f*.

profile ['proufail] *n* Profil *neut*. *v* profilieren.

profit ['profit] *n (comm)* Gewinn *m*, Profit *m*; *(advantage)* Vorteil *m*. *v* **profit from** Nutzen ziehen aus. **profitable** *adj* rentabel; *(advantageous)* vorteilhaft. **profiteer** *n* Profitmacher *m*; *v* sich bereichern.

program ['prougram] *n (computer)* Programm *neut*. *v* programmieren. **programmer** *n* Programmierer(in).

programme ['prougram] *n* Programm *neut*; *(TV, radio: broadcast)* Sendung *f*. *v* planen.

progress ['prougres] *n* Fortschritt *m*; *(development)* Entwicklung *f*. *v* fortschreiten, sich entwickeln. **in progress** im Gange. **progression** *n* Fortbewegung *f*. **progressive** *adj* fortschrittlich.

prohibit [prǝ'hibit] *v* verbieten. **prohibition** *n* Verbot *neut*; *(of drinking)* Alkoholverbot *neut*. **prohibitive** *adj* verbietend; *(excessively high)* untragbar.

project ['prodʒekt; *v* prǝ'dʒekt] *n* Projekt *neut*, Plan *m*; *(school)* Planaufgabe *f*. *v* *(film, etc.)* projizieren; *(plan)* planen. **projection** *n* Projektion *f*. **projector** *n* Projektionsapparat *m*.

proletariat [proulǝ'teǝriǝt] *n* Proletariat *neut*. **proletarian** *adj* proletarisch. *n* Proletarier(in).

proliferate [prǝ'lifǝreit] *v* sich vermehren, wuchern. **proliferation** *n* Wucherung *f*.

prolific [prǝ'lifik] *adj* fruchtbar.

prologue ['proulog] *n* Prolog *m*.

prolong [prǝ'loŋ] *v* verlängern. **prolonged** *adj* anhaltend. **prolongation** *n* Verlängerung *f*.

promenade [promǝ'naːd] *n* Promenade *f*; *(walk)* Spaziergang *m*. *v* promenieren, spazieren.

prominent ['prominǝnt] *adj* *(person)* prominent, maßgebend. **prominence** *n* Prominenz *f*, hervorragende Bedeutung *f*.

promiscuous [prǝ'miskjuǝs] *adj* promiskuitiv. **promiscuity** *n* Promiskuität *f*.

promise ['promis] *n* Versprechen *neut*. *v* versprechen. **promising** *adj* vielversprechend.

promontory ['promǝntǝri] *n* Landspitze *f*.

promote [prǝ'mout] *v (person)* befördern; *(encourage, support)* fördern, Vorschub leisten (+ *dat*); *(comm)* Reklame machen für. **promoter** *n (sport)* Promoter *m*. **pro-**

motion n Beförderung; (*publicity*) Werbung f, Reklame f.

prompt [prompt] *adj* sofortig, prompt. v (*theatre*) soufflieren; (*cause*) hervorrufen. **promptness** n Pünktlichkeit f.

prone [proun] *adj* hingestreckt. **prone to** geneigt zu.

prong [proŋ] n Zinke f. **pronged** *adj* gezinkt.

pronoun ['prounaun] n Pronomen *neut*.

pronounce [prə'nauns] v aussprechen. **pronouncement** n Ausspruch m. **pronunciation** n Aussprache f.

proof [pruːf] n Beweis m, Nachweis m; (*printing*) Korrekturabzug m. *adj* undurchlässig, fest. **proof against** sicher vor. **proof-reader** n Korrektor(in).

prop[1] [prop] n Stütze f. v **prop up** stützen.

prop[2] [prop] n (*theatre*) Requisit *neut*.

propaganda [propə'gandə] n Propaganda f. **propagandist** n Propagandist(in).

propagate ['propəgeit] v fortpflanzen. **propagation** n Fortpflanzung f.

propel [prə'pel] v (an)treiben. **propellant** n Treibstoff m. **propeller** n Propeller m.

proper ['propə] *adj* (*fitting*) richtig, passend, geeignet; (*thorough*) ordentlich. **properly** *adv* richtig, wie es sich gehört.

property ['propəti] n Eigentum *neut*; (*characteristic*) Eigenschaft f; (*real estate*) Immobilien *pl*.

prophecy ['profəsi] n Weissagung f. **prophesy** v prophezeien. **prophet** n Prophet m. **prophetic** *adj* prophetisch.

proportion [prə'poːʃən] n Verhältnis *neut*; (*part*) Anteil m; (*measurement*) Ausmaß *neut*. **in proportion to** im Verhältnis zu. **be out of proportion to** in keinem Verhältnis stehen zu. **well-proportioned** *adj* wohlgestaltet. **proportional** *adj* verhältnismäßig, proportional.

propose [prə'pouz] v vorschlagen; (*a motion*) beantragen; (*marriage*) einen Heiratsantrag machen (+ *dat*). **proposal** n Vorschlag m; (*offer*) Angebot *neut*; (*marriage*) Heiratsantrag m. **proposer** n Antragsteller m. **proposition** n Vorschlag m; (*project*) Projekt *neut*, Plan m.

proprietor [prə'praiətə] n Besitzer(in), Inhaber(in).

propriety [prə'praiəti] n Schicklichkeit f, Anstand m.

propulsion [prə'pʌlʃən] n Antrieb m.

prose [prouz] n Prosa f. *adj* Prosa-.

prosecute ['prosikjuːt] v (*law*) gerichtlich verfolgen. **prosecution** n Verfolgung f; (*law*) Anklage f.

prospect ['prospekt; v prə'spekt] n Aussicht f. v **prospect for** (*gold, etc.*) graben nach. **prospective** *adj* künftig, voraussichtlich.

prospectus [prə'spektəs] n (Werbe-)Prospekt m.

prosper ['prospə] v gedeihen. **prosperity** n Wohlstand m. **prosperous** *adj* erfolgreich, wohlhabend.

prostitute ['prostitjuːt] n Prostituierte f. v prostituieren. **prostitution** n Prostitution f.

prostrate ['prostreit; v pro'streit] *adj* hingestreckt. v zu Boden werfen. **prostrate oneself** sich demütigen (vor).

protagonist [prou'tagənist] n Hauptfigur f.

protect [prə'tekt] v (be)schützen. **protection** n Schutz m. **protectionism** n Schutzzollpolitik f. **protective** *adj* (be)schützend. **protector** n Beschützer m. **protectorate** n Schutzgebiet *neut*.

protégé ['protəʒei] n Schützling m.

protein ['proutiːn] n Protein *neut*, Eiweiß *neut*.

protest ['proutest; v prə'test] n Protest m, Einspruch m. v protestieren, Einspruch erheben (auf).

Protestant ['protistənt] n Protestant(in). *adj* protestantisch. **Protestantism** n Protestantismus m.

protocol ['proutəkol] n Protokoll *neut*.

prototype ['proutətaip] n Prototyp m.

protractor [prə'traktə] n Winkelmesser m.

protrude [prə'truːd] v herausstehen, hervorstehen.

proud [praud] *adj* stolz (auf); (*arrogant*) hochmütig.

prove [pruːv] v beweisen. **prove to be** sich erweisen als.

proverb ['provəːb] n Sprichwort *neut*. **proverbial** *adj* sprichwörtlich.

provide [prə'vaid] v versehen, versorgen. **provide for** sorgen für. **provided** *conj* vorausgesetzt.

provident ['providənt] *adj* fürsorglich. **providence** n Vorsehung f. **providential** *adj* glücklich.

province ['provins] n Provinz f. **provincial** *adj* Provinz-, provinzial; (*limited, narrow*) provinziell.

provision [prə'viʒən] *n* Vorrichtung *f*; (*regulation*) Vorschrift *f*. **provisions** *pl* Vorrat *m*. **provisional** *adj* vorläufig, provisorisch.

proviso [prə'vaizou] *n* Vorbehalt *m*, Klausel *f*.

provoke [prə'vouk] *v* (*cause*) veranlassen; (*person*) provozieren; (*annoy*) ärgern. **provocation** *n* Provokation *f*; (*challenge*) Herausforderung *f*.

prow [prau] *n* Bug *m*.

prowess ['prauis] *n* Tüchtigkeit *f*.

prowl [praul] *v* herumstreichen. **prowler** *n* Herumtreiber *m*.

proximity [prok'siməti] *n* Nähe *f*.

proxy ['proksi] *n* Vollmacht *f*; (*person*) Bevollmächtigte(r).

prude [pruːd] *n* prüder Mensch *m*. **prudery** *n* Prüderie *f*. **prudish** *adj* prüde.

prudent ['pruːdənt] *adj* vernünftig, umsichtig. **prudence** *n* Klugheit *f*.

prune[1] [pruːn] *n* Backpflaume *f*.

prune[2] [pruːn] *v* (*tree*) beschneiden.

pry [prai] *v* herumschnuffeln. **pry into die** Nase stecken in. **prying** *adj* neugierig.

psalm [saːm] *n* Psalm *m*.

pseudonym ['sjuːdənim] *n* Pseudonym *neut*, Deckname *m*.

psychedelic [‚saikə'delik] *adj* psychedelisch.

psychiatry [sai'kaiətri] *n* Psychiatrie *f*. **psychiatric** *adj* psychiatrisch. **psychiatrist** *m* Psychiater(in).

psychic ['saikik] *adj* psychisch.

psychoanalysis [‚saikouə'naləsis] *n* Psychoanalyse *f*. **psychoanalyst** *n* Psychoanalytiker(in).

psychology [sai'kolədʒi] *n* Psychologie *f*. **psychological** *adj* psychologisch. **psychologist** *n* Psycholog(in).

psychopath ['saikəpaθ] *n* Psychopath(in).

psychosomatic [‚saikəsə'matik] *adj* psychosomatisch.

pub [pʌb] *n* (*coll*) Kneipe *f*.

puberty ['pjuːbəti] *n* Pubertät *f*, Geschlechtsreife *f*.

pubic ['pjuːbik] *adj* Scham-.

public ['pʌblik] *adj* öffentlich; (*national*) Volks-, national. *n* Öffentlichkeit *f*, Publikum *neut*. **public house** *n* Wirtshaus *neut*. **public school** *n* Privatschule *f* **public-spirited** *adj* gemeinsinnig. **publication** *n* Veröffentlichung *f*, Publikation *f*. **publicity** *n* Reklame *f*, Werbung *f*. **publicize** *v* veröffentlichen.

publish ['pʌbliʃ] *v* (*publicize*) veröffentlichen; (*book*) herausbringen. **publisher** *n* Verleger(in), Herausgeber(in); (*firm*) Verlag *m*. **publishing** *n* Verlagswesen *neut*.

pucker ['pʌkə] *v* runzeln; (*mouth*) spitzen.

pudding ['pudiŋ] *n* Pudding *m*. **black pudding** *n* Blutwurst *f*.

puddle ['pʌdl] *n* Pfütze *f*, Lache *f*.

puerile ['pjuərail] *adj* pueril.

puff [pʌf] *n* Hauch *m*; (*on cigar, etc.*) Zug *m*. *v* blasen, pusten. **powder puff** Puderquaste *f*. **puffed-up** *adj* (*coll*) aufgeblasen. **puff pastry** Blätterteig *m*. **puffy** *adj* angeschwollen.

pull [pul] *v* ziehen; (*tug*) zerren; (*rip*) reißen. *n* Zug *m*. **pull through** (*survive*) durchkommen.

pulley ['puli] *n* Rolle *f*.

pullover ['pul‚ouvə] *n* Pullover *m*.

pulp [pʌlp] *n* Brei *m*; (*fruit*) Fruchtfleisch *neut*; (*paper*) Pulpe *f*. **pulpy** *adj* breiig, weich.

pulpit ['pulpit] *n* Kanzel *f*.

pulsate [pʌl'seit] *v* pulsieren. **pulsation** *n* Pulsieren *neut*.

pulse [pʌls] *n* Puls *m*, Pulsschlag *m*. *v* pulsieren.

pulverize ['pʌlvəraiz] *v* pulverisieren, zermahlen. **pulverization** *n* Pulverisierung *f*.

pump [pʌmp] *n* Pumpe *f*. *v* pumpen.

pumpkin ['pʌmpkin] *n* Kürbis *m*.

pun [pʌn] *n* Wortspiel *neut*.

punch[1] [pʌntʃ] *n* (*blow*) (Faust)Schlag *m*. *v* (mit der Faust) schlagen.

punch[2] [pʌntʃ] *n* (*drink*) Punsch *m*. **punchbowl** *n* Punschbowle *f*.

punch[3] [pʌntʃ] *n* (*tool*) Locher *m*, Lochzange *f*. *v* lochen; (*tickets*) knipsen. **punchcard** *n* Lochkarte *f*.

punctual ['pʌŋktʃuəl] *adj* pünktlich. **punctuality** *n* Pünktlichkeit *f*

punctuate ['pʌŋktʃueit] *v* interpunktieren; (*fig*) unterbrechen. **punctuation** *n* Interpunktion *f*.

puncture ['pʌŋktʃə] *v* durchstechen, perforieren; (*tyre*) platzen. *n* Loch *neut*; (*tyre*) Reifenpanne *f*.

pungent ['pʌndʒənt] *adj* scharf.

punish ['pʌniʃ] *v* (be)strafen. **punishment** *n* Strafe *f*.

puny ['pjuːni] *adj* schwächlich.

pupil¹ ['pjuːpl] *n* Schüler(in).
pupil² ['pjuːpl] *n* (*eye*) Pupille *f*.
puppet ['pʌpit] *n* Marionette *f*. **puppet show** Puppenspiel *neut*, Marionettentheater *neut*.
puppy ['pʌpi] *n* junger Hund *m*, Welpe *m*.
purchase ['pɔːtʃəs] *n* Einkauf *m*. *v* (ein)kaufen. **purchaser** *n* Käufer(in).
pure ['pjuə] *adj* rein. **purebred** *adj* reinrassig. **purify** *v* reinigen; (*tech*) klären. **purification** *n* Reinigung *f*; Klärung *f*. **purity** *n* Reinheit *f*.
purée ['pjuərei] *n* Purée *neut*.
purgatory ['pɔːgətəri] *n* Fegefeuer *neut*.
purge [pɔːdʒ] *v* reinigen, säubern. *n* Reinigung *f*; (*pol*) Säuberung *f*.
puritan ['pjuəritən] *n* Puritaner(in). **puritanical** *adj* puritanisch. **puritanism** *n* Puritanismus *m*.
purl [pɔːl] *n* Linksstricken *neut*. *v* linksstricken.
purple ['pɔːpl] *adj* purpurn, purpurrot. *n* Purpur *m*.
purpose ['pɔːpəs] *n* Zweck *m*, Ziel *neut*. **for the purpose of** zwecks (+ *gen*). **on purpose** absichtlich. **purposeful** *adj* zielbewußt. **purposeless** *adj* zwecklos. **purposely** *adv* absichtlich.
purr [pɔː] *v* schnurren, summen. *n* Schnurren *neut*.
purse [pɔːs] *n* Portemonnaie *neut*, Geldbeutel *m*; Handtasche *f*; (*prize*) Börse *f*. *v* (*lips*) spitzen.
purser ['pɔːsə] *n* Zahlmeister *m*.
pursue [pə'sjuː] *v* verfolgen; (*studies*) betreiben; (*continue*) fortfahren in. **pursuit** *n* Verfolgung *f*; (*activity*) Beschäftigung *f*; (*of happiness, etc.*) Jagd *f*, Suche *f*.
pus [pʌs] *n* Eiter *m*.
push [puʃ] *n* Stoß *m*, Schub *m*. **get the push** (*coll*) entlassen werden. *v* stoßen, schieben; (*button*) drücken; (*in crowd*) drängen. **be pushed for time** keine zeit haben. **push aside** beiseite schieben. **push open/to** (*door*) auf/zuschieben. **push off** (*coll*) abhauen. **push through** durchsetzen. **pushbike** *m* (*coll*) Rad *neut*. **pushbutton** *n* Druckknopf *m*. **pushchair** *n* Kinderwagen. **pusher** *n* (*drugs*) Pusher *m*. **pushing** *adj* aufdringlich.
pussy ['pusi] *n* (*coll*) Mieze *f*.
*put [put] *v* stellen, setzen, legen; (*express*) ausdrücken; (*shot*) werfen. **put away** weglegen. **put back** (*clock*) nach-

stellen; (*postpone*) aufschieben. **put by** aufsparen. **put down** hinlegen; (*revolt*) unterdrücken; (*animal*) töten. **put off** verschieben; (*discourage*) davon abraten (+ *dat*). **put through** durchführen; (*phone*) verbinden. **put up** (*coll*) unterbringen. **put up with** dulden, ausstehen.
putrid ['pjuːtrid] *adj* verfault.
putt [pʌt] *v* putten.
putty ['pʌti] *n* Kitt *m*.
puzzle ['pʌzl] *n* Rätsel *neut*; (*jigsaw*) Puzzlespiel *neut*. *v* verwirren. **puzzlement** *n* Verwirrung *f*. **puzzling** *adj* rätselhaft.
pyjamas [pə'dʒaːməz] *n* Schlafanzug *m*.
pylon ['pailən] *n* (*elec*) Leitungsmast *m*.
pyramid ['pirəmid] *n* Pyramide *f*.
python ['paiθən] *n* Pythonschlange *f*.

Q

quack¹ [kwak] *n* (*duck*) Quaken *neut*. *v* quaken.
quack² [kwak] *n* (*doctor*) Quacksalber *m*. *adj* quacksalberisch.
quadrangle ['kwodraŋgl] *n* Viereck *neut*; Hof *m*. **quadrangular** *adj* viereckig.
quadrant ['kwodrənt] *n* Quadrant *m*.
quadrilateral [kwodrə'latərəl] *adj* vierseitig.
quadruped ['kwodruped] *n* Vierfüßer *m*.
quadruple [kwod'ruːpl] *adj* vierfach, vierfältig. *v* vervierfachen.
quagmire ['kwagmaiə] *n* Morast *m*.
quail¹ [kweil] *n* (*bird*) Wachtel *f*.
quail² [kweil] *v* verzagen, den Mut verlieren.
quaint [kweint] *adj* kurios, merkwürdig.
quake [kweik] *v* beben. *n* Erdbeben *neut*.
qualify ['kwolifai] *v* (sich) qualifizieren; (*limit*) einschränken. **qualification** *n* Qualifikation *f*; Einschränkung *f*. **qualified** *adj* qualifiziert, geeignet; eingeschränkt.
quality ['kwoləti] *n* Qualität *f*; (*property*) Eigenschaft *f*; (*type*) Sorte *f*. *adj* erstklassig, guter Qualität *f*.
qualm [kwaːm] *n* Skrupel *m*.
quandary ['kwondəri] *n* Verlegenheit *f*.
quantify ['kwontifai] *v* messen, (quantitativ) bestimmen.

quantity ['kwontəti] *n* Quantität *f*, Menge *f*.

quarantine ['kworəntiːn] *n* Quarantäne *f*. *v* unter Quarantäne stellen.

quarrel ['kworəl] *n* Streit *m*, Zank *m*. *v* (sich) streiten, (sich) zanken. **quarrelsome** *adj* streitsüchtig, zankig.

quarry[1] ['kwori] *n* (*hunting*) Jagdbeute *f*; (*fig*) Opfer *neut*.

quarry[2] ['kwori] *n* Steinbruch *m*. *v* brechen, hauen.

quart [kwoːt] *n* Quart *neut*.

quarter ['kwoːtə] *n* (*fourth, of town, etc.*) Viertel *neut*; (*of year*) Quartal *neut*, Vierteljahr *neut*. *v* vierteln; (*to house*) unterbringen. **quarter of an hour** Viertelstunde *f*. **quarter to/past** Viertel vor/nach. **quarterdeck** *n* Achterdeck *neut*. **quarter-final** *n* Viertelfinale *neut*. **quarterly** *adj* vierteljährlich.

quartet [kwoːˈtet] *n* Quartett *neut*.

quartz [kwoːts] *n* Quartz *m*.

quash [kwoʃ] *v* annullieren; (*resistance etc.*) unterdrücken.

quaver ['kweivə] *v* zittern. *n* (*music*) Achtelnote *f*.

quay [kiː] *n* Kai *m*.

queasy ['kwiːzi] *adj* übel. *I feel queasy* mir ist übel.

queen [kwiːn] *n* Königin *f*; (*cards, chess*) Dame *f*. **queen bee** Bienenkönigin *f*. **queen mother** Königinmutter *f*.

queer [kwiə] *adj* seltsam, sonderbar; (*odd*) komisch; (*coll: homosexual*) schwul. *n* (*coll*) Homo *m*, Schwule(r).

quell [kwel] *v* unterdrücken.

quench [kwentʃ] *v* löschen.

query ['kwiəri] *n* Frage *f*, Erkundigung *f*. *v* in Frage stellen.

quest [kwest] *n* Suche *f* (nach).

question ['kwestʃən] *n* Frage *f*. *v* (be)fragen. **put** *or* **ask a question** eine Frage stellen. **out of the question** ausgeschlossen. **the question is** es handelt sich darum. **questionable** *adj* fragwürdig. **questioning** *adj* fragend. *n* Befragung *f*. **questionnaire** *n* Fragebogen *m*.

queue [kjuː] *n* Schlange *f*. *v* Schlange stehen, sich anstellen.

quibble ['kwibl] *v* Haare spalten, spitzfindig sein.

quick [kwik] *adj* schnell; (*nimble*) flink; (*temper*) hitzig; (*ear, eye*) scharf. **quicken** *v* beschleunigen. **quickness** *n* Schnel-

ligkeit *f*. **quicksand** *n* Treibsand *m*. **quicksilver** *n* Quecksilber *neut*. **quick-tempered** *adj* hitzig, reizbar. **quick-witted** *adj* scharfsinnig.

quid [kwid] *n* (*coll*) Pfund *neut*.

quiet ['kwaiət] *adj* ruhig, still. **quieten** *v* beruhigen. **quietness** *n* Ruhe *f*, Stille *f*.

quill [kwil] *n* Feder *f*.

quilt [kwilt] *n* Steppdecke *f*.

quinine [kwi'niːn] *n* Chinin *neut*.

quinsy ['kwinzi] *n* Mandelentzündung *f*.

quintet [kwin'tet] *n* Quintett *neut*.

quirk [kwəːk] *n* Eigenart *f*.

***quit** [kwit] *v* (*stop*) aufhören; (*leave*) verlassen; (*job*) aufgeben. **notice to quit** Kündigung *f*. **quits** *adj* (*coll*) quitt.

quite [kwait] *adv* (*fairly*) ziemlich; (*wholly*) ganz, durchaus.

quiver[1] ['kwivə] *v* zittern.

quiver[2] ['kwivə] *n* (*arrows*) Köcher *m*.

quiz [kwiz] *n* Quiz *neut*. *v* (aus)fragen. **quizzical** ['kwizikl] *adj* spöttisch.

quota ['kwouta] *n* Quote *f*, Anteil *m*.

quote [kwout] *v* zitieren. **quotation** *n* Zitat *f*; (*comm*) Preisangabe *f*. **quotation marks** Anführungszeichen *pl*.

R

rabbi ['rabai] *n* Rabbiner *m*.

rabbit ['rabit] *n* Kaninchen *neut*. **rabbit hutch** Kaninchenstall *m*.

rabble ['rabl] *n* Pöbel *m*.

rabies ['reibiːz] *n* Tollwut *f*. **rabid** *adj* tollwütig; (*coll: angry*) wütend.

race[1] [reis] *n* Rennen *neut*, Wettlauf *m*. *v* um die Wette laufen (mit), rennen. **the races** Pferderennen *pl*. **racecourse** *n* Rennbahn *f*. **racehorse** *n* Rennpferd *neut*. **racing** *n* Pferderennen *neut*; *adj* Renn-. **racing driver** Rennfahrer *m*.

race[2] [reis] *n* (*group*) Rasse *f*. **racial** *adj* rassisch, Rassen-. **racialism** *or* **racism** *n* Rassismus *m*. **racialist** *or* **racist** *n* Rassist(in); *adj* rassistisch.

rack [rak] *n* Gestell *neut*; (*luggage*) Gepäcknetz *neut*. *v* **rack one's brains** sich den Kopf zerbrechen.

racket[1] ['rakit] *n* (*sport*) Rakett *neut*, Schläger *m*.

racket² ['rakit] n (*noise*) Krach m, Trübel m; (*coll: swindle*) Schwindel m. **racketeer** n Schwindler m, Gangster m.

radar ['reidɑː] n Radar m or neut.

radial ['reidiəl] adj radial. n (*tyre*) Gürtelreifen m.

radiant ['reidiənt] adj strahlend. **radiance** n Strahlung f.

radiate ['reidieit] v ausstrahlen. **radiation** n Strahlung f. **radiator** n (*house*) Heizkörper m; (*mot*) Kühler m.

radical ['radikəl] adj radikal. n Radikale(r). **radicalism** n Radikalismus m.

radio ['reidiou] n (*set*) Radio neut; (*network*) Rundfunk m. v senden, durchgeben. **radio ham** (*coll*) Funkamateur m. **radio station** Sender m, Funkstation f. **radio wave** Radiowelle f.

radioactive [reidiou'aktiv] adj radioaktiv. **radioactivity** n Radioaktivität f.

radiology [reidi'olədʒi] n Radiologie f, Röntgenlehre f. **radiologist** n Radiologe m.

radiotherapy [reidiou'θerəpi] n Radiotherapie f, Strahlenbehandlung f.

radish ['radiʃ] n Radieschen neut.

radium ['reidiəm] n Radium neut.

radius ['reidiəs] n Radius m.

raffia ['rafiə] n Raffiabast m.

raffle ['rafl] n Tombola f. v verlosen.

raft [rɑːft] n Floß neut.

rafter ['rɑːftə] n Dachsparren m.

rag¹ [rag] n Fetzen m, Lumpen m; (*coll: newspaper*) Blatt neut. **rag doll** Stoffpuppe f. **ragged** adj zerfetzt.

rag² [rag] v (*coll: tease*) necken, piesacken.

rage [reidʒ] n Wut f. v wüten. **in a rage** wütend. **be all the rage** die große Mode sein.

raid [reid] n Angriff m, Überfall m; (*police*) Razzia f. v überfallen; eine Razzia machen auf.

rail [reil] n Riegel m, Schiene f. **by rail** mit der Bahn. **railing** n Geländer neut.

railway or **railroad** n Eisenbahn f. **railway station** Bahnhof m.

rain [rein] n Regen m. v regnen. **rainbow** n Regenbogen m. **raincoat** n Regenmantel m. **rainfall** n Niederschlag m. **rainproof** adj wasserdicht. **rainstorm** n Regenguß. **rainy** adj regnerisch.

raise [reiz] v erheben, aufrichten; (*provoke*) hervorrufen; (*money*) beschaffen. n (*in pay*) Erhöhung f. **raised** adj erhöht.

raisin ['reizən] n Rosine f.

rake [reik] n Rechen m. v rechen.

rally ['rali] n (*meeting*) (Massen)Versammlung f; (*mot*) Sternfahrt f, Rallye f. v (*wieder*) sammeln; (*spirits*) sich erholen. **rally round** sich scharen um.

ram [ram] n (*zool*) Widder m; (*tech*) Ramme f. v rammen.

ramble ['rambl] v wandern; (*speech*) drauflos reden. n Wanderung f, Bummel m. **rambler** n Wanderer m; (*rose*) Kletterrose f. **rambling** adj wandernd; (*speech*) unzusammenhängend, weitschweifig.

ramp [ramp] n Rampe f.

rampage [ram'peidʒ] v (herum)toben.

rampant ['rampənt] adj üppig, wuchernd.

rampart ['rampɑːt] n Festungswall m.

ramshackle ['ramʃakl] adj wackelig.

ran [ran] V **run**.

ranch [rɑːntʃ] n Ranch f.

rancid ['ransid] adj ranzig.

rancour ['raŋkə] n Erbitterung f, Böswilligkeit f.

random ['randəm] adj zufällig. n **at random** wahllos, aufs Geratewohl.

randy ['randi] adj (*coll*) geil, wollüstig.

rang [raŋ] V **ring²**.

range [reindʒ] n Reihe f; (*mountains*) Kette f; (*reach*) Tragweite f. v anordnen; (*vary*) variieren, schwanken; (*rove*) wandern.

rank¹ [raŋk] n (*status*) Rang m; (*row*) Reihe f. v **rank with** zählen zu. **the ranks** (*mil*) die Mannschaften pl.

rank² [raŋk] adj (*plants*) üppig; (*offensive*) widerlich; (*coarse*) grob.

rankle ['raŋkl] v nagen.

ransack ['ransak] v plündern, durchwühlen.

ransom ['ransəm] n Lösegeld neut. v loskaufen.

rap [rap] n Klopfen neut. v klopfen.

rape [reip] n Vergewaltigung f. v vergewaltigen. **rapist** n Vergewaltiger m.

rapid ['rapid] adj schnell, rasch. **rapidity** n Schnelligkeit f. **rapids** pl n Stromschnelle f.

rapier ['reipiə] n Rapier neut.

rapture ['raptʃə] n Verzückung f, Begeisterung f. **rapturous** adj hingerissen.

rare¹ ['reə] *adj* selten, rar; *(air)* dünn.
rarely *adv* selten. **rarity** *n* Seltenheit *f.*
rare² ['reə] *adj* *(cookery)* nicht durchgebraten, englisch.
rascal ['rɑːskəl] *n* Schurke *m.* **rascally** *adj* schurkisch.
rash¹ [raʃ] *n* *(on skin)* Hautausschlag *m.*
rash² [raʃ] *adj* hastig, übereilt. **rashness** *n* Hast *f.*
rasher ['raʃə] *n* (Schinken)Schnitte *f.*
raspberry ['raɪzbəri] *n* Himbeere *f.*
rat [rat] *n* Ratte *f.* *v* **rat on** *(coll)* verraten.
rate [reit] *n* *(comm)* Satz *m,* Kurs *m;* *(charge)* Gebühr *f;* *(speed)* Geschwindigkeit *f;* *v* schätzen. **rates** *pl* Gemeindesteuer *f.* **birth rate** Geburtenziffer *f.* **at any rate** auf jeden Fall. **first-rate** *adj* erstklassig. **second-rate, third-rate,** *etc. adj* minderwertig.
rather ['rɑːðə] *adv* *(quite)* ziemlich, etwas; *(preferably)* lieber, eher. *I would rather* ich möchte lieber.
ratify ['ratifai] *v* ratifizieren. **ratification** *n* Ratifizierung *f.*
ratio ['reiʃiou] *n* Verhältnis *neut.*
ration ['raʃən] *n* Ration *f.* *v* rationieren. **rations** *pl* Verpflegung *f sing.*
rational ['raʃənl] *adj* rational, vernünftig. **rationale** *n* Grundprinzip *neut.* **rationalization** *n* Rationalisierung *f.* **rationalize** *v* rationalisieren.
rattle ['ratl] *v* klappern, rasseln. *n* Gerassel *neut,* Klappern *neut.* **rattlesnake** *n* Klapperschlange *f.*
raucous ['rɔːkəs] *adj* rauh, heiser.
ravage ['ravidʒ] *v* verwüstern. *n* Verwüstung. **ravages of time** Zahn der Zeit *m.*
rave [reiv] *v* irre reden, toben. **rave about** *(coll)* schwärmen von. **raving** *adj* delirierend. **ravings** *pl* *n* Fieberwahn *m,* Delirien *pl.*
raven ['reivən] *n* Rabe *m.*
ravenous ['ravənəs] *adj* heißhungrig.
ravine [rə'viːn] *n* Schlucht *f.*
ravish ['raviʃ] *v* *(delight)* hinreißen; *(rape)* vergewaltigen. **ravishing** *adj* entzückend.
raw [rɔː] *adj* roh; *(voice)* rauh; *(sore)* wund. **rawhide** *n* Rohleder *neut.* **rawness** *n* Rohzustand *m.*
ray [rei] *n* Strahl *m.* **ray of light** Lichtstrahl *m.*
rayon ['reiɔn] *n* Kunstseide *f.*
razor ['reizə] *n* Rasiermesser *neut.* **electric razor** Elektrorasierer *m.* **razor blade**

Rasierklinge *f.* **razor-sharp** *adj* messerscharf.
reach [riːtʃ] *v* *(arrive at)* erreichen; *(stretch to)* sich erstrecken (bis). *n* Reichweite *f.* **reach (out) for** reichen *or* greifen nach.
react [ri'akt] *v* reagieren. **reaction** *n* Reaktion *f.* **reactionary** *adj* reaktionär; *n* Reaktionär(in).
*read [riːd] *v* lesen; *(interpret)* auslegen, deuten. **read aloud** vorlesen. **read through** durchlesen. **readable** *adj* leserlich; *(worth reading)* lesenswert. **reader** *n* Leser(in); *(university)* Dozent *m.* **readership** *n* Leserkreis *m.* **reading** *n* Lesen *neut;* *(public)* Vorlesung *f.* **reading matter** Lektüre *f.*
readjust [riːə'dʒʌst] *v* wieder in Ordnung bringen; *(tech)* wieder einstellen; *(person)* (sich) wieder anpassen (an). **readjustment** *n* Wiederanpassung *f.*
ready ['redi] *adj* bereit, fertig; *(quick)* prompt. **get** *or* **make ready** sich vorbereiten, *(thing)* fertig machen. **readiness** *n* Bereitschaft *f.* **ready-made** *adj* Fertig-.
ready-reckoner *n* Rechentabelle *f.* **readily** *adv* ohne weiteres.
real [riəl] *adj* wirklich, wahr; *(genuine)* echt. **real estate** Immobilien *pl.* **realism** *n* Realismus *m.* **realist** *n* Realist(in). **realistic** *adj* realistisch. **reality** *n* Wirklichkeit *f,* Realität *f.* **really** *adv* tatsächlich, in der Tat; *(very, actually)* wirklich.
realize ['riəlaiz] *v* begreifen, erkennen; *(bring about)* verwirklichen. **realizable** *adj* durchführbar. **realization** *n* Erkenntnis *f;* Verwirklichung *f.*
realm [relm] *n* Königreich *neut;* *(sphere)* Gebiet *neut.*
reap [riːp] *v* ernten, mähen. **reaper** *n* Mäher(in).
reappear [riːə'piə] *v* wieder erscheinen. **reappearance** *n* Wiedererscheinen *neut.*
rear¹ [riə] *adj* hinter, Hinter-. *n* Hinterseite *f,* Rückseite *f.* **rear lamp** Schlußlicht *neut.* **rear wheel** Hinterrad *neut.*
rear² [riə] *v* *(child)* erziehen; *(animals)* züchten.
rearrange [riːə'reindʒ] *v* neu ordnen, umordnen; *(date, etc.)* ändern. **rearrangement** *n* Neuordnung *f;* Änderung *f.*
reason ['riːzn] *n* Grund *m;* *(good sense)* Vernunft *f.* *v* folgern. **for this reason** aus diesem Grund. **by reason of** wegen (+ *gen*). **reason with** zu überzeugen ver-

suchen. **reasonable** adj vernünftig. **reasonableness** n Vernünftigkeit. **reasonably** adv vernünftigerweise; (fairly) ziemlich.
reasoning n Schlußfolgerung f, Argument neut.
reassure [riə'ʃuə] v beruhigen. **reassurance** n Beruhigung f.
rebate ['riːbeit] n Rabatt m.
rebel ['rebl] n Rebell(in), Aufrührer(in). adj aufrührerisch. v rebellieren. **rebellion** n Aufstand m. **rebellious** adj aufrührerisch.
rebound [ri'baund; n 'riːbaund] v zurückprallen. n Rückprall m.
rebuff [ri'bʌf] v abweisen. n Abweisung f.
***rebuild** [riː'bild] v wiederaufbauen.
rebuke [ri'bjuːk] v zurechtweisen, rüffeln. n Rüffel m.
recall [ri'kɔːl] v (call back) zurückrufen; (remember) sich erinnern an. n Rückruf m; Erinnerung f.
recap [riːkap] v kurz zusammenfassen. n Zusammenfassung f.
recede [ri'siːd] v zurückgehen, zurückweichen.
receipt [rə'siːt] n (of letter) Empfang m; (of goods) Annahme f; (bill) Quittung f. **receipts** pl Einnahmen pl. **acknowledge receipt** Empfang bestätigen.
receive [rə'siːv] v empfangen, bekommen. **receiver** n (phone) Hörer m; (comm) Konkursverwalter m; (radio) Empfänger m. **receivership** n Konkursverwaltung f.
recent ['riːsnt] adj neu, modern, neulich entstanden. **recently** adv neulich, vor kurzem.
receptacle [rə'septəkl] n Behälter m, Gefäß neut.
reception [rə'sepʃən] n Empfang m. **receptionist** n Empfangsdame f. **reception room** Empfangszimmer neut.
recess [ri'ses] n Pause f, Unterbrechung f; (holiday) Ferien pl; (niche) Nische f. **recession** [rə'seʃən] n (comm) Rezession f.
recharge [riː'tʃaɪdʒ] v (battery) wieder aufladen.
recipe ['resəpi] n Rezept neut.
recipient [rə'sipiənt] n Empfänger(in).
reciprocate [rə'siprəkeit] v erwidern. **reciprocal** adj gegenseitig. **reciprocation** n Erwiderung f.
recite [rə'sait] v vortragen, rezitieren. **piano/song recital** Klavier-/Liederabend m.

reckless ['rekləs] adj rücksichtslos. **recklessness** n Rücksichtslosigkeit f.
reckon ['rekən] v rechnen, zählen; (believe) meinen. **reckon on** sich verlassen auf. **reckon with** rechnen mit. **reckoning** n Abrechnung f.
reclaim [ri'kleim] v (ask for back) zurückfordern; (land from sea) gewinnen.
recline [rə'klain] v sich zurücklehnen (an).
recluse [rə'kluːs] n Einsiedler(in).
recognize ['rekəgnaiz] v (wieder) erkennen; (acknowledge) anerkennen; (concede) zugeben. **recognition** n (Wieder)Erkennen neut; Anerkennung f. **recognizable** adj erkennbar.
recoil [rə'koil; n 'riːkoil] v zurückprallen; (in fear) zurückschrecken. n Rückprall m.
recollect [rekə'lekt] n sich erinnern an. **recollection** n Erinnerung f.
recommence [riːkə'mens] v wieder beginnen.
recommend [rekə'mend] v empfehlen. **to be recommended** empfehlenswert. **recommendation** n Empfehlung f; (suggestion) Vorschlag m.
recompense ['rekəmpens] n Belohnung f. v belohnen.
reconcile ['rekənsail] v versöhnen. **reconcile oneself to** sich abfinden mit. **reconcilable** adj vereinbar (mit). **reconciliation** n Versöhnung f.
reconstruct [riːkən'strʌkt] v wiederaufbauen; (events) rekonstruieren. **reconstruction** n Wiederaufbau m; Rekonstruktion f.
record [ri'kɔːd; n 'rekɔːd] v (film, tape) aufnehmen; (write down) aufschreiben, eintragen. n (disc) Schallplatte f; (of proceedings, etc.) Protokoll neut, Bericht m; (sport) Rekord m. **break the record** den Rekord brechen. **off the record** inoffiziell. **recorder** n (music) Blockflöte f. **recording** n Aufnahme f. **record-player** n Plattenspieler m.
recount [ri'kaunt] v (narrate) erzählen.
recoup [ri'kuːp] v (loss) wieder einholen.
recover [rə'kʌvə] v zurückgewinnen; (get better) sich erholen. **recovery** n Zurückgewinnung f; Erholung f.
recreation [rekri'eiʃən] n Erholung f, Entspannung f. **recreation ground** n Spielplatz neut.

recrimination [rɪˌkrɪmiˈneɪʃən] *n* Gegenbeschuldigung *f*.

recruit [rəˈkruːt] *n* Rekrut *m*. *v* rekrutieren. **recruitment** *n* Rekrutierung *f*.

rectangle [ˈrektæŋgl] *n* Rechteck *neut*. **rectangular** *adj* rechteckig.

rectify [ˈrektifaɪ] *v* richtigstellen, korrigieren; (*elec*) gleichrichten. **rectification** *n* Richtigstellung *f*, Korrektur *f*.

rectum [ˈrektəm] *n* Mastdarm *m*. **rectal** *adj* rektal.

recuperate [rəˈkjuːpəreit] *v* sich erholen. **recuperation** *n* Erholung *f*.

recur [rɪˈkəː] *v* wieder auftreten, sich wiederholen. **recurrence** *n* Wiederauftreten *neut*. **recurrent** *adj* wiederkehrend.

red [red] *adj* rot. *n* Rot *neut*. **red tape** Amtsschimmel *m*. **redden** *v* erröten, rot werden. **redness** *n* Röte *f*. **red-handed** *adj* auf frischer Tat.

redeem [rəˈdiːm] *v* (*pledge*) einlösen; (*prisoner*) loskaufen; (*promise*) einhalten. **redemption** *n* Ablösung *f*; Rückkauf *m*.

redevelop [ˌriːdiˈveləp] *v* neu entwickeln; (*town*) umbauen.

redress [rəˈdres] *n* (*legal*) Rechtshilfe *f*; (*compensation*) Wiedergutmachung *f*. *v* wiedergutmachen. **redress the balance** das Gleichgewicht wiederherstellen.

reduce [rəˈdjuːs] *v* vermindern, verringern; (*prices*) herabsetzen; (*tech*) reduzieren; (*slim*) eine Abmagerungskur machen. **in reduced circumstances** verarmt. **reduction** *n* Verminderung *f*; Herabsetzung *f*; (*tech*) Reduktion *f*.

redundant [rəˈdʌndənt] *adj* überflüssig; (*jobless*) arbeitslos. **be made redundant** entlassen werden. **redundancy** *n* Überflüssigkeit *f*; (*worker*) Entlassung *f*.

reed [riːd] *n* Rohr *neut*; (*music*) (Rohr)Blatt *neut*. **reedy** *adj* (*voice*) piepsig.

reef [riːf] *n* (Felsen)Riff *neut*.

reek [riːk] *v* stinken (nach). *n* Gestank *m*.

reel[1] [riːl] *n* Spule *f*; (*cotton*) Rolle *f*.

reel[2] [riːl] *v* taumeln, schwanken.

refectory [rəˈfektəri] *n* Speisesaal *m*; (*university*) Mensa *f*.

refer [rəˈfəː] *v* **refer to** hinweisen auf, sich beziehen auf; (*mention*) erwähnen; (*a book*) nachschlagen in. **reference** *n* Bezug *m*, Hinweis *m*; Erwähnung *f*; (*in book*) Verweis *m*. **with reference to** in Bezug auf, hinsichtlich (+*gen*). **reference book** Nachschlagewerk *neut*.

referee [refəˈriː] *n* Schiedsrichter *m*.

referendum [refəˈrendəm] *n* Volksentscheid *m*.

refill [riːˈfil] *n* (ˈriːfil) *v* nachfüllen. *n* (*for pen*) Ersatzmine *f*.

refine [rəˈfain] *v* (*tech*) raffinieren; (*improve*) verfeinern. **refined** *adj* raffiniert; (*person, etc.*)kultiviert **refinement** *n* Verfeinerung *f*; (*good breeding*) Kultiviertheit *f*. **refinery** *n* Raffinerie *f*.

reflation [rəˈfleiʃn] *n* Wirtschaftsbelebung *f*.

reflect [rəˈflekt] *v* widerspiegeln; (*consider*) nachdenken. **reflection** *n* Widerspiegelung *f*. (*thought*) Überlegung *f*; (*remark*) Bemerkung *f*. **reflective** *adj* zurückstrahlend; (*thoughtful*) nachdenklich. **reflector** *n* (*mot*) Rückstrahler *m*.

reflex [ˈriːfleks] *n* Reflex *m*.

reform [rəˈfoːm] *n* Reform *f*, Verbesserung *f*. *v* reformieren, (ver)bessern. **reformation** *n* Verbesserung *f*; (*history*) Reformation *f*. **reformatory** *n* Besserungsanstalt *f*. **reformed** *adj* verbessert. **reformer** *n* Reformer(in).

refract [rəˈfrakt] *v* brechen.

refrain[1] [rəˈfrein] *v* **refrain from** sich enthalten (+*gen*).

refrain[2] [rəˈfrein] *n* Refrain *m*.

refresh [rəˈfreʃ] *v* erfrischen; (*memory*) auffrischen. **refresher course** Wiederholungskurs *m*. **refreshing** *adj* erfrischend. **refreshment** *n* Erfrischung *f*. **refreshments** *pl* Imbiß *m sing*.

refrigerator [rəˈfridʒəreitə] *n* Kühlschrank *m*. **refrigerate** *v* kühlen. **refrigeration** *n* Kühlung *f*.

refuel [riːˈfjuəl] *v* tanken.

refuge [ˈrefjuːdʒ] *n* Zuflucht *f*, Schutz *m*. **refugee** *n* Flüchtling *m*.

refund [ˈriːfʌnd]; *v* riˈfʌnd] *n* Rückvergütung *f*. *v* zurückzahlen.

refuse[1] [rəˈfjuːz] *v* ablehnen, verweigern. **refusal** *n* Verweigerung *f*, Ablehnung *f*.

refuse[2] [ˈrefjuːs] *n* Abfall *m*, Müll *m*. **refuse collection** Müllabfuhr *f*.

refute [riˈfjuːt] *v* widerlegen.

regain [riˈgein] *v* wiedergewinnen.

regal [ˈriːgəl] *adj* königlich.

regard [rəˈgaːd] *v* ansehen, betrachten. *n* (*esteem*) (Hoch)Achtung *f*; (*consideration*) Rücksicht *f*, Hinblick *m*. **in this regard** in dieser Hinsicht. **with regard to** in bezug auf. **as regards** was … betrifft. **regarding** *prep* hinsichtlich (+*gen*), bezüglich (+*gen*). **regardless** *adj* ohne Rücksicht (auf).

regatta [rə'gatə] *n* Regatta *f*.

regent ['riːdʒənt] *n* Regent(in).

regime [rei'ʒiːm] *n* Regime *f*.

regiment ['redʒimənt] *n* Regiment *neut*.

region ['riːdʒən] *n* Gebiet *neut*, Gegend *f*. **in the region of** etwa, ungefähr. **regional** *adj* regional, örtlich.

register ['redʒistə] *v* registrieren; (*report*) sich eintragen lassen. *n* Register *neut*. **registered** *adj* eingetragen. **registered letter** Einschreibebrief *m*. **send by registered post** per Einschreiben schicken. **registrar** *n* (*births*, *etc*.) Standesbeamte(r); (*hospital*, *etc*.) Direktor *m*. **registration** *n* Registrierung *f*. **registration number** (*mot*) polizeiliches Kennzeichen *neut*. **registry office** Standesamt *neut*.

regress [ri'gres] *v* zurückgehen. **regression** *n* Regression *f*. **regressive** *adj* rückläufig.

regret [rə'gret] *v* bedauern. *n* Reue *f*, Bedauern *neut*. **regrettable** *adj* bedauerlich.

regular ['regjulə] *adj* regelmäßig; (*normal*) gewöhnlich; (*correct*) ordnungsgemäß. **regular** (*customer*) Stammgast *m*. **regularity** *n* Regelmäßigkeit *f*.

regulate ['regjuleit] *v* regeln, ordnen. **regulation** *n* (*rule*) Vorschrift *f*; (*tech*) Regelung *f*. **regulator** *n* Regler *m*.

rehabilitate [riːhə'biliteit] *n* rehabilitieren. **rehabilitation** *n* Rehabilitation *f*.

rehearse [rə'həːs] *v* proben. **rehearsal** *n* Probe *f*.

reign [rein] *n* Regierung(szeit) *f*. *v* regieren, herrschen.

reimburse [riːim'bəːs] *v* (*person*) entschädigen. **reimbursement** *n* Entschädigung *f*.

ein [rein] *n* Zügel *m*.

eincarnation [riːinkaːˈneiʃən] *n* Reinkarnation *f*, Wiederverkörperung *f*.

reindeer ['reindiə] *n* Ren(tier) *neut*.

reinforce [riːin'foːs] *v* verstärken; (*concrete*) armieren. **reinforcement** *n* Verstärkung *f*.

reinstate [,riːin'steit] *v* wiedereinsetzen. **reinstatement** *n* Wiedereinsetzung *f*.

reinvest [riːin'vest] *v* wiederinvestieren.

reissue [riːˈiʃuː] *v* neu herausgeben. *n* Neuausgabe *f*.

reject [rə'dʒekt; *n* 'riːdʒekt] *v* ablehnen,

verwerfen. **rejection** *n* Ablehnung *f*, Verwerfung *f*. *n* Ausschußartikel *m*.

rejoice [rə'dʒois] *v* sich freuen. **rejoicing** *adj* froh; *n* Freude *f*.

rejoin [rə'dʃoin] *v* sich wieder anschließen; (*reply*) erwidern. **rejoinder** *n* Erwiderung *f*.

rejuvenate [rə'dʒuːvəneit] *v* verjüngen. **rejuvenation** *n* Verjüngung *f*.

relapse [rə'laps] *v* zurückfallen; (*med*) einen Rückfall bekommen. *n* Rückfall *m*.

relate [rə'leit] *v* (*tell*) erzählen; (*link*) verbinden. **related** *adj* verwandt. **relating to** in bezug auf.

relation [rə'leiʃn] *n* Verhältnis *neut*; (*business*) Beziehung *f*; (*person*) Verwandte(r). **relationship** *n* Verhältnis *neut*; (*family*) Verwandtschaft *f*.

relative ['relətiv] *n* Verwandte(r). *adj* relativ, verhältnismäßig. **relatively** *adv* verhältnismäßig. **relativity** *n* Relativität *f*.

relax [rə'laks] *v* entspannen. **relaxation** *n* Entspannung *f*.

relay ['riːlei; *v* ri'lei] *n* (*race*) Staffellauf *m*; (*tech*) Relais *neut*. *v* weitergeben.

release [rə'liːs] *v* freilassen, entlassen; (*film*, *etc*.) freigeben; (*news*) bekanntgeben; (*let go*) loslassen. *n* Entlassung *f*; Freigabe *f*.

relent [rə'lent] *v* nachgiebig werden. **relentless** *adj* unbarmherzig.

relevant ['reləvənt] *adj* erheblich, relevant; (*appropriate*) entsprechend. **relevance** *n* Relevanz *f*.

reliable [ri'laiəbl] *adj* zuverlässig. **reliability** *n* Zuverlässigkeit *f*. **reliance** *n* Vertrauen *neut*.

relic ['relik] *n* Überbleibsel *neut*; (*rel*) Reliquie *f*.

relief [rə'liːf] *n* Erleichterung *f*; (*mil*) Ablösung *f*; (*help*) Hilfe *f*; (*geog*) Relief *neut*. **tax relief** Steuerbegünstigung *f*.

relieve [rə'liːv] *v* erleichtern; (*from burden*) entlasten; (*person*) ablösen; (*reassure*) beruhigen.

religion [rə'lidʒən] *n* Religion *f*. **religious** *adj* religiös.

relinquish [rə'liŋkwiʃ] *v* aufgeben, verzichten auf.

relish ['reliʃ] *v* sich erfreuen an. *n* (*fig*) Vergnügen *neut*; (*sauce*) Soße *f*.

reluctant [rə'lʌktənt] *adj* widerwillig. **be reluctant to do** ungern tun. **reluctance** *n* Widerstreben *neut*. **reluctantly** *adv* ungern.

report

rely [rə'lai] *v* sich verlassen (auf).
remain [rə'mein] *v* bleiben; (*be left over*)
übrigbleiben. **remains** *pl n* Überreste *pl*;
(*person*) die sterblichen Überreste *pl*.
remainder *n* Rest *m*, Restbestand *m*.
remaining *adj* übriggeblieben.
remand [rə'maind] *v* in Untersuchungs-
haft zurückschicken.
remark [rə'maik] *n* Bemerkung *f. v*
bemerken. **remarkable** *adj* bemerkenswert.
remarry [riː'mari] *v* wieder heiraten.
remedy ['remədi] *n* Gegenmittel *neut*,
(*med*) Heilmittel *neut. v* berichtigen.
remember [ri'membə] *v* sich erinnern an.
remember me to your mother grüße
deine Mutter von mir. **remembrance** *n*
Erinnerung *f.*
remind [rə'maind] *v* erinnern (an); (*someone to do something*) mahnen. **reminder** *n*
Mahnung *f.*
reminiscence [remə'nisəns] *n* Erinnerung
f. **be reminiscent of** erinnern an.
remiss [rə'mis] *adj* nachlässig.
remit [rə'mit] *v* überweisen. **remittance** *n*
Überweisung *f.*
remnant ['remnənt] *n* (Über)Rest *m*,
Überbleibsel *neut.*
remorse [rə'mois] *n* Gewissensbisse *pl*,
Reue *f.* **remorseful** *n* reumütig. **remorse-
less** *adj* unbarmherzig.
remote [rə'mout] *adj* fern, entfernt.
remote control Fernsteuerung *f.* **remote-
ness** *n* Ferne *f.*
remove [rə'muiv] *v* beseitigen, entfernen;
(*move house*) umziehen. **removal** *n* Beseitigung *f*; Umzug *m*. **remover** *n*
(Möbel)Spediteur *m.*
remunerate [rə'mjuinəreit] *v* belohnen.
remuneration *n* Lohn *m*, Vergütung *f.*
renaissance [rə'neisəns] *n* Renaissance *f.*
rename [riː'neim] *v* umbenennen.
render ['rendə] *v* (*make*) machen; (*give
back*) wiedergeben; (*service*) leisten.
rendezvous ['rondivuː] *n* Verabredung *f*,
Stelldichein *neut.*
renegade ['renigeid] *n* Abtrünnige(r). *adj*
abtrünnig.
renew [rə'njuː] *v* erneuern; (*contract*)
verlängern. **renewal** *n* Erneuerung *f.*
renounce [ri'nauns] *v* verzichten auf;
(*person*) verleugnen; (*beliefs*)
abschwören.
renovate ['renəveit] *v* erneuern, renovier-

en, **renovation** *n* Renovierung *f*,
Erneuerung *f.*
renown [rə'naun] *n* Ruhm *m*,
Berühmtheit *f.* **renowned** *adj* berühmt.
rent [rent] *n* Miete *f. v* mieten; (*let*)
vermieten. **rental** *n* Mietbetrag *m.*
renunciation [ri,nʌnsi'eifən] *n* (*rejection*)
Ablehnung *f.*
reopen [riː'oupən] *v* wieder öffnen; (*shop,
etc.*) wiedereröffnen.
reorganize [riː'oigənaiz] *v* reorganisieren,
neugestalten. **reorganization** *n* Reor-
ganisation *f.*
rep [rep] *n* (*coll: representative*) Ver-
treter(in).
repair [ri'peə] *v* reparieren, ausbessern;
(*clothes*) flicken. *n* Reparatur *f.* **in good
repair** in gutem Zustand. **in need of
repair** reparaturbedürftig. **repair kit**
Flickzeug *neut.* **reparation** *n*
Wiedergutmachung *f.*
repartee [repaː'tiː] *n* Schlagabtausch *m.*
repatriate [riː'patrieit] *v* repatriieren.
repatriation *n* Repatriierung *f.*
*repay [ri'pei] *v* zurückzahlen; (*kindness*)
erwidern. **repayable** *adj* rückzahlbar.
repayment *n* Rückzahlung *f.*
repeal [rə'piːl] *v* aufheben, widerrufen. *n*
Aufhebung *f.*
repeat [rə'piːt] *v* wiederholen. *n*
Wiederholung *f.* **repeated** *adj* wiederholt.
repel [rə'pel] *v* abweisen. **repellent** *adj*
abstoßend, widerlich.
repent [rə'pent] *v* bereuen. **repentance** *n*
Reue *f.* **repentant** *adj* bußfertig.
repercussions [riipə'kʌfənz] *pl n*
Rückwirkungen *pl.*
repertoire ['repətwaɪ] *n* Repertoire *neut.*
repetition [repə'tifn] *n* Wiederholung *f.*
repetitive *adj* sich wiederholend.
replace [rə'pleis] *v* ersetzen. **replacement**
n Ersatz *m.* **replacement part** Ersatzteil
neut.
replay ['riiplei] *n* (*sport*) Wiederholungs-
spiel *neut*; (*tape*) Wiedergabe *f.*
replenish [rə'plenif] *v* ergänzen.
replica ['replikə] *n* Kopie *f.*
reply [rə'plai] *v* antworten, erwidern. *n*
Antwort *f*, Erwiderung *f.* **reply to** (*person*) antworten (+*dat*); (*question, letter*)
antworten auf. **in reply to** in Erwiderung
auf.
report [rə'poit] *n* Bericht *m*; (*factual
statement*) Meldung *f. v* berichten;

(*denounce*) melden; (*present oneself*) sich melden. **reporter** *n* Reporter *m*.

repose [rə'pouz] *n* Ruhe *f*. *v* ruhen.

represent [reprə'zent] *v* darstellen; (*act as representative*) vertreten. **representation** *n* Darstellung *f*; Vertretung *f*. **representative** *n* Vertreter(in). *adj* (*typical*) typisch.

repress [rə'pres] *v* unterdrücken; (*psychol*) verdrängen. **repression** *n* Unterdrückung *f*; Verdrängung *f*.

reprieve [rə'priːv] *v* begnadigen. *n* Strafaufschub *m*; (*fig*) Gnadenfrist *f*.

reprimand ['reprimaind] *v* rügen. *n* Rüge *f*. Verweis *m*.

reprint [riː'print; *n* 'riːprint] *v* neu drucken. *n* Neudruck *m*.

reprisal [rə'praizəl] *n* Repressalie *f*.

reproach [rə'prouʧ] *n* Vorwurf *m*, Tadel *m*. *v* Vorwürfe machen (+*dat*). **reproachful** *adj* vorwurfsvoll.

reproduce [riːprə'djuːs] *v* (sich) fortpflanzen; (*copy*) kopieren. **reproduction** *n* Fortpflanzung *f*; (*copy*) Reproduktion *f*.

reproof [rə'pruːf] *n* Verweis *m*, Rüge *f*. **reprove** *v* rügen.

reptile ['reptail] *n* Reptil *neut*, Kriechtier *neut*.

republic [rə'pʌblik] *n* Republik *f*. **republican** *adj* republikanisch; *n* Republikaner(in).

repudiate [rə'pjuːdieit] *v* zurückweisen, nicht anerkennen. *n* Nichtanerkennung *f*.

repugnant [rə'pʌgnənt] *adj* widerlich, widerwärtig.

repulsion [rə'pʌlʃn] *n* Abscheu *m*. **repulsive** *adj* widerwärtig, abscheulich.

repute [rə'pjuːt] *n* Ruf *m*. **reputation** *n* Ruf *m*. **reputed** *adj* angeblich. **be reputed** betrachtet sein (als).

request [ri'kwest] *n* Bitte *f*. *v* bitten (um). **on request** auf Wunsch.

requiem ['rekwiəm] *n* Requiem *neut*.

require [rə'kwaiə] *v* (*need*) brauchen; (*person*) verlangen (von); (*call for*) erfordern. **be required** erforderlich sein. **requirement** *n* Anforderung *f*; (*need*) Bedürfnis *neut*.

requisite ['rekwizit] *adj* erforderlich, notwendig.

re-route [riː'ruːt] *v* umleiten.

resale [riː'seil] *n* Weiterverkauf *m*.

rescue ['reskjuː] *v* retten, befreien. *n* Rettung *f*. **come to the rescue of** zur Hilfe kommen (+*dat*). **rescuer** *n* Retter *m*.

research [ri'səːʧ] *n* Forschung *f*. *v* forschen. **researcher** *n* Forscher *m*.

resemble [rə'zembl] *v* ähnlich sein (+*dat*). **resemblance** *n* Ähnlichkeit *f*.

resent [ri'zent] *v* übelnehmen. **resentful** *adj* ärgerlich (auf). **resentment** *n* Groll *m*, Unwille *m*.

reserve [rə'zəːv] *v* reservieren (lassen). *n* Reserve *f*; (*for animals*) Schutzgebiet *neut*; (*sport*) Ersatzmann *m*. **reserved** *adj* reserviert. **reservation** *n* Vorbehalt *m*; Reservierung *f*.

reservoir ['rezəvwaɪ] *n* Reservoir *neut*.

reside [rə'zaid] *v* wohnen. **residence** *n* Wohnung *f*; (*domicile*) Wohnsitz *m*. **resident** *adj* wohnhaft. **residential** *adj* Wohn-.

residue ['rezidjuː] *n* Rest *m*, Rückstand *m*. **residual** *adj* übrig, Rest-.

resign [rə'zain] *v* zurücktreten. **resign oneself to** sich abfinden mit. **resignation** *n* Rücktritt *m*; (*mood*) Resignation *f*. **hand in one's resignation** seinen Rücktritt einreichen. **resigned** *adj* resigniert, ergeben.

resilient [rə'ziliənt] *adj* elastisch; (*person*) unverwüstlich.

resin ['rezin] *n* Harz *neut*.

resist [rə'zist] *v* widerstehen. **resistance** *n* Widerstand *m*. **resistant** *adj* widerstehend, beständig.

***resit** [riː'sit] *v* (*exam*) wiederholen.

resolute ['rezəluːt] *adj* entschlossen. **resolution** *n* (*determination*) Entschlossenheit *f*; (*decision*) Beschluß *m*.

resolve [rə'zolv] *v* (*problem*) lösen; (*tech*) auflösen; (*decide*) beschließen. *n* (*determination*) Entschlossenheit *f*. **resolved** *adj* entschlossen.

resonant ['rezənənt] *adj* widerhallend; (*voice*) volltönend. **resonance** *n* Resonanz *f*.

resort [rə'zoːt] *n* (*hope*) Ausweg *m*; (*place*) Ferienort *m*; (*use*) Anwendung *f*. **seaside resort** Seebad *neut*. *v* **resort to** zurückgreifen auf.

resound [rə'zaund] *v* widerhallen.

resource [rə'zoːs] *n* Mittel *neut*. **natural resources** Bodenschätze *pl*. **resourceful** *adj* findig.

respect [rə'spekt] *v* (hoch)achten; (*take account of*) berücksichtigen. *n* (*for person*) Hochachtung *f*, Respekt *m*; Rücksicht *f*. **in this respect** in dieser Hinsicht. **respectable** *adj* ansehnlich, respektabel.

147 reverberate

respectful *adj* achtvoll. **respective** *adj*
entsprechend. **respectively** *adv*
beziehungsweise.
respiration [respə'reiʃn] *n* Atmung *f*.
respite ['respait] *n* **without respite** ohne
Unterlaß.
respond [rə'spond] *v* **respond to** (*question*)
antworten (auf); (*react*) reagieren (auf).
response *n* Antwort *f*; Reaktion *f*.
responsible [rə'sponsəbl] *adj* verantwortlich. **responsibility** *n* Verantwortung *f*;
(*commitment*) Verpflichtung *f*.
rest[1] [rest] *n* Ruhe *f*. **day of rest** Ruhetag
m. **have a rest** sich ausruhen. **without rest**
unaufhörlich. *v* ruhen. **rested** *adj* aus-
geruht. **restful** *adj* ruhig. **restive** *adj*
unruhig. **restless** *adj* ruhelos. **restlessness**
n Unruhe *f*.
rest[2] [rest] *n* (*remainder*) Rest *m*.
restaurant ['restront] *n* Restaurant *neut*,
Gaststätte *f*. **restaurant car** Speisewagen
m.
restore [rə'stoɪ] *v* wiederherstellen. **restoration** *n* Wiederherstellung *f*; (*of painting, etc.*) Restauration *f*.
restrain [rə'strein] *v* zurückhalten.
restrained *adj* zurückhaltend. **restraint** *n*
Zurückhaltung *f*; (*limitation*) Einschränkung *f*.
restrict [rə'strikt] *v* einschränken,
beschränken. **restricted** *adj* eingeschränkt, beschränkt. **restriction** *n* Einschränkung *f*, Beschränkung *f*. **restrictive**
adj einschränkend.
result [rə'zʌlt] *n* Ergebnis *neut*, Resultat
neut; (*consequence*) Folge *f*. *v* sich
ergeben. **result in** enden mit. **resultant**
adj daraus enstehend.
resume [rə'zjuːm] *v* wieder beginnen;
(*work*) wieder aufnehmen. **resumption** *n*
Wiederaufnahme *f*.
résumé ['reizumei] *n* Resümee *neut*.
resurgence [ri'səːdʒəns] *n* Wiederaufstieg
m.
resurrect [rezə'rekt] *v* (*thing*) ausgraben,
wieder einführen. **resurrection** *n* Auferstehung *f*.
resuscitate [rə'sʌsəteit] *v* wiederbeleben.
resuscitation *n* Wiederbelebung *f*.
retail ['riːteil] *n* Einzelhandel *m*. *adj*
Einzelhandels-. **retail price** Ladenpreis
m. **retail shop** Einzelhandelsgeschäft
neut. *v* im Einzelhandel verkaufen. **retailer** *n* Einzelhändler(in).

retain [rə'tein] *v* behalten. **retention** *n*
Beibehaltung *f*.
retaliate [rə'talieit] *v* sich rächen. **retaliation** *n* Vergeltung *f*. **relaliatory** *adj*
Vergeltungs-.
retard [rə'taɪd] *v* hindern. **retarded** *adj*
zurückgeblieben.
reticent ['retisənt] *adj* schweigsam. **reti-
cence** *n* Schweigsamkeit *f*, Zurückhaltung *f*.
retina ['retinə] *n* Netzhaut *f*.
retinue ['retinjuɪ] *n* Gefolge *neut*.
retire [rə'taiə] *v* sich zurückziehen; (*from
work*) in den Ruhestand treten. **retired**
adj pensioniert. **retirement** *n* Ruhestand
m; (*resignation*) Rucktritt *m*. **retiring** *adj*
zurückhaltend.
retort[1] [rə'toɪt] *v* (scharf) erwidern. *n*
(schlagfertige) Antwort *f*.
retort[2] [rə'toɪt] *n* (*vessel*) Retorte *f*.
retrace [ri'treis] *v* zurückverfolgen.
retract [rə'trakt] *v* (*draw in*) einziehen;
(*take back*) zurücknehmen, widerrufen.
retractable *adj* einziehbar.
retreat [rə'triːt] *v* sich zurückziehen. *n*
Rückzug *m*; (*place*) Zufluchtsort *m*.
retrieve [rə'triːv] *v* wiederfinden, her-
ausholen. **retriever** *n* Apporthund *m*.
retrograde ['retrəgreid] *adj* rückläufig.
retrospect ['retrəspekt] *n* Rückblick *m*. **in
retrospect** rückschauend. **retrospective**
adj rückwirkend.
return [rə'təɪn] *v* zurückkommen,
wiederkehren; (*give back*) zurückgeben;
(*answer*) erwidern. *n* Rückkehr *f*; (*ticket*)
Rückfahrkarte *f*; (*comm*) Ertrag *m*. **tax
return** Steuererklärung *f*. **many happy
returns** herzlichen Glückwunsch.
reunite [riːju'nait] *v* wiedervereinigen.
reunion *n* Wiedervereinigung *f*; (*meeting*)
Treffen *neut*.
rev [rev] *v* (*coll*: *mot*) auf Touren bringen.
revs *pl n* Drehzahl *f* sing.
reveal [rə'viːl] *v* enthüllen, offenbaren;
(*display*) zeigen. **revealing** *adj*
aufschlußreich. **revelation** *n* Enthüllung
f, Offenbarung *f*.
revel ['revl] *v* feiern. **revel in** schwelgen
in. **reveller** *n* Feiernde(r). **revelry** *n*
Festlichkeit *f*.
revenge [rə'vendʒ] *n* Rache *f*. *v* rächen.
take revenge on sich rächen an.
revenue ['revinjuɪ] *n* Einnahmen *pl*.
reverberate [rə'vəːbəreit] *v* (*sound*)

widerhallen. **reverberation** n Widerhall m.

reverence ['revərəns] n Verehrung f, Ehrfurcht f. **revere** v (ver)ehren. **reverend** adj ehrwürdig. **reverent** adj ehrerbietig.

reverse [rə'vəis] v umkehren; (mot) rückwärts fahren. n (opposite) Gegenteil neut; (of coin, etc.) Rückseite f; (mot) Rückwärtsgang m. **reverse-charge call** R-Gespräch neut. **reversible** adj (coat) wendbar; (law) umstoßbar.

revert [rə'vəit] v zurückkehren.

review [rə'vjui] n Nachprüfung f; (magazine) Rundschau f; (troops) Parade f. v nachprüfen. **reviewer** n Kritiker m.

revise [rə'vaiz] v revidieren; (book) überarbeiten. **revision** n Revision f; Überarbeitung f.

revive [rə'vaiv] v wiederbeleben. **revival** n Wiederbelebung f; (play) Wiederaufführung f.

revoke [rə'vouk] n widerrufen. **revocable** adj widerruflich. **revocation** n Widerruf m.

revolt [rə'voult] n Aufruhr m, Aufstand m. v revoltieren, sich empören; (disgust) abstoßen. **revolting** adj abstoßend.

revolution [revə'luiʃən] n (pol) Revolution f; (turning) Umdrehung f, Rotation f. **revolutions per minute** Drehzahl f. **revolutionary** adj revolutionär; n Revolutionär(in).

revolve [rə'volv] v (sich) drehen. **revolver** n Revolver m. **revolving** adj drehbar.

revue [rə'vjui] n Revue f.

revulsion [rə'vʌlʃən] n Ekel m.

reward [rə'woid] n Belohnung f; v belohnen. **rewarding** adj lohnend.

rhetoric ['retərik] n Rhetorik f; (empty) Redeschwall m. **rhetorical** adj rhetorisch.

rheumatism ['ruimətizəm] n Rheumatismus m. **rheumatic** adj rheumatisch.

rhinoceros [rai'nosərəs] n Nashorn neut.

rhododendron [roudə'dendrən] n Rhododendron m or neut.

rhubarb ['ruibaib] n Rhabarber m.

rhyme [raim] n Reim m v reimen. **nursery rhyme** Kinderreim n.

rhythm ['riðəm] n Rhythmus m. **rhythmic** adj rhythmisch.

rib [rib] n Rippe f. **ribbed** adj (material) gerippt.

ribbon ['ribən] n Band neut; (typewriter) Farbband neut. **ribbons** pl (rags) Fetzen pl. **ribboned** adj gestreift.

rice [rais] n Reis m.

rich [ritʃ] adj reich, wohlhabend; (earth) fruchtbar; (food) schwer. **rich man/woman** Reiche(r). **the rich** die Reichen. **riches** pl n Reichtum m. **richness** n Reichtum m; (food) Schwere f; (finery) Pracht f.

rickety ['rikəti] adj (wobbly) wackelig.

*** rid** [rid] v befreien, frei machen. **be rid of** los sein (+acc). **get rid of** loswerden (+acc). **good riddance to him!** Gott sei Dank ist man ihn los!

ridden ['ridn] V ride.

riddle ['ridl] n Rätsel neut.

riddled ['ridld] adj durchlöchert.

*** ride** [raid] v reiten; (bicycle, motor cycle) fahren. **riding whip** Reitpeitsche f. n Ritt m; Fahrt f. **take for a ride** (coll) übers Ohr hauen. **rider** n Reiter(in); (cycle) Fahrer(in). **riding** n Reitsport m.

ridge [ridʒ] n Kamm m, Grat m; (roof) First m.

ridicule ['ridikjuil] n Spott m. v verspotten, lächerlich machen. **ridiculous** adj lächerlich.

rife [raif] adj **be rife** vorherrschen, grassieren. **rife with** voll von.

rifle[1] ['raifl] n (gun) Gewehr neut. **rifle-range** n Schießstand m.

rifle[2] ['raifl] v ausplündern.

rift [rift] n Spalte f, Riß m.

rig [rig] n Takelung f; (coll) Vorrichtung f, Anlage f. v auftakeln. **rig out** (coll) ausstatten. **rigging** n Takelwerk neut.

right [rait] adj (correct) recht, richtig; (proper) angemessen; (right-hand) recht. **all right** in Ordnung. **be right** (thing) recht sein; (person) recht haben. **feel all right** sich wohl befinden. **right-handed** adj rechtshändig. **right-wing** adj Rechts-. adv (correctly) recht, richtig; (completely) ganz; (to the right) (nach) rechts. **right away** sofort. n Recht neut. **right of way** (mot) Vorfahrt f. v berichtigen. **rightly** adv mit Recht.

righteous ['raitʃəs] adj rechtschaffen, gerecht.

rigid ['ridʒid] adj starr, steif; (person) streng, unbeugsam. **rigidity** n Starrheit f.

rigmarole ['rigməroul] n (coll) Theater neut.

rigour ['rigə] n Strenge f, Härte f. **rigorous** adj streng.

rim [rim] n Rand m.

rind [raind] n (cheese) Rinde f; (bacon) Schwarte f.

ring[1] [riŋ] n Ring m; (comm) Kartell neut. **wedding ring** n Trauring m. **ringleader** n Rädelsführer m.

***ring**[2] [riŋ] v (sound) läuten, klingeln; (echo) widerhallen. n (Glocken)Klang m, Klingeln neut. **there's a ring at the door** es klingelt. **ring (up)** (coll: phone) anrufen. **ringing** n Läuten neut.

rink [riŋk] n (ice) Eisbahn f.

rinse [rins] v ausspülen. n Spülung f.

riot ['raiət] n Aufruhr m, Tumult m. v randalieren. **rioter** n Aufrührer(in). **riotous** adj aufrührerisch; (laughter) zügellos.

rip [rip] v reißen, zerreißen. n Riß m. **ripcord** n Reißleine f.

ripe [raip] adj reif. **ripen** v reifen, reif werden.

ripple ['ripl] n Kräuselung f; (noise) Platschern neut. v (sich) kräuseln.

***rise** [raiz] v sich erheben; (get up) aufstehen; (meeting) vertagen; (prices) steigen. n Aufstieg m; (prices) Steigen neut; (increase) Zuwachs m; (pay) Erhöhung f. **give rise to** hervorrufen, veranlassen. **rising** adj steigend.

risen ['rizn] V rise.

risk [risk] n Risiko neut; (danger) Gefahr f. v riskieren. **take a risk** ein Risiko eingehen. **risky** adj riskant.

rissole ['risoul] n Boulette f, Frikadelle f.

rite [rait] n Ritus m, Zeremonie f.

ritual ['ritjuəl] n Ritual neut. adj rituell.

rival ['raivəl] n Rivale m, Rivalin f. adj rivalisierend. v rivalisieren or wetteifern mit. **rivalry** n Rivalität f.

river ['rivə] n Fluß m. **down river** stromabwärts. **up river** stromaufwärts. **riverside** n Flußufer neut; Ufer-.

rivet ['rivit] n Niet m. v vernieten; (captivate) fesseln.

road [roud] n Straße f; (esp. fig) Weg m. **main road** Landstraße f. **on the road to** auf dem Wege zu. **road accident** Verkehrsunfall m. **road block** Straßensperre f. **road sign** Straßenschild neut. **roadworks** pl n Straßenbauarbeiten pl.

roam [roum] v (umher)wandern.

roar [roɪ] v brüllen; (person) laut schreien; (wind) toben. n Gebrüll neut. **roaring** adj (coll) enorm, famos.

roast [roust] v braten, rösten. n Braten m.

rob [rob] v rauben. **robber** n Räuber m. **robbery** n Raub m.

robe [roub] n Talar m. **bathrobe** Bademantel m. v kleiden.

robin ['robin] n Rotkehlchen neut.

robot ['roubot] n Roboter m.

robust [rə'bʌst] adj robust, kräftig. **robustness** n Robustheit f.

rock[1] [rok] n (stone) Fels m, Felsen m; (naut) Klippe f. **steady as a rock** felsenfest on the rocks (fig) gescheitert; (drink) mit Eis. **rockery** n Steingarten m **rocky** adj felsig.

rock[2] [rok] v schaukeln; (baby) wiegen. **rocking-horse** n Schaukelpferd neut. **rock 'n' roll** n Rock and Roll m.

rocket ['rokit] n Rakete f. v hochschießen.

rod [rod] n Rute f.

rode [roud] V ride.

rodent ['roudənt] n Nagetier neut.

roe [rou] n Rogen m.

rogue [roug] n Schurke m. **roguish** adj schurkisch.

role [roul] n Rolle f.

roll [roul] v rollen. **roll out** ausrollen. **roll over** sich herumdrehen. **roll up** aufwickeln, aufrollen. **roller** n Walze f. **roller blind** Rouleau neut. **roller-skate** n Rollschuh. **rolling-pin** n Nudelholz neut. **roll-neck** n Rollkragen m. n Rolle f; (bread) Brötchen neut; (meat) Roulade f. **roll-call** n Namensaufruf m.

romance [rou'mans] n Romanze f. **romantic** romantisch; n Romantiker(in).

Rome [roum] n Rom neut. **Roman** adj römisch. n Römer(in). **Roman Catholic** römisch-katholisch.

romp [romp] v sich herumbalgen. **romp through** leicht hindurchkommen.

roof [ruɪf] n (pl -s) Dach neut. v bedachen. **roofing** n Dachwerk neut.

rook[1] [ruk] n Saatkrähe f. v (coll) schwindeln, betrügen.

rook[2] [ruk] n (chess) Turm m.

room [ruɪm] n (house) Zimmer neut; (space) Raum m, Platz m. v logieren (bei). **rooms** pl Wohnung f. **room-mate** n Zimmergenosse m, -genossin f. **roomy** adj geräumig.

roost [ruɪst] n Hühnerstall m. v (bird) auf der Stange sitzen, schlafen. **rooster** n Hahn m.

root¹ [ruːt] *n* Würzel *f*; (*source*) Quelle *f*. **take root** Wurzel schlagen. **rooted** *adj* eingewürzelt. **rootless** *adj* wurzellos.

root² [ruːt] *v* **root for** (*pigs*) wühlen nach. **root out** ausgraben.

rope [roup] *n* Seil *neut*; (*naut*) Tau *neut*. *v* festbinden. **know the ropes** sich auskennen. **ropeladder** *n* Strickleiter *f*. **ropy** *adj* (*coll*) kläglich, schäbig.

rosary ['rouzəri] *n* Rosenkranz *m*.

rose¹ [rouz] *V* **rise**.

rose² [rouz] *n* Rose *f*. **rosebush** *n* Rosenstrauch *m*. **rose-coloured** *adj* rosenrot. **through rose-coloured spectacles** durch eine rosarote Brille. **rosette** *n* Rosette *f*. **rosy** *adj* rosig.

rosemary ['rouzməri] *n* Rosmarin *m*.

rot [rot] *v* verfaulen. *n* Fäulnis *f*; (*nonsense*) Quatsch *m*. **rotten** *adj* faul, verfault; (*corrupt*) morsch, faul. **rottenness** *n* Fäule *f*. **rotter** *n* (*coll*) Schweinehund *m*.

rota ['routə] *n* Turnus *m*.

rotate [rou'teit] *v* sich drehen, rotieren; (*crops*) wechseln lassen. **rotary** *adj* rotierend, kreisend. **rotation** *n* Umdrehung *f*, Rotation *f*; (*crops, etc.*) Abwechselung *f*. **rotor** *n* Rotor *m*.

rouge [ruːʒ] *n* (*make-up*) Rouge *neut*.

rough [rʌf] *adj* rauh; (*sea*) stürmisch; (*hair*) struppig; (*person*) grob, roh; (*approximate*) ungefähr. **roughage** *n* Ballaststoffe *pl*. **roughen** *v* aufrauhen. **roughly** *adv* ungefähr. **roughness** *n* Rauhheit *f*.

roulette [ruː'let] *n* Roulette *f*.

round [raund] *adj* rund. *adv* rundherum. *n* Runde *f*. *v* runden; (*corner*) (herum)fahren um. **round off** abrunden. **round up** (*cattle*) zusammentreiben; (*criminals*) ausheben. **round trip** (Hin-und) Rückfahrt *f*. **roundabout** *n* Karussell *neut*; (*mot*) Kreisverkehr *m*; *adj* weitschweifig. **roundly** *adv* gründlich. **roundness** *n* Rundheit *f*.

route [ruːt] *n* Weg *m*, Route *f*.

routine [ruː'tiːn] *n* Routine *f*. *adj* üblich.

rove [rouv] *v* herumwandern. **rover** *n* Wanderer *m*.

row¹ [rou] *n* Reihe *f*. **in rows** reihenweise.

row² [rou] *v* (*boat*) rudern. **rowing** *n* Rudern *neut*; (*sport*) Rudersport *m*. **rowing boat** Ruderboot *neut*.

row³ [rau] *n* (*quarrel*) Streit *m*; (*noise*) Krach *m*. *v* sich streiten, zanken.

rowdy ['raudi] *adj* lärmend, flegelhaft. *n* Rowdy *m*.

royal ['roiəl] *adj* königlich. **royalist** *n* Royalist *m*. **royalty** *n* Königtum *neut*. **royalties** *pl* Tantieme *f*.

rub [rʌb] *v* reiben. **rub off** abreiben. **rub out** (*erase*) ausradieren. *n* Reiben *neut*.

rubber ['rʌbə] *n* Gummi *m*; (*eraser*) Radiergummi *m*. **rubber band** Gummiband *neut*. **rubber stamp** Gummistempel *m*.

rubbish ['rʌbiʃ] *n* Abfall *m*, Müll *m*; (*nonsense*) Quatsch *m*. **rubbishy** *adj* wertlos.

rubble ['rʌbl] *n* Trümmer *pl*, Schutt *m*.

ruby ['ruːbi] *n* Rubin *m*. *adj* (*colour*) rubinrot.

rucksack ['rʌksak] *n* Rucksack *m*.

rudder ['rʌdə] *n* Ruder *neut*.

rude [ruːd] *adj* grob, unverschämt; (*rough*) roh, wild. **rudeness** *n* Grobheit *f*; Roheit *f*.

rudiment ['ruːdimənt] *n* Rudiment *neut*. **rudiments** *pl* Grundlagen *pl*.

rueful ['ruːfəl] *adj* kläglich, traurig. **ruefulness** *n* Traurigkeit *f*.

ruff [rʌf] *n* Krause *f*; (*bird's*) Halskrause *f*.

ruffian ['rʌfiən] *n* Schurke *m*, Raufbold *m*.

ruffle ['rʌfl] *v* kräuseln. *n* Krause *f*.

rug [rʌg] *n* (*floor*) Vorleger *m*; (*blanket*) Wolldecke *f*.

rugby ['rʌgbi] *n* Rugby *neut*.

rugged ['rʌgid] *adj* wild, rauh; (*face*) runzelig. **ruggedness** *n* Rauheit *f*.

ruin ['ruːin] *n* Verfall *m*, Vernichtung *f*; (*building*) Ruine *f*. *v* vernichten, ruinieren. **ruins** *pl* Trümmer *pl*. **ruinous** *adj* ruinierend.

rule [ruːl] *n* Regel *f*; (*pol*) Regierung *f*; (*drawing*) Lineal *neut*. **rule of thumb** Faustregel *f*. *v* (*govern*) regieren; (*decide*) entscheiden. **ruler** *n* (*pol*) Herrscher(in); (*drawing*) Lineal *neut*. **ruling** *adj* herrschend; *n* Entscheidung *f*.

rum [rʌm] *n* Rum *m*.

Rumania [ruː'mainjə] *n* Rumänien *neut*. **Rumanian** *n* Rumäne *m*, Rumänin *f*; *adj* rumänisch.

rumble ['rʌmbl] *v* poltern, knurren. *n* Dröhnen *neut*, Gepolter *neut*.

rummage ['rʌmidʒ] *v* **rummage through** durchsuchen, herumwühlen in.

rumour ['ruːmə] *n* Gerücht *neut*.

rump [rʌmp] *n* Hinterteil *neut.* **rump steak** Rumpsteak *neut.*

*run [rʌn] *v* rennen, laufen; (*river*) fließen; (*machine*) laufen, in Gang sein; (*nose*) laufen. **run away** weglaufen. **run down** (*person*) heruntermachen. **run-down** *adj* erschöpft. **run out** zu Ende laufen. **run out of** knapp werden mit. **run over** (flüchtig) durchsehen. **runway** *n* Rollbahn *f*. *n* Lauf *m*, Rennen *neut*. **in the long run** auf die Dauer. **on the run** auf der Flucht. **runner** *n* Läufer(in). **running** *adj* laufend; (*water*) fließend.

rung¹ [rʌŋ] *V* ring².

rung² [rʌŋ] *n* Sprosse *f.*

rupture ['rʌptʃə] *n* Bruch *m*. *v* brechen, zerreißen.

rural ['ruərəl] *adj* ländlich, Land-.

rush¹ [rʌʃ] *v* stürzen, rasen. *n* Stürzen *neut*. **be in a rush** es eilig haben. **rush hour** Hauptverkehrszeit *f.*

rush² [rʌʃ] *n* (*bot*) Binse *f.*

rusk [rʌsk] *n* Zwieback *m.*

Russia ['rʌʃə] *n* Rußland *neut*. **Russian** *adj* russisch; *n* Russe *m*, Russin *f.*

rust [rʌst] *n* Rost *m*. *v* rosten, rostig werden. **rust-coloured** *adj* rostfarben. **rust-proof** *adj* rostfrei. **rusty** *adj* rostig.

rustic ['rʌstik] *adj* ländlich, bäuerlich. *n* Bauer *m.*

rustle ['rʌsl] *v* rascheln, rauschen. *n* Rascheln *neut.*

rut [rʌt] *n* Furche *f.* **be stuck in a rut** beim alten Schlendrian verbleiben.

ruthless ['ruːθlis] *adj* unbarmherzig, rücksichtslos. **ruthlessness** *n* Unbarmherzigkeit *f.*

rye [rai] *n* Roggen *m.*

S

Sabbath ['sabəθ] *n* Sabbat *m.*

sabbatical [sə'batikəl] *adj* **sabbatical year** Urlaubsjahr *neut.*

sable ['seibl] *n* Zobel *m*; (fur) Zobelpelz *m*. *adj* Zobel-.

sabotage ['sabətaːʒ] *n* Sabotage *f.* *v* sabotieren. **saboteur** *n* Saboteur *m.*

sabre ['seibə] *n* Säbel *m.*

saccharin ['sakərin] *n* Saccharin *neut.*

sachet ['saʃei] *n* Kissen *neut*, Täschchen *neut.*

sack [sak] *n* Sack *m*. *v* entlassen. **get the sack** (*coll*) entlassen werden.

sacrament ['sakrəmənt] *n* Sakrament *neut.* **sacramental** *adj* sakramental.

sacred ['seikrid] *adj* heilig.

sacrifice ['sakrifais] *v* opfern. *n* Opfer *neut*. **sacrificial** *adj* Opfer-.

sacrilege ['sakrəlidʒ] *n* Sakrileg *neut*. **sacrilegious** *adj* gotteslästerlich.

sad [sad] *adj* traurig. **sadden** *v* traurig machen. **sadness** *n* Traurigkeit *f.*

saddle ['sadl] *n* Sattel *m*, (*meat*) Rücken *m*. *v* satteln; (*with task*) belasten. **saddlebag** *n* Satteltasche *f.* **saddler** *n* Sattler *m.*

sadism ['seidizəm] *n* Sadismus *m*. **sadist** *n* Sadist(in). **sadistic** *adj* sadistisch.

safe [seif] *adj* (*secure*) sicher; (*not dangerous*) ungefährlich; (*careful*) vorsichtig; (*dependable*) verläßlich. *n* Safe *m*, Geldschrank *m*. **safe and sound** gesund und munter. **safe conduct** Geleitbrief *m*. **safeguard** *n* Sicherung *f*, Vorsichtsmaßnahme *f.* **safety** *n* Sicherheit *f.* **safety belt** Sicherheitsgurt *m*. **safety pin** Sicherheitsnadel *f.*

saffron ['safrən] *n* Safran *m*. *adj* safrangelb.

sag [sag] *v* absacken, herabhängen.

saga ['saɪgə] *n* Saga *f.*

sage¹ [seidʒ] *adj* weise. *n* Weise(r). **sagacious** *adj* scharfsinnig, klug. **sagacity** *n* Klugheit *f.*

sage² [seidʒ] *n* (*bot*) Salbei *f.*

Sagittarius [sadʒi'teəriəs] *n* Schütze *m.*

sago ['seigou] *n* Sago *m.*

said [sed] *V* say.

sail [seil] *n* Segel *neut*. *v* segeln; (*depart*) fahren. **sailing** *n* Segelsport *m.* **sailing boat** *n* Segelboot *neut*. **sailor** *n* Matrose *m.*

saint [seint] *n* Heilige(r). **saintliness** *n* Heiligkeit *f.* **saintly** *adj* fromm.

sake [seik] *n* **for the sake of** wegen (+*gen*), um ... (+*gen*) willen. **for heaven's sake** um Himmels willen. **for my sake** um meinetwillen.

salad ['saləd] *n* Salat *m*. **salad dressing** Salatsoße *f.*

salami [sə'laɪmi] *n* Salami *f.*

salary ['saləri] *n* Gehalt *neut*. **salaried employee** Gehaltsempfänger(in). **salary increase** Gehaltserhöhung *f.*

sale [seil] *n* Verkauf *m*; (*end of season*) Schlußverkauf *m*. **on** *or* **for sale** zu verkaufen. **sales** *pl* Absatz *m*, Umsatz *m*. **sales department** Verkaufsabteilung *f*. **salesgirl** *or* **saleswoman** *n* Verkäuferin. **salesman** *n* Verkäufer *m*; (*travelling*) Geschäftsreisende(r).

saline ['seilain] *adj* salzig. **salinity** *n* Salzigkeit *f*.

saliva [sə'laivə] *n* Speichel *m*. **salivary** *adj* Speichel-.

sallow ['salou] *adj* bläßlich.

salmon ['samən] *n* Lachs *m*. *adj* (*colour*) lachsrot.

salon ['salon] *n* Salon *m*.

saloon [sə'luɪn] *n* Saal *m*, Salon *m*; (*bar*) Kneipe *f*, Ausschank *m*.

salt [soɪlt] *n* Salz *neut*. *v* salzen; (*pickle*) einsalzen. **salt beef** gepökeltes Rindfleisch *neut*. **salt cellar** Salzfäßchen *neut*. **salted** *adj* gesalzen. **saltiness** *n* Salzigkeit *f*. **salt water** Salzwasser *neut*. **salty** *adj* salzig.

salute [sə'luɪt] *v* grüßen. *n* Gruß *m*; (*of guns*) Salut *m*.

salvage ['salvidʒ] *n* Bergung *f*, Rettung *f*. *v* bergen, retten.

salvation [sal'veiʃən] *n* Rettung *f*, Heil *neut*. **Salvation Army** Heilsarmee *f*.

same [seim] *pron*, *adj* derselbe, dieselbe, dasselbe; der/die/das gleiche. **all the same** trotzdem. **it's all the same to me** es ist mir gleich *or* egal. **the same old story** die alte Leier *f*. **sameness** *n* Gleichheit *f*; (*monotony*) Eintönigkeit *f*.

sample ['saɪmpl] *n* Muster *neut*, Probe *f*. *v* probieren.

sanatorium [sanə'toɪriəm] *n* Sanatorium *neut*.

sanction ['saŋkʃən] *n* Sanktion *f*. *v* billigen.

sanctity ['saŋktəti] *n* Heiligkeit *f*.

sanctuary ['saŋktʃuəri] *n* Heiligtum *neut*; (*place of safety*) Asyl *neut*.

sand [sand] *n* Sand *m*. *v* **sand down** abschmirgeln. **sandbag** *n* Sandsack *m*. **sandbank** *n* Sandbank *f*. **sandpaper** *n* Sandpapier *neut*. **sand-pit** *n* Sandgrube *f*. **sandy** *adj* sandig.

sandal ['sandl] *n* Sandale *f*.

sandwich ['sanwidʒ] *n* Sandwich *neut*.

sane [sein] *adj* geistig gesund. **sanity** *n* geistige Gesundheit *f*.

sang [saŋ] *V* sing.

sanitary ['sanitəri] *adj* hygienisch. **sanitary towel** Damenbinde *f*. **sanitation** *n* Sanierung *f*, sanitäre Einrichtungen *pl*.

sank [saŋk] *V* sink.

sap [sap] *n* Saft *m*. **sapling** *n* junger Baum *m*.

sapphire ['safaiə] *n* Saphir *m*.

sarcasm ['saɪkazəm] *n* Sarkasmus *m*. **sarcastic** *adj* sarkastisch, höhnisch.

sardine [saɪ'diɪn] *n* Sardine *f*.

sardonic [saɪ'donik] *adj* sardonisch, zynisch.

sash[1] [saʃ] *n* (*garment*) Schärpe *f*.

sash[2] [saʃ] *n* (*window*) Fensterrahmen *m*. **sash window** Fallfenster *neut*.

sat [sat] *V* sit.

satchel ['satʃəl] *n* Schulmappe *f*.

satellite ['satəlait] *n* Satellit *m*; (*pol*) Satellitenstaat *m*.

satin ['satin] *n* Satin *m*. *adj* Satin-.

satire ['sataiə] *n* Satire *f*. **satirical** *adj* satirisch. **satirist** *n* Satiriker(in).

satisfy ['satisfai] *v* befriedigen. **satisfaction** *n* Befriedigung *f*; (*contentment*) Zufriedenheit *f*. **satisfactory** *adj* befriedigend. **satisfied** *adj* zufrieden.

saturate ['satʃəreit] *v* sättigen. **saturation** *n* Sättigung *f*.

Saturday ['satədi] *n* Sonnabend *m*, Samstag *m*.

Saturn ['satən] *n* Saturn *m*. **saturnine** *adj* (*person*) stillschweigend, verdrießlich.

sauce [soɪs] *n* Soße *f*; (*cheek*) Frechheit *f*. **sauce-boat** *n* Soßenschüssel *f*. **saucepan** ['soɪspən] *n* Kochtopf *m*, Kasserolle *f*.

saucer ['soɪsə] *n* Untertasse *f*. **flying saucer** fliegende Untertasse *f*.

saucy ['soɪsi] *adj* frech, keck.

sauna [soɪnə] *n* Sauna *f*.

saunter [soɪntə] *v* schlendern.

sausage ['sosidʒ] *n* Wurst *f*.

savage ['savidʒ] *adj* (*animal*) wild; (*tribe, etc.*) primitiv, barbarisch; (*behaviour*) brutal, roh. *n* Wilde(r). **savageness** *n* Wildheit *f*. **savagery** *n* Unzivilisiertheit *f*.

save[1] [seiv] *v* (*rescue*) (er)retten; (*money*) sparen; (*avoid*) ersparen; (*time*) gewinnen; (*protect*) schützen. *n* (*football*) Abwehr *f*. **saving** *n* Ersparnis *f*. **savings** *pl* Ersparnisse *pl*. **savings account** Sparkonto *neut*. **savings bank** Sparkasse *f*. **savings book** Sparbuch *neut*.

save[2] [seiv] *prep*, *conj* außer (+*dat*), mit Ausnahme von (+*dat*).

saviour ['seivjə] n Retter m.
savoir-faire [savwaːˈfɛə] n Gewandtheit f, Feingefühl neut.
savoury ['seivəri] adj wohlschmeckend, würzig. n (piquant) Vorspeise f.
saw[1] [soː] V see[1].
***saw**[2] [soː] n Säge f. v sägen. **sawdust** n Sägemehl neut. **sawmill** n Sägewerk neut.
sawn [soːn] V saw[2].
saxophone ['saksəfoun] n Saxophon neut. **saxophonist** n Saxophonist(in).
***say** [sei] v sagen; (maintain) behaupten. **saying** n Sprichwort neut. **have one's say** seine Meinung äußern. **it goes without saying** selbstverständlich.
scab [skab] n Schorf m; (strike-breaker) Streikbrecher m.
scaffold ['skafəld] n (execution) Schafott m. **scaffolding** n Baugerüst neut, Gestell neut.
scald [skoːld] v verbrühen. n Verbrühung f. **scalding** adj brühheiß.
scale[1] [skeil] n (fish, etc.) Schuppe f; (kettle) Kesselstein m. v schuppen. **scaly** adj schuppig.
scale[2] [skeil] n also **scales** pl Waage f.
scale[3] [skeil] n (gradation) Skala f; (music) Tonleiter f; (proportion) Maßstab m. v (climb) erklettern. **to scale** maßstabgetreu. **scale model** maßstabgetreues Modell neut.
scallop ['skaləp] n Kammuschel f.
scalp [skalp] n Kopfhaut f; (as trophy) Skalp m. v skalpieren.
scalpel ['skalpəl] n Skalpell neut.
scampi ['skampi] pl n Scampi pl.
scan [skan] v (carefully) prüfen, genau untersuchen; (briefly) (flüchtig) überblicken.
scandal ['skandl] n Skandal m. **scandalize** v schockieren. **scandalous** adj skandalös. **scandalmonger** n Lästermaul neut.
scant [skant] adj knapp, spärlich. **scanty** adj knapp; (insufficient) unzulänglich.
scapegoat ['skeipgout] n Sündenbock m.
scar [skaː] n Narbe f. v vernarben.
scarce [skeəs] adj knapp, selten. **scarcely** adv kaum. **scarcity** n Mangel m.
scare [skeə] v erschrecken, in Schrecken versetzen. n Schreck m. **scarecrow** n Vogelscheue f. **scary** adj erschreckend.
scarf [skaːf] n Halstuch neut, Schal m.
scarlet ['skaːlit] adj scharlachrot. **scarlet fever** Scharlachfieber neut.

scathing ['skeiðiŋ] adj (fig) verletzend, beißend.
scatter ['skatə] v (ver)streuen; bestreuen (mit). **scatterbrain** n Wirrkopf n.
scavenge ['skavindʒ] v durchsuchen, herumwühlen (in). **scavenger** n (zool) Aasfresser m.
scene [siːn] n Szene f; (situation) Ort m. **scenery** n Landschaft f; (theatre) Bühnenbild neut. **scenic** adj malerisch.
scent [sent] n Duft m; (perfume) Parfüm neut. v (smell) riechen; (perfume) parfümieren. **scented** adj parfümiert.
sceptic ['skeptik] n Skeptiker(in). **sceptical** adj skeptisch. **scepticism** n Skeptizismus m.
sceptre ['septə] n Zepter neut.
schedule ['ʃedjuːl] n Plan m; (list) Verzeichnis neut; (trains) Fahrplan m. v planen.
scheme [skiːm] n Schema neut, (plan) Plan m, Programm neut. v (coll) intrigieren. **schemer** n Ränkeschmied m.
schizophrenia [ˌskitsəˈfriːniə] n Schizophrenie f. **schizophrenic** adj schizophren; n Schizophrene(r).
scholar ['skolə] n Gelehrte(r); (pupil) Schüler(in). **scholarly** adj gelehrt. **scholarship** n Gelehrsamkeit f; (grant) Stipendium neut.
scholastic [skəˈlastik] adj akademisch.
school[1] [skuːl] n Schule f. v schulen. **schoolboy** n Schüler m. **schoolgirl** n Schülerin f. **schooling** n Unterricht m.
schoolteacher n Lehrer(in).
school[2] [skuːl] n (fish) Zug m; (whales) Schar f.
schooner ['skuːnə] n Schoner m; (glass) Humpen m.
sciatica [saiˈatikə] n Ischias m or neut.
science ['saiəns] n Wissenschaft f; (natural science) Naturwissenschaft f. **scientific** adj wissenschaftlich. **scientist** n Wissenschaftler(in).
scissors ['sizəz] pl n Schere f sing.
scoff[1] [skof] v spotten (über). n Spott m, Hohn m.
scoff[2] [skof] v (coll: eat) fressen, hinunterschlingen.
scold [skould] v schimpfen. **give a scolding** ausschelten (+acc).
scone [skon] n Teegebäck neut.
scoop [skuːp] n Schaufel f, Schöpfer m; (newspaper) (sensationelle) Erstmeldung f. v schöpfen.

scooter ['skuːtə] n Roller m.
scope [skoup] n Umfang m, Gebiet neut.
scorch [skɔːtʃ] v verbrennen. scorching adj (weather) brennend.
score [skɔː] n (score) Punktzahl f, Spielergebnis neut; (20) zwanzig (Stück); (music) Partitur f. v (points) zählen, machen. know the score (coll) Bescheid wissen. scoreboard n Anzeigetafel f.
scorn [skɔːn] n Verachtung f, Spott m. v verachten. scornful adj verächtlich.
scorpion ['skɔːpiən] n Skorpion m.
Scotland ['skɔtlənd] n Schottland neut. Scotch n (schottischer) Whisky m. Scotsman n Schotte m. Scotswoman n Schottin f. Scottish adj schottisch.
scoundrel ['skaundrəl] n Schurke m, Schuft m.
scour¹ [skauə] v (clean) scheuern, schrubben. scourer n Scheuerlappen m.
scour² [skauə] v (search) durchsuchen.
scout [skaut] n (mil) Späher m; (boy scout) Pfadfinder m.
scowl [skaul] v finster (an)blicken. n finsterer Blick m.
scramble ['skrambl] v krabbeln, klettern; (eggs) rühren. scramble for balgen um. scrambled egg(s) Rührei neut.
scrap [skrap] n (piece) Stück neut, Fetzen m; (metal) Schrott m; (fight) Prügelei f. v (metal) verschrotten; (plan) verwerfen. scrapbook n Sammelalbum neut, Einklebebuch neut.
scrape [skreip] v schaben, kratzen. n Kratzen neut; (coll) Klemme f.
scratch [skratʃ] v (zer)kratzen. n Kratzstelle f, Riß m; (wound) Schramme f. scratchy adj kratzend.
scrawl [skrɔːl] v kritzeln. n Gekritzel neut.
scream [skriːm] n Schrei m. v schreien. it's a scream es ist zum Schreien.
screech [skriːtʃ] n Gekreisch neut; (cry) (durchdringender) Schrei m. v kreischen.
screen [skriːn] n (Schutz)Schirm m, (Schutz)Wand f; (film) Leinwand f; (TV) Bildschirm m. v abschirmen. screenplay n Drehbuch neut.
screw [skruː] n Schraube f. v schrauben. screwdriver n Schraubenzieher m.
scribble ['skribl] n Gekritzel neut. v kritzeln. scribbler n Kritzler m.
script [skript] n Schrift f; (handwriting) Handschrift f; (film) Drehbuch neut.
scripture ['skriptʃə] n Heilige Schrift f.

scroll [skroul] n Schriftrolle f; (decoration) Schnörkel m.
scrounge [skraundʒ] v (coll) schmarotzen, schnorren. scrounger n Schmarotzer m.
scrub¹ [skrʌb] v schrubben, scheuern. n Schrubben neut. scrubbing brush n Scheuerbürste f.
scrub² [skrʌb] n (bush) Gestrüpp neut, Busch m.
scruffy ['skrʌfi] adj schäbig.
scruple ['skruːpl] n Skrupel m. scrupulous adj peinlich, voller.
scrutiny ['skruːtəni] n (genaue) Untersuchung f. scrutinize v genau untersuchen.
scuffle ['skʌfl] n Rauferie f. v sich raufen.
sculpt [skʌlpt] v formen, schnitzen. sculptor n Bildhauer m. sculpture n Skulptur f.
scum [skʌm] n Abschaum m.
scurf [skəːf] n Schorf m; (dandruff) Schuppen pl.
scurvy ['skəːvi] n Skorbut m.
scuttle ['skʌtl] n Kohleneimer m.
scythe [saið] n Sense f. v (ab)mähen.
sea [siː] n See f, Meer neut. at sea auf See. all at sea (coll) perplex, im Dunkeln. on the high seas auf hoher see. go to sea zur See gehen.
seabed ['siːbed] n Meeresgrund m.
sea front n Strandpromenade f.
seagoing ['siːgouiŋ] adj Hochsee-.
seagull ['siːgʌl] n Möwe f.
seahorse ['siːhɔːs] n Seepferdchen neut.
seal¹ [siːl] n Siegel neut. v besiegeln. seal up versiegeln. sealing wax Siegellack m.
seal² [siːl] n (zool) Robbe f, Seehund m. sealskin n Seehundsfell neut.
sea-level n Meeresspiegel m.
sea-lion n Seelöwe m.
seam [siːm] n Saum m, Naht f; (minerals) Flöz neut. v säumen.
seaman ['siːmən] n Seemann m, Matrose m. seamanlike adj seemännisch. seamanship n Seemannskunst f.
search [səːtʃ] v suchen, forschen (nach); (for criminal) fahnden (nach); (person, place) durchsuchen (nach). searchlight n Scheinwerfer m. search party Suchtrupp m. search warrant Haussuchungsbefehl m. n Suche f; Untersuchung f. searcher n Sucher m, Forscher m. searching adj (enquiry) gründlich.
sea-shore n Seeküste f.

seasick ['siːsik] *adj* seekrank. **seasickness** *n* Seekrankheit *f*.

seaside ['siːsaid] *n* See *f*. **at the seaside** an der See. **to the seaside** an die See. **seaside town** Küstenstadt *f*.

season ['siːzn] *n* Jahreszeit *f*; (*comm*) Saison *f*. *v* (*cookery*) würzen; (*wood*) ablagern. **seasonal** *adj* saisonbedingt. **seasoning** *n* Würze *f*. **season-ticket** *n* Zeitkarte *f*; (*theatre*) Abonnement *neut*.

seat [siːt] *n* Sitz *m*; (*train, theatre*) Platz *m*; (*residence*) Wohnsitz *m*. *v* setzen. *please be seated!* bitte setzen Sie sich! **seating** *n* Sitzgelegenheit *f*.

seaweed ['siːwiːd] *n* Tang *m*, Alge *f*.

seaworthy ['siːwəːði] *adj* seetüchtig.

secluded [si'kluːdid] *adj* abgelegen. **seclusion** *n* Zurückgezogenheit *f*.

second[1] ['sekənd] *n* (*time*) Sekunde *f*. *wait a second!* moment mal!

second[2] ['sekənd] *adj* zweit; (*next*) nächst, folgend. *adv* an zweiter Stelle. *n* Zweite(r). **for the second time** zum zweiten Mal. **on second thoughts** bei näherer Überlegung. **play second fiddle** die Nebenrolle spielen. **secondary** *adj* nebensächlich, sekundär. **secondary school** Sekundarschule *f*. **second-best** *adj* zweitbest. **second-class** *adj* zweitrangig. **second-hand** *adj* gebraucht, Gebraucht-. **secondly** *adv* zweitens. **second-rate** *adj* minderwertig.

secret ['siːkrit] *adj* geheim, heimlich **keep secret** geheimhalten. *n* Geheimnis *neut*. **in secret** *or* **secretly** *adv* heimlich. **secrecy** *n* Verborgenheit *f*, Heimlichkeit *f*. **secretive** *adj* verschlossen. **secretiveness** *n* Verschlossenheit *f*.

secretary ['sekrətəri] *n* Sekretär(in). **secretarial** *adj* Sekretär-. **secretary general** Generalsekretär *m*.

secrete [si'kriːt] *v* absondern. **secretion** *n* Absonderung *f*.

sect [sekt] *n* Sekte *f*. **sectarian** *adj* sektiererisch.

section ['sekʃən] *n* (*part*) Teil *m*; (*of firm*) Abteilung *f*; (*of book, document*) Abschnitt *m*. *v* **section off** abteilen.

sector ['sektə] *n* Sektor *m*.

secular ['sekjulə] *adj* weltlich. **secularism** *n* Säkularismus *f*.

secure [si'kjuə] *adj* sicher. *v* sichern; (*affix*) festmachen (an); (*procure*) sich beschaffen. **security** *n* Sicherheit *f*; (*bond*) Bürgschaft *f*. **securities** *pl* (*comm*) Wertpapiere *pl*.

sedate [si'deit] *adj* ruhig, gelassen. **sedateness** *n* Gelassenheit *f*. **sedative** *n* Beruhigungsmittel *neut*. **sedation** *n* (Nerven)Beruhigung *f*.

sediment ['sedimənt] *n* Sediment *neut*. **sedimentation** *n* Sedimentation *n*.

seduce [si'djuːs] *v* verführen. **seducer** *n* Verführer *m*. **seduction** *n* Verführung *f*. **seductive** *adj* verlockend.

*see[1] [siː] *v* sehen; (*understand*) einsehen, verstehen; (*consult*) konsultieren, besuchen. **see home** (*person*) nach Hause begleiten. **seeing that** da. **see through** (*understand*) durchschauen; (*finish*) zu Ende führen. **see to** sich kümmern um. **see to it that** darauf achten, daß. **wait and see** abwarten.

see[2] [siː] *n* Bistum *neut*.

seed [siːd] *n* Same *m*; (*pip*) Kern *m*. **seedy** *adj* schäbig.

*seek [siːk] *v* suchen. **seeker** *n* Sucher(in).

seem [siːm] *v* scheinen. **seeming** *adj* scheinbar. **seemly** *adj* schicklich.

seen [siːn] *V* see[1].

seep [siːp] *v* (durch)sickern.

seesaw ['siːsɔː] *n* Wippe *f*. *v* schaukeln.

seethe [siːð] *v* sieden. **seething** *adj* (*coll*) wütend.

segment ['segmənt] *n* Abschnitt *m*, Segment *neut*.

segregate ['segrigeit] *v* trennen, absondern. **segregation** *n* Absonderung *f*; (*racial*) Rassentrennung *f*.

seize [siːz] *v* ergreifen. **seize up** festfahren. **seizure** *n* Ergreifung *f*; (*med*) Anfall *m*.

seldom ['seldəm] *adv* selten.

select [sə'lekt] *v* auswählen, auslesen. *adj* exklusiv. **selected** *adj* ausgewählt. **selection** *n* Auswahl *f*. **selective** *adj* auswählend.

self [self] *n* Selbst *neut*, Ich *neut*.

self-assured *adj* selbstsicher. **self-assurance** *n* Selbstsicherheit *f*.

self-centred *adj* ichbezogen.

self-confident *adj* selbstbewußt, selbstsicher. **self-confidence** *n* Selbstbewußtsein *neut*.

self-conscious *adj* gehemmt, befangen. **self-consciousness** *n* Befangenheit *f*.

self-contained *adj* (*flat*) separat; (*person*) zurückhaltend.

self-control *n* Selbstbeherrschung *f*.
self-defence *n* Selbstverteidigung *f*.
self-denial *n* Selbstverleugnung *f*.
self-discipline *n* Selbstdisziplin *f*.
self-employed *adj* selbständig.
self-esteem *n* Selbstachtung *f*.
self-evident *adj* selbstverständlich.
self-important *adj* wichtigtuerisch.
self-indulgent *adj* selbstgefällig.
self-interest *n* Eigennutz *m*. **self-interested** *adj* eigennützig.
selfish ['selfiʃ] *adj* selbstisch, selbstsüchtig. **selfishness** *n* Egoismus *m*.
selfless ['selflis] *adj* selbstlos.
self-made *adj* **self-made man** Emporkömmling *m*.
self-pity *n* Selbstmitleid *neut*.
self-portrait *n* Selbstporträt *neut*.
self-respect *n* Selbstachtung *f*.
self-righteous *adj* selbstgerecht.
self-sacrifice *n* Selbstaufopferung *f*. **self-sacrificing** *adj* aufopferungsvoll.
selfsame ['selfseim] *adj* ebenderselbe, ebendieselbe, ebendasselbe.
self-satisfied *adj* selbstzufrieden.
self-service *adj* Selbstbedienung *f*. *adj* Selbstbedienungs-.
self-sufficient *adj* unabhängig; (*person*) selbstgenügsam.
self-will *n* Eigensinn *m*. **self-willed** *adj* eigensinnig.
*sell [sel] *v* verkaufen. **seller** *n* Verkäufer(in). **sell out** (*betray*) verraten. **sold out** ausverkauft.
Sellotape ® ['seləteip] *n* Tesa-Film *m*.
semantic [sə'mantik] *adj* semantisch. **semantics** *n* Semantik *f*.
semaphore ['seməfoɪ] *n* Semaphor *m*.
semen ['siːmən] *n* Samen *m*, Sperma *neut*.
semicircle ['semisəɪkl] *n* Halbkreis *m*. **semicircular** *adj* halbkreisförmig.
semicolon [ˌsemi'koulən] *n* Strichpunkt *m*.
semi-detached (house) *adj* halbfreistehend.
semifinal [semi'fainl] *n* Vorschlußrunde *f*; Halbfinale *neut*.
seminal ['seminl] *adj* Samen-; (*influential*) einflußreich, wichtig.
seminar ['seminaɪ] *n* Seminar *neut*.
semiprecious [semi'preʃəs] *adj* halbedel.
semolina [ˌseməˈliːnə] *n* Grieß *m*; (*pudding*) Grießbrei *m*.
senate ['senit] *n* Senat *m*. **senator** *n* Senator *m*. **senatorial** *adj* senatorisch.

*send [send] *v* schicken, senden. **send away** fortschicken. **send for** (*person*) schicken nach. **send off** (*letter*) absenden. **send-off** *n* Abschiedsfeier *f*. **sender** *n* Absender(in).
senile ['siːnail] *adj* senil. **senility** *n* Senilität *f*.
senior ['siːnjə] *adj* älter; (*school*) Ober-. *n* Ältere(r).
sensation [sen'seiʃən] *n* Gefühl *neut*, Empfindung *f*; (*excitement*) Sensation *f*. **sensational** *adj* sensationell. **sensationalism** *n* Effekthascherei *f*.
sense [sens] *n* Sinn *m*; (*feeling*) Gefühl *neut*. **common sense** Vernunft *f*. **make sense** sinnvoll sein. **sense of humour** Sinn für Humor *m*. *v* empfinden, spüren. **senseless** *adj* sinnlos.
sensible ['sensəbl] *adj* vernünftig. **sensibility** *n* Sensibilität *f*. **sensibleness** *n* Vernünftigkeit *f*.
sensitive ['sensitiv] *adj* empfindlich (gegen). **sensitivity** *n* Empfindlichkeit *f*; (*appreciativeness*) Sensibilität *f*, Feingefühl *neut*.
sensual ['sensjuəl] *adj* sinnlich. **sensuality** *n* Sinnlichkeit *f*.
sensuous ['sensjuəs] *adj* sinnlich. **sensuousness** *n* Sinnlichkeit *f*.
sent [sent] *V* send.
sentence ['sentəns] *n* Satz *m*; (*punishment*) Strafe *f*, Urteil *neut*. *v* verurteilen.
sentiment ['sentimənt] *n* Empfindsamkeit *f*; (*feeling*) Gefühl *neut*. **sentiments** *pl* Meinungen *pl*, Gesinnung *f sing*. **sentimental** *adj* sentimental. **sentimentality** *n* Sentimentalität *f*.
sentry ['sentri] *n* Wachposten *m*.
separate ['sepərət] *v* ['sepəreit] *adj* getrennt. *v* trennen; (*couple*) sich trennen. **separable** *adj* trennbar. **separateness** *n* Getrenntheit *f*. **separation** *n* Trennung *f*.
September [sep'tembə] *n* September *m*.
septic ['septik] *adj* septisch.
sequel ['siːkwəl] *n* (*novel, etc.*) Fortsetzung *f*; (*consequence*) Folge *f*.
sequence ['siːkwəns] *n* (Reihen)Folge *f*, Reihe *f*; (*film*) Szene *f*. **sequential** *adj* (aufeinander)folgend.
sequin ['siːkwin] *n* Paillette *f*.
serenade [serə'neid] *n* Serenade *f*.
serene [sə'riːn] *adj* heiter, gelassen. **serenity** *n* Heiterkeit *f*.

shallot

serf [səːf] n Leibeigene(r). **serfdom** n Leibeigenschaft f.

sergeant ['saːdʒənt] n (mil) Feldwebel m; (police) Wachtmeister m.

serial ['siəriəl] n (book) Fortsetzungsroman m; (TV, radio) Sendereihe f. adj Fortsetzungs-. **serial number** Seriennummer f.

series ['siəriz] n Serie f.

serious ['siəriəs] adj ernst(haft); (illness) gefährlich. **seriously** adv ernstlich, im Ernst; (injured) schwer. **seriousness** n Ernst m.

sermon ['səːmən] n Predigt f.

serpent ['səːpənt] n Schlange f.

servant ['səːvənt] n Diener(in). **domestic servant** Hausangestellte(r). **public servant** n Beamte(r), Beamtin f.

serve [səːv] v dienen (+dat); (customer) bedienen; (food) servieren; (tennis) aufschlagen. **serve no purpose** nichts nützen. **it serves him right** es geschieht ihm recht.

service ['səːvis] n Dienst m; (shop, restaurant) Bedienung f; (after-sales) Kundendienst m; (mot) Inspektion; (favour) Gefallen m; (church) Gottesdienst m. **military service** Wehrdienst m. **service station** Tankstelle f. v (mot) warten, überholen. **serviceable** adj brauchbar.

serviette [ˌsəːviˈet] n Serviette f.

servile ['səːvail] adj servil. **servility** n Unterwürfigkeit f.

session ['seʃən] n Sitzung f; (university) Semester neut.

***set** [set] v setzen, stellen; (date, etc.) festsetzen; (table) decken; (sun) untergehen; (become solid) gerinnen. **set aside** aufheben. **setback** n Rückschlag m. **set fire to** in Brand stecken. **set off** (on journey) sich auf den Weg machen, aufbrechen. **set one's heart on** sein Herz hängen an. **set to** darangehen. **setting** n Hintergrund m. n Satz m; (crockery) Service f; (radio) Apparat m; (clique) Kreis m, Clique f.

settee [seˈtiː] n Sofa neut.

settle ['setl] v (arrange) festsetzen; (dispute) schlichten; (debt) bezahlen; (come to rest) sich niederlassen; (subside) sich senken; (in place) sich ansiedeln. **settle down** (calm down) sich beruhigen; (in place) sich niederlassen. **settle for** (coll)

annehmen. **settle in** sich einleben. **settle up** bezahlen. **settled** adj abgemacht, erledigt. **settlement** n (place) Siedlung f; (agreement) Übereinkommen neut. **settler** n Siedler(in).

seven ['sevn] adj sieben. n Sieben f. **seventh** adj siebt, siebent; n Siebtel neut.

seventeen [sevn'tiːn] adj siebzehn. n Siebzehn f. **seventeenth** adj siebzehnt.

seventy ['sevnti] adj siebzig. n Siebzig f.

sever ['sevə] v trennen. **severance** n Trennung f. **severance pay** Abfindungsentschädigung f.

several ['sevrəl] adj mehrere; (separate) getrennt. **severally** adv getrennt.

severe [sə'viə] adj streng, hart; (weather) rauh; (difficult) schwierig. **severity** n Strenge f; Härte f; (seriousness) Ernst m.

***sew** [sou] v nähen. **sewing** n Näharbeit f. **sewing machine** Nähmaschine f.

sewage ['sjuːdʒ] n Abwasser neut. **sewer** n Abwasserkanal m. **sewerage** n Kanalisation f.

sewn [soun] V see **sew**.

sex [seks] n Geschlecht neut, Sex m. adj Geschlechts-, sexual. **sexual** adj sexual. **sexual intercourse** Geschlechtsverkehr m. **sexuality** n Sexualität f. **sexy** adj sexy.

sextet [seks'tet] n Sextett neut.

shabby ['ʃabi] adj schäbig.

shack [ʃak] n Hütte f.

shackle ['ʃakl] v fesseln. **shackles** pl n Fesseln pl.

shade [ʃeid] n Schatten m. v beschatten; (protect) schützen; (drawing) schattieren. **shading** n Schattierung f. **shady** adj schattig; (dubious) fragwürdig.

shadow ['ʃadou] n Schatten m. **without a shadow of doubt** ohne den geringsten Zweifel. **shadow cabinet** Schattenkabinett neut. **shadowy** adj schattig.

shaft [ʃaːft] n (handle) Schaft m; (lift) Schacht m; (tech) Welle f.

shaggy ['ʃagi] adj zottig.

***shake** [ʃeik] v schütteln; (shock) erschüttern; (tremble) zittern; (hand) drücken. **shake hands with** die Hand geben (+dat). **shake off** (coll) loswerden. n Schütteln neut. **shaky** adj wackelig.

shall [ʃal] v (to form future) werden; (implying permission) sollen, dürfen. I **shall go** ich werde gehen. **shall I go?** soll ich gehen?

shallot [ʃə'lot] n Schalotte f.

shallow ['ʃalou] adj flach, seicht; (superficial) oberflächlich, seicht. **shallows** pl n Untiefe f. **shallowness** n Seichtheit f.
sham [ʃam] n Betrug m; (person) Schwindler m. adj falsch.
shambles ['ʃamblz] n Durcheinander neut.
shame [ʃeim] n Scham f, Schamgefühl neut; (scandal) Schande f. **it's a shame that ...** schade, daß ... **shame-faced** adj verschämt. **shamefacedness** n Verschämtheit f. **what a shame!** (wie) shade! v schämen. **shameful** adj schändlich. **shamefulness** n Schändlichkeit f. **shameless** adj schamlos. **shamelessness** n Schamlosigkeit f.
shampoo [ʃam'puː] n Shampoo neut, Haarwaschmittel neut. v shampooieren.
shamrock ['ʃamrok] n Kleeblatt neut.
shanty[1] ['ʃanti] n (hut) Hütte f. **shanty town** Elendsviertel neut.
shanty[2] ['ʃanti] n (song) Matrosenlied neut.
shape [ʃeip] n Gestalt f, Form f. v gestalten, formen. **shaped** adj geformt. **shapeless** adj formlos. **shapelessness** n Formlosigkeit f. **shapely** adj wohlgeformt.
share [ʃeə] n (An)Teil m; (comm) Aktie f. v teilen. **shareholder** n Aktionär m.
shark [ʃaːk] n Hai(fisch) m.
sharp [ʃaːp] adj scharf; (pointed) spitz; (outline) deutlich. adv (coll) pünktlich. **look sharp!** mach schnell! **sharpen** v (knife) schleifen; (pencil) spitzen. **sharp-eyed** adj scharfsichtig. **sharpness** n Schärfe f. **sharpshooter** n Scharfschütze m. **sharp-witted** adj scharfsinnig.
shatter ['ʃatə] v zerschmettern; (glass) zersplittern. **shattered** adj (coll) erschüttert.
shave [ʃeiv] v (sich) rasieren. **clean-shaven** adj glattrasiert. **shaving brush** Rasierpinsel m. **shaving soap** Rasierseife f. **shaving foam** Rasierschaum m. n Rasur f. **shaver** n Rasierapparat m.
shawl [ʃoːl] n Schal m.
she [ʃiː] pron sie.
sheaf [ʃiːf] n (pl sheaves) Garbe f.
***shear** [ʃiə] v scheren. **shears** pl n Schere f sing. **shearer** n Scherer m. **shearing** n Schur f.
sheath [ʃiːθ] n Scheide f. **sheathe** v (sword) in die Scheide stecken. **sheathed** adj (tech) verkleidet.
***shed**[1] [ʃed] v (tears, blood) vergießen; (leaves) abwerfen.

shed[2] [ʃed] n (hut) Schuppen m; (cows) Stall m.
sheen [ʃiːn] n Glanz m, Schimmer m.
sheep [ʃiːp] n (pl sheep) Schaf neut. **sheepdog** n Schäferhund. **sheepskin** n Schaffell neut. **sheepish** adj einfältig, verlegen.
sheer [ʃiə] adj (pure) bloß; (steep) steil.
sheet [ʃiːt] n (bed) Bettuch neut, (Bett)Laken neut; (paper, metal) Blatt neut.
shelf [ʃelf] n (pl shelves) Regal neut, Fach neut. **on the shelf** sitzengeblieben.
shell [ʃel] n Schale f; (snail) Schneckenhaus neut; (mil) Granate f. **shellfish** n Schalentier neut. **shell-shock** n Kriegsneurose f. v (egg) schälen; (nuts) enthülsen. **shelling** n (mil) Artilleriefeuer neut.
shelter ['ʃeltə] n Obdach neut; (little hut) Schutzhütte f. v beschützen; (take shelter) Schutz suchen.
shelve [ʃelv] v (plan) auf die lange Bank schieben, aufschieben.
shepherd ['ʃepəd] n Schäfer m, Hirt m. **shepherdess** n Schäferin f, Hirtin f.
sheriff ['ʃerif] n Sheriff m.
sherry ['ʃeri] n Sherry m.
shield [ʃiːld] n Schild m; (fig) Schutz m. v beschirmen.
shift [ʃift] v (sich) verschieben; (get rid of) beseitigen; (coll: move fast) schnell fahren; (gear) schalten. n Verschiebung f; (work) Schicht f. **shifty** adj schlau.
shimmer ['ʃimə] n Schimmer m. v schimmern.
shin [ʃin] n Schienbein neut. v **shin up** hinaufklettern.
***shine** [ʃain] v scheinen, leuchten; (shoes) putzen. n Glanz m. **shiny** adj glänzend, strahlend.
shingle ['ʃiŋgl] n (on beach) Strandkies m.
shingles ['ʃiŋglz] n (med) Gürtelrose f.
ship [ʃip] n Schiff neut. **shipowner** n Reeder m. **shipwreck** n Schiffbruch m **be shipwrecked** Schiffbruch erleiden. **shipyard** n Werft f. v verschiffen, spedieren. **shipment** n Verladung f. **shipper** n Spediteur m.
shirk [ʃəːk] v sich drücken (vor). **shirker** n Drückeberger(in).
shirt [ʃəːt] n Hemd neut. **shirty** adj (coll) verdrießlich.
shit [ʃit] n (vulgar) Scheiße f. v scheißen. **shitty** adj beschissen.

shiver ['ʃivə] v zittern. n Zittern neut.

shoal [ʃoul] n Schwarm m, Zug m.

shock [ʃok] v (impact) Stoß m, Anprall m; (fright) Schreck m, Schock m; (med) Nervenschock m; (elec) Schlag m. v schockieren, entsetzen. shocked adj schockiert. shocking adj schockierend.

shod [ʃod] V shoe.

shoddy ['ʃodi] adj schäbig.

*shoe [ʃuː] n Schuh m; (horse) Hufeisen neut. shoe-horn n Schuhlöffel m. shoelace n Schnürsenkel m. v beschuhen. shoemaker n Schuhmacher m.

shone [ʃon] V shine.

shook [ʃuk] V shake.

*shoot [ʃuːt] v schießen; (hit) anschießen; (kill) erschießen; (film) drehen. shoot down (aeroplane) abschießen. shooting n (game, etc.) Jagd f. shooting star Sternschnuppe f.

shop [ʃop] n Laden m, Geschäft neut; (factory) Werkstatt f. shop assistant Verkäufer(in). shopkeeper n Ladenbesitzer m. shop-lifting n Ladendiebstahl m. shop-steward n Betriebsrat m. shop-window n Schaufenster neut. v (also go shopping) einkaufen gehen. shopper n Einkäufer(in). shopping n Einkäufe pl.

shore [ʃoɪ] n Küste f, Strand m.

shorn [ʃoɪn] V shear.

short [ʃoɪt] adj kurz; (person) klein. adv plötzlich. short of knapp an.

shortage ['ʃoɪtidʒ] n Mangel m, Knappheit f.

shortbread ['ʃoɪtbred] n Mürbekuchen m.

short-circuit n Kurzschluß m. v kurzschließen.

shortcoming ['ʃoɪtkʌmiŋ] n Fehler m, Unzulänglichkeit f.

short cut n Abkürzung f.

shorthand ['ʃoɪthand] n Kurzschrift f. shorthand typist Stenotypist(in).

short list v in die engere Wahl ziehen.

short-lived adj kurzlebig.

shortly ['ʃoɪtli] adv bald, in kurzer Zeit.

short-sighted adj kurzsichtig. shortsightedness n Kurzsichtigkeit f.

shorts [ʃoɪts] pl n kurze Hose f sing.

short-tempered adj reizbar.

short-term adj kurzfristig.

short-time adj short-time work Kurzarbeit f.

short-wave adj Kurzwellen-.

shot [ʃot] V shoot. n Schuß m; (pellets)

Schrot m; (sport) Kugel f; (films) Aufnahme f; (injection) Spritze f. adj (coll) erschüttert. have a shot (coll) versuchen. shotgun n Schrotflinte f. shot put Kugelstoß m.

should [ʃud] v sollen. I should go ich sollte gehen. I should like (to) Ich möchte.

shoulder ['ʃouldə] n Schulter f, Achsel f. shoulder-blade n Schulterblatt neut.

shout [ʃaut] v rufen, schreien. n Schrei m, Ruf m. shouting n Geschrei neut.

shove [ʃʌv] v schieben, stoßen. n Stoß m, Schub m.

*show v zeigen; (goods, etc.) ausstellen. showcase n Schaukasten m. showman n Schausteller m. show off angeben, sich großtun. show-off n Angeber m, Großtuer m. showpiece n Paradestück neut. showroom n Ausstellungsraum m. n Ausstellung f; (theatre) Vorstellung f. mere show leerer Schein m.

shower ['ʃauə] n (rain) Schauer m; (bath) Dusche f. v sich duschen.

shown [ʃoun] V show.

shred [ʃred] n Fetzen m. v zerfetzen. not a shred of keine Spur von.

shrew [ʃruɪ] n Spitzmaus f; (woman) zankisches Weib neut.

shrewd [ʃruɪd] adj scharfsinnig, schlau. shrewdness n Scharfsinn m.

shriek [ʃriɪk] n Schrei m, Gekreisch neut. v schreien, kreischen.

shrill [ʃril] adj schrill, gellend.

shrimp [ʃrimp] n Garnele f.

shrine [ʃrain] n Schrein m.

*shrink [ʃriŋk] v einschrumpfen. shrink from zurückweichen von. shrinkage n Schrumpfung f.

shrivel ['ʃrivl] v runzelig werden, schrumpfen.

shroud [ʃraud] n Leichentuch neut. v (fig) umhüllen.

Shrove Tuesday [ʃrouv] n Fastnachtsdienstag m.

shrub [ʃrʌb] n Strauch m, Busch m. shrubbery n Gebüsch neut.

shrug [ʃrʌg] v zucken. n (Achsel)Zucken neut.

shrunk [ʃrʌŋk] V shrink.

shudder ['ʃʌdə] v schaudern. n Schauder m.

shuffle ['ʃʌfl] v (mit den Füßen) scharren, schlurfen; (cards) mischen. n Schlurfen neut; (cards) (Karten)Mischen neut.

shun [ʃʌn] v vermeiden.
shunt [ʃʌnt] v (rail) rangieren.
***shut** [ʃʌt] v schließen, zumachen; (book)
zuklappen. **shut down** stillegen. **shut off**
abstellen. **shut out** aussperren. **shut up**
(be silent) den Mund halten. adj geschlossen, zu.
shutter ['ʃʌtə] n Fensterladen m; (phot)
Verschluß m.
shuttle ['ʃʌtl] n Pendelverkehr m.
shuttlecock ['ʃʌtlkok] n Federball m.
shy [ʃai] adj schüchtern. v (horse)
scheuen. **shy away from** zurückschrecken
vor. **shyness** n Schüchternheit f.
sick [sik] adj krank. I feel sick mir ist
übel. **sick humour** schwarzer Humor m.
sicken v erkranken; (disgust) anekeln.
sickening adj ekelhaft. **sick leave**
Krankheitsurlaub m. **sickly** adj kränklich. **sickness** n Krankheit f; (vomiting)
Erbrechen neut.
sickle ['sikl] n Sichel f.
side [said] n Seite f; (edge) Rand m;
(team) Mannschaft f. adj seitlich, Seiten-.
sideboard n Buffet neut. **sideboards** or
sideburns pl n Koteletten pl. **sidelight** n
(mot) Standlicht neut. **sideline** n
Nebenbeschäftigung f. **sidelong** adj seitlich. **sideshow** n Jahrmarktsbude f. **siding**
n Nebengleis neut.
sidle ['saidl] v sich schlängeln. **sidle up to**
heranschleichen an.
siege [siidʒ] n Belagerung f. **lay siege to**
belagern.
sieve [siv] n Sieb neut. v (durch)sieben.
sift [sift] v (durch)sieben; (evidence, etc.)
sorgfältig überprüfen.
sigh [sai] v seufzen. n Seufzer m.
sight [sait] n (power of) Sehvermögen
neut; (instance of seeing) Anblick m;
(range of vision) Sicht f; (of gun) Visier
neut; (place of interest) Sehenswürdigkeit
f. **at sight** (comm) bei Sicht. **at first sight**
beim ersten Anblick. **sighted** adj sichtig.
sightless adj blind. **go sightseeing** die
Sehenswürdigkeiten besichtigen.
sign [sain] n Zeichen neut; (noticeboard,
etc.) Schild neut. v unterschreiben. **sign-
writer** n Schriftmaler m. **signpost** n
Wegweiser m.
signal ['signəl] n Signal neut. v signalisier-
en.
signature ['signətʃə] n Unterschrift f. **signature tune** Kennmelodie f. **signatory** n
Unterzeichner m; (pol) Signatar m.

signify ['signifai] v bedeuten. **significance**
n Bedeutung f. **significant** adj wichtig.
silence ['sailəns] n Ruhe f, Stille f;
(absence of talking, etc.) Schweigen neut.
v zum Schweigen bringen.
silent ['sailənt] adj still, ruhig;
stillschweigend. **be** or **fall silent**
schweigen. **silent film** Stummfilm m.
silhouette [silu'et] n Silhouette f.
silk [silk] n Seide f. adj Seiden-.
sill [sil] n Fensterbrett neut; (door)
Schwelle f.
silly ['sili] adj dumm, albern. **silly season**
Sauregurkenzeit f.
silt [silt] n Schlamm m. v **silt up**
verschlammen.
silver ['silvə] n Silber neut. adj silbern,
Silber-. **silver plate** Tafelsilber neut. **sil-
ver-plated** adj versilbert.
similar ['similə] adj ähnlich (+dat). **similarity** n Ähnlichkeit f. **similarly** adv
gleichermaßen.
simile ['siməli] n Gleichnis neut.
simmer ['simə] v leicht kochen (lassen).
simple ['simpl] adj einfach. **simple-minded**
adj einfältig. **simpleton** n Einfaltspinsel
m. **simplicity** n Einfachheit f. **simplify** v
vereinfachen. **simply** adv einfach.
simulate ['simjuleit] v simulieren. **simulation** n Simulation f. **simulator** n Simulator m.
simultaneous [siməl'teinjəs] adj gleichzeitig.
sin [sin] n Sünde f. v sündigen. **sinful** adj
sündig. **sinner** n Sünder(in).
since [sins] prep seit. I've been living here
since 1960 ich wohne hier seit 1960. conj
(time) seit(dem); (because) da. adv
seitdem, seither; (in the meantime)
inzwischen.
sincere [sin'siə] adj aufrichtig, ehrlich.
yours sincerely mit freundlichen Grüßen.
sincerity n Aufrichtigkeit f.
sinew ['sinjui] n Sehne f. **sinewy** adj
sehnig.
***sing** [siŋ] v singen. **singer** n Sänger(in).
singing n Singen neut, Gesang m.
singe [sindʒ] v (ver)sengen.
single ['siŋgl] adj einzig; (individual)
einzeln; (room, bed, etc.) Einzel-;
(unmarried) ledig. v **single out** auslesen.
single ticket einfache Fahrkarte f. **single-
handed** adj eigenhändig. **single-minded**
adj zielstrebig. **singly** adv einzeln, allein.

161   **slant**

singular ['siŋgjulə] *adj* einzigartig;
(*gramm*) im Singular. *n* (*gramm*) Singular *m*.
sinister ['sinistə] *adj* drohend, unheilvoll.
***sink** [siŋk] *v* sinken; (*cause to sink*)
senken. *n* Spülbecken *neut*.
sinuous ['sinjuəs] *adj* gewunden, sich
windend.
sinus ['sainəs] *n* (Nasen) Nebenhöhle *f*.
sinusitis *n* Nebenhöhlenentzündung *f*.
sip [sip] *v* nippen an, schlürfen. *n*
Schlückchen *neut*.
siphon ['saifən] *n* Heber *m*; (*soda*) Siphon
m, *v* aushebern.
sir [sət] *n* (mein) Herr. **Dear Sir** (*in letters*) sehr geehrter Herr!
siren ['saiərən] *n* Sirene *f*.
sirloin ['sətloin] *n* Lendenstück *neut*.
sister ['sistə] *n* Schwester *f*; (*nurse*)
Oberschwester *f*. **sister-in-law** *n*
Schwägerin *f*. *adj* Schwester-. **sisterly** *adj*
schwesterlich.
***sit** [sit] *v* sitzen; (*exam*) machen; (*hen*)
brüten. **sit down** sich (hin)setzen. **sitting**
n Sitzung *f*. **sitting duck** leichtes Opfer
neut. **sitting-room** *n* Wohnzimmer *neut*.
site [sait] *n* Stelle *f*. **building site** Baustelle
f. *v* placieren.
situation [sitju'eiʃən] *n* Lage *f*; (*state of
affairs*) Situation *f*, (Sach)Lage *f*; (*job*)
Stelle *f*, Posten *m*. **situated** *adj* gelegen.
six [siks] *adj* sechs. *n* Sechs *f*. **sixth** *adj*
sechst; *n* Sechstel *neut*. **sixth form** Prima
f.
sixteen [siks'tiːn] *adj* sechzehn. *n*
Sechzehn *f*.
sixty ['siksti] *adj* sechzig. *n* Sechzig *f*.
size [saiz] *n* Größe *f*. *v* **size up** (*coll*)
abschätzen.
sizzle ['sizl] *v* zischen.
skate¹ [skeit] *n* (*ice*) Schlittschuh *m*; (*roller*) Rollschuh *m*. *v* Schlitt-
schuh/Rollschuh laufen. **skater** *n*
Eisläufer(in); Rollschuhläufer(in).
skate² [skeit] *n* (*fish*) Rochen *m*.
skeleton ['skelitn] *n* Skelett *neut*,
Knochengerüst *neut*. **skeleton key** Dietrich *m*.
sketch [sketʃ] *n* Skizze *f*; (*theatre*) Sketch
m. *v* skizzieren. **sketchy** *adj* oberflächlich.
skewer ['skjuə] *n* Fleischspieß *m*. *v*
spießen.
ski [skiː] *n* Ski *m*. *v* Ski laufen. **skier** *n*
Skiläufer(in), Skifahrer(in). **skiing** *n* Ski-
laufen *neut*, Skifahren *neut*.

skid [skid] *v* schleudern. *n* Schleudern
neut.
skill [skil] *n* (*skilfulness*) Geschicklichkeit
f, Gewandtheit *f*; (*expertise*) Fachkennt-
nis *f*. **skilled** *adj* geschickt. **skilled worker**
Facharbeiter *m*. **skilful** *adj* geschickt.
skim [skim] *v* abschöpfen; (*milk*)
entrahmen. **skim through** (*read*) überfliegen. **skim milk** Magermilch *f*.
skimp [skimp] *v* geizen (mit); (*work*)
nachlässig machen.
skin [skin] *n* Haut *f*; (*animal*) Fell *neut*.
Pelz *m*; (*fruit*) Schale *f*, Rinde *f*. **skin
deep** *adj* oberflächlich. **skin-diving** *n*
Schwimmtauchen *neut*. **skinflint** *n*
Geizhals *m*. **skin-tight** *adj* hauteng. *v*
enthäuten. **skinny** *adj* mager.
skip [skip] *v* hüpfen; (*with rope*) seil-
springen; (*miss*) auslassen. **skip through**
(*read*) überfliegen. *n* Sprung *m*. **skipping-
rope** *n* Hüpfseil *neut*.
skipper ['skipə] *n* (*coll*: *naut*) Kapitän *m*.
skirmish ['skəmiʃ] *n* Gefecht *neut*.
skirt [skət] *n* Rock *m*. *v* (*go around*)
herumgehen um. **skirting board** Wand-
leiste *f*.
skittle ['skitl] *n* Kegel *m*. **play skittles**
kegeln. **skittle alley** Kegelbahn *f*.
skull [skʌl] *n* Schädel *m*. **skull-cap** *n*
Käppchen *neut*.
skunk [skʌŋk] *n* Skunk *m*, Stinktier *neut*.
sky [skai] *n* Himmel *m*. **sky-blue** *adj* him-
melblau. **sky-high** *adj*, *adv* himmelhoch.
skylark *n* Lerche *f*. **skylight** *n* Dachfen-
ster *neut*. **skyscraper** *n* Hochhaus *neut*,
Wolkenkratzer *m*.
slab [slab] *n* (*stone*) (Stein)Platte *f*; (*chocolate*) Tafel *f*.
slack [slak] *adj* schlaff, locker; (*person*)
nachlässig; (*trade*) flau. **slacken** *v* lockern, entspannen; (*pace, etc.*) vermindern.
slackness *n* Schlaffheit *f*.
slacks [slaks] *pl n* Hose *f sing*.
slag [slag] *n* Schlacke *f*. **slagheap** *n* Halde
f.
slalom ['slaɪləm] *n* Slalom *m*.
slam [slam] *v* (*door*) zuknallen. *n* Knall
m.
slander ['slaɪndə] *n* Verleumdung *f*. *v*
verleumden. **slanderer** *n* Verleumder *m*.
slanderous *adj* verleumderisch.
slang [slaŋ] *n* Jargon *m*. *v* beschimpfen.
slant [slaɪnt] *n* Schräge *f*; (*attitude*) Einstellung *f*. *v* schräg liegen. **slant-eyed** *adj*

mit schräggestellten Augen. **slanting** *adj* schräg.

slap [slap] *v* klapsen, schlagen. *n* Klaps *m*, Schlag *m*. **slapdash** *adj* schlampig.

slash [slaʃ] *v* schlitzen, zerfetzen. *n* Schnitt *m*, Schlitz *m*.

slat [slat] *n* Latte *f*, Leiste *f*.

slate [sleit] *n* Schiefer *m*; (*writing*) Schiefertafel *f*; (*on roof*) Dachschiefer *m*. *v* (*coll*) heftig tadeln, kritisieren.

slaughter [ˈslɔːtə] *v* schlachten. *n* Schlachten *neut*. **slaughterhouse** *n* Schlachthaus *neut*. **slaughterer** *n* Schlächter *m*.

slave [sleiv] *n* Sklave *m*, Sklavin *f*. **slavedriver** *n* Leuteschinder *m*. *v* **slave away** schuften. **slavery** *n* Sklaverei *f*. **slavish** *adj* sklavisch.

sledge [sledʒ] *n* Schlitten *m*.

sledgehammer [ˈsledʒˌhamə] *n* Schmiedehammer *m*, Schlägel *m*.

sleek [sliːk] *adj* glatt. **sleekness** *n* Glätte *f*.

*sleep [sliːp] *v* schlafen; (*spend the night*) übernachten. *n* Schlaf *m*. **go to sleep** einschlafen. **sleeper** *n* Schläfer(in); (*railway*) Schwelle *f*. **sleeping bag** Schlafsack *m*. **sleeping car** Schlafwagen *m*. **sleepless** *adj* schlaflos. **sleeplessness** *n* Schlaflosigkeit *f*. **sleepwalker** *n* Nachtwandler *m*. **sleepy** *adj* schläfrig, müde.

sleet [sliːt] *n* Schneeregen *m*.

sleeve [sliːv] *n* Ärmel *m*. **sleeved** *adj* mit Ärmeln. **sleeveless** *adj* ärmellos.

sleigh [slei] *n* Schlitten *m*.

slender [ˈslendə] *adj* schlank, schmal. **slenderness** *n* Schlankheit *f*.

slept [slept] *V* sleep.

slice [slais] *n* Scheibe *f*, Schnitte *f*. *v* aufschneiden. **sliced** *adj* geschnitten, in Scheiben. **slicer** *n* Schneidemaschine *f*.

slick [slik] *adj* glatt; (*person*) raffiniert. **slicker** *n* Gauner *m*.

slid [slid] *V* slide.

*slide [slaid] *v* gleiten, rutschen. **slide rule** Rechenschieber *m*. **sliding door** Schiebetür *f*. **sliding scale** gleitende Skala *f*. *n* (*phot*) Dia(positiv) *neut*; (*playground*) Schlitterbahn *f*.

slight [slait] *adj* gering, unbedeutend, klein; (*person*) schmächtig, dünn. **not in the slightest** nicht im geringsten. *v* (*person*) kränken. *n* Beleidigung *f*. **slightly** *adv* leicht, ein bißchen.

slim [slim] *adj* schlank, dünn; (*chance, etc.*) gering. *v* eine Schlankheitskur machen, abnehmen. **slimness** *n* Schlankheit *f*.

slime [slaim] *n* Schleim *m*. **slimy** *adj* schleimig.

*sling [sliŋ] *n* (*weapon*) Schleuder *m*; (*arm*) Schlinge *f*. *v* schleudern.

*slink [sliŋk] *v* schleichen.

slip [slip] *n* Fehltritt *m*; (*underskirt*) Unterrock *m*. *v* gleiten, rutschen. **slip away** sich davonmachen. **slip off** (*clothes*) ausziehen. **slip on** (*clothes*) anziehen. **slip up** sich irren, sich vertun. **slipknot** *n* Laufknoten *m*. **slipshod** *adj* schlampig.

slipper [ˈslipə] *n* Pantoffel *m*.

slippery [ˈslipəri] *adj* schlüpfrig, glitschig; (*person*) aalglatt.

*slit [slit] *n* Schlitz *m*. *v* aufschlitzen. **slit-eyed** *adj* schlitzäugig.

slither [ˈsliðə] *v* rutschen, schlittern. **slithery** *adj* schlüpfrig.

slobber [ˈslobə] *v* sabbern, geifern. *n* Geifer *m*. **slobbery** *adj* sabbernd.

sloe [slou] *n* Schlehe *f*.

slog [slog] *v* hart schlagen; (*work hard*) schuften. *n* (harter) Schlag *m*.

slogan [ˈslougən] *n* Slogan *m*, Schlagwort *neut*.

slop [slop] *v* verschütten. *n* Pfütze *f*. **slops** *pl n* Abwasser *neut*.

slope [sloup] *n* Abhang *m*. *v* abfallen. **sloping** *adj* schräg.

sloppy [ˈslopi] *adj* matschig; (*slapdash*) schlampig. **sloppiness** *n* Matschigkeit *f*; Schlampigkeit *f*.

slot [slot] *n* Schlitz *m*; (*for coin*) Münzeinwurf *m*.

slouch [slautʃ] *v* latschen. **slouching** *adj* latschig.

slovenly [ˈslʌvnli] *adj* schlampig.

slow [slou] *adj* langsam; (*boring*) langweilig. *v* also **slow down** or **up** (sich) verlangsamen. **slow-down** *n* Verlangsamung *f*. **slow motion** Zeitlupentempo *neut*. **slowness** *n* Langsamkeit *f*; (*wits*) Schwerfälligkeit *f*.

sludge [slʌdʒ] *n* Schlamm *m*.

slug [slʌg] *n* Schnecke *f*.

sluggish [ˈslʌgiʃ] *adj* träge, schwerfällig; (*river*) langsam fließend. **sluggishness** *n* Schwerfälligkeit *f*.

sluice [sluːs] *n* Schleuse *f*. *v* ausspülen.

slums [slʌmz] *pl n* Elendsviertel *neut.*
slumber ['slʌmbə] *v* schlummern. *n*
Schlummer *m.*
slump [slʌmp] *v* hinplumpsen; (*prices*)
stürzen. *n* (*comm*) Geschäftsrückgang *m,*
Wirtschaftskrise *f.*
slung [slʌŋ] *V* sling.
slunk [slʌŋk] *V* slink.
slur [sləɪ] *v* (*words*) verschlucken, undeutlich aussprechen. *n* Vorwurf *m.*
slush [slʌʃ] *n* Matsch *m;* (*snow*)
Schneematsch *m;* (*sentimentality*)
Schmalz *m.* **slushy** *adj* matschig;
schmalzig.
slut [slʌt] *n* Schlampe *f.* **sluttish** *adj*
schlampig.
sly [slaɪ] *adj* schlau, hinterhältig. **slyness**
n Schlauheit *f.*
smack[1] [smak] *n* Klaps *m,* Klatsch *m.* *v*
schlagen, einen Klaps geben (+ *dat*).
smack[2] [smak] *n* (*flavour*) Geschmack *m.*
v schmecken (nach).
small [smɔɪl] *adj* klein; (*number, extent*)
gering. **small change** Kleingeld *neut.*
small talk Geplauder *neut.* **smallness** *n*
Kleinheit *f.*
smallpox ['smɔɪlpoks] *n* Pocken *pl.*
smart [smaɪt] *adj* schick, gepflegt; (*coll:
clever*) gescheit, raffiniert. **smart aleck**
(*coll*) Naseweis *m.* *v* (*suffer*) leiden.
smarten up zurechtmachen.
smash [smaʃ] *v* zerschmettern,
zerschlagen; (*enemy, etc.*) vernichten. *n*
(*mot*) Zusammenstoß *m.* **smash hit**
Bombenerfolg *m.* **smashing** *adj* (*coll*) toll,
sagenhaft.
smear [smɪə] *v* (be)schmieren. *n*
(*Schmutz*) Fleck *m;* (*med*) Abstrich *m.*
smear campaign Verleumdung-
skampagne *f.*
***smell** [smel] *n* Geruch *m;* (*pleasant*)
Duft *m.* *v* riechen. **smell of** riechen nach.
smelly *adj* übelriechend.
smelt [smelt] *V* smell.
smile [smaɪl] *v* lächeln. *n* Lächeln *neut.*
smiling *adj* lächelnd.
smirk [smɜɪk] *v* schmunzeln.
smock [smok] *n* Kittel *m.*
smog [smog] *n* Smog *m,* Rauchnebel *m.*
smoke [smouk] *v* rauchen; (*meat, fish*)
räuchern. *n* Rauch *m.* **smokescreen** *n*
Nebelvorhang *m.* **smokestack** *n* Schornstein *m.* **smoker** *n* Raucher(in); (*train*)
Raucherabteil *m.* **smoking** *n* Rauchen
neut. **no smoking** Rauchen verboten.

smooth [smuɪð] *adj* glatt. **smoothness** *n*
Glätte *f.* **smooth-tongued** *adj*
schmeichlerisch. *v* glätten.
smother ['smʌðə] *v* ersticken; (*with gifts,
etc.*) überhäufen.
smoulder ['smouldə] *v* schwelen.
smudge [smʌdʒ] *n* Schmutzfleck *m,*
Klecks *m.* *v* beschmutzen.
smug [smʌg] *adj* selbstgefällig.
smuggle ['smʌgl] *v* schmuggeln. **smuggler**
n Schmuggler *m.* **smuggling** *n* Schmuggel
m.
snack [snak] *n* Imbiß *m.* **snack bar**
Imbißstube *f.*
snag [snag] *n* (*difficulty*) Haken *m.*
snail [sneil] *n* Schnecke *f.* **at a snail's pace**
im Schneckentempo.
snake [sneik] *n* Schlange *f.*
snap [snap] *v* (*break*) (zer)brechen; (*dog*)
schnappen; (*noise*) knacken; (*phot*) knipsen. **snap at** (*person*) anschnauzen. **snap-
dragon** *n* Löwenmaul *neut.* **snap-fastener**
n Druckknopf *m.* **snapshot** *n* Schnapp-
schuß *m.* **snappy** *adj* (*coll*) schnell,
lebhaft.
snare [sneə] *n* Schlinge *f.* *v* fangen.
snare drum *n* Schnarrtrommel *f.*
snarl [snaɪl] *n* Knurren *neut.* *v* knurren.
snatch [snatʃ] *v* schnell ergreifen. **snatch
at** greifen nach.
sneak [sniɪk] *v* schleichen; (*tell tales*)
petzen. *n* Petzer *m.* **sneakers** *pl n* Turn-
schuhe *pl.* **sneaking** *adj* heimlich. **sneaky**
adj heimtückisch.
sneer [snɪə] *v* spötteln (über). *v* höhnisch
lächeln. *n* Hohnlächeln *neut.*
sneeze [sniɪz] *v* niesen. *n* Niesen *neut.*
sniff [snif] *v* schnüffeln. *n* Schnüffeln
neut.
snigger ['snigə] *v* kichern. *n* Kichern *neut.*
snip [snip] *v* schneiden. *n* Schnitt *m.*
snipe [snaip] *n* Schnepfe *f.* *v* aus dem
Hinterhalt schießen. **sniper** *n* Hecken-
schütze *m.*
snivel ['snivl] *v* wimmern. **snivelling** *adj*
weinerlich.
snob [snob] *n* Snob *m.* **snobbery** *n* Snob-
ismus *m.* **snobbish** *adj* snobistisch.
snooker ['snuɪkə] *n* Snooker *neut.*
snoop [snuɪp] *v* herumschnüffeln. *n*
Schnüffler *m.*
snooty ['snuɪti] *adj* hochnäsig.
snooze [snuɪz] *n* Nickerchen *neut.* *v* ein
Nickerchen machen.

snore [snɔɪ] v schnarchen. n Schnarchen neut.

snorkel ['snɔɪkəl] n Schnorchel m.

snort [snɔɪt] n Schnauben neut. v schnauben.

snout [snaut] n Schnauze f.

snow [snou] n Schnee m. **snowball** n Schneeball m; v (develop) lawinenartig anwachsen. **snowdrift** n. Schneewehe f. **snowdrop** n Schneeglöckchen neut. v schneien.

snub [snʌb] n Rüffel m, Verweis m. v rüffeln. adj stumpf.

snuff [snʌf] n Schnupftabak m. **take snuff** schnupfen.

snug [snʌg] adj gemütlich, bequem.

snuggle ['snʌgl] v sich schmiegen (an).

so [sou] adv so; (very) sehr. conj also, daher. **so that** damit. **so am/do I** ich auch. **so what?** na und? I think so ich glaube schon.

soak [souk] v durchtränken; (washing) einweichen. **soaking wet** triefend naß.

soap [soup] n Seife f. v (ein)seifen. **soapy** adj seifig. **soapy water** Seifenwasser neut.

soar [sɔɪ] v (fly up) hochfliegen; (rise) hoch aufsteigen.

sob [sob] v schluchzen. n Schluchzen neut.

sober ['soubə] adj nüchtern. v **sober up** nüchtern werden. **sobriety** n Nüchternheit f.

sociable ['souʃəbl] adj gesellig. **sociability** n Geselligkeit f.

social ['souʃəl] adj (animals) gesellig; (gathering) gesellschaftlich, gesellig; (of society) Gesellschafts-, Sozial-, gesellschaftlich. **social security** Sozialversicherung f. **social services** soziale Einrichtungen pl. **social worker** Sozialarbeiter(in). **socialism** n Sozialismus m. **socialist** n Sozialist(in).

society [sə'saiəti] n Gesellschaft f.

sociology [sousi'olədʒi] n Soziologie f. **sociological** adj soziologisch. **sociologist** n Soziologe m.

sock [sok] n Socke f.

socket ['sokit] n (elec) Steckdose f; (eye) Höhle f; (bone) Gelenkpfanne f.

soda ['soudə] n Soda; also **soda water** Soda(wasser) neut.

sodden ['sodn] adj durchnäßt.

sofa ['soufə] n Sofa neut.

soft [soft] adj weich; (voice, etc.) leise; (gentle) sanft, mild. **soften** v weich machen or werden; (water) enthärten. **soft-hearted** adj weichherzig.

soggy ['sogi] adj feucht.

soil¹ [soil] n Boden m, Erde f.

soil² [soil] n (dirt) Schmutz m. v beschmutzen.

solar ['soulə] adj Sonnen-.

sold [sould] V sell.

solder ['soldə] v löten. n Lot neut. **soldering iron** Lötkolben m.

soldier ['souldʒə] n Soldat m.

sole¹ [soul] adj (only) einzig, alleinig.

sole² [soul] n (of shoe) Sohle f. v besohlen.

sole³ [soul] n (fish) Seezunge f.

solemn ['soləm] adj feierlich; (person) ernst. **solemnity** n Feierlichkeit f.

solicitor [sə'lisitə] n (law) Anwalt m.

solicitous [sə'lisitəs] adj fürsorglich; (eager) eifrig.

solid ['solid] adj (not liquid) fest; (pure) massiv. **solidarity** n Solidarität f. **solidify** v fest werden.

solitary ['solitəri] adj (person) einsam; (single) einzeln.

solitude ['solitjuɪd] n Einsamkeit f.

solo ['soulou] n Solo neut. adj Solo-, Allein-. adv allein. **soloist** n Solist(in).

solstice ['solstis] n Sonnenwende f.

solve [solv] v lösen. **soluble** adj löslich; (problem) lösbar. **solution** n Lösung f. **solvent** n Lösungsmittel neut; adj (comm) zahlungsfähig.

sombre ['sombə] adj düster.

some [sʌm] adj (several) einige; (a little) etwas; (some ... or other) (irgend)ein; (approx.) ungefähr. **somebody** or **someone** pron jemand. **some day** eines Tages. **something** pron etwas. **sometime** adv irgendwann. **sometimes** adv manchmal. **somewhat** adv ziemlich. **somewhere** adv irgendwo(hin).

somersault ['sʌməsoɪlt] n Purzelbaum m. v (person) einen Purzelbaum schlagen; (thing) sich überschlagen.

son [sʌn] n Sohn m. **son-in-law** n Schwiegersohn m.

sonata [sə'naɪtə] n Sonata f.

song [soŋ] n Lied neut, Gesang m. **songbird** n Singvogel m.

sonic ['sonik] adj Schall-. **sonic barrier** Schallgrenze f.

sonnet ['sonit] n Sonett neut.

soon [suɪn] adv bald. **as soon as** sobald. **as soon as possible** so bald wie möglich. **sooner** adv früher.

soot [sut] *n* Ruß *m.* sooty *adj* rußig.
soothe [suːð] *v* beruhigen; *(pain)* lindern.
soothing *adj* lindernd, besänftigend.
sophisticated [səˈfistikeitid] *adj (person)* kultiviert; *(machinery, etc.)* kompliziert, hochentwickelt. sophistication *n* Kultiviertheit *f.*
sopping [ˈsopiŋ] *adj* patschnaß.
soprano [səˈprainou] *n* Sopranistin *f;* *(voice)* Sopran *m. adj* Sopran-.
sordid [ˈsoidid] *adj* schmutzig, gemein.
sore [soi] *adj* wund; *(inflamed)* entzündet; *(coll: annoyed)* verärgert. *n* Wunde *f.* sorely *adv* äußerst. soreness *n* Empfindlichkeit *f.*
sorrow [ˈsorou] *n* Kummer *m,* Leid *neut;* *(regret)* Reue *f.* sorrowful *adj* betrübt, traurig.
sorry [ˈsori] *adj* traurig, betrübt; *(sight, etc.)* jämmerlich, traurig. *interj* Verzeihung! *I am sorry* es tut mir leid. *I am/feel sorry for you* Sie tun mir leid.
sort [soit] *n* Sorte *f.* Art *f;* *(brand)* Marke *f.* all sorts of allerlei. a sort of eine Art. sort of *(coll)* gewissermaßen. that sort of thing so etwas. *v* sortieren.
soufflé [ˈsuflei] *n* Auflauf *m.*
sought [soit] *V* seek. sought-after *adj* gesucht.
soul [soul] *n* Seele *f.* not a soul kein Mensch. soul-destroying *adj* seelentötend. soulful *adj* seelenvoll. soulless *adj* seelenlos.
sound¹ [saund] *n* Schall *m;* *(noise)* Geräusch *neut,* Klang *m.* soundproof *adj* schalldicht. sound wave Schallwelle *f. v* klingen. sound the alarm den Alarm schlagen. sound the horn hupen. soundless *adj* geräuschlos.
sound² [saund] *adj (healthy)* gesund; *(safe)* sicher; *(reasoning)* stichhaltig.
sound³ [saund] *v* loten, sondieren.
soup [suip] *n* Suppe *f,* Brühe *f.*
sour [saua] *adj* sauer.
source [sois] *n* Quelle *f.*
south [sauθ] *n* Süden *m. adj also* southerly, southern südlich, Süd-. *adv also* southwards nach Süden, südwärts. South America Sudamerika *neut.* south-east *n* Südosten. South Pole Südpol *m.* southwest *n* Südwesten *m.*
souvenir [suivəˈniə] *n* Andenken *neut.*
sovereign [ˈsovrin] *n* Souverän *m. adj* souverän. sovereignty *n* Souveränität *f.*
Soviet Union [ˈsouviət] *n* Sowjetunion *f.*

*sow¹ [sou] *v* säen; *(field)* besäen. sower *n* Säer *m.*
sow² [sau] *n* Sau *f.*
sown [soun] *V* sow¹.
soya [ˈsoiə] *n* Sojabohne *f.*
spa [spai] *n* Badekurort *m.*
space [speis] *n* Raum *m;* *(gap)* Zwischenraum *m,* Abstand *m;* *(astron)* Weltraum *m.* space flight Raumflug *m* spaceship *n* Raumschiff *neut. v* (räumlich) einteilen. spacious *adj* geräumig.
spade¹ [speid] *n* Spaten *m.* spadework *n* *(fig)* Vorarbeit *f.*
spade² [speid] *n (cards)* Pik *neut.*
Spain [spein] *n* Spanien *neut.* Spaniard *n* Spanier(in). Spanish *adj* spanisch.
span [span] *n (arch)* Spannweite *f;* *(time)* Zeitspanne *f.*
spaniel [ˈspanjəl] *n* Spaniel *m.*
spank [spaŋk] *v* verhauen, prügeln.
spanner [ˈspanə] *n* Schraubenschlüssel *m.*
spare [speə] *adj* Ersatz-; *(over)* übrig; *(thin)* hager, dürr. spare time Freizeit *f.* spare tyre Ersatzreifen *m.* spare rib Rippenspeer *m. v (pains, expense)* scheuen; *(give)* übrig haben (für); *(feelings, etc.)* verschonen. sparing *adj* sparsam. *n also* spare part Ersatzteil *m.*
spark [spaik] *n* Funke *m. v* funkeln. spark *or* sparking plug Zündkerze *f.*
sparkle [ˈspaikl] *v* funkeln, glänzen. *n* Funkeln *neut,* Glanz *m.* sparkler *n* Wunderkerze *f.* sparkling *adj* funkelnd; *(wine)* schäumend.
sparrow [ˈsparou] *n* Spatz *m,* Sperling *m.*
sparse [spais] *adj* spärlich, dünn. sparseness *n* Spärlichkeit *f.*
spasm [ˈspazəm] *n (med)* Krampf *m;* *(fig)* Anfall *m.* spasmodic *adj (fig)* sprunghaft.
spastic [ˈspastik] *adj* spastisch. *n* Spastiker(in).
spat [spat] *V* spit¹.
spatial [ˈspeiʃl] *adj* räumlich.
spatula [ˈspatjulə] *n* Spachtel *m.*
spawn [spoin] *n* Laich *m. v (eggs)* ablegen; *(fig)* hervorbringen.
*speak [spiik] *v* sprechen, reden. speak out frei herausreden. speak to reden mit. speak up laut sprechen. speak up for sich einsetzen für. speaker *n* Redner *m.*
spear [spiə] *n* Speer *m. v* aufspießen.
special [ˈspeʃəl] *adj* besonder, speziell; *(train, case)* Sonder-. specialist *n* Fachmann *m.* speciality *n* Spezialität *f.* specialization *n* Spezialisierung *f.* special-

ize v spezialisieren. **specially** adv besonders.

species ['spiːʃiːz] n Art f; (biol) Spezies f.

specify ['spesifai] v spezifizieren, im einzeln angeben. **specific** adj spezifisch. **specifications** n pl (tech) technische Daten pl.

specimen ['spesimin] n Muster neut, Probe f.

speck [spek] n Fleck m. **speckle** v flecken.

spectacle ['spektəkl] n Schauspiel neut. **spectacles** pl Brille f sing. **spectacular** adj sensationell.

spectator [spek'teitə] n Zuschauer(in).

spectrum ['spektrəm] n Spektrum neut.

speculate ['spekjuleit] v nachdenken; (comm) spekulieren. **speculation** n Mutmaßung f, Annahme f; (comm) Spekulation f. **speculative** adj spekulativ. **speculator** n Spekulant m.

sped [sped] V **speed**.

speech [spiːtʃ] n Sprache f; (a talk) Rede f. **make a speech** eine Rede halten.

***speed** [spiːd] n Geschwindigkeit f, Tempo neut. v rasen, eilen; (exceed limit) (zu) schnell fahren. **speed up** beschleunigen. **speed limit** Geschwindigkeitsbegrenzung f. **speedboat** n Schnellboot neut. **speedometer** n Tachometer m. **speedy** adj schnell.

***spell**[1] [spel] v (name the letters in) buchstabieren; (signify) bedeuten. **how do you spell ... ?** wie schreibt man ... ? **spell out** (fig) deutlich erklären. **spelling** n Rechtschreibung f.

spell[2] [spel] n (magic) Zauber m, Zauberspruch m. **cast a spell on** bezaubern. **spellbound** adj fasziniert.

spell[3] [spel] n (period) Periode f, Weile f. **spelt** [spelt] V **spell**[1].

***spend** [spend] v (money) ausgeben; (time) verbringen. **spending money** Taschengeld neut. **spendthrift** n Verschwender(in); adj verschwenderisch.

spent [spent] V **spend**.

sperm [spəːm] n Sperma neut. **sperm whale** n Pottwal m.

spew [spjuː] v (vulgar) sich erbrechen, kotzen. **spew out** ausspeien.

sphere [sfiə] n Kugel f; (fig) Bereich m. **spherical** adj kugelförmig.

spice [spais] n Gewürz neut. v würzen. **spiced** adj gewürzt. **spicy** adj pikant, scharf.

spider ['spaidə] n Spinne f. **spider's web** Spinngewebe neut. **spidery** adj spinnenartig.

spike [spaik] n Spitze f, Dorn m.

***spill** [spil] v verschütten; (blood) vergießen. n (coll) Sturz, Fall m. **spilt** [spilt] V **spill**.

***spin** [spin] v (thread, web) spinnen; (turn) (herum)wirbeln, spinnen; (washing) schleudern. n (coll: in car, etc.) Spazierfahrt f. **spin-dryer** n Wäscheschleuder f. **spinning wheel** Spinnrad neut.

spinach ['spinidʒ] n Spinat m.

spindle ['spindl] n Spindel f. **spindly** adj spindeldürr.

spine [spain] n (thorn, etc.) Stachel m; (anat) Rückgrat neut, Wirbelsäule f. **spiny** adj stachelig.

spinster ['spinstə] n unverheiratete Frau f; (elderly) alte Jungfer f.

spiral ['spaiərəl] adj schraubenförmig, spiral. **spiral staircase** Wendeltreppe f. n Spirale f.

spire ['spaiə] n Turmspitze f.

spirit ['spirit] n Geist m. **spirits** pl (drinks) Spirituosen pl, Alkohol m. **high spirits** Frohsinn m, gehobene Stimmung f. v **spirit away** hinwegzaubern. **spirited** adj lebhaft. **spiritual** adj geistig, geistlich.

***spit**[1] [spit] n (saliva) Spucke f, Speichel m. v spucken.

spit[2] [spit] n (roasting) (Brat)Spieß m; (geog) Landzunge f.

spite [spait] n Boshaftigkeit f. **in spite of** trotz (+gen). **spiteful** adj boshaft.

splash [splaʃ] v (be)spritzen. n Spritzen neut; (mark) Fleck m.

spleen [spliːn] n Milz f.

splendid ['splendid] adj prächtig, herrlich. **splendour** n Pracht f.

splice [splais] v (ropes) spleißen; (tapes, films) zusammenfügen.

splint [splint] n Schiene f. **splinter** n Splitter m. v zersplittern. **splinter group** Splittergruppe f.

***split** [split] v (zer)spalten, sich spalten. **split up** sich trennen. **split hairs** Haarspalterei treiben. **splitting headache** rasende Kopfschmerzen pl. n Spalt m, Riß m. adj gespalten.

splutter ['splʌtə] v stottern.

***spoil** [spoil] v verderben; (child) verwöhnen. **spoils** pl n Beute f. **spoilsport** n Spielverderber(in).

spoke[1] [spouk] V **speak**.
spoke[2] [spouk] n (wheel) Speiche f.
spoken ['spoukn] V **speak**.
spokesman ['spouksmən] n Sprecher m.
sponge [spʌndʒ] n Schwamm m. v **sponge down** (mit einem Schwamm) abwaschen. **sponge-cake** n Sandtorte f. **sponger** n (coll) Schmarotzer m. **spongy** adj schwammig.
sponsor ['sponsə] n Förderer m, Schirmherr m; (radio, TV) Sponsor m. v unterstützen, fördern. **sponsorship** n Schirmherrschaft f.
spontaneous [spon'teinjəs] adj spontan. **spontaneity** n Freiwilligkeit f, Spontaneität f.
spool [spuːl] n Spule f.
spoon [spuːn] n Löffel m. v **spoon out** auslöffeln. **spoon-feed** v verhätscheln. **spoonful** n Löffelvoll m.
sporadic [spə'radik] adj verstreut, sporadisch.
sport [spoːt] n Sport m; (fun) Spaß m. **play sports** Sport treiben. **sportscar** n Sportwagen m. **sportsman** n Sportler m. **sportswoman** n Sportlerin f. v scherzen; (wear) tragen. **sporting** adj sportlich.
spot [spot] n (mark) Fleck m; (place) Stelle f; (pimple) Pickel m. **spot check** Stichprobe f. **spotlight** n Scheinwerfer m. **spotless** adj fleckenlos. v beflecken; (notice) entdecken, erspähen. **spotted** adj fleckig. **spotty** adj pickelig.
spouse [spaus] n Gatte m, Gattin f, Gemahl(in).
spout [spaut] n Tülle f, Schnauze f. v (coll) deklamieren.
sprain [sprein] n Verrenkung f. v verrenken.
sprang [spraŋ] V **spring**.
sprawl [sproːl] v (person) sich rekeln; (town) sich ausbreiten.
spray[1] [sprei] v (be)sprühen. n (aerosol, etc.) Sprühdose f, Spray m; (sea) Schaum m.
spray[2] [sprei] n (of flowers) Blütenzweig m.
*spread [spred] v ausbreiten; (butter, etc.) streichen; (rumour) (sich) verbreiten. n Ausbreitung f; (extent) Umfang m, Spanne f; (for bread) Aufstrich m.
spree [spriː] n (shopping) Einkaufsbummel m.
sprig [sprig] n Schößling m.

sprightly ['spraitli] adj lebhaft, munter.
*spring [spriŋ] n (season) Frühling m; (tech) Feder f; (water) Brunnen m, Quelle f. **springboard** n Sprungbrett neut. v springen. **spring a leak** ein Leck bekommen. **springing** n Federung f. **springy** adj elastisch.
sprinkle ['spriŋkl] v sprenkeln. **sprinkler** n Brause f. **a sprinkling of** ein bißchen.
sprint [sprint] n Sprint m. v sprinten. **sprinter** n Sprinter m.
sprout [spraut] v sprießen. n Sprößling m. (Brussels) **sprouts** Rosenkohl m sing.
spruce [spruːs] n (tree) Fichte f.
sprung [sprʌŋ] V **spring**.
spur [spəː] n Sporn m; (fig) Ansporn m. v (horse) die Sporen geben (+dat); (fig) anspornen.
spurious ['spjuəriəs] adj falsch, unecht.
spurn [spəːn] v zurückweisen.
spurt [spəːt] v (water) hervorspritzen. n (sport) Spurt m.
spy [spai] v (espy) erspähen; (pol) spionieren. n Spion(in). **spy-glass** n Fernglas neut. **spying** n Spionage f.
squabble ['skwobl] v sich zanken. n Kabbelei f, Zank m.
squad [skwod] n Gruppe f; (mil) Zug m; (police) Kommando neut. **flying squad** Überfallkommando neut. **squad car** Streifenwagen m.
squadron ['skwodrən] n (naut) Geschwader neut; (aero) Staffel f. **squadron leader** Major m.
squalid ['skwolid] adj schmutzig. **squalor** n Schmutz m.
squall [skwoːl] n heftiger Windstoß m; (storm) Gewitter neut.
squander ['skwondə] v verschwenden, vergeuden.
square [skweə] n Quadrat neut, Viereck neut; (in town) Platz m. adj viereckig, quadratisch.
squash [skwoʃ] n (people) Gedränge neut; (game) Squash neut. v zerquetschen. **fruit squash** Fruchtsaft m.
squat [skwot] v hocken; (ein Haus) unberechtigt besetzen. adj gedrungen. **squatter** n Squatter m.
squawk [skwoːk] n Kreischen neut. v kreischen.
squeak [skwiːk] v (wheel, etc.) quietschen; (mouse, etc.) piepsen. n Quietschen neut; Piepsen neut. **squeaky** adj quietschend.

squeal [skwiːl] v schreien, quieken; (criminal) pfeifen. n Schrei m, Quieken neut.

squeamish ['skwiːmiʃ] adj überempfindlich. **squeamishness** n Überempfindlichkeit f.

squeeze [skwiːz] v drücken; (fruit) auspressen, ausquetschen. n Druck m. **credit squeeze** Kreditbeschränkung f. **squeezer** n Presse f.

squid [skwid] n Tintenfisch m.

squiggle ['skwigl] n Kritzelei f.

squint [skwint] n Schielen neut. v schielen. **squint-eyed** adj schielend.

squire ['skwaiə] n Junker m, Gutsherr m.

squirm [skwəːm] v sich winden.

squirrel ['skwirəl] n Eichhörnchen neut.

squirt [skwəːt] v spritzen. n Spritze f.

stab [stab] v (kill) erstechen. n Stich m. **stab wound** Stichwunde f. **make a stab at** versuchen.

stabilize ['steibilaiz] v stabilisieren. **stability** n Stabilität f. **stabilization** n Stabilisierung f.

stable[1] ['steibl] n Stall m. v einstallen. **stable-lad/man** n Stallknecht m.

stable[2] ['steibl] adj stabil.

staccato [stə'kaːtou] adj, adv staccato.

stack [stak] n Schober m; (wood, etc.) Stapel m. v aufschobern.

stadium ['steidiəm] n Stadion neut.

staff [staːf] n (stick) Stock m; (work force) Personal neut; (mil) Stab m. adj Personal-; stabs-.

stag [stag] n Rothirsch m. **stag party** Herrengesellschaft f.

stage [steidʒ] n (of development, etc.) Stufe f, Stadium neut; (theatre) Bühne. **stage fright** Lampenfieber neut. **stage-manager** n Inspizient m. v (play) aufführen; (fig) veranstalten.

stagger ['stagə] v schwanken, taumeln; (amaze) verblüffen. **staggering** adj taumelnd; phantastisch.

stagnant ['stagnənt] adj stillstehend, stagnierend. **stagnate** v stagnieren. **stagnation** n Stagnation f.

staid [steid] adj gesetzt, seriös.

stain [stein] adj Fleck m; (for wood, etc.) Färbung f. v beflecken; färben. **stainless** adj (steel) rostfrei.

stair [steə] n Treppenstufe f. (flight of) **stairs** Treppe f. **stair-carpet** n Treppenläufer m.

stake[1] [steik] n (post) Pfahl m, Pfosten m.

stake a claim (to) Anspruch erheben (auf).

stake[2] [steik] n (betting) Einsatz m; (share) Anteil m. v (money) setzen. **put at stake** aufs Spiel setzen.

stale [steil] adj (bread) alt, altbacken; (beer, etc.) abgestanden; (thing) abgedroschen.

stalemate ['steilmeit] n (chess) Patt neut; (fig) Stillstand m. v pattsetzen.

stalk[1] [stɔːk] n (bot) Stiel m.

stalk[2] [stɔːk] v sich anpirschen an.

stall[1] [stɔːl] n (stable) Stand m; (market) Bude f. **stalls** pl (theatre) Parkett neut sing. v (engine) aussetzen; (car) stehenbleiben.

stall[2] [stɔːl] v (delay) ausweichen, Ausflüchte machen.

stallion ['staljən] n Hengst m.

stamina ['staminə] n Durchhaltevermögen neut, Ausdauer f.

stammer ['stamə] v stottern, stammeln. n Stottern neut, Gestammel neut. **stammerer** n Stotterer m. **stammering** adj stotternd.

stamp [stamp] v (with foot) stampfen; (rubber stamp) stempeln; (letters) frankieren. n Stempel m; (letter) Briefmarke f. **stamp album** Briefmarkenalbum neut. **stamp collector** Briefmarkensammler m.

stampede [stam'piːd] n wilde Flucht f.

*****stand** [stand] n (sales, etc.) Bude f, Stand m; (attitude) Standpunkt m; (for spectators) (Zuschauer)Tribüne f; (resistance) Widerstand m. v stehen. I can't stand him ich kann ihn nicht ausstehen. I can't stand it ich kann es nicht aushalten. **as things stand** unter den Umständen. **my offer stands** mein Angebot gilt noch. **stand aside** beiseite treten. **stand back** zurücktreten. **stand by** (be loyal to) treu bleiben (+ dat). **stand for** (mean) bedeuten, stehen für; (tolerate) sich gefallen lassen; (parliament) kandidieren. **stand in for** einspringen für. **stand up** aufstehen. **stand up to** sich verteidigen gegen. **standby** n Stütze f; (alert) Alarmbereitschaft f. **standing** n Stand m, Rang m. **standing order** (bank) Dauerauftrag m. **stand-offish** adj hochmütig.

standard ['standəd] n Standard m, Norm f. (flag) Standarte f. adj Normal-; (usual) gewöhnlich, normal. **standardize** v

normen, standardisieren. **standardization**
n Normung *f*.
stank [stæŋk] *V* stink.
stanza ['stænzə] *n* Strophe *f*, Stanza *f*.
staple[1] [steipl] *n* Heftklammer *f*. *v* heften.
stapler *n* Heftmaschine *f*.
staple[2] [steipl] *adj* Haupt-.
star [staɪ] *n* Stern *m*; (*films, etc.*) Star *m*.
starlight *n* Sternenlicht *neut*. *v* die Hauptrolle spielen. **starring** in der Hauptrolle.
starry *adj* (*sky*) Sternen ; (*night*)
sternhell.
starboard ['staɪbəd] *n* Steuerbord *neut*.
adj Steuerbord-.
starch [staɪtʃ] *n* (Wäsche)Stärke *f*. *v*
stärken. **starched** *adj* gestärkt. **starchy**
adj (*person*) steif, förmlich.
stare [steə] *n* starrer Blick *m*, Starrblick
m. *v* starren. **stare at** anstarren.
stark [staɪk] *adj* kahl, öde. *adv* **stark
naked** splitternackt. **stark-staring mad**
total verrückt.
starling ['staɪliŋ] *n* Star *m*.
start [staɪt] *v* anfangen, beginnen; (*leave*)
abfahren; (*arise*) entstehen; (*sport*)
starten (lassen); (*engine*) anlassen;
(*jump*) hochschrecken. *n* Anfang *m*,
Beginn *m*; (*sport*) Start *m*; (*journey*)
Abreise *f*. **from the start** vom Anfang an.
starter *n* (*sport*) Starter *m*. **starter motor**
Anlaßmotor *m*.
startle ['staɪtl] *v* erschrecken, überraschen.
startling *adj* erschreckend.
starve [staɪv] *v* verhungern. **starvation** *n*
Hungern *neut*, Verhungern *neut*.
state [steit] *n* (*pol*) Staat *m*; (*condition*)
Zustand *m*; (*situation*) Lage *f*. *v* erklären,
behaupten. *adj* Staats-, staatlich. **stated**
adj angegeben. **stateless** *adj* staatenlos.
stately *adj* stattlich. **statement** *n*
Erklärung *f*. **statement of account**
Kontoauszug *m*. **statesman** *n* Staatsmann
m. **statesmanship** *n* Staatskunst *f*.
static ['stætik] *adj* statisch. *n* statische
Elektrizität *f*.
station ['steiʃən] *n* Platz *m*, Posten *m*;
(*rail*) Bahnhof *m*; (*standing*) Stand *m*.
station master Bahnhofsvorsteher *m*. **station wagon** Kombi(wagen) *m*. *v* station-
ieren.
stationary ['steiʃənəri] *adj* stillstehend,
stationär.
stationer ['steiʃənə] *n* Schreibwarenhänd-
ler *m*. **stationery** *n* Schreibwaren *pl*;
(*office*) Büromaterial *neut*.

statistics [stə'tistiks] *n* Statistik *f*. **statistical** *adj* statistisch.
statue ['stætjuɪ] *n* Standbild *neut*, Statue *f*.
stature ['stætʃə] *n* Körpergröße *f*, Statur *f*;
(*moral, etc.*) Kaliber *neut*.
status ['steitəs] *n* Status *m*; (*rank*) Stand
m, Rang *m*. **status quo** Status quo *m*.
status symbol Statussymbol *neut*.
statute ['stætjuɪt] *n* Gesetz *neut*. **statutory**
adj gesetzlich (vorgeschrieben).
staunch [stɔɪntʃ] *adj* getreu, zuverlässig.
stay [stei] *v* bleiben; (*in hotel*) logieren,
unterkommen; (*with friends, etc.*) zu
Besuch sein (bei). **stay the night**
übernachten. **stay behind** zurückbleiben.
stay in zu Hause bleiben. *n* Aufenthalt
m; Besuch *m*.
steadfast ['stedfaɪst] *adj* fest, treu.
steady ['stedi] *adj* sicher, fest, stabil; (*regular*) regelmäßig, gleichmäßig; (*cautious*)
vorsichtig. *v* festigen. **steady on!** langsam!, vorsichtig! **steadiness** *n* Festigkeit
f, Sicherheit *f*.
steak [steik] *n* Steak *neut*.
*steal [stiɪl] *v* stehlen. **steal away** sich
davonstehlen.
stealthy ['stelθi] *adj* heimlich. **stealth** *n*
Heimlichkeit *f*.
steam [stiɪm] *n* Dampf *m*. *v* dampfen;
(*food*) dünsten. **steam-boiler** *n*
Dampfkessel *m*. **steamer** *n* (*naut*)
Dampfer *m*, Dampfschiff *neut*; (*cookery*)
Dampfkochtopf *m*. **steam-roller** *n*
Dampfwalze *f*; *v* (*opposition*)
niederwalzen. **steamy** *adj* dampfig.
steel [stiɪl] *n* Stahl *m*. *adj* stählern, Stahl-.
steelworks *pl* *n* Stahlwerk *neut* *sing*.
steely *adj*.
steep[1] [stiɪp] *adj* steil, jäh; (*coll: improbable*) unwahrscheinlich; (*prices*) gepfeffert.
steep[2] [stiɪp] *v* (*soak*) einweichen.
steeple ['stiɪpl] *n* Kirchturm *m*, Spitzturm
m.
steeplechase ['stiɪpltʃeis] *n* Steeplechase *f*.
steeplejack *n* Turmarbeiter *m*.
steer [stiə] *v* steuern, lenken. **steering column** Lenksäule *f*. **steering lock** Len-
kradschloß *m*. **steering wheel** Lenkrad
neut, Steuer *neut*.
stem[1] [stem] *n* (*stalk*) Stiel *m*; (*line of
descent*) Stamm *m*. *v* **stem from** stammen
von, zurückgehen auf.
stem[2] [stem] *v* eindämmen; (*blood*) stillen.

stench [stentʃ] *n* Gestank *m*.
stencil ['stensl] *n* Schablone *f*. *v* schablonieren.
step [step] *v* treten, schreiten. *n* Schritt *m*; (*measure*) Maßnahme *f*; (*stage, gradation*) Stufe *f*. **step by step** Schritt für Schritt. **step on it** (*coll*) Gas geben. **step aside** zur seite treten. **step-ladder** *n* Trittleiter *f*. **stepping-stone** *n* Trittstein *m*; (*fig*) Sprungbrett *neut*.
stepbrother ['stepbrʌðə] *n* Stiefbruder *m*.
stepdaughter ['stepdɔ:tə] *n* Stieftochter *f*.
stepfather ['stepfɑːðə] *n* Stiefvater *m*.
stepmother ['stepmʌðə] *n* Stiefmutter *f*.
stepsister ['stepsɪstə] *n* Stiefschwester *f*.
stepson ['stepsʌn] *n* Stiefsohn *m*.
stereo ['steriou] *n* Stereoanlage *f*. *adj* Stereo-. **stereophonic** *adj* stereophonisch.
stereotyped ['steriətaipt] *adj* stereotyp.
sterile ['sterail] *adj* steril. **sterility** *n* Sterilität *f*.
sterling ['stə:lɪŋ] *n* Sterling *m*.
stern[1] [stə:n] *adj* streng, hart. **sternness** *n* Strenge *f*. Härte *f*.
stern[2] [stə:n] *n* (*naut*) Heck *neut*.
stethoscope ['steθəskoup] *n* Stethoskop *neut*.
stew [stju:] *n* Eintopfgericht *neut*. *v* schmoren. **stewed** *adj* geschmort.
steward ['stjuəd] *n* (*ship, aeroplane*) Steward *m*; (*race, etc.*) Ordner *m*. **stewardess** *n* Stewardeß *f*.
stick[1] [stik] *n* (*wood*) Stock *m*; (*hockey*) Schläger *m*.
*stick[2] [stik] *v* (*with glue, etc.*) kleben *or* heften (an); (*pointed instrument*) stecken; **stick out** (*tongue*) herausstrecken; (*protrude*) hervorstehen. **stick to** (*remain with*) bleiben bei. **stick up for** sich einsetzen für. **be stuck** steckenbleiben. **stuck-up** *adj* hochnäsig. **sticking plaster** Heftpflaster *neut*. **sticky** *adj* klebrig.
stiff [stif] *adj* steif, starr; (*drink*) stark; (*difficult*) schwierig. *n* (*coll*) Leiche *f*. **stiffen** *v* (ver)steifen, (ver)stärken. **stiffnecked** *adj* halsstarrig. **stiffness** *n* Steife *f*, Starrheit *f*.
stifle ['staifl] *v* ersticken. **stifling** *adj* zum Ersticken.
stigma ['stigmə] *n* Brandmal *neut*, Stigma *neut*.
stile [stail] *n* Zauntritt *m*.
still[1] [stil] *adj* still. *adv* (immer)noch. *conj* und doch, dennoch. *v* beruhigen. **still**

birth Totgeburt *f*. **stillborn** *adj* totgeboren. **stillness** *n* Stille *f*.
still[2] [stil] *n* (*for spirits*) Brennerei *f*.
stilt [stilt] *n* Stelze *f*. **stilted** *adj* gespreizt.
stimulus ['stimjuləs] *n* (*pl* **-i**) Stimulus *m*. **stimulant** *n* Reizmittel *neut*. **stimulate** *v* anregen. **stimulating** *adj* anregend. **stimulation** *n* Anreiz *m*.
*sting [stiŋ] *v* (*insect*) stechen; (*be painful*) brennen; (*remark*) kränken. *n* Stich *m*. **stinging** *adj* brennend; schmerzend. **stinging nettle** Brennessel *f*.
stingy ['stindʒi] *adj* geizig.
*stink [stiŋk] *v* stinken, übel riechen. *n* Gestank *m*; (*coll: scandal*) Skandal *m*.
stint [stint] *v* knausern mit. *n* (*of work*) Schicht *f*.
stipulate ['stipjuleit] *v* festsetzen; (*insist on*) bestehen auf. **stipulation** Bedingung *f*.
stir [stə:] *v* (*liquids*) (an)rühren; (*move*) sich rühren *or* bewegen; (*excite*) aufrühren, bewegen. *n* Rühren *neut*; (*sensation*) Sensation *f*. **stirring** *adj* aufregend.
stirrup ['stirəp] *n* Steigbügel *m*.
stitch [stitʃ] *n* Stich *m*; (*knitting*) Masche *f*; (*pain*) Stechen *m*. *v* nähen. **stitch up** vernähen. **stitching** *n* Näherei *f*.
stoat [stout] *n* Hermelin *neut*.
stock [stɔk] *n* (*of goods*) Vorrat *m*, Lager *neut*; (*cookery*) Brühe; (*descent*) Stamm *m*. **stocks** *pl* (*comm*) Aktien *pl*. **stockbroker** *n* Börsenmakler *m*. **stock exchange** Börse *f*. **stockpile** *v* aufstapeln. **stock-still** *adj* bewegungslos. **stocktaking** *n* Bestandaufnahme *f*. *v* (*goods*) führen, vorrätig haben.
stocking ['stɔkiŋ] *n* Strumpf *m*.
stocky ['stɔki] *adj* stämmig, untersetzt.
stodge [stɔdʒ] *n* schwerverdauliches Zeug *neut*. **stodgy** *adj* schwer(verdaulich).
stoical ['stouikl] *adj* stoisch.
stoke [stouk] *v* schüren. **stoker** *n* Heizer *m*.
stole[1] [stoul] *V* steal.
stole[2] [stoul] *n* Stola *f*.
stolen ['stoulən] *V* steal.
stomach ['stʌmək] *n* Magen *m*; (*coll: abdomen*) Bauch *m*; (*taste for*) Appetit (zu) *f*. *v* ertragen. **stomach-ache** *n* Magenschmerzen *pl*.
stone [stoun] *n* Stein *m*; (*fruit*) Kern *m*. *adj* steinern, Stein-. *v* (*fruit*) entkernen; (*to death*) steinigen. **stone age** Steinzeit *f*.

stoned adj (coll) besoffen. **stone-deaf** adj stocktaub. **stonemason** n Steinmetz m. **stony** adj steinig.
stood [stud] V **stand**.
stool [stuɪl] n Hocker m, Stuhl m; (med) Stuhlgang m.
stoop [stuɪp] v sich bücken; (posture) gebeugt gehen. n Beugen neut, krumme Haltung f.
stop [stop] v (activity) aufhören; (motion) anhalten, stoppen; (clock) stehenbleiben; (put a stop to) einstellen; (bus, train) anhalten; (pipe, etc.) verstopfen. n Halt m, Stillstand m; (break) Pause f; (bus) Haltestelle f. **stoppage** n Stillstand m. **stopper** n Stöpsel m. **stop-watch** n Stoppuhr f.
store [stoɪ] v aufbewahren. n Vorrat m, Lager neut; (shop) Laden m. **storage** n Lagerung f. **storekeeper** n (shop) Ladenbesitzer m.
storey ['stoɪri] n Stockwerk neut. **four-storied** adj vierstöckig.
stork [stoɪk] n Storch m.
storm [stoɪm] n Sturm m, Unwetter neut; (thunderstorm) Gewitter neut. **storm-tossed** adj sturmgepeitscht. v stürmen. **storm-troops** Sturmtruppen pl. **stormy** adj stürmisch.
story ['stoɪri] n Geschichte f, Erzählung f. **to cut a long story short** um es ganz kurz zu sagen. **story-book** n Märchenbuch neut. **story-teller** n Erzähler(in).
stout [staut] adj dick, beleibt; (strong) kräftig. n dunkles Bier neut, Malzbier neut.
stove [stouv] n Ofen m; (cooking) Kochherd m. **stove-pipe** Ofenrohr neut.
stow [stou] v verstauen. **stowaway** blinder Passagier m.
straddle ['stradl] v (sitting) rittlings sitzen auf.
straggle ['stragl] v umherstreifen. **straggle behind** nachhinken. **straggler** n Nachzügler m.
straight [streit] adj gerade; (hair) glatt; (candid) offen, freimütig. adv gerade, direkt. **get straight** (clarify) klarstellen. **think straight** logisch denken. **straight on** or **ahead** gerade aus. **straightaway** adv sofort. **straighten** v gerademachen. **straighten out** (put in order) in Ordnung bringen. **straightforward** adj (thing) einfach, schlicht; (person) offen, aufrichtig. n (sport) Gerade f.

strain¹ [strein] v spannen; (muscle) zerren; (tech) verzerren; (filter) sieben, filtern. **strain oneself** sich (über)anstrengen. n Überanstrengung f; (emotional) Streß m, Anspannung f; (med) Zerrung. **strained** adj (relations, etc.) gespannt.
strain² [strein] n (race) Abstammung f, Rasse f.
straits [streits] pl n Straße f, Meerenge f. **dire straits** Notlage f. **strait-jacket** n Zwangsjacke f.
strand¹ [strand] n (rope) Strang m; (hair) Strähne f, (thought) Faden m.
strand² [strand] n (shore) Strand m, Ufer neut. v stranden. **stranded** adj gestrandet.
strange [streindʒ] adj (odd) seltsam, sonderbar; (alien) fremd. **strangeness** n Seltsamkeit f; Fremdartigkeit f. **stranger** n Fremde(r). **be a stranger to** nicht vertraut sein mit. **strangely** adv seltsamerweise.
strangle ['strangl] v erwürgen, erdrosseln. **strangulation** n Würgen m.
strap [strap] n Riemen m; (dress) Träger m. v festschnallen. **strapless** adj trägerlos. **strapping** adj stramm.
strategy ['stratədʒi] n Strategie f. **strategic** adj strategisch.
stratum ['straitəm] n (pl -a) Schicht f.
straw [stroɪ] n Stroh neut; (single) Strohhalm m; (drinking) Trinkhalm m. adj Stroh-. **straw hat** Strohhut m.
strawberry ['stroɪbəri] n Erdbeere f.
stray [strei] v sich verirren; (from path, etc.) abgehen (von); (attention) wandern. adj verirrt. n verirrtes Tier neut.
streak [striɪk] n Streifen neut; (in character) Einschlag m. **streak of lightning** Blitzstrahl m. v streifen; (race, fly) rasen, sausen. **streaked** adj gestreift.
stream [striɪm] n Bach m; (current) Strom m, Strömung f. v strömen. **streamer** n (party) Papierschlange f. **streamline** v (fig) rationalisieren. **streamlined** adj windschnittig.
street [striɪt] n Straße f. **streetcar** n Straßenbahn f. **street lamp** Straßenlaterne f. **street-walker** n Straßendirne f.
strength [streŋθ] n Stärke f, Kraft f, Kräfte pl; (liquids) Stärke f; (mil) Macht f, Schlagkraft f. **strengthen** v (ver)stärken. **strengthening** n Verstärkung f.

strenuous ['strenjuəs] *adj* anstrengend.

stress [stres] *n (emphasis)* Nachdruck *m*; *(psychological)* Streß *m*; *(pronunciation)* Akzent *m*. *v* betonen. **stressful** *adj* belastend.

stretch [stretʃ] *v* (aus)strecken, ausdehnen; *(person)* sich strecken; *(e.g. land, town)* sich erstrecken. *n (time)* Zeitspanne *f*; *(place)* Strecke *f*. **stretcher** *n* Tragbahre *f*. **stretchy** *adj* dehnbar.

stricken ['strikən] *adj (sickness)* befallen (von); *(emotion)* ergriffen (von).

strict [strikt] *adj* streng. **strictness** *n* Strenge *f*.

stridden ['stridn] *V* **stride**.

***stride** [straid] *v* schreiten. *n* Schritt *m*. **make great strides** Fortschritte machen. **get into one's stride** in Schwung kommen.

strident ['straidənt] *adj* grell.

strife [straif] *n* Kampf *m*.

***strike** [straik] *v* schlagen; *(target)* treffen; *(workers)* streiken; *(match)* entzünden. **it strikes me** es fällt mir ein. **strike off** streichen von. *n* Schlag *m*, Stoß *m*; *(labour)* Streik *m*. **striking** *adj* auffallend.

***string** [striŋ] *n* Schnur *f*, Bindfaden *m*; *(instrument)* Saite *f*. **strings** *pl (mus)* Streicher *pl*. *v (instrument)* besaiten. **string together** verknüpfen. **stringed instrument** Streichinstrument *neut*.

stringent ['strindʒənt] *adj* streng. **stringency** *n* Strenge *f*.

strip¹ [strip] *v* abziehen; *(clothes)* ausziehen.

strip² [strip] *n (narrow piece)* (schmaler) Streifen *m*.

stripe [straip] *n* Streifen *m*, Strich *m*. *v* streifen. **striped** *adj* gestreift.

***strive** [straiv] *v (for)* streben (nach); *(to do)* sich anstrengen (zu).

striven ['strivn] *V* **strive**.

strode [stroud] *V* **stride**.

stroke¹ [strouk] *n (blow)* Schlag *m*; *(pen)* Strich *m*; *(med)* Schlaganfall *m*.

stroke² [strouk] *v* streicheln.

stroll [stroul] *v* schlendern. *n* Bummel *m*, Spaziergang *m*.

strong [stroŋ] *adj (person, thing)* stark; *(person)* kräftig; *(flavour, etc.)* scharf. **be going strong** wohlauf sein. **strong-room** *n* Tresor *m*. **strong-willed** *adj* willensstark. **strongly** *adv* kräftig.

strove [strouv] *V* **strive**.

struck [strʌk] *V* **strike**.

structure ['strʌktʃə] *n* Struktur *f*. **structural** *adj* strukturell.

struggle ['strʌgl] *v* kämpfen, ringen. *n* Kampf *m*.

strum [strʌm] *v* klimpern (auf).

strung [strʌŋ] *V* **string**.

strut¹ [strʌt] *v* (herum)stolzieren. **strutting** *adj* prahlerisch.

strut² [strʌt] *n* Stütze *f*, Spreize *f*.

stub [stʌb] *n* Stumpf *m*; *(cheque)* Kontrollabschnitt *m*, Talon *m*; *(cigarette)* (Zigaretten)Stummel *m*. *v* **stub out** ausdrücken.

stubble ['stʌbl] *n* Stoppel *f*; *(beard)* Stoppeln *pl*. **stubbly** *adj* stoppelig.

stubborn ['stʌbən] *adj* hartnäckig, eigensinnig. **stubbornness** *n* Hartnäckigkeit *f*.

stuck [stʌk] *V* **stick²**.

stud¹ [stʌd] *n* Beschlagnagel *m*; *(button)* Knopf *m*.

stud² [stʌd] *n (farm)* Gestüt *neut*; *(horse)* Zuchthengst *m*.

student ['stjuːdənt] *n* Student(in); *(at school, also fig)* Schüler(in).

studio ['stjuːdiou] *n* Studio *neut*.

study ['stʌdi] *n* Studium *neut*; *(piece of research, etc.)* Studie *f*, Untersuchung *f*; *(room)* Studierzimmer *neut*. *v* studieren.

stuff [stʌf] *n* Stoff *m*; *(coll)* Zeug *neut*, Kram *m*. *v* vollstopfen; *(taxidermy)* ausstopfen; *(cookery)* füllen. **stuffing** *n* Füllung *f*.

stuffy ['stʌfi] *adj (air)* dumpf, schwül; *(thing)* langweilig; *(person)* pedantisch; *(nose)* verstopft.

stumble ['stʌmbl] *v* stolpern. **stumbling-block** *n* Hindernis *neut*.

stump [stʌmp] *n* Stumpf *m*. *v (coll)* verblüffen. **stumpy** *adj* stumpfartig.

stun [stʌn] *v* betäuben; *(fig)* bestürzen. **stunning** *adj (coll)* phantastisch.

stung [stʌŋ] *V* **sting**.

stunk [stʌŋk] *V* **stink**.

stunt¹ [stʌnt] *v (growth)* hindern, hemmen. **stunted** *adj* verkümmert.

stunt² [stʌnt] *n (feat)* Kunststück *neut*.

stupid ['stjuːpid] *adj* dumm, blöd. **stupidity** *n* Dummheit *f*.

stupor ['stjuːpə] *n* Erstarrung *f*; *(dullness)* Stumpfsinn *m*.

sturdy ['stəːdi] *adj* robust, kräftig.

sturgeon ['stəːdʒən] *n* Stör *m*.

stutter ['stʌtə] *n* Stottern *neut.* *v* stottern.
stutterer *n* Stotterer *m.*
sty [stai] *n* Schweinestall *m.*
style [stail] *n* Stil *m.* *v* (*name*) benennen; (*shape*) formen. **latest style** neueste Mode *f.* **hairstyle** *n* Frisur *f.* **stylish** *adj* elegant.
stylus ['stailəs] *n* Griffel *m;* (*record-player*) Nadel *f.*
suave [swaɪv] *adj* weltmännisch, zuvorkommend.
subconscious [sʌb'kɒnʃəs] *adj* unterbewußt. *n* das Unterbewußte *neut.*
subcontract [sʌbkən'trakt] *n* Nebenvertrag *m.* **subcontractor** *n* Unterkontrahent *m.*
subdue [səb'djuɪ] *v* unterwerfen. **subdued** *adj* (*person*) zurückhaltend; (*lights*) gedämpft.
subject ['sʌbdʒikt; *v* səb'dʒekt] *n* (*school, etc.*) Fach *neut;* (*theme*) Thema *neut,* Gegenstand *m;* (*gramm*) Subjekt *neut;* (*citizen*) Staatsangehörige(r). *adj* (*to ruler*) untertan (+*dat*); (*liable*) geneigt (zu); (*exposed*) ausgesetzt (+*dat*). *v* unterwerfen; (*expose*) aussetzen (+*dat*). **subjection** *n* Unterwerfung *f.* **subjective** *adj* subjektiv.
subjunctive [səb'dʒʌŋktiv] *n* Konjunktiv *m.*
*sublet [sʌb'let] *n* untervermieten.
sublime [sə'blaim] *adj* sublim, erhaben.
submarine ['sʌbmərɪn] *n* Unterseeboot (U-Boot) *neut. adj* Untersee-.
submerge [səb'məidʒ] *v* (ein)tauchen. **submerged** *adj* untergetaucht.
submit [səb'mit] *v* sich unterwerfen; (*maintain*) behaupten; (*hand in*) einreichen, vorlegen. **submission** *n* Unterwerfung *f;* (*documents*) Vorlage *f.* **submissive** *adj* gehorsam.
subnormal [sʌb'noɪməl] *adj* (*child, etc.*) minderbegabt.
subordinate [sʊ'bɔidinət] *v* unterordnen. *adj* untergeordnet. *n* Untergebene(r).
subscribe [səb'skraib] *v* (*money*) zeichnen. **subscribe to** (*newspaper*) abonnieren auf; (*view, etc.*) billigen. **subscriber** *n* Abonnent(in); (*phone*) Teilnehmer(in). **subscription** *n* Abonnement *neut.*
subsequent ['sʌbsɪkwənt] *adj* (nach)folgend. **subsequently** *adv* nachher, hinterher.
subservient [səb'səɪvɪənt] *adj* unterwürfig. **subservience** *n* Unterwürfigkeit *f.*

subside [səb'said] *v* (*noise, etc.*) nachlassen, abnehmen; (*sink*) sich senken. **subsidence** *n* (Boden)Senkung *f.*
subsidiary [səb'sidiəri] *adj* Hilfs-, Neben-. *n* (*company*) Tochtergesellschaft.
subsidize ['sʌbsidaiz] *v* subventionieren. **subsidy** *n* Subvention *f.*
subsist [səb'sist] *v* existieren. **subsist on** sich ernähren von. **subsistence** *n* Existenz *f.*
substance ['sʌbstəns] *n* Substanz *f,* Stoff *m;* (*of argument, etc.*) Gehalt *neut,* Kern *m.* **substantial** *adj* beträchtlich. **substantiate** *v* begründen.
substitute ['sʌbstitjuɪt] *n* Ersatz *m;* (*sport*) Ersatzspieler(in). *adj* Ersatz-. *v* ersetzen. **substitution** *n* Einsetzung *f.*
subtitle ['sʌbtaitl] *n* Untertitel *m.*
subtle ['sʌtl] *adj* fein, subtil. **subtlety** *n* Feinheit *f.*
subtract [səb'trakt] *v* abziehen. **subtraction** *n* Abziehen *neut;* (*thing subtracted*) Abzug *m.*
suburb [sʌbəɪb] *n* Vorort *m.* **suburban** *adj* Vororts-; (*coll: provincial*) kleinstädtisch.
subvert [səb'vəɪt] *v* (*government*) stürzen; (*morals*) untergraben. **subversion** *n* Sturz *m;* Untergrabung *f.* **subversive** *adj* umstürzlerisch.
subway ['sʌbwei] *n* (*in UK*) Fußgängerunterführung *f;* (*in US*) U-Bahn *f.*
succeed [sək'siɪd] *v* (*follow*) folgen auf, nachfolgen (+*dat*); (**be successful**) Erfolg haben, erfolgreich sein; gelingen (*impers*). *I succeeded in doing it* es gelang mir, es zu tun. **success** *n* Erfolg *m.* **successful** *adj* erfolgreich. **succession** *n* Reihenfolge *f,* Folge *f.* **successive** *adj* (aufeinander)folgend. **successor** *n* Nachfolger(in).
succinct [sək'siŋkt] *adj* kurz(gefaßt).
succulent ['sʌkjulənt] *adj* saftig. *n* (*bot*) Sukkulente *f.* **succulence** *n* Saftigkeit *f.*
succumb [sə'kʌm] *v* nachgeben (+*dat*).
such [sʌtʃ] *adj* solch, derartig. *such a big house* ein so großes Haus. **no such thing** nichts dergleichen. **such as** wie zum Beispiel. **as such** an sich. *such is life* so ist das Leben.
suck [sʌk] *v* saugen; (*sweet, thumb*) lutschen. **sucker** *n* (*coll*) Gimpel *m;* (*bot*) Wurzelschößling *m.* **sucking pig** *n* Spanferkel *neut.* **suckle** *v* stillen. **suckling** *n* Säugling *m.*

suction ['sʌkʃən] v Saugwirkung f, Sog m.
sudden ['sʌdən] adj plötzlich. **suddenness** n Plötzlichkeit f.
suds [sʌdz] n Seifenlauge f.
sue [suɪ] v verklagen (auf).
suede [sweid] n Wildleder neut.
suet ['suɪt] n Nierenfett neut, Talg m.
suffer ['sʌfə] v leiden (an). **sufferer** n Leidende(r). **suffering** n Leiden neut; adj leidend (an).
sufficient [sə'fiʃənt] adj genügend, ausreichend.
suffocate ['sʌfəkeit] v ersticken. **suffocating** adj erstickend. **suffocation** n Ersticken neut.
sugar ['ʃugə] n Zucker m. v zuckern; süßen. **sugar cane** n Zuckerrohr neut. **sugared** adj gezuckert. **sugary** adj süßlich; (fig) zuckersüß.
suggest [sə'dʒest] v vorschlagen; (maintain) behaupten; (indicate) hindeuten auf. **suggestion** n Vorschlag m; (trace) Spur f. **suggestive** adj anzüglich, zweideutig. **be suggestive of** deuten auf.
suicide ['suɪsaid] n Selbstmord m. **suicidal** adj selbstmörderisch.
suit [suɪt] n (man's) Anzug m; (woman's) Kostüm neut; (cards) Farbe f; (law) Klage f. **follow suit** dasselbe tun. **suitcase** n Handkoffer m. v (an)passen; (clothes) (gut) stehen (+dat); (food) bekommen (+dat). **suitable** adj geeignet, passend.
suite [swiɪt] n (furniture) Garnitur f; (rooms) Zimmerflucht f.
sulk [sʌlk] v schmollen, trotzen. **sulky** adj mürrisch, schmollend.
sullen ['sʌlən] adj mürrisch.
sulphur ['sʌlfə] n Schwefel m. **sulphurous** adj schwefelig; (fig) hitzig.
sultan ['sʌltən] n Sultan m.
sultana [sʌl'taɪnə] n (dried fruit) Sultanine f.
sultry ['sʌltri] adj schwül. **sultriness** n Schwüle f.
sum [sʌm] n Summe f; (money) Betrag m; (calculation) Rechenaufgabe f. v **sum up** zusammenfassen.
summarize ['sʌməraiz] v zusammenfassen. **summary** n Zusammenfassung f.
summer ['sʌmə] n Sommer m. adj sommerlich, Sommer-. **summerhouse** n Gartenhaus neut. **summery** adj sommerlich.
summit ['sʌmit] n Gipfel m. **summit conference** Gipfelkonferenz f.

summon ['sʌmən] v aufrufen, kommen lassen; (meeting) einberufen; (courage) fassen. **summons** n Berufung f; (law) (Vor)Ladung f. **take out a summons against** vorladen lassen.
sump [sʌmp] n Ölwanne f.
sumptuous ['sʌmptʃuəs] adj prächtig, kostspielig.
sun [sʌn] n Sonne f. v **sun oneself** sich sonnen.
sunbathe ['sʌnbeið] v ein Sonnenbad nehmen, sich sonnen.
sunbeam ['sʌnbiːm] n Sonnenstrahl m.
sunburn ['sʌnbəːn] n Sonnenbrand m. **sunburnt** adj sonnenverbrannt.
sundae ['sʌndei] n Eisbecher m.
Sunday ['sʌndi] n Sonntag m. **Sunday best** Sonntagskleider pl.
sundial ['sʌndaiəl] n Sonnenuhr f.
sundry ['sʌndri] pl adj verschiedene, diverse. **sundries** pl n Verschiedenes neut sing.
sunflower ['sʌn,flauə] n Sonnenblume f.
sung [sʌŋ] V **sing**.
sun-glasses pl n Sonnenbrille f sing.
sunk [sʌŋk] V **sink**.
sunlight ['sʌnlait] n Sonnenlicht neut.
sunny ['sʌni] adj sonnig.
sunrise ['sʌnraiz] n Sonnenaufgang m.
sunset ['sʌnset] n Sonnenuntergang m.
sunshine ['sʌnʃain] n Sonnenschein m.
sunstroke ['sʌnstrouk] n Sonnenstich m.
sun-tan n (Sonnen)Bräune f.
super ['suɪpə] adj (coll) prima.
superannuation [,suɪpərʌnjuˈeiʃən] n (contribution) Altersversicherungsbeitrag m; (pension) Pension f. **superannuated** adj pensioniert.
superb [suɪ'pəːb] adj herrlich, prächtig.
supercilious [,suɪpə'siliəs] adj herablassend, hochmütig.
superficial [,suɪpə'fiʃəl] adj oberflächlich.
superfluous [su'pəːfluəs] adj überflüssig.
superhuman [suɪpə'hjuːmən] adj übermenschlich.
superimpose [,suɪpərim'pouz] v legen (auf); (add) hinzufügen (zu). **superimposed** adj darübergelegt.
superintendent [,suɪpərin'tendənt] n Inspektor m, Vorsteher m.
superior [suɪpiəriə] adj überlegen; (higher) höherliegend; (quality) hervorragend, erlesen. n Überlegene(r). **mother superior** Oberin f. **superiority** n Überlegenheit f.

superlative [suːˈpɜːlətiv] *adj* unübertrefflich, hervorragend. *n* Superlativ *m*.

supermarket [ˈsuːpəˌmaːkit] *n* Supermarkt *m*.

supernatural [ˌsuːpəˈnatʃərəl] *adj* übernatürlich. *n* das Übernatürliche *neut*.

supersede [ˌsuːpəˈsiːd] *v* ersetzen.

supersonic [ˌsuːpəˈsonik] *adj* Überschall-.

superstition [suːpəˈstiʃən] *n* Aberglaube *m*. **superstitious** *adj* abergläubig.

supervise [ˈsuːpəvaiz] *v* beaufsichtigen, kontrollieren. **supervision** *n* Beaufsichtigung *f*, Kontrolle *f*. **supervisor** *n* Aufseher *m*, Kontrolleur *m*. **supervisory** *adj* Aufsichts-.

supper [ˈsʌpə] *n* Abendessen *neut*.

supple [ˈsʌpl] *adj* geschmeidig, biegsam. **suppleness** *n* Geschmeidigkeit *f*.

supplement [ˈsʌpləmənt] *n* Ergänzung *f*; *(newspaper)* Beilage *f*. **supplementary** *adj* ergänzend, Zusatz-.

supply [səˈplai] *v* liefern, versorgen; *(n need)* decken. *n* Lieferung *f*. *(stock)* Vorrat *m*; *(water, electricity, etc.)* Versorgung *f*. **supply and demand** Angebot und Nachfrage. **supplies** *pl n* Zufuhren *pl*. **supplier** *n* Lieferant *m*.

support [səˈpoːt] *v* tragen, stützen; *(withstand)* ertragen; *(family)* unterhalten; *(cause)* befürworten. *n* *(tech)* Stütze *f*; Unterstützung *f*. **supporter** *n* Anhänger *m*.

suppose [səˈpouz] *v* annehmen, sich vorstellen; *(believe, think)* meinen. **supposed** *adj* angenommen. **be supposed to** sollen. **supposition** *n* Vermutung *f*, Annahme *f*.

suppository [səˈpozitri] *n* (Darm-)Zäpfchen *neut*.

suppress [səˈpres] *v* unterdrücken; *(truth)* verheimlichen. **suppression** *n* Unterdrückung *f*; Verheimlichung *f*.

supreme [suˈpriːm] *adj* oberst, höchst. **supremacy** *n* Obergewalt *neut*.

surcharge [ˈsɜːtʃaːdʒ] *n* Zuschlag *m*.

sure [ʃuə] *adj* sicher, gewiß. *adv* *(coll)* sicherlich. **for sure** gewiß. **make sure** sich vergewissern. **you can be sure** du kannst dich darauf verlassen. **sure-fire** *adj* todsicher. **surely** *adv* sicherlich. **sureness** *n* Sicherheit *f*. **surety** *n* Bürge *f*.

surf [sɜːf] *n* Brandung *f*. *v* wellenreiten. **surfboard** *n* Wellenreiterbrett *neut*. **surfer** *n* Wellenreiter(in).

surface [ˈsɜːfis] *n* Oberfläche *f*. *adj* oberflächlich. *v* auftauchen. **surface mail** gewöhnliche Post *f*.

surfeit [ˈsɜːfit] *n* Übermaß *neut*. *v* übersättigen.

surge [sɜːdʒ] *n* *(water)* Woge *f*; *(emotion)* Aufwallung *f*. *v* *(waves)* branden; *(crowd)* (vorwärts)drängen.

surgeon [ˈsɜːdʒən] *n* Chirurg *m*. **surgery** *n* Chirurgie *f*; *(consulting room)* Sprechzimmer *neut*. **surgical** *adj* chirurgisch.

surly [ˈsɜːli] *adj* verdrießlich, mürrisch. **surliness** *n* Verdrießlichkeit *f*.

surmount [səˈmaunt] *v* überwinden. **surmountable** *adj* überwindlich.

surname [ˈsɜːneim] *n* Familienname *m*, Zuname *m*.

surpass [səˈpaːs] *v* übertreffen. **surpass oneself** sich selbst übertreffen.

surplus [ˈsɜːpləs] *n* Überschuß *m*. *adj* überschüssig.

surprise [səˈpraiz] *v* überraschen. *n* Überraschung *f*. *adj* unerwartet. **surprised** *adj* überrascht. **surprising** *adj* erstaunlich.

surrealism [səˈriəlizəm] *n* Surrealismus *m*. **surrealist** *n* Surrealist(in). **surrealistic** *adj* surrealistisch.

surrender [səˈrendə] *v* sich ergeben, kapitulieren; *(office)* aufgeben; *(prisoner)* ausliefern. *n* Kapitulation *f*; Auslieferung *f*.

surreptitious [ˌsʌrəpˈtiʃəs] *adj* erschlichen; *(stealthy)* heimlich.

surround [səˈraund] *v* umgeben, umringen. *n* Einfassung *f*. **surrounding** *adj* umgebend. **surroundings** *pl n* Umgebung *f*.

survey [ˈsɜːvei; *v* səˈvei] *n* Überblick *m*; *(land, house, etc.)* Vermessung *f*; *(questionnaire)* Umfrage *f*. *v* überblicken; vermessen. **surveyor** *n* Landmesser *m*.

survive [səˈvaiv] *v* *(outlive)* überleben; *(continue to exist)* weiterleben, weiterbestehen. **survival** *n* Überleben *neut*. **survivor** *n* Überlebende(r).

susceptible [səˈseptəbl] *adj* anfällig, empfänglich (für). **susceptibility** *n* Anfälligkeit *f*, Empfänglichkeit *f*.

suspect [səˈspekt; *n* ˈsʌspekt] *v* verdächtigen; *(believe)* vermuten. *n* Verdachtsperson *f*. *adj* verdächtig.

suspend [səˈspend] *v* aufhängen; *(person)* suspendieren; *(regulation)* (zeitweilig) aufheben. **suspended** *adj* ausgesetzt, verschoben. **suspender** *n* Strumpfhalter *m*. **suspenders** *pl* *(for trousers)* Hosenträger *pl.* **suspense** *n* Spannung *f.* **suspension** *n* (*mot*) Federung *f*; (*person*) Suspension *f.* **suspension bridge** Hängebrücke *f.* **suspension railway** Schwebebahn *f.*

suspicion [sə'spiʃən] *n* Verdacht *m*; (*mistrust*) Mißtrauen *neut*; (*trace*) Spur *f.* **suspicious** *adj* mißtrauisch; (*behaviour*) verdächtig. **suspiciousness** *n* Mißtrauen *neut.*

sustain [sə'stein] *v* (*suffer*) erleiden; (*family*) ernähren. **sustained** *adj* anhaltend. **sustenance** *n* Ernährung *f.*

suture ['suːtʃə] *n* Naht *f. v* vernähen.

swab [swob] *n* (*med*) Abstrich *m.*

swagger ['swagə] *v* (herum)stolzieren. **swaggering** *adj* stolzierend.

swallow[1] ['swolou] *v* schlucken. *n* Schluck *m.*

swallow[2] ['swolou] *n* (*bird*) Schwalbe *f.*

swam [swam] *V* **swim.**

swamp [swomp] *n* Sumpf *m*, Moor *neut. v* überschwemmen. **swampy** *adj* sumpfig.

swan [swon] *n* Schwan *m.*

swank [swaŋk] *v* protzen, prahlen. **swanky** *adj* protzig.

swap [swop] *v* (aus)tauschen. *n* Tausch *m.*

swarm [swoːm] *n* Schwarm *m. v* schwärmen.

swarthy ['swoːði] *adj* dunkelhäutig, schwärzlich.

swat [swot] *v* zerquetschen.

sway [swei] *v* schwanken, schaukeln. *n* Schwanken *neut*; (*power*) Macht *f*, Einfluß *m.*

swear [sweə] *v* schwören; (*bad language*) fluchen. **swearword** *n* Fluch *m*, Fluchwort *neut.*

sweat [swet] *n* Schweiß *m. v* schwitzen. **sweater** *n* Pullover *m.* **sweaty** *adj* verschwitzt.

swede [swiːd] *n* Kohlrübe *f.* **Sweden** ['swiːdn] *n* Schweden *neut.* **Swede** *n* Schwede *m*, Schwedin *f.* **Swedish** *adj* schwedisch.

sweep [swiːp] *v* kehren, fegen; (*mines*) suchen. **sweep aside** beiseite schieben, abtun. **sweepstake** *n* Toto *neut. n* Schornsteinfeger *m.* **make a clean sweep** reinen Tisch machen. **sweeper** *n* Kehrer *m.* **sweeping** *adj* radikal, weitreichend. **sweepings** *pl* Kehricht *m sing.*

sweet [swiːt] *adj* süß; (*kind*) nett. **sweet corn** Mais *m.* **sweeten** *v* süßen. **sweetheart** *n* Schatz *m.* **sweet-tempered** *adj*

gutmütig. *n* Bonbon *m*; (*dessert*) Nachspeise *f.* **sweetshop** *n* Süßwarengeschäft *neut.* **sweetness** *n* Süßigkeit *f*; (*person*) Lieblichkeit *f.*

swell [swel] *v* (auf)schwellen. *n* (*sea*) Wellengang *m. adj* (*coll*) prima. **swelling** *n* (*med*) Schwellung *f.*

swelter ['sweltə] *v* vor Hitze kochen. **sweltering** *adj* schwül.

swept [swept] *V* **sweep.**

swerve [swəːv] *v* ausscheren.

swift [swift] *n* (*zool*) Segler *m. adj* schnell, rasch. **swift-footed** *adj* schnellfüßig. **swiftness** *n* Schnelligkeit *f.*

swill [swil] *n* Schweinefutter *neut. v* spülen.

swim [swim] *v* schwimmen. *my head is swimming* mir ist schwindlig. *n* Schwimmen *neut*, Bad *neut.* **in the swim** auf dem laufenden. **swimmer** *n* Schwimmer(in). **swimming** *n* Schwimmen *neut.* **swimming pool** Schwimmbad *neut.*

swindle ['swindl] *v* betrügen. *n* Schwindel *m*, Betrug *m.* **swindler** *n* Schwindler(in).

swine [swain] *n* (*pl* **swine**) Schwein *neut.*

swing [swiŋ] *v* schwingen. *n* (*child's*) Schaukel *f.* **swing a door open/shut** eine Tür auf/zustoßen.

swipe [swaip] *v* hauen; (*coll: steal*) klauen. *n* Hieb *m.*

swirl [swəːl] *v* wirbeln. *n* Wirbel *m.*

swish [swiʃ] *v* rascheln. *n* Rascheln *neut.*

Swiss [swis] *n* Schweizer(in). *adj* schweizerisch. **Swiss German** Schweizerdeutsch *neut.*

switch [switʃ] *n* Schalter *m*; (*change*) Wechsel *m*; (*whip*) Rute *f.* **on/off-switch** *n* Ein/Ausschalter *m. v* (*change*) wechseln. **switchboard** *n* (*phone*) Vermittlung *f.* **switch on** einschalten. **switch off** ausschalten. **switch over to** übergehen zu.

Switzerland ['switsələnd] *n* die Schweiz *f.*

swivel ['swivl] *v* (sich) drehen.

swollen ['swoulən] *V* **swell.** *adj* geschwollen. **swollen-headed** *adj* eingebildet, aufgeblasen.

swoop [swuːp] *v* niederschießen, sich stürzen (auf).

swop [swop] *V* **swap.**

sword [soːd] *n* Schwert *neut.* **swordfish** *n* Schwertfisch *m.* **swordsman** *n* Fechter *m.*

swore [swoː] *V* **swear.**

sworn [swoːn] *V* **swear.** *adj* vereidigt; (*enemy*) geschworen.

swot [swɒt] *v* (*coll*) büffeln, pauken. *n* Büffler *m*.

swum [swʌm] *V* swim.

swung [swʌŋ] *V* swing.

sycamore ['sikəmɔɪ] *n* Sykamore *f*.

syllable ['siləbl] *n* Silbe *f*.

syllabus ['siləbəs] *n* Lehrplan *m*.

symbol ['simbl] *n* Sinnbild *neut*, Symbol *neut*. **symbolic** *adj* sinnbildlich, symbolisch (für). **symbolism** *n* Symbolik *f*. **symbolize** *v* symbolisieren.

symmetry ['simitri] *n* Symmetrie *f*. **symmetrical** *adj* symmetrisch.

sympathy ['simpəθi] *n* Mitleid *neut*, Mitgefühl *neut*. **sympathetic** *adj* mitleidend.

symphony ['simfəni] *n* Sinfonie *f*. **symphonic** *adj* sinfonisch.

symposium [sim'pouziəm] *n* Symposion *neut*.

symptom ['simptəm] *n* Symptom *neut*. **symptomatic** *adj* symptomatisch.

synagogue ['sinəgɒg] *n* Synagoge *f*

synchromesh ['siŋkroumeʃ] *n* Synchrongetriebe *neut*.

synchronize ['siŋkrənaiz] *v* synchronisieren.

syndicate ['sindikit] *n* Syndikat *neut*. **syndication** *n* Syndikatsbildung *f*.

syndrome ['sindroum] *n* (*med*) Syndrom *neut*.

synonym ['sinənim] *n* Synonym *neut*. **synonymous** *adj* synonym.

synopsis [si'nopsis] *n* (*pl* -ses) Synopse *f*, Zusammenfassung *f*. **synoptic** *adj* synoptisch.

syntax ['sintaks] *n* Syntax *f*. **syntactic** *adj* syntaktisch.

synthesis ['sinθisis] *n* (*pl* -ses) Synthese *f*. **synthetic** *adj* synthetisch, Kunst-.

syphilis ['sifilis] *n* Syphilis *f*.

syringe [si'rindʒ] *n* Spritze *f*.

syrup ['sirəp] *n* Sirup *m*, Zuckersaft *m*. **syrupy** *adj* sirupartig.

system ['sistəm] *n* System *neut*; (*geol*) Formation *f*. **systematic** *adj* systematisch.

T

tab [tab] *n* (*in garment*) Aufhänger *m*; (*label*) Etikett *neut*; (*coll*: *bill*) Rechnung *f*.

table ['teibl] *n* Tisch *m*; (*math, etc.*) Tabelle *f*. **table of contents** Inhaltsverzeichnis *neut*. **table-cloth** *n* Tischtuch *neut*. **table-spoon** *n* Eßlöffel *m*.

table d'hôte [taɪblə'dout] *n* Table d'hôte *f*.

tablet ['tablit] *n* Tablette *f*; (*stone*) Tafel *f*.

taboo [ta'buɪ] *adj* tabu. *n* Tabu *neut*.

tacit ['tasit] *adj* stillschweigend. **taciturn** *adj* schweigsam.

tack [tak] *n* Reißnagel *m*; (*naut*) Lavieren *neut*; (*sewing*) Heftstich *m*. *v* lavieren; heften. **tacky** *adj* klebrig.

tackle ['takl] *n* (*naut*) Takel *neut*; (*equipment, etc.*) Zeug *neut*, Ausrüstung *f*. *v* (*sport*) angreifen; (*person*) angehen; (*problem*) anpacken.

tact [takt] *n* Takt *m*. **tactful** *adj* taktvoll. **tactless** *adj* taktlos.

tactics ['taktiks] *pl n* Taktik *f*. **tactical** *adj* taktisch.

tadpole ['tadpoul] *n* Kaulquappe *f*.

taffeta ['tafitə] *n* Taft *m*.

tag [tag] *n* (*loop*) Anhänger *m*, (*label*) Etikett *neut*. **price-tag** Preiszettel *m*.

tail [teil] *n* Schwanz *m*. *v* (*coll*: *follow*) beschatten. **tail end** Schluß *m*. **tailcoat** *n* Frack *m*. **tail-lamp** *n* Schlußlicht *neut*.

tailor ['teilə] *n* Schneider *m*. *v* schneidern. **tailor-made** *adj* nach Maß angefertigt.

taint [teint] *n* Fleck *m*, Makel *m*. *v* verderben.

*take [teik] *v* nehmen; (*something somewhere*) bringen; (*prisoner*) fassen; (*photo, exam*) machen. **how long does it take?** wie lange dauert es? wie lange braucht man? **take aback** verblüffen. **take along** mitnehmen. **take away** wegnehmen; (*subtract*) abziehen. **take back** (*retract*) zurücknehmen. **take down** (*on paper*) aufschreiben. **take off** (*clothes*) ausziehen; (*mimic*) nachäffen. **take over** übernehmen. **take up** aufnehmen.

taken ['teikn] *V* take.

talcum powder ['talkəm] *n* Talkumpuder *m*.

tale [teil] *n* Erzählung *f*. **old wives' tale** Ammenmärchen *neut*.

talent ['talənt] *n* Talent *neut*, Begabung *f*. **talented** *adj* begabt.

talk [tɔɪk] *n* Rede *neut*; (*conversation*) Gespräch *neut*; (*chat*) Unterhaltung *f*; (*lecture*) Vortrag *m*. *v* reden, sprechen. **talk over** besprechen. **talkative** *adj* geschwätzig.

tall [tɔɪl] *adj* groß, hoch. **tallness** *n* Größe, Höhe *f*. **tall story** unglaubliche Geschichte *f*.

tally ['tali] *v* (*coll*) übereinstimmen (mit), entsprechen (+*dat*).

talon ['talən] *n* Klaue *f*.

tambourine [tambə'riɪn] *n* Tamburin *neut*.

tame [teim] *adj* zahm, gezähmt. *v* zähmen.

tamper ['tampə] *v* herumpfuschen (an), sich einmishcen (in).

tampon ['tampon] *n* Tampon *m*.

tan [tan] *v* gerben; (*skin*) sich bräunen. *n* (*colour*) Gelbbraun *neut*; (*skin*) Sonnenbräunung *f*.

tandem ['tandəm] *n* Tandem *neut*.

tangent ['tandʒənt] *n* Tangente *f*.

tangerine [tandʒə'riɪn] *n* Mandarine *f*.

tangible ['tandʒəbl] *adj* greifbar.

tangle ['taŋgl] *n* Gewirr *neut*. *v* verwickeln.

tank [taŋk] *n* Tank *m*, Behälter *m*; (*mil*) Panzer *m*. **tanker** *n* (*ship*) Tanker *m*.

tankard ['taŋkəd] *n* Krug *m*.

tantalize ['tantəlaiz] *v* quälen.

tantamount ['tantəmaunt] *adj* **be tantamount to** gleichkommen (+*dat*).

tantrum ['tantrəm] *n* Wutanfall *m*.

tap[1] [tap] *v* leicht schlagen, klopfen. *n* leichter Schlag *m*. **tap-dance** *n* Steptanz *m*.

tap[2] [tap] *n* Hahn *m*. *v* anzapfen. **taproom** *n* Schankstube *f*.

tape [teip] *n* Band *neut*, Streifen *m*; (*recording*) Tonband *neut*; (*sport*) Zielband *m*. *v* heften. **adhesive tape** Klebestreifen. **tape measure** *n* Metermaß *m*. **tape-recorder** *n* Tonbandgerät *neut*. **tape-recording** *n* Bandaufnahme *f*.

taper ['teipə] *n* (dünne) Wachskerze *f*. *v* spitz zulaufen. **tapered** *adj* spitz (zulaufend).

tapestry ['tapəstri] *n* Wandteppich *m*.

tapioca [tapi'oukə] *n* Tapioka *f*.

tar [taɪ] *n* Teer *m*.

tarantula [tə'rantjulə] *n* Tarantel *f*.

target ['taɪgit] *n* (*sport*) Zielscheibe *f*; (*ambition*) Ziel *neut*.

tariff ['tarif] *n* (*imports*) Zolltarif *m*; (*price list*) Preisverzeichnis *neut*.

tarmac ® ['taɪmak] *n* Asphalt *m*; (*runway*) Rollbahn *f*.

tarnish ['taɪniʃ] *v* (*metal*) anlaufen; (*reputation*) beflecken.

tarpaulin [taɪ'pɔɪlin] *n* Persenning *f*.

tarragon ['tarəgon] *n* Estragon *m*.

tart[1] [taɪt] *n* Torte *f*; (*prostitute*) Dirne *f*.

tart[2] [taɪt] *adj* sauer, herb.

tartan ['taɪtən] *n* Tartan *m*, Schottenmuster *neut*.

tartar ['taɪtə] *n* Weinstein *m*; (*teeth*) Zahnstein *m*.

task [taɪsk] *n* Aufgabe *f*. **take to task** zur Rede stellen.

tassel ['tasəl] *n* Quaste *f*.

taste [teist] *n* Geschmack *neut*; (*sample*) Kostprobe *f*; (*liking*) Neigung *f*. *v* schmecken. **tasteful** *adj* geschmackvoll. **tasteless** *adj* geschmacklos. **tasty** *adj* schmackhaft.

tattered ['tatəd] *adj* zerrissen.

tattoo [tə'tuɪ] *n* Tätowierung *f*. *v* tätowieren.

taught [tɔɪt] *V* teach.

taunt [tɔɪnt] *v* sticheln, verspotten. *n* Stichelei *f*.

Taurus ['tɔɪrəs] *n* Stier *m*.

taut [tɔɪt] *adj* stramm, straff.

tavern ['tavən] *n* Taverne *f*, Kneipe *f*.

tax [taks] *n* Steuer *f*. **tax-free** *adj* steuerfrei. **taxpayer** *n* Steuerzahler(in). **tax return** *n* Steuererklärung *f*. *v* besteuern; (*test*) anstrengen. **taxable** *adj* steuerpflichtig.

taxi ['taksi] *n* Taxi *neut*. **taxi-driver** *n* Taxifahrer *m*.

tea [tiɪ] *n* Tee *m*; (*meal*) Abendbrot *neut*. **tea-cloth** *n* Geschirrtuch *neut*. **teacup** *n* Teetasse *f*. **teapot** *n* Teekanne *f*. **teaspoon** *n* Teelöffel *m*.

***teach** [tiɪtʃ] *v* lehren; (*animals*) dressieren. **teacher** *n* Lehrer(in). **teaching** *n* Unterricht *m*. **teachings** *pl* Lehre *f sing*.

teak [tiɪk] *n* Teakholz *neut*.

team [tiɪm] *n* (*sport*) Mannschaft *f*; (*horses*) Gespann *neut*. *v* **team up** sich zusammentun (mit). **teamwork** *n* Zusammenarbeit *f*.

***tear**[1] [teə] *v* reißen, zerreißen. *n* Riß *m*. **tear away** wegreißen. **tear oneself away** sich losreißen.

tear[2] [tiə] *n* Träne *f*. **tear gas** *n* Tränengas *neut*. **tearful** *adj* weinerlich.

tease [tiːz] v necken.

teat [tiːt] n (bottle) Sauger m; (anat) Brustwarze f; (zool) Zitze f.

technical ['teknikəl] adj technisch. technician n Techniker m. technique n Technik f. technological adj technologisch. technology n Technologie f.

tedious ['tiːdiəs] adj langweilig. tedium n Langeweile f.

tee [tiː] n (golf) Abschlagstelle f.

teem [tiːm] v wimmeln (von).

teenage ['tiːneidʒ] adj Jugend-. teenager n Teenager m.

teeth [tiːθ] V tooth.

teethe [tiːð] v zahnen. teething troubles (fig) Kinderkrankheiten pl.

teetotal [tiːˈtoutl] adj abstinent. teetotaller n Abstinenzler(in).

telecommunications [ˌtelikəmjuːniˈkeiʃənz] pl n Fernmeldewesen neut sing.

telegram ['teligram] n Telegramm neut. by telegram telegraphisch.

telegraph ['teligraːf] n Telegraph m. v telegraphieren. telegraphic adj telegraphisch.

telepathy [təˈlepəθi] n Telepathie f, Gedankenübertragung f. telepathic adj telepathisch.

telephone ['telifoun] n Fernsprecher m, Telefon neut. v anrufen, telefonieren. by telephone telefonisch. telephone booth Telefonzelle f. telephone call Telefongespräch neut, Anruf m. telephone directory Telefonbuch neut. telephone exchange (Telefon)Zentrale f. telephonist n Telefonist(in).

telescope ['teliskoup] n Fernrohr neut, Teleskop neut. telescopic adj teleskopisch.

television ['teliviʒən] n Fernsehen neut. televize v (im Fernsehen) übertragen. on television im Fernsehen.

telex ['teleks] n Fernschreiber m, Telex neut. v (durch Telex) übertragen.

*tell [tel] v sagen; (story) erzählen; (recognize) erkennen. telltale n Klatschbase f. tell the truth die Wahrheit sagen. teller n Kassierer m. telling adj wirkungsvoll.

temper ['tempə] n Wut f, Zorn m; (mood) Laune f. lose one's temper in Wut geraten. v mildern; (steel) härten. temperament n Temperament neut. temperamental adj temperamentvoll. temperance n

Mäßigkeit f. temperate adj maßvoll; (climate) gemäßigt. tempered adj gehärtet.

temperature ['temprətʃə] n Temperatur f. have a temperature Fieber haben. take (a person's) temperature die Temperatur messen (+dat).

tempestuous [temˈpestjuəs] adj stürmisch.

temple[1] ['templ] n (arch) Tempel m.

temple[2] ['templ] n (anat) Schläfe f.

tempo ['tempou] n Tempo neut.

temporary ['tempərəri] adj provisorisch, vorläufig.

tempt [tempt] v verlocken. temptation n Verlockung f. tempting adj verlockend; (food) appetitanregend.

ten [ten] adj zehn. n Zehn f. tenth adj zehnt; n Zehntel neut.

tenable ['tenəbl] adj haltbar.

tenacious [təˈneiʃəs] adj zäh. tenacity n Zähigkeit f.

tenant ['tenənt] n Mieter m. tenancy n Mietverhältnis neut.

tend[1] [tend] v (be inclined) neigen (zu), eine Tendenz haben (zu).

tend[2] [tend] v (care for) bedienen, sich kümmern um.

tendency ['tendənsi] n Tendenz f.

tender[1] ['tendə] adj zart; (affectionate) zärtlich. tender-hearted adj weichherzig. tenderloin n Filet neut. tenderness n Zartheit f, Zärtlichkeit f.

tender[2] ['tendə] v anbieten; (comm) ein Angebot machen. n Angebot neut.

tendon ['tendən] n Sehne f.

tendril ['tendril] n Ranke f.

tenement ['tenəmənt] n Mietshaus neut.

tennis ['tenis] n Tennis neut. tennis ball Tennisball m. tennis court Tennisplatz m. tennis racket (Tennis)Schläger m.

tenor ['tenə] n Tenor m. adj Tenor-.

tense[1] [tens] adj gespannt. v (sich) straffen. tensile adj dehnbar. tension n Spannung f.

tense[2] [tens] n (gramm) Zeitform f, Tempus neut.

tent [tent] n Zelt neut.

tentacle ['tentəkl] n Tentakel m, Fühler m; (octopus) Fangarm m.

tentative ['tentətiv] adj versuchend, Versuchs-; (temporary) vorläufig. tentatively adv versuchsweise.

tenterhooks ['tentəhuks] n be on tenterhooks wie auf heißen Kohlen sitzen.

tenuous ['tenjuəs] adj dünn; (argument) schwach.

tepid 180

tepid ['tepid] *adj* lauwarm. **tepidness** *n* Lauheit *f*.

term [tɜːm] *n* (*expression*) Ausdruck *m*; (*period of time*) Frist *f*; (*academic, two per year*) Semester *neut*; (*academic, three per year*) Trimester *neut*. **end of term** (*school*) Schulschluß *m*. **terms** *pl* Bedingungen *pl*. **be on good terms with** gut auskommen mit. **come to terms with** sich abfinden mit.

terminal ['tɜːminəl] *adj* End-, Schluß-; (*med*) unheilbar. *n* Terminal *neut*.

terminate ['tɜːmineit] *v* beendigen; (*contract*) kündigen. **termination** *n* Ende *neut*, Schluß *m*.

terminology [tɜːmi'nolədʒi] *n* Terminologie *f*.

terminus ['tɜːminəs] *n* Endstation *f*.

terrace ['terəs] *n* Terrasse *f*; (*houses*) Häuserreihe *f*.

terrain [tə'rein] *n* Terrain *neut*, Gelände *neut*.

terrestrial [tə'restriəl] *adj* irdisch.

terrible ['terəbl] *adj* schrecklich, furchtbar. **terribleness** *n* Schrecklichkeit *f*, Fürchterlichkeit *f*.

terrier ['teriə] *n* Terrier *m*.

terrify ['terifai] *v* erschrecken. **terrific** *adj* (*coll*) klasse, unwahrscheinlich. **terrified** *adj* erschrocken. **be terrified of** sich fürchten vor.

territory ['teritəri] *n* Gebiet *neut*, Territorium *neut*; (*pol*) Staatsgebiet *neut*. **territorial waters** Hoheitsgewässer *pl*.

terror ['terə] *n* Schrecken *m*, Entsetzen *neut*; (*pol*) Terror *m*. **terrorism** *n* Terrorismus *m*. **terrorist** *n* Terrorist(in); *adj* terroristisch.

test [test] *n* Versuch *m*, Probe *f*; (*examination*) Prüfung *f*. *v* prüfen, erproben. **test-case** *n* Präzedensfall *m*.

testament ['testəmənt] *n* Testament *neut*.

testicle ['testikl] *n* Hoden *m*.

testify ['testifai] *v* bezeugen.

testimony ['testiməni] *n* Zeugnis *neut*. **testimonial** *n* Zeugnis *neut*, Empfehlungsschreiben *n*.

tetanus ['tetənəs] *n* Wundstarrkrampf *m*, Tetanus *m*.

tether ['teðə] *n* Haltestrick *m*. **be at the end of one's tether** mit seiner Geduld am Ende sein. *v* anbinden.

text [tekst] *n* Text *m*. **textbook** *n* Lehrbuch *neut*. **textual** *adj* textlich.

textile ['tekstail] *n* Gewebe *neut*, Faserstoff *m*. **textiles** *pl* Textilien *pl*.

texture ['tekstjuə] *n* Textur *f*.

than [ðən] *conj* als.

thank [θaŋk] *v* danken (+*dat*), sich bedanken bei. **thanks** *pl* *n* Dank *m sing*. *interj* danke! **thankful** *adj* dankbar. **thankless** *adj* undankbar. **thank you!** danke! **many thanks!** dankeschön! **thank goodness!** Gott sei Dank!

that [ðat] *adj* der, die, das; jener, jene, jenes. *pron* das; (*who, which*) der, die, das, welch. **that is** (i.e.) das heißt (d.h.). **that's it!** so ist es! **like that** so. **that which** das, was. *the man that I saw* der Mann, den ich sah. **in order that** damit. *conj* daß. *adv* (*coll*) so, dermaßen.

thatch [θatʃ] *n* Dachstroh *neut*. **thatched roof** Strohdach *neut*.

thaw [θɔː] *v* tauen. *n* Tauwetter *neut*.

the [ðə] *art* der, die, das *sing*; die *pl*.

theatre ['θiətə] *n* Theater *neut*; (*operating*) Operationssaal *m*. **theatre-goer** *n* Theaterbesucher(in). **theatrical** *adj* theatralisch.

theft [θeft] *n* Diebstahl *m*.

their [ðeə] *poss adj* ihr, ihre, ihr. **theirs** *pron* der/die/das ihrige. *a friend of theirs* ein Freund von ihnen.

them [ðem] *pron* (*acc*) sie; (*dat*) ihnen.

theme [θiːm] *n* Thema *neut*.

then [ðen] *adv* (*at that time*) damals; (*next*) dann, darauf. *conj* also. *adj* damalig.

theology [θi'olədʒi] *n* Theologie *f*. **theologian** *n* Theologe *m*. **theological** *adj* theologisch.

theorem ['θiərəm] *n* Theorem *m*.

theory ['θiəri] *n* Theorie *f*. **theoretical** *adj* theoretisch. **theorist** *n* Theoretiker(in). **theorize** *v* theoretisieren.

therapy ['θerəpi] *n* Therapie *f*, Behandlung *f*. **therapeutic** *adj* therapeutisch. **therapist** *n* Therapeut(in).

there [ðeə] *adv* dort, da; (*to that place*) dahin, dorthin. **here and there** hier und da. **over there** da drüben. **thereabouts** *adv* so ungefähr. **thereafter** *adv* danach. **there and back** hin und zurück. **there are** es sind, es gibt. **there is** es ist, es gibt. **up there** da oben. *interj* na!

thermal ['θɔːməl] *adj* thermal, Wärme-. *n* (*aero*) Thermik *f*.

thermodynamics [θɔːmoudai'namiks] *n* Thermodynamik *f*.

thermometer [θə'mɒmɪtə] *n* Thermometer *neut.*

thermonuclear [θəɪmou'njukliə] *adj* thermonuklear.

thermos ® ['θəɪməs] *n* Thermosflasche *f.*

thermostat ['θəɪməstat] *n* Thermostat *m.*

these [ðiɪz] *pl adj, pron* diese. **one of these days** eines Tages. **these are** dies sind.

thesis ['θiɪsis] *n* (*pl* -ses) These *f*, Satz *m*; (*university*) Dissertation *f.*

they [ðei] *pl pron* sie. **they say** man sagt.

thick [θik] *adj* dick; (*hair, woods*) dicht; (*coll: stupid*) dumm. **thicken** *v* dick machen *or* werden, (sich) verdicken; (*cookery*) legieren. **thickness** *n* Dicke *f*, Stärke *f*. **thick-skinned** *adj* (*fig*) dickfellig.

thief [θiɪf] *n* (*pl* **thieves**) Dieb(in). **thieve** *v* stehlen. **thievish** *adj* diebisch.

thigh [θai] *n* (Ober)Schenkel *m*. **thighbone** *n* Schenkelknochen *m.*

thimble ['θimbl] *n* Fingerhut *m.*

thin [θin] *adj* dünn, (*person*) mager; (*weak*) schwach. *v* dünn machen *or* werden; (*cookery*) verdünnen. **thinner** *n* Verdünner *m*. **thinness** *n* Dünne *f*; Magerkeit *f*. **thin-skinned** *adj* empfindlich.

thing [θiŋ] *n* Ding *neut.* **things** *pl* Sachen *pl*, Zeug *neut sing. how are things?* wie geht es?

*****think** [θiŋk] *v* denken; (*hold opinion*) denken, meinen. **think about** denken an; (*consider*) überlegen, nachdenken über. **think of** (*doing*) daran denken, vorhaben. *what do you think of it?* was halten sie davon? *I think so* ich glaube schon. **thinker** *n* Denker(in). **thinking** *n* (*opinion*) Meinung *f.*

third [θəɪd] *adj* dritt. *n* Drittel *neut.* **third party** Dritte(r). **third-party insurance** Haftpflichtversicherung *f*. **third-rate** *adj* (*coll*) minderwertig.

thirst [θəɪst] *n* Durst (nach) *m*. **die of thirst** verdursten. *v* dursten. **thirsty** *adj* durstig. **be thirsty** Durst haben.

thirteen [θəɪ'tiɪn] *adj* dreizehn. *n* Dreizehn *f*. **thirteenth** *adj* dreizehnt.

thirty ['θəɪti] *adj* dreißig. *n* Dreißig *f*. **thirtieth** *adj* dreißigst.

this [ðis] *adj* (*pl* **these**) dieser, diese, dieses, *pron* dies, das. **like this** so, folgendermaßen. **this morning** heute früh. **this year** dieses Jahr.

thistle ['θisl] *n* Distel *f.*

thorn [θɔin] *n* Dorn *m*. **thorny** *adj* dornig.

thorough ['θʌrə] *adj* gründlich; (*person*) genau, sorgfältig. **thoroughbred** *n* Vollblut *neut. adj* Vollblut-. **thoroughfare** *n* Durchgangsstraße *f*. **thoroughness** *n* Gründlichkeit *f.*

those [ðouz] *pl adj, pron* jene.

though [ðou] *conj* obwohl, obgleich. *adv* aber, dennoch, jedoch. **as though** als ob. **even though** wenn ... auch.

thought [θɔit] *V* **think**. *n* Gedanke *m*; (*thinking*) Denken *neut*; (*reflection*) Überlegung *f*. **thoughtful** *adj* gedankenvoll; (*considerate*) rücksichtsvoll. **thoughtless** *adj* gedankenlos; rücksichtslos.

thousand ['θauzənd] *adj* tausend. *n* Tausend *neut*. **thousandth** *adj* tausendst; *n* Tausendstel *neut.*

thrash [θraʃ] *v* verdreschen; (*defeat*) heftig schlagen. **thrash about** hin und her schlagen. **thrashing** *n* Prügel *pl*, Dresche *f.*

thread [θred] *n* Faden *m*; (*screw*) Gewinde *neut*. **threadbare** *adj* fadenscheinig. *v* (*needle*) einfädeln; (*beads*) einreihen. **thread one's way through** sich winden (durch).

threat [θret] *n* Drohung *f*; (*danger*) Gefahr *f*, Bedrohung *f*. **threaten** *v* bedrohen; (*endanger*) gefährden. **threatening** *adj* drohend.

three [θriɪ] *adj* drei. *n* Drei *f*. **three-cornered** dreieckig. **three-dimensional** *adj* dreidimensional. **threefold** *adv, adj* dreifach. **three-ply** *adj* dreifach. **three-quarters of an hour** eine Dreiviertelstunde *f.*

thresh [θreʃ] *v* dreschen.

threshold ['θreʃould] *n* (Tür)Schwelle *f.*

threw [θruɪ] *V* **throw**.

thrift [θrift] *n* Sparsamkeit *f*. **thrifty** *adj* sparsam.

thrill [θril] *v* erregen, begeistern. *n* Zittern *neut*, Erregung *f*. **thriller** *n* Reißer *m*. **thrilling** *adj* sensationell.

thrive [θraiv] *v* gedeihen. **thriving** *adj* blühend.

throat [θrout] *n* Kehle *f*, Rachen *m*; (*neck*) Hals *m*. **throaty** *adj* rauh.

throb [θrob] *v* pulsieren, klopfen. *n* Pulsieren *neut.*

thrombosis [θrom'bousis] *n* Thrombose *f.*

throne [θroun] *n* Thron *m.*

throng [θroŋ] *n* Gedränge *neut. v* sich scharen.

throttle ['θrotl] *v* erwürgen. *n* (*tech*) Drosselklappe *f.* **open the throttle** (*mot*) Gas geben.

through [θruː] *prep, adv* durch. **fall through** (*coll*) ins Wasser fallen. **get through** fertig sein mit; (*exam*) bestehen. **go through with** zu Ende führen. **wet through** durchnäßt. **throughout** *adv* (*place*) überall in. **throughout the night** die ganze Nacht hindurch. *adj* (*ticket, train*) durchgehend.

*throw [θrou] *v* werfen. **throw away** wegwerfen; (*chance*) verpassen. **throwback** *n* Rückkehr *f.* **throw up** (*coll*) kotzen. **throw-in** (*sport*) Einwurf *m. n* Wurf *m.*

thrush [θrʌʃ] *n* Drossel *f.*

*thrust [θrʌst] *v* stecken, schieben. *n* Stoß *m,* Hieb *m;* (*tech*) Schubkraft *f.*

thud [θʌd] *n* (dumpfer) Schlag *m. v* dumpf schlagen.

thumb [θʌm] *n* Daumen *m. v* **thumb through** durchblättern. **thumb a lift** per Anhalter fahren. **thumbtack** Reißnagel *m.*

thump [θʌmp] *n* Puff *m,* Schlag *m. v* puffen.

thunder ['θʌndə] *n* Donner *m. v* donnern. **thunderbolt** *n* Blitz *m.* **thunderclap** *n* Donnerschlag *m.* **thunderstorm** *n* Gewitter *neut.* **thunderstruck** *adj* wie vom Blitz getroffen.

Thursday ['θəːzdi] *n* Donnerstag *m.* **on Thursdays** donnerstags.

thus [ðʌs] *adv* so, folgendermaßen. **thus far** bis jetzt, soweit.

thwart [θwoːt] *v* (*person*) entgegenarbeiten (+*dat*); (*plan*) vereiteln.

thyme [taim] *n* Thymian *m.*

thyroid ['θairoid] *n* Schilddrüse *f. adj* Schilddrüsen-.

tiara [ti'airə] *n* Tiara *f.*

tick¹ [tik] *v* (*clock*) ticken; (*with pen*) abhaken. **tick over** (*mot*) im Leerlauf sein. *n* Ticken *neut;* Häkchen *neut.*

tick² [tik] *n* (*parasite*) Zecke *f.*

ticket ['tikit] *n* (*label*) Etikett *neut,* Zettel *m;* (*travel*) Fahrkarte *f,* Fahrschein *m;* (*theatre*) Karte *f.* **ticket-collector** *m* Schaffner *m.* **ticket-office** *n* Fahrkartenschalter *m.*

tickle ['tikl] *v* kitzeln; (*fig*) amüsieren. *n* Kitzel *m,* Juckreiz *m.* **ticklish** *adj* kitzlig.

tide [taid] *n* Gezeiten *pl,* Ebbe und Flut *f.* **high tide** Flut *f,* Hochwasser *neut.* **low tide** Ebbe *f,* Niedrigwasser *neut.* **tidal** *adj* Gezeiten-, Flut-.

tidy ['taidi] *adj* ordentlich, sauber. *v* in Ordnung bringen. **tidy up** aufräumen.

tie [tai] *v* (an)binden, festbinden; (*knot*) machen; (*necktie*) binden. **tie in with** übereinstimmen mit. **tie up** verbinden. **be tied up** nicht abkömmlich sein. *n* (*necktie*) Schlips *m,* Krawatte *m;* (*sport*) Unentschieden *neut;* (*obligation*) Verpflichtung *f.* Last *f.*

tier [tiə] *n* Reihe *f,* Rang *m.*

tiger ['taigə] *n* Tiger *m.* **tigress** *n* Tigerin *f.*

tight [tait] *v* fest, stramm; (*clothes*) eng, knapp; (*watertight, etc.*) dicht; (*in short supply*) knapp; (*coll: mean*) geizig. **tighten** *v* festziehen, straffen. **tight-fisted** *adj* geizig. **tights** *pl n* Strumpfhose *f sing. adv* **hold tight** festhalten. **sit tight** sitzenbleiben.

tile [tail] *n* (*roof*) (Dach)Ziegel *m;* (*wall*) Fliese *f.*

till¹ [til] *V* until.

till² [til] *n* (*in shop*) Kasse *f.*

till³ [til] *v* (*land*) bebauen, pflügen.

tiller ['tilə] *n* (*naut*) (Ruder)Pinne *f.*

tilt [tilt] *v* kippen, (sich) neigen. *n* Neigung *f,* Schräglage *f.* **tilt over** umkippen.

timber ['timbə] *n* (Bau)Holz *neut.* **timber forest** Hochwald *m.*

time [taim] *n* Zeit *f;* (*occasion*) Mal *neut;* (*era*) Zeitalter *neut,* (*music*) Takt *m.* **at all times** stets. **at this time** zu dieser Zeit. **behind the times** rückständig. **have a good time** sich gut unterhalten. **in good time** rechtzeitig. **time limit** *n* Frist *f.* **timepiece** *n* Uhr *f.* **timetable** *n* (*bus, train*) Fahrplan *m;* (*school*) Stundenplan *m.* **what time is it?** wieviel Uhr ist es? *or* wie spät ist es? *v* (mit der Uhr) messen, zeitlich abstimmen. **timeless** *adj* ewig. **timely** *adj* rechtzeitig.

timid ['timid] *adj* ängstlich, schüchtern. **timidity** *n* Ängstlichkeit *f,* Schüchternheit *f.*

tin [tin] *n* Zinn *neut;* (*can*) Dose *f,* Büchse *f. adj* zinnern, Zinn-. **tin can** Blechdose *f.* **tin foil** *n* Stanniol *neut.* **tin-opener** *n* Dosenöffner *m.*

183   **tool**

tinge [tɪndʒ] v (leicht) färben. n Färbung
f; (fig) Anstrich m.
tingle ['tɪŋgl] v prickeln, kribbeln. n
Prickeln neut.
tinker ['tɪŋkə] n Kesselflicker m. v tinker
with herumbasteln an.
tinkle ['tɪŋkl] v klingeln. n Klingeln neut,
Geklingel neut.
tinsel ['tɪnsəl] n Lametta neut.
tint [tɪnt] n Farbton m. v tönen, leicht
färben.
tiny ['taɪni] adj winzig.
tip[1] [tɪp] n (sharp end) Spitze f; (summit)
Gipfel m. **tipped** adj (cigarette) Filter-.
on tiptoe auf den Zehenspitzen.
tip[2] [tɪp] n (for rubbish) (Müll)Abladeplatz
m. v kippen. **tip over** umkippen.
tip[3] [tɪp] n (gratuity) Trinkgeld neut; (hint)
Wink m, Tip m. v ein Trinkgeld geben
(+ dat); einen Tip geben (+ dat). **tip off**
n rechtzeitiger Wink m.
tipsy ['tɪpsi] adj (coll) beschwipst.
tire[1] ['taɪə] v ermüden; (become tired)
müde werden. **tire out** erschöpfen. **tired**
adj müde. **tiredness** n Müdigkeit f. **tire-**
less adj unermüdlich. **tiresome** adj lästig.
tire[2] ['taɪə] (US) V tyre.
tissue ['tɪʃu] n Gewebe neut; (paper handkerchief) Papiertaschentuch neut. **tissue**
paper n Seidenpapier neut.
tit [tɪt] n (bird) Meise f.
title ['taɪtl] n Titel m; (right) Rechtstitel
m. **titled** adj betitelt. **title-deed** Eigen-
tumsurkunde f. **title-holder** n (sport)
Titelverteidiger(in). **title-role** Titelrolle f.
to [tu] prep zu; (motion, travel) nach;
(time of day) vor; (in order to) um zu. adv
(shut) zu, geschlossen. **to and fro** auf und
ab. **fix to the wall** an die Wand befestigen. **go to bed/the movies/school** ins
Bett/ins Kino/in die Schule gehen. **go to**
Berlin nach Berlin fahren. I gave it to
him ich gab es ihm. **ten to one** (o'clock)
zehn vor eins; (odds) zehn gegen eins. **to-**
do n Getue neut.
toad [toud] n Kröte f. **toadstool** n Pilz m.
toast [toust] n Toast m; (drink) Trink-
spruch m, Toast m. v toasten. **toaster** n
Toaster m. **toastmaster** n Toastmeister
m.
tobacco [tə'bakou] n Tabak m. **tobacco-**
nist n Tabakhändler m.
toboggan [tə'bogən] n Schlitten m,
Rodel(schlitten) m. v rodeln.
today [tə'dei] n, adv heute. **today's** or of

today heutig, von heute; (of nowadays)
der heutigen Zeit.
toddler ['todlə] n Kleinkind neut.
toe [tou] n Zehe f. **on one's toes** auf
Draht. **toe-cap** n Kappe f. **toe-nail** n
Zehennagel m.
toffee ['tofi] n Karamelle f.
together [tə'geðə] adv zusammen; (at the
same time) gleichzeitig. **get together** (coll)
sich treffen.
toil [toil] n Mühe f, schwere Arbeit f. v
mühselig arbeiten, schuften (an).
toilet ['toilit] n (all senses) Toilette f;
(WC) Klosett neut. **toilet-paper**
Klosettpapier neut. **toilet soap** Toiletten-
seife f.
token ['toukən] n Zeichen neut, Beweis
m; (voucher) Gutschein m, Bon m. adj
nominell.
told [tould] V tell.
tolerate ['toləreit] v dulden, tolerieren.
tolerable adj erträglich. **tolerance** n
Toleranz f. **tolerant** adj duldsam, tolerant.
toll[1] [toul] n Zoll m.
toll[2] [toul] v (bell) läuten.
tomato [tə'maːtou] n (pl tomatoes)
Tomate f.
tomb [tuːm] n Grabmal neut, Grab neut.
tombstone n Grabstein m.
tomorrow [tə'morou] n, adv morgen.
tomorrow morning morgen früh. **tomor-**
row's or of tomorrow morgig, von morgen. **the day after tomorrow** übermorgen.
ton [tʌn] n Tonne f.
tone [toun] n Ton m; (muscle) Tonus m.
tone down v mildern. **tonal** adj tonal.
tongs [toŋz] pl n Zange f sing.
tongue [tʌŋ] n Zunge f; (language)
Sprache f. **tongue-tied** adj zungenlahm.
tongue-twister n Zungenbrecher m.
tonic ['tonik] adj tonisch, Ton-. **tonic**
water Tonic neut. n Tonikum neut.
tonight [tə'nait] adv heute abend, heute
nacht.
tonsil ['tonsil] n Mandel f. **tonsillectomy** n
Mandelentfernung f. **tonsillitis** n
Mandelentzündung f.
too [tuː] adv (excessively) zu, allzu; (as
well) auch, ebenfalls.
took [tuk] V take.
tool [tuːl] n Werkzeug neut. **toolbox** n
Werkzeugkasten m. **tooling** n
Bearbeitung f.

tooth [tuːθ] n (pl **teeth**) Zahn m. **toothache** n Zahnweh neut. **toothbrush** n Zahnbürste f. **toothless** adj zahnlos. **toothpaste** n Zahnpasta f. **toothpick** n Zahnstocher m.

top[1] [top] n oberes Ende neut, obere Seite f; (hill) Gipfel m; (lid) Deckel m; (page) Kopf m. **on top of** oben auf; (besides) über. **top hat** Zylinder m. **top-heavy** adj kopflastig. **topsoil** n Ackerkrume f. adj oberst, höchst; (chief) Haupt-. v krönen.

top[2] [top] n (toy) Kreisel m.

topaz ['toupaz] n Topas m.

topic ['topik] n Thema neut, Gegenstand m. **topical** adj aktuell.

topography [tə'pogrəfi] n Topographie f.

topple ['topl] v (um)kippen.

topsy-turvy [topsi'təːvi] adv durcheinander, in Unordnung.

torch [toːtʃ] n Fackel f; (elec) Taschenlampe f.

tore [toː] V tear[1].

torment [toː'ment; n 'toːment] v quälen. n Qual f. **tormentor** n Quälgeist m.

torn [toːn] V tear[1]. adj zerrissen.

tornado [toː'neidou] n Tornado m, Wirbelsturm m.

torpedo [toː'piːdou] n Torpedo m.

torrent ['torənt] n Wildbach m; (of abuse, etc.) Strom m, Ausbruch m. **torrential** adj strömend. **torrential rain** Wolkenbruch m.

torso ['toːsou] n Torso m.

tortoise ['toːtəs] n Schildkröte f. **tortoiseshell** n Schildpatt m.

tortuous ['toːtʃuəs] adj gekrümmt.

torture ['toːtʃə] n Folter f, Folterung f; Tortur f. v foltern. **torturer** n Folterer m.

toss [tos] v (hoch)werfen; (coin) hochwerfen; tossed about by the waves von den Wellen hin und her geworfen.

tot[1] [tot] n (whisky, etc.) Schlückchen neut; (child) Knirps m.

tot[2] [tot] v tot up zusammenzählen.

total ['toutəl] adj total, ganz, Gesamt-. n Summe f, Gesamtbetrag m. **in total** als Ganzes. **totalitarian** adj totalitär. **totalisator** n Totalisator m. v sich belaufen auf; (person) zusammenzählen. **totality** n Gesamtheit f. **totally** adv völlig, total.

totter ['totə] v taumeln, wanken. **tottering** adj wackelig.

touch [tʌtʃ] v anrühren, anfassen; (feel) betasten; (border on) grenzen an; (emotionally) berühren. **touch down** landen.

touching adj rührend. **touchline** n Marklinie f. **touchstone** n Prüfstein m. n Berührung f, Anrühren neut; (sense) Tastsinn m, (trace) Spur f. **be/keep in touch with** in Verbindung stehen/bleiben mit. **touchy** adj empfindlich, reizbar.

tough [tʌf] adj zäh; (person) zäh, robust; (difficult) schwierig, sauer. **toughen** v zäher machen or werden. **toughness** n Zähigkeit f, Härte f.

toupee ['tuːpei] n Toupet neut.

tour [tuə] n Tour f, Rundreise f, (of inspection) Rundgang m; (theatre) Tournee f. v bereisen. **touring** adj Touren-. **tourism** n Tourismus m. **tourist** n Tourist(in).

tournament ['tuənəmənt] n Turnier neut.

tow [tou] v bugsieren, schleppen. n Schlepptau neut. **have in tow** im Schlepptau haben. **towline** or **towrope** n Schlepptau neut.

towards [tə'woːdz] prep (place) auf ... zu, nach ... hin; (behaviour, attitude) gegen(über). **towards midday** gegen Mittag.

towel ['tauəl] n Handtuch neut. **towelling** n Handtuchstoff m.

tower ['tauə] n Turm m. v (hoch)ragen.

town [taun] n Stadt f. adj Stadt-. **town council** Stadtrat m. **town hall** Rathaus neut. **town planning** Stadtplanung f.

toxic ['toksik] adj giftig, toxisch. **toxin** n Toxin neut.

toy [toi] n Spielzeug neut. **toys** pl Spielwaren pl. v **toy with** spielen mit.

trace [treis] n Spur f. v nachspüren, verfolgen; (draw) pausen, durchzeichnen. **tracing** n Pause f. **tracing paper** Pauspapier neut.

track [trak] n Spur f, Fährte f; (rail) Gleis neut; (road) Weg m, Pfad m; (sport) Bahn f. **track suit** Trainingsanzug m.

tract[1] [trakt] n (land) Strecke f. **digestive tract** Verdauungssystem neut.

tract[2] [trakt] n (treatise) Traktat neut.

tractor ['traktə] n Traktor m.

trade [treid] n Handel m; (job, skill) Gewerbe neut. **trade balance** n Handelsbilanz f. **trade fair** Messe f. **trademark** n Warenzeichen neut. **tradesman** n Lieferant m. **trade union** n Gewerkschaft f. **trade-unionist** n Gewerkschaftler(in). v handeln; (exchange) eintauschen. **trader** n Händler m.

tradition [trə'diʃən] *n* Tradition *f*. **traditional** *adj* traditionell.
traffic ['trafik] *n* Verkehr *m*. **traffic jam** Verkehrsstockung *f*. **trafficker** *n* Händler *m*. **traffic lights** Verkehrsampel *f sing*.
tragedy ['tradʒədi] *n* (*theatre*) Tragödie *f*; (*fig*) Unglück *neut*. **tragic** *adj* tragisch.
trail [treil] *n* Spur *f*. Fährte *f*. *v* schleifen, (nach)schleppen; (*follow*) verfolgen; (*lag behind*) nachhinken.
train [trein] *n* Zug *m*; (*of dress*) Schleppe *f*. *v* (*person for job, etc.*) ausbilden; (*sport*) trainieren; (*child*) schulen; (*animal*) dressieren. **trainee** *n* Lehrling *m*. **trainer** *n* (*sport*) Trainer *m*. **training** *n* Ausbildung *f*; (*sport*) Training *neut*.
trait [treit] *n* Zug *m*, Merkmal *neut*.
traitor ['treitə] *n* Verräter(in). **traitorous** *adj* verräterisch.
tram [tram] *n* Straßenbahn *f*.
tramp [tramp] *n* Landstreicher *m*. *v* stampfen.
trample ['trampl] *v* trampeln.
trampoline ['trampəliːn] *n* Trampoline *f*.
trance [trains] *n* Trance *f*.
tranquil ['traŋkwil] *adj* ruhig, friedlich. **tranquillity** *n* Ruhe *f*. **tranquillizer** *n* Beruhigungsmittel *neut*.
transact [tran'zakt] *v* durchführen. **transaction** *n* Geschäft *neut*, Transaktion *f*.
transcend [tran'send] *v* überschreiten. **transcendental** *adj* transzendental.
transcribe [tran'skraib] *v* abschreiben. **transcription** *n* Abschrift *f*.
transept ['transept] *n* Querschiff *neut*.
transfer [trans'fəː; *n* 'transfəː] *v* übertragen; (*money*) überweisen; (*trains*) umsteigen. *n* Übertragung *f*; Überweisung *f*; Umsteigen *neut*; (*design*) Abziehbild *neut*. **transferable** *adj* übertragbar. **transferred-charge call** R-Gespräch *neut*.
transform [trans'fɔːm] *v* umwandeln. **transformation** *n* Umwandlung *f*. **transformer** *n* (*elec*) Transformator *m*.
transfuse [trans'fjuːz] *v* (*blood*) übertragen. **transfusion** *n* (*blood*) Blutübertragung *f*.
transient ['tranziənt] *adj* vorübergehend.
transistor [tran'zistə] *n* Transistor *m*.
transit ['transit] *n* Durchfahrt *f*; (*of goods*) Transport *f*. *adj* Durchgangs-. **in transit** unterwegs.
transition [tran'ziʃən] *n* Übergang *m*. **transitional** *adj* Übergangs-.

transitive ['transitiv] *adj* transitiv.
translate [trans'leit] *v* übersetzen. **translation** *n* Übersetzung *f*. **translator** *n* Übersetzer(in).
translucent [trans'luːsnt] *adj* lichtdurchlässig.
transmit [tranz'mit] *v* übersenden; (*radio, TV*) senden. **transmitter** *n* (*radio, TV*) Sender *m*. **transmission** *n* (*mot*) Getriebe *neut*; (*radio, TV*) Sendung *f*.
transparent [trans'peərənt] *adj* durchsichtig, transparent; (*fig*) offensichtlich. **transparency** *n* Durchsichtigkeit *f*; (*phot*) (Dia)Positiv *neut*.
transplant [trans'plaint; *n* 'transplaint] *v* verpflanzen; (*med*) transplantieren. *n* (*operation*) Transplantation *f*; (*actual organ*) Transplantat *neut*. **transplantation** *n* Verpflanzung *f*.
transport [trans'pɔːt; *n* 'transpɔːt] *v* befördern, transportieren. *n* Beförderung *f*, Transport *m*. **transportable** *adj* transportierbar. **transportation** *n* Transport *m*.
transpose [trans'pouz] *v* umstellen, versetzen.
transverse ['tranzvəːs] *adj* quer, Quer-.
trap [trap] *n* Falle *f*. **lay a trap** eine Falle stellen. **shut your trap!** (*impol*) halt die Klappe! **trapdoor** *n* Falltür *f*. *v* fangen. **trapper** *n* Trapper *m*.
trapeze [trə'piːz] *n* Trapez *neut*.
trash [traʃ] *n* Abfall *m*; (*film, book, etc.*) Kitsch *m*. **trash-can** *n* Abfalleimer *m*. **trashy** *adj* wertlos.
trauma ['trɔːmə] *n* Trauma *neut*. **traumatic** *adj* traumatisch.
travel ['travl] *v* reisen. *n* Reisen *neut*. **travel agency** Reisebüro *neut*. **traveller** *n* Reisende(r). **travelling** *adj* Reise-. **travelling expenses** Reisespesen *pl*.
travesty ['travəsti] *n* Travestie *f*.
trawl [trɔːl] *n* Grundschleppnetz *neut*, Trawl *neut*. **trawler** *n* Trawler *m*.
treachery ['tretʃəri] *n* Verrat *m*. **treacherous** *adj* verräterisch; (*dangerous*) gefährlich.
treacle ['triːkl] *n* Sirup *m*, Melasse *f*.
*tread [tred] *n* Tritt *m*, Schritt *m*; (*tyre*) Profil *neut*; (*ladder*) Sprosse *f*. *v* treten. **treadmill** *n* Tretmühle *f*.
treason ['triːzn] *n* Verrat *m*.
treasure ['treʒə] *n* Schatz *m*. *v* hochschätzen. **treasurer** *n* Schatzmeister(in); (*club*) Kassenwart *m*. **treasury** *n*

Schatzkammer *f*. **Treasury** *n* (*pol*) Finanzministerium *neut*.
treat [triːt] *v* behandeln. **treat someone to something** jemandem zu etwas einladen. *n* (*coll*) Genuß *m*, Vergnügen *neut*. **treatment** *n* Behandlung *f*.
treatise ['triːtiz] *n* Abhandlung *f*.
treaty ['triːti] *n* Vertrag *m*, Pakt *m*.
treble ['trebl] *adj* dreifach; (*music*) Diskant-. *v* (sich) verdreifachen.
tree [triː] *n* Baum *m*. **family tree** Stammbaum *m*.
trek [trek] *n* Treck *m*. *v* trecken.
trellis ['trelis] *n* Gitter *neut*, Gitterwerk *neut*.
tremble ['trembl] *v* zittern. *n* Zittern *neut*.
tremendous [trəˈmendəs] *adj* enorm, kolossal; (*coll*: *excellent*) ausgezeichnet.
tremor ['tremə] *n* Beben *neut*.
trench [trentʃ] *n* Graben *m*; (*mil*) Schützengraben *m*. **trench coat** *n* Trenchcoat *m*.
trend [trend] *n* Tendenz *f*, Trend *m*. **trendy** *adj* (neu)modisch.
trespass ['trespəs] *v* unbefugt betreten. **trespasser** *n* Unbefugte(r). **trespassers will be prosecuted** Eintritt bei Strafe verboten.
trestle ['tresl] *n* Gestell *m*.
trial ['traiəl] *n* Probe *f*, Versuch *m*; (*legal*) Prozeß *m*. *adj* Probe-. **on trial** vor Gericht.
triangle ['traiaŋgl] *n* Dreieck *neut*; (*music*) Triangel *m*. **triangular** *adj* dreieckig.
tribe [traib] *n* Stamm *m*. **tribal** *adj* Stammes-. **tribesman** *n* Stammesangehörige(r).
tribunal [traiˈbjuːnl] *n* Gerichtshof *m*, Tribunal *neut*.
tributary ['tribjutəri] *n* Nebenfluß *m*.
tribute ['tribjuːt] *n* Tribut *m*. **pay tribute** (*fig*) Anerkennung zollen.
trick [trik] *n* Trick *m*, Kniff *m*; (*practical joke*) Streich *m*; (*cards*) Stich *m*. *adj* Trick-. *v* betrügen. **trickery** *n* Betrügerei *f*. **trickster** *n* Schwindler(in). **tricky** *adj* knifflig.
trickle ['trikl] *v* tröpfeln, sickern. *n* Tröpfeln *neut*.
tricycle ['traisikl] *n* Dreirad *neut*.
tried [traid] *adj* erprobt, bewährt.
trifle ['traifl] *n* Kleinigkeit *f*; (*cookery*) Trifle *m*, (süßer) Auflauf *m*. **a trifle** ein bißchen. *v* spielen. **trifling** *adj* belanglos.
trigger ['trigə] *n* Abzug *m*. **pull the trigger** abdrücken. *v* **trigger off** auslösen.

trigonometry [trigəˈnomətri] *n* Trigonometrie *f*.
trilby ['trilbi] *n* weicher Filzhut *m*.
trim [trim] *adj* gepflegt, nett; (*slim*) schlank. *v* zurechtmachen; (*hair*, *etc*.) ausputzen, beschneiden. **trimming** *n* Verzierung *f*.
trinket ['triŋkit] *n* Schmuckstück *neut*.
trio ['triːou] *n* Trio *neut*.
trip [trip] *n* Reise *f*, Ausflug *m*; (*stumble*) Fehltritt *m*, Stolpern *neut*. *v* stolpern; (*dance*) tänzeln, trippeln. **trip up** (*someone else*) ein Bein stellen (+ *dat*). **tripper** *n* Ausflügler(in).
tripe [traip] *n* Kaldaunen *pl*; (*coll*: *nonsense*) Quatsch *m*.
triple ['tripl] *adj* dreifach, Drei-. *v* verdreifachen. **triplet** *n* Drilling *m*. **triplex glass** Sicherheitsglas *neut*.
tripod ['traipod] *n* Dreifuß *m*; (*phot*) Stativ *neut*.
trite [trait] *adj* platt, banal.
triumph ['traiʌmf] *n* Triumph *m*; Sieg *m*. *v* triumphieren. **triumphal** *adj* Triumph-, Sieger-. **triumphant** *adj* triumphierend, siegreich.
trivial ['triviəl] *adj* geringfügig, trivial. **triviality** *n* Trivialität *f*.
trod [trod] *V* **tread**.
trodden ['trodn] *V* **tread**.
trolley ['troli] *n* (*supermarket*) Einkaufswagen *m*; (*tea*) Servierwagen *m*; (*airport*, *etc*.) Kofferkuli *m*; (*tram*) Straßenbahn *f*. **trolleybus** *n* O-Bus *m*.
trombone [tromˈboun] *n* Posaune *f*. **trombonist** *n* Posaunist(in).
troop [truːp] *n* Trupp *m*. **troops** *pl* Truppen *pl*. **trooping the colour** Fahnenparade *f*.
trophy ['troufi] *n* (*sport*) Preis *m*; (*mil*, *hunting*) Trophäe *f*.
tropic ['tropik] *n* Wendekreis *m*. **tropics** *pl* Tropen *pl*. **tropical** *adj* tropisch.
trot [trot] *n* Trott *m*, Trab *m*. *v* trotten, traben.
trouble ['trʌbl] *n* Schwierigkeiten *pl*; (*effort*) Mühe *f*; (*burden*) Belästigung *f*; (*tech*) Störung *f*. *v* beunruhigen, stören. **troubles** *pl* (*pol*) Unruhe *f*, Aufruhr *f*. **be in trouble** Schwierigkeiten haben. **be troubled** bekümmert sein. **get into trouble** Ärger bringen (+ *dat*) *or* bekommen. **take (the) trouble** sich die Mühe geˈˀn. **trouble-maker** *n* Unruhestifter(in). **trou-**

ble-shooter n Störungssucher(in). **troub-lesome** adj lästig.

trough [trof] n Trog m.

trousers ['trauzəz] pl n Hose f sing.

trout [traut] n Forelle f.

trowel ['trauəl] n Kelle f; (gardening) Pflanzenheber m.

truant ['truːənt] n Schwänzer(in). **play truant** (die Schule) schwänzen. **truancy** n Schwänzerei f.

truce [truːs] n Waffenstillstand m.

truck [trʌk] n (road) Lastkraftwagen (Lkw) m; (rail) Güterwagen m. **truckdriver** n Lastwagenfahrer m.

trudge [trʌdʒ] v sich mühsam schleppen.

true [truː] adj wahr; (genuine) echt; (loyal) treu; (rightful) rechtmäßig. **truism** n Binsenwahrheit f. **truly** adv wirklich, in der Tat. **yours truly** hochachtungsvoll.

truffle ['trʌfl] n Trüffel f.

trump [trʌmp] n Trumpf m. **trump card** Trumpfkarte f. v (über)trumpfen. **trumped up** falsch, erdichtet.

trumpet ['trʌmpit] n Trompete f. v trompeten. **trumpeter** n Trompeter m.

truncheon ['trʌntʃən] n Knüppel m.

trunk [trʌŋk] n (tree) Baumstamm m; (anat) Leib m; (case) Schankkoffer m. (mot) n Kofferraum m. **trunks** pl Badehose f sing. **trunk-call** Ferngespräch neut. **trunk-road** Fernstraße f.

truss [trʌs] n (med) Bruchband neut. v zusammenbinden; (cookery) dressieren.

trust [trʌst] v trauen (+dat); (hope) hoffen. n Vertrauen neut; (expectation) Erwartung f; (comm) Trust m. **hold in trust** als Treuhänder verwalten. **trustee** n Treuhänder m. **trusting** adj vertrauensvoll. **trustworthy** adj vertrauenswürdig. **trusty** adj treu.

truth [truːθ] n Wahrheit f. **truthful** adj wahr, wahrhaftig. **truthfulness** n Wahrhaftigkeit f.

try [trai] v (attempt) versuchen; (test, sample) probieren; (law) vor Gericht stellen, verhandeln gegen (wegen). **try on** (clothes) anprobieren. **try out** probieren. n Versuch m. **trying** adj peinlich, schwierig; (person) belästigend.

tsar [zaː] n Zar m.

T-shirt ['tiːʃəːt] n T-Shirt neut.

tub [tʌb] n (Bade)Wanne f; (barrel) Faß neut, Tonne f. **tubby** adj (coll) rundlich.

tuba ['tjuːbə] n Tuba f.

tube [tjuːb] n Rohr neut, Röhre f; (of tyre) (Luft)Schlauch m; (coll: underground railway) U-Bahn f.

tuber ['tjuːbə] n Knolle f.

tuberculosis [tjubəːkjuˈlousis] n Tuberkulose f.

tuck [tʌk] n Einschlag m. v **tuck in** (shirt) einstecken; (food) einhauen, zugreifen; (sheet) feststecken; (person) warm zudecken.

Tuesday ['tjuːzdi] n Dienstag m. **on Tuesdays** dienstags.

tuft [tʌft] n Büschel neut, Schopf m.

tug [tʌg] v ziehen, zerren; (boat) schleppen. n Zerren neut, Zug m; (boat) Schlepper m, Bugsierdampfer m.

tuition [tjuˈiʃən] n Unterricht m.

tulip ['tjuːlip] n Tulpe f.

tumble ['tʌmbl] v hinfallen, umstürzen. **tumbledown** adj baufällig. **tumble-dryer** (Wäsche)Trockner m. n Fall m, Sturz m. **tumbler** n Glas neut.

tummy ['tʌmi] n (coll) Bauch m, Bäuchlein neut. **tummy-ache** n Bauchweh neut.

tumour ['tjuːmə] n Geschwulst f, Tumor m.

tumult ['tjuːmʌlt] n Tumult m, Lärm m. **tumultuous** adj stürmisch.

tuna ['tjuːnə] n Thunfisch m.

tune [tjuːn] n Melodie f. **in/out of tune** gestimmt/verstimmt. **to the tune of** (coll) im Ausmaß von. v (ab)stimmen. **tune in to** einstellen auf. **tuneful** adj melodisch, wohlklingend. **tuner** n (pianos, etc.) Stimmer m.

tunic ['tjuːnik] n (school) Kittel m. (mil) Uniformrock m.

tunnel ['tʌnl] n Tunnel m, Unterführung f. v **tunnel through** einen Tunnel bauen durch.

tunny ['tʌni] V tuna.

turban ['təːbən] n Turban m.

turbine ['təːbain] n Turbine f.

turbot ['təːbət] n Steinbutt m.

turbulent ['təːbjulənt] adj unruhig, stürmisch. **turbulence** n Turbulenz f.

tureen [təˈriːn] n Terrine f.

turf [təːf] n Rasen m; (sport) Turf m, Rennbahn f. v **turf out** (coll) hinausschmeißen.

turkey ['təːki] n (cock) Truthahn m; (hen) Truthenne f.

Turkey ['təːki] n die Türkei f. **Turk** n Türke m, Türkin f. **Turkish** adj türkisch.

turmeric 188

turmeric ['təːmərik] *n* Gelbwurz *f*.
turmoil ['təːmoil] *n* Aufruhr *m*.
turn [təːn] *v* (sich) drehen; (*become*) werden. **turn around** *or* **round** (*person*) sich umdrehen; (*thing*) herumdrehen. **turn back** umkehren. **turn down** (*offer*) ablehnen; (*radio*) leiser stellen. **turning** *n* (*mot*) Abzweigung *f*. **turning point** Wendepunkt *m*. **turn left/right** links/rechts abbiegen. **turn loose** freilassen. **turn off** (*light*) ausschalten; (*radio*) abstellen; (*mot*) abbiegen. **turn on** einschalten. **turn out** (*expel*) ausweisen; (*produce*) herstellen. **turn-out** *n* (*spectators*) Teilnahme *f*. **turn over** (sich) umdrehen. **turnover** *n* (*comm*) Umsatz *m*. **turnstile** *n* Drehkreuz *neut*. **turntable** *n* (*records*) Plattenteller *m*. **turn up** (*appear*) auftauchen; (*radio*) lauter stellen. **turn-up** *n* (*trousers*) Umschlag *m*. *n* Umdrehung *f*; (*change of direction*) Wendung *f*. **it's my turn** ich bin an der Reihe. **do someone a good turn** jemandem einen Gefallen tun.
turnip ['təːnip] *n* (weiße) Rübe *f*.
turpentine ['təːpəntain] *n* Terpentin *neut*.
turquoise ['təːkwoiz] *n* Türkis *m*. *adj* (*colour*) türkisblau.
turret ['tʌrit] *n* Türmchen *neut*; (*gun*) Geschützturm *m*, Panzerturm *m*.
turtle ['təːtl] *n* Schildkröte *f*. **turtle dove** Turteltaube *f*.
tusk [tʌsk] *n* Stoßzahn *m*.
tussle ['tʌsl] *n* Balgerei *f*, Ringen *neut*. *v* sich balgen, kämpfen.
tutor ['tjuːtə] *n* Privatlehrer *m*; (*university*) Tutor *m*.
tuxedo [tʌk'siːdou] *n* Smoking *m*.
tweed [twiːd] *n* Tweed *m*.
tweezers ['twiːzəz] *pl n* Pinzette *f sing*.
twelve [twelv] *adj* zwölf. *n* Zwölf *f*. **twelfth** *adj* zwölft.
twenty ['twenti] *adj* zwanzig. *n* Zwanzig *f*. **twentieth** *adj* zwanzigst.
twice [twais] *adv* zweimal. **twice as much** zweimal so viel. **think twice about** sich gründlich überlegen.
twiddle ['twidl] *v* herumdrehen, spielen mit.
twig [twig] *n* Zweig *m*.
twilight ['twailait] *n* (Abend)Dämmerung *f*, Zwielicht *neut*. *adj* Zwielicht-.
twin [twin] *n* Zwilling *m*. *adj* Zwillings-. **twin-cylinder engine** Zweizylindermotor *m*.

twine [twain] *n* Bindfaden *m*, Schnur *f*. *v* (*threads*) zusammendrehen. **twine around** winden um.
twinge [twindʒ] *n* Stich *m*, Stechen *neut*. **twinge of conscience** Gewissensbiß *m*. *v* zwicken, kneifen.
twinkle ['twiŋkl] *v* glitzern, funkeln; (*eyes*) blinzeln. *n* Glitzern *neut*; Blinzeln *neut*. **in a twinkle** im Nu.
twirl [twəːl] *v* wirbeln. *n* Wirbel *m*.
twist [twist] *v* (sich) drehen, (sich) winden; (*meaning*) verdrehen; (*features*) verzerren. **twist one's ankle** sich den Fuß verrenken. **twisted** *adj* (*person*) verschroben. **twisting** *adj* sich windend. *n* Drehung *f*, Windung *f*; (*in story*) Wendung *f*.
twit [twit] *n* (*coll*) Dummkopf *m*.
twitch [twitʃ] *v* zucken. *n* Zucken *neut*.
twitter ['twitə] *v* zwitschern. *n* Gezwitscher *neut*, Zwitschern *neut*.
two [tuː] *adj* zwei. **two-faced** *adj* heuchlerisch. **twofold** *adj* zweifach. **two-stroke engine** Zweitaktmotor *m*. *n* Zwei *f*; (*pair*) Paar *neut*.
tycoon [tai'kuːn] *n* Industriemagnat *m*.
type [taip] *n* Typ *m*, Sorte *f*, Klasse *f*; (*person*) Typ *m*; (*print*) Druck *m*, Druckschrift *f*. *v* (mit der Maschine) schreiben, tippen. **typed** *adj* maschinengeschrieben. **typewriter** *n* Schreibmaschine *f*. **typing error** Tippfehler *m*. **typist** *n* Typist(in).
typhoid ['taifoid] *n* Typhus *m*.
typhoon [tai'fuːn] *n* Taifun *m*.
typical ['tipikəl] *adj* typisch. **typify** *v* verkörpern.
tyrant ['tairənt] *n* Tyrann(in). **tyrannical** *adj* tyrannisch. **tyrannize** *v* tyrannisieren. **tyranny** *n* Tyrannei *f*.
tyre ['taiə] *or US* **tire** *n* Reifen *m*.

U

ubiquitous [ju'bikwitəs] *adj* überall zu finden(d).
udder ['ʌdə] *n* Euter *neut*.
ugly ['ʌgli] *adj* häßlich. **ugliness** *n* Häßlichkeit *f*.
ulcer ['ʌlsə] *n* Geschwür *neut*.

ulterior [ʌl'tiəriə] *adj* **ulterior motives** Hintergedanken *pl.*

ultimate ['ʌltimət] *adj* allerletzt; *(conclusive)* endgültig, entscheidend. **ultimately** *adv* schließlich. **ultimatum** *n* Ultimatum *neut.*

ultraviolet [ʌltrə'vaiələt] *adj* ultraviolett.

umbilical [ʌm'bilikəl] *n* Nabelschnur *f.*

umbrella [ʌm'brelə] *n* Regenschirm *m.*

umlaut ['umlaut] *n* Umlaut *m.*

umpire ['ʌmpaiə] *n* Schiedsrichter *m.*

umpteen [ʌmp'tiːn] *adj* zahllos. **umpteen times** x-mal.

unable [ʌn'eibl] *adj* unfähig. **be unable** nicht können.

unacceptable [ʌnək'septəbl] *adj* unannehmbar.

unaccompanied [ʌnə'kʌmpənid] *adj* unbegleitet; *(music)* ohne Begleitung.

unanimous [ju'naniməs] *adj* einstimmig. **unanimity** *n* Einstimmigkeit *f.*

unannounced [ʌnə'naunst] *adj* unangekündigt.

unarmed [ʌn'aːmd] *adj* unbewaffnet.

unassuming [ʌnə'sjuːmiŋ] *adj* bescheiden.

unattractive [ʌnə'traktiv] *adj* reizlos, nicht anziehend.

unauthorized [ʌn'oːθəraizd] *adj* unbefugt.

unavoidable [ʌnə'voidəbl] *adj* unvermeidlich.

unaware [ʌnə'weə] *adj* **be unaware of** sich nicht bewußt sein (+*gen*). **unawares** *adv* **take unawares** überraschen.

unbalanced [ʌn'balənst] *adj* unausgeglichen; *(mentally disturbed)* geistesgestört.

unbearable [ʌn'beərəbl] *adj* unerträglich.

unbelievable [ʌnbi'liːvəbl] *adj* unglaublich. **unbeliever** *n* Ungläubige(r). **unbelieving** *adj* ungläubig.

***unbend** [ʌn'bend] *v (person)* freundlicher werden. **unbending** *adj* unbeugsam.

unbounded [ʌn'baundid] *adj* unbegrenzt, grenzenlos.

unbreakable [ʌn'breikəbl] *adj* unzerbrechlich.

unbridled [ʌn'braidld] *adj* zügellos.

unbroken [ʌn'broukn] *adj (continuous)* ununterbrochen.

uncalled-for [ʌn'koːldfoː] *adj* unangebracht.

uncanny [ʌn'kani] *adj* unheimlich.

uncertain [ʌn'səːtn] *adj* unsicher, ungewiß. **uncertainty** *n* Unsicherheit *f,* Ungewißheit *f.*

uncle ['ʌŋkl] *n* Onkel *m.*

unclean [ʌn'kliːn] *adj* unrein.

uncomfortable [ʌn'kʌmfətəbl] *adj* unbequem; *(fact, etc.)* beunruhigend.

uncommon [ʌn'komən] *adj* ungewöhnlich, selten. **uncommonly** *adv (extremely)* außerordentlich.

unconditional [ʌnkən'diʃənl] *adj* bedingungslos, uneingeschränkt.

unconfirme [ʌnkən'fəːmd]d *adj* unbestätigt.

unconscious [ʌn'konʃəs] *adj (unknowing)* unbewußt; *(med)* bewußtlos. **unconsciousness** *n* Bewußtlosigkeit *f.*

uncontrollable [ʌnkən'trouləbl] *adj* unbeherrscht, unkontrollierbar.

unconventional [ʌnkən'venʃənl] *adj* unkonventionell.

unconvinced [ʌnkən'vinst] *adj* nicht überzeugt. **unconvincing** *adj* nicht überzeugend.

uncooked [ʌn'kukt] *adj* roh, ungekocht.

uncork [ʌn'koːk] *v* entkorken.

uncouth [ʌn'kuːθ] *adj* ungehobelt, unfein.

uncover [ʌn'kʌvə] *v* aufdecken.

uncut [ʌn'kʌt] *adj (gem)* ungeschliffen; *(grass)* ungemäht; *(book)* unabgekürzt.

undecided [ʌndi'saidid] *adj (thing)* unentschieden; *(person)* unentschlossen.

undeniable [ʌndi'naiəbl] *adj* unbestreitbar.

under ['ʌndə] *prep* unter; *(less than)* weniger als. **under age** minderjährig. **under construction** im Bau. **under cover of** im Schutz (+*gen*). *adv* unten. **go under** zugrunde gehen. *adj* Unter-.

undercharge [ʌndə'tʃaidʒ] *v* zu wenig berechnen.

underclothes ['ʌndəklouðz] *pl n* Unterwäsche *f sing.*

undercoat ['ʌndəkout] *n* Grundierung *f,* Grundanstrich *m.*

undercover [ʌndə'kʌvə] *adj* Geheim-.

***undercut** [ʌndə'kʌt] *v (comm)* unterbieten.

underdeveloped [ʌndədi'veləpt] *adj* unterentwickelt. **underdeveloped country** Entwicklungsland *neut.*

underdone [ʌndə'dʌn] *adj (meat)* nicht durchgebraten.

underestimate [ʌndə'estimeit] *adj* unterschätzen

underexpose [ʌndərik'spouz] *v* unterbelichten. **underexposure** *n* Unterbelichtung *f.*

underfoot [ʌndə'fut] *adv* am Boden.
***undergo** [ʌndə'gou] *v* erleben; *(operation)* sich unterziehen (+*dat*).
undergraduate [ʌndə'grædjuət] *n* Student(in).
underground ['ʌndəgraund; *adv* ʌndə'graund] *adj* unterirdisch, Untergrund-; *(pol)* geheim, Untergrund-. *n* *(rail)* Untergrundbahn *f*. *(coll)* U-Bahn *f*. *adv* unter der Erde. **go underground** *(hide)* untertauchen.
undergrowth ['ʌndəgrouθ] *n* Unterholz *neut*.
underhand [ʌndə'hand] *adj* heimlich, hinterlistig.
***underlie** [ʌndə'lai] *v* zugrunde liegen (+*dat*).
underline [ʌndə'lain] *v* unterstreichen; *(stress)* betonen.
undermine [ʌndə'main] *v* unterminieren, untergraben.
underneath [ʌndə'niːθ] *prep* unter, unterhalb. *adv* unten, darunter.
underpants ['ʌndəpants] *pl n* Unterhose *f sing*.
underpass ['ʌndəpaɪs] *n* Unterführung *f*.
underprivileged [ʌndə'privilidʒd] *adj* benachteiligt.
underrate [ʌndə'reit] *v* unterschätzen.
***understand** [ʌndə'stand] *v* verstehen. **understandable** *adj* verständlich. **understanding** *n* Verständnis *neut*; *(agreement)* Verständigung *f*; *adj* verständnisvoll.
understate [ʌndə'steit] *v* untertreiben. **understatement** *n* Untertreibung *f*.
understudy ['ʌndəstʌdi] *n* Ersatzschauspieler(in).
***undertake** [ʌndə'teik] *v* übernehmen. **undertaker** *n* Leichenbestatter *m*. **undertaking** *n* Unternehmen *neut*; *(promise)* Versprechen *neut*.
undertone ['ʌndətoun] *n* Unterton *m*.
underwear ['ʌndəweə] *n* Unterwäsche *f*.
underweight [ʌndə'weit] *adj* untergewichtig.
underworld ['ʌndəwəɪld] *n* Unterwelt *f*.
***underwrite** [ʌndə'rait] *v* unterzeichnen, versichern. **underwriter** *n* Versicherer *m*.
undesirable [ʌndi'zaiərəbl] *adj* nicht wünschenswert, unerwünscht.
***undo** [ʌn'duɪ] *v* *(package)* öffnen, aufmachen; *(coat, knot)* aufknöpfen; *(work)* zunichte machen. **undoing** *n* Ruin *m*, Vernichtung *f*.

undoubted [ʌn'dautid] *adj* unbestritten. **undoubtedly** *adv* ohne Zweifel.
undress [ʌn'dres] *v* (sich) ausziehen. **undressed** *adj* unbekleidet.
undue [ʌn'djuɪ] *adj* übermäßig, übertrieben; *(improper)* unschicklich. **unduly** *adv* übertrieben.
undulate ['ʌndjuleit] *v* wogen, wallen. **undulation** *n* Wallen *neut*.
unearth [ʌn'əɪθ] *v* ausgraben; *(fig)* ans Tageslicht bringen.
uneasy [ʌn'iɪzi] *adj* *(person)* beunruhigt, ängstlich; *(feeling)* unbehaglich.
uneducated [ʌn'edjukeitid] *adj* ungebildet.
unemployed [ʌnem'ploid] *adj* arbeitslos. **unemployment** *n* Arbeitslosigkeit *f*.
unending [ʌn'endiŋ] *adj* endlos.
unequal [ʌn'iːkwəl] *adj* ungleich. **unequalled** *adj* unübertroffen.
uneven [ʌn'iɪvn] *adj* uneben. **unevenness** *n* Unebenheit *f*.
uneventful [ʌni'ventfəl] *adj* ereignislos.
unexpected [ʌneks'pektid] *adj* unerwartet.
unfailing [ʌn'feiliŋ] *adj* unfehlbar.
unfair [ʌn'feə] *adj* ungerecht, unfair. **unfairness** *n* Unbilligkeit *f*.
unfaithful [ʌn'feiθfəl] *adj* untreu. **unfaithfulness** *n* Untreue *f*.
unfamiliar [ʌnfə'miljə] *adj* unbekannt.
unfasten [ʌn'faisn] *v* aufmachen, losbinden.
unfit [ʌn'fit] *adj* ungeeignet; *(sport)* nicht fit.
unfold [ʌn'fould] *v* (sich) entfalten.
unforeseen [ʌnfoɪ'siɪn] *adj* unvorhergesehen.
unforgettable [ʌnfə'getəbl] *adj* unvergeßlich.
unfortunate [ʌn'foɪtʃənət] *adj* unglücklich; *(regrettable)* bedauerlich. *n* Unglückliche(r). **unfortunately** *adv* unglücklicherweise, leider.
unfurnished [ʌn'fəɪniʃd] *adj* unmöbliert.
ungrateful [ʌn'greitfəl] *adj* undankbar.
unhappy [ʌn'hapi] *adj* unglücklich; *(with something)* unzufrieden. **unhappily** *adv* leider. **unhappiness** *n* Unglück *neut*.
unhealthy [ʌn'helθi] *adj* *(person)* ungesund; *(damaging to health)* gesundheitsschädlich.
unhurt [ʌn'həɪt] *adj* unverletzt.
unicorn ['juɪnikoɪn] *n* Einhorn *m*.

uniform ['juːnifoːm] *n* Uniform *f*, Dienstkleidung *f*. *adj* einförmig, gleichförmig.
uniformity *n* Gleichheit *f*.
unify ['juːnifai] *v* vereinigen. **unification** *n* Vereinigung *f*.
unilateral [juːni'latərəl] *adj* einseitig.
uninhabited [ʌnin'habitid] *adj* unbewohnt. **uninhabitable** *adj* unbewohnbar.
unintelligible [ʌnin'telidʒəbl] *adj* unverständlich.
uninterested [ʌn'intristid] *adj* uninteressiert. **uninteresting** *adj* uninteressant.
union ['juːnjən] *n* Vereinigung *f*; (*pol*) Staatenbund *m*; (*agreement*) Eintracht *f*; (*trade union*) Gewerkschaft *f*. **unionize** *v* gewerkschaftlich organisieren.
unique [juː'niːk] *adj* einzigartig; (*only*) einzig.
unison ['juːnisn] *n* Einklang *m*.
unit ['juːnit] *n* Einheit *f*.
unite [juː'nait] *v* (sich) vereinigen. **united** *adj* vereint, vereinigt. **unity** *n* Einheit *f*; (*accord*) Einigkeit *f*.
United Kingdom *n* Vereinigtes Königreich.
United Nations *pl n* Vereinte Nationen.
United States of America *n* Vereinigte Staaten von Amerika.
universe ('juːnivəːs] *n* Weltall *neut*, Universum *neut*. **universal** *adj* universal.
university [juːni'vəːsəti] *n* Universität *f*, Hochschule *f*. *adj* Universitäts-, Hochschul-.
unjust [ʌn'dʒʌst] *adj* ungerecht.
unkempt [ʌn'kempt] *adj* ungepflegt.
unkind [ʌn'kaind] *adj* unfreundlich. **unkindness** *n* Unfreundlichkeit *f*.
unknown [ʌn'noun] *adj* unbekannt. *n* das Unbekannte.
unlawful [ʌn'loːfəl] *adj* rechtswidrig, unzulässig.
unless [ʌn'les] *conj* wenn ... nicht, es sei denn.
unlike [ʌn'laik] *adj*, *prep* unähnlich. (*in contrast to*) im Gegensatz zu. **unlikely** *adv* unwahrscheinlich.
unload [ʌn'loud] *v* (*goods*) abladen; (*truck*, *etc*.) entladen.
unlock [ʌn'lok] *v* aufschließen, öffnen. **unlocked** *adj* unverschlossen.
unlucky [ʌn'lʌki] *adj* unglücklich.
unmarried [ʌn'marid] *adj* ledig, unverheiratet.
unnatural [ʌn'natʃərəl] *adj* unnatürlich.

unnecessary [ʌn'nesəsəri] *adj* unnötig, nicht notwendig.
unobtainable [ʌnəb'teinəbl] *adj* unerhältlich.
unoccupied [ʌn'okjupaid] *adj* unbesetzt; (*house*) unbewohnt; (*person*) unbeschäftigt.
unofficial [ʌnə'fiʃəl] *adj* inoffiziell.
unorthodox [ʌn'oːθədoks] *adj* unorthodox.
unpack [ʌn'pak] *v* auspacken.
unpleasant (ʌn'pleznt] *adj* unangenehm. **unpleasantness** *n* Unannehmlichkeit *f*.
unpopular [ʌn'popjulə] *adj* unbeliebt.
unprecedented [ʌn'presidentid] *adj* unerhört.
unpretentious [ʌnpri'tenʃəs] *adj* anspruchslos.
unravel [ʌn'ravəl] *v* auftrennen; (*fig*) enträtseln.
unreal [ʌn'riəl] *adj* unwirklich. **unrealistic** *adj* unrealistisch.
unreasonable [ʌn'riːzənəbl] *adj* übertrieben, übermäßig; (*person*) unvernünftig.
unrelenting [ʌnri'lentiŋ] *adj* unerbittlich.
unreliable [ʌnri'laiəbl] *adj* unzuverlässig. **unreliability** *n* Unzuverlässigkeit *f*.
unrest [ʌn'rest] *n* Unruhe *f*.
unruly [ʌn'ruːli] *adj* unlenksam.
unsafe [ʌn'seif] *adj* unsicher, gefährlich.
unsatisfactory [ʌnsatis'faktəri] *adj* unbefriedigend. **unsatisfied** *adj* unzufrieden.
unscrew [ʌn'skruː] *v* aufschrauben.
unsettle [ʌn'setl] *v* beunruhigen. **unsettled** *adj* unruhig.
unsightly [ʌn'saitli] *adj* unansehnlich.
unskilled [ʌn'skild] *adj* ungelernt.
unsound [ʌn'saund] *adj* (*advice*, *etc*.) unzuverlässig. **of unsound mind** geistesgestört.
unspeakable [ʌn'spiːkəbl] *adj* unbeschreiblich; (*horrible*) scheußlich, entsetzlich.
unstable [ʌn'steibl] *adj* nicht fest, schwankend; (*person*) labil.
unsteady [ʌn'stedi] *adj* wackelig, unsicher.
unsuccessful [ʌnsək'sesfəl] *adj* erfolglos.
unsuitable [ʌn'suːtəbl] *adj* ungeeignet.
untangle [ʌn'taŋgl] *v* entwirren.
untidy [ʌn'taidi] *adj* unordentlich. **untidiness** *n* Unordentlichkeit *f*.

untie [ʌn'tai] v losbinden.

until [ən'til] prep, conj bis. **not until** erst.

untoward [ʌntə'wɔːd] adj ungünstig.

untrue [ʌn'truː] adj unwahr, falsch; (friend) untreu. **untruth** n Unwahrheit f, Falschheit f. **untruthful** adj unwahr, unaufrichtig.

unusual [ʌn'juːʒuəl] adj ungewöhnlich, außergewöhnlich.

unwell [ʌn'wel] adj unwohl.

unwieldy [ʌn'wiːldi] adj unhandlich.

*unwind [ʌn'waind] v loswickeln, abspulen; (rest) sich entspannen, (sich) ausruhen.

unworthy [ʌn'wəːði] adj unwürdig.

unwrap [ʌn'rap] v auswickeln.

up [ʌp] prep auf, hinauf. adv auf, hoch; hinauf, herauf; (out of bed) auf; (sun) aufgegangen. **it's up to me** es liegt an mir. **up to now** bis jetzt. **up for trial** vor Gericht. **what's up?** was ist los?

upbringing ['ʌpbriŋiŋ] n Erziehung f.

update [ʌp'deit] v modernisieren; (book) neu bearbeiten.

upheaval [ʌp'hiːvl] n Umwälzung f.

uphill [ʌp'hil] adv bergauf. adj (fig) mühsam.

*uphold [ʌp'hould] v unterstützen, billigen.

upholster [ʌp'houlstə] v (auf)polstern. **upholsterer** n Polsterer m. **upholstery** n Polsterung f.

upkeep ['ʌpkiːp] n Instandhaltung f; (cost) Unterhaltskosten pl.

uplift [ʌp'lift] v erbauen.

upon [ə'pon] prep auf. **once upon a time** es war einmal.

upper ['ʌpə] adj ober, höher. **uppermost** adj oberst, höchst. n (shoe) Oberleder neut.

upright ['ʌprait] adj, adv gerade, aufrecht; (honest) aufrecht, aufrichtig.

uprising ['ʌpraiziŋ] n Aufstand m.

uproar ['ʌprɔː] n Aufruhr m, Tumult m.

uproot [ʌp'ruːt] v ausreißen, entwurzeln.

*upset [ʌp'set; n 'ʌpset] v (person) bestürzen, beunruhigen; (plan) vereiteln; (tip over) umkippen. adj bestürzt, außer Fassung; (stomach) verstimmt. n (stomach) Verstimmung f.

upshot ['ʌpʃot] n Ergebnis neut.

upside down [ʌpsai'daun] adv verkehrt herum, mit dem Kopf nach unten. **turn upside down** sich auf den Kopf stellen.

upstairs [ʌp'steəz] adv (go) nach oben, die Treppe hinauf; (be) oben. adj (room) obere(r).

upstream [ʌp'striːm] adv stromaufwärts.

uptight ['ʌptait] adj (coll) nervös, aufgeregt.

up-to-date [ʌptə'deit] adj modern, aktuell.

upward ['ʌpwəd] adj nach oben (gerichtet). **upward glance** Blick nach oben m. adv also **upwards** aufwärts, nach oben.

uranium [ju'reiniəm] n Uran neut.

Uranus [juə'reinəs] n Uranus m.

urban ['əːbən] adj städtisch, Stadt-. **urbanization** n Verstädterung f. **urbanize** v verstädtern.

urchin ['əːtʃin] n (boy) Bengel m.

urge [əːdʒ] v (implore) (dringend) bitten, raten (+dat); (insist on) bestehen auf. **urge on** antreiben. n Drang m, (An)Trieb m.

urgent ['əːdʒənt] adj dringend. **urgency** n Dringlichkeit f.

urine ['juːrin] n Urin m, Harn m. **urinal** n Urinbecken neut, Pissoir neut. **urinary** adj Urin-. **urinate** v urinieren.

urn [əːn] n Urne f.

us [ʌs] pron uns. **both of us** wir beide. **all of us** wir alle.

usage ['juːzidʒ] n Brauch m, Gebrauch m.

use [juːz; v n juːs] v benutzen, gebrauchen; (apply) anwenden; (coll: exploit) ausbeuten. n Gebrauch m, Verwendung f. **be of use** von Nutzen sein, helfen. **for the use of** zum Nutzen von. **it's no use** es hilft nichts. **make use of** Gebrauch machen von. **use up** verbrauchen. I used to live here ich wohnte (früher) hier. she used to say sie hat immer gesagt, sie pflegte zu sagen. **useful** adj nützlich, brauchbar. **usefulness** n Nützlichkeit f. **useless** adj nutzlos, unnütz. **user** Benutzer(in). **uselessness** n Nutzlosigkeit f.

usher ['ʌʃə] n Platzanweiser(in). v **usher in** (fig) einleiten.

usual ['juːzuəl] adj üblich, gewöhnlich. **usually** adv gewöhnlich, normalerweise.

usurp [ju'zəːp] v gewaltsam nehmen, usurpieren. **usurpation** n Usurpation f. **usurper** n Usurpator m.

utensil [ju'tensl] n Gerät neut, Werkzeug neut; (pl) Utensilien pl.

uterus ['juːtərəs] n Gebärmutter f, Uterus m. **uterine** adj Gebärmutter-.

utility [ju'tiləti] n Nutzen m. **public utility** n öffentlicher Versorgungsbetrieb m.

utilize ['juːtilaiz] v verwenden. **utilization** n Verwendung f.

utmost ['ʌtmoust] adj äußerst. **do one's utmost** sein möglichstes tun.

utter¹ ['ʌtə] v äußern, aussprechen. **utterance** n Äußerung f.

utter² ['ʌtə] adj rein, bloß, höchst.

U-turn ['juːtəːn] n Wende f; (pol) Kehrtwendung f.

V

vacant ['veikənt] adj leer. **vacancy** n Leere f; (job) freie Stelle. **vacate** v verlassen; (seat) freimachen. **vacation** n Urlaub m.

vaccine ['vaksiːn] n Impfstoff m. **vaccinate** v impfen. **vaccination** n Impfung f.

vacillate ['vasileit] v schwanken. **vacillation** n Schwanken neut.

vacuum ['vakjum] n Vakuum neut. **vacuum-cleaner** n Staubsauger m. v (coll) mit dem Staubsauger reinigen. **vacuous** adj leer.

vagina [və'dʒainə] n Scheide f, Vagina f.

vagrant ['veigrənt] n Vagabund m, Landstreicher m.

vague [veig] adj vage, undeutlich; (person) zerstreut. **vagueness** n Verschwommenheit f.

vain [vein] adj (person) eitel, eingebildet; (thing) eitel, leer; (effort) vergeblich. **in vain** umsonst, vergeblich.

valiant ['valiənt] adj tapfer, heroisch.

valid ['valid] adj gültig. **validate** v für gültig erklären. **validity** n Gültigkeit f.

valley ['vali] n Tal neut.

value ['valjuː] n Wert neut. **value-added tax (VAT)** Mehrwertsteuer (Mwst) f. v (establish value of) einschätzen; (treasure) bewerten. **valuable** adj wertvoll, kostbar. **valuables** pl n Wertsachen pl. **valuation** n Schätzung f. **valued** adj hochgeschätzt. **valueless** adj wertlos.

valve [valv] n Ventil neut; (anat) Klappe f; (elec) Röhre f.

vampire ['vampaiə] n Vampir m.

van [van] n Lastwagen m, Lieferwagen m. **luggage van** Gepäckwagen m.

vandal ['vandl] n Vandale m, Vandalin f. **vandalism** n Vandalismus m.

vanilla [və'nilə] n Vanille f.

vanish ['vaniʃ] v verschwinden. **vanishing cream** Tagescreme f.

vanity ['vanəti] n Eitelkeit f. **vanity bag** Kosmetiktasche f.

vapour ['veipə] n Dampf m. **vaporize** v verdampfen.

varicose veins ['varikous] pl n Krampfadern pl.

varnish ['vaːniʃ] n Lack m, Firnis m. v lackieren.

vary ['veəri] v (modify) (ab)ändern, variieren; (become changed) sich ändern, variieren. **variable** adj veränderlich. **variation** n Veränderung; (music, biology) Variation f. **varied** adj verschiedenartig, abwechslungsvoll. **variety** n Verschiedenheit, Mannigfaltigkeit f; (species) Art f, Varietät f. **variety show** Variété neut. **various** adj verschieden; (several) mehrere. **varying** adj wechselnd, unterschiedlich.

vase [vaːz] n Vase f.

vasectomy [və'sektəmi] n Vasektomie f.

vast [vaːst] adj ungeheuer, riesig; (wide) weit, ausgedehnt. **vast majority** überwiegende Mehrheit f. **vast numbers of** zahllos(e). **vastly** n gewaltig. **vastness** n Weite f.

vat [vat] n großes Faß neut.

vault¹ [voːlt] n (ceiling) Gewölbe neut; (cellar) Keller m; (safe) Stahlkammer f.

vault² [voːlt] v (jump) springen (über). n Sprung m. **vaulting-horse** n Sprungpferd neut.

veal [viːl] n Kalbfleisch neut.

veer [viə] v sich drehen; (mot) ausscheren.

vegetable ['vedʒtəbl] n Gemüse neut. adj pflanzlich. **vegetarian** n Vegetarier(in); adj vegetarisch. **vegetation** n Pflanzenwuchs m, Vegetation f.

vehement ['viːəmənt] adj heftig, gewaltig.

vehicle ['viəkl] n Fahrzeug neut; (medium) Mittel neut, Vehikel neut.

veil [veil] n Schleier m. v verschleiern. **veiled** adj verschleiert.

vein [vein] n Vene f; (mood) Stimmung f; (in rock) Ader f. **veined** adj geädert.

velocity [və'losəti] n Geschwindigkeit f.

velvet ['velvit] n Samt m. adj Samt-. **velvety** adj samtweich, samtartig.

vending machine ['vendiŋ] *n* (Verkaufs)Automat *m*.

veneer [və'niə] *n* Furnier *neut*; (*fig*) Anstrich *m*. *v* furnieren.

venerate ['venəreit] *v* verehren, bewundern. **venerable** *adj* ehrwürdig. **veneration** *n* Verehrung *f*.

venereal disease [və'niəriəl] *n* Geschlechtskrankheit *f*.

Venetian blind [və'niːʃən] *n* Jalousie *f*.

vengeance ['vendʒəns] *n* Rache *f*. **take vengeance on** sich rächen an. **vengeful** *adj* rachsüchtig.

venison ['venisn] *n* Reh *neut*, Wildbret *neut*.

venom ['venəm] *n* (Tier)Gift *neut*. **venomous** *adj* giftig.

vent [vent] *n* Öffnung *f*, Luftloch *neut*; (*in jacket*) Schlitz *m*. *v* lüften; (*feelings*) freien Lauf lassen (+ *dat*), äußern.

ventilate ['ventileit] *v* ventilieren, lüften. **ventilation** *n* Ventilation *f*, Lüftung *f*. **ventilator** *n* Ventilator *m*, Lüftungsanlage *f*.

venture ['ventʃə] *n* (*risk*) Risiko *neut*, Wagnis *neut*; (*undertaking*) Unternehmen *neut*. *v* wagen.

venue ['venjuː] *n* Schauplatz *m*; (*meeting place*) Treffpunkt *m*.

Venus ['viːnəs] *n* Venus *f*.

verb [vəːb] *n* Verbum *neut*, Zeitwort *neut*. **verbal** *adj* mündlich. **verbalize** *v* formulieren. **verbatim** *adv* wortwörtlich. **verbose** *adj* wortreich.

verdict ['vəːdikt] *n* Urteil *neut*.

verge [vəːdʒ] *n* Rand *m*, Grenze *f*; (*grass*) Grasstreifen *m*. **verge on** grenzen an.

verify ['verifai] *v* beweisen, bestätigen, beglaubigen. **verification** *n* Beglaubigung *f*.

vermin ['vəːmin] *pl n* Schädlinge *pl*.

vermouth ['vəːməθ] *n* Wermut *m*.

vernacular [və'nakjulə] *n* Volkssprache *f*.

versatile ['vəːsətail] *adj* (*person*) vielseitig. **versatility** *n* Vielseitigkeit *f*.

verse [vəːs] *n* (*stanza*) Strophe *f*; (*line*) Vers *m*; (*poetry*) Poesie *f*, Dichtung *f*. **versed** *adj* versiert.

version ['vəːʃən] *n* Fassung *f*, Version *f*; (*Bible, etc.*) Übersetzung *f*.

versus ['vəːsəs] *prep* gegen.

vertebra ['vəːtibrə] *n* (*pl* -ae) Wirbel *m*. **vertebral column** Wirbelsäule *f*. **vertebrate** *n* Wirbeltier *neut*.

vertical ['vəːtikl] *adj* senkrecht, lotrecht. *n* Senkrechte *f*.

vertigo ['vəːtigou] *n* Schwindelgefühl *neut*.

very ['veri] *adj* sehr. *very best* allerbest. *adj that very day* an ebendemselben Tag. *at the very beginning* gerade am Anfang.

vessel ['vesl] *n* Gefäß *neut*; (*ship*) Schiff *neut*.

vest [vest] *n* (*undershirt*) Unterhemd *neut*; (*waistcoat*) Weste *f*.

vestige ['vestidʒ] *n* Spur *f*.

vestments ['vestmənts] *pl n* (*rel*) Amtstracht *f*.

vestry ['vestri] *n* Sakristei *f*.

vet [vet] *n* (*animals*) Tierarzt *m*. *v* prüfen, überholen.

veteran ['vetərən] *n* Veteran *m*.

veterinary ['vetərinəri] *n* Tierarzt *m*.

veto ['viːtou] *n* Veto *neut*, Einspruch *m*. *v* Veto einlegen gegen.

vex [veks] *v* ärgern, belästigen. **vexation** *n* Ärger *m*. **vexed** *adj* ärgerlich; (*question*) strittig.

via [vaiə] *prep* über.

viable ['vaiəbl] *adj* lebensfähig; (*practicable*) durchführbar.

viaduct ['vaiədʌkt] *n* Viadukt *m*.

vibrate [vai'breit] *v* vibrieren. **vibration** *n* Vibrieren *neut*, Vibration *f*.

vicar ['vikə] *n* Pfarrer *m*. **vicarage** *n* Pfarrhaus *neut*.

vicarious [vi'keəriəs] *adj* aus zweiter Hand.

vice¹ [vais] *n* (*evil*) Laster *neut*, Untugend *f*.

vice² [vais] *n* (*tool*) Schraubstock *m*, Zwinge *f*.

vice-chancellor [vais'tʃaɪnsələ] *n* (*university*) Rektor *m*.

vice-president [vais'prezidənt] *n* Vizepräsident *m*.

vice versa [vaisi'vəːsə] *adv* umgekehrt.

vicinity [vi'sinəti] *n* Nähe *f*, Nachbarschaft *f*.

vicious ['viʃəs] *adj* bösartig, gemein; (*blow, etc*) heftig, gewaltig. **vicious circle** Teufelskreis *m*. **viciousness** *n* Gemeinheit *f*.

victim ['viktim] *n* Opfer *neut*. **victimize** *v* ungerecht behandeln.

victor ['viktə] *n* Sieger(in). **victorious** *adj* siegreich. **victory** *n* Sieg *m*.

video-tape ['vidiouteip] *n* Magnetbildband *neut*.

view [vjuː] *n* Ausblick *m*, Aussicht *f*; *(picture, opinion)* Ansicht *f*. **in view** in Sicht. **viewfinder** *n* Sucher *m*. **viewpoint** *n* Gesichtspunkt *m*, Standpunkt *m*. **with a view to** mit der Absicht, zu. *v* ansehen, betrachten. **viewer** *n (TV)* Zuschauer(in).

vigil ['vidʒil] *n* Wachen *neut*. **keep vigil** wachen. **vigilance** *n* Wachsamkeit *f*. **vigilant** *adj* wachsam.

vigour ['vigə] *n* Kraft *f*, Vitalität *f*. **vigorous** *adj* kräftig, energisch.

vile [vail] *adj* gemein, ekelerregend, widerlich.

villa ['vilə] *n* Villa *f*.

village ['vilidʒ] *n* Dorf *neut*. *adj* dörflich, Dorf-. **villager** *n* Dorfbewohner(in).

villain ['vilən] *n* Schurke *m*; *(coll)* Schelm *m*. **villainous** *adj* schurkisch. **villainy** *n* Schurkerei *f*.

vindictive [vin'diktiv] *adj* rachsüchtig. **vindictiveness** *n* Rachsucht *f*.

vine [vain] *n* Rebe *f*, Weinstock *m*. **vineleaf** *n* Weinblatt *m*. **vineyard** *n* Weinberg *m*. **viniculture** *n* Weinbau *m*.

vinegar ['vinigə] *n* Essig *m*. **vinegary** *adj* sauer.

vintage ['vintidʒ] *n* Weinernte *f*; *(particular year)* Jahrgang *m*.

vinyl ['vainil] *n* Vinyl *neut*. *adj* Vinyl-.

viola [vi'oulə] *n* Viola *f*.

violate ['vaiəleit] *v (law)* übertreten; *(woman)* vergewaltigen. **violation** *n* Übertretung *f*.

violence ['vaiələns] *n* Gewalt *f*, Gewalttätigkeit *f*. **violent** *adj (blow)* heftig, gewaltig; *(person, action)* gewaltsam.

violet ['vaiəlit] *n* Veilchen *neut*. *adj* violett.

violin [vaiə'lin] *n* Geige *f*, Violine *f*. **violinist** *n* Geiger(in).

viper ['vaipə] *n* Viper *f*, Natter *f*.

virgin ['vəːdʒin] *n* Jungfrau *f*. *adj* jungfräulich; *(soil)* unbebaut. **virginity** *n* Jungfernschaft *f*.

Virgo ['vəːgou] *n* Jungfrau *f*.

virile ['virail] *adj* männlich, kräftig. **virility** *n* Männlichkeit *f*.

virtual ['vəːtʃuəl] *adj* eigentlich; *(coll)* praktisch. **virtually** *adv* praktisch.

virtue ['vəːtʃuː] *n* Tugend *f*. **by virtue of** wegen (+ *gen*). **virtuous** *adj* tugendhaft, rechtschaffen.

virtuoso [,vəːtju'ouzou] *n* Virtuose *m*, Virtuosin *f*. **virtuosity** *n* Virtuosität *f*.

virus ['vaiərəs] *n* Virus *neut*.

visa ['viːzə] *n* Visum *neut*.

viscount ['vaikaunt] *n* Vicomte *m*.

viscous ['viskəs] *adj* zähflüssig. **viscosity** *n* Viskosität *f*.

visible ['vizəbl] *adj* sichtbar. **visibility** *n* Sichtbarkeit *f*. **visibly** *adj* offenbar.

vision ['viʒən] *n (power of sight)* Sehvermögen *neut*; *(insight)* Einsicht *f*; *(mystical, etc.)* Vision *f*. **field of vision** Blickfeld *neut*. **visionary** *adj* phantastisch; *n* Hellseher(in).

visit ['vizit] *v* besuchen. *n* Besuch *m*. **visitation** *n* Besuchen *neut*. **visiting** *adj* Besuchs-. **visitor** *n* Besucher(in). **visitor's book** Gästebuch *neut*.

visor ['vaizə] *n* Visier *neut*; *(peak)* Schirm *m*.

visual ['viʒuəl] *adj* visuell. **visual aids** Anschauungsmaterial *neut*. **visualize** *v* vergegenwärtigen.

vital ['vaitl] *adj* lebenswichtig. **vitality** *n* Lebenskraft *f*.

vitamin ['vitəmin] *n* Vitamin *neut*.

vivacious [vi'veiʃəs] *adj* lebhaft, munter. **vivacity** *n* Lebhaftigkeit *f*.

vivid ['vivid] *adj (description)* lebendig; *(colour)* leuchtend; *(imagination)* lebhaft.

vixen ['viksn] *n* Füchsin *f*.

vocabulary [və'kabjuləri] *n* Wortschatz *m*; *(glossary)* Wörterverzeichnis *neut*.

vocal ['voukəl] *adj* stimmlich; *(music)* Vokal-. **vocal cords** *pl* Stimmbänder *pl*. **vocalist** *n* Sänger(in).

vocation [vou'keiʃən] *n (rel)* Berufung *f*; *(occupation)* Beruf *m*. **vocational** *adj* Berufs-.

vociferous [və'sifərəs] *adj* brüllend, lärmend.

vodka ['vodkə] *n* Wodka *m*.

voice [vois] *n* Stimme *f*. *v* ausdrücken, äußern.

void [void] *adj* leer; *(invalid)* nichtig, ungültig.

volatile ['volətail] *adj* flüchtig; *(person)* wankelmutig, sprunghaft.

volcano [vol'keinou] *n* Vulkan *m*. **volcanic** *adj* vulkanisch. **volcanic eruption** Vulkanausbruch *m*.

volley ['voli] *n (mil)* Salve *f*; *(tennis)* Flugschlag *m*.

volt [voult] *n* Volt *neut*. **voltage** *n* Spannung *f*.

volume ['voljum] *n* Volumen *neut*, Inhalt *m*; *(book)* Band *m*; *(noise level)* Lautstärke *f*.

voluntary ['volǝntri] *adj* freiwillig.
volunteer [volǝn'tiǝ] *n* Freiwillige(r). *adj* Freiwilligen-. *v* sich freiwillig melden.
voluptuous [vǝ'lʌptʃuǝs] *adj* wollüstig.
voluptuousness *n* Wollust *f*.
vomit ['vomit] *v* (sich) erbrechen.
voodoo ['vuːduː] *n* Wodu *m*.
voracious [vǝ'reiʃǝs] *adj* gierig.
vote [vout] *n* (*individual*) Stimme *f*; (*right to vote*) Stimmrecht *neut*; (*election*) Abstimmung *f*, Wahl *f*. **vote of no confidence** Mißtrauensvotum *neut*. *v* abstimmen. **vote for** stimmen für. **voter** *n* Wähler(in).
vouch [vautʃ] *v* (sich) bürgen für. **voucher** *n* Gutschein *m*. **vouchsafe** *v* gewähren.
vow [vau] *n* Gelübde *neut*. *v* schwören, geloben.
vowel ['vauǝl] *n* Vokal *m*. *adj* vokalisch.
voyage ['voiidʒ] *n* Reise *f*. *v* reisen. **voyager** *n* Reisende(r).
vulgar ['vʌlgǝ] *adj* vulgär, ordinär. **vulgarity** *n* Ungezogenheit *f*.
vulnerable ['vʌlnǝrǝbl] *adj* verwundbar.
vulture ['vʌltʃǝ] *n* Geier *m*.

W

wad [wod] *n* Bausch *m*; (*money*) Rolle *f*.
waddle ['wodl] *v* watscheln.
wade [weid] *v* waten.
wafer ['weifǝ] *n* Waffel *f*; (*rel*) Hostie *f*. **wafer-thin** *adj* hauchdünn.
waffle ['wofl] *n* Waffel *f*.
waft [woft] *v* wehen.
wag [wag] *v* **wag one's head** mit dem Kopf wackeln. **wag one's tail** wedeln.
wage [weidʒ] *n also* **wages** Lohn *m*. **wage agreement** Tarifvertrag *m*. **wage-earner** *n* Lohnempfänger(in). **wage freeze** *n* Lohnstopp *m*. **wage-packet** *n* Lohntüte *f*. *v* (*war*) führen.
waggle ['wagl] *v* wackeln (mit).
wagon ['wagǝn] *n* Wagen *m*; (*rail*) Waggon *m*.
waif [weif] *n* verwahrlostes Kind *neut*.
wail [weil] *v* jammern, wehklagen. **wailing** *n* Jammern *neut*.
waist [weist] *n* Taille *f*. **waistband** *n* Bund *m*. **waistcoat** *n* Weste *f*.
wait [weit] *v* warten. **no waiting** Parken verboten. **wait and see** abwarten. **wait for** warten auf. **waiting-room** *n* Wartesaal *m*. **wait on** bedienen. *n* Wartezeit *f*. **waiter** *n* Kellner *m*. **waitress** *n* Kellnerin *f*.
waive [weiv] *v* verzichten auf.
***wake** [weik] *v also* **waken** *or* **wake up** aufwachen, erwachen; (*awaken*) (auf)wecken, erwecken. **wakeful** *adj* wachsam. **waking** *adj* wach.
walk [woːk] *v* laufen, (zu Fuß) gehen. **walk out** streiken. **walk out on** im Stich lassen. **walk-over** *n* leichter Sieg *m*, Spaziergang *m*. **walk** Spaziergang *m*; (*path*) Weg *m*. **go for a walk** einen Spaziergang machen, spazierengehen. **walk of life** Lebensstellung *f*.
wall [woːl] *n* Mauer *f*; (*internal*) Wand *f*. **wallpaper** *n* Tapete *f*; *v* tapezieren.
wallet ['wolit] *n* Brieftasche *f*, Geldtasche *f*.
wallop ['wolǝp] *v* prügeln. *n* (heftiger) Schlag *m*.
wallow ['wolou] *v* sich wälzen.
walnut ['woːlnʌt] *n* Walnuß *f*.
walrus ['woːlrǝs] *n* Walroß *neut*.
waltz [woːlts] *n* Walzer *m*. *v* Walzer tanzen, walzen.
wand [wond] *n* Rute *f*; (*magic*) Zauberstab *m*.
wander ['wondǝ] *v* wandern. **wander about** umherwandern. **wanderlust** *n* Wanderlust *f*. **wanderer** *n* Wanderer *m*. **wandering** *n* Wandern *neut*. *adj* wandernd.
wane [wein] *v* abnehmen.
wangle ['waŋgl] *v* organisieren, (hintenherum) beschaffen. **wangler** *n* Schieber *m*.
want [wont] *v* wollen; (*need*) benötigen; (*wish*) wünschen. **wants** *pl n* Bedürfnisse *pl*. **wanted** *adj* gesucht. **be found wanting** den Erwartungen nicht entsprechen.
wanton ['wontǝn] *adj* lüstern; (*cruelty, etc.*) rücksichtslos.
war [woː] *n* Krieg *m*. **be at war with** Krieg führen mit. **prisoner-of-war** Kriegsgefangene(r). **war crime** *n* Kriegsverbrechen *neut*. **warfare** *n* Kriegführung *f*. **warlike** *adj* kriegerisch. **war memorial** Kriegerdenkmal *neut*.
warble ['woːbl] *v* trillern.
ward [woːd] *n* (*town*) Bezirk *n*; (*hospital*) Station *f*; (*of court*) Mündel *neut*. *v* **ward off** abwehren. **warden** *n* Vorsteher *m*. **warder** *n* Gefängniswärter *m*.

wardrobe ['wɔːdroub] *n* Kleiderschrank *m*; (*clothes*) Garderobe *f*.

wares [weəz] *pl n* Waren *pl*.

warehouse ['weəhaus] *n* Lager(haus) *neut*.

warm [wɔːm] *adj* warm. **warm-blooded** *adj* warmblütig. **warm-hearted** *adj* warmherzig. *v* (auf)wärmen. **warm up** *v* (*become warm*) warm werden; (*engine*) warmlaufen (lassen). **warmish** *adj* lauwarm. **warmth** *n* Wärme *f*.

warn [wɔːn] *v* warnen. **warn off** verwarnen. **warning** *n* Warnung *f*. *adj* warnend. **warning light** Warnlicht *neut*.

warp [wɔːp] *v* sich verziehen, krumm werden. **warped** *adj* verzogen.

warrant ['wɔrənt] *n* Vollmacht *f*, Berechtigung *f*. **warrant of arrest** Haftbefehl *m*.

warren ['wɔrən] *n* Kaninchengehege *neut*.

warrior ['wɔriə] *n* Krieger *m*.

wart [wɔːt] *n* Warze *f*.

wary ['weəri] *adj* vorsichtig, behutsam. **wary of** auf der Hut vor.

was [wɔz] *v* be.

wash [wɔʃ] *v* waschen; (*oneself*) sich waschen; (*dishes*) spülen. **washbasin** *n* Waschbecken *neut*. **wash down** abwaschen. **washed-out** *adj* verblaßt; (*coll*) ermüdet. **washed-up** *adj* (*coll*) ruiniert, fertig. **washing** *n* (*laundry*) Wäsche *f*. **washing machine** Waschmaschine *f*. **washing powder** Waschmittel *neut*. **wash up** (ab)spülen, abwaschen. *n* Waschen *neut*, Wäsche *f*. **washable** *adj* waschecht. **washer** *n* (*tech*) Scheibe *f*, Dichtungsring *m*.

wasp [wɔsp] *n* Wespe *f*. **waspish** *adj* reizbar.

waste [weist] *v* verschwenden, vergeuden. **waste away** abnehmen, verfallen. *n* Verschwendung *f*; (*rubbish*) Abfall *m*. **waste of time** Zeitverschwendung *f*. *adj* (*land*) wüst; Abfall-. **lay waste** verwüsten. **waste-bin** *n* Abfalleimer *m*. **wastepaper basket** *n* Papierkorb *neut*. **wasteful** *adj* verschwenderisch.

watch [wɔtʃ] *v* (*guard*) bewachen; (*observe*) zusehen, beobachten; (*pay attention to*) achtgeben auf. **watch out!** paß auf! **watch out for** auf der Hut sein vor. **watch television** fernsehen. *n* Wache *f*; (*wristwatch*) Armbanduhr *f*. **keep watch** Wache halten. **watchdog** *n* Wachhund *m*. **watchman** *n* Wächter *m*. **watchful** *adj* wachsam.

water ['wɔːtə] *n* Wasser *neut*. *v* wässern. **water down** verwässern.

water-closet *n* (Wasser)Klosett *neut*, WC *neut*.

water-colour *n* Aquarell *neut*. *adj* Aquarell-.

watercress ['wɔːtəkres] *n* Brunnenkresse *f*.

waterfall ['wɔːtəfɔːl] *n* Wasserfall *m*.

watering-can *n* Gießkanne *f*.

water-lily *n* Seerose *f*, Wasserlilie *f*.

waterlogged ['wɔːtəlɔgd] *adj* vollgesogen.

watermark ['wɔːtəmaːk] *n* (*in paper*) Wasserzeichen *neut*.

water-melon *n* Wassermelone *f*.

water-mill *n* Wassermühle *f*.

waterproof ['wɔːtəpruːf] *adj* wasserdicht. *n* Regenmantel *m*. *v* imprägnieren.

watershed ['wɔːtəʃed] *n* Wasserscheide *f*.

water-ski *n* Wasserski *m*. *v* Wasserski fahren.

watertight ['wɔːtətait] *adj* wasserdicht; (*argument*) unanfechtbar.

water-way *n* Wasserstraße *f*.

waterworks ['wɔːtəwəːks] *pl n* Wasserwerk *neut sing*.

watery ['wɔːtəri] *adj* wässerig; (*eyes*) tränend.

watt [wɔt] *n* Watt *neut*. **wattage** *n* Wattleistung *f*.

wave [weiv] *n* Welle *f*; (*gesture*) Wink *m*. **waveband** *n* Wellenband *neut*. **wavelength** *n* Wellenlänge *f*. *v* winken; (*hair*) in Wellen legen. **wavy** *adj* wellig; (*hair*) gewellt.

waver ['weivə] *v* schwanken.

wax[1] [waks] *n* Wachs *neut*. *v* (*floor*) bohnern. **waxen** *adj* wächsern. **waxwork** *n* Wachsfigur *f*.

wax[2] [waks] *v* (*increase*) wachsen; (*become*) werden.

way [wei] *n* Weg *m*; (*direction*) Richtung *f*; (*method*) Art *f*, Weise *f*; (*respect*) Hinsicht *f*, Beziehung *f*. **by the way** übrigens. **on the way** unterwegs. **out-of-the-way** *adj* abgelegen; (*odd*) ungewöhnlich.

*waylay ['wei'lei] *v* auflauern (+ *dat*).

wayward ['weiwəd] *adj* eigensinnig. **waywardness** *n* Eigensinn *m*.

we [wiː] *pl pron* wir.

weak [wiːk] *adj* schwach; (*liquids*) dünn. **weak-minded** *adj* charakterschwach. **weaken** *v* schwächen. *n* Schwächling *m*. **weakly** *adj*, *adv* schwächlich. **weakness** *n* Schwäche *f*; (*disadvantage*) Nachteil *m*; (*liking*) Vorliebe *f*.

wealth [welθ] *n* Reichtum *m*; (*fortune*)
Vermögen *neut*. **wealthy** *adj* reich,
wohlhabend.
wean [wiːn] *v* entwöhnen.
weapon ['wepən] *n* Waffe *f*.
*wear [weə] *v* tragen; (*wear out*)
abnutzen; (*become worn*) abgenutzt werden; *n* Tragen *neut*; (*wear and tear*)
Abnutzung *f*, Verschleiß *m*. **wear off** (*fig*)
sich verlieren. **wear out** (*person*)
ermüden.
weary ['wiəri] *adj* müde; (*task*) lästig. *v*
ermüden; (*become tired of*) müde werden
(+*gen*). **weariness** *n* Müdigkeit *f*. **weari-
some** *adj* ermüdend, langweilig.
weasel ['wiːzl] *n* Wiesel *neut*.
weather ['weðə] *n* Wetter *neut*. **weather-
beaten** *adj* verwittert. **weathercock** *n*
Wetterhahn *m*. **weather forecast** Wettervorhersage *f*. **weatherman** *n* (*coll*)
Meteorologe *m*. **weather-proof** *adj* wet-
terfest.
*weave [wiːv] *v* weben. **weave into** einflechten in. **weaving** *n* Weberei *f*; *adj*
Web-.
web [web] *n* (*spider's*) Spinngewebe *neut*.
webbed foot Schwimmfuß *m*. **webbing** *n*
Gewebe *neut*. **web-footed** *adj*
schwimmfüßig.
wedding ['wedin] *n* Hochzeit *f*. **wedding
cake** Hochzeitskuchen *m*. **wedding day**
Hochzeitstag *m*. **wedding ring** Trauring
m.
wedge [wedʒ] *n* Keil *m*; (*of cheese*) Ecke
f. **wedge-shaped** *adj* keilförmig. *v*
einkeilen.
Wednesday ['wenzdi] *n* Mittwoch *m*. **on
Wednesdays** mittwochs.
weed [wiːd] *n* Unkraut *neut*. *v* (Unkraut)
jäten. **weedy** *adj* (*coll*) schmächtig.
week [wiːk] *n* Woche *f*. **weekday** *n*
Wochentag *m*. **weekend** *n* Wochenende
neut. **weekly** *adj* wöchentlich; *n* (*magazine*) Wochenzeitschrift *f*.
*weep [wiːp] *v* weinen. **weeping** *adj*
weinend; *n* Weinen *neut*. **weeping willow**
Trauerweide *f*.
weigh [wei] *v* wiegen. **weigh one's words**
seine Worte abwägen. **weigh up**
abschätzen. **weight** *n* Gewicht *neut*. **carry
weight with** viel gelten bei. **lose weight**
abnehmen. **put on weight** zunehmen.
weight-lifting *n* Gewichtheben *neut*.
weighty *adj* schwerwiegend.
weir [wiə] *n* Wehr *neut*.

weird [wiəd] *adj* unheimlich.
welcome ['welkəm] *n* Willkommen *neut*.
adj, *interj* willkommen. **you're welcome**
(*coll*) bitte, nichts zu danken. *v* willkommen heißen; (*fig*) begrüßen.
weld [weld] *v* (ver)schweißen. *n*
Schweißstelle *f*, Schweißnaht *f*. **welder** *n*
Schweißer *m*. **welding** *n* Schweißen *neut*.
welfare ['welfeə] *n* Wohlfahrt *f*. **welfare
state** Wohlfahrtsstaat *m*.
well[1] [wel] *n* (*for water*) Brunnen *m*,
Quelle *f*.
well[2] [wel] *adv* gut. **as well** auch. **as well
as** sowohl ... als auch. **you may well ask**
du kannst wohl fragen. *adj* (*healthy*)
wohl, gesund. **feel well** sich wohl fühlen.
I'm not well mir ist nicht wohl. *interj* na,
schön.
well-being *n* Wohlergehen *neut*.
well-behaved *adj* artig.
well-bred *adj* wohlerzogen.
well-built *adj* gut gebaut; (*person*) kräftig
gebaut.
well-done *adj* (*meat*) gut durchgebraten.
wellingtons ['welintənz] *pl n* Gummis-
tiefel *pl*.
well-known *adj* (wohl)bekannt.
well-meaning *adj* wohlmeinend.
well-off *adj* wohlhabend.
well-paid *adj* gut bezahlt.
well-spoken *adj* höflich.
well-to-do *adj* wohlhabend.
well-worn *adj* abgenutzt; (*phrase*)
abgedroschen.
went [went] *V* go.
wept [wept] *V* weep.
west [west] *n* Westen *m*. *adj also* **westerly**
westlich, West-. *adv also* **westwards** nach
Westen; westwärts. **western** *adj* westlich;
n Wildwestfilm *m*.
wet [wet] *adj* naß. **wet through** durchnäßt.
wet weather Regenwetter *neut*. *n* Nässe *f*.
v anfeuchten, naßmachen. **wetness** *n*
Nässe *f*.
whack [wak] *v* schlagen, verhauen. *n*
Schlag *m*.
whale [weil] *n* Wal *m*, Walfisch *m*. **whaler**
n Walfänger *m*. **whaling** *n* Walfang *m*.
wharf [woːf] *n* Kai *m*.
what [wot] *pron* was. **so what?** na und?
what about ... ? wie wäre es mit ... ?
whatever *pron* was auch immer. **nothing
whatever** überhaupt nichts. **what for?**
wozu? **what's up?** was ist los? **what's your**

name? wie heißt du? *or (polite)* wie ist Ihr Name? *adj* was für ein, welch.

wheat [wiːt] *n* Weizen *m*.

wheel [wiːl] *n* Rad *neut*; *(steering)* Lenkrad *neut*. **at the wheel** am Steuer. *v* rollen. **wheelbarrow** *n* Schubkarren *m*. **wheelchair** *n* Rollstuhl *m*.

wheeze [wiːz] *n* Keuchen *neut*; *(coll)* Plan *m*. *v* keuchen, schnaufen.

whelk [welk] *n* Wellhornschnecke *f*.

when [wen] *adv (question)* wann. *conj (with past tense)* als; *(with present tense)* wenn. **whenever** *conj* wann auch immer.

where [weə] *adv*, *conj* wo; *(motion)* wohin. **where from?** woher? **where to?** wohin? *where do you come from?* wo kommen Sie her? *where are you going?* wo gehen Sie hin? **whereabouts** *adv* wo; *n* Verbleib *m*. **whereas** *conj* wohingegen, während. **whereby** *adv* wodurch, womit. **whereupon** *adv* woraufhin. **wherever** *adv* wo auch immer.

whether ['weðə] *conj* ob.

which [witʃ] *pron (question)* welch, *(the one that)* welch, der/die/das.

whiff [wif] *n* Hauch *m*.

while [wail] *conj* während; *(whereas)* wogegen. *n* Weile *f*. **a long while ago** schon lange her. **for a while** eine Zeitlang. **in a while** bald. *v* **while away the time** sich die Zeit vertreiben.

whim [wim] *n* Laune *f*, Einfall *m*.

whimper ['wimpə] *n* Wimmer *neut*. *v* wimmern.

whimsical ['wimzikl] *adj* launenhaft.

whine [wain] *n* Gewinsel *neut*. *v* winseln. **whining** *adj* weinerlich.

whip [wip] *n* Peitsche *f*. *v* peitschen; *(cream)* schlagen. **whipped cream** Schlagsahne *f*. **whipping** *n* Peitschen *neut*. **whip-round** *n* *(coll)* Geldsammlung *f*.

whippet ['wipit] *n* Whippet *m*.

whirl [wəːl] *n* Wirbel *m*. *v* wirbeln. **whirlwind** *n* Wirbelwind *m*.

whisk [wisk] *n* Schneebesen *m*. *v* schlagen. **whisk away/off** *v* wegzaubern.

whiskers ['wiskəz] *pl n (animals)* Schnurrhaare *pl*; *(man's)* Barthaare *pl*.

whisky ['wiski] *n* Whisky *m*.

whisper ['wispə] *v* flüstern. *n* Flüstern *m*.

whist [wist] *n* Whist *neut*.

whistle ['wisl] *v* pfeifen. *n* Pfiff *m*; *(instrument)* Pfeife *f*.

white [wait] *adj* weiß; *(pale)* blaß. **white**

bread Weißbrot *neut*. **white lie** Notlüge *f*. **white man** Weiße(r) *m*. **whitewash** *v* tünchen. **white wine** Weißwein *m*. *n* Weiß *neut*; *(person)* Weiße(r). **whiten** *v* weiß machen; *(bleach)* bleichen. **whiteness** *n* Weiße *f*.

whiting ['waitiŋ] *n* Weißfisch *m*.

Whitsun ['witsn] *n* Pfingsten *neut sing*.

whiz [wiz] *v* zischen.

who [huː] *pron (question)* wer; *(the one which, that)* wer, welch, der/die/das. **whoever** *pron* wer auch immer.

whole [houl] *adj* ganz; *(undamaged)* heil, unverletzt. *n* das Ganze *neut*; *(collective)* Gesamtheit *f*. **on the whole** im großen und ganzen.

whole-hearted *adj* rückhaltlos.

wholemeal ['houlmiːl] *adj* Vollkorn-.

wholesale ['houlseil] *adv* en gros; *(fig)* unterschiedslos. *adj* Großhandels-. *n* Großhandel *m*. **wholesaler** *n* Großhändler *m*.

wholesome ['houlsəm] *adj* bekömmlich, gesund.

whom [huːm] *pron (question) (acc)* wen, *(dat)* wem; *(that, the one whom)* den, dem.

whooping cough ['huːpiŋ] *n* Keuchhusten *m*.

whore [hoː] *n* Hure *f*. *v* huren.

whose [huːz] *pron (question)* wessen; *(of whom)* dessen, deren. *whose is this?* wem gehört dies?

why [wai] *adv* warum. *interj* nun, ja. **that is why** deshalb. **the reason why** der Grund, weshalb.

wick [wik] *n* Docht *m*.

wicked ['wikid] *adj* böse. **wickedness** *n* Bosheit *f*.

wicker ['wikə] *adj* Weiden-, Korb-. **wickerwork** *n* Korbwaren *pl*.

wicket ['wikit] *n* *(gate)* Pförtchen *neut*.

wide [waid] *adj* breit. *adv* weit. **far and wide** weit und breit. **wide awake** hellwach. **widespread** *adj* weitverbreitet. **widely** *adv* weit. **widely known** allgemein bekannt. **widen** *v* breiter machen *or* werden. **wideness** *n* Breite *f*.

widow ['widou] *n* Witwe *f*. **widowed** *adj* verwitwet. **widower** *n* Witwer *m*. **widowhood** *n* Witwenstand *m*.

width [widθ] *n* Breite *f*, Weite *f*.

wield [wiːld] *v* *(weapon)* handhaben; *(influence)* ausüben.

wife [waif] n (pl **wives**) Frau f.
wig [wig] n Perücke f.
wiggle ['wigl] v wackeln. n Wackeln neut.
wild [waild] adj wild; (coll: angry) wütend. **be wild about** (coll) schwärmen für. **wildcat strike** wilder Streik m. **wild flower** Feldblume f. **Wildness** n Wildheit f.
wilderness ['wildənəs] n Wüste f.
wilful ['wilfəl] adj eigensinnig. **wilfulness** n Eigensinn m.
will[1] [wil] v (to form future) werden; (expressing wish or determination) wollen.
will[2] [wil] n Wille m; (testament) Testament neut. **will-power** n Willenskraft f.
willing ['wiliŋ] adj bereit. **willingly** adv bereitwillig. **willingness** n Bereitschaft f.
willow ['wilou] n Weide f.
wilt [wilt] v verwelken.
wily ['waili] adj schlau, listig.
*****win** [win] v gewinnen; (mil) siegen. n Seig m.
wince [wins] v zusammenzucken. n (Zusammen)Zucken neut.
winch [wintʃ] n Winde f.
wind[1] [wind] n Wind m. **wind instrument** Blasinstrument neut.
*****wind**[2] [waind] v (sich) winden; (yarn) aufwickeln; (clock) aufziehen. **wind up** (come to a close) Schluß machen. (business) auflösen. **winder** n Winde f. **winding** adj sich windend, schlängelnd.
windlass ['windləs] n Winde f.
windmill ['wind‚mil] n Windmühle f.
windpipe ['windpaip] n Luftröhre f.
window ['windou] n Fenster neut; (ticket office, etc.) Schalter m; (shop) Schaufenster neut. **window-box** n Blumenkasten m. **window-frame** n Fensterrahmen m. **window-pane** n Fensterscheibe f. **window-shopping** n Schaufensterbummel m. **window-sill** Fensterbrett neut.
windshield ['windʃiːld] n Windschutzscheibe f. **windshield-wiper** Scheibenwischer m.
windy ['windi] adj windig.
wine [wain] n Wein m. **wine bar** Weinstube f. **wineglass** n Weinglas neut.
wing [wiŋ] n Flügel m; (theatre) Kulisse f; (mot) Kotflügel m. **on the wing** im Fluge. **winged** adj geflügelt. **winger** n (sport) Außenstürmer m. **wing-nut** n Flügelmutter f.
wink [wiŋk] n Zwinkern neut. v **wink at** zuzwinkern (+dat).

winkle ['wiŋkl] n Strandschnecke f.
winner ['winə] n Sieger(in), Gewinner(in). **winnings** pl n Gewinn m sing.
winter ['wintə] n Winter m. v überwintern. **wintry** adj winterlich.
wipe [waip] v wischen. **wipe out** (destroy) ausrotten. **wipe up** (dishes) abtrocknen. **wiper** n Wischer m.
wire [waiə] n Draht m; (telegram) Telegramm neut. **wire netting** Maschendraht m. v (house, etc.) Leitungen legen in. **wireless** n Radio neut. **wiring** n Leitungsnetz neut.
wiry ['waiəri] adj (person) sehnig, zäh, (hair) borstig.
wisdom ['wizdəm] n Weisheit f. **wisdom tooth** n Weisheitszahn m.
wise [waiz] adj weise, klug. **wise guy** (coll) Besserwisser m. **wise man/woman** Weise(r).
wish [wiʃ] v wünschen. **wish for** sich wünschen. I wish to know ich möchte wissen. **wished-for** adj erwünscht. n Wunsch m.
wisp [wisp] n (hair) Strähne f. **wispy** adj (hair) wuschelig.
wistful ['wistfəl] adj sehnsüchtig. **wistfulness** n Sehnsucht f.
wit [wit] n Witz m, Esprit m. **wits** pl Verstand m.
witch [witʃ] n Hexe f. **witchcraft** n Hexerei f. **witch-doctor** n Medizinmann m.
with [wið] prep mit; (among people) bei. **weep with joy** vor Freude weinen. **stay with** bleiben bei.
*****withdraw** [wið'drɔː] v (sich) zurückziehen; (remark) zurücknehmen; (money) abheben. **withdrawal** n Zurückziehung f; Zurücknahme f; Abhebung f. **withdrawn** adj zurückgezogen.
wither ['wiðə] v verdorren, verwelken. **withered** adj welk.
*****withhold** [wið'hould] v zurückhalten.
within [wi'ðin] prep innerhalb (+gen). adv darin, innen. **within a short time** binnen kurzem.
without [wi'ðaut] prep ohne (+acc).
*****withstand** [wið'stand] v widerstehen (+dat).
witness ['witnis] n Zeuge m, Zeugin f. **bear witness to** Zeuge ablegen von. **witness-box** n Zeugenstand m. v bezeugen; (be present at) erleben, sehen.

wrap

witty ['witi] *adj* witzig. **witticism** *n* Witz *m*.

wizard ['wizəd] *n* Zauberer *m*. **wizardry** *n* Zauberei *f*.

wobble ['wobl] *v* wackeln, schwanken. *n* Wackeln *neut*. **wobbly** *adj* wackelig.

woke [wouk] *V* **wake**.

woken ['woukn] *V* **wake**.

wolf [wulf] *n* (*pl* **wolves**) Wolf *m*. *v* (*gobble*) verschlingen. **she-wolf** *n* Wölfin *f*.

woman ['wumən] *n* (*pl* **women**) Frau *f*. **woman doctor** Ärztin *f*. **womanly** *adj* weiblich, fraulich.

womb [wuːm] *n* Gebärmutter *f*

won [wʌn] *V* **win**.

wonder ['wʌndə] *n* (*marvel*) Wunder *neut*; (*astonishment*) Erstaunen *neut*, Verwunderung *f*. **no wonder** kein Wunder. *v* (*be surprised*) sich wundern; (*ask oneself, muse*) sich fragen, gespannt sein. **wonderful** *adj* wunderbar. **wondrous** *adj* erstaunlich.

wonky ['woŋki] *adj* wackelig.

wood [wud] *n* Holz *neut*; (*forest*) Wald *m*. **wooden** *adj* hölzern, Holz-.

woodcock ['wudkok] *n* Waldschnepfe *f*.

woodpecker ['wudpekə] *n* Specht *m*.

wood-pigeon *n* Ringeltaube *f*.

woodwind ['wudwind] *n* Holzblasinstrument *neut*; Holzbläser *m*.

woodwork ['wudwəːk] *n* Holzarbeit *f*, Tischlerei *f*.

woodworm ['wudwəːm] *n* Holzwurm *m*.

woody ['wudi] *adj* Holz-, holzig; (*countryside*) Wald-, waldig.

wool [wul] *n* Wolle *f*. **woollen** *adj* wollen, Woll-. **woolly** *adj* wollig.

word [wəːd] *n* Wort *neut*. **break/keep one's word** sein Wort brechen/halten. **wording** *n* Fassung *f*. **wordy** *adj* wortreich, langatmig.

wore [woː] *V* **wear**.

work [wəːk] *n* Arbeit *f*; (*piece of work, art, music, etc.*) Werk *neut*. **works** *pl* Werk *neut*. *v* arbeiten; (*of machine*) laufen, funktionieren; (*succeed*) klappen; (*land*) bebauen; (*metal*) schmieden; (*operate (machine)*) bedienen. **work off** (*debt*) abarbeiten; (*feelings*) abreagieren. **work out** ausrechnen. **out of work** arbeitslos. **worked-up** *adj* aufgeregt, aufgebracht. **worker** *n* Arbeiter(in). **working** *adj* Arbeits-; (*person*) berufstätig. **working class** Arbeiterklasse *f*; *adj* Arbeiter-. **in working order** betriebsfähig.

working party Arbeitsgruppe *f*. **workman** *n* Handwerker *m*. **work-to-rule** *n* Bummelstreik *m*.

world [wəːld] *n* Welt *f*. **not for all the world** nicht um alles in der Welt. **the world to come** das Jenseits *neut*. **world champion** Weltmeister(in). **world-famous** *adj* weltberühmt. **worldly-wise** *adj* weltklug. **world-wide** *adj* weitverbreitet. **worldly** *adj* irdisch.

worm [wəːm] *n* Wurm *m*.

worn [woːn] *v* **wear**. *adj* (*worn out*) abgenutzt. **worn out** *adj* (*thing*) abgenutzt; (*person*) todmüde.

worry ['wʌri] *v* (*bother*) beunruhigen; (*be worried*) sich Sorgen machen, sich beunruhigen. *n* Sorge *f*, Besorgnis *f*. **worrying** *adj* beunruhigend. **worried** *adj* beunruhigt, besorgt.

worse [wəːs] *adj*, *adv* schlimmer, schlechter. **worse and worse** immer schlechter. **worsen** *v* (sich) verschlechtern *or* verschlimmern.

worship ['wəːʃip] *n* Anbetung *f*, Verehrung *f*; (*in church*) Gottesdienst *m*. *v* anbeten, verehren. **worshipful** *adj* ehrwürdig. **worshipper** *n* Anbeter(in).

worst [wəːst] *adj* schlechtest, schlimmst *adv* am schlechtesten *or* schlimmsten. **at the worst** im schlimmsten Falle.

worsted ['wustid] *n* Kammgarn *neut*.

worth [wəːθ] *n* Wert *m*. *adj* wert. *it's worth ten marks* es ist zehn Mark wert. *it's not worth it* es lohnt sich nicht. **worthless** *adj* wertlos. **worthwhile** *adj* der Mühe wert. **worthy** *adj* würdig, wert.

would [wud] *v* (*to form conditional*) würde, würdest, etc. (*used to*) pflegte, pflegtest, etc; (*expressing desire, volition*) wollte, wolltest, etc. *he would go* (*if*) er würde gehen(wenn). *I would like* ich möchte. *he would come in the summer* er pflegte im Sommer zu kommen. *he would not come* er wollte durchaus nicht kommen.

wound[1] [waund] *V* **wind**[2].

wound[2] [wuːnd] *n* Wunde *f*. *v* verwunden. **wounded** *adj* verletzt.

wove [wouv] *V* **weave**.

woven ['wouvn] *V* **weave**.

wrangle ['raŋgl] *v* zanken, streiten. *n* Zank *m*, Streit *m*.

wrap [rap] *v* wickeln. **wrap up** einwickeln. *n* Schal *m*. **wrapper** *n* Umschlag *m*. **wrap-**

ping n Verpackung f. **wrapping paper** Einwickelpapier neut.

wreath [riθ] n Kranz m.

wreck [rek] n wrack neut; (naut) Schiffbruch m. v zerstören. **wreckage** n Trümmer pl.

wren [ren] n Zaunkönig m.

wrench [rentʃ] v zerren, ziehen. n (tool) Schraubenschlüssel m.

wrestle ['resl] v ringen. **wrestler** n Ringer m. **wrestling** n Ringkampf m, Ringen neut.

wretch [retʃ] n Elende(r), armes Wesen neut. **wretched** adj unglücklich, elend.

wriggle ['rigl] v sich schlängeln. n Schlängeln neut.

***wring** [riŋ] v (hands) ringen; (clothes) auswringen. **wringer** n Wringermaschine f. **wringing wet** triefend naß.

wrinkle ['riŋkl] n (face, brow) Runzel f, Falte f; (paper) Knitter m. **wrinkled** adj runzlig.

wrist [rist] n Handgelenk neut. **wristwatch** n Armbanduhr f.

writ [rit] n (law) (Vor)Ladung f. **Holy Writ** Heilige Schrift f.

***write** [rait] v schreiben. **write down** aufschreiben. **write off** abschreiben. **write out** (cheque) ausstellen. **writer** n Schriftsteller(in). **writing** n Schreiben neut. **in writing** schriftlich. **writing-paper** n Schreibpapier neut.

written ['ritn] V write. adj schriftlich.

writhe [raið] v sich winden.

wrong [roŋ] adj (incorrect) falsch; (bad, immoral) unrecht. **be wrong** sich irren, unrecht haben. **what's wrong with ...?** was ist los mit ...? **that was wrong of you** das war unrecht von dir. **go wrong** (mech) kaputtgehen; (plan) schiefgehen. **get it wrong** es ganz falsch verstehen. **wrongdoer** n Missetäter(in). **wrongdoing** n Missetat f. **wrongly** adv mit Unrecht.

wrote [rout] V write.

wrought iron [,rɔit'aiən] n Schweißeisen neut.

wrung [rʌŋ] V wring.

wry [rai] adj verschroben.

X

xenophobia [,zenə'foubiə] n Fremdenfeindlichkeit f.

Xerox ® ['ziəroks] n Fotokopiergerät neut. v fotokopieren.

X-ray [eks'rei] n Röntgenstrahl m; (picture) Röntgenbild neut. v röntgen. adj Röntgen-.

xylophone ['zailəfoun] n Xylophon neut.

Y

yacht [jot] n Jacht f. **yachting** n Segeln neut.

yank [jaŋk] v (coll) heftig ziehen (an). n Ruck m.

yap [jap] v kläffen; (coll) schwätzen. n Kläffen neut.

yard¹ [jaid] n (measure) Yard neut. **yardstick** n Maßstab m.

yard² [jaid] n Hof m.

yarn [jain] n Garn neut; (story) Geschichte f.

yawn [jom] n Gähnen neut. v gähnen.

year [jiə] n Jahr neut. **5 years old** fünf Jahre alt. **for years** jahrelang. **yearbook** n Jahrbuch neut. **yearly** adj jährlich.

yearn [jəin] v sich sehnen (nach). **yearning** n Sehnsucht f.

yeast [jiist] n Hefe f.

yell [jel] v (gellend) aufschreien. n Schrei m.

yellow ['jelou] adj gelb. n Gelb neut.

yelp [jelp] v jaulen. n Jaulen neut.

yes [jes] adv ja, jawohl. **yes-man** n Jasager m.

yesterday ['jestədi] n, adv gestern. **yesterday morning** gestern früh. **yesterday's** or **of yesterday** gestrig, von gestern. **the day before yesterday** vorgestern.

yet [jət] adv noch, immer noch. conj aber.

yew [jui] n Eibe f.

yield [jiild] n Ertrag m. **yielding** adj ergiebig.

yoga ['jougə] n Joga m.

yoghurt ['jogət] n Joghurt m.

yoke [jouk] n Joch m. v verbinden.

yolk [jouk] n Eidotter m, Eigelb neut.

yonder ['jondə] adv da, dort drüben. adj jene(r).

you [juː] *pron* (*fam sing*) du; (*fam pl*) ihr; (*polite sing or pl*) Sie; (*impers, one*) man. *acc*: dich; euch; Sie; einen. *dat*: dir; euch; Ihnen; einem.

young [jʌŋ] *adj* jung. *n* (Tier)Junge *pl.* **young children** kleine Kinder *pl.*

your [jɔː] *adj* (*fam sing*) dein; (*fam pl*) euer; (*polite sing or pl*) Ihr; (*impers, one's*) sein. **yours** (der/die/das) deine *or* eure *or* Ihre *or* seine. *a friend of yours* ein Freund von dir.

youth [juːθ] *n* Jugend *f*; (*lad*) Jüngling *m*. *adj* Jugend-. **youth hostel** Jugendherberge *f*. **youthful** *adj* jugendlich, jung.

Yugoslavia [juːgou'slaːvjə] *n* Jugoslawien *neut*. **Yugoslav** *n* Jugoslawe *m*, Jugoslawin *f*. *adj* jugoslawisch.

Z

zeal [ziːl] *n* Eifer *m*. **zealous** *adj* eifrig.

zebra ['zebrə] *n* Zebra *neut*. **zebra crossing** *n* Zebrastreifen *m*.

zero ['ziərou] *n* Null *f*.

zest [zest] *n* Lust *f*, Begeisterung *f*.

zigzag ['zigzag] *adj* Zickzack-. *n* Zickzack *m*.

zinc [ziŋk] *n* Zink *neut*.

zip [zip] *n also* **zipper** Reißverschluß *m*. **zip code** Postleitzahl *f*.

zodiac ['zoudiak] *n* Tierkreis *m*. **signs of the zodiac** Tierkreiszeichen *pl.*

zone [zoun] *n* Zone *f*.

zoo [zuː] *n* Zoo *m*. **zoological** *adj* zoologisch. **zoologist** *n* Zoologe *m*. **zoology** *n* Zoologie *f*, Tierkunde *f*.

zoom [zuːm] *v* summen, brummen; (*coll*: *rush*) sausen; (*prices*) Hochschnellen. **zoom lens** *n* Zoom (objektiv) *neut*.

German—Englisch

abfertigen

A

Aal [aːl] *m* (*pl* -e) eel.
ab [ap] *adv* off; *prep* (*abwärts, nach unten*)
from; (*weg, fort*) from. **ab und zu** now
and again, from time to time. **auf und ab**
up and down, to and fro.
abänderlich ['apɛndərliç] *adj* variable.
abändern *v* change, modify. **Abänderung**
f modification; (*Pol*) amendment.
abarbeiten ['aparbaitən] (*Schuld*) work
off; (*Werkzeug*) wear out. **sich die Finger
abarbeiten** work one's fingers to the
bone.
Abbau ['apbau] *m* (*unz.*) demolition;
(*Personal*) reduction of staff, staff-cut.
abbauen *v* demolish; (*Personal*) cut.
abbestellen ['apbəʃtɛlən] *v* cancel.
***abbiegen** ['apbiːgən] *v* deflect, turn
aside; (*Straße*) bend; (*Mot*) turn off.
Abbild ['apbilt] *neut* image, likeness.
abbilden *v* illustrate, depict. **Abbildung** *f*
illustration, drawing.
abblenden ['apblɛndən] *v* (*Mot*) dip one's
headlights.
***abbrechen** ['apbrɛçən] *v* break off;
(*Blumen, Obst*) pick; (*abbauen*) demolish; (*Lager*) break.
***abbringen** ['apbriŋən] *v* dissuade, put
off; (*entfernen*) remove.
Abbruch ['apbrux] *m* (*unz.*) (*Haus*) demolition; (*Einstellung*) stop, cessation.
abdanken ['apdaŋkən] *v* (*König*) abdicate; (*Beamter*) resign. **Abdankung** *f* (*pl*
-en) abdication; resignation.
abdecken ['apdɛkən] *v* uncover; (*Tisch*)

clear; (*schützen*) shield, cover; (*Verlust*)
make good.
abdichten ['apdiçtən] *v* seal up; (*wasserdicht machen*) make watertight.
Abdomen [ap'doːmən] *neut* abdomen.
abdominal *adj* abdominal.
abdrehen ['apdreːən] *v* unscrew, twist off;
(*Hals*) wring.
Abdruck ['apdruk] *m* reprint, new
impression; (*Finger-*) print. **abdrucken** *v*
print.
abdrücken ['apdrykən] *v* (*Pistole*) fire.
Abend ['aːbənt] *m* (*pl* -e) evening. **gestern
abend** yesterday evening, last night.
–brot *or* **–essen** *neut* supper, dinner.
–land *neut* West, Occident. **–mahl** *neut*
Holy Communion. **abends** *adv* in the
evening(s).
Abenteuer ['aːbəntɔyər] *neut* (pl -) adventure. **abenteuerlich** *adj* adventurous.
Abenteurer *m* adventurer.
aber ['aːbər] *conj* but; (*jedoch*) however.
das ist aber schrecklich! that's just awful!
Aberglaube ['aːbərglaubə] *m* superstition.
abergläubisch *adj* superstitious.
aberkennen ['apɛrkɛnən] *v* deprive, dispossess.
abermals ['aːbərmals] *adv* again, once
more.
***abfahren** ['apfaːrən] *v* set off, depart;
(*Mot*) drive off. **Abfahrt** *f* departure;
(*Ski*) descent, downhill run.
Abfall ['apfal] **1** (*unz.*) falling off, decline;
(*Neigung*) slope. **2** *m* waste, rubbish.
–eimer *m* dustbin. **abfallen** *v* fall off,
decline. **abfällig** *adj* disparaging.
abfassen ['apfasən] *v* compose, draw up,
formulate. **Abfassung** *f* wording.
abfertigen ['apfɛrtigən] *v* (*Güter*) (prepare
for) dispatch; (*Fahrzeug*) check over,
prepare (for departure); (*Kundschaft*) see
to.

abfinden ['apfɪndən] v pay off. **sich abfinden mit** come to terms with (auch fig) **Abfindung** f (pl **-en**) settlement, agreement.

*abfliegen ['apfliːɡən] fly away; (Flugzeug) take off.

*abfließen ['apfliːsən] flow away, drain off.

Abflug ['apfluːk] m (Flugzeug) take-off.

Abfluß ['apfluːs] m outflow, draining off. **-rohr** neut waste-pipe.

Abfuhr ['apfuːr] m removal. **abführen** v lead away. **Abführmittel** n laxative.

Abgabe ['apɡaːbə] f delivery, handing over; (Steuer) tax, duty. **Abgaben** pl (Verkauf) sales. **abgabenfrei** adj tax-free, duty-free.

Abgang ['apɡaŋ] m (Zug, usw.) departure; (Abtreten) retirement; (Verlust) loss, depreciation.

Abgas ['apɡaːs] neut exhaust gas.

*abgeben ['apɡeːbən] v give up, hand over; (Stimme) cast.

abgedroschen ['apɡədrɔʃən] adj commonplace, hackneyed.

abgegriffen ['apɡəɡrifən] adj (Münze) worn; (Buch) dog-eared, well-thumbed.

*abgehen ['apɡeːən] v go away, depart; (Straße) branch off; (Knopf, usw.) come off.

abgemacht ['apɡəmaxt] adj agreed.

Abgeordnete(r) ['apɡəɔrdnətə(r)] delegate; (Parlament) Member of Parliament; (US) congressman. **Abgeordnetenhaus** neut parliament; (GB) House of Commons.

abgesehen ['apɡəzeːən] prep **abgesehen von** apart from, except for.

abgestanden ['apɡəʃtandən] adj stale; (Bier, usw.) flat.

abgestorben ['apɡəʃtɔrbən] adj numb.

Abgott ['apɡɔt] m idol.

abgrenzen ['apɡrɛntsən] v (Gebiete) limit, mark off. **Abgrenzung** f demarcation, definition.

Abgrund ['apɡrunt] m abyss.

abhalten ['aphaltən] v keep away; (hindern) hinder, stop; (Versammlung, usw.) hold.

Abhandlung ['aphandluŋ] f essay, written report.

Abhang ['aphaŋ] m slope.

abhauen ['aphauən] v cut off; (umg.) go away, (umg.) buzz off.

abhelfen ['aphɛlfən] v remedy, correct.

abholen ['apho:lən] v call for, pick up.

abhören ['aphœːrən] v (Platte) listen to; (Gespräch) eavesdrop on; (Telef) monitor, listen in, tap; (Zeugen) question. **Abhörgerät** neut (electronic) listening device, bug.

Abitur [abi'tuːr] neut school-leaving exam, 'A'-levels.

abkanzeln ['apkantsəln] v scold, reprimand.

abkehren ['apkeːrən] v sweep up. **sich abkehren** turn away.

abknöpfen ['apknœpfən] v unbutton.

Abkommen ['apkɔmən] neut (pl **-**) agreement, settlement.

abkühlen ['apkyːlən] v cool, cool off.

Abkunft ['apkunft] f descent, lineage.

abkürzen ['apkyrtsən] v shorten; (Wort) abbreviate. **Abkürzung** f abbreviation; (Weg) short cut.

*abladen ['aplaːdən] v unload.

Ablauf ['aplauf] m (Abfluß) outlet, drain; (Verlauf) sequence of events; (Ende) expiry, end. **ablaufen** v drain, flow off; (Zeit) elapse; (Schuhe) wear out.

ablegen ['apleːɡən] v put down; (Kleider) take off; (Gewohnheiten) give up.

ablehnen ['apleːnən] v reject, refuse; (Einladung) decline. **Ablehnung** f (pl **-en**) refusal.

ableiten ['aplaitən] v divert, lead away; (Flüssigkeit) draw off. **Ableitung** f diversion.

ablenken ['aplɛŋkən] v turn away, divert.

abliefern ['apliːfərn] v deliver. **Ablieferung** f delivery.

ablösen ['aplœːzən] v (Person) relieve, replace; (Schuld) settle; (loslösen) loosen, free. **Ablösung** f relief; loosening.

abmachen ['apmaxən] v detach; (Geschäft) arrange, agree about. **Abmachung** f (pl **-en**) arrangement, agreement.

abmelden ['apmɛldən] v **sich abmelden** v give notice (of one's departure).

*abmessen ['apmɛsən] v measure off; (Grundstück) survey; (Worte) weigh. **Abmessung** f measurement, dimension.

Abnahme ['apnaːmə] f (pl **-n**) reduction, decrease; (Entfernung) removal.

*abnehmen ['apneːmən] v take off, take away; (sich vermindern) decrease; (schlanker werden) lose weight, grow slim. **Abnehmer** m (pl **-**) customer, consumer.

Abneigung ['apnaiguŋ] ƒ dislike, aversion.

abnorm [ap'nɔrm] adj abnormal. **Abnormität** ƒ (pl -en) abnormality.

abnutzen ['apnutsən] v wear out. **Abnutzung** ƒ wear (and tear).

Abonnement [abɔn'mã] neut (pl -s) subscription. **Abonnent** m (pl -en) subscriber. **abonnieren** v subscribe.

Abort [a'bɔrt] m (pl -e) lavatory.

abquälen ['apkvɛɪlən] v sich abquälen take great pains.

abraten ['apraɪtən] v advise against, dissuade from.

abräumen ['aprɔymən] v clear away.

abrechnen ['aprɛçnən] v settle; (abziehen) deduct. **abrechnen mit** settle up with.

Abrede ['apreɪdə] ƒ agreement. **in Abrede stellen** deny. **abreden** v agree.

abreiben ['apraibən] v rub off; (trocknen) rub down.

Abreise ['apraizə] ƒ departure. **abreisen** v depart, leave.

***abreißen** ['apraisən] v tear off; (Haus) demolish, tear down; (sich abfrnu) break off.

Abrieb ['apriɪp] m abrasion, wear.

***abrufen** ['apruɪfən] v cancel, call off; (Person) recall.

abrüsten ['aprystən] v disarm. **Abrüstung** ƒ disarmament.

Absage ['apza·gə] ƒ (pl -n) refusal. **absagen** v cancel, call off; (Einladung) decline, refuse.

Absatz ['apzats] 1 m (Pause) stop, break; (Schuh) heel; paragraph. 2 m (unz.) (Waren) sales (pl), turnover.

abschaffen ['apʃafən] v abolish, do away with. **Abschaffung** ƒ abolition.

abschalten ['apʃaltən] v switch off.

abschätzen ['apʃɛtsən] v estimate, appraise. **Abschätzung** ƒ estimate, assessment.

Abscheu ['apʃɔy] m or ƒ horror, revulsion. **abscheulich** adj horrible, revolting.

abschicken ['apʃikən] v send off or away.

Abschied ['apʃiɪt] m (pl -e) departure, leaving. **Abschied nehmen von** say goodbye to, take one's leave of.

***abschießen** ['apʃiɪsən] v (Gewehr) fire; (Flugzeug) shoot down.

Abschlag ['apʃlaɪk] m reduction, rebate. **abschlagen** v strike off; (ablehnen) refuse.

***abschließen** ['apʃliɪsən] v lock up; (Geschäft, Vertrag) conclude, settle; end, close.

Abschluß ['apʃlus] m conclusion; (Geschäft, Vertrag) settlement. **–prüfung** ƒ final exam(s), finals.

abschnallen ['apʃnalən] v unbuckle.

***abschneiden** ['apʃnaidən] v cut off.

Abschnitt ['apʃnit] m section, part; (Kontroll-) counterfoil.

abschrauben ['apʃraubən] v unscrew.

abschrecken ['apʃrɛkən] v scare off, deter. **–d** adj deterrent. **Abschreckung** ƒ deterrence. **–smittel** neut deterrent.

***abschreiben** ['apʃraibən] v copy out, write out; (Verlust, usw.) abschreiben; (plagiieren) plagiarize.

Abschrift ['apʃrift] ƒ copy.

Abschuß ['apʃus] m (Gewehr) firing; (Flugzeug) shooting down.

***absehen** ['apzeɪən] v see, perceive; (voraussehen) foresee. **absehbar** adj within sight; (Zeit) foreseeable.

abseits ['apzaits] adv aside.

***absenden** ['apzɛndən] v send (off). **Absender** m (pl -) sender.

absetzen ['apzɛtsən] v set down; (verkaufen) sell; (entlassen) dismiss; (aussteigen lassen) drop off.

Absicht ['apziçt] ƒ (pl -en) intention, purpose. **absicht∥lich** adj deliberate; adv on purpose, deliberately. **–slos** adj unintentional.

absolut [apzo'luɪt] adj absolute.

absondern ['apzɔndərn] v isolate, cut off, separate; (Med, Bot) secrete. **Absonderung** ƒ (pl -en) isolation.

absorbieren [apzɔr'biɪrən] v absorb. **Absorption** ƒ absorption.

absperren ['apʃpɛrən] v block off; (Gas, Strom) cut off; (Straße) block, cordon off.

abspielen ['apʃpiɪlən] v (Schallplatte, usw.) play; (Musik) sight-read; (Ball) pass.

***abspringen** ['apʃpriŋən] v jump down (from), jump off; (Flugzeug) bale out, (Splitter) chip or break off; (Farbe) flake off.

abspülen ['apʃpyɪlən] v wash, wash up. **Abspülwasser** neut dishwater.

abstammen ['apʃtamən] v be descended from. **Abstammung** ƒ descent, lineage.

Abstand ['apʃtant] m distance. **Abstand halten** keep one's distance.

abstatten ['apʃtatən] v (Besuch) pay; (Dank) give.

*absteigen ['apʃtaigən] v climb down, descend; (vom Pferd) dismount.

abstellen ['apʃtɛlən] v (Gerät, Licht) turn off; (niederlegen) put down; (Mot) park.

Abstieg ['apʃtiːk] m (pl -e) descent.

abstimmen ['apʃtimən] v vote, (Instrument, Radio) tune. **sich abstimmen** agree. **aufeinander abstimmen** collate, coordinate. **Abstimmung** f vote, poll.

Abstinenz [apsti'nɛnts] f abstinence; (Alkohol) teetotalism. **–ler** m (pl -) abstainer; teetotaller.

abstoßend ['apʃtoːsənt] adj repulsive, repellent.

abstrakt [ap'strakt] adj abstract.

Absturz ['apʃturts] m fall; (Flugzeug) crash; (Abgrund) precipice. **abstürzen** v fall, plummet; (Flugzeug) crash.

absurd [ap'zurt] adj absurd.

Abszeß [aps'tsɛs] m (pl Abszesse) abcess.

Abt [apt] m (pl Äbte) abbott. **Abtei** f (pl -en) abbey.

Abteil [ap'tail] neut (pl -e) compartment. **abteilen** v separate, divide off. **Abteilung** f (auch Mil) division; (einer Firma) department. **–sleiter** m head of department.

Äbtissin [ɛp'tisin] f (pl -nen) abbess.

*abtreiben ['aptraibən] v drive away; (Med) abort. **Abtreibung** f (pl -en) (induced) abortion.

Abtritt ['aptrit] m departure; (Theater) exit.

abtrocknen ['aptrɔknən] v wipe dry; (Geschirr) wipe up, dry.

abtrünnig ['aptryniç] adj disloyal, rebellious.

*abtun ['aptuːn] put aside; (Kleider) take off; (erledigen) close, settle; (Tier) put down.

abwandeln ['apvandəln] v vary. **Abwandlung** f variation.

abwarten ['apvartən] v wait for, expect; wait and see.

abwärts ['apvɛrts] adv downwards, down.

abwaschen ['apvaʃən] v wash off; (Geschirr) wash up.

Abwasser ['apvasər] neut waste water, effluent.

abwechseln ['apvɛksəln] v take turns; (wechseln) change, vary. **–d** adj alternating. adv alternately, in turns. **Abwechslung** f change.

Abwehr ['apveːr] f defence; (Widerstand) resistance. **abwehren** v ward off; (Feind) repel.

*abweichen ['apvaiçən] v deviate. **–d** adj discrepant, anomalous; (Meinung) dissenting.

*abweisen ['apvaisən] v turn away, refuse; (Bewerber) turn down. **–d** adj unfriendly, dismissive.

*abwenden ['apvɛndən] v turn away or aside; (Gefahr) avert, prevent.

*abwerfen ['apvɛrfən] v throw off; (Bomben) drop; (Zinsen) yield.

abwerten ['apvɛrtən] v devalue. **Abwertung** f devaluation.

abwesend ['apveːzənt] adj absent; (zerstreut) absent-minded. **Abwesenheit** f absence.

abzahlen ['aptsaːlən] v pay off.

abzählen ['aptsɛːlən] v count; (Geld) count out.

abzäunen ['aptsɔynən] v fence off.

Abzeichen ['aptsaiçən] neut badge; (Kennzeichen) mark.

*abziehen ['aptsiːən] v draw off, remove; (Math) subtract; (fortgehen) go away, withdraw.

Abzug ['aptsuːk] m departure; (Geld) deduction; (Foto) print; (Abdruck) copy.

abzweigen ['aptsvaigən] v branch off. **Abzweigung** f (pl -en) branch; (Mot) turning.

ach! [ax] interj oh! ah!

Achse ['aksə] f (pl -n) (Rad) axle; (Math, Pol) axis.

Achsel ['aksəl] f (pl -n) shoulder. **–bein** neut shoulder-blade. **–höhle** f armpit. **–zucken** neut (pl -) shrug (of the shoulders).

acht [axt] adj eight. **(heute) vor acht Tagen** a week ago (today).

Acht [axt] f (unz.) attention. **außer acht lassen** ignore, disregard. **sich in acht nehmen** be careful, take care. **acht‖en** v esteem. **–en auf** pay attention to, heed. **–geben** v pay attention. **–los** adj careless. **–sam** adj attentive. **Achtung** f attention; (Wertschätzung) esteem; interj watch out! look out!

achtzig ['axtsiç] adj eighty.

ächzen ['ɛçtsən] v groan.

Acker ['akər] m (pl Äcker) field. **–bau** m agriculture, farming.

addieren [a'diːrən] v add (up). **Addiermaschine** f adding machine.

Adel ['aɪdəl] *m* nobility, aristocracy.
ad(e)lig *adj* noble, aristocratic.
Ad(e)lige(r) noble(man), aristocrat.
Ader ['aɪdər] *f* (*pl* -n) blood vessel; vein, artery.
Adjektiv ['atjɛktiːf] *neut* (*pl* -e) adjective.
Adler ['aɪdlər] *m* (*pl* -) eagle.
Admiral [atmi'raɪl] *m* (*pl* -e) admiral. **–ität** *f* admiralty.
adoptieren [adɔp'tiːrən] *v* adopt. **Adoptiv**- adopted, adoptive.
Adrenalin [adrena'liːn] *neut* adrenaline.
Adresse [a'drɛsə] *f* (*pl* -n) address. **Adreßbuch** *neut* address book, directory. **adressieren** *v* address.
Advokat [atvo'kaɪt] *m* (*pl* -en) lawyer.
Affäre [a'fɛɪrə] *f* (*pl* -n) affair; (*Liebes*-) (love) affair.
Affe ['afə] *m* (*pl* -n) ape, monkey.
affektiert [afɛk'tiɪrt] *adj* affected, conceited.
äffen ['ɛfən] *v* ape, imitate.
Afrika ['aɪfrika] *neut* Africa. **Afrikaner** *m* African. **afrikanisch** *adj* African.
After ['aftər] *m* (*pl* -) anus.
Agent [a'gɛnt] *m* (*pl* -en) agent. **–ur** *f* (*pl* -en) agency.
Agnostiker [a'gnɔstikər] *m* (*pl* -) agnostic. **agnostisch** *adj* agnostic.
Ägypten [ɛ'gyptən] *neut* Egypt. **Ägypter** *m* (*pl* -) Egyptian. **ägyptisch** *adj* Egyptian.
Ahn [aɪn] *m* (*pl* -en) ancestor.
ähneln ['ɛɪnəln] *v* look like, resemble.
ahnen ['aɪnən] *v* suspect, guess.
ähnlich ['ɛɪnliç] *adj* like, similar (to). **Ähnlichkeit** *f* (*pl* -en) likeness, similarity.
Ahorn ['aɪhɔrn] *m* (*pl* -e) maple.
Ähre ['ɛɪrə] *f* (*pl* -n) ear (of corn).
Akadem‖ie [akade'miː] *f* (*pl* -n) academy; (*Hochschule, Fachschule*) college. **–iker** *m* (*pl* -) university graduate. **akademisch** *adj* academic.
Akkord [a'kɔrt] *m* (*pl* -e) agreement; (*Musik*) chord. **–arbeit** *f* piece-work.
Akrobat [akro'baɪt] *m* (*pl* -en) acrobat. **akrobatisch** *adj* acrobatic.
Akt [akt] *m* (*pl* -e) act, action, deed; document; (*Kunst*) nude.
Akte ['aktə] *f* (*pl* -n) file, dossier. **zu den Akten legen** file (away). **Akten‖schrank** *m* filing cabinet. **–tasche** *f* briefcase.
Aktie ['aktsiə] *f* (*pl* -n) share. **Aktien‖gesellschaft** *f* joint-stock company. **–makler** *m* stockbroker.

Aktionär [aktsio'nɛɪr] *m* (*pl* -e) shareholder.
aktiv [ak'tiɪf] *adj* active. **–ieren** *v* activate.
aktuell [aktu'ɛl] *adj* current, contemporary, up-to-date.
Akzent [ak'tsɛnt] *m* (*pl* -e) accent. **akzeptieren** [aktsɛp'tiɪrən] *v* accept.
Alarm [a'larm] *m* (*pl* -e) alarm. **alarm‖bereit** *adj* standing by, on the alert. **–ieren** *v* alarm.
albern ['albərn] *adj* silly, foolish.
Album ['album] *neut* (*pl* **Alben**) album.
Alge ['algə] *f* (*pl* -n) seaweed.
Algebra ['algebra] *f* algebra.
Alimente [ali'mɛntə] *pl* alimony *sing.*
Alkohol [alko'hoɪl] *m* (*pl* -e) alcohol. **alkoholfrei** *adj* non-alcoholic. **Alkoholiker** *m* alcoholic. **alkoholisch** *adj* alcoholic.
all [al] *pron, adj* all. **All** *neut* universe. **alle** *pl* all; everybody *sing.* **alle beide** both. **wir alle** we all, all of us. **die Milch ist alle** the milk is all gone. **alle zwei Tage** every other day. **alles** everything. **alledem** *pron* trotz alledem nevertheless.
Allee [a'leɪ] *f* (*pl* -n) avenue.
Allegorie [alego'riː] (*pl* -n) allegory. **allegorisch** *adj* allegorical.
allein [a'lain] *adj, adv* alone; (*ohne Hilfe*) (by) oneself. *conj* but. **alleinstehend** *adj* (*Haus*) detached; (*Person*) single.
allemal ['aləmaɪl] *adv* always. **ein für allemal** once and for all.
allenfalls ['alənfals] *adv* if need be; (*höchstens*) at most.
aller‖best ['alərbɛst] *adj* very best, best of all. **–dings** *adv* certainly, surely, indeed. **–erst** *adj* first of all, very first. **–höchst** *adj* supreme, highest of all. **–lei** *adj* (*undeklinierbar*) various, all kinds of. **–liebst** *adj* (most) delightful, dearest. **–wenigst** *adj* very least.
allezeit ['alətsait] *adv* always, at any time.
allgemein ['algəmain] *adj* common, general. **im allgemeinen** in general.
Alliierte(r) [ali'iːrtə(r)] *m* ally.
alljährlich [al'jɛɪrliç] *adj* annual.
allmächtig [al'mɛçtiç] *adj* all-powerful, almighty.
allmählich [al'mɛɪliç] *adj* gradual.
allseitig ['alzaitiç] *adj* universal, comprehensive.
alltäglich ['al'tɛɪkliç] *adj* everyday. *adv* every day.

allzu ['altsuː] *adv* much too, all too.
Almanach ['almanax] *m* (*pl* -e) almanac.
Alpen ['alpən] *pl* Alps *pl*.
Alphabet [alfa'beɪt] *neut* (*pl* -e) alphabet. **alphabetisch** *adj* alphabetical.
Alptraum ['alptraum] *m* nightmare.
als [als] *conj* as; (*da, zu der Zeit*) when; (*nach Komparativen*) than. **als ob** as if. **nichts als** nothing but. *als dein Freund möchte ich sagen ...* as your friend, I would like to say ... *als ich noch ein Kind war* when I was a child.
also ['alzo] *conj* so, therefore.
alt [alt] *adj* old.
Alt [alt] *m* (*unz.*) alto (voice).
Altar [al'taɪr] *m* (*pl* Altäre) altar.
Alter ['altər] *neut* (*unz.*) age; (*hohes Alter*) old age. **Alters‖fürsorge** *f* care of the aged. **–heim** *neut* old people's home. **altersschwach** *adj* (*Person*) senile, feeble. **Altertum** *neut* (*unz.*) antiquity. **altertümlich** *adj* ancient, archaic.
Aluminium [alu'miːnium] *neut* aluminium.
am [am] *prep* + *art* an dem.
Amboß ['ambɔs] *m* (*pl* Ambosse) anvil.
Ameise ['aɪmaizə] *f* (*pl* -n) ant.
Amerika [a'meɪrika] *neut* America. **Amerikaner** *m* American. **amerikanisch** *adj* American.
Ampel ['ampəl] *f* (*pl* -n) (*Verkehrs-*) traffic light; (*Hängelampe*) hanging lamp.
Amsel ['amzəl] *f* (*pl* -n) blackbird.
Amt [amt] *neut* (*pl* Ämter) office; (*Stellung*) official position, post; (*Telef*) exchange. *das Auswärtige Amt* the Foreign Office. *das Amt antreteten* take office. **amtieren** *v* officiate. **amtlich** *adj* official. **Amts‖geheimnis** *neut* offical secret. **–gericht** *neut* district court. **–zeichen** *neut* dial tone.
amüsant [amy'zant] *adj* amusing. **amüsieren** *v* amuse. **sich amüsieren** amuse *or* enjoy oneself.
an [an] *prep* at; (*nahe*) near; (*auf*) on. *adv* on. *an diesem Tag* on this day. *an diesem Ort* at this place. *der Ort, an dem* the place where. *an der Wand* on the wall. *an die Tür klopfen* knock at *or* on the door. *von heute an* from today. *von jetzt an* from now on. *sie hat nichts an* she has nothing on.
analog [ana'loɪk] *adj* analagous. **Analogie** *f* analogy. **analogisch** *adj* analogous.

Analphabet [analfa'beɪt] *m* (*pl* -en) illiterate.
Analyse [ana'lyɪzə] *f* (*pl* -n) analysis. **analysieren** *v* analyse. **Analytiker** *m* analyst. **analytisch** *adj* analytical.
Ananas ['ananas] *f* (*pl* -se) pineapple.
Anarchie [anar'çiɪ] *f* (*pl* -n) anarchy. **Anarchist** *m* (*pl* -en) anarchist.
Anatomie [anato'miɪ] *f* (*pl* -n) anatomy. **anatomisch** *adj* anatomical.
Anbau ['anbau] **1** *m* (*unz.*) cultivation, tillage. **2** *m* extension, annexe.
*anbeißen ['anbaisən] *v* bite into; (*Fisch*) bite, take the bait.
anbelangen ['anbəlaŋən] *v* concern, relate to. *was mich anbelangt* as to me, as far as I am concerned.
anbeten ['anbeɪtən] *v* worship, adore.
*anbieten ['anbiɪtən] *v* offer.
Anblick ['anblik] *m* sight, view; (*Aussehen*) appearance. **anblicken** *v* look at, gaze at.
*anbrechen ['anbrɛçən] *v* (*Essen, Vorrat*) break into, begin; (*Tag*) dawn, break; (*Nacht*) fall.
*anbrennen ['anbrɛnən] *v* (*Speisen*) burn; (*Zigarette, Lampe*) light.
*anbringen ['anbriŋən] *v* bring, place; (*befestigen*) attach; (*Klage*) lodge, bring.
Anbruch ['anbrux] *m* (*unz.*) beginning. *bei Anbruch der Nacht* at nightfall.
Andacht ['andaxt] *f* (*pl* -en) devotion.
Andenken ['andɛŋkən] *neut* (*pl* -) memory, remembrance; (*Erinnerungstück*) souvenir.
ander ['andər] *adj, pron* other, different. **ein andermal** *adv* another time.
ändern ['ɛndərn] *v* alter, change. **Änderung** *f* (*pl* -en) alteration, change.
ander‖thalb ['andərthalp] *adj* one-and-a-half. **–nfalls** *adv* otherwise, else. **–s** *adv* differently. **–seits** *adv* on the other hand. **–swo** *adv* elsewhere.
andeuten ['andɔytən] *v* indicate, point to; (*anspielen*) imply, suggest, allude to. **Andeutung** *f* indication; suggestion, allusion.
andrehen ['andreɪən] *v* turn on, switch on; (*Mot*) start up; (*umg.*) wangle, fix up.
andrer ['andrər] *pron* anderer. *V* ander.
aneignen ['anaignən] *v* **sich aneignen** appropriate; (*Kenntnisse*) acquire. **Aneignung** *f* (*pl* -en) appropriation; acquisition.

aneinander [anain'andər] *adv* to *or* against one another, together. **–liegend** *adj* neighbouring, adjacent. **–schließen** *v* join together.

*anerkennen ['anɛrkɛnən] *v* recognize, acknowledge. **Anerkennung** *f* recognition, approval.

*anfahren ['anfaɪrən] *v* begin (to move); (*bringen*) convey, carry; (*ankommen*) arrive; (*zusammenstoßen*) drive into. **Anfahrt** *f* arrival; (*Zufahrtsstraße*) drive. **Anfall** ['anfal] *m* attack.

Anfang ['anfaŋ] *m* beginning, start. **anfangen** *v* begin, start. **Anfänger** *m* (*pl* -) beginner. **anfangs** *adv* at first, initially. **Anfangsbuchstabe** *m* (*pl* -n) initial letter.

anfassen ['anfasən] *v* touch; (*ergreifen*) hold, grasp; (*Aufgabe*) set *or* go about.

*anfecht‖en ['anfɛçtən] *v* contest, dispute; (*beunruhigen*) trouble; (*Versuchung*) tempt. **– bar** *adj* questionable, contestable.

Anforderung ['anfordəruŋ] *f* demand, claim; (*Bedürfnis*) requirement.

Anfrage ['anfraɪgə] *f* inquiry.

anfühlen ['anfyɪlən] *v* touch, feel. **sich anfühlen** feel (to the touch).

anführen ['anfyɪrən] *v* lead, command; (*Worte*) quote, state; (*täuschen*) trick, deceive. **Anführungszeichen** *pl* quotation marks.

anfüllen ['anfylən] *v* fill (up).

Angabe ['angaɪbə] *f* declaration, statement. **–n** *pl* specifications, data. **nähere Angaben** details, particulars.

*angeben ['angeɪbən] *v* state, declare; (*anzeigen*) inform against; (*vorgeben*) pretend; (*prahlen*) brag, boast, show off. **Angeber** *m* (*pl* -) informer; (*Prahler*) show off, boaster. **angeblich** *adj* supposed, alleged.

angeboren ['angəboɪrən] *adj* innate, inherent.

Angebot ['angəboɪt] *neut* (*pl* -e) offer. **Angebot und Nachfrage** supply and demand.

*angehen ['angeɪən] *v* begin; (*angreifen*) attack; (*betreffen*) concern. *das geht mich nichts an* that is none of my business.

angehören ['angəhœɪrən] *v* belong (to). **Angehörige(r)** member.

Angeklagte(r) ['angəklaɪktə(r)] (*Jur*) (the) accused, defendant.

Angelegenheit ['angəleɪgənhait] *f* matter, concern, business.

angeln ['aŋəln] *v* fish, angle. **Angeln** *neut* angling, fishing. **Angelrute** *f* fishing rod.

Angelsachse ['aŋəlzaksə] *m* Anglo-Saxon. **angelsächsisch** *adj* Anglo-Saxon.

angemessen ['angəmesən] *adj* proper, suitable.

angenehm ['angəneɪm] *adj* pleasant, agreeable.

angenommen ['angənɔmən] *adj* supposing, assuming.

angesehen ['angəzeɪən] *adj* respected.

Angesicht ['angəziçt] *neut* face, countenance. **angesichts** *prep* considering, in view of.

Angestellte(r) ['angəʃtɛltə(r)] employee, office worker.

angewandt ['angəvant] *adj* applied, practical.

angewöhnen ['angəvœɪnən] *v* accustom. **sich angewöhnen** get used to, make a habit of. **Angewohnheit** *f* habit, custom.

Angler ['aŋlər] *m* (*pl* -) angler, fisherman.

*angreifen ['angraifən] *v* (*anfassen*) take hold of; (*feindlich*) attack; (*unternehmen*) set about. **Angreifer** *m* (*pl* -) aggressor, attacker.

angrenzen ['angrɛntsən] *v* border on, adjoin.

Angriff ['angrif] *m* attack. **angriffslustig** *adj* aggressive.

Angst [aŋst] *f* (*pl* **Ängste**) fear, anxiety. **Angst haben vor** be afraid of.

ängst‖igen ['ɛŋstigən] *v* frighten. **–lich** *adj* fearful, timid, (*peinlich*) scrupulous, (over-)careful.

*anhaben ['anhaɪbən] *v* wear, have on.

Anhalt ['anhalt] *m* support, prop; (*fig*) clue. **anhalten** *v* stop; (*andauern*) continue, last. **Anhalter** *m* hitchhiker. **per Anhalter fahren** hitchhike.

Anhang ['anhaŋ] *m* appendix, supplement. **anhängen** *v* hang on, attach; (*hinzufügen*) add. **Anhänger** *m* follower; (*Fußball*) supporter; (*Mot*) trailer. **Anhängeschloß** *neut* padlock. **anhänglich** *adj* affectionate.

Anhöhe ['anhœɪə] *f* (low) hill.

anhören ['anhœɪrən] *v* listen (to).

Ankauf ['ankauf] *m* purchase. **ankaufen** *v* purchase, buy.

Anker ['aŋkər] *m* (*pl* -) anchor. **den Anker lichten/werfen** weigh/cast anchor. **ankern** *v* anchor.

Anklage ['anklaːgə] *f* accusation, charge.
–**bank** *f* dock. **anklagen** *v* accuse.
Ankläger *m* plaintiff.
Anklang ['anklaŋ] *m* approval, recognition; (*Spur*) touch, echo.
anknüpfen ['anknypfən] *v* fasten (on), tie (on); (*fig*) take up, establish.
*****ankommen** ['ankɔmən] *v* arrive; (*abhängen*) depend (on). **es kommt darauf an** it depends.
ankündigen ['ankyndigən] *v* announce, publicize. **Ankündigung** *f* announcement.
Ankunft ['ankunft] *f* (*pl* **Ankünfte**) arrival.
Anlage ['anlaːgə] *f* installation; (*Entwurf*) plan, layout; park, gardens *pl*; (*Brief*) enclosure; (*Begabung*) talent; (*Neigung*) tendency, susceptibility; (*Komm*) investment; (*Fabrik*) plant, works.
anlangen ['anlaŋən] *v* (*ankommen*) arrive; (*betreffen*) concern.
Anlaß ['anlas] *m* (*pl* **Anlässe**) occasion, cause. **Anlaß geben** cause, give rise to.
anlassen *v* leave on; (*Mot*) start.
anläßlich *prep* on the occasion of.
Anlasser *m* (*pl* -) (*Mot*) starter-motor.
Anlauf ['anlauf] *m* start; (*kurzer Lauf*) run, dash. **anlaufen** *v* run at, rush at; (*Hafen*) put into; (*wachsen*) rise, increase.
anlegen ['anleːgən] *v* put on *or* against; (*Gewehr*) aim at; (*gründen*) found; (*Geld*) invest; (*Schiff*) lie alongside.
Anleihe ['anlaiə] *f* (*pl* -n) loan.
Anleitung ['anlaituŋ] *f* instruction.
*****anliegen** ['anliːgən] *v* (*Schiff*) lie beside; (*Kleidung*) fit well. **Anliegen** *neut* (*pl* -) request. **anliegend** *adj* adjoining.
anlocken ['anlɔkən] *v* entice, attract.
anmachen ['anmaxən] *v* attach; (*Speisen*) prepare; (*Feuer*) kindle; (*Licht*) turn on.
Anmarsch ['anmarʃ] *m* advance, approach. **anmarschieren** *v* advance on, march on.
anmaßen ['anmaːsən] *v* **sich anmaßen, zu** presume to, take it upon oneself to. **Anmaßung** *f* presumptuousness.
anmelden ['anmɛldən] *v* announce, report. **sich anmelden** *v* report; (*polizeilich*) register (with the police). **Anmeldung** *f* announcement; (*polizeilich*) registration.
anmerken ['anmɛrkən] *v* note, observe. **Anmerkung** *f* note, observation.
Anmut ['anmuːt] *f* grace, charm, elegance. **anmutig** *adj* graceful.

annähern ['annɛːərn] *v* bring closer; (*ähnlich machen*) make similar. **sich annähern** approach. **annähernd** *adj* approaching. *adv* almost, close to.
Annahme ['annaːmə] *f* (*pl* -n) acceptance; (*Vermutung*) assumption.
*****annehm‖en** ['anneːmən] *v* accept, take; (*vermuten*) assume, suppose. –**bar** *adj* acceptable.
anonym [ano'nyːm] *adj* anonymous. **Anonymität** *f* anonymity.
anordnen ['anɔrdnən] *v* put in order, arrange; (*befehlen*) direct, command. **Anordnung** *f* arrangement; (*Befehl*) order, instruction.
anpacken ['anpakən] *v* grasp, seize.
anpassen ['anpasən] *v* fit, adapt. **sich anpassen** *v* adapt, adjust. **Anpassung** *f* adaptation, adjustment. **anpassungsfähig** *adj* adaptable. **Anpassungsfähigkeit** *f* adaptability.
anrechnen ['anrɛçnən] *v* charge; (*hochschätzen*) value, esteem highly.
Anrede ['anreːdə] *f* speech, address. **anreden** *v* address, speak to.
anregen ['anreːgən] *v* stimulate, incite; (*geistig*) excite, inspire. –**d** *adj* exciting. **Anregung** *f* excitement.
anrichten ['anriçtən] *v* (*Schaden*) cause, do; (*Essen*) prepare.
Anruf ['anruːf] *m* call, shout; (*Telef*) call. **anrufen** *v* call, hail; (*Telef*) ring up, call.
anrühren ['anryːrən] *v* touch, handle; (*Küche*) stir.
ans [ans] *prep* + *art* **an das**.
Ansage ['anzaːgə] *f* announcement; (*Kartenspiel*) bidding. **ansagen** *v* announce, declare; bid. **Ansager** *m* (*pl* -) announcer.
ansammeln ['anzaməln] *v* collect. **sich ansammeln** gather. **Ansammlung** *f* collection, accumulation; (*Menge*) crowd, gathering.
Ansatz ['anzats] *m* (*Anfang*) start, beginning; (*Zusatzstück*) (added) piece, fitting. –**punkt** *m* starting point.
anschaffen ['anʃafən] *v* procure, obtain.
anschalten ['anʃaltən] *v* switch, turn on.
anschau‖en ['anʃauən] *v* look at, view. –**lich** *adj* obvious, evident.
Anschein ['anʃain] *m* (*unz.*) (outer) appearance. **allem Anschein nach** to all appearances.

Anschlag ['anʃlaɪk] m (Med) stroke, attack; (Plakat) poster; (Kosten-) estimate; (Angriff) (criminal) attack, outrage.

***anschließen** ['anʃliːsən] v connect; (anketten) chain up. **-d** adj subsequent.

Anschluß ['anʃlus] m connection; (pol) annexation.

anschnallen ['anʃnalən] v fasten, buckle.

Anschove [an'ʃoːvə] f (pl -n), **Anschovis** f (pl -) anchovy.

Anschrift ['anʃrɪft] f address.

anschuldigen ['anʃuldɪgən] v accuse (of), charge (with).

***ansehen** ['anzeːən] v look at, consider. **Ansehen** neut appearance; (Hochachtung) respect, esteem. **ansehnlich** adj notable.

ansetzen ['anzɛtsən] v put on, attach; (Gewicht) put on; (anfangen) begin; (versuchen) try.

Ansicht ['anzɪçt] f view, sight, (Meinung) opinion.

Anspiel ['anʃpiːl] neut (Tennis) service; (Fußball) kick-off. **anspielen** v play first; (Tennis) serve; (Fußball) kick off. **anspielen auf** hint at, allude to. **Anspielung** f (pl -en) allusion.

ansprechen ['anʃprɛçən] v speak to, address; (auf der Straße, usw.) accost. **Anspruch** ['anʃprux] m claim. **Anspruch haben auf** have a right to. **in Anspruch nehmen** lay claim to, claim; (Zeit) take up. **Ansprüche stellen** make demands. **anspruchsvoll** adj demanding.

Anstalt ['anʃtalt] f (pl -en) (Heim) institution; (Schule) institute; (Vorbereitung) arrangement.

Anstand ['anʃtant] m (unz.) decency. **anständig** adj decent, proper. **Anstandsdame** f chaperone.

anstatt ['anʃtat] prep instead of. **anstatt daß** rather than.

anstecken ['anʃtɛkən] v pin on (to); (Ring) put on; (Med) infect; (Feuer) light. **-d** adj infectious. **Ansteckung** f infection.

anstellen ['anʃtɛlən] v carry out, do; (Person) appoint, employ; (Mot) start; (Radio) switch on. **Anstellung** f appointment.

anstiften ['anʃtɪftən] v cause, instigate.

Anstoß ['anʃtoːs] m impulse; (Sport) kick-off. **Anstoß geben/nehmen** give/take offence (US offense). **anstoßen** v knock against; (Haus, usw.) adjoin.

anstrengen ['anʃtrɛŋən] v strain, exert; (Prozeß) bring in. **sich anstrengen** strain or exert oneself; make an effort.

Antarktika [an'tarktika] f Antarctica. **Antarktis** f Antarctic. **antarktisch** adj antarctic.

antasten ['antastən] v touch, handle; (Thema) touch on; (Recht, usw.) injure.

Anteil ['antail] m share, portion; (Mitgefühl) sympathy. **-nahme** f sympathy.

Antenne [an'tɛnə] f (pl -n) aerial.

Antibiotikum [antibi'oːtikum] neut (pl -biotika) antibiotic.

antik [an'tiːk] adj ancient, classical.

Antikörper ['antikœrpər] m antibody.

Antiquität [antikvi'tɛːt] f (pl -en) antique. **-enhändler** m antique dealer.

antisemitisch [antize'miːtiʃ] adj antisemitic.

Antiseptikum [anti'sɛptikum] m (pl -septika) antiseptic. **antiseptisch** adj antiseptic.

Antrag ['antraːk] m (pl Anträge) offer, proposal; (Pol) motion. **einen Antrag stellen** propose a motion. **Antragsteller** m applicant; (Pol) mover (of a motion).

***antreffen** ['antrɛfən] v encounter.

***antreiben** ['antraibən] v drive, propel; (Person) urge; (ans Ufer) drift ashore.

***antreten** ['antreːtən] v (Amt) enter, take over; (Reise) set out on.

Antrieb ['antriːp] m drive, impulse; (Tech) drive. **aus eigenem Antrieb** of one's own free will.

Antritt ['antrit] m beginning; (Amt) entrance.

***antun** ['antuːn] v (Kleidung) put on; (Verletzung) do, inflict.

Antwort ['antvort] f (pl -en) answer, reply. **antworten** v answer, reply (to).

anvertrauen ['anfertrauən] v entrust.

Anwalt ['anvalt] m (pl Anwälte) (defending) lawyer, solicitor.

anwärmen ['anvɛrmən] v warm (up).

***anweisen** ['anvaisən] v (zuweisen) assign; (anleiten) direct, show; (Geld) transfer. **Anweisung** f instruction, order; (Geld) remittance, transfer.

***anwend∥en** ['anvɛndən] v employ, use; (Gewalt, Methode, Wissenschaft, usw.) apply. **-bar** adj applicable. **Anwendung** f. application.

anwesend ['anveɪzənt] *adj* present.
Anwesenheit *f* presence.
Anzahl ['antsaɪl] *f* number. **Anzahlung** *f* deposit, down payment.
Anzeichen ['antsaiçən] *neut* mark, sign.
Anzeige ['antsaigə] *f* (*pl* -n) announcement; (*Inserat*) advertisement; (*bei der Polizei*) report. –**blatt** *neut* advertiser, advertising journal. **anzeig‖en** *v* announce; (*person*) inform against, report (to the police). –**epflichtig** *adj* notifiable.
***anziehen** ['antsiɪən] *v* (*Kleider*) put on; (*Schraube*) tighten; (*Person*) dress; (*heranlocken*) attract. **sich anziehen** get dressed. **anziehend** *adj* attractive. **Anziehung** *f* attraction. –**skraft** *f* power of attraction; (*Person*) attractiveness.
Anzug ['antsuɪk] **1** *m* (*unz.*) approach. **2** *m* suit.
anzünden ['antsyndən] *v* light, ignite.
Apfel ['apfəl] *m* (*pl* **Äpfel**) apple. –**baum** *m* apple tree. –**garten** *m* apple orchard. –**kuchen** *m* apple cake. –**mus** *neut* apple sauce. –**saft** *m* apple juice. –**sine** *f* orange. –**wein** *m* cider.
Apostel [a'pɔstəl] *m* (*pl* -) apostle. –**geschichte** *f* Acts of the Apostles.
Apostroph [apo'stroɪf] *m* (*pl* -e) apostrophe.
Apotheke [apo'teɪkə] *f* (*pl* -n) chemist's (shop), pharmacy. –**r** *m* (*pl* -) chemist, pharmacist. –**rkunst** *f* pharmacy, pharmaceutics.
Apparat [apa'raɪt] *m* (*pl* -e) apparatus; (*Vorrichtung*) appliance, device; (*Foto*) camera; (*Telef*) telephone, handset. **am Apparat!** speaking! **am Apparat bleiben** hold the line.
appellieren [apɛ'liɪrən] *v* appeal.
Appetit [ape'tiɪt] *m* (*pl* -e) appetite.
Aprikose [apri'koɪzə] *f* (*pl* -n) apricot.
April [a'pril] *m* (*pl* -e) April. **der erste April** April Fools' Day.
Aquarell [akva'rɛl] *neut* (*pl* -e) water-colour.
Aquarium [a'kvaɪrium] *neut* (*pl* **Aquarien**) aquarium.
Äquator [ɛ'kvaɪtɔr] *m* equator. **äquatorial** *adj* equatorial.
Arab‖er ['arabər] *m* (*pl* -) Arab. –**ien** *neut* Arabia. **arabisch** *adj* Arab, Arabian.
Arbeit ['arbaɪt] *f* (*pl* -en) work; (*Beschäftigung*) job. **arbeiten** *v* work. **Arbeiter** *m*

worker, workman. –**klasse** *f* working class. **Arbeitgeber** *m* employer. **Arbeits‖amt** *neut* employment office. –**erlaubris** *f* work permit. **arbeits‖fähig** *adj* able to work. –**los** *adj* unemployed. –**losenunterstützung** *f.* unemployment benefit. –**losigkeit** *f* unemployment.
Archäolog‖ie [arçeolo'giɪ] *f* archaeology. –**e** *m* archaeologist. **archäologisch** *adj* archaeological.
Architekt [arçi'tɛkt] *m* (*pl* -en) architect. –**ur** *f* (*pl* -en) architecture.
Archiv [ar'çiɪf] *neut* (*pl* -e) archives *pl*, records *pl*.
arg [ark] *adj* bad, evil; (*ernst*) serious.
Ärger ['ɛrgər] *m* (*unz.*) (*Verdruß*) annoyance, irritation; (*Zorn*) anger. **ärgerlich** *adj* (*Person*) angry, annoyed; (*Sache*) annoying. **ärgern** *v* annoy, irritate. **sich ärgern über** be angry about.
Argument [argu'mɛnt] *neut* (*pl* -e) argument, reasoning.
Argwohn ['arkvoɪn] *m* (*unz.*) distrust, suspicion. **argwöhnisch** *adj* suspicious, mistrustful.
Aristokrat [aristo'kraɪt] *m* (*pl* -en) aristocrat. –**ie** *f* aristocracy. **aristokratisch** *adj* aristocratic.
Arithmetik [arit'mɛttik] *f* arithmetic. **arithmetisch** *adj* arithmetical.
Arktis ['arktis] *f* Arctic. **arktisch** *adj* arctic.
arm [arm] *adj* poor. –**arm** *adj* poor in .... **nikotinarm** *adj* low-nicotine.
Arm [arm] *m* (*pl* -e) arm; (*Fluß*) branch, tributary.
Armaturenbrett [arma'tuɪrənbrɛt] *neut* dashboard, instrument panel.
Armband ['armbant] *neut* bracelet. –**uhr** *f* (wrist)watch.
Armee [ar'meɪ] *f* (*pl* -n) army.
Ärmel ['ɛrməl] *m* (*pl* -) sleeve. –**kanal** *m* English Channel.
ärmlich ['ɛrmliç] *adj* poor, miserable.
armselig ['armzɛliç] *adj* wretched, miserable.
Arm‖sessel *m* armchair. –**stuhl** *m* armchair.
Armut ['armuɪt] *f* poverty.
Arrest [a'rɛst] *m* (*pl* -e) arrest, detention.
Arsch [arʃ] *m* (*pl* **Ärsche**) (*vulgär*) arse.
Art [art] *f* (*pl* -en) type, kind, sort; (*Weise*) way, method; (*Biol*) species; (*Brauch*) habit.

artig ['artiç] *adj* (*Kind*) good, well-behaved.
-artig [-artiç] *adj* -like.
Artikel [ar'tiːkəl] *m* (*pl* -) article.
Artillerie [artilə'riː] *f* (*pl* -n) artillery.
Artischocke [arti'ʃɔkə] *f* (*pl* -n) artichoke.
Artist [ar'tist] *m* (*pl* -en) artiste.
Arznei [arts'nai] *f* (*pl* -en) medicine, medicament, drug. **-mittel** *neut* medicine.
Arzt [artst] *m* (*pl* Ärzte) doctor, physician.
Ärztin ['ɛrtstin] *f* (*pl* -nen) (woman) doctor. **ärztlich** *adj* medical.
As [as] *neut* (*pl* -se) ace.
Asbest [as'bɛst] *m* asbestos.
Asche ['aʃə] *f* (*pl* -n) ash. **-nbecher** *m* ashtray.
Aspekt [as'pɛkt] *m* (*pl* -e) aspect.
Asphalt [as'falt] *m* asphalt, tarmac.
Assistent [asis'tɛnt] *m* (*pl* -en) assistant.
Ast [ast] *m* (*pl* Äste) bough, branch.
ästhetisch [ɛs'teːtiʃ] *adj* aesthetic.
Astronaut [astro'naut] *m* (*pl* -en) astronaut. **-ik** *f* astronautics. **astronautisch** *adj* astronautical.
Astronom [astro'noːm] *m* (*pl* -en) astronomer. **-ie** *f* astronomy. **astronomisch** *adj* astronomical.
Asyl [a'zyːl] *neut* (*pl* -e) asylum.
Atelier [atə'ljeː] *neut* (*pl* -s) studio.
Atem ['aːtəm] *m* (*pl* -) breath. **Atem holen** take breath.
Atheis∥mus [ate'ismus] *m* atheism. **-t** *m* (*pl* -en) atheist.
Äther ['ɛːtər] *m* ether. **ätherisch** *adj* ethereal.
Athlet [at'leːt] *m* (*pl* -en) athlete. **-ik** *f* athletics. **athletisch** *adj* athletic.
Atlantik [at'lantik] *m* Atlantic (Ocean).
Atlas[1] ['atlas] *m* (*pl* Atlanten) (*Buch*) atlas.
Atlas[2] *m* (*pl* -se) (*Stoff*) satin.
atmen ['aːtmən] *v* breathe.
Atmosphäre [atmos'fɛːrə] *f* (*pl* -n) atmosphere.
Atmung ['aːtmuŋ] *f* respiration, breathing. **-sapparat** *m* respirator.
Atom [a'toːm] *neut* (*pl* -e) atom. **-abfall** *m* atomic waste. **-antrieb** *m* nuclear propulsion. **-bombe** *f* atom bomb. **-kraft** *f* nuclear power. **-kraftwerk** *f* nuclear power station.
Attentat [atɛn'taːt] *neut* (*pl* -e) assassination (attempt). **Attentäter** *m* assassin, assailant.

ätzen ['ɛtsən] *v* corrode; (*Med*) cauterize; (*Kupferstich*) etch. **-d** *adj* corrosive, caustic.
Aubergine [obɛr'ʒiːnə] *f* (*pl* -n) aubergine.
auch [aux] *conj* also, too; (*sogar*) even; (*tatsächlich*) indeed, but. **nicht nur ... sondern auch ...** not only ... but also .... **sowohl ... als auch ...** both ... and .... **auch wenn** even if, (even) though. **ich auch!** me too! **ich auch nicht** nor me, me neither. **was er auch sagen mag** whatever he may say. **wer auch immer** whoever.
Audienz [audi'ɛnts] *f* (*pl* -en) audience, interview.
auf [auf] *prep* on. *adv* up; (*offenstehend*) open. **auf und ab** up and down. *auf den Tisch stellen* put on the table. *auf dem Tisch finden* find on the table. *auf die Schule gehen* go to school. *auf der Schule sein* be at school. *auf deutsch* in German. **auf einmal** at once.
Aufbau ['aufbau] *m* (*unz.*) building, construction; structure.
aufbessern ['aufbɛsərn] *v* improve; (*Gehalt*) increase. **Aufbesserung** *f* improvement; (*Gehalt*) increase, rise.
aufbewahren ['aufbəvaːrən] *v* store (up), keep. **Aufbewahrung** *f* storage, safe-keeping.
*aufblasen ['aufblaːzən] *v* blow up, inflate.
aufblicken ['aufblikən] *v* look up.
aufbrauchen ['aufbrauxən] *v* use up.
*aufbrechen ['aufbrɛçən] *v* break open; (*Knospen, Wunden*) open; (*abreisen*) set off.
*aufbringen ['aufbriŋən] *v* bring up, raise; (*ärgern*) imitate, provoke.
Aufbruch ['aufbrux] *m* departure, start.
aufdecken ['aufdɛkən] *v* uncover, reveal; (*Tisch*) spread. **Aufdeckung** *f* revealing, unveiling.
aufdrehen ['aufdreːən] *v* switch *or* turn on; (*Schraube*) unscrew.
aufdringlich ['aufdriŋliç] *adj* intrusive, importunate.
aufeinander [aufain'andər] *adv* (one) after another; (*gegeneinander*) one against the other. **-folgen** *v* follow (one after another). **-folgend** *adj* successive. **-stoßen** *v* (*Mot*) collide; (*Meinungen*) clash. **-treffen** *v* meet.

Aufenthalt ['aufənthalt] *m* (*pl* **-e**) (*kurze Wartezeit*) delay, stop; (*längerer Besuch usw.*) stay. **-serlaubnis** *f* residence permit.

auferlegen ['aufɛrleɪgən] *v* impose.

***auferstehen** ['aufɛrʃteɪən] *v* rise from the dead. **Auferstehung** *f* resurrection.

***auffahren** ['auffaɪrən] *v* rise, go up; (*herauffahren*) draw up; (*aufspringen*) start, jump; (*zornig werden*) flare up; (*wagen*) collide. **Auffahrt** *f* ascent; (*in den Himmel*) Ascension; (*Zufahrtsweg*) drive.

***auffallen** ['auffalən] *v* strike, come to one's attention. **es fiel mir ein** it struck me, I realized. **auffallend** *or* **auffällig** *adj* striking, remarkable.

auffassen ['auffasən] *v* pick up; (*begreifen*) understand; (*deuten*) interpret. **Auffassung** *f* comprehension; (*Auslegung*) interpretation; (*Meinung*) opinion.

***auffliegen** ['auffliːgən] *v* fly up; (*Flugzeug*) take off; (*Tür*) fly open; (*explodieren*) explode.

auffordern ['auffɔrdərn] *v* challenge; (*einladen*) ask, invite. **Aufforderung** *f* challenge; (*Recht*) summons; (*Einladung*) invitation, request.

***auffressen** ['auffresən] *v* devour.

auffrischen ['auffriʃən] *v* freshen up; (*Kenntnisse*) refresh.

aufführen ['auffyɪrən] *v* (*Theater*) put on, perform; (*Film*) show; (*Konzert*) give; (*zitieren*) cite; (*aufbauen*) erect. **Aufführung** *f* performance; (*Film*) showing; (*Benehmen*) behaviour.

Aufgabe ['aufgaɪbə] *f* task, duty; (*Übergabe*) handing in.

Aufgang ['aufgaŋ] *m* rise, ascent.

***aufgeben** [aufgeɪbən] *v* give up; (*Gepäck*) check in.

aufgeblasen ['aufgəblaɪzən] *adj* arrogant, conceited.

aufgeklärt ['aufgəklɛɪrt] *adj* enlightened.

aufgelegt ['aufgəlɛɪkt] *adj* inclined, in the mood. **gut/schlecht aufgelegt** in a good/bad mood.

aufgeregt ['aufgərɛɪkt] *adj* excited.

aufgeschlossen ['aufgəʃlɔsən] *adj* enlightened, open-minded.

***aufhalten** ['aufhaltən] *adj* keep open; (*anhalten*) stop; (*hinhalten*) delay. **sich aufhalten** stay.

***aufhängen** ['aufhɛŋən] *v* hang up.

***aufheben** ['aufheɪbən] *v* lift, raise; (*aufbewahren*) store, keep; (*abschaffen*) abolish, cancel. **Aufhebung** *f* raising, abolition.

aufheitern ['aufhaitərn] *v* cheer up. **sich aufheitern** (*Wetter*) brighten up.

aufhören ['aufhœɪrən] *v* stop, cease.

aufklären ['aufkleɪrən] *v* (*Person*) enlighten; (*Sache*) clarify, explain. **Aufklärung** *f* clarification; (the) Enlightenment.

aufkleben ['aufkleɪbən] *v* stick on, paste on.

aufknöpfen ['aufknœpfən] *v* unbutton.

***aufkommen** ['aufkɔmən] *v* arise. **aufkommen für** take responsibility for.

***aufladen** ['auflaɪdən] *v* load.

Auflage ['auflaɪgə] *f* (*Buch*) edition; (*Zeitung*) circulation.

***auflassen** ['auflasən] *v* leave open.

Auflauf ['auflauf] *m* riot; (*Speise*) trifle, soufflé. **auflaufen** *v* run up; (*Schiff*) run aground; (*Geld*) increase.

auflegen ['aufleɪgən] *v* put on; (*Buch*) print, publish; (*Telef*) hang up.

auflösbar ['auflœɪzbaɪr] *adj* soluble. **auflösen** *v* (*Knoten*) loosen; (*in Wasser, usw.*) dissolve; (*Rätsel*) solve; (*Vertrag*) cancel; (*Geschäft*) close down; (*Ehe*) break up. **Auflösung** *f* loosening; solution; cancellation; closure; break-up.

***aufmachen** ['aufmaxən] *v* open; (*Knoten, Knöpfe*) undo. **sich aufmachen** set off. **Aufmachung** *f* outward appearance.

aufmerksam ['aufmɛrkzam] *adj* attentive. **jemanden auf etwas aufmerksam machen** draw something to someone's attention. **Aufmerksamkeit** *f* attentiveness, attention.

aufmuntern ['aufmuntərn] *v* encourage, cheer up.

Aufnahme ['aufnaɪmə] *f* (*pl* **-n**) taking up; (*Foto*) shot, picture; (*Tonband, usw.*) recording; (*Zulassung*) admission; (*Empfang*) reception. **aufnahmefähig** *adj* receptive. **Aufnahmeprüfung** *f* entrance exam.

***aufnehmen** ['aufneɪmən] *v* take up; (*zulassen*) admit; (*empfangen*) receive; (*Radio*) pick up; (*Foto*) photograph; (*Protokoll, Tonband*) record.

aufopfern ['aufɔpfərn] *v* sacrifice.

aufpassen ['aufpasən] *v* pay attention; (*vorsichtig sein*) take care. **aufpassen auf** take care of, look after.

Aufprall ['aufpral] *m* (*pl* -e) impact, collision. **aufprallen** *v* strike, collide.

aufputzen ['aufputsən] *v* dress up, adorn; (*reinigen*) clean up.

aufräumen ['aufrɔymən] *v* tidy up, clean up; (*wegschaffen*) clear away. **Aufräumung** *f* cleaning up.

aufrecht ['aufrɛçt] *adj* upright, erect; (*fig*) upright, honest. **–erhalten** *v* maintain, keep up.

aufregen ['aufreigən] *v* excite, upset, **sich aufregen** get excited *or* upset. **Aufregung** *f* excitement, agitation.

aufrichten ['aufrɪçtən] *v* erect, set up; (*trösten*) console.

aufrichtig ['aufrɪçtɪç] sincere, honest. **Aufrichtigkeit** *f* sincerity, honesty.

aufrücken ['aufrykən] *v* move up; (*Dienstgrad*) be promoted.

Aufruf ['aufruːf] *m* call, appeal. **aufrufen** *v* call out.

Aufruhr ['aufruːr] *m* (*pl* -e) tumult; (*Erhebung*) revolt. **aufrühren** *v* stir up; (*Erhebung*) incite to revolt. **Aufrührer** *m* (*pl* -) agitator, rebel. **aufrührerisch** *adj* rebellious, riotous.

aufrüsten ['aufrystən] *v* (re)arm. **Aufrüstung** *f* (re)armament.

aufs [aufs] *prep* + *urt* auf das.

aufsagen ['aufzagən] *v* recite, repeat.

Aufsatz ['aufzats] *m* essay; (*Tech*) top (piece); (*Tafel*) centre-piece.

*aufsaugen ['aufzaugən] *v* suck up. **–d** *adj* absorbent.

*aufschieben ['aufʃiːbən] *v* push open; (*fig*) put off, delay. **Aufschiebung** *f* postponement, delay.

Aufschlag ['aufʃlaːk] *m* surcharge, extra charge; (*Hose*) turn-up; (*Jacke*) lapel; (*Auftreffen*) impact; (*Tennis*) service. **aufschlagen** *v* (*Preis*) raise; (*Stoff*) turn up; (*auftreffen*) hit; (*Buch*) open, consult; (*Tennis*) serve.

*aufschließen ['aufʃliːsən] *v* open up, unlock; (*erklären*) explain. **Aufschluß** ['aufʃlus] *m* unlocking; (*Erklärung*) explanation. **aufschlußreich** *adj* informative.

*aufschneiden ['aufʃnaidən] *v* cut open; (*Fleisch*) carve. **Aufschnitt** ['aufʃnit] *m* (cold) sliced meat. **Aufschrei** ['aufʃrai] *m* scream, shriek; (*fig*) outcry.

*aufschreiben ['aufʃraibən] *v* write down, note.

Aufschrift ['aufʃrit] *f* (*Briefumschlag*) address; (*Etikett*) labelling, information; (*Inschrift*) inscription.

Aufschub ['aufʃuːp] *m* delay, deferment.

Aufschwung ['aufʃvuŋ] *m* swinging up, rising up; (*Komm*) boom, upturn (in economy).

*aufsehen ['aufzeiən] *v* look up. **Aufsehen** *neut* (*unz.*) stir, sensation. **Aufseher** *m* (*pl* -) overseer, inspector.

aufsetzen ['aufzɛtsən] *v* put on; (*Schriftliches*) draft, draw up.

Aufsicht ['aufziçt] *f* supervision, control; (*Verantwortung*) charge, care. **–srat** *m* board of directors.

*aufspringen ['aufʃpriŋən] *v* spring up; (*Tür*) fly open; (*Riß*) crack, open.

Aufstand ['aufʃtant] *m* revolt, rebellion.

aufstapeln ['aufʃtaːpəln] *v* stack up, pile up.

aufstauen ['aufʃtauən] *v* dam (up).

*aufstehen ['aufʃteiən] *v* stand up; (*morgens, usw.*) get up, rise; (*revoltieren*) revolt; (*offenstehen*) stand open.

*aufsteigen ['aufʃtaigən] *v* climb up, ascend, rise; (*Pferd*) mount.

aufstellen ['aufʃtɛlən] *v* set up; (*Kandidat*) nominate; (*Mil*) draw up; (*Theorie, usw.*) propose, advance.

Aufstieg ['aufʃtiːk] *m* ascent, rise.

aufsuchen ['aufzuːxən] *v* (*Arzt, Gasthaus*) visit; (*Person*) visit, look up.

auftanken ['auftaŋkən] *v* refuel.

auftauchen ['auftauxən] *v* (*aus Wasser*) emerge; (*fig*) turn up, crop up.

auftauen ['auftauən] *v* thaw (out), melt.

aufteilen ['auftailən] *v* divide up; (*verteilen*) share out.

Auftrag ['auftraːk] *m* (*pl* **Aufträge**) (*Komm*) order; (*Aufgabe*) task. **auftragen** *v* (*Farbe*) apply; (*Essen*) serve. **Auftrag‖geber** *m* customer, purchaser. **–nehmer** *m* contractor, supplier.

*auftreiben ['auftraibən] *v* (*auffinden*) hunt out, find; (*Staub*) stir up; (*Geld*) raise.

*auftreten ['auftreːtən] *v* come forward, appear.

Auftritt ['auftrit] *m* (*Szene*) scene; (*Schauspieler*) appearance, entrance.

*auftun ['auftuːn] *v* open.

aufwachen ['aufvaxən] *v* wake up.

*aufwachsen ['aufvaksən] grow up.

Aufwand ['aufvant] *m* (*unz.*) expenditure.
aufwärmen ['aufvɛrmən] *v* (*Sport*) warm up; (*speisen*) heat up.
aufwärts ['aufvɛrts] *adv* up(wards).
aufwecken ['aufvɛkən] *v* wake up.
***aufwend‖en** ['augvɛndən] *v* (*Geld*) spend; (*Zeit*) devote; (*Energie*) expend. **–ig** *adj* expensive. **Aufwendung** *f* expenditure.
***aufwerfen** ['aufvɛrfən] *v* throw up.
aufwerten ['aufvɛrtən] *v* raise the value of, revalue. **Aufwertung** *f* revaluation.
***aufwinden** ['aufvindən] *v* wind up; (*mit der Winde*) winch up.
aufwirbeln ['aufvirbəln] *v* whirl up.
aufwischen ['aufviʃən] *v* wipe up.
aufwühlen ['aufvyːlən] *v* root up; (*fig*) stir up, agitate.
aufzählen ['auftsɛːlən] *v* count out.
aufzeichnen ['auftsaiçnən] *v* sketch; (*niederschreiben*) write down.
***aufziehen** ['auftsiːən] *v* (*Kind, Tier, Flagge*) raise; (*Vorhang*) open; (*Pflanze*) grow; (*necken*) tease.
Aufzug ['auftsuːk] *m* lift, (*US*) elevator; (*Festzug*) procession, parade; (*Theater*) act.
Augapfel ['aukapfəl] *m* eyeball.
Auge ['augə] *neut* (*pl* **-n**) eye. **unter vier Augen** in private. **ins Auge fallen** be conspicuous, catch the eye. **Augen‖arzt** *m* oculist, ophthalmologist. **–blick** *m* moment, instant. **–braue** *f* eyebrow. **–lid** *neut* eyelid. **–loch** *neut* eye socket.
August [au'gust] *m* (*pl* **-e**) August.
Aula ['aula] *f* (*pl* **Aulen**) (great) hall.
Au-pair-Mädchen [o'pɛirmɛitçən] *neut* au-pair girl.
aus [aus] *prep* from. *adv* out; (*vorbei*) over, finished. *aus London* from London. *aus dem Fenster* out of the window. *aus Liebe zu* for love of. *aus Holz* (made) of wood, wooden. *von mir aus* as far as I'm concerned. *es ist aus* it's over.
ausarbeiten ['ausarbaitən] *v* work out; (*vervollkommnen*) perfect, finish off. **Ausarbeitung** *f* working out; finishing off, completion.
ausarten ['ausairtən] *v* degenerate.
ausatmen ['ausaitmən] *v* exhale, breathe out.
ausbaggern ['ausbagərn] *v* dredge.
Ausbau ['ausbau] *m* (*pl* **-ten**) extension; (*Fertigstellung*) completion.

ausbauchen ['ausbauxən] *v* bulge. **Ausbauchung** *f* bulge.
ausbessern ['ausbesərn] *v* repair, mend.
Ausbeute ['ausbɔytə] *f* profit, gain; (*Ernte*) crop, yield. **ausbeuten** *v* exploit. **Ausbeut‖er** *m* exploiter. **–ung** *f* exploitation.
ausbilden ['ausbildən] *v* educate; (*Lehrling*) train; (*gestalten*) develop, shape. **Ausbildung** *f* education; training; (*Gestaltung*) development, shaping.
***ausbleiben** ['ausblaibən] *v* stay away; (*aufhören*) stop.
Ausblick ['ausblik] *m* view; (*fig*) prospect, outlook.
***ausbrechen** ['ausbrɛçən] *v* break out.
ausbreiten ['ausbraitən] *v* spread (out), stretch (out), extend.
Ausbruch ['ausbrux] *m* outbreak; (*vom Gefängnis*) escape, break-out; (*Zorn, Vulkan*) eruption.
***ausbrüten** ['ausbryːtən] *v* hatch.
Ausdauer ['ausdauər] *f* endurance, perseverance. **ausdauern** *v* persevere, endure.
ausdehnen ['ausdeːnən] *v* extend; (*Metall*) expand. **Ausdehnung** *f* extension; expansion.
***ausdenken** ['ausdɛŋkən] *v* invent, think out; (*sich vorstellen*) imagine.
ausdrehen ['ausdreːən] *v* turn off, switch off; (*Gelenk*) dislocate.
Ausdruck ['ausdruk] *m* expression, phrase. **ausdrück‖en** *f* express; (*auspressen*) squeeze out. **–lich** *adj* express, explicit. **ausdrucks‖los** *adj* expressionless, vacant. **–voll** *adj* expressive.
auseinander [ausain'andər] *adv* apart. **–bauen** *v* take apart, dismantle. **–fallen** *v* fall to pieces. **–gehen** *v* break up; (*sich trennen*) part. **–nehmen** *v* take apart. **–setzen** *v* explain. **Auseinandersetzung** *f* (vigorous) discussion; (*Streit*) argument.
auserlesen ['ausɛrleɪzən] *adj* selected.
ausersehen ['ausɛrzeɪən] *v* choose, select.
auserwählen ['ausɛrvɛːlən] *v* choose, select.
***ausfahren** ['ausfaɪrən] *v* drive out; (*Person*) take for a drive *or* walk. **Ausfahrt** *f* exit; (*Ausflug*) excursion; (*Ausfahren*) departure.
Ausfall ['ausfal] *m* loss; (*Fehlbetrag*) deficiency, deficit; (*Ergebnis*) result; (*Mil*) attack, sally. **ausfallen** *v* fall out; (*unterbleiben*) fail, be wanting; attack.

ausfertigen ['ausfɛrtigən] v (*Schriftliches*) draw up; (*ausstellen*) issue.

ausfindig ['ausfindiç] adj **ausfindig machen** find out.

Ausflug ['ausfluːk] m excursion, outing.

ausfragen [ausfraɪgən] v question, interrogate.

Ausfuhr ['ausfuːr] f (*pl* -en) export.

ausführ‖en ['ausfyːrən] v carry out, perform; (*Waren*) export; (*erklären*) explain, set out (in detail). **-bar** adj feasible. **-lich** adj detailed, extensive; adv in full. **Ausführung** f execution, performance; (*Darstellung*) explanation.

ausfüllen ['ausfylən] v fill; (*Formular*) fill out.

Ausgabe ['ausgaɪbə] f expenditure, expense; (*Buch*) edition.

Ausgang ['ausgaŋ] m going out; (*Tür*) way out, exit; (*Ergebnis*) result, issue; (*freier Tag*) day off.

*ausgeben ['ausgeɪbən] v (*Geld*) spend; (*herausgeben*) distribute; (*Karten*) deal. **sich ausgeben für** pose as.

ausgeglichen ['ausgəglɪçən] adj (well-)balanced.

*ausgehen ['ausgeɪən] v go out; (*enden*) come to an end; (*Vorrat*) run out. **Ausgehverbot** neut curfew.

ausgelassen ['ausgəlasən] adj wild, unrestrained, boisterous.

ausgemacht ['ausgəmaxt] adj agreed, settled.

ausgenommen ['ausgənomən] prep except for.

ausgeprägt ['ausgəprɛikt] adj marked, distinct.

ausgerechnet ['ausgərɛçnət] adv precisely, just.

ausgeschlossen ['ausgəʃlɔsən] adj impossible, out of the question.

ausgesprochen ['ausgəʃprɔxən] adj pronounced, distinct. adv distinctly, very.

ausgewachsen ['ausgəvaksən] adj fullgrown.

ausgezeichnet ['ausgətsaiçnət] adj excellent.

*ausgießen ['ausgiːsən] v pour out.

Ausgleich ['ausglaiç] m (*pl* -e) settlement; (*Entschädigung*) compensation; (*Sport*) equalizer. **ausgleichen** v equalize, make even; (*Verlust*) compensate; (*Konto*) balance.

Ausguß ['ausgus] m outlet; (*Kanne*) spout.

*aushalten ['aushaltən] v bear, endure; (*durchhalten*) persevere.

*ausheben ['ausheɪbən] v pull out, lift out; (*Truppen*) enlist. **Aushebung** f enlistment; (*Wehrdienst*) conscription.

*aushelfen ['aushɛlfən] v help (out), assist.

Aushilfe ['aushilfə] f (temporary) help, assistance.

aushöhlen ['aushœːlən] v hollow out, excavate.

*auskennen ['auskɛnən] v **sich auskennen** (*umg.*) know what's what; (*in einer Sache*) know well.

auskleiden ['ausklaidən] v line. **sich auskleiden** undress.

*auskommen ['auskɔmən] v (*mit etwas*) manage or cope with; (*mit einer Person*) get on well with.

Auskunft ['auskunft] f (*pl* **Auskünfte**) information.

auslachen ['auslaxən] v laugh at.

*ausladen ['auslaidən] v unload.

Auslage ['auslaɪgə] f display; (*Schaufenster*) shop window. **-n** pl expenses pl.

Ausland ['auslant] neut foreign country or countries. **ins** or **im Ausland** abroad. **Ausländer** m (*pl* -), **Ausländerin** f (*pl* -nen) foreigner. **ausländisch** adj foreign.

*auslassen ['auslasən] v omit, leave out; (*Butter*) melt; (*Kleider*) let down. **Auslassung** f omission; (*Äußerung*) utterance. **-szeichen** neut apostrophe.

Auslauf ['auslauf] m outflow; (*Schiff*) sailing, departure; (*Bewegungsfreiheit*) room to move. **auslaufen** v run out; (*Schiff*) put to sea.

ausleeren ['ausleɪrən] v empty. **Ausleerung** f emptying, draining.

auslegen ['ausleɪgən] v lay out; (*Geld*) spend; (*erklären*) explain, interpret. **Auslegung** f display; (*Erklärung*) interpretation.

Auslese ['ausleɪzə] f (*pl* **-n**) selection; (*Wein*) choice wine. **auslesen** v select; (*Buch*) read to the end.

ausliefern ['ausliːfərn] v deliver; (*Verbrecher*) extradite. **Auslieferung** f delivery; extradition.

auslösen ['auslœːzən] v loosen; (*Gefangene*) ransom; (*veranlassen*) cause, spark off.

ausmachen ['ausmaxən] v (*Feuer, Licht*) put out; (*betragen*) amount to; (*ver-

abreden) agree, fix. **das macht nichts aus** that doesn't matter.

Ausmaß ['ausmaɪs] *neut* scale, extent.

Ausnahme ['ausnaɪmə] *f* (*pl* **-n**) exception. **mit Ausnahme von** excepting, with the exception of. **–fall** *m* exception, special case. **–zustand** *m* (*Pol*) state of emergency. **ausnahms‖los** *adj* without exception. **–weise** *adv* by way of exception, just for once.

*****ausnehmen** ['ausneɪmən] *v* take out; (*ausschließen*) exclude, make an exception of.

ausnutzen ['ausnutsən] *v* take advantage of.

auspacken ['auspakən] *v* unpack.

ausprobieren ['ausprobiːrən] *v* try (out), test.

Auspuff ['auspuf] *m* (*pl* **-e**) exhaust. **–rohr** *neut* exhaust pipe. **–topf** *m* silencer.

ausradieren ['ausradiːrən] *v* erase, rub out.

ausräumen ['ausrɔymən] *v* clear out, clean out.

ausrechnen ['ausrɛçnən] *v* calculate, work out. **Ausrechnung** *f* calculation.

Ausrede ['ausreɪdə] *f* excuse.

ausreichen ['ausraɪçən] *v* be enough *or* sufficient. **–d** *adj* sufficient, enough.

Ausreise ['ausraɪzə] *f* outward journey; (*Grenzübertritt*) departure, exit. **ausreisen** *v* depart.

ausrichten ['ausrɪçtən] *v* adjust, align; (*durchsetzen*) accomplish, do; (*Botschaft*) convey.

ausrotten ['ausrɔtən] *v* stamp out, root out.

Ausruf ['ausruːf] *m* cry, exclamation; (*Bekanntmachung*) proclamation. **ausrufen** *v* cry out, exclaim; (*Namen*) call out. **Ausrufung** *f* exclamation. **–zeichen** *neut* exclamation mark.

ausruhen ['ausruːən] *v* rest.

ausrüsten ['ausrystən] *v* equip; (*Mil*) arm. **Ausrüstung** *f* equipment; (*Mil*) armament.

Aussage ['auszaɪgə] *f* (*pl* **-n**) statement, declaration; (*Jur*) evidence, testimony. **aussagen** *v* declare, state; (*Jur*) give evidence, make a statement, testify.

ausschalten ['ausʃaltən] *v* switch off; (*fig*) exclude.

Ausschank ['ausʃaŋk] *m* (*Ausgabe*) service

(of alcoholic drinks); (*Kneipe*) bar, pub. **Ausschank über die Straße** off-sales, off-licence.

*****ausscheiden** ['ausʃaɪdən] *v* withdraw, retire; (*absondern*) separate. **Ausscheidung** *f* withdrawal; separation.

ausschicken ['ausʃɪkən] *v* send out.

ausschiffen ['ausʃɪfən] *v* disembark, land. **Ausschiffung** *f* disembarkation.

ausschimpfen ['ausʃɪmpfən] *v* scold, abuse.

*****ausschlafen** ['ausʃlaɪfən] *v* lie in, sleep until completely rested.

Ausschlag ['ausʃlaːk] *m* (*Med*) rash; (*Bot*) shoot; (*Zeiger*) deflection. **ausschlagen** *v* knock out; (*ablehnen*) refuse; (*Pferd*) kick out.

*****ausschließen** ['ausʃliːsən] *v* shut out, lock out; (*fig*) exclude. **ausschließlich** *adj* exclusive; *prep* excluding, exclusive of. **Ausschließung** *f* exclusion; (*Arbeiter*) lock-out.

*****ausschneiden** ['ausʃnaɪdən] *v* cut out.

Ausschnitt ['ausʃnɪt] *m* (*Teil*) section; (*Zeitung*) press cutting; (*Kleid*) low neckline.

ausschöpfen ['ausʃœpfən] *v* (*Wasser*) scoop out; (*Boot*) bail out; (*Möglichkeiten*) exhaust.

*****ausschreiben** ['ausʃraɪbən] *v* write out, copy out; (*Formular*) fill out; (*ankündigen*) announce.

Ausschreitung ['ausʃraɪtuŋ] *f* excess, transgression.

Ausschuß ['ausʃus] **1** *m* committee, board. **2** *m* (*unz.*) (*Abfall*) refuse, rejects *pl*.

ausschweifen ['ausʃwaifən] *v* (*moralisch*) lead a dissolute life; (*von Thema*) digress. **Ausschweifung** *f* debauchery, immorality; digression.

*****aussehen** ['auszeɪən] *v* appear, look. *sie sieht hübsch aus* she looks pretty. *es sieht nach Regen aus* it looks like rain.

außen ['ausən] *adv* (to the) outside, outwards. **Außenbordmotor** *m* outboard motor.

*****aussenden** ['auszɛndən] *v* send out; (*Strahlen*) emit; (*Radio*) transmit.

Außen‖handel *m* foreign trade. **–läufer** *m* wing-half. **–minister** *m* foreign minister. **–politik** *f* foreign policy; (*allgemein*) foreign affairs. **–seite** *f* outside. **–seiter** outsider. **–stürmer** *m* wing (forward).

außer ['ausər] *prep (räumlich)* out of, outside; *(ausgenommen)* except. außer Betrieb out of order.

äußer ['ɔysər] *adj* external, exterior, outer.

außer||dem *adv* besides. –halb *adv, prep* outside.

äußerlich ['ɔysərliç] *adj* external.

äußern ['ɔysərn] *v* express, utter; *(zeigen)* manifest, reveal.

außerordentlich [ausər'ɔrdəntliç] *adj* extraordinary.

äußerst ['ɔysərst] *adj* the utmost.

aussetzen ['auszɛtzən] *v (Pflanze)* plant out; *(Kind)* abandon; *(Tier)* set free; *(Geld)* offer; *(einer Gefahr, dem Spott, usw.)* expose (to); *(aufhören)* stop; *(Mot)* stall.

Aussicht ['ausziçt] *f* outlook, prospect; *(Blick)* view. aussichts||los *adj* unpromising, hopeless. –voll *adj* promising.

aussondern ['auszɔndərn] *(auswählen)* select; excrete. Aussonderung *f* separation; selection; excretion.

ausspeien ['ausʃpaiən] *v* spit out; *(Rauch)* belch out.

Aussprache ['ausʃpraixə] *f* pronunciation. *ausprechen ['ausʃprɛçən] *v* pronounce.

Ausspruch ['ausʃprux] *m* remark, saying; *(Jur)* verdict.

ausspülen ['ausʃpy:lən] *v* wash out, rinse.

Ausstand ['ausʃtant] *m* strike.

ausstatten ['ausʃtatən] *v* equip, furnish; *(Tochter)* provide with a dowry. Ausstattung *f (pl -en)* equipment, outfit; dowry.

*ausstehen ['ausʃteːən] *v* be missing; *(Geld)* be owed; *(ertragen)* endure, bear. ich kann ihn nicht ausstehen I can't stand him.

*aussteigen ['ausʃtaigən] *v* get off, alight.

ausstellen ['ausʃtɛlən] *v* display, exhibit; *(Paß, Urkunde)* issue; *(Quittung)* write out. Aussteller *m (pl -)* exhibitor. Ausstellung *f* exhibition; issue; writing out.

*aussterben ['ausʃtɛrbən] *v* die out.

Ausstieg ['ausʃtiːg] *m (pl -e)* exit door.

*ausstoßen ['ausʃtoːsən] *v* push out, thrust out; *(Schrei)* give.

ausstrahlen ['ausʃtraːlən] *v* radiate.

ausstrecken ['ausʃtrɛkən] *v* stretch out, extend.

*ausstreichen ['ausʃtraiçən] *v (Wort)* strike out, cross out; *(Teig)* roll out.

ausströmen ['ausʃtrœːmən] *v (Flüssigkeit)* pour out; *(Gas)* escape.

aussuchen ['auszuːxən] *v* search (out), select.

Austausch ['austauʃ] *m* exchange. austauschen *v* exchange.

austeilen ['austailən] *v* distribute, share out.

Auster ['austər] *f (pl -n)* oyster.

Austrag ['austraːk] *m (pl Austräge)* decision, end, result. austragen *v* carry out; *(Kampf)* decide; *(Post)* deliver.

Australi||en [au'straːliən] *neut* Australia. –er *m (pl -)*, –erin *f (pl -nen)* Australian. australisch *adj* Australian.

*austreiben ['austraibən] *v* expel.

*austreten ['austrɛtən] *v* leave, withdraw (from); *(Schuhe, usw.)* wear out.

*austrinken ['austriŋkən] *v* drain, drink off.

Austritt ['austrit] *m* leaving, departure.

ausüben ['ausʔyːbən] *v* practise; *(Druck, Einfluß)* exert; *(Macht)* wield. –d *adj* practising. Ausübung *f* practice, exercise.

Ausverkauf ['ausfɛrkauf] *m* (clearance) sale. ausverkauft *adj* sold out.

Auswahl ['ausvaːl] *f* choice, selection.

Auswanderer ['ausvandərər] *m* emigrant. auswandern *v* emigrate. Auswanderung *f* emigration.

auswärtig ['ausvɛrtiç] *adj* foreign. das Auswärtige Amt the Foreign Office.

auswärts ['ausvɛrts] *adv* outwards; *(nach draußen)* outside.

auswechseln ['ausvɛksəln] *v* change (for), exchange.

Ausweg ['ausveːk] *m* way out.

*ausweichen ['ausvaiçən] *v* make way; *(Frage)* evade, dodge. –d *adj* evasive, elusive. Ausweichung *f* evasion.

Ausweis ['ausvais] *m (pl -e)* identity card or papers; *(Paß)* passport. ausweisen *v* expel, turn out. Ausweisung *f* expulsion.

auswendig ['ausvɛndiç] *adj* external. auswendig lernen learn by heart.

*auswerfen ['ausvɛrfən] *v* throw out; *(Anker)* cast.

auswirken ['ausvirkən] *v* obtain. sich auswirken auf have an effect on. Auswirkung *f* effect.

auswischen ['ausviʃən] *v* wipe out.

Auswuchs ['ausvuks] *m* growth; *(Nebenerscheinung)* (unwelcome) product, side-effect.

auszahlen ['austsaːlən] *v* pay out. Auszahlung *f* payment.

auszeichnen ['austsaiçnən] v (*Ware*) label; (*ehren*) honour; (*hervorheben*) distinguish, mark out. **sich auszeichnen** distinguish oneself. **Auszeichnung** f distinction, honour, award.

***ausziehen** ['austsiːən] v pull out, extract; (*Person*) undress; (*aus einer Wohnung*) move out. **sich ausziehen** undress.

Auszug ['austsuːk] m removal; (*Abmarsch*) departure; (*Exzerpt*) excerpt.

authentisch [au'tɛntiʃ] adj authentic.

Auto ['auto] neut (pl -s) car, automobile. **–ausstellung** f motor show. **–bahn** f motorway. **–fahrer** m driver, motorist.

Autogramm [auto'gram] neut (pl -e) autograph.

Automat [auto'maːt] m (pl -en) vending machine. **automatisch** adj automatic. **automatisieren** v automate.

autonom [auto'noːm] adj autonomous.

Autor ['autɔr] m (pl -en) author.

autoritär [autori'tɛːr] adj authoritarian. **Autorität** f authority.

Auto‖unfall m road accident. **–vermietung** f car hire.

avantgardistisch [avãgar'distiʃ] adj avant-garde.

Axt [akst] f (pl Äxte) axe.

B

Baby ['beːbi] neut (pl -s) baby.

Bach [bax] m (pl Bäche) stream, brook.

Backbord ['bakbɔrt] neut (naut) port (side).

Backe ['bakə] f (pl -n) cheek.

backen ['bakən] v bake.

Bäcker ['bɛkər] m (pl -) baker. **–ei** f (pl -en) bakery.

Back‖ofen m oven. **–pulver** neut baking powder. **–stein** m brick.

Bad [baːt] neut (pl Bäder) bath; (*Badeort*) spa. **Bade‖anstalt** f baths, swimming pool. **–anzug** m bathing costume. **–hose** f bathing trunks pl. **baden** v bathe. **Bade‖wanne** f bath tub. **–zimmer** neut bathroom.

Bagger ['bagər] m (pl -) dredger, excavator. **baggern** v dredge, excavate.

Bahn [baːn] f (pl -en) railway; (*Weg*) path. **–brecher** m pioneer. **bahnen** v den **Weg bahnen** pave the way (for).

Bahn‖hof m (railway) station. **–steig** m (railway) platform.

Bahre ['baːrə] f (pl -n) stretcher; (*Toten-*) bier.

Bai [bai] f (pl -en) (*Bucht*) bay.

Bajonett [bajo'nɛt] neut (pl -e) bayonet.

Bakterium [bak'teːrium] neut (pl Bakterien) bacterium (pl -a).

balancieren [balã'siːrən] v balance.

bald [balt] adv soon. **–ig** adj early, quick. **–möglichst** adv as soon as possible.

Balken ['balkən] m (pl -) beam.

Balkon [nal'kõ] m (pl -e) balcony.

Ball[1] [bal] m (pl Bälle) ball.

Ball[2] m (pl Bälle) (*Tanz*) dance, ball.

Ballade [ba'laːdə] f (pl -n) ballad.

ballen ['balən] v (*Faust*) clench. **sich ballen** cluster, clump together.

Ballen ['balən] m (pl -) bale, bundle; (*Anat*) palm. **–entzündung** f bunion.

Ballett [ba'lɛt] neut (pl -e) ballet. **Ballett‖tänzer** m (pl -), **–tänzerin** f (pl -nen) ballet dancer. **Balletteuse** f (pl -n) ballerina.

Ballistik [ba'listik] f (unz.) ballistics. **ballistisch** adj ballistic.

Ballon [ba'lõ] m (pl -e) balloon.

Balsam ['balzaːm] m (pl -e) balsam; (*fig*) balm. **balsamieren** v embalm.

baltisch ['baltiʃ] adj Baltic.

Bambus ['bambus] m (pl -se) bamboo.

Banane [ba'naːnə] f (pl -n) banana.

Band[1] [bant] 1 neut (pl Bänder) tape; (*Haar*) ribbon; (*Anat*) ligament; (*Radio*) waveband. 2 neut (pl -e) bond, tie.

Band[2] m (pl Bände) (*Buch*) volume.

Band[3] [bɛnt] f (pl -s) (*Jazz*) band.

Bandage [ban'daːʒə] f (pl -n) bandage. **bandagieren** v bandage.

Bandaufnahme ['bantaufnaːmə] f tape recording.

Bande ['bandə] f (pl -n) gang, band.

bändigen ['bɛndigən] v tame, subdue; (*Wut*) control.

Bandit [ban'diːt] m (pl -en) bandit.

Bandscheibe ['bantʃaibə] f (*Anat*) disc. **–nverfall** m slipped disc.

bang(e) ['baŋ(ə)] adj afraid, anxious. **bangen** v be afraid or anxious.

Bank[1] [baŋk] f (pl Bänke) (*zum Sitzen*) bench, seat.

Bank[2] f (pl -en) (*Komm*) bank.

Bankett [baŋ'kɛt] neut (pl -e) banquet.

bankrott [baŋ'rɔt] adj bankrupt. **Bankrott** m (pl -e) bankruptcy. **Bankrott machen**

223   bebauen

go bankrupt. **Bankrotteur** *m* (*pl* **-e**) bankrupt.

Bank‖konto *neut* bank account. −**note** *f* banknote.

Bann [ban] *m* (*pl* **-e**) ban; (*Kirche*) excommunication; (*Zauber*) spell.

bar [baɪr] *adj* bare; (*Geld*) ready, in cash. **für bare Münze nehmen** accept, take at face value.

Bar [baɪr] *f* (*pl* **-s**) bar, tavern.

Bär [bɛɪr] *m* (*pl* **-en**) bear.

Barbar [bar'baɪr] *m* (*pl* **-en**) barbarian. **Barbarei** *f* (*pl* **-en**) barbarism. **barbarisch** *adj* barbarian.

barfuß ['baɪrfuɪs] *adv* barefoot. **barfüßig** *adj* barefoot.

Bargeld ['baɪrgɛlt] *neut* cash.

Bariton ['bariton] *m* (*pl* **-e**) baritone.

Barmädchen ['baɪrmɛtçən] *neut* barmaid.

barmherzig [barm'hɛrtsiç] *adj* merciful, compassionate. **Barmherzigkeit** *f* mercifulness, mercy.

Barock [ba'rɔk] *neut* or *m* baroque.

Barometer [ba'romɛtər] *neut* barometer.

Baron [ba'roɪn] *m* (*pl* **-e**) baron. −**in** *f* (*pl* **-nen**) baroness.

Barre [barə] *f* (*pl* **-n**) bar; (*Gold*) ingot.

Barriere [bari'ɛɪrə] *f* (*pl* **-n**) barrier, gate.

barsch [barʃ] *adj* rude, brusque.

Bart [baɪrt] *m* (*pl* **Bärte**) beard. **bärtig** ['bɛɪrtiç] *adj* bearded.

Base¹ ['baɪzə] *f* (*pl* **-n**) (female) cousin.

Base² *f* (*pl* **-n**) alkali, base.

Basel ['baɪzəl] *neut* Basle, Bâle.

basieren [ba'ziɪrən] *v* be based (on). **Basis** *f* (*pl* **Basen**) basis (*pl* **-ses**), base.

Baß [bas] *m* (*pl* **Bässe**) bass. −**geige** *f* double-bass.

Bassist [ba'sist] *m* (*pl* **-en**) (*Sänger*) bass (singer); (*Baßgeigenspieler*) double-bass (player).

Bastard ['bastart] *m* (*pl* **-e**) bastard.

basteln ['bastəln] *v* put together, rig up; (*umg.*) do-it-yourself. *er bastelt gern* he loves to tinker around. **Bastler** *m* (*pl* **-**) handyman, tinkerer.

Bataillon [batai'ljoɪn] *neut* (*pl* **-e**) battalion.

Batterie [batə'riɪ] *f* (*pl* **-n**) battery.

Bau [bau] **1** *m* (*unz.*) building, construction; (*Getreide, usw.*) cultivation, growing. **2** *m* (*pl* **-e**) (*Bergwerk*) mine; (*Tiere*) burrow. **3** *m* (*pl* **-ten**) building. −**arbeiter** *m* construction worker.

Bauch [baux] *m* (*pl* **Bäuche**) belly, abdomen. **bauchig** *adj* bellied, bulging, convex. **Bauchweh** *neut* or **Bauchschmerzen** *pl* stomach-ache.

bauen ['bauən] build; (*Bot*) grow, cultivate.

Bauer ['bauər] *m* (*pl* **-n**) (small) farmer, peasant; (*Schach*) pawn.

Bäuerin ['bɔyərin] *f* (*pl* **-nen**) farmer's wife, peasant woman. **bäuerlich** *adj* rustic, rural.

Bauern‖haus *neut* farmhouse. −**hof** *m* farm(yard).

baufällig ['baufɛliç] *adj* dilapidated.

Bau‖genossenschaft *f* building society. −**ingenieur** *m* structural or civil engineer. −**stelle** *f* building site.

Baum [baum] *m* (*pl* **Bäume**) tree; (*Schiff*) boom. −**garten** *m* orchard. −**wolle** *f* cotton.

Bayer ['baiər] *m* (*pl* **-**) Bavarian. −**n** *neut* Bavaria. **bay(e)risch** *adj* Bavarian.

beabsichtigen [bə'apziçtigən] *v* intend, propose.

beachten [bə'axtən] *v* pay attention to. **beachtungswert** *adj* noteworthy. **Beachtung** *f* attention, notice.

Beamte(r) [bə'amtə(r)] *m*, **Beamtin** *f* (*Staats-*) civil servant, official, (*Privat-*) officer, representative.

beängstigen [bə'ɛŋstigən] *v* worry, frighten.

beanspruchen [bə'anʃpruxən] *v* claim, demand; (*Person*) make demands on. **Beanspruchung** *f* claim; (*Belastung*) strain, load.

*beantragen [bə'antraɪgən] *v* propose.

beantworten [bə'antvɔrtən] *v* answer, reply to.

bearbeiten [bə'arbaitən] *v* work on; (*Metall, Holz, Land*) work; (*Buch*) edit, revise; (*Musik*) arrange; (*Theaterstück*) adapt. **Bearbeiter** *m* editor, reviser; arranger. **Bearbeitung** *f* working; (*Verbesserung*) revision, adaptation; (*Musik*) arrangement.

beaufsichtigen [bə'aufziçtigən] *v* supervise, control. **Beaufsichtigung** *f* supervision, control.

*beauftragen [bə'auftraɪgən] *v* commission, authorize. **Beauftragte(r)** *m* deputy, agent.

bebauen [bə'bauən] *v* (*Gelände*) build on; (*Land*) cultivate. **bebaute Fläche** *f* built-up area.

beben ['beɪbən] v tremble, shake.
Becher ['bɛçər] m (pl -) tumbler, glass.
–**glas** neut (laboratory) beaker.
Becken ['bɛkən] neut (pl -) basin; (Anat) pelvis; (Musik) cymbal.
bedacht [bə'daxt] adj thoughtful, mindful. **Bedacht** m consideration; (Überlegung) deliberation. **bedächtig** adj thoughtful, careful.
Bedarf [bə'darf] m (unz.) need; (Nachfrage) demand.
bedauerlich [bə'dauərliç] adj regrettable, unfortunate. **bedauern** v (Sache) regret, deplore; (Person) be or feel sorry for.
bedecken [bə'dɛkən] v cover. **bedeckt** adj (Himmel) overcast. **Bedeckung** f (pl -en) cover(ing).
*****bedenken** [bə'dɛŋkən] v consider, think over. **sich bedenken** deliberate, weigh the consequences (of).
bedeuten [bə'dɔytən] v mean, signify. –**d** adj important. **Bedeutung** f meaning; (Wichtigkeit) significance, importance. **bedeutungs‖los** adj meaningless. –**voll** adj significant.
bedienen [bə'diːnən] v serve, wait on; (Maschine) operate, work. **Bedienung** f service; (Maschine) operation; (Diener) staff, servants pl.
bedingt [bə'dɪŋkt] adj conditional, limited. **Bedingung** f (pl -en) condition.
Bedrängnis [bə'drɛŋnis] f (pl -se) distress, trouble.
bedrohen [bə'droːən] v threaten. **Bedrohung** f (pl -en) threat.
*****bedürfen** [bə'dʏrfən] v need, require. **Bedürfnis** neut (pl -se) need, requirement. **Bedürfnisanstalt** f public toilet.
beeilen [bə'aɪlən] v sich beeilen hurry.
beeindrucken [bə'aɪndrukən] v impress.
beeinflussen [bə'aɪnflusən] v influence, have an influence or effect on.
beeinträchtigen [bə'aɪntrɛçtigən] v reduce, inhibit, be detrimental to.
beendigen [bə'ɛndigən] v end, finish. **Beendigung** f end, termination.
Beerdigung [bə'eɪrdiguŋ] f burial, funeral.
Beere ['beɪrə] f (pl -n) berry.
Beet [beɪt] neut (pl -e) bed; (Blumen-) flowerbed; (Gemüse) vegetable patch.
befähigen [bə'fɛːigən] v enable, make fit. **befähigt** adj able, qualified. **Befähigung** f (pl -en) capacity, fitness.

befahrbar [bə'faːrbaɪr] adj passable, usable. **befahren** v travel or drive on.
*****befallen** [bə'falən] v befall; (Krankheit) attack, strike.
befangen [bə'faŋən] adj shy, self-conscious; (parteiisch) biased.
befassen [bə'fasən] v sich befassen mit engage in, occupy oneself with.
*****befehlen** [bə'feɪlən] v command, order. **Befehl** m (pl -e) command, order. **Befehlshaber** m (pl -) commander, commanding officer.
befestigen [bə'fɛstigən] v fasten; (stärken) strengthen; (Mil) fortify. **Befestigung** f (pl -en) fastening; strengthening; (Mil) fortification.
*****befinden** [bə'findən] v find. **sich befinden** be, be situated; (Person) be, find oneself. **sich wohl befinden** feel well. **befindlich** adj present, to be found.
beflecken [bə'flɛkən] v stain, soil.
befolgen [bə'fɔlgən] v obey, follow.
befördern [bə'fœdərn] v convey, dispatch; (Rang) promote. **Beförderung** f (pl -en) transport, conveyance; promotion.
befragen [bə'fraɪgən] v question. **sich befragen** enquire, inquire.
befreien [bə'fraɪən] v liberate, free. **Befreier** m (pl -) liberator. **Befreiung** f (pl -en) liberation; (Entlastung) exemption.
befreunden [bə'frɔyndən] v sich befreunden mit make friends with. **befreundet** adj friendly (with); intimate. **eng befreundet sein mit** be a close friend of.
befriedigen [bə'friːdigən] v satisfy. –**d** adj satisfactory. **Befriedigung** f (pl -en) satisfaction.
befruchten [bə'fruxtən] v fertilize; (anregen) stimulate. **Befruchtung** f (pl -en) fertilization.
befugen [bə'fuːgən] v authorize, empower. **Befugnis** f (pl -se) authority, right.
befürchten [bə'fʏrçtən] v fear; (vermuten) suspect. **Befürchtung** f (pl -en) fear, apprehension.
befürworten [bə'fʏrvɔrtən] v recommend, advocate.
begabt [bə'gaɪpt] adj talented, gifted. **Begabung** f talent, gift.
begatten [bə'gatən] v sich begatten mate, copulate. **Begattung** f (pl -en) mating, copulation.
*****begeben** [bə'geɪbən] v sich begeben go, proceed; (verzichten) renounce, give up.

begegnen [bə'geignən] v meet, encounter.
Begegnung f (pl -en) meeting, encounter.
*begehen [bə'geiən] (Unrecht) commit,
do; (gehen auf) walk on.
begehren [bə'geirən] v desire, covet.
begeistern [bə'gaistərn] v inspire, fill with
enthusiasm. begeistert adj inspired,
enthusiastic. Begeisterung f enthusiasm.
Begier [bə'giir], f (unz.), also Begierde f
(pl -n) desire, craving. begierig adj desirous, covetous.
begießen [bə'giisən] v water, sprinkle;
(Braten) baste.
Beginn [bə'gin] m (unz.) beginning.
beginnen v begin.
beglaubigen [bə'glaubigən] v certify,
attest. Beglaubigung f (pl -en) certification.
begleiten [bə'glaitən] v accompany.
Begleit||er m (pl -) attendant; (Musik)
accompanist. –schreiben neut covering
letter. –ung f (pl -en) attendants pl,
escort; (Musik) accompaniment.
beglücken [bə'glykən] v make happy.
beglückwünschen v congratulate.
Beglückwünschung f (pl -en) congratulations pl.
begnadigen [bə'gnaidigən] v pardon.
begnügen [bə'gnyigən] v sich begnügen
mit content oneself with, be satisfied
with.
*begraben [bə'graibən] v bury. Begräbnis
neut (pl -se) burial, funeral.
*begreifen [bə'graifən] v understand,
grasp, apprehend. begreiflich adj comprehensible.
begrenzt [bə'grentst] adj restricted, limited.
Begriff [bə'grif] m (pl -e) concept, idea.
Begriffsvermögen neut comprehension.
begründen [bə'gryndən] v found, establish; (Behauptung) substantiate.
Begründer m founder.
begrüßen [bə'gryisən] v greet, welcome.
begünstigen [bə'gynstigən] v (vorziehen)
favour; (fördern) promote, further.
begütert [bə'gyitərt] adj wealthy, well-to-
do.
begütigen [bə'gyitigən] v placate, appease.
behäbig [bə'he:biç] adj (beleibt) portly,
corpulent; (bequem, langsam) comfort
able.
behagen [bə'haigən] v please, suit.
Behagen neut (pl -) ease, comfort. behaglich adj comfortable, at ease.

*behalten [bə'haltən] v keep, retain; (im
Gedächtnis) remember. Behälter m (pl -)
container; (Flüssigkeiten) tank.
behandeln [bə'handəln] v treat, handle.
Behandlung f treatment, handling; (Med)
treatment, therapy.
beharren [bə'harən] v persist. beharrlich
adj persistent, pertinacious.
behaupten [bə'hauptən] v maintain, asset,
state. Behauptung f (pl -eu) statement,
assertion.
behend(e) [bə'hent, bə'he:ndə] adj, also
behendig nimble, agile. Behendigkeit f
agility.
beherbergen [bə'herbergən] v rule, govern.
beherrschen [bə'herfən] v (Zorn, usw.)
control; (meistern, können) master. sich
beherrschen control oneself. Beherrschung f rule, control; mastery.
beherzigen [bə'hertsigən] v take to heart.
behilflich [bə'hilfliç] adj helpful.
behindern [bə'hindərn] v hinder,
obstruct. Behinderung f (pl -en) hindrance.
Behörde [bə'hoerdə] f (pl -n) authority,
authorities pl.
behüten [bə'hyitən] v guard, protect.
Behüter m (pl -) protector, guard.
bei [bai] prep at; (neben) near. bei mir at
(my) home; (in der Tasche) on me. bei
Herrn Schmidt at Herr Schmidt's
(house). bei der Post arbeiten work for
the Post Office. bei der Hand nehmen
take by the hand. beim Aussteigen while
or when getting out. bei Nacht at night.
bei Tag during the day. bei der Arbeit at
work. bei weitem by far. bei Shakespeare
in Shakespeare.
*beibehalten ['baibəhaltən] v retain;
keep.
*beibringen ['baibriŋən] v bring forward;
(Verlust, Wunde) inflict; (lehren) teach.
Beichte ['baiçtə] f (pl -n) (Rel) confession.
beichten v confess. Beichtvater m confes-
sor.
beide ['baidə] adj, pron both. alle beide
both. einer von beiden either of two. in
beiden Fällen in either case. wir beide
both of us. zu beiden Seiten on both
sides. beider||lei adj of both sorts. –sei-
tig adj mutual, reciprocal. –seits adv
mutually. beidhändig adj ambidextrous.

Beifahrer ['baifaːrər] m (pl -) passenger.
Beifall ['baifal] m (unz.) applause; (Billigung) approval. **Beifall klatschen** applaud.
beifügen ['baifyːgən] v enclose, attach.
*****beigeben** ['baigeːbən] v add. **klein beigeben** draw in one's horns, yield.
Beigeschmack ['baigəʃmak] m (after)taste; (fig) tinge.
Beihilfe ['baihilfə] f financial aid, subsidy; (Jur) aiding and abetting.
*****beikommen** ['baikɔmən] v get at, get near, reach.
Beil [bail] neut (pl -e) (Holz) hatchet; (Fleisch) cleaver.
Beilage ['bailaɪgə] f enclosure, insert; (Zeitung) supplement.
beiläufig ['bailɔyfiç] adj incidental. adv incidentally, by the way.
beilegen ['baileːgən] v add; (zuschreiben) attribute, ascribe; (schlichten) settle.
Beileid ['bailait] neut (unz.) condolence.
beiliegend ['bailiːgənt] adj enclosed.
beim [baim] prep + art **bei dem**.
*****beimessen** ['baimɛsən] v attribute, credit with.
Bein [bain] neut (pl -e) leg; (Knochen) bone.
beinah(e) ['bainaɪ(ə)] adv almost, nearly.
Beiname ['bainaɪmə] m nickname. **mit dem Beinamen ... known as ... , called ...**
beirren [bəˈirən] v **sicht nicht beirren lassen** stick to one's opinions, not be misled.
beisammen [baiˈzamən] adv together.
Beischlaf ['baiʃlaːf] m (sexual) intercourse.
beiseite [baiˈzaitə] adv to one side, aside. **-legen** v put aside or by.
Beispiel ['baiʃpiːl] neut (pl -e) example. **zum Beispiel** for example or instance. **beispielsweise** adv for instance, as an example.
*****beißen** ['baisən] v bite. **beißend** adj biting; (Säure) caustic. **Beiß‖zahn** m incisor. **-zange** f pincers.
Beistand ['baiʃtant] m help, assistance.
*****beistehen** ['baiʃteːən] v help, assist.
beistimmen ['baiʃtimən] v agree, consent. **Bestimmung** f agreement, consent.
Beitrag ['baitraɪk] m (pl Beiträge) contribution; (Klub) subscription. **beitragen** v contribute. **Beiträger** m (pl -) contributor.

*****beitreten** ['baitreɪtən] v join; (Meinung) agree to, accept.
Beiwagen ['baivaɪgən] m sidecar.
beiwohnen ['baivoːnən] v be present at, attend; (beischlafen) have sex with.
beizeiten [baiˈtsaitən] adv early.
beizen ['baitsən] v (Holz) stain; (Metall) etch; (Fleisch) salt, pickle.
bejahen [bəˈjaːən] v affirm, agree to.
bejahrt [bəˈjaɪrt] adj aged.
bekämpfen [bəˈkɛmpfən] v fight (against), combat.
bekannt [bəˈkant] adj known. **bekannt werden mit** become acquainted with. **sich bekanntmachen mit** acquaint oneself with. **Bekannt‖e(r)** acquaintance. **-gabe** f announcement, notification. **bekannt‖geben** v make known, disclose. **-lich** adv as is well known. **Bekanntschaft** f acquaintance.
bekehren [bəˈkeːrən] v convert. **Bekehr‖te(r)** convert. **-ung** f conversion.
*****bekennen** [bəˈkɛnən] v acknowledge, confess. **Bekenntnis** neut (pl -se) confession; (Glaube) faith, creed.
beklagen [bəˈklaɪgən] v lament, deplore. **-swert** adj lamentable. **Baklagte(r)** m accused, defendant.
bekleiden [bəˈklaidən] v clothe; (beziehen) coat; (Amt) occupy. **Bekleidung** f clothing; (Material) coating.
*****beklemmen** [bəˈklɛmən] v oppress, frighten; (ersticken) stifle. **Angst beklemmt mich** I am seized by fear.
*****bekommen** [bəˈkɔmən] v obtain, get, receive; (Zug) catch; (Krankheit) catch, get. **bekömmlich** adj wholesome, beneficial.
bekräftigen [bəˈkrɛftigən] v confirm, strengthen.
bekreuzigen [bəˈkrɔytsigən] v **sich bekreuzigen** cross oneself.
bekümmern [bəˈkymərn] v trouble, distress. **bekümmert sein** be anxious or troubled.
bekunden [bəˈkundən] v state; (zeigen) show, manifest.
*****beladen** [bəˈlaɪdən] v load.
Belag [bəˈlaɪk] m (pl Beläge) covering, coating; (Aufstrich) spread. **Butterbrot mit Belag** sandwich.
belagern [bəˈlaɪgərn] v besiege. **Belagerung** f siege.

belangen [bə'laŋɡən] v concern; (*Jur*) prosecute. **belanglos** adj unimportant.

belasten [bə'lastən] v burden; (*Konto*) debit, charge; (*Jur*) accuse.

belästigen [bə'lɛstiɡən] v pester, bother; (*umg.*) bug. **Belästigung** f bother, annoyance.

Belastung [bə'lastuŋ] f (*pl* -en) load; (*Konto*) debit, charge.

*****belaufen** [bə'laufən] v **sich belaufen auf** amount to, total.

belauschen [bə'lauʃən] v eavesdrop on, listen to (secretly).

beleben [bə'leibən] v animate; (*Med*) revive. **belebt** adj animated, lively; (*Ort*) crowded, bustling. **Beleb‖theit** f liveliness. **–ung** f animation; revival.

Beleg [bə'leik] m (*pl* -e) proof, evidence; (*Urkunde*) voucher. **belegen** v cover; (*Platz*) reserve; (*Kursus*) enrol for, (*Brot*) spread. **belegtes Brötchen** filled roll, sandwich. **Belegschaft** f personnel, staff.

belehren [bə'leirən] v instruct, teach.

beleibt [bə'laipt] adj portly, stout.

beleidigen [bə'laidiɡən] v insult. **beleidigend** adj insulting, offensive. **Beleidigung** f (*pl* -en) insult.

beleuchten [bə'lɔyçtən] v illuminate, light (up). **Beleuchtung** f lighting, illumination.

Belgien ['bɛlɡiən] neut Belgium. **Belgier** m (*pl* -), **Belgierin** f (*pl* -nen) Belgian. **belgisch** adj Belgian.

belichten [bə'liçtən] v (*Foto*) expose. **Belichtung** f (*pl* -en) exposure. **Belichtungsmesser** m light meter.

belieben [bə'liibən] v (*gefallen*) please; (*wünschen*) like, wish. **Belieben** neut pleasure, will. **nach Belieben** at will, as you like. **beliebig** adj any (you like), whatever. **beliebt** adj loved, popular.

bellen ['bɛlən] v bark.

belohnen [bə'loinən] v reward, recompense. **Belohnung** f reward, recompense.

belüften [bə'lyftən] v ventilate. **Belüftung** f ventilation.

belustigen [bə'lustiɡən] v amuse. **Belustigung** f amusement.

bemächtigen [bə'mɛçtiɡən] v **sich bemächtigen** seize, take possession of.

bemerkbar [bə'mɛrkbair] adj noticeable, observable. **bemerken** v notice; (*sagen*) remark. **–swert** adj remarkable, noteworthy. **Bemerkung** f (*pl* -en) remark.

*****bemessen** [bə'mɛsən] v measure. adj restricted.

bemitleiden [bə'mitlaidən] v pity, feel sorry for.

bemühen [bə'myiən] v trouble (oneself), take pains. **Bemühen** neut or **Bemühung** f (*pl* -en) effort, exertion.

benachbart [bə'naxbairt] adj neighbouring.

benachrichtigen [bə'naxriçtiɡən] v inform. **Benachrichtigung** f report.

benannt [bə'nant] adj named.

*****benehmen** [bə'neimən] v **sich benehmen** behave. **Benehmen** neut behaviour.

beneiden [bə'naidən] v envy.

*****benennen** [bə'nɛnən] v name, call. **Benennung** f (*pl* -en) name, title.

Bengel ['bɛŋəl] m (*pl* -) brat, little rascal.

benommen [bə'nɔmən] adj confused.

benötigen [bə'nœitiɡən] v need, require.

benutzen [bə'nutsən] v use, make use of. **Benutzung** f use, employment.

Benzin [bɛn'tsiin] neut petrol, (*US*) gasoline. **–uhr** f petrol or fuel gauge. **–verbrauch** m fuel consumption.

beobachten [bə'oibaxtən] v observe, watch; (*bemerken*) notice. **Beobach‖ter** m (*pl* -) observer, onlooker. **–tung** f (*pl* -en) observation.

bepflanzen [bə'pflantsən] v plant.

bequem [bə'kveim] adj comfortable; (*mühelos*) convenient. **bequemlich** adj lazy, comfort-loving.

*****beraten** [bə'raitən] v advise. **sich beraten** confer. **beratend** adj advisory. **Berater** m adviser, counsellor. **Beratung** f consultation.

berauben [bə'raubən] v rob or deprive of.

berauschen [bə'rauʃən] v intoxicate.

berechenbar [bə'reçənbair] adj calculable. **berechnen** v calculate, evaluate. **berechnend** adj (*Person*) selfish, calculating. **Berechnung** f calculation, evaluation.

berechtigen [bə'reçtiɡən] v entitle, authorize. **berechtigt** adj entitled. **Berechtigung** f authorization, entitlement.

bereden [bə'reidən] v persuade. **beredsam** adj eloquent.

Bereich [bə'raiç] m (*pl* -e) region, domain; (*fig*) field, sphere, realm.

bereichern [bə'raiçərn] v enrich. **sich bereichern** acquire wealth, get rich.

bereit [bə'rait] adj ready, prepared. **bereiten** v prepare, make ready. **bereit‖halten** v keep in readiness. **–machen**

v make ready. **Bereitschaft** f readiness. **bereit‖stehen** v be ready. **–stellen** v make ready, prepare. **Bereitung** f (pl **-en**) preparation. **bereitwillig** adj ready.

bereuen [bə'rɔyən] v regret, repent.

Berg [bɛrk] m (pl **-e**) mountain. **bergab** adv downhill. **Bergarbeiter** m miner. **bergauf** adv uphill. **Bergbau** m mining.

***bergen** ['bɛrgən] v conceal; (schützen) protect; (Güter) recover.

Bergführer ['bɛrkfyrər] m mountain guide.

bergig ['bɛrgiç] adj mountainous, hilly.

Berg‖leute pl miners. **–mann** m miner. **bergmännisch** adj mining. **Berg‖rutsch** m landslide. **–steigen** neut mountain climbing. **–steiger** m (mountain) climber, mountaineer.

Bergung ['bɛrguŋ] f (pl **-en**) rescue; (Schiff) salvage. **–sarbeiten** f pl salvage or rescue operations.

Bergwerk ['bɛrkvɛrk] neut mine, pit.

Bericht [bə'riçt] m (pl **-e**) report, account. **berichten** v report, give an account. **Berichterstatter** m (pl **-**) reporter; (Radio) commentator, correspondent.

berichtigen [bə'riçtigən] v correct, amend; (Schulden) pay. **Berichtigung** f correction; (Schulden) settlement.

beritten [bə'ritən] adj mounted.

Bernstein ['bɛrnʃtain] m amber.

berüchtigt [bə'ryçtiçt] adj notorious, infamous.

berücksichtigen [bə'rykziçtigən] v keep in mind, consider, take account of. **Berücksichtigung** f consideration.

Beruf [bə'ruːf] m (pl **-e**) occupation, job, profession; (Gewerbe) trade. **beruf‖en** v appoint; (kommen lassen) summon, send for. **–lich** adj professional, vocational. **Berufs‖ausbildung** f vocational training. **–krankheit** f occupational disease. **–schule** f vocational school, technical college. **berufstätig** adj employed. **Berufstätigkeit** f employment, professional activity; (Jur) appeal. **Berufung** f (pl **-en**) appointment; (Jur) appeal.

beruhen [bə'ruːən] v rest (on), be founded (on).

beruhigen [bə'ruːigən] v pacify, calm. **beruhigend** adj calming. **Beruhigung** f calming, pacification. **Beruhigungsmittel** neut sedative.

berühmt [bə'ryːmt] adj famous, celebrat-

ed. **Berühmtheit** f fame; (Person) celebrity.

berühren [bə'ryːrən] v touch, handle; (angrenzen) border; (angehen) concern; (erwähnen) touch on.

besäen [bə'zɛːən] v sow.

besänftigen [bə'zɛnftigən] v soothe, calm (down).

Besatzung [bə'zatsuŋ] f (Mil) garrison; (Schiff, Flugzeug) crew; (Pol) occupation. **–szone** f occupied area (of a country).

beschädigen [bə'ʃɛːdigən] v damage. **Beschädigung** f damage.

beschaffen [bə'ʃafən] v get, procure. adj constituted.

beschäftigen [bə'ʃɛftigən] v employ; (zu tun geben) occupy, keep busy. **beschäftigt** adj employed; occupied, busy. **Beschäftigung** f (pl **-en**) employment, occupation.

beschämen [bə'ʃɛːmən] v shame.

beschatten [bə'ʃatən] v shade; (verfolgen) shadow.

beschauen [bə'ʃauən] v look at; (prüfen) examine, look over. **Beschauer** m (pl **-**) spectator, inspector. **beschaulich** adj contemplative.

Bescheid [bə'ʃait] m (pl **-e**) information; (Entscheidung) decision, ruling. **Bescheid geben/sagen** give information, inform. **Bescheid wissen** know the situation, be well informed.

bescheinigen [bə'ʃainigən] v certify, attest. **Bescheinigung** f (pl **-en**) certificate; (Quittung) receipt.

beschenken [bə'ʃɛnkən] v give a present to, present (with).

bescheren [bə'ʃeːrən] v give presents. **Bescherung** f giving (of presents). **eine schöne Bescherung** a fine mess.

***beschießen** [bə'ʃiːsən] v fire on, shell. **Beschießung** f shelling, bombardment.

beschimpfen [bə'ʃimpfən] v insult.

Beschlag [bə'ʃlaːk] m (pl **Beschläge**) clasp, catch; (Jur) seizure. **in Beschlag nehmen** seize, confiscate. **beschlagen** v cover, fit; (Pferd) shoe. **Beschlagnahme** f (pl **-n**) confiscation, seizure. **beschlagnahmen** v seize, confiscate.

beschleunigen [bə'ʃlɔynigən] v accelerate. **Beschleunigung** f acceleration.

***beschließen** [bə'ʃliːsən] v decide, resolve; (beendigen) terminate, end.

Beschluß [bə'ʃlus] *m* (*pl* **Beschlüsse**) decision, resolution; (*Ende*) end, close.
beschmutzen [bə'ʃmutsən] *v* dirty, soil.
***beschneiden** [bə'ʃnaidən] *v* cut, prune, clip; (*Kind*) circumcize. **Beschneidung** *f* circumcision.
beschränken [bə'ʃrɛnkən] *v* restrict, limit. **beschränkt** *adj* limited, confined. **Beschränkung** *f* limitation.
***beschreiben** [bə'ʃraibən] *v* describe. **Beschreibung** *f* description.
beschuldigen [bə'ʃuldigən] *v* accuse. **Beschuldigte(r)** *m* accused, defendant. **Beschuldigung** *f* accusation.
beschützen [bə'ʃytsən] *v* protect.
Beschwerde [bə'ʃveɪrdə] *f* (*pl* -n) complaint. **beschweren** *v* burden. **sich beschweren über** complain about. **beschwerlich** *adj* troublesome; (*mühselig*) tedious.
beschwichtigen [bə'ʃviçtigən] *v* appease, pacify. **Beschwichtigung** *f* allaying, appeasement.
beschwipst [bə'ʃvipst] *adj* (*umg.*) tipsy.
***beschwören** [bə'ʃvœɪrən] *v* swear (on oath); (*Person*) implore, beg; (*Erinnerungen, Geister*) conjure up.
***besehen** [bə'zeɪən] *v* look at, inspect.
beseitigen [bə'zaitigən] *v* remove, get rid of, eliminate; (*Schwierigkeiten*) overcome. **Beseitigung** *f* removal, elimination.
Besen ['beɪzən] *m* (*pl* -) broom.
besessen [bə'zɛsən] *adj* possessed.
besetzen [bə'zɛtsən] *v* (*Platz*) occupy, take, (*Mil*) occupy, (*Kleid*) trim, decorate; (*Posten*) fill. **besetzt** *adj* (*Theater*) full; (*Platz*) taken; (*WC*) occupied, engaged; (*Telef*) engaged. **Besetzung** *f* occupation; (*Theater*) casting.
besichtigen [bə'ziçtigən] *v* inspect, view. **Besichtigung** *f* inspection; (*Sehenswürdigkeiten*) sightseeing.
besiedeln [bə'ziːdəln] *v* colonize.
besiegen [bə'ziːgən] *v* conquer.
***besinnen** [bə'zinən] *v* **sich besinnen** remember, recollect. **Besinnen** *neut* reflection, consideration. **Besinnung** *f* contemplation; (*Bewußtsein*) consciousness. **besinnunglos** *adj* unconscious, senseless.
Besitz [bə'zits] *m* (*pl* -e) possession. **besitzen** *v* possess, own. **Besitzer** *m* (*pl* -) owner.
besoffen [bə'zɔfən] *adj* (*vulgär*) drunk.

Besoldung [bə'zɔldun] *f* (*pl* -en) salary, wages *pl*.
besonder [bə'zɔndər] *adj* special, particular. **besonders** *adv* especially, particularly. **nichts Besonderes** nothing special, not up to much.
besonnen [bə'zɔnən] *adj* sensible, prudent. **Besonnenheit** *f* prudence.
besorgen [bə'zɔrgən] *v* take care of, see to; (*beschaffen*) obtain. **Besorgnis** *f* (*pl* -se) apprehension, anxiety. **besorgniserregend** *adj* giving cause for worry. **besorgt** *adj* anxious, worried. **Besorgung** *f* (*pl* -en) management; (*Einkauf*) purchase.
bespannen [bə'ʃpanən] *v* (*verkleiden*) cover; (*Fahrzeug*) harness; (*Musik*) string. **Bespannung** *f* (*pl* -en) covering; (*Pferde*) team (of horses).
***besprechen** [bə'ʃprɛçən] *v* discuss; (*Buch, Film*) review. **Besprechung** *f* discussion; (*Buch, Film*) review.
besser ['bɛsər] *adj* better. **desto besser** so much the better. **um so besser** all the better. **er ist besser dran** he is better off. **bessern** *v* improve, make better. **Besserung** *f* (*pl* -en) improvement.
best [bɛst] *adj* best. **am besten** *adv* best. **aufs Beste** in the best possible way. **besten Dank!** many thanks!
Bestand [bə'ʃtant] *m* (*pl* **Bestände**) continuance, duration; (*Vorrat*) stock, supply.
beständig [bə'ʃtendiç] *adj* constant, lasting. **Bestandteil** [bə'ʃtanttail] *m* component, part.
bestärken [bə'ʃtɛrkən] *v* strengthen; (*bestätigen*) confirm. **Bestärkung** *f* strengthening; confirmation.
bestätigen [bə'ʃtɛtigən] *v* confirm, verify. **bestätigend** *adj* confirmatory. **Bestätigung** *f* (*pl* -en) confirmation.
bestatten [bə'ʃtatən] *v* bury. **Bestattung** *f* (*pl* -en) funeral, burial.
***bestechen** [bə'ʃtɛçən] *v* bribe, corrupt. **bestechlich** *adj* corrupt, bribable. **Bestechung** *f* bribery, corruption.
Besteck [bə'ʃtɛk] *neut* (*pl* -e) cutlery; knife, fork, and spoon; (*Med*) (medical) instruments *pl*.
***bestehen** [bə'ʃteɪən] *v* exist, be; (*überstehen*) undergo; (*Examen*) pass; (*fortdauern*) endure, survive. **bestehen auf** insist on. **bestehen aus** consist of.

*besteigen [bə'ʃtaigən] v climb, ascend; (*Pferd*) mount. **Besteigung** f ascent; mounting.

bestellen [bə'ʃtɛlən] v (*Waren*) order; (*Zimmer*) reserve; (*Boden*) cultivate. **Bestellung** f order; reservation; cultivation.

bestenfalls ['bɛstənfals] adv at best. **bestens** adv in the best manner.

besteuern [bə'ʃtɔyərn] v tax. **Besteuerung** f taxation.

Bestie ['bɛstiə] f (*pl* -n) beast.

bestimmen [bə'ʃtimən] v determine, fix; (*ernennen*) appoint. **bestimmt** adj definite, certain. **Bestimmung** f determination; (*Vorschrift*) regulation; (*Ernennung*) appointment.

bestrafen [bə'ʃtraɪfən] v punish. **Bestrafung** f punishment.

Bestrahlung [bə'ʃtraɪluŋ] f radiation; (*Med*) radiotherapy.

bestreben [bə'ʃtreɪbən] v **sich bestreben** strive, endeavour. **Bestreben** neut or **Bestrebung** f endeavour, exertion.

*bestreiten [bə'ʃtraitən] v dispute, contest.

bestürmen [bə'ʃtyrmən] v assault, storm.

bestürzen [bə'ʃtyrtsən] v startle, disconcert. **bestürzt** adj taken aback, dismayed.

Besuch [bə'zuːx] m (*pl* -e) visit, call. **Besuch haben** have visitors. *ich bin zu Besuch hier* I am visiting, I am a visitor. **besuchen** v visit, see; (*Schule*) go to, attend. **Besucher** m (*pl* -) visitor, caller; (*Gast*) guest.

betagt [bə'taːkt] adj aged, elderly.

betasten [bə'tastən] v finger, touch.

betätigen [bə'tɛːtigən] v put into action; (*Maschine*) operate; (*Bremse*) apply. **sich betätigen** occupy oneself, work; (*activ sein*) be active, participate. **Betätigung** f operation; (*Teilnahme*) participation.

betäuben [bə'tɔybən] v stun; (*narkotisieren*) anaesthetize. **Betäubung** f anaesthesia. **Betäubungsmittel** neut anaesthetic.

Bete ['beːtə] f beet, beetroot.

beteiligen [bə'tailigən] v give a share to. **sich beteiligen** participate in. **beteiligt sein an** be involved in. **Beteiligung** f (*pl* -en) participation; (*Anteil*) share.

beten ['beːtən] v pray.

beteuern [bə'tɔyərn] v affirm, declare; (*Unschuld*) protest. **Beteuerung** f (*pl* -en) affirmation, declaration.

Beton [be'tɔ̃] m concrete.

betonen [bə'toːnən] v stress, emphasize. **Betonung** f stress, emphasis.

Betracht [bə'traxt] m (*unz.*) consideration. **außer Betracht lassen** leave aside, not consider. **in Betracht ziehen** take into consideration. **betrachten** v look at; (*ansehen als*) consider. **beträchtlich** adj considerable. **Betrachtung** f consideration.

Betrag [bə'traɪk] m (*pl* **Beträge**) amount. **betragen** v amount to. **sich betragen** behave. **Betragen** neut behaviour.

betrauen [bə'trauən] v entrust.

Betreff [bə'trɛf] m (*unz.*) **in Betreff** with regard to, concerning. **betreff‖en** v concern; (*befallen*) befall; (*erwischen*) surprise. **–end** adj in question. **prep** concerning. **–s** prep concerning.

*betreiben [bə'traibən] v carry on, follow; (*Studien*) pursue; (*Maschine*) operate.

*betreten [bə'treːtən] v tread on; (*eintreten*) enter. adj surprised, disconcerted.

Betrieb [bə'triːp] m (*pl* -e) firm, concern, business; (*Wirken*) running; (*Verkehr*) bustle, activity. **außer Betrieb** out of order. **in Betrieb** in operation, working, in use. **in Betrieb setzen** put into operation. **Betriebs‖anlage** f industrial plant, works. **–anweisung** f operating instructions pl. **–führer** m works manager. **–kosten** pl operating costs. **–rat** m works council. **–unfall** m industrial accident.

*betrinken [bə'triŋkən] v **sich betrinken** get drunk.

betroffen [bə'trɔfən] adj perplexed, disconcerted.

betrüben [bə'tryːbən] v grieve, depress. **betrübt** adj sad.

Betrug [bə'truːk] m (*unz.*) fraud, swindle, deception. **betrügen** v cheat, deceive. **Betrüger** m (*pl* -) cheat, swindler. **betrügerisch** adj deceitful.

betrunken [bə'truŋkən] adj drunk. **Betrunkenheit** f drunkenness.

Bett [bɛt] neut (*pl* -en) bed. **ins Bett gehen** go to bed. **–decke** f bedspread.

betteln ['bɛtəln] v beg.

bettlägerig ['bɛtlɛːgəriç] adj bedridden.

Bettler ['bɛtlər] m (*pl* -) beggar.

Bett‖wäsche f bed linen. **–zeug** neut bedding.

beugen ['bɔygən] v bend; (Gramm) inflect. **sich beugen** bow; (sich fügen) submit. **Beugung** f bow, bend(ing).

Beule ['bɔylə] f (pl -n) swelling, lump; (Metall) dent.

beunruhigen [bə'unruːigən] v disturb, make anxious. **beunruhigt sein** be anxious or alarmed. **Beunruhigung** f agitation, uneasiness.

beurkunden [bə'uɪrkundən] v certify, attest. **Beurkundung** f certification.

beurlauben [bə'uɪrlaubən] v grant leave to, send on holiday.

beurteilen [bə'uɪrtailən] v judge. **Beurteilung** f judgment.

Beute ['bɔytə] f (unz.) booty, loot.

Beutel ['bɔytəl] m (pl -) bag; (Geld) purse; (Zool) pouch. **beuteln** v be baggy, bulge. **Beuteltier** neut marsupial.

bevölkern [bə'fœlkərn] v populate. **dicht/spärlich bevölkert** densely/sparsely populated. **Bevölkerung** f population.

bevollmächtigen [bə'fɔlmeçtigən] v authorize. **bevollmächtigt** adj authorized. **Bevollmächtigte(r)** m authorized agent or representative; (Jur) attorney.

bevor [bə'foːr] conj before.

***bevorstehen** [bə'foːrʃteɪən] v be imminent, be at hand.

bevorzugen [bə'foːrtsuːgən] v favour, prefer.

bewachen [bə'vaxən] v guard.

bewaffnen [bə'vafnən] v arm. **bewaffnet** adj armed. **Bewaffnung** f armament.

bewahren [bə'vaɪrən] v keep, preserve.

bewähren [bə'veɪrən] v **sich bewähren** prove true. **bewährt** adj tried, proved.

Bewahrung [bə'vaɪruŋ] f (pl -en) preservation.

Bewährung [bə'veɪruŋ] f trial, test; (Jur) probation. **-sfrist** f probation (period).

bewältigen [bə'veltigən] v overpower; (Schwierigkeit) master, overcome.

bewässern [bə'vɛsərn] v irrigate. **Bewässerung** f irrigation.

***bewegen** [bə'veɪgən] v move; (rühren) move, touch; (überreden) persuade. **sich bewegen** move. **Beweggrund** m motive. **beweglich** adj movable, mobile. **bewegt** adj excited; (gerührt) touched, moved. **Bewegung** f (pl -en) motion, movement, (Rührung) emotion. **in Bewegung setzen** set in motion.

Beweis [bə'vais] m (pl -e) proof, evidence.

beweisen v prove, demonstrate.

Beweis‖führung f reasoning, demonstration. **-stück** neut (piece of) evidence, exhibit.

bewerben [bə'vɛrbən] v **sich bewerben um** apply for. **Bewerber** m applicant, candidate. **Bewerbung** f application, candidacy.

bewerkstelligen [bə'vɛrkʃtɛligən] v accomplish, achieve.

bewerten [bə'veɪrtən] v value, rate.

bewilligen [bə'viligən] v allow, grant. **Bewilligung** f (pl -en) grant, permission.

bewirken [bə'virkən] v bring about, cause.

bewirten [bə'virtən] v entertain. **bewirtschaften** v manage, administer. **Bewirtung** f hospitality.

bewohnbar [bə'voɪnbaɪr] adj inhabitable. **bewohnen** v live in, inhabit. **Bewohner** m (pl -) inhabitant, resident.

bewölken [bə'vœlkən] v **sich bewölken** (Himmel) become cloudy. **bewölkt** adj overcast, cloudy.

Bewunderer [bə'vundərər] m (pl -) admirer. **bewundern** v admire. **bewundernswert** adj admirable. **Bewunderung** f admiration.

bewußt [bə'vust] adj conscious, deliberate; (klar) aware, conscious. **ich bin mir meines Fehlers bewußt** I am aware of my mistake. **Bewußtheit** f awareness. **bewußtlos** adj unconscious. **Bewußt‖losigkeit** f unconsciousness. **-sein** neut consciousness. **zu Bewußtsein kommen** regain consciousness.

bezahlen [bə'tsaɪlən] v pay for; (Rechnung) pay. **Bezahlung** f payment, settlement.

bezaubern [bə'tsaubərn] v enchant, charm, bewitch. **Bezauberung** f spell.

bezeichnen [bə'tsaiçnən] v designate; (Zeichen) mark. **Bezeichnung** f (Beschreibung) description; (Name) designation; (Zeichen) mark.

bezeugen [bə'tsɔygən] v testify (to), provide evidence of.

***beziehen** [bə'tsiːən] v cover; (Geige) string; (Wohnung) move into; (Posten) take up; (Gehalt) draw; (erhalten, kaufen) procure. **das Bett frisch beziehen** change the sheets. **sich beziehen auf** refer to, relate to. **Beziehung** f relation(ship). **in Beziehung auf** with regard or respect to. **beziehungsweise** adv respectively, or.

Bezirk [bə'tsɪrk] *m* (*pl* -e) district, area.
Bezug [bə'tsuːk] *m* (*pl* **Bezüge**) covering;
(*Kopfkissen*) pillow-case; (*Waren*) supply, purchase. **bezüglich** *prep* concerning,
relating to.
bezweifeln [bə'tsvaifəln] *v* doubt.
***bezwingen** [bə'tsvɪŋən] *v* conquer, overcome. **sich bezwingen** control *or* restrain
oneself.
Bibel ['biːbəl] *f* (*pl* -n) Bible. **-stelle** *f*
(biblical) text *or* passage.
Biber ['biːbər] *m* (*pl* -) beaver.
Bibliographie [bibliogra'fiː] *f* (*pl* -n) bibliography. **bibliographisch** *adj* bibliographic.
Bibliothek [biblio'teːk] *f* (*pl* -en) library.
-ar *m* (*pl* -e) librarian.
biblisch ['biːbliʃ] *adj* biblical.
bieder ['biːdər] *adj* honest, upright,
respectable. **Biedermann** *m* honest man
or fellow.
***biegen** ['biːgən] *v* bend; (*beim Fahren,
usw.*) turn. **biegsam** *adj* supple; (*f*
-*ügsam*) yielding. **Biegung** *f* (*pl* -en)
bend; curve.
Biene ['biːnə] *f* (*pl* -n) bee. **Bienen‖stich**
m bee sting; (*Kuchen*) almond pastry.
-stock *m* beehive. **-wabe** *f* honeycomb.
-zucht *f* beekeeping. **-züchter** *m* beekeeper.
Bier [biːr] *neut* (*pl* -e) beer. **-faß** *neut*
beer barrel, cask. **-garten** *m* beer garden.
Biest [biːst] *neut* (*pl* -er) beast; (*fig*)
brute.
***bieten** ['biːtən] *v* offer; (*Versteigerung*)
bid.
Bigamie [biga'miː] *f* bigamy. **bigamisch**
adj bigamous.
bigott [bi'gɔt] *adj* bigoted.
Bikini [bi'kiːniː] *m* (*pl* -s) bikini.
Bilanz [bi'lants] *f* (*pl* -en) balance (sheet),
annual accounts.
Bild [bilt] *neut* (*pl* -er) picture; (*Buch*)
illustration; (*Vorstellung*) idea.
bilden ['bildən] *v* form, shape; (*erziehen*)
educate; (*darstellen*) constitute.
Bilder‖buch *neut* picture book. **-galerie**
f (picture) gallery. **Bild‖feld** *neut* field of
vision. **-hauer** *m* sculptor. **bildhübsch**
adj very pretty, lovely. **Bildnis** *neut* (*pl*
-se) image, likeness. **bildsam** *adj* plastic,
flexible; (*fig*) docile. **Bildsäule** *f* statue.
Bildung ['bildʊŋ] *f* (*pl* -en) formation;
(*Erziehung*) education.

Billard ['biljart] *neut* (*pl* -e) billiards;
(*Tisch*) billiard table. **-stock** *m* cue.
Billett [bil'jet] *neut* (*pl* -s *or* -e) ticket;
(*Zettel*) note.
billig ['biliç] *adj* cheap, inexpensive; (*gerecht*) fair. **-en** *v* approve. **Billig‖keit** *f*
cheapness, fairness. **-ung** *f* approval.
Billion [bil'joːn] *f* (*pl* -en) billion, (*US*)
trillion.
Bimsstein ['bimsʃtain] *m* pumice stone.
binär [bi'nɛːr] *adj* binary.
Binde ['bində] *f* (*pl* -n) bandage; (*Arm*)
sling. **-haut** *f* conjunctiva.
***binden** ['bindən] *v* bind, tie.
Bind‖estrich *m* hyphen. **-faden** *m* string.
-ung *f* binding; (*Verpflichtung*) obligation.
binnen ['binən] *prep* within. **Binnenhandel**
m internal trade.
Biograph [bio'graːf] *m* (*pl* -en) biographer. **-ie** *f* biography. **biographisch** *adj*
biographical.
Biologe [bio'loːgə] *m* (*pl* -n) biologist.
Biologie *f* biology. **biologisch** *adj* biological.
Birke ['birkə] *f* (*pl* -n) birch.
Birne ['birnə] *f* (*pl* -n) pear; (*Glühbirne*)
light-bulb.
bis [bis] *prep* (*räumlich*) as far as, (up) to;
(*zeitlich*) until, till, to. *conj* until, till. **bis
an, bis nach,** *or* **bis zu** up to, as far as. **bis
jetzt** until now. **bis morgen** by tomorrow; (*Gruß*) see you tomorrow.
Bischof ['biʃɔf] *m* (*pl* **Bischöfe**) bishop.
bischöflich *adj* episcopal.
bisher [bis'heːr] *adv* until now, hitherto.
-ig *adj* until now, previous.
Biß [bis] *m* (*pl* **Bisse**) bite. **ein bißchen** a
bit, a little.
bisweilen [bis'vailən] *adv* occasionally,
sometimes.
bitte ['bitə] *interj* please. **Bitte** *f* request.
bitten *v* request, ask; (*anflehen*) beg,
implore.
bitter ['bitər] *adj* bitter. **Bitter‖keit** *f* bitterness. **-salz** *neut* Epsom salts. **bittersüß** *adj* bittersweet.
Bizeps ['bitseps] *m* (*pl* -e) biceps.
Blamage [bla'maːʒə] *f* (*pl* -n) disgrace.
blamieren *v* disgrace, compromise.
blank [blaŋk] *adj* bright, polished; (*rein*)
clean; (*bloß*) bare.
blanko ['blaŋko] *adj* blank. **Blankoscheck**
m blank cheque.

Blase ['blaːzə] *f* (*pl* **-n**) bubble; (*Haut*) blister; (*Harn*) bladder. **blasen** *v* blow.
blasiert [bla'ziːrt] *adj* blasé, conceited.
Blasinstrument ['blaːzɪnstrumɛnt] *neut* wind instrument.
blaß [blas] *adj* pale. **Blässe** *f* paleness, pallor. **bläßlich** *adj* pale, palish.
Blatt [blat] *neut* (*pl* **Blätter**) leaf; (*Papier*) sheet; (*Zeitung*) newspaper; (*Klinge*) blade. **blätterabwerfend** *adj* deciduous. **blättern** *v* (*Buch*) leaf through. **Blätterteig** *m* puff pastry. **Blatt‖grün** *neut* chlorophyll. **–laus** *f* greenfly, aphid.
blau [blau] *adj* blue; (*umg.*) drunk. **blaues Auge** black eye. **Blau** *neut* blue.
Blech [blɛç] *neut* (*pl* **-e**) sheet metal, tin. **–bläser** *pl* (*Musik*) brass (section). **–dose** *f* tin-can.
blecken ['blɛkən] show, bare (teeth).
Blei [blaɪ] *neut* (*pl* **-e**) lead.
***bleiben** ['blaɪbən] *v* remain, stay. **bleiben bei** keep or stick to.
bleich [blaɪç] *adj* pale, faded. **Bleiche** *f* paleness. **bleichen** *v* black; (*farblos werden*) grow pale, fade. **Bleich‖mittel** *neut* bleach(ing agent). **–sucht** *f* anaemia. **bleichsüchtig** *adj* anaemic.
Bleistift ['blaɪʃtɪft] *m* (*pl* **-e**) pencil.
Blende ['blɛndə] *f* (*pl* **-n**) blind, shutter; (*Foto*) shutter. **blenden** *v* blind, dazzle. **–d** *adj* dazzling, brilliant.
Blick [blɪk] *m* (*pl* **-e**) glance, look; (*Aussicht*) view. **blicken** *v* look.
blind [blɪnt] *adj* blind. **Blind‖darm** *m* (*Anat*) appendix. **–darmentzündung** *f* appendicitis. **–e(r)** *m* blind man. **–enhund** *m* guide dog. **–enschrift** *f* braille. **–gänger** *m* dud (bomb or shell). **–heit** *f* blindness. **blindlings** *adv* blindly.
blinken ['blɪŋkən] *v* sparkle, twinkle, glitter. **Blinker** *m* (*Mot*) indicator. **Blinklicht** *neut* flashing light.
blinzeln ['blɪntsəln] *v* blink, wink.
Blitz [blits] *m* (*pl* **-e**) lightning. **blitzen** *v* flash, emit flashes. **Blitzlicht** *neut* (*Foto*) flash, flashlight. **blitz‖sauber** *adj* spruce, very clean. **–schnell** *adj* quick as lightning. **Blitzschlag** *m* flash of lightning.
Block [blɔk] *m* (*pl* **Blöcke**) block; (*Papier*) pad. **–ade** *f* blockade. **–flöte** *f* (*Musik*) recorder. **blockieren** *v* blockade, block. **Blockschrift** *f* block letters.
blöd(e) [blœːt, 'blœːdə] *adj* silly, daft. **Blöd‖heit** *f* stupidity, silliness. **–sinn** *m* idiocy. **blödsinnig** *adj* idiotic, silly.

blöken ['blœːkən] *v* bleat.
blond [blɔnt] *adj* blond, fair-haired. **Blondine** *f* blonde.
bloß [bloːs] *adj* bare, simple. *adv* only, merely.
Blöße ['blœːsə] *f* nakedness; (*fig*) weakness.
bloßlegen ['bloːsleːgən] *v* reveal, expose.
blühen ['blyːən] *v* bloom, flower. **blühend** *adj* blooming; (*fig*) flourishing.
Blume ['bluːmə] *f* (*pl* **-n**) flower; (*Wein*) bouquet. **Blumen‖beet** *neut* flowerbed. **–blatt** *neut* petal. **–kohl** *m* cauliflower. **–muster** *neut* floral pattern. **–strauß** *m* bunch of flowers, bouquet. **–topf** *m* flowerpot. **–zwiebel** *f* bulb.
Bluse ['bluːzə] *f* (*pl* **-n**) blouse.
Blut [bluːt] *neut* blood. **–druck** *m* blood pressure. **blutdurstig** *adj* bloodthirsty.
Blüte ['blyːtə] *f* (*pl* **-n**) blossom, bloom.
bluten ['bluːtən] *v* bleed. **Blut‖gefäß** *neut* blood vessel. **–gerinnsel** *neut* blood clot. **–gruppe** *f* blood group. **blutig** *adj* bloody. **Blut‖übertragung** *f* blood transfusion. **–untersuchung** *f* blood test.
Bö [bœː] *f* (*pl* **-en**) squall, gust of wind.
Bock [bɔk] *m* (*pl* **Böcke**) (*Schaf-*) ram; (*Ziegen-, Reh-*) buck; (*Sport*) horse. **bockig** *adj* obstinate. **Bockwurst** *f* saveloy, large Frankfurter.
Boden ['boːdən] *m* (*pl* **Böden**) (*Erde*) ground; (*Fuß-*) floor; (*Dach-*) loft; (*Fluß-, Meeres-*) bottom, bed. **bodenlos** *adj* bottomless.
Bogen ['boːgən] *m* (*pl* **-**) curve, arch; (*Waffe, auch für Geige*) bow. **–schießen** *neut* archery. **–schütze** *m* archer.
Bohne ['boːnə] *f* (*pl* **-n**) bean.
bohren ['boːrən] *v* bore, drill. **Bohrer** *m* (*pl* **-**) borer, drill. **Bohrmaschine** *f* drill.
Boje ['boːjə] *f* (*pl* **-n**) buoy.
Bollwerk ['bɔlvɛrk] *neut* (*pl* **-e**) bulwark.
Bolzen ['bɔltsən] *m* (*pl* **-**) peg; (*Tech*) bolt; (*Pfeil*) arrow, bolt.
bombardieren [bɔmbaɪr'diːrən] *v* bombard.
Bombe ['bɔmbə] *f* (*pl* **-n**) bomb. **Bomben‖angriff** *m* bombing raid. **–anschlag** *m* (terrorist) bombing. **–flugzeug** *neut* bomber.
Bonbon [bõ'bõ] *neut* (*pl* **-s**) sweet, (*US*) candy.
Boot [boːt] *neut* (*pl* **-e**) boat.

Bord¹ [bɔrt] *neut* (*pl* -e) board.
Bord² *m* (*pl* -e) edge, rim. **an Bord gehen** go aboard, board.
Bordell [bɔr'dɛl] *neut* (*pl* -e) brothel.
borgen ['bɔrgən] *v* (*entleihen*) borrow; (*verleihen*) lend. **Borger** *m* (*pl* -) (*Entleiher*) borrower; (*Verleiher*) lender.
Borke ['bɔrkə] *f* (*pl* -n) bark.
Börse ['bœrzə] *f* (*pl* -n) stock exchange; (*Beutel*) purse. **-nmakler** *m* stockbroker.
Borste ['bɔrstə] *f* (*pl* -n) bristle.
bös(e) ['bøːz(ə)] *adj* bad; (*Mensch*) wicked; (*Geist*) evil; (*Kind*) naughty; (*wütend*) cross. **bösartig** *adj* malicious; (*Med*) malignant. **Böse** *neut* mischief; *m* evil person, devil.
boshaft ['boːshaft] *adj* malicious, spiteful.
Boß [bɔs] *m* (*pl* **Bosse**) boss.
böswillig ['bœːzvɪlɪç] *adj* malicious, malevolent. **Böswilligkeit** *f* malice.
Botanik [bo'taːnik] *f* botany. **-er** *m* (*pl* -) botanist. **botanisch** *adj* botanical.
Bote ['boːtə] *m* (*pl* -n) messenger. **Bot‖engang** *m* errand. **-schaft** *f* message; (*Gesandschaft*) embassy. **-schafter** *m* ambassador.
Bottich ['bɔtɪç] *m* (*pl* -e) tub, vat.
Bowle ['boːlə] *f* (*pl* -n) (*Getränk*) punch, fruit cup; (*Gefäß*) punchbowl.
boxen ['bɔksən] *v* box. **Boxer** *m* (*pl* -) boxer. **Boxkampf** *m* boxing match.
brach [braːx] *adj* fallow, untilled.
Branche ['brãʃə] *f* (*pl* -n) (*Geschäftszweig*) line of business, trade; (*Abteilung*) department.
Brand [brant] *m* (*pl* **Brände**) fire, blaze; (*Med*) gangrene; (*Bot*) mildew. **-bombe** *f* incendiary bomb. **brandmarken** *v* brand, stigmatize. **Brand‖stifter** *m* arsonist, fire-raiser. **-stiftung** *f* arson.
Brandung ['brandʊŋ] *f* (*pl* -en) surf, breakers *pl*.
Branntwein ['brantvain] *m* brandy.
***braten** ['braːtən] *v* roast; (*in der Pfanne*) fry; (*auf dem Rost*) grill. **Braten** *m* roast (meat), joint. **Brat‖fisch** *m* fried fish. **-hähnchen** *neut* roast chicken. **-kartoffeln** *pl* fried potatoes. **-pfanne** *f* frying pan. **-wurst** *f* fried sausage.
Bräu [brɔy] *neut* brew; (*Brauerei*) brewery.
Brauch [braux] *m* (*pl* **Bräuche**) custom, usage. **brauchbar** *adj* serviceable; usable; (*nützlich*) useful. **brauchen** *v* need, require; (*gebrauchen*) use.

brauen ['brauən] *v* brew. **Brauerei** *f* brewery.
braun [braun] *adj* brown. **Braun** *neut* brown.
Braunschweig ['braunʃvaik] *neut* Brunswick.
Brause ['brauzə] *f* (*pl* -n) (*Dusche*) shower; (*Gießkanne*) rose; (*Limonade*) lemonade, pop. **-bad** *neut* shower.
Braut [braut] *f* (*pl* **Bräute**) (*am Hochzeitstag*) bride; (*Verlobte*) fiancée.
Bräutigam [brɔytigam] *m* bridegroom.
Braut‖jungfer *f* bridesmaid. **-kleid** *neut* wedding dress.
bräutlich [brɔytlɪç] *adj* bridal.
brav [braːf] *adj* honest, worthy; (*tapfer*) brave; (*artig*) good, well-behaved.
***brechen** ['brɛçən] *v* break; (*Marmor*) quarry. **Bahn brechen** (*fig*) blaze a trail. **Brech‖bohne** *f* French bean. **-mittel** *neut* emetic.
Brei [brai] *m* (*pl* -e) paste, pulp.
breit [brait] *adj* broad, wide. **Breite** *f* breadth, width; (*Geog*) latitude.
Bremse¹ ['brɛmzə] *f* (*pl* -n) brake. **bremsen** *v* brake. **Brems‖licht** *f* brake light, stop light. **-pedal** *neut* brake pedal.
Bremse² *f* (*pl* -n) horse-fly.
brennbar ['brɛnbaːr] *adj* combustible, inflammable. **brennen** *v* burn; (*Branntwein*) distill. **Brenn‖erei** *f* distillery. **-nessel** *f* stinging nettle. **-punkt** *m* focus. **-stoff** *m* fuel.
Brett [brɛt] *neut* (*pl* -er) board; (*Regal*) shelf.
Brezel ['breːtsəl] *f* (*pl* -n) pretzel.
Brief [briːf] *m* (*pl* -e) letter. **-kasten** *m* letterbox. **-kopf** *m* letterhead. **brieflich** *adj* written. **Brief‖marke** *f* (postage) stamp. **-tasche** *f* wallet, pocket book. **-träger** *m* postman.
Brigade [bri'gaːdə] *f* (*pl* -n) brigade.
brillant [bril'jant] *adj* brilliant.
Brille ['brɪlə] *f* (*pl* -n) spectacles, glasses; (*Schutz*) goggles.
***bringen** ['brɪŋən] *v* bring; (*mitnehmen, begleiten*) take; (*Zeitung*) print, publish; (*Theater*) present, put on. **es weit bringen** do well, go far. **ans Licht bringen** bring to light.
Brite ['briːtə] *m* (*pl* -n), **Britin** *f* (*pl* -nen) Briton.
bröckelig ['brœkəlɪç] *adj* crumbly. **bröckeln** *v* crumble.

Bündel

Brocken ['brɔkən] *m* (*pl* -) crumb; (*pl*) scraps, bits and pieces.
Brombeere ['brɔmbeːrə] *f* blackberry.
Brombeerstrauch *m* blackberry bush, bramble.
Bronze ['brõːsə] *f* (*pl* -n) bronze. **bronzefarben** *adj* bronze(-coloured).
Brosche ['brɔʃə] *f* (*pl* -n) brooch.
Broschüre [brɔˈʃyːrə] *f* (*pl* -n) brochure.
Brot [broːt] *neut* (*pl* -e) bread; (*Laib*) loaf.
Brötchen ['brøːtçən] *neut* bread roll.
Brot||schnitte *f* slice (of bread). **–verdiener** *m* bread-winner.
Bruch [brux] *m* (*pl* **Brüche**) break; (*Knochen*) fracture; (*Math*) fraction; (*Versprechen, Vertrag*) breech; (*Gesetz*) violation, breech. **bruchfest** *adj* unbreakable.
brüchig ['bryçiç] *adj* brittle.
Bruch||landung *f* crash landing. **–stück** *neut* fragment. **–teil** *m* fraction.
Brücke ['brykə] *f* (*pl* -n) bridge.
Bruder ['bruːdər] *m* (*pl* **Brüder**) brother. **brüderlich** ['bryːdərliç] *adj* brotherly. **Brüderschaft** *f* brotherhood.
Brühe ['bryːə] *f* (*pl* -n) broth; (*Suppengrundlage*) stock. **brühen** *v* scald. **brühheiß** *adj* boiling hot.
brüllen ['brylən] *v* bellow; (*Sturm, Raubtier*) roar. **Brüllfrosch** *m* bullfrog.
brummen ['brumən] growl; (*Insekten*) buzz, hum; (*mürrisch sein*) grumble; (*umg.*) go to prison, do time.
brünett [bryˈnɛt] *adj* brunette, dark brown. **Brünette** *f* brunette.
Brunnen ['brunən] *m* (*pl* -) well; (*Quelle*) spring.
Brunst [brunst] *f* (*pl* **Brünste**) lust, ardour; (*Tier*) heat. **brünstig** *adj* lusty; (*Tier*) in heat.
Brüssel ['brysəl] *neut* Brussels.
Brust [brust] *f* (*pl* **Brüste**) breast, chest; (*Frauen*) breast. **–kasten** *m* chest. **–krebs** *m* breast cancer. **–schwimmen** *neut* breaststroke. **–warze** *f* nipple.
brutal [bruˈtaːl] *adj* brutal.
brüten ['bryːtən] *v* brood.
brutto ['bruto] *adj* gross. **Bruttogewicht** *neut* gross weight. **Bruttosozialprodukt** *neut* gross national product.
Bube ['buːbə] *m* (*pl* -n) boy, lad; (*Karten*) jack, knave.
Buch [buːx] *neut* (*pl* **Bücher**) book.
Buche ['buːxə] *f* (*pl* -n) beech (tree).

buchen ['buːxən] *v* record, enter (in a book).
Bücherei ['byçərai] *f* (*pl* -en) library. **Bücherschrank** *m* bookcase.
Buchfink [buçfiŋk] *m* chaffinch.
Buch||halter *m* book-keeper. **–haltung** *f* book-keeping; accounts department. **–händler** *m* bookseller. **–handlung** *f* bookshop. **–macher** *m* bookmaker.
Büchse ['byksə] *f* (*pl* -n) box; (*Blechdose*) tin, can; (*Gewehr*) rifle.
Buchstabe ['buːxʃtaːbə] *f* (*pl* -n) letter (of the alphabet). **buchstabieren** *v* spell. **Buchstabierung** *f* spelling. **buchstäblich** *adj* literal.
Bucht [buxt] *f* (*pl* -en) bay.
Buckel ['bukəl] *m* (*pl* -) hump, mound; (*am Rücken*) humpback. **buckelig** *adj* hunchbacked.
bücken ['bykən] *v* **sich bücken** stoop, bow.
Bude ['buːdə] *f* (*pl* -n) booth; (*Markt*) stall; (*umg.*) lodgings, digs, room(s).
Budget [byˈdʒeː] *neut* (*pl* -s) budget.
Büfett [byˈfɛt] *neut* (*pl* -s) sideboard, dresser. **kaltes Büfett** cold buffet.
Büffel ['byfəl] *m* (*pl* -) buffalo.
Bug [buːk] *m* (*pl* -e) (*Schiff*) bow; (*Flugzeug*) nose; (*Pferd*) shoulder.
Bügel ['byːgəl] *m* (*pl* -) hoop, handle; (*Kleider-*) hanger; (*Steig-*) stirrup. **–brett** *neut* ironing board. **–eisen** *neut* iron. **bügelt** *adj* permanent press, non-iron. **bügeln** *v* iron.
bugsieren ['bugziːrən] *v* tow. **Bugsierer** *m* tugboat.
Bühne ['byːnə] *f* (*pl* -n) stage. **Bühnen||bild** *neut* set, scenery. **–dichter** *m* playwright. **–deutsch** *neut* high German, standard German.
Bulgare [bulˈgaːrə] *m* (*pl* -n), **Bulgarin** *f* (*pl* -nen) Bulgarian. **Bulgarien** *neut* Bulgaria. **bulgarisch** *adj* Bulgarian.
Bulle ['bulə] *m* (*pl* -n) bull; (*umg.*) cop.
Bummel ['buməl] *m* (*pl* -) stroll. **bummeln** *v* stroll; (*nichts tun*) loaf, loiter. **Bummel||streik** *m* work-to-rule, go-slow. **–zug** *m* slow train, local (train).
Bund¹ [bunt] *neut* (*pl* -e) bundle; (*Schlüssel, Radieschen, usw.*) bunch.
Bund² *m* (*pl* **Bünde**) band; (*Verein*) association, league; (*Staat*) federation.
Bündel ['byndəl] *neut* (*pl* -) bundle, bunch. **bündeln** bundle (up).

Bundes‖bahn f federal railway, West German railway. **–haus** parliament buildings. **–präsident** m federal (West German) president. **–rat** m (BRD, Österreich) upper house (of parliament); (Schweiz) (Swiss) government. **–republik Deutschland (BRD)** f Federal Republic of Germany, West Germany. **–tag** m West German parliament, federal parliament. **–staat** m federal state.

Bündnis ['byntnis] neut (pl -se) alliance.

Bunker ['bunkər] m (pl -) bunker.

bunt [bunt] adj brightly coloured, gay.

Bürde ['byrdə] f (pl -n) burden.

Burg [burk] f (pl -en) castle; (Festung) fort.

Bürge ['byrgə] m (pl -n) surety, guarantor. **bürgen** v guarantee, vouch for; (Jur) stand bail for.

Bürger ['byrgər] m (pl -) citizen; (Stadt) townsman; bourgeois. **–krieg** m civil war. **bürgerlich** adj bourgeois, middle-class; (Küche) simple, plain; (zivil) civilian. **Bürger‖meister** m mayor. **–recht** neut civil rights. **–schaft** f citizenry, citizens. **–stand** m middle class(es). **–steig** m pavement, (US) sidewalk.

Bürgschaft ['byrgʃaft] f (pl -en) surety, bond.

Büro [by'roː] neut (pl -s) office. **–klammer** f paperclip. **–krat** m (pl -en) bureaucrat. **–kratie** f bureaucracy. **bürokratisch** adj bureaucratic.

Bursche ['burʃə] m (pl -n) lad, fellow.

Bürste ['byrstə] f (pl -n) brush. **bürsten** v brush.

Busch [buʃ] m (pl Büsche) bush, shrub.

Büschel ['byʃəl] neut (pl -) bunch; (Haare) tuft.

buschig ['buʃiç] adj bushy.

Busen ['buːzən] m (pl -) breast. **–freund** m bosom friend.

Buße ['buːsə] f (pl -n) penance; (Geld) fine.

büßen ['byːsən] v do penance (for).

Büste ['byːstə] f (pl -n) bust. **–nhälter** m brassière.

Butter ['butər] f (unz.) butter. **–blume** f buttercup. **–brot** neut (slice of) bread and butter. **–brotpapier** neut greaseproof paper.

C

Café [ka'feː] neut (pl -s) café, coffee house.

campen ['kɛmpən] v camp. **Camper** m camper. **Camping** neut camping. **–platz** m camp(ing) site.

Caravan ['karavaɪn] m (pl -s) caravan; (Kombiwagen) estate car.

Cellist [tʃɛ'list] m (pl -en), **Cellistin** f (pl -nen) cellist. **Cello** neut cello.

Cembalo ['tʃɛmbalo] neut (pl -s) harpsichord.

Champagner [ʃam'panjər] m (pl -) champagne.

Champignon ['ʃampinjɔ] m (pl -s) mushroom.

Chance ['ʃãːsə] f (pl -n) chance. **Chancengleichheit** f equality of opportunity.

Chaos ['kaːɔs] neut (unz.) chaos. **chaotisch** adj chaotic.

Charakter ['karaktər] m (pl -e) character. **charakterisieren** v characterize. **charakteristisch** adj characteristic.

Chauffeur [ʃɔ'fœːr] m (pl -e) driver, chauffeur.

Chaussee [ʃɔ'seː] f (pl -n) highway, main road.

Chef [ʃɛf] m (pl -s) boss, head; (Arbeitgeber) employer.

Chemie [çe'miː] f (unz.) chemistry. **Chemikalien** f pl chemicals. **Chemiker** m (pl -) (industrial or research) chemist. **chemisch** adj chemical. **–e Reinigung** f dry cleaning.

China ['çiːna] neut China. **Chinese** m (pl -n), **Chinesin** f (pl -nen) Chinese (person). **chinesisch** adj Chinese.

Chirurg [çi'rurk] m (pl -en) surgeon. **–ie** f surgery. **chirurgisch** adj surgical.

Chlor [kloːr] neut (unz.) chlorine. **Chloroform** neut chloroform. **Chlorophyll** neut chlorophyll. **Chlorwasser** neut chlorinated water.

Cholera ['kolera] f (unz.) cholera.

Chor [koːr] m (pl Chöre) choir; (Gesang) chorus. **–direktor** m choirmaster.

Christ [krist] m (pl -en) Christian. **christlich** adj Christian. **Christ‖nacht** f Christmas Eve. **–us** m Christ.

Chrom [kroːm] neut (unz.) chromium; (Verchromung) chrome, chrome-plating. **chromiert** adj chrome-plated.

Chronik ['kroːnik] f (pl -en) chronicle. **chronisch** adj chronic.

Computer [kɔm'pjuɪtər] *m* (*pl* -) computer.

Coupé [ku'peɪ] *neut* (*pl* -s) railway carriage.

Cousin [ku'zɛ̃] *m* (*pl* -s) (male) cousin. **-e** *f* (female) cousin.

Creme [kreɪm] *f* (*pl* -s) cream; (*Süßspeise*) cream pudding; (*Hautsalbe*) handcream, skincream.

D

da [da] *adv* (*örtlich*) there; (*zeitlich*) then. *conj* because, since. **da draußen/drinnen** out/in there. **da sein** be present. **da bin ich** here I am. **da siehst Du!** see! **da hingegen** whereas.

dabei [da'bai] *adv* close (by), near; (*bei diesem*) thereby; (*außerdem*) moreover. **dabei sein** be present. **es bleibt dabei** that is *or* remains settled. **was ist dabei?** what does it matter? **dabei sein, es zu tun** be on the point of doing it. **dabei bleiben** stick to one's opinion.

Dach [dax] *neut* (*pl* **Dächer**) roof. **-boden** *m* attic. **-fenster** *neut* skylight. **-gesellschaft** *f* holding company. **-kammer** *f* attic, garret. **-rinne** *f* gutter.

Dachs [daks] *m* (*pl* -e) badger. **-hund** *m* dachshund.

Dachziegel ['daxtsiːgəl] *m* roof tile.

dadurch [da'durç] *adv* for this reason, in this way. **dadurch daß** because, since.

dafür [da'fyɪr] *adv* for that; (*Gegenleistung*) in return. **dafür sein** be in favour (of it). **er kann nichts dafür** he can't help it.

dagegen [da'geɪgən] *adv* against it; (*Vergleich*) in comparison. *conj* on the contrary, however. **ich habe nichts dagegen** I have no objections. **er stimmt dagegen** he is voting against it.

daher [da'heɪr] *adv* from there. *conj* hence, accordingly. **daher kommt es** hence it follows. **daher, daß** since, because.

dahin [da'hin] *adv* there, to that place.

dahinten [da'hintən] *adv* back there.

dahinter [da'hintər] *adv* behind it *or* that. **-kommen** *v* find out (about it), get to the bottom of it. **-stecken** *v* lie behind, be the cause.

damals ['daɪmaɪls] *adv* then, at that time.

Dame ['daɪmə] *f* (*pl* -n) lady; (*Karten*) queen. **-brett** *neut* draughtboard, (*US*) checker-board. **Damen‖binde** *f* sanitary towel. **-toilette** *f* ladies' lavatory. **-wäsche** *f* lingerie. **Dame‖spiel** *neut* draughts. **-stein** *m* draughtsman, (*US*) checker.

Damm [dam] *m* (*pl* **Dämme**) dam; dike; (*Bahn-, Straßen-*) embankment.

dämmen ['dɛmən] *v* dam (up).

dämmern ['dɛmərn] *v* (*morgens*) dawn, grow light; (*abends*) grow dark. **es dämmert** dawn is breaking. **Dämmerung** *f* (*pl* -en) (*morgens*) dawn; (*abends*) twilight, dusk.

Dampf [dampf] *m* (*pl* **Dämpfe**) steam, vapour. **dampfen** *v* steam; (*Rauch*) smoke, fume.

dämpfen ['dɛmpfən] *v* (*Ofen*) damp down, (*Schall*) muffle; (*Licht*) soften; (*Küche*) steam.

Dampf‖er ['dampfər] *m* (*pl* -) steamer, steamship. **-kessel** *m* boiler. **-kochtopf** *m* pressure cooker. **-maschine** *f* steam engine. **-schiff** *neut* steamship, steamer.

danach [da'naɪx] *adv* after it; (*darauf*) afterwards; (*entsprechend*) accordingly.

Däne ['dɛɪnə] *m* (*pl* -n). **Dänin** (-nen) Dane. **Dänemark** *neut* Denmark. **dänisch** *adj* Danish.

daneben [da'neɪbən] *adv* beside (it); (*außerdem*) besides.

Dank [daŋk] *m* (*unz.*) thanks. **dankbar** *adj* grateful, thankful. **Dankbarkeit** *f* gratitude. **danken** *v* thank.

dann [dan] *adv* then.

daran [da'ran] *adv* on *or* at *or* by it. **nahe daran sein zu** be on the point of. **nahe daran** close by. **gut daran sein** be well off.

darauf [da'rauf] *adv* on it; (*nachher*) afterwards. **es kommt darauf an (ob)** it depends (whether). **wie kommt er darauf?** why does he think so?

daraus [da'raus] *adv* out of it, from it. **es ist nichts daraus geworden** nothing has come of that.

*darbieten ['daɪrbiɪtən] *v* offer, present.

darein [da'rain] *adv* in(to) it; (*hierin*) therein.

darin [da'rin] *adv* in it, within; (*hierin*) therein.

darlegen ['daɪrleɪgən] *v* explain, expound. **Darlegung** *f* explanation.

Darlehen ['daːrleːən] *neut* (*pl* -) loan.
Darm [darm] *m* (*pl* **Därme**) intestines *pl*.
–verstopfung *f* constipation.
darstellen ['daːrʃtɛlən] *v* represent. **Darsteller** *m* (*Theater*) actor, performer. **Darstellung** *f* exhibition.
darüber [da'ryːbər] *adv* over it; (*davon*) about it; (*hinüber*) across. **darüber hinaus** over and above that, furthermore.
darum [da'rum] *adv* around *or* about it, for it. *conj* therefore.
darunter [da'runtər] *adv* under *or* beneath it; (*dazwischen*) among them; (*weniger*) less.
das [das] *art* the. *pron* which, that.
Dasein ['daːzaɪn] *neut* (*unz.*) existence, being; (*Vorhandensein*) presence. **Daseinskampf** *m* struggle for existence.
daß [das] *conj* that.
Daten ['daːtən] *neut pl* data *pl*. **-verarbeitung** *f* data processing.
datieren [da'tiːrən] *v* date.
Datum ['daːtum] *neut* (*pl* **Daten**) date; (*Tatsache*) datum, fact.
Dauer ['dauər] *f* (*unz.*) period (of time), duration. **–auftrag** *m* (*Bank*) standing order. **dauerhaft** *adj* lasting, durable. **Dauerkarte** *f* season ticket. **dauern** *v* last, continue. **-d** *adj* lasting, permanent. **Dauerwelle** *f* perm, permanent wave.
Daumen ['daumən] *m* (*pl* -) thumb.
Daunendecke ['daunəndɛkə] *f* eiderdown, continental quilt.
davon [da'fɔn] *adv* of *or* from it; (*weg*) away; (*darüber*) about it. **–kommen** *v* escape. **sich davonmachen** *v* (*umg.*) make one's escape, slide off.
davor [da'foːr] *adv* (*örtlich*) before it, in front of it; (*zeitlich*) before that *or* then. **Angst haben davor** be afraid of it. **eine Stunde davor** an hour earlier.
dawider [da'viːdər] *adv* against it.
dazu [da'tsuː] *adv* to it; (*Zweck*) for this (purpose), to that end; (*überdies*) in addition.
dazwischen [da'tsviʃən] *adv* between *or* among them. **–treten** *v* intervene.
Debatte [de'batə] *f* (*pl* -n) debate. **debattieren** *v* debate.
Debet ['deːbɛt] *neut* (*pl* -s) debit.
Debüt [de'byː] *neut* (*pl* -s) début.
Deck [dɛk] *neut* (*pl* -e) deck.
Decke ['dɛkə] *f* (*pl* -n) cover(ing); (*Bett*) blanket; (*Zimmer*) ceiling. **–l** *m* lid.
decken *v* cover; set (the table).

Deck‖mantel *m* pretext. **–name** *m* pseudonym. **–ung** *f* cover(ing); (*Verteidigung*) protection.
definieren [defi'niːrən] *v* define. **definitiv** *adj* definite.
Defizit ['deːfitsit] *neut* (*pl* -e) deficit.
degenerieren [degene'riːrən] *v* degenerate.
dehnbar ['deːnbaːr] *adj* elastic, malleable; (*Begriff*) loose, vague. **Dehnbarkeit** *f* elasticity, malleability. **dehnen** *v* stretch. **Dehnung** *f* stretching, expansion.
Deich [daɪç] *m* (*pl* -e) dike.
Deichsel ['daɪksəl] *f* (*pl* -n) shaft, pole. **deichseln** *v* (*umg.*) wangle.
dein [daɪn] *adj* your. *pron* yours. **deinerseits** *adv* on *or* for your part. **deinesgleichen** *pron* your likes, people like you. **deinethalben**, **deinetwegen**, *or* **deinetwillen** *adv* for your sake. **deinige** *pron* **der, die, das deinige** yours.
dekadent [deka'dɛnt] *adj* decadent. **Dekadenz** *f* decadence.
Dekan [de'kaːn] *m* (*pl* -e) dean.
deklamieren [dekla'miːrən] *v* declaim.
deklarieren [dekla'riːrən] *v* declare.
Deklination [deklinatsi'oːn] *f* (*pl* -en) declension. **deklinieren** *v* decline.
Dekor [de'koːr] *m* (*pl* -s) decoration(s). **dekorieren** *v* decorate.
Dekret [de'kreːt] *neut* (*pl* -e) decree.
delegieren [dele'giːrən] *v* delegate. **Delegierte(r)** *m* delegate.
delikat [deli'kaːt] *adj* (*Person, Angelegenheit*) delicate; (*Speise*) delicious. **Delikatesse** *f* (*pl* -n) delicacy.
Delikt [de'likt] *neut* (*pl* -e) crime.
Delphin [dɛl'fiːn] *m* (*pl* -e) dolphin.
dem [deːm] *art* to the. *pron* to this *or* that (one); (*wem*) to whom, to which.
Dementi [de'mɛnti] *neut* (*pl* -s) (official) denial. **dementieren** *v* deny.
demgemäß ['deːmɡəmɛːs] *adv* accordingly.
Demission [demisi'oːn] *f* (*pl* -en) resignation. **demissionieren** *v* resign.
demnach [deːm'naːx] *adv* accordingly.
demnächst ['deːmnɛːçst] *adv* shortly, soon.
Demokrat [demo'kraːt] *m* (*pl* -en) democrat. **–ie** *f* democracy. **demokratisch** *adj* democratic.
demolieren [demo'liːrən] *v* demolish.
Demonstrant [demɔn'strant] *m* (*pl* -en) demonstrator. **Demonstration** *f* (*pl* -en)

demonstration. **demonstrieren** v demonstrate. **demonstrativ** adj demonstrative.

Demut ['deːmuːt] f (unz.) humility. **demütig** adj humble. **-en** v humiliate, humble. **Demütigung** f (pl -en) humiliation.

demzufolge ['deːmtsufɔlgə] adv accordingly. pron according to which.

den [deɪn] art the. pl to the. pron whom, which. pl to these. **denen** pron to whom or which.

Denkart ['deŋkaɪrt] f way of thinking. **denk∥bar** adj conceivable, thinkable. **-en** v think. **Denk∥en** neut thinking, thought. **-er** m (pl -) thinker. **-freiheit** f freedom of thought. **-mal** neut monument. **denkwürdig** adj memorable. **Denkzettel** m lesson, punishment.

dennoch ['dennɔx] conj nevertheless.

Denunziant [denuntsi'ant] m (pl -en) informer. **denunzieren** v denounce, inform against.

Depesche [de'pɛʃə] f (pl -n) telegram, dispatch.

deponieren [depo'niːrən] v deposit.

Depot [de'poː] neut (pl -s) warehouse, storehouse, depot.

Depression [depresi'oːn] f (pl -en) depression. **depressiv** adj depressed.

deprimieren [depri'miːrən] v depress. **-d** adj depressing.

der [deɪr] art the; (to) the; pl of the. pron who, which; (to) whom or which.

derart ['deɪraɪt] adv in such a way, so. **-ig** adj of such a type, such, of that kind.

derb [dɛrp] adj crude, coarse; (Person) rough, tough. **Derbheit** f crudeness; (Person) roughness.

deren ['deɪrən] pron whose, of which. **derenthalben, derentwegen,** or **derentwillen** adv on whose account, for whose sake.

dergleichen [deɪr'glaiçən] adv suchlike, of the kind.

derjenige ['deɪrjeɪnigə] **diejenige, dasjenige** pron he who, she who, that which.

dermaßen ['deɪrmaɪsən] adv to such a degree, in such a way.

derselbe [deɪr'zɛlbə] pron **dieselbe, dasselbe** the same.

derzeitig ['deɪrtsaitiç] adj present; (damalig) of that time.

des [dɛs] art of the.

desgleichen [dɛs'glaiçən] adv likewise.

deshalb ['dɛshalp] adv therefore.

Desillusion [dɛziluzi'oːn] f disillusionment.

Desinfektion [dɛzinfɛktsi'oːn] f disinfection. **-smittel** neut disinfectant. **desinfizieren** v disinfect.

dessen ['dɛsən] pron whose, of which.

destillieren [dɛsti'liːrən] v distil.

desto ['dɛsto] adv the, all the, so much. **je ... desto ...** the ... the ... .

deswegen ['dɛsveɪgən], **deswillen** adv therefore.

Detail [de'tai] neut (pl -s) detail, item. **-geschäft** neut retail firm or business. **-handel** m retail trade. **detaillieren** v detail, particularize.

deuten ['dɔytən] v explain, interpret. **deuten auf** point to, indicate, suggest. **deutlich** adj clear, plain. **Deutlichkeit** f clearness, distinctness.

deutsch [dɔytʃ] adj German. **Deutsch** neut German (language). **Deutsche(r)** German. **Deutschland** neut Germany.

Devise [de'viːzə] f (pl -n) motto; pl foreign currency or exchange. **Devisenkurs** m rate of exchange.

Dezember [de'tsɛmbər] m (pl -) December.

dezimal [detsi'maːl] adj decimal.

Dia ['diːa] neut (pl -s), also **Diapositiv** slide, transparency.

Dialekt [dia'lɛkt] m (pl -e) dialect.

Dialog [dia'loːk] m (pl -e) dialogue.

Diamant [dia'mant] m (pl -en) diamond. **diamanten** adj diamond.

Diät [di'ɛːt] f (pl -en) diet.

dich [diç] pron sing you.

dicht [diçt] adj dense; (Wald, Nebel, Stoff) thick; (nahe) close (by); (wasserdicht) watertight.

dichten[1] ['diçtən] v seal, make watertight or airtight.

dichten[2] v write (poetry); (erträumen) invent. **Dichter** m (pl -), **Dichterin** f (pl -nen) poet. **dichterisch** adj poetic.

Dichtheit [diçthait] or **Dichtigkeit** f density.

Dichtung ['diçtuŋ] f poetry, literature.

dick [dik] adj think; (Person) fat. **Dick∥darm** m large intestine. **-e** f fatness, thickness. **-icht** neut thicket.

die [diː] art the; pron who, which.

Dieb [diːp] m (pl -e) thief. **diebisch** adj thieving. **Diebstahl** m theft.

Diele ['diːlə] f (pl -n) board, plank; (Vor-

raum) hall, vestibule; (*Eis-*) ice-cream parlour. **Dielenbrett** *neut* floorboard.

dienen ['diːnən] *v* serve. **Diener** *m* (*pl* -), **Dienerin** *f* (*pl* -**nen**) servant. **Dienerschaft** *f* servants *pl*, domestics *pl*. **Dienst** *f* (*pl* -**e**) service; (*Amt*) duty.

Dienstag ['diːnstaːk] *m* Tuesday.

Dienst‖entlassung *f* dismissal. –**grad** *m* rank. –**leistung** *f* service. **dienstlich** *adj*, *adv* official(ly). **Dienst‖mädchen** *neut* (serving) maid. –**pflicht** *f* conscription. –**stunden** *f pl* working hours. –**wohnung** *f* official residence.

dieser ['diːzər] **diese, dieses** *pron*, *adj* this. **dies‖jährig** *adj* this year's. –**mal** *adv* this time. –**seits** *adv* on this side.

Dietrich ['diːtriç] *m* (*pl* -**e**) skeleton key.

diffizil [difiˈtsiːl] *adj* difficult, awkward.

Diktat [dikˈtaːt] *neut* (*pl* -**e**) dictation. **Diktator** *m* (*pl* -**en**) dictator. **diktatorisch** *adj* dictatorial. **Diktatur** *f* (*pl* -**en**) dictatorship. **diktieren** *v* dictate. **Diktiergerät** *neut* dictaphone, dictating machine.

Diner [diˈneː] *neut* (*pl* -**s**) dinner, dinner-party.

Ding [diŋ] *neut* (*pl* -**e**) thing. **vor allen Dingen** above all. **Dingelchen** *neut* (pretty) little thing. **Dingsbums** *neut* (*umg.*) what's-it's-name, what's-his-name.

Diplom [diˈploːm] *neut* (*pl* -**e**) diploma. –**at** *m* (*pl* -**en**) diplomat. –**atie** *f* diplomacy. **diplomatisch** *adj* diplomatic. **Diplomingenieur** *m* graduate engineer.

dir [diːr] *pron sing* to you.

Dirigent [diriˈgɛnt] *m* (*pl* -**en**) (*Musik*) conductor. **dirigieren** *v* conduct.

Dirne ['dirnə] *f* (*pl* -**n**) prostitute, whore; wench.

diskontieren [diskɔnˈtiːrən] *v* discount. **Diskontsatz** *m* bank-rate.

Diskothek [diskoˈteːk] *f* (*pl* -**en**) disco(theque).

diskriminieren [diskrimiˈniːrən] *v* discriminate (against). **Diskriminierung** *f* discrimination.

Diskussion [diskusiˈoːn] *f* (*pl* -**en**) discussion. **diskutieren** *v* discuss.

disponieren [dispoˈniːrən] *v* arrange, dispose (of). **disponieren über** have at one's disposal.

Dissident [disiˈdɛnt] *m* (*pl* -**en**) dissident, dissenter.

Distel ['distəl] *f* (*pl* -**n**) thistle.

Disziplin [distsiˈpliːn] *f* (*pl* -**en**) discipline.

disziplinarisch *adj* disciplinary. **Disziplinarverfahren** *neut* disciplinary action.

D-Mark ['deːmark] *f* (*pl* -) (West) German mark.

doch [dɔx] *conj* nevertheless, yet, but; *adv* indeed, oh yes.

Docht [dɔxt] *m* (*pl* -**e**) wick.

Dock [dɔk] *neut* (*pl* -**e**) dock. –**arbeiter** *m* docker, (*US*) longshoreman.

Dogge ['dɔgə] *f* (*pl* -**n**) Great Dane; bulldog.

Dogma ['dɔgma] *f* (*pl* **Dogmen**) Dogma. **dogmatisch** *adj* dogmatic.

Doktor ['dɔktɔr] *m* (*pl* -**en**) doctor. –**arbeit** *f* doctoral *or* PhD thesis. –**at** *neut* doctorate, PhD.

Dolch [dɔlç] *m* (*pl* -**e**) dagger.

dolmetschen ['dɔlmɛtʃən] *v* interpret. **Dolmetscher** *m* interpreter.

Dom [doːm] *m* (*pl* -**e**) cathedral. –**herr** *m* canon. –**pfaff** (*Zool*) *m* bullfinch.

Domino ['doːmino] *neut* (*pl* -**s**) dominoes. –**stein** *m* domino.

Donau ['doːnau] *f* Danube.

Donner ['dɔnər] *m* (*pl* -) thunder. **donnern** *v* thunder.

Donnerstag ['dɔnərstaːk] *m* Thursday.

Donnerwetter ['dɔnərvɛtər] *neut* thunderstorm. *interj* damn!

doof [doːf] *adj* (*umg.*) daft, dumb, stupid.

Doppel ['dɔpəl] *neut* (*pl* -) duplicate. **Doppel-** *adj* double-. **Doppel‖bett** *neut* double bed. –**ehe** *f* bigamy. –**gänger** *m* ghostly double; doppelgänger **doppeln** *v* double. **Doppel‖punkt** *m* colon. –**sinn** *m* ambiguity. **doppelt** *adj* double(d).

Dorf [dɔrf] *neut* (*pl* **Dörfer**) village. –**bewohner** *m* villager.

Dorn [dɔrn] *m* (*pl* -**en**) thorn. –**röschen** *neut* Sleeping Beauty.

Dorsch [dɔrʃ] *m* (*pl* -**e**) cod.

dort [dɔrt] *adv* there. –**her** *adv* (from) there. –**herum** *adv* around there. –**hin** (to) there. –**ig** *adj* of that place.

Dose ['doːzə] *f* (*pl* -**n**) tin, box; (*Konserven-*) tin, can. **Dosenöffner** *m* tin-opener, can-opener.

dosieren [doˈziːrən] *v* measure out (a dose of). **Dosis** *f* (*pl* **Dosen**) dose.

Dotter ['dɔtə] *m* (*pl* -) (egg) yolk.

Dozent [doˈtsɛnt] *m* (*pl* -**en**) university *or* college lecturer.

Drache ['draxə] *m* (*pl* -**n**) dragon.

Drachen ['draxən] *m* (*pl* -) kite.
Draht [draɪt] *m* (*pl* **Drähte**) wire, (*Kabel*) cable. **–anschrift** *f* telegraphic address. **–seil** *neut* cable. **–seilbahn** *f* cable car, funicular.
Drama ['draɪma] *neut* (*pl* **Dramen**) drama. **–tiker** *m* (*pl* -) dramatist. **dramatisch** *adj* dramatic.
dran [dran] *V* **daran.**
Drang [draŋ] *m* (*pl* **Dränge**) drive, urge; (*Druck*) pressure.
drängeln ['drɛŋəln] *v* jostle, shove.
drängen ['drɛŋən] *v* press, urge.
drapieren [dra'piːrən] *v* drape.
drastisch ['drastiʃ] *adj* drastic.
drauf [drauf] *V* **darauf.**
draußen ['drausən] *adv* outside, out of doors.
Dreck [drɛk] *m* (*unz.*) filth, dirt; (*Kot*) excrement; (*Kleinigkeit*) trifle. **dreckig** *adj* filthy, dirty.
Dreh [dreɪ] *m* (*pl* -e) turn. **den Dreh heraushaben** get the hang *or* knack of it. **–bank** *f* lathe. **–buch** *neut* film script, scenario. **drehen** *v* turn, rotate. **Dreh‖punkt** *m* pivot. **–ung** *f* (*pl* -en) turn, rotation, revolution. **–zahl** *f* revolutions per minute, rpm.
drei [drai] *adj* three. **Dreieck** *neut* triangle. **dreieckig** *adj* triangular. **dreifach** *adj* triple, treble. **Dreifuß** *m* tripod. **dreimal** *adv* three times. **Dreirad** *neut* tricycle.
dreißig ['draisiç] *adj* thirty.
dreist [draist] *adj* cheeky, impudent.
dreiviertel ['draifirtəl] *adj* three-quarter. *adv* three-quarters. **Dreiviertelstunde** *f* three-quarters of an hour.
dreizehn ['draitseɪn] *adj* thirteen.
***dreschen** ['drɛʃən] *v* thresh.
dressieren [drɛ'siːrən] *v* train.
Drillich ['driliç] *m* (*pl* -e) (*Stoff*) drill, canvas.
Drilling ['driliŋ] *m* (*pl* -e) triplet.
drin [drin] *V* **darin.**
***dringen** ['driŋən] *v* penetrate. **dringen auf** insist on. **dringen in** implore, urge.
dritte ['dritə] *adj* third. **Drittel** *neut* (*pl* -) third.
Droge ['droɪgə] *f* (*pl* -n) drug. **Drogerie** *f* (*pl* -n) chemist's (shop), pharmacy. **Drogist** *m* (*pl* -en) pharmacist, chemist.
drohen ['droɪən] *v* threaten. **–d** *adj* threatening; (*Gefahr, usw.*) impending, imminent.
Drohne ['droɪnə] *f* (*pl* -n) drone.

dröhnen ['drœɪnən] *v* roar; (*Kanone*) boom; (*Donner*) rumble.
Drohung ['droɪuŋ] *f* (*pl* -en) threat.
Droschke ['drɔʃkə] *f* (*pl* -n) taxi; (*Pferde-*) cab.
Drossel ['drɔsəl] *f* (*pl* -n) (*Vogel*) thrush; (*Mot*) throttle. **–ader** *f* jugular vein. **drosseln** *v* throttle.
drüben ['dryɪbən] *adv* over there.
Druck[1] [druk] *m* (*pl* **Drücke**) pressure.
Druck[2] *m* (*pl* -e) print; (*Auflage*) impression. **drucken** *v* print.
drücken ['drykən] *v* press, push; (*Hand*) shake; (*bedrücken*) oppress. **sich drücken** get out of, avoid.
Druck‖er ['drukər] *m* (*pl* -) printer. **–erei** *f* (*pl* -en) printing plant, press. **–fehler** *m* misprint. **–knopf** *m* push button; (*Kleidung*) snap fastener. **–luft** *f* compressed air. **–messer** *m* pressure gauge. **–sache** *f* printed matter. **–schrift** *f* publication; (*Buchstaben*) block letter.
drum [drum] *V* **darum.**
drunter ['druntər] *V* **darunter.**
Drüse ['dryɪzə] *f* (*pl* -n) gland.
Dschungel ['dʒuŋəl] *m* (*pl* -) jungle.
du [duɪ] *pron* you.
Dübel ['dyɪbəl] *m* (*pl* -) dowel, wall-plug.
ducken ['dukən] *v* humble, humiliate. **sich ducken** duck; (*fig*) cower.
Dudelsack ['duɪdəlzak] *m* bagpipes *pl.*
Duell [du'ɛl] *neut* (*pl* -e) duel. **–ant** *m* duellist.
Duett [du'ɛt] *neut* (*pl* -e) duet.
Duft [duft] *m* (*pl* **Düfte**) fragrance, aroma; (*Blumen*) scent. **dufte** *adj* (*umg.*) splendid, fine. **duften** *v* smell (sweet), be fragrant. **–d** *adj* fragrant, aromatic.
dulden ['duldən] *v* endure; (*erlauben*) tolerate, allow. **duldsam** *adj* tolerant, patient.
dumm [dum] *adj* stupid. **–heit** *f* stupidity; (*Tat*) foolish action, blunder. **–kopf** *m* idiot, fool.
dumpf [dumpf] *adj* (*Klang*) dull, hollow, muffled; (*schwül*) close, sultry; (*muffig*) musty.
Düne ['dyɪnə] *f* (*pl* -n) dune.
Düngemittel ['dyŋəmitəl] *neut* fertilizer. **düngen** *v* fertilize, manure. **Dünger** *m* manure.
dunkel ['duŋkəl] *adj* dark; (*düster*) gloomy, dim; (*ungewiß*) obscure. **Dunkel‖heit** *f* darkness, obscurity.

−**kammer** f (*Foto*) darkroom. **dunkeln** v es dunkelt it is growing dark.
Dünkel ['dyŋkəl] m arrogance.
dünn [dyn] adj thin. **Dünn**‖**darm** m small intestine.
Dunst [dunst] m (pl **Dünste**) haze, mist. **dunsten** v steam.
dünsten ['dynstən] v steam; (*Küche*) stew.
Dur [duːr] neut (*Musik*) major (key).
durch [durç] prep through; (*mittels*) by, through; (*Zeit*) during. adv through(out). **durch Zufall** by chance. **durch und durch** thoroughly.
durchaus [durç'aus] adv completely, thoroughly.
durchblättern [durç'blɛtərn] v leaf through, skim through.
durchbohren ['durçboːrən] v pierce, bore through.
*****durchbrechen** ['durçbrɛçən] v break through. **Durchbruch** m break-through; (*Öffnung*) breach.
*****durchdringen** ['durçdriŋən] v penetrate; ['driŋən] (*durchsickern*) permeate.
durcheinander [durçain'andər] adv in confusion, in disorder, in a mess. **Durcheinander** neut muddle. **durcheinanderbringen** v muddle up; (*aufregen*) upset, excite.
Durchfahrt ['durçfaːrt] f passage; (*Tor*) gate. **keine Durchfahrt** no thoroughfare.
Durchfall ['durçfal] m failure; (*Med*) diarrhoea. **durchfallen** v fall through; (*Prüfung*) fail.
durchführen ['durçfyːrən] v carry out, perform; (*begleiten*) lead through. **Durchführung** f implementation, execution.
Durchgabe ['durçgaːbə] f transmission.
Durchgang ['durçgaŋ] m passage.
durchgeben ['durçgeːbən] v transmit, pass on.
durchgehen ['durçgeːən] v walk or go through, (*fliehen*) run away; (*durchdringen*) penetrate. −**d** adj continuous; (*Zug*) through.
*****durchkommen** ['durçkɔmən] v come or pass through.
*****durchlaufen** ['durçlaufən] v run through.
durchleuchten [durç'lɔyçtən] v (*Med*) x-ray.
durchmachen ['durçmaxən] v endure, live through.
Durchmesser ['durçmɛsər] m diameter.

Durchreise ['durçraizə] f journey through, passage, transit.
durchs [durçs] prep + art **durch das**.
Durchsage ['durçzaːgə] f announcement. **durchsagen** v announce.
Durchschlag ['durçʃlaːk] m carbon (copy); (*Sieb*) strainer, sieve. −**papier** neut carbon paper.
Durchschnitt ['durçʃnit] m cutting through; (*Querschnitt*) cross-section; (*Mittelwert*) mean, average. **durchschnittlich** adj average. **Durchschnittsmensch** m average person, man in the street.
Durchschrift ['durçʃrift] f (carbon) copy.
*****durchsehen** ['durçzeːən] v look or see through; (*prüfen*) look through or over.
Durchsicht ['durçziçt] f (pl -en) perusal, inspection. **durchsichtig** adj transparent.
durchsuchen ['durçzuːxən] v search.
durchtrieben [durç'triːbən] adj cunning, sly.
*****durchwinden** ['durçvindən] v **sich durchwinden** struggle through.
*****durchziehen** ['durçtsiːən] v pass through; (*etwas durch etwas*) pull or draw through; [-'tsiːən] traverse; (*durchdringen*) fill, permeate.
*****dürfen** ['dyrfən] v be allowed or permitted to, may. **darf ich?** may I? **wenn ich bitten darf** if you please. **du darfst nicht** you may or must not.
dürftig ['dyrftiç] adj needy, poor. **Dürftigkeit** f poverty.
dürr [dyr] adj arid, dry; (*hager*) lean. **Dürre** f drought; (*Magerkeit*) leanness.
Durst [durst] m thirst. **durst**‖**en** v be thirsty. −**ig** adj thirsty. −**stillend** adj thirst-quenching.
Dusche ['duʃə] f (pl -n) shower. **duschen** v shower, have or take a shower.
Düse ['dyːzə] f (pl -n) jet, nozzle. **Düsen**‖**antrieb** m jet propulsion. −**flugzeug** neut jet (plane).
düster ['dyːstər] adj dark; (*fig*) gloomy.
Dutzend ['dutsənt] neut (pl -e) dozen.
duzen ['duːtsən] v address familiarly (using **du**), be on first-name terms with.
Dynamik [dy'naːmik] f dynamics. **dynamisch** adj dynamic.
Dynamit [dyna'miːt] neut (unz.) dynamite.
Dynamo [dy'naːmo] m (pl -s) dynamo.
Dynastie [dynas'tiː] f (pl -n) dynasty.
D-Zug ['deːtsuk] m (pl **D-Züge**) express train.

E

Ebbe ['ɛbə] *f (pl -n)* ebb; (*Niedrigwasser*) low tide. **ebben** *v* ebb.

eben ['eɪbən] *adj* level, even. *adv* just. *ich war eben abgereist* I had just left. **eben deswegen** for that very reason. **Ebenbild** *neut* image. **ebenbürtig** *adj* equal (in rank). **Ebene** *f (pl -n)* plain; (*Math*) plane. **ebenfalls** *adv* likewise. **Eben∥heit** *f* evenness, smoothness. **–holz** *neut* ebony. **ebenso** *adv* just so. **–gut** *adv* just as well. **–viel** *adv* just as much.

Eber ['eɪbər] *m (pl -)* boar.

ebnen ['eɪbnən] *v* level, smooth.

Echo ['ɛço] *neut (pl -s)* echo.

echt [ɛçt] *adj* genuine, real. **Echtheit** *f* genuineness, authenticity.

Eck [ɛk] *neut (pl -e)* corner. **–ball** *m* corner (kick). **–e** *f* corner, angle. **eckig** *adj* angular. **Eckzahn** *m* eyetooth.

edel ['eɪdəl] *adj* noble. **Edel∥mann** *m* nobleman. **–metall** *neut* precious metal. **–stein** *m* precious stone, gemstone.

Edikt [e'dikt] *neut (pl -e)* edict.

Efeu ['eɪfɔy] *m* ivy.

Effekten [ɛ'fɛktən] *pl* effects, personal belongings; (*Komm*) bonds, shares. **Effekthascherei** *f* sensationalism. **effekt∥iv** *adj* effective, actual. **–voll** *adj* effective.

egal [e'gaɪl] *adj* equal, (all) the same. *das ist mir ganz egal* it's all the same to me.

Egoismus [ego'ismus] *m (pl Egoismen)* selfishness, egotism. **Egoist** *m* egotist. **egoistisch** *adj* egotistic, selfish.

ehe ['eɪə] *conj, adv* before. **–malig** *adj* former.

Ehe ['eɪə] *f (pl -n)* marriage. **–brecher** *m* adulterer. **–brecherin** *f* adulteress. **ehebrecherisch** *adj* adulterous. **Ehe∥bruch** *m* adultery. **–frau** *f* wife, married woman. **ehe∥lich** *adj* matrimonial, conjugal. **–los** *adj* unmarried, single. **Ehe∥mann** *m* husband. **–paar** *neut* married couple.

eher ['eɪər] *adv* sooner; (*lieber*) rather.

Ehre ['eɪrə] *f (pl -n)* honour. **ehren** *v* honour. **–haft** *adj* honourable. **Ehrenmal** *neut* war memorial. **ehrenvoll** *adj* honourable.

Ehrfurcht ['eɪrfurçt] *f* awe. **ehrfürchtig** *adj* full of awe *or* reverence.

Ehr∥gefühl *neut* sense of honour, self-respect. **–geiz** *m* ambition. **ehrgeizig** *adj* ambitious.

ehrlich ['eɪrliç] *adj* honest, sincere. **Ehrlichkeit** *f* honesty. **ehrlos** *adj* dishonourable. **Ehrung** *f (pl -en)* honour, award. **ehrwürdig** *adj* venerable.

Ei [ai] *neut (pl -er)* egg. **–abstoßung** *f* ovulation. **–dotter** *m* yolk.

Eiche ['aiçə] *f (pl -n)* oak. **Eich∥el** *f* acorn. **–hörnchen** *neut* squirrel.

Eid [ait] *m (pl -e)* oath. **einen Eid ablegen** swear an oath.

Eidechse ['aidɛksə] *f (pl -n)* lizard.

Eidgenosse *m* confederate. **–nschaft** *f* confederacy; (*Schweiz*) Switzerland. **eidgenössisch** *adj* confederate; (*schweizerisch*) Swiss.

Eier∥becher ['aiərbɛçər] *m* eggcup. **–kuchen** *m* omelette. **–schale** *f* eggshell. **–stock** *m* ovary.

Eifer ['aifər] *m (unz.)* fervour, zeal. **–sucht** *f* jealousy. **eifersüchtig** *adj* jealous. **eifrig** *adj* eager, zealous. **Eifrigkeit** *f* zeal.

Eigelb ['aigɛlp] *neut (pl -e)* (egg) yolk.

eigen ['aigən] *adj* own; (*eigentümlich*) particular; (*eigenartig*) peculiar. **sich etwas zu eigen machen** get *or* acquire something. **etwas auf eigene Faust unternehmen** do something of one's own accord. **Eigenart** *f (pl -en)* peculiarity. **eigenartig** *adj* peculiar. **eigen∥händig** *adj* by oneself. **–mächtig** *adj* arbitrary. **Eigen∥name** *m* proper name. **–nutz** *m* self-interest. **Eigenschaft** *f (pl -en)* quality, attribute, trait. **–swort** *neut* adjective. **Eigensinn** *m* obstinacy. **eigensinnig** *adj* obstinate, headstrong. **eigen∥ständig** *adj* independent. **–süchtig** *adj* egoistic. **eigentlich** ['aigəntliç] *adv* actually, really. *adj* real, actual. **Eigentum** ['aigəntuːm] *neut (pl Eigentümer)* property. **Eigentümer** *m* owner. **eigentümlich** *adj* peculiar.

eignen ['aignən] *v* **sich eignen für** *or* **zu** be suited for.

Eil∥bote ['ailboːtə] *m (pl -n)* courier, express messenger. **–brief** *m* express letter.

Eile ['ailə] *f* haste, hurry. **eilen** *v* hurry, hasten. **eilig** *adj* hasty, fast. **Eil∥sendung** *f*

(*Post*) special delivery. **–zug** *m* fast train, limited-stop train.
Eimer ['aimər] *m* (*pl* -) bucket, pail.
ein [ain], **eine**, **ein** *art* a, an. *pron*, *adj* one.
einander [ain'andər] *pron* each other, one another.
einatmen ['ainaɪtmən] *v* inhale, breathe in. **Einatmung** *f* inhalation.
Einbahnstraße ['ainbaɪnʃtraɪsə] *f* one-way street.
einbalsamieren [ainbaɪlza'miɪrən] *v* embalm.
Einband ['ainbant] *m* binding, cover (of book).
Einbau ['ainbau] *m* installation. **einbauen** *v* install, build in; (*fig*) incorporate (into).
***einbegreifen** ['ainbəgraifən] *v* include, comprise. **mit einbegriffen** included.
***einbiegen** ['ainbiɪgən] *v* bend in; (*Straße*) turn into.
einbilden ['ainbildən] *v* **sich einbilden** imagine. **Einbildung** *f* imagination; (*Dünkel*) conceit. **–svermögen** *neut* (power of) imagination.
Einblick ['ainblik] *m* insight.
***einbrechen** ['ainbrɛçən] *v* break open; (*Haus*) break into, burgle. **Einbrecher** *m* burglar. **Einbruch** *m* break-in, burglary; (*Mil*) invasion. **–sdiebstahl** *m* burglary.
einbürgern ['ainbyrgən] *v* naturalize. **sich einbürgen** become naturalized; (*Wort, usw.*) come into use, gain acceptance. **Einbürgerung** *f* naturalization.
eindeutig ['aindɔytiç] *adj* unequivocal, clear.
***eindringen** ['aindriɲən] *v* enter by force; (*Mil*) invade. **eindringlich** *adj* urgent.
Eindruck ['aindruk] *m* impression. **eindrücken** *v* press in. **sich eindrücken** leave an impression. **eindrucksvoll** *adj* impressive.
einerlei ['ainərlai] *adj* of one kind. **est ist einerlei** it makes no difference.
einerseits ['ainərzaits] *adv* on (the) one hand.
einfach ['ainfax] *adj* simple; (*nicht doppelt*) single. **Einfachheit** *f* simplicity.
***einfahren** ['ainfaɪrən] *v* drive in; (*Mot*) run in; (*einbringen*) bring in. **Einfahrt** *f* entrance, way in; (*Hineinfahren*) arrival, entrance.
Einfall ['ainfal] *m* idea, inspiration; (*Mil*) invasion, assault. **einfallen** *v* fall in;

(*idee*) occur (to). *es fällt mir ein* it strikes me.
einfältig ['ainfɛltiç] *adj* naive, artless. **Einfältigkeit** *f* naivety, artlessness.
einfetten ['ainfɛtən] *v* grease, lubricate.
***einfinden** ['ainfindən] *v* **sich einfinden** appear, turn up.
***einflechten** ['ainflɛçtən] *v* interweave; (*Wort*) put in.
Einflug ['ainfluːk] *m* incursion; (*Aero*) approach.
Einfluß ['ainflus] *m* influence. **einflußreich** *adj* influential.
einförmig ['ainfœrmiç] *adj* monotonous, uniform.
einfügen ['ainfyɪgən] *v* fit in.
einfühlen ['ainfyɪlən] *v* **sich einfühlen in** sympathize with, get into the spirit of. **Einfühlung** *f* sympathizing, sympathy.
Einfuhr ['ainfuːr] *f* (*pl* -en) import. **einführen** *v* bring in; (*Waren*) import; (*Gebrauch*) introduce. **Einfuhrhandel** *m* import trade. **Einführung** *f* introduction. **Einfuhrverbot** *neut* import ban.
Eingang ['aingaɲ] *m* way in; (*Ankunft*) arrival; (*Einleitung*) introduction.
eingebildet ['aingəbildət] *adj* conceited; (*erfunden*) imaginary.
eingeboren ['aingəbɔɪrən] *adj* native; (*angeboren*) innate. **Eingeborene(r)** *m* native.
Eingebung ['aingɛɪbuɲ] *f* (*pl* -en) inspiration.
***eingehen** ['aingeɪən] *v* go *or* enter into; (*aufhören*) stop; (*welken*) decay; (*Risiko*) run; (*zustimmen*) agree. **–d** *adj* thorough, detailed.
eingemacht ['aingəmaxt] *adj* bottled; canned; (*Fleisch*) potted.
eingenommen ['aingenɔmən] *adj* biased (in favour of).
Eingeweide ['aingəvaidə] *neut* (*pl* -) intestines *pl*, entrails *pl*.
Eingeweihte(r) ['aingəvaitə(r)] *m* (*pl* -) initiate.
eingewöhnen ['aingəvœnən] *v* accustom. **sich eingewöhnen** become accustomed (to).
***eingießen** ['aingiɪsən] *v* pour in *or* out.
eingliedern ['aingliɪdərn] *v* incorporate; (*einordnen*) classify. **Eingliederung** *f* incorporation; classification.
***eingreifen** ['aingraifən] *v* catch (hold of); (*einmischen*) interfere. **Eingriff** *m*

catch; interference; (*Übergriff*) encroachment.

*einhalten ['ainhaltən] *v* restrain, check; observe; stop.

einhändig ['ainhɛndig] *adj* with one hand. **–en** *v* hand in.

einheimisch ['ainhaimiʃ] *adj* native, indigenous.

Einheit ['ainhait] *f* (*pl* -en) unit; (*Pol*) unity. **einheitlich** *adj* uniform.

einholen ['ainhoilən] *v* collect; (*einkaufen*) shop, buy; (*erreichen*) catch up with.

einig [aiᵢnɪç] *adj* united, at one. **einig sein** be in agreement. **–en** *v* unite. **sich einigen** agree.

einiger ['ainigər], **einige, einiges** *pron* some, any. **einigermaßen** *adv* to some extent.

Einigkeit *f* (*unz.*) unity; (*Eintracht*) agreement. **Einigung** *f* unification; agreement.

einjährig ['ainjɛiriç] *adj* one-year-old; (*Bot*) annual.

einkassieren [ainkasiirən] *v* cash (in).

Einkauf ['ainkauf] *m* (*pl* **Einkäufe**) purchase. **einkaufen** *v* buy, purchase. **einkaufen gehen** go shopping.

einkehren ['ainkeirən] *v* call in (at).

Einklang ['ainklaŋ] *m* (*pl* **Einklänge**) harmony.

*einkommen ['ainkɔmən] *v* come in, arrive. **Einkommen** *neut* income.

einkreisen ['ainkraisən] *v* encircle.

Einkünfte ['ainkynftə] *pl* revenue, income *sing.*

*einladen ['ainlaidən] *v* invite. **Einladung** *f* (*pl* -en) invitation.

Einlage ['ainlaigə] *f* (*pl* -n) lining, filler; (*Brief*) enclosure; (*Geld*) deposit.

Einlaß ['ainlas] *m* (*pl* **Einlässe**) admission; (*Öffnung*) inlet. **einlassen** *v* let in, admit.

*einlaufen ['ainlaufən] *v* arrive; (*Wasser*) run in.

einleben ['ainleibən] *v* **sich einleben in** accustom oneself to.

einlegen ['ainleigən] *v* enclose, insert; (*Beschwerde*) file; (*Fleisch*) salt, pickle.

einleiten ['ainlaitən] *v* introduce, initiate; (*beginnen*) start. **Einleitung** *f* introduction.

einlösen ['ainlœizən] *v* redeem. **Einlösung** *f* payment, redemption.

einmachen ['ainmaxən] *v* (*Obst*) preserve, bottle.

einmal ['ainmal] *adv* once. **auf einmal** all at once. **noch einmal** (once) again. **nicht einmal** not even. **–ig** *adj* unique.

Einmarsch ['ainmarʃ] *m* (*pl* **Einmärsche**) marching in, entry. **einmarschieren** *v* enter, march in (to).

einmischen ['ainmiʃən] *v* **sich einmischen in** interfere *or* meddle in.

einmünden ['ainmyndən] *v* run *or* flow (into), join.

Einnahme ['ainnaimə] *f* (*pl* -n) receipts *pl*, takings *pl*, revenue.

*einnehmen ['ainneimən] *v* take (in); (*Geld*) receive.

Einöde ['ainœidə] *f* (*pl* -n) desert, wasteland.

einölen ['ainœilən] *v* oil.

einordnen ['ainɔrdnən] *v* order, arrange; (*Mot*) get in lane.

einpacken ['ainpakən] *v* pack, wrap up.

einpökeln ['ainpœikəln] *v* pickle.

einprägen ['ainpreigən] *v* imprint. **jemandem etwas einprägen** impress something on somebody.

einrahmen ['ainraimən] *v* frame.

einräumen ['ainrɔymən] *v* tidy up, put away; (*zugeben*) concede; (*einrichten*) furnish; (*Platz*) vacate, give up.

Einrede ['ainreidə] *f* (*pl* -n) objection. **einreden** *v* persuade; (*widersprechen*) contradict.

einreichen ['ainraiçən] *v* hand over *or* in.

Einreise ['ainraisə] *f* (*pl* -n) entry.

einrichten ['ainriçtən] *v* arrange, set up; (*gründen*) establish; (*Zimmer*) furnish. **Einrichtung** *f* establishment; arrangement; (*Anstalt*) institution; (*Zimmer*) fittings *pl*, furnishings *pl*.

einrücken ['ainrykən] *v* enter.

eins [ains] *pron* one.

einsam ['ainzaim] *adj* lonely, solitary. **Einsamkeit** *f* loneliness.

Einsatz ['ainzats] *m* (*pl* **Einsätze**) insertion; insert, filling; (*Spiel*) stake; (*Mil*) mission, operation.

einschalten ['ainʃaltən] *v* switch on; (*einfügen*) insert, put in. **Einschaltung** *f* switching on; insertion.

einschiffen ['ainʃifən] *v* bring on board, load (into a ship). **sich einschiffen** go on board, embark.

*einschlafen ['ainʃlaifən] *v* go to sleep, fall asleep.

Einschlag ['ainʃlaık] *m* (*pl* **Einschläge**) impact; (*Umschlag*) wrapper. **einschlagen** *v* drive in, break; (*einwickeln*) wrap; (*Weg*) take, follow; (*Hände*) shake hands; (*zustimmen*) agree.

*einschließen ['ainʃliːsən] *v* lock up *or* in; (*umfassen*) comprise, include; (*umzingeln*) encircle. **einschließlich** *adj* inclusive; *prep* including, inclusive of. **Einschluß** *m* (*pl* **Einschlüsse**) inclusion.

einschmeicheln ['ainʃmaiçəln] *v* **sich einschmeicheln bei** ingratiate oneself with.

einschränken ['ainʃrɛnkən] *v* restrict, limit. **Einschränkung** *f* restriction, limitation.

Einschreibebrief ['ainʃraibəbriːf] *m* registered letter. **einschreiben** *v* register; (*eintragen*) inscribe, write in. **per Einschreiben** *adv* (by) registered mail. **Einschreibung** *f* registration.

einschüchtern ['ainʃyçtərn] *v* intimidate.

*einsehen ['ainzeːən] *v* inspect, look over; (*prüfen*) examine; (*begreifen*) realize.

einseitig ['ainzaitiç] *adj* one-sided; (*Pol*) unilateral.

einsenden ['ainzɛndən] *v* send in.

einsetzen ['ainzɛtsən] *v* set in, put in; (*Amt*) install; begin; (*Geld*) deposit.

Einsicht ['ainziçt] *f* (*pl* -en) insight; (*Verständnis*) understanding. **einsichtsvoll** *adj* judicious, sensible.

Einsiedler ['ainziːdlər] *m* (*pl* -) hermit.

einspannen ['ainʃpanən] *v* (*Pferd*) harness; (*mit Rahmen*) stretch.

einsperren ['ainʃpɛrən] *v* lock in *or* up; (*Gefängnis*) imprison, jail.

einspritzen ['ainʃpritsən] *v* inject.

Einspruch ['ainʃprux] *m* (*pl* **Einsprüche**) objection, protest. **Einspruch erheben gegen** raise an objection against.

einst [ainst] *adv* (*Vergangenheit*) once, at one time; (*Zukunft*) some day, one day.

einstecken ['ainʃtɛkən] *v* put in; (*in die Tasche*) pocket.

*einsteigen ['ainʃtaigən] *v* (*Auto, Schiff, usw.*) get in, get on, board.

einstellen ['ainʃtɛlən] *v* cease, stop; (*tech*) adjust; (*phot*) focus; (*radio, usw.*) tune. **–bar** *adj* adjustable. **Einstellung** *f* stop, suspension; adjustment; (*Ansicht*) attitude.

einstig ['ainstiç] *adj* former.

einstimmen ['ainʃtimən] *v* agree; join (in). **einstimmig** *adj* unanimous.

einstmalig ['ainstmaːliç] *adj* former.

einstöckig ['ainʃtœkiç] *adj* one-storeyed.

*einstoßen ['ainʃtoːsən] *v* push *or* drive in(to); (*Tür*) knock *or* break down.

einströmen ['ainʃtrœːmən] *v* flow *or* stream in(to).

einstufen ['ainʃtuːfən] *v* classify, grade.

einstürmen ['ainʃtyrmən] *v* rush in; (*angreifen*) attack.

Einsturz ['ainʃturts] *m* (*pl* **Einstürze**) downfall, collapse. **einstürzen** *v* collapse; (*niederreißen*) knock down, demolish.

einstweilen ['ainstvailən] *adv* meanwhile, for the time being. **einstweilig** *adj* temporary, provisional.

eintägig ['ainteːgiç] *adj* one-day.

Eintausch ['aintauʃ] *m* exchange. **eintauschen** *v* exchange, trade.

einteilen ['aintailən] *v* divide up, classify; (*Skala*) graduate; (*Arbeit*) plan out.

eintönig ['aintøːniç] *adj* monotonous.

Eintopf ['aintɔpf] *m* stew, casserole.

Eintracht ['aintraxt] *f* (*unz.*) harmony, unity.

Eintrag ['aintraık] *m* (*pl* **Einträge**) (*Komm*) entry; (*Schaden*) damage. **eintragen** *v* carry in; (*einschreiben*) enter; (*einbringen*) yield. **einträglich** *adj* profitable. **Eintragung** *f* entry.

*eintreten ['aintreːtən] *v* come in; (*eindrücken*) kick in; (*beitreten*) join; (*geschehen*) occur.

Eintritt ['aintrit] *m* entrance; (*Anfang*) beginning. **–skarte** *f* admission ticket.

einverleiben ['ainfɛrlaibən] *v* incorporate.

einverstanden ['ainfɛrʃtandən] *adj* in agreement. **einverstanden sein mit** agree with, approve of.

Einwand ['ainvant] *m* (*pl* **Einwände**) objection. **einwandfrei** *adj* perfect, faultless.

Einwanderer ['ainvandərər] *m* (*pl* -) immigrant. **einwandern** *v* immigrate. **Einwanderung** *f* immigration.

einwärts ['ainvɛrts] *adv* inwards.

einwechseln ['ainvɛksəln] *v* change; exchange.

Einwegflasche ['ainveːkflaʃə] *f* non-returnable bottle.

einweichen ['ainvaiçən] *v* soak, steep.

einweihen ['ainvaiən] *v* inaugurate; (*Person*) initiate; (*Kirche*) consecrate. **Einweihung** *f* inauguration; initiation; consecration.

Einwendung ['ainvɛnduŋ] *f* (*pl* -en) objection.

einwickeln ['ainvikəln] *v* wrap (up).

einwilligen ['ainviligən] *v* consent, agree. **Einwilligung** *f* consent.

einwirken ['ainvirkən] *v* **einwirken auf** influence, affect. **Einwirkung** *f* influence.

Einwohner ['ainvoːnər] *m* (*pl* -) inhabitant.

Einzahl ['aintsaːl] *f* (*unz.*) (*Gramm*) singular.

einzahlen ['aintsaːlən] *v* pay in, deposit.

Einzel‖erscheinung ['aintsəlɛrʃainuŋ] *f* (isolated) phenomenon. **–fall** *m* individual case. **–handel** *m* retail trade. **–handelsgeschäft** *neut* retail shop. **–händler** *m* retailer. **–haus** *neut* detached house. **–heit** *f* detail. **–kind** *neut* only child. **einzeln** *adj* single; (*getrennt*) isolated; (*alleinstehend*) detached. **einzelnstehend** *adj* detached. **Einzelzimmer** *neut* single room.

einziehen ['aintsiːən] *v* pull *or* draw in; (*einkassieren*) collect; (*beschlagnahmen*) confiscate; (*Rekruten*) draft; (*Wohnung*) move in.

einzig ['aintsiç] *adj* only, single.

Einzug ['aintsuːk] *m* entry, entrance; (*Wohnung*) moving in.

Eis [ais] *neut* (*unz.*) ice; (*Speise*) ice-cream. **–bahn** *f* ice/skating rink. **–bär** *m* polar bear. **–bein** *neut* knuckle of pork. **–berg** *m* iceberg.

Eischale ['aiʃaːlə] *f* eggshell.

Eisen ['aizən] *neut* (*pl* -) iron. **–bahn** *f* railway. **–händler** *m* ironmonger. **–waren** *f pl* ironmongery.

eisern ['aizərn] *adj* iron.

eisig ['aiziç] *adj* icy. **eiskalt** *adj* ice-cold.

Eis‖lauf *m* skating. **–läufer** *m* (*pl* -) skater. **–laufbahn** *f* skating rink. **–meer** *neut* polar sea. **–regen** *m* freezing rain. **–tüte** *f* ice-cream cone/cornet. **–vogel** *m* kingfisher. **–würfel** *m* ice cube. **–zapfen** *m* icicle.

eitel ['aitəl] *adj* vain. **Eitelkeit** *f* vanity.

Eiter ['aitər] *m* (*unz.*) pus. **eitern** *v* fester, suppurate.

Eiweiß ['aivais] *neut* (*pl* -e) egg-white; protein; albumen. **–stoff** *m* protein.

Ekel ['eːkəl] *m* (*unz.*) disgust, repugnance. **ekelhaft** *adj* loathsome, disgusting. **sich ekeln** be disgusted by.

Ekzem [ɛk'tseːm] *neut* (*pl* -e) eczema.

elastisch [e'lastiʃ] *adj* elastic.

Elefant [ele'fant] *m* (*pl* -en) elephant.

elegant [ele'gant] *adj* elegant. **Eleganz** *f* elegance.

elektrifizieren [elɛktrifi'tsiːrən] *v also* **elektrisieren** electrify. **Elektriker** *m* electrician. **elektrisch** *adj* electric(al). **Elektrizität** *f* electricity.

Elektro‖gerät [e'lɛktrogərɛit] *neut* electric appliance. **–installateur** *m* electrician. **–motor** *m* electric motor.

Elektronik [elɛk'troːnik] *f* electronics. **elektronisch** *adj* electronic.

Elektrotechnik [elɛktro'teçnik] *f* electrical engineering.

Element [ele'mɛnt] *neut* (*pl* -e) element; (*Zelle*) battery. **elementar** *adj* elementary.

elend ['eːlɛnt] *adj* miserable. **Elend** *neut* misery. **–sviertel** *neut* slums *pl*.

elf [ɛlf] *pron, adj* eleven.

Elf [ɛlf] *m* (*pl* -en) elf, fairy.

Elfenbein ['ɛlfənbain] *neut* (*unz.*) ivory.

elfte ['ɛlftə] *adj* eleventh.

Elite [e'liːtə] *f* (*pl* -n) elite.

Ellbogen ['ɛlboːgən] *m* (*pl* -) elbow.

Ellipse [ɛ'lipsə] *f* (*pl* -n) ellipse. **elliptisch** *adj* elliptical.

Elsaß ['ɛlsas] *neut* Alsace. **Elsässer** *m* (*pl* -), **Elsässerin** *f* (*pl* -nen) Alsatian. **elsässisch** *adj* Alsatian.

Elster ['ɛlstər] *f* (*pl* -n) magpie.

Eltern ['ɛltərn] *pl* parents. **elterlich** *adj* parental.

Email [e'maːj] *neut* (*pl* -s) enamel.

emanzipieren [emantsi'piːrən] *v* emancipate. **Emanzipation** *f* emancipation.

Empfang [ɛm'pfaŋ] *m* (*pl* **Empfänge**) welcome, reception. **empfangen** *v* welcome, receive; (*Kind*) conceive. **Empfänger** *m* receiver. **empfänglich** *adj* susceptible. **Empfängnis** *f* conception. **–verhütung** *f* contraception.

***empfehlen** [ɛm'pfeːlən] *v* recommend. **–swert** *adj* to be recommended. **Empfehlung** *f* recommendation. **–sschreiben** letter of recommendation.

empfinden [ɛm'pfindən] *v* feel. **empfindlich** *adj* sensitive; (*reizbar*) touchy. **Empfindung** *f* feeling; (*Wahrnehmung*) perception.

empor [ɛm'poːr] *adv* up(wards). **–ragen** *v* tower (up/over). **–streben** *v* struggle up(wards).

empören [ɛm'pœrən] v shock, revolt; (*erregen*) stir up. **sich empören** rebel.

emsig ['ɛmziç] adj diligent, industrious.

Ende ['ɛndə] neut (pl **-n**) end.

endemisch [ɛn'deːmiʃ] adj endemic.

enden ['ɛndən] v finish, end. **end‖gültig** adj final. **–lich** adv finally, at last; adj final; (*beschränkt*) finite. **–los** adj endless, infinite.

End‖punkt m end (point). **–spiel** neut (*Sport*) final. **–station** f terminus. **–zweck** m (ultimate) goal or purpose.

Energie [enɛr'giː] f (pl **-n**) energy. **–krise** energy crisis. **energisch** adj energetic.

eng [ɛŋ] adj narrow; (*dicht*) tight, close; (*Freund*) close. **Enge** f narrowness; tightness; (*Klemme*) difficulty.

Engel ['ɛŋəl] m (pl **-**) angel. **engelhaft** adj angelic.

England ['ɛŋlant] neut England. **Engländer** m (pl **-**) Englishman. **Engländerin** f (pl **-nen**) Englishwoman. *ich bin Engländer(in)* I am English. **englisch** adj English.

Engpaß ['ɛŋpas] m narrow pass; (*verkehr*) bottleneck; (*Klemme*) difficulty, tight spot.

engros [ã'groː] adv wholesale.

engstirnig ['ɛŋʃtirniç] adj narrow-minded.

Enkel ['ɛŋkəl] m (pl **-**) grandson. **–in** f granddaughter. **–kind** neut grandchild.

enorm [e'nɔrm] adj enormous.

entarten [ɛnt'aːrtən] v degenerate. **Entartung** f degeneracy, degeneration.

entbehrlich [ɛnt'beːrliç] adj dispensable, (to) spare.

***entbinden** [ɛnt'bindən] v release, set free; (*eine Frau*) deliver. **Entbindung** f release, setting free; (*Geburt*) delivery.

entblößen [ɛnt'blœsən] v uncover; (*berauben*) deprive, rob.

entdecken [ɛnt'dɛkən] v discover. **Entdecker** m discoverer. **Entdeckung** f discovery.

Ente ['ɛntə] f (pl **-n**) duck; (*Falschmeldung, Lüge*) hoax, canard.

entehren [ɛnt'eːrən] v dishonour, disgrace.

enteignen [ɛnt'aignən] v expropriate, dispossess. **Enteignung** f expropriation; seizure.

enterben [ɛnt'ɛrbən] v disinherit.

***entfallen** [ɛnt'falən] v fall or slip from; (*Gedächtnis*) slip, escape.

entfalten [ɛnt'faltən] v unfold; (*zeigen*) display. (*Mil*) deploy; **Entfaltung** f

unfolding; display; deployment; development.

entfernen [ɛnt'fɛrnən] v remove. **sich entfernen** go away, withdraw. **Entfernung** f distance; (*Wegbringen*) removal.

entflammen [ɛnt'flamən] v inflame, kindle.

***entfliehen** [ɛnt'fliːən] v flee from.

entfremden [ɛnt'frɛmdən] v alienate, estrange. **Entfremdung** f alienation, estrangement.

entführen [ɛnt'fyːrən] v abduct; (*Flugzeug*) hijack. **Entführer** m abductor, kidnapper; hijacker. **Entführung** f abduction, kidnapping; hijacking.

entgegen [ɛnt'geːgən] prep against, contrary to; (*hinzu*) towards. adv towards. **–kommen** v meet; (*Kompromiß*) make concessions. **–sehen** v look forward to. **–treten** v move towards; (*widerstehen*) oppose. **–wirken** v work against.

entgegnen [ɛnt'geːgnən] v retort, answer back.

***entgehen** [ɛnt'geːən] v escape from.

Entgelt [ɛnt'gɛlt] neut (*unz.*) compensation.

entgiften [ɛnt'giftən] v decontaminate.

entgleisen [ɛnt'glaizən] v be or become derailed. **Entgleisung** f derailment.

entgräten [ɛnt'grɛːtən] v bone; fillet (fish).

enthaaren [ɛnt'haːrən] v remove hair from, depilate.

***enthalten** [ɛnt'haltən] v hold, contain. **sich enthalten** refrain (from). **enthaltsam** adj abstemious. **Enthaltung** f abstention.

enthaupten [ɛnt'hauptən] v behead, decapitate.

enthüllen [ɛnt'hylən] v uncover, reveal.

Enthusiasmus [ɛntuzi'asmus] m (*unz.*) enthusiasm. **enthusiastisch** adj enthusiastic.

entkernen [ɛnt'kɛrnən] v (*Obst*) stone.

entkleiden [ɛnt'klaidən] v (*Person*) undress, strip; (*wegnehmen*) divest. **sich entkleiden** undress.

***entkommen** [ɛnt'kɔmən] v escape.

entkuppeln [ɛnt'kupəln] v disconnect; (*Mot*) declutch.

entladen [ɛnt'laːdən] v unload; (*Gewehr, Batterie*) discharge.

entlang [ɛnt'laŋ] prep, adv along. **–fahren** v travel along. **–gehen** v walk along.

***entlassen** [ɛnt'lasən] v dismiss, discharge, (*umg.*) fire, sack; (*Gefangene*) release. **entlassen werden** be dismissed, (*coll*) get the sack. **Entlassung** *f* dismissal, discharge; release.

entlasten [ɛnt'lastən] *v* unburden; (*erleichtern*) relieve; (*Bank*) credit; (*Verdachtsperson*) clear, exonerate.

entleeren [ɛnt'leːrən] *v* empty. **sich entleeren** relieve oneself.

entlegen [ɛnt'leːgən] *adj* remote.

entmilitarisieren [ɛntmilitariˈziːrən] *v* demilitarize.

entmutigen [ɛnt'muːtigən] *v* discourage. **Entmutigung** *f* discouragement.

Entnahme [ɛnt'naːmə] *f* (*unz.*) taking *or* drawing out; (*Geld*) withdrawal; (*Strom*) use.

entnazifizieren [ɛntnatsifiˈtsiːrən] *v* denazify.

*****entnehmen** [ɛnt'neːmən] *v* take away *or* out; (*folgern*) conclude, infer; (*Geld*) withdraw; (*Strom*) use. **Entnehmer** *m* (*Komm*) drawer (of bills); (*Strom*) user.

entrahmen [ɛnt'raːmən] *v* skim (milk).

entrüsten [ɛnt'rystən] *v* irritate, anger. **Entrüstung** *f* indignation, anger.

entsagen [ɛnt'zaːgən] *v* renounce, give up.

entschädigen [ɛnt'ʃɛːdigən] *v* compensate. **Entschädigung** *f* compensation.

Entscheid [ɛnt'ʃait] *m* (*pl* -e) decision. **entscheiden** *v* decide. **sich entscheiden** decide, resolve, make up one's mind. **entscheidend** *adj* decisive. **Entscheidung** *f* decision; (*Urteil*) sentence.

entschieden [ɛnt'ʃiːdən] *adj* determined, resolute. *adv* decidedly. **Entschiedenheit** *f* determination.

*****entschließen** [ɛnt'ʃliːsən] *v* **sich entschließen** decide, determine.

entschlossen [ɛnt'ʃlɔsən] *adj* determined, resolute.

Entschluß [ɛnt'ʃlus] *m* (*pl* **Entschlüsse**) decision. **-kraft** *f* power of decision, decisiveness.

entschuldigen [ɛnt'ʃuldigən] *v* excuse, pardon. **sich entschuldigen** apologize, excuse oneself. **entschuldigen Sie! excuse me! Entschuldigung** *f* apology; *interj* I'm sorry! pardon me!

entsetzen [ɛnt'zɛtsən] *v* horrify, appal; (*von einem Posten*) dismiss; (*Mil*) relieve. **Entsetzen** *neut* horror. **entsetzlich** *adj* dreadful, horrible. **entsetzt** *adj* horrified, shocked.

entspannen [ɛnt'ʃpanən] *v* relax, release. **sich entspannen** relax, calm down. **Entspannung** *f* relaxation; (*Pol*) détente.

*****entsprechen** [ɛnt'ʃprɛçən] *v* correspond (to); (*Anforderung*) comply with. **entsprechend** *adj* corresponding, appropriate.

*****entspringen** [ɛnt'ʃpriŋən] *v* escape from, run away from.

entstammen [ɛnt'ʃtamən] *v* descend (from).

*****entstehen** [ɛnt'ʃteːən] *v* arise, originate. **Entstehung** *f* origin.

enttäuschen [ɛnt'tɔyʃən] *v* disappoint. **enttäuscht** *adj* disappointed. **Enttäuschung** *f* disappointment.

entvölkern [ɛnt'fœlkərn] *v* depopulate.

*****entwachsen** [ɛnt'vaksən] *v* grow out of.

entwaffnen [ɛnt'vafnən] *v* disarm.

entwässern [ɛnt'vɛsərn] *v* drain; (*austrocknen*) dehydrate. **Entwässerung** *f* drainage; dehydration.

entweder [ɛnt'veːdər] *conj* either.

*****entweichen** [ɛnt'vaiçən] *v* escape.

entweihen [ɛnt'vaiən] *v* desecrate, profane.

*****entwerfen** [ɛnt'vɛrfən] *v* design, plan; (*skizzieren*) sketch; (*Fassung*) draft, draw up.

entwerten [ɛnt'veːrtən] *v* devalue; (*Briefmarke*) cancel. **Entwertung** *f* devaluation; cancellation.

entwickeln [ɛnt'vikəln] *v* develop. **sich entwickeln** develop. **Entwicklung** *f* development. **Entwicklungs||land** *neut* developing country. **-lehre** *f* theory of evolution.

entwirren [ɛnt'virən] *v* disentangle.

entwischen [ɛnt'viʃən] *v* slip *or* steal away from.

entwürdigen [ɛnt'vyrdigən] *v* degrade, debase.

Entwurf [ɛnt'vurf] *m* (*pl* **Entwürfe**) design, plan; (*Skizze*) sketch; (*Fassung*) draft.

entwurzeln [ɛnt'vurtsəln] *v* uproot; (*vernichten*) eradicate.

*****entziehen** [ɛnt'tsiːən] *v* take away, withdraw; (*rauben*) deprive.

entziffern [ɛnt'tsifərn] *v* decipher, make out.

entzücken [ɛnt'tsykən] *v* delight, enchant. **Entzücken** *neut* delight, enchantment. **entzückt** *adj* delighted, enchanted. **entzückend** *adj* delightful, enchanting.

entzündbar [ɛnt'tsyntbaɪr] *adj* inflammable. **entzünden** *adj* kindle, light. **sich entzünden** catch fire. **Entzündung** *f* ignition; (*med*) inflammation.

entzwei [ɛnt'tsvai] *adv* in two, asunder.
–brechen *v* break in two.

Enzyklopädie [ɛntsyklope'diː] *f* (*pl* -n) encyclopedia.

Epidemie [epide'miː] *f* (*pl* -n) epidemic. epidemisch *adj* epidemic.

Epilepsie [epilɛp'siː] *f* (*unz.*) epilepsy. Epileptiker *m* epileptic. epileptisch *adj* epileptic.

Episode [epi'zoːdə] *f* (*pl* -n) episode.

er [ɛr] *pron* he.

erachten [ɛr'axtən] *v* think, consider. Erachten *neut* opinion, judgment. meines Erachtens in my opinion.

Erbarmen [ɛr'barmən] *neut* (*unz.*) pity, compassion. erbärmlich *adj* pitiful, pitiable. erbarmungs||los *adj* merciless, pitiless. –voll *adj* compassionate, merciful.

erbauen [ɛr'bauən] *v* build, erect.

Erbe ['ɛrbə] *m* (*pl* -n) heir; *neut* (*unz.*) inheritance. Erbeinheit *f* gene. erben *v* inherit. Erb||fehler *m* hereditary defect. –feind *m* traditional enemy. –gut *neut* inheritance; (*Erbhof*) ancestral estate. erblich *adj* hereditary.

erbittern [ɛr'bitərn] *v* embitter. erbittert *adj* embittered, bitter.

erblassen [ɛr'blasən] *v* grow pale.

erblicken [ɛr'blikən] *v* glimpse, catch sight of.

erblinden [ɛr'blindən] *v* blind.

*erbrechen [ɛr'brɛçən] *v* sich erbrechen vomit.

Erbschaft ['ɛrpʃaft] *v* (*pl* -en) legacy, inheritance.

Erbse ['ɛrpsə] *f* (*pl* -n) pea.

Erd||beben ['ɛrtbeibən] *neut* (*pl* -) earthquake. –beere *f* strawberry. –boden *m* earth, soil.

Erde ['ɛrdə] *v* (*pl* -n) earth. erden *v* (*Strom*) earth.

*erdenken [ɛr'dɛŋkən] *v* think of, think out; (*erfinden*) invent.

Erdgas *neut* natural gas.

erdichten [ɛr'diçtən] *v* fabricate, invent. Erdichtung *f* fabrication, invention.

Erd||kreis *m* globe, earth. –kunde *f* geography. erdkundlich *adj* geographic(al). Erd||nuß *f* peanut. –öl *neut* oil, petroleum.

erdrosseln [ɛr'drɔsəln] *v* strangle.

erdulden [ɛr'duldən] *v* endure.

ereignen [ɛr'aignən] *v* sich ereignen happen. Ereignis *neut* event, occurrence.

*erfahren [ɛr'fairən] *v* experience; (*hören, lernen*) learn, hear of. *adj* experienced, proficient. Erfahrung *f* experience.

erfassen [ɛr'fasən] *v* seize; (*einschließen*) include; (*begreifen*) understand, grasp.

*erfinden [ɛr'findən] *v* invent. Erfinder *m* inventor. erfinderisch *adj* inventive. Erfindung *f* invention.

Erfolg [ɛr'fɔlk] *m* (*pl* -e) success; (*Ergebnis*) result, outcome. Erfolg haben achieve success, succeed. erfolgen *v* result, follow. erfolg||los *adj* unsuccessful. –reich *adj* successful.

erforderlich [ɛr'fɔrdərliç] *adj* necessary. erfordern *v* require, need; (*verlangen*) demand. Erfordernis *neut* necessity; (*Voraussetzung*) requirement.

erforschen [ɛr'fɔrʃən] *v* investigate. Erforsch||er *m* investigator. –ung *f* investigation.

erfreuen [ɛr'frɔyən] *v* delight. sich erfreuen an enjoy, take delight in. erfreulich *adj* gratifying. erfreut *adj* gratified.

*erfrieren [ɛr'friːrən] *v* freeze to death. Erfrierung *f* frostbite.

erfrischen [ɛr'friʃən] *v* refresh. –d *adj* refreshing. Erfrischung *f* refreshment.

erfüllen [ɛr'fylən] *v* fill; (*Aufgabe*) carry out; (*Bitte, Forderung*) comply with, fulfil. Erfüllung *f* accomplishment, fulfilment.

ergänzen [ɛr'gɛntsən] *v* supplement, add to; (*vervollständigen*) complete. Ergänzung *f* supplement; completion.

*ergeben [ɛr'geibən] *v* yield. sich ergeben surrender; (*folgen*) result. Ergebenheit *f* devotion; (*Fügsamkeit*) submissiveness. Ergebnis *neut* result.

*ergehen [ɛr'geiən] *v* (*Gesetz*) be promulgated, come out.

ergiebig [ɛr'giːbiç] *adj* productive, profitable.

*ergreifen [ɛr'graifən] *v* grasp, seize; (*rühren*) touch, move (deeply). –d *adj* touching, affecting. Ergreifung *f* seizure.

erhaben [ɛr'haibən] *adj* exalted, sublime.

*erhalten [ɛr'haltən] *v* receive, obtain; (*bewahren*) preserve, maintain. erhältlich *adj* available, obtainable. Erhaltung *f* preservation, maintenance.

*erheben [ɛr'heibən] *v* lift up; (*Einspruch*) raise. sich erheben risé (up). Anspruch erheben auf lay claim to. erheblich *adj* considerable. Erhebung *f* uprising.

251

erörtern

erheitern [ɛr'haitərn] v cheer up; (*unterhalten*) amuse. **sich erheitern** (*Himmel*) brighten, clear up.

erhitzen [ɛr'hitsən] v heat (up); (*Person*) inflame.

erhöhen [ɛr'hœiən] v raise, heighten. **Erhöhung** f raising, heightening.

erholen [ɛr'hoilən] v **sich erholen** recover, get better; (*sich ausruhen*) rest. **Erholung** f recovery; rest; (*Unterhaltung*) recreation.

erinnern [ɛr'inərn] v remind. **sich erinnern an remember. Erinnerung** f (*pl* -en) memory, remembrance.

erkälten [ɛr'kɛltən] v cool. **sich erkälten** catch (a) cold. **Erkältung** f (*pl* -en) (*Med*) cold.

erkennbar [ɛr'kɛnbair] *adj* recognizable. **erkennen** v recognize; (*Fehler*) acknowledge; (*merken*) perceive.

Erkenntnis¹ [ɛr'kɛntnis] *neut* (*pl* -se) judgment, sentence.

Erkenntnis² f (*pl* -se) recognition; (*Einsicht*) understanding.

Erkenn‖ung [ɛr'kɛnuŋ] f (*pl* -en) recognition. **–ungswort** *neut* password. **–ungszeichen** *neut* distinguishing mark.

Erkerfenster ['ɛrkərfɛnstər] *neut* bay window.

erklären [ɛr'klɛirən] v explain; (*aussprechen*) declare. **sich erklären** declare oneself. **Erklärung** f explanation; declaration.

erkranken [ɛr'kraŋkən] v fall ill, become sick.

erkundigen [ɛr'kundigən] v **sich erkundigen (nach)** inquire (about). **Erkundigung** f inquiry.

erlangen [ɛr'laŋən] v obtain, acquire; (*erreichen*) get to, reach.

Erlaß [ɛr'las] *m* (*pl* **Erlässe**) decree, edict. ***erlassen** [ɛr'lasən] v issue; (*befreien*) release, absolve.

erlauben [ɛr'laubən] v permit. **Erlaubnis** f permission.

erläutern [ɛr'lɔytərn] v explain, elucidate. **Erläuterung** f explanation; *pl* commentary, notes.

erleben [ɛr'leibən] v live through, experience. **Erlebnis** *neut* (*pl* -se) experience.

erledigen [ɛr'leidigən] v take care of, deal with; (*beenden*) finish (off). **erledigt** *adj* settled; (*erschöpft*) exhausted. **Erledigung** f (*pl* -en) carrying out, execution.

erlegen [ɛr'leigən] v kill.

erleichtern [ɛr'laiçtərn] v ease, aid, lighten. **Erleichterung** f (*pl* -en) relief.

*erleiden [ɛr'laidən] v suffer, undergo.

erlernen [ɛr'lɛrnən] v learn, acquire.

Erlös [ɛr'lœis] *m* (*pl* -e) proceeds *pl*.

*erlöschen [ɛr'lœʃən] v go *or* die out.

ermächtigen [ɛr'mɛçtigən] v authorize, empower.

ermahnen [ɛr'mainən] v admonish.

Ermangelung [ɛr'maŋəluŋ] f (*pl* -) **in Ermangelung** in the absence *or* default (of).

ermäßigen [ɛr'mɛisigən] v reduce, lower. **Ermäßigung** f reduction.

ermitteln [ɛr'mitəln] v ascertain, find out.

ermöglichen [ɛr'mœikliçən] v enable, render possible.

ermorden [ɛr'mordən] v murder, assassinate.

ermüden [ɛr'myidən] v tire out; grow tired.

ermuntern [ɛr'muntərn] v encourage, cheer up.

ermutigen [ɛr'muitigən] v encourage. **Ermutigung** f encouragement.

ernähren [ɛr'nɛirən] v feed, nourish. **sich ernähren** support oneself. **Ernährer** *m* breadwinner. **Ernährung** f nourishment.

*ernennen [ɛr'nɛnən] v appoint, designate. **Ernennung** f appointment.

erneuern [ɛr'nɔyərn] v renew; renovate, restore. **Erneuerung** f renewal; renovation. **erneut** *adj* repeated; *adv* again.

erniedrigen [ɛr'niidrigən] v lower; (*degradieren*) degrade, humble.

ernst [ɛrnst] *adj* serious, grave. **Ernst** *m* seriousness, gravity. **im Ernst** in earnest. **ernsthaft** *adj* earnest, serious. **–lich** *adj* serious.

Ernte ['ɛrntə] f (*pl* -n) harvest; (*Wein*) vintage. **ernten** v harvest, reap.

ernüchtern [ɛr'nyçtərn] v disillusion, disenchant; (*vom Rausch*) sober (up). **sich ernüchtern** sober up. **Ernüchterung** f disillusionment; sobering up.

Eroberer [ɛr'oibərər] *m* (*pl* -) conqueror. **erobern** v conquer. **Eroberung** f conquest.

eröffnen [ɛr'œfnən] v open; (*anfangen*) open, begin. **Eröffnung** f opening, beginning.

erörtern [ɛr'œrtərn] v discuss. **Erörterung** f discussion.

Erotik [e'roːtik] *f* (*unz.*) eroticism.
erotisch *adj* erotic.
erpressen [ɛr'prɛsən] *v* (*Sache*) extort; (*Person*) blackmail. **Erpresser** *m* blackmailer. **erpresserisch** *adj* extortionate. **Erpressung** *f* blackmail, extortion.
erproben [ɛr'proːbən] *v* try (out), test. **Erprobung** *f* trial, test.
*****erraten** [ɛr'raːtən] *v* guess.
errechnen [ɛr'rɛçnən] *v* calculate.
erregen [ɛr'reːgən] *v* excite; (*hervorrufen*) create, produce. **erregbar** *adj* excitable. **erregend** *adj* exciting. **erregt** *adj* excited. **Erregung** *f* excitement.
erreichen [ɛr'raiçən] *v* attain, reach. **erreichbar** *adj* attainable. **Erreichung** *f* attainment.
errichten [ɛr'riçtən] *v* erect, build; (*gründen*) set up, establish.
erröten [ɛr'rœːtən] *v* blush.
Errungenschaft [ɛr'rʊŋənʃaft] *f* (*pl* **-en**) achievement.
Ersatz [ɛr'zats] *m* (*unz.*) substitute; (*Wiedergutmachung*) compensation; (*Nachschub*) reinforcements *pl*. **–kaffee** *m* coffee substitute. **–rad** *neut* spare wheel. **–spieler** *m* (*Sport*) substitute. **–teil** *neut* spare part.
*****erschaffen** [ɛr'ʃafən] *v* create. **Erschaffer** *m* creator. **Erschaffung** *f* creation.
*****erscheinen** [ɛr'ʃainən] *v* appear. **Erscheinung** *f* phenomenon; (*Aussehen*) appearance.
*****erschießen** [ɛr'ʃiːsən] *v* shoot (dead). **Erschießungskommando** *neut* firing squad.
*****erschließen** [ɛr'ʃliːsən] *v* open up; (*folgern*) infer, deduce.
erschöpfen [ɛr'ʃœpfən] *v* exhaust, use up; (*Person*) exhaust, tire out. **erschöpft** *adj* exhausted. **Erschöpfung** *f* exhaustion.
*****erschrecken** [ɛr'ʃrɛkən] *v* scare, frighten; be frightened or scared. **Erschrecken** *neut* fright. **erschreckend** *adj* frightening. **erschrocken** [ɛr'ʃrɔkən] *adj* frightened, terrified. **Erschrockenheit** *f* fright, terror.
erschüttern [ɛr'ʃytərn] *v* shake; (*Person*) shake, disturb, shock. **Erschütterung** *f* shock.
erschweren [ɛr'ʃveːrən] *v* make (more) difficult, aggravate.
*****ersehen** [ɛr'zeːən] *v* perceive, see.
ersetzen [ɛr'zɛtsən] *v* replace; (*Schaden*) make good. **ersetzlich** *adj* replaceable, renewable.

ersichtlich [ɛr'ziçtliç] *adj* evident.
*****ersinnen** [ɛr'zinən] *v* contrive, devise.
ersparen [ɛr'ʃpaːrən] *v* save.
erst [ɛirst] *adj* first. *adv* at first; (*nur*) only, just.
erstarren [ɛr'ʃtarən] *v* stiffen, become rigid; (*Flüssigkeit*) congeal, solidify. **Erstarrung** *f* stiffness.
erstatten [ɛr'ʃtatən] *v* restore; (*ersetzen*) replace. **Bericht erstatten** report, make a report. **Erstattung** *f* restitution.
Erstaufführung ['eirstauffyːruŋ] *f* (*pl* **-en**) première, first performance.
erstaunen [ɛr'ʃtaunən] *v* astonish; be astonished. **Erstaunen** *neut* astonishment, amazement. **erstaunlich** *adj* astonishing.
erste(r) ['eirstə(r)], **erste**, **erste(s)** *adj* first.
erstens ['eirstəns] *adv* first(ly).
ersticken [ɛr'ʃtikən] *v* suffocate; (*fig*) stifle. **erstickend** *adj* suffocating. **Erstickung** *f* suffocation; stifling.
erst‖klassig *adj* first-class. **–malig** *adj* for the first time, first-time.
erstrecken [ɛr'ʃtrɛkən] *v* **sich erstrecken** stretch, extend.
ertappen [ɛr'tapən] *v* catch, surprise. **auf frischer Tat ertappen** catch red-handed.
Ertrag [ɛr'traik] *m* (*pl* **Erträge**) profit; (*Boden*) yield. **ertragen** *v* bear, stand. **erträglich** *adj* bearable, tolerable.
ertränken [ɛr'trɛŋkən] *v* (cause to) drown.
*****ertrinken** [ɛr'triŋkən] *v* drown, be drowned.
erwachen [ɛr'vaxən] *v* awake, wake up.
*****erwachsen** [ɛr'vaksən] *v* grow up. **Erwachsene(r)** *m* adult.
erwägen [ɛr'vɛigən] *v* consider, weigh. **Erwägung** *f* consideration.
erwähnen [ɛr'veinən] *v* mention. **Erwähnung** *f* mention.
erwärmen [ɛr'vɛrmən] *v* warm, heat.
erwarten [ɛr'vartən] *v* expect. **über Erwarten** better than expectation. **wider Erwarten** contrary to expectation. **Erwartung** *f* (*pl* **-en**) expectation.
erwecken [ɛr'vɛkən] *v* awaken; (*erregen*) arouse, rouse.
*****erweisen** [ɛr'vaizən] *v* prove; (*Dienst*) render, do; (*Ehrung*) pay. **sich erweisen als** prove to be.
erweitern [ɛr'vaitərn] *v* enlarge, widen, extend. **Erweiterung** *f* (*pl* **-en**) extension, enlargement.

Erwerb [ɛr'vɛrp] *m* (*pl* **-e**) acquisition;
(*Lohn*) earnings. **erwerben** *v* acquire;
(*Verdienen*) earn. **erwerbstätig** *adj* (gain-
fully) employed. **Erwerbung** *f* acquisition.
erwidern [ɛr'viːdərn] *v* reply; (*vergelten*)
retaliate. **Erwiderung** *f* reply.
erwischen [ɛr'viʃən] *v* (*Person*) catch.
erwünscht [ɛr'vynʃt] *adj* desired, wished-
for.
erwürgen [ɛr'vyrgən] *v* strangle.
Erz [ɛrts] *neut* (*pl* **-e**) ore.
erzählen [ɛr'tsɛːlən] *v* tell, relate. **Erzähler**
m narrator; story-teller. **erzählerisch** *adj*
narrative. **Erzählung** *f* story.
Erz‖bischof *n* archbishop. —**engel** *m*
archangel.
erzeugen [ɛr'tsɔygən] *v* (*herstellen*) produce; (*Strom*) generate; (*Kinder*) procreate. **Erzeuger** *m* producer; father, pro-
creator. **Erzeugnis** *neut* product(ion);
(*Boden*) produce.
Erz‖feind *m* arch-enemy. —**herzog** *m*
archduke. —**herzogin** *f* archduchess.
***erziehen** [ɛr'tsiːən] *v* (*Tiere, Menschen*)
bring up; (*Bildung*) educate. **Erzieher** *m*
educator. **erzieherisch** *adj* educational.
Erziehung *f* upbringing; (*Bildung*) education.
erzogen [ɛr'tsoːgən] *adj* **gut/schlecht
erzogen** well/badly brought up.
es [ɛs] *pron* it.
Esche ['ɛʃə] *f* (*pl* **-n**) ash (tree).
Esel ['eːzəl] *m* (*pl* **-**) donkey, ass. **eselhaft**
adj asinine. **Eselsohr** *neut* dog's-ear (on
page).
esoterisch [ezo'teːriʃ] *adj* esoteric.
Essay ['ɛse] *m*, *neut* (*pl* **-s**) essay.
eßbar ['ɛsbar] *adj* edible.
essen ['ɛsən] *v* eat. **zu Mittag essen** lunch,
have lunch. **zu Abend essen** dine, have
supper. **Essen** *neut* food; (*Mahlzeit*)
meal.
Essig ['ɛsiç] *m* (*pl* **-e**) vinegar. —**gurke** *f*
pickled cucumber, gherkin.
Eß‖kastanie *f* sweet chestnut. —**löffel** *m*
tablespoon. —**tisch** *m* dinner table.
—**zimmer** *neut* dining room.
etablieren [eta'bliːrən] *v* establish.
Etage [e'taːʒə] *f* (*pl* **-n**) storey, floor.
—**nwohnung** *f* flat, (*US*) apartment.
Etat [e'taː] *m* (*pl* **-s**) budget; (*Komm*) bal-
ance-sheet.
Ethik ['eːtik] *f* (*unz.*) ethics. **ethisch** *adj*
ethical.

ethnisch ['ɛtniʃ] *adj* ethnic.
Etikett [eti'kɛt] *neut* (*pl* **-e**) tag, label.
Etikette [eti'kɛtə] *f* (*pl* **-n**) etiquette.
etliche ['ɛtliçə] *pron pl* some, several.
Etui [ɛt'viː] *neut* (*pl* **-s**) (small) case;
(*Zigaretten*) cigarette-case; (*Brillen*)
spectacles-case.
etwa ['ɛtva] *adv* about, around; (*vielleicht*)
perhaps.
etwas ['ɛtvas] *pron* something, anything.
adj some, any, a little.
Etymologie [etymolo'giː] *f* (*pl* **-n**) etymology.
euch [ɔyç] *pron* you; (*to*) you.
euer ['ɔyər] *pl adj* your. *pron* yours.
Eule ['ɔylə] *f* (*pl* **-n**) owl.
Eunuch [ɔy'nuːx] *m* (*pl* **-en**) eunuch.
Europa [ɔy'roːpa] *neut* Europe. **Europäer**
m European. **europäisch** *adj* European.
Europäische Gemeinschaften (*EG*) European Community. **Europäische Wirtschaftsgemeinschaft** (*EWG*) European
Economic Community (EEC).
evakuieren [evaku'iːrən] *v* evacuate.
evangelisch [evan'geːliʃ] *adj* Protestant.
Evangelium *neut* gospel.
eventuell [evɛntu'ɛl] *adj* possible. *adv*
possibly, if necessary.
ewig ['eːviç] *adj* eternal, everlasting. **auf
ewig** for ever. **Ewigkeit** *f* eternity.
exakt [ɛ'ksakt] *adj* exact, accurate.
Examen [ɛ'ksaːmən] *neut* (*pl* **-**, *or*
Examina) exam(ination).
Exempel [ɛ'ksɛmpəl] *neut* (*pl* **-**) example.
Exemplar [ɛksɛm'plaːr] *neut* (*pl* **-e**) specimen; (*Buch*) copy.
Exil [ɛ'ksiːl] *neut* (*pl* **-e**) exile.
Existenz [ɛksis'tɛnts] *f* (*pl* **-en**) existence;
(*Unterhalt*) livelihood. **existieren** *v* exist.
exklusiv [ɛksklu'ziːf] *adj* exclusive.
exkommunizieren [ɛkskɔmuni'tsiːrən] *v*
excommunicate.
exotisch [ɛ'ksoːtiʃ] *adj* exotic.
Expedition [ɛkspeditsi'oːn] *f* (*pl* **-en**)
expedition; (*Versendung*) dispatching.
Experiment [ɛksperi'mɛnt] *neut* (*pl* **-e**)
experiment. **experimentell** *adj* experi-
mental. **experimentieren** *v* experiment.
explodieren [ɛksplo'diːrən] *v* explode.
Explosion *f* explosion. **explosiv** *adj*
explosive.
Export [ɛks'pɔrt] *m* (*pl* **-e**) export. —**eur**
m exporter. —**handel** *m* export trade.
exportieren *v* export.

extrem [ɛks'treɪm] *adj* extreme.
Extrem‖ismus *m* extremism. **–ist(in)**
extremist.
Exzentriker [ɛk'tsɛntrikər] *m* (*pl* -) eccentric. **exzentrisch** *adj* eccentric.

F

Fabel ['faɪbəl] *f* (*pl* -n) fable; (*Handlung-
sablauf*) plot. **fabelhaft** *adj* fabulous,
marvellous.
Fabrik [fa'briːk] *f* (*pl* -en) factory. **–ant** *m*
(*pl* -en) manufacturer. **–arbeiter(in)** factory worker. **–at** *neut* (*pl* -e) manufacture. **fabrizieren** *v* manufacture.
Fach [fax] *neut* (*pl* **Fächer**) (*Abteil*) compartment, pigeonhole; (*Wissensgebiet*)
subject; speciality. **–arbeiter** *m* skilled
worker. **–arzt** *m* medical specialist.
fächeln ['fɛçəln] *v* fan. **Fächer** *m* (*pl* -)
fan.
Fach‖mann *m* specialist. **–schule** *f* technical college *or* school. **–sprache** *f* technical language, jargon. **–wort** *neut* technical term. **–zeitschrift** *f* technical journal.
Fackel ['fakəl] *f* (*pl* -n) torch.
fade ['faɪdə] *adj* insipid, boring; (*Essen*)
tasteless.
Faden ['faɪdən] *m* (*pl* **Fäden**) thread.
Fagott [fa'gɔt] *neut* (*pl* -e) bassoon.
fähig ['fɛːɪç] *adj* capable, able. **Fähigkeit** *f*
(*pl* -en) ability.
fahl [faɪl] *adj* pale, sallow.
Fahne ['faɪnə] *f* (*pl* -n) flag, standard;
(*mil*) colours. **Fahnen‖flucht** *f* desertion.
–flüchtige(r) *m* deserter. **–stock** *m*
flagstaff.
Fahrbahn ['faɪrbaɪn] *f* (*Mot*) lane. **fahrbar**
adj passable; (*Wasser*) navigable;
(*beweglich*) mobile.
Fähre ['fɛɪrə] *f* (*pl* -n) ferry.
*fahren ['faɪrən] *v* go, travel; (*Mot, Zug*)
drive; (*Rad, Motorrad*) ride. **Fahrer** *m*
driver.
Fahr‖gast *m* passenger. **–geld** *neut* fare.
–gestell *neut* (*Mot*) chassis; (*Flugzeug*)
undercarriage. **–karte** *f* ticket. **–karten-
schalter** *m* ticket office.
fahrlässig ['faɪrlɛsɪç] *adj* careless, negligent.
Fahr‖plan *m* timetable. **–preis** *m* fare.

–prüfung *f* driving test. **–rad** *neut* bicy-
cle. **–schein** *m* ticket. **–schule** *f* driving
school. **–stuhl** *m* lift, (*US*) elevator.
Fahrt [faɪrt] *f* (*pl* en) drive, journey.
Fährte ['fɛɪrtə] *f* (*pl* -n) track, trail.
Fahrzeug ['faɪrtsɔyk] *neut* vehicle.
Faktur [fak'tuːr] *f* (*pl* -en) *also* **Faktura**
invoice. **fakturieren** *v* invoice.
Fakultät [fakul'tɛːt] *f* (*pl* -en) faculty.
Falke ['falkə] *m* (*pl* -n) hawk, falcon.
Fall [fal] *m* (*pl* **Fälle**) (*Sturz*) fall;
(*Angelegenheit*) case. **–beil** *neut* guillotine. **–brücke** *f* drawbridge.
Falle ['falə] *f* (*pl* -n) trap, snare; (*umg.*)
bed. **in die Falle gehen** go to bed.
*fallen ['falən] *v* fall. **Fallen** *neut* fall,
decline.
fällen ['fɛlən] *v* cut down; (*Urteil*) pass;
(*Chem*) precipitate.
fällig ['fɛlɪç] *adj* due.
falls [fals] *conj* if, in case.
Fall‖schirm *m* (*pl* -e) parachute.
–schirmjäger *m* paratrooper. **–sucht** *f*
epilepsy. **–tür** *f* trapdoor.
falsch [falʃ] *adj* false.
fälschen ['fɛlʃən] *v* falsify, fake; (*Geld*)
counterfeit. **Fälscher** *m* (*pl* -) counterfeit-
er, forger.
Falschheit ['falʃhait] *f* (*pl* -en) falsehood.
Fälschung ['fɛʃuŋ] *f* (*pl* -en) falsification;
(*Geld*) forgery, counterfeiting.
Falte ['faltə] *f* (*pl* -n) crease, fold. **falten** *v*
crease; (*zusammenlegen*) fold.
familiär [famil'jɛɪr] *adj* familiar.
Familie [fa'miːliə] *f* (*pl* -n) family. **–stand**
m personal *or* marital status. **–zulage** *f*
family allowance. **Familien‖name** *m* surname.
famos [fa'mois] *adj* splendid, excellent.
Fanatiker [fa'naɪtikər] *m* (*pl* -) fanatic.
fanatisch *adj* fanatical.
Fanfare [fan'faɪrə] *f* (*pl* -n) fanfare.
Fang [faŋ] *m* (*pl* **Fänge**) catch. **fangen** *v*
catch.
Farbe ['faɪrbə] *f* (*pl* -n) colour. **Farbe
bekennen** show one's colours; (*Karten*)
follow suit.
färben ['fɛrbən] *v* colour, tint; (*Stoff*) dye.
farbenblind ['faɪrbanblint] *adj* colour
blind. **Farb‖fernsehen** *neut* colour television. **-film** *m* colour film. **-stoff** *m* dye.
farbig *adj* coloured. **Farbiger(r)** *m* coloured (man). **farblos** *adj* colourless.
Fasan [fa'zaɪn] *m* (*pl* -e) pheasant.

Fasching ['faʃɪŋ] *m* (*pl* -e) carnival.
Faschismus [fa'ʃɪsmus] *m* (*unz.*) fascism.
Faschist *m* (*pl* -en) fascist. **faschistisch** *adj* fascist.
Faser ['faɪzər] *f* (*pl* -n) fibre; (*fein*) filament. **-stoff** *m* synthetic fibre, man-made material.
Faß [fas] *neut* (*pl* **Fässer**) barrel, cask, vat. **-bier** *neut* draught beer.
Fassade [fa'saɪdə] *f* (*pl* -n) façade.
fassen ['fasən] *v* grasp, seize; (*begreifen*) understand. **sich fassen** pull oneself together; (*ausdrücken*) express oneself.
Fassung *f* (*Kleinod*) mounting; (*Gemütsruhe*) composure; (*Wortlaut*) wording; (*Verständnis*) comprehension. **-skraft** *f* (power of) comprehension.
fast [fast] *adv* almost, nearly.
fasten ['fastən] *v* fast. **Fasten** *neut* fasting. **-zeit** *f* Lent. **Fastnacht** *f* Shrove Tuesday.
fatal [fa'taɪl] *adj* disastrous; (*peinlich*) awkward.
faul [faul] *adj* rotten; (*person*) lazy. **-en** *v* rot. **-enzen** *v* idle, be lazy. **Faul‖enzer** *m* loafer. **-heit** *f* laziness, sloth.
Fäulnis ['fɔylnɪs] *f* rottenness, putrefaction.
Faust [faust] *f* (*pl* **Fäuste**) fist. **-handschuh** *m* mitten.
Februar ['feɪbruaɪr] *m* (*pl* -e) February.
*fechten ['fɛçtən] *v* fence, fight (with swords).
Feder ['feɪdər] *f* (*pl* -n) feather; (*tech*) spring; (*schreiben*) pen. **-bett** *neut* featherbed. **-gewicht** *neut* featherweight. **federleicht** *adj* light as a feather. **Federung** *f* suspension, springs *pl*.
Fee [feɪ] *f* (*pl* -n) fairy.
fegen ['feɪgən] *v* sweep.
Fehde ['feɪdə] *f* (*pl* -n) feud.
fehlbar ['feɪlbaɪr] *adj* fallible. **Fehl‖betrag** *m* deficit. **-druck** *m* misprint; (*Briefmarken*) error. **fehlen** *v* (*mangeln*) be missing *or* lacking; (*abwesend*) be absent; (*irren*) make a mistake. **-d** *adj* missing, absent.
Fehler ['feɪlər] *m* (*pl* -) mistake; (*Schwäche*) weakness; (*Mangel*) defect. **fehler‖frei** *adj* flawless. **-haft** *adj* faulty, defective.
Fehlgeburt ['feɪlgəburt] *f* miscarriage. **fehlschlagen** *v* fail, not succeed. **Fehl‖tritt** *m* false move *or* step, slip. **-zündung** *f* (*Mot*) misfire.

Feier ['faiər] *f* (*pl* -n) festival. **Feierabend** *m* evening leisure time, free time. **Feierabend machen** finish work (for the day). **feierlich** *adj* solemn, ceremonial. **feiern** *v* celebrate. **Feiertag** *m* holiday; (*Festtag*) festival.
feige ['faigə] *adj* cowardly.
Feige ['faigə] *f* (*pl* -n) fig.
Feig‖heit *f* (*unz.*) cowardice. **-ling** *m* coward.
feil [fail] *adj* for sale; (*bestechlich*) venal, corrupt.
Feile ['failə] *f* (*pl* -n) file. **feilen** *v* file.
feilschen ['failʃən] *v* haggle.
fein [fain] *adj* fine.
Feind [faint] *m* (*pl* -e) enemy. **feindlich** *adj* hostile. **Feindschaft** *f* enmity, hostility. **feind/schaftlich** *adj* inimical. **-selig** *adj* hostile.
Fein‖gehaltsstempel *m* hallmark (stamp). **-heit** *f* fineness. **-schmecker** *m* gourmet.
Feld [fɛlt] *neut* (*pl* -er) field; (*Schach*) square. **-bau** *m* agriculture. **-blume** *f* wild flower. **-früchte** *f pl* crops. **-herr** *m* commander(-in-chief). **-messer** *m* surveyor. **-zug** *m* campaign.
Fell [fɛl] *neut* (*pl* -e) skin, hide.
Fels [fɛls] *m* (*pl* -en) rock, boulder. **-enklippe** *f* cliff. **-sturz** *m* rockfall.
Femininum [femi'niːnum] *neut* (*pl* **Feminina**) (*Gramm*) feminine (gender).
Fenster ['fɛnstər] *neut* (*pl* -) window.
Ferien ['feɪrjən] *neut pl* holiday. **in die Ferien gehen** go on holiday. **-kolonie** *f* holiday-camp. **-ort** *m* holiday resort.
Ferkel ['fɛrkəl] *neut* (*pl* -) piglet.
Ferment [fɛr'mɛnt] *neut* (*pl* -e) enzyme, ferment.
fern [fɛrn] *adj* far(away), distant. **-bleiben** *v* stay away. **Ferne** *f* distance. **ferner** *adj* farther; *adv* further; *conj* in addition. **-hin** *adv* in future.
Fern‖gespräch *neut* (*phone*) long-distance call. **-glas** *neut* telescope. **-laster** *m* long-distance lorry. **-lenkung** *f* remote control. **-meldedienst** *m* telecommunications. **-rohr** *neut* telescope. **-schreiber** *m* teletype machine; Telex. **-sehapparat** *m* television (set). **-sehen** *neut* television. *v* watch television. **-sprecher** *m* telephone. **-straße** *f* trunk-road. **-zug** *m* long-distance train.
Ferse ['fɛrzə] *f* (*pl* -n) heel.

fertig ['fɛrtiç] *adj* (*bereit*) ready; (*beendet*) finished. **–en** *v* produce. **Fertigkeit** *f* (*pl* -en) skill, proficiency. **fertigmachen** *v* finish; (*umg.*) beat (into submission).

Fessel ['fɛsəl] *f* (*pl* -n) fetter, chain. **fesseln** *v* fetter, chain. **–d** *adj* fascinating; (*bezaubernd*) enchanting.

fest [fɛst] *adj* firm, secure; (*dicht*) solid.

Fest [fɛst] *neut* (*pl* –e) festival. **–essen** *neut* banquet.

*festhalten ['fɛsthaltən] *v* hold (tight); (*Bild, Buch*) portray; (*anpacken*) seize. **festigen** *v* make firm *or* secure. **Festland** *neut* continent. **festlegen** *v* lay down, fix. **sich festlegen** commit oneself.

festlich ['fɛstliç] *adj* festive. **Festlichkeit** *f* festivity.

fest‖machen *v* fasten; (*vereinbaren*) agree, arrange. **–nehmen** *v* arrest, capture. **–setzen** *v* settle, fix. **Festsetzung** *f* settling, establishment. **fest‖stehen** *v* stand fast. **–stellen** *v* settle; (*herausfinden*) establish, ascertain. **Feststellung** *f* establishment, ascertaining.

Festtag ['fɛsttaɪk] *m* holiday.

Festung ['fɛstuŋ] *f* (*pl* -en) fortress.

Festzug ['fɛsttsuɪk] *m* procession.

fett [fɛt] *adj* fat; (*schmierig*) greasy. **Fett** *neut* (*pl* -e) fat; grease. **fettig** *adj* fatty; greasy.

Fetzen ['fɛtsən] *m* (*pl* -) rag, shred.

feucht [fɔyçt] *adj* damp, moist. **–en** *v* dampen, moisten. **Feuchtigkeit** *f* dampness, moisture.

Feuer ['fɔyər] *neut* (*pl* -) fire. **–alarm** *m* fire alarm. **feuer‖beständig** *or* **–fest** *adj* fireproof. **–gefährlich** *adj* inflammable. **Feuerlöscher** *m* fire extinguisher. **feuern** *v* fire. **Feuer‖schaden** *m* fire damage. **–spritze** *f* fire engine. **–stein** *m* flint. **–waffe** *f* gun. **–wehr** *f* fire brigade, (*US*) fire department. **–wehrmann** *m* fireman. **–zeug** *neut* (cigarette) lighter.

Feuilleton ['fœjətɔ̃] *neut* (*pl* -s) newspaper supplement, review section.

feurig ['fɔyriç] *adj* fiery.

Fiber ['fiːbər] *f* (*pl* -n) fibre.

Fichte ['fiçtə] *f* (*pl* -n) fir, spruce (tree).

Fieber ['fiːbər] *neut* (*pl* -) fever. **fieberartig** *adj* feverish. **fieberhaft** *adj* feverish.

Fiedel ['fiːdəl] *f* (*pl* -n) fiddle, violin. **fiedeln** *v* (play the) fiddle.

Figur [fi'guːr] *f* (*pl* -en) figure; (*Schach*) piece, chessman.

fiktiv [fik'tiːf] *adj* fictitious.

Filiale [fili'aːlə] *f* (*pl* -n) (*Komm*) branch.

Film [film] *m* (*pl* -e) film.

Filter ['filtər] *m* (*pl* -) filter. **filtrieren** *v* filter.

Filz [filts] *m* (*pl* -e) felt; (*Geizhals*) miser.

Finanz [fi'nants] *f* (*pl* -en) finance. **–amt** *neut* tax office, Inland Revenue. **finanziell** *adj* financial. **Finanzier** *m* (*pl* -s) financier. **finanzieren** *v* finance. **Finanz‖jahr** *m* financial year. **–minister** *m* finance minister.

*finden ['findən] *v* find; (*glauben*) think, believe. **Finder** *m* (*pl* -) finder. **findig** *adj* clever, resourceful.

Finger ['fiŋər] *m* (*pl* -) finger. **–abdruck** *m* fingerprint. **–hut** *m* thimble; (*Bot*) foxglove. **–nagel** *m* fingernail. **–spitze** *f* fingertip.

Fink [fiŋk] *m* (*pl* -en) finch.

Finne ['finə] *m* (*pl* -), **Finnin** *f* (*pl* -nen) Finn. **finnisch** *adj* Finnish. **Finnland** *neut* Finland. **Finnländer(in)** *f* Finn.

finster ['finstər] *adj* dark; (*düster*) gloomy; (*drohend*) foreboding. **Finsternis** *f* darkness; gloom.

Firma ['firmə] *f* (*pl* **Firmen**) firm, business.

Firnis ['firnis] *m* (*pl* -se) varnish.

Fisch [fiʃ] *m* (*pl* -e) fish. **Fische** *pl* (*Astrol*) Pisces. **fischen** *v* fish. **Fischer** *m* (*pl* -) fisherman. **–boot** *neut* fishing boat. **–ei** *f* fishing. **–korb** *m* creel. **–otter** *m or f* otter. **–reiher** *m* heron. **–zeug** *neut* (*fishing*) tackle.

fix [fiks] *adj* firm; (*fig*) quick.

flach [flax] *adj* flat, even; (*nicht tief*) shallow; (*uninteressant*) dull.

Fläche ['flɛçə] *f* (*pl* -n) flatness; (*Gebiet*) area; (*Oberfläche*) surface. **–ninhalt** *m* surface area.

Flachs [flaks] *m* (*unz.*) flax.

flackerig ['flakəriç] *adj* flickering. **flackern** *v* flicker, flare.

Flagge ['flagə] *f* (*pl* -n) flag.

Flamme ['flamə] *f* (*pl* -n) flame. **flammen** *v* flame, blaze.

Flanell [fla'nɛl] *m* (*pl* -e) flannel.

Flanke ['flaŋkə] *f* (*pl* -n) flank. **flankieren** *v* (out)flank.

Flasche ['flaʃə] *f* (*pl* -n) bottle. **Flaschen–** *adj* cylindrical. **Flaschenöffner** *m* bottle-opener.

flattern ['flatərn] *v* flutter.

flau [flau] *adj* weak; (*Getränke*) flat; (*Komm*) slack, dull.

Flaum [flaum] *m* (*unz.*) down. **flaumig** *adj* downy.

Flaute ['flautə] *f* (*pl* -n) lull, calm; (*Wirtschaft*) recession.

Flechte ['flɛçtə] *f* (*pl* -n) braid; (*Bot*) lichen; (*Med*) ringworm, herpes. **flechten** *v* braid, interweave; (*Korb*) weave. **Flechtkorb** *m* wicker basket.

Fleck [flɛk] *m* (*pl* -e) stain, spot; (*Makel*) blemish, flaw. **flecken** *v* stain.

Fledermaus ['fleːdərmaus] *f* bat.

flehen ['fleːən] *v* implore, entreat (for). **-tlich** *adj* imploring.

Fleisch [flaiʃ] *neut* (*unz.*) meat. **-brühe** *f* (meat) stock. **Fleischer** *m* (*pl* -) butcher. **-ei** *f* (*pl* -en) butcher's (shop). **fleisch||farbig** *adj* flesh-coloured. **-fressend** *adj* carnivorous. **-ig** *adj* fleshy. **-lich** *adj* carnal. **Fleisch||topf** *m* meat saucepan; (*fig*) fleshpot. **-werdung** *f* (*Rel*) Incarnation. **-wolf** *m* mincer.

Fleiß [flais] *m* (*unz.*) diligence, industry. **fleißig** *adj* industrious, hard-working.

Flick [flik] *n* (*pl* -en) patch. **-arbeit** *f* patching; (*Pfuscherei*) botch. **flicken** *v* mend, patch.

Fliege ['fliːgə] *f* (*pl* -n) fly. **fliegen** *v* fly. **Flieger** *m* (*pl* -) aviator, flier. **-abwehr** *f* anti-aircraft defence.

*fliehen ['fliːən] *v* flee.

Fließband ['fliːsbant] *neut* conveyor belt, assembly line. **fließen** *v* flow. **fließend** *adj* flowing, running.

flimmern ['flimərn] *v* glimmer, twinkle.

flink [fliŋk] *adj* nimble, agile.

Flinte ['flintə] *f* (*pl* -n) musket; (*Schrot*) shotgun.

flirten ['flirtən] *v* flirt.

Flitterwochen ['flitərvɔxən] *f pl* honeymoon *sing*.

Flocke ['flɔkə] *f* (*pl* -n) flake; (*Wolle, Haar*) flock, tuft. **flocken** *v* fall in flakes. **flockig** *adj* flaky; (*Haar, usw.*) fluffy.

Floh [floː] *m* (*pl* Flöhe) flea. **-stich** *m* fleabite.

Floskel ['flɔskəl] *f* (*pl* -n) flowery *or* fine phrase.

Floß [floːs] *neut* (*pl* Flöße) raft.

Flosse ['flɔsə] *f* (*pl* -n) fin.

Flöte ['flœːtə] *f* (*pl* -n) flute. **flöten** *v* play the flute. **Flötist(in)** flautist.

flott [flɔt] *adj* brisk; (*Schnell*) fast;

(*schick*) smart; (*schwimmend*) afloat. **Flotte** *f* fleet, navy.

Flöz [flœːts] *neut* (*pl* -e) (*Mineralien*) seam.

Fluch [fluːx] *m* (*pl* Flüche) curse; (*Fluchwort*) swear-word. **fluchen** *v* swear, curse.

Flucht [fluxt] *f* (*pl* -en) flight, escape; (*Reihe*) row.

flüchtig ['flyçtiç] *adj* fleeting, cursory. **Flüchtling** *m* (*pl* -e) refugee.

Flug [fluːk] *m* (*pl* Flüge) flight, flying; (*Vögel*) flock. **-bahn** *f* trajectory. **-blatt** *neut* handbill, pamphlet. **Flügel** ['flyːgəl] *m* (*pl* -) wing; (*Klavier*) grand piano. **-fenster** *neut* French window.

Flug||gast *m* air passenger. **-hafen** *m* airport. **-post** *f* air-mail. **-schiff** *m* flyingboat. **-schrift** *f* pamphlet. **-wesen** *neut* aviation, flying. **-zeug** *neut* aeroplane. **-zeug-halle** *f* hangar. **-zeug-träger** *m* aircraft-carrier.

flunkern ['fluŋkərn] *v* fib, lie; (*übertreiben*) exaggerate, brag.

Flur [fluːr] *m* (*pl* -e) floor; (entrance) hall.

Fluß [flus] *m* (*pl* Flüsse) river. **fluß||abwärts** *adv* downstream. **-aufwärts** *adv* upstream. **Flussfisch** *m* fresh-water fish.

flüssig ['flysiç] *adj* liquid. **Flüssigkeit** *f* liquid.

flüstern ['flystərn] *v* whisper.

Flut [fluːt] *f* (*pl* -en) flood; (*Hochwasser*) (high) tide. **Ebbe und Flut** ebb and flow. **fluten** *v* flood.

Fohlen ['foːlən] *neut* (*pl* -) foal.

Föhn [fœn] *m* (*pl* -e) (warm) south wind.

Folge ['fɔlgə] *f* (*pl* -n) succession; (*Wirkung*) consequence. **folgen** *v* follow; (*gehorchen*) obey. **folgend** *adj* (the) following. **-ermaßen** *adv* as follows. **folgerichtig** *adj* consistent, logical. **folgern** *v* conclude, infer. **Folgerung** *f* (*pl* -en) conclusion, inference. **folgewidrig** *adj* inconsistent, illogical. **folglich** *adv* consequently.

Folter ['fɔltər] *f* (*pl* -n) torture; (*Gerät*) rack. **foltern** *v* torture. **Folterung** *f* torture, torturing.

Fön [fœn] *m* (*pl* -e) hairdrier.

Fonds [fɔ̃] *m* (*pl* -) fund.

Förderer ['fœrdərər] *m* (*pl* -) promoter, sponsor. **förderlich** *adj* useful, beneficial.

fordern ['fɔrdərn] *v* demand; (*beanspruchen*) claim.

fördern ['fœirdərn] *v* further, promote.

Forderung ['fɔrdəruŋ] *f* (*pl* -en) demand.

Förderung ['fœirdəruŋ] *f* (*pl* -en) furtherance, advancement; (*Komm*) promotion; (*Kohle*) mining.

Forelle [fo'rɛlə] *f* (*pl* -n) trout.

Form [fɔrm] *f* (*pl* -en) form; (tech, Kuchen) mould. **in Form** (*sport*) fit, on form. **Formel** *f* (*pl* -n) formula. **form‖ell** *adj* formal. –**en** *v* form, shape. –**los** *adj* shapeless, formless. **Formular** *neut* (*pl* -e) (question) form, (*US*) blank. **formulieren** *v* formulate.

forschen ['fɔrʃən] *v* investigate; (*fragen*) inquire; (*Wissenschaft*) do research. **forschend** *adj* searching. **Forscher** *m* (*pl* -) investigator, enquirer; researcher. **Forschung** *f* (*pl* -en) investigation; research.

Forst [fɔrst] *m* (*pl* -e) forest.

Förster ['fœirstər] *m* (*pl* -) forester.

Forstwirtschaft ['fɔrstvirtʃaft] *f* forestry.

fort [fɔrt] *adv* away; (*vorwärts*) forward(s); (*weiter*) on.

fortan [fɔrt'an] *adv* from now on.

*****fortbestehen** ['fɔrtbəʃteiən] *v* continue (to exist), live on, survive.

Fortbildung ['fɔrtbilduŋ] *f* further education.

*****fortbleiben** ['fɔrtblaibən] *v* remain away.

fortdauern ['fɔrtdauərn] *v* last, continue. –**d** *adj* continual, incessant.

*****fortfahren** ['fɔrtfairən] *v* drive away, depart; (*weitermachen*) proceed, continue.

*****fortgehen** ['fɔrtgeiən] *v* go away.

fortgeschritten ['fɔrtgəʃritən] *adj* advanced.

*****fortkommen** ['fɔrtkɔmən] *v* escape; (*fig*) prosper, make progress.

*****fortlaufen** ['fɔrtlaufən] *v* run away; (*fortkommen*) escape; (*weiterlaufen*) continue. –**d** *adj* continuous.

fortleben ['fɔrtleibən] *v* survive. **Fortleben** *neut* survival; (*nach dem Tode*) afterlife.

fortpflanzen ['fɔrtpflantsən] *v* **sich fortpflanzen** reproduce, multiply; (*Krankheit*) spread.

*****fortschreiten** ['fɔrtʃraitən] *v* go forward, proceed.

Fortschritt ['fɔrtʃrit] *m* (*pl* -e) progress. **fortschrittlich** *adj* progressive.

fortsetzen ['fɔrtzɛtsən] *v* continue. **Fortsetzung** *f* continuation.

fortwährend ['fɔrtvɛirənt] *adj* continuous, incessant.

Fossil [fɔ'siil] *neut* (*pl* -ien) fossil.

Foto ['foito] *neut* (*pl* -s) (*umg.*) photo.

Fötus ['fœtus] *m* (*pl* -se) foetus.

Fracht [fraxt] *f* (*pl* -en) freight. –**brief** *m* consignment *or* dispatch note. –**gut** *neut* cargo, goods. –**schiff** *neut* merchantman.

Frack [frak] *m* (*pl* **Fräcke**) dresscoat, tails. –**hemd** *neut* dress shirt. –**zwang** *m* obligatory evening dress, formal dress.

Frage ['fraigə] *f* (*pl* -n) question. –**bogen** *m* questionnaire. **fragen** *v* ask. **Fragezeichen** *neut* question mark. **frag‖lich** *adj* in question, doubtful. –**los** *adj* unquestionable.

Fragment [frag'mɛnt] *neut* (*pl* -e) fragment.

fragwürdig [fraikvurdiç] *adj* questionable.

Fraktion [fraktsi'oin] *f* (*pl* -en) (*Pol*) parliamentary party, faction.

Fraktur [frak'tuir] *f* (*pl* -en) fracture; (*Druck*) Gothic type *or* script.

frankieren [fraŋ'kiirən] *v* (*Brief*) stamp; (*Päckchen*) pre-pay. **franko** *adv* post paid.

Frankreich ['fraŋkraiç] *neut* France.

Franse ['franzə] *f* (*pl* -n) fringe. **fransig** *adj* fringed; (*ausgefasert*) frayed.

Franzose [fran'tsoizə] *m* (*pl* -n) Frenchman. **Französin** *f* (*pl* -nen) Frenchwoman. **französisch** *adj* French.

Fratze ['fratsə] *f* (*pl* -n) grimace. **Fratzen schneiden** make *or* pull faces.

Frau [frau] *f* (*pl* -en) woman; (*Ehefrau*) wife; (*Titel*) Mrs. **Frauen‖arzt** *m* gynaecologist. –**befreiung** *f* women's liberation. **frauenhaft** *adj* womanly. **Frauen‖rechtlerin** *f* (*pl* -nen) feminist. –**welt** *f* womankind, women *pl*.

Fräulein ['frɔylain] *neut* (*pl* -) young lady; (*Titel*) Miss.

frech [frɛç] *adj* cheeky, insolent. **Frechheit** *f* cheek, insolence.

frei [frai] *adj* free; (*nicht besetzt*) vacant, unoccupied; (*offen*) candid.

Freibad ['fraibat] *neut* outdoor swimming pool.

freiberuflich ['fraibərufliç] *adj* freelance, self-employed, professional.

Freibrief ['fraibriif] *m* charter.

Freie ['fraiə] *neut* (*unz.*) outdoors, open air. **im Freien** in the open air.

Freigabe ['fraigaɪbə] *f* release.
*freigeben ['fraigeɪbən] *v* set free;
(*Straße, usw.*) open; (*Waren, Arznei*)
pass, approve, decontrol. **freigebig** *adj*
generous.
Freihandel ['fraihandəl] *m* free-trade.
Freiheit ['fraihait] *f* (*pl* -en) freedom, liberty. **freiheitlich** *adj* liberal.
Freiherr ['fraihɛr] *m* (*pl* -) baron. −in *f*
(*pl* -nen) baroness.
Freikarte ['fraikaɪrtə] *f* complimentary
ticket.
*freilassen ['frailasən] *v* set free.
freilich ['frailɪç] *adv* certainly, indeed, of
course.
freimachen ['fraimaxən] *v* deliver (from
captivity), release.
Freimaurer ['fraimaurər] *m* (*pl* -) freemason.
Freimut ['fraimuːt] *m* (*unz.*) candour,
frankness. **freimütig** *adj* candid, frank.
*freisprechen ['fraiʃprɛçən] *v* acquit, discharge.
Freitag ['fraitaɪk] *m* Friday.
freiwillig ['fraivilɪç] *adj* voluntary.
Freizeit ['fraitsait] *f* leisure time, spare
time.
fremd [frɛmt] *adj* strange; (*ausländisch*)
foreign. **Fremde(r)** stranger; foreigner.
Fremd‖enzimmer *neut* guest room. −**heit**
f strangeness. −**körper** *m* foreign body.
−**sprache** *f* foreign language. −**wort** *neut*
foreign word, loan word.
Frequenz [fre'kvɛnts] *f* (*pl* -en) frequency.
*fressen ['frɛsən] *v* eat, devour.
Freude ['frɔydə] *f* (*pl* -n) joy; (*Vergnügen*)
delight. −**ntag** *m* red-letter day. **freudig**
adj joyful, joyous.
freuen ['frɔən] *v* give pleasure to. **es freut
mich** I am glad *or* pleased. **sich freuen** be
glad, rejoice. **sich freuen auf** look forward to.
Freund [frɔynt] *m* (*pl* -e) friend;
(*Liebhaber*) boyfriend. −**in** *f* (*pl* -nen)
(girl) friend. **freundlich** *adj* friendly;
(*liebenswürdig*) kind. **Freund‖lichkeit** *f*
friendliness. −**schaft** *f* friendship. **freundschaftlich** *adj* friendly.
Frevel ['freːfəl] *m* (*pl* -) sacrilege.
frevelhaft *adj* sacrilegious.
Friede(n) ['friːdə(n)] *m* (*pl* -) peace.
Friedens‖bruch *m* breach of the peace.
−**stifter** *m* peacemaker. −**vertrag** *m*
peace (treaty). **Friedhof** *m* cemetary
friedlich *adj* peaceful.

*frieren ['friːrən] *v* freeze.
Frikadelle [frika'dɛlə] *f* (*pl* -n) rissole.
frisch [friʃ] *adj* fresh; (*lebhaft*) lively.
Frische *f* freshness; liveliness.
Friseur [fri'zœːr] *m*, (*pl* -e) **Friseuse** *f* (*pl*
-n) hairdresser; (*nur für Herren*) barber.
frisieren *v* cut *or* style hair; (*Bücher*)
cook, falsify; (*Mot*) soup up. **Frisiersalon**
m hairdressing salon.
Frist [frist] *f* (*pl* -en) period, time;
(*Termin*) time limit, deadline.
Frisur [fri'zuːr] *f* (*pl* en) hairstyle; (*umg.*)
hairdo.
froh [froː] *adj* glad, cheerful, happy.
fröhlich ['frœːlɪç] *adj* cheerful, joyous.
Fröhlichkeit *f* cheerfulness.
frohlocken ['froːlɔkən] *v* rejoice. **Frohsinn**
m gaiety.
fromm [frɔm] *adj* pious, religious.
frömmelnd ['frœməlnd] *adj* religiose, hypocritical. **Frömmler** *m* hypocritic.
Fronleichnam [froːn'laiçnaɪm] *m* Corpus
Christi Day.
Front [frɔnt] *f* (*pl* -en) front, face; (*Pol*)
front. −**antrieb** *m* front-wheel drive.
Frosch [frɔʃ] *m* (*pl* **Frösche**) frog;
(*Feuerwerk*) squib, banger.
Frost [frɔst] *m* (*pl* **Fröste**) frost; (*Kälte*)
coldness, chill. −**beule** *f* chilblain. **frostig**
adj chilly, frosty. **Frostschutzmittel** *neut*
antifreeze.
Frucht [fruxt] *f* (*pl* **Früchte**) fruit.
fruchtbar *adj* fertile. **Fruchtbarkeit** *f* fertility. **fruchtlos** *adj* fruitless. **Fruchtsaft** *m*
fruit juice.
früh [fryː] *adj* early. **Frühe** *f* early hour,
early morning. **früher** *adj* earlier;
(*ehemalig*) former. **frühestens** *adv* earliest.
Früh‖geburt *f* premature birth. −**jahr**
neut spring. −**ling** *m* spring. −**reife** *f* pre-
cocity. −**stück** *neut* breakfast.
früh‖stücken *v* breakfast. −**zeitig** *adj*
premature, untimely; (*rechtzeitig*) early,
in good time.
Fuchs [fuks] *m* (*pl* **Füchse**) fox.
Füchsin ['fyçsin] *f* (*pl* -nen) vixen.
Fuge ['fuɪgə] *f* (*pl* -n) joint; (*Musik*)
fugue.
fügen ['fyɪgən] *v* join together; (*ordnen*)
dispose. **sich fügen** submit. **fügsam** *adj*
submissive, obedient.
fühlen ['fyːlən] *v* touch, feel. **sich fühlen**
feel. **sich glücklich fühlen** feel *or* be hap-

py. **Fühlen** *neut* feeling. **Fühler** *m* feeler.
Fühlung *f* touch.
führen ['fyɪrən] *v* lead, direct; (*Waren*)
stock, carry; (*Bücher*) keep. **–d** *adj*
prominent, leading. **Führer** *m* leader,
guide. **–haus** *neut* (*Zug*) driver's cab.
–schaft *f* leadership. **–schein** *m* driving
licence, (*US*) driver's license. **–sitz** *m*
driver's *or* pilot's seat. **Führung** *f* command, management.
Fülle ['fylə] *f* (*pl* **-n**) abundance, plenty.
Hülle und Fülle plentiful, in plenty. **fül-
len** *v* fill (up). **Füll**||**feder** *f* fountain-pen.
–ung *f* (*pl* **–en**) filling.
Fundament [fundaˈmɛnt] *neut* (*pl* **-e**)
foundation, base.
fünf [fynf] *adj* five. **fünft** *adj* fifth. **Fünftel**
neut fifth. **fünf**||**zehn** *pron, adj* fifteen.
fungieren [fuŋˈgiɪrən] *v* function (as), act
(as).
Funk [fuŋk] *m* (*unz.*) radio, wireless. **–e**
m (*pl* **-n**) spark. **funkeln** *v* sparkle. **Funksendung** *f* (*Radio*) programme transmission.
Funktion [fuŋktsiˈoɪn] *f* (*pl* **-en**) function.
–är *m* (*pl* **-e**) functionary. **funktionieren**
v function.
für [fyɪr] *prep* for.
Furche ['furçə] *f* (*pl* **-n**) furrow; (*Runzel*)
wrinkle. **furchen** *v* furrow.
Furcht [furçt] *f* (*unz.*) fear. **furchtbar** *adj*
frightful.
fürchten ['fyɪrçtən] *v* fear. **sich fürchten
vor** be afraid of. **fürchterlich** *adj* terrible,
dreadful.
Furnier [furˈniɪr] *neut* (*pl* **-e**) veneer.
Fürsorge ['fyɪrzɔrgə] *f* care; (*Hilfstä-
tigkeit*) welfare work; (*Geld*) social security. **–arbeit** *f* social work.
Fürsprecher ['fyɪrʃprɛçər] *m* advocate.
fürsprechen *v* intercede.
Fürst [fyrst] *m* (*pl* **-en**) prince. **–in** *f* (*pl*
-nen) princess. **fürstlich** *adj* princely.
Furz [furts] *m* (*pl* **Fürze**) (*vulgär*) fart.
furzen *v* fart.
Fuß [futs] *m* (*pl* **Füße**) foot. **–ball** *m*
football. **–boden** *m* floor. **–bremse** *f*
footbrake. **–gänger** *m* pedestrian.
–pflege *f* chiropody. **–steig** *m* pavement, (*US*) sidewalk. **–tritt** *m* kick;
(*Gang*) step. **–volk** *neut* infantry. **–weg**
m footpath.
Futter ['futər] *neut* (*pl* **-**) feed, fodder;
(*Kleider*) lining.

füttern ['fytərn] *v* feed; line. **Fütterung** *f*
feeding, fodder; lining.

G

Gabe ['gaɪbə] *f* (*pl* **-n**) gift.
Gabel ['gaɪbəl] *f* (*pl* **-n**) fork. **gabeln** *v*
fork. **Gabelung** *f* fork, branching.
gackern ['gakərn] *v* cackle.
gähnen ['gɛɪnən] *v* yawn.
galant [gaˈlant] *adj* polite, gallant.
Galeere [gaˈleɪrə] *f* (*pl* **-n**) galley.
Galerie [galəˈriɪ] *f* (*pl* **-n**) gallery.
Galgen ['galgən] *m* (*pl* **-**) gallows *pl*.
Galle ['galə] *f* (*pl* **-n**) gall, bile; (*fig*) rancour.
Gallen||**blase** ['galənˌblaɪzə] *f* gallbladder.
–stein *m* gallstone.
Galopp [gaˈlɔp] *m* (*pl* **-e**) gallop. **galoppieren** *v* gallop.
galvanisieren [galvaniˈziɪrən] *v* galvanize.
Gang [gaŋ] *m* (*pl* **Gänge**) walk; (*Gangart*)
gait; (*Flur*) corridor; (*Essen*) course;
(*Mot*) gear. **im Gang** in motion.
Gang||**art** *f* gait. **–schalter** *m* gear lever.
Gans [gans] *f* (*pl* **Gänse**) goose.
Gänse||**blume** ['gɛnzəbluɪmə] *f* daisy.
–braten *m* roast goose. **–füßchen** *pl*
quotation marks. **–rich** *m* gander.
ganz [gants] *adj* whole, all; (*vollständig*)
complete. *adv* quite; (*vollends*) fully.
Ganze *neut* whole.
gar [gaɪr] *adj* (*Kochen*) done, cooked. *adv*
very. **gar nicht** not at all. **gar keiner** none
whatever.
Garantie [garanˈtiɪ] *f* (*pl* **-n**) guarantee.
Garde ['gardə] *f* (*pl* **-n**) guard.
Garderobe [gardəˈroɪbə] *f* (*pl* **-n**) cloakroom; (*Kleider*) wardrobe.
Gardine [garˈdiɪnə] *f* (*pl* **-n**) curtain.
*gären ['gɛɪrən] *v* ferment.
garnieren [garˈniɪrən] *v* garnish;
(*Kleidung*) trim.
Garnison [garniˈzoɪn] *f* (*pl* **-en**) garrison.
Garnitur [garniˈtuɪr] *f* (*pl* **-en**)
(*Verzierung*) trimming; (*Satz*) set; (*Aus-
rüstung*) equipment.
Garten ['gartən] *m* (*pl* **Gärten**) garden.
–bau *m* horticulture. **–haus** *neut* sum-
mer house. **–laube** *f* arbour.
Gärtner ['gɛrtnər] *m* (*pl* **-**) gardener. **–ei**
f (*pl* **-en**) nursery.

Gärung ['gɛːruŋ] *f* (*pl* -en) fermentation.
Gas [gaɪs] *neut* (*pl* -e) gas. **-flasche** *f* gas cylinder *or* bottle. **-hebel** *m* accelerator. **-hahn** *m* gas cock. **-herd** *m* gas cooker.
Gasse ['gasə] *f* (*pl* -n) alley, lane.
Gast [gast] *m* (*pl* Gäste) guest. **gastfreundlich** *adj* hospitable. **Gast‖freundschaft** *f* hospitality. **-geber** *m* (*pl* -) host. **-geberin** *f* (*pl* -nen) hostess. **-hof** *m* hotel, inn. **-mahl** *neut* banquet. **-stätte** *f* restaurant, café. **-wirt** *m* landlord, innkeeper.
Gatte ['gatə] *m* (*pl* -n) spouse, husband, **gatten** *v* match. **Gattin** *f* (*pl* -nen) spouse, wife.
Gattung ['gatuŋ] *f* (*pl* -en) sort, kind; (*Biol*) species.
gaukeln ['gaukəln] *v* perform tricks, juggle.
Gaul [gaul] *m* (*pl* Gäule) nag.
Gaumen ['gaumən] *m* (*pl* -) palate.
Gauner ['gaunər] *m* (*pl* -) swindler, trickster.
Gaze ['gaɪzə] *f* (*pl* -n) gauze.
Gazelle [ga'tsɛlə] *f* (*pl* -n) gazelle.
geartet [gə'aɪrtət] *adj* constituted, composed.
Gebäck [gə'bɛk] *neut* (*pl* -e) pastry, cakes; (*Keks*) biscuit.
Gebärde [gə'bɛɪrdə] *f* (*pl* -n) gesture.
***gebären** [gə'bɛɪrən] *v* give birth to, bear. **Gebärmutter** *f* womb.
Gebäude [gə'bɔydə] *neut* (*pl* -) building.
***geben** ['geɪbən] *v* give. **sich geben** relent, abate. **es gibt** there is/are. **was gibt es?** what is the matter? **sich zufrieden geben** be content. **das gibt's nicht!** that's impossible! **Geben** *neut* giving. **Geber** *m* (*pl* -), **Geberin** *f* (*pl* -nen) giver, donor.
Gebet [gə'beɪt] *neut* (*pl* -e) prayer. **-buch** *neut* prayerbook.
Gebiet [gə'biɪt] *neut* (*pl* -e) (*Staats-*) territory; (*Gegend*) area, district; (*fig*) field, sphere.
Gebilde [gə'bildə] *neut* (*pl* -) (*Erzeugnis*) product; (*Form*) structure, shape.
gebildet [gə'bildət] *adj* educated, cultured.
Gebirge [gə'birgə] *neut* (*pl* -) mountain range, mountains *pl*.
Gebiß [gə'bis] *neut* (*pl* Gebisse) (set of) teeth; (*Zaum*) bit; (*künstlich*) denture.
Gebläse [gə'blɛɪzə] *neut* (*pl* -) blower, bellows *pl*; (*Mot*) supercharger.
geboren [gə'bɔɪrən] *adj* born. *geborener*

Hamburger native of Hamburg. *Frau Maria Müller, geborene (geb.) Schmidt* Mrs. Maria Müller, *nee* Schmidt.
Gebot [gə'boɪt] *neut* (*pl* -e) order. **die zehn Gebote** the Ten Commandments.
Gebrauch [gə'braux] *neut* (*pl* Gebräuche) custom; (*Benutzen*) use. **gebrauchen** *v* use. **gebräuchlich** *adj* customary. **Gebrauchs‖anweisung** *f or* **-anleitung** *f* instructions (for use). **Gebrauchtwagen** *m* second-hand car.
gebrechlich [gə'brɛçliç] *adj* (*Gegenstand*) fragile; (*Person*) frail.
Gebrüder [gə'bryɪdər] *m pl* brothers. **Gebrüder Schmidt** Schmidt Bros.
Gebrüll [gə'bryl] *neut* (*unz.*) roar, roaring.
Gebühr [gə'byɪr] 1 *f* (*pl* -en) fee, charge. 2 *f* (*unz.*) decency, propriety. **nach Gebühr** duly. **gebühren** *v* be due. **sich gebühren** be fitting *or* decent. **gebührend** *adj* seemly, proper.
gebunden [gə'bundən] *adj* bound.
Geburt [gə'burt] *f* (*pl* -en) birth. **Geburten‖beschränkung** *f or* **-regelung** *f* birth control. **gebürtig** *adj* born (in). **Geburts‖fehler** *m* congenital defect. **-helfer** *m* obstetrician. **-helferin** *f* midwife; (*Ärztin*) obstetrician. **-hilfe** *f* obstetrics. **-mal** *neut* mole. **-ort** *m* birthplace. **-schein** *m* birth certificate. **-tag** *m* birthday.
Gebüsch [gə'byʃ] *neut* (*pl* -e) (clump of) bushes.
Gedächtnis [gə'dɛçtnis] *neut* (*pl* -se) memory. **-feier** *f* commemoration. **-schwund** *m* loss of memory, amnesia.
Gedanke [gə'daŋkə] *m* (*pl* -n) thought. **sich Gedanken machen über** worry about. **gedankenlos** *adj* thoughtless. **gedanklich** *adj* mental.
Gedeck [gə'dɛk] *neut* (*pl* -e) cover, place-setting; menu.
***gedeihen** [gə'daiən] *v* flourish, thrive.
***gedenken** [gə'dɛŋkən] *v* think (of); (*vorhaben*) intend. **Gedenkfeier** *f* commemoration.
Gedicht [gə'diçt] *neut* (*pl* -e) poem. **-sammlung** *f* anthology (of verse).
gediegen [gə'diɪgən] *adj* (*echt*) genuine; (*rein*) pure; (*solide*) solid; (*sorgfältig*) thorough.
Gedränge [gə'drɛŋə] *neut* (*unz.*) crowd, press; (*Notlage*) difficulty. **gedrängt** *adj* narrow, close; (*Stil*) terse, concise.

gedruckt [gə'drukt] *adj* printed.
gedrückt [gə'drykt] *adj* depressed.
Geduld [gə'dult] *f* patience. **geduldig** *adj* patient. **Geduldspiel** *neut* puzzle.
geehrt [gə'eɪrt] *adj* honoured. **sehr geehrter Herr (Smith)** Dear Sir (Dear Mr Smith).
geeignet [gə'aignət] *adj* suitable, adapted (to).
Gefahr [gə'faɪr] *f* (*pl* **-en**) danger. **gefährden** *v* endanger, jeopardize. **gefährlich** *adj* dangerous. **gefahr‖los** *adj* safe, without risk. **-voll** *adj* dangerous.
Gefährte [gə'fɛɪrtə] *m* (*pl* **-n**), **Gefährtin** *f* (*pl* **-nen**) companion.
***gefallen** [gə'falən] *v* please. **es gefällt mir** I like it. **sich nicht gefallen lassen** not put up with.
Gefallen¹ [gə'falən] *neut* (*unz.*) pleasure.
Gefallen² *m* (*pl* **-**) favour. **tun Sie mir den Gefallen und ...** Do me the favour of . . . .
gefällig [gə'fɛliç] *adj* pleasing; obliging.
gefangen [gə'faŋən] *adj* captive. **Gefangene(r)** *m* prisoner, captive. **Gefangenschaft** *f* captivity.
Gefängnis [gə'fɛŋnis] *neut* (*pl* **-se**) prison. **-wärter** *m* warder, prison officer.
Gefäß [gə'fɛis] *neut* (*pl* **-e**) container, vessel.
gefaßt [gə'fast] *adj* collected, calm, (*bereit*) ready.
Gefecht [gə'fɛçt] *neut* (*pl* **-e**) fight, combat.
Gefieder [gə'fiːdər] *neut* (*unz.*) feathers *pl*, plumage.
Geflügel [gə'flyɪgəl] *neut* (*unz.*) poultry.
Gefolge [gə'fɔlgə] *neut* (*pl* **-**) followers *pl*, entourage.
gefräßig [gə'frɛisiç] *adj* voracious, gluttonous.
Gefrier‖punkt [gə'friɪrpuŋkt] *m* freezing point. **-schutzmittel** *neut* antifreeze.
gefügig [gə'fyɪgiç] *adj* pliant, submissive.
Gefühl [gə'fyɪl] *neut* (*pl* **-e**) feeling. **gefühllos** *adj* unfeeling. **Gefühlssinn** *m* sense of touch. **gefühlvoll** *adj* full of feeling, emotional.
gegebenenfalls [gə'geɪbənənfals] *adv* if need be, should the need arise.
Gegebenheit *f* (*pl* **-en**) reality.
gegen ['geɪgən] *prep* against; (*in Richtung*) towards; (*ungefähr*) about; compared with; (*Tausch*) in exchange for.

Gegen‖angriff *m* counterattack. **-besuch** *m* return visit. **-bild** *neut* counterpart.
Gegend ['geɪgənt] *f* (*pl* **-en**) district, area.
gegeneinander ['geɪgənainandər] *adv* against one another. **-stoßen** *v* collide.
Gegen‖gift *neut* antidote. **-leistung** *f* return (service). **-mittel** *neut* remedy. **-satz** *m* opposite, contrary. **gegen‖sätzlich** *adj* opposite, contrary. **-seitig** *adj* reciprocal, mutual. **Gegen‖stand** *m* object; (*Thema*) subject. **-stück** *neut* counterpart. **-teil** *neut* opposite, contrary. **im Gegenteil zu** contrary to, in contrast to.
gegenüber ['geɪgənybər] *adv*, *prep* opposite. **-liegend** *adj* opposite. **-stehen** *v* stand opposite. **Gegenüberstellung** *f* confrontation; antithesis.
Gegenwart ['geɪgənvaɪrt] *f* (*unz.*) present; (*Anwesenheit*) presence. **gegenwärtig** *adj* present, current.
Gegner ['geɪgnər] *m* (*pl* **-**) opponent, enemy. **gegnerisch** *adj* antagonistic, hostile.
Gehalt¹ [gə'halt] *m* (*unz.*) contents *pl*; (*Wert*) worth, value.
Gehalt² *neut* (*pl* **Gehälter**) salary, pay. **Gehalts‖empfänger** *m* salaried employee. **-erhöhung** *f* rise (in salary).
gehässig [gə'hɛsiç] *adj* spiteful, malicious.
Gehäuse [gə'hɔyzə] *neut* (*pl* **-**) case, box; (*Tech*) casing.
geheim [gə'haim] *adj* secret. **Geheim‖agent** *m* secret agent. **-dienst** *m* secret *or* intelligence service. **geheimhalten** *v* keep secret. **Geheimnis** *neut* (*pl* **-se**) secret; (*unerklärbar*) mystery. **geheimnisvoll** *adj* mysterious. **Geheim‖polizei** *f* secret police. **-schrift** *f* code, cipher. **geheimtuerisch** *adj* secretive.
***gehen** ['geɪən] *v* walk, go (on foot); (*Maschine*) go, work. **wie geht es Ihnen?** how are you? **es geht** it's all right. **es geht nicht** it can't be done, that's no good. **sie geht mit ihm** she is going out with him. **an die Arbeit gehen** set to work.
Gehilfe [gə'hilfə] *m* (*pl* **-n**) assistant, help.
Gehirn [gə'hirn] *neut* (*pl* **-e**) brain. **-erschütterung** *f* concussion. **-schlag** *m* cerebral apoplexy. **-wäsche** *f* brainwashing.
gehoben [gə'hoɪbən] *adj* high, elevated.
Gehör [gə'hœɪr] *neut* (*unz.*) hearing; (*Musik*) ear.

gehorchen [gə'hɔrçən] v obey.
gehören [gə'hœːrən] v belong (to). **es gehört sich** it is proper or fitting. **gehörig** adj fit, proper.
gehorsam [gə'hoːrzaım] adj obedient. **Gehorsam** m obedience. **–sverweigerung** f insubordination.
Geh‖steig ['geːʃtaik] m (pl -e) pavement. **–werk** neut movement, works.
Geier ['gaiər] m (pl -) vulture.
Geifer ['gaifər] m (unz.) spittle, slaver; (fig) venom. **geifern** v slaver; (fig) rave, foam with rage.
Geige [gaigə] f (pl -n) violin, fiddle. **–r** m violinist.
Geisel ['gaizəl] m (pl -) hostage.
Geist [gaist] 1 m (unz.) mind; (Witzigkeit) wit; (nichtmaterielle Eigenschaften) spirit. 2 m (pl -er) (Genius) genius; (Gespenst) ghost, spirit. **geistesabwesend** adj absent-minded. **Geistes‖blitz** m brainwave. **–freiheit** f freedom of thought. **geisteskrank** adj mentally ill, insane. **Geisteskranke(r)** m mental patient. **geist‖ig** adj intellectual; (nicht körperlich) spiritual; (Getränke) alcoholic. **–lich** adj spiritual, religious; (kirchlich) clerical. **Geistliche(r)** m cleric, clergyman. **geistreich** adj clever, ingenious.
Geiz [gaits] m (unz.) avarice, miserliness. **geizig** adj miserly, avaricious.
Gekicher [gə'kiçər] neut (unz.) giggling.
Geklapper [ge'klapər] neut (unz.) clatter(ing).
Geklimper [gə'klimpər] neut (unz.) jingling, chinking; (Instrument) strumming.
Geklingel [gə'kliŋəl] neut (unz.) tinkling, ringing.
gekünstelt [gə'kynstəlt] adj artificial, affected.
Gelächter [gə'leçtər] neut (pl -) laughter.
geladen [gə'laidən] adj loaded; (Batterie) charged.
Gelände [gə'lɛndə] neut (pl -) tract of land, area; (Bau-) site; (Sport-) grounds pl. **–lauf** m cross-country (running).
Geländer [gə'lɛndər] neut (pl -) railing, banister.
gelangen [gə'laŋən] v reach, arrive at; (Ziel) attain.
gelassen [gə'lasən] adj calm, composed.
geläufig [gə'lɔyfiç] adj familiar; (Sprache) fluent.
gelaunt [gə'launt] adj disposed. **gut**

gelaunt sweet-tempered. **schlecht** or **übel gelaunt** bad-tempered.
gelb [gɛlp] adj yellow. **Gelb** neut yellow. **–sucht** f jaundice. **gelbsüchtig** adj (Med) jaundiced.
Geld [gɛlt] neut (pl -er) money. **–ausgabe** f expenditure. **–beutel** m purse. **–geber** m financial backer. **geldlich** adj pecuniary. **Geld‖nehmer** m borrower. **–strafe** f fine. **–stück** neut coin. **–sucht** f avarice.
Gelee [ʒe'leː] neut (pl -s) jelly.
gelegen [gə'leːgən] adj situated; (günstig) convenient, opportune. **Gelegenheit** f (pl -en) opportunity, occasion. **Gelegenheits‖arbeit** f casual work. **–kauf** m bargain. **gelegentlich** adj occasional.
gelehrig [gə'leːriç] adj eager to learn; (klug) intelligent. **gelehrt** adj learned. **Gelehrte(r)** m scholar.
Geleit [gə'lait] neut (pl -) escort, entourage. **–brief** m (letter of) safe conduct. **geleiten** v escort, accompany.
Gelenk [gə'lɛŋk] neut (pl -e) joint. **–entzündung** f arthritis.
gelernt [gə'lɛrnt] adj skilled, trained.
Geliebte(r) [gə'liːptə] m beloved, sweetheart.
gelinde [gə'lində] adj gentle, mild.
gelingen [gə'liŋən] v succeed, be successful. **es gelingt mir, zu ...** I am able to ....
geloben [gə'loːbən] v vow, promise solemnly.
*gelten [gɛltən] v be worth, cost; (gültig sein) be valid; (betreffen) concern. **–d** adj valid. **geltend machen** urge, insist (on).
Gelübde [gə'lypdə] neut (pl -) vow.
Gemach [gə'max] neut (pl Gemächer) room, chamber.
Gemahl [gə'maːl] m (pl -e) husband. **–in** f (pl -nen) wife.
Gemälde [gə'mɛːldə] neut (pl -) painting, picture. **–galerie** f picture gallery.
gemäß [gə'mɛːs] prep in accordance with. adj suitable.
gemein [gə'main] adj common; (öffentlich) public; vulgar, low; (böse) nasty, mean.
Gemeinde [gə'maində] f (pl -n) community; (Kommune) municipality, town; (Kirche) congregation. **–rat** m local council; (Person) councillor. **–schule** f village school. **–steuer** f rates pl.

Gemeine(r) [gə'mainə(r)] *m* (*Mil*) private.
Gemeinheit *f* meanness, nastiness; (*Tat*)
mean trick, piece of spite. **gemein‖nützig**
adj charitable. **–sam** *adj* joint, common.
Gemeinschaft *f* community; (*Komm*)
partnership. **–serziehung** *f* coeducation.
–sschule *f* coeducational school.
Gemenge [gə'mɛŋə] *neut* (*pl* -n) mixture;
(*Gewühl*) scuffle.
gemessen [gə'mɛsən] *adj* measured,
sedate.
Gemisch [gə'miʃ] *neut* (*pl* -e) mixture.
gemischt *adj* mixed.
Gemurmel [gə'murməl] *neut* (*unz.*) mur-
muring.
Gemüse [gə'myːzə] *neut* (*pl* -) vegeta-
ble(s). **–gärtner** *m* market gardener.
–händler *m* greengrocer.
Gemüt [gə'myːt] *neut* (*pl* -er) disposition,
temperament, heart. **gemütlich** *adj* comfortable, cosy; (*leutselig*) good-natured.
Gemütlichkeit *f* cosiness, comfortable-
ness; good-nature.
Gen [gɛn] *neut* (*pl* -e) gene.
genannt [gə'nant] *adj* named, called.
genau [gə'nau] *adj* precise, exact.
Genauigkeit *f* precision, exactness.
genehmigen [gə'neːmigən] *v* authorize,
permit. **Genehmigung** *f* (*pl* -en) authorization, permission.
geneigt [gə'naikt] *adj* disposed, inclined.
General [gene'raːl] *m* (*pl* -e) general.
–police *f* comprehensive insurance policy. **–probe** *f* dress rehearsal. **–sekretär**
m secretary-general. **–versammlung** *f*
general meeting.
Generation [generatsi'oːn] *f* (*pl* -en) generation.
***genesen** [gə'neːzən] *v* recover, conval-
lesce, get better. **Genesung** *f* recovery.
–sheim *neut* convalescent home.
Genetik [ge'neːtik] *f* genetics. **genetisch**
adj genetic.
Genf [gɛnf] *neut* Geneva.
genial [geni'aːl] *adj* (*Person*) brilliant, gifted; (*Sache*) ingenious, inspired.
Genick [gə'nik] *neut* (*pl* -e) (nape of the)
neck.
Genie [ʒe'niː] *neut* (*pl* -s) genius.
genieren [ʒe'niːrən] *v* bother, trouble. **sich**
genieren be embarrassed.
genießbar [gə'niːsbaːr] *adj* enjoyable;
(*Essen, Trinken*) palatable. **genießen** *v*
enjoy; eat; drink. **Genießer** *m* (*pl* -) epicure, gourmet.

Genitalien [geni'taːliən] *pl* genitals.
Genosse [gə'nɔsə] *m* (*pl* -n), **Genossin** *f*
(*pl* -nen) comrade; (*Kollege*) colleague.
Genossenschaft *f* cooperative (society).
genossenschaftlich *adj* cooperative.
genug [gə'nuːk] *adv*, *adj* enough, suffi-
cient(ly). **genügen** *v* be enough, suffice.
–d *adj* sufficient, enough. **genügsam** *adj*
easily satisfied. **Genugtuung** *f* satisfaction.
Genuß [gə'nus] *m* (*pl* **Genüsse**) pleasure,
enjoyment.
Geograph [geo'graːf] *m* (*pl* -en) geographer. **–ie** *f* geography. **geographisch** *adj*
geographical.
Geologe [geo'loːgə] *m* (*pl* -n) geologist.
Geologie *f* geology. **geologisch** *adj* geo-
logical.
Geometrie [geome'triː] *f* (*pl* -n) geometry.
geometrish *adj* geometrical.
Gepäck [gə'pɛk] *neut* (*unz.*) baggage, luggage. **–aufbewahrung** *f* left-luggage
office. **–netz** *neut* luggage rack. **–träger**
m porter.
gepflegt [gə'pfleːkt] *adj* well-tended; (*Person*) well-groomed, well-dressed.
gepanzert [gə'pantsərt] *adj* armoured.
Gepflogenheit [gə'pfloːgənhait] *f* (*pl* -en)
habit, custom.
Geplapper [gə'plapər] *neut* (*unz.*) chatter.
Geplauder [gə'plaudər] *neut* (*unz.*) chat,
small talk.
Gepräge [gə'prɛːgə] *neut* (*pl* -) stamp;
(*Münze*) coinage; (*Eigenart*) character.
Geprassel [gə'prasəl] *neut* (*unz.*) clatter.
gerade [gə'raːdə] *adj* straight; (*direkt*)
direct; (*Haltung*) erect; (*Zahl*) even. *adv*
just; (*genau*) exactly, precisely; (*direkt*)
straight, directly. **–aus** *adv* straight on *or*
ahead. **–so** *adv* just so, just the same.
–stehen *v* stand erect, stand up straight.
–swegs *adv* immediately; (*ohne
Umwege*) directly. **–zu** *adv* directly;
(*freimütig*) plainly, flatly; (*durchaus*)
sheer, downright. **Geradheit** *f* straight-
ness; (*Ehrlichkeit*) honesty. **gerad‖läufig**
adj straight. **–zahlig** *adj* even(-num-
bered).
Geranie [ge'raːniə] *f* (*pl* -n) geranium.
Gerassel [gə'rasəl] *neut* (*unz.*) clatter, rattle.
Gerät [gə'rɛːt] *neut* (*pl* -e) tool, implement; (*kompliziert*) instrument; (*Maschine*) device, appliance; (*Radio, TV*)
set; (*Ausrüstung*) equipment.

*geraten [gə'raɪtən] v come upon; (gel-ingen) turn out well; (gedeihen) thrive. **in Schwierigkeiten geraten** get into difficulties. **in Zorn geraten** fly into a rage. **über etwas geraten** come across, stumble upon something.

Geratewohl [gə'raɪtəvoɪl] neut **aufs Geratewohl** at random.

geräumig [gə'rɔymiç] adj roomy, spacious.

Geräusch [gə'rɔyʃ] neut (pl -e) noise.

gerben ['gɛrbən] v tan. **Gerber** m (pl -) tanner. **Gerberei** f (pl -en) tannery.

gerecht [gə'rɛçt] adj just, fair; (geeignet) suitable. **-fertigt** adj justified; (legitim) legitimate **Gerechtigkeit** f justice; (Rechtschaffenheit) righteousness.

Gerede [gə'reɪdə] neut (unz.) gossip.

Gericht[1] [gə'riçt] neut (pl -e) (Essen) dish; (Gang) course.

Gericht[2] neut (pl -e) law-court; (fig) justice, judgment. **gerichtlich** adj judicial, legal. **Gerichts‖hof** m (law) court. **-kosten** pl (legal) costs. **-medizin** f forensic medicine. **-saal** m courtroom. **-schreiber** m clerk (of the court). **-verfahren** neut legal proceedings pl. **-vollzieher** m bailiff.

gerieben [gə'riːbən] adj grated.

Gerinnsel neut clot.

gering [gə'riŋ] adj small; (Vorrat) short; (Preis) low; (unbedeutend) unimportant, insignificant. **-fügig** adj trivial, insignificant. **-schätzen** v think little of, despise. **-schätzig** adj disdainful.

gerinnen [gə'rinən] v congeal; (Blut) clot.

Gerippe [gə'ripə] neut (pl -) skeleton.

Germane [gɛr'maɪnə] m (pl -n), **Germanin** f (pl -nen) German; pl Germanic (tribes or peoples). **germanisch** adj Germanic.

gern(e) ['gɛrn(ə)] adv willingly, gladly, readily. **gern haben** or **mögen** be fond of, like. **gern tun** like to do. **ich möchte gern . . .** I should like . . . **gut und gern** easily.

Gerste ['gɛrstə] f barley.

Geruch [gə'ruːx] m (pl Gerüche) smell, odour. **-sinn** m (sense of) smell.

Gerücht [gə'ryçt] neut (pl -e) rumour.

Gerümpel [gə'rympəl] neut junk, trash.

Gerüst [gə'ryst] neut (pl -e) scaffolding.

gesamt [gə'zamt] adj whole, entire. **Gesamt‖betrag** m total (amount). **-heit** f whole, totality. **-schule** comprehensive

school. **-übersicht** f overall view. **-versicherung** f comprehensive insurance. **-zahl** f total (number).

Gesandte(r) [gə'zantə] m (pl -n) ambassador. **Gesandtschaft** f embassy.

Gesang [gə'zaŋ] m (pl Gesänge) song; (Singen) singing. **-buch** neut songbook; (Kirche) hymnbook.

Gesäß [gə'zeːs] neut (pl -e) seat, bottom.

Geschäft [gə'ʃɛft] neut (pl -e) business; (Laden) shop; (Handel) deal. **das Geschäft blüht** business is booming. **ein unsauberes Geschäft** a dirty business. **ein gutes Geschäft machen** get a bargain. **geschäftlich** adj commercial, business. **Geschäfts‖freund** m business associate, customer. **-führer** m manager; (Verein) secretary. **-haus** neut firm. **-jahr** neut business year. **-mann** m businessman. **-raum** m or **-räume** pl office(s). **geschäftsmäßig** adj businesslike. **Geschäfts‖reisende(r)** m commercial traveller, representative. **-schluß** m closing time. **-stunden** pl office hours.

*geschehen [gə'ʃeɪən] v happen.

gescheit [gə'ʃaɪt] adj clever, smart.

Geschenk [gə'ʃɛŋk] neut (pl -e) present, gift.

Geschichte [gə'ʃiçtə] f (pl -n) (Erzählung) story; (Vergangenheit) history, (Angelegenheit) affair. **Geschichtenbuch** neut story book. **geschichtlich** adj historical. **Geschichts‖buch** neut history book. **-forscher** m (research) historian, **-schreiber** m historian.

Geschick [gə'ʃik] neut (pl -e) aptitude; (Schicksal) fate. **-lichkeit** f skill. **geschickt** adj able, skilful.

geschieden [gə'ʃiːdən] adj divorced.

Geschirr [gə'ʃir] neut (pl -e) crockery, dishes; (Pferde) harness. **-tuch** neut dishcloth. **-spülmaschine** f dishwasher.

Geschlecht [gə'ʃlɛçt] neut (pl -er) sex; (Art) kind, sort; (Familie) family, house; (Gramm) gender. **geschlechtlich** adj sexual. **Geschlechts‖krankheit** f venereal disease. **-reife** f puberty. **-teile** pl genitals. **-verkehr** m sexual intercourse.

geschlossen [gə'ʃlɔsən] adj closed.

Geschmack [gə'ʃmak] m (pl Geschmäcke) taste. **geschmacklos** adj tasteless. **Geschmacks‖sache** f matter of taste. **-sinn** m sense of taste. **geschmackvoll** adj tasteful.

Geschnatter [gə'ʃnatər] *neut* (*unz.*) cackling.
Geschöpf [gə'ʃœpf] *neut* (*pl* -e) creature.
Geschoß [gə'ʃɔs] *neut* (*pl* **Geschosse**) projectile, missile; (*Kanone*) shell; (*Stockwerk*) floor, storey.
Geschrei [gə'ʃrai] *neut* (*pl* -e) cry, shouting, crying; (*fig*) fuss, noise.
Geschütz [gə'ʃyts] *neut* (*pl* -e) gun, cannon.
Geschwätz [gə'ʃvɛts] *neut* idle talk, prattle. **geschwätzig** *adj* talkative.
geschweige [gə'ʃvaigə] *conj* **geschweige denn** let alone, to say nothing of.
geschwind [gə'ʃvint] *adj* quick, fast. **Geschwindigkeit** *f* speed, velocity. **Geschwindigkeits‖grenze** *f* speed limit. **—messer** *m* speedometer.
Geschwister [gə'ʃvistər] *pl* brother(s) and sister(s); siblings. **haben Sie Geschwister?** have you any brothers and sisters?
Geschworene(r) [gə'ʃvoirənə] *m* (*pl* -n) juror. **Geschworenengericht** *neut* (trial by) jury.
Geschwür [gə'ʃvyir] *neut* (*pl* -e) ulcer, sore.
Geselle [gə'zɛlə] *m* (*pl* -n) comrade, companion; (*Bursche*) lad, fellow; (*gelehrter Handwerker*) journeyman. **gesellig** *adj* sociable. **Gesellschaft** *f* society; (*Firma*) company; (*Verein*) society, association; (*Abend-, usw.*) party, social gathering; (*Begleitung*) company. **gesellschaftlich** *adj* social. **Gesellschaftsanzug** *m* evening dress. **gesellschaftsfeindlich** *adj* antisocial. **Gesellschafts‖kleid** *neut* party dress. **—steuer** *f* corporation tax. **—tanz** *m* society dance, ball.
Gesetz [gə'zɛts] *neut* (*pl* -e) law. **—buch** *neut* statute book, law code. **—entwurf** *m* bill. **gesetzgebend** *adj* legislative. **Gesetzgebung** *f* legislation. **gesetz‖lich** *adj* legal, lawful. **—los** *adj* lawless. **—mäßig** *adj* legal, lawful.
gesetzt [gə'zɛtst] *adj* sedate, quiet.
gesetzwidrig [gə'zɛtsviidriç] *adj* illegal, unlawful.
Gesicht [gə'ziçt] *neut* (*pl* -er) face; (*Miene*) expression. **Gesichts‖ausdruck** *m* (facial) expression. **—farbe** *f* complexion. **—feld** *neut* field of vision. **—punkt** *m* viewpoint.
gesinnt [gə'zint] *adj* disposed, minded. **Gesinnung** *f* opinion, mind, conviction. **gesinnungslos** *adj* unprincipled.

Gespann [gə'ʃpan] *neut* (*pl* -e) (*Pferden*) (team of) horses.
gespannt [gə'ʃpant] *adj* tense; (*Verhältnis*) strained. **gespannt sein** be eager *or* anxious.
Gespenst [gə'ʃpɛnst] *neut* (*pl* -er) ghost. **gespenstig** *adj* ghostly.
Gespräch [gə'ʃprɛiç] *neut* (*pl* -e) conversation, talk. **Gespräche** *pl* talks, discussion *sing.* **gesprächig** *adj* talkative.
Gestalt [gə'ʃtalt] *f* (*pl* -en) form, shape; (*Körper-*) figure, build; (*Literatur*) character. **gestalt‖en** *v* form, shape. **—et** *adj* formed, shaped. **—los** *adj* shapeless. **Gestaltung** *f* (*unz.*) shaping, formation.
Geständnis [gə'ʃtɛntnis] *neut* (*pl* -se) confession.
Gestank [gə'ʃtaŋk] *m* stink, stench.
gestatten [gə'ʃtatən] *v* permit, allow.
Geste ['gɛstə] *f* (*pl* -n) gesture.
*gestehen [gə'ʃteiən] *v* confess.
Gestell [gə'ʃtɛl] *neut* (*pl* -e) (*Rahmen*) frame, stand; (*Bock*) trestle; (*Regal*) shelf; (*Bett-*) bedstead.
gestern ['gɛstərn] *adv* yesterday.
Gesträuch [gə'ʃtrɔyç] *neut* (*unz.*) shrubbery, bushes *pl.*
gestrichen [gə'ʃtriçən] *adj* painted. **frisch gestrichen** newly painted; wet paint.
gestrig ['gɛstriç] *adj* yesterday's.
Gestrüpp [gə'ʃtryp] *neut* undergrowth, scrub.
Gesuch [gə'zuiç] *neut* (*pl* -e) petition. **gesucht** *adj* in demand; (*Person*) wanted.
gesund [gə'zunt] *adj* healthy, well. **Gesundheit** *f* health. *interj* bless you! **gesundheitlich** *adj* sanitary. **gesundheitsförderlich** *adj* wholesome, healthy. **Gesundheitslehre** *f* hygiene. **gesundheitsschädlich** *adj* insanitary, unhealthy.
Getränk [gə'trɛŋk] *neut* (*pl* -e) drink.
Getreide [gə'traidə] *neut* (*pl* -) grain, cereals *pl*
getreu [gə'trɔy] *adj* loyal, faithful.
Getriebe [gə'triibə] *neut* (*pl* -) commotion, bustle; (*Tech*) transmission, gears *pl.* **—gehäuse** *neut* gearbox.
getrost [gə'troist] *adj* confident. *adv* without hesitation.
Getto ['getoi] *neut* (*pl* -s) ghetto.
geübt [gə'ypt] *adj* practised, skilful.
Gewächs [gə'vɛks] *neut* (*pl* -e) plant; (*Med*) growth.

gewachsen [gə'vaksən] *adj* grown.
gewachsen sein be equal (to), be up (to).
gewagt [gə'vaikt] *adj* bold, daring.
gewählt [gə'veilt] *adj* select(ed), choice.
Gewähr [gə'veir] *f* (*unz.*) guarantee, surety. **gewähren** *v* allow, grant. **gewährleisten** *v* guarantee, vouch for.
Gewalt [gə'valt] *f* (*pl* -en) force; (*Macht*) power; (*Obrigkeit*) authority; (*Gewalttätigkeit*) violence. **-herrscher** *m* tyrant. **gewalt||ig** *adj* forceful, powerful; enormous; (*gewalttätig*) violent. **- los** *adj* powerless. **-sam** *adj* violent; *adv* by force. **-tätig** *adj* violent.
Gewand [gə'vant] *neut* (*pl* **Gewänder**) garment, robe.
gewandt [gə'vant] *adj* skilled, skilful. **Gewandtheit** *f* dexterity, skill.
Gewässer [gə'vesər] *neut* (*pl* -) water(s).
Gewebe [gə'veibə] *neut* (*pl* -) material, textile; (*Biol*) tissue; (*Lügen, usw.*) web, network.
geweckt [gə'vekt] *adj* bright, lively.
Gewehr [gə'veir] *neut* (*pl* -e) rifle, gun. **-kugel** *f* (rifle) bullet.
Geweih [gə'vai] *neut* (*pl* -e) antlers *pl.*
Gewerbe [gə'verbə] *neut* (*pl* -) trade. **-schule** *f* technical school. **gewerb||lich** *adj* industrial. **-smäßig** *adj* professional.
Gewerkschaft [gə'verkʃaft] *f* (*pl* -en) (trade) union. **-ler** *m* (trade) unionist. **gewerkschaftlich** *adj* trade-union.
Gewicht [gə'viçt] *neut* (*pl* -e) weight; (*fig*) importance. **-heben** *neut* weight-lifting. **gewichtig** *adj* heavy; (*fig*) important.
Gewimmel [gə'viməl] *neut* (*pl* -) crowd, swarm.
Gewinde [gə'vində] *neut* (*pl* -) (*Schraube*) thread.
Gewinn [gə'vin] *m* (*pl* -e) profit; (*Ertrag*) yield, returns; (*Preis*) prize; (*Erwerben*) gaining. **-beteiligung** *f* profit-sharing. **gewinn||bringend** *adj* profitable. **-en** *v* (*Preis*) win; (*erwerben*) gain, acquire; (*siegen*) win. **-süchtig** *adj* acquisitive.
Gewirr [gə'vir] *neut* (*pl* -e) confusion, tangle.
gewiß [gə'vis] *adj* certain, sure. *adv* certainly. *ein gewisser Herr Schmidt* a certain Mr Schmidt. *ein gewisses Etwas* a certain something.
Gewissen [gə'visən] *neut* (*unz.*) conscience. **gewissen||haft** *adj* conscientious. **-los** *adj* unscrupulous. **Gewissens||bisse**

pl pangs of conscience. **-konflikt** *m* conflict of conscience.
gewissermaßen [gə'visərmaisən] *adv* to some extent.
Gewißheit [gə'vishait] *f* (*unz.*) certainty.
Gewitter [gə'vitər] *neut* (*pl* -) thunderstorm. **gewitterhaft** *adj* stormy.
gewogen [gə'voigən] *adj* well disposed, favourably inclined.
gewöhnen [gə'vœinən] *v* accustom. **sich gewöhnen an** become accustomed to, get used to. **Gewohnheit** *f* (*pl* -en) habit; (*Brauch*) custom. **gewohnheitsmäßig** *adj* customary. **gewöhnlich** *adj* usual, ordinary; (*unfein*) vulgar. *adv* usually. **gewohnt** *adj* used (to).
Gewölbe [gə'vœlbə] *neut* (*pl* -) vault. **gewölbt** *adj* arched, vaulted.
Gewühl [gə'vyil] *neut* (*unz.*) crowd, tumult.
Gewürz [gə'vyrts] *neut* (*pl* -e) spice, seasoning. **gewürzig** *adj* spicy. **gewürzt** *adj* spiced, seasoned.
gezackt [gə'tsakt] *adj* serrated; (*Fels*) jagged.
geziemend [gə'tsiimənt] *or* **geziemlich** *adj* seemly.
geziert [gə'tsiirt] *adj* affected.
gezwungen [gə'tsvuŋən] *adj* forced; (*steif*) formal, stiff.
Gicht [giçt] *f* (*unz.*) gout.
Giebel ['giibəl] *m* (*pl* -) gable. **-dach** *neut* gabled roof.
Gier [giir] *f* greed; (*nach etwas*) craving, burning desire (for). **gierig** *adj* greedy.
*gießen ['giisən] *v* pour; (*Pflanzen*) water; (*schmelzen*) cast. **Gleß||erei** *f* (*pl* -en) foundry. **-kanne** *f* watering can.
Gift [gift] *neut* (*pl* -e) poison. **-gas** *neut* poison gas. **giftig** *adj* poisonous. **Giftschlange** *f* poisonous snake.
Ginster ['ginstər] *m* (*pl* -) (*Bot*) broom.
Gipfel ['gipfəl] *m* (*pl* -) peak, summit. **-gespräche** *pl* summit talks. **-leistung** *f* record.
Gips [gips] *m* (*pl* -e) gypsum; (*erhitzt*) plaster (of Paris). **-verband** *m* plaster cast.
Giraffe [gi'rafə] *f* (*pl* -n) giraffe.
Giro ['dʒiiroi] *neut* (*pl* -s) giro. **-konto** *neut* current account.
Gitarre [gi'tarə] *f* (*pl* -n) guitar.
Gitter ['gitər] *neut* (*pl* -) grille, grating; (*Fenster*) bars; (*Spalier*) trellis.

Glanz [glants] *m* (*unz.*) shine, brilliance, brightness; (*fig*) splendour.

glänzen ['glɛntsən] *v* gleam, shine; (*fig*) excel, shine. **−d** *adj* brilliant.

Glas [glaɪs] *neut* (*pl* **Gläser**) glass. **−haus** *neut* greenhouse, hothouse. **−perle** *f* bead. **−scheibe** *f* (window) pane. **glasieren** *v* glaze; (*Kuchen*) ice. **Glasur** *f* glaze; (*Kuchen*) icing.

glatt [glat] *adj* smooth; (*glitschig*) slippery. **Glatteis** *neut* (*Mot*) black ice. **glattrasiert** *adj* clean-shaven.

Glaube ['glaubə] *m* (*unz.*) belief; (*Rel*) faith. **glauben** *v* believe; (*vermuten*) think, suppose; (*vertrauen*) trust. **glaubhaft** *adj* credible.

gläubig ['glɔybiç] *adj* believing; (*fromm*) pious. **Gläubige(r)** *m* believer; (*Komm*) creditor.

glaublich ['glaupliç] *adj* credible. **glaubwürdig** *adj* (*Person*) trustworthy; (*Sache*) credible.

gleich [glaiç] *adj* (the) same, equal; (*eben*) level. *adv* equally; (*sofort*) at once; (*schon*) just. **von gleichem Alter** of the same age. **das ist mir gleich** it makes no difference to me. **das gleiche gilt für Dich** the same goes for you. **Ich komme gleich** I'm just coming. **gleich viel** just as much. **gleich‖artig** *adj* similar. **−bedeutend** *adj* synonymous. **−berechtigt** *adj* having equal rights.

*gleichen ['glaiçən] *v* equal; (*ähnlich sein*) resemble.

gleichermaßen ['glaiçərmasən] *or* **gleicherweise** *adv* likewise.

gleich‖falls *adv* also, likewise. **−gesinnt** *adj* like-minded.

Gleichgewicht ['glaiçgəviçt] *neut* equilibrium, balance.

gleichgültig ['glaiçgyltiç] *adj* unconcerned, indifferent. **Gleichgültigkeit** *f* indifference.

Gleich‖heit *f* equality. **−maß** *neut* proportion, symmetry. **−mut** *m* equanimity. **−nis** *neut* (*pl* **-se**) simile; (*Erzählung*) parable.

gleichschalten ['glaiçʃaltən] *v* coordinate; (*Tech*) synchronize.

Gleichschritt ['glaiçʃrit] *m* **Gleichschritt halten** keep step.

Gleich‖strom *m* direct current. **−ung** *f* (*pl* **-en**) equation.

gleich‖viel *adv* no matter. **−wertig** *adj*

equivalent, of the same value. **−wohl** *adv* nonetheless. **−zeitig** *adj* simultaneous.

Gleis [glais] *neut* (*pl* **-e**) track, platform. ***gleiten** ['glaitən] *v* slide, slip. **Gleitflugzeug** *neut* glider, sailplane.

Gletscher ['glɛtʃər] *m* (*pl* **-**) glacier. **Gletscherspalte** *f* crevasse.

Glied [gliɪt] *neut* (*pl* **-er**) limb; (*Kette*) link. **gliedern** *v* organize, arrange; divide into. **Gliederung** *f* (*pl* **-en**) organization, arrangement.

Glocke ['glɔkə] *f* (*pl* **-n**) bell. **Glocken‖blume** *f* bluebell. **−turm** *m* belltower.

glorreich ['glɔrraiç] *adj* glorious.

Glossar [glɔ'saɪr] *neut* (*pl* **-e**, **-ien**) glossary. **Glosse** *f* (*pl* **-n**) comment.

glotzen ['glɔtsən] *v* stare.

Glück [glyk] *neut* luck; (*Geschick*) fortune; (*Freude*) happiness. **glück‖lich** *adj* happy, fortunate. **−licherweise** *adv* fortunately, luckily. **−selig** *adj* blissful. **Glücks‖fall** *m* lucky chance. **−spiel** *neut* game of chance.

glühen ['glyɪən] *v* glow. **Glüh‖hitze** *f* white heat. **−wein** *m* mulled wine.

Glut [gluɪt] *f* (*pl* **-en**) glow. **−asche** *f* embers *pl*.

Gnade ['gnaɪdə] *f* (*pl* **-n**) grace, mercy. **Gnaden‖frist** *f* reprieve, period of grace. **−stoß** *m* coup de grâce.

gnädig ['gnɛɪdiç] *adj* gracious; kind. **gnädige Frau** Madam.

Gold [gɔlt] *neut* (*unz.*) gold. **−barren** *m* gold bar *or* ingot. **gold‖en** *adj* golden. **−ig** *adj* sweet, lovely.

Golf¹ [gɔlf] *m* (*pl* **-e**) gulf.

Golf² *neut* (*unz.*) (*Sport*) golf.

gönnen ['gœnən] *v* not begrudge; grant, allow. **Gönner** *m* (*pl* **-**) patron, sponsor. **gönnerhaft** *adj* patronizing; condescending.

Gosse ['gɔsə] *f* (*pl* **-n**) gutter.

Gott [gɔt] *m* God; (*pl* **Götter**) god. **grüß Gott!** greetings! God be with you! **Gott sei dank!** thank God! **um Gottes willen!** for God's sake! **Gottes‖dienst** *m* (church) service. **−lästerung** *f* blasphemy. **Gottheit** *f* godhead, divinity.

Göttin ['gœtin] *f* (*pl* **-nen**) goddess. **göttlich** *adj* divine.

Götze ['gœtsə] *m* (*pl* **-n**) idol, false god.

Grab [graɪp] *neut* (*pl* **Gräber**) grave. **graben** *v* dig. **Graben** *m* ditch, trench. **Grab‖schrift** *f* epitaph. **−stätte** *f* grave. **−stein** *m* tombstone.

Grad [graːt] *m* (*pl* -e) degree; (*Rang*) rank, grade. **-messer** *m* (*fig*) indication, sign.
graduieren [gradu'iːrən] *v* graduate.
Graduierte(r) *m* graduate.
Graf [graːf] *m* (*pl* -en) count.
Gräfin ['grɛːfɪn] *f* (*pl* -en) countess.
Grafschaft ['graːfʃaft] *f* (*pl* -en) county.
Gram [graːm] *m* (*unz*.) grief.
Gramm [gram] *neut* (*pl* -e) gram(me).
Grammatik [gra'matik] *f* (*pl* -en) grammar.
Granatapfel [gra'naːtapfəl] *m* (*pl* Granatäpfel) pomegranate.
Granate [gra'naːtə] *f* (*pl* -n) shell, grenade.
Granit [gra'niːt] *m* (*pl* -e) granite.
Graphik ['graːfik] *f* (*unz*.) graphics. **-er** *m* (*pl* -) designer, commercial artist. **graphisch** *adj* graphic. **graphische Darstellung** graph.
Gras [graːs] *neut* (*pl* Gräser) grass. **grasen** *v* graze.
gräßlich ['grɛslɪç] *adj* horrible, ghastly.
Grat [graːt] *m* (*pl* -e) ridge, edge.
Gräte ['grɛːtə] *f* (*pl* -n) fishbone. **-nmuster** *neut* herringbone pattern.
gratulieren [gratu'liːrən] *v* congratulate.
grau [grau] *adj* grey. **Graubrot** *neut* ryebread.
grauen ['grauən] *v* be horrible. *es graut mir vor* I have a horror of. **-haft** *adj* dreadful, horrible.
Graupe ['graupə] *f* (*pl* -n) groats *pl*, pearl barley.
graupeln ['graupəln] *pl* sleet *sing*.
grausam ['grauzaɪm] *adj* cruel. **Grausamkeit** *f* cruelty. **grausig** *adj* fearful, dreadful.
gravieren [gra'viːrən] *v* engrave.
greif‖en ['graifən] *v* seize, grasp. **-bar** *adj* (*Waren*) available, at hand; (*fig*) tangible. **greifen an** touch. **greifen in** dip into.
Greis [grais] *m* (*pl* -e) old man.
grell [grɛl] *adj* (*Ton*) shrill, harsh; (*Farbe*) glaring.
Grenze ['grɛntsə] *f* (*pl* -n) (*eines Staates*) border, frontier; (*einer Stadt, Zone*) boundary; (*fig*) limit. **grenzen** border (on). **Grenz‖fall** *m* borderline case. **-übergang** *m* crossing (of a frontier).
Greuel ['grɔyəl] *m* (*pl* -) (*Abscheu*) horror; (*Scheußlichkeit*) atrocity, abomination

Grieche ['griːçə] *m* (*pl* -n) Greek (man). **Griechenland** *neut* Greece. **Griechin** *f* (*pl* -nen) Greek (woman). **griechisch** *adj* Greek.
Grieß [griːs] *m* (*unz*.) (*Essen*) semolina; (*Kies*) gravel. **-pudding** *m* semolina pudding.
Griff [grif] *m* (*pl* -e) (*Henkel, Knopf, usw.*) handle; (*Greifen*) hold, grip.
Grille ['grilə] *f* (*pl* -n) (*Insekt*) cricket; (*Laune*) whim.
Grimasse [gri'masə] *f* (*pl* -n) grimace.
grimmig ['grimiç] *adj* furious.
grinsen ['grinzən] *v* grin.
Grippe ['gripə] *f* (*pl* -n) influenza.
grob [groːp] *adj* coarse; (*Benehmen*) coarse, rude; (*Scherz*) crude, coarse; (*Fehler*) gross, serious. **Grobheit** *f* coarseness, rudeness.
Groll [grɔl] *m* animosity, rancour. **grollen** *v* be resentful, be angry.
gros [groː] **en gros** wholesale.
Gros¹ [groː] *neut* (*pl* -) (*Armee*) main body.
Gros² [grɔs] *neut* (*pl* -e) gross, twelve dozen.
Groschen ['grɔʃən] *m* (*pl* -) (*Österreich*) Groschen; (*BRD*) ten-pfennig piece; (*fig*) penny.
groß [groːs] *adj* big, large; (*wichtig*) great, grand; (*hoch*) tall. **im großen und ganzen** on the whole. **-artig** *adj* splendid, grand.
Großbritannien [groːsbri'taniən] *neut* Great Britain.
Großbuchstabe ['groːsbuːxʃtaibə] *m* capital (letter).
Großeltern ['groːseltern] *pl* grandparents.
großenteils ['groːsentails] *adv* mostly, for the most part.
Groß‖handel *m* wholesale trade. **-händler** *m* wholesaler.
großherzig ['groːshɛrtsiç] *adj* magnanimous.
Groß‖industrie *f* large-scale industry. **-macht** *f* great power. **-maul** *neut* braggart, big-mouth. **-mutter** *f* grandmother. **-stadt** *f* large town, city.
größtenteils ['grœːstəntails] *adv* mostly, largely.
Groß‖teil *m* bulk. **-tuer** *m* show-off, big-head. **-vater** *m* grandfather.
großzügig ['groːstsyːgiç] *adj* generous; (*weittragend*) large-scale. **Großzügigkeit** *f* generosity; largeness.

grotesk [gro'tɛsk] *adj* grotesque.
Grübchen ['gryːpçən] *neut* (*pl* -) dimple.
Grube ['gruːbə] *f* (*pl* -n) pit, hole;
(*Bergbau*) mine, pit; (*Höhle, Bau*) hole,
burrow; (*Falle*) snare.
grübeln ['gryːbəln] *v* brood, ponder.
grün [gryːn] *adj* green. **Grün** *neut* green.
–anlage *f* public park, open space.
Grund [grunt] *m* (*pl* Gründe) (*Erdboden*)
ground, soil; (*Veranlassung*) reason,
grounds *pl*; (*Grundlage*) basis, base;
(*Grundbesitz*) land; (*eines Meeres*) bottom. **–bau** *m* foundation. **–besitz** *m*
landed property, real estate. **im Grunde
(genommen)** basically.
gründen ['gryndən] *v* found, establish.
sich gründen auf be based on. **Gründer** *m*
(*pl* -) founder.
Grund||gesetz *neut* basic law; (*Verfas-
sung*) constitution. **–lage** *f* basis, foundation.
gründlich ['gryntliç] *adj* thorough.
grundlos ['gruntloːs] *adj* unfounded, base-
less.
Grund||maß *neut* standard of measure-
ment. **–riß** *m* outline, design. **–satz** *m*
principle, axiom. **grundsätzlich** *adj* fundamental.
Grund||schule *f* primary school. **–stoff** *m*
raw material; (*Chem*) element. **–stück**
neut lot of land.
Gründung ['grynduŋ] *f* (*pl* -en) establishment, foundation.
Grund||unterschied *m* basic difference.
–zahl *f* cardinal number. **–zug** *m* characteristic, feature.
Grünkohl ['gryːnkoːl] *m* kale.
grunzen ['gruntsən] *v* grunt.
Grünzeug ['gryːntsɔyk] *neut* greens *pl*,
green vegetables *pl*.
Gruppe ['grupə] *f* (*pl* -n) group. **–nführer**
m section leader. **gruppieren** *v* group.
gruselig ['gruːzəliç] *adj* gruesome; (*umg.*)
creepy.
Gruß [gruːs] *m* (*pl* Grüße) greeting; (*Mil*)
salute. **herzliche Grüße** kind regards,
best wishes.
grüßen ['gryːsən] *v* greet; (*Mil*) salute.
gucken ['gukən] *v* (take a) look, peep.
Gulasch ['guːlaʃ] *neut, m* (*pl* -e) goulash.
gültig ['gyltiç] *adj* valid; (*Gesetz*) in force.
Gültigkeit *f* validity, currency. **–sdauer** *f*
(period of) validity.
Gummi ['gumi] *neut* (*pl* -s) rubber; (*Kleb-*

stoff) gum; (*Kau-*) (chewing) gum.
–band *neut* rubber band. **gummiert** *adj*
(*Briefmarke, usw.*) gummed.
Gunst [gunst] *f* (*unz.*) favour.
günstig ['gynstiç] *adj* favourable, advantageous.
gurgeln ['gurgəln] *v* gargle. **Gurgelwasser**
neut gargle.
Gurke ['gurkə] *f* (*pl* -n) cucumber; (*saure*)
gherkin.
Gurt [gurt] *m* (*pl* -e) belt; (*Pferd*) girth.
Gürtel ['gyrtəl] *m* (*pl* -) belt; (*Geog*) zone.
–reifen *m* radial-ply tyre, (*umg.*) radial.
Guß [gus] *m* (*pl* Güsse) (*Regen*) downpour, gush; (*Metall*) casting, founding.
gut [guːt] *adj* good. *adv* well. **gut sein mit**
be on good terms with. **es wird schon
alles gut werden** everything will be all
right. **das tut mir gut** that does me good.
schon gut! that's all right. **gut aussehen**
look good; (*gesund*) look well. **Gut** *neut*
(*pl* Güter) possession; (*Land*) landed
estate; (*Ware*) commodity. **gutartig** *adj*
good-natured. **Gutdünken** *neut* discretion. **nach (Ihrem) Gutdünken** at your
discretion.
Güte ['gyːtə] *f* (*unz.*) kindness, goodness;
(*Qualität*) quality.
Güter||flugzeug *neut* cargo plane. **–zug**
m freight train.
gut||gelaun *adj* good-humoured. **–gesinnt**
adj friendly, well-disposed. **–gläubig** *adj*
acting in good faith, bona-fide; *adv* in
good faith.
Guthaben ['guːthaːbən] *neut* credit (balance).
*gut||heißen *v* approve. **–herzig** *adj*
kind-hearted.
gütig ['gyːtiç] *adj* kind.
gutmachen ['guːtmaxən] *v* **wieder
gutmachen** make amends for, make
good.
gutmütig ['guːtmyːtiç] *adj* good-natured.
Gutschein ['guːtʃain] *m* (*pl* -e) voucher,
credit-note.
Gymnasium [gym'naːzium] *neut* (*pl*
Gymnasien) grammar school.
Gymnastik [gym'nastik] *f* gymnastics.
gymnastisch *adj* gymnastic.

H

Haag, Den [dein'haik] *m* The Hague.
Haar [hair] *neut* (*pl* -e) hair. **sich die Haare schneiden lassen** have a haircut. **haarig** *adj* hairy. **Haar‖nadelkurve** *f* hairpin bend. **–schnitt** *m* haircut. **haarsträubend** *adj* hair-raising.
Habe ['haibə] *f* (*unz.*) property, possessions *pl.* **haben** *v* have. **habsüchtig** *adj* greedy, (*umg.*) grasping.
Hackbrett ['hakbrɛt] *neut* chopping board. **hacken** *v* chop, hack; (*Fleisch*) mince. **Hackfleisch** *neut* mince, minced meat.
Hafen ['haifən] *m* (*pl* Häfen) port, harbour. **–arbeiter** *m* docker. **–damm** *m* pier, mole. **–sperre** *f* embargo. **–stadt** *f* port.
Hafer ['haifər] *m* (*pl* -) oats *pl.* **–flocken** *f pl* rolled oats, oat-flakes.
Haft [haft] *f* arrest, detention, custody. **haften** *v* adhere, cling. **haften für** be liable for, answer for. **Haftpflichtversicherung** *f* (compulsory) third-party insurance.
Hagel [haigəl] *m* (*pl* -) hail. **–korn** *neut* hailstone. **hageln** *v* **es hagelt** it is hailing.
hager ['haigər] *adj* lean, haggard.
Hahn [hain] *m* (*pl* Hähne) cock; (*Wasser-, usw.*) tap. **Hahnenkamm** *m* cockscomb.
Hähnchen [hɛinçən] *neut* (*pl* -) cock; (*Wasser-, usw.*) tap.
Hai [hai] *m* (*pl* -e) *or* **Haifisch** *m* shark.
Hain [hain] *m* (*pl* -e) grove.
Häkelarbeit ['hɛikəlairbait] *f* crochet work. **häkeln** *v* crochet.
haken ['haikən] *v* hook. **sich haken an** catch on, get caught on. **Haken** *m* (*pl* -) hook; (*fig*) snag. **–kreuz** *neut* swastika.
halb [halp] *adj* half. **um halb drei** at half past two. **eine halbe Stunde** half an hour. **–jährlich** *adj* half-yearly. **Halb‖kreis** *m* semicircle. **–kugel** *f* hemisphere. **–messer** *m* radius. **–starke(r)** *m* hooligan. **halbwegs** *adv* halfway. **Halbzeit** *f* half-time.
Hälfte ['hɛlftə] *f* (*pl* -n) half.
Halfter ['halftər] *f or neut* (*pl* -n) halter.
Hall [hal] *m* (*pl* -e) sound, peal.
Halle ['halə] *f* (*pl* -n) hall; (*Hotel*) lobby; (*Flugzeug-*) hangar.
hallen ['halən] *v* sound, resound.
Hallenbad ['halənbait] *neut* indoor swimming-pool *or* baths.
Halm [halm] *m* (*pl* -e) stalk; (*Gras*) blade.

Hals [hals] *m* (*pl* Hälse) neck; (*innerer Hals, Kehle*) throat. **–band** *neut* (*Hund*) collar; (*Frauen*) necklace, choker. **–binde** *f* tie. **–kette** *f* necklace. **–weh** *neut* sore throat.
Halt [halt] *m* (*pl* -e) (*Anhalten*) stop, halt; (*Stütze*) hold, support; (*Standhaftigkeit*) steadiness, firmness. **haltbar** *adj* durable, lasting. **haltbar bis ...** (*Speisen*) use by ... . **halten** *v* hold; (*bewahren*) keep; (*dauern*) last, keep; (*Gebot, usw.*) observe; (*anhalten*) stop. **viel halten von** think highly of. **halten für** consider (to be), think of as. **Halte‖stelle** *f* (*Bus*) bus-stop. **–tau** *neut* guy-rope. **haltmachen** *v* stop. **Haltung** *f* (*pl* -en) attitude; (*Körper-*) bearing, posture.
hämisch ['hɛimiʃ] *adj* spiteful, sardonic.
Hammelfleisch ['haməlflaiʃ] *neut* mutton.
Hammer ['hamər] *m* (*pl* Hämmer) hammer.
hämmern ['hɛmərn] *v* hammer.
Hämorrhoiden [hɛmɔrɔ'iidən] *pl* piles, haemorrhoids *pl.*
Hamster ['hamstər] *m* (*pl* -) hamster. **hamstern** *v* hoard.
Hand [hant] *f* (*pl* Hände) hand. **an Hand von** with the aid of. **bei der Hand** ready, at hand. **mit der Hand** by hand. **von Hand gemacht** hand-made. **zur linken/rechten Hand** on the left/right hand side. **Hand‖arbeit** *f* handiwork; (*Nadelarbeit*) needlework. **–becken** *neut* hand basin. **–bremse** *f* handbrake. **–buch** *neut* manual, handbook.
Händedruck ['hɛndədruk] *m* handshake.
Handel ['handəl] *m* trade, commerce; (*Geschäft*) transaction, deal. **handeln** *v* act. **handeln mit** (*Person*) trade *or* deal with; (*Waren*) trade *or* deal in. **handeln von** treat, deal with. **Handels‖beziehungen** *pl* trade relations. **–bilanz** *f* balance of trade. **–schule** *f* business *or* commercial school. **–sperre** *f* (trade) embargo.
handfest ['hantfest] *adj* sturdy, strong.
Hand‖fläche *f* palm. **–gebrauch** *m* everyday use. **–gelenk** *neut* wrist. **–gepäck** *neut* hand luggage.
handhaben ['hanthaibən] *v* (*gebrauchen*) use, employ; (*fig*) handle.
Händler ['hɛntlər] *m* (*pl* -) trader, dealer.
handlich [hantliç] *adj* handy.

Handlung

Handlung ['hantluŋ] f (pl -en) deed, act; (Roman, usw.) plot; (Geschäft) business, firm; (Laden) shop.
Hand‖schellen pl handcuffs pl. **–schuh** m glove. **–tasche** f handbag. **–tuch** neut towel. **–werk** neut craft, trade. **–werker** m craftsman, workman.
Hang [haŋ] m (pl Hänge) slope; (Neigung) tendency.
Hängematte ['hɛŋəmatə] f hammock.
***hängen¹** [hɛŋən] v be suspended, hang; (sich neigen) slope; (unentschieden) be pending, remain undecided; (abhängen) depend.
hängen² v hang, suspend; (hinrichten) hang.
Hannover [ha'nɔɪfər] neut Hanover.
hantieren [han'tiːrən] v busy oneself, potter around.
Happen ['hapən] m (pl -) mouthful, bite.
Harfe ['harfə] f (pl -n) harp.
harmlos ['harmlɔɪs] adj harmless.
Harmonie [harmɔ'niː] f (pl -n) harmony. **harmonisch** adj harmonic. **harmonisieren** v harmonize.
Harn [harn] m urine. **–blase** f (Anat) bladder.
Harnisch ['harnɪʃ] m (pl -e) armour; harness.
Harpune [har'puːnə] f (pl -n) harpoon.
harren ['harən] v wait for, await.
hart [hart] adj hard; (fig) harsh, rough.
Härte ['hɛrtə] f (pl -n) hardness; (Strenge) severity; (Grausamkeit) cruelty. **härten** v harden; (Metall) temper.
hart‖gekocht adj hard-boiled. **–näckig** adj stubborn.
Harz [harts] neut (pl -e) resin.
Haschisch ['haʃɪʃ] neut hashish.
Hase ['haɪzə] m (pl -n) hare.
Haselnuß ['haɪzəlnus] f hazelnut.
Haspe ['haspə] f (pl -n) hinge.
Haß [has] m hate.
hassen ['hasən] v hate. **–swert** adj hateful, odious.
häßlich ['hɛslɪç] adj ugly; (fig) wicked, nasty. **Häßlichkeit** f ugliness; (fig) wickedness.
Hast [hast] f haste. **hasten** v hasten. **hastig** adj hasty.
hätscheln ['hɛtʃəln] v (liebkosen) caress, fondle; (verwöhnen) pamper.
Haube ['haubə] f (pl -n) bonnet, cap; (Mot) bonnet, (US) hood.

Hauch [haux] m (pl -e) breath; (fig) touch, trace.
Haue ['hauə] f (pl -n) pick; (umg.) beating, spanking. **hauen** v hew; (zerhacken) chop up; (umg.) beat, belt.
Haufen ['haufən] m (pl -) heap, pile; (umg.) heaps of, lots of.
häufen ['hɔyfən] v heap (up), accumulate.
häufig ['hɔyfɪç] adj frequent, numerous. adv frequently.
Haupt [haupt] neut (pl Häupter) head; (Führer) leader, chief. **–bahnhof** m main railway station, central station. **–buch** neut ledger. **–film** m feature film, main film. **–leitung** f (Gas, Strom) mains pl. **–mann** m (Mil) captain. **–rolle** f (Theater) leading part or role.
Hauptsache ['hauptzaxə] f main thing or point. **hauptsächlich** adj essential. adv principally, mainly.
Haupt‖sitz m head office. **–stadt** f capital (city). **–straße** f main street. **–wort** neut noun.
Haus [haus] neut (pl Häuser) house; (Heim) home. **zu Hause** at home. **–arbeit** f housework; (Schule) homework. **–aufgaben** pl (Schule) homework sing.
Häuschen ['hɔsçən] neut (pl -) cottage, small house.
Haus‖frau f housewife. **–halt** m household; (Budget) budget. **–hälterin** f housekeeper. **–haltsplan** m budget.
hausieren [hau'ziːrən] v peddle, hawk.
häuslich ['hɔyslɪç] adj domestic.
Haus‖mädchen neut housemaid. **–meister** m caretaker. **–tür** f front door. **–wart** m caretaker. **–wirt** m landlord. **–wirtin** f landlady. **–wirtschaft** f housekeeping.
Haut [haut] f (pl Häute) skin; (Tier) hide, pelt. **–auschlag** m rash. **–krem** m skin cream.
Hebamme ['heɪpamə] f (pl -n) midwife.
Hebel ['heɪbəl] m (pl -) lever.
***heben** ['heɪbən] v lift, raise; (Steuer) raise, levy. **sich heben** rise. **Hebung** f raising; (Beseitigung) removal.
Hecht [hɛçt] m (pl -e) pike.
Heck [hɛk] neut (pl -e) stern; (eines Autos) rear. **–klappe** f (Mot) hatchback, tailgate.
Hecke ['hɛkə] f (pl -n) hedge; (Brut) brood, hatch. **–nschütze** m sniper.

Heer [heɪr] *neut* (*pl* -e) army.
Hefe ['heɪfə] *f* yeast.
Heft [hɛft] *neut* (*pl* -e) notebook, exercise book; (*Zeitschrift*) issue; (*Griff*) handle, haft.
heftig ['hɛftɪç] *adj* violent; (*leidenschaftlich*) passionate, vehement.
hegen ['heɪɡən] *v* (*hätscheln*) cherish; (*schützen*) protect; (*Gedanken*) nurture.
Heide[1] ['haɪdə] *m* (*pl* -n) heathen, pagan.
Heide[2] *f* (*pl* -n) heath, moor. **-kraut** *neut* heather.
Heidelbeere ['haɪdəlbɛɪrə] *f* bilberry.
heidnisch ['haɪtnɪʃ] *adj* heathen, pagan.
heikel ['haɪkəl] *adj* delicate, awkward.
heil [haɪl] *adj* safe, uninjured; (*geheilt*) healed; (*ganz*) whole. **Heil** *neut* welfare; (*Kirche*) salvation. **-and** *m* saviour.
heil‖bringend *adj* salutary. **-en** *v* heal, cure.
heilig ['haɪlɪç] *adj* holy, sacred. **Heiliger Abend** Christmas Eve. **Heilige(r)** *m* saint. **Heiligenschein** *m* halo.
Heil‖kunde *f* medicine, medical science. **-mittel** *neut* remedy, cure.
heim [haɪm] *adv* home(ward). **Heim** *neut* (*pl* -e) home.
Heimat ['haɪmaɪt] *f* (*unz.*) home(land), native place. **-land** *neut* homeland. **heimatlos** *adj* homeless. **Heimatstadt** *f* home town.
heimisch *adj* domestic; (*heimatlich*) native. **Heimkehr** *f* return (home).
heim‖lich *adj* secret. **-suchen** *v* plague, afflict. **-tückisch** *adj* malicious, insidious.
Heimweh ['haɪmveɪ] *neut* homesickness. **Heimweh haben** be homesick.
Heirat ['haɪraɪt] *f* (*pl* -en) marriage. **heiraten** *v* marry.
heiser ['haɪzər] *adj* hoarse.
heiß [haɪs] *adj* hot.
***heißen** ['haɪsən] *v* be called *or* named; (*bedeuten*) mean. **wie heißt Du?** what's your name? **das heißt (d.h.)** that is (i.e.).
heiter ['haɪtər] *adj* (*Person*) serene; (*Erählung*) happy; (*Wetter*) bright, clear. **Heiterkeit** *f* serenity.
Heiz‖apparat ['haɪtsaparaɪt] *m* (*pl* -e) heater. **-decke** *f* electric blanket. **heizen** *v* heat. **Heiz‖ung** *f* heating. **-material** *neut* fuel.
Hektar [hɛk'taɪr] *neut* (*pl* -e) hectare.

Held [hɛlt] *m* (*pl* -en) hero. **Helden‖mut** *m* heroism. **-tat** *f* heroic deed, exploit.
Heldin *f* (*pl* -nen) heroine.
helfen ['hɛlfən] *v* help, assist; (*nützen*) help, do good. **Helfer** *m* (*pl* -), **Helferin** *f* (*pl* -nen) helper, assistant.
hell [hɛl] *adj* (*Licht*) bright; (*Farbe*) light; (*Klang*) clear. **hellblau** *adj* light blue. **Hellseher** *m* (*pl* -), **Hellseherin** *f* (*pl* -nen) clairvoyant.
Helm [hɛlm] *m* (*pl* -e) helmet; (*Naut*) rudder; (*Kuppel*) dome.
Hemd [hɛmt] *neut* (*pl* -en) shirt. **-särmel** *m* shirtsleeve.
hemmen ['hɛmən] *v* restrain, hinder, inhibit; (*Psychol*) inhibit. **Hemmung** *f* (*pl* -en) hindrance, stoppage; (*Psychol*) inhibition. **hemmungslos** *adj* unrestrained.
Hengst [hɛŋst] *m* (*pl* -e) stallion.
Henkel ['hɛŋkəl] *m* (*pl* -) handle.
Henker ['hɛŋkər] *m* (*pl*-) hangman.
her [heɪr] *adv* (to) here; (*zeitlich*) ago, since; (*von*) from. **hin und her** to and fro, back and forth. **komm her!** come here! **wo kommen Sie her?** where do you come from? **schon lange her** a long time ago. **von weit her** from afar.
herab [he'rap] *adv* down(wards). **-hängen** *v* hang down. **-lassen** *v* lower. **sich herablassen** condescend. **herab‖lassend** *adj* patronizing. **-setzen** *v* reduce; (*Person*) degrade. **-setzend** *adj* contemptuous. **-würdigen** *v* debase, degrade.
heran [he'ran] *adv* near, up to; (*hierher*) (to) here. **-gehen** *v* go up to, approach. **-kommen** *v* approach, draw near.
herauf [he'rauf] *adv* (up) here, (*hinauf*) upwards. **-beschwören** *v* conjure up. **-ziehen** *v* pull up.
heraus [he'raus] *adv* out; (*draußen, aus dem Hause*) outside. **-fordern** *v* challenge. **Herausforderung** *f* challenge. **herausgeben** *v* give out; (*Buch, usw.*) publish. **Herausgeber** *m* publisher. **herauswachsen aus** *v* grow out of.
herb [hɛrp] *adj* sharp, tart; (*Wein*) dry; (*fig*) harsh.
herbei [hɛr'baɪ] *adv* (to) here, this way. **-führen** *v* cause.
Herberge ['hɛrbɛrɡə] *f* (*pl* -n) hostel.
Herbst [hɛrpst] *m* (*pl* -e) autumn, (*US*) fall. **herbstlich** *adj* autumnal.
Herd [heɪrt] *m* (*pl* -e) cooker, stove.
Herde ['heɪrdə] *f* (*pl* -n) herd.

herein [hɛ'rain] *adv* in, inside, in here.
−**führen** *v* usher in. −**treten** *v* enter.
***hergeben** ['hɛɪrgeɪbən] *v* hand over.
hergebracht ['hɛɪrgəbraxt] *adj* traditional,
customary.
Hering ['heriŋ] *m* (*pl* -e) herring.
***herkommen** ['hɛɪrkɔmən] *v* come here;
(*abstammen*) come from. **herkommen von**
be caused by, be due to. **herkömmlich**
adj customary, traditional.
Herkunft ['hɛrkunft] *f* (*unz*) origin; (*Person*) birth, descent.
herleiten ['hɛɪrlaɪtən] *v* lead here; (*fig*)
derive, deduce. **Herleitung** *f* derivation.
Hermelin [hɛrmə'liɪn] *neut* (*pl* -e) ermine.
hernach [hɛr'naɪx] *adv* afterwards, after
this.
Heroin [hero'iɪn] *neut* heroin.
Herr [hɛr] *m* (*pl* -en) (*Anrede*) Mr; (*Herrscher*) master, lord. **der Herr Gott** Lord
God. **dieser Herr** this gentleman. **Her-
ren‖artikel** *pl* men's clothing. −**haus** *neut*
manor house. −**toilette** *f* men's lavatory.
herrichten ['hɛrɪçtən] *v* prepare, arrange.
Herrin ['hɛrin] *f* (*pl* -nen) lady, mistress.
herr‖isch *adj* overbearing, domineering.
−**lich** *adj* splendid, magnificent.
Herr‖lichheit *f* splendour, magnificence.
−**schaft** *f* power, rule; (*fig*) mastery.
herrschen *v* rule, govern; (*vorhanden
sein*) prevail. **Herrscher** *m* (*pl* -) ruler.
her‖rühren *v* originate (from). −**stammen**
v descend (from). −**stellen** *v* manufacture, make; (*reparieren*) repair. **Hersteller** *m* manufacturer, maker. **Herstellung** *f*
manufacture.
herüber [hɛ'ryɪbər] *adv* across, over here.
herum [hɛ'rum] *adv* (a)round, about.
−**fahren** *v* drive around. −**pfuschen** *v*
tinker, mess around (with). −**streichen** *v*
roam about, wander around.
herunter [hɛ'runtər] *adv* downwards,
down (here). −**kommen** *v* come down;
(*sinken*) decline.
hervor [hɛr'foɪr] *adv* forth, out. −**bringen**
v produce; (*Worte*) utter. −**heben** *v* make
prominent, bring out. −**ragen** *v* stand
out, jut out. −**ragend** *adj* outstanding.
−**rufen** *v* arouse; (*verursachen*) cause.
−**treten** *v* come forward.
Herz [hɛrts] *neut* (*pl* -en) heart. −**anfall** *m*
heart attack. **herz‖erfreuend** *adj* hearten-
ing, cheering. −**erschütternd** *adj* appalling. −**haft** *adj* stout-hearted. −**ig** *adj*

lovely. −**lich** *adj* hearty. −**los** *adj* heart-
less.
Herzog ['hɛrtsoɪk] *m* (*pl* **Herzöge**) duke.
−**in** *f* (*pl* -nen) duchess. **Herzogtum** *neut*
duchy, dukedom.
herzu [hɛr'tsuɪ] *adv* (to) here, towards.
Hessen ['hɛsən] *neut* Hesse.
Hetze ['hɛtsə] *f* (*pl* -n) hounding, baiting;
(*Eile*) mad rush, dash; (*Jagd*) hunt.
hetzen *v* hound; rush, dash; hunt.
Heu [hɔy] *neut* hay. **Heu‖fieber** *neut* hay
fever. −**gabel** *f* pitchfork. −**schober** *m*
haystack. −**schrecke** *f* grasshopper,
locust.
Heuchelei [hɔyçə'lai] *f* (*pl* -en) hypocrisy.
heucheln *v* be hypocritical. **Heuchler** *m*
(*pl* -), **Heuchlerin** *f* (*pl* -nen) hypocrite.
heuchlerisch *adj* hypocritical.
heulen ['hɔylən] *v* cry, howl.
heute ['hɔytə] *adv* today. **heutig** *adj*
today's; (*gegenwärtig*) present, current.
heutzutage *adv* nowadays, these days.
Hexe ['hɛksə] *f* (*pl* -n) witch.
Hieb [hiɪp] *m* (*pl* -e) blow, stroke;
(*Schnitt*) cut, slash.
hier [hiɪr] *adv* here. **hier und da** now and
then. **hier und dort** here and there.
hier‖auf *adv* then, upon this. −**aus** *adv*
from this. −**bei** *adv* hereby, herewith;
(*Brief*) enclosed. −**für** *adv* for this.
hi-fi ['haifai] *adj* hi-fi.
Hilfe ['hilfə] *f* (*pl* -n) help, assistance.
−**ruf** *m* cry for help. **hilf‖los** *adj* helpless.
−**reich** *adj* helpful. −**sbereit** *adj* eager to
help. **Hilfs‖lehrer** *m* assistant teacher.
−**mittel** *neut* remedy, aid.
Himbeere ['himbeirə] *f* raspberry.
Himmel ['himəl] *m* (*pl* -) sky; (*Paradies*)
heaven. −**fahrt** *f* Ascension. −**reich** *neut*
heaven. −**skörper** *m* celestial body.
himmlisch ['himliʃ] *adj* celestial, heavenly.
hin [hin] *adv* (to) there, from here,
towards. **hin und her** to and fro, back
and forth. **hin und wieder** now and
again. **hin und zurück** there and back.
vor sich hin to oneself. **es ist noch lange
hin** there's a long time to go.
hinab [hi'nap] *adv* down(wards). −**lassen**
v lower, let down. −**steigen** *v* descend.
hinan [hi'nan] *adv* up (to), upwards.
hinauf [hi'nauf] *adv* up (there), upwards.
die Treppe hinauf up the stairs. −**setzen**
v put up. −**ziehen** *v* pull up, (*umziehen*)
move up.

hinaus [hi'naus] *adv* out, forth. **–gehen** *v* go out. **hinausgehen über** surpass, exceed. **hinaus‖kommen** *v* come out. **–werfen** *v* throw out.

Hinblick ['hinblik] *m* **im Hinblick auf** with regard to.

hinderlich ['hindərliç] *adj* restrictive, hindering. **hindern** *v* hinder; (*verhindern*) prevent. **Hindernis** *neut* (*pl* -se) obstacle, hindrance.

hindeuten ['hindɔytən] *v* point (at); (*fig*) hint (at).

hindurch [hin'durç] *adv* through, across; (*zeitlich*) throughout.

hinein [hi'nain] *adv* in(to). **sich hineindrängen** *v* force one's way in. **hineinziehen** *v* draw in; (*fig: verwickeln*) involve; (*umziehen*) move to.

hinfahren ['hinfaɪrən] *v* drive there; (*hinbringen*) take there. **Hinfahrt** *f* outward journey, way there.

*****hinfallen** ['hinfalən] *v* fall down. **hinfällig** *adj* feeble, frail; (*Meinung*) untenable, invalid.

Hingabe ['hingaɪbə] *f* devotion.

*****hingeben** ['hingeɪbən] *v* give up. **sich hingeben** devote oneself (to).

hingegen ['hingeɪgən] *conj* on the other hand, whereas.

*****hingehen** ['hingeɪən] *v* go there; (*Zeit*) pass, elapse. **etwas hingehen lassen** let something pass.

hinken ['hiŋkən] *v* limp.

hin‖kommen *v* arrive, get there; (*umg.*) manage. **–langen** *v* reach. **–länglich** *adj* sufficient. **–legen** *v* put down. **sich hinlegen** lie down. **hin‖nehmen** *v* put up with, bear. **–reichend** *adj* sufficient.

Hinreise ['hinraizə] *f* outward journey, way there.

hinreißen ['hinraisən] *v* carry along; (*entzücken*) charm, transport. **–d** *adj* charming, enchanting.

hinrichten ['hinriçtən] *v* (*Person*) execute. **Hinrichtung** *f* execution.

*****hinschreiben** ['hinʃraibən] *v* write down.

Hinsicht ['hinziçt] *f* **in Hinsicht auf** with regard to. **in dieser Hinsicht** in this regard. **hinsichtlich** *adv* with regard to.

hinten ['hintən] *adv* behind, at the back. **nach hinten** to the back, backwards. **von hinten** from behind.

hinter ['hintər] *prep* behind, after. *adj* rear, back. **Hinter‖achse** *f* rear axle. **–bein** *neut* hind leg. **Hintere(r)** *m* back

part; (*Körper*) bottom, backside. **hintergehen** *v* deceive, fool.

Hinter‖grund *m* background. **–halt** *m* ambush. **aus dem Hinterhalt überfallen** ambush. **Hinterhof** *m* rear court, back yard.

hinter‖lassen *v* leave (behind). **–legen** *v* deposit.

Hintern ['hintərn] *m* (*pl* -) bottom, backside.

Hinter‖schiff *neut* stern. **–teil** *m* back part. **–tür** *f* back door.

hinterziehen [hintər'tsiːən] *v* (*Steuern*) evade. **Hinterziehung** *f* (tax) evasion.

hinüber [hi'nyːbər] *adv* over, across, to the other side. **–gehen** *v* cross (over).

hinunter [hi'nuntər] *adv* downwards, down (there). **die Treppe hinunter** downstairs.

hinweg [hin'vɛk] *adv* away (from here), off. **Hinweg** *m* outward journey. **hinwegkommen über** get over.

Hinweis ['hinvais] *m* (*pl* -e) indication, hint. **hinweisen** *v* point out, show; (*Person*) direct; (*anspielen*) refer, allude.

*****hinziehen** ['hintsiːən] *v* draw, attract; (*verzögern*) drag out.

hinzu [hin'tsuː] *adv* in addition, as well. **–fügen** *v* add. **–kommen** *v* be added. **–kommend** *adj* additional. **–ziehen** *v* draw *or* bring in; (*Fachmann*) consult.

Hirn [hirn] *neut* (*pl* -e) brain.

Hirsch [hirʃ] *m* (*pl* -e) stag. **–fleisch** *neut* venison. **–kalb** *neut* fawn. **–kuh** *f* doe, hind.

Hirt [hirt] *m* (*pl* -en) shepherd, herdsman. **–in** *f* (*pl* -nen) shepherdess.

hissen ['hisən] *v* hoist.

Historiker [hi'stoːrikər] *m* (*pl* -) historian. **historisch** *adj* historical; (*bedeutend*) historic.

Hitze ['hitsə] *f* (*unz.*) heat; (*Leidenschaft*) passion. **hitzebeständig** *adj* heat-resistant. **hitzig** *adj* hot; (*fig*) fiery, passionate. **Hitz‖kopf** *m* hothead. **–schlag** *m* heat-stroke.

hoch [hoːx] (**hoher, hohe, hohes, höher, höchst**) *adj* high; (*Baum*) tall; (*Alter*) old, advanced. *adv* highly, greatly. **hohe Blüte** full bloom. **hohe See** high *or* open sea. **10 hoch 4** 10 to the power of 4. **Hoch** *neut* (*pl* -s) cheer; (*Hochdruckgebiet*) high-pressure area. **Dreimal hoch** three cheers.

Hochachtung ['hoːxaxtuŋ] f respect, esteem. **hochachtungsvoll** respectfully, yours faithfully.

hochdeutsch ['hoxdɔytʃ] adj high German, standard German.

Hoch‖druck m high pressure. −**ebene** f plateau. −**flut** f high tide. −**frequenz** f high frequency.

*****hochhalten** ['hoːxhaltən] v think highly of, esteem.

Hoch‖haus neut tall building, high-rise block. −**konjunktur** f boom. −**land** neut highland(s). −**leistung-** adj heavy-duty. −**mut** m pride, arrogance. **hochmütig** adj proud, arrogant.

Hoch‖ruf m cheer. −**schätzung** f (high) esteem. −**schule** f college, university; (technische) polytechnic. −**spannung** f high tension, high voltage. −**sprung** m high jump. −**verrat** m high treason. −**wasser** neut high tide, high water; (Überschwemmung) flooding. **Hochzeit** f wedding. **hochzeitlich** adj nuptial, bridal. **Hochzeitskleid** neut wedding dress.

höchst [hœːxst] adj highest, greatest. adv very (much), greatly, highly.

hochstehend ['hoxʃteːənt] adj high-ranking, eminent.

höchstens [hœxstəns] adv at most, at best.

Höchst‖geschwindigkeit f maximum speed. −**preis** m maximum price.

hocken ['hɔkən] v squat, crouch. **Hocker** m (pl -) stool.

Hode ['hoːdə] f (pl -n) or **Hoden** m (pl -) testicle.

Hof [hoːf] m (pl **Höfe**) (court)yard; (Landwirtschaft) farm; (fürstlich) court.

hoffen ['hɔfən] v hope. **hoffentlich** adv I hope (so); let us hope (that). **Hoffnung** f (pl -en) hope. **hoffnungs‖los** adj hopeless. −**voll** adj hopeful.

höflich ['hœflɪç] adj polite, courteous. **Höflichkeit** f courtesy, politeness.

hohe(r) ['hoːə(r)] V hoch.

Höhe ['hœːə] f (pl -n) height; (Gipfel) top; (Geog) latitude; (Hügel) hill.

Hoheit ['hoːhait] f (unz.) grandeur, greatness; (Titel) Highness. −**sgewässer** pl territorial waters.

Höhepunkt ['hœːəpuŋkt] m climax.

höher ['hœːər] V hoch.

hohl [hoːl] adj hollow, (Linse) concave.

Höhle ['hœːlə] f (pl -n) cave; (Loch) hole;

(eines Tiers) burrow, hole. **höhlen** v hollow (out).

höhnen ['hœːnən] v mock, taunt. **höhnisch** adj mocking, scornful.

hold [hɔlt] adj charming, gracious. −**selig** adj most charming, most gracious.

holen ['hoːlən] v fetch. **Atem holen** draw breath. **sich Rat holen bei** ask for advice.

Holländer ['hɔlɛndər] m (pl -) Dutchman. −**in** f (pl -nen) Dutchwoman. **holländisch** adj Dutch.

Hölle ['hœlə] f (pl -n) hell.

Holunder [ho'lundər] m (pl -) elder (tree). −**beere** f elderberry.

Holz [hɔlts] neut (pl **Hölzer**) wood. −**blasinstrument** neut woodwind instrument.

hölzern ['hœltsərn] adj wooden; (fig) stiff, awkward, clumsy.

holzig ['hɔltsɪç] adj woody.

Holz‖klotz m wooden block. −**kohle** f charcoal. −**schnitt** m woodcut. −**weg** m **auf dem Holzwege sein** to be on the wrong track. **Holzwurm** m woodworm.

Homosexualität [homozɛksuali'tɛit] f homosexuality. **homosexuell** adj homosexual. **Homosexuelle(r)** m homosexual.

Honig ['hoːnɪç] m honey. −**biene** f honeybee.

Honorar [hono'raːr] neut (pl -e) fee, honorarium; (eines Autors) royalties pl.

Hopfen ['hɔpfən] m (pl -) hops pl.

hörbar ['hœːrbaːr] adj audible.

horchen ['hɔrçən] v listen (to); (heimlich) eavesdrop.

Horde ['hɔrdə] f (pl -n) horde.

hören ['hœːrən] v hear; (Radio) listen to. **Hören** neut (sense of) hearing. −**sagen** neut hearsay. **Hörer** m hearer; (Radio) listener; (Telef) receiver; (pl) audience. −**schaft** f audience. **Hörgerät** neut hearing aid.

Horizont [hori'tsɔnt] m (pl -e) horizon. **horizontal** adj horizontal.

Hormon [hɔr'moːn] neut (pl -e) hormone.

Horn [hɔrn] neut (pl **Hörner**) horn. −**brille** f horn-rimmed spectacles. −**haut** f (Anat) cornea.

Horoskop [horo'skoːp] neut (pl -e) horoscope.

Hör‖probe f audition. −**saal** m lecture hall. −**spiel** neut radio play.

Hose ['hoːzə] f (pl -n) trousers. **Hosen‖schlitz** m flies, (US) fly. −**träger** pl braces, (US) suspenders.

Höschen ['hœɪsçən] *neut* (*pl* -) knickers *pl*; panties *pl*.
Hotel [ho'tɛl] *neut* (*pl* -s) hotel.
Hub [huːp] *m* (*pl* Hübe) lift; (*Mot*) stroke. **–raum** *m* cylinder capacity.
hübsch [hypʃ] *adj* pretty, nice; (*Mann*) good-looking.
Hubschrauber ['hupʃraubər] *m* (*pl* -) helicopter.
Huf [huːf] *m* (*pl* -e) hoof. **–eisen** *neut* horseshoe.
Hüftbein ['hyftbain] *neut* hipbone. **Hüfte** *f* hip.
Hügel ['hyːgəl] *m* (*pl* -) hill. **hügelig** *adj* hilly.
Huhn [huːn] *neut* (*pl* Hühner) hen; (*Küche*) chicken.
Hühner‖auge *neut* (*Med*) corn. **–braten** *m* roast chicken. **–brühe** *f* chicken broth. **–ei** *neut* hen's egg. **–stall** *m* henhouse.
huldigen ['huldɪgən] *v* pay homage to; (*Ansicht*) hold, subscribe to. **Huldigung** *f* homage.
Hülle ['hylə] *f* covering, wrapping; (*Umschlag*) envelope. (*Buch*) jacket, cover. **in Hülle und Fülle** in abundance. **hüllen** *v* wrap, cover.
Hülse ['hylzə] *f* (*pl* -n) husk, shell; (*Erbse*) pod; (*aus Papier, usw.*) case, casing.
human [hu'maːn] *adj* humane. **Humanist** *m* (*pl* -en) humanist. **humanitär** *adj* humanitarian.
Hummel ['huməl] *f* (*pl* -n) bumblebee.
Hummer ['humər] *m* (*pl* -) lobster.
Humor [hu'moːr] *m* (sense of) humour. **humorvoll** *adj* humorous.
humpeln ['humpəln] *v* hobble, limp.
Hund [hunt] *m* (*pl* -e) dog. **Hunde‖hütte** *f* kennel. **–leine** *f* leash.
hundert ['hundərt] *adj, pron* hundred. **Hundert‖füßler** *m* centipede. **–jahrfeier** *f* centenary. **hundert‖mal** *adv* a hundred times. **–prozentig** *adj* one-hundred-per-cent, complete.
Hündin ['hyndin] *f* (*pl* -nen) bitch.
Hunger ['huŋər] *m* hunger. **Hunger haben** be hungry. **–lohn** *m* starvation wages *pl*; pittance. **hungern** *v* starve; be hungry. **Hungersnot** *f* famine. **Hungerstreik** *m* hungerstrike. **hungrig** *adj* hungry.
Hupe ['huːpə] *f* (*pl* -n) (*Mot*) horn. **hupen** *v* sound the horn, beep.
hüpfen ['hypfən] *v* hop, skip.
Hürde ['hyrdə] *f* (*pl* -n) hurdle; (*Schafe*) fold, pen.

Hure ['huːrə] *f* (*pl* -n) whore.
hurra [hu'raː] *interj* hurrah!
husten ['huːstən] *v* cough. **Husten** *m* (*pl* -) cough.
Hut¹ [huːt] *m* (*pl* Hüte) hat.
Hut² *f* (*unz.*) (*Schutz*) protection; (*Vorsicht*) care; (*Aufsicht*) guard. **auf der Hut sein** (**vor**) be on one's guard (against).
hüten ['hyːtən] *v* guard. **sich hüten** (**vor**) be careful *or* wary (of).
Hütte ['hytə] *f* (*pl* -n) hut, cabin; (*Metall*) foundry, ironworks. **–nkäse** *m* cottage cheese.
Hyäne [hy'ɛːnə] *f* (*pl* -n) hyena.
Hydraulik [hy'draulik] *f* hydraulics. **hydraulisch** *adj* hydraulic.
Hygiene [hygi'eːnə] *f* hygiene. **hygienisch** *adj* hygienic.
Hymne ['hymnə] *f* (*pl* -n) hymn.
Hypnose [hyp'noːzə] *f* (*pl* -n) hypnosis. **hypno‖tisch** *adj* hypnotic. **–tisieren** *v* hypnotize.
Hypothek [hypo'teːk] *f* (*pl* -en) mortgage.
Hypothese [hypo'teːzə] *f* (*pl* -n) hypothesis. **hypothetisch** *adj* hypothetical.
Hysterie [hyste'riː] *f* hysteria. **hysterisch** *adj* hysterical. **hysterische Anfälle** *pl* hysterics.

I

ich [iç] *pron* I. **Ich** *neut* self, ego. **ichbezogen** *adj* egocentric.
ideal [ide'aːl] *adj* ideal. **Ideal** *neut* (*pl* -e) ideal. **Idealismus** *m* idealism.
Idee [i'deː] *f* (*pl* -n) idea.
identifizieren ['dɛntifi'tsiːrən] *v* identify. **identisch** *adj* identical. **Identität** *f* identity.
Idiot [idi'oːt] *m* (*pl* -en) idiot. **idiotisch** *adj* idiotic.
Igel ['iːgəl] *m* (*pl* -) hedgehog.
ignorieren [igno'riːrən] *v* ignore.
ihm [iːm] *pron* (*Person*) (to) him; (*Sache*) (to) it.
ihn [iːn] *pron* (*Person*) him; (*Sache*) it.
ihnen ['iːnən] *pron* (to) them. **Ihnen** *pron* (to) you.
ihr [iːr] *pron* you; (*Dat*) (to) her. *pron, adj* (*Person*) her; its; their. **Ihr** *pron, adj* your. **ihrer, ihre, ihres** *pron* hers; its; theirs. **Ihrer, Ihre, Ihres** yours. **ihrerseits** *adv* for your part. **ihr‖esgleichen** *adv* like

her (it, them). **–etwegen** or **–etwillen** on her (its, their) account. **der, die, das ihrige** pron hers; its; theirs.

Illusion [iluzi'oɪn] f (pl **-en**) illusion. **illusorisch** adj illusory.

illustrieren [ilu'striɪrən] v illustrate. **Illustrierte** f (illustrated) magazine.

im [im] prep+art in dem.

Imbiß ['imbis] m (pl **Imbisse**) snack. **–stube** f snack bar.

Immatrikulation [imatrikulatsi'oɪn] f (pl **-en**) matriculation, registration.

immer ['imər] adv always. **immer mehr** more and more. **immer noch** still. **immer wieder** again and again. **wenn auch immer** although. **auf immer** forever. **–fort** adv constantly. **–grün** adj evergreen. **–hin** adv nevertheless. **–zu** adv all the time.

Immigrant [imi'grant] m (pl **-en**) immigrant.

Immobilien [imo'biɪliən] pl real estate sing.

Imperialismus [imperia'lismus] m imperialism. **Imperialist** m (pl **-en**) imperialist.

impfen ['impfən] v inoculate, vaccinate. **Impfung** f (pl **-en**) inoculation, vaccination.

imponieren [impo'niɪrən] v impress. **–d** adj impressive.

Import [im'pɔrt] m (pl **-e**) import(ation); (Ware) import. **–eur** m (pl **-e**) importer. **–handel** m import trade. **importieren** v import.

impotent ['impotɛnt] adj impotent.

imprägnieren [imprɛg'niɪrən] v impregnate, saturate.

improvisieren [improvi'ziɪrən] v improvise. **improvisiert** adj improvized, ad-lib.

imstande [im'ʃtandə] adv **imstande sein** be able or capable.

in [in] prep (+Dat) in; (+Acc) into, in; (Zeit) (with)in.

Inanspruchnahme [in'anʃpruxnaɪmə] f demands pl.

Inbegriff ['inbəgrif] m essence, epitome. **mit Inbegriff von** inclusive of. **inbegriffen** adj, adv (Steuer) included, inclusive(ly).

Inbrunst ['inbrunst] f ardour, fervour.

indem [in'deɪm] conj (dadurch daß) in that, by; (während) while.

Inder ['indər] m (pl **-**) (Asian) Indian.

indessen [in'dɛsən] conj (inzwischen) meanwhile, in the meantime; (immerhin) however, nevertheless.

Indianer [indi'aɪnər] m (pl **-**) (American) Indian. **indianisch** adj (American) Indian.

Indien ['indiən] neut India.

indirekt ['indirɛkt] adj indirect.

indisch ['indiʃ] adj (Asian) Indian.

indiskret ['indiskrɛt] adj indiscreet, tactless.

Individualist [individua'list] m (pl **-en**) individualist. **individualistisch** adj individualist(ic). **individuell** adj individual. **Individuum** neut (pl **-duen**) individual.

industrialisieren [industriali'ziɪrən] v industrialize. **Industrie** f (pl **-n**) industry. **–gebiet** neut industrial region. **industriell** adj industrial. **Industrielle(r)** m industrualist.

ineinander [inain'andər] adv in(to) each other. **–greifen** v (Tech) engage; (fig) overlap.

Infanterie [infantə'riɪ] f infantry. **Infanterist** m (pl **-en**) infantryman.

infiltrieren [infil'triɪrən] v infiltrate.

infizieren [infi'tsiɪrən] v infect. **sich infizieren** become infected, catch a disease.

Inflation [inflatsi'oɪn] f (Komm) inflation. **inflationär, inflationistisch** adj inflationary.

infolge [in'fɔlgə] prep on account of, owing to. **–dessen** adv consequently.

Information [infɔrmatsi'oɪn] f (pl **-en**) information. **eine Information** a piece of information.

informell ['infɔrmɛl] adj informal.

informieren [infɔr'miɪrən] v inform, instruct. **sich informieren über** find out about, gather information about.

Ingenieur [inʒe'njœɪr] m (pl **-e**) engineer. **–schule** f engineering college. **–wesen** neut engineering.

Ingwer ['iŋvɛɪr] m ginger.

Inhaber ['inhaɪbər] m (pl **-**) owner; (Titel, Paß, Patent) holder.

inhalieren [inha'liɪrən] v inhale.

Inhalt ['inhalt] m (pl **-e**) contents pl; (Bedeutung) meaning, content. **–sverzeichnis** neut table of contents.

Initiative [initsia'tiɪvə] f (unz.) initiative. **die Initiative ergreifen** take the initiative.

inklusive [inklu'ziɪvə] prep including, inclusive of.

inkonsequent ['inkɔnzekvɛnt] adj inconsistent.

Inkontinenz ['inkɔntinɛnts] *f* incontinence.

inkorporieren [inkɔrpɔ'riːrən] *v* incorporate.

Inkrafttreten [in'kraftreitən] *neut* coming into effect.

Inland ['inlant] *neut* inland, interior.

inmitten [in'mitən] *prep* in the midst of, among.

inne ['inə] *adv* within.

innen ['inən] *adv* within, inside. **nach innen** inwards. **Innen‖ausstattung** *f* interior decoration, decor. **–minister** *m* Home Secretary, Minister of the Interior. **–politik** *f* domestic policy. **innenpolitisch** *adj* (relating to) internal affairs. **Innenraum** *m* interior.

inner ['inər] *adj* internal, inner. **Innereien** *pl* offal. **Innere(s)** *neut* (*pl* -(e)n) interior. **inner‖halb** *prep* within. **–lich** *adj* inward, internal. **innerst** *adj* innermost.

innewohnen ['inəvoːnən] *v* be inherent (in).

innig ['iniç] *adj* (*Gefühle*) sincere; (*Freunde*) intimate.

ins [ins] *prep* + *art* in das.

Insasse ['inzasə] *m* (*pl* -n) inmate.

insbesondere [insbə'zɔndərə] *adv* particularly

Inschrift ['inʃrift] *f* inscription.

Insekt [in'zɛkt] *neut* (*pl* -en) insect. **–enpulver** *neut* insect powder. **–izid** *neut* insecticide.

Insel ['inzəl] *f* (*pl* -n) island.

Inserat [inze'raːt] *neut* (*pl* -e) (newspaper) advertisement.

insgesamt [insgə'zamt] *adv* altogether.

insofern [inzo'fɛrn] *conj* so far as; [in'zofɛrn] (*bis zu diesem Punkt*) to that extent. **insofern als** inasmuch as.

insoweit [inzo'vait] *adv* to that extent.

Inspektor [inspɛk'tɔr] *m* (*pl* -en) inspector.

instand halten [in'ʃtant haltən] *v* maintain (in good order). **instand setzen** *v* repair, overhaul; (*Person*) enable. **Instandhaltung** *f* upkeep, maintenance.

Instanz [in'stants] *f* (*pl* -en) authority. **durch die Instanzen** through official channels.

instinktiv [instiŋk'tiːf] *adj* instinctive.

Institut [insti'tuːt] *neut* (*pl* -e) institute.

Instrument [instru'mɛnt] *neut* (*pl* -e) instrument.

inszenieren [instse'niːrən] *v* (*Film,*

Schauspiel) produce; (*fig*) create, engineer.

integrieren [inte'griːrən] *v* integrate. **Integration** *f* integration.

intellektuell [intɛlɛktu'ɛl] *adj* intellectual. **intelligent** [intɛli'gɛnt] *adj* intelligent, clever.

interessant [intərɛ'sant] *adj* interesting. **Interesse** *neut* interest. **interessieren** *v* interest. **sich interessieren für** take an interest in, be interested in.

intern [in'tɛrn] *adj* internal.

Internat [intər'naːt] *neut* (*pl* -e) boarding school.

international [intərnatsio'naːl] *adj* international.

Interview [intər'vjuː] *neut* (*pl* -s) interview. **interviewen** *v* interview. **Interviewer** *m* interviewer. **Interviewte(r)** interviewee.

intim [in'tiːm] *adj* intimate.

Intrige [in'triːgə] *f* (*pl* -n) intrigue. **intrigieren** *v* plot, scheme.

Invalide(r) [inva'liːdə(r)] *m* invalid. **Invaliden‖heim** *neut* home for the disabled. **–rente** *f* disability pension. **invalid** *adj* invalid.

Inventar [invɛn'taːr] *neut* (*pl* -e) inventory.

Inventur [invɛn'tuːr] *f* (*pl* -en) stock-taking.

inwendig ['invɛndiç] *adj* inner.

inwiefern [invir'fɛrn] *conj* to what extent, how far.

inzwischen [in'tsviʃən] *adv* meanwhile.

irdisch ['irdiʃ] *adj* earthly, worldly.

Ire ['iːrə] *m* (*pl* -n) Irishman. **Irin** *f* (*pl* -nen) Irishwoman.

irgend ['irgənt] *adv* perhaps, ever. *pron* some, any. **irgend etwas** something, anything. **irgend jemand** someone, anyone. **irgend‖ein** *adj* some, any. **–wann** *adv* (at) sometime (or other). **–was** *pron* something, anything. **–wie** *adv* somehow, anyhow. **–wo** *adv* somewhere, anywhere.

Iris ['iːris] *f* (*pl* -) (*Anat*) iris.

irisch ['iːriʃ] *adj* Irish.

Irland ['irlant] *neut* Ireland. **Irländer** *m* (*pl* -) Irishman. **Irländerin** *f* (*pl* -nen) Irishwoman. **irländisch** *adj* Irish.

Ironie [iro'niː] *f* (*pl* -n) irony. **ironisch** *adj* ironic; (*spöttisch*) ironical.

irre ['irə] *adj* (*geistesgestört*) insane, mad; (*verwirrt*) confused. *adv* (*von Ziel weg*) astray. **irr werden** go insane. **irren** *v* err.

Irre(r) madman/woman). **irreführen** v lead astray; (täuschen) mislead. **Irrenanstalt** f mental home. **Irrglaube** m heresy. **irrig** adj erroneous. **Irrsinn** m insanity, madness. **irrsinnig** adj insane. **Irrtum** m (pl **Irrtümer**) error. **irrtümlich** adj erroneous, wrong.

Isolierband [izo'liːrbant] neut insulating tape; **isolieren** v isolate; (Elek) insulate. **Isolierung** f isolation; insulation.

Italien [i'taːliən] neut Italy. **Italiener** m (pl -). **Italienerin** f (pl -nen) Italian. **italienisch** adj Italian.

J

ja [ja] adv yes. **ja doch** to be sure, but yes. **ja freilich** yes indeed. **wenn ja** if so.

Jacht [jaxt] f (pl -en) yacht.

Jacke ['jakə] f (pl -n) jacket.

Jagd [jaːkt] f (pl -en) hunt; (Jagen) hunting. **-flugzeug** neut fighter plane. **-hund** m hound. **-schloß** neut hunting lodge.

jagen ['jaːgən] v hunt; (treiben) drive (away); (verfolgen) pursue; (eilen) rush, race.

Jäger ['jɛːgər] m (pl -) hunter; (Flugzeug) fighter.

jäh [jɛː] adj steep; (plötzlich) sudden.

Jahr [jaːr] neut (pl -e) year. **-buch** neut yearbook. **jahrelang** adv for years. **Jahres∥einkommen** neut annual income. **-ende** neut end of the year. **-tag** m anniversary. **-viertel** neut quarter. **-wende** f New Year, turn of the year. **-zeit** f season. **jahreszeitlich** adj seasonal. **Jahrhundert** neut century.

jährig ['jɛːriç] adj lasting a year. **dreijährig** adj three-year-old.

jährlich ['jɛːrliç] adj yearly, annual.

Jahr∥markt m fair. **-zehnt** neut decade.

Jalousie [ʒalu'ziː] f (pl -n) venetian blind.

Jammer ['jamər] m (unz.) wailing; (Elend) misery; (Verzweiflung) despair.

jämmerlich ['jɛmərliç] adj pitiable.

jammern ['jamərn] v wail; (klagen) complain.

Januar ['januaːr] m (pl -e) January.

Japan ['jaːpan] neut Japan. **-er** m (pl -), **Japanerin** f (pl -nen) Japanese. **japanisch** adj Japanese.

jauchzen ['jauxtsən] v shout joyfully, rejoice.

jawohl [ja'voːl] adv, interj yes indeed, certainly.

Jazz [dʒɛs] m jazz.

je [jeː] adv ever. **je und je** always. **je zwei** two each. conj **je mehr, desto besser** the more, the better. **je nachdem** that depends.

jedenfalls ['jeːdənfals] adv in any case.

jeder ['jeːdər], **jede, jedes** pron, adj each, every. **jedermann** pron everybody.

jederzeit adv always, (at) any time.

jedesmal ['jeːdəsmaːl] adv each time.

jedoch [je'dɔx] adv however, yet.

jemals ['jeːmaːls] adv ever, at any time.

jemand ['jeːmant] pron someone; (Fragen) anyone.

jener ['jeːnər], **jene, jenes** pron, adj that, pl those; (zuerst erwähnt) the former.

jenseits adv on the other side. prep on the other side of, across.

jetzig ['jɛtsiç] adj current, present. **jetzt** adv now, at present.

jeweilig ['jeːvailiç] adj at the time; (Vergangenheit) at that time, then. **jeweils** adv at a(ny) given time.

Jiddisch ['jidiʃ] neut Yiddish (language).

Joch [jɔx] neut (pl -e) yoke.

Jockei ['dʒɔki] m (pl -s) jockey.

Jod [joːt] neut iodine.

jodeln ['joːdəln] v yodel.

Joghurt ['joːgurt] neut (pl -s) yoghurt.

Johannisbeere [jo'hanisbeːrə] f redcurrant. **schwarze Johannisbeere** blackcurrant.

Journalismus [ʒurna'lismus] m journalism. **Journalist** m (pl -en) journalist. **journalistisch** adj journalistic.

Jubel ['juːbəl] m rejoicing, jubilation. **jubeln** v rejoice. **Jubiläum** neut (pl -äen) anniversary, jubilee.

jucken ['jukən] v itch. **Jucken** neut itch.

Jude ['juːdə] m (pl -n), **Jüdin** f (pl -nen) Jew. **jüdisch** adj Jewish.

Judo ['juːdo] neut judo.

Jugend ['juːgənt] f (unz.) youth. **-gericht** neut juvenile court. **-herberge** f youth hostel. **-kriminalität** f juvenile delinquency. **jugendlich** adj youthful, young, juvenile. **jugendlicher Verbrecher** m juvenile delinquent. **Jugendliche(r)** m youth, juvenile.

Jugoslawe [jugo'slaːvə] m, **Jugoslawin** f Yugoslav. **Jugoslawien** neut Yugoslavia. **jugoslawisch** adj Yugoslav.

Juli ['juːli] m (pl -s) July.
jung [juŋ] adj young. Junge m (pl -n)
boy; (Lehrling) apprentice; (Karten)
jack. jungenhaft adj boyish.
jünger ['jyŋər] adj younger, junior. Jünger m (pl -) disciple.
Junges ['juŋəs] neut (pl Jungen) young
(animal), offspring.
Jung‖fer f (pl -n) virgin; (Mädchen) girl.
alte Jungfer old maid, spinster. –frau f
virgin. jungfräulich adj maidenly, chaste.
Junggeselle m bachelor.
Jüngling ['jyŋliŋ] m (pl -e) youth, young
man. –salter neut youth, adolescence.
jüngst [jyŋst] adj youngest, (letzt) latest.
das jüngste Gericht the Last Judgment.
Juni ['juːni] m (pl -s) June.
Junker ['juŋkər] m (pl -) squire; (jung)
young aristocrat.
Jura¹ ['juːra] f law sing. Jura studieren
study law.
Jura² m (pl -s) the Jura, Jura Mountains.
Jurist [ju'rist] m (pl -en) lawyer.
just [just] adv just, exactly.
Justiz [jus'tiːts] f (unz.) justice, administration of the law. –irrtum m miscarriage of justice. –wesen neut legal
affairs, the law.
Juwel [ju'veːl] neut (pl -en) jewel. –ier m
(pl -e) jeweller.
Jux [juks] m (pl -e) joke, prank. aus Jux
as a joke, for fun.

K

Kabarett [kaba'rɛt] neut (pl -e) cabaret.
Kabel ['kaːbəl] neut (pl -) cable.
Kabeljau ['kaːbəljau] m (pl -e) cod.
kabeln ['kaːbəln] v cable, wire.
Kabine [ka'biːnə] f (pl -n) (Schiff) cabin;
(Umkleide-) cubicle; (Seilbahn) cable-
car.
Kabinett [kabi'nɛt] neut (pl -e) (Pol) cabi-
net; (Zimmer) closet.
Kadaver [ka'daːvər] m (pl -) carcass.
Kadett [ka'dɛt] m (pl -en) cadet.
Käfer ['kɛːfər] m (pl -) beetle.
Kaffee [ka'feː] m (pl -s) coffee. –bohne f
coffee bean. –kanne f coffee-pot.
–mühle f coffee-grinder. –satz m coffee
grounds pl.
Käfig ['kɛːfiç] m (pl -e) cage.
kahl [kaːl] adj bald; (Landschaft) bare,

barren. Kahlheit f baldness. kahlköpfig
adj bald-headed.
Kahn [kaːn] m (pl Kähne) small boat,
punt; (Last-) barge.
Kai [kai] m (pl -e) quay, wharf.
Kaiser ['kaizər] m (pl -) emperor. –in f
empress. kaiserlich adj imperial. Kaiser-
reich neut empire.
Kakao [ka'kao] m cocoa.
Kaktee [kak'teː] f, Kaktus m (pl Kakteen)
cactus.
Kalb [kalp] neut (pl Kälber) calf. –fleisch
neut veal. –sbraten m roast veal.
Kalender [ka'lɛndər] m (pl -) calendar.
Kaliber [ka'liːbər] neut (pl -) calibre.
Kalk [kalk] m (pl -e) lime. –stein m
limestone.
Kalorie [kalo'riː] f (pl -n) calorie.
kalt [kalt] adj cold. –blütig adj cold-
blooded.
Kälte ['kɛltə] f (unz.) cold(ness).
Kamel [ka'meːl] neut (pl -e) camel.
Kamera ['kaˈmeːra] f (pl -s) camera.
–mann m cameraman.
Kamerad [kame'rat] m (pl -en) companion, comrade. –schaft f companionship,
comradeship.
Kamin [ka'miːn] m (pl -e) (Feuerstelle)
hearth, fireplace; (Schornstein) chimney.
–feger m chimneysweep. –gesims neut
mantelpiece. –vorsatz m fireguard, fender.
Kamm [kam] m (pl Kämme) comb;
(Vogel) crest; (Berg) ridge, crest.
kämmen ['kɛmən] v comb. sich kämmen
comb one's hair.
Kammer ['kamər] f (pl -n) small room,
chamber; (Mil, Pol) chamber. –frau f
chambermaid. –herr m chamberlain.
–musik f chamber music.
Kampf [kampf] m (pl Kämpfe) fight,
struggle; (Schlacht) battle.
kämpfen ['kɛmpfən] v fight, struggle.
Kämpfer m (pl -) fighter.
Kampf‖handlung f (Mil) engagement;
action. –platz m battlefield. –wagen m
(Mil) tank.
Kanada ['kanada] neut Canada. Kanadier
m (pl -), Kanadierin f (pl -nen) Canadian.
kanadisch adj Canadian.
Kanal [ka'nal] m (pl Kanäle) canal;
(natürlicher, auch Radio, fig) channel;
(Abwasser) drain, sewer. –inseln pl
Channel Islands.

Kanarienvogel

Kanarienvogel [ka'naːriənfoːɡəl] *m* canary.

Kandidat [kandi'daɪt] *m* (*pl* **-en**) candidate. **kandidieren** *v* (*Wahl*) stand (for election); (*Posten*) apply (for).

Känguruh [kɛŋɡu'ruː] *neut* (*pl* **-s**) kangaroo.

Kaninchen [ka'niːnçən] *neut* (*pl* **-**) rabbit. **-stall** *m* rabbit hutch.

Kanne ['kanə] *n* (*pl* **-n**) can; (*Kaffee, Tee*) pot; (*Krug*) jug, pitcher.

Kannibale [kani'baːlə] *m* (*pl* **-n**) cannibal. **kannibalisch** *adj* cannibal.

Kanon ['kanɔn] *m* (*pl* **-s**) canon.

Kanone [ka'noːnə] *f* (*pl* **-n**) cannon, gun. **Kanonen‖feuer** *neut* bombardment. **-kugel** *f* cannonball.

Kante ['kantə] *f* (*pl* **-n**) edge.

Kantine [kan'tiːnə] *f* (*pl* **-n**) canteen.

Kanton [kan'tɔɪn] *m* (*pl* **-e**) canton.

Kanzel ['kantsəl] *f* (*pl* **-n**) pulpit. **-rede** *f* sermon.

Kanzlei [kants'laɪ] *f* (*pl* **-en**) (*Büro*) office; (*Behörde*) chancellery. **-papier** *neut* foolscap.

Kanzler ['kantslər] *m* (*pl* **-**) chancellor.

Kap [kap] *neut* (*pl* **-s**) cape, headland.

Kapazität [kapatsi'tɛɪt] **1** *f* (*unz.*) capacity. **2** *f* (*pl* **-en**) (*Könner*) authority, expert.

Kapelle [ka'pɛlə] *f* (*pl* **-n**) chapel; (*Musik*) band.

Kaper ['kaɪpər] *f* (*pl* **-n**) (*Gewürz*) caper.

kapieren [ka'piːrən] *v* (*umg.*) understand, catch on, (*umg.*) get.

Kapital [kapi'taɪl] *neut* (*Komm*) capital. **-ismus** *m* capitalism. **-ist** *m* capitalist. **kapitalistisch** *adj* capitalist.

Kapitän [kapi'tɛɪn] *m* (*pl* **-e**) (ship's) captain.

Kapitel [ka'pitəl] *neut* (*pl* **-**) chapter.

kapitulieren [kapitu'liːrən] *v* capitulate, surrender. **Kapitulation** *f* (*pl* **-en**) capitulation, surrender.

Kaplan [ka'plan] *m* (*pl* **Kapläne**) chaplain.

Kappe ['kapə] *f* (*pl* **-n**) cap; (*Deckel*) top; (*Arch*) dome; (*Schuh*) toecap.

Kapriole [kapri'oɪlə] *f* (*pl* **-n**) caper, cartwheel.

kaputt [ka'put] *adj* broken, (*umg.*) bust; (*erschöpft*) exhausted, (*umg.*) shattered. **-machen** *v* break, ruin.

Kapuze [ka'puɪtsə] *f* (*pl* **-n**) hood.

Karaffe [ka'rafə] *f* (*pl* **-n**) carafe.

Karamelle [kara'mɛlə] *f* (*pl* **-n**) toffee.

Karat [ka'raɪt] *neut* (*pl* **-e**) carat.

Karate [ka'raɪtə] *neut* karate.

Karawane [kara'vaɪnə] *f* (*pl* **-n**) caravan.

Kardinal [kardi'naɪl] *m* (*pl* **Kardinäle**) cardinal.

Karfreitag [kaɪr'fraitak] *m* Good Friday.

karg [kark] *adj* meagre, poor; (*geizig*) miserly.

kärglich ['kɛrkliç] *adj* scanty, poor.

kariert [ka'riərt] *adj* chequered, checked.

Karies ['kaɪriːs] *f* (*Med*) caries.

Karikatur [karika'tuɪr] *f* (*pl* **-en**) caricature.

karmesin [karme'ziɪn] *adj* crimson.

Karneval ['karnɛval] *m* (*pl* **-s**) (Shrovetide) carnival.

Karo ['kaɪro] *neut* (*pl* **-s**) square; (*Karten*) diamonds.

Karosserie [karɔsə'riɪ] *f* (*pl* **-n**) body, coachwork.

Karotte [ka'rɔtə] *f* (*pl* **-n**) carrot.

Karpfen ['karpfən] *m* (*pl* **-**) carp.

Karre ['karə] *f* (*pl* **-n**), **Karren** *m* (*pl* **-**) cart.

Karriere [kari'ɛɪrə] *f* (*pl* **-n**) rise, (successful) career; (*Pferd*) full gallop.

Karte ['kartə] *f* (*pl* **-n**) (*Blatt*) card; (*Land-*) map; (*Eintritt, Reise*) ticket.

Kartei [kar'tai] *f* (*pl* **-en**) card file, card index.

Kartell [kar'tɛl] *neut* (*pl* **-e**) cartel, combine.

Karten‖ausgabe *f* ticket office. **-spiel** *neut* card game.

Kartoffel [kar'tɔfəl] *f* (*pl* **-n**) potato. **-chips** *pl* potato crisps (*US* chips). **-püree** *neut* mashed potatoes *pl*. **-puffer** *m* potato pancake. **-salat** *m* potato salad.

Karton [kar'tɔɪr] *m* (*pl* **-s**) cardboard; (*Schachtel*) cardboard box, carton; (*Skizze*) cartoon.

Kartusche [kar'tuʃə] *f* (*pl* **-n**) cartridge.

Karussell [karu'sɛl] *neut* (*pl* **-s**) roundabout, merry-go-round.

Kaschmir [kaʃ'miɪr] *neut* cashmere.

Käse [kɛɪzə] *m* (*pl* **-**) cheese.

Kaserne [ka'zɛrnə] *f* (*pl* **-n**) barracks *pl*.

Kasino [ka'ziɪno] *neut* (*pl* **-s**) casino; (*Mil*) (officers') mess; (*Gesellschaftshaus*) club.

Kasse ['kasə] *f* (*pl* **-n**) cash box, till; (*Laden, Supermarkt*) cash-desk; (*Kino, Theater*) box office; (*Bank*) cashier's window, counter. **gut/schlecht bei Kasse sein** be flush/hard up. **Kassen‖buch** *neut* cash book. **-wart** *m* treasurer.

Kassette [ka'sɛtə] *f* (*pl* -n) small box, casket; (*Geld*) strong-box; (*Tonband*) cassette. –**nrecorder** *m* cassette recorder.
kassieren [ka'siːrən] *v* (*Geld*) receive; (*Scheck*) cash; (*Urteil*) annul, reverse; (*Mil*) cashier, dismiss. **Kassierer** *m* cashier.
Kastanie [ka'staːniə] *f* (*pl* -n) chestnut. **kastanienbraun** *adj* chestnut, auburn.
Kasten ['kastən] *m* (*pl* **Kästen**) box, chest; (*Schrank*) cupboard.
kastrieren [ka'striːrən] castrate.
Kasus ['kaːzus] *m* (*pl* -n) (*Gramm*) case.
Katalog [kata'loːg] *m* (*pl* -e) catalogue.
Katarakt[1] [kata'rakt] *m* (*pl* -e) rapids, waterfall.
Katarakt[2] *f* (*pl* -e) (*Med*) cataract.
Katarrh [ka'tar] *m* (*pl* -e) catarrh.
katastrophal [katastro'faːl] *adj* catastrophic. **Katastrophe** *f* (*pl* -n) catastrophe.
Kategorie [katego'riː] *f* (*pl* -n) category. **kategorisch** *adj* categorical.
Kater ['kaːtər] *m* (*pl* -) tom cat; (*Katzenjammer*) hangover.
Kathedrale [kate'draːlə] *f* (*pl* -n) cathedral.
Katholik(in) [kato'liːk(in)] Catholic. **katholisch** *adj* Catholic. **Katholizismus** *m* Catholicism.
Kätzchen ['kɛtsçən] *neut* kitten.
Katze ['katsə] *f* (*pl* -n) cat. **katzenartig** *adj* feline, cat-like. **Katzen‖auge** *neut* (*Rückstrahler*) rear reflector. –**jammer** *m* hangover.
Kauderwelsch ['kaudərvɛlʃ] *neut* gibberish.
kauen ['kauən] *v* chew.
kauern ['kauərn] *v* cower.
Kauf [kauf] *m* (*pl* **Käufe**) purchase. **einen guten Kauf machen** make a good buy, get a bargain. **kaufen** *v* buy, purchase.
Käufer ['kɔyfər] *m* (*pl* -) buyer.
Kauf‖haus *neut* department store. –**kraft** *f* purchasing power.
käuflich ['kɔyflıç] *adj* saleable, purchasable; (*bestechlich*) corrupt, venal.
Kaufmann *m* businessman; (*Kleinhandel*) shopkeeper; (*Großhandel*) merchant. **kaufmännisch** *adj* commercial, mercantile. **Kaufpreis** *m* purchase price.
kaum [kaum] *adv* hardly, scarcely.
Kaution [kau'tsioːn] *f* (*pl* -en) security, deposit. **gegen Kaution freilassen** release on bail.

Kauz [kauts] *m* (*pl* **Käuze**) screech owl; (*fig*) odd fellow.
Kavaller‖ie [kavalə'riː] *f* (*pl* -n) cavalry. –**ist** *m* cavalryman.
Kaviar ['kaviar] *m* (*pl* -e) caviar.
keck [kɛk] *adj* pert, cheeky.
Kegel ['keːgəl] *m* (*pl* -) cone; (*Spiel*) skittle. –**bahn** *f* bowling alley. **kegel‖förmig** *adj* conical. –**n** *v* play skittles, go bowling. **Kegelspiel** *neut* skittles, bowling.
Kehle ['keːlə] *f* (*pl* -n) throat. **Kehlkopf** *m* larynx. –**entzündung** *f* laryngitis.
kehren[1] [keːrən] *v* sweep, brush.
kehren[2] *v* turn. **sich kehren** turn (round). **sich kehren an** pay attention to.
Kehricht ['keːrıçt] *m* (*unz.*) sweepings *pl*.
Kehr‖reim *m* refrain. –**seite** *f* reverse, other side.
Keil [kail] *m* (*pl* -e) wedge; (*Arch*) keystone. **keilen** *v* wedge; (*werben*) win over. **sich keilen** scuffle.
Keiler ['kailər] *m* (*pl* -) (wild) boar
Keilriemen ['kailriːmən] *m* (*Mot*) fanbelt.
Keim [kaim] *m* (*pl* -e) germ; (*Bot*) bud; embryo; (*Anfang*) origin. **keimen** *v* germinate; bud. **Keim‖träger** *m* carrier. –**ung** *f* germination.
kein [kain] **keine, kein** *pron, m, f* no one, nobody; *neut* nothing, none. *adj* no, not any. **kein anderer als** none other than. **keine Ahnung!** (I've) no idea! **keiner von beiden** neither (of the two). **keinerlei** *adj* of no sort. **keines‖falls** *adv* on no account. –**wegs** *adv* not at all.
Keks [keks] *m* (*pl* -e) biscuit.
Keller ['kɛlər] *m* (*pl* -) cellar. –**ei** *f* wine cellar. –**geschoß** *neut* basement.
Kellner ['kɛlnər] *m* (*pl* -) waiter. –**in** *f* waitress.
*****kennen** ['kɛnən] *v* know. –**lernen** *v* get to know, become acquainted with. **Kenner** *m* (*Wein, Kunst*) connoisseur; (*Fachmann*) expert. **kenntlich** *adj* distinguishable, distinct. **Kenntnis** *f* knowledge. **kenntnisreich** *adj* experienced. **Kennwort** *neut* password. **kennzeichnen** *v* (*fig*) characterize, distinguish. –**d** *adj* characteristic. **Kennziffer** *f* reference *or* code number; (*Math*) index.
kentern ['kɛntərn] *v* capsize.
Kerbe ['kɛrbə] *f* (*pl* -n) notch.
Kerker ['kɛrkər] *m* (*pl* -) dungeon.

Kerl [kɛrl] *m* (*pl* -e) fellow.
Kern [kɛrn] *m* (*pl* -e) kernel; (*Obst*) stone, pit; (*Atom*) nucleus; (*fig*) core, essence. **kerngesund** *adj* thoroughly healthy. **Kern‖haus** *neut* core. **–reaktion** *f* nuclear reaction. **–waffe** *f* nuclear weapon. **–kraftwerk** *neut* nuclear power station.
Kerze ['kɛrtsə] *f* (*pl* -n) candle. **Kerzen‖leuchter** *neut* candlestick. **–licht** *neut* candlelight.
Kessel ['kɛsəl] *m* (*pl* -) kettle; (*Tech*) boiler; (*Geog*) depression, hollow.
Kette ['kɛtə] *f* (*pl* -n) chain. **ketten** *v* chain, link. **Ketten‖gebirge** *neut* mountain range. **–geschäft** *neut* chain store. **–raucher** *m* chain smoker. **–reaktion** *f* chain reaction.
Ketzer ['kɛtsər] *m* (*pl* -) heretic. **–ei** *f* (*pl* -en) heresy. **ketzerisch** *adj* heretical.
keuchen ['kɔyçən] *v* gasp, pant. **Keuchhusten** *m* whooping cough.
Keule ['kɔylə] *f* (*pl* -n) club, bludgeon; (*Fleisch*) leg.
keusch [kɔyʃ] *adj* chaste, modest. **Keuschheit** *f* chastity.
kichern ['kɪçərn] *v* giggle.
Kiefer¹ ['kiːfər] *m* (*pl* -) (*Anat*) jaw.
Kiefer² *f* (*pl* -n) (*Bot*) pine.
Kieferknochen ['kiːfərknɔxən] *m* jawbone.
Kiefern‖holz *neut* pinewood. **–wald** *m* pine forest.
Kiel [kiːl] *m* (*pl* -e) keel.
Kieme ['kiːmə] *f* (*pl* -n) gill.
Kies [kiːs] *m* (*pl* -e) gravel. **Kiesel** *m* (*pl* -) pebble, flint. **–stein** *m* pebble. **Kiesgrube** *f* gravelpit.
Kilo ['kiːlo] *neut* (*pl* -) kilo, kilogram(me). **–gramm** *neut* (*pl* -) kilogram(me). **Kilometer** *neut* kilometre. **–zähler** *m* milometer, odometer.
Kind [kint] *neut* (*pl* -er) child. **ein Kind bekommen/erwarten** have/expect a baby.
Kinder‖arzt *m* paediatrician. **–bett** *neut* cot, crib. **–buch** *neut* children's book. **–heilkunde** *f* paediatrics. **–jahre** *pl* childhood *sing*. **–lähmung** *f* polio. **–spiel** *neut* children's game; (*fig*) child's play. **–wagen** *m* pram, (*US*) baby carriage.
Kindheit *f* childhood. **kindisch** *adj* childish. **kindlich** *adj* childlike.
Kinn [kin] *neut* (*pl* -e) chin.
Kino ['kiːno] *neut* (*pl* -s) cinema.

Kiosk ['kiːɔsk] *m* (*pl* -e) kiosk.
kippen ['kipən] *v* tip, tilt. **Kippwagen** *m* tipper, tip cart.
Kirche ['kirçə] *f* (*pl* -n) church. **Kirchen‖gemeinde** *f* parish. **–lied** *neut* hymn. **–schändung** *f* desecration, profanation. **Kirch‖gänger** *m* church-goer. **–hof** *m* churchyard. **kirchlich** *adj* ecclesiastical, church.
Kirsch [kirʃ] *m* kirsch, cherry brandy. **–e** *f* (*pl* -n) cherry.
Kissen ['kisən] *neut* (*pl* -) cushion; (*Kopf-*) pillow; (*pl*) bedding.
Kiste ['kistə] *f* (*pl* -n) chest, case, box.
Kitsch [kitʃ] *m* (tasteless) trash, kitsch. **kitschig** *adj* trashy.
Kittel ['kitəl] *m* (*pl* -) smock.
Kitzel ['kitsəl] *m* (*pl* -) tickle. **kitzeln** *v* tickle. **kitzlig** *adj* ticklish.
klaffen ['klafən] *v* gape, yawn. **–d** *adj* gaping.
Klage ['klaːgə] *f* (*pl* -n) complaint, grievance; (*Jur*) action, lawsuit. **klagen** *v* complain, (*Jur*) bring an action. **Klagende(r)** plaintiff.
kläglich ['klɛːklɪç] *adj* miserable, pitiful.
Klammer ['klamər] *f* (*pl* -n) clamp; (*kleine*) clip; (*Wäsche*) peg. **klammern** *v* clamp; (*befestigen*) fasten. **sich klammern an** cling to.
Klamotten [kla'mɔtən] *pl* (*umg.*) gear *sing*, clothes *pl*.
Klang [klaŋ] *m* (*pl* **Klänge**) sound.
klapp‖en ['klapən] flap, clap; (*umg.*) work out, be all right. **–bar** *adj* collapsible, folding. **Klappe** *f* flap; (*umg.*) mouth, trap. **halt die Klappe!** (*vulgär*) shut up!
Klapper ['klapər] *f* (*pl* -n) rattle. **klapperig** *adj* clattering, rattling. **klappern** *v* rattle, clatter.
Klapp‖messer *neut* jack-knife. **–stuhl** *m* folding chair. **–tür** *f* trapdoor.
klar [klaːr] *adj* clear.
klären ['klɛːrən] *v* clarify.
Klarheit ['klaːrhait] *f* clarity, clearness.
Klarinette [klari'nɛtə] *f* (*pl* -n) clarinet. **Klarinettist** *m* clarinettist.
klarlegen ['klaːrleːgən] *v* clear up.
Klärung ['klɛːruŋ] *f* clarification.
klarwerden ['klaːrveːrdən] *v* become clear.
klasse ['klasə] *adj* (*umg.*) marvellous, splendid. **Klasse** *f* class. **ein Musiker von Klasse** an excellent musician. **ein Restaurant erster Klasse** a first-class restaurant.

klassenbewußt *adj* class-conscious. **Klassenzimmer** *neut* classroom.
Klassik ['klasɪk] *f* classical era; (*Literatur, Musik*) classicism. **–er** *m* classicist. **klassisch** *adj* classical.
Klatsch [klatʃ] *m* (*pl* **-e**) slap, smack; (*Gerede*) gossip, chatter. **–base** *f* gossip, chatterbox. **klatschen** *v* clap; (*reden*) gossip, chatter.
Klaue ['klauə] *f* (*pl* **-n**) claw; (*Raubvogel*) talon. **klauen** *v* (*umg.*) steal, pinch.
Klausel ['klauzəl] *f* (*pl* **-n**) clause.
Klavier [klaviːr] *neut* (*pl* **-e**) piano. **–spieler(in)** pianist.
Klebeband ['kleːbəbant] *neut* (adhesive) tape. **kleben** *v* glue, paste; (*anhaften*) stick. **klebrig** *adj* sticky. **Klebstoff** *m* glue.
Klecks [klɛks] *m* (*pl* **-e**) blot, spot.
Klee [kleː] *m* clover. **–blatt** *neut* cloverleaf.
Kleid [klaɪt] *neut* (*pl* **-er**) garment; (*Frau*) dress; (*pl*) clothes. **kleiden** *v* clothe. **Kleider‖bügel** *m* coat-hanger. **–bürste** *f* clothes brush. **–schrank** *m* wardrobe. **Kleidung** *f* clothing, clothes. **–sstück** *neut* article of clothing, garment.
klein [klaɪn] *adj* small, little. **der kleine Mann** the ordinary man. **klein stellen** turn down, put on low. **im kleinen** in miniature; (*Komm*) retail.
Klein‖anzeige *f* classified advertisement. **–asien** *neut* Asia Minor. **–bürger** *m* petty bourgeois. **–geld** *neut* (small) change. **–handel** *m* retail trade. **Kleinigkeit** *f* (*pl* **-en**) trifle, trivial matter. **Klein‖kind** *neut* infant. **–lebewesen** *neut* microorganism. **klein‖lich** *adj* petty. **–mütig** *adj* fainthearted, cowardly.
Kleinod ['klaɪnoːt] *neut* (*pl* **-ien**) jewel, gem.
Kleister ['klaɪstər] *m* (*pl* **-**) paste, gum.
Klemme ['klɛmə] *f* (*pl* **-n**) clamp; (*Haar*) grip; (*Klammer*) clip. **in der Klemme sitzen** be in a dilemma *or* tight corner. **klemmen** *v* squeeze, pinch.
Klempner ['klɛmpnər] *m* (*pl* **-**) plumber; (*Metall*) metalworker. **–ei** *f* plumbing. **klempnern** *v* do plumbing.
Kleriker ['kleːrikər] *m* (*pl* **-**) cleric, clergyman. **Klerus** *m* (*unz.*) clergy.
Kletterer ['klɛtərər] *m* (*pl* **-**) climber. **klettern** *v* climb. **Kletterpflanze** *f* climbing plant, creeper.
Klima ['kliːma] *f* (*pl* **-te**) climate. **–anlage**

f air-conditioning (equipment). **klimatisch** *adj* climatic.
Klinge ['klɪŋə] *f* (*pl* **-n**) blade.
Klingel ['klɪŋəl] *f* (*pl* **-n**) (door)bell. **klingeln** *v* ring the bell, ring.
klingen ['klɪŋən] *v* sound; ring.
Klinik ['kliːnik] *f* (*pl* **-en**) clinic, hospital. **klinisch** *adj* clinical.
Klinke ['klɪŋkə] *f* (*pl* **-n**) doorhandle, latch.
Klippe ['klɪpə] *f* (*pl* **-n**) cliff; (*im Meer*) rocks *pl*, reef.
klirren ['klɪrən] *v* tinkle, jangle.
Klischee [kli'ʃeː] *neut* (*pl* **-s**) (*fig*) cliché.
Klo [kloː] *neut* (*pl* **-s**) (*umg.*) toilet, loo.
Kloake [klo'aːkə] *f* (*pl* **-n**) sewer.
klopfen ['klɔpfən] *v* (*Tür*) knock; (*Herz*) beat; (*Schulter*) tap, pat. **Klopfen** *neut* knocking; beating.
Klosett [klo'zɛt] *neut* (*pl* **-s**) toilet. **–papier** *neut* toilet paper.
Kloß [kloːs] *m* (*pl* **Klöße**) dumpling; (*Fleisch*) meatball.
Kloster ['kloːstər] *neut* (*pl* **Klöster**) monastery, abbey, convent. **–gang** *m* cloister.
Klotz [klɔts] *m* (*pl* **Klötze**) block, log.
Klub [klup] *m* (*pl* **-s**) club, association.
Kluft [kluft] *m* (*pl* **Klüfte**) cleft; (*Abgrund*) chasm, abyss; (*fig*) rift.
klug [kluːk] *adj* clever, prudent; (*Ansicht, Rat*) sensible, prudent. **Klugheit** *f* cleverness, intelligence.
Klumpen ['klumpən] *m* (*pl* **-**) lump; (*Gold*) nugget.
knabbern ['knabərn] *v* nibble.
Knabe ['knaːbə] *m* (*pl* **-n**) boy. **–nalter** *neut* boyhood, youth. **knabenhaft** *adj* boyish.
Knäckebrot ['knɛkəbroːt] *neut* crispbread.
knacken ['knakən] *v* crack.
Knall [knal] *m* (*pl* **-e**) bang; explosion. **–bonbon** *m* cracker. **knallen** *v* crack, bang; explode. **Knallfrosch** *m* banger, jumping jack.
knapp [knap] *adj* scant, insufficient; (*Kleidung*) tight. **knapp sein** be in short supply. **knapp werden** be running short *or* out. **knapp bei Kasse sein** be hard up. *knapp drei Meter* just under (*or* barely) three metres.
knarren ['knarən] *v* creak.
knattern ['knatərn] *v* crackle, rattle.
Knebel ['kneːbəl] *m* (*pl* **-**) gag. **knebeln** *v* gag.

Knecht [knɛçt] *m* (*pl* -e) (farm) worker; (*Diener*) servant.
***kneifen** ['knaifən] *v* pinch, nip. **Kneifzange** *f* pincers.
Kneipe ['knaipə] *f* (*pl* -n) pub, bar. **kneipen** *v* go boozing.
kneten ['kneitən] *v* knead; (*Körper*) massage.
Knick ['knik] *m* (*pl* -e) crack; (*Kniff*) crease; (*Kurve*) sharp bend. **knicken** *v* break, crack; fold, crease.
Knicks [kniks] *m* (*pl* -e) curtsey.
Knie [kniː] *neut* (*pl* -) knee. **knien** *v* kneel. **-d** *adj* kneeling, on one's knees. **Kniescheibe** *f* kneecap.
Kniff [knif] *m* (*pl* -e) pinch; (*Falte*) crease; trick. **den Kniff heraushaben** get the hang of it.
knipsen ['knipsən] *v* punch, clip; (*Foto*) snap.
knirschen ['knirʃən] *v* gnash.
Knitter ['knitər] *m* (*pl* -) crease. **knitterfrei** *adj* crease-resistant. **-n** *v* crease.
Knoblauch ['knoiplaux] *m* garlic.
Knöchel ['knœçəl] *m* (*pl* -) (*Finger*) knuckle; (*Bein*) ankle.
Knochen ['knɔxən] *m* (*pl* -) bone. **-bruch** *m* fracture. **-gerüst** *neut* skeleton. **-mark** *neut* (bone) marrow. **knochig** *adj* bony.
Knödel ['knœidəl] *m* (*pl* -) dumpling.
Knolle ['knɔlə] *f* (*pl* -n) tuber; (*Zwiebel*, *Tulpe*) bulb.
Knopf [knɔpf] *m* (*pl* Knöpfe) button. **knöpfen** ['knœpfən] *v* button.
Knorpel ['knɔrpəl] *m* (*pl* -) cartilage; (*bei gekochtem Fleisch*) gristle.
Knospe ['knɔspə] *f* (*pl* -n) bud. **knospen** *v* bud.
Knoten ['knoitən] *m* (*pl* -) knot; (*Tech*) node. **knoten** *v* knot. **Knotenpunkt** *m* junction.
knüpfen ['knypfən] *v* join, tie.
knusprig ['knuspriç] *adj* crisp.
Koalition [koali'tsioin] *f* (*pl* -en) coalition.
Kobold ['koibɔlt] *m* (*pl* -e) goblin.
Koch [kɔx] *m* (*pl* Köche) cook. **-buch** *neut* cookery book. **kochen** *v* cook; (*sieden*) boil. **-d** boiling. **Kocher** *m* cooker. **Kochherd** *m* kitchen range.
Köchin ['kœçin] *f* (*pl* -nen) (female) cook.
Koch||platte *f* hotplate, ring. **-topf** *m* saucepan, pot.
Köder ['kœidər] *m* (*pl* -) bait. **ködern** *v* lure, entice.

Koexistenz [koiɛksi'stɛnts] *f* coexistence. **koexistieren** *v* coexist.
Koffer ['kɔfər] *m* (*pl* -) suitcase; (*Schrankkoffer*) trunk. **-kuli** *m* (luggage) trolley. **-raum** *m* (*Mot*) trunk.
Kohl [koil] *m* (*pl* -e) cabbage.
Kohle ['koilə] *f* (*pl* -n) coal; (*Holzkohle*) charcoal. **Kohlen||bergwerk** *neut* coal mine, pit. **-säure** *f* carbonic acid; (*in Getränken*) carbon dioxide. **-hydrat** *neut* carbohydrate. **-stoff** *m* carbon. **Kohle||papier** *neut* carbon paper. **-stift** *m* charcoal crayon.
Kohl||rabi [koil'rabi] *m* (*pl* -s) kohlrabi. **-rübe** *f* swede.
Koje ['koijə] *f* (*pl* -n) bunk, berth; (*Zimmer*) cabin.
kokett [ko'kɛt] *adj* coquettish. **-ieren** *v* flirt.
Kokosnuß ['koikɔsnus] *f* coconut.
Koks ['koiks] *m* (*pl* -e) coke.
Kolben ['kɔlbən] *m* (*pl* -) club; (*Gewehr*) butt; (*Zylinder*) piston.
Kollege [kɔ'leigə] *m* (*pl* -n) **Kollegin** *f* (*pl* -nen) colleague.
kollektiv [kɔlɛk'tiːf] *adj* collective.
Köln [kœln] *neut* Cologne. **-ischwasser** *neut* eau de Cologne.
Kolon ['koilən] *neut* (*pl* -s) colon.
kolonial [kɔlo'niaːl] *adj* colonial. **Kolonialwaren** *pl* groceries. **-händler** *m* grocer.
Kolonne [kɔ'lɔnə] *f* (*pl* -n) column.
Kombi ['kɔmbi] *m* (*pl* -s) estate car.
Kombination [kɔmbina'tsioin] *f* (*pl* -en) combination; (*Sport*) teamwork; (*Unterkleidung*) combinations *pl*; (*Schützkleidung*) one-piece suit; (*Ideen*) conjecture. **kombinieren** *v* combine.
Komet [ko'meit] *m* (*pl* -en) comet.
Komfort [kɔm'foir] *m* (*unz.*) comfort. **komfortabel** *adj* comfortable.
Komiker ['koimikər] *m* (*pl* -) comedian, comic. **komisch** *adj* funny; (*seltsam*) strange.
Komitee [kɔmi'teː] *neut* (*pl* -s) committee.
Komma ['kɔma] *neut* (*pl* -s) comma.
Kommandant [kɔman'dant] *m* (*pl* -en) commander. **kommandieren** *v* command.
Kommanditgesellschaft (**KG**) [kɔman'diitgəzɛlʃaft (ka'geː)] *f* limited-liability company.
Kommando [kɔ'mandoi] *neut* (*pl* -s) order, command; (*Abteilung*) squad, detachment, detail. **-truppe** *f* commando (unit).

*kommen ['kɔmən] v come. kommen lassen send for. um etwas kommen lose something. hinter etwas kommen get to the bottom of something. Kommen neut arrival, coming. kommend adj coming. Kommentar [kɔmɛn'taɪr] m (pl -e) commentary. kommentieren v comment on. Kommerz [kɔ'mɛrts] m commerce. komerziell adj commercial. Kommisar [kɔmi'saɪr] m (pl -e) commissioner; (Polizei) inspector. Kommission f commission. kommun [kɔ'muɪn] adj common. -al adj municipal. Kommune f (pl -n) commune; (Gemeinde) municipality. Kommunikation [komunika'tsioɪn] f (pl -en) communication. Kommuniqué [kɔmyni'keɪ] neut (pl -s) communiqué. Kommunismus [kɔmu'nizmus] m communism. Kommunist(in) communist. kommunistisch adj communist. Komödie [kɔ'mœɪdiə] f (pl -n) comedy; (Dreigns) farce. Kompaß ['kɔmpas] m (pl Kompasse) compass. -strich m point of the compass. kompetent [kɔmpe'tɛnt] adj competent. Komplex [kɔm'plɛks] m (pl -e) complex. Kompliment [kɔmpli'mɛnt] neut (pl -e) compliment. komplizieren [kɔmpli'tsiɪrən] v complicate. kompliziert adj complicated, complex. Komplott [kɔm'plɔt] neut (pl -e) plot, conspiracy. komponieren [kɔmpo'niɪrən] v compose. Komponist m (pl -en) composer. Kompott [kɔm'pɔt] neut (pl -e) stewed fruit, compote. Kompresse [kɔm'prɛsə] f (pl -n) compress. Kompromiß [kɔmpro'mis] m (pl Kompromisse) compromise. kompromittieren v compromise. kondensieren [kɔndɛn'siɪrən] v condense. Kondensmilch f condensed milk. Konditorei [kɔndito'rai] (pl -en) patisserie, cake shop. -waren pl pastries, cakes. Kondom [kɔn'doɪm] m (pl -e) condom. Konferenz [kɔnfe'rɛnts] f (pl -en) conference. Konfession [kɔnfe'sioɪn] f (pl -en) confession, creed, faith. Konflikt [kɔn'flikt] m (pl -e) conflict.

konform [kɔn'fɔrm] adj in agreement, in accordance. Konfrontation [kɔnfrɔnta'tsioɪn] f (pl -en) confrontation. konfrontieren v confront. konfus [kɔn'fuɪs] adj confused, muddled. Konfusion f confusion. Kongreß [kɔŋ'grɛs] m (pl Kongresse) congress. König ['kœɪniç] m (pl -e) king. -in f (pl -nen) queen. -inmutter m queen mother. königlich adj royal, regal. Königreich neut kingdom, realm. Konjunktur [kɔnjuŋk'tuɪr] f (pl -en) (state of the) economy, economic trends pl; (Aufschwung) boom. Konkurrent [kɔnku'rɛnt] m (pl -en) competitor. Konkurrenz f (unz.) competition. konkurrenzfähig adj competitive. konkurrieren v compete. Konkurs [kɔn'kurs] m (pl -e) bankruptcy, insolvency. in Konkurs gehen become bankrupt. *können ['kœnən] v can, be able (to); (dürfen) may, be allowed (to); (gelernt haben) know. tun können know how to do. eine Sprache können speak a language. Ich kann nicht mehr! I can't go on. das kann sein it may be so. er kann nichts dafür it's not his fault, he can't help it. Können neut ability. konsequent [kɔnzɛ'kvɛnt] adj consistent. Konsequenz f consistency; (Folge) consequence. die Konsequenzen tragen bear the consequences. Konsequenzen ziehen draw conclusions. konservativ [kɔnzɛrva'tiɪf] adj conservative. Konservative(r) conservative. Konserve [kɔn'zɛrvə] f (pl -n) preserve, tinned or bottled food. Konservenbüchse f tin (of preserves). konservieren v preserve. konsolidieren [kɔnzɔli'diɪrən] v consolidate. Konsonant [kɔnzo'nant] m (pl -en) consonant. konstant [kɔn'stant] adj constant. konstruieren [kɔnstru'iɪrən] v construct. Konstruktion f (pl -en) construction; (Entwurf) design. Konsul [kɔn'zuɪl] m (pl -n) consul. -at neut (pl -e) consulate. Konsum [kɔn'zuɪm] m consumption. -gesellschaft f consumer society. konsumieren v consume. Konsumverein m co-operative society.

Kontakt [kɔn'takt] *m* (*pl* -e) contact.

Kontinent [kɔnti'nɛnt] *m* (*pl* -e) continent.

Konto ['kɔnto] *neut* (*pl* **Konten**) account. **-auszug** *m* (bank) statement. **-buch** *neut* passbook. **-inhaber** *m* accountholder.

Kontrabaß ['kɔntrabas] *m* double bass.

konträr [kɔn'trɛː] *adj* adverse.

Kontrast [kɔn'trast] *m* (*pl* -e) contrast. **kontrastieren** *v* contrast.

Kontrolle [kɔn'trɔlə] *f* (*pl* -n) control, supervision. **-abschnitt** *m* counterfoil. **-eur** *m* controller. **kontrollieren** *v* control, supervise. **Kontrollpunkt** *m* checkpoint. **unter Kontrolle** under control.

konventionell [kɔnvɛntsio'nɛl] *adj* conventional.

Konversation [kɔnvɛrza'tsioɪn] *f* (*pl* -en) conversation. **-slexikon** *neut* encyclopedia.

konvertieren [kɔnvɛr'tiːrən] *v* convert.

konvex [kɔn'vɛks] *adj* convex.

Konzentrat [kɔntsən'traɪt] *neut* (*pl* -e) concentrate. **-ion** *f* (*pl* -en) concentration. **-ionslager** *neut* concentration camp. **konzentrieren** *v* concentrate.

Konzept [kɔn'tsɛpt] *neut* (*pl* -e) rough draft.

Konzert [kɔn'tsɛrt] *neut* (*pl* -e) concert; (*Stück*) concerto.

Kopf [kɔpf] *m* (*pl* **Köpfe**) head. **auf den Kopf stellen** turn upside down. **pro Kopf** per capita, each. **im Kopf haben** be preoccupied with. **-ball** *m* (*Sport*) header. **köpfen** ['kœpfən] *v* behead, decapitate. **Kopf‖haut** *f* scalp. **-hörer** *m* headphone. **-kissen** *neut* pillow. **-putz** *m* headdress. **-salat** *m* lettuce. **-schmerzen** *pl* headache *sing.* **-sprung** *m* header. **-stand** *m* headstand. **kopfüber** *adv* headlong, head first.

Kopie [ko'piː] *f* (*pl* -n) copy. **kopieren** *v* copy.

Kopulation [kɔpula'tsioɪn] *f* (*pl* -en) copulation. **kopulieren** *v* copulate; (*Bäume*) graft.

Koralle [ko'ralə] *f* (*pl* -n) coral. **-nriff** *neut* coral reef.

Korb [kɔrp] *m* (*pl* **Körbe**) basket. **-ball** *m* basketball. **-geflecht** *neut* basketwork.

Kord [kɔrt] *or* **Kordsamt** *m* cord(uroy).

Kordhose *f* corduroy trousers; (*umg.*) cords.

Korinthe [ko'rintə] *f* (*pl* -n) currant.

Kork [kɔrk] *m* (*pl* -e) cork. **-enzieher** *m* corkscrew.

Korn [kɔrn] *neut* (*pl* **Körner**) grain, corn.

Körnchen ['kœrnçən] *neut* (*pl* -) granule.

Koronarthrombose [koro'naɪrtrɔmbɔɪzə] *f* (*pl* -n) coronary thrombosis.

Körper [kœrpər] *m* (*pl* -) body. **-bau** *m* physique, build. **körperbehindert** *adj* physically handicapped. **Körper‖bildung** *f* body-building. **-geruch** *m* body odour. **-gewicht** *neut* weight. **-haltung** *f* posture.

körperlich ['kœrpərliç] *adj* bodily, physical; (*Strafe*) corporal.

Körper‖maß *neut* cubic measure. **-pflege** *f* hygiene. **-schaft** *f* (*pl* -en) corporation.

Korporal [kɔrpo'raɪl] *m* (*pl* -e) corporal.

korrekt [ko'rɛkt] *adj* correct. **Korrektur** *f* (*pl* -en) correction; (*Druck*) proof.

Korrespondent [kɔrɛspɔn'dɛnt] *m* (*pl* -en) correspondent. **Korrespondenz** *f* correspondence.

korrigieren [kɔri'giːrən] *v* correct; (*gedrucktes*) proofread.

Kosename ['koːzənaɪmə] *m* pet name.

Kosmetik [kɔz'mɛɪtik] *f* (*unz.*) cosmetics *pl*. **kosmetisch** *adj* cosmetic.

Kosmos ['kɔsmɔs] *m* (*pl* **Kosmen**) cosmos, universe. **kosmisch** *adj* cosmic.

Kost [kɔst] *f* (*unz.*) food, fare. **Kost und Wohnung** board and lodging. **kräftige Kost** rich diet.

kostbar ['kɔstbaɪr] *adj* expensive; (*sehr wertvoll*) precious.

kosten¹ ['kɔstən] *v* (*probieren*) taste, try, sample.

kosten² *v* cost. **Kosten** *pl* costs. **auf meine Kosten** at my expense. **kostenlos** *adj* free (of charge).

köstlich ['kœstliç] *adj* delicious; (*reizend*) charming; (*wertvoll*) precious.

kostspielig ['kɔstʃpiːliç] *adj* expensive.

Kostüm [kɔs'tyɪm] *neut* (*pl* -e) costume; (*Damen-*) suit. **-ball** *m* fancy-dress ball. **-probe** *f* dress rehearsal.

Kot [koɪt] *m* dung, droppings *pl*; (*Schmutz*) dirt, mud.

Kotelett [kɔtə'lɛt] *neut* (*pl* -e) chop, cutlet. **-en** *pl* sideburns, mutton-chop whiskers.

Kotflügel ['koɪtflyːgəl] *m* mudguard; fender.

kotzen ['kɔtsən] *v* (*vulgär*) puke, be sick. **zum Kotzen** enough to make you sick.
Krabbe ['krabə] *f* (*pl* -n) shrimp.
krabbeln ['krabəln] *v* scuttle, scurry.
Krach [krax] *m* (*pl* -e) noise; (*Streit*) quarrel, row; (*Knall*) crash.
krächzen ['krɛçtsən] *v* croak.
kraft [kraft] *prep* on the strength of, by virtue of. **Kraft** *f* (*pl* **Kräfte**) strength; (*Macht*) power. **-fahrer** *m* driver. **-fahrzeug** *neut* motor vehicle.
kräftig ['krɛftiç] *adj* strong; (*mächtig*) powerful; (*Essen*) substantial. **-en** *v* strengthen. **-end** *adj* invigorating.
kraftlos *adj* powerless. **Kraft‖probe** *f* trial of strength. **-rad** *neut* motorcycle. **-stoff** *m* fuel. **-wagen** *m* motor vehicle. **-werk** *neut* power station.
Kragen ['kraɪgən] *m* (*pl* -) collar.
Krähe ['krɛɪə] *f* (*pl* -n) crow. **krähen** *v* crow.
Kralle ['kralə] *f* (*pl* -n) claw. **krallen** *v* claw. **sich krallen an** clutch.
Kram [kraɪm] *m* stuff, trash; (*umg.*) things, stuff.
Krampf [krampf] *m* (*pl* **Krämpfe**) cramp, spasm. **krampfhaft** *adj* convulsive; (*heftig*) frenzied, frantic.
Kran [kraɪn] *m* (*pl* **Kräne**) (*Mech*) crane.
Kranich ['kraɪniç] *m* (*pl* -e) (*Zool*) crane.
krank [kraŋk] *adj* sick, ill, unwell. **Kranke(r)** patient.
kränken ['krɛŋkən] *v* vex, annoy.
Kranken‖haus *neut* hospital. **-kasse** *f* health insurance (company). **-schein** *m* medical certificate. **-schwester** *f* nurse. **-versicherung** *f* health insurance. **-wagen** *m* ambulance. **krankhaft** *adj* diseased, unhealthy. **Krankheit** *f* (*pl* -en) disease, illness.
Kranz [krants] *m* (*pl* **Kränze**) wreath, garland.
Krapfen ['krapfən] *m* (*pl* -) fritter; doughnut.
kraß [kras] *adj* crass, gross.
kratzen ['kratsən] *v* scratch. **Kratzwunde** *f* scratch.
kraulen ['kraulən] *or* **kraulschwimmen** *v* swim the crawl. **Kraulstil** *m* crawl.
kraus [kraus] *adj* curly, crinkled.
Kraut [kraut] *neut* (*pl* **Kräuter**) herb; (*Kohl*) cabbage; (*grüne Pflanzen*) vegetation.
Kräuter‖buch ['krɔytərbuɪx] *neut* herbal. **-tee** *m* herb tea.

Krawall [kra'val] *m* (*pl* -e) brawl.
Krawatte [kra'vatə] *f* (*pl* -n) (neck)tie.
Krebs [kreɪps] *m* (*pl* -e) crab; (*Med*) cancer; (*Astrol*) Cancer.
Kredit [kre'diɪt] *m* (*pl* -e) (*Komm*) credit. **-brief** *m* letter of credit. **kreditieren** *v* credit.
Kreide ['kraidə] *f* (*pl* -n) chalk. **-fels** *m* chalk cliff.
Kreis ['krais] *m* (*pl* -e) circle; (*Gebiet*) district, area. **-bahn** *f* orbit. **-bewegung** *f* rotation, revolution. **-bogen** *m* arc (of a circle).
kreischen ['kraiʃən] *v* screech, shriek.
Kreisel ['kraizəl] *m* (*pl* -) (spinning) top. **kreiseln** *v* spin (like a top).
kreis‖en *v* revolve, rotate. **-förmig** *adj* circular. **Kreis‖lauf** *m* circulation. **-säge** *f* circular saw. **-umfang** *m* circumference.
Krem [kreɪm] *f* (*pl* -s) cream.
Krematorium [krema'toɪrium] *neut* (*pl* **Krematorien**) crematorium.
Kreml ['kreməl] *m* Kremlin.
Krempel ['krɛmpəl] *m* junk, rubbish.
krepieren [kre'piɪrən] *v* burst; (*umg.*) die.
Kresse ['krɛsə] *f* (*pl* -n) cress.
Kreuz [krɔyts] *neut* (*pl* -e) cross; (*Karten*) club(s); (*Anat*) small of the back. **kreuz und quer** in all directions. **kreuzen** *v* cross; (*Schiff*) cruise. **sich kreuzen** intersect. **Kreuzer** *m* (*pl* -) cruiser. **Kreuz‖fahrer** *m* crusader. **-fahrt** *f* (*Schiff*) cruise; (*Kreuzzug*) crusade.
kreuzigen ['krɔytsigən] *v* crucify. **Kreuzigung** *f* (*pl* -en) crucifixion.
Kreuzung ['krɔytsuŋ] *f* (*pl* -en) crossing.
Kreuz‖verhör *neut* cross-examination. **-verweis** *m* cross-reference. **-weg** *m* crossroads. **-worträtsel** *neut* crossword puzzle. **-zug** *m* crusade.
***kriechen** ['kriːçən] *v* creep, crawl; (*fig*) cringe, grovel. **kriecherisch** *adj* cringing, servile.
Krieg [kriːk] *m* (*pl* -e) war. **den Krieg erklären/führen** declare/wage war. **Krieger** *m* (*pl* -) warrior. **kriegführend** *adj* belligerent. **Kriegs‖dienstverweigerer** *m* conscientious objector. **-gefangene(r)** prisoner of war. **-gericht** *neut* court-martial. **-hetzer** *m* warmonger. **-verbrecher** *m* war criminal. **-zeit** *f* wartime.
Krimi ['krimi] *neut* (*pl* -s) detective novel, thriller.

kriminal [krimi'naɪl] *adj* criminal.
Kriminal‖polizei *f* detective force, CID.
–roman *m* detective novel, thriller.
Krippe ['kripə] *f* (*pl* -n) crib; (*Kinder-*)
crèche.
Krise ['kriːzə] *f* (*pl* -n) crisis.
Kristall [kri'stal] *m* (*pl* -e) crystal. **kristall-
lisieren** *v* crystallize.
Kritik [kri'tiːk] *f* (*pl* -en) criticism. **–er** *m*
critic. **kritisch** *adj* critical. **kritisieren** *v*
criticize; (*Buch, Film*) review.
Krokodil [kroko'diːl] *neut* (*pl* -e) croco-
dile.
Krone ['kroːnə] *f* (*pl* -n) crown.
krönen ['krœːnən] *v* crown. **Krönung** *f*
coronation.
Kröte ['krœːtə] *f* (*pl* -n) toad.
Krücke ['krykə] *f* (*pl* -n) crutch.
Krug [kruːk] *m* (*pl* **Krüge**) jug; (*Becher*)
mug.
Krume ['kruːmə] *f* (*pl* -n) crumb.
Krümel [kryməl] *m* (*pl* -) crumb.
krümelig ['kryməliç] *adj* crumbly.
krumm [krum] *adj* crooked. **–beinig** *adj*
bow-legged.
Krumme ['krumə] *f* (*pl* -n) sickle.
Krümmung ['krymun] *f* curve, bend.
Krüppel ['krypəl] *m* (*pl* -) cripple.
Kruste ['krustə] *f* (*pl* -n) crust. **–ntier**
neut crustacean.
Kruzifix [kruːtsi'fiks] *neut* (*pl* -e) crucifix.
Kubikinhalt [ku'biːkinhalt] *m* volume.
Küche ['kyçə] *f* (*pl* -n) kitchen; cookery,
cuisine.
Kuchen ['kuːxən] *m* (*pl* -) cake.
Küchen‖schabe *f* cockroach. **–schrank**
m kitchen cupboard.
Kuckuck ['kukuk] *m* (*pl* -e) cuckoo.
Kugel ['kuːgəl] *f* (*pl* -n) ball; (*Gewehr*)
bullet; (*Math*) sphere. **kugel‖fest** *adj* bul-
let-proof. **–förmig** *adj* spherical.
Kugel‖lager *neut* ball-bearing. **–schrei-
ber** *m* ball(point) pen.
Kuh [kuː] *f* (*pl* **Kühe**) cow.
kühl [kyːl] *adj* cool. **Kühle** *f* coolness.
kühlen *v* cool. **Kühl‖schrank** *m* refrigerator. **–ung** *f* cooling.
kühn [kyːn] *adj* daring, bold, audacious.
Kühnheit *f* daring, boldness, audacity.
Kuhstall ['kuːʃtal] *m* cowshed.
Kulissen [ku'lisən] *pl* (*Theater*) scenery
sing. **hinter den Kulissen** (*fig*) behind the
scenes.
Kult [kult] *m* (*pl* -e) cult; (*Verehrung*)
worship.

kultivieren [kulti'viːrən] *v* cultivate.
Kultur [kul'tuːr] *f* (*pl* -en) culture;
(*Boden*) cultivation; (*Bakterien*) culture.
kulturell *adj* cultural.
Kümmel ['kyməl] *m* caraway (seed).
Kummer ['kumər] *m* (*unz.*) sorrow, distress.
kümmerlich ['kymərliç] *adj* miserable,
poor. **kümmern** *v* grieve; (*angehen*) concern. **sich kümmern um** take care of,
look after.
Kumpel ['kumpəl] *m* (*pl* -s) (**umg.**) mate,
buddy; (*Bergmann*) miner.
kund [kunt] *adj* (generally) known.
Kunde¹ ['kundə] *f* information,
(*Nachrichten*) news.
Kunde² *m*, **Kundin** *f* customer, client.
Kundendienst ['kundəndiːnst] *m* after-
sales service.
*kundgeben ['kuntgeːbən] *v* make known,
declare. **Kundgebung** *f* demonstration;
(*Kundgeben*) declaration.
kündigen ['kyndigən] *v* give notice.
Kündigung *f* notice.
Kundschaft ['kuntʃaft] *f* (*unz.*) customers
pl, clientele.
künftig ['kynftiç] *adj* future.
Kunst [kunst] *f* (*pl* **Künste**) art; (*Fertigkeit*) skill. **–akademie** *f* art college.
kunstfertig *adj* skilled. **Kunst‖gegenstand**
m objet d'art. **–griff** *m* trick, dodge.
–handwerker *m* craftsman.
Künstler ['kynstlər] *m* **Künstlerin** *f* artist.
künstlerisch *adj* artistic.
künstlich ['kynstliç] *adj* artificial.
künstliche Atmung *f* artificial respiration.
Kunst‖stück [*neut* stunt, trick. **–werk**
neut work of art.
Kupfer ['kupfər] *neut* (*pl* -) copper. **kup-
fer‖farben** *adj* copper(-coloured). **–n** *adj*
copper.
Kuppel ['kupəl] *f* (*pl* -n) dome, cupola.
Kuppelei [kupə'lai] ·*f* (*unz.*) procuring,
pimping. **kuppeln** *v* unite, couple; (*Mot*)
declutch. **Kuppler** *m* procurer. **Kupplerin**
f procuress. **Kupplung** *f* coupling; (*Mot*)
clutch.
Kur [kuːr] *f* (*pl* -en) (course of) treatment.
–anstalt *f* sanatorium.
Kurbel ['kurbəl] *f* (*pl* -n) crank, handle.
–welle *f* crankshaft.
Kürbis ['kyrbis] *m* (*pl* -se) pumpkin.
Kurfürst ['kuːrfyrst] *m* elector, electoral
prince.

Kurort *m* spa.

Kurs [kurs] *m* (*pl* -e) course; (*Komm*) rate. **–buch** *neut* railway timetable.

kursiv [kur'ziːf] *adv* in italics.

Kurve ['kurvə] *f* (*pl* -n) curve; (*Straße*) bend.

kurz [kurts] *adj* short. **kurze Hose** shorts *pl*. **kurz und gut** in a word, in short. **sich kurz fassen** be brief, make it short. **Kurz‖arbeit** *f* short time (work). **–ausgabe** *f* abridged edition.

Kürze ['kyrtsə] *f* shortness; (*Zeit*) brevity. **kürzen** *v* shorten. **kürzlich** *adv* recently, lately.

Kurz‖meldung *f* news flash. **–schluß** *m* short circuit. **–schrift** *f* shorthand. **kurzsichtig** *adj* nearsighted, shortsighted.

Kürzung ['kyrtsuŋ] *f* (*pl* -en) shortening, reduction.

Kurz‖waren *f pl* haberdashery. **–welle** *f* shortwave.

Kusine [ku'ziːnə] *f* (*pl* -n) (female) cousin.

Kuß [kus] *m* (*pl* Küsse) kiss.

küssen ['kysən] *v* kiss.

Küste ['kystə] *f* (*pl* -n) coast, shore. **–nwache** *f* coastguard.

Kutsche ['kutʃə] *f* (*pl* -n) carriage, coach. **–r** *m* (*pl* -) coachman.

L

labil [la'biːl] *adj* unstable; (*oft krank*) delicate, sickly.

Labor [la'boːr] *neut* (*pl* -s) (*umg.*) lab.

Laboratorium [labora'toːrium] *neut* (*pl* **Laboratorien**) laboratory, (*umg.*) lab.

lächeln ['leçəln] *v* smile. **Lächeln** *neut* smile.

lachen ['laxən] *v* laugh. **Lachen** *neut* laughter, laugh. **zum Lachen bringen** make laugh. **das ist zum Lachen** that's ridiculous.

lächerlich ['leçərliç] *adj* ridiculous.

Lachs [laks] *m* (*pl* -e) salmon.

Lack [lak] *m* (*pl* -e) lacquer; (*mit Farbstoff*) (enamel) paint. **–farbe** *f* (enamel) paint. **–leder** *neut* patent leather.

*laden¹ ['laːdən] *v* load.

*laden² *v* invite; (*Jur*) summon.

Laden ['laːdən] *m* (*pl* Läden) shop; (*Fenster*) shutter. **–diebstahl** *m* shoplifting. **–schluß** *m* closing time. **–tisch** *m* counter.

Lade‖platz *m* loading place; (*Schiff*) wharf. **–raum** *m* hold. **Ladung** (*pl* -en) *f* load; (*Schiffe*) cargo.

Lage ['laːgə] *f* (*pl* -n) situation, position. **in der Lage sein zu** be in a position to.

Lager ['laːgər] *neut* (*pl* -) camp; (*Speicher*) store(s); (*Tier*) lair; (*Geol*) stratum, layer; (*Tech*) bearing. **–feuer** *neut* campfire. **–haus** *neut* warehouse. **lagern** *v* (*im Freien rasten*) camp; (*aufbewahren*) store; (*einlegen*) lay down, place; (*aufbewahrt werden*) be stored.

Lagune [la'guːnə] *f* (*pl* -n) lagoon.

lahm [laːm] *adj* crippled; (*müde*) exhausted; (*schwach*) lame, feeble.

lähmen ['leːmən] *v* cripple, paralyze; (*fig*) obstruct. **Lähmung** *f* (*pl* -en) paralysis.

Laib [laip] *m* (*pl* -e) loaf.

Laie ['laiə] *m* (*pl* -n) layman. **Laien‖priester** *m* lay preacher. **–stand** *m* laity.

Lakritze [la'kritsə] *f* (*pl* -n) liquorice.

Lamm [lam] *neut* (*pl* Lämmer) lamb. **–fleisch** *neut* lamb. **–wolle** *f* lambswool.

Lampe ['lampə] *f* (*pl* -n) lamp.

Land [lant] **1** *neut* (*unz.*) (*Erdboden, Grundstück, Festland*) land; (*Landschaft*) country(side). **2** *neut* (*pl* Länder) land, country; (*Provinz*) state, province. **an Land gehen** go ashore, disembark. **Hügeliges Land** hilly country *or* terrain. **auf dem Lande** in the country. **Land‖arbeiter** *m* farmworker. **–besitz** *m* land, property. **landen** *v* land; (*umg.*) land up, end up. **Landenge** *f* isthmus.

Landes‖bank *f* national bank; regional bank. **–flagge** *f* national flag. **–verrat** *m* high treason.

Land‖gut *neut* (landed) estate. **–haus** *neut* country house. **–karte** *f* map. **–leute** *pl* country folk.

ländlich ['lentliç] *adj* rural.

Land‖mann *m* countryman; (*Bauer*) farmer. **–messer** *m* surveyor. **–mine** *f* landmine. **–schaft** *f* countryside; (*Malerei*) landscape; (*Gebiet*) area, region. **–schule** *f* village school. **–smann** *m* fellow countryman. **–spitze** *f* cape, headland. **–straße** *f* highway, main road. **–streicher** *m* tramp, vagrant.

Landung ['landuŋ] *f* (*pl* -en) landing. **–ssteg** *m* gangway, landing ramp.

Landweg ['lantveːk] *m* land route. **auf dem Landwege** by land.

Landwirt ['lantviːrt] *m* farmer. **landwirt-schaftlich** *adj* agricultural.

lang [laŋ] *adj* long; (*Mensch*) tall. **viele Jahre lang** for many years. **lange** *adv* (for) a long time.

Länge ['lɛŋə] *f* (*pl* -n) length; (*Mensch*) height; (*Größe*) size; (*Geog*) longitude.

langen ['laŋən] *v* suffice. **langen nach** reach for.

länger ['lɛŋər] *adj* longer; taller. **länger machen** lengthen, extend. **auf längere Zeit** for a considerable period.

Langeweile ['laŋəvailə] *f* boredom.

lang||jährig *adj* of long standing. **–lebig** *adj* long-lived.

länglich ['lɛŋliç] *adj* oblong, longish. **–rund** *adj* oval, elliptical.

längs [lɛŋs] *prep* along.

langsam ['laŋzaɪm] *adj* slow. **Langsamkeit** *f* slowness.

Langspielplatte ['laŋʃpiːlplatə] *f* long-playing record, LP.

längst [lɛŋst] *adj* longest. *adv* long ago. **–ens** *adv* (*höchstens*) at the most; (*spätestens*) at the latest.

langweilen ['laŋvailən] *v* bore. **sich langweilen** be bored. **langweilig** *adj* boring, tedious.

Lanze ['lantsə] *f* (*pl* -n) lance.

Lappen ['lapən] *m* (*pl* -) rag, (cleaning) cloth; (*Anat, Bot*) lobe. **lappig** *adj* (*umg.*) flabby; (*Anat, Bot*) lobed.

Lärche ['lɛrçə] *f* (*pl* -n) larch.

Lärm [lɛrm] *m* (*unz.*) noise, din. **lärmen** *v* make a noise. **–d** *adj* noisy.

Laser ['leɪzər] *m* (*pl* -) laser.

*lassen ['lasən] *v* (*erlauben*) let, allow; (*unterlassen*) leave, stop; (*überlassen*) leave. **außer Acht lassen** disregard. **bleiben lassen** leave alone. **fallen lassen** (let) drop. **kommen lassen** send for. **sich machen lassen** have done *or* made. **lassen von** renounce. **sich nicht beschreiben lassen** be indescribable *or* beyond words. **laß mich gehen!** let me go! **laß mich in Ruhe!** leave me alone. **es läßt sich nicht machen** it can't be done.

lässig ['lɛsiç] *adj* careless, negligent.

Last [last] *f* (*pl* -en) load; (*Bürde*) burden; (*Gewicht*) weight; (*Fracht*) cargo.

Laster[1] ['lastər] *m* (*pl* -) (*umg.*) lorry, truck.

Laster[2] *neut* (*pl* -) vice. **lasterhaft** *adj* immoral.

lästern ['lɛstərn] slander. **Lästerung** *f* slander.

lästig ['lɛstiç] *adj* irksome, bothersome.

Last||kahn *m* barge, lighter. **–kraftwagen** (**Lkw**) *m* lorry, truck. **–pferd** *neut* packhorse.

Latein [la'tain] *neut* Latin (language). **–amerika** *neut* Latin America. **lateinisch** *adj* Latin.

Laterne [la'tɛrnə] *f* (*pl* -n) lantern. **–npfahl** *m* lamppost.

Latte ['latə] *f* (*pl* -n) lath.

lau [lau] *adj* lukewarm, tepid; (*Wetter*) mild.

Laub [laup] *neut* (*pl* -e) foliage. **–baum** *m* deciduous tree. **–säge** *f* fretsaw. **–wald** *m* deciduous forest. **–werk** *neut* foliage.

Lauch [laux] *m* (*pl* -e) leek.

lauern ['lauərn] *v* lurk, lie in ambush; (*umg.*) hang around, wait impatiently.

Lauf [lauf] *m* (*pl* Läufe) run; (*Sport*) race; (*Fluß*) course; (*Gewehr*) barrel; (*Maschine*) running, operation. **–bahn** *f* career. **laufen** *v* (*Maschine, Wasser, Weg, usw.*) run; (*zu Fuß gehen*) walk. **laufend** *adj* current, running; (*Zahl*) consecutive. **auf dem laufenden** up to date.

Läufer ['lɔyfər] *m* (*pl* -) (*Sport*) runner; (*Schach*) bishop.

läufig ['lɔyfiç] *adj* (*Hündin*) in heat.

Lauf||planke *f* gangway. **–werk** *neut* mechanism, drive.

Lauge ['laugə] *f* (*pl* -n) lye; (*Seifen-*) suds. **laugenartig** *adj* alkaline, (*Chem*) basic.

Laune ['launə] *f* (*pl* -n) mood, temper; (*Grille*) whim. **launenhaft** *adj* capricious, whimsical. **launig** *adj* humorous, funny. **launisch** *adj* moody, capricious.

Laus [laus] *f* (*pl* Läuse) louse.

lauschen ['lauʃən] *v* listen (to); (*heimlich*) listen in, eavesdrop.

lausig ['lauziç] *adj* lousy.

laut[1] [laut] *adj* loud. *adv* aloud.

laut[2] *prep* according to.

Laut [laut] *m* (*pl* -e) sound.

Laute ['lautə] *f* (*pl* -n) lute.

lauten ['lautən] *v* read, say; (*klingen*) sound.

läuten ['lɔytən] *v* ring, sound.

lauter ['lautər] *adj* pure; (*echt*) genuine; (*nichts als*) nothing but, sheer.

Laut||sprecher *m* loudspeaker. **–stärke** *f* volume, loudness.

lauwarm ['lauvarm] *adj* lukewarm.

Lawine [la'viːnə] *f* (*pl* -n) avalanche.
lax [laks] *adj* lax.
leben ['leːbən] *v* live. **von . . . leben** live on
. . . . **Es lebe die Königin!** Long live the
Queen! **Leben** *neut* (*pl* -) life; (*Geschäf-
tigkeit*) activity, bustle. **am Leben** alive.
ums Leben kommen lose one's life, die.
lebend *adj* living, alive. **-ig** *adj* alive, living; (*munter*) lively.
Lebens‖art *f* lifestyle. **-freude** *f* joy of
life. **-funktion** *f* vital function. **-gefahr** *f*
danger to life. **-haltungskosten** *pl* cost of
living *sing*. **-jahr** *neut* year of one's life.
im 16. Lebensjahr during the sixteenth
year of his/her life.
lebenslänglich ['leːbənsleŋliç] *adj* life-
long; *Jury* for life
Lebens‖lauf *m* curriculum vitae, c.v.
-mittel *pl* food *zing*. **-standard** *m* standard of living. **-stil** *m* lifestyle.
-unterhalt *m* livelihood. **-versicherung** *f*
life insurance. **-weise** *f* way of life.
Leber ['leːbər] *f* (*pl* -n) liver. **-fleck** *m*
birthmark. **-wurst** *f* liver sausage.
Lebe‖wesen *neut* living creature, organism. **-wohl** *neut* farewell.
lebhaft ['leːphaft] *adj* lively. **Lebhaftigkeit**
f liveliness.
leblos ['leːploːs] *adj* lifeless.
leck [lɛk] *adj* leaky. **Leck** *neut* (*pl* -e)
leak.
lecken ['lɛkən] *v* lick.
lecker ['lɛkər] *adj* delicious. **-bissen** *m*
delicacy, titbit.
Leder ['leːdər] *neut* (*pl* -) leather. **-hose** *f*
leather shorts *pl*. **ledern** *adj* leather; (*fig*)
dry, boring. **Leder‖riemen** *m* leather
strap. **-waren** *pl* leather goods.
ledig ['leːdiç] *adj* single, unmarried; (*frei*)
free (of). **lediger Stand** *m* celibacy. **ledig-
lich** *adv* solely.
Lee [leː] *f* lee.
leer [leːr] *adj* empty; (*unbesetzt*) unoccupied; (*Stellung*) open; (*Seite*) blank.
Leere *f* emptiness; (*Physik*) vacuum.
leeren *v* empty. **Leer‖lauf** *m* (*Mot*)
idling, tick-over. **-ung** *f* (*pl* -en) emptying; (*Post*) collection.
legal [le'gaːl] *adj* legal.
legen ['leːgən] *v* lay, place, put (down);
(*Eier*) lay; (*installieren*) install, fit. **sich
legen** lie down; (*wind*) abate.
Legende [le'gɛndə] *f* (*pl* -n) legend.
legieren [le'giːrən] *v* (*Metalle*) alloy;
(*Suppe*) thicken.

legitim [lɛgi'tiːm] *adj* legitimate.
Lehm [leːm] *m* (*pl* -e) loam.
Lehne ['leːnə] *f* (*pl* -n) support, prop;
(*Stuhl*) back. **lehnen** *v* lean, rest. **sich
lehnen** lean, rest. **Lehn‖sessel** or **-stuhl**
m armchair, easy chair.
Lehrbuch ['leːrbuːx] *neut* textbook. **Lehre**
f (*pl* -n) teaching; (*Lehrzeit*) training.
lehren *v* teach. **Lehrer** *m* (*pl* -) teacher,
schoolmaster. **-in** *f* (*pl* -nen) teacher,
schoolmistress. **Lehr‖film** *m* educational
film. **-gang** *m* curriculum, course of
instruction. **-ling** *m* (*pl* -e) apprentice.
lehrreich *adj* instructive. **Lehr‖satz** *m*
rule, proposition. **-zeit** *f* training,
apprenticeship.
Leib [laip] *m* (*pl* -er) body. **Leibes‖frucht**
f foetus. **-übung** *f* physical exercise.
Leiche ['laiçə] *f* (*pl* -n) corpse.
Leichen‖halle *neut* mortuary. **-schau** *f*
postmortem, autopsy. **Leichnam** *m* (*pl*
-e) corpse.
leicht [laiçt] *adj* light; (*einfach*) easy.
leicht zugänglich easily accessible. **es sich
leicht machen** take it easy. **Leichtathletik**
f athletics. **leichtfertig** *adj* superficial;
(*Antwort*) glib. **Leichtgewichtler** *m* light-
weight. **leichtgläubig** *adj* credulous.
Leichtigkeit *f* lightness; (*Mühelosigkeit*)
ease. **leichtlebig** *adj* easy-going. **-sinnig**
adj thoughtless.
leid [lait] *adj* disagreeable, painful. **es ist
(or es tut) mir leid** I am sorry. **Leid** *neut*
(*unz.*) sorrow, grief; (*Schaden*) harm. **leiden** *v* suffer; (*erlauben*) tolerate, allow.
leiden an suffer from. **ich kann ihn nicht
leiden** I can't stand him. **leidend** *adj* suffering; (*kränklich*) sickly.
Leidenschaft ['laidənʃaft] *f* (*pl* -en) passion. **leidenschaft‖lich** *adj* passionate.
-slos *adj* dispassionate.
leider ['laidər] *adv* unfortunately. **leider
muß ich . . .** I am afraid I have to . . . .
leidig [laidiç] *adj* tiresome, disagreeable.
leidlich ['laitliç] *adj* tolerable.
Leier ['laiər] *f* (*pl* -n) lyre. **die alte Leier**
the same old story. **leiern** *v* (*sprechen*)
drawl.
leihen ['laiən] *v* lend; (*borgen*) borrow.
Leihbibliothek *f* lending library.
Leim [laim] *m* (*pl* -e) glue.
Lein [lain] *m* (*pl* -e) flax.
Leine ['lainə] *f* (*pl* -n) line, cord; (*Hund*)
leash.

leinen ['lainən] *adj* linen. **Leinen** *neut* linen.

leise ['laizə] *adj* quiet; (*sanft*) gentle, soft.

Leiste ['laistə] *f* (*pl* -n) (*Anat*) groin.

leisten ['laistən] *v* do; (*schaffen*) accomplish, achieve; (*ausführen*) carry out. **Hilfe leisten** help, assist. **sich leisten** allow oneself. *ich kann mir einen neuen Wagen nicht leisten* I cannot afford a new car. **Leistung** *f* (*pl* -en) achievement, accomplishment; (*Tat*) deed; (*Arbeit*) output. **leistungsfähig** *adj* capable; productive. **Leistungsfähigkeit** *f* ability (to work); productivity.

leiten ['laitən] *v* (*führen*) (*Elek, Musik*) conduct. **-d** *adj* guiding, leading; (*Person*) prominent, senior.

Leiter¹ ['laitər] *m* (*pl* -) leader; manager.

Leiter² *f* (*pl* -n) ladder.

Leit‖faden *m* clue; (*Lehrbuch*) guide, textbook. **-satz** *m* guiding principle. **-ung** *f* (*pl* -en) (*Führung*) leadership; (*Verwaltung*) management; (*Elek*) circuit; (*Draht*) wire; (*Wasser*) pipes *pl*, mains *pl*.

Lektüre lɛk'tyːrə] *f* (*pl* -n) reading; (*Lesestoff*) reading material, literature.

Lende ['lɛndə] *f* (*pl* -n) (*Anat*) lumbar region; (*Fleisch*) loin.

lenken ['lɛŋkən] *v* steer; (*führen*) direct. **Lenk‖er** *m* guide; (*Flugzeug*) pilot; (*Leiter*) manager. **-rad** *neut* steering wheel. **-ung** *f* (*pl* -en) (*Mot*) steering; (*Leitung*) direction.

Leopard [leo'part] *m* (*pl* -en) leopard.

lepra ['leːpra] *f* leprosy. **-kranke(r)** leper.

Lerche ['lɛrçə] *f* (*pl* -n) lark.

lernen ['lɛrnən] *v* learn. **Lernen** *neut* (*unz.*) learning.

lesbar ['leːsbaːr] *adj* readable. **Lese** *f* (*pl* -n) vintage. **Lesebuch** *neut* reading book. **lesen** *v* read; lecture; (*sammeln, ernten*) gather, harvest. **Leser** *m* (*pl* -), **Leserin** *f* (*pl* -en) reader. **leserlich** *adj* legible. **Leserschaft** *f* readership, readers. **Lesesaal** *m* reading room.

letzt [lɛtst] *adj* last; (*spätest*) latest, final. **letzte Nummer** current issue. **letztens** *adv* lately; (*zum Schluß*) lastly.

Leuchte ['lɔyçtə] *f* (*pl* -n) light, lamp. **leuchten** *v* emit light, shine. **-d** *adj* shining, luminous. **Leuchter** *m* (*pl* -) candlestick. **Leuchtturm** *m* lighthouse.

leugnen ['lɔygnən] *v* deny.

Leukämie [lɔykɛ'miː] *f* leukaemia.

Leute ['lɔytə] *pl* people.

Leutnant ['lɔytnant] *m* (*pl* -e) lieutenant.

leutselig ['lɔytzɛːliç] *adj* affable, sociable.

Lexikon ['lɛksikɔn] *neut* (*pl* **Lexika**) dictionary.

Libelle [li'bɛlə] *f* (*pl* -n) (*Insekt*) dragonfly; (*Tech*) (spirit) level.

liberal [libe'raɪl] *adj* liberal.

licht [liçt] *adj* bright; (*Farbe*) light; (*Wald*) sparse, thin. **Licht** *neut* (*pl* -er) light; (*Kerze*) candle. **-bild** *neut* photograph. **lichtdurchlässig** *adj* translucent.

lichten ['liçtən] *v* (*Wald*) clear; (*Anker*) weigh.

Licht‖jahr *neut* lightyear. **-pause** *f* blueprint. **-signal** *neut* light signal. **lichtundurchlässig** *adj* opaque.

Lichtung ['liçtuŋ] *f* (*pl* -en) glade, clearing.

Lid [liːt] *neut* (*pl* -er) eyelid.

lieb [liːb] *adj* dear; (*nett*) nice; (*angenehm*) agreeable. *ein liebes Kind* a good child. *es wäre ihm lieb* he would appreciate it. *das ist lieb von Ihnen* that is most kind of you.

Liebchen ['liːpçən] *neut* (*pl* -) darling.

Liebe ['liːbə] *f* (*pl* -n) love. **Liebelei** *f* (*pl* -en) flirtation. **lieben** *v* love. **liebens‖wert** *adj* lovable. **-würdig** *adj* amiable, helpful, kind.

lieber ['liːbər] *adj* dearer. *adv* rather; (*besser*) better. **lieber haben** prefer. **lieber als** rather than. **Ich gehe lieber zu Fuß** I prefer to walk. *das hättest Du lieber nicht sagen sollen* you had better not say that.

Liebes‖affäre *f* (love) affair. **-brief** *m* love letter. **-paar** *neut* lovers *pl*, couple.

liebevoll ['liːbəfɔl] *adj* affectionate, loving.

*liebhaben ['liːphaɪbən] *v* love, like. **Liebhaber** *m* (*pl* -), **Liebhaberin** *f* (*pl* -nen) lover.

lieb‖kosen *v* caress, fondle. **-lich** *adj* lovely. **Lieb‖ling** *m* darling; (*Günstling*) favourite. **-reiz** *m* charm, attraction.

liebst [liːpst] *adj* favourite, best-loved. *adv* **am liebsten haben** like best of all. **am liebsten machen** like doing best.

Lied [liːt] *neut* (*pl* -er) song. **-erbuch** *neut* songbook; (*Rel*) hymnbook.

liederlich *adj* slovenly; (*sittenlos*) debauched, dissipated.

Lieferant [liːfə'rant] *m* (*pl* -en) supplier. **liefern** *v* deliver, supply; (*Ertrag*) yield. **Lieferung** *f* (*pl* -en) delivery, supply.

Liege ['liːgə] *f* (*pl* -n) couch. **liegen** *v* lie. −**bleiben** *v* remain; (*Waren*) be unsold; (*Arbeit*) remain unfinished; (*Panne haben*) break down. −**lassen** *v* leave (behind). **Liege∥platz** *m* berth. −**stuhl** *m* deckchair.

Liga ['liːga] *f* (*pl* **Ligen**) league.

Likör *m* (*pl* -e) liqueur.

lila ['liːla] *adj* lilac, purple. **Lila** *neut* lilac, purple.

Lilie ['liːliə] *f* (*pl* -n) lily.

Limonade [limo'naːdə] *f* (*pl* -n) lemonade, soda-pop.

Linde ['lində] *f* (*pl* -n) lime tree.

lindern ['lindərn] *v* alleviate, mitigate.

Lineal [line'aːl] *neut* (*pl* -e) ruler, rule.

Linie ['liːniə] *f* (*pl* -n) line.

Linke ['liŋkə] *f* (*pl* -n) left, left(-hand) side; (*Pol*) the Left. **linkisch** *adj* clumsy. **links** *adv* (on *or* to the) left. **Linkshänder** *m* left-hander. **linkshändig** *adj* left-handed. **Links∥radikale(r)** *m* (radical) left-winger. −**steuerung** *f* left-hand drive.

Linse ['linzə] *f* (*pl* -n) (*Foto, Anat*) lens; (*Küche*) lentil.

Lippe ['lipə] *f* (*pl* -n) lip. −**nstift** *m* lipstick.

lispeln ['lispəln] *v* lisp.

Lissabon ['lissabon] *neut* Lisbon.

List [list] *f* (*pl* -en) (*Schlauheit*) cunning; trick, ruse.

Liste ['listə] *f* (*pl* -n) list.

listig ['listiç] *adj* cunning.

Litanei [lita'nai] *f* (*pl* -en) litany.

Liter ['liːtər] *neut or m* (*pl* -) litre.

literarisch [lite'raːriʃ] *adj* literary. **Literatur** *f* literature.

Live-Sendung ['laifzɛnduŋ] *f* live *or* direct broadcast.

Lizenz [li'tsɛnts] *f* (*pl* -en) licence. −**inhaber** *m* licensee.

Lob [loːp] *neut* (*pl* -e) praise. **loben** *v* praise. **Lob∥gesang** *m* song of praise. −**hudelei** *f* adulation.

Loch [lɔx] *neut* (*pl* **Löcher**) hole; (*Reifen*) puncture. **lochen** *v* pierce, punch; (*perforieren*) perforate.

löcherig ['lœçəriç] *adj* full of holes.

Lochung ['lɔxuŋ] *f* (*pl* -en) perforation.

Locke ['lɔkə] *f* (*pl* -n) curl, lock.

locken ['lɔkən] *v* lure, entice.

locker ['lɔkər] *adj* loose; (*Lebensart*) lax, slack. **lockern** *v* loosen (up). **sich lockern** *v* become loose; (*entspannen*) relax.

lockig ['lɔkiç] *adj* curly.

Lock∥speise *f* bait. −**vogel** *m* decoy.

lodern ['loːdərn] *v* blaze (up); (*fig*) glow, smoulder.

Löffel ['lœfəl] *m* (*pl* -) spoon.

Loge ['loːʒə] *f* (*pl* -n) (*Theater*) box; (*Freimaurer*) lodge.

logieren [lo'ʒiːrən] *v* lodge.

Logik ['loːgik] *f* logic. **logisch** *adj* logical.

Lohn [loːn] *m* (*pl* **Löhne**) (*Gehalt, Bezahlung*) wages *pl*, pay; (*Belohnung*) reward; (*verdiente Strafe*) deserts *pl*. **arbeiter** *m* wage-earner, (*weekly-paid*) worker. **lohnen** *v* reward. **es lohnt sich** (**nicht**) it's (not) worth it. **Lohn∥forderung** *f* wage claim. −**schreiber** *m* hack (writer). −**stopp** *m* wage freeze. −**tag** *m* payday.

lokal [lo'kaːl] *adj* local. **Lokal** *neut* (*pl* -e) pub, tavern.

Lokomotive [lokomo'tiːvə] *f* (*pl* -n) locomotive.

Lorbeer ['lɔrbeːr] *m* (*pl* -en) laurel. −**blatt** *neut* bay leaf. −**kranz** *m* laurel wreath.

los [loːs] *adj* free; (*nicht fest*) loose. *adv* away, off. **los!** go on! off you go! **was ist los?** what's going on? **was ist mit dir los?** what's the matter (with you)? **etwas/jemanden los sein/werden** be/get rid of something/someone.

Los *neut* (*pl* -e) (*Schicksal*) fate, lot; (*Lotterie*) lottery ticket. **das Los ziehen** draw lots.

lösbar ['lœsbaːr] *adj* soluble.

*****los∥binden** *v* untie. −**brechen** *v* break loose.

löschen ['lœʃən] *v* (*Feuer*) put out, extinguish; (*Licht*) turn off, switch off; (*Schuld*) cancel, write off; (*Tinte*) blot; (*Firma*) liquidate; (*Durst*) quench. **Löscher** *m* (*Feuer*) extinguisher; (*Tinte*) blotter.

lose ['loːzə] *adj* loose.

Lösegeld ['lœzəgɛlt] *neut* ransom.

lösen ['lœːzən] *v* loosen; (*Knoten*) unravel (a plot); (*Verschluß*) unfasten; (*Rätsel, Problem*) solve; (*abtrennen*) detach; (*Chem*) dissolve.

*****los∥fahren** *v* drive off. −**gehen** *v* set out, get going. −**knüpfen** *v* untie. −**kommen** *v* get away *or* free. −**lassen** *v* let go.

löslich ['lœːzliç] *adj* soluble.

los∥lösen *v* free, detach. −**machen** *v* unfasten, release. −**reißen** *v* tear away. −**sagen** *v* **sich lossagen von** renounce.

los‖schießen v fire away/off. **–schrauben** v unscrew. **–sprechen** v acquit, release.
Losung ['loːzuŋ] f (pl -en) password.
Lösung ['løːzuŋ] f (pl -en) solution; (Lösen) loosening. **–smittel** neut solvent.
los‖werden v get rid of. **–ziehen** v set out.
Lot [loːt] neut (pl -e) plumbline; (zum Löten) solder. **loten** v take soundings.
löten v solder.
lotrecht ['loːtrɛçt] adj perpendicular, vertical.
Lotse ['loːtsə] f (pl -n) (Schiff) pilot.
Lotterie [lɔteˈriː] f (pl -n) lottery.
Löwe ['løːvə] m (pl -n) lion. **–nzahn** m dandelion. **Löwin** f lioness.
Luchs [luks] m (pl -e) lynx.
Lücke ['lykə] f (pl -n) gap; (Auslassung) omission; (eines Gesetzes) loophole. **–nbüßer** m stopgap. **lückenhaft** adj defective; (fig) patchy, full of gaps.
Luft [luft] f (pl Lüfte) air. **–ansicht** f aerial view. **–bild** neut aerial photograph. **–bremse** f air brake.
–brücke f airlift. **luftdicht** adj airtight.
lüften ['lyftən] v ventilate, air.
Luftfahrt ['luftfaːrt] f aviation. **luftgekühlt** adj air-cooled. **Lufthafen** m airport. **luftig** adj airy, breezy. **Luft‖krankheit** f airsickness. **–krieg** m aerial warfare. **–post** f airmail. **–reifen** m pneumatic tyre, (US tire). **–röhre** f windpipe. **–schiff** neut airship.
Lüftung ['lyftuŋ] f (pl -en) ventilation.
Luftverkehr ['luftvɛrkeːr] m air traffic. **–sgesellschaft** f airline.
Lüge ['lyːgə] f (pl -n) lie. **lügen** v (tell a) lie. **–haft** adj lying. **Lügner** m liar.
Lump [lump] m (pl -) rag. **–händler** m rag-and-bone man.
Lunge ['luŋə] f (pl -n) lung. **Lungen‖entzündung** f pneumonia. **–krebs** m lung cancer.
Lupe ['luːpə] f (pl -n) magnifying glass. **unter die Lupe nehmen** scrutinize, examine closely.
Lust [lust] f (pl Lüste) delight, pleasure; (Verlangen) desire; (Wollust) lust. **Lust haben an** take pleasure in. **Lust haben (zu tun)** feel like (doing). **keine Lust haben (zu tun)** not be in the mood (to do), not feel like (doing).
lüstern ['lystərn] adj (geil) lascivious, lecherous.

Lustfahrt ['lustfaːrt] f pleasure trip. **lustig** adj merry, joyful; (unterhaltend) amusing, funny. **sich lustig machen über** make fun of. **Lustigkeit** f gaiety, merriment. **lustlos** adj dull, inactive. **Lust‖mord** m sex murder. **–spiel** neut comedy.
lutschen ['lutʃən] v suck. **Lutscher** m (baby's) dummy, (US) pacifier.
Luxus ['luksus] m luxury. **–artikel** m luxury item; pl luxuries.
Luzern ['luːtsɛrn] neut Lucerne.
lyrisch ['lyːriʃ] adj lyrical.

M

Maat [maːt] m (pl -e) mate; (Kriegsmarine) petty officer.
machen ['maxən] v make; do; (Rechnung) come to. **eine Prüfung machen** sit an exam **fertig machen** get ready. **Licht machen** switch on a light. **(das) macht nichts**, it doesn't matter, never mind. **mach's gut!** good luck! all the best!
Macht [maxt] f (pl Mächte) power.
mächtig ['mɛçtiç] adj powerful; mighty; (riesig) immense.
Machtkampf m power struggle. **machtlos** adj powerless. **Machtprobe** f trial of strength.
Mädchen ['mɛːtçən] neut (pl -) girl. **mädchenhaft** adj girlish. **Mädchenname** m maiden name.
Made ['maːdə] f (pl -n) maggot.
Mädel ['mɛːdəl] neut (pl -) girl.
Magazin [magaˈtsiːn] neut (pl -e) store(house); (Zeitschrift, auch Gewehr-) magazine.
Magd [maːkt] f (pl Mägde) maid(servant).
Magen ['maːgən] m (pl -Mägen) stomach. **–brennen** neut heartburn. **–schmerzen** pl stomach-ache sing.
mager ['maːgər] adj thin, lean.
Magie [maˈgiː] f magic. **magisch** adj magic(al).
Magnet [magˈneːt] m (pl -en) magnet. **magnetisch** adj magnetic.
Mahagoni [mahaˈgoːni] neut (pl -s) mahogany.
Mähdrescher ['mɛːdrɛʃər] m combine harvester. **mähen** v mow.
Mahl [maːl] neut (pl -e) meal.
*mahlen ['maːlən] v mill, grind.

Mahl‖zahn m molar. **–zeit** f meal; interj good appetite!

Mähne ['mɛːnə] f (pl -n) mane.

mahnen ['maːnən] v remind, admonish; warn. **Mahnung** f reminder, warning.

Mai [mai] m (pl -e) May. **–blume** f lily of the valley.

Mais [mais] m maize, (US) corn. **–kolben** m cob of corn. **–mehl** neut cornflour.

Majestät [majɛsˈtɛːt] f (pl -en) majesty. **majestätisch** adj majestic.

Majoran [majoˈraːn] m marjoram.

Makel ['maːkəl] m (pl -) stain, spot; (Fehler) defect, fault. **makellos** adj spotless; faultless.

Makler ['maːklər] m (pl -) broker.

Makrele [maˈkreːlə] f (pl -n) mackerel.

mal [maːl] adv (Math) times; (einmal) once, just. **drei mal fünf** three times five. **hör' mal!** just listen!

Mal¹ [maːl] neut (pl -e) time. **zum ersten Mal** for the first time.

Mal² neut (pl -e or Mäler) mark, sign; (Denkmal) monument; (Grenzstein) boundary stone.

Malaria [maˈlaːria] f malaria.

malen ['maːlən] v paint; (zeichnen) draw. **Maler** m (pl -) painter. **Malerei** f (pl -en) painting. **malerisch** adj picturesque.

Malz [malts] neut (pl -e) malt. **–bier** neut malt beer, stout.

Mama [maˈmaː] f (pl -s) mamma.

man [man] pron one, you; (die Leute) people. **man sagt** people say, it is said. **man tut das nicht** that is not done, you shouldn't do that.

Manager ['mɛnidʒər] m (pl -) manager.

manch [manç] pron, adj many a, some. **manche** pl several, many. **–mal** adv sometimes.

Mandat [manˈdaːt] neut (pl -e) mandate.

Mandel ['mandəl] f (pl -n) almond; (Anat) tonsil. **–entfernung** f tonsillectomy. **–entzündung** f tonsillitis.

Mangel¹ ['maŋəl] f (pl -n) mangle.

Mangel² [m (pl Mängel) lack, want; (Knappheit) shortage; (Fehler) fault.

mangeln ['maŋəln] v lack, want. **es mangelt mir an** I lack.

Manie [maˈniː] f (pl -n) mania.

Manier [maˈniːr] f (pl -en) manner, way; (Stil) style. **Manieren** pl manners. **maniert** adj affected, mannered. **manierlich** adj well-mannered, civil.

Manifest [maniˈfɛst] neut (pl -e) manifesto.

manisch ['maːniʃ] adj manic.

Mann [man] m (pl Männer) man; (Ehemann) husband.

Männchen ['mɛnçən] neut (pl -) little man; (Tier) male.

Mannesalter ['manəsaltər] neut (age of) manhood. **mannhaft** adj manly.

Mannequin [manəˈkɛ̃] neut (pl -s) mannequin, fashion model.

mannigfaltig ['maniçfaltiç] adj varied, manifold.

männlich ['mɛnliç] adj male; (fig, Gramm) masculine. **Männlichkeit** f manhood; masculinity.

Mannschaft ['manʃaft] f (pl -en) crew; (Sport) team; (Belegschaft) personnel. **–sführer** m (Sport) captain.

Manöver [maˈnœvər] neut (pl -) manoeuvre. **manövrieren** v manoeuvre.

Manschette [manˈʃɛtə] f (pl -n) cuff.

Mantel ['mantəl] m (pl -Mäntel) coat; (Umhang) cloak.

Manuskript [manuˈskript] neut (pl -e) manuscript.

Mappe ['mapə] f (pl -n) briefcase; (Aktenmappe) folder, portfolio.

Märchen ['mɛːrçən] neut (pl -) fairytale. **märchenhaft** adj fairytale, magical.

Margarine [margaˈriːnə] f (pl -n) margarine.

Marien‖bild neut (picture of the) Madonna. **–käfer** m ladybird.

Marine [maˈriːnə] f (pl -n) (Kriegsmarine) navy; (Handelsmarine) merchant navy. **–soldat** m marine.

marinieren [mariˈniːrən] v marinate.

Marionette [marioˈnɛtə] f (pl -n) marionette.

Mark¹ [mark] neut (unz.) (bone) marrow. **bis ins Mark** (fig) to the core.

Mark² f (pl -) (Geld) mark.

Mark³ f (pl -en) boundary; (Grenzgebiet) marches pl, border-country.

Marke ['markə] f (pl -n) (Zeichen) mark, stamp; (Fabrikat, Sorte) brand; (Handelszeichen) trademark; (Briefmarke) (postage) stamp; (Wertschein) token. **–nname** m tradename, brand-name.

Markt [markt] m (pl Märkte) market. **–halle** f covered market, market hall. **platz** m marketplace. **–tag** m market day. **–wirtschaft** f (free) market economy.

Marmelade [marmə'laɪdə] f (pl -n) jam.
Marmor ['marmɔr] m (pl -e) marble.
Mars [maɪrs] m Mars. **–bewohner** m
Martian.
Marsch[1] [marʃ] m (pl **Märsche**) march.
Marsch[2] [marʃ] f (pl -en) marsh.
Marschall ['marʃal] m (pl **Marschälle**)
marshal.
marschieren [marr'ʃɪirən] v march.
Märtyrer ['mɛrtyrər] m (pl -) martyr.
–tum neut martyrdom.
Märtyrin [mɔɪr'tyrin] f (pl -nen) martyr.
Marxismus [mar'ksismus] m (unz.) Marx-
ism.
März [mɛrts] m (pl -e) March.
Masche ['maʃə] f (pl -n) mesh; (Stricken)
stitch; (Trick) trick.
Maschine [ma'ʃiinə] f (pl -en) machine;
(Mot) engine. **Maschinen‖bau** m
mechanical engineering. **–fabrik** f engineering works. **–gewehr** neut machine-
gun. **–schreiben** neut typewriting, typ-
ling. **–schreiber(in)** m typist.
Maske ['maskə] f (pl -n) mask. **Mas-
ken‖ball** m fancy-dress ball. **–kostüm**
neut fancy dress (costume).
Maß [maɪs] neut (pl -e) measure;
(Mäßigung) moderation; (Grenze) limit;
(Umfang) extent. **in hohem Maße** to a
great extent. **Maß halten** be moderate.
Masse ['masə] f (pl -n) mass; (Jur) estate,
assets. **die Massen** the masses. **Mas-
sen‖erzeugung** f mass production.
–karambolage f multiple collision,
(umg.) pile-up. **–versammlung** f mass
meeting. **massenweise** adv wholesale, in
large numbers.
Maßgabe ['maɪsgaɪbə] f standard.
maßgeblich adj authoritative.
mäßig ['mɛɪsiç] adj moderate. **mäßigen** v
moderate. **Mäßigung** f modulation.
massiv [ma'siɪf] adj massive.
maßlos ['maɪslos] adj immoderate.
Maßnahme f (pl -n) measure, step.
Maßnahmen treffen take steps. **Maßstab**
m measure; (Tech) scale; (fig) yardstick.
Mast [mast] m (pl -e or -en) mast.
mästen ['mɛstən] v fatten.
Material [materi'aɪl] neut (pl -ien) material. **–ismus** m materialism. **materialistisch**
adj materialist(ic).
Materie [ma'teɪriə] f (pl -n) matter, stuff,
substance.
Mathematik [matema'tiik] f (unz.) mathe-

matics. **-er** m (pl -) mathematician.
mathematisch adj mathematical.
Matratze [ma'tratsə] f (pl -n) mattress.
Mätresse [mɛ'tresə] f (pl -n) mistress.
Matrize [ma'triitsə] f (pl -n) (Druck) sten-
cil; (Math) matrix.
Matrose [ma'troɪzə] m (pl -n) sailor.
Matsch [matʃ] m mud; (Schnee-) slush.
matschig adj muddy; (breiig) squashy.
matt [mat] adj faint, weary; (glanzlos)
dull, matt; (Licht) dim; (Schach) mate.
Matte ['matə] f (pl -n) mat.
Mattheit ['mathait] f weariness; dullness.
mattherzig adj fainthearted.
Mauer ['mauər] f (pl -n) wall. **mauern** v
build (a wall). **Mauerwerk** neut masonry.
Maul [maul] neut (pl **Mäuler**) (animals)
mouth, snout, muzzle; (vulgär) (person's)
mouth.
Maurer ['maurər] m (pl -) bricklayer,
building worker.
Maus [maus] f (pl **Mäuse**) mouse.
Mause‖falle f mousetrap. **–loch** neut
mousehole.
maximal [maksi'maɪl] adj maximum.
Maximum neut maximum.
Mechanik [me'çaɪnik] **1** f (unz.) mechanics. **2** (pl -en) (Mechanismus) mechanism.
–er m mechanic. **mechanisch** adj
mechanical.
meckern ['mɛkərn] v bleat; (nörgeln)
grumble, moan.
Medaille [me'daijə] f (pl -n) medal.
Medikament [medika'mɛnt] neut (pl -e)
medicine.
Medizin [medi'tsiin] f (pl -en) medicine.
-er m doctor, physician; (student) medical student. **medizinisch** adj medical.
Meer [meɪr] neut (pl -e) sea. **–enge** f
straits pl. **Meeres‖boden** m sea bed.
–spiegel m sea level.
Mehl [meɪl] neut (pl -e) flour. **mehlig** adj
floury, mealy.
mehr [meɪr] adv, adj more. **mehr als** more
than. **nicht mehr** no longer. **immer mehr**
more and more. **noch mehr** still more.
Mehrbetrag m surplus. **mehrdeutig** adj
ambiguous.
mehrere ['meɪrərə] pl pron, adj several.
mehrfach adj multiple.
Mehr‖gepäck neut excess baggage.
–gewicht neut excess weight. **–heit** f
majority.
mehr‖mals adv repeatedly, several times.
–seitig adj many-sided; (Math) polygo-

nal. **−sprachig** *adj* multilingual. **−stöckig** *adj* multistoreyed.

Mehr‖wertsteuer (MwSt) *f* value added tax (VAT). **−zahl** *f* majority; (*Gramm*) plural.

*meiden ['maidən] *v* avoid.

Meierei ['maiərai] *f* (*pl* **-en**) farm; (*Milchwirtschaft*) dairy farm.

Meile ['mailə] *f* (*pl* **-n**) mile.

mein [main] *adj, pron* my; mine. **meinerseits** *adv* for my part. **meinesgleichen** *pron* people like me, the likes of me. **meinethalben, meinetwegen, meinetwillen** *adv* for my sake. **meinige** *pron* (**der, die, das meinige**) mine.

Meineid ['mainait] *m* (*pl* **-e**) perjury.

meinen ['mainən] *v* mean; (*denken*) think; (*äußern*) say; (*beabsichtigen*) intend. **Meinung** *f* opinion. **Ich bin der Meinung, daß** I am of the opinion that. **meiner Meinung nach** in my opinion. **Meinungs‖forschung** *f* opinion research. **−umfrage,** *f* opinion poll. **−verschiedenheit** *f* difference of opinion.

Meißel ['maisəl] *m* (*pl* **-**) chisel. **meißeln** *v* chisel.

meist [maist] *adj* most. **die meisten(Leute)** most people. **am meisten** for the most part. **Meistbietende(r)** *m* highest bidder. **meistens** *adv* mostly.

Meister ['maistər] *m* (*pl* **-**) master; (*Sport*) champion. **meisterhaft** *adj* masterly. **Meisterin** *f* (*Sport*) champion. **meistern** *v* master. **Meister‖schaft** *f* mastery; (*Sport*) championship. **−schaftsspiel** *neut* championship match. **−stück** *or* **−werk** *neut* masterpiece.

meistgekauft ['maistgəkauft] *adj* best-selling.

Meldeamt ['mɛldəamt] *neut* registration office. **melden** *v* inform; (*ankündigen*) announce. **sich melden** report, present oneself; (*Stelle*) apply. **Meldung** *f* report; (*ankündigung*) announcement; (*bei der Polizei, usw.*) registration.

*melken ['mɛlkən] *v* milk. **Melkmaschine** *f* milking machine.

Melodie [melo'diː] *f* (*pl* **-n**) melody. **melodisch** *adj* melodious.

Melone [me'loːnə] *f* (*pl* **-n**) melon.

Membran(e) [mem'brain] *f* (*pl* **Membranen**) membrane.

Menge ['mɛŋə] *f* (*pl* **-n**) quantity; (*Menschen*) crowd. **eine (ganze) Menge** a lot

(of), lots (of). **mengen** *v* mix. **sich mengen in** meddle.

Mensa ['mɛnsa] *f* (*pl* **Mensen**) student refectory.

Mensch [mɛnʃ] *m* (*pl* **-en**) human (being), man, person. **Menschenfeind** *m* misanthrope. **menschenfeindlich** *adj* misanthropic. **Menschenfreund** *m* philanthropist. **menschenfreundlich** *adj* philanthropic; (*gütig*) affable. **Menschen‖kunde** *f* anthropology. **−leben** *neut* human life; (*Lebenszeit*) lifetime. **−liebe** *f* human kindness. **−rechte** *pl* human rights. **−würde** *f* human dignity.

Menschheit ['mɛnʃhait] *f* mankind, human race. **menschlich** *adj* human; (*human*) humane. **Menschlichkeit** *f* humanity.

menstrual [mɛnstru'ail] *adj* menstrual. **Menstruation** *f* (*pl* **-nen**) menstruation. **menstruieren** *v* menstruate.

Mentalität [mɛntali'tɛit] *f* (*pl* **-en**) mentality.

merkbar ['mɛrkbair] *adj* noticeable. **merken** *v* notice, note. **sich etwas merken** make a mental note of something. **merklich** *adj* evident. **Merkmal** (*pl* **-e**) *neut* characteristic, attribute. **merkwürdig** *adj* remarkable, peculiar.

Meßband ['mɛsbant] *neut* tape measure. **meßbar** *adj* measurable.

Messe ['mɛsə] *f* (*pl* **-n**) (*Rel*) mass; (*Ausstellung*) (trade) fair.

*messen ['mɛsən] *v* measure. **sich messen mit** compete with.

Messer¹ ['mɛsər] *m* (*pl* **-**) (*Gerät*) gauge, meter.

Messer² *neut* (*pl* **-**) knife.

Messing ['mɛsiŋ] *neut* (*pl* **-**) brass.

Messung ['mɛsuŋ] *f* (*pl* **-en**) measurement; (*Messen*) measuring.

Metall [me'tal] *neut* (*pl* **-e**) metal. **metallisch** *adj* metallic.

Meteor [mete'oir] *neut* (*pl* **-e**) meteor. **−ologe** *m* meteorologist. **−ologie** *f* meteorology. **meteorologisch** *adj* meteorologist.

Meter ['meitər] *neut* (*pl* **-**) metre.

Methode [me'toidə] *f* (*pl* **-n**) method. **methodisch** *adj* methodical.

metrisch ['meitriʃ] *adj* metric.

Mettwurst ['mɛtvurst] *f* a type of German sausage.

metzen ['mɛtsəln] *v* massacre, slaughter.

Metzger *m* (*pl* -) butcher. **-ei** *f* (*pl* -en) butcher's shop.
Meuchelmord ['mɔyçəlmɔrt] *m* assassination.
Meuterei [mɔytə'rai] *f* (*pl* -en) mutiny. **meutern** *v* mutiny.
mich [miç] *pron* me.
Mieder ['miːdər] *neut* (*pl* -) bodice.
Miene ['miːnə] *f* (*pl* -n) expression, look.
mies [miːs] *adj* (*umg.*) nasty, wretched.
Miete ['miːtə] *f* (*pl* -n) hire; (*für Wohnung*) rent. **mieten** *v* (*Haus, Wohnung*) rent; (*Wagen, usw.*) hire. **Mieter** *m* (*pl* -), **Mieterin** *f* (*pl* -nen) tenant, lessee. **Miet‖shaus** *neut* block of flats, tenement. **-wagen** *m* hired car. **-wohnung** *f* rented apartment.
Mikrophon [mikro'foːn] *neut* (*pl* -e) microphone.
Mikroskop [mikro'skoːp] *neut* microscope. **mikroskopisch** *adj* microscopic.
Milbe ['milbə] *f* (*pl* -n) mite.
Milch [milç] *f* milk. **milchig** *adj* milky. **Milchstraße** *f* Milky Way.
mild [milt] *adj* mild; (*sanft*) soft, gentle. **Milde** *f* mildness; gentleness. **mildern** *v* alleviate, moderate. **Milderung** *f* (*pl* -en) alleviation. **mildtätig** *adj* charitable.
Militär [mili'tɛːr] **1** *neut* (*unz.*) army, military. **2** *m* (*pl* -s) military man, soldier.
Milliarde [mil'jardə] *f* (*pl* -n) thousand million, (*US*) billion.
Million [mil'joːn] *f* (*pl* -en) million. **-är** *m* (*pl* -e) millionaire.
Mimik ['miːmik] *f* (*pl* -en) mimicry, miming. **-er** *m* (*pl* -) mimic.
minder ['mindər] *adj* lesser, smaller. *adv* less.
Minderheit *f* minority. **Minderjährige(r)** minor. **minderjährig** *adj* under age. **minderwertig** *adj* inferior. **Minderwertigkeit** *f* inferiority.
mindest ['mindəst] *adj* least; (*kleinst*) smallest. **-ens** *adv* at least. **Mindestzahl** *f* minimum number; (*Pol*) quorum.
Mine ['miːnə] *f* (*pl* -n) mine.
Mineral [mine'raːl] *neut* (*pl* -ien) mineral. **-wasser** *neut* mineral water.
Miniatur [minia'tuːr] *f* (*pl* -en) miniature.
minimal [mini'maːl] *adj* minimum. **Minimum** *neut* minimum.
Minister [mi'nistər] *m* (*pl* -) minister. **-ium** *neut* ministry. **-präsident** *m* prime minister.

minus ['miːnus] *adv* minus, less.
Minute [mi'nuːtə] *f* (*pl* -n) minute.
mir [miːr] *pron* (to) me.
mischen ['miʃən] *v* mix, blend. **sich mischen in** meddle or interfere in. **Misch‖ling** *m* (*Pflanze*) hybrid; (*Tier*) mongrel; (*Mensch*) half-breed. **-sprache** *f* pidgin. **-ung** *f* (*pl* -en) mixture.
mißach‖ten [mis'axtən] *v* disregard. **Mißachtung** *f* disregard.
Mißbildung ['misbilduŋ] *f* deformity.
mißbilligen ['misbiligən] *v* disapprove (of), object (to). **Mißbilligung** *f* disapproval.
Mißbrauch ['misbraux] *m* misuse, abuse. **mißbrauchen** *v* misuse, abuse.
mißdeuten [mis'dɔytən] *v* misinterpret, misunderstand. **Mißdeutung** *f* misinterpretation.
Mißerfolg ['misɛrfɔlk] *m* failure.
Missetat ['misətaːt] *f* misdeed. **Missetäter** *m* wrong-doer; (*Verbrecher*) criminal.
*mißfallen [mis'falən] *v* displease. **Mißfallen** *neut* displeasure.
Mißgeschick ['misgəʃik] *neut* misfortune.
mißgestaltet ['misgəʃtaltət] *adj* misshapen.
mißhandeln [mis'handəln] *v* maltreat. **Mißhandlung** *f* maltreatment.
Mission [misi'oːn] *f* (*pl* -en) mission. **-ar** *m* (*pl* -e) missionary.
Mißklang ['misklaŋ] *m* discord.
mißlich ['misliç] *adj* awkward, embarrassing.
*mißlingen *v* fail. **mißlungen** *adj* failed, unsuccessful.
mißtrauen [mis'trauən] *v* distrust. **Mißtrauen** *neut* distrust. **-svotum** *neut* vote of no confidence.
Mißverständnis ['misfɛrʃtɛntnis] *neut* misunderstanding. **mißverstehen** *v* misunderstand.
Mist [mist] *m* (*pl* -e) dung, manure.
Mistel ['mistəl] *f* (*pl* -n) mistletoe.
mit [mit] *prep* with; (*mittels*) by; (*Zeit*) at. *adv* along with; (*außerdem*) also, as well. *kommst du mit?* are you coming (with us)? *mit 10 Jahren* at the age of ten. **mit einemmal** suddenly. **mit dabei sein** be concerned or involved.
Mitarbeiter ['mitarbaitər] *m* colleague, fellow worker; (*Zeitschrift*) contributor.
Mitbestimmung ['mitbəʃtimuŋ] *f* worker participation, co-determination.

mitbeteiligt ['mɪtbətailiçt] *adj* participating, taking part.

***mitbringen** ['mɪtbrɪŋən] *v* bring along.

miteinander [mɪtain'andər] *adv* together, with each other.

miteinbegriffen [mit'ainbəgrifən] *adj* included.

Mitgefühl ['mɪtgəfyːl] *neut* sympathy.

Mitglied ['mɪtgliːt] *neut* member. **–schaft** *f* membership.

mithin [mɪt'hin] *adv* consequently, therefore.

***mitkommen** ['mɪtkɔmən] *v* come along (with); keep up.

Mitlaut ['mɪtlaut] *m* consonant.

Mitleid ['mɪtlait] *neut* pity, sympathy. **mitleid haben mit** have pity on, be sorry for.

mitmachen ['mɪtmaxən] *v* take part in, join in; *(erleben)* go *or* live through.

Mitmensch ['mɪtmɛnʃ] *m* fellow man.

***mitnehmen** ['mɪtneːmən] *v* take (along); *(im Auto)* give a lift to; *(erschöpfen)* exhaust. **Essen zum Mitnehmen** food to take away.

mitnichten [mɪt'nɪçtən] *adv* by no means.

***mitreißen** ['mɪtraisən] *v* drag along; *(fig)* sweep along, transport.

Mittag ['mɪtaːk] *m* noon, midday. **–essen** *neut* lunch, midday meal. **mittags** *adv* at noon. **Mittagspause** *f* lunch hour.

Mitte ['mɪtə] *f (pl* -n) middle, centre; *(Math)* mean.

mitteilen ['mɪttailən] *v* communicate, inform of, tell. **jemandem etwas mitteilen** inform *or* notify someone of something. **Mitteilung** *f* communication, report.

Mittel ['mɪtəl] *neut (pl* -) means, way; *(Ausweg)* remedy; *(Durchschnitt)* average, mean. **–alter** *neut* Middle Ages. **mittelalterlich** *adj* medieval.

Mittel‖amerika *f* Central America. **–gewichtler** *m* middleweight.

mittelgroß ['mɪtəlgroːs] *adj* of medium size.

Mittelläufer ['mɪtəlbyfər] *m (Fußball)* centre-half.

mittel‖los *adj* destitute. **–mäßig** *adj* mediocre.

Mittel‖meer *neut* Mediterranean (Sea). **–punkt** *m* centre.

mittels ['mɪtəls] *prep* by (means of).

Mittel‖stand *m* middle classes *pl*. **–stürmer** *m (Fußball)* centre-forward.

mitten ['mɪtən] *adv* in the middle, midway. **mitten in/auf/unter** in the middle of. **mitten drin** in the middle.

Mitternacht ['mɪtərnaxt] *f* midnight.

mittler ['mɪtlər] *adj* in **mittlerem Alter** middle-aged. **mittlerweile** *adv* in the meantime.

Mittwoch ['mɪtvɔx] *m (pl* -e) Wednesday.

mitwirken ['mɪtvirkən] *v* cooperate, take part, participate. **–d** *adj* participating, contributing.

Möbel ['møːbəl] *neut (pl* -) piece of furniture; *(pl)* furniture *sing*.

mobil [mo'biːl] *adj* movable, mobile; *(flink)* active, lively.

möblieren [mœ'bliːrən] *v* furnish. **möbliert** *adj* furnished.

Mode ['moːdə] *f (pl* -n) fashion, vogue. **in Mode sein** be in fashion. **aus der Mode kommen** become unfashionable. **Modeartikel** *pl* fancy goods, fashions.

Modell [mo'dɛl] *neut (pl* -e) model; *(Muster)* pattern. **Modellbogen** *m* cutting-out pattern. **modellieren** *v* model.

Modenschau ['moːdənʃau] *f* fashion show. **Modezeichner** *m* dress *or* fashion designer.

Moder ['moːdər] *m* decay, mould. **moderig** *adj* mouldy, putrid. **modern** *v* rot, decay.

modern [mo'dɛrn] *adj* modern. **modernisieren** *v* modernize.

modifizieren [modifi'tsiːrən] *v* modify.

modisch ['moːdiʃ] *adj* fashionable.

mogeln ['moːgəln] *v* cheat.

***mögen** ['møːgən] *v* like; *(wünschen)* wish; *(können)* may, might. **nicht mögen** dislike. *Ich mag ihn* I like him. *das mag sein* that may be so. *Wer mag das sein?* who might that be? *Ich möchte* I would like. *Ich möchte lieber* I would prefer. *Er mag ruhig warten!* let him wait!

möglich ['møːgliç] *adj* possible. **–erweise** *adv* possibly. **Möglichkeit** *f* possibility. **möglichst** *adv* as ... as possible.

Mohammedaner [mohame'daːnər] *m (pl* -) Muslim, Mohammedan. **mohammedanisch** *adj* Muslim, Mohammedan.

Mohn [moːn] *m (pl* -e) poppy; *(Samen)* poppyseed.

Mohr [moːr] *m (pl* -en) moor, black(man).

Möhre ['møːrə] *f (pl* -n) carrot.

Mohrrübe ['moːrryːbə] *f (pl* -n) carrot.

Molekül [mole'ky:l] *neut* (*pl* -e) molecule.
molekular *adj* molecular.
Molkerei [mɔlkə'rai] *f* (*pl* -en) dairy.
Moll [mɔl] *neut* (*unz.*) (*Musik*) minor.
Moment¹ [mo'mɛnt] *m* (*pl* -e) moment, instant. **Moment mal!** Just a moment!
Moment² *neut* (*unz.*) (*Physik*) moment; (*Anlaß*) motive; (*Umstand*) factor.
Monarch [mo'narç] *m* (*pl* -en) monarch. **-ie** *f* (*pl* -n) monarchy. **-ist** *m* (*pl* -en) monarchist.
Monat ['mo:nat] *m* (*pl* -e) month. **monatelang** *adv* for months. **monatlich** *adj* monthly. **Monats‖blutung** *f* menstruation. **-karte** *f* (monthly) season ticket.
Mönch [mœnç] *m* (*pl* -e) monk.
Mond [mo:nt] *m* (*pl* -e) moon. **-finsternis** *f* lunar eclipse. **-schein** *m* moonlight. **-strahl** *m* moonbeam.
Monogramm [mono'gram] *neut* (*pl* -e) monogram, initials.
Monopol [mono'po:l] *neut* (*pl* -e) monopoly. **monopolisieren** *v* monopolize.
Montag ['mo:nta:k] *m* Monday. **montags** *adv* (on) Mondays.
Montage [mɔn'ta:ʒə] *f* (*pl* -n) assembly; installation. **-band** *neut* assembly line.
Monteur [mɔn'tœ:r] *m* (*pl* -e) mechanic, fitter. **montieren** *v* install, assemble.
Moor [mo:r] *neut* (*pl* -e) marsh, moor.
Moos [mo:s] *neut* (*pl* -e) moss.
Moped ['mo:pɛt] *neut* (*pl* -s) moped.
Moral [mo'ra:l] *f* (*pl*-en) moral; (*Sittlichkeit*) morality; (*Zuversicht*) morale. **moralisieren** *v* moralize.
Mord [mɔrt] *m* (*pl* -e) murder.
Mörder ['mœrdər] *m* (*pl* -) murderer. **mörderisch** *adj* murderous.
morgen ['mɔrgən] *adv* tomorrow. **morgen früh** tomorrow morning. **Morgen** *m* (*pl* -) morning. **-dämmerung** *f* dawn. **-land** *neut* Orient. **-stern** *m* morning star, Venus.
Morphium ['mɔrfium] *neut* morphine.
morsch [mɔrʃ] *adj* rotten.
Morseschrift ['mɔrzəʃrift] *f* Morse code.
Mörtel ['mœrtəl] *m* (*pl* -) mortar, cement.
Mosaik [moza'i:k] *neut* (*pl* -e) mosaic.
Moschee [mɔ'ʃei] *f* (*pl* -n) mosque.
Mosel ['mo:zəl] *f* Moselle.
Moskau ['mɔskau] *neut* Moscow.
Most [mɔst] *m* (*pl* -e) new wine, must.
Motiv [mo'ti:f] *neut* (*pl* -e) (*Antrieb*) motive; (*Kunst, Dichtung*) theme, motif. **motivieren** *v* motivate.
Motor ['mo:tɔr] *m* (*pl* -en) motor, engine. **-ausfall** *m* engine failure. **-boot** *neut* motorboat. **-haube** *f* bonnet, (*US*) hood. **-rad** *neut* motorcycle. **-roller** *m* (motor) scooter.
Motte ['mɔtə] *f* (*pl* -n) moth.
Möwe ['mœ:və] *f* (*pl* -n) seagull.
Mücke ['mykə] *f* (*pl* -n) midge, gnat. **Mücken‖netz** *neut* mosquito net. **-stich** *m* midge *or* gnat bite.
müde ['my:də] *adj* tired. **Müdigkeit** *f* tiredness, fatigue.
Muff¹ [muf] *m* (*unz.*) musty smell.
Muff² *m* (*pl* -e) (**Pelz**) muff.
Muffel ['mufəl] *m* (*pl* -) grumpy person. **muffelig** *adj* grumpy, sullen.
muffig ['mufiç] *adj* (*moderig*) musty.
Mühe ['my:ə] *f* (*pl* -n) trouble, pains *pl.* **sich Mühe geben** take pains. **nicht der Mühe wert** not worth the trouble. **mühelos** *adj* effortless. **sich mühen** trouble oneself, take pains. **mühevoll** *adj* laborious, troublesome.
Mühle ['my:lə] *f* (*pl* -n) mill.
mühsam ['my:za:m] *adj* also **mühselig** troublesome; (*schwierig*) difficult.
Mulde ['muldə] *f* (*pl* -n) trough; (*Landschaft*) depression, hollow.
Mull [mul] *m* (*pl* -e) muslin.
Müll [myl] *m* refuse, rubbish, (*US*) garbage. **-abfuhr** *f* refuse disposal. **-eimer** *m* dustbin.
Müller ['mylər] *m* (*pl* -) miller.
Multiplikation [multiplikatsi'o:n] *f* (*pl* -en) multiplication. **multiplizieren** *v* multiply.
Mumie ['mu:miə] *f* (*pl* -n) mummy.
Mummenschanz ['mumənʃants] *m* (*pl* -e) masquerade.
München ['mynçən] *neut* Munich. **Münchner** *adj* (of) Munich.
Mund [munt] *m* (*pl* **Münder**) mouth. **-art** *f* dialect.
münden ['myndən] *v* **münden in** (*Fluß*) flow into; (*Straße*) run into, join.
mund‖faul *adj* taciturn. **-fertig** *adj* glib. **-gerecht** *adj* appetizing. **Mund‖geruch** *m* bad breath, halitosis. **-harmonika** *f* mouth organ, harmonica.
mündig ['myndiç] *adj* of age. **mündig werden** come of age. **Mündigkeit** *f* majority, full legal age.

mündlich ['myntlıç] *adj* oral.
Mundstück ['muntʃtyk] *neut* mouthpiece.
Mündung ['myndʊŋ] *f* (*pl* -en) (*Fluß*) estuary.
Munition [munitsi'oːn] *f* (*pl* -en) ammunition.
munter ['muntər] *adj* lively, cheerful, merry. **Munterkeit** *f* liveliness, cheer.
Münze ['myntsə] *f* (*pl* -n) coin; (*Anstalt*) mint. **für bare Münze nehmen** take at face value. **Münz||einwurf** *m* coin-slot. **–fernsprecher** *m* pay phone, call box.
mürbe ['myrbə] *adj* (*Fleisch*) tender; (*morsch*) rotten, soft; (*brüchig*) brittle; (*Gebäck*) crumbly. **Mürbeteig** *m* short pastry.
murmeln ['murməln] *v* murmur.
murren ['murən] *v* grumble.
mürrisch ['myrıʃ] *adj* morose, grumpy.
Mus [muːs] *neut* purée.
Muschel ['muʃəl] *f* (*pl* -n) mussel; (*Telef*) (telephone) receiver. **–tier** *neut* mollusc.
Museum [mu'zeːum] *neut* (*pl* Museen) museum.
Musical ['mjuːzikəl] *neut* (*pl* -s) musical.
Musik [mu'ziːk] *f* music; (*Kapelle*) band. **musikalisch** *adj* musical. **Musik||antenknochen** *m* (*umg.*) funnybone. **–er** *m* (*pl* -) musician. **–freund** *m* music-lover. **–instrument** *m* musical instrument.
Muskat [mus'kaːt] *m* (*pl* -e) nutmeg. **–blüte** *f* mace. **–nuß** *f* nutmeg.
Muskel ['muskəl] *m* (*pl* -n) muscle. **–kraft** *f* muscular strength. **–krampf** *m* muscle spasm. **–zerrung** *f* pulled muscle.
Muße ['muːsə] *f* leisure. **müßig** *adj* idle.
*müssen ['mysən] *v* must, have to. **ich mußgehen** I must go. **ich muß nicht gehen** I don't have to go. **ich muß fort** I must leave. **ich müßte** I ought to.
Muster ['mustər] *net* (*pl* -) model, pattern; (*Stoffverzierung*) pattern, design; (*warenprobe*) sample. **–stück** *neut* sample, specimen. **–zeichnung** *f* design.
Mut [muːt] *m* courage. **mutig** *adj* brave, courageous. **mutlos** *adj* discouraged, despondent.
mutmaßen ['muːtmaːsən] *v* suppose, surmise. **Mutmaßung** *f* (*pl* -en) conjecture.
Mutter¹ ['mutər] *f* (*pl* Mütter) mother.
Mutter² *f* (*pl* -n) (*Tech*) nut.
mütterlich ['mytərlıç] *adj* motherly.

–erseits *adv* on one's mother's side, maternal.
Mutter||liebe *f* mother-love. **–mal** *neut* birthmark. **–schaft** *f* motherhood. **–sprache** *f* mother tongue, native language.
Mütze ['mytsə] *f* (*pl* -n) cap.
mysteriös [mysteri'øːs] *adj* mysterious.
Mystik ['mystik] *f* (*unz.*) mysticism. **–er** *m* mystic. **mystisch** *adj* mystical.
Mythe ['myːtə] *f* (*pl* -n) myth. **mythisch** *adj* mythical.

N

na [na] *interj* well! (come) now!
Nabe ['naːbə] *f* (*pl* -n) hub.
Nabel ['naːbəl] *m* (*pl* -) navel. **–schnur** *f* umbilical cord.
nach [naːx] *prep* after; (*örtlich*) to, towards; (*gemäß*) according to, by. *adv* after. **nach und nach** gradually. **der Größe nach** by size. **nach außen** externally.
nachahmen ['naːxaːmən] *v* imitate. **Nachahmung** *f* imitation.
Nachbar ['naːxbaːr] *m* (*pl* -n) neighbour. **–land** *neut* neighbouring country. **–schaft** *f* neighbourhood.
Nachbildung ['naːxbıldʊŋ] *f* copy, replica.
nachdem [naːx'deːm] *adv* afterwards. *conj* after. **je nachdem** according as.
*nachdenken ['naːxdɛŋkən] *v* think (over), reflect. **Nachdenken** *neut* reflection, thinking over. **nachdenklich** *adj* reflective, thoughtful.
Nachdruck ['naːxdruk] *m* (*Betonung*) emphasis, stress; (*Festigkeit*) vigour. **nachdrücklich** *adj* emphatic; forceful.
nacheifern ['naːxaifərn] *v* emulate.
nacheinander ['naːxainandər] *adv* one after another.
Nachfolge ['naːxfɔlgə] *f* succession. **nachfolgen** *v* succeed, follow. **Nachfolger** *m* successor.
Nachfrage ['naːxfraːgə] *f* (*Erkundigung*) inquiry; (*Komm*) demand.
*nachgehen ['naːxgeːbən] *v* give way *or* in.
Nachgeburt ['naːxgəburt] *f* afterbirth.
*nachgehen ['naːxgeːən] *v* follow; (*untersuchen*) investigate; (*Uhr*) be slow.

nachgemacht ['naɪxgəmaxt] *adj* imitated, false.

Nachgeschmack ['naɪxgəʃmak] *m* aftertaste.

nachgiebig ['naɪxgiːbiç] *adj* pliable, flexible; (*Person*) compliant, yielding.

nachher [naɪx'heɪr] *adv* afterwards.

Nachhilfe ['naɪxhilfə] *f* help, assistance. **–stunden** *pl* coaching *sing*, private tuition *sing*.

nachholen ['naɪxhoɪlən] *v* fetch later; (*fig*) make up for, catch up on.

Nach‖hut ['naɪxhuɪt] *f* rearguard. **–klang** *m* echo, resonance.

Nachkomme ['naɪxkɔmə] *m* (*pl* **-n**) descendant. **nachkommen** *v* follow, come after; (*Verpflichtung*) fulfil. **Nachkommenschaft** *f* posterity, descendants *pl*.

Nachkriegszeit ['naɪxkriːkstsait] *f* postwar era.

Nachlaß ['naɪxlas] *m* (*pl* **Nachlässe**) (*Preis*) reduction, discount; (*Erbschaft*) inheritance, estate. **nachlassen** *v* slacken, abate; (*aufhören*) cease; (*Strafe*) remit; (*Preis*) reduce. **nachlässig** *adj* careless, negligent.

nachmachen ['naɪxmaxən] *v* copy, imitate.

Nachmittag ['naɪxmitaɪk] *m* afternoon. **nachmittags** *adv* in the afternoon(s).

Nachnahme ['naɪxnaɪmə] *f* **gegen** *or* **per Nachnahme** cash on delivery (COD).

Nachname ['naɪxnaɪmə] *m* (*pl* **-n**) surname.

nachprüfen ['naɪxpryɪfən] *v* verify, check again.

Nachricht ['naɪxriçt] *f* (*pl* **-en**) report, (item of) news. **Nachrichten** *pl* news *sing*. **Nachrichten‖büro** *neut* news agency. **–dienst** *m* (*Radio*) news service; (*Mil*) intelligence service.

Nachruf ['naɪxruɪf] *m* (*Zeitung*) obituary; (*Rede*) memorial address.

***nachschlagen** ['naɪxʃlaɪgən] *v* (*Buch*) look up, consult. **Nachschlagebuch** *neut* reference book.

Nach‖schrift ['naɪxʃrift] *f* (*Brief*) postscript; (*eines Vortrages*) transcript. **–schub** *m* (*Mil*) reinforcement(s); (*Material*) supplies *pl*.

***nach‖sehen** ['naɪxzeɪən] *v* (*nachblicken*) watch, follow with one's eyes; (*prüfen*) examine, check; (*nachschlagen*) consult; (*verzeihen*) overlook. **–senden** *v* send on; (*Post*) forward.

Nach‖sicht ['naɪxziçt] *f* leniency. **–sorge** *f* (medical) aftercare. **–spiel** *neut* epilogue, sequel. **–speise** *f* dessert.

nächst [nɛɪçst] *adj* next; (*Entfernung*) nearest; (*Verwandte*) close, closest; (*umg: kürzest*) shortest. *adv* next. *prep* next to. **am nächsten** next. **nächste Woche** next week. *das nächste Dorf liegt 10 km von hier entfernt* the nearest village is 10 km away. **Nächste(r)** fellowman, neighbour.

***nach‖stehen** ['naɪxʃteɪən] *v* be inferior to. **–stellen** re-adjust; (*Uhr*) put back; (*Frau*) molest, bother.

Nächstenliebe ['nɛɪçstənliːbə] *f* charity, love of one's fellow men. **nächstens** *adv* shortly.

Nacht [naxt] *f* (*pl* **Nächte**) night. **heute Nacht** tonight. **über Nacht** overnight.

Nachteil ['naɪxtail] *m* disadvantage; (*Schaden*) damage, detriment. **nachteilig** *adj* disadvantageous, unfavourable.

Nachthemd ['naxthɛmt] *neut* nightshirt, nightgown.

Nachtigall ['naxtigal] *f* (*pl* **-en**) nightingale.

Nach‖tisch ['naɪxtiʃ] *m* dessert. **–trag** *m* supplement. **nachträglich** *adj* subsequent, later.

nachts [naxts] *adv* at *or* by night. **Nachtwächter** *m* nightwatchman. **nachtwandeln** *v* sleepwalk.

Nach‖untersuchung ['naɪxuntərzuɪxuŋ] *f* check-up. **–wahl** *f* by-election. **–weis** *m* proof, evidence. **nachweisen** *v* prove, demonstrate.

Nach‖wirkung ['naɪxvirkuŋ] *f* after-effect. **–wort** *neut* epilogue. **–wuchs** *m* new *or* young generation.

***nachziehen** ['naɪxtsiːən] *v* drag, draw along; (*nachzeichnen*) trace; (*folgen*) follow.

Nachzügler ['naɪxtsyɪklər] *m* (*pl* **-**) straggler, late-comer.

Nacken ['nakən] *m* (*pl* **-**) (nape of the) neck.

nackt [nakt] *adj* naked, bare. **Nacktheit** *f* nakedness.

Nadel ['naɪdəl] *f* (*pl* **-n**) needle; (*Stecknadel*) pin. **–baum** *m* conifer. **–öhr** *neut* eye (of a needle). **–wald** *m* coniferous forest.

Nagel ['naɪgəl] *m* (*pl* **Nägel**) nail. **–feile** *f* nail-file. **–haut** *f* cuticle. **–lack** *m* nail varnish. **nageln** *v* nail. **nagelneu** *adj* brand-new. **Nagelschere** f nail scissors pl.

nagen ['na:gən] v gnaw.

Nagetier ['na:gəti:r] neut rodent.

nah(e) ['na:(ə)] adj, adv near, close. prep near to. **einer Person zu nahe treten** offend a person. **nahe dabei** or **gelegen** nearby. **nahe Freundschaft** close friendship.

Nahaufnahme ['na:aufna:mə] f (Foto) close-up.

Nähe ['nɛ:ə] f nearness; (Sicht-, Hörweite) vicinity. **in der Nähe** close by, in the vicinity.

*****nahe||kommen** v approach. **–liegend** adj obvious; (örtlich) close, nearby.

nähen ['nɛ:ən] v sew, stitch.

näher ['nɛ:ər] adj nearer, closer; (ausführlicher) more detailed. **nähere Angaben** further details. **nähere Umstände** exact circumstances. **Nähere(s)** neut particulars pl, details pl. **nähern** v bring near. **sich nähern** approach, draw near.

nahe||stehend adj close, friendly. **–zu** adv nearly, almost.

Näh||kasten m sewing box. **–machine** f sewing machine. **–nadel** f sewing needle.

nähren ['nɛ:rən] v nourish; (unterhalten) support. **sich nähren von** live on.

nahrhaft ['na:rhaft] adj nutritious.

Nährmittel ['nɛ:rmitəl] pl foodstuffs, food sing.

Nahrung ['na:ruŋ] f (unz.) food; (Unterhalt) support. **–smittel** pl foodstuffs.

Naht ['na:t] f (pl Nähte) seam; (Med) suture.

naiv [na:i:f] adj naive.

Name ['na:mə] or **Namen** m (pl Namen) name. **namens** adv named, by the name of.

nämlich ['nɛ:mliç] adv that is (to say), namely.

Napf [napf] m (pl Näpfe) basin, bowl.

Narbe ['narbə] f (pl -n) scar.

Narkose [nar'ko:zə] f (pl -n) (Betäubung) anaesthesia. **Narkotikum** neut (pl Narkotika) narcotic. **narkotisch** adj narcotic.

Narr [nar] m (pl -en) fool. **zum Narren haben** make a fool of. **Narrheit** f folly, foolishness.

närrisch ['nɛriʃ] adj foolish, crazy, silly.

Nase ['na:zə] f (pl -n) nose. **die Nase voll haben von** be fed up with. **Nasen||loch**

neut nostril. **–höhle** f (anat) sinus. **–spitze** f tip of the nose. **naseweis** adj cheeky.

naß [nas] adj wet; (feucht) moist, damp. **Nässe** ['nɛsə] f wet, wetness.

Nation [natsi'o:n] f (pl -en) nation. **national** adj national. **National||flagge** f national flag. **–hymne** f national anthem.

nationalisieren [natsiona:li'zi:rən] v nationalize. **Nationalisierung** f nationalization. **Nationalismus** m nationalism. **nationalistisch** adj nationalist(ic).

National||mannschaft f national team. **–sozialismus** m national socialism, Nazism. **–tracht** f national costume.

Natter ['natər] f (pl -n) adder.

Natur [na'tu:r] f (pl -en) nature. **–anlage** f temperament, disposition. **–forscher** m scientist, naturalist. **–kunde** f natural history. **natürlich** adj natural. **Natur||schutz** m preservation (of nature). **–trieb** m instinct. **–wissenschaft** f natural science.

Nazi ['na:tsi] m (pl -s) Nazi.

Nebel ['ne:bəl] m (pl -) fog; (dünner) mist. **–horn** neut foghorn. **nebelig** adj foggy; misty.

neben ['ne:bən] prep near (to), beside; (im Vergleich zu) compared with, next to. **–an** adv next door. **–bei** adv by the way; (außerdem) besides. **Neben||beschäftigung** f second job, sideline. **–buhler** m rival.

nebeneinander ['ne:bənainandər] adv side by side. **–stellen** v juxtapose.

Neben||fach neut subsidiary subject. **–fluß** m tributary. **–gebäude** neut annexe. **–kosten** pl extras, additional expenses.

nebensächlich ['ne:bənsɛçliç] adj incidental.

necken ['nɛkən] v tease.

Neffe ['nɛfə] m (pl -n) nephew.

negativ ['ne:gati:f] adj negative.

Neger ['ne:gər] m (pl -) Negro, Black. **–in** f (pl -nen) Black (woman).

*****nehmen** ['ne:mən] v take.

Neid [nait] m envy, jealousy. **neid||en** v envy. **–isch** adj envious, jealous.

Neige ['naigə] f (pl -n) slope, incline. **neigen** v incline. **neigen zu** tend (to), be inclined (to). **sich neigen** incline, slope. **Neigung** f slope; (fig) inclination.

nein 306

nein [nain] *adv* no.
Nelke ['nɛlkə] *f* (*pl* -n) carnation; (*Gewürz*) clove.
***nennen** ['nɛnən] *v* call, name. **Nenn‖er** *m* denominator. **–ung** *f* naming; (*Sport*) entry. **–wert** *m* nominal value.
Nerv [nɛrf] *m* (*pl* -en) nerve. **Nerven‖kitzel** *m* thrill. **–krankheit** *f* nervous disease. **nervös** *adj* nervous.
Nessel ['nɛsəl] *f* (*pl* -n) nettle.
Nest [nɛst] *neut* (*pl* -er) nest.
nett [nɛt] *adj* nice; (*gepflegt*) neat.
netto ['nɛto] *adv* net. **Netto‖gewinn** *m* net profit. **–preis** *m* net price.
Netz [nɛts] *neut* (*pl* -e) net; (*System*) grid, network. **–haut** *f* retina. **–werk** *neut* network.
neu [nɔy] *adj* new; (*modern*) modern. **–artig** *adj* novel.
Neu‖ausgabe *f* new edition. **–bau** *n* new building.
neuerdings ['nɔyərdiŋs] *adv* recently, lately.
Neuerer ['nɔyərər] *m* (*pl* -) innovator.
Neuerscheinung ['nɔyɛrʃainuŋ] *f* (*pl* -en) new book.
Neu‖erung ['nɔyəruŋ] *f* (*pl* -en) innovation.
neuestens ['nɔyəstəns] *adv* of late.
neu‖geboren *adj* new-born. **–gestalten** *v* reorganize.
Neugier(de) ['nɔygiɪr(də)] *f* (*unz.*) curiosity. **neugierig** *adj* curious.
Neu‖heit *f* (*pl* -en) novelty. **–igkeit** *f* (*pl* -en) (item of) news. **–jahr** *neut* New Year. **–jahrstag** *m* New Year's Day.
neulich ['nɔyliç] *adv* recently, lately.
neun [nɔyn] *pron, adj* nine. **neunte** *adj* ninth. **neunzehn** *pron, adj* nineteen. **neunzig** *pron, adj* ninety.
Neu‖ordnung *f* reorganization. **–reiche(r)** nouveau riche, wealthy parvenu.
Neurologe [nɔyroˈloɪgə] *m* (*pl* -n) neurologist. **Neurologie** *f* neurology. **neurologisch** *adj* neurological.
Neurose [nɔyˈroɪzə] *f* (*pl* -n) neurosis. **neurotisch** *adj* neurotic.
Neuseeland [nɔyˈzeɪlant] *neut* New Zealand.
neutral [nɔyˈtraɪl] *adj* neutral. **neutralisieren** *v* neutralize. **Neutralität** *f* neutrality.
neuzeitlich ['nɔytsaitliç] *adj* modern.
nicht [niçt] *adv* not. **durchaus nicht** not at all. **nicht einmal** not even. **bitte nicht** please don't. **nicht mehr** no longer. **nicht wahr?** isn't it? don't you agree?
Nicht‖achtung *f* disregard. **–annahme** *f* nonacceptance. **–beachtung** *f* nonobservance.
Nichte ['niçtə] *f* (*pl* -n) niece.
Nicht‖einmischung *f* nonintervention. **–erscheinen** *neut* nonappearance.
nichtig ['niçtiç] *adj* futile, empty; (*ungültig*) null, void. **Nichtigkeit** *f* futility; invalidity.
Nicht‖mitglied *neut* non-member. **–raucher** *m* non-smoker. **–raucherabteil** *neut* no-smoking compartment.
nichts [niçts] *pron* nothing. **nichts daraus machen** not take seriously. **(es) macht nichts** it doesn't matter. **nichts dergleichen** nothing of the kind. **Nichts** *neut* nothing(ness).
nichts‖sagend *adj* meaningless. **–würdig** *adj* worthless, base.
Nicht‖vorhandensein *neut* lack, absence. **–zutreffende(s)** *neut* (that which is) nonapplicable.
Nickel ['nikəl] *neut* nickel.
nicken ['nikən] *v* nod, bow; doze, nod off. **Nickerchen** *neut* nap.
nie [niɪ] *adv* never.
nieder ['niɪdər] *adj* low; (*fig*) inferior. *adv* down.
***nieder‖brennen** *v* burn down. **–drücken** *v* depress. **–fallen** *v* fall down.
Nieder‖frequenz *f* low frequency. **–gang** *m* decline, downfall; (*Sonne*) setting.
***nieder‖gehen** *v* go down; (*Aero*) land. **–geschlagen** *adj* depressed.
Niederlage ['niɪdərlaɪgə] *f* defeat.
Niederlande ['niɪdərlandə] *pl* Netherlands. **Niederländer** *m* Dutchman. **–in** *f* Dutchwoman. **niederländisch** *adj* Dutch.
***niederlassen** ['niɪdərlasən] *v* lower. **sich niederlassen** settle down; (*Vogel*) land, settle. **Niederlassung** *f* (*pl* -en) settlement; (*Komm*) branch.
niederlegen ['niɪdərleɪgən] *v* lay down.
Niedersachsen ['niɪdəzaksən] *neut* Lower Saxony.
Niederschlag ['niɪdərʃlaɪk] *m* (*Regen, usw.*) precipitation; (*auf Fensterscheiben*) condensation; (*Chem*) sediment, precipitation; (*Boxen*) knock-down.
***niederschlagen** *v* knock down; (*Augen*) lower; (*Aufstand*) suppress.

nieder‖schmettern v strike down. **–schreiben** v write down. **–setzen** v put down. **–werfen** v throw down. **sich niederwerfen** prostrate oneself.

niedlich ['niːdliç] adj nice, (umg.) cute, dainty.

niedrig ['niːdriç] adj low. **Niedrigkeit** f lowness. **Niedrigwasser** neut low water, low tide.

niemals ['niːmaɪls] adv never.

niemand ['niːmant] pron no one, nobody. **Niemandsland** neut no-man's-land.

Niere ['niːrə] f (pl -n) kidney.

nieseln ['niːzəln] v drizzle.

niesen ['niːzən] v sneeze. **Niesen** neut sneeze.

Niet [niːt] neut (pl -e) rivet.

Niete ['niːtə] f (pl -n) (Lotterie) blank (ticket); (Person) nonentity, failure; (Theater) flop.

Nikotin [niko'tiːn] neut nicotine.

Nilpferd ['niːlpfeɪrt] neut hippopotamus.

nimmer ['nimər] adv never. **–mehr** adv never again.

nippen ['nipən] v sip.

nirgends ['nirgənts] or **nirgendwo** adv nowhere.

Nische ['niːʃə] f (pl -n) niche, alcove.

nisten ['nistən] v (build a) nest.

Niveau [ni'voː] neut (pl -s) level; (fig) standard; (geistig) culture, good education. **Niveau haben** be cultured or sophisticated.

noch [nox] adv (außerdem) in addition. conj nor. **noch nicht** not yet. **noch einmal** once again. **noch etwas?** anything else? **noch dazu** in addition. **weder ... noch ... neither ... nor ....** **nochmals** adv once again.

Nockenwelle ['nɔkənvɛlə] f camshaft.

Nomade [no'maɪdə] m (pl -n) nomad.

Nominativ ['nominatiːf] m (pl -e) nominative.

nominell [nomi'nɛl] adj nominal.

Nonne ['nɔnə] f (pl -n) nun. **–nkloster** neut convent, nunnery.

Nord [nɔrt] m north. **–amerika** f North America. **–en** m north. **nordisch** adj northern; (Skandinavisch) nordic. **Nordländer 1** m (pl -) Northerner. **2** pl northern countries.

nördlich ['nœrtliç] adj northern. adv northwards. **prep** to the north of.

Nordost(en) ['nɔrtɔst(ən)] m northeast. **nordöstlich** adj northeast(ern).

Nord‖pol m North Pole. **–rhein-Westfalen** neut North Rhine-Westphalia. **–see** f North Sea. **nordwärts** adv northwards.

Nordwest(en) ['nɔrtvɛst(ən)] m northwest. **nordwestlich** adj northwest(ern).

nörgeln ['nœrgəln] v grumble, grouse.

Norm [nɔrm] f (pl -en) standard, norm. **normal** adj normal. **–erweise** adv normally. **normalisieren** v normalize. **–maß** neut standard measure. **normgerecht** adj conforming to a standard.

Norwegen ['nɔrveɪgən] neut Norway. **Norweger** m (pl -), **Norwegerin** f (pl -nen) Norwegian. **norwegisch** adj Norwegian.

Not [noːt] f (pl Nöte) (Armut) need, want; (Gefahr) danger; (Bedrängnis) distress; (Knappheit) lack, shortage.

Notar [no'taɪr] m (pl -e) notary.

Not‖ausgang m emergency exit. **–bremse** f emergency brake. **–durft** f call of nature. **–dürftig** adj scanty; hard up.

Note ['noːtə] f (pl -n) note; (Schul-) mark, grade; banknote, (US) bill; (Musik) note. **–nständer** m music stand.

Not‖fall m emergency. **–hilfe** f emergency service.

notieren [no'tiːrən] v note.

nötig ['nœːtiç] adj necessary. **–en** v compel, force.

Notiz [no'tiːts] f (pl -en) notice; (Vermerk) note. **–buch** neut notebook.

Not‖lage f distress, predicament. **–landung** f emergency landing. **–lüge** f white lie. **notleidend** adj distressed; (arm) needy, destitute.

notorisch [no'tɔriʃ] adj notorious.

Not‖ruf m distress call; (Telef) emergency call. **–stand** m emergency.

notwendig [nɔɪtvɛndiç] adj necessary. **Notwendigkeit** f necessity.

Notzucht ['nɔɪtsuxt] f rape.

Novelle [no'vɛlə] f (pl -n) short story, short novel.

November [no'vɛmbər] m (pl -) November.

Novize [no'viːtsə] m (pl -n) novice.

Nuance [ny'ãsə] f (pl -n) nuance.

Nüchternheit ['nyçtərnhait] f sobriety; (fig) realism, clear-headedness.

Nudeln ['nuɪdəln] pl noodles.

null [nul] adj nil, zero, (ungültig) null. **null und nichtig** null and void. **Null** f (pl -en) nought, zero.

numerieren [numeˈriːrən] *v* number.
numerisch *adj* numerical.
Nummer [ˈnumər] *f* (*pl* -n) number. **Nummern‖scheibe** *f* (telephone) dial. **–schild** *neut* number plate.
nun [nuːn] *adv* now. *interj* well! **was nun?** what now? **nun also** why then. **–mehr** *adv* (by) now.
nur [nuːr] *adv* only, merely; (*eben*) just. **conj** nevertheless, but. **nur noch** only, still. **nicht nur ... sondern auch ...** not only ... but also ... .
Nürnberg [ˈnyrnbɛrk] *neut* Nuremberg.
Nuß [nus] *f* (*pl* **Nüsse**) nut. **–baum** *m* walnut tree. **Nuß‖knacker** *m* nutcracker. **–schale** *f* nutshell.
nutz [nuts] *adj* useful. **–bar** *adj* useful. **–bringend** *adj* profitable.
nutzen [ˈnutsən] *or* **nützen** *v* be of use, be useful; (*gebrauchen*) make use of, use. **Nutzen** *m* (*pl* -) use; (*Vorteil*) profit, advantage. **Nutzen ziehen aus** derive advantage from, benefit from. **zum Nutzen von** for the benefit of. **Nutzfahrzeug** *neut* commercial vehicle.
nützlich [ˈnytsliç] *adj* useful. **Nützlichkeit** *f* usefulness.
nutzlos [ˈnutsloːs] *adj* useless. **Nutz‖losigkeit** *f* uselessness. **–nießer** *m* beneficiary. **–ung** *f* use, utilization.
Nylon [ˈnailɔn] *neut* (*pl* -s) nylon.

O

Oase [oˈaːzə] *f* (*pl* -n) oasis.
ob [ɔp] *conj* whether. **als ob** as if, as though.
Obdach [ˈɔpdax] *neut* (*unz.*) shelter. **obdachlos** *adj* homeless.
oben [ˈoːbən] *adv* above, at the top; (*Haus*) upstairs. **oben auf** on top of. **von oben** from above.
ober [ˈoːbər] *adj* upper, higher; (*fig*) superior; (*Dienstgrad*) senior, principal. **Ober** *m* (*pl* -) (head) waiter. **die Oberen** those in authority.
Ober‖arm *m* upper arm. **–befehlshaber** *m* commander-in-chief. **–bürgermeister** *m* (lord) mayor. **–fläche** *f* surface (area). **oberflächlich** *adj* superficial.
oberhalb [ˈoːbərhalp] *adv*, *prep* above.
Ober‖hand *f* upper hand, ascendancy. **–haupt** *m* chief, head. **–hemd** *neut* shirt.

–in *f* (*pl* -nen) (*Rel*) mother superior; (*Krankenschwester*) matron.
oberirdisch [ˈoːbərˈirdiʃ] *adj* above ground; (*Leitung*) overhead.
Ober‖kellner *m* head waiter. **–klasse** *f* upper class. **–schicht** *f* ruling class, upper classes *pl*. **–schule** *f* secondary school. **–schwester** *f* (*Med*) sister. **–seite** *f* upper side.
oberst [ˈoːbərst] *adj* highest, uppermost; (*fig*) supreme. **Oberst** *m* (*pl* -en) colonel.
obgleich [ɔpˈglaiç] *conj* although.
Obhut [ˈɔphuːt] *f* (*unz.*) care, protection. **in seine Obhut nehmen** take care of, take under one's wing.
obig [ˈoːbiç] *adj* above-mentioned, foregoing.
Objekt [ɔpˈjɛkt] *neut* (*pl* -e) object. **objektiv** *adj* objective.
*obliegen [ˈɔpliːgən] *v* (*einer Aufgabe*) perform, carry out. **es liegt ihm ob, zu** it is his job *or* duty to. **Obliegenheit** *f* duty.
obligatorisch [ɔbligaˈtoːriʃ] *adj* obligatory, compulsory.
Obmann [ˈɔpman] *m* foreman; (*Vorsitzender*) chairman; (*Sprecher*) spokesman.
Oboe [oˈboːə] *f* (*pl* -n) oboe. **Oboist** *m* oboist.
Obrigkeit [ˈoːbriçkait] *f* (*pl* -en) authorities *pl*, government.
obschon [ɔpˈʃoːn] *conj* although.
Observatorium [ɔpzɛrvaˈtoːrium] *neut* (*pl* **Observatorien**) observatory.
obskur [ɔpsˈkuːr] *adj* obscure.
Obst [oːpst] *neut* (*unz.*) fruit. **–baum** *m* fruit tree. **–garten** *m* orchard. **–händler** *m* fruiterer.
obszön [ɔpsˈtsœːn] *adj* obscene.
obwohl [ɔpˈvoːl] *conj* although.
Ochse [ˈɔksə] *m* (*pl* -n) ox. **Ochsen‖fleisch** *neut* beef. **–schwanz** *m* oxtail.
Ode [ˈoːdə] *f* (*pl* -n) ode.
öde [ˈøːdə] *adj* desolate, bleak; (*fig*) dull, bleak. **Öde** *f* (*unz.*) desert, wasteland; (*fig*) dullness, tedium.
oder [ˈoːdər] *conj* or.
Ofen [ˈoːfən] *m* (*pl* **Öfen**) stove; (*Back-, Tech*) oven.
offen [ˈɔfən] *adj* open; (*freimütig*) open, frank; (*Stellung*) vacant. **–bar** *adj* obvious. **–baren** *v* reveal, disclose. **Offenheit** *f* openness, frankness. **offen‖herzig** *adj* open-hearted. **–kundig** *adj* evident. **–sichtlich** *adj* obvious, evident.

offensiv [ɔfɛnˈziːf] *adj* offensive. **Offensive** *f* (*pl* **-n**) offensive.

offenstehend [ˈɔfənʃteːənt] *adj* open; (*Schuld*) outstanding.

öffentlich [ˈœfəntliç] *adj* public. **Öffentlichkeit** *f* publicity; (*das Volk*) public.

offiziell [ɔfiˈtsjɛl] *adj* official.

Offizier [ɔfiˈtsiːr] *m* (*pl* **-e**) officer. **Offiziers‖messe** *f* officers' mess. **–patent** *neut* (officer's) commission.

offiziös [ɔfitsiˈœːs] *adj* semi-official.

öffnen [ˈœfnən] *v* open. **Öffnung** *f* opening. **–szeiten** *pl* opening hours.

oft [ɔft] *adv* often; frequently. **wie oft?** how many times?

öfter [ˈœftər] *adj* frequent. *adv* more often *or* frequently. **öfters** *adv* often.

Oheim [ˈoːhaim] *m* (*pl* **-e**) uncle.

ohne [ˈoːnə] *prep*, *conj* without. **ohne daß ich es wußte** without my knowledge. **ohne‖dies** *or* **–hin** *adv* all the same, besides.

Ohnmacht [ˈoːnmaxt] *f* unconsciousness, faint. **ohnmächtig** *adj* unconscious. **ohnmächtig werden** *v* faint.

Ohr [oːr] *neut* (*pl* **-en**) ear. **die Ohren spitzen** prick up one's ears. **ganz Ohr sein** be all ears.

Öhr [œːr] *neut* (*pl* **-e**) eye (of a needle).

Ohren‖schmalz *neut* ear wax. **–schmerz** *m* earache. **Ohrfeige** *f* slap across the face. **ohrfeigen** *v* slap (across the face). **Ohr‖läppchen** *neut* ear lobe. **–muschel** *f* (external) ear. **–ring** *m* earring.

Ökonom [œkoˈnoːm] *m* (*pl* **-en**) (*Hausverwalter*) caretaker, steward; (*Wirtschaftswissenschaftler*) economist. **–ie** *f* housekeeping; economics. **ökonomisch** *adj* economic; (*sparsam*) economical.

Oktave [ɔkˈtaːvə] *f* (*pl* **-n**) octave.

Oktober [ɔkˈtoːbər] *m* (*pl* **-**) October.

Okzident [ˈɔktsidɛnt] *m* occident.

Öl [œːl] *neut* (*pl* **-e**) oil, **–baum** *m* olive tree. **ölen** *v* oil, lubricate. **Ölfarbe** *f* oil paint.

Olive [oˈliːvə] *f* (*pl* **-n**) olive. **olivengrün** *adj* olive-green. **olivenöl** *neut* olive oil. **Öl‖leitung** *f* (oil) pipeline. **–meßstab** *m* dipstick.

Olympiade [olympiˈaːdə] *f* (*pl* **-n**) Olympiad, Olympic games. **olympisch** *adj* Olympic.

Ölzweig [ˈœːltsvaik] *m* olive branch.

Oma [ˈoːma] *f* (*pl* **-s**) granny, grandma.

Omelett [ɔməˈlɛt] *neut* (*pl* **-e**) *or* **Omelette** *f* (*pl* **-n**) omelette.

Ondulieren [ɔnduˈliːrən] *v* wave.

Onkel [ˈɔŋkəl] *m* (*pl* **-**) uncle.

Opa [ˈoːpa] *m* (*pl* **-s**) grandad, grandpa.

Opal [oˈpaːl] *m* (*pl* **-e**) opal.

Oper [ˈoːpər] *f* (*pl* **-n**) opera; (*Opernhaus*) opera house.

Operation [operatsiˈoːn] *f* (*pl* **-en**) operation. **–ssaal** *m* operating theatre. **operieren** *v* operate.

Opfer [ˈɔpfər] *neut* (*pl* **-**) (*Verzicht, Gabe*) sacrifice; (*Geopfertes*) victim. **opfern** *v* sacrifice, offer. **Opferung** *f* sacrifice.

Opium [ˈoːpium] *neut* opium.

opportun [ɔpɔrˈtuːn] *adj* opportune.

Opposition [ɔpozitsiˈoːn] *f* (*pl* **-n**) opposition. **–sführer** *m* leader of the opposition.

Optik [ˈɔptik] *f* optics. **–er** *m* optician.

optimal [ɔptiˈmaːl] *adj* optimum. **Optimismus** *m* optimism. **Optimist** *m* optimist. **optimistisch** *adj* optimistic.

optisch [ˈɔptiʃ] *adj* optic(al).

Orange [oˈrãːʒə] *f* (*pl* **-n**) orange. **orange** *adj* orange. **Orangensaft** *m* orange juice.

Orchester [ɔrˈkɛstər] *neut* (*pl* **-**) orchestra.

Orchidee [ɔrçiˈdeːə] *f* (*pl* **-n**) orchid.

Orden [ˈɔrdən] *m* (*pl* **-**) (*Gesellschaft*) order; (*Ehrenzeichen*) decoration, order. **Ordens‖bruder** *m* member of an order; (*Rel*) monk, friar. **–schwester** *f* nun.

ordentlich [ˈɔrdəntliç] *adj* (*ordnungsgemäß*) orderly; (*ordnungsliebend, geordnet*) tidy; (*anständig, auch umg.*) proper, decent. **Ordentlichkeit** *f* orderliness; decency, respectability.

ordinär [ɔrdiˈnɛːr] *adj* common, vulgar. **Ordinarius** [ɔrdiˈnaːrius] *m* (*pl* **Ordinarien**) professor.

Ordination [ɔrdinaˈtsioːn] *f* (*pl* **-en**) ordination. **ordinieren** *v* ordain.

ordnen [ˈɔrdnən] *v* put in order, arrange, classify. **Ordner** *m* (*pl* **-**) organizer; (*Versammlungen*) steward; (*Mappe*) file. **Ordnung** *f* (*pl* **-en**) order; (*Regel*) regulation. **ordnungs‖gemäß** *or* **–mäßig** *adj* orderly, lawful. *adv* properly, duly. **–widrig** *adj* irregular, illegal.

Organ [ɔrˈgaːn] *neut* (*pl* **-e**) organ. **–isation** *f* organization. **organ‖isch** *adj* organic. **–isieren** *v* organize. **Organismus** *m* (*pl* **Organismen**) organism.

Orgasmus [ɔr'gazmus] *m* (*pl* **Orgasmen**) orgasm.

Orgel ['ɔrgəl] *f* (*pl* **-n**) organ. **-spieler** *m* (*pl* **-**), **-spielerin** *f* (*pl* **-nen**) organist.

Orgie ['ɔrgiə] *f* (*pl* **-n**) orgy.

Orient ['ɔːriɛnt] *m* Orient. **Orientale** *m* (*pl* **-n**), **Orientalin** (*pl* **-nen**) Oriental. **orientalisch** *adj* oriental.

orientieren [ɔriɛn'tiːrən] *v* locate. **sich orientieren** orientate oneself. **Orientierung** *f* orientation. **Orientierungs‖punkt** *m* reference point. **-vermögen** *neut* sense of direction.

original [origi'naːl] *adj* original. **Original** *neut* (*pl* **-e**) original.

originell [origi'nɛl] *adj* original, novel; (*eigenartig*) peculiar.

Orkan [ɔr'kaɪn] *m* (*pl* **-e**) hurricane.

Ornat [ɔr'nat] *m* (*pl* **-e**) (official) robes.

Ort [ɔrt] *m* (*pl* **-e**) place; (*Ortschaft*) town; (*Dorf*) village; (*Punkt*) point.

orthodox [ɔrto'dɔks] *adj* orthodox.

Orthopädie [ɔrtopɛ'diː] *f* orthopaedics.

örtlich ['œrtliç] *adj* local.

Orts‖gespräch *neut* local call. **-verkehr** *m* local traffic. **-zeit** *f* local time.

Öse ['œːzə] *f* (*pl* **-n**) eye(let). **Haken und Ösen** hooks and eyes.

Ost(en) ['ɔst(ən)] *m* east. **der Nahe/Ferne Osten** the Middle/Far East. **Ostblock** *m* Eastern bloc, Eastern Europe.

Oster‖ei *neut* Easter egg. **-hase** *m* Easter bunny.

Ostern ['ɔɪstərn] *neut pl* Easter.

Österreich ['œːstərraiç] *neut* Austria. **Österreicher** *m* (*pl* **-**), *f* **Österreicherin** (*pl* **-nen**) Austrian. **österreichisch** *adj* Austrian.

Osteuropa ['ɔstɔyropa] *f* Eastern Europe.

östlich ['œstliç] *adj* east(ern).

Ost‖politik *f* East policy, policy towards the Eastern bloc. **-see** *f* Baltic Sea.

Otter ['ɔtər] *m* (*pl* **-**) or *f* (*pl* **-n**) otter.

Ouvertüre [uvɛr'tyːrə] *f* (*pl* **-n**) overture.

Ovarium [o'vaɪrium] *neut* (*pl* **Ovarien**) ovary.

oval [o'vaɪl] *adj* oval.

Oxyd [ɔ'ksyːt] *neut* (*pl* **-e**) oxide. **oxydieren** *v* oxidize.

Ozean ['ɔɪtseaɪn] *m* (*pl* **-e**) ocean. **ozeanisch** *adj* oceanic.

P

paar [paɪr] *adj* **ein paar** a few. **Paar** *neut* (*pl* **-e**) pair, couple. **paaren** *v* (*Tiere*) pair, couple; (*vereinigen*) join. **sich paaren** couple, mate. **Paarung** *f* (*pl* **-en**) mating. **paarweise** *adv* in couples.

Pacht [paxt] *f* (*pl* **-en**) lease; (*Entgelt*) rent. **-brief** *m* lease. **pachten** *v* lease.

Pächter ['pɛçtər] *m* (*pl* **-**) leaseholder; (*Bauer*) tenant farmer.

Pack [pak] *m* (*pl* **Päcke**) pack; packet; bundle.

Päckchen ['pɛkçən] *neut* (*pl* **-**) packet, small parcel.

packen ['pakən] *v* grasp, seize; (*einpacken*) pack. **-d** *adj* thrilling, fascinating. **Pack‖kasten** *m* packing case. **-pferd** *neut* pack-horse. **-esel** *m* (*fig*) drudge. **-stoff** *m* packing (material). **Packung** *f* (*pl* **-en**)package.

Pädagogik [peda'goɪgik] *f* pedagogy, education. **pädagogisch** *adj* pedagogic. **pädagogische Hochschule** teacher-training college.

Paddel ['padəl] *neut* (*pl* **-**) paddle. **paddeln** *v* paddle.

Page ['paɪʒə] *m* (*pl* **-n**) page(boy).

Paket [pa'keɪt] *neut* (*pl* **-e**) packet, parcel.

Pakt [pakt] *m* (*pl* **-e**) pact, agreement.

Palast [pa'last] *m* (*pl* **Paläste**) palace.

Palästina [palɛ'stiːna] *neut* Palestine.

Palette [pa'lɛtə] *f* (*pl* **-n**) palette.

Palme ['palmə] *f* (*pl* **-n**) palm. **Palmsonntag** *m* Palm Sunday.

Pampelmuse ['pampəlmuːzə] *f* (*pl* **-n**) grapefruit.

Panda ['panda] *m* (*pl* **-**) panda.

Paneel [pa'neɪl] *neut* (*pl* **-e**) panel, panelling.

paniert [pa'niɪrt] *adj* coated with breadcrumbs.

Panik ['paɪnik] *f* (*pl* **-en**) panic. **panisch** *adj* panic-stricken, panicky.

Panne ['panə] *f* (*pl* **-n**) breakdown.

Pantoffel [pan'tɔfəl] *m* (*pl* **-n**) slipper.

Pantomime [panto'miːmə] *f* (*pl* **-n**) pantomime.

Panzer ['pantsər] *m* (*pl* **-**) armour; (*Panzerwagen*) tank; (*Tiere*) shell. **-hemd** *neut* coat of mail. **panzern** *v* armour. **Panzer‖ung** *f* (*pl* **-en**) armour-plating. **-wagen** *m* tank, armoured car. **-weste** *f* bullet-proof vest.

311   **Pastille**

Papa [pa'paɪ, 'papa] *m* (*pl* -s) daddy, papa.
Papagei [papa'gaɪ] *m* (*pl* -en) parrot.
Papier [pa'piːr] *neut* (*pl* -e) paper.
–**bogen** *m* sheet of paper. –**korb** *m*
wastepaper basket. –**tüte** *f* paper bag.
–**waren** *pl* stationery *sing.*
Pappe ['papə] *f* (*pl* -n) cardboard.
Pappel ['papəl] *f* (*pl* -n) poplar.
pappen ['papən] *v* paste (together).
Pappschachtel ['papʃaxtəl] *f* cardboard
box.
Paprika ['paprika] *m* (*pl* -s) paprika.
–**schote** *f* green or red pepper, capsicum.
Papst [paɪpst] *m* (*pl* Päpste) pope.
päpstlich ['pɛɪpstliç] *adj* papal.
Parabel [pa'raɪbəl] *f* (*pl* -n) parable;
(*Math*) parabola.
Parade [pa'raɪdə] *f* (*pl* -n) parade.
paradieren *v* parade; (*fig*) make a show,
show off.
Paradies [para'diːs] *neut* (*pl* -e) paradise.
paradox [para'dɔks] *adj* paradoxical.
Paradoxie *f* paradox.
Paragraph [para'graɪf] *m* (*pl* -en) paragraph, section.
parallel [para'leɪl] *adj* parallel. **Parallele** *f*
parallel.
Paralyse [para'lyːzə] *f* (*pl* -n) paralysis.
paralysieren *v* paralyse. **Paralytiker** *m*
paralytic. **paralytisch** *adj* paralytic.
Paranuß ['paranus] *f* Brazil nut.
Parasit [para'ziːt] *m* (*pl* -en) parasite.
Pärchen ['pɛɪrçən] *neut* (*pl* -) couple, lovers.
Parenthese [parɛn'teɪzə] *f* (*pl* -n) parenthesis.
Parfüm [par'fyːm] *neut* (*pl* -e) perfume.
parfümieren *v* perfume, scent.
parieren [pa'riːrən] *v* (*Angriff*) parry;
(*Pferd*) rein (in); (*gehorchen*) obey, toe
the line.
Parität [pari'tɛɪt] *f* (*pl* -en) parity.
Park [park] *m* (*pl* -s) park. –**anlagen** *f pl*
park, public gardens. **parken** *v* park.
Parkett [par'kɛt] *neut* (*pl* -e) (*Fußboden*)
parquet; (*Theater*) stalls.
Park||**platz** *m* car park, (*US*) parking lot.
–**uhr** *f* parking meter.
Parlament [parla'mɛnt] *neut* (*pl* -e) parliament. –**arier** *m* (*pl* -) parliamentarian.
parlamentarisch *adj* parliamentary.
Parodie [paro'diː] *f* (*pl* -n) parody.
parodieren *v* parody.

Partei [par'taɪ] *f* (*pl* -en) (*Pol, Jur*) party.
–**führer** *m* party leader. **partei**||**isch** *or*
–**lich** *adj* biased, partial. –**los** *adj* impar-
tial. **Partei**||**politik** *f* party politics. –**tag**
m party conference.
Parterre [par'tɛr] *neut* (*pl* -s) ground
floor; (*Theater*) pit. –**wohnung** *f* ground-
floor flat.
Partie [par'tiː] *f* (*pl* -n) (*Teil, Musik*) part;
(*Spiel, Heirat*) match; (*Jagd*-) party.
Partikel [par'tiːkəl] *f* (*pl* -n) particle.
Partisan [parti'zaɪn] *m* (*pl* -en) partisan.
Partitur [parti'tuːr] *f* (*pl* -en) (*Musik*)
score.
Partizip [parti'tsiːp] *neut* (*pl* -ien) partici-
ple.
Partizipation [parrtisipa'tsioɪn] *f* partici-
pation. **partizipieren** *v* participate.
Partner ['parrtnər] *m* (*pl* -) partner.
Partnerschaft *f* partnership.
Party ['parrti] *f* (*pl* -s) party.
Parzelle [par'tsɛlə] *f* (*pl* -n) plot (of land).
Paß [pas] *m* (*pl* Pässe) (*Reisepaß*) passport; (*Durchgang*) pass.
passabel [pa'saɪbəl] *adj* tolerable, passable.
Passage [pa'saɪʒə] *f* (*pl* -n) passage. **Passagier** *m* (*pl* -e) passenger.
Passant [pa'sant] *m* (*pl* -en) passer-by.
Paßbild ['pasbilt] *neut* passport photograph.
passen ['pasən] *v* fit, suit; (*Kartenspiel*)
pass. **gut zueinander passen** go well
together. **das paßt mir nicht** that doesn't
suit me. **passend** *adj* fitting, suitable.
passieren [pa'siːrən] *v* (*geschehen*) happen; (*vorübergehen*) pass; (*überqueren*)
cross. **Passierschein** *m* permit, pass.
Passion [pasi'oɪn] *f* (*pl* -en) passion. **sich
passionieren für** be enthusiastic about.
passioniert enthusiastic, dedicated. **Pas-
sions**||**spiel** *neut* Passion Play. –**woche** *f*
Holy Week.
passiv ['pasiːf] *adj* passive. **Passiv** *neut*
passive.
Paßkontrolle ['paskɔntrɔlə] *f* passport
inspection.
Pastellfarbe [pa'stɛlfaɪrbə] *f* pastel colour.
Pastete [pa'steɪtə] *f* (*pl* -n) (*savoury*) pie,
pasty.
pasteurisieren [pastœri'ziːrən] *v* pasteurize.
Pastille [pa'stilə] *f* (*pl* -n) lozenge.

Pastor ['pastɔr] *m* (*pl* -en) pastor, priest.
Pate ['paːtə] *m* (*pl* -n) godfather. –**nkind** *neut* godchild.
Patent [pa'tɛnt] *neut* (*pl* -e) patent; (*Erlaubnis*) licence; (*Mil*) commission. **patentieren** *v* patent. **Patentinhaber** *m* patentee.
pathetisch [pa'teːtiʃ] *adj* (*feierlich*) solemn, lofty; (*übertrieben*) rhetorical, flowery.
Pathologe [pato'loːgə] *m* (*pl* -n) pathologist. **Pathologie** *f* pathology. **pathologisch** *adj* pathological.
Patient [patsi'ɛnt] *m* (*pl* -en) patient.
Patin ['paːtin] *f* (*pl* -nen) godmother.
Patriot [patri'oːt] *m* (*pl* -en) patriot. **patriotisch** *adj* patriotic. **Patriotismus** *m* patriotism.
Patron [pa'troːn] *m* (*pl* -e) patron; (*umg.*) fellow, customer.
Patrone [pa'troːnə] *f* (*pl* -n) cartridge.
Patrouille [pa'truljə] *f* (*pl* -n) patrol.
Patt [pat] *neut* (*pl* -s) stalemate.
Pauke ['paukə] *f* (*pl* -n) kettledrum. **pauken** *v* (*umg.*) cram, swot. **Pauker** *m* drummer; (*umg.*) crammer.
pausbackig ['pausbakiç] *adj* chubby(-faced).
pauschal [pau'ʃaːl] *adj* all-inclusive. **Pauschalsumme** *f* lump sum.
Pause ['pauzə] *f* (*pl* -n) pause, break; (*Theater*) interval. **Pause machen** take a break. **pausenlos** *adj* uninterrupted, continuous.
Pavian ['paːviaːn] *m* (*pl* -e) baboon.
Pazifik [pa'tsiːfik] *m* Pacific Ocean. **pazifisch** *adj* Pacific.
Pazifismus [patsi'fismus] *m* pacifism. **Pazifist** *m* (*pl* -en) pacifist.
Pech [pɛç] *neut* (*pl* -e) pitch; (*fig*) bad luck. **Pech haben** be unlucky. **pechdunkel** *adj* pitch dark.
Pedal [pe'daːl] *neut* (*pl* -e) pedal.
Pedant [pe'dant] *m* (*pl* -en) pedant. **pedantisch** *adj* pedantic.
peilen ['pailən] *v* take (one's) bearings; (*loten*) sound out.
Pein [pain] *f* (*unz.*) pain, torment, agony. **pein||igen** *v* torment. –**lich** *adj* awkward, embarrassing; (*genau*) (over-)careful, fussy.
Peitsche ['paitʃə] *f* (*pl* -n) whip, lash.
Pelikan ['peːlikaːn] *m* (*pl* -e) pelican.
Pelle ['pɛlə] *f* (*pl* -n) peel, skin.

Pellkartoffel *pl* potatoes (boiled) in their jackets.
Pelz [pɛlts] *m* (*pl* -e) fur, pelt. **pelzig** *adj* furry. **Pelzmantel** *m* fur coat.
Pendel ['pɛndəl] *neut* (*pl* -) pendulum. **pendeln** *v* swing, oscillate; (*fig*) commute. **Pendler** *m* commuter.
penibel [pe'niːbəl] *adj* meticulous.
pennen ['pɛnən] *v* (*umg.*) doss, kip down. **Penne** *f* (*umg.*) school. **Penner** *m* dosser.
Pension [pã'sjoːn] *f* (*pl* -en) guest house, boarding house; (*Ruhegehalt*) pension. **pensionieren** *v* pension off. **Pensionierte(r)** pensioner.
per [pɛr] *prep* by, per. **per Adresse** care of, c/o.
perfekt [pɛr'fɛkt] *adj* perfect. **einen Vertrag perfekt machen** clinch a deal.
perforieren [pɛrfo'riːrən] *v* perforate. **Perforation** *f* perforation.
Pergament [pɛrga'mɛnt] *neut* (*pl* -e) parchment. –**papier** *neut* greaseproof paper.
Periode [peri'oːdə] *f* (*pl* -n) period. **periodisch** *adj* periodic.
Perle ['pɛrlə] *f* (*pl* -n) pearl; (*Glas-*) bead. **perlen** *v* sparkle. **Perl||enkette** *f* string of pearls. –**mutter** *f* mother-of-pearl.
permanent [pɛrma'nɛnt] *adj* permanent.
perplex [pɛr'plɛks] *adj* perplexed, confused.
Person [pɛr'zoːn] *f* (*pl* -en) person.
Personal [pɛrzo'naːl] *neut* staff, personnel. –**abteilung** *f* personnel department. –**ausweis** *m* pass, ID card. –**chef** *m* personnel manager.
Personen||kraftwagen (Pkw) *m* (passenger) car. –**verzeichnis** *neut* (*Theater*) dramatis personae. –**zug** *m* (local) passenger train.
persönlich [pɛr'zœnliç] *adj* personal. **Persönlichkeit** *f* personality.
Perspektive [pɛrspɛk'tiːvə] *f* (*pl* -n) perspective.
Perücke [pe'rykə] *f* (*pl* -n) wig.
pervers [pɛr'vɛrs] *adj* perverse. **Perversion** *f* perversion.
Pessimismus [pɛsi'mismus] *m* pessimism. **Pessimist** *m* (*pl* -en) pessimist. **pessimistisch** *adj* pessimistic.
Pest [pɛst] *f* (*pl* -en) plague.
Petersilie [petər'ziːliə] *f* (*pl* -n) parsley.
Petroleum [pe'troːleum] *neut* petroleum; (*Kerosin*) paraffin, (*US*) kerosene.

petzen ['pɛtsən] v (umg.) tell tales, sneak.
Pfad [pfaɪt] m (pl -e) path. −**finder** m Boy Scout.
Pfahl [pfaɪl] m (pl **Pfähle**) post, stake; (Stange) pole. −**werk** neut paling, palisade.
Pfalz [pfalts] f Palatinate.
Pfand [pfant] neut (pl **Pfänder**) pledge, security; (Flaschen, usw.) deposit. −**brief** m mortgage (deed). −**leiher** m pawnbroker.
Pfanne ['pfanə] f (pl -n) pan. **Pfannkuchen** m pancake.
Pfarrbezirk ['pfarrbətsirk] m parish **Pfarrer** m parson. **Pfarrhaus** neut parsonage.
Pfau [pfau] m (pl -en) peacock.
Pfeffer ['pfɛfər] m (pl -) pepper. −**kuchen** m gingerbread. −**minz** neut (pl -e) peppermint (sweet). −**minze** f (Bot) peppermint.
Pfeife ['pfaɪfə] f (pl -n) pipe. **pfeifen** v whistle. **Pfeifer** m whistler; (Pfeife) piper.
Pfeil [pfaɪl] m (pl -e) arrow.
Pfeiler ['pfaɪlər] m (pl -) pillar.
pfeilschnell ['pfaɪlʃnɛl] adj swift as an arrow. **Pfeilschütze** m archer.
Pfennig ['pfɛnɪç] m (pl -e) pfennig; (fig) penny.
Pferch [pfɛrç] m (pl -e) fold, pen. **pferchen** v pen.
Pferd [pfeɪrt] neut (pl -e) horse. **Pferde‖bremse** f horsefly. −**knecht** m groom. −**rennbahn** f race course. −**rennen** neut horseracing. −**stall** m stable. −**stärke** (Ps) f horsepower (hp).
Pfiff [pfɪf] m (pl -e) (Ton) whistle; (Kniff) trick.
Pfifferling ['pfɪfərlɪŋ] m (pl -e) (Bot) chanterelle (edible mushroom). **das ist keinen Pfifferling wert** that's (worth) nothing.
Pfingsten ['pfɪŋstən] neut (pl -) Whitsun(tide).
Pfirsich ['pfɪrzɪç] m (pl -e) peach.
Pflanze ['pflantsə] f (pl -n) plant. **pflanzen** v plant. −**fressend** adj herbivorous. **Pflanzen‖fresser** m herbivore. −**öl** neut vegetable oil. −**reich** neut vegetable kingdom.
Pflaster ['pflastər] neut (pl -) (Straße) pavement; (Wunden) plaster. −**stein** m paving stone.
Pflaume ['pflaumə] f (pl -n) plum

Pflege ['pfleɪgə] f (pl -n) care. −**dienst** m service. −**eltern** pl foster parents. −**kind** neut foster child. −**mutter** f foster mother. **pflegeleicht** adj easy-care.
pflegen ['pfleɪgən] v care for; (Kranken) nurse; (Pflanzen) cultivate; (gewohnt sein) be accustomed to. **er pflegte zu sagen** he used to say. **Pfleger** m male nurse; (vormund) guardian. **Pflegerin** f nurse, sister.
Pflege‖sohn m foster son. −**mutter** f foster mother. −**tochter** f foster daughter. −**vater** m foster father.
pflichtig ['pfleɪklɪç] adj careful. **pfleglich behandeln** handle with care.
Pflicht [pflɪçt] f (pl -en) duty. **pflicht‖bewußt** adj conscientious. −**gemäß** adj dutiful, in accordance with duty. −**getreu** adj dutiful, conscientious.
Pflock [pflɔk] m (pl **Pflöcke**) peg, pin.
pflücken ['pflʏkən] v pluck; gather.
Pflug [pfluːk] m (pl **Pflüge**) plough.
pflügen ['pflyːgən] v plough.
Pflüger ['pflyːgər] m ploughman.
Pforte ['pfɔrtə] f (pl -n) door, gate.
Pförtner ['pfœrtnər] m (pl -) doorkeeper, porter.
Pfosten ['pfɔstən] m (pl -) post, stake.
Pfote ['pfoɪtə] f (pl -n) paw.
Pfropf [pfrɔpf] m (pl -e oder **Pfröpfe**) (Blutgerinsel) blood clot; (Watte) wad (of cotton wool). **pfropfen** v (Flasche) cork, stopper; (Bäume) graft; (stopfen) pack, stuff. **Pfropf‖en** m (pl -) cork, stopper. −**reis** neut graft.
pfui [pfuɪ] interj pooh, ugh.
Pfund [pfunt] neut (pl -e) pound.
pfuschen ['pfuʃən] v botch, bungle, make a mess. **Pfuscher** m botcher, bungler. −**ei** f bungling; (Arbeit) botch-job, botch-up.
Pfütze ['pfʏtsə] f (pl -n) puddle.
Phänomen [fɛnoˈmeɪn] neut (pl -e) phenomenon.
Phantasie [fantaˈziː] f (pl -n) (Einbildungskraft) imagination; (Trugbild) fantasy. **phantasie‖los** adj unimaginative. −**reich** adj imaginative. −**ren** v fantasize, daydream; (Med) be delirious. **phantastisch** adj fantastic.
Phantom [fanˈtoɪm] neut (pl -e) phantom.
Phase ['faɪzə] f (pl -n) phase.
Philister [fiˈlistər] m (pl -) philistine. **philisterhaft** adj philistine, narrow-minded.

Philosoph [filo'zoːf] *m* (*pl* **-en**) philosopher. **-ie** *f* philosophy. **philosophisch** *adj* philosophical.
Phonetik [fo'neːtik] *f* (*unz.*) phonetics. **phonetisch** *adj* phonetic.
Phosphor ['fɔsfɔr] *m* (*unz.*) phosphorus.
Photo ['foːto] *neut* (*pl* **-s**) photo, photograph. **-album** *neut* photograph album. **-apparat** *m* camera. **photogen** *adj* photogenic. **Photograph** *m* (*pl* **-en**) photographer. **-ie** *f* photography. **photograph‖ieren** *v* photograph. **-isch** *adj* photographic.
Phrase ['fraːzə] *f* (*pl* **-n**) phrase; (*fig*) empty talk, fine phrases.
Physik [fy'ziːk] *f* physics. **-er** *m* physicist.
Physiologie [fyzjolo'giː] *f* physiology. **physiologisch** *adj* physiological.
physisch ['fyːziʃ] *adj* physical.
Pianist [pia'nist] *m* (*pl* **-en**), **Pianistin** *f* (*pl* **-nen**) pianist.
Pickel[1] ['pikəl] *m* (*pl* **-**), **Picke** *f* (*pl* **-n**) pickaxe.
Pickel[2] ['pikəl] *m* (*pl* **-**) (*Med*) pimple, spot.
piep [piːp] *interj* cheep. **nicht piep sagen** not say a word. **Piep** *m* (*pl* **-se**) peep, chirp. **piep‖en** *v* chirp. **-sen** *v* (*Maus*) squeak.
Pietät [pie'tɛːt] *f* piety; (*Ehrfurcht*) reverence.
Pik [piːk] *neut* (*pl* **-s**) spades *pl*.
pikant [pi'kant] *adj* spicy; (*fig*) suggestive, racy.
Pikkoloflöte ['pikoloflœːtə] *f* piccolo.
Pilger ['pilgər] *m* (*pl* **-**), **Pilgerin** *f* (*pl* **-nen**) pilgrim. **Pilgerfahrt** *f* pilgrimage.
Pille ['pilə] *f* (*pl* **-n**) pill. **die Pille** (*umg.*) the (contraceptive) pill.
Pilot [pi'loːt] *m* (*pl* **-en**) pilot.
Pilz [pilts] *m* (*pl* **-e**) mushroom.
Pinguin [piŋgu'iːn] *m* (*pl* **-e**) penguin.
Pinie ['piːniə] *f* (*pl* **-n**) stone pine. **-nnuß** *f* pine kernel.
Pinne ['pinə] *f* (*pl* **-n**) pin, peg; (*Ruder-*) tiller.
Pinsel ['pinzəl] *m* (*pl* **-**) brush; (*Farbe*) paintbrush. **pinseln** *v* paint, daub.
Pionier [pio'niːr] *m* (*pl* **-e**) pioneer.
Pirat [pi'raːt] *m* (*pl* **-en**) pirate.
Piste ['pistə] *f* (*pl* **-n**) track; (*Ski*) ski-run; (*Flugzeug*) runway.
Pistole [pi'stoːlə] *f* (*pl* **-n**) pistol.
pissen ['pisən] *v* (*vulgär*) piss.

Plackerei [plakə'rai] *f* (*pl* **-en**) drudgery, toil.
plädieren [plɛ'diːrən] *v* plead. **Plädoyer** *neut* (*pl* **-s**) (*Jur*) plea.
Plage ['plaːgə] *f* (*pl* **-n**) nuisance, bother, vexation. **plagen** *v* torment, annoy.
Plagiat [plagi'aːt] *neut* (*pl* **-e**) plagiarism. **plagiieren** *v* plagiarize.
Plakat [pla'kaːt] *neut* (*pl* **-e**) poster, placard.
Plan [plaːn] *m* (*pl* **Pläne**) (*Absicht*) plan, intention; (*Zeichnung*) plan, diagram; (*Stadt*) map; (*Skizze*) design, scheme.
Plane ['plaːnə] *f* (*pl* **-n**) awning.
planen ['plaːnən] *v* plan.
Planet [pla'neːt] *m* (*pl* **-en**) planet. **-arium** *neut* (*pl* **-arien**) planetarium.
planieren [pla'niːrən] *v* plane, level, smooth. **Planierraupe** *f* grader, bulldozer.
Planke ['plaŋkə] *f* (*pl* **-n**) plank.
Plänkelei [plɛŋkə'lai] *f* (*pl* **-en**) (*Gefecht*) skirmish; (*Wortstreit*) bantering.
planmäßig ['plaːnmɛːsiç] *adj* systematic; (*nach einem Plan*) according to plan. *der Zug fährt planmäßig um drei Uhr ab* the train is scheduled to leave at 3 o'clock.
Plantage [plan'taːʒə] *f* (*pl* **-n**) plantation.
Planung ['plaːnuŋ] *f* planning. **Planwirtschaft** *f* planned economy.
plappern ['plapərn] *v* chatter.
plärren ['plɛrən] *v* blubber, cry, sob.
Plastik ['plastik] *f* (*pl* **-en**) (*Kunst*) sculpture; (*Med*) plastic surgery; (*Kunststoff*) plastic. **plastisch** *adj* plastic.
Platin [pla'tiːn] *neut* platinum.
plätschern ['plɛtʃərn] *v* (*Bach*) babble; (*Regen*) splash, patter; (*planschen*) paddle.
platt [plat] *adj* flat, level; (*Redensart*) silly, trite; (*erstaunt*) tongue-tied, flabbergasted. **Plattdeutsch** *neut* Low German.
Platte ['platə] *f* (*pl* **-n**) plate, dish; (*Stein*) flag; (*Metall, Holz*) sheet, slab; (*Tisch*) leaf; (*Schallplatte*) record, disc. **-nspieler** *m* record-player.
Platz [plats] *m* (*pl* **Plätze**) place; (*Sitz*) seat; (*Raum*) space, room; (*Stadt*) square. **-anweiser** *m* usher. **-anweiserin** *f* usherette.
platzen ['platsən] *v* burst, split; (*explodieren*) explode; (*Scheck*) bounce.
Platz‖karte *f* seat-reservation ticket. **-patrone** *f* blank cartridge. **-regen** *m* downpour, heavy shower.

plaudern ['plaudərn] v chat.
plausibel [plau'ziːbəl] adj plausible.
Plazenta [pla'sɛnta] f (pl -s or **Plazenten**) placenta.
pleite ['plaitə] adj bankrupt; (umg.) broke. **Pleite** f bankruptcy; (fig) flop, wash-out.
plombieren [plɔm'biːrən] v seal; (Zahn) fill.
plötzlich ['plœtsliç] adj sudden.
plump [plump] adj (grob) coarse; (ungeschickt) clumsy. **plumps** Interj bump, thud. **plumpsen** v fall down (with a thud), plump down.
plündern ['plyndərn] v plunder.
Plural ['pluːraɪl] m (pl -e) plural.
pneumatisch [pnɔy'maːtiʃ] adj pneumatic.
Pöbel ['pœibəl] m mob, rabble.
pochen ['pɔxən] v knock, tap; (Herz) beat.
Pocken ['pɔkən] pl smallpox sing.
Pokal [po'kaɪl] m (pl -e) (Sport) cup. **-endspiel** neut (Sport) cup final. **-spiel** neut cup tie.
Pökel ['pœikəl] m (pl -) brine (for pickling). **pökeln** v pickle, salt.
Pol [poɪl] m (pl -e) pole. **polar** adj polar. **Polarmeer** neut Arctic Ocean. **südliches Polarmeer** Antarctic Ocean.
Polemik [po'leːmik] f (pl -en) polemic, controversy. **polemisch** adj polemic(al).
Polen ['poːlən] neut Poland. **Pole** m (pl -n), **Polin** f (pl -nen) Pole. **polnisch** adj Polish.
Police [po'liːs, po'liːsə] f (pl -n) (insurance) policy.
polieren [po'liːrən] v polish. **Poliermittel** neut polish.
Politik [poli'tiːk] f (unz.) (Staatskunst) politics; (Verfahren, Programm) policy. **-er** m (pl -) politician. **politisch** adj political.
Politur [poli'tuːr] f (pl -en) polish.
Polizei [poli'tsai] f (pl -en) police. **-hund** m police dog. **-kommisar** or **-kommissär** m police inspector. **polizeilich** adj police. **Polizei||präsident** m chief constable, commissioner. **-stunde** f closing time. **-wache** f police station. **Polizist** m (pl -en) policeman. **-in** f (pl -nen) policewoman.
Polster ['polstər] neut (pl -) cushion; (Polsterung) upholstery. **polstern** v upholster. **Polsterung** f upholstery.

Poltergeist ['pɔltərgaist] m poltergeist, hobgoblin.
Polyp [po'lyːp] m (pl -en) (umg.) copper.
Polytechnikum [poly'tɛçnikum] neut (pl **Polytechniken**) technical college.
Pommern ['pɔmərn] neut (unz.) Pomerania.
Pommes frites [pɔm'friːt] pl (potato) chips, (US) French fries.
Pomp [pɔmp] m pomp. **pomphaft** adj stately, with pomp.
Pony ['pɔni] neut (pl -s) pony; (Frisur) fringe.
Pop-Musik ['pɔp muˈziːk] f pop (music).
populär [popu'lɛːr] adj popular. **popularisieren** v popularize.
Pore ['poːrə] f (pl -n) pore.
Pornographie [pɔrnogra'fiː] f pornography. **pornographisch** adj pornographic.
porös [pɔ'rœːs] adj porous.
Porree ['pɔre] m (pl -s) leek.
Portion [pɔrtsi'oːn] f (pl -en) portion, helping.
Porto ['pɔrto] neut (pl -s) postage. **portofrei** adv post-free.
Porträt [pɔr'trɛɪ, pɔr'trɛɪt] neut (pl -s) portrait.
Portugal ['pɔrtugal] neut Portugal. **Portugiese** m (pl -n), **Portugiesin** f (pl -nen) Portuguese. **portugiesisch** adj Portuguese.
Porzellan [pɔrtsɛ'laɪn] neut (pl -e) porcelain, china.
Posaune [po'zaunə] f (pl -n) trombone.
Pose ['poːzə] f (pl -n) pose, attitude.
Poseur m poseur. **posieren** v (strike a) pose.
Position [pozitsi'oːn] f (pl -en) position.
positiv ['poːzitiːf] adj positive.
Posse ['pɔsə] f (pl -n) (Theater) farce.
Possen m (pl -) prank, practical joke, trick. **possenhaft** adj farcical.
possessiv ['pɔsɛsiːf] adj possessive.
Post [pɔst] f (pl -en) post (office), postal service; (Briefe) post, mail. **-amt** neut post office. **-anweisung** f postal order. **-beamte(r)** m post office official. **-bote** m postman.
Posten ['pɔstən] m (pl -) place, post; (Stellung) position, post; (Mil) sentry; (Ware) item; (Streik-) picket.
Post||fach ['pɔstfax] neut post-office box, PO box. **-gebühr** f postage. **-karte** f postcard.
postlagernd ['pɔstlaɪgərnt] adj poste restante, (US) general delivery.

post‖leitzahl f postal code. **–sparkasse** f post-office savings bank. **–stempel** m postmark.

Postulat [pɔstu'laɪt] neut (pl **-e**) postulate. **postulieren** v postulate.

postwendend ['pɔstvɛndənt] adj by return (of) post. **Postwertzeichen** neut postage stamp.

potent [po'tɛnt] adj capable; (Med) potent.

potential [potɛntsi'aɪl] adj potential. **Potential** neut potential. **potentiell** adj potential, possible.

Potenz [po'tɛnts] f (pl **-en**) power.

Pottasche ['pɔtaʃə] f potash.

Pracht [praxt] f splendour, magnificence. **prächtig** ['prɛçtiç] adj splendid, magnificent.

Prag [praɪk] neut Prague.

Präge ['prɛɪgə] f (pl **-n**) mint. **prägen** v stamp; (Münze) mint, coin.

pragmatisch [prag'maɪtiʃ] adj pragmatic. **Pragmatiker** m (pl **-**) pragmatist.

prägnant [prɛg'nant] adj precise, terse.

prahlen ['praɪlən] v brag, boast. **Prahler** m (pl **-**)braggart. **prahlerisch** adj boastful.

Praktikant [prakti'kant] m (pl **-en**), **Praktikantin** f (pl **-nen**) trainee, probationer. **Praktik‖er** m experienced person, expert. **–um** neut (pl **-a**) training course, field course. **praktisch** adj practical; (zweckmäßig) useful; (Person) handy.

prall [pral] adj (rund) plump, chubby; (straff) tight; (sonne) blazing. **Prall** m (pl **-e**) collision, impact. **prallen** v (Ball) bounce, rebound. **prallen gegen** collide with, bump into.

Prämie ['prɛmiə] f (pl **-n**) bonus; (Versicherungs-) premium.

Prämisse [prɛ'misə] f (pl **-n**) premise.

Präparat [prɛpa'raɪt] neut (pl **-e**) preparation; (Med) medicament.

präsentieren [prɛɪzɛn'tiɪrən] v present. **Präsenz** f (pl **-en**) presence.

Präsident [prɛzi'dɛnt] m (pl **-en**) president. **–enwahl** f presidential election. **–schaft** f presidency. **präsidieren** v preside, act as chairman.

prasseln ['prasəln] v clatter; (Regen) patter, drum; (Feuer) crackle.

präventiv [prɛvɛn'tiɪf] adj preventive. **Präventiv‖maßnahme** f preventive measure. **–mittel** neut contraceptive.

Praxis ['praksis] f (pl **Praxen**) practice.

Präzedenzfall [prɛtse'dɛntsfal] m precedent.

präzis [prɛ'tsiːs] adj precise.

predigen ['preɪdigən] v preach. **Prediger** m (pl **-**) preacher. **Predigt** f (pl **-en**) sermon.

Preis [prais] m (pl **-e**) price; (Belohnung) prize; (Lob) praise.

Preißelbeere ['praisəlbeɪrə] f cranberry.

preisgeben ['praisgeɪbən] v give up, abandon; (opfern) sacrifice. **Preisgebung** f surrender; sacrifice.

Preis‖liste f price list. **–senkung** f price reduction. **–steigerung** f price rise. **–stopp** m price freeze. **–sturz** m slump or fall in prices. **preiswert** adj cheap. **Preiszettel** m price tag.

prellen ['prɛlən] v (betrügen) swindle, cheat; (Ball) bounce.

Premiere [prem'jeɪrə] f (pl **-n**) première, first night.

Premierminister [prem'jeɪrministər] prime minister, premier.

Presse ['prɛsə] f (pl **-n**) (Zeitungen) the press; (Druckmaschine) press; (Saft) squeezer. **–agentur** f press agency. **–freiheit** f freedom of the press. **pressen** v press.

Preß‖holz neut chipboard. **–kohle** f briquette. **–luftbohrer** m pneumatic drill.

Preuße ['prɔysə] m (pl **-n**), **Preußin** f (pl **-nen**) Prussian. **Preußen** neut Prussia. **preußisch** adj Prussian.

prickeln ['prikəln] v prickle, tingle. **–d** adj tingling.

Priester ['priːstər] m (pl **-**) priest. **–in** f priestess. **priesterlich** adj priestly.

prima ['priːma] adj (umg.) first-rate, excellent. **Prima** f sixth form.

primär [pri'mɛɪr] adj primary.

Primarschule [pri'maɪrʃuɪlə] f primary school (in Switzerland).

Primel ['priːməl] f (pl **-n**) primrose.

primitiv [primi'tiɪf] adj primitive.

Prinz [prints] m (pl **-en**) prince. **-essin** f (pl **-nen**) princess.

Prinzip [prin'tsiɪp] f (pl **-ien**) principle. **aus Prinzip** on principle. **im Prinzip** in principle, theoretically. **Prinzipal** m principal.

Priorität [priori'tɛɪt] f (pl **-en**) priority.

Prise ['priːzə] f (pl **-n**) pinch.

Prisma ['prisma] neut (pl **Prismen**) prism.

privat [pri'vaɪt] adj private. **Privat‖adresse**

f home address. **–angelegenheit** *f* personal matter.
Privileg [privi'leɪk] *neut* (*pl* **-ien**) privilege. **privilegiert** *adj* privileged.
Probe ['proːbə] *f* (*pl* **-n**) (*Versuch*) test, trial; (*Theater*) rehearsal; (*Muster*) sample, specimen. **auf Probe** on approval. **auf die Probe stellen** put to the test. **Probe‖abzug** *m* (*Druck*) proof. **–zeit** *f* probationary period. **probieren** *v* (*versuchen*) try, attempt; (*Speise*) taste, sample.
Problem [pro'bleɪm] *neut* (*pl* **-e**) problem. **problematisch** *adj* problematic.
Produkt [pro'dukt] *neut* (*pl* **-e**) product; (*Landwirtschaft*) produce. **–ion** *f* production. **produktiv** *adj* productive. **Produzent** *m* producer; (*Landwirtschaft*) grower. **produzieren** *v* produce.
Professor [pro'fɛsɔr] *m* (*pl* **-en**) professor. **professorisch** *adj* professorial. **Professur** *f* (*pl* **-en**) professorship.
Profil [pro'fiːl] *f* (*pl* **-e**) profile; (*Reifen*) tread. **profilieren** *v* outline, sketch.
Profit [pro'fiːt] *m* (*pl* **-e**) profit. **profit‖abel** *adj* profitable. **–ieren** *v* profit, gain. **Profitmacher** *m* profiteer.
Prognose [pro'gnoːzə] *f* (*pl* **-n**) (*Med*) prognosis; (*Wetter*) outlook, forecast.
Programm [pro'gram] *neut* (*pl* **-e**) programme. **programmgemäß** *adj* according to plan. **programmieren** *v* (*Computer*) program. **Programm‖ierer** *m* (*pl* **-**), **–iererin** *f* (*pl* **-nen**) programmer. **–ierung** *f* programming.
Projekt [pro'jɛkt] *neut* (*pl* **-e**) (*Plan*) plan; (*Entwurf*) scheme. **projektieren** *v* plan; scheme. **Projektionsapparat** *m* projector. **projizieren** [proji'tsiːrən] *v* project.
proklamieren [prokla'miːrən] *v* proclaim.
Proletariat [proletaːri'aːt] *neut* (*pl* **-e**) proletariat. **Proletarier** *m* proletarian. **proletarisch** *adj* proletarian.
Prolog [pro'loːk] *m* (*pl* **-e**) prologue.
Promenade [promə'naːdə] *f* (*pl* **-n**) promenade.
Promotion [promotsi'oːn] *f* (*pl* **-en**) (awarding of a) doctorate; (*Komm*) (sales) promotion. **promovieren** *v* be awarded a doctorate.
prompt [prompt] *adj* prompt.
Propaganda [propa'ganda] *f* propaganda. **Propagandist** *m* (*pl* **-en**) propagandist.
Propeller [pro'pɛlər] *m* (*pl* **-**) propeller.
Prophet [pro'feːt] *m* (*pl* **-en**) prophet. **–ie**

f prophecy. **prophe‖tisch** *adj* prophetic. **–zeien** *v* prophesy. **Prophezeiung** *f* (*pl* **-en**) prophecy.
Proportion [proportsi'oːn] *f* (*pl* **-en**) proportion. **proportional** *adj* proportional.
Prosa ['proːza] *f* prose.
prosit ['proːzit] *interj* cheers! your health! **prosit Neujahr!** a Happy New Year!
Prospekt [pro'spɛkt] *m* (*pl* **-e**) prospectus, leaflet; (*Ansicht*) prospect.
prostituieren [prostitu'iːrən] *v* prostitute. **Prostituierte** *f* (*pl* **-n**) prostitute. **Prostitution** *f* prostitution.
Protest [pro'tɛst] *m* (*pl* **-e**) protest.
Protestant [prote'stant] *m* (*pl* **-en**) Protestant. **protest‖antisch** *adj* protestant. **–ieren** *v* protest.
Prothese [pro'teːzə] *f* (*pl* **-n**) prosthesis; (*Arm-, Bein-*) artificial limb; (*Zahn-*) denture.
Protokoll [proto'kɔl] *neut* (*pl* **-e**) (*Jur*) record; (*einer Versammlung*) minutes *pl*; (*Diplomatie*) protocol.
Protz [prɔts] *m* (*pl* **-en**) snob. **protzen** *v* put on airs, swagger. **–haft** *adj* snobbish.
Proviant [provi'ant] *m* provisions *pl*, victuals *pl*.
Provinz [pro'vints] *f* (*pl* **-en**) province. **provinzial** *adj* provincial, regional. **provinziell** *adj* provincial, narrow-minded.
Provision [provizi'oːn] *f* (*pl* **-en**) (*Komm*) commission.
provisorisch [provi'zoːriʃ] *adj* provisional.
provozieren [provo'tsiːrən] *v* provoke.
Prozedur [protse'duːr] *f* (*pl* **-en**) procedure.
Prozent [pro'tsɛnt] *neut* (*pl* **-e**) percent. **–satz** *m* percentage.
Prozeß [pro'tsɛs] *m* (*pl* **Prozesse**) (*Jur*) lawsuit, trial; (*Vorgang*) process.
Prozession [protsɛsi'oːn] *f* (*pl* **-en**) procession.
prüde ['pryːdə] *adj* prudish.
prüfen ['pryːfən] *v* (*Kenntnisse*) examine, test; (*erproben*) try, test; (*untersuchen*) inspect, check. **Prüf‖ling** *m* (*pl* **-e**) (examination) candidate. **–stein** *m* touchstone. **–ung** *f* (*pl* **-en**) examination, test.
Prügel ['pryːgəl] *m* (*pl* **-**) cudgel, club; *pl* beating. **prügeln** *v* beat, thrash. **Prügelstrafe** *f* corporal punishment.
Prunk [pruŋk] *m* pomp, show, splendour. **prunken** *v* show off. **Prunkstück** *neut*

showpiece. **prunk**||**süchtig** *adj* ostentatious. −**voll** *adj* magnificent, gorgeous.

Psalm [psalm] *m* (*pl* -en) psalm.

Pseudonym [psɔydo'nyɪm] *neut* (*pl* -e) pseudonym.

Psychiater [psyki'aɪtər] *m* (*pl* -) psychiatrist. **Psychiatrie** *f* psychiatry. **psychiatrisch** *adj* psychiatric. **psychisch** *adj* psychic.

Psycho||**analyse** [psyçoana'lyɪzə] *f* psychoanalysis. −**loge** *m* (*pl* -n) psychologist. **psychologisch** *adj* psychological.

Psycho||**path** *m* (*pl* -en) psychopath. −**therapeut** *m* (*pl* -en) psychotherapist. −**therapie** *f* psychotherapy.

Pubertät [pubɛr'tɛɪt] *f* puberty.

Publikum ['puɪblikum] *neut* public; (*Zuhörer*) audience.

publizieren [publi'tsiɪrən] *v* publish. **Publizist** *m* journalist.

Pudding ['pudiŋ] *m* (*pl* -s) pudding.

Pudel ['puɪdəl] *m* (*pl* -) poodle.

Puder ['puɪdər] *m* (*pl* -) powder.

Puff¹ [puf] 1. *m* (*pl* Püffe) push, thump. 2. *m* (*pl* -e) pouffe.

Puff² *neut* (*Spiel*) backgammon.

puffen [pufən] *v* shove, thump; (*knallen*) pop. **Puffer** *m* buffer; (*Kartoffel*-) pancake, fritter. **Puff**||**mais** *m* popcorn. −**spiel** *neut* backgammon.

Pulli ['puli] *m* (*pl* -s) pullover. **Pullover** *m* (*pl* -) pullover.

Puls [puls] *m* (*pl* -) pulse. **pulsieren** *v* pulsate, throb. **Puls**||**schlag** *m* pulse. −**zahl** *f* pulse rate.

Pult [pult] *neut* (*pl* -e) desk. -**dach** *neut* lean-to roof.

Pulver ['pulvər] *neut* (*pl* -) powder. **pulver**||**artig** *adj* powdery. −**isieren** *v* pulverize.

Pumpe ['pumpə] *f* (*pl* -n) pump. **pumpen** *v* pump.

Pumpernickel ['pumpərnikəl] *m* black (rye) bread.

Punkt [puŋkt] *m* (*pl* -e) point; (*Ort*) place, spot; (*Gramm*) full stop. **punktieren** *v* punctuate; (*Med*) puncture; (*tüpfeln*) dot. **punktiert** *adj* dotted.

pünktlich ['pyŋktliç] *adj* punctual, on time. **Pünktlichkeit** *f* punctuality.

Pupille [pu'piɪlə] *f* (*pl* -n) (*Anat*) pupil.

Puppe ['pupə] *f* (*pl* -n) doll; (*Theater*) puppet; (*Insekten*) pupa, chrysalis. **Puppen**||**haus** *neut* doll's house. −**theater** *neut* puppet show.

pur [puɪr] *adj* pure, unadulterated; (*Getränk*) neat.

Puritaner [puri'taɪnər] *m* (*pl* -) Puritan. **puritanisch** *adj* puritan.

Purpur ['purpur] *m* purple. **purpurn** *adj* purple.

Purzelbaum *m* somersault. **purzeln** *v* somersault.

Pustel ['pustəl] *f* (*pl* -n) pustule.

Pute ['puɪtə] *f* (*pl* -n) turkey (hen). **Puter** *m* (*pl* -) turkey (cock).

Putsch [putʃ] *m* (*pl* -e) putsch, uprising. **putschen** *v* revolt, rise.

Putz ['puts] *m* (*pl* -e) (*Kleidung*) finery, fine dress; (*Zierat*) ornaments *pl*, trimmings *pl*; (*Bewurf*) plaster. **putzen** *v* clean; (*Schuhe*) polish. **sich putzen** dress up. **sich die Nase putzen** wipe one's nose. **Putzer** *m* (*pl* -), **Putzerin** *f* (*pl* -nen) cleaner. **Putz**||**frau** *f* charwoman, cleaner. −**tuch** *f* polishing cloth.

Pyjama [pi'dʒaɪma] *m* (*pl* -s) pyjamas *pl*.

Pyramide [pyra'miɪdə] *f* (*pl* -n) pyramid.

Q

quabbelig ['kvabəliç] *adj* flabby, wobbly. **quabbeln** *v* wobble, quiver.

Quacksalber ['kvakzalbər] *m* (*pl* -) quack, charlatan.

Quadrat [kva'draɪt] *neut* (*pl* -e) square. −**meter** *neut* square metre. −**wurzel** *f* square root. −**zahl** *f* (*Math*) square. **quadrieren** *v* (*Math*) square.

quäken ['kvɛɪkən] *v* squeak.

Qual [kvaɪl] *f* (*pl* -en) torment, pain.

quälen ['kvɛɪlən] *v* torment; (*foltern*) torture. **sich quälen** toil. **quälerisch** *adj* tormenting.

Qualifikation [kvalifikatsi'oɪn] *f* (*pl* -en) qualification; (*Fähigkeit*) ability, fitness. **qualifizieren** *v* qualify. **sich qualifizieren** be fit (for).

Qualität [kvali'tɛɪt] *f* (*pl* -en) quality.

Qualle ['kvalə] *f* (*pl* -n) jellyfish.

Qualm [kvalm] *m* dense smoke; (*Wasser*) vapour, steam. **qualmen** *v* smoke; (*Wasser*) steam.

qualvoll ['kvaɪlfɔl] *adj* painful; agonizing.

Quantität [kvanti'tɛɪt] *f* (*pl* -en) quantity.

Quarantäne [kvaran'tɛɪnə] *f* (*pl* -n) quarantine.

Quark [kvark] *m* curds *pl*, curd cheese; (*fig*) tripe, rubbish. −**käse** *m* curd cheese.
Quartal [kvar'taːl] *neut* (*pl* -e) quarter (of a year).
Quartett [kvar'tɛt] *neut* (*pl* -e) quartet.
Quartier [kvar'tiːr] *neut* (*pl* -e) accommodation; (*Mil*) quarters *pl*; (*Stadt*) quarter, district.
Quarz [kvarts] *m* (*pl* -e) quartz.
quasi ['kvaːzi] *adv* as it were, in a way.
Quatsch [kvatʃ] *m* (*umg.*) rubbish, nonsense. **quatschen** *v* babble, talk nonsense.
Quecksilber ['kvɛkzilbər] *neut* quicksilver, mercury.
Quelle [kvɛlə] *f* (*pl* -n) (*Wasser*) spring; (*Herkunft*) source, origin; (*Öl*) well. **aus guter Quelle** on good authority. **quellen** *v* spring, gush; arise.
quer [kveːr] *adj* cross, transverse; (*seitlich*) lateral. *adv* across, crosswise. **kreuz und quer** hither and thither. **Quer‖balken** *m* crossbeam. −**baum** *m* crossbar. **querdurch** *adv* (right) across.
quetschen ['kvɛtʃən] *v* squeeze, squash. **Quetschung** *f* (*pl* -en) bruise.
quietschen ['kviːtʃən] *v* (*Person, Bremsen*) squeal; (*Tür*) squeak.
Quintett [kvin'tɛt] *neut* (*pl* -e) quintet.
Quirl [kvirl] *m* (*pl* -e) whisk, beater. **quirlen** *v* whisk, beat.
quitt [kvit] *adj* quits, even.
Quitte [kvitə] *f* (*pl* -n) quince.
quittieren [kvi'tiːrən] *v* (*aufgeben*) abandon; (*Rechnung*) give a receipt for. **Quittung** *f* (*pl* -en) receipt.

R

Rabatt [ra'bat] *m* (*pl* -e) discount, rebate.
Rabbiner [ra'biːnər] *m* (*pl* -) rabbi.
Rabe ['raːbə] *m* (*pl* -n) raven. **rabenschwarz** *adj* jet-black.
rabiat [rabi'aːt] *adj* furious, raging.
Rache ['raxə] *f* revenge, vengeance. **Rache nehmen an** revenge oneself on.
Rachen ['raxən] *m* (*pl* -) throat; (*Maul*) jaws *pl*, mouth.
rächen ['rɛçən] *v* avenge. **sich rächen an** take revenge on.
Rad [raːt] *neut* (*pl* Räder) wheel.
Radar ['raːdaːr] *neut or m* radar.
Rädchen ['rɛːtçən] *neut* (*pl* -) caster

Rädelsführer ['rɛːdəlzfyːrər] *m* ringleader.
***radfahren** ['raːtfaːrən] *v* cycle. **Radfahrer** *m* (*pl* -), **Radfahrerin** *f* (*pl* -nen) cyclist.
radieren [ra'diːrən] *v* erase, rub out; (*Kupfer*) etch. **Radiergummi** *m* rubber, eraser.
Radieschen [ra'diːsçən] *neut* (*pl* -) radish.
radikal [radi'kaːl] *adj* radical. **Rakikal‖e(r)** radical. −**ismus** *m* radicalism.
Radio ['raːdio] *neut* (*pl* -s) radio. **radioaktiv** *adj* radioactive. **Radioaktivität** *f* radioactivity.
Radium ['raːdium] *neut* radium. −**therapie** *f* radiotherapy.
raffen ['rafən] *v* snatch (up); (*Stoff*) gather; (*langes Kleid*) take up.
raffinier‖en [rafi'niːrən] *v* refine. −**t** *adj* refined; (*fig*) clever, crafty.
ragen ['raːgən] *v* project, tower up.
Rahm [raːm] *m* cream.
rahmen ['raːmən] *v* frame. **Rahmen** *m* (*pl* -) frame; (*fig*) framework limit, (*Umgebung*) surroundings *pl*, setting. **im Rahmen von** in the context of.
Rakete [ra'keːtə] *f* (*pl* -n) rocket.
Rakett [ra'kɛt] *neut* (*pl* -s) (*Sport*) racket.
Ramme ['ramə] *f* (*pl* -n) pile-driver.
Rampe ['rampə] *f* (*pl* -n) ramp; (*Bühne*) apron. −**nlicht** *neut* footlight.
***ran** [ran] *V* heran.
Rand [rant] *m* (*pl* Ränder) edge; (*Seite*) margin; (*Gefäß, Hut*) brim; (*Grenze*) border, boundary. −**bemerkung** *f* marginal note.
Rang [raŋ] *m* (*pl* Ränge) rank, class; (*Theater*) circle.
rangieren [rãˈʒiːrən] *v* rank; (*Eisenbahnwagen*) shunt.
Ranke ['raŋkə] *f* (*pl* -n) tendril, shoot.
Ränke ['rɛŋkə] *pl* intrigues *pl*, machinations *pl*.
Ranzen ['rantsən] *m* (*pl* -) knapsack; (*Schule*) satchel.
ranzig ['rantsiç] *adj* rancid.
rar [raːr] *adj* rare, scarce. **Rarität** *f* (*pl* -en) rarity.
rasch [raʃ] *adj* rapid, swift.
rascheln ['raʃəln] *v* rustle.
Raschheit ['raʃhait] *f* swiftness.
rasen ['raːzən] *v* rage, storm; (*eilen*) race.
Rasen ['raːzən] *m* (*pl* -) lawn, grass.
rasend ['raːzənt] *adj* furious, raving. **rasend werden** go mad, (*umg.*) blow one's top.

rasieren [ra'ziːrən] v shave. **Rasierapparat** f safety razor. **elektrischer Rasierapparat** electric razor. **sich rasieren** shave (oneself). **Rasier‖klinge** f razor blade. **–krem** f shaving cream. **–messer** neut razor. **–pinsel** m shaving brush.

Raspel ['raspəl] f (pl -n) rasp; (Küche) grater.

Rasse ['rasə] f (pl -n) race; (Tiere) breed. **Rassehund** m pedigree dog.

Rassel ['rasəl] f (pl -n) rattle. **rasseln** v rattle, clatter.

Rassen‖diskriminierung f racial discrimination. **–haß** m racial hatred. **–integration** f racial integration. **–kreuzung** f cross-breeding. **–trennung** f racial segregation.

rassig ['rasiç] adj purebred; (schwungvoll) racy.

rassisch ['rasiʃ] adj racial. **Rassismus** m racialism, (US) racism, **rassistisch** adj racialist, (US) racist.

Rast [rast] f (pl -en) rest; (Pause) halt, break. **rasten** v rest. **rastlos** adj restless; (unermüdlich) unwearying. **Raststätte** f (motorway) service area.

Rasur [razuːr] f (pl -en) (Radieren) erasure; (Rasieren) shave.

Rat [raːt] 1 m (unz.) advice. 2 (pl Räte) (Versammlung) council; (Beamter) councillor. **um Rat fragen** ask for advice. **sich Rat holen bei** consult. **Rat wissen** know what has to be done.

Rate [raːtə] f (pl -en) instalment, payment.

*raten ['raːtən] v advise; (mutmaßen) guess.

Ratenkauf ['raːtənkauf] m hire purchase. **ratenweise** adv by instalments.

Rat‖geber(in) adviser, counsellor. **–haus** neut town hall.

ratifizieren [ratifi'tsiːrən] v ratify. **Ratifizierung** f ratification.

Ration [ra'tsioːn] f (pl -en) ration.

rationalisieren [ratsionali'ziːrən] v rationalize. **Rationalisierung** f rationalization. **rationell** adj rational.

rationieren [ratsio'niːrən] v ration.

rat‖los ['raːtloːs] adj helpless, perplexed. **–sam** adj advisable; (nützlich) useful; (förderlich) expedient. **Ratschlag** m (piece of) advice. **ratschlagen** v deliberate, consult together.

Rätsel ['rɛːtsəl] neut (pl -) puzzle, riddle; (Geheimnis) mystery. **rätselhaft** adj puzzling; mysterious.

Rats‖herr ['raːtshɛr] m (town) councillor. **–keller** m town-hall restaurant. **–versammlung** f council meeting.

Ratte ['ratə] f (pl -n) rat.

Raub [raup] m robbery; (Beute) loot. **–anfall** m (armed) raid. **rauben** v rob; (Person) abduct; (plündern) plunder.

Räuber ['rɔybər] m (pl -) robber.

raubgierig ['raupɡiːriç] adj rapacious. **Raub‖tier** m beast of prey. **–vogel** m bird of prey.

Rauch [raux] m smoke. **–rauchen** v smoke. **Rauchen** neut smoking. **Raucher** m (pl -) smoker.

räuchern ['rɔyçərn] v cure, smoke.

Rauch‖fang m chimney. **–fleisch** neut smoked meat. **rauch‖frei** adj smokeless. **–ig** adj smokey.

'rauf [rauf] V herauf.

Raufbold ['raufbɔlt] f (pl -e) ruffian, rowdy. **raufen** v (Haare) tear out. **sich raufen mit** brawl with. **Rauferei** f (pl -en) fight, brawl. **raufustig** adj quarrelsome.

rauh [rau] adj rough; (grob) coarse; (Klima) inclement. **Rauheit** f roughness; coarseness; harshness.

Raum [raum] 1 m (unz.) room, space. 2 m (pl Räume) room; (Gebiet) area.

räumen ['rɔymən] v evacuate, remove; (Zimmer) vacate.

Raum‖fahrt f space travel. **–inhalt** m volume, capacity.

räumlich ['rɔymliç] adj spatial, of space. **Raumschiff** ['raumʃif] neut space ship.

Räumung ['rɔymun] f (pl -en) evacuation, removal; (Gebiet) cleaning.

Raupe [raupə] f (pl -n) caterpillar. **–nkette** f caterpillar track.

'raus [raus] V heraus.

Rausch [rauʃ] m (pl Räusche) intoxication.

rauschen ['rauʃən] v (Blätter) rustle; (Bach) babble, murmur.

Rauschgift ['rauʃɡift] neut drug, narcotic. **–sucht** f drug addiction. **–süchtige(r)** (drug) addict.

Reagenzglas [rea'ɡɛntsɡlaːs] neut test tube.

reagieren [rea'ɡiːrən] v react.

Reaktion [reaktsi'oːn] f (pl -en) reaction. **reaktionär** adj reactionary.

real [re'aːl] adj real. **–isieren** v realize. **Real‖ismus** m realism. **–ist** m (pl -en) realist. **realistisch** adj realistic.

Rebe ['reɪbə] *f* (*pl* -n) vine.
Rebell [re'bɛl] *m* (*pl* -en) rebel. **rebellieren**
v rebel. **Rebellion** *f* (*pl* -en) rebellion.
rebellisch *adj* rebellious.
Rebhuhn ['rɛphuːn] *neut* partridge.
Rebstock ['reɪpʃtɔk] *m* vine.
rechen ['rɛçən] *v* rake. **Rechen** *m* (*pl* -)
rake.
Rechen‖fehler *m* miscalculation. **–kunst**
f arithmetic. **–maschine** *f* calculating
machine. **–schaft** *f* (*unz.*) account.
rechnen ['rɛçnən] *v* calculate. **rechnen auf**
count on. **rechnen mit** reckon with.
Rechnen *neut* arithmetic. **Rechner** *m* calculator **Rechnung** *f* calculation; (*Waren*)
invoice; (*Gaststätte*) bill.
Rechnungs‖abschluß *m* balancing of
accounts. **–führer** *m* accountant, book-
keeper. **–prüfer** *m* auditor. **–wesen** *neut*
accountancy, accounting.
recht [rɛçt] *adj* right. *adv* (*sehr*) quite,
very *mir ist das recht* that suits me. **recht
haben** be (in the) right. **ganz recht!** just
so! **Recht** *neut* (*pl* -e) right; (*Gesetze*)
law. **–e** *f* right (side), right-hand side;
(*Pol*) the Right. **–eck** *neut* rectangle.
Rechtfertigung *f* justification.
recht‖fertigen *v* justify. **–gläubig** *adj*
orthodox. **Rechthaber** *m* (*pl* -) dogmatic
person, (*umg.*) know all. **recht‖haberisch**
adj dogmatic, obstinate. **–lich** *adj* legal,
of law; (*ehrlich*) honest, just. **–mäßig** *adj*
legal, lawful.
rechts [rɛçts] *adv* on *or* to(wards) the
right.
Rechtsanwalt *m* lawyer.
Rechtschreibung *f* spelling.
Rechts‖fall *m* law suit, case. **–gleichheit**
f equality before the law. **–händer** *m*
right-handed person, right-hander.
rechts‖händig *adj* right-handed. **–kräftig**
adj legally binding, legal.
Rechtsprechung *f* (*pl* -en) judicial decision, verdict; (*Gerichtsbarkeit*) jurisdiction.
rechtsradikal *adj* extreme right-wing.
Rechts‖radikale(r) *m* right-wing radical.
–spruch *m* (*Urteil*) verdict, judgment;
(*Strafe*) sentence. **–steuerung** *f* right-
hand drive. **–streit** *m* law suit. **rechtswidrig** *adj* illegal.
recht‖winklig *adj* right-angled. **–zeitig**
adj timely, opportune; *adv* in (good)
time.

recken ['rɛkən] *v* stretch.
Redakt‖eur [redak'tœɪr] *m* (*pl* -) editor.
–ion *f* editing; (*Arbeitskräfte*) editorial
staff.
Rede ['reɪdə] *f* (*pl* -n) speech, talk.
redefertig *adj* fluent, eloquent.
Rede‖freiheit *f* freedom of speech.
–kunst *f* rhetoric.
reden ['reɪdən] *v* speak, talk. **offen reden**
speak out. **mit sich reden lassen** be open
to persuasion, listen to reason. **Reden**
neut speech, talking. **–sart** *f* expression,
idiom. **Redewendung** *f* turn of speech,
idiom.
redigieren [redi'giːrən] *v* edit.
redlich ['reɪdliç] *adj* honest, upright, just.
Redlichkeit *f* honesty.
Redner ['reɪdnər] *m* (*pl* -) speaker, orator.
reduzieren [redu'tsiːrən] *v* reduce,
decrease, **sich reduzieren** diminish, be
reduced.
Reeder ['reɪdər] *m* (*pl* -) shipowner.
reell [re'ɛl] *adj* respectable, honest, reliable.
Referat [refe'raɪt] *neut* (*pl* -e) lecture,
talk; (*Gutachten*) report, review. **Referent**
m lecturer, speaker; (*Fachmann*) expert
adviser, reviewer.
reflektieren [reflɛk'tiːrən] *v* reflect.
Reflex [re'flɛks] *m* (*pl* -e) reflex.
–bewegung *f* reflex action.
Reform [re'fɔrm] *f* (*pl* -en) reform. **–ation**
f reformation. **–er** *m* (*pl* -) reformer.
–haus *neut* health-food shop, **reformier-
en** *v* reform.
Regal [re'gaɪl] *neut* (*pl* -e) (book)shelf.
rege ['reɪgə] *adj* active, lively.
Regel ['reɪgəl] *f* (*pl* -n) rule. **regel‖los** *adj*
irregular (*unordentlich*) chaotic. **–mäßig**
adj regular. **regelmäßigkeit** *f* regularity.
regeln *v* regulate, arrange. **Regelung** *f*
regulation, arrangement. **regelwidrig** *adj*
against the rule(s). **Regelwidrigkeit** *f*
irregularity; (*Sport*) foul.
Regen ['reɪgən] *m* rain. **–bogen** *m* rainbow. **–fall** *m* rainfall. **–mantel** *m* raincoat. **–tropfen** *m* raindrop. **–wetter** *neut*
rainy weather. **–wurm** *m* earthworm.
–zeit *f* rainy season, rains *pl*.
Regie [re'ʒiː] *f* (*pl* -n) (*Theater, Film*)
direction; (*Verwaltung*) administration,
management.
regieren [re'giːrən] *v* rule, govern.
Regierung *f* government.

Regiment [regi'mɛnt] *neut* (*pl* -er) regiment.

Regisseur [reʒi'sœːr] *m* (*pl* -e) (theatre *or* film) director.

Register [re'gistər] *neut* (*pl* -) register; (*Buch*) index. **registrieren** *v* register. **Registrierkasse** *f* cash register.

Regler ['reiglər] *m* (*pl* -) regulator.

regnen ['reignən] *v* rain. **regnerisch** *adj* rainy.

regulieren [regu'liːrən] *v* regulate.

Regung ['reiguŋ] *f* (*pl* -en) motion; (*Gefühle*) stirring, emotion; (*Antrieb*) impulse.

Reh [rei] *neut* (*pl* -e) roe deer. −**bock** *m* roebuck. **rehfarben** *adj* fawn. **Reh||fleisch** *neut* venison. −**kalb** *neut* fawn. −**ziege** *f* doe.

***reiben** ['raibən] *v* rub; (*Käse, usw.*) grate. **Reibung** *f* rubbing; (*fig, Tech*) friction; (*Käse*) grating.

reich [raiç] *adj* rich.

Reich [raiç] *neut* (*pl* -e) empire; (*fig*) realm; (*Tier-, Pflanzen*) kingdom.

reichen ['raiçən] *v* reach; (*überreichen*) pass, hand; (*anbieten*) offer; (*genügen*) be enough.

reich||haltig *adj* copious; (*Programm*) full. −**lich** *adj* plentiful, ample.

Reichs||adler *m* (German) imperial eagle. −**tag** *m* (German) Imperial Parliament (1871 − 1934).

Reichtum ['raiçtuːm] *m* (*pl* **Reichtümer**) wealth, riches *pl*; (*Fülle*) abundance.

Reichweite ['raiçvaitə] *f* range.

reif [raif] *adj* (*Frucht*) ripe; (*Person*) mature.

Reif [raif] *m* hoarfrost.

Reife ['raifə] *f* (*Frucht*) ripeness; (*Person*) maturity. **reifen** *v* mature.

Reifen ['raifən] *m* (*pl* -) ring, hoop; (*Mot*) tyre. −**druck** *m* tyre pressure.

Reihe ['raiə] *f* (*pl* -n) row; (*Satz*) series, set. *ich bin an der Reihe* it is my turn. **eine ganze Reihe** (**von**) a lot (of), a whole series (of). **reihen** *v* line up, put in a row; (*Perlen*) string; (*Stoff*) gather; (*heften*) tack. **Reihenfolge** *f* order, sequence.

Reiher ['raiər] *m* (*pl* -) heron.

Reim [raim] *m* (*pl* -e) rhyme. **reimen** *v* rhyme. **sich reimen** make sense.

rein [rain] *adj* pure; (*sauber*) clean; (*vollkommen*) perfect; (*Komm*) net. **ins Reine bringen** clear up, settle. *adv* completely. **die reine Wahrheit** the plain truth.

***rein** [rain] *V* **herein**.

Reinemachen ['rainəmaxən] *neut* cleaning. **Reinheit** *f* purity; cleanness, cleanliness. **reinigen** *v* clean; (*fig*) purify, cleanse. **Reinigung** *f* cleaning; purification. **chemische Reinigung** *f* dry cleaning. **rein||lich** *adj* clean, neat, tidy. −**rassig** *adj* purebred; (*Pferd*) thoroughbred.

Reis [rais] *m* rice.

Reise ['raizə] *f* (*pl* -n) trip, journey; (*See*) voyage. −**büro** *neut* travel agency. −**leiter(in)** courier. **reisen** *v* travel. −**d** *adj* itinerant, travelling. **Reisende(r)** traveller. **Reise||paß** *m* passport. −**tasche** *f* travelling bag. −**scheck** *m* traveller's cheque.

Reißbrett ['raisbrɛt] *neut* drawing board. **reißen** *v* tear, rip; (*zerren*) pull. **sich reißen um** fight for. **reißend** *adj* rapid; (*Schmerz*) sharp, shooting. **Reiß||kohle** *f* charcoal. −**verschluß** *m* zip, zipper.

***reiten** ['raitən] *v* ride. **Reit||en** *neut* riding. −**er** *m* rider, horseman. −**erin** *f* rider, horsewoman. −**kunst** *f* horsemanship, equitation.

Reiz [raits] *m* (*pl* -e) charm, attractiveness; (*Erregung*) stimulation. **reiz||bar** *adj* irritable. −**en** *v* excite, stimulate; (*anziehen*) attract, charm; (*zornig machen*) irritate. −**end** *adj* charming, enchanting.

Reklame [re'klaːmə] *f* (*pl* -n) advertising, publicity; (*einzelne*) advertisement. **Reklame machen für** promote, advertise.

Rekord [re'kɔrt] *m* (*pl* -e) record.

Rekrut [re'kruːt] *m* (*pl* -en) recruit. **rekrutieren** *v* recruit.

Rektor [re'ktor] *m* (*pl* -en) (*Universität*) vice-chancellor; (*andere Schulen*) principal, head.

relativ [rela'tiːf] *adj* relative. **Relativität** *f* relativity.

Relief [rə'ljɛf] *neut* (*pl* -s) (*Kunst*) relief.

Religion [religi'oːn] *f* (*pl* -en) religion. −**sbekenntnis** *neut* confession of faith. **religiös** *adj* religious.

Ren [rɛn] *neut* (*pl* -e) reindeer.

Rennbahn ['rɛnbain] *f* racecourse. **rennen** *v* run; (*Sport*) race. **Renn||en** *neut* running; race. −**pferd** *neut* racehorse. −**wagen** *m* racing car.

renovieren [reno'viːrən] *v* renovate.

rentabel [rɛn'taɪbəl] *adj* profitable.
Rentabilität *f* profitability. **Rente** *f*
(*Alters-*) pension; (*Versicherung*) annui-
ty. **rentieren** *v* **sich rentieren** be profitable. **Rentner** *m* (*pl* -) **Rentnerin** *f* (*pl*
-nen) pensioner.
Reparatur [repara'tuːr] *f* (*pl* -en) repair.
–**werkstatt** *f* repair shop. **reparieren** *v*
repair.
Report [re'pɔrt] *m* (*pl* -e) report. –**age** *f*
(*pl* -n) (eye-witness) report. –**er** *m* (*pl* -)
reporter.
Repressalien [repre'saɪliən] *pl* reprisals.
Reproduktion [reproduk'tsioɪn] *f* (*pl* -en)
reproduction. **reproduzieren** *v* reproduce.
Reptil [rep'tiɪl] *neut* (*pl* -ien) reptile.
Republik [re'publik] *f* (*pl* -en) republic.
–**aner** *m* (*pl* -) republican. **republikanisch**
adj republican.
Reserve [re'zɛrvə] *f* (*pl* -n) reserve. –**rad**
neut spare wheel. **reservier**∥**en** *v* reserve,
book. –**t** *adj* reserved.
Residenz [rezi'dɛnts] *f* (*pl* -en) residence.
Resonanz [rezo'nants] *f* (*pl* -en)
resonance.
Respekt [re'spɛkt] *m* respect.
respekt∥**abel** *adj* respectable. –**ieren** *v*
respect. –**los** *adj* disrespectful. –**voll** *adj*
respectful.
Rest [rɛst] *m* (*pl* -e) remainder, rest.
Restaurant [resto'rãː] *neut* (*pl* -s) restaurant.
Restbetrag *m* balance, remainder.
restlich *adj* remaining.
Resultat [rezul'taɪt] *neut* (*pl* -e) result.
retablieren [reta'bliːrən] *v* re-establish.
Retorte [re'tɔrtə] *f* (*pl* -n) retort.
retten ['rɛtən] *v* save. **Retter** *m* (*pl* -) rescuer; (*Rel*) Saviour. **Rettung** *f* (*pl* -en)
rescue, deliverance. **Rettungs**∥**boot** *neut*
lifeboat. –**gürtel** *m* lifebelt.
Reue ['rɔyə] *f* remorse, regret. **reuen** *v*
regret. *es reut mich, daß ich es getan habe*
I regret doing that, I am sorry I did that.
Revanche [re'vãːʃə] *f* (*pl* -n) revenge, vengeance. **sich revanchieren** *v* take one's
revenge.
Revers[1] [re'vɛrs] *m* (*pl* -e) (*Rückseite*)
reverse, back.
Revers[2] [re'vɛːr] *m or neut* (*pl* -) (*Jacke*)
lapel.
Revers[3] [re'vɛrs] *m* (*pl* -e) written undertaking, bond.
reversibel [revɛr'siɪbəl] *adj* (*Med, Chem*)
reversible.

revidieren [revi'diːrən] *v* revise.
Revier [re'viɪər] *neut* (*pl* -e) district;
(*Polizei*) beat; (*Wache*) station.
Revis∥**ion** [revizi'oɪn] *f* (*pl* -en) revision,
(*Jur*) appeal; (*Komm*) auditing. –**or** *m*
auditor.
Revolte [re'vɔltə] *f* (*pl* -n) revolt, insurrec-
tion.
Revolution [revolutsi'oɪn] *f* (*pl* -en) revo-
lution. **revolutionär** *adj* revolutionary.
Revolutionär *m* (*pl* -e) revolutionary.
revolutionieren *v* revolutionize.
Revolver [re'vɔlvər] *m* (*pl* -) revolver.
rezensieren [retsɛn'ziːrən] *v* review.
Rezept [re'tsɛpt] *neut* (*pl* -e) recipe;
(*Med*) prescription.
Rhabarber [ra'barbər] *m* rhubarb.
Rhapsodie [rapso'diɪ] *f* (*pl* -n) rhapsody.
Rhein [raɪn] *m* Rhine. –**hessen** *neut*
Rhenish Hesse. **rheinisch** *adj* Rhine,
Rhenish. **Rheinland** *neut* Rhineland. –**-**
Pfalz *f* Rhineland-Palatinate. **Rheinwein**
m hock, Rhine wine.
rhetorisch [re'toɪriʃ] *adj* rhetorical.
Rheumatismus [rɔyma'tizmus] *m* (*pl*
Rheumatismen) rheumatism.
Rhinozeros [ri'noɪtserɔs] *neut* (*pl* -se) rhinoceros.
rhythmisch ['rytmiʃ] *adj* rhythmic(al).
Rhythmus *m* (*pl* **Rhythmen**) rhythm.
richten ['riçtən] *v* (*zurechtmachen*)
arrange, prepare; (*einstellen*) adjust, set;
(*reparieren*) repair; (*Frage, Brief*)
address; (*Gewehr*) aim; (*Jur*) judge. **sich**
richten an address oneself to. **sich richten**
nach follow. **Richter** *m* (*pl* -) judge.
richtig ['riçtiç] *adj* correct, right. *ein rich-
tiger Berliner* a real Berliner. **Richtigkeit**
f correctness, rightness. **richtigstellen** *v*
correct, set right.
Richt∥**linie** *f* guideline. –**preis** *m* recommended price.
Richtung [riçtuŋ] *f* (*pl* -en) direction;
(*Neigung*) trend, tendency.
Richtweg ['riçtvɛk] *m* short cut.
***riechen** ['riːçən] *v* smell. **riechen nach**
smell of. **gut/übel riechen** smell
good/bad.
Riegel ['riːgəl] *m* (*pl* -) bolt, bar; (*Seife,
Schokolade*) bar. **riegeln** *v* bolt, bar.
Riemen ['riːmən] *m* (*pl* -) strap, belt;
(*Gürtel*) belt.
Riese ['riːzə] *m* (*pl* -n) giant. **Riesen-** *adj*
colossal, huge. **Riesenerfolg haben** be a
great success, (*umg.*) be a smash hit.

riesengroß or **riesig** adj gigantic, huge.
Riesin f (pl -nen) giantess.
Riff [rɪf] neut (pl -e) reef.
Rille ['rɪlə] f (pl -n) groove; (Furche) furrow.
Rind [rɪnt] neut (pl -er) (Ochse) ox; (Kuh) cow.
Rinde ['rɪndə] f (pl -n) (Baum) bark; (Käse) rind; (Brot) crust.
Rind‖erbraten m roast beef. **–fleisch** neut beef. **–vieh** neut cattle.
Ring [rɪŋ] m (pl -e) ring; (Straße) ring road; (Komm) combine, cartel; (Kettenglied) link. **–elchen** neut (pl -) ringlet.
*ringen ['rɪŋən] v wrestle; (Hände) wring. **ringen um** struggle for. **Ringen** neut struggle, battle.
Ringfinger m ring finger. **ringförmig** adj ring-shaped.
Ringkampf m wrestling (match).
rings [rɪŋs] adv around. **–herum** adv all around.
Ringstraße f ring road.
Rinne ['rɪnə] f (pl -n) channel, groove; (Dach-) gutter.
Rippchen ['rɪpçən] neut (pl -) cutlet, chop. **Rippe** f (pl -n) rib.
Risiko ['riːziko] neut (pl -s or Risiken) risk. **risk‖ant** adj risky. **–ieren** v risk.
Riß [rɪs] m (pl Risse) (Stoff, Haut) tear; (Mauer) crack; (fig) breach, rift; (Zeichnung) technical drawing, plan.
rissig ['rɪsɪç] adj cracked; (Haut) chapped.
Ritt [rɪt] m (pl -e) ride.
Ritter ['rɪtər] m (pl -) knight. **ritterlich** adj chivalrous. **Ritterlichkeit** f chivalry.
rittlings ['rɪtlɪŋs] adv astride.
rituell [ritu'ɛl] adj ritual. **Ritus** m (pl Riten) rite.
Ritz [rɪts] m (pl -e) or **Ritze** f (pl -n) crack; (Schramme) scratch.
Robbe ['rɔbə] f (pl -n) seal.
Roboter ['rɔbotər] m (pl -) robot.
Rock [rɔk] m (pl Röcke) (Frauen) skirt; (Obergewand) cloak; (Jacke) jacket, coat.
Rodel ['roːdəl] m (pl -) toboggan. **rodeln** v toboggan.
roden ['roːdən] v clear (land). **Rodung** f (pl -en) cleared land.
Rogen ['roːgən] m (pl -) (fish) roe.
Roggen ['rɔgən] m rye. **–brot** neut ryebread.
roh [roː] adj raw; (grausam) cruel, brutal; (Stein, Person) rough. **rohe Gewalt** brute force. **Roheit** f rawness; brutality; rough-

ness. **Roh‖gewicht** neut gross weight. **–öl** neut crude oil.
Rohr [roːr] neut (pl -e) tube, pipe; (Gewehr) barrel; (Bot) seed.
Röhre ['røːrə] f (pl -n) tube, pipe; (Radio) valve; (Leitung) conduit, duct.
Rohr‖leitung f pipeline. **–leitungen** pl pipes, plumbing sing. **–stock** m cane, bamboo. **–stuhl** m cane chair. **–zucker** m cane sugar.
Rohstoff m raw material.
Rolladen ['rɔlaːdən] m (pl - or **Rolläden**) rolling shutter.
Rollbahn f runway.
Rolle ['rɔlə] f (pl -n) roll; (Theater, Film) role; (Tech) pulley. **eine Rolle spielen** play a part. **keine Rolle spielen** make no difference, not matter.
rollen ['rɔlən] v roll; (Flugzeug) taxi.
Roll‖mops m pickled herring. **–schuh** m roller skate. **–schuhlaufen** neut roller-skating. **–stuhl** m wheelchair. **–treppe** f escalator. **–tür** f sliding door.
Rom [roːm] neut Rome.
Roman [ro'maːn] m (pl -e) novel.
Romantik [ro'mantik] f Romanticism. **–er** m (pl -) romantic. **romantisch** adj romantic.
Römer ['røːmər] m (pl -) Roman. **römisch** adj Roman. **römisch-katholisch** adj Roman Catholic.
röntgen [ˈrœntgən] v x-ray. **Röntgen‖behandlung** f radiation therapy. **–bild** neut x-ray (photograph) **–strahlen** pl x-rays.
rosa ['roːza] adj pink, rose.
Rose ['roːzə] f (pl -n) rose. **Rosen‖busch** m rose bush. **–kohl** m Brussels sprouts pl. **–kranz** m rose garland; (Rel) rosary.
Rosine [roˈziːnə] f (pl -n) raisin.
Rosmarin [rozmaˈriːn] m rosemary.
Roß [rɔs] neut (pl Rosse) steed, horse. **–kastanie** f horse chestnut.
Rost[1] [rɔst] m (pl -e) grate; (Kochen) grill.
Rost[2] m rust.
rost‖beständig adj rustproof. **–braun** adj rust(-brown).
Röstbrot ['rœstbroːt] neut toast.
rosten ['rɔstən] v rust.
rösten ['rœstən] v roast; (Brot) toast.
rot [roːt] adj red. **Rot** neut red.
Röte ['røːtə] f red(ness).
Röteln ['røːtəln] pl German measles, rubella.

rot‖glühend adj red-hot. **–haarig** adj red-haired. **Rot‖käppchen** neut Little Red Riding Hood. **–kehlchen** neut robin.

rötlich ['rœtlɪç] adj reddish.

Rotte ['rɔtə] f (pl -n) gang, band; (Tiere) pack. **sich rotten** v band together, gang up.

Roulade [ru'laɪdə] f (pl -n) rolled meat; (Musik) trill.

Rübe ['ryɪbə] f (pl -n) (Bot) rape. **weiße/gelbe/rote Rübe** turnip/carrot/beetroot.

Rubin [ru'biɪn] m (pl -e) ruby.

Rubrik ['ruɪbrɪk] f (pl -en) (Titel) title, heading; (Spalte) column; (fig) category.

ruchbar ['ruɪxbaɪr] adj notorious.

Ruck [ruk] m (pl -e) jolt, jerk, start.

Rück‖ansicht f rear view. **–blende** f flashback. **–blick** m glance back; (fig) retrospect.

rücken ['rykən] v move, shift; (Platz machen) move up, shift up.

Rücken ['rykən] m (pl -) back. **–lehne** f back (of a chair). **–mark** neut spinal cord. **–schmerzen** pl backache sing. **–schwimmen** neut backstroke.

Rück‖erstattung f return; (Geld) repayment. **–fahrkarte** f return ticket. **–fahrt** f return journey. **–gabe** f return, restoration. **–gang** m decline, retrogression. **rückgängig** adj retrograde. **rückgängig machen** cancel, annul. **Rück‖grat** neut backbone. **–griff** m recourse. **–halt** m support. **–handschlag** m (Tennis) backhand (stroke). **–kehr** f return. **–licht** neut rear light.

Rucksack ['rukzak] m rucksack, pack.

Rück‖schlag m set-back, reverse. **–schritt** m retrogression, relapse. **–seite** f reverse (side), back.

Rücksicht f consideration, regard. **Rücksicht nehmen auf** take into consideration; (Person) show consideration to. **mit Rücksicht auf** with respect to. **Rücksichtnahme** f consideration, regard. **rücksichtslos** adj inconsiderate (hart) ruthless. **Rücksichtslosigkeit** f lack of consideration; ruthlessness.

Rück‖sitz m back seat. **–spiegel** m rearview mirror. **–spiel** neut return match.

Rückstand m rest, remainder. **im Rückstand** in arrears. **rückständig** adj in arrears; (altmodisch) old-fashioned, backward.

Rücktritt m resignation; (in den Ruhestand) retirement.

rückwärts adv back(wards). **–gehen** v decline, retrogress.

Rück‖wirkung f reaction, repercussion. **–zug** m retreat. **–zahlung** f repayment, reimbursement.

Rudel ['ruːdəl] neut (pl -) (Schar) troop; (Hunde) pack; (Rehe, Schafe) herd.

Ruder ['ruːdər] neut (pl -) oar; (Steuer) rudder. **–boot** neut rowing boat. **rudern** v row. **Rudersport** m rowing.

Ruf [ruːf] m (pl -e) call, shout; (Tier) cry; (Vogel) call; (Ruhm) reputation, good name; (Aufforderung) summons. **rufen** v call, shout, cry. **Rufnummer** f telephone number.

Rüge ['ryːgə] f (pl -n) rebuke, reprimand. **rügen** v rebuke, reprimand.

Ruhe ['ruːə] f quiet, stillness; (Erholung) rest; (Gefaßtsein) composure, calm. **in Ruhe lassen** leave alone. **zur Ruhe gehen** go to bed, ruhelos adj restless. **Ruhelosigkeit** f restlessness. **ruhen** v rest; (schlafen) sleep; (begründet sein) be based. **–d** adj resting; (Tech) latent. **Ruhe‖pause** f break, rest period. **–platz** m resting place. **–stand** m retirement. **–stätte** f resting place. **–störung** f breach of the peace. **–tag** m day of rest.

ruhig ['ruːɪç] adj still, quiet; (gefaßt) calm, composed.

Ruhm [ruːm] m fame, glory. **rühmen** ['ryːmən] v praise. **sich rühmen** boast. **rühmlich** adj glorious.

Ruhr [ruːr] f dysentery.

Rührei ['ryːraɪ] neut scrambled egg(s). **rühren** v (bewegen) move; (vermischen) stir; (innerlich) move, affect. **sich rühren** stir, move. **rühr‖end** adj (fig) touching, moving. **–selig** adj sentimental. **Rührung** f (unz.) feeling, emotion.

Ruine [ru'iɪnə] f (pl -n) ruin. **ruinieren** v ruin.

Rülps [rylps] m (pl -e) belch. **rülpsen** v belch.

Rum [rum] m (pl -s) rum.

Rumäne [ru'mɛːnə] m (pl -n) Rumanian. **Rumänien** n Rumania. **Rumänin** f (pl -nen) Rumanian (woman). **rumänisch** adj Rumanian.

Rummel ['rumə]] m (unz.) (umg.) bustle, activity; (Lärm) hubbub, racket. **–platz** m fairground.

Rumpf

Rumpf [rumpf] *m* (*pl* **Rümpfe**) trunk, torso; (*Tier*) carcass; (*Schiff*) hull; (*Flugzeug*) fuselage.
rümpfen [rympfən] *v* turn up (one's nose).
rund [runt] *adj* round. *adv* about. **Rundblick** *m* panorama. **Runde** *f* (*pl* **-n**) circle; (*Boxen*) round; (*Rennen*) lap; (*Sport*) heat; (*Polizist*) beat. **runden** *v* round (off).
Rund‖fahrt *f* (circular) tour. **–frage** *f* questionnaire. **–funk** *m* radio; (*Übertragung*) broadcasting. **–funksendung** *f* radio programme. **–gang** *m* tour (of inspection); (*Spaziergang*) stroll. **–heit** *f* roundness.
rund‖heraus *adv* frankly, flatly. **–lich** *adj* rotund, plump.
Rund‖schau *f* panorama; (*Zeitschrift*) review. **–schreiben** *neut* circular. **–ung** *f* curve.
'runter ['runtər] *V* **herunter.**
Runzel ['runtsəl] *f* (*pl* **-n**) wrinkle. **runzelig** *adj* wrinkled. **runzeln** *v* wrinkle. **die Stirn runzeln** frown.
rupfen ['rupfən] *v* pluck.
Ruß [rus] *m* soot.
Russe ['rusə] *m* (*pl* **-n**) Russian.
rußig ['rusiç] *adj* sooty.
Russin ['rusin] *f* (*pl* **-nen**) Russian (woman). **russisch** *adj* Russian.
Rußland ['ruslant] *neut* Russia.
rüsten ['rystən] *v* prepare; (*Mil*) arm, prepare for war. **sich rüsten (auf)** get ready (for). **Rüstung** *f* armament; (*Kriegsvorbereitung*) arming; **Rüstungs‖fabrik** *f* armaments factory. **–wettbewerb** *m* arms race.
Rute ['rutə] *f* (*pl* **-n**) rod; (*Gerte*) switch; (*Anat*) penis.
Rutsch [rutʃ] *m* (*pl* **-e**) slide; (*Erde*) landslip. **rutsch‖en** *v* slip; (*gleiten*) slide. **–ig** *adj* slippery.
rütteln ['rytəln] *v* shake (up); (*beim Fahren*) jolt.

S

Saal [zaːl] *m* (*pl* **Säle**) hall, large room.
Saat [zaːt] *f* (*pl* **-en**) (*Samen*) seed; (*Säen*) sowing; (*grün*) green corn. **–korn** *neut* seed corn.

Sabbat ['zabat] *m* (*pl* **-e**) Sabbath.
Säbel ['zɛːbəl] *m* (*pl* **-**) sabre.
Sabotage [zabo'taːʒə] *f* sabotage. **sabotieren** *v* sabotage.
Saccharin [zaxa'riːn] *neut* saccharine.
Sachbearbeiter ['zaxbəarbaitər] *m* executive, official in charge. **Sache** *f* thing; (*Angelegenheit*) affair, matter; (*Tat*) fact. **Sachen** *pl* things, belongings; (*Kleider*) things, clothes. **Sach‖kundige(r)** expert. **–lage** *f* situation, state of affairs. **sachlich** *adj* businesslike, matter-of-fact; (*objektiv*) objective.
Sachse ['zaksə] *m* (*pl* **-n**) Saxon. **Sachsen** *neut* Saxony.
Sächsin ['zɛksin] *f* (*pl* **-nen**) Saxon (woman). **sächsisch** *adj* Saxon.
sacht(e) [zaxt(ə)] *adv* softly, gently.
Sack [zak] *m* (*pl* **Säcke**) sack, bag. **–gasse** *f* cul-de-sac, (*US*) dead end.
Sadismus [za'dizmus] *m* sadism. **Sadist** *m* (*pl* **-en**) sadist. **sadistisch** *adj* sadistic.
säen ['zɛːən] *v* sow.
Safari [za'faːri] *f* (*pl* **-s**) safari.
Safe [seɪf] *m* (*pl* **-s**) safe.
Saft [zaft] *m* (*pl* **Säfte**) juice; (*Baum*) sap; (*umg.: Strom, Benzin*) juice. **saftig** *adj* juicy; (*Witz*) spicy.
Sage ['zaːgə] *f* (*pl* **-n**) legend, fable.
Säge ['zɛːgə] *f* (*pl* **-n**) saw. **–maschine** *f* mechanical saw. **–mehl** *neut* sawdust.
*sagen ['zaːgən] *v* say; (*mitteilen*) tell. *was Sie nicht sagen!* you don't say! *sagen wir* let's say, suppose. *wie gesagt* as I said. *das sagt mir etwas* that means something to me.
sägen ['zɛːgən] *v* saw.
sagenhaft ['zaːgənhaft] *adj* legendary; (*umg.*) splendid, great.
Sahne ['zaːnə] *f* cream. **–kuchen** *m* cream cake. **sahnig** *adj* creamy.
Saison [zɛ'zɔ̃] *f* (*pl* **-s**) season. **stille Saison** off-season.
Saite ['zaitə] *f* (*pl* **-n**) string. **–ninstrument** *neut* stringed instrument.
Sakrament [zakra'mɛnt] *neut* (*pl* **-e**) sacrament.
Salat [za'laːt] *m* (*pl* **-e**) salad; (*Kopfsalat*) lettuce. **–kopf** *m* head of lettuce.
Salbe ['zalbə] *f* (*pl* **-n**) ointment, salve.
Salbei [zal'bai] *f or m* (*Bot*) sage.
salben ['zalbən] *v* anoint.
Saldo ['zaldo] *m* (*pl* **Salden**) (*Komm*) balance.

Salon [za'lõ] *m* (*pl* -e) drawing room.
salonfähig *adj* presentable (in society).
Salut [za'luːt] *m* (*pl* -e) salute. **salutieren** *v* salute.
Salve ['zalvə] *f* (*pl* -n) volley.
Salz [zalts] *neut* (*pl* -e) salt. **salzen** *v* salt. **Salzfaß** *neut* salt cellar. **salzig** *adj* salty.
Salz‖kartoffeln *pl* boiled potatoes. **–wasser** *neut* salt water.
Samen ['zaːmən] *m* (*pl* -) seed; (*Tiere*) sperm. **–erguß** *m* ejaculation. **–händler** *m* seed merchant. **–pflanze** *f* seedling. **–staub** *m* pollen.
Sämischleder ['zɛːmɪʃleɪdər] *neut* chamois (leather).
sammeln ['zaməln] *v* gather; (*Hobby*) collect. **Samm‖elplatz** *m* assembly point. **–ler** *m* collector. **–lung** *f* collection.
Samstag ['zamstaɪk] *m* Saturday. **samstags** *adv* on Saturdays.
samt [zamt] *prep* (together) with, including.
Samt [zamt] *m* (*pl* -e) velvet.
sämtlich ['zɛmtlɪç] *adj* complete, entire; (*alle*) all, (*Werke*) complete.
Sand [zant] *m* (*pl* -e) sand.
Sandale [zan'daːlə] *f* (*pl* -n) sandal.
Sandbank *f* sandbank. **sandfarben** *adj* sandy(-coloured). **Sand‖papier** *neut* sandpaper. **–stein** *m* sandstone.
sanft [zanft] *adj* gentle, soft. **Sanftheit** *f* gentleness, softness. **sanftmütig** *adj* gentle, mild.
Sänger ['zɛŋər] *m* (*pl* -), **Sängerin** *f* (*pl* -nen) singer.
sanieren [za'niːrən] *v* heal; (*Betrieb*) rationalize, make viable; (*Stadt, Viertel*) redevelop. **Sanierung** *f* (*Komm*) reorganization; (*Gebäude*) renovation.
sanitär [zani'tɛːr] *adj* sanitary, hygienic. **sanitäre Anlagen** *pl* sanitation *sing*.
Sankt [zaŋkt] *adj* Saint.
Sanktion [zaŋk'tsioːn] *f* (*pl* -en) sanction. **sanktionieren** *v* sanction.
Saphir ['zafiːr] *m* (*pl* -e) sapphire.
Sardelle [zar'dɛlə] *f* (*pl* -n) anchovy.
Sardine [zar'diːnə] *f* (*pl* -n) sardine.
Sarg [zark] *m* (*pl* Särge) coffin.
sarkastisch [zar'kastɪʃ] *adj* sarcastic.
Satan ['zaːtan] *m* (*pl* -e) Satan; (*böser Mensch*) devil, demon. **satanisch** *adj* satanic.
Satellit [zate'liːt] *m* (*pl* -en) satellite.
Satin [za'tɛ̃] *m* (*pl* -s) satin.

Satire [za'tiːrə] *f* (*pl* -n) satire. **Satiriker** *m* (*pl* -) satirist. **satirisch** *adj* satirical.
satt [zat] *adj* satisfied, satiated; (*Farbe*) deep, rich. **satt sein** have had enough; (*nach dem Essen*) be full. **satt haben** have had enough of, be tired of.
Sattel ['zatəl] *m* (*pl* Sättel) saddle. **satteln** *v* saddle. **Sattel‖schlepper** *m* (tractor for an) articulated truck. **–tasche** *f* saddlebag.
Satz [zats] *m* (*pl* Sätze) (*Sprung*) leap, jump; (*Gramm*) sentence; (*Sammlung, Math*) set; (*Musik*) movement; (*Bodensatz*) sediment; (*Wein*) dregs *pl*; (*Grundsatz*) principle; (*Geld*) price, rate; (*Druck*) composition, setting. **–lehre** *f* syntax.
Satzung ['zatsuŋ] *f* (*pl* -en) statute; (*Vorschrift*) rule. **satzungs‖gemäß** or **–mäßig** *adj* statutory.
Sau [zau] *f* (*pl* Säue) sow.
sauber ['zaubər] *adj* clean; (*hübsch*) pretty, nice; (*ordentlich*) tidy. **Sauberkeit** *f* cleanliness, niceness; tidiness.
säuberlich ['zɔybərlɪç] *adj* clean; (*ordentlich*) tidy; (*anständig*) proper.
saubermachen *v* clean (up).
sauer ['zauər] *adj* (*Geschmack*) sour; (*säurehältig*) acid. **Sauerbraten** *m* roast marinated beef.
Sauerei *f* (*pl* -en) (*Unanständigkeit*) smuttiness; (*Pfuscherei*) mess.
Sauerkraut ['zauərkraut] *neut* pickled cabbage, sauerkraut.
Sauerstoff *m* oxygen. **sauersüß** *adj* bittersweet; (*Speise*) sweet-and-sour.
***saufen** ['zaufən] *v* drink; (*umg.*) drink, booze.
Säufer ['zɔyfər] *m* (*pl* -) heavy drinker, boozer.
***saugen** ['zaugən] *v* suck; (*einziehen*) absorb. **Saugen** *neut* suction, sucking.
säugen ['zɔygən] *v* suckle, nurse. **Säug‖en** *neut* suckling, nursing. **–etier** *neut* mammal. **–ling** *m* baby.
Säule ['zɔylə] *f* (*pl* -n) column, pillar.
Saum [zaum] *m* (*pl* Säume) seam, hem; (*Rand*) border, margin.
säumen[1] ['zɔymən] *v* (*Kleid*) hem; (*allgemein*) edge; (*fig*) skirt, fringe.
säumen[2] *v* (*zögern*) delay, hesitate.
Säumnis ['zɔymnɪs] *f* (*pl* -se) or *neut* (*pl* -e) delay.
Saumpferd ['zaumpfert] *neut* packhorse.

Sauna ['zauna] *f* (*pl* -s) sauna.
Säure ['zɔyrə] *f* (*pl* -n) acid; sourness.
Sauregurkenzeit [zaurə'gurkəntsait] *f* silly season.
sausen ['zauzən] *v* (*eilen*) rush, dash, zoom; (*Wind*) howl, whistle.
Saxophon [zakso'foːn] *neut* (*pl* -e) saxophone.
schaben ['ʃaːbən] *v* scrape; (*Fleisch*) cut into strips.
schäbig ['ʃɛːbiç] *adj* shabby.
Schablone [ʃa'bloːnə] *f* (*pl* -n) stencil, pattern, model.
Schach [ʃax] *neut* (*Spiel*) chess; (*Warnruf*) check. **in Schach halten** keep in check. **Schachbrett** *neut* chessboard.
Schacherei [ʃaxə'rai] *f* haggling, bargaining.
Schachfigur *f* chessman.
Schacht [ʃaxt] *m* (*pl* -e) shaft.
Schachtel ['ʃaxtəl] *f* (*pl* -n) box.
schade ['ʃaːdə] *adv* a pity. *es ist schade* it's a pity, it's a shame. *schade, daß Sie ... what a pity that you ... . wie schade!* what a pity!
Schädel ['ʃɛːdəl] *m* (*pl* -) skull.
schaden ['ʃaːdən] *v* harm, injure, hurt. **Schaden** *m* damage; (*Verlust*) loss; (*körperlich*) injury, harm. **-ersatz** *m* compensation. **-freude** *f* malicious joy, gloating. **schadenfroh** *adj* malicious, gloating. **schadhaft** *adj* damaged.
schädigen ['ʃɛːdigən] *v* harm, damage; (*körperlich*) injure. **Schädigung** *f* damage; injury. **schädlich** *adj* dangerous, injurious.
Schaf [ʃaːf] *neut* (*pl* -e) sheep.
Schäfer ['ʃɛːfər] *m* (*pl* -) shepherd. **-hund** *m* sheepdog; (*deutscher*) Alsatian (dog). **-in** *f* (*pl* -nen) shepherdess.
Schaffell *neut* sheepskin, fleece.
***schaffen**[1] ['ʃafən] *v* (*hervorbringen, gestalten*) create.
schaffen[2] *v* (*bringen*) bring, convey; (*fertigbringen*) manage, accomplish; (*arbeiten*) work.
Schaffner ['ʃafnər] *m* (*pl* -) (*Zug*) guard; (*Bus*) conductor. **-in** *f* (*pl* -nen) guard; conductress.
Schaf‖**pelz** *m* sheepskin. **-stall** *m* sheepfold.
Schaft [ʃaft] *m* (*pl* **Schäfte**) shaft; (*Griff*) handle; (*Gewehr*) stock; (*Baum*) trunk.
Schale ['ʃaːlə] *f* (*pl* -n) (*Schüssel*) bowl,

basin; (*Ei, Nuß*) shell; (*Frucht, Gemüse*) peel, skin; (*fig*) cover(ing).
schälen ['ʃɛːlən] *v* shell; peel.
Schalk [ʃalk] *m* (*pl* -e) rogue, knave. **schalkhaft** *adj* roguish.
Schall [ʃal] *m* (*pl* -e) sound. **-dämpfer** *m* silencer. **schallen** *v* sound, resound; (*Glocke*) ring, peal. **Schall**‖**platte** *f* (gramophone) record. **-welle** *f* soundwave.
schalten ['ʃaltən] *v* switch; (*Mot*) change (gear). **Schalt**‖**er** *m* (*Bank, usw.*) counter, window; (*Elek*) switch. **-hebel** *m* control lever, switch; (*Mot*) gear lever. **-jahr** *neut* leap year. **-plan** *m* circuit diagram. **-ung** *f* wiring; (*Mot*) gear-change.
Scham [ʃaːm] *f* shame; (*Scheu*) modesty.
schämen ['ʃɛːmən] *v* **sich schämen** *v* be ashamed.
scham‖**haft** *adj* bashful, modest. **-los** *adj* shameless, immodest.
Schampoo [ʃam'puː] *neut* shampoo. **schampoonieren** *v* shampoo.
Schande ['ʃandə] *f* (*pl* -n) disgrace, shame.
schänden ['ʃɛndən] *v* disgrace; (*verderben*) spoil; (*entheiligen*) desecrate; (*Frau*) rape, violate.
Schandfleck ['ʃantflɛk] *m* blemish, stain.
schändlich ['ʃɛntliç] *adj* shameful, disgraceful.
Schandtat ['ʃanttaɪt] *f* misdeed, crime.
Schank ['ʃank] *m* (*pl* **Schänke**) bar.
Schanze ['ʃantsə] *f* (*pl* -n) fortification; (*Erdwall*) earthworks *pl*; (*Skilauf*) skijump.
Schar [ʃaːr] *f* (*pl* -en) troop, band; (*Gänse*) flock; (*Hunde*) pack. **sich scharen** *v* gather, congregate.
scharf [ʃarf] *adj* sharp; (*Gewürze*) spicy, hot.
Schärfe ['ʃɛrfə] *f* (*pl* -n) sharpness, edge; (*Ätzkraft*) acidity; (*Klarheit*) clarity. **schärfen** *v* sharpen.
Scharfschütze *m* marksman, sharpshooter. **scharfsichtig** *adj* sharpsighted. **Scharfsinn** *m* shrewdness. **scharfsinnig** *adj* shrewd.
Scharlachfieber ['ʃarlaxfiːbər] *neut* scarlet fever. **scharlachrot** *adj* scarlet.
Scharm [ʃarm] *m* charm. **scharmant** *adj* charming, delightful.
Scharnier ʃar'niːr] *neut* (*pl* -e) hinge.
scharren ['ʃarən] *v* scrape, scratch.

Schatten ['ʃatən] *m* (*pl* -) shadow; (*Dunkel*) shade. **in den Schatten stellen** overshadow. **Schattenbild** *neut* silhouette. **schatten‖haft** *adj* shadowy. **-ig** *adj* shaded.

Schatz [ʃats] *m* (*pl* Schätze) treasure; (*fig*) darling. **-amt** *neut* treasury.

schätzen ['ʃetsən] *v* value; (*ungefähr*) estimate. **-swert** *adj* valuable, estimable.

Schatz‖kammer *f* treasury. **-meister** *m* treasurer.

Schätzung ['ʃetsuŋ] *f* (*pl* -en) estimate; (*Hochschätzung*) esteem. **schätzungsweise** *adv* approximately; at a guess.

Schau [ʃau] *f* (*pl* -en) show; (*Ausstellung*) exhibition; (*Überblick*) survey, review. **zur Schau stellen** exhibit.

schaudern ['ʃaudərn] *v* shudder, shiver. **-haft** *adj* horrible.

schauen ['ʃauən] *v* look (at), observe.

Schauer ['ʃauər] *m* (*pl* -) (*Regen*) shower; (*Schrecken*) horror; (*Zittern*) thrill.

Schaufel ['ʃaufəl] *f* (*pl* -n) shovel; (*Tech*) blade.

Schaufenster *neut* shop window.

Schaukel ['ʃaukəl] *f* (*pl* -n) (child's) swing. **-pferd** *neut* rocking horse. **-stuhl** *m* rocking-chair.

Schaum [ʃaum] *m* (*pl* Schäume) foam; (*Seife*) lather.

schäumen ['ʃɔymən] *v* foam; (*Wein*) sparkle.

schaumig ['ʃaumiç] *adj* foamy.

Schauspiel *neut* play; drama; (*fig*) spectacle. **-er** *m* (*pl* -) actor. **-erin** *f* (*pl* -nen) actress. **-haus** *neut* theatre.

Scheck [ʃɛk] *m* (*pl* -s) check. **-buch** *neut* check book.

Scheibe ['ʃaibə] *f* (*pl* -n) disc; (*Brot, Wurst*) slice; (*Glas*) pane. **Scheiben‖bremse** *f* disc brake. **-wischer** *m* windshield wiper.

Scheide ['ʃaidə] *f* (*pl* -n) sheath; (*Anat*) vagina; (*Grenze*) limit. **scheiden** *v* separate; (*Ehepartner*) divorce. **sich scheiden** part, separate. **sich scheiden lassen** get a divorce. **Scheideweg** *m* crossroads.

Scheidung *f* separation; (*Ehe*) divorce.

Schein [ʃain] *m* (*pl* -e) (*Aussehen*) appearance; (*Licht*) light; (*Glanz*) shine; (*Geld*) bill (*US*); banknote; (*Bescheinigung*) certificate. **schein‖bar** apparent, ostensible. **-en** *v* (*aussehen*) appear, seem; (*leuchten*) shine. **-heilig** *adj* sanctimoni-

ous. **Schein‖heilige(r)** hypocrite. **-krankheit** *f* feigned sickness. **-werfer** *m* (*pl* -) searchlight; (*Reflektor*) reflector; (*Theater*) spotlight; (*Mot*) headlight.

Scheiße ['ʃaisə] *f* (*vulgär*) shit. **scheißen** *v* shit.

Scheitel ['ʃaitəl] *m* (*pl* -) top; (*Kopf*) crown, top of the head; (*Haar*) parting.

scheitern ['ʃaitərn] *v* fail, come to nought; (*Schiff*) be wrecked.

Schelle ['ʃɛlə] *f* (*pl* -n) small bell; (*Hand-*) handcuff.

Schellfisch ['ʃɛlfiʃ] *m* haddock.

Schelm [ʃɛlm] *m* (*pl* -e) rogue.

Schema ['ʃema] *neut* (*pl* -ta *or* Schemen) scheme; (*Muster*) pattern; (*Darstellung*) diagram.

Schenkel ['ʃɛŋkəl] *m* (*pl* -) thigh. **-knochen** *m* thigh-bone, femur.

schenken ['ʃɛŋkən] *v* give, present; (*Getränk*) pour (out). **Schenk‖er** *m* (*pl* -) donor, giver. **-ung** *f* donation.

Scherbe ['ʃɛrbə] *f* (*pl* -n) fragment.

Schere ['ʃeirə] *f* (*pl* -n) scissors *pl*; (*große*) shears *pl*; (*Krebs*) claw. **scheren** *v* (*Wolle*) shear; (*Haare*) cut; (*Hecke*) cut, trim; (*Rasen*) mow.

Scherz [ʃɛrts] *m* (*pl* -e) joke; (*Unterhaltung*) fun. **scherz‖en** *v* joke, have fun. **-haft** *adj* joking.

scheu [ʃɔy] *adj* shy.

Scheuche ['ʃɔyçə] *f* (*pl* -n) scarecrow.

scheuen ['ʃɔyən] *v* shy away from, avoid; (*Pferd*) shy; (*Mühe, usw.*) spare. **sich scheuen vor** be afraid of.

Scheuerbürste ['ʃɔyərbyrstə] *f* scrubbing brush. **scheuern** *v* scrub, scour.

Scheune ['ʃɔynə] *f* (*pl* -n) barn.

Scheusal ['ʃɔyzal] *neut* (*pl* -e) monster.

scheußlich ['ʃɔysliç] *adj* horrible, hideous. **Scheußlichkeit** *f* hideousness.

Schicht [ʃiçt] *f* (*pl* -en) layer; (*Arbeit*) shift; (*Gesellschaft*) class. **-arbeit** *f* shift work. **-holz** *neut* plywood. **-ung** *f* stratification; (*fig*) classification.

schick [ʃik] *adj* elegant, chic, smart.

schicken ['ʃikən] *v* send. **sich schicken** (*sich gehören*) suit, be becoming; (*sich entwickeln*) happen.

schicklich ['ʃikliç] *adj* becoming, fit, proper. **Schicklichkeit** *f* fitness, propriety.

Schicksal ['ʃikzal] *neut* (*pl* -e) fate, destiny. **-sschlag** *m* stroke of fate, blow.

Schiebedach ['ʃiːbədax] *neut* sliding roof; (*Mot*) sun-roof. **schieben** *v* push; (*Schuld*) pass on; (*Arbeit*) put off. **Schiebetür** *f* sliding door.

Schieds‖gericht ['ʃiːtsgərɪçt] *neut* arbitration court, tribunal. **–richter** *m* arbitrator; (*Sport*) referee, umpire. **–spruch** *m* arbitration, award.

schief [ʃiːf] *adj* slanting, sloping; (*fig*) wrong, amiss.

schiefgehen *v* go wrong *or* amiss.

schielen ['ʃiːlən] *v* squint. **Schielen** *neut* (*Med*) strabismus, squint.

Schienbein ['ʃiːnbain] *neut* shin(bone).

Schiene ['ʃiːnə] *f* (*pl* -n) rail; (*Med*) splint.

schießen ['ʃiːsən] *v* shoot. **Schieß‖en** *neut* shooting. **–erei** *f* gunfight.

Schiff [ʃɪf] *neut* (*pl* -e) ship; (*Kirche*) nave. **–ahrt** *f* navigation; (*Verkehr*) shipping. **–bau** *m* shipbuilding. **–bruch** *m* shipwreck. **–brüchig** *adj* shipwrecked. **Schiffs‖küche** *f* galley. **–raum** *m* hold; (*Inhalt*) tonnage. **–verkehr** *m* shipping. **–werft** *f* shipyard.

Schikane [ʃiˈkaːnə] *f* (*pl* -n) chicanery. **schikanieren** *v* make trouble for.

Schild¹ [ʃɪlt] *m* (*pl* -e) shield.

Schild² *neut* (*pl* -er) sign; (*Namen-*) name-plate; (*Flasche*) label; (*Mütze*) peak.

schildern ['ʃɪldərn] *v* depict, describe. **Schilderung** *f* depiction, description.

Schildkröte *f* turtle; (*Land*) tortoise.

Schilf [ʃɪlf] *neut* (*pl* -e) reed.

Schilling ['ʃɪlɪŋ] *m* (*pl* -e) (Austrian) Schilling.

Schimmel ['ʃɪməl] *m* (*pl* -) mildew, mould. **schimmel‖ig** *adj* mouldy. **–n** *v* become mouldy.

Schimmer ['ʃɪmər] *m* (*pl* -) glimmer, gleam. **schimmern** *v* gleam, shine.

Schimpanse [ʃɪmˈpanzə] *m* (*pl* -n) chimpanzee.

Schimpf [ʃɪmpf] *m* (*pl* -e) abuse, insult. **schimpfen** *v* swear, curse; (*umg.: tadeln*) curse, scold. **Schimpfwort** *neut* swearword.

schinden ['ʃɪndən] *v* (*ausnützen*) exploit. **sich schinden** work hard, slave.

Schinken ['ʃɪŋkən] *m* (*pl* -) ham.

Schippe ['ʃɪpə] *f* (*pl* -n) shovel; (*Karten*) spade(s).

Schirm [ʃɪrm] *m* (*pl* -e) (*Regen-*) umbrella; (*Lampen-*) shade; (*Bild-*) screen; (*Mütze*) peak; (*fig: Schutz*) protection. **schirmen** *v* protect, screen.

schizophren [ʃitsoˈfreɪn] *adj* schizophrenic. **Schizophrenie** *f* schizophrenia.

Schlacht [ʃlaxt] *f* (*pl* -en) battle. **schlachten** *v* slaughter.

Schlächter ['ʃlɛçtər] *m* (*pl* -) butcher.

Schlacht‖feld *neut* battlefield. **–hof** *m* slaughterhouse. **–schiff** *neut* battleship.

Schlaf [ʃlaːf] *m* sleep. **–anzug** *m* pyjamas *pl*. **schlafen** *v* sleep. **–d** *adj* sleeping; (*fig*) dormant. **Schlafenszeit** *f* bedtime.

Schläfer ['ʃlɛːfər] *m* (*pl* -) sleeper.

schlaff [ʃlaf] *adj* slack; (*fig*) lax; (*welk*) limp.

Schlaf‖losigkeit *f* sleeplessness, insomnia. **–mittel** *neut* sleeping pill.

schläfrig ['ʃlɛːfrɪç] *adj* sleepy.

Schlaf‖wagen *m* sleeping car. **–zimmer** *neut* bedroom.

Schlag [ʃlaːk] *m* (*pl* **Schläge**) blow, stroke; (*Elek*) shock; (*Med*) stroke; (*Art*) sort, kind. **schlagen** *v* hit, strike; (*besiegen*) beat, defeat; (*mit der Faust*) punch; (*Vögel*) warble, sing; (*Wurzel*) take root. **kurz und klein schlagen** smash to pieces. **Alarm schlagen** sound the alarm. **nach jemandem schlagen** take after someone. **Schlagen** *neut* striking, hitting. **schlagend** *adj* striking; (*fig*) impressive; (*entscheidend*) decisive.

Schlager *m* (*pl* -) (great) success, hit; (*Musik*) hit (song).

Schläger ['ʃlɛːɡər] *m* (*pl* -) (*Tennis*) racket; (*Golf*) club; (*Kochen*) beater; (*Raufbold*) rowdy.

schlagfertig ['ʃlaːkfɛrtɪç] *adj* quick-witted.

Schlag‖instrument *neut* percussion instrument. **–sahne** *f* whipped cream. **–wort** *neut* slogan. **–zeile** *f* headline. **–zeug** *neut* percussion (instruments) *pl*.

Schlamm [ʃlam] *m* (*pl* -e) mud. **schlammig** *adj* muddy.

Schlampe ['ʃlampə] *f* (*pl* -n) slut. **schlampig** *adj* slovenly.

Schlange ['ʃlaŋə] *f* (*pl* -n) snake; (*Reihe Menschen*) queue, (*US*) line. **Schlange stehen** *v* queue, (*US*) line up. **Schlangen‖gift** *neut* snake venom. **–leder** *neut* snakeskin.

schlank [ʃlaŋk] *adj* slender, slim. **Schlank‖heit** *f* slenderness, slimness. **–skur** *f* (reducing) diet.

schlapp [ʃlap] *adj* slack, limp.
schlau [ʃlau] *adj* cunning, sly, clever. **Schlauheit** *f* cunning, slyness.
Schlauch [ʃlaux] *m* (*pl* **Schläuche**) hose; (*Reifen*) inner tube.
schlecht [ʃlɛçt] *adj* bad; (*unwohl*) ill; (*Qualität*) poor, inferior; (*Luft*) stale, foul. **mir ist schlecht** I feel ill. **–gelaunt** *adj* bad-tempered. **Schlechtigkeit** *f* wickedness. **Schlechtheit** *f* badness.
schlechthin *adv* simply, plainly.
Schlegel [ʃleɪgəl] *m* (*pl* -) (wooden) mallet; (*Trommel*) drumstick.
*schleichen [ʃlaiçən] *v* creep; (*heimlich*) slink, sneak.
Schleier [ʃlaiər] *m* (*pl* -) veil.
Schleife [ʃlaifə] *f* (*pl* -n) loop, slip-knot; (*Band*) bow.
*schleifen¹ [ʃlaifən] *v* slide, glide, slip.
schleifen² *v* (*schleppen*) drag; (*Messer*) sharpen, grind; (*Edelstein*) cut.
Schleim [ʃlaim] *m* (*pl* -e) slime; (*Med*) mucus. **schleimig** *adj* slimy; mucous.
*schleißen [ʃlaisən] *v* slit; (*spalten*) split; (*reißen*) rip, tear.
schlendern [ʃlɛndərn] *v* saunter. **Schlendrian** *m* (*pl* -) (*umg.*) old routine.
Schleppboot [ʃlɛpboːt] *neut* tug(boat).
schleppen *v* drag, pull; (*tragen*) carry, lug. **sich schleppen** *v* drag oneself along.
Schlesien [ʃleːziən] *neut* Silesia.
Schleuder [ʃlɔydər] *f* (*pl* -n) sling, catapult; (*Wäsche*) spin-drier, spinner; (*Zentrifuge*) centrifuge. **–preis** *m* cut-price, give-away price. **schleudern** *v* sling, hurl; (*Mot*) skid; (*Wäsche*) spin-dry; (*Komm*) dump, sell off cheap.
schleunig [ʃlɔyniç] *adj* prompt, speedy.
Schleuse [ʃlɔyzə] *f* (*pl* -n) sluice; (*Kanal*) lock.
schlicht [ʃliçt] *adj* simple, plain; (*bescheiden*) modest. **–en** *v* (*glätten*) smooth; (*ebnen*) level; (*Streit*) settle. **Schlichtung** *f* (*pl* -en) settlement.
*schließen [ʃliːsən] *v* close, shut; (*mit dem Schlüssel*) lock; (*zum Schluß bringen*) close, end, conclude; (*folgern*) conclude, infer. **Schließfach** *neut* (*Bank*) safe-deposit box. **schließlich** *adv* finally, (at) last.
schlimm [ʃlim] *adj* bad. **schlimmstenfalls** *adv* at worst.
Schlinge [ʃliŋə] *f* (*pl* -n) noose, loop; (*Jagd, fig*) snare, trap.

*schlingen¹ [ʃliŋən] *v* wind; (*flechten*) twist; (*verknüpfen*) tie, knot.
*schlingen² *v* (*schlucken*) swallow; (*gierig essen*) devour, wolf.
Schlitten [ʃlitən] *m* (*pl* -) sledge. **Schlittschuh** *m* skate. **Schlittschuh laufen** skate.
Schlitz [ʃlits] *m* (*pl* -e) slit; (*Münzeinwurf*) slot; (*Hosen-*) fly.
Schloß [ʃlɔs] *neut* (*pl* **Schlösser**) lock; (*Burg*) castle.
Schlosser [ʃlɔsər] *m* (*pl* -) fitter, mechanic, locksmith.
Schlot [ʃloːt] *m* (*pl* -e) chimney.
schlott(e)rig [ʃɔt(ə)riç] *adj* (*wackelig*) wobbly, shaky; (*schlaff*) loose; (*kleider*) baggy.
Schluck [ʃluk] *m* (*pl* -e) sip, gulp, mouthful. **–auf** *m* hiccup. **schlucken** *v* swallow.
Schlund [ʃlunt] *m* (*pl* **Schlünde**) throat; (*geog*) abyss, gorge; (*fig*) gulf.
schlüpfen [ʃlypfən] *v* slip, slide. **Schlüpfer** *m* knickers *pl.* **schlüpfrig** *adj* slippery; (*fig*) lewd.
Schlupfwinkel [ʃlupfviŋkəl] *m* hiding place.
Schluß [ʃlus] *m* (*pl* **Schlüsse**) end, close; (*Folgerung*) inference, conclusion. **zum Schluß** finally. **Schluß machen** stop, finish.
Schlüssel [ʃlysəl] *m* (*pl* -) key; (*Musik*) clef; (*Tech*) spanner, (*US*) wrench. **–bein** *neut* collarbone. **–bund** *m* bunch of keys. **–loch** *neut* keyhole. **–ring** *m* keyring.
Schluß‖prüfung *f* final examination, finals *pl.* **–runde** *f* (*Sport*) final. **–verkauf** *m* end-of-season sale.
Schmach [ʃmax] *f* disgrace, dishonour.
schmächtig [ʃmɛçtiç] *adj* slim, slender.
schmackhaft [ʃmakhaft] *adj* appetizing, delicious.
schmal [ʃmaːl] *adj* narrow, thin, slender; (*fig*) scanty, poor.
Schmalz [ʃmalts] *neut* (*pl* -e) fat, grease, dripping; (*fig*) sentimentality.
schmarotzen [ʃmaˈrɔtsən] *v* (*umg.*) sponge, scrounge. **Schmarotzer** *m* (*Tier, Pflanze*) parasite; (*Person*) scrounger, parasite.
schmatzen [ʃmatsən] *v* smack one's lips, eat noisily; (*küssen*) give a smacking kiss.
schmecken [ʃmɛkən] *v* taste; (*gut*) taste good. **schmecken nach** taste of. (**wie**)

schmeckt es? do you like it? **es schmeckt (mir)** I like it, it's good.

Schmeichelei [ʃmaiçəˈlai] *f* (*pl* -en) flattery. **schmeicheln** *v* flatter. **Schmeichler** *m* (*pl* -) flatterer. **schmeichlerisch** *adj* flattering.

***schmeißen** [ˈʃmaisən] *v* throw, cast; (*umg.*) chuck; (*Schlagen*) strike, smash.

Schmelz [ʃmɛlts] *m* (*pl* -e) (*Email*) enamel; (*Glasur*) glaze; (*Stimme, Töne*) mellowness, sweetness. **schmelzen** *v* melt; (*Erz*) smelt.

Schmerz [ʃmɛrts] *m* (*pl* -en) pain; (*seelisch*) grief, pain. **Schmerzen haben** be in pain. **schmerzen** *v* hurt; (*seelisch*) grieve, pain. **schmerz‖haft** *adj* painful. –**lich** *adj* painful, hurtful. –**los** *adj* painless.

Schmetterling [ˈʃmɛtərliŋ] *m* (*pl* -e) butterfly. –**sschwimmen** *neut* butterfly (stroke).

Schmied [ʃmiːt] *m* (*pl* -e) (black)smith. **Schmiede** *f* (*pl* -n) forge, smithy. –**eisen** *neut* wrought iron. **schmieden** *v* forge; (*Pläne*) devise.

Schmiere [ˈʃmiːrə] *f* (*pl* -n) grease; (*Theater, umg.*) small (touring) company. **schmieren** *v* (*fetten*) grease; (*ölen*) oil, lubricate; (*streichen*) spread. **Schmierung** *f* (*pl* -en) lubrication.

Schminke [ˈʃmiŋkə] *f* (*pl* -n) make-up. **schminken** *v* make up. **sich schminken** put on make-up; make oneself up.

Schmorbraten [ˈʃmɔːrbraːtən] *m* stewed steak, pot roast. **schmoren** *v* stew, braise.

Schmuck [ʃmuk] *m* (*pl* -e) ornament, decoration; (*Juwelen*) jewellery. **schmücken** [ˈʃmykən] *v* adorn, decorate; (*Kleider*) trim.

schmuggeln [ˈʃmugəln] *v* smuggle. **Schmuggelware** *f* contraband. **Schmuggler** *m* (*pl* -) smuggler.

Schmus [ʃmuːs] *m* (*umg.*) (empty) chatter, soft-soap; **schmusen** *v* chatter, soft-soap.

Schmutz [ʃmuts] *m* dirt, filth. **schmutzig** *adj* dirty, filthy. **Schmutzpresse** *f* gutter press.

Schnabel [ˈʃnaːbəl] *m* (*pl* **Schnäbel**) bill, beak.

Schnalle [ˈʃnalə] *f* (*pl* -n) clasp; (*Schuh, Gürtel*) buckle; (*Tür*) latch. **schnallen** *v* buckle.

schnappen [ˈʃnapən] *v* snap; (*erwischen*) grab, catch. **nach Luft schnappen** gasp for air.

Schnaps [ʃnaps] *m* (*pl* **Schnäpse**) liqueur, schnaps, brandy.

schnarchen [ˈʃnarçən] *v* snore.

schnattern [ˈʃnatərn] *v* (*Geflügel*) cackle; (*Menschen*) prattle.

schnaufen [ˈʃnaufən] *v* pant, puff.

Schnauze [ˈʃnautsə] *f* (*pl* -n) snout, muzzle; (*Kanne*) spout. **halt die Schnauze!** (*vulgär*) shut up! belt up!

Schnecke [ˈʃnɛkə] *f* (*pl* -n) snail; (*nackte*) slug.

Schnee [ʃneː] *m* snow. –**glöckchen** *neut* snowdrop. –**lawine** *f* avalanche. –**mann** *m* snowman. –**schläger** *m* egg whisk. –**schuh** *m* ski. –**sturm** *m* blizzard. –**wehe** *f* snowdrift.

Schneide [ˈʃnaidə] *f* (*pl* -n) (cutting) edge. **schneiden** *v* cut; (*Braten*) carve. **Schneider** *m* (*pl* -) tailor. –**ei** *f* (*pl* -en) tailor's shop. –**in** *f* (*pl* -nen) dressmaker, seamstress.

schneien [ˈʃnaiən] *v* snow.

schnell [ʃnɛl] *adj* fast, quick. **mach schnell!** hurry up! get a move on! **Schnellboot** *neut* speedboat. **schnellen** *v* jerk, spring. **Schnell‖gaststätte** *f* fast-food restaurant, cafeteria. –**igkeit** *f* speed. –**imbiß** *m* snack. –**zug** *m* express train.

schnippisch [ˈʃnipiʃ] *adj* pert, saucy.

Schnitt [ʃnit] *m* (*pl* -e) cut; (*Scheibe*) slice; (*Art*) style; (*Math*) intersection; (*Zeichnung*) (cross-)section. –**lauch** *m* chive(s). –**ling** *m* (*Bot*) cutting.

Schnitzel [ˈʃnitsəl] *neut* (*pl* -) chip, shaving; (*Fleisch*) cutlet, escalope.

schnitzen [ˈʃnitsən] *v* carve (wood). **Schnitzer** *m* carver; (*Fehler*) blunder, bloomer.

Schnörkel [ˈʃnœrkəl] *m* (*pl* -) flourish; (*Kunst, Architektur*) scroll.

schnüffeln [ˈʃnyfəln] *v* snuffle, sniff; (*fig*) snoop, nose around.

Schnuller [ˈʃnulər] *m* (*pl* -) (baby's) dummy, (*US*) pacifier.

schnupfen [ˈʃnupfən] *v* take snuff. **Schnupfen** *m* (*pl* -) catarrh, (head) cold. **einen Schnupfen bekommen/haben** catch/have a cold. **Schnupftabak** *m* snuff.

Schnur [ʃnuːr] *f* (*pl* **Schnüre**) string, cord; (*Elek*) flex, wire.

schnüren [ˈʃnyːrən] *v* tie (up), fasten.

schüchtern

schnurgerade ['ʃnuːrgəraɪdə] adj, adv (as) straight (as a die).

Schnurrbart ['ʃnurbaːrt] m moustache.

schnurren ['ʃnurən] v hum, buzz; (Katze) purr.

Schock [ʃɔk] m (pl -s or -e) shock. schokieren v shock, scandalize.

Schokolade [ʃokoˈlaɪdə] f (pl -n) chocolate.

Scholle ['ʃɔlə] f (pl -n) (Erde) clod, clump; (Eis) floe; (Fisch) plaice; (fig) native soil, home.

schon [ʃoːn] adv already; (bestimmt) certainly; (zwar) indeed. schon lange for a long time, schon lange her a long time ago. ich komme schon! I'm coming! schon wieder yet again. schon der Name the mere name, the name alone.

schön [ʃøːn] adj beautiful, pretty; (Wetter) fine, fair. danke schön thank you. bitte schön (if you) please. schön machen beautify.

schonen ['ʃoːnən] v spare; treat carefully, go carefully with. -d adj considerate, careful.

Schönheit [ˈʃøːnhaɪt] f (pl -en) beauty. Schönheits‖fehler m blemish, flaw. -königin f beauty queen. -pflege f beauty treatment.

Schonkost ['ʃoːnkɔst] f (bland) diet.

Schopf [ʃɔpf] m (pl Schöpfe) shock, tuft.

schöpfen ['ʃœpfən] v scoop, ladle; (Atem) take, draw; (Mut) take.

Schöpfer[1] ['ʃœpfər] m (pl -) creator.

Schöpfer[2] m (pl -) (zum Schöpfen) scoop.

schöpferisch ['ʃœpfəriʃ] adj creative.

Schöpflöffel ['ʃœpflœfəl] m ladle.

Schöpfung [ˈʃœpfuŋ] f creation.

Schornstein ['ʃɔrnstaɪn] m chimney. -feger m chimney-sweep. -kappe f chimney-pot.

Schoß[1] [ʃoːs] m (pl Schöße) lap; (fig) bosom. -hund m lap-dog.

Schoß[2] [ʃɔs] m (pl Schosse) (Bot) shoot, sprout.

Schote ['ʃoːtə] f (pl -n) pod. Schoten pl (green) peas.

Schotte ['ʃɔtə] m (pl -n) Scot, Scotsman. Schottin f (pl -nen) Scot, Scotswoman. schottisch adj Scottish, Scots. Schottland neut Scotland.

schräg [ʃrɛːk] adj sloping, slanting, oblique.

Schrank [ʃraŋk] m (pl Schränke) cupboard; (Kleider) wardrobe.

Schranke ['ʃraŋkə] f (pl -n) barrier, bar. schrankenlos adj limitless, boundless.

Schraube ['ʃraubə] f (pl -n) screw. Schraubdeckel m screw-cap. Schrauben‖schlüssel m spanner, (US) wrench. -zieher m screwdriver.

Schrebergarten ['ʃreːbərgartən] m allotment (garden).

Schreck [ʃrɛk] m (pl -e) or Schrecken m (pl -) fright, terror. einen Schreck bekommen/kriegen receive/get a fright. schrecken v terrify, frighten. schrecklich adj terrible, frightful.

Schrei [ʃrai] m (pl -e) cry, shout, scream. schreien v cry, shout; (kreischen) shriek, screech; (weinen) cry, weep.

*schreiben ['ʃraibən] v write; (buchstabieren) spell. schreibfaul adj lazy about writing (letters). Schreib‖fehler m spelling error. -krampf m writer's cramp. -maschine f typewriter. -tisch m desk. -ung f (pl -en) spelling. -waren pl stationery ring

Schrein [ʃrain] m (pl -e) (Kasten) chest, box; (Reliquien) shrine. -er m (pl -) joiner, carpenter.

*schreiten ['ʃraitən] v stride, step.

Schrift [ʃrift] f (pl -en) writing; (Handschrift) handwriting; (Geschriebenes) pamphlet, paper; (Art) script, type. schriftlich adj in writing, written. Schrift‖steller m (pl -), Schriftstellerin f (pl -nen) writer, author. -stück neut document, paper.

Schritt [ʃrit] m (pl -e) step, stride; (Gangart) gait; (Tempo) pace. Schritt halten mit keep pace with. Schrittmacher m (fig, Med) pacemaker. schrittweise adv step-by-step.

schroff [ʃrɔf] adj steep, precipitous; (fig) gruff, surly.

Schrot [ʃroːt] m or neut (pl -e) (Getreide) groats pl; (Bleikügelchen) (buck)shot. -brot neut wholemeal bread.

Schrott [ʃrɔt] m (pl -e) scrap (metal).

schrubben ['ʃrubən] v scrub.

schrumpfen ['ʃrumpfən] v shrink. Schrumpfung f shrinking, contraction.

Schub [ʃuːp] m (pl Schübe) shove, push; (Tech) thrust. -fach neut drawer. -karren m wheelbarrow. -lade f drawer.

schüchtern ['ʃyçtərn] adj shy. Schüchternheit f shyness.

Schuft [ʃuft] m (pl -e) rascal, rogue. **schuften** v (umg.) toil, sweat, graft.
Schuh [ʃuɪ] m (pl -e) shoe. –**krem** f shoe polish. –**macher** m shoemaker. –**werk** neut footwear.
Schul‖arbeit f homework, task. –**buch** neut school book.
schuld [ʃult] adj guilty. **schuld haben** be guilty. **Schuld** f (pl -en) (Geld, fig) debt; (Rel, Jur) guilt. **schuld sein an** be to blame for. **Schulden haben** be in debt. **die Schuld schieben auf** push the blame onto. **schulden** v owe. **Schuldgefühl** neut sense of guilt. **schuldig** adj guilty; (Geld) indebted. **Schuldig‖e(r)** guilty person, culprit. –**keit** f (unz.) obligation; (Pflicht) duty. –**sprechung** f conviction, verdict of guilty.
Schuldirektor m headmaster. –**in** f headmistress.
schuldlos [ˈʃultloɪs] adj innocent. **Schuld‖ner** m (pl -), –**nerin** f (pl -nen) debtor. –**schein** m promissory note, IOU.
Schule [ˈʃuɪlə] f (pl -n) school. **schulen** v school, train.
Schüler [ˈʃyɪlə] m (pl -) schoolboy; (bei einem Meister) pupil; (Rel) disciple. –**in** f (pl -nen) schoolgirl; pupil; disciple.
Schul‖fach neut (school) subject. –**ferien** pl school holidays. **schulfrei haben** have a holiday. **Schul‖freund** m school friend. –**geld** neut school fees. –**hof** m (school) playground. –**junge** m schoolboy. –**lehrer** m (pl -), –**lehrerin** f (pl -nen) schoolteacher. –**mädchen** neut schoolgirl. –**schluß** m end of term, breaking-up.
Schulter [ˈʃultər] f (pl -en) shoulder. –**blatt** neut shoulder blade.
Schulung [ˈʃuɪluŋ] f (pl -en) schooling, training. **Schul‖wesen** neut educational system. –**zimmer** neut classroom, schoolroom.
Schund [ʃunt] m trash, rubbish.
Schuppe [ˈʃupə] f (pl -n) scale. **Schuppen** pl dandruff. **schuppig** adj scaly.
schüren [ˈʃyɪrən] v stir up, incite; (Feuer) poke, stoke.
schürfen [ˈʃyrfən] v (Haut) scratch, graze; (Metall) prospect. **Schürfung** f (pl -en) graze, abrasion; prospecting.
Schurke [ˈʃurkə] m (pl -n) villain, scoundrel.
Schürze [ˈʃyrtsə] f (pl -n) apron.

Schuß [ʃus] m (pl Schüsse) shot. –**loch** neut bullet-hole. –**waffe** f firearm. –**weite** f range. –**wunde** f gunshot wound.
Schüssel [ˈʃysəl] f (pl -n) bowl, dish.
Schuster [ˈʃuɪstər] m (pl -) cobbler, shoemaker.
Schutt [ʃut] m (Trümmer) debris; (Abfall) refuse.
schütteln [ˈʃytəln] v shake.
schütten [ˈʃytən] v pour (out). **es schüttet** it's pouring (with rain).
schüttern [ˈʃytərn] v tremble, shake.
Schutz [ʃuts] m (pl -e) protection; (Obdach) shelter; (Schirm) screen. –**anzug** m protective clothing. –**brille** f goggles pl.
Schütze [ˈʃytsə] m (pl -n) marksman, sharpshooter; (Bogen) archer. **schützen** v protect, defend; (behüten) guard.
Schutz‖farbe f camouflage. –**heilige(r)** m patron saint.
Schützling [ˈʃytsliŋ] m (pl -e) protégé(e), charge.
schutzlos [ˈʃutsloɪs] adj defenceless. **Schutz‖mann** m policeman. –**maßnahme** f precaution, preventive measure. –**mittel** neut preservative. –**umschlag** m (Book) jacket, dust cover.
Schwabe [ˈʃvaɪbə] m (pl -n) Swabian (man). –**n** neut Swabia.
Schwäbin [ˈʃvɛɪbin] f (pl -nen) Swabian woman. **schwäbisch** adj Swabian.
schwach [ʃvax] adj weak; (kränklich) delicate, sickly; (klein) small; (gering) scanty, poor.
Schwäche [ˈʃvɛçə] f (pl -n) weakness. **schwächen** v weaken.
Schwachheit [ˈʃvaxhait] f (pl -en) weakness.
schwächlich [ˈʃvɛçliç] adj feeble, sickly, delicate.
Schwachsinn [ˈʃvaxzin] m feeblemindedness. **schwachsinnig** adj feebleminded.
Schwager [ˈʃvaɪgər] m (pl Schwäger) brother-in-law.
Schwägerin [ˈʃvɛɪgərin] f (pl -nen) sister-in-law.
Schwalbe [ˈʃvalbə] f (pl -n) (Vogel) swallow.
Schwall [ʃval] m (pl -e) flood, torrent.
Schwamm [ʃvam] m (pl Schwämme) sponge.
Schwan [ʃvaɪn] m (pl Schwäne) swan.

schwanger ['ʃvaŋər] *adj* pregnant.
Schwangere *f* (*pl* -n) pregnant woman.
Schwangerschaft *f* pregnancy. –**vorsorge**
f ante-natal care.
schwanken ['ʃvaŋkən] *v* sway, swing;
(*taumeln*) stagger, reel; (*zögern*) waver;
(*Preise*) fluctuate. –**d** *adj* (*Person*) wavering. **Schwankung** *f* (*pl* en) swaying,
wavering, fluctuation.
Schwanz [ʃvants] *m* (*pl* **Schwänze**) tail.
Schwarm [ʃvarm] *m* (*pl* **Schwärme**)
swarm; (*Vogel*) flock; (*Fische*) shoal;
(*Rind, Schaf*) herd; (*Menschen*) crowd;
(*fig*) craze.
schwärmen ['ʃvermən] *v* swarm; (*Mil*)
deploy. **schwärmen für** rave about, gush
over. **schwärmerisch** *adj* wildly enthusiastic.
schwarz [ʃvarts] *adj* black. **Schwarz** *neut*
black (colour). –**brot** *neut* black bread.
–**e(r)** Black, Negro.
Schwärze ['ʃvertsə] *f* (*pl* -n) blackness;
(*Druck*) printer's ink. **schwärz||en** *v*
blacken. –**lich** *adj* blackish, darkish.
Schwarz||markt *m* black market. –**wald**
m Black Forest. **schwarzweiß** *adj* black-
and-white.
schwatzen ['ʃvatsən] *v* also **schwätzen**
chatter, prattle; (*Geheimnisse*) gossip.
Schwebe ['ʃveibə] *f* suspense. **in der
Schwebe** undecided, pending.
schweben *v* float, hover; (*hängen*) hang,
be suspended; (*fig*) remain undecided.
Schwede ['ʃveidə] *m* (*pl* -n), **Schwedin** *f*
(*pl* -nen) Swede. **Schweden** *neut* Sweden.
schwedisch *adj* Swedish.
Schwefel ['ʃveifəl] *m* sulphur.
schweifen ['ʃvaifən] *v* roam, wander.
*****schweigen** ['ʃvaigən] *v* be silent. **ganz zu
schweigen von** to say nothing of.
Schweigen *neut* silence. **schweigsam** *adj*
silent; (*fig*) secretive.
Schwein [ʃvain] *neut* (*pl* -e) pig; (*fig*)
(good) luck. **Schweine||braten** *m* roast
pork. –**fett** *neut* lard. –**fleisch** *neut* pork.
–**hund** *m* (*vulgär*) bastard, swine. –**rei** *f*
filthy mess; (*fig*) dirty trick. –**stall** *m*
pigsty. **Schweinsrippchen** *neut* pork
chop.
Schweiß [ʃvais] *m* (*pl* -e) sweat, perspiration. **schweißen** *v* weld; (*Wild*) bleed.
Schweiz [ʃvaits] *f* **die Schweiz** Switzerland. **Schweizer** *m* (*pl* -). **Schweizerin** *f*
(*pl* -nen) Swiss. **schweizerisch** *adj* Swiss.

Schwelle ['ʃvelə] *f* (*pl* -n) threshold;
(*Eisenbahn*) sleeper.
*****schwellen** ['ʃvelən] *v* swell.
schwemmen ['ʃvemən] *v* wash down;
(*Vieh*) water.
Schwengel ['ʃveŋəl] *m* (*pl* -) (*Glocke*)
clapper; (*Pumpe*) pump handle.
schwenken ['ʃveŋkən] *v* turn; (*Fahne,
Hut*) wave, flourish.
schwer [ʃveir] *adj* heavy; (*schwierig*) difficult; (*ernst*) serious. **es ist 2 Kilo schwer**
it weighs two kilos. **schwere Arbeit** hard
work. –**beschädigt** *adj* seriously disabled. **Schwere** *f* weight. **schwerfällig** *adj*
clumsy, awkward. **Schwergewichtler** *m*
heavyweight. **schwerhörig** *adj* hard of
hearing. **Schwer||industrie** *f* heavy indus-
try. –**kraft** *f* gravity. **schwer||lich** *adj*
with difficulty, hardly. –**mütig** *adj* melancholy, sad.
Schwert [ʃveirt] *neut* (*pl* -er) sword.
Schwester ['ʃvestər] *f* (*pl* -n) sister.
schwesterlich *adj* sisterly. **Schwestern-
schaft** *f* sisterhood.
Schwieger||eltern *pl* parents-in-law;
(*umg.*) in-laws. –**mutter** *m* mother-in-
law. –**sohn** *m* son-in-law. –**tochter** *f*
daughter-in-law. –**vater** *m* father-in-law.
schwierig ['ʃviiriç] *adj* difficult, hard.
Schwierigkeit *f* (*pl* -en) difficulty.
Schwimmbad ['ʃvimbait] *neut* swimming
pool. **Schwimmbecken** *neut* swimming
pool. **schwimmen** *v* swim; (*Gegenstand*)
float. **Schwimmen** *neut* swimming.
schwimmend *adj* swimming; floating.
Schwimmer *m* (*pl* -) swimmer; float.
Schwindel ['ʃvindəl] *m* (*pl* -) giddiness;
(*Täuschung*) swindle, fraud.
schwindel||haft *adj* giddy; fraudulent.
–**ig** *adj* giddy, dizzy. **schwindeln** *v* cheat,
swindle. **mir schwindelt** I feel giddy.
Schwindler *m* (*pl* -) swindler, cheat.
*****schwingen** ['ʃviŋən] *v* swing; (*Fahne,
Waffe*) wave, flourish. **Schwingung** *f* (*pl*
-en) oscillation, vibration.
schwitzen ['ʃvitsən] *v* sweat.
*****schwören** ['ʃvœirən] *v* swear.
schwul [ʃvuil] *adj* (*vulgär*) queer, homosexual.
schwül [ʃvyil] *adj* sultry, hot and humid.
Schwulst [ʃvulst] *m* (*pl* **Schwülste**) bombast, pomposity. **schwülstig** *adj* bombast-
ic, pompous.
Schwund [ʃvunt] *m* contraction,
shrinkage; (*Med*) atrophy.

Schwung [ʃvuŋ] *m* (*pl* **Schwünge**) impetus, momentum; (*fig*) drive, vitality, verve. **–kraft** *f* centrifugal force; (*fig*) verve. **–rad** *neut* flywheel.
Schwur [ʃvuːr] *m* (*pl* **Schwüre**) oath. **–gericht** *neut* court with jury.
sechs [zɛks] *pron, adj* six. **sechst** *adj* sixth. **Sechstel** *neut* sixth (part).
sechzehn [ˈzɛçtseɪn] *pron, adj* sixteen. **sechzehntel** *adj* sixteenth.
sechzig [ˈzɛçtsiç] *pron, adj* sixty. **die sechziger Jahre** the '60s. **sechzigst** *adj* sixtieth.
See [seɪ] **1** *m* (*pl* **-n**) lake. **2** *f* (*pl* **-n**) sea. **–fahrt** *f* voyage. **–jungfer** *f* mermaid. **seekrank** *adj* seasick.
Seele [ˈzeɪlə] *f* (*pl* **-n**) soul, spirit. **seelisch** *adj* spiritual.
See‖löwe *m* sealion. **–räuber** *m* pirate. **–wasser** *neut* sea water.
Segel [ˈzeɪgəl] *neut* (*pl* **-**) sail. **–boot** *neut* sailing boat. **–flugzeug** *neut* glider, sailplane. **segeln** *v* sail. **Segeltuch** *neut* canvas.
Segen [ˈzeɪgən] *m* (*pl* **-**) blessing; (*Tischgebet*) grace. **segnen** *v* bless. **Segnung** *f* (*pl* **-en**) blessing.
*sehen [ˈzeɪən] *v* see; (*anblicken*) look; (*beobachten*) watch, observe. **sehen lassen** display, show. **Sehen** *neut* (eye)sight, vision. **–würdigkeit** *f* (tourist) sight. **Seh‖feld** *neut* field of vision. **–kraft** *f* eyesight, vision.
Sehne [ˈzeɪnə] *f* (*pl* **-n**) sinew, tendon; (*Bogen*) string.
sehnen [ˈzeɪnən] *v* **sich sehnen nach** long for.
sehr [zeɪr] *adv* very.
Sehweite [ˈzeɪvaɪtə] *f* range of vision.
seicht [zaɪçt] *adj* shallow.
Seide [ˈzaɪdə] *f* (*pl* **-n**) silk.
Seife [ˈzaɪfə] *f* (*pl* **-n**) soap. **Seifen‖schaum** *m* lather. **–wasser** *neut* suds *pl*, soapy water.
Seil [zaɪl] *neut* (*pl* **-e**) rope; (*Kabel*) cable. **–bahn** *f* funicular.
sein[1] [zaɪn] *adj, pron* his, its. **seinerseits** *adv* on or for his part. **seinesgleichen** *pron* the likes of him *pl*, people like him *pl*. **seinethalben, seinetwegen,** *or* **seinetwillen** *adv* for his sake. **seinige** *pron* **der, die, das seinige** his.
*sein[2] *v* be. **es sei denn, daß** unless. **kann sein** perhaps. **sein lassen** leave alone. **mir ist kalt/warm** I feel cold/warm.

seit [zaɪt] *prep* since. **–dem** *conj* since; *adv* since then. **seit damals** since then. **seit wann?** since when? **seit zwei Jahren** for two years.
Seite [ˈzaɪtə] *f* (*pl* **-n**) side; (*Buch*) page. **auf die Seite bringen** put aside. **von seiten** on the part (of). **Seiten‖lampe** *f* side lamp. **–schiff** *neut* aisle. **–straße** *f* side street. **–wagen** *m* sidecar.
seither [zaɪtˈheɪr] *adv* since then.
seitlich [ˈzaɪtliç] *adj* lateral, side. **seitwärts** *adv* sideways.
Sekretär [zekreˈtɛɪr] *m* (*pl* **-e**) secretary; (*Schreibschrank*) bureau, locking desk. **–in** *f* (*pl* **-nen**) secretary.
Sekt [zɛkt] *m* (*pl* **-e**) sparkling wine.
Sekte [ˈzɛktə] *f* (*pl* **-n**) sect. **sektiererisch** *adj* sectarian.
sekundär [zekunˈdɛɪr] *adj* secondary.
Sekunde [zeˈkundə] *f* (*pl* **-n**) second.
selber [ˈzɛlbər] *V* **selbst**.
selbst [zɛlpst] *pron* self. *adv* even. **ich selbst** I myself. **von selbst** on one's own accord; (*Sache*) by itself. **sie kann es selbst machen** she can do it by herself. **selbst wenn** even though. **Selbst** *neut* self. **–achtung** *f* self-respect.
selbständig [ˈzɛlpstendiç] *adj* independent. **Selbständigkeit** *f* independence.
Selbst‖bedienung *f* self-service. **–beherrschung** *f* self-control. **–mitleid** *f* self-pity. **–bestimmung** *f* self-determination.
selbstbewußt *adj* self-confident; (*eingebildet*) conceited. **Selbstbewußtsein** *neut* self-confidence; conceit.
Selbsterkenntnis *f* self-knowledge.
selbst‖gebacken *adj* home-made. **–gefällig** *adj* self-satisfied. **–gerecht** *adj* self-righteous.
Selbsthilfe *f* self-help; (*Jur*) self-defence.
selbst‖klebend *adj* adhesive, gummed. **–los** *adj* selfless.
Selbst‖mord *m* suicide. **–mörder** *m* suicide. **–schutz** *m* self-defence.
selbstsicher *adj* self-confident. **Selbstsicherheit** *f* self-confidence.
Selbstsucht *f* selfishness. **selbstsüchtig** *adj* selfish.
Selbst‖täuschung *f* self-deception. **–versorgung** *f* self-sufficiency.
selbstverständlich *adj* self-evident. *adv* obviously, naturally.
Selbstvertrauen *neut* self-confidence.

selig ['zeːliç] *adj* blessed; (*verstorben*) late, deceased; (*überglücklich*) blissful, delighted.

Sellerie ['zɛləriː] *f* (*pl* -n) *or m* (*pl* -s) celeriac. **–stangen** *pl* celery *sing.*

selten ['zɛltən] *adj* rare. *adv* rarely, seldom.

seltsam ['zɛltzaɪm] *adj* strange, odd, curious.

Semester [ze'mɛstər] *neut* (*pl* -) semester, (half-yearly) session.

Seminar [zemi'naɪr] *neut* (*pl* -e) training college; tutorial group.

Semit [ze'miːt] *m* (*pl* -en) Semite. **semitisch** *adj* Semitic.

Semmel ['zɛməl] *f* (*pl* -n) bread roll.

Senat [ze'naɪt] *m* (*pl* -e) senate. **–or** *m* (*pl* -en) senator.

*senden ['zɛndən] *v* send; (*Funk*) transmit, broadcast. **Sender** *m* (*pl* -) (*Gerät*) transmitter; (*Anstalt*) station. **Sendung** *f* (*pl* -en) package; (*Waren*) consignment; (*Funk*) broadcast.

Senf [zɛnf] *m* (*pl* -e) mustard.

sengen ['zɛŋən] *V* singe.

Senkblei ['zɛŋkblaɪ] *neut* plumb-line.

Senkel ['zɛŋkəl] *m* (*pl* -) (shoe)lace.

senken ['zɛŋkən] *v* lower; (*Kopf*) bow; (*Preise*) reduce. **sich senken** sink. **senkrecht** *adj* vertical, perpendicular. **Senkung** *f* (*pl* -en) sinking; (*Preise*) reduction; (*Vertiefung*) depression.

Sensation [zɛnzatsi'oːn] *f* (*pl* -en) sensation. **sensationell** *adj* sensational.

Sense ['zɛnzə] *f* (*pl* -n) scythe.

sensibel [zɛn'ziːbəl] *adj* sensitive.

sentimental [zɛntimen'taɪl] *adj* sentimental.

separieren [zɛpa'riːrən] *v* separate.

September [zɛp'tɛmbər] *m* (*pl* -) September.

septisch ['zɛptiʃ] *adj* septic.

Serie ['zeɪriə] *f* (*pl* -n) series. **–nherstellung** *f* mass production.

seriös [zeɪri'øːs] *adj* serious, earnest; (*Firma*) reliable, honourable.

Service¹ [zɛr'viːs] *neut* (*pl* -) (dinner) service.

Service² *neut or m* (*pl* -s) (customer) service.

servieren [zɛr'viːrən] *v* serve. **Servierwagen** *m* trolley. **Serviette** *f* (*pl* -n) (table) napkin.

Sesam ['zɛzaɪm] *m* sesame.

Sessel ['zɛsəl] *m* (*pl* -) armchair. **–lift** *m* chairlift.

seßhaft ['zɛshaft] *adj* settled, established; (*ansässig*) resident.

setzen ['zɛtsən] *v* set, put, place; (*einpflanzen*) plant; (*Druck*) compose, set; (*Spiel*) wager, bet. **in Bewegung setzen** set in motion. **außer Kraft setzen** invalidate. **in die Welt setzen** give birth to. **sich setzen** sit down. **sich in Verbindung setzen mit** get in contact with.

Seuche ['zɔyçə] *f* (*pl* -n) epidemic.

seufzen ['zɔyftsən] *v* sigh. **Seufzer** *m* (*pl* -) sigh.

Sex [zɛks] *m* (*pl* -) sex. **Sexualität** *f* sexuality. **–aufklärung** *f* sex education. **sexuell** *adj* sexual. **sexy** *adj* sexy.

sezieren [ze'tsiːrən] *v* dissect.

sich [ziç] *pron* himself, herself, itself, yourself, oneself, yourselves; themselves; (*miteinander*) (with) one another, each other. **an (und für) sich** in itself. **bei sich haben** have with one. **sich die Hände waschen** wash one's hands. **sie lieben sich** they love each other.

Sichel ['ziçəl] *f* (*pl* -n) sickle; (*Mond-*) crescent.

sicher ['ziçər] *adj* safe, secure; (*gewiß*) sure, certain. *adv* surely, certainly. **Sicherheit** *f* safety; certainty; trustworthiness; (*Pol, Psychol*) security. **Sicherheits‖bestimmungen** *pl* safety regulations. **–gurt** *m* safety belt. **–nadel** *f* safety pin. **sicher‖lich** *adv* surely, certainly. **–n** *v* secure; (*schützen*) protect. **–stellen** *v* secure, guarantee. **Sicherung** *f* (*pl* -en) protection; (*Elek*) fuse; (*Tech*) safety device.

Sicht [ziçt] *f* (*unz.*) sight; (*Aussicht*) view; (*Sichtbarkeit*) visibility. **sichtbar** *adj* visible. **Sichtbarkeit** *f* visibility.

sickern ['zikərn] *v* trickle, seep.

sie [ziː] *pron* she, it; her; they; them. **Sie** *pron* you.

Sieb [ziːp] *neut* (*pl* -e) sieve; (*Tee*) strainer.

sieben¹ ['ziːbən] *v* sift, sieve.

sieben² *pron, adj* seven. **siebent or siebt** *adj* seventh.

siebzehn ['ziːptseɪn] *pron, adj* seventeen. **siebzehnt** *adj* seventeenth.

siebzig ['ziːptsiç] *pron, adj* seventy. **siebzigt** *adj* seventieth.

siedeln ['ziːdəln] *v* settle, colonize.

*sieden ['ziːdən] v boil. **Siedepunkt** m boiling point.

Siedler ['ziːdlər] m (pl -) settler. **Siedlung** f (pl -en) settlement (place); (am Stadtrand) housing estate.

Sieg [ziːk] m (pl -e) victory.

Siegel ['ziːgəl] neut (pl -) seal, signet.

siegen ['ziːgən] v win, triumph, be victorious. **Sieger** m (Mil) conqueror, victor; (Sport) winner. **siegreich** adj victorious.

Signal [zig'naːl] neut (pl -e) signal. **-feuer** neut beacon. **-rakete** f rocket-flare.

Signatur [zigna'tuːr] f (pl -en) mark, symbol; (Unterschrift) signature.

Silbe ['zilbə] f (pl -n) syllable.

Silber ['zilbər] neut silver. **silbern** adj silver.

Silvesterabend [zil'vɛstəraibənt] m New Year's Eve.

simpel ['zimpəl] adj simple.

Sims [zims] neut (pl -e) (Fenster) window-sill.

simulieren [zimu'liːrən] v pretend; (Krankheit) malinger; (Tech) simulate.

Sinfonie [zinfo'niː] f (pl -n) symphony.

*singen ['ziŋən] v sing. **Singvogel** m songbird.

*sinken ['ziŋkən] v sink; (fig) diminish; (Preise) fall. **Sinken** neut fall, drop; (Werte) depreciation; (fig) decline.

Sinn [zin] m (pl -e) sense; (Gedanken) mind, thoughts pl. es hat keinen Sinn it makes no sense. es kam mir in den Sinn, daß ... it crossed my mind that ... . **Sinn für Humor** sense of humour. **Sinn für Literatur** interest in literature. **Sinnbild** neut symbol. **sinn‖bildlich** adj symbolic. **-en** v reflect, think (over). **-lich** adj sensual. **-los** adj senseless. **Sinnspruch** m epigram, maxim.

Sippe ['zipə] f (pl -n) tribe; (Verwandte) kin.

Sirup ['ziːrup] m (pl -e) syrup.

Sitte ['zitə] f (pl -n) custom; (Gewohnheit) habit. **Sitten** pl morals. **Sittenlehre** f ethics. **sittenlos** adj immoral. **sittlich** adj moral. **Sittlichkeit** f morality. **-sverbrechen** neut indecent assault.

Situation [zituatsi'oːn] f (pl -en) situation.

Sitz [zits] m (pl -e) seat; (Kleidung) fit. **-bank** f bench. **sitzen** v sit; (Kleidung) fit. **-bleiben** v remain seated. **Sitzung** f (pl -en) sitting; (Versammlung) session.

Skala ['skaːla] f (pl Skalen) scale. **Skalenscheibe** f dial.

Skandal [skan'daːl] m (pl -e) scandal. **skandalös** adj scandalous.

Skandinavien [skandi'naːviən] neut Scandinavia. **Skandinavier** m (pl -), **Skandinavierin** f (pl -nen) Scandinavian. **skandinavisch** adj Scandinavian.

Skelett [ske'lɛt] neut (pl -e) skeleton.

Skeptiker ['skɛptikər] m (pl -) sceptic. **skeptisch** adj sceptical.

Ski [ʃiː] m (pl -er)· ski. **-fahrer(in)** skier.

Skizze ['skitsə] f (pl -n) sketch. **skizzieren** v sketch.

Sklave ['sklaːvə] m (pl -n) slave. **Sklaverei** f slavery. **Sklavin** f (pl -nen) (female) slave, slave girl.

Skorpion ['skorpiən] m (pl -e) (Tier) scorpion; (Astrol) Scorpio.

Skrupel ['skruːpəl] m (pl -) scruple. **skrupellos** adj unscrupulous. **skrupulös** adj scrupulous.

Skulptur [skulp'tuːr] f (pl -en) sculpture.

Smaragd [sma'rakt] m (pl -e) emerald. **smaragdgrün** adj emerald(-green).

Smoking ['smoːkiŋ] m (pl -s) dinner jacket, (US) tuxedo.

so [zoː] adv thus, so, in this way. conj consequently, therefore. **so daß** so that. **so ein** such a. **so sehr** so much. **so ... wie ...** as ... as ... . **um so besser** all the better. **-bald** conj as soon as.

Socke ['zɔkə] f (pl -n) sock.

Sockel ['zɔkəl] m (pl -) pedestal, base.

sodann [zo'dan] adv, conj then, in that case.

Sodawasser ['zoːdavasər] neut soda water.

Sodbrennen ['zoːtbrɛnən] neut heartburn.

soeben [zo'eːbən] adv just (now).

Sofa ['zoːfa] neut (pl -s) sofa.

sofern [zo'fɛrn] conj as or so far as.

sofort [zo'fɔrt] adv at once, immediately. **-ig** adj immediate.

Sog [zoːk] m (pl -e) suction; (Boot) wake.

sogar [zo'gaɪr] adv even.

sogenannt ['zoːgənant] adj so-called.

Sohle ['zoːlə] f (pl -n) (Fuß, usw.) sole. **sohlen** v sole.

Sohn [zoːn] m (pl Söhne) son.

solang(e) [zo'laŋ(ə)] conj as long as; (während) while.

solch [zɔlç] pron, adj such. **solcher‖art** adv of this sort, along these lines. **-lei** adj of such a kind. **-weise** adv in such a way.

Soldat [zɔl'daıt] *m* (*pl* **-en**) soldier. **Soldat werden** enlist, join up.
Söldner ['zœldnər] *m* (*pl* **-**) mercenary.
solid [zo'liːt] *adj* also **solide** (*Person*) reliable, decent; (*Leben*) decent, respectable; (*Gegenstand*) solid, robust. **-arisch** *adj* united, unanimous. **Solidarität** *f* solidarity.
Solist [zo'list] *m* (*pl* **-en**), **Solistin** *f* (*pl* **-nen**) soloist.
Soll [zɔl] *neut* (*pl* **-s**) (*Komm*) debit; (*Produktion*) target. **sollen** *v* ought to, have to, should; (*angeblich*) be supposed to be. *ich sollte* I should. *was soll das?* what is this supposed to be *or* mean? *sie soll reich sein* she is said to be rich. *Kinder sollen gehorchen* children should be obedient. *du sollst nicht töten* thou shalt not kill.
Solo ['zoːlo] *neut* (*pl* **-s** *or* **Soli**) solo. **-sänger** *m* soloist, solo singer.
Sommer ['zɔmər] *m* (*pl* **-**) summer. **-ferien** *pl* summer holidays. **-sprosse** *f* freckle.
Sonate [zo'naːtə] *f* (*pl* **-n**) sonata.
Sonde ['zɔndə] *f* (*pl* **-n**) (*Tech*) probe.
Sonder‖angebot *neut* special offer. **-ausgabe** *f* special edition. **sonder‖bar** *adj* strange, peculiar. **-lich** *adj* remarkable, special.
sondern[1] ['zɔndərn] *v* separate.
sondern[2] *conj* but. **nicht nur ... sondern auch ...** not only ... but also ....
Sonder‖preis *m* special price. **-ung** *f* (*pl* **-en**) separation.
Sonnabend ['zɔnaːbənt] *m* Saturday. **sonnabends** *adv* on Saturdays.
Sonne ['zɔnə] *f* (*pl* **-n**) sun. **sonnen** *v* air, put out in the sun. **sich sonnen** sun oneself, lie in the sun.
Sonnen‖aufgang *m* sunrise. **-blume** *f* sunflower. **-brand** *m* sunburn. **-bräune** *f* suntan. **-finsternis** *f* solar eclipse. **-schein** *m* sunshine. **-stich** *m* sunstroke. **-system** *neut* solar system. **-untergang** *m* sunset.
sonnig ['zɔnɪç] *adj* sunny.
Sonntag ['zɔntaːk] *m* Sunday. **sonntags** *adv* on Sundays.
sonst [zɔnst] *adv* otherwise, else. **sonst etwas?** anything else? **sonst nichts** nothing else. **wer sonst?** who else? **wie sonst** as usual. **-ig** *adj* other, miscellaneous. **-wie** *adv* some other way. **-wo** *adv* elsewhere.

Sopran [zo'praːn] *m* (*pl* **-e**) soprano. **-istin** *f* (*pl* **-nen**) soprano (singer).
Sorge ['zɔrgə] *f* (*pl* **-n**) (*Kummer*) care, worry; (*Pflege*) care. **sich Sorgen machen (um)** worry (about). **sorgen für** take care of. **dafür sorgen, daß** make sure that, see to it that. **sich sorgen** be anxious, worry. **sorgen‖frei** *or* **-los** *adj* carefree. **-voll** *adj* careworn. **sorg‖lich** *adj* careful, caring. **-los** *adj* careless. **-sam** *adj* careful, cautious.
Sorte ['zɔrtə] *f* (*pl* **-n**) sort, kind; (*Ware*) brand. **sortieren** *v* sort (out). **Sortiment** *neut* (*pl* **-e**) assortment.
Soße ['zoːsə] *f* (*pl* **-n**) sauce; (*für Fleisch*) gravy.
Souveränität [suvərεni'tɛːt] *f* sovereignty.
soviel ['zofiːl] *conj* as far as. *adv* as *or* so much. **soviel wie** as much as. **soweit** *conj* as *or* so far as. *adv* so far. **sowenig(wie)** *conj* as little (as). **sowie** *conj* as soon as; (*außerdem*) as well as, and also. **sowieso** *adv* in any case.
Sowjet [zɔ'vjet] *m* (*pl* **-e**) Soviet. **sowjetisch** *adj* Soviet. **Sowjetunion** *f* Soviet Union.
sowohl [zo'voːl] *conj* as well as. **sowohl ... als auch ...** both ... and ....
sozial [zɔtsi'aːl] *adj* social. **Sozial‖abgaben** *pl* national insurance contributions. **-demokrat** *m* social democrat. **-einrichtungen** *pl* social services. **-fürsorge** *f* (social) welfare.
Sozialismus [zɔtsia'lizmus] *m* socialism. **Sozialist** *m* socialist. **sozialistisch** *adj* socialist.
Sozial‖politik *f* social policies *pl*. **-produkt** *neut* (gross) national product. **-unterstützung** *f* social security.
Soziologe [zɔtsio'loːgə] *m* (*pl* **-n**) sociologist. **Soziologie** *f* sociology. **soziologisch** *adj* sociological.
sozusagen [zɔtsu'zaːgən] *adv* so to speak.
spähen ['ʃpɛːən] *v* look out, watch; (*Mil*) scout.
Spalt [ʃpalt] *m* (*pl* **-e**) crack, slit. **-e** *f* (*Druck*) column; crack, crevice. **spalten** *v* split.
Span [ʃpaːn] *m* (*pl* **Späne**) chip, shaving; (*Splitter*) splinter.
Spange ['ʃpaŋə] *f* (*pl* **-n**) clasp; (*Schnalle*) buckle.
Spanien ['ʃpaːniən] *neut* Spain. **Spanier** *m* (*pl* **-**), **Spanierin** *f* (*pl* **-nen**) Spaniard. **spanisch** *adj* Spanish.

Spann [ʃpan] *m* (*pl* -e) instep.
Spanne ['ʃpanə] *f* (*pl* -n) span.
spannen ['ʃpanən] *v* stretch; (*straff ziehen*) tighten. **-d** *adj* thrilling, exciting.
Spann‖seil *neut* guy(-rope). **-ung** *f* (*pl* -en) tension.
sparen ['ʃpaɪrən] *v* save; (*sparsam sein*) economize. **Sparer** *m* (*pl* -) saver.
Spargel ['ʃpargəl] *m* (*pl* -) asparagus. **-kohl** *m* broccoli.
Sparkasse ['ʃpaɪrkasə] *f* savings bank. **-nbuch** *neut* deposit book.
spärlich ['ʃpɛːlɪç] *adj* scanty, meagre. **Spärlichkeit** *f* scarcity.
Sparmaßnahme ['ʃpaɪrmaɪsnaɪmə] *f* economy measure.
Spaß [ʃpaɪs] *m* (*pl* Späße) fun; (*Scherz*) joke. **Spaß haben an** enjoy. *es macht uns Spaß* it amuses us, it is fun. **spaß‖en** *v* make fun, joke. **-haft** *or* **-ig** *adj* comical. **Spaßvogel** *m* joker, clown.
spät [ʃpɛːt] *adj* late. *wie spät ist es?* what is the time?
Spaten ['ʃpaɪtən] *m* (*pl* -) spade.
später ['ʃpɛːtər] *adj* later. **spätestens** *adv* at the latest.
Spatz [ʃpats] *m* (*pl* -en) sparrow.
spazieren [ʃpa'tsiɪrən] *v* go for a walk, stroll. **-fahren** *v* go for a drive. **-gehen** *v* go for a walk, walk. **Spazier‖fahrt** *f* drive. **-gang** *m* walk, stroll.
Specht [ʃpɛçt] *m* (*pl* -e) woodpecker.
Speck [ʃpɛk] *m* (*pl* -e) bacon; (*Schmalz*) lard, fat. **speckig** *adj* greasy.
spedieren [ʃpe'diɪrən] *v* forward, transport, ship. **Spediteur** *m* (*pl* -e) shipping agent, haulier, carrier. **Spedition** *f* (*pl* -en) shipping (agency).
Speer [ʃpeɪr] *m* (*pl* -e) spear.
Speichel ['ʃpaiçəl] *m* spittle, saliva.
Speicher ['ʃpaiçər] *m* (*pl* -) warehouse, storehouse; (*Getreide*) granary; (*Computer*) memory. **speichern** *v* store.
Speise ['ʃpaizə] *f* (*pl* -n) food; (*Gericht*) dish. **-eis** *neut* ice cream. **-karte** *f* menu. **speisen** *v* dine, eat. **Speise‖röhre** *f* gullet. **-saal** *m* dining room. **-wagen** *m* dining car.
Spektakel [ʃpɛk'taɪkəl] *m* (*pl* -) spectacle; (*Aufregung*) uproar.
Spekulation [ʃpekulatsi'oɪn] *f* (*pl* -en) speculation. **spekulieren** *v* speculate.
Spende ['ʃpɛndə] *f* (*pl* -n) donation. **spenden** *v* contribute, donate. **Spender** *m* (*pl* -). **Spenderin** *f* (*pl* -nen) donor.

Sperre ['ʃpɛrə] *f* (*pl* -n) barrier; (*Verbot*) ban. **sperren** *v* close, bar; (*untersagen*) ban; (*Strom*) cut off. **Sperr‖riegel** *m* (door) bolt. **-kette** *f* door chain. **-klinke** *f* safety catch. **-ung** *f* blocking, barring. **-zeit** *f* closing time.
Spesen ['ʃpeɪzən] *pl* expenses.
Spezialfach [ʃpeɪtsi'aɪlfax] *neut* speciality. **spezialisieren** *v* specialize. **Spezialist** *m* specialist. **speziell** *adj* special.
spezifisch [ʃpe'tsiɪfiʃ] *adj* specific.
Sphäre ['sfɛːrə] *f* (*pl* -n) sphere.
Spiegel ['ʃpiɪgəl] *m* (*pl* -) mirror; (*Schiff*) stern. **-ei** *neut* fried egg. **-glas** *neut* plate glass. **spiegeln** *v* reflect; (*glänzen*) shine. **Spiegelung** *f* (*pl* -en) reflection.
Spiel [ʃpiɪl] *neut* (*pl* -e) game; (*Theater*) play; (*Glücksspiel*) gambling. **aufs Spiel setzen** put at stake. **auf dem Spiel stehen** be at stake. **-automat** *m* slot machine. **-bank** *f* casino. **-brett** *neut* board.
spielen ['ʃpiɪlən] *v* play; (*Geld*) gamble.
Spieler ['ʃpiɪlər] *m* (*pl* -), **Spielerin** *f* (*pl* -nen) player; (*Schauspieler*) actor *m*, actress *f*; (*Geld*) gambler. **Spielergebnis** *neut* result, (final) score. **spielerisch** *adj* playful. **Spiel‖feld** *neut* playing field. **-karte** *f* playing card. **-platz** *m* playground. **-zeug** *neut* toy.
Spieß [ʃpiːs] *m* (*pl* -e) spear; (*Bratspieß*) spit. **-bürger** *m* philistine.
Spinat [ʃpi'naɪt] *m* (*pl* -e) spinach.
Spindel ['ʃpindəl] *f* (*pl* -n) spindle, axle.
Spinne ['ʃpinə] *f* (*pl* -n) spider. **spinnen** *v* spin; (*umg.*) talk nonsense. *du spinnst ja!* you're crazy!
Spion [ʃpi'oɪn] *m* (*pl* -e) spy. **-age** *f* espionage. **spionieren** *v* spy.
Spirale [ʃpi'raɪlə] *f* (*pl* -n) spiral.
Spirituosen [ʃpiritu'oɪzən] *pl* spirits, liquor *sing*.
spitz [ʃpits] *adj* sharp, pointed. **Spitze** *f* (*pl* -n) point, tip. **Spitzen** *pl* (*Gewebe*) lace *sing*. **spitzen** *v* sharpen. **Spitzen‖geschwindigkeit** *f* top speed. **-leistung** *f* maximum performance, record. **Spitzer** *m* (*pl* -) pencil-sharpener. **spitzfindig** *adj* shrewd, ingenious; (*haarspalterisch*) over-critical, hair-splitting. **Spitzname** *m* nickname.
Splitter ['ʃplitər] *m* (*pl* -) splinter. **-gruppe** *f* splinter group.
spontan [ʃpɔn'taɪn] *adj* spontaneous.

Spore ['ʃpɔːrə] *f* (*pl* -n) spore.
Sporn [ʃpɔrn] *m* (*pl* **Sporen**) spur.
spornen *v* spur.
Sport [ʃpɔrt] *m* (*pl* -e) sport. **Sport treiben** go in for sport(s). **Sport||feld** *neut* sports ground. **–ler** *m* (*pl* -) sportsman. **–lerin** *f* (*pl* -nen) sportswoman. **sportlich** *adj* sporting.
Spott [ʃpɔt] *m* ridicule. **spottbillig** *adj* dirt cheap. **spotten über** ridicule, deride.
spöttisch ['ʃpœtiʃ] *adj* mocking, scornful.
Sprache ['ʃpraːxə] *f* (*pl* -n) language, speech. **Sprachfehler** *m* speech defect; (*Gramm*) grammatical error. **sprach||lich** *adj* linguistic. **–los** *adj* speechless.
*sprechen ['ʃpreçən] *v* speak. **sprechen mit** talk to, speak with. **Sprecher** *m* (*pl* -), **Sprecherin** *f* (*pl* -nen) speaker; (*offiziell*) spokesman.
sprengen ['ʃprenjən] *v* explode, blow up; (*aufbrechen*) burst open; (*bespritzen*) sprinkle. **Spreng||kopf** *m* warhead. **–stoff** *m* explosive.
Sprichwort ['ʃpriçvɔrt] *neut* (*pl* **Sprichwörter**) proverb.
*sprießen [ʃpriːsən] *v* sprout.
Spring [ʃpriŋ] *m* (*pl* -e) spring. **–brunnen** *m* fountain. **springen** *v* jump, spring; (*Ball*) bounce; (*platzen*) burst, break; (*Schwimmen*) dive. **Springen** *neut* jumping; (*Schwimmen*) diving. **Springer** *m* (*pl* -) jumper; (*Schach*) knight. **Spring||feder** *f* spring. **–seil** *neut* skipping rope.
Sprit [ʃprit] *m* (*pl* -e) (*umg.*) gas, juice.
Spritze ['ʃpritsə] *f* (*pl* -n) syringe; (*Einspritzung*) injection; (*Tech*) spray. **spritzen** *v* squirt (*bespregen*) sprinkle; (*Med*) inject.
spröde ['ʃprøːdə] *adj* brittle; (*Person*) reserved, cool.
Sproß [ʃprɔs] *m* (*pl* **Sprosse**) shoot, sprout.
Spruch [ʃprux] *m* (*pl* **Sprüche**) saying, aphorism; (*Jur*) sentence.
Sprudel ['ʃpruːdəl] *m* (*pl* -) spring, source (of water); mineral water. **sprudeln** *v* bubble up; (*Mineralwasser, usw.*) sparkle. **–d** *adj* bubbling; sparkling. **Sprudelwasser** *neut* mineral water.
Sprühdose ['ʃpryːdoːzə] *f* spray can, aerosol pack. **sprühen** *v* spray; (*Regen*) drizzle. **Sprühregen** *m* drizzle.
Sprung [ʃpruŋ] *m* (*pl* **Sprünge**) leap, jump; (*Schwimmen*) dive; (*Riß*) crack, split. **–brett** *neut* diving board.

spucken ['ʃpukən] *v* spit.
Spuk [ʃpuːk] *m* (*pl* -e) ghost.
Spülbecken ['ʃpyːlbekən] *neut* sink.
Spule ['ʃpuːlə] *f* (*pl* -n) spool; (*Elek*) coil. **spulen** *v* wind.
spülen ['ʃpyːlən] *v* rinse, wash; (*Geschirr*) wash up; (*WC*) flush. **Spül||ung** *f* rinsing, washing; flushing. **–wasser** *neut* dishwater.
Spur [ʃpuːr] *f* (*pl* -en) track, trail; (*fig*) trace.
spürbar ['ʃpyːrbaːr] *adj* perceptible, noticeable. **spüren** *v* trace; (*folgen*) track; (*fühlen*) feel. **Spürsinn** *m* shrewdness.
Staat [ʃtaːt] *m* (*pl* -e) state. **staatlich** *adj* state. **Staats||angehörige(r)** *m* citizen, national. **–angehörigkeit** *f* nationality. **–anwalt** *m* public prosecutor. **–bürger** *m* citizen. **–mann** *m* statesman. **–streich** *m* coup d'état.
Stab [ʃtaːp] *m* (*pl* **Stäbe**) staff; (*Metall*) bar; (*Holz*) stick, pole.
stabil [ʃtaˈbiːl] *adj* stable. **–isieren** *v* stabilize. **Stabilität** *f* stability.
Stachel ['ʃtaxəl] *m* (*pl* -n) spike, prickle; (*Biene*) sting. **–beere** *f* gooseberry. **–draht** *m* barbed wire. **stachel||ig** *adj* prickly; stinging. **–n** *v* prick; sting. **Stachelschwein** *neut* porcupine.
Stadion ['ʃtaːdiɔn] *neut* (*pl* **Stadien**) stadium.
Stadt [ʃtat] *f* (*pl* **Städte**) town, city.
städtisch ['ʃtɛtiʃ] *adj* urban; (*Verwaltung*) municipal.
Stadt||mitte *f* town centre. **–plan** *m* town map. **–rat** *m* town council; (*Person*) councillor.
Staffel ['ʃtafəl] *f* (*pl* -n) rung, step; (*Mil*) detachment; (*Lauf*) relay. **–ei** *f* (*pl* -en) easel.
Stahl [ʃtaːl] *m* (*pl* -e) steel.
Stall [ʃtal] *m* (*pl* **Ställe**) (*Pferde*) stable; (*Hunde*) kennel; (*Schweine*) sty; (*Kuhe*) cowshed.
Stamm [ʃtam] *m* (*pl* **Stämme**) (*Volk*) tribe; (*Baum*) trunk; (*Stengel*) stalk, stem. **–baum** *m* family tree, genealogy; (*Hund*) pedigree. **stammen (von)** *v* (*Ort*) come (from); (*Familie*) be descended (from); (*fig, Gramm*) be derived (from).
stampfen ['ʃtampfən] *v* stamp; (*zerstampfen*) mash, crush.
Stand [ʃtant] *m* (*pl* **Stände**) stand; (*Markt*) stall; (*Höhe*) level, height; (*Stellung*) position, situation.

Standard ['ʃtandart] *m* (*pl* -s) standard.
Standbild ['ʃtantbilt] *neut* statue.
Ständer ['ʃtɛndər] *m* (*pl* -) stand.
Standesamt ['ʃtandəzamt] *neut* registry office.
standhaft ['ʃtandhaft] *adj* steadfast. **Standhaftigkeit** *f* steadfastness. **standhalten** *v* stand firm.
ständig ['ʃtɛndiç] *adj* permanent; (*laufend*) constant.
Stand‖ort *m* position, station. **–punkt** *m* standpoint.
Stange ['ʃtaŋə] *f* (*pl* -n) pole, bar.
Stanniol [ʃtani'oːl] *neut* (*pl* -e) tinfoil.
Stapel ['ʃtaːpəl] *m* (*pl* -) pile, heap, stack. **stapeln** *v* pile up.
Star[1] [ʃtaːr] *m* (*pl* -e) (*Vogel*) starling.
Star[2] *m* (*pl* -s) (*Film*) star.
Star[3] *m* (*pl* -e) (*Med*) cataract.
stark [ʃtark] *adj* strong; (*Zahl*) numerous; (*dick*) thick(set). **starke Erkältung** severe cold. **stark gesucht** in great demand.
Stärke ['ʃtɛrkə] *f* (*pl* -n) strength; (*Dicke*) stoutness; (*Gewalt*) violence; (*Wäsche-, Chem*) starch. **stärken** *v* strengthen.
starr [ʃtar] *adj* rigid; (*Blick*) fixed, staring. **starren** *v* stare. **Starrheit** *f* rigidity; (*Charakter*) obstinacy.
Start [ʃtart] *m* (*pl* -e) start; (*Flugzeug*) take-off. **starten** *v* start; take off. **Starter** *m* (*pl* -) (*Mot, Sport*) starter. **–klappe** *f* (*Mot*) choke.
Station [ʃtatsi'oːn] *f* (*pl* -en) station; (*Krankenhaus*) ward.
Statistik [ʃta'tistik] *f* (*pl* -en) statistics. **statistisch** *adj* statistical.
statt [ʃtat] *prep* instead of. **Statt** *f* place, stead.
Stätte ['ʃtɛtə] *f* (*pl* -n) place, spot.
*****statt‖finden** *v* take place. **–haft** *adj* allowed, permissible. **–lich** *adj* stately; (*Summe*) considerable.
Statut [ʃta'tuːt] *neut* (*pl* -en) statute.
Staub [ʃtaup] *m* dust. **staubig** *adj* dusty. **Staubtuch** *neut* duster.
stauen ['ʃtauən] *v* dam (up); (*Ladung*) stow (away). **sich stauen** accumulate, pile up.
staunen ['ʃtaunən] *v* be astonished. **Staunen** *neut* (*pl* -) astonishment.
Steak [steɪk] *neut* (*pl* -s) steak.
*****stechen** ['ʃtɛçən] *v* (*Insekt*) sting; (*Dorn*) prick; (*mit einer Waffe*) stab, jab. **–d** *adj* stinging; (*fig*) piercing. **Stechpalme** *f* holly.

Steck‖brief *m* warrant (for arrest). **–dose** *f* (*Elek*) socket.
stecken ['ʃtɛkən] *v* put, place, insert; (*sich befinden*) be, lie. **etwas in die Tasche stecken** put something in one's pocket. **in Brand stecken** set fire to. **da steckt er!** there he is! that's where he's hiding! **es steckt etwas dahinter** there's more to it than meets the eye. **steckenbleiben** *v* be or get stuck. **Steck‖enpferd** *neut* hobbyhorse; (*fig*) hobby. **–er** *m* (*pl* -) (*Elek*) plug. **–nadel** *f* pin.
Steg [ʃteɪk] *m* (*pl* -e) (foot)path; (*Brücke*) (foot)bridge; (*Geige*) bridge.
*****stehen** ['ʃteɪən] *v* stand; (*sein*) be (situated). **in Verdacht stehen** be suspected. **offen stehen** be open. **das Kleid steht dir (gut)** the dress suits you. **stehen‖bleiben** *v* (*nicht weitergehen*) come to a standstill, stop; (*nicht umfallen*) remain standing. **–d** *adj* standing; (*ständig*) permanent.
*****stehlen** ['ʃteɪlən] *v* steal. **Stehlen** *neut* (*unz.*) stealing, theft.
steif [ʃtaif] *adj* stiff. **Steifheit** *f* stiffness.
Steig [ʃtaik] *m* (*pl* -e) path. **–bügel** *m* stirrup. **steigen** *v* rise; (*klettern*) climb. **–d** *adj* rising; (*wachsend*) growing.
steigern ['ʃtaigərn] *v* raise, increase. **Steigerung** *f* (*pl* -en) rise, increase.
Steigung ['ʃtaiguŋ] *f* (*pl* -en) rise, incline.
steil [ʃtail] *adj* steep.
Stein [ʃtain] *m* (*pl* -e) stone. **–bock** *m* (*Tier*) ibex; (*Astrol*) Capricorn. **–bruch** *m* quarry. **steinern** *adj* stone. **Steingut** *neut* stoneware, pottery. **steinigen** *v* stone (to death). **Steinzeit** *f* Stone Age.
Stelle ['ʃtɛlə] *f* (*pl* -n) place; (*Arbeit*) job, position; (*in einem Buch*) passage. **an Ort und Stelle** on the spot. **an Stelle von** in place of. **eine Stelle bekleiden** hold a position.
stellen ['ʃtɛlən] *v* put, place; (*Frage*) ask; (*Forderung*) make. **zufriedenstellen** satisfy. **eine Falle stellen** set a trap. **sich stellen** present oneself; (*vortäuschen*) pretend, feign.
Stellen‖angebot *neut* vacancy, vacant position. **–nachweis** *m* employment agency.
Stellung ['ʃtɛluŋ] *f* (*pl* -en) position; (*Arbeit*) post, position; (*Ansicht*) attitude, opinion; (*Körperhaltung*) posture. **–nahme** *f* comment, opinion.

stopfen

stellvertretend adj deputy, delegated. **Stellvertret||er** m deputy, representative. **-ung** f representation.
Stelze ['ʃtɛltsə] f (pl -n) stilt.
Stempel ['ʃtɛmpəl] m (pl -) stamp. **-geld** neut (umg.) dole money. **stempeln** v stamp. **stempeln gehen** (umg.) go on the dole.
Stengel ['ʃtɛŋəl] m (pl -) stalk.
Stenograph [ʃtenoˈgraːf] m (pl -en) stenographer. **-ie** f shorthand. **Stenotypist(in)** shorthand typist.
Steppe ['ʃtɛpə] f (pl -n) steppe, prairie.
Sterbe||bett neut deathbed. **-fall** m a death.
***sterben** ['ʃtɛrbən] v die. **Sterben** neut death. **sterblich** adj mortal. **Sterblichkeit** f mortality.
Stereoanlage ['ʃtereoanlaːgə] f stereo (system).
steril [ʃteˈriːl] adj sterile. **-isieren** v sterilize.
Stern [ʃtɛrn] m (pl -e) star. **-bild** neut constellation. **-chen** neut asterisk. **-kunde** f astronomy.
stet [ʃteːt] or **stetig** adj constant, continual. **stets** adv always, constantly.
Steuer ['ʃtɔyər] f (pl -n) tax.
Steuer||behörde f inland revenue, (US) internal revenue. **-berater** m tax consultant. **-erklärung** f tax return. **-hinterziehung** f tax evasion.
steuern ['ʃtɔyərn] v steer.
steuerpflichtig ['ʃtɔyərpfliçtiç] adj taxable, subject to taxation.
Steuer||rad neut steering wheel. **-säule** f steering column.
Steuerung ['ʃtɔyəruŋ] f (pl -en) steering. **Steuerzahler** ['ʃtɔyərtsaːlər] m tax-payer.
Stich [ʃtiç] m (pl -e) prick; (Insekt) sting; (Messer) stab; (Nähen) stitch; (Kartenspiel) trick. **im Stich lassen** abandon, leave in the lurch.
sticken ['ʃtikən] v embroider. **Stickerei** f embroidery.
Stickstoff ['ʃtikʃtɔf] m nitrogen.
Stiefbruder ['ʃtiːfbruːdər] m stepbrother.
Stiefel ['ʃtiːfəl] m (pl -) boot.
Stief||eltern pl step-parents. **-kind** neut stepchild. **-mutter** f stepmother. **-mütterchen** neut pansy. **-schwester** f stepsister. **-sohn** m stepson. **-tochter** f stepdaughter. **-vater** m stepfather.
Stiel [ʃtiːl] m (pl -e) handle; (Bot) stalk.

Stier [ʃtiːr] m (pl -e) bull. **-kampf** m bullfight.
Stift¹ [ʃtift] m (pl -e) peg; (Bleistift) pencil; (Pflocke) pin.
Stift² neut (pl -e or -er) (charitable) foundation; (Kloster) monastery.
stiften ['ʃtiftən] v donate; (gründen) found, establish; (Frieden) make. **Stifter** m founder. **Stiftung** f (pl -en) (charitable) foundation, institution; (geschenktes Vermögen) endowment, bequest.
Stil [ʃtiːl] m (pl -e) style.
still [ʃtil] adj quiet, still; (schweigend) silent. **Stille** f quiet, stillness, silence. **stillen** v allay, stop; (Schmerz) soothe; (Durst) quench; (Säugling) nurse. **stillschweigen** v be silent. **-d** adj silent; (fig) implicit, tacit. **Stillstand** m standstill. **stillstehen** v stand still; (aufhören) stop.
Stimme ['ʃtimə] f (pl -n) voice; (Wahl) vote; (Musik) part. **seine Stimme abgeben** cast one's vote. **sich der Stimme enthalten** abstain (from voting). **stimmen** v (richtig sein) be right or true, tally; (Wahl) vote; (Instrument) tune. **hier stimmt etwas nicht!** something's wrong here! **stimmt schon!** that's all right. **Stimm||enthaltung** f abstention. **-recht** neut franchise. **-ung** f (pl -en) mood, atmosphere; (Musik) tuning.
***stinken** ['ʃtiŋkən] v stink.
Stipendium [ʃtiˈpɛndium] neut (pl Stipendien) scholarship, (student) grant.
Stirn [ʃtirn] f (pl -en) forehead. **die Stirn runzeln** frown.
stöbern ['ʃtøːbərn] v rummage (about).
Stock [ʃtɔk] m (pl Stöcke) stick, rod; (Musik) baton; (Etage) storey. **stockdunkel** adj pitch dark.
stocken ['ʃtɔkən] v stoop, come to a standstill; (Milch) curdle. **Stockung** f (pl -en) standstill, stop; (Verkehr) congestion, jam.
Stockwerk ['ʃtɔkvɛrk] neut floor, storey.
Stoff [ʃtɔf] m (pl -e) matter; (Gewebe, fig) material.
stöhnen ['ʃtøːnən] v groan.
Stolle ['ʃtɔlə] f (pl -n) or **Stollen** m (pl -) (German) Christmas cake.
stolpern ['ʃtɔlpərn] v stumble.
stolz [ʃtɔlts] adj proud. **Stolz** m pride.
stopfen ['ʃtɔpfən] v stuff, fill; (Strümpfe) darn; (sättigen) fill up; (Med) constipate.

Stopp [ʃtɔp] *m* (*unz.*) hitchhiking.
Stoppel ['ʃtɔpəl] *f* (*pl* -n) stubble.
stoppen ['ʃtɔpən] *v* stop. **Stopplicht** *neut* brake light.
Stöpsel ['ʃtœpsəl] *m* (*pl* -) stopper; (*Elek*) plug.
Storch [ʃtɔrç] *m* (*pl* **Störche**) stork.
stören ['ʃtœɪrən] *v* disturb; (*belästigen*) bother, trouble; (*Radio*) interfere. **–d** *adj* disturbing, troublesome. **Störenfried** *m* troublemaker. **Störung** *f* (*pl* -en) disturbance; trouble; (*Radio*) interference.
Stoß [ʃtoɪs] *m* (*pl* **Stöße**) push, shove; (*Schlag*) blow; (*Tritt*) kick; (*Haufen*) heap. **–dämpfer** *m* shock-absorber. **stoßen** *v* push, shove; knock; (*fig*) take offence. **stoßen an** run across. **sich stoßen an** bump into *or* against; (*fig*) take offence at. **Stoß||stange** *f* bumper. **–zahn** *m* tusk.
stottern ['ʃtɔtərn] *v* stutter, stammer.
Straf||anstalt *f* prison, penal institution. **–arbeit** *f* (*Schule*) punishment, lines *pl*. **strafbar** *adj* punishable.
Strafe ['ʃtraɪfə] *f* (*pl* -n) punishment; (*fig*) penalty; (*Jur*) sentence. **strafen** *v* punish.
Straferlaß *m* pardon; (*allgemeiner*) amnesty.
straff [ʃtraf] *adj* tight, taught; (*fig*) strict, stern.
Straf||geld *neut* fine. **–gericht** *neut* criminal court.
sträflich ['ʃtrɛɪfliç] *adj* punishable. **Sträfling** *m* prisoner.
Straf||recht *neut* criminal law. **–tat** *f* offence.
Strahl [ʃtraɪl] *m* (*pl* -en) ray, beam; (*Blitz*) flash; (*Wasser*) jet. **strahlen** *v* radiate; (*fig*) beam. **–d** *adj* beaming.
Strahlmotor *m* jet engine. **Strahlung** *f* radiation.
Strand [ʃtrant] *m* (*pl* -e) beach, shore. **stranden** *v* run aground; (*fig*) founder.
strapazieren [ʃtrapa'tsiɪrən] *v* fatigue, tire; (*abnutzen*) wear out.
Straße ['ʃtraɪsə] *f* (*pl* -n) street. **Straßen||bahn** *f* tram, (*US*) street car. **–kreuzung** *f* crossing. **–laterne** *f* street lamp. **–sperre** *f* roadblock. **–überführung** *f* overpass. **–unterführung** *f* underpass.
sträuben ['ʃtrɔybən] *v* ruffle (up). **sich sträuben** (*Haare*) stand up on end; (*fig*) struggle (against), resist.
Strauch [ʃtraux] *m* (*pl* **Sträucher**) bush.

Strauß¹ [ʃtraus] *m* (*pl* -e) (*Vogel*) ostrich.
Strauß² *m* (*pl* **Sträuße**) bouquet, bunch (of flowers).
streben ['ʃtreɪbən] *v* strive.
Strecke ['ʃtrɛkə] *f* (*pl* -n) stretch, distance; (*Math*, *Sport*) distance; (*Teilschnitt*) section. **strecken** *v* stretch (out), extend.
Streich [ʃtraiç] *m* (*pl* -e) stroke, blow; (*Peitsche*) lash; (*Possen*) trick, prank.
streicheln ['ʃtraiçəln] *v* stroke, pet.
*streichen ['ʃtraiçən] *v* stroke, rub; (*Farbe*) paint; (*gehen*) wander, ramble. **Streich||instrument** *neut* string instrument. **–musik** *f* string music. **–quartett** *neut* string quartet.
Streife ['ʃtraifə] *f* (*pl* -n) patrol; (*Streifzug*) stroll, look around.
Streifen ['ʃtraifən] *m* (*pl* -) stripe; (*Land*) strip.
streifen ['ʃtraifən] *v* streak, stripe; (*berühren*) brush (against), touch; (*wandern*) wander, roam.
Streik [ʃtraik] *m* (*pl* -s) strike. **–brecher** *m* strike-breaker; (*umg.*) scab. **streiken** *v* (go on) strike.
Streit [ʃtrait] *m* (*pl* -e) dispute, quarrel; (*Kampf*) conflict; (*Schlägerei*) fight, brawl. **streiten** *v* dispute, quarrel. **sich streiten um** quarrel about, fight over. **Streitfrage** *f* matter in dispute. **streit||ig** *adj* contested; (*fraglich*) controversial. **–lustig** *adj* quarrelsome, aggressive.
streng [ʃtrɛŋ] *adj* stern, severe, strict. **Strenge** *f* severity, strictness.
streuen ['ʃtrɔyən] *v* scatter, spread.
Strich [ʃtriç] *m* (*pl* -e) stroke, line; (*Vogel*) flight; (*Gebiet*) district; (*Kompaß*) compass point. **–punkt** *m* semicolon.
Strick [ʃtrik] *m* (*pl* -e) cord, string, (thin) rope; (*Kind*) rascal. **–arbeit** *f* knitting; (*Artikel*) knitwear. **stricken** *v* knit. **Strick||maschine** *f* knitting machine. **–nadel** *f* knitting needle. **–zeug** *neut* knitting.
strittig ['ʃtritiç] *adj* questionable, debatable; (*Angelegenheit*) disputed.
Stroh [ʃtroɪ] *neut* straw. **–dach** *neut* thatched roof.
Strolch [ʃtrɔlç] *m* (*pl* -e) tramp, vagabond. **strolchen** *v* roam, stroll about.
Strom [ʃtroɪm] *m* (*pl* **Ströme**) (*Fluß*) (large) river; (*Strömung*, *Elek*) current;

(*fig*) stream. **strom‖abwärts** *adv* downstream. **–aufwärts** *adv* upstream.
strömen [ˈʃtrœɪmən] *v* stream, flow; (*Regen*) pour.
Strom‖erzeuger *m* generator. **–sperre** *f* power cut.
Strömung [ˈʃtrœɪmuŋ] *f* (*pl* -en) current.
Struktur [ʃtrukˈtuːr] *f* (*pl* -en) structure.
Strumpf [ʃtrumpf] *m* (*pl* **Strümpfe**) stocking; (*Socke*) sock.
Stube [ˈʃtuːbə] *f* (*pl* -n) room, chamber. **stubenrein** *adj* house-trained.
Stück [ʃtyk] *neut* (*pl* -e) piece; (*Theater*) play; (*Vieh*) head. **in Stücke gehen** fall to pieces. **Stückchen** *neut* bit, little piece; (*Papier*) scrap. **stückeln** *v* cut *or* chop into pieces.
Student [ʃtuˈdɛnt] *m* (*pl* -en) student. **–enheim** *neut* hall of residence, (*US*) dorm(itory). **Studentin** *f* (*pl* -nen) (woman) student.
Studien‖direktor *m* headmaster, (*US*) principal. **–plan** *m* syllabus.
studieren [ʃtuˈdiːrən] *v* study. **Studio** *neut* studio. **Studium** *neut* studies *pl*; (*Untersuchung*) study.
Stufe [ˈʃtuːfə] *f* (*pl* -n) step; (*Leiter*) rung; (*fig*) stage. **stufen‖los** *adj* infinitely variable. **–weise** *adv* gradually.
Stuhl [ʃtuːl] *m* (*pl* **Stühle**) chair; (*ohne Lehne*) stool. **–gang** *m* bowel movement.
stumm [ʃtum] *adj* mute, dumb; (*schweigend*) silent. **Stumme(r)** *m* mute, dumb person.
Stummel [ˈʃtuməl] *m* (*pl* -) stump. **Stumm‖film** *m* silent film. **–heit** *f* dumbness.
stumpf [ʃtumpf] *adj* blunt; (*Mensch*) dull. **Stumpf‖heit** *f* bluntness; dullness. **–sinn** *m* stupidity. **stumpfsinnig** *adj* stupid, dull-witted.
Stunde [ˈʃtundə] *f* (*pl* -n) hour; (*Unterricht*) lesson. **Stunden‖plan** *m* timetable. **–satz** *m* hourly rate.
stupid [ʃtuˈpiːt] *adj* half-witted, idiotic.
stur [ʃtuːr] *adj* stubborn.
Sturm [ʃturm] *m* (*pl* **Stürme**) storm; (*Angriff*) attack.
stürmen [ˈʃtyrmən] *v* storm; (*Wind*) blow. **Stürmer** *m* (*pl* -) assailant; (*Fußball*) forward. **stürmisch** *adj* stormy.
Sturz [ʃturts] *m* (*pl* **Stürze**) fall; (*Zusammenbruch*) collapse.
stürzen [ˈʃtyrtsən] *v* (*fallen*) fall (down); (*umkippen*) overturn; (*Regierung*) over-

throw; (*eilen*) dash, rush. **sich stürzen auf** rush at.
Sturzhelm [ˈʃturtshɛlm] *m* crash-helmet.
Stute [ˈʃtuːtə] *f* (*pl* -n) mare. **–nfüllen** *neut* foal, filly.
Stütze [ˈʃtytsə] *f* (*pl* -n) prop, support.
stutzen¹ [ˈʃtutsən] *v* stop short, be startled.
stutzen² *v* (*schneiden*) clip, trim; (*Schwanz*) dock.
stützen [ˈʃtytsən] *v* prop, support. **Stützpunkt** *m* fulcrum; (*Mil*) stronghold.
subjektiv [subjɛkˈtiːf] *adj* subjective.
subtil [zupˈtiːl] *adj* subtle.
Subvention [zupvɛntsiˈoːn] *f* (*pl* -en) subsidy.
Suche [ˈzuːxə] *f* (*pl* -n) search. **suchen** *v* look for, search for. **Sucher** *m* (*pl* -) searcher. **Sucht** *f* (*pl* **Süchte**) addiction; (*fig*) craving, passion.
süchtig [ˈzyçtiç] *adj* addicted. **Süchtige(r)** *m* addict.
Süd(en) [zyːt (ˈzyːdən)] *m* south. **Süd‖afrika** *neut* South Africa. **–amerika** *neut* South America. **–länder(in)** southerner.
südlich [ˈzyːtliç] *adj* southern.
Südost(en) [zyːdˈɔst(ən)] *m* southeast. **südöstlich** *adj* southeast(ern); (*Wind, Richtung*) southeasterly.
Südpol [ˈzyːtpoːl] *m* South Pole.
südwärts [ˈzyːtverts] *adv* southwards.
Südwest(en) [zyːdˈvɛst(ən)] *m* southwest. **südwestlich** *adj* southwest(ern); (*Wind, Richtung*) southwesterly.
Sühne [ˈzyːnə] *f* (*pl* -n) atonement. **sühnen** *v* atone for.
Sultanine [zultaˈniːnə] *f* (*pl* -n) sultana.
Sülze [ˈzyltsə] *f* (*pl* -n) brawn.
Summe [ˈzumə] *f* (*pl* -n) sum total; (*Geld*) sum, amount.
summen [ˈzumən] *v* buzz, hum.
summieren [zuˈmiːrən] *v* add up. **Summierung** *f* summation.
Sumpf [zumpf] *m* (*pl* **Sümpfe**) swamp, marsh.
Sund [zunt] *m* (*pl* -e) sound, channel.
Sünde [ˈzyndə] *f* (*pl* -n) sin. **–nbock** *m* scapegoat. **Sünder(in)** sinner. **sündhaft** *adj* sinful.
Suppe [ˈzupə] *f* (*pl* -n) soup.
süß [zyːs] *adj* sweet. **Süße** *f* sweetness. **süßen** *v* sweeten. **Süßigkeit** *f* sweetness. **Süßigkeiten** *pl* sweets, (*US*) candy *sing*. **süßlich** *adj* sweetish; (*fig*) slushy, senti-

mental. **Süß||waren** *pl* sweets, (*US*) candy *sing*. **-wasser** *neut* fresh water.

Symbol [zym'boːl] *neut* (*pl* -e) symbol. **symbol||isch** *adj* symbolic. **-isieren** *v* symbolize.

sympathisch [zym'paːtiʃ] *adj* likeable, congenial.

Symptom [zymp'toːm] *neut* (*pl* -e) symptom.

Synagoge [zyna'goːgə] *f* (*pl* -n) synagogue.

synchron ['zynkron] *adj* synchronous. **-isieren** *v* synchronize.

Synthese [zyn'teːzə] *f* (*pl* -n) synthesis. **Syphilis** ['zyːfilis] *f* syphilis.

System [zys'teːm] *neut* (*pl* -e) system. **systematisch** *adj* systematic.

Szene ['stseːnə] *f* (*pl* -n) scene.

T

Tabak ['taːbak] *m* (*pl* -e) tobacco.

Tabelle [ta'bɛlə] *f* (*pl* -n) table, list. **tabellenförmig** *adj* tabular.

Tablette [ta'blɛtə] *f* (*pl* -n) pill, tablet.

Tadel ['taːdəl] *m* blame; reproach, reprimand; (*Schule*) bad mark. **tadellos** *adj* faultless. **tadeln** *v* reproach, scold, criticize.

Tafel ['taːfəl] *f* (*pl* -n) board; (*Schule*) blackboard; (*Schokolade*) bar; (*Tabelle*) table, chart. **die Tafel decken** lay the table.

Tag [taːk] *m* (*pl* -e) day. **am Tag** by day. **Tages||anbruch** *m* dawn, daybreak. **-licht** *neut* daylight. **-zeitung** *f* daily (newspaper). **täglich** *adj* daily.

Taille ['taljə] *f* waist.

Takelwerk ['taːkəlvɛrk] *neut* rigging.

Takt [takt] *m* (*Musik*) time, beat; (*Tech*) stroke; (*Höflichkeit*) tact. **Zweitaktmotor** *m* two-stroke engine.

Taktik ['taktik] *f* (*pl* -en) tactics *pl*. **taktisch** *adj* tactical.

taktlos ['taktloːs] *adj* tactless.

Tal [taːl] *neut* (*pl* **Täler**) valley, vale.

Talent [ta'lɛnt] *neut* (*pl* -e) talent, gift. **talentiert** *adj* talented, gifted.

Talk [talk] *m* talcum.

Tampon [tã'põ] *m* (*pl* -s) (*Med*) swab; (*für Frauen*) tampon.

tändeln ['tɛndəln] *v* flirt; (*langsam gehen*,

usw.) dawdle, dally. **Tändelei** *f* (*pl* -en) flirtation.

Tang [taŋ] *m* (*pl* -e) seaweed.

Tank [taŋk] *m* (*pl* -e) tank. **tanken** *v* (*Mot*) refuel, fill up. **Tank||schiff** *neut* tanker. **-stelle** *f* petrol station.

Tanne ['tanə] *f* fir. **Tannen||baum** *m* fir-tree. **-zapfen** *m* fir-cone.

Tante ['tantə] *f* (*pl* -n) aunt.

Tanz [tants] *m* (*pl* **Tänze**) dance; (*Tanzen*) dancing. **tanzen** *v* dance. **Tänzer** *m* (*pl* -), **Tänzerin** *f* (*pl* -nen) dancer. **Tanz||lokal** *neut* dancehall. **-platz** *m* dance-floor.

Tapete [ta'peːtə] *f* (*pl* -n) wallpaper. **tapezieren** *v* paper, decorate.

tapfer ['tapfər] *adj* brave, courageous. **Tapferkeit** *f* bravery, courage.

tappen ['tapən] *v* grope, fumble about.

Tarif [ta'riːf] *m* (*pl* -e) price list. **-verhandlungen** *pl* collective bargaining *sing*.

tarnen ['tarnən] *v* camouflage. **Tarnung** *f* camouflage.

Tasche ['taʃə] *f* (*pl* -n) pocket; suitcase; handbag; (*Schule*) satchel; (*Aktentasche*) briefcase. **Taschen||dieb** *m* pickpocket. **-geld** *neut* pocket money. **-lampe** *f* torch. **-messer** *neut* penknife.

Tasse ['tasə] *f* (*pl* -n) cup. **eine Tasse Kaffee** a cup of coffee.

Taste ['tastə] *f* (*pl* -n) (*Klavier, Schreibmaschine*) key; (push)button. **tasten** *v* feel, touch. **Tastbrett** (*Musik*) *neut also* **Tastatur** keyboard.

Tat [taːt] *f* (*pl* -en) deed, act. **in der Tat** in reality, really.

tätig ['tɛːtiç] *adj* active, busy, employed. **tätig sein als** be employed as, practise. **tätig sein bei** work for. **Tätigkeit** *f* (*pl* -en) activity; (*Beruf*) work, occupation.

tätowieren [tɛto'viːrən] *v* tattoo. **Tätowierung** *f* (*pl* -en) tattoo.

Tatsache ['taːtzaxə] *f* (*pl* -n) fact. **tatsächlich** *adj* real, actual. *adv* really, actually. *interj* really? is that so?

Tatze ['tatsə] *f* (*pl* -n) paw.

Tau¹ [tau] *neut* (*pl* -e) (*Seil*) rope, cable.

Tau² *m* (*unz.*) dew. **Tauwetter** *neut* thaw.

taub [taup] *adj* deaf.

Taube ['taubə] *f* (*pl* -n) pigeon, dove.

taubstumm ['taupʃtum] *adj* deaf and dumb. **Taubstumme(r)** deaf mute.

tauchen ['tauxən] *v* dive, plunge; immerse, dip. **Tauchen** *neut* diving. **Taucher** *m* (*pl* -) diver.

tauen ['tauən] v thaw, melt.
Taufe ['taufə] f (pl -n) baptism, christening. **taufen** v baptize, christen. **Taufname** m Christian name.
taugen ['taugən] v **taugen zu** be good or fit for. **zu nichts taugen** be useless or worthless. **Taugenichts** m (pl -e) good-for-nothing.
taumeln ['tauməln] v stagger, reel.
Tausch [tauʃ] m (pl -e) exchange. **tausch‖bar** adj exchangeable. **–en** v exchange, swap.
täuschen ['tɔyʃən] v deceive, delude. **–d** adj deceptive.
Tauschhandel ['tauʃhandəl] m barter.
Täuschung ['tɔyʃuŋ] f (pl -en) delusion, illusion; (Schwindel) deception, fraud.
tausend ['tauzənt] adj thousand.
Taxe ['taksə] f (pl -n) charge, fee; (Schätzung) valuation. **taxieren** v value, assess.
Taxi ['taksi] neut or m (pl -s) taxi. **–fahrer** m taxi-driver.
Technik ['tɛçnik] f (pl -n) technique; engineering, technology. **–er** m (pl -) technician. **Technologie** f technology. **technologisch** technological.
Tee [teː] m tea. **–kanne** f teapot. **–löffel** m teaspoon. **–service** neut tea-set.
Teer [teːr] m (pl -e) tar, pitch.
Teich [taiç] m (pl -e) pond.
Teig [taik] m (pl -e) dough; (flüssig) batter. **–waren** pl noodles pl.
Teil [tail] m or neut (pl -e) part; share, portion. **teilbar** adj divisible. **Teil‖beschäftigung** f part-time work. **–chen** neut particle. **teil‖en** v divide; share out. **–haben** take part (in). **Teilnahme** f participation; interest; (Mitleid) sympathy. **teil‖nehmen** v take part in. **–s** adv partly. **Teilung** f (pl -en) division, partition; sharing out, distribution. **teilweise** adj partial. adv partly.
Telegramm [tele'gram] neut (pl -e) telegram.
Telephon [tele'foːn] neut (pl -e) telephone. **–buch** neut telephone directory. **telephonieren** v telephone, ring up. **Telephon‖zelle** f call box. **–zentrale** f telephone exchange.
Teleskop [tele'skɔp] neut (pl -e) telescope.
Teller ['tɛlər] m (pl -) plate; (Tech) disc.
Tempel ['tɛmpəl] m (pl -) temple.

Temperament [tɛmpera'mɛnt] neut (pl -e) temperament, disposition. **temperamentvoll** adj high-spirited, lively.
Temperatur [tɛmpera'tuːr] f temperature.
Tempo ['tɛmpo] neut (pl -s or -pi) pace, tempo.
temporär [tɛmpo'rɛːr] adj temporary.
Tendenz [tɛn'dɛnts] f (pl -en) tendency, propensity.
Tennis ['tɛnis] neut tennis. **–platz** m tennis court. **–schläger** m tennis racket.
Tenor [te'noːr] m (pl -e) tenor.
Teppich ['tɛpiç] m (pl -e) carpet, rug; (Wand) tapestry.
Termin [tɛr'miːn] m (pl -e) fixed date; closing date, deadline. **–geschäft** neut (Komm) futures pl.
Terpentinöl [tɛrpɛn'tiːnøːl] neut turpentine.
Terrasse [tɛ'rasə] f (pl -n) terrace.
Terror ['tɛrɔr] m terror. **–ismus** m terrorism. **–ist(in)** terrorist. **terroristisch** adj terrorist.
Testament [tɛsta'mɛnt] neut (pl -e) will; (Bibel) testament, **Testaments‖bestätigung** f probate. **–vollstrecker** m executor.
testieren [tɛs'tiːrən] v make one's will; bequeath.
teuer ['tɔyər] adj expensive, dear; (lieb) dear, cherished. adv dearly. **Teuerung** f (pl -en) rising prices pl, increase in the cost of living. **Teuerungszulage** f cost-of-living bonus.
Teufel ['tɔyfəl] m devil, Satan. **Teufels‖beschwörung** f exorcism. **–skreis** m vicious circle. **teuflisch** adj devilish, diabolical.
Text [tɛkst] m (pl -e) text; (Lied) lyrics pl; (Oper) libretto. **–buch** neut libretto.
Textilien [tɛks'tiːliən] or **Textilwaren** pl textiles.
Theater [te'aːtər] neut (pl -) theatre; (umg.) fuss, to do. **theatralisch** adj theatrical.
Thema ['teːma] neut (pl Themen) theme, subject.
Theologe [teo'loːgə] m (pl -n) theologian. **Theologie** f theology. **theologisch** adj theological.
Theoretiker [teo'reːtikər] m (pl -) theorist. **theoretisch** adj theoretical. **Theorie** f (pl -n) theory.
Therapie [tera'piː] f (pl -n) therapy.

thermisch ['tɛrmɪʃ] *adj* thermal.
Thermometer [tɛrmo'mɛitər] *neut (pl -)* thermometer.
Thermosflasche ['tɛrmɔsflaʃə] *f* vacuum flask, thermos .
Thermostat [tɛrmo'ʃtait] *m (pl -en)* thermostat.
These [teizə] *f (pl -n)* thesis.
Thrombose [trɔm'boizə] *f (pl -n)* thrombosis.
Thron [troin] *m (pl -e)* throne. **−erbe** *m* heir to the throne.
Thunfisch ['tuinfɪʃ] *m* tuna.
Thüringen ['tyriŋən] *neut* Thuringia.
Thymian ['tymian] *m* thyme.
ticken ['tikən] *v* tick.
tief [tiif] *adj* deep; (*Musik*) low(-pitched), bass; (*Stimme*) deep; (*Sinn*) profound; extreme. *adv* deep; (*Atmen*) deeply. **aus tiefstem Herzen** from the bottom of one's heart. **tief in der Nacht** at dead of night. **tiefbewegt** *adj* deeply moved. **Tief‖druckgebeit** *neut* low-pressure area. **−e** *f* depth. **−ebene** *f* lowlands *pl.* **tief‖gekühlt** *adj* deep-frozen. **−greifend** *adj* far-reaching. **Tief‖kühltruhe** *f* freezer, deep freeze. **−punkt** *m* low(est) point.
Tiegel ['tiigəl] *m (pl -)* saucepan.
Tier [tiir] *neut (pl -e)* animal, beast. **hohes Tier** (*umg.*) big shot. **Tier‖arzt** *m* veterinary surgeon, (*umg.*) vet. **−garten** *m* zoological gardens *pl.* **tierisch** *adj* animal; (*brutal*) bestial, brutal. **Tier‖kreis** *m* zodiac. **−welt** *f* animal kingdom, fauna. **−zucht** *f* livestock breeding.
Tiger ['tiigər] *m (pl -)* tiger.
tilgen ['tilgən] *v* (*streichen*) delete, erase; (*ausrotten*) exterminate; (*Schuld*) pay off. **Tilgung** *f (pl -en)* deletion; extermination; discharge, repayment.
Tinte ['tintə] *f* ink. **−nklecks** *m* ink-stain.
Tip [tip] *m (pl -s)* hint; (*Sport*) tip.
tippen ['tipən] *v* tap; (*mit der Schreibmaschine*) type. **Tippfehler** *m* typing error.
Tisch [tiʃ] *m (pl -e)* table. **den Tisch decken/abdecken** lay/clear the table. **Tich‖gast** *m* diner, guest (at table). **−gesellschaft** *f* dinner party.
Tischler ['tiʃlər] *m* carpenter, cabinet-maker. **−arbeit** *f* carpentry.
Titel ['tiitəl] *m (pl -)* title. **−bild** *neut* frontispiece. **−kopf** *m* heading.
Toast [toist] *m (pl -e)* toast. **toasten** *v* toast. **Toaster** *m (pl -)* toaster.

toben ['toibən] *v* rage, rave. **tobsüchtig** *adj* raving, frantic.
Tochter ['tɔxtər] *f (pl Töchter)* daughter.
Tod [toit] *m (pl -e)* death. **Todes‖anzeige** *f* obituary. **−fall** *m* (a case of) death. **−kampf** *m* death throes *pl.* **−strafe** *f* death penalty. **−wunde** *f* mortal wound. **Todfeind** *m* deadly enemy. **tödlich** *adj* deadly, fatal, lethal. **todmüde** *adj* dead tired.
Toilette [toa'lɛtə] *f (pl -n)* toilet, lavatory; toilette; dressing-table. **−papier** *neut* toilet paper.
tolerant [tole'rant] *adj* tolerant. **Toleranz** *f* toleration. **tolerieren** *v* tolerate.
toll [tɔl] *adj* raving mad, crazy, wild; (*umg.*) fantastic. **Toll‖heit** *f (pl -en)* madness; fury. **−wut** *f* rabies.
Tölpel ['tœlpəl] *m (pl -e)* awkward person; oaf, boor.
Tomate [to'maitə] *f (pl -n)* tomato.
Ton¹ [toin] *m (pl -e)* clay.
Ton² *m (pl Töne)* sound; (*Musik*) tone, note; accent, stress; tone, fashion. **−art** *f* (*Musik*) key, pitch. **−band** *neut* magnetic tape. **−bandgerät** *neut* tape-recorder. **−blende** *f* tone control.
tönen ['tœinən] *v* ring, resound; (*Foto*) shade, tint.
Ton‖fall *m* intonation; (*Musik*) cadence. **−fülle** *f* volume (of sound). **−leiter** *f* (musical) scale. **−spur** *f* soundtrack.
Tonne ['tɔnə] *f (pl -n)* ton; cask, barrel.
Topf [tɔpf] *m (pl Töpfe)* pot.
Töpfchen ['tœpfçən] *neut (pl -)* (child's) potty. **Töpfer** *m (pl -)* potter. **−waren** *pl* pottery *sing.*
Tor¹ [toir] *m (pl -en)* fool.
Tor² *neut (pl -e)* gate; (*Sport*) goal. **−schütze** *m* (football) scorer.
Torf [tɔrf] *m* peat.
Torheit ['tɔrhait] *f (pl -en)* folly.
töricht ['tœriçt] *adj* foolish. **Törin** *f (pl -nen)* fool, foolish woman.
torkeln ['tɔrkəln] *v* stagger, reel.
Torpedo [tɔr'peido] *m (pl -s)* torpedo. **−boot** *neut* torpedo boat.
Torte ['tɔrtə] *f (pl -n)* (fruit) flan, tart, gâteau.
Tor‖waächter *m (pl -)* gatekeeper. **−wart** *m* goalkeeper.
tot [toit] *adj* dead.
total [to'tail] *adj* total, complete.
Tote(r) ['toitə(r)] dead person.

töten ['tœɪtən] v kill.
Toten‖bett neut deathbed. **–gräber** m gravedigger. **–hemd** neut shroud. **–wagen** m hearse.
totgeboren ['toɪtɡəbɔɪrən] adj stillborn. **sich totlachen** v split one's sides laughing. **totschießen** v shoot dead.
Totschlag ['toɪtʃlak] m manslaughter. **tot‖schlagen** v slay, kill; (Zeit) waste (time). **–schweigen** v hush up. **–sicher** adj absolutely or dead certain.
Tötung ['tœɪtuŋ] f (pl -en) killing.
Tour [tuɪr] f (pl -en) tour, trip. **–ismus** m tourism. **–ist** m (pl -en) tourist.
Trab [traɪp] m trot. **traben** v trot.
Tracht [traxt] f (pl -en) costume, dress.
Tradition [traditsi'oɪn] f (pl -en) tradition. **traditionell** adj traditional.
träge ['trɛɪɡə] adj (faul) lazy; (langsam) ponderous, slow; (schläfrig) sleepy.
*tragen ['traɪɡən] v carry; (Kleider) wear; (stützen) support; (ertragen) endure, bear.
Träger ['trɛɪɡər] m (pl -) carrier; (Mensch) porter; (Balken) girder.
Trägheit ['trɛɪkhaɪt] f laziness; (Langsamkeit) slowness.
tragisch ['traɪɡiʃ] adj tragic. **Tragödie** f (pl -n) tragedy.
Trainer ['trɛɪnər] m (pl -) (Sport) coach, trainer. **trainieren** v train. **Training** neut training. **–sanzug** m track suit.
Traktor ['traktɔr] m (pl -en) tractor.
trampeln ['trampəln] v trample, stamp.
trampen ['trɛmpən] v hitchhike.
Tran [traɪn] m (pl -e) whale oil.
tranchieren [trãˈʃiɪrən] v carve. **Tranchiermesser** neut carving knife.
Träne ['trɛɪnə] f (pl -n) tear.
Trank [traŋk] m (pl Tränke) drink.
tränken ['trɛŋkən] v water; (durchtränken) soak.
transatlantisch [transatˈlantiʃ] adj transatlantic.
Transmission [transmisi'oɪn] f (pl -en) transmission.
Transport [transˈpɔrt] m (pl -e) transportation. **transportieren** v transport. **Transportunternehmen** neut haulage or shipping company.
Tratte ['tratə] f (pl -n) bill of exchange, draft.
Traube ['traʊbə] f (pl -n) grape; bunch of grapes. **Trauben‖lese** f vintage. **–saft** m grape juice. **–zucker** m glucose.

trauen ['traʊən] v trust; (Ehepaar) marry, join in wedlock. **sich trauen** dare.
Trauer ['traʊər] f sorrow, grief; (für Tote) mourning. **–anzeige** f death notice. **trauern** v grieve, mourn. **Trauer‖spiel** neut tragedy. **–weide** f weeping willow. **traurig** adj sad.
Traufe ['traʊfə] f (pl -n) eaves pl. **aus dem Regen in die Traufe** out of the frying pan into the fire. **Traufrinne** f gutter.
traulich ['traʊliç] adj snug, cosy, comfortable.
Traum [traʊm] m (pl Träume) dream. **–bild** neut vision.
träumen ['trɔʏmən] v dream. **Träumer** m (pl -) dreamer. **–ei** f (pl -en) daydream, reverie. **träumerisch** adj dreamy.
Trau‖ring m wedding ring.
*treffen ['trɛfən] v (begegnen) meet; (erreichen) hit; (betreffen) concern; (Vorkehrungen) make; (Maßnahmen) take. **sich treffen** meet; (zufällig geschehen) happen. **Treffen** neut meeting. **treffend** adj striking; (Antwort) pertinent. **Treffpunkt** m meeting place.
*treiben ['traɪbən] v drive, move; (drängen) urge, impel; (Metall) work; (Pflanzen) force; (tun) do, occupy oneself with; (Blüte) blossom; (im Wasser) float. **treibend** adj driving; (im Wasser) floating. **Treib‖er** m driver; (Vieh) drover. **–haus** neut hothouse. **–kraft** f moving force. **–stoff** m fuel.
trennbar ['trɛnbaɪr] adj separable. **trennen** v separate; (abtrennen) sever, cut; (Telef) cut off. **sich trennen** part, separate. **Trennung** f (pl -en) separation.
Treppe ['trɛpə] f (pl -n) staircase, stairs pl. **–ngeländer** neut handrail, banister.
*treten ['treɪtən] v tread, step; (betreten) step on; (stoßen) kick. **Trethebel** m treadle.
treu [trɔʏ] adj loyal, faithful, true; (redlich) honest, sincere. **Treubruch** m disloyalty, breach of faith. **Treue** f loyalty, faithfulness. **treu‖lich** adj loyal, faithful. **–los** adj disloyal, faithless.
Tribüne [triˈbyɪnə] f (pl -n) platform; (für Zuschauer) gallery.
Trichter ['triçtər] m (pl -) funnel; (Bombe) crater.
Trick [trik] m (pl -s) trick. **–film** m animated cartoon.

Trieb [triːp] *m* (*pl* -e) force, drive; (*Antrieb*) impulse; (*Bot*) shoot; (*Instinkt*) instinct.
*triefen [ˈtriːfən] *v* trickle, drip. **triefnaß** *adj* dripping wet.
triftig [ˈtriftiç] *adj* convincing, plausible.
Triller [ˈtrilər] *m* (*pl* -) trill. **trillern** *v* trill.
trinkbar [ˈtriŋkbaːr] *adj* drinkable, potable. **trinken** *v* drink. **Trink‖er** *m* (*pl* -) drinker. **-geld** *neut* tip. **-halm** *m* (drinking) straw. **-spruch** *m* toast.
Tripper [ˈtripər] *m* (*pl* -) gonorrhoea.
Tritt [trit] *m* (*pl* -e) step, tread; (*Stoß*) kick; (*Fußspur*) footprint. **-leiter** *f* stepladder.
Triumph [triˈumf] *m* (*pl* -e) triumph.
trocken [ˈtrɔkən] *adj* dry. **Trockenheit** *f* dryness. **trocknen** *v* dry. **Trockner** *m* (*pl* -) drier.
Trödel [ˈtrœdəl] *m* junk, rubbish. **trödeln** *v* dawdle; (*handeln*) trade in old junk.
Trommel [ˈtrɔməl] *f* (*pl* -n) drum. **-fell** *neut* drumskin; (*Anat*) eardrum. **trommeln** *v* drum. **Trommler** *m* (*pl* -) drummer.
Trompete [trɔmˈpeːtə] *f* (*pl* -n) trumpet.
Tropen [ˈtroːpən] *pl* tropics.
tröpfeln [ˈtrœpfəln] *v* trickle, drip.
Tropfen [ˈtrɔpfən] *m* (*pl* -) drop.
tropisch [ˈtroːpiʃ] *adj* tropical.
Trost [troːst] *m* consolation, solace, comfort.
trösten [ˈtrœstən] *v* console, solace, comfort. **sich trösten mit** take comfort in.
trostlos [ˈtroːstloːs] *adj* disconsolate.
Tröstung [ˈtrœstuŋ] *f* (*pl* -en) consolation, comfort.
Trott [trɔt] *m* (*pl* -e) trot.
Trottel [ˈtrɔtəl] *m* (*pl* -) idiot, fool.
trotz [trɔts] *prep* despite, in spite of. **Trotz** *m* defiance; (*Eigensinn*) obstinacy. **trotzdem** *conj*, *adv* nevertheless. **trotzen** *v* defy; (*widersetzlich sein*) be obstinate. **trotzig** *adj* defiant, obstinate.
trüb(e) [ˈtryːb(ə)] *adj* cloudy, opaque; (*glanzlos*) dull; (*fig*) gloomy. **trüben** *v* cloud, dim, darken. **Trübsinn** *m* gloom, depression. **trübsinnig** *adj* gloomy, miserable.
Trug [truːk] *m* (*Täuschung*) fraud, deceit; (*Sinnes*) delusion.
*trügen [ˈtryːgən] *v* be deceptive; (*betrügen*) deceive. **trügerisch** *adj* treacherous, deceitful.

Truhe [ˈtruːə] *f* (*pl* -n) chest, trunk.
Trümmer *pl* ruins, debris *sing*.
Trumpf [trumpf] *m* (*pl* **Trümpfe**) trump. **-karte** *f* trump (card).
Trunk [truŋk] *m* (*pl* **Trünke**) drink. **-enheit** *f* drunkenness, intoxication. **-sucht** *f* alcoholism.
Trupp [trup] *m* (*pl* -s) troop, gang, band. **Truppe** *f* (*pl* -n) (*Theater*) company; (*Mil*) (combat) troops *pl*. **Truppen** *pl* troops.
Truthahn [ˈtruːthaːn] *m* turkey-cock.
Tscheche [ˈtʃɛçə] *m* (*pl* -n), **Tschechin** *f* (*pl* -nen) Czech. **tschechisch** *adj* Czech. **Tschechoslowakei** *f* Czechoslovakia.
Tuberkulose [tubɛrkuˈloːzə] *f* tuberculosis, TB.
Tuch [tuːx] **1** *neut* (*pl* -e) cloth, fabric. **2** *neut* (*pl* **Tücher**) (piece of) cloth; (*zum Trocknen*) towel. **-händler** *m* draper.
tüchtig [ˈtyçtiç] *adj* capable, able; (*leistungsfähig*) efficient; (*fleißig*) hard-working; (*klug*) clever. **Tüchtigkeit** *f* ability; efficiency; cleverness.
Tücke [ˈtykə] *f* (*pl* -n) spite, malice. **tückisch** *adj* spiteful.
Tugend [ˈtuːgənt] *f* (*pl* -en) virtue. **tugendhaft** *adj* virtuous.
Tulpe [ˈtulpə] *f* (*pl* -n) tulip.
*tun [tuːn] *v* do; (*machen*) make. **tun als ob** pretend to. **nur so tun** pretend. **zu tun haben** be busy, have things to do. **groß tun** boast. **etwas in etwas tun** put something into something.
Tünche [ˈtynçə] *f* (*pl* -n) whitewash, distemper.
Tunke [ˈtuŋkə] *f* (*pl* -n) sauce. **tunken** *v* dip, dunk.
Tunnel [ˈtunəl] *m* (*pl* -) tunnel.
Tupfen [ˈtupfən] *m* (*pl* -) dot, spot. **tupfen** *v* dot.
Tür [tyːr] *f* (*pl* -en) door.
Türkis [tyrˈkiːs] *m* (*pl* -e) turquoise.
Türklinke [ˈtyːrkliŋkə] *f* doorhandle.
Turm [turm] *m* (*pl* **Türme**) tower; (*Schach*) rook, castle; (*Elek*) pylon. **-spitze** *f* spire, steeple.
turnen [ˈturnən] *v* do gymnastics. **Turnen** *neut* gymnastics. **Turnhalle** *f* gymnasium.
Turnier [turˈniːr] *neut* (*pl* -e) tournament.
Türschwelle [ˈtyːrʃvelə] *f* threshold.
Tusche [ˈtuʃə] *f* (*pl* -n) Indian ink, drawing ink.
tuscheln [ˈtuʃəln] *v* whisper.

Tüte ['tyːtə] *f (pl* -n) paperbag.
tuten ['tuːtən] *v* hoot, honk.
Typ [tyːp] *m (pl* -en) type. **-e** *f (Druck)*
type.
Typhus ['tyːfus] *m* typhoid (fever).
typisch ['tyːpiʃ] *adj* typical.
Tyrann [ty'ran] *m (pl* -en) tyrant. **-ei** *f*
tyranny. **tyrann||isch** *adj* tyrannical.
-isieren *v* tyrannize.

U

U-Bahn ['uːbaːn] *f* underground (railway). *(US)* subway.
übel ['yːbəl] *adj* evil, wicked; *(schlecht)*
bad; *(unwohl)* sick, ill. *mir wird übel* I
feel sick. *übel daran sein* be in a bad
way. **Übel** *neut (pl* -) evil; *(Mißgeschick)*
misfortune; *(Krankheit)* sickness.
übel||gelaunt *adj* bad-tempered. **-gesinnt**
adj evil-minded. **-nehmen** *v* be offended
by, take amiss. **-riechen** *v* smell bad.
üben ['yːbən] *v* practise.
über ['yːbər] *prep* over, above; *(quer über)*
across; *(während)* during. *(betreffend)*
about; *(mehrals)* over; *(weg)* via.
überall [yːbər'al] *adv* everywhere.
überanstrengen [yːbər'anʃtrɛŋən] *v* overwork. **sich überanstrengen** overexert oneself. **Überanstrengung** *f* overexertion.
überarbeiten [yːbər'arbaitən] *v* revise.
sich überarbeiten *v* overwork, work too
hard.
überbelichten ['yːbərbəliçtən] *v (Foto)*
overexpose.
*****überbieten** [yːbər'biːtən] *v* outbid; *(fig)*
surpass, beat.
Überbleibsel ['yːbərblaipsəl] *neut (pl* -)
remainder.
Überblick ['yːbərblik] *m* survey, overall
view.
*****überbringen** [yːbər'briŋən] *v* deliver.
überbrücken [yːbər'brykən] *v* bridge.
überdies [yːbər'diːs] *adv* besides.
überdrüssig ['yːbərdrusiç] *adj* sick (of),
disgusted (with).
übereifrig ['yːbəraifriç] *adj* too eager,
over-zealous.
übereilen [yːbər'ailən] *v* rush, hurry too
much. **übereilt** *adj* hasty. *(Benehmen)*
inconsiderate.
übereinander [yːbərain'andər] *adv* one

upon another. **-greifen** *v* overlap.
-legen *v* lay one upon another.
*****übereinkommen** [yːbər'ainkəmən] *v*
agree. **Überein||kommen** *neut (pl* -) *or*
kunft *f* agreement.
übereinstimmen [yːbər'ainʃtimən] *v* concur, agree; *(zueinander passen)* correspond, tally. **Übereinstimmung** *f* agreement, concord.
überempfindlich ['yːbərɛmpfintliç] *adj*
hypersensitive.
*****überfahren** ['yːbərfaːrən] *v* take *or* drive
across. *(Mot)* run over. **Überfahrt** *f* crossing.
Überfall ['yːbərfal] *m* (sudden) attack,
assault. **überfallen** *v* attack (suddenly).
Überfallkommando *neut* flying squad.
Überfluß ['yːbərflus] *m* excess, overabun-
dance. **überflüssig** *adj* superfluous.
überführen ['yːbərfyːrən] *v* transport,
convey. **-**['ryːrən] *(Jur)* convict.
Überführung *f* transport; *(Brücke)* viaduct, overpass.
Übergabe ['yːbərgaːbə] *f* surrender, hand-
ing-over.
Übergang ['yːbərgaŋ] *m* crossing, passage; *(fig)* transition.
*****übergeben** ['yːbərgeːbən] *v* deliver, hand
over; *(Mil)* surrender. **sich übergeben**
vomit.
übergehen ['yːbərgeːən] *v* cross (over);
(werden) pass into, become, [-'geːən]
omit, overlook.
Übergewicht ['yːbərgeviçt] *neut* overweight.
*****übergreifen** ['yːbərgraifən] *v* overlap.
übergreifen auf encroach on.
*****überhandnehmen** [yːbər'hantneːmən] *v*
increase (rapidly).
überhaupt [yːbər'haupt] *adv* in general.
wenn überhaupt if at all. **überhaupt nicht**
not at all. **überhaupt kein** ... no ...
whatever.
*****überheben** [yːbər'heːbən] *v* exempt,
spare. **einer Mühe überheben** spare the
trouble. **überheblich** *adj* presumptuous,
arrogant.
überholen [yːbər'hoːlən] *v* overtake;
(Tech) overhaul. **überholt** *adj* outmoded.
überhören [yːbər'høːrən] *v* not hear;
(ignorieren) ignore, let pass.
überirdisch ['yːbərirdiʃ] *adj* celestial;
(übernatürlich) supernatural.
überkochen ['yːbərkɔxən] *v* boil over.

*überlassen [y:bər'lasən] v leave.
überlaufen ['y:bərlaufən] v overflow;
(Mil) defect.
überleben [y:bər'le:bən] v survive.
überlegen [y:bər'le:gən] v consider,
reflect. adj superior. **Überlegenheit** f
superiority. **überlegt** adj considered,
deliberate. **Überlegung** f consideration,
reflection.
überleiten ['y:bərlaitən] v lead on to; (fig)
convert.
überliefern [y:bər'li:fərn] v deliver; (der
Nachwelt) pass on, hand down.
Übermacht ['y:bərmaxt] f superiority.
übermächtig adj overwhelming, too powerful.
Übermaß ['y:bərmais] neut excess.
übermäßig adj excessive.
Übermensch ['y:bərmɛnʃ] m superman.
übermenschlich adj superhuman.
übermitteln [y:bər'mitəln] v convey.
übermorgen ['y:bərmɔrgən] adv the day
after tomorrow.
übermüdet [y:bər'my:dət] adj overtired.
Übermut ['y:bərmu:t] m arrogance; (Aus-
gelassenheit) high spirits pl. **übermütig**
adj arrogant; high-spirited.
übernächst [y:bərnɛiçst] adj the next but
one, the one after.
übernachten [y:bər'naxtən] v spend the
night, stay overnight.
übernatürlich ['y:bərnatu:rliç] adj supernatural.
*übernehmen [y:bər'ne:mən] v take over;
(Pflicht) undertake.
überprüfen [y:bər'pry:fən] v verify, check,
examine. **Überprüfung** f verification,
check.
überqueren [y:bər'kve:rən] v cross.
überragen [y:bər'ra:gən] v rise above,
tower above; (fig) surpass, outdo. **-d** adj
excellent.
übersinnlich ['y:bərzinliç] adj spiritual,
transcendental.
überspannen [y:bər'ʃpanən] v overstretch,
overtighten; (fig) go too far, exaggerate;
(bedecken) stretch over. **überspannt** adj
eccentric.
*überspringen [y:bar'ʃpriŋən] v jump
over; (auslassen) omit, skip.
*überstehen [y:bər'ʃte:ən] v survive.
*übersteigen [y:bər'ʃtaigən] v climb over,
surmount; (fig) exceed.
Überstunden ['y:bərʃtundən] pl overtime

sing. **Überstunden machen** v work overtime. **überstürzen** [y:bər'ʃtyrtsən] v rush,
hurry. **sich überstürzen** rush, act too
hastily. **überstürzt** adj hasty.
Übertrag ['y:bərtraik] m (pl **Überträge**)
balance brought forward. **übertragen** v
carry over; (Komm) bring forward;
(befördern) transport; (übersetzen) translate; (Radio, Med) transmit. **Übertragung**
f transfer; (Radio, Med) transmission;
(Übersetzung) translation.
*übertreffen [y:bər'trɛfən] v excel, surpass.
*übertreiben [y:bər'traibən] v exaggerate.
Übertreibung f exaggeration.
*übertreten [y:ber'tre:tən] v overstep.
['y:bər-] (Fluß) overflow; (Sport) step
over.
übertrieben [y:bər'tri:bən] adj exaggerated.
Übervölkerung [y:bər'fœlkəruŋ] f over-
population
überwachen [y:bər'vaxən] v supervise.
Überwachung f supervision.
überwältigen [y:bər'vɛltigən] v overpower, overwhelm. **-d** adj overwhelming.
Überwältigung f overpowering, conquest.
*überweisen [y:bər'vaizən] v transfer.
Überweisung f transfer; (Post-) money
order.
überwiegend [y:bər'vi:gənt] adj preponderant. adv primarily, mainly.
*überwinden [y:bər'vindən] v overcome.
sich überwinden (zu) bring oneself (to).
Überwindung f overcoming, conquest.
überwuchern [y:bər'vuxərn] v overrun,
overgrow.
überzeugen [y:bər'tsɔygən] v convince.
-d adj convincing. **überzeugt** adj con-
vinced, sure. **Überzeugung** f conviction.
*überziehen ['y:bərtsi:ən] v pull over, put
on. [-'tsi:ən] cover; (Konto) overdraw;
(Bett) change (the sheets of).
Überziehung f overdraft.
Überzug ['y:bərtsu:k] m cover(ing).
üblich ['y:pliç] adj usual.
U-Boot ['u:bo:t] neut submarine.
übrig ['y:briç] adj remaining, left(-over).
die Übrigen the rest, the others. **übrig**
haben have left (over). **-bleiben** v
remain, be left (over). **-ens** adv by the
way, incidentally.
Übung ['y:buŋ] f (pl -en) exercise; (Üben)
practice.

Ufer ['uːfər] *neut* (*pl* -) bank, shore.
-damm *m* embankment.
Uhr [uːr] *f* (*pl* -en) clock; (*Armbanduhr*) watch; (*Gas, usw.*) meter; (*Kraftstoff*) gauge. **-armband** *neut* watch strap.
-werk *neut* clockwork. **-zeiger** *m* (clock) hand. **-zeigersinn** *m* clockwise direction. **im Uhrzeigersinn** *adv* clockwise. **entgegen dem Uhrzeigersinn** *adv* anticlockwise (*US*) counterclockwise.
Ulk [ulk] *m* (*pl* -e) fun, lark. **ulkig** *adj* funny.
Ulme ['ulmə] *f* (*pl* -n) elm.
um [um] *prep* (*zeitlich, örtlich*) around, about; (*wegen*) for; (*Maßangeben*) by; (*ungefähr*) about. *adv* about. *conj* in order to. **um zu** (in order) to. **um diese Zeit** around this time. **um so besser** so much the better. **bitten um** ask for. **um 2 cm länger** longer by 2 cm.
umändern ['umɛndərn] *v* change, alter. **Umänderung** *f* change, alteration.
umarmen [um'armən] *v* embrace. **Umarmung** *f* embrace.
Umbau ['umbau] *m* alteration, rebuilding, conversion. **umbauen** *v* rebuild, alter, convert.
umbilden ['umbildən] *v* transform, remodel. **Umbildung** *f* transformation.
*****umbinden** ['umbindən] *v* tie (up), tie around (oneself), put on.
Umblick ['umblik] *m* panorama, survey. **umblicken** *v* (*sich umblicken*) look around.
*****umbringen** ['umbriŋən] *v* kill. (*sich umbringen*) commit suicide.
umdrehen ['umdreiən] *v* turn over *or* around. **sich umdrehen** rotate, spin; (*Person*) turn around. **Umdrehung** *f* turn, rotation.
*****umfahren** ['umfaːrən] *v* run over, knock down; [-'faːrən] drive around.
*****umfallen** ['umfalən] *v* fall over.
Umfang ['umfaŋ] *m* (*pl* **Umfänge**) (*Kreis*) circumference; (*Ausdehnung*) extent; (*Größe*) size. **umfangreich** *adj* extensive.
umfassen [um'fasən] *v* put one's arm around, hold, clasp; (*fig*) embrace, cover; (*Mil*) encircle. **-d** *adj* comprehensive.
Umfrage ['umfraːgə] *f* poll, inquiry.
Umgang ['umgaŋ] *m* circuit, turn; (*Verkehr*) intercourse, (social) contact. **umgänglich** *adj* sociable.
*****umgeben** [um'geːbən] *v* surround.

Umgebung *f* surroundings *pl*, environment.
*****umgehen** *v* ['umgeiən] go around; (*behandeln*) handle, deal with; (*mit Menschen*) associate (with). [-'geiən] go around; (*vermeiden*) avoid.
umgekehrt ['umgəkeirt] *adv* the other way round. *adj* inverted, reverse(d).
umgestalten ['umgəʃtaltən] *v* alter, transform; (*umorganisieren*) reorganize. **Umgestaltung** *f* alteration, transformation; reorganization.
Umhang ['umhaŋ] *m* wrap, cape.
umher [um'heir] *adv* about, (a)round. **-blicken** *v* look around. **-laufen** run around.
umhüllen [um'hylən] *v* wrap up.
Umkehr ['umkeir] *f* turning back, return; (*fig*) change, conversion. **umkehren** *v* turn back, return; (*umdrehen*) turn over; (*fig*) reform.
umkippen ['umkipən] *v* tip over.
umklammern [um'klamərn] *v* clasp.
umkleiden ['umklaidən] *v* **sich umkleiden** change (one's clothes). **Umkleideraum** *m* changing room.
*****umkommen** ['umkomən] *v* die, perish, be killed; (*verderben*) go bad.
Umkreis ['umkrais] *m* neighbourhood, vicinity. **umkreisen** *v* (en)circle.
Umlauf ['umlauf] *m* circulation. **im Umlauf** in circulation.
Umlaut ['umlaut] *m* vowel modification.
umleiten ['umlaitən] *v* divert. **Umleitung** *f* diversion.
umlernen ['umlɛrnən] *v* learn anew, relearn.
umliegend ['umliːgənt] *adj* surrounding.
umordnen ['umɔrdnən] *v* rearrange.
umpflanzen ['umpflantsən] *v* transplant.
umrahmen [um'raːmən] *v* frame.
umrechnen ['umrɛçnən] *v* convert, (ex)change. **Umrechnung** *f* conversion. **-skurs** *m* rate of exchange.
*****umreißen** ['umraisən] *v* pull down, demolish. [-'raisən] sketch, outline.
umringen [um'riŋən] *v* surround.
Umriß ['umris] *m* sketch, outline. **umrissen** *adj* defined.
umrühren [um'ryːrən] *v* stir.
ums [ums] *prep* + *art* um das.
Umsatz ['umzats] *m* turnover, sales.
umsäumen ['umzɔymən] *v* hem. [-'zɔymən] enclose, surround.

umschalten ['umʃaltən] v (*fig*) switch or change over. **Umschaltung** f (*fig*) change-over, switch.

umschauen ['umʃauən] v **sich umschauen** look around.

umschiffen [um'ʃifən] v circumnavigate; trans-ship. **Umschiffung** f circumnavigation.

Umschlag ['umʃlaɪk] m cover; (*Brief*) envelope; (*Buch*) wrapper, jacket; (*Hose*) turn-up; (*Kleid*) hem; (*Veränderung*) change; (*Komm*) turnover. **umschlagen** v change (*Boot*) capsize; (*Wind*) veer; (*umwenden*) turn over; (*umwerfen*) knock down.

*umschließen [um'ʃliːsən] v surround, enclose.

*umschreiben ['umʃraibən] v rewrite; transcribe. [- 'ʃraibən] paraphrase.

umschulen ['umʃuːlən] v retrain; (*neue Schule*) send to a new school. **Umschulung** f retraining.

Umschwung ['umʃvuŋ] m turn; (*fig*) sudden change, reversal.

*umsehen ['umzeːən] v **sich umsehen** look around; (*rückwärts*) look round.

umsetzen ['umzɛtsən] v transpose; (*Pflanze*) transplant; (*verkaufen*) sell.

Umsicht ['umziçt] f prudence, circumspection. **umsichtig** adj prudent, circumspect.

umsiedeln ['umziːdəln] v resettle. **Umsiedlung** f resettlement.

umsonst [um'zɔnst] adv free (of charge); (*vergebens*) in vain.

Umstand ['umʃtant] m circumstance. **in anderen Umständen** (*umg.*) expecting, in the family way. **ohne Umstände** without fuss. **nähere Umstände** further particulars. **unter diesen Umständen** in these circumstances.

*umsteigen ['umʃtaigən] v change (trains, buses, etc.). **Umsteiger** m through-ticket.

*umstoßen ['umʃtoːsən] v overturn, knock over; (*ungültig machen*) revoke; (*Pläne*) upset.

Umsturz ['umʃturts] m overthrow; (*Pol*) revolution. **umstürzen** v overturn; (*Regierung*) overthrow; (*umfallen*) fall over.

Umtausch ['umtauʃ] m exchange. **umtauschen** v exchange, (*umg.*) swap.

umwälzen ['umvɛltsən] v roll over; (*gründlich ändern*) revolutionize.

umwandeln ['umwandəln] v change, transform; (*Elek*) transform, (*Komm*) convert.

Umweg ['umveɪk] m detour, long way round.

Umwelt ['umvɛlt] f environment. **umweltfreundlich** adj non-polluting, conservationist. **Umweltverschmutzung** f (environmental) pollution.

*umwenden ['umvɛndən] v turn over; (*Wagen*) turn round.

*umwerben [um'vɛrbən] v court.

*umwerfen ['umvɛrfən] v upset, overturn; (*Kleider*) wrap round oneself.

umwickeln [um'vikəln] v wrap round.

umzäunen [um'tsɔynən] v fence in.

*umziehen ['umtsiːən] v move (house); (*Kind*) change (clothes). **sich umziehen** change (clothes).

Umzug ['umtsuːk] m move, removal; procession.

unabänderlich [unap'ɛndərliç] adj unalterable.

unabhängig ['unaphɛŋiç] adj independent. **Unabhängig||e(r)** (*Pol*) independent. **-keit** f independence.

unabkömmlich ['unapkœmliç] adj indispensable.

unablässig ['unaplɛsiç] adj incessant.

unabsichtlich ['unapziçtliç] adj unintentional.

unachtsam ['unaxtsaim] adj careless.

unähnlich ['unɛːnliç] adj unlike, dissimilar (to).

unangemessen ['unaŋəmɛsən] adj unsuitable; (*Forderung*) unreasonable.

unangenehm ['unaŋəneɪm] adj unpleasant; (*peinlich*) awkward.

Unannehmlichkeit ['unanneɪmliçkait] f unpleasantness; (*lästige Mühe*) inconvenience.

unansehnlich ['unanzeɪnliç] adj unsightly.

unanständig ['unanʃtɛndiç] adj indecent, improper. **Unanständigkeit** f indecency.

unartig ['unaɪrtiç] adj badly-behaved, rude.

unauffällig ['unaufɛliç] adj inconspicuous.

unaufgefordert ['unaufɡəfɔrdət] adj unbidden, unasked.

unaufhörlich ['unaufhœɪrliç] adj incessant.

unaufmerksam ['unaufmɛrkzaɪm] adj inattentive.

unaufrichtig ['unaufriçtiç] *adj* insincere.

unausgeglichen ['unausgəglıçən] *adj* uneven, unbalanced.

unbändig ['unbɛndiç] *adj* tremendous.

unbeabsichtigt ['unbəapziçtiçt] *adj* unintentional.

unbeachtet ['unbəaxtət] *adj* unnoticed, unheeded.

unbedacht ['unbədaxt] *adj* inconsiderate, thoughtless, rash.

unbedeutend ['unbədɔytənt] *adj* unimportant, insignificant.

unbedingt [unbədıŋt] *adj* absolute, unconditional. *adv* by all means.

unbefahrbar ['unbəfairbair] *adj* impassable.

unbefriedigend ['unbəfriidigənt] *adj* unsatisfactory.

unbefugt ['unbəfukt] *adj* unauthorized.

unbegreiflich ['unbəgraifliç] *adj* incomprehensible, inconceivable.

Unbehagen ['unbəhaigən] *neut* uneasiness, discomfort. **unbehaglich** *adj* uneasy, uncomfortable.

unbeholfen ['unbəhɔlfən] *adj* clumsy, awkward.

unbekannt ['unbəkant] *adj* unknown.

unbekümmert [unbə'kymərt] *adj* unconcerned.

unbemerkt ['unbəmɛrkt] *adj* unnoticed, unobserved.

unbemittelt ['unbəmitəlt] *adj* poor, without means.

unbequem ['unbəkveim] *adj* uncomfortable.

umberechenbar ['unbəreçənbair] *adj* incalculable.

unberechtigt ['unbəreçtiçt] *adj* (*ungerechtfertigt*) unjustified; (*unbefugt*) unauthorized. *adv* without authority.

unberührt ['unbəryirt] *adj* untouched, intact.

unbeschränkt ['unbəʃrɛnkt] *adj* unlimited, unrestricted.

unbeschreiblich ['unbəʃraipliç] *adj* indescribable.

unbesonnen ['unbəzɔnən] *adj* imprudent; (*unüberlegt*) rash, hasty.

unbeständig ['unbəʃtɛndiç] *adj* unsettled, unstable; (*nicht dauernd*) inconstant.

unbestimmt ['unbəʃtimt] *adj* indefinite.

unbestreitbar [unbə'ʃtraitbair] *adj* indisputable.

unbestritten ['unbəʃtritən] *adj* undisputed, uncontested.

unbeteiligt ['unbətailiçt] *adj* unconcerned; (*nicht beteiligt*) uninvolved.

unbeweglich ['unbəveikliç] *adj* immovable; (*bewegungslos*) motionless.

unbewußt ['unbəvust] *adj* unconscious.

unbiegsam ['unbiikzaim] *adj* unbending.

unbrauchbar ['unbrauxbair] *adj* useless.

und [unt] *conj* and.

undankbar ['undaŋkbair] *adj* ungrateful; (*Arbeit*) thankless. **Undankbarkeit** *f* ingratitude.

undenkbar [un'dɛŋkbair] *adj* unthinkable.

undeutlich ['undɔytliç] *adj* unclear, indistinct.

undurchdringlich ['undurçdriŋliç] *adj* impenetrable.

undurchlässig ['undurçlɛsiç] *adj* impermeable; (*Wasser-*) water-proof.

undurchsichtig ['undurçziçtiç] *adj* opaque; (*Person*) inscrutable.

uneben ['uneibən] *adj* uneven, rough.

unecht ['uneçt] *adj* not genuine, false; (*künstlich*) artificial.

unehelich ['uneiliç] *adj* illegitimate.

unehrlich ['uneirliç] *adj* dishonest. **Unehrlichkeit** *f* dishonesty.

unendlich [un'ɛntliç] *adj* endless, infinite.

unentbehrlich [unɛnt'beirliç] *adj* indispensable.

unentschieden ['unɛntʃiidən] *adj* undecided; (*Fussball*) drawn. **Unentschiedenheit** *f* indecision.

unentschlossen ['unɛntʃlɔsən] *adj* undecided, irresolute. **Unentschlossenheit** *f* indecision, irresolution.

unentwickelt ['unɛntvikəlt] *adj* undeveloped.

unentzündbar ['unɛntzyntbair] *adj* nonflammable.

unerbittlich [unɛr'bitliç] *adj* relentless.

unerfahren ['unɛrfairən] *adj* inexperienced.

unerhört [unɛr'hœirt] *adj* unheard-of, outrageous.

unerklärbar [unɛrkleirbair] *adj* inexplicable.

unerläßlich [unɛr'lɛsliç] *adj* indispensable.

unerlaubt ['unɛrlaupt] *adj* not permitted; (*ungesetzlich*) forbidden, illegal.

unermeßlich [unɛr'mɛsliç] *adj* immense, immeasurable.

unermüdlich [unɛr'myitliç] *adj* indefatigable, untiring.

unerreichbar ['unɛraiçbaɪr] *adj* unattainable. **unerreicht** *adj* unequalled, unrivalled.
unersättlich ['unɛrzɛtliç] *adj* insatiable.
unerschrocken ['unɛrʃrɔkən] *adj* fearless, undaunted.
unerschütterlich ['unɛrʃytərliç] *adj* imperturbable, unshakeable.
unersetzlich ['unɛrzɛtsliç] *adj* irreplaceable.
unerträglich ['unɛrtrɛikliç] *adj* unbearable, intolerable.
unerwartet ['unɛrvaɪrtət] *adj* unexpected.
unfähig ['unfɛːiç] *adj* incapable; (*nicht instande*) unable. **Unfähigkeit** *f* incapacity; inability.
unfair ['unfɛɪr] *adj* unfair.
Unfall ['unfal] *m* accident. **–station** *f* first-aid post. **–verhütung** *f* accident prevention.
unfaßbar ['unfasbaɪ] *adj* inconceivable.
unfehlbar [un'feɪlbaɪr] *adj* infallible.
unflätig ['unflɛɪtiç] *adj* filthy, coarse.
unfreundlich ['unfrɔyntliç] *adj* unfriendly; (*barsch*) rude; (*Wetter*) disagreeable, inclement. **Unfreundlichkeit** *f* unfriendliness, unkindness.
Unfug ['unfuɪk] *m* misconduct; (*Dummheiten*) mischief.
unfühlbar [un'fyɪlbaɪr] *adj* intangible, impalpable.
Ungar ['uŋar] *m* (*pl* **-n**), **Ungarin** *f* (*pl* **-nen**) Hungarian. **ungarisch** *adj* Hungarian. **Ungarn** *neut* Hungary.
ungastlich ['ungastliç] *adj* inhospitable.
ungeachtet ['ungəaxtət] *adj* overlooked, disregarded. *prep* notwithstanding.
ungebeten ['ungəbeɪtən] *adj* uninvited.
ungebildet ['ungəbildət] *adj* uneducated; (*Benehmen*) ill-mannered.
ungebührend ['ungəbyɪrənt] *or* **ungebührlich** *adj* improper, unbecoming.
ungebunden ['ungəbundən] *adj* unbound; (*fig*) unrestrained, free.
Ungeduld ['ungədult] *f* impatience. **ungeduldig** *adj* impatient.
ungeeignet ['ungəaiknət] *adj* unsuitable.
ungefähr ['ungəfɛɪr] *adv* approximately, about, roughly. *adj* approximate.
ungefährlich ['ungəfɛɪrliç] *adj* not dangerous.
ungeheuer ['ungəhɔyər] *adj* enormous. **Ungeheuer** *neut* (*pl* **-**) monster.
ungehorsam ['ungəhɔɪrzaɪm] *adj* disobedient. **Ungehorsam** *m* disobedience.

ungekünstelt ['ungəkyɪnstəlt] *adj* unaffected, natural.
ungelegen ['ungəleɪgən] *adj* inconvenient.
ungelernt ['ungəlɛrnt] *adj* unskilled.
ungemächlich ['ingəmɛçliç] *adj* uncomfortable, unpleasant.
ungemein ['ungəmain] *adj* uncommon, extraordinary.
ungemütlich ['ungəmyɪtliç] *adj* uncomfortable; (*grob*) unpleasant, nasty.
ungenannt ['ungənant] *adj* unnamed.
ungeniert ['unʒəniɪrt] *adj* free and easy, relaxed and informal.
ungenießbar ['ungəniɪsbaɪr] *adj* inedible, unenjoyable.
ungenügend ['ungənygənt] *adj* insufficient; (*Qualität*) inadequate.
ungeraten ['ungəraɪtən] *adj* (*Kind*) spoiled.
ungerecht ['ungərɛçt] *adj* unjust.
ungereimt ['ungəraimt] *adj* (*fig*) nonsensical, absurd.
ungern ['ungɛrn] *adv* unwillingly, reluctantly.
Ungeschick ['ungəʃik] *neut* ineptitude, clumsiness. **ungeschickt** *adj* clumsy, awkward.
ungesellig ['ungəzɛliç] *adj* unsociable.
ungesetzlich ['ungəzɛtsliç] *adj* illegal, unlawful.
ungestüm ['ungəʃtyɪm] *adj* impetuous.
ungesund ['ungəzunt] *adj* unhealthy, unwell.
ungewiß ['ungəvis] *adj* uncertain. **Ungewißheit** *f* uncertainty.
ungewöhnlich ['ungəvœɪnliç] *adj* unusual, uncommon. **ungewohnt** *adj* unaccustomed.
Ungeziefer ['ungətsiɪfər] *neut* vermin.
ungezogen ['ungətsoɪgən] *adj* rude; (*Kind*) naughty.
ungezwungen ['ungətsvuŋən] *adj* free, natural, uninhibited.
ungläubig ['unglɔybiç] *adj* incredulous, disbelieving; (*Rel*) unbelieving. **Ungläubige(r)** *m* sceptic; (*Rel*) unbeliever.
unglaublich ['unglaupliç] *adj* incredible, unbelievable. **unglaubwürdig** *adj* (*Person*) untrustworthy, unreliable; (*Sache*) incredible.
ungleich ['unglaiç] *adj* unequal, uneven; (*verschieden*) different; (*unähnlich*) unlike; (*Zahl*) odd. **Ungleichheit** *f* inequality; difference.

Unglück ['unglyk] *neut* misfortune; (*Katastrophe*) disaster, catastrophe; (*Pech*) bad luck. **unglücklich** *adj* unlucky; (*traurig*) unhappy. **–erweise** *adv* unfortunately. **Unglücksfall** *m* accident.

Ungnade ['ungnaɪdə] *f* disgrace, displeasure. **ungnädig** *adj* ungracious, churlish.

ungünstig ['ungynstiç] *adj* unfavourable.

unhaltbar ['unhaltbaɪr] *adj* untenable.

Unheil ['unhail] *neut* mischief, harm. **unheil∥bar** *adj* incurable. **–bringend** *adj* unlucky, fateful.

unheimlich ['unhaimliç] *adj* weird, sinister, uncanny. *adv* (*umg*.) tremendously.

unhöflich ['unhœɪfliç] *adj* impolite, rude. **Unhöflichkeit** *f* rudeness, incivility.

unhörbar ['unhœɪrbaɪr] *adj* inaudible.

uniform [uni'fɔrm] *adj* uniform. **Uniform** *f* (*pl* -en) uniform.

uninteressant [unintərɛsant] *adj* uninteresting. **uninteressiert** *adj* disinterested.

universal [univer'saɪl] *or* **universell** *adj* universal.

Universität [univerzi'tɛɪt] *f* (*pl* -en) university.

Universum [uni'verzum] *neut* universe.

unkenntlich ['unkentliç] *adj* unrecognizable. **Unkenntnis** *f* ignorance.

unklar ['unklaɪr] *adj* unclear, obscure; (*trübe*) muddy, cloudy.

unklug ['unkluɪk] *adj* unwise, unintelligent.

Unkosten ['unkɔstən] *pl* expenses, costs; (*Komm*) overheads.

Unkraut ['unkraut] *neut* weed.

unlängst ['unlɛŋst] *adv* recently, lately.

unlauter ['unlautər] *adj* impure; (*nicht ehrlich*) unfair, dishonest. **unlauterer Wettbewerb** unfair competition.

unlesbar ['unleɪzbaɪr] *adj* illegible, unreadable.

unlogisch ['unloɪgiʃ] *adj* illogical.

unlösbar ['unlœɪsbaɪr] *adj* insoluble.

unmäßig ['unmeɪsiç] *adj* immoderate.

Unmenge ['unmɛŋə] *f* huge quantity.

Unmensch ['unmɛnʃ] *m* brute, monster, barbarian. **unmenschlich** *adj* inhuman, brutal. **Unmenschlichkeit** *f* inhumanity.

unmittelbar ['unmitəlbaɪr] *adj* immediate, direct.

unmodisch ['unmoɪdiʃ] *adj* unfashionable.

unmöglich ['unmœɪkliç] *adj* impossible. **Unmöglichkeit** *f* impossibility.

unmoralisch ['unmoraɪliʃ] *adj* immoral.

unmündig ['unmyndiç] *adj* under age.

unnachgiebig ['innaxgiɪbiç] *adj* unyielding, uncompromising.

unnatürlich ['unnatyrliç] *adj* unnatural.

unnötig ['unnœɪtiç] *adj* unnecessary.

unnütz ['unnyts] *adj* useless, unprofitable.

unordentlich ['unɔrdəntliç] *adj* disorderly, untidy. **Unord∥entlichkeit** *f* untidiness, disorderliness. **–nung** *f* disorder.

unorganisch ['unɔrgainiʃ] *adj* inorganic.

unpaar ['unpaɪr] *adj* odd.

unparteiisch ['unpartaiiʃ] *or* **unparteilich** *adj* impartial, unbiased. **Unparteilichkeit** *f* impartiality.

unpassend ['unpasənt] *adj* unsuitable, inappropriate; (*unschicklich*) improper.

unpersönlich ['unperzœɪnliç] *adj* impersonal.

unpolitisch ['unpoliɪtiʃ] *adj* nonpolitical.

Unrat ['unraɪt] *m* refuse, dirt.

unratsam ['unraɪtzaɪm] *adj* inadvisable.

unrecht ['unreçt] *adj* wrong; (*ungerecht*) unjust. **Unrecht** *neut* wrong; (*Ungerechtigkeit*) injustice. **unrechtmäßig** *adj* illegal, unlawful, illegitimate.

unregelmäßig ['unreɪgəlmeɪsiç] *adj* irregular. **Unregelmäßigkeit** *f* irregularity.

unreif ['unraif] *adj* unripe; (*Mensch*) immature.

unrein ['unrain] *adj* dirty, unclean; (*fig*) impure.

unrentabel ['unrentaɪbəl] *adj* unprofitable.

unrichtig ['unriçtiç] *adj* incorrect.

Unruhe ['unruɪə] *f* restlessness; (*Aufruhr*) unrest. (*Uhr*) balance(-wheel). **unruhig** *adj* restless.

uns [uns] *pron* (to) us; (*Reflexiv*) (to) ourselves.

unsauber ['unzaubər] *adj* unclean, dirty; (*unfair*) unfair.

unschätzbar ['unʃɛtsbaɪr] *adj* inestimable.

unscheinbar ['unʃainbaɪr] *adj* inconspicuous.

unschicklich ['unʃikliç] *adj* improper, unseemly.

unschlüssig ['unʃlysiç] *adj* irresolute.

unschön ['unʃœɪn] *adj* unlovely, unpleasant.

Unschuld ['unʃult] *f* innocence. **unschuldig** *adj* innocent.

unselbständig ['unzɛlpʃtɛndiç] *adj* dependent.

unselig ['unzeɪlɪç] *adj* unfortunate, fatal.
unser ['unzər] *adj* our. *pron* ours. **unser(er) seits** *adv* for our part, as for us.
unser(es)gleichen *pron* people like us. *pron* **der, die, das uns(e)rige** ours.
unserthalben, unsertwegen, unsertwillen for our sakes.
unsicher ['unziçər] *adj* unsafe, insecure; (*zweifelhaft*) uncertain. **Unsicherheit** *f* insecurity, uncertainty.
unsichtbar ['unzɪçtbaɪr] *adj* invisible.
Unsinn ['unzin] *adj* nonsense. **unsinnig** *adj* nonsensical.
unsittlich ['unzɪtlɪç] *adj* indecent, immoral. **Unsittlichkeit** *f* immorality.
unsre ['unzrə] *V* **unser**.
unsrige ['unzrɪgə] *V* **unser**.
unsterblich ['unʃterplɪç] *adj* immortal. **Unsterblichkeit** *f* immortality.
unstet ['unʃtɛtt] *adj* unsteady, inconstant.
Unstimmigkeit ['unʃtimɪçkaɪt] *f* (*pl* -en) inconsistency; (*Meinungsverschiedenheit*) disagreement.
unsympathisch ['unzympaɪtɪʃ] *adj* disagreeable, unpleasant.
Untat ['untaɪt] *f* outrage, crime.
untätig ['untɛɪtɪç] *adj* inactive, idle. **Untätigkeit** *f* inactivity, idleness.
untauglich ['untauklɪç] *adj* unfit; (*Sache*) unusable.
unten ['untən] *adv* below, at the bottom; (*im Hause*) downstairs. **nach unten** downwards. **von oben bis unten** from top to bottom. **von unten an** from the bottom (up).
unter ['untər] *prep* below, under; (*zwischen*) between, among. *adj* lower. **unter allen Umständen** under any circumstances. **unter uns** between you and me. **unter vier Augen** in private. **unter der Hand** secretly.
Unterarm ['untərarm] *m* forearm.
Unterbau ['untərbau] *m* foundations *pl*.
unterbelichten ['untərbəlɪçtən] *v* (*Foto*) underexpose.
unterbevölkert ['untərbəfœlkərt] *adj* underpopulated.
unterbewußt ['untərbəvust] *adj* subconscious. **Unterbewusstsein** *neut* subconsciousness.
***unterbleiben** [untər'blaibən] *v* not occur.
***unterbrechen** [untər'brɛçən] *v* interrupt; (*Telef*) cut off, disconnect. **Unterbrechung** *f* interruption.

***unterbringen** ['untərbriŋən] *v* accommodate, lodge, shelter; (*lagern*) store.
unterdrücken [untər'drykən] *v* suppress. **Unterdrückung** *f* suppression.
untereinander [untərain'andər] *adv* with each other, with one another.
unterentwickelt ['untərɛntvikəlt] *adj* underdeveloped.
Unterführung [untər'fyɪruŋ] *f* underpass.
Untergang ['untərgaŋ] *m* (*Sonne*) setting; (*Schiff*) sinking, wreck; (*fig*) decline, fall.
Untergebene(r) [untər'geɪbənə(r)] *m* subordinate.
***untergehen** ['untərgeɪən] *v* sink; (*Sonne*) set; (*fig*) perish, be lost.
untergeordnet ['untərgəɔrdnət] *adj* subordinate.
Untergestell ['untərgəʃtɛl] *neut* undercarriage.
Untergewicht ['untərgəviçt] *neut* short weight. **Untergewicht haben** be underweight.
***untergraben** [untər'graɪbən] *v* undermine.
Untergrund ['untərgrunt] *m* subsoil. **-bahn** *f* underground (railway), (*US*) subway.
unterhalb ['untərhalp] *prep* below, under(neath).
Unterhalt ['untərhalt] *m* support, keep; (*Instandhaltung*) maintenance.
unterhalten *v* (*Person*) keep, support; (*Instand halten*) maintain; (*zerstreuen*) entertain. **sich unterhalten** enjoy oneself; (*reden (mit)*) converse (with), talk (to).
unterhaltsam *adj* entertaining, amusing.
Unterhaltung *f* entertainment, amusement; (*Instandhaltung*) maintenance.
-skosten *pl* maintenance costs.
unterhandeln [untər'handəln] *v* negotiate.
Unterhaus ['untərhaus] *neut* lower chamber (of parliament).
Unterhemd ['untərhɛmt] *neut* vest, (*US*) undershirt.
Unterholz ['untərhɔlts] *neut* undergrowth.
Unterhose ['untərhoɪzən] *f* underpants *pl*.
unterirdisch ['untərirdɪʃ] *adj* underground.
***unterkommen** ['untərkɔmən] *v* find accommodation *or* shelter; (*Arbeit*) find work.
Unterkunft ['untərkunft] *f* accommodation, lodgings *pl*.

Unterlage ['untərlaıgə] *f* base, basis, foundation; (*Beweisstück*) (documentary) evidence.

Unterlaß ['untərlas] *m* **ohne Unterlaß** incessantly, unceasingly.

unterlassen [untər'lasən] *v* neglect, fail (to do), omit. **Unterlassung** *f* omission.

unterlegen [untər'leıgən] *adj* inferior.

Unterleib ['untərlaıp] *m* abdomen.

unterliegen [untər'liːgən] *v* be defeated. **es unterliegt keinem Zweifel** it is not open to doubt.

Untermieter [untərmiːtər] *m* lodger.

unternehmen [untər'neːmən] *v* undertake, attempt. **Unternehmen** *neut* undertaking, enterprise; (*Firma*) firm. **Unternehmer** *m* entrepreneur, contractor. **unternehmungslustig** *adj* enterprising.

Unteroffizier ['untərɔfitsiːr] *m* noncommissioned officer, NCO.

Unterredung [untər'reːduŋ] *f* (*pl* -en) conversation, discussion.

Unterricht ['untərriçt] *m* (*pl* -e) instruction, lessons *pl*, teaching. **Unterricht geben** teach, give lessons. **unterrichten** *v* teach, give lessons. **unterrichten** *v* instruct, teach; (*benachrichtigen*) inform.

Unterrock ['untərrɔk] *m* slip, petticoat.

unters ['untərs] *prep + art* **unter das.**

untersagen [untər'zaːgən] *v* forbid, prohibit.

unterscheiden [untər'ʃaıdən] *v* distinguish. **sich unterscheiden** differ.

unterschieben [untər'ʃiːbən] *v* attribute (to); substitute.

Unterschied ['untərʃiːt] *m* (*pl* -e) difference. **unterschiedlich** *adj* different.

unterschlagen [untər'ʃlaːgən] *v* (*Geld*) embezzle; (*Nachricht*) suppress. **Unterschlagung** *f* embezzlement; suppression.

Unterschlupf ['untərʃlupf] *m* (*pl* **Unterschlüpfe**) refuge, hiding place.

unterschreiben [untər'ʃraıbən] *v* sign. **Unterschrift** ['untərʃrift] *f* signature.

Unterseeboot ['untərzeːboːt] *neut* submarine. **unterseeisch** *adj* submarine.

unterst ['untərst] *adj* lowest, bottom, undermost.

unterstehen [untər'ʃteːən] *v* be subordinate (to). **sich unterstehen** dare.

unterstreichen [untər'ʃtraıçən] *v* underline.

unterstützen [untər'ʃtytsən] *v* support,

assist. **Unterstützung** *f* (*pl* -en) support, assistance.

untersuchen [untər'zuːxən] *v* examine. **Untersuchung** *f* examination. –**shaft** *f* imprisonment on remand.

Untertan ['untərtaːn] *m* (*pl* -en) subject.

Untertasse ['untərtasə] *f* saucer.

untertauchen ['untərtauxən] *v* dive; (*verschwinden*) disappear.

Unterteil ['untərtaıl] *m* bottom (part).

Untertitel ['untərtiːtəl] *m* (*Film*) subtitle.

unterwärts ['untərverts] *adv* downwards.

Unterwäsche ['untərvɛʃə] *f* underwear.

unterwegs [untər'veːks] *adv* on the way, en route.

unterweisen [untər'vaizən] *v* instruct, teach. **Unterweisung** *f* instructions *pl*.

Unterwelt ['untərvelt] *f* underworld.

unterwerfen [untər'verfən] *v* subject (to); (*besiegen*) subjugate. **sich unterwerfen** submit, surrender. **unterworfen** *adj* subject (to).

unterwürfig [untər'vyrfiç] *adj* obsequious.

unterzeichnen [untər'tsaıçnən] *v* sign. **Unterzeichnung** *f* signature.

unterziehen [untər'tsiːən] *v* subject. **sich unterziehen** undergo, submit (to).

untief ['untiːf] *adj* shallow.

untreu ['untrɔy] *adj* unfaithful.

untrüglich [un'tryːkliç] *adj* infallible, certain.

untüchtig ['untyçtiç] *adj* incompetent, incapable.

Untugend ['untuːgənt] *f* vice.

unüberlegt ['unyːbərleːkt] *adj* ill-considered, hasty.

unüberwindlich ['unyːbərvintliç] *adj* impregnable; insurmountable, insuperable.

ununterbrochen ['ununtərbrɔxən] *adj* uninterrupted.

unveränderlich ['unferendərliç] *adj* unchangeable.

unverantwortlich [unfer'antvortliç] *adj* irresponsible. **Unverantwortlichkeit** *f* irresponsibility.

unverbesserlich [unfer'besərliç] *adj* incorrigible.

unverbindlich ['unferbintliç] *adj* not binding; (*Komm*) without obligation.

unverdaulich ['unferdauliç] *adj* indigestible.

unverderblich ['unferderpliç] *adj* incorruptible.

unverdient ['unfɛrdiːnt] *adj* unearned, undeserved.

unvereinbar [unfɛr'ainbaːr] *adj* incompatible.

unverfroren ['unfɛrfroːrən] *adj* impudent, brazen. **Unverfrorenheit** *f* impudence.

unvergänglich ['unfɛrgɛsliç] *adj* imperishable; immortal.

unvergeßlich [unfɛr'gɛsliç] *adj* unforgettable.

unverhältnismäßig ['unfɛrhɛltnismɛːsiç] *adj* disproportionate.

unverheiratet ['unfɛrhairaːtət] *adj* unmarried.

unvermeidlich [unfɛr'maitliç] *adj* unavoidable.

unvermittelt ['unfɛrmitəlt] *adj* sudden, unexpected.

Unvermögen ['unfɛrmœːgən] *neut* inability, powerlessness.

unvermutet ['unfɛrmuːtət] *adj* unexpected.

unvernünftig ['unfɛrnynftiç] *adj* unreasonable.

unverschämt ['unfɛrʃɛːmt] *adj* impudent, impertinent. **Unverschämtheit** *f* impudence, impertinence.

unversehens ['unfɛrzeːəns] *adv* suddenly, unexpectedly.

unversöhnlich ['unfɛrsœːnliç] *adj* irreconcilable.

unverständlich ['unfɛrʃtɛntliç] *adj* unintelligible.

unverträglich ['unfɛrtrɛːkliç] *adj* incompatible; unsociable.

unverzagt ['unfɛrtsakt] *adj* undaunted, fearless.

unverzüglich ['unfɛrtsykliç] *adj* immediate, instant.

unvollkommen ['unfɔlkɔmən] *adj* imperfect.

unvoreingenommen ['unfɔraingənɔmən] *adj* unprejudiced.

unvorsichtig ['unfɔrziçtiç] *adj* careless, incautious; (*unklug*) imprudent.

unvorstellbar ['unfɔrʃtɛlbaːr] *adj* unimaginable.

unvorteilhaft ['unfɔrtailhaft] *adj* unfavourable.

unwahr ['unvaːr] *adj* untrue. **–haftig** *adj* untruthful. **Unwahrheit** *f* untruth, falsehood. **unwahrscheinlich** *adj* unlikely, improbably; (*umg.*) fantastic, incredible. *adv* (*umg.*) incredibly.

unweit ['unvait] *prep, adv* near, not far (from).

Unwetter ['unvɛtər] *neut* storm.

unwichtig ['unviçtiç] *adj* unimportant. **Unwichtigkeit** *f* unimportance; (*Sache*) trifle.

unwiderruflich [unviːdər'ruːfliç] *adj* irrevocable.

unwiderstehlich [unviːdər'ʃteːliç] *adj* irresistible.

unwillig ['unviliç] *adj* indignant; (*widerwillig*) unwilling, reluctant.

unwillkürlich ['unvilkyːrliç] *adj* involuntary; instinctive.

unwirksam ['unviːrkzaːm] *adj* ineffective.

unwissend ['unvisənt] *adj* ignorant. **Unwissenheit** *f* ignorance. **unwissentlich** *adv* unconsciously, unwittingly.

unwürdig ['unvyrdiç] *adj* unworthy.

Unzahl ['untsaːl] *f* endless number.

unzählbar ['untsɛːlbaːr] *or* **unzählig** *adj* innumerable.

unzeitgemäß ['untsaitgəmɛːs] *adj* inopportune; (*unmodisch*) outdated. **unzeitig** *adj* premature; (*Obst*) unripe.

unzerbrechlich [untsɛr'brɛçliç] *adj* unbreakable.

unzertrennlich [untsɛr'trɛnliç] *adj* inseparable.

unziemlich ['untsiːmliç] *adj* unseemly.

Unzucht ['untsuxt] *f* lechery, fornication; (*Jur*) sexual offence. **unzüchtig** *adj* lewd, lecherous.

unzufrieden ['untsufriːdən] *adj* dissatisfied.

unzugänglich ['untsuːgɛŋliç] *adj* inaccessible.

unzulänglich ['untsuːlɛŋliç] *adj* inadequate, insufficient.

unzulässig ['untsuːlɛsiç] *adj* inadmissible.

unzureichend ['untsuraiçənt] *adj* insufficient, inadequate.

unzuverlässig ['untsuferlɛsiç] *adj* unreliable.

unzweifelhaft ['untsfaifəlhaft] *adj* undoubted.

üppig ['ypiç] *adj* abundant, luxuriant; (*blühend*) exuberant; (*wollüstig*) voluptuous.

uralt ['uːralt] *adj* very old, ancient.

Uran [u'raːn] *neut* uranium.

uranfänglich ['uranfɛŋliç] *adj* original, premordial.

Uraufführung ['uːraufyːruŋ] *f* first performance, première.

urban [ur'baɪn] adj urbane.
urbar ['uɪrbaɪr] adj arable.
Ureinwohner ['uɪrainvoɪnər] m aboriginal.
Ureltern ['uɪrɛltərn] pl ancestors.
Urenkel ['uɪrɛŋkəl] m (Kind) greatgrandchild, (Junge) great-grandson. **-in** f great-granddaughter.
Urgeschichte ['uɪrgəʃɪçtə] f prehistory.
Urgroß||eltern ['uɪrgroɪsɛltərn] pl greatgrandparents. **-mutter** f great-grandmother. **-vater** m great-grandfather.
Urheber ['uɪrheɪbər] m (pl -) author, creator. **-recht** neut copyright.
Urin [u'riɪn] m urine. **urinieren** v urinate.
Urkunde ['uɪrkundə] f document, deed; (Zeugnis) certificate. **urkundlich** adj documentary.
Urlaub ['uɪrlaup] m (pl -e) leave (of absence); (Ferien) holiday, vacation. **im** or **auf Urlaub** on holiday, on vacation.
Urmensch ['uɪrmɛnʃ] m primitive man.
Urne ['uɪrnə] f (pl -n) urn.
Ursache ['uɪrzaxə] f cause. **keine Ursache!** don't mention it!
Ursprung ['uɪrʃpruŋ] m source, origin. **ursprünglich** adj original. **Ursprungsland** neut country of origin.
Urteil ['urtaɪl] neut judgment, verdict; (Strafmaß) sentence; (Urteilskraft) judgment. **urteilen** v judge. **Urteils||kraft** f (power of) judgment, discernment. **-spruch** m verdict, sentence.
Urvater ['uɪrfaɪtər] m forefather.
Urwelt ['uɪrvɛlt] f primeval world.
Urzeit ['uɪrtsait] f prehistory, earliest times pl. **urzeitlich** adj primordial, primeval.
Utopie [uto'piɪ] f (pl -n) Utopia. **utopisch** adj utopian.

V

vag [vaɪk] adj vague.
Vagabund [vaga'bunt] m (pl -en) vagabond, tramp.
vakant [va'kant] adj vacant.
Vakuum ['vaɪkuum] neut (pl Vakua) vacuum.
validieren [vali'diɪrən] v make valid, validate.
Valuta [va'luɪtə] f (pl Valuten) (Wert) value; (Währung) currency.

Vampir ['vampiɪr] m (pl -e) vampire.
Vandale [van'daɪlə] m (pl -n) vandal. **Vandalismus** m vandalism.
Vanille [va'niljə] f vanilla.
Varietät [varie'tɛɪt] f (pl -en) variety.
Variation [variatsi'oɪn] f (pl -en) variation.
Vase ['vaɪzə] f (pl -en) vase.
Vater ['faɪtər] m (pl Väter) father. **-land** neut native land, fatherland. **väterländisch** adj national; patriotic. **väterlich** ['fɛɪtərliç] adj paternal, fatherly. **väterlicherseits** adv on the father's side.
Vaterschaft ['faɪtərʃaft] f (pl -en) paternity.
Vegetarier [vege'taɪriər] m (pl -) vegetarian. **vegetarisch** adj vegetarian.
Veilchen ['failçən] neut (pl -) violet. **veilchenblau** adj violet.
Vene ['veɪnə] f (pl -n) vein. **Venenentzündung** f (Med) phlebitis.
Venedig [ve'neɪdɪç] neut Venice. **venezianer** m (pl -), **Venezianerin** f (pl -nen) Venetian. **venezianisch** adj Venetian.
Ventil [vɛn'tiɪl] neut (pl -e) valve. **-ator** m (pl -en) ventilator; (Mot) fan; (Elek) electric fan.
verabreden [fɛr'apreɪdən] v agree (upon); (Ort, Zeitpunkt) fix, appoint. **Verabredung** f agreement; appointment.
verabscheuen [fɛr'apʃɔyən] v abhor, detest.
verabschieden [fɛr'apʃiɪdən] v dismiss; (Gesetze) pass. **sich verabschieden von** take one's leave of, say goodbye to.
verachten [fɛr'axtən] v despise. **verächtlich** adj contemptible. **Verachtung** f contempt.
verallgemeinern [fɛralgə'mainərn] v generalize. **Verallgemeinerung** f generalization.
veralten [fɛr'altən] v become outmoded, go out of use. **veraltet** adj out-of-date.
veränderlich [fɛr'ɛndərliç] adj changeable. **verändern** v change, alter. **sich verändern** change, alter. **Veränderung** f change, alteration.
Verankern [fɛr'aŋkərn] v moor, anchor.
veranlagt [fɛr'anlaɪkt] adj talented, gifted.
veranlassen [fɛr'anlasən] v cause, bring about. **Veranlassung** f cause; (Beweggrund) motive.
veranschaulichen [fɛr'anʃauliçən] v make clear.

veranstalten [fɛr'anʃtaltən] *v* organize, arrange. **Veranstalt‖er** *m* (*pl* -) organizer. **–ung** *f* (*pl* -en) event, function; (*Veranstalten*) organization.

verantworten [fɛr'antvɔrtən] *v* take responsibility for, answer for. **verantwortlich** *adj* responsible. **Verantwort‖lichkeit** *f* responsibility. **–ung** *f* (*pl* -en) responsibility; (*Rechtfertigung*) justification.

verarbeiten [fɛr'arbaitən] *v* manufacture, make; (*bearbeiten*) work, process; (*durchdenken*) assimilate. **Verarbeitung** *f* manufacture; working; assimilation.

verargen [fɛr'argən] *v* blame.

verärgern [fɛr'ɛrgərn] *v* annoy, vex.

verarmen [fɛr'armən] *v* become poor. **verarmt** *adj* impoverished.

Verb [vɛrp] *neut* (*pl* -en) verb.

Verband [fɛr'bant] *m* (*pl* Verbände) (*Med*) bandage, dressing; (*Verein*) association, society.

verbannen [fɛr'banən] *v* banish. **Verbann‖te(r)** exile. **–ung** *f* banishment, exile.

*verbergen [fɛr'bɛrgən] *v* hide.

verbessern [fɛr'bɛsərn] *v* improve; (*berichtigen*) correct. **Verbesserung** *f* (*pl* -en) improvement; correction.

verbeugen [fɛr'bɔygən] *v* **sich verbeugen** bow.

*verbieten [fɛr'biːtən] *v* forbid, prohibit.

*verbinden [fɛr'bindən] *v* connect, join; (*Med*) bandage, dress; (*Telef*) connect, put through. **sich verbinden mit** join up with, combine with. **verbindlich** *adj* binding, obligatory; (*zuvorkommend*) obliging. **Verbindung** *f* connection; (*Med*) bandage, dressing; (*Telef*) connection. **in Verbindung mit** in association with. **im Verbindung treten mit** get in touch with. **im Verbindung stehen mit** be in contact with. **in Verbindung setzen mit** put in contact with.

verbissen [fɛr'bisən] *adj* grim, dogged.

verbittern [fɛr'bitərn] *v* embitter. **Verbitterung** *f* bitterness.

verblassen [fɛr'blasən] *v* turn *or* grow pale; (*Farbe, Erinnerung*) fade.

Verbleib [fɛr'blaip] *m* whereabouts. **verbleiben** *v* remain.

verblenden [fɛr'blɛndən] *v* blind, dazzle, delude; (*Mauerwerk*) face. **Verblendung** *f* blindness, delusion.

verblüffen [fɛr'blyfən] *v* dumbfound, nonplus. **verblüfft** *adj* dumbfounded, non-

plussed. **Verblüffung** *f* amazement, stupefaction.

verbluten [fɛr'bluːtən] *v* bleed to death.

verbohrt [fɛr'boːrt] *adj* stubborn.

verborgen [fɛr'bɔrgən] *adj* hidden. **Verborgenheit** *f* concealment, secrecy.

Verbot [fɛr'boːt] *neut* (*pl* -e) prohibition, ban. **verboten** *adj* prohibited, forbidden.

Verbrauch [fɛr'braux] *m* consumption, use. **verbrauchen** *v* consume, use up. **Verbraucher** *m* (*pl* -) consumer. **Verbrauchsgüter** *pl* consumer goods *pl*.

Verbrechen [fɛr'brɛçən] *neut* crime. **–er** *m* criminal. **verbrechen** *v* commit a crime. **verbrecherisch** *adj* criminal.

verbreiten [fɛr'braitən] *v* spread. **weit verbreitet** *adj* widespread.

*verbrennen [fɛr'brɛnən] *v* burn; (*Leichen*) cremate. **Verbrennung** *f* burning; cremation. **–smotor** *m* internal combustion engine.

*verbringen [fɛr'briŋən] *v* spend (time).

verbrühen [fɛr'bryːən] *v* scald.

Verbum ['vɛrbum] *neut* (*pl* Verben) verb.

verbünden [fɛr'byndən] *v* **sich verbünden mit** ally oneself with. **Verbündete(r)** *m* ally.

verchromt [fɛr'kroːmt] *adj* chromiumplated. **Verchromung** *f* chromium plating.

Verdacht [fɛr'daxt] *m* (*pl* -e) suspicion. **in Verdacht kommen** arouse suspicion, be suspected. **verdächtig** *adj* suspicious. **–en** *v* suspect.

verdammen [fɛr'damən] *v* condemn, damn. **verdammt** *adj* damned. *interj* damn! **Verdammung** *f* damnation.

verdampfen [fɛr'dampfən] *v* evaporate, vaporize. **Verdampfung** *f* evaporation, vaporization.

verdanken [fɛr'daŋkən] *v* owe.

verdauen [fɛr'dauən] *v* digest. **verdaulich** *adj* digestible. **Verdauung** *f* digestion.

Verdeck [fɛr'dɛk] *neut* (*pl* -e) canopy, covering; (*Mot*) roof; (*Schiff*) deck. **verdecken** *v* cover, conceal. **verdeckt** *adj* masked, concealed.

Verderb [fɛr'dɛrp] *m* ruin, destruction. **verderben** *v* spoil, ruin; (*verführen*) corrupt; (*Speisen*) spoil, go bad; (*Menschen*) come to grief, perish. **Verderben** *neut* ruin, destruction. **verderblich** *adj* destructive, pernicious; (*Waren*) perishable. **verderbt** *adj* corrupt(ed).

verdeutlichen [fɛr'dɔytliçən] v make clear, elucidate.

verdichten [fɛr'diçtən] v compress. **Verdichtung** f compression.

verdicken [fɛr'dikən] v thicken.

verdienen [fɛr'diːnən] v (Geld) earn; (Beachtung, Lob) deserve. **er hat es verdient** he deserves it; (negativ) it serves him right. **Verdienst 1** m (pl -e) earnings pl, gains pl. **2** neut (pl -e) deserts pl. **-spanne** f margin (of profit).

verdingen [fɛr'diŋən] v hire out.

verdoppeln [fɛr'dɔpəln] v double. **Verdoppelung** f doubling.

verdorben [fɛr'dɔrbən] adj spoilt; (fig) corrupted.

verdrängen [fɛr'drɛŋən] v displace, push out; (vertreiben) drive away; (Psychol) repress.

verdrehen [fɛr'dreːən] v distort, twist.

*verdrießen [fɛr'driːsən] v vex, annoy. **verdrießlich** adj sullen, disgruntled; tiresome irksome.

verdrossen [fɛr'drɔsən] adj sullen.

Verdruß [fɛr'drus] m annoyance.

verdummen [fɛr'dumən] v stupefy; (dumm werden) grow stupid.

verdunkeln [fɛr'duŋkəln] v darken.

verdünnen [fɛr'dynən] v dilute, thin.

veredeln [fɛr'eːdəln] v ennoble; (fig) improve, refine.

verehren [fɛr'eːrən] v (Rel) worship; (lieben) adore; (hochschätzen) venerate, respect. **Verehr||er** m worshipper; adorer; admirer. **-ung** f worship; adoration; veneration.

Verein [fɛr'ain] m (pl -e) society, association; (Klub) club. **vereinbar** adj reconcilable, compatible. **vereinbar||en** v agree upon. **-t** adj agreed (upon). **Vereinbarung** f (pl -en) agreement.

vereinfachen [fɛr'ainfaxən] v simplify.

vereinheitlichen [fɛr'ainhaitliçən] v unify, standardize.

vereinigen [fɛr'ainigən] v unite, join. **sich vereinigen** unite. **vereinigt** adj united. **die Vereinigten Staaten** pl the United States. **Vereinigung** f (pl -en) union; association, society; (Zusammenschluß) combination. **-spunkt** m meeting point.

vereint [fɛr'aint] adj united.

vereiteln [fɛr'aitəln] v frustrate. **Vereitelung** f frustration.

vererben [fɛr'ɛrbən] v leave, bequeath;

(Krankheit, Eigenschaft) transmit. **vererblich** adj hereditary. **Vererbung** f heredity.

verewigen [fɛr'eːvigən] v immortalize.

verfahren [fɛr'faːrən] v act, proceed. **sich verfahren** lose one's way. **Verfahren** neut procedure; (Methode) method; (Tech) process.

Verfall [fɛr'fal] m ruin; (allmählich) decline, decay. **verfallen** v decline, decay.

verfälschen [fɛr'fɛlʃən] v falsify. **Verfälschung** f falsification.

verfassen [fɛr'fasən] v compose, write; (Urkunde) draw up. **Verfasser** m (pl -), **Verfasserin** f (pl -nen) author, writer.

*verfechten [fɛr'feçtən] v fight for, defend.

verfehlen [fɛr'feːlən] v miss, not reach; (versäumen) fail. **Verfehlung** f mistake, lapse.

verfeinern [fɛr'fainərn] v refine.

verflechten [fɛr'flɛçtən] v interweave; (fig) involve.

fluchen [fɛr'fluːxən] v curse. **verflucht** adj cursed, damned. interj damn (it)!

verfolgen [fɛr'fɔlgən] v pursue; (beobachten) follow; (gerichtlich) prosecute; (plagen) persecute. **Verfolger** m pursuer; persecutor. **Verfolgung** f pursuit; prosecution; persecution.

Verformung [fɛr'fɔrmuŋ] f distortion, warping.

verfügbar [fɛr'fyːkbaːr] adj available. **verfügen** v order, decree. **verfügen über** have at one's disposal, dispose of. **Verfügung** f disposal; (Anordnung) order. **zur Verfügung stehen/stellen** be/put at the disposal (of).

verführen [fɛr'fyːrən] v seduce; (verleiten) lead astray. **Verführ||er** m seducer; tempter. **-ung** f seduction; temptation.

vergangen [fɛr'gaŋən] adj past. **Vergangenheit** f past. **vergänglich** adj transitory, impermanent.

Vergaser [fɛr'gaːzər] m (pl -) carburettor.

*vergeben [fɛr'geːbən] v (verzeihen) forgive; (verschenken) give away; (verteilen) distribute. **vergeb||ens** adv in vain. **-lich** adj vain. adv in vain. **Vergebung** f forgiveness. interj pardon me!

vergegenwärtigen [fɛrgeːgənˈvɛrtigən] v represent.

*vergehen [fɛr'geːən] v pass. **vergehen vor** die of. **sich vergehen** v commit an offence, err. **Vergehen** neut misdeed.

*vergelten [fɛrˈgɛltən] v pay back. **Vergeltung** f reward; retaliation.

*vergessen [fɛrˈgɛsən] v forget. **Vergessenheit** f oblivion. **vergeßlich** adj forgetful.

vergeuden [fɛrˈgɔydən] v waste, squander. **Vergeudung** f waste, dissipation.

vergewaltigen [fɛrgəˈvaltigən] v rape. **Vergewaltiger** m rapist. **Vergewaltigung** f rape.

*vergießen [fɛrˈgiːsən] v shed, spill.

vergiften [fɛrˈgiftən] v poison. **Vergiftung** f poisoning.

Vergißmeinnicht [fɛrˈgismainniçt] neut (pl -e) forget-me-not.

verglasen [fɛrˈglaːzən] v glaze.

Vergleich [fɛrˈglaiç] m (pl -e) comparison; (Redewendung) simile; (Abkommen) agreement, settlement. **einen Vergleich schließen** come to an agreement. **im Vergleich mit/zu** in comparison with/to. **vergleichbar** adj comparable. **vergleichen** v compare; settle, agree.

Vergnügen [fɛrˈgnyːgən] neut enjoyment. **vergnügen** v amuse. **sich vergnügen** amuse oneself. **vergnügt** adj merry, happy. **Vergnügung** f pleasure, enjoyment. **–spark** m amusement park.

vergoldet [fɛrˈgɔldət] adj (Metall) gold-plated; (Holz) gilt.

vergöttern [fɛrˈgœtərn] v deify; (fig) idolize.

vergraben [fɛrˈgraːbən] v bury.

vergriffen [fɛrˈgrifən] adj sold out; (Buch) out of print.

vergrößern [fɛrˈgrøːsərn] v enlarge, magnify. **Vergrößerung** f (pl -en) enlargement.

Vergünstigung [fɛrˈgynstiguŋ] f (pl -en) privilege; (Rabatt) discount.

vergüten [fɛrˈgyːtən] v compensate (for); (Unkosten) reimburse. **Vergütung** f (pl -en) compensation; reimbursement.

verhaften [fɛrˈhaftən] v arrest. **verhaftet** adj arrested; (fig) bound, connected. **Verhaftung** f (pl -en) arrest.

*verhalten [fɛrˈhaltən] v hold back. **sich verhalten** behave, act; (Sache) be. **Verhalten** neut behaviour.

Verhältnis [fɛrˈhɛltnis] neut (pl -se) relation, proportion; (Beziehungen) relation; (Liebesaffäre) relationship; liaison. **im Verhältnis zu** in comparison with. **Verhältnisse** pl circumstances. **Verhältn-**

ismäßig adj proportional. adv relatively, comparatively.

verhandeln [fɛrˈhandəln] v negotiate. **Verhandlung** f negotiation.

Verhängnis [fɛrˈhɛŋnis] neut (pl -se) fate, destiny. **verhängnisvoll** adj fateful.

verhaßt [fɛrˈhast] adj odious, hated.

verheeren [fɛrˈheːrən] v devastate, lay waste.

verheimlichen [fɛrˈhaimliçən] v conceal, keep secret.

verheiraten [fɛrˈhairaitən] v marry. **sich verheiraten** get married, marry.

*verheißen [fɛrˈhaisən] v promise.

*verhelfen [fɛrˈhɛlfən] v assist, help.

verherrlichen [fɛrˈhɛrliçən] v glorify. **Verherrlichung** f glorification.

verhindern [fɛrˈhindərn] v prevent. **Verhinderung** f prevention.

verhöhnen [gɛrˈhœːnən] v ridicule, mock.

Verhör [fɛrˈhœːr] neut (pl -e) interrogation, examination. **verhören** v interrogate, examine. **sich verhören** hear wrongly, misunderstand.

verhungern [fɛrˈhuŋərn] v starve (to death).

verhüten [fɛrˈhyːtən] v prevent, ward off. **–d** adj preventive. **Verhütung** f prevention. **–smittel** neut contraceptive.

verirren [fɛrˈirən] v **sich verirren** go astray, get lost.

verjüngen [fɛrˈjyŋən] v rejuvenate; (erneuern) renew. **Verjüngung** f rejuvenation; renewal.

Verkauf [fɛrˈkauf] m sale. **verkaufen** v sell. **Verkäufer** m seller; (Angestellter) salesman; (im Laden) sales assistant. **–in** f saleswoman, sales assistant. **verkäuflich** adj for sale. **Verkaufs‖abteilung** f sales department. **–automat** m vending machine. **–bedingungen** (pl) terms of sale. **–förderung** f sales promotion. **–preis** m selling price.

Verkehr [fɛrˈkeːr] m traffic; (Umgang) intercourse; (Handel) trade. **verkehren** v (Bus) run; (verdrehen) distort; (besuchen) frequent; (Menschen) associate (with). **Verkehrs‖ampeln** f pl traffic lights. **–ordnung** f traffic regulation. **–spitze** f rush hour. **–stockung** f traffic jam. **–unfall** m road accident. **verkehrt** adj inverted, wrong way round; (falsch) wrong.

*verkennen [fɛrˈkɛnən] v mistake, misjudge; (Person) not recognize.

365 **vermeintlich**

verklagen [fɛr'klaɪgən] v (*Jur*) sue (for); (*umg.*) inform against.
verklären [fɛr'klɛːrən] v transfigure; (*fig*) illumine. Verklärung f transfiguration; illumination.
verkleiden [fɛr'klaɪdən] v cover, mask; (*Wand*) face. sich verkleiden disguise oneself. Verkleidung f (pl -en) disguise; facing, lining.
verkleinern [fɛr'klaɪnərn] v reduce, diminish. Verkleinerung f (pl -en) reduction, diminution.
verknüpfen [fɛr'knypfən] v knot (together), join; (*fig*) connect. verknüpft adj connected.
*verkommen [fɛr'kɔmən] v (*Person*) degenerate, (*umg.*) go to the dogs; (*speisen*) go bad; (*Gebäude*) decay, be neglected.
verkörpern [fɛr'kœrpərn] v embody. Verkörperung f embodiment, incarnation.
verkrümmen [fɛr'krymən] v bend, make crooked. Verkrümmung f (pl -en) crookedness, distortion; (*Rückgrat*) curvature.
verkrüppeln [fɛr'krypəln] v cripple.
verkünden [fɛr'kyndən] v announce, proclaim; (*Urteil*) pronounce. verkündigen v proclaim. Mariä Verkündigung Annunciation, Lady Day.
verkürzen [fɛr'kyrtsən] v shorten, abbreviate; (*Buch*) abridge. sich verkürzen shrink, diminish. Verkürzung f shortening; (*Buch*) abridgment.
*verladen [fɛr'laːdən] v load; (*verschicken*) dispatch. Verladung f loading.
Verlag [fɛr'laːk] m (pl -e) publishing house, publisher.
verlangen [fɛr'laŋən] v demand; (*benötigen*) require. verlangen nach long for. Verlangen neut demand; (*Wunsch*) desire. auf Verlangen on demand.
verlängern [fɛr'lɛŋərn] v extend, lengthen; (*Gültigkeit, usw.*) extend. Verlängerung f (pl -en) extension.
verlangsamen [fɛr'laŋzaɪmən] v · slow down.
Verlaß [fɛr'las] m trustworthiness, reliability. verlassen v leave; (*im Stich lassen*) desert, abandon. adj abandoned, forsaken. sich verlassen auf rely on. verläßlich adj reliable.
Verlauf [fɛr'lauf] m course. verlaufen v (*Zeit*) pass; (*Angelegenheit*) go, turn out; (*Weg*) run, to. es ist alles gut verlaufen

everything went very well. sich verlaufen lose one's way.
verlautbaren [fɛr'lautbaɪrən] v notify.
verlegen [fɛr'leːgən] v misplace; (*Platz ändern*) transfer, remove; (*Buch*) publish; (*Termin*) postpone. adj embarrassed. Verleg∥enheit f embarrassment; (*Schwierigkeit*) difficulty. –er m (pl -) publisher.
*verleihen [fɛr'laɪən] v lend; (*Preise*) confer, bestow.
verleiten [fɛr'laɪtən] v lead astray, mislead.
verlernen [fɛr'lɛrnən] v forget.
*verlesen [fɛr'leːzən] v read out; (*auslesen*) pick. sich verlesen misread.
verletzen [fɛr'lɛtsən] v injure, wound; (*kränken*) hurt, offend; (*Gesetze*) infringe. verletzlich adj vulnerable; (*fig*) sensitive, touchy. Verletzung f (pl -en) injury; (*Vergehen*) offence.
verleugnen [fɛr'lɔygnən] v deny; (*Kind, Freunde*) disown.
verleumden [fɛr'lɔymdən] v slander. Verleumder m (pl -) slanderer. verleumderisch adj slanderous. Verleumdung f (pl -en) slander.
verlieben [fɛr'liːbən] v sich verlieben in fall in love with.
*verlieren [fɛr'liːrən] v lose. sich verlieren get lost.
verloben [fɛr'loːbən] v sich verloben mit get engaged to. Verlobte f (pl -n) fiancée. Verlobter m (pl -en) fiancé. Verlobung f (pl -en) engagement.
verlocken [fɛr'lɔkən] v tempt, entice. –d adj tempting. Verlockung f (pl -en) enticement, temptation.
verlogen [fɛr'loːgən] adj untruthful, lying.
verloren [fɛr'loːrən] adj lost. –gehen v be lost.
Verlust [fɛr'lust] m (pl -e) loss. verlustbringend adj detrimental.
vermachen [fɛr'maxən] v bequeath, leave. Vermächtnis neut (pl -se) (*Testament*) will; (*Vermachtes*) legacy, bequest.
vermehren [fɛr'meːrən] v also sich vermehren increase. Vermehrung f (pl -en) increase.
*vermeiden [fɛr'maɪdən] v avoid. vermeidlich adj avoidable. Vermeidung f avoidance.
vermeintlich [fɛr'maɪntliç] adj supposed, presumed.

Vermerk [fɛr'mɛrk] *m* (*pl* -e) note, remark. **vermerken** *v* note, remark.

***vermessen** [fɛr'mɛsən] *v* measure; (*Land*) survey. *adj* presumptuous. **Vermess||er** *m* surveyor. —**ung** *f* measurement; (*Land*) survey.

vermieten [fɛr'miːtən] *v* let, rent (out). **Vermiet||er** *m* landlord. —**ung** *f* letting.

vermindern [fɛr'mindərn] *v* reduce, decrease. **Verminderung** *f* reduction, decrease.

vermischen [fɛr'miʃən] *v* mix, blend.

vermissen [fɛr'misən] *v* miss. **vermißt** *adj* missing.

vermitteln [fɛr'mitəln] *v* mediate, negotiate; (*verschaffen*) procure, obtain. **Vermittl||er** *m* mediator, go-between; (*Komm*) agent. —**ung** *f* (*pl* -en) mediation, negotiation; (*Telef*) exchange.

***vermögen** [fɛr'mœːgən] *v* be able (to). —**d** *adj* well-to-do. **Vermögen** *neut* fortune, wealth, property; (*Fähigkeit*) ability. —**sverwalter** *m* trustee (of an estate).

vermuten [fɛr'muːtən] *v* suppose, suspect. **vermutlich** *adj* supposed. *adv* probably, presumably. **Vermutung** *f* (*pl* -en) supposition, suspicion.

vernachlässigen [fɛr'naxlɛsigən] *v* neglect.

vernarren [fɛr'narən] *v* **sich vernarren in** become infatuated with; (*Kind*) dote on.

***vernehmen** [fɛr'neːmən] *v* perceive; (*Gefangene*) interrogate. **vernehmlich** *adj* perceptible.

verneinen [fɛr'nainən] *v* deny; (*Frage*) say no, answer in the negative. **Verneinung** *f* denial; negation.

vernichten [fɛr'niçtən] *v* destroy, annihilate. —**d** *adj* annihilating, crushing. **Vernichtung** *f* destruction, annihilation.

vernieten [fɛr'niːtən] *v* rivet.

Vernunft [fɛr'nunft] *f* reason; (*Besonnenheit*) sense, commonsense. **zur Vernunft kommen** come to one's senses. **vernünftig** *adj* sensible, reasonable.

veröden [fɛr'œːdən] *v* become desolate.

veröffentlichen [fɛr'œfəntliçən] *v* publish. **Veröffentlichung** *f* publication.

verordnen [fɛr'ɔrdnən] *v* order; (*Med*) prescribe. **Verordnung** *f* order; prescription.

verpachten [fɛr'paxtən] *v* lease, let.

verpacken [fɛr'pakən] *v* pack.

verpassen [fɛr'pasən] *v* miss.

verpfänden [fɛr'pfɛndən] *v* pawn, pledge.

verpflegen [fɛr'pfleːgən] *v* feed. cater for. **Verpflegung** *f* food, board.

verpflichten [fɛr'pfliçtən] *v* oblige, commit. **sich verpflichten** bind *or* commit oneself. **Verpflichtung** *f* obligation, commitment, duty.

verpfuschen [fɛr'pfuʃən] *v* bungle, botch, make a mess of.

verprügeln [fɛr'pryːgəln] *v* thrash, beat.

verputzen [fɛr'putsən] *v* plaster; (*umg.*) scoff, put away.

Verrat [fɛr'raɪt] *m* (*unz.*) treachery; (*Pol*) treason; (*eines Geheimnisses*) betrayal. **verraten** *v* betray. **Verräter** *m* (*pl* -) traitor. **verräterisch** *adj* treacherous.

verrechnen [fɛr'rɛçnən] *v* reckon up. **sich verrechnen** miscalculate. **Verrechnung** *f* miscalculation.

verreisen [fɛr'raizən] *v* go away (on a journey).

verrenken [fɛr'rɛŋkən] *v* dislocate, sprain. **Verrenkung** *f* (*pl* -en) dislocation, sprain.

verrichten [fɛr'riçtən] *v* perform, do, execute.

verriegeln [fɛr'riːgəln] *v* bolt, bar.

verringern [fɛr'riŋərn] *v* reduce, lessen.

verrotten [fɛr'rɔtən] *v* rot. **verrottet** *adj* rotten.

verrücken [fɛr'rykən] *v* shift, displace. **verrückt** *adj* crazy.

Verruf [fɛr'ruːf] *m* ill repute, disrepute. **in Verruf bringen/kommen** bring/fall into disrepute.

Vers [fɛrs] *m* (*pl* -e) line; (*Strophe*) verse.

versagen [fɛr'zaigən] *v* fail; (*verweigern*) refuse. **Versager** *m* (*pl* -) failure.

versammeln [fɛr'zaməln] *v* assemble, gather. **sich versammeln** meet. **Versammlung** *f* (*pl* -en) meeting, assembly, convention.

Versand [fɛr'zant] *m* dispatch, shipment, forwarding. —**handel** *m* mail-order (trading).

versäumen [fɛr'zɔymən] *v* neglect, fail; (*verpassen*) miss. **Versäumnis** *f* neglect, omission.

verschaffen [fɛr'ʃafən] *v* obtain, procure.

verschämt [fɛr'ʃɛimt] *adj* bashful, ashamed.

Verschanzung [fɛr'ʃantsuŋ] *f* (*pl* -en) fortification, entrenchment.

verschärfen [fɛr'ʃɛrfən] *v* sharpen, intensify.

***verscheiden** *v* die. **verschieden** *adj* dead.

verschicken [fɛr'ʃikən] v send off, dispatch.

*verschieben [fɛr'ʃiːbən] v move, shift; (*Termin*) postpone. **Verschiebung** f displacement; postponement.

verschieden [fɛr'ʃiːdən] adj different. –**artig** adj various. **Verschiedenheit** f difference.

verschiffen [fɛr'ʃifən] v ship.

verschimmeln [fɛr'ʃiməln] v moulder, grow mouldy.

*verschlafen [fɛr'ʃlaːfən] v oversleep; (*Sorgen*) sleep off. adj sleepy.

Verschlag [fɛr'ʃlaɪk] m shed.

verschlechtern [fɛr'ʃlɛçtərn] v make worse, aggravate. **sich verschlechtern** deteriorate, get worse. **Verschlechterung** f deterioration.

verschleiern [fɛr'ʃlaiərn] v veil; (*fig*) camouflage, conceal.

Verschleiß [fɛr'ʃlais] m (pl -e) wear and tear. **verschließen** v wear out.

verschleudern [fɛr'ʃləydərn] v waste, squander.

verschließbar [fɛr'ʃliːsbaɪr] adj lockable. **verschließen** v lock; (*Sachen*) lock up or away.

verschlimmern [fɛr'ʃlimərn] v make worse, aggravate. **sich verschlimmern** become worse, deteriorate. **Verschlimmerung** f deterioration.

*verschlingen [fɛr'ʃliŋən] v devour, gorge; (*verflechten*) twist, intertwine.

verschlossen [fɛr'ʃləsən] adj locked; (*Person*) reserved, withdrawn.

verschlucken [fɛr'ʃlukən] v swallow.

Verschluß [fɛr'ʃlus] m fastening; (*Propfen*) stopper, plug; (*Phot*) shutter.

verschmähen [fɛr'ʃmɛːən] v disdain, scorn.

*verschmelzen [fɛr'ʃmɛltsən] v melt, fuse; (*ineinander*) merge.

*verschneiden [fɛr'ʃnaidən] v trim, prune; (*Wein*) mix, adulterate; (*kastrieren*) castrate.

verschollen [fɛr'ʃələn] adj missing.

verschonen [fɛr'ʃoːnən] v spare.

verschönern [fɛr'ʃøːnərn] v beautify.

verschränken [fɛr'ʃrɛŋkən] v fold, cross.

verschulden [fɛr'ʃuldən] v fall into or be in debt; (*Übel*) be to blame for. **Verschulden** neut guilt, fault. **verschuldet** adj in debt.

*verschweigen [fɛr'ʃvaigən] v keep secret, hide. **Verschweigung** f concealment.

verschwenden [fɛr'ʃvɛndən] v waste, squander. **verschwenderisch** adj wasteful. **Verschwendung** f waste.

verschwiegen [fɛr'ʃviːgən] adj discreet; (*Platz*) secluded, quiet. **Verschwiegenheit** f discretion.

*verschwinden [fɛr'ʃvindən] v disappear.

verschwommen [fɛr'ʃvəmən] adj blurred, hazy.

verschwören [fɛr'ʃvøːrən] v renounce, abjure. **sich verschwören** conspire, plot. **Verschwör\|er** m conspirator, plotter. –**ung** f conspiracy.

*versehen [fɛr'zeːən] v (*versorgan*) provide, supply; (*Dienst*) discharge; (*Haus, usw.*) look after. **sich versehen** make a mistake. **Versehen** neut mistake; (*Übersehen*) oversight. **versehentlich** adv by mistake.

*versenden [fɛr'zɛndən] v send, dispatch.

versengen [fɛr'zɛŋən] v singe, scorch.

versenken [fɛr'zɛŋkən] v lower, (*unter Wasser*) submerge; (*Schiff*) sink. **sich versenken in** become absorbed in.

versessen [fɛr'zɛsən] adj **versessen auf** mad about or on.

versetzen [fɛr'zɛtsən] v move, transfer; (*verpfänden*) pawn; (*umg.*) leave in the lurch, jilt. **Versetzung** f removal, transfer.

verseuchen [fɛr'zɔyçən] v contaminate.

versichern [fɛr'ziçərn] v insure; (*überzeugen*) assure. **sich versichern** make certain. **Seien Sie versichert, daß** you may rest assured that. **Versicherung** f insurance. –**spolice** f insurance policy.

versiegeln [fɛr'ziːgəln] v seal.

versöhnen [fɛr'zøːnən] v reconcile. **sich versöhnen mit** become reconciled with. **versöhnlich** adj conciliatory. **Versöhnung** f reconciliation.

versorgen [fɛr'zɔrgən] v (*Kind, usw.*) provide for. **versorgen mit** provide or supply with. **Versorgung** f care, provision; (*staatlich*) maintenance, (public) assistance.

verspäten [fɛr'ʃpɛːtən] v delay. **verspätet** adj late, delayed. **Verspätung** f (pl -en) delay. **10 Minuten Verspätung haben** be running 10 minutes late.

versperren [fɛr'ʃpɛrən] v bar, obstruct.

verspielen [fɛr'ʃpiːlən] v gamble away, lose.

verspotten [fɛr'ʃpɔtən] v scoff at, ridicule. Verspottung f ridicule.

*versprechen [fɛr'ʃprɛçən] v promise. sich versprechen make a (verbal) mistake. Versprechen neut (pl -) promise.

versprengen [fɛr'ʃprɛŋən] v (Mil) scatter, disperse.

versprochen [fɛr'ʃprɔxən] adj promised.

verstaatlichen [fɛr'ʃtaːtliçən] v nationalize. Verstaatlichung f nationalization.

Verstand [fɛr'ʃtant] m understanding; (Geist) mind, intelligence. den Verstand verlieren lose one's reason, go out of one's mind. verständig adj intelligent; sensible. verständigen v inform. sich verständigen mit (über) come to an understanding with (about). Verständigung f understanding, arrangement. verständlich adj intelligible. Verständnis neut understanding, comprehension. verständnis‖los adj uncomprehending, unappreciative. –voll adj understanding, sympathetic.

verstärken [fɛr'ʃtɛrkən] v strengthen; (Ton) amplify; (Farbe, Spannung) intensify. Verstärk‖er m amplifier. –ung f strengthening; (Ton) amplification; (Mil) reinforcements pl.

Versteck [fɛr'ʃtɛk] neut (pl -e) hiding place. verstecken v hide. sich verstecken hide. versteckt adj hidden; (Anspielung) veiled, implied.

*verstehen [fɛr'ʃteːən] v understand. zu verstehen geben give to understand. sich verstehen mit come to an understanding with.

Versteigerer [fɛr'ʃtaigərər] m (pl -) auctioneer. versteigern v (sell by) auction. Versteigerung f (pl -en) auction.

versteinern [fɛr'ʃtainərn] v petrify. versteinert adj petrified.

verstellbar [fɛr'ʃtɛlbair] adj adjustable, movable. verstellen v adjust; (versperren) block, bar; (unkenntlich machen) disguise. sich verstellen feign, dissemble. Verstellung f (pl -en) adjustment; (fig) pretence.

verstimmt [fɛr'ʃtimt] adj (Musik) out of tune; (Person) bad-tempered; (Magen) upset.

verstockt [fɛr'ʃtɔkt] adj stubborn.

verstohlen [fɛr'ʃtoːlən] adj furtive, stealthy.

verstopfen [fɛr'ʃtɔpfən] v plug, stop up;

(Med) constipate. Verstopfung f obstruction; (Med) constipation.

verstorben [fɛr'ʃtɔrbən] adj deceased, late. Verstorbene(r) the deceased.

Verstoß [fɛr'ʃtɔs] m offence. verstoßen v offend; (von sich stoßen) reject.

verstricken [fɛr'ʃtrikən] v entangle, ensnare.

verstümmeln [fɛr'ʃtyməln] v mutilate, maim.

Versuch [fɛr'zuːx] m (pl -e) attempt; (Probe) test, trial; (Experiment) experiment. versuchen v attempt, try; (kosten) taste, try. Versuchs‖fahrt f trial run. –kaninchen neut (fig) guinea pig.

vertagen [fɛr'taːgən] v adjourn.

vertauschen [fɛr'tauʃən] v exchange.

verteidigen [fɛr'taidigən] v defend. Verteidig‖er m (pl -) defender; (Jur) defence counsel. –ung f (pl -en) defence.

verteilen [fɛr'tailən] v distribute; (zerteilen) divide. Verteil‖er m (pl -) distributor. –ung f (pl -en) distribution.

vertiefen [fɛr'tiːfən] v deepen. sich vertiefen in be absorbed in. vertieft adj sunk; (fig) absorbed. Vertiefung f depression, hollow; (fig) absorption.

vertikal [vɛrti'kaːl] adj vertical.

vertilgen [fɛr'tilgən] v exterminate; (vernichten) destroy. Vertilgung f extermination; destruction.

Vertrag [fɛr'traːk] m (pl Verträge) contract; (Pol) treaty. vertragen v bear, endure. sich vertragen mit get on well with. vertraglich adj stipulated, agreed.

verträglich [fɛr'trɛːkliç] adj (Person) good-natured, obliging; (Speise) light, digestible.

Vertrags‖bruch m breach of contract. –nehmer m contractor.

vertrauen [fɛr'trauən] v trust. vertrauen auf trust in, have confidence in. Vertrauen neut trust, confidence. Vertrauens‖sache f confidential affair. –votum neut vote of confidence. vertrauens‖voll adj trustful, trusting. –würdig adj trustworthy. vertraulich adj confidential. vertraut adj familiar.

*vertreiben [fɛr'traibən] v expel, drive away; (verkaufen) sell. Vertreibung f (pl -en) expulsion.

*vertreten [fɛr'treːtən] v represent; (vorübergehend) replace, stand in for; (eintreten für) advocate. Vertret‖er m (pl

-) representative; (*Komm*) sales representative; **–ung** *f* (*pl* **-en**) representation.
Vertrieb [fɛr'triːp] *m* (retail) sale.
*vertun [fɛr'tuːn] *v* squander, spend.
vertuschen [fɛr'tuʃən] *v* hush up.
verunglimpfen [fɛr'unɡlɪmpfən] *v* defame, revile.
verunglücken [fɛr'unɡlyːkən] *v* be involved in an accident; (*Angelegenheit*) fail.
verunreinigen [fɛr'untainiɡən] *v* pollute, soil.
verunstalten [fɛr'unʃtaltən] *v* disfigure.
veruntreuen [fɛr'untrɔyən] *v* embezzle.
verursachen [fɛr'uːrzaxən] *v* cause, bring about.
verurteilen [fɛr'uːrtailən] *v* condemn; (*Jur*) sentence. **Verurteilung** *f* condemnation; conviction.
vervielfältigen [fɛr'fiːlfɛltiɡən] *v* duplicate, copy. **Vervielfältigung** *f* reproduction, duplication.
vervollkommnen [fɛr'fɔlkɔmnən] *v* perfect.
vervollständigen [fɛr'fɔlʃtɛndiɡən] *v* complete.
*verwachsen [fɛr'vaksən] *v* grow together; (*Wunde*) heal up; (*bucklig werden*) become deformed; (*sich verbinden*) be tied to. *adj* deformed.
verwahren [fɛr'vaːrən] *v* keep; (*schützen*) protect, preserve.
verwahrlosen [fɛr'vaːrloːzən] *v* neglect. **verwahrlost** *adj* neglected; (*Kind*) scruffy, unkempt.
verwalten [fɛr'valtən] *v* administer, manage. **Verwalter** *m* administrator; (*Fabrik, Büro*) manager; (*Gut, Haus*) steward. **Verwaltung** *f* administration; management.
verwandeln [fɛr'vandəln] *v* transform; (*ändern*) change. **Verwandlung** *f* transformation; change.
verwandt [fɛr'vant] *adj* related. **Verwandt||e(r)** relative, relation. **–schaft** *f* relationship; (*Verwandte*) relatives *pl*.
verwechseln [fɛr'vɛksəln] *v* confuse. **verwechseln mit** mistake for, confuse with. **Verwechslung** *f* confusion.
verwegen [fɛr'veɡən] *adj* bold, audacious.
verweichlicht [fɛr'vaiçlɪçt] *adj* effeminate.
verweigern [fɛr'vaiɡərn] *v* refuse. **Verweigerung** *f* refusal.
verweilen [fɛr'vailən] *v* linger, stay.
Verweis [fɛr'vais] *m* (*pl* **-e**) reprimand,

rebuke; (*Hinweis*) reference. **verweisen** *v* reprimand, rebuke; (*verbannen*) exile, banish. **verweisen auf** refer to.
*verwenden [fɛr'vɛndən] *v* use, employ; apply; (*Zeit*) spend. **Verwendung** *f* use; application.
*verwerfen [fɛr'vɛrfən] *v* throw away; (*zurückweisen*) reject.
verwesen¹ [fɛr'veːzən] *v* (*verwalten*) administer.
verwesen² *v* (*verfaulen*) decay.
verwickeln [fɛr'vikəln] *n* entangle. **sich verwickeln in** become involved in. **verwickelt** *adj* complicated. **Verwicklung** *f* (*pl* **-en**) entanglement, complication.
verwirken [fɛr'virkən] *v* forfeit.
verwirklichen [fɛr'virkliçən] *v* realize. **sich verwirklichen** come true, materialize. **Verwirklichung** *f* realization.
*verwirren [fɛr'virən] *v* confuse, bewilder. **verwirrt** *adj* confused. **Verwirrung** *f* confusion.
verwischen [fɛr'viʃən] *v* blur, smear; (*fig*) cover up, wipe out.
verwitwet [fɛr'vitvət] *adj* widowed.
verwöhnen [fɛr'vœːnən] *v* spoil. **verwöhnt** *adj* pampered, spoiled.
verworfen [fɛr'vɔrfən] *adj* depraved.
verworren [fɛr'vɔrən] *adj* confused.
verwundbar [fɛr'vuntbaːr] *adj* vulnerable. **verwunden** *v* wound, hurt. **verwundet** *adj* wounded. **Verwundete(r)** injured person; (*Mil*) casualty. **Verwundung** *f* wound, injury.
verwunderlich [fɛr'vundaːrliç] *adj* surprising. **verwundern** *v* surprise, astonish. **sich verwundern über** be astonished by, wonder about. **Verwunderung** *f* astonishment.
verwünschen [fɛr'vynʃən] *v* curse. **verwünscht** *adj* cursed, bewitched.
verwüsten [fɛr'vyːstən] *v* devastate. **Verwüstung** *f* devastation.
verzagt [fɛr'tsaɪkt] *adj* downcast, despondent.
verzaubern [fɛr'tsaubərn] *v* enchant, charm. **verzaubert** *adj* enchanted, magic.
Verzehr [fɛr'tseːr] *m* consumption (of food and drink). **verzehren** *v* consume, take, eat.
verzeichnen [fɛr'tsaiçnən] *v* note, enter, write down. **Verzeichnis** *neut* (*pl* **-se**) list, catalogue; (*Buch*) index; (*Register*) register.

*verzeihen [fɛr'tsaiən] v pardon, forgive.
verzeihen Sie! pardon (me)! I'm sorry!
Verzeihung f pardon, forgiveness. *interj* I
beg your pardon! excuse me!
verzerren [fɛr'tsɛrən] v distort.
Verzicht [fɛr'tsiçt] m (pl -e) renunciation.
verzichten auf renounce, do without.
verziehen [fɛr'tsiːən] v distort; (*Kinder*)
spoil.
verzieren [fɛr'tsiːrən] v decorate, adorn.
verzögern [fɛr'tsœːɡərn] v delay.
Verzögerung f (pl -en) delay.
verzollen [fɛr'tsɔlən] v pay duty on.
verzücken [fɛr'tsukən] v enrapture.
verzückt adj enraptured, ecstatic.
Verzückung f (pl -en) rapture, ecstasy.
verzuckern [fɛr'tsukərn] v sugar.
Verzug [fɛr'tsuk] m (unz.) delay.
verzweifeln [fɛr'tsvaifəln] v despair.
verzweifelt adj desperate. **Verzweiflung** f
despair.
verzwickt [fɛr'tsvikt] adj complicated, difficult.
veterinär [veteri'nɛːr] adj veterinary.
Veterinär m (pl -e) veterinary surgeon.
Vetter ['fɛtər] m (pl -n) (male) cousin.
Vibration [vibratsi'oːn] f (pl -en) vibration. **vibrieren** v vibrate.
Vieh [fiː] 1 neut (unz.) cattle pl. 2 neut (pl
Viecher) beast. **viehisch** adj bestial, brutal. **Vieh‖stall** m cowshed. **–treiber** m
drover. **–zucht** f cattle-breeding.
viel [fiːl] adj much. **viele** pl adj many. **so
viel** so much. **viel besser** much better.
viel mehr als far more than. **recht viel** a
great deal. **viel halten von** think much or
highly of. **viel‖fach** adj multiple. adv frequently, many times. **–fältig** adj various,
manifold.
vielleicht [fi'laiçt] adv perhaps.
viel‖mal(s) adv often, many times.
–mehr adv, conj rather. **–seitig** adj
many-sided. **–versprechend** adj (very)
promising.
vier [fiːr] pron, adj four. **Viereck** neut
square, rectangle. **viereckig** adj square,
rectangular. **viermal(s)** adv four times.
viert adj fourth. **Viertaktmotor** m four-
stroke engine. **Viertel** neut quarter.
–stunde f quarter (of an) hour. **viertens**
adv fourthly.
vierzehn ['fiːrtsein] pron, adj fourteen.
vierzehn Tage fortnight. **vierzehnt** adj
fourteenth.

vierzig ['fiːrtsiç] pron, adj forty. **vierzigst**
adj fortieth.
Villa ['vila] f (pl **Villen**) villa.
Viola [vi'oːla] f (pl **Violen**) viola. **Viol‖ine**
f violin. **–inist** m (pl -), **–inistin** f (pl
-nen) violinist. **–oncello** neut violoncello,
cello.
Virtuose [virtu'oːzə] m (pl -n) virtuoso.
Visite [vi'ziːtə] f (pl -n) visit. **–nkarte** f
visiting card.
Visum ['viːzum] neut (pl **Visa**) visa.
Vitamin [vita'miːn] neut (pl -e) vitamin.
Vlies [fliːs] neut (pl -e) fleece.
Vogel ['foːɡəl] m (pl **Vögel**) bird. **–gesang**
m bird-song. **–haus** neut aviary. **–kunde**
f ornithology. **–perpektive** f or **–schau** f
bird's-eye view.
vokal [vo'kaːl] adj vocal. **Vokal** m vowel.
Volk [fɔlk] neut (pl **Völker**) people, folk;
nation.
Völker‖kunde f ethnology. **–schaft** people, tribe. **völkisch** adj national.
Volks‖eigentum neut public property.
–entscheid m plebiscite, referendum.
–gruppe f ethnic group. **–lied** neut
(traditional) folksong. **–menge** f crowd.
–schule f primary school. **–staat** m
republic. **–tanz** m folk dance. **–tracht** f
national costume.
volkstümlich ['fɔlkstyːmliç] adj popular.
Volkswirt ['fɔlksvirt] m economist.
–schaft f (political) economy. **volkswirt-
schaftlich** adj economic.
voll [fɔl] adj full. adv fully. der Topf ist
voll Wasser the pot is full of water. ein
Glas voll Milch a glassful of milk. in voller Blüte in full bloom. volles Gesicht
round face. **voll‖auf** adv in abundance.
–automatisch adj fully automatic. **–berechtigt** adj fully authorized. **–beschäftigt**
adj fully employed. **–blütig** adj full-
blooded.
*vollbringen [fɔ'briŋən] v accomplish.
Vollbringung f accomplishment.
vollenden [fɔl'ɛndən] v finish, end, complete. **vollendet** adj completed;
(vervollkomnet) perfect. **Vollendung** f
completion; perfection.
voller ['fɔlər] adj or **voll von** full (of).
völlig ['fœliç] adj complete, entire, whole.
vollkommen ['fɔlkɔmən] adj perfect,
finished. **Vollkommenheit** f perfection.
Voll‖kornbrot neut wholemeal bread.
–macht f power of attorney, authority.
–milch f whole milk.

voll‖ständig *adj* complete. **–stopfen** *v* stuff.

vollstrecken [fɔl'ʃtrɛkən] *v* execute, carry out. **Vollstreck‖er** *m* (*pl* -), **–erin** *f* (*pl* -nen) executor. **–ung** *f* (*pl* -en) execution.

*vollziehen [fɔl'tsiːən] *v* carry out, execute.

Volontär [volɔn'tɛːr] *m* (*pl* -e) volunteer (worker), unpaid helper.

vom [fɔm] *prep* + *art* von dem.

von [fɔn] *prep* from; (*einer Person gehörig*) of; (*einer Person stammend*) by. *das Buch von Peter* Peter's book. *ein Buch von Greene* a book by Greene. *ein Freund von ihm* a friend of his. **von ... an** starting, from. **von nun an** from now on. *von mir aus* as far as I am concerned. **von selbst** by itself, automatically.

vor [foːr] *prep* in front of; (*zeitlich*) before. *vor acht Tagen* a week ago. *vor allem* above all, *nach wie vor* as ever, *nicht vor* not until. **Viertel vor 12** (a) quarter to twelve. **vor Zeiten** formerly.

Vorabend ['foːraːbənt] *m* eve.

Vorahnung ['foːraːnuŋ] *f* presentiment.

voran [fo'ran] *adv* at the head, in front, first. **–gehen** *v* go ahead, precede. **–kommen** *v* make progress.

Voranschlag ['foːr'anʃlaːk] *m* rough estimate.

Vorarbeiter ['foːrarbaitər] *m* foreman, supervisor.

voraus [fo'raus] *adv* ahead, in front. **im voraus** in advance. **vorausbestimmen** *v* predetermine. **vorausgesetzt daß** provided that. **Voraussage** *f* prediction. **voraus‖sagen** *v* predict, forecast. **–sehen** *v* foresee. **Voraus‖setzung** *f* assumption; (*Vorbedingung*) prerequisite. **–sicht** *f* foresight. **voraussichtlich** *adv* probably. **Vorauszahlung** *f* advance payment.

vorbedacht ['foːrbədaxt] *adj* premeditated. **Vorbedacht** *m* forethought. **mit Vorbedacht** on purpose, advisedly.

Vorbedingung ['foːrbədiŋuŋ] *f* precondition, prerequisite.

Vorbehalt ['foːrbəhalt] *m* (*pl* -e) reservation, proviso. **vorbehalten** *v* hold in reserve, withhold.

vorbei [fɔr'bai] *adv* (*örtlich*) past, by; (*zeitlich*) past, over. **vorbei sein** be all over. **vorbei‖gehen** *v* go past, pass. **–kommen** *v* pass by. **–marschieren** *v* march past.

vorbereiten ['foːrbəraitən] *v* prepare. **Vorbereitungen** *pl* preparations.

vorbestellen ['foːrbəʃtɛlən] *v* book in advance.

Vorbestrafte(r) ['foːrbəʃtraːftə(r)] *m* person with previous conviction.

vorbeugen ['foːrbɔygən] *v* prevent. **Vorbeugung** *f* prevention.

Vorbild ['foːrbilt] *neut* model, example. **vorbildlich** *adj* model, exemplary.

*vorbringen ['foːrbriŋən] *v* bring up, put forward.

vorder ['fɔrdər] *adj* fore(most), front. **Vorder‖bein** *neut* foreleg. **–grund** *m* foreground. **–radantrieb** *m* front-wheel drive. **–seite** *f* façade; obverse; face (of coin). **–teil** *m* front (part). **–tür** *f* front door.

*vordringen ['foːrdriŋən] *v* advance, press forward. **vordringlich** *adj* urgent, pressing.

voreilig ['foːrailiç] *adj* premature, hasty, precipitate.

voreingenommen ['foːraingənɔmən] *adj* prejudiced. **voreingenommen gegen** prejudiced against. **voreingenommen für** biased in favour of. **Voreingenommenheit** *f* prejudice.

*vorenthalten ['foːrenthaltən] *v* hold back, withhold.

vorerst ['foːrerst] *adv* for the time being.

vorerwähnt ['foːrervɛːnt] *adj* above-mentioned, already mentioned, aforesaid.

Vorfahr ['foːrfaːr] *m* (*pl* -en) ancestor.

Vorfahrt ['foːrfaːrt] *f* right-of-way.

Vorfall ['foːrfal] *m* incident.

vorführen ['foːrfyːrən] *v* bring forward, present; (*zeigen*) show; (*Film*) project. **Vorführung** *f* presentation, demonstration; (*Film*) showing.

Vorgang ['foːrgaŋ] *m* event, incident; (*Tech*) process; (*Komm*) file, record. **Vorgänger** *m* predecessor.

*vorgeben ['foːrgeːbən] *v* pretend.

Vorgebirge ['foːrgəbirgə] *neut* foothills *pl*; (*Kap*) promontory.

vorgeblich ['foːrgeːpliç] *adj* alleged, ostensible.

vorgefaßt ['foːrgəfast] *adj* preconceived.

Vorgefühl ['foːrgəfyːl] *neut* presentiment.

*vorgehen ['foːrgeːən] *v* go forward; (*handeln*) act, proceed; (*geschehen*) occur; (*Uhr*) be fast; (*wichtiger sein*) take precedence; (*führen*) lead (on). **Vorgehen** *neut* advance; proceedings *pl*.

vorgenannt ['foɪrgənant] *adj* above-mentioned.

Vorgeschichte ['foɪrgəʃɪçtə] *f* previous history; *(Urgeschichte)* prehistory.

Vorgeschmack ['foɪrgəʃmak] *m* foretaste.

Vorgesetzte(r) ['foɪrgəzɛtstə] superior.

vorgestern ['foɪrgɛstərn] *adv* the day before yesterday.

*vorhaben ['foɪrhaɪbən] *v* intend, plan. **haben Sie heute etwas vor?** have you anything arranged for today?

Vorhalle ['foɪrhalə] *f* vestibule, entrance (hall).

vorhanden ['foɪrhandən] *adj* existing, available. **Vorhandensein** *neut* existence, availability.

Vorhang ['foɪrhaŋ] *m* (*pl* **Vorhänge**) curtain.

vorher [foɪr'heɪr] *adv* before(hand), previously. **Vorhersage** *f* prediction. **vorher‖sagen** *v* predict. **–sehen** *v* foresee.

vorherrschend ['foɪrhɛrʃənt] *adj* predominant.

vorhin ['foɪrhin] *adv* a short while ago, just now.

Vorhut ['foɪrhuɪt] *f* (*pl* **-en**) vanguard.

vorig ['foɪriç] *adj* previous.

Vorjahr ['foɪrjaɪr] *neut* last year. **vorjährig** *adj* last year's.

vorjammern ['foɪrjamərn] *v* lament, complain.

Vorkämpfer ['foɪrkɛmpfər] *m* (*pl* **-**) advocate, champion.

Vorkehrung ['foɪrkeɪruŋ] *f* (*pl* **-en**) precaution.

Vorkenntnis ['foɪrkɛntnis] *f* previous knowledge. **Vorkenntnisse** *pl* rudiments, basic knowledge *sing*.

*vorkommen ['foɪrkɔmən] *v* *(geschehen)* happen, take place; *(sich finden)* occur, be found; *(nach vorn kommen)* come forward; *(scheinen)* seem, appear.

*vorladen ['foɪrlaɪdən] *v* summon. **Vorladung** *f* summons.

Vorlage ['foɪrlaɪgə] *f* submission, presentation; *(Muster)* model; *(Gesetz)* bill.

Vorläufer ['fɔɪrlɔyfər] *m* forerunner. **vorläufig** *adv* provisional, temporary.

vorlaut ['foɪrlaut] *adj* forward, nosy.

vorlegen ['foɪrleɪgən] *v* present; *(Essen)* serve.

*vorlesen ['foɪrleɪzən] *v* read out, read aloud. **Vorlesung** *f* (*pl* **-en**) lecture.

vorletzt ['foɪrlɛtst] *adj* last but one, penultimate.

Vorliebe ['foɪrliːbə] *f* preference, liking.

*vorliegen ['foɪrliːgən] *v* be, exist; *(Arbeit)* be in hand. **der vorliegende Fall** the case in point, the case in question.

Vormachtstellung ['foɪrmaxtʃtɛluŋ] *f* hegemony.

vormals ['foɪrmaɪls] *adv* formerly.

Vormittag ['foɪrmitaɪk] *m* morning. **vormittags** *adv* in the morning.

Vormund ['foɪrmunt] *m* guardian.

vorn [fɔrn] *adv* in front, ahead. **nach vorn** forward. **von vorn** from the start.

Vorname ['foɪrnaɪmə] *m* first name, Christian name.

vornehm ['foɪrneɪm] *adj* *(von höherem Stand)* distinguished; *(edel)* noble; elegant, *(umg.)* posh.

vornherein ['fɔrnherain] *adv* **von vornherein** from the start.

Vorort ['foɪrɔrt] *m* outpost.

Vorrang ['foɪrraŋ] *m* precedence, priority.

Vorrat ['foɪrraɪt] *m* supply, stock. **vorrätig** *adj* in stock.

Vorrecht ['foɪrreçt] *neut* privilege.

Vorrede ['foɪrreɪdə] *f* introduction; *(Buch)* preface.

Vorrichtung ['fɔɪrriçtuŋ] *f* (*pl* **-en**) device.

vorrücken ['foɪrrykən] *v* move forward, advance.

Vorsatz ['foɪrzats] *m* intention, purpose. **vorsätzlich** *adj* intentional.

Vorschau ['foɪrʃau] *f* preview; *(Film)* trailer.

*vorschieben ['foɪrʃiːbən] *v* push forward; *(Entschuldigung)* plead (as an excuse).

vorschiessen ['foɪrʃiːsən] *v* advance (money).

Vorschlag ['foɪrʃlaɪk] *m* suggestion, proposal. **vorschlagen** *v* suggest, propose.

Vorschlußrunde ['foɪrʃlusrundə] *f* semifinal.

vorschneiden ['fɔɪrʃnaidən] *v* carve.

vorschreiben ['foɪrʃraibən] *v* prescribe, order.

Vorschrift ['foɪrʃrift] *f* rule, regulation; *(Befehl)* order; *(Med)* prescription. **vorschrifts‖gemäß** *adj*, *adv* in accordance with regulations. **–widrig** *adj*, *adv* contrary to regulations.

Vorschub ['foɪrʃuɪp] *m* assistance, support. **Vorschub leisten** assist, support.

Vorschule ['foɪrʃuɪlə] *f* prep school.

Vorschuß ['foɪrʃus] *m* (cash) advance.

vorschützen ['fɔːrʃytsən] *v* pretend. **Unwissenheit vorschützen** plead ignorance.

vorsehen ['fɔːrzeɪən] *v* assign, earmark. **sich vorsehen** take care, mind. **Vorsehung** *f* providence.

vorsetzen ['fɔːrzɛtsən] *v* put (forward); (*anbieten*) offer, put before.

Vorsicht ['fɔːrziçt] *f* caution, care. *interj* be careful! take care! **vorsichtig** *adj* careful, cautious. **Vorsichtsmaßnahme** *f* precaution.

Vorsitz ['fɔːrzits] *m* chair(manship). **den Vorsitz führen** be in the chair, preside. **Vorsitzende(r)** chairman.

Vorsorge ['fɔːrzɔrgə] *f* (*unz.*) provision, precaution, advance measure. **versorglich** *adj* provident. *adv* as a precaution.

Vorspeise ['fɔːrʃpaizə] *f* hors d'oeuvre, starter.

vorspiegeln ['fɔːrʃpiːgəln] *v* **jemandem etwas vorspiegeln** delude someone with something. **Vorspiegelung** *f* misrepresentation.

Vorspiel ['fɔːrʃpiːl] *neut* prelude.

****vorspringen** ['fɔːrʃpriŋən] *v* leap forward; (*hervorragen*) protrude.

Vorsprung ['fɔːrʃpruŋ] *m* (*Vorteil*) lead, advantage; (*Arch*) projection.

Vorstadt ['fɔːrʃtat] *f* suburb.

Vorstand ['fɔːrʃtant] *m* board of directors, management.

****vorstehen** ['fɔːrʃteːən] *v* protrude; (*leiten*) manage, be head of. **-d** *adj* protruding; (*vorangehend*) preceding. **Vorsteher** *m* chief, superintendant, manager. **-in** *f* manageress.

vorstellbar ['fɔːrʃtɛlbaːr] *adj* imaginable. **vorstellen** *v* put forward; (*Person*) introduce; (*bedeuten*) mean. **sich vorstellen** introduce oneself. **sich etwas vorstellen** imagine something. **Vorstellung** *f* introduction; (*Begriff*) idea; (*Theater*) performance. **-skraft** *f* (power of) imagination.

vorstrecken ['fɔːrʃtrɛkən] *v* stretch out.

Vorstufe ['fɔːrʃtuːfə] *f* first stage.

Vorteil ['fɔrtail] *m* advantage. **vorteilhaft** *adj* advantageous, favourable.

Vortrag ['fɔːrtraːk] *m* (*pl* **Vorträge**) (*Vorlesung*) talk, lecture; (*Komm*) balance carried forward. **vortragen** *v* lecture; (*Gedicht*) recite; (*Meinung*) express;

(*Rede*) deliver. **Vortragssaal** *m* lecture hall.

vortrefflich [fɔːr'trefliç] *adj* excellent.

****vortreten** ['fɔːrtreːtən] *v* step forward; (*hervorragen*) protrude.

Vortritt ['fɔːrtrit] *m* precedence.

vorüber [fo'ryːbər] *adv* past; (*Zeit*) over, past. **-gehen** *v* pass. **-gehend** *adj* passing, temporary.

Vorurteil ['fɔːrurtail] *neut* prejudice. **vorurteilsfrei** *adj* unprejudiced.

Vorverkauf ['fɔːrfɛrkauf] *m* advance sale; (*Theater*) advance booking.

Vorwahl ['fɔːrvail] *f* preliminary election, (*US*) primary. **Vorwahlnummer** *f* (*Telef*) area code.

Vorwand ['fɔːrvant] *f* pretence, pretext, excuse.

vorwärts ['fɔːrvɛrts] *adv* forward(s), onward(s). **-bringen** *v* promote, further. **-gehen** *v* go ahead. **-kommen** *v* make progress.

vorweg [for'vɛk] *adv* in advance. **-nehmen** *v* anticipate, forestall.

****vorwerfen** ['fɔːrvɛrfən] *v* reproach with.

vorwiegend ['fɔːrviːsənd] *adj* preponderant. *adv* chiefly, mostly.

Vorwissen ['fɔːrvisən] *neut* foreknowledge, prescience.

Vorwort ['fɔːrvɔrt] *neut* (*pl* **-e**) preface, foreword.

Vorwurf ['fɔːrvurf] *m* reproach.

Vorzeichen ['fɔːrtsaiçən] *neut* omen; (*Math*) sign.

****vorzeigen** ['fɔːrtsaigən] *v* produce, display.

Vorzeit ['fɔːrtsait] *f* antiquity. **vorzeitig** *adj* premature, too early.

****vorziehen** ['fɔːrtsiːən] *v* (*bevorzugen*) prefer; (*hervorziehen*) pull forward.

Vorzug ['fɔːrtsuːk] *m* preference, (*Vorteil*) advantage; (*Eigenschaft*) merit, good quality. **vorzüglich** *adj* excellent, superb. **Vorzugsrecht** *neut* priority.

vulgär [vul'gɛːr] *adj* vulgar.

Vulkan [vul'kaːn] *m* (*pl* **-e**) volcano. **vulkanisch** *adj* volcanic.

W

Waage ['vaɪgə] *f* (*pl* **-n**) scales *pl*. **waage-recht** *adj* horizontal.

wabbelig ['vabəlɪç] *adj* wobbly, flabby.

Wabe ['vaɪbə] *f* (*pl* **-n**) honeycomb.

wach [vax] *adj* awake. **Wache** *f* (*pl* **-n**) watch, guard; (*Polizei*) station. **wachen** *v* be awake; (*Wache halten*) keep watch. **wachen über** watch over.

Wachs [vaks] *neut* (*pl* **-e**) wax.

wachsam ['vaxzaɪm] *adj* watchful, alert. **Wachsamkeit** *f* watchfulness, vigilance.

*wachsen ['vaksən] *v* grow. **-d** *adj* increasing, growing. **Wachstum** *neut* growth.

Wacht [vaxt] *f* (*pl* **-en**) watch, guard.

Wachtel ['vaxtəl] *f* (*pl* **-n**) quail.

Wächter [veçtər] *m* (*pl* **-**) watchman, guard. **Wacht‖hund** *neut* watchdog. **-meister** *m* sergeant-major; (*Polizist*) constable. **-turm** *m* watchtower.

wackelig ['vakəlɪç] *adj* wobbly, shaky. **wackeln** *v* wobble, shake.

wacker ['vakər] *adj* brave, stout; (*anständig*) worthy.

Wade ['vaɪdə] *f* (*pl* **-n**) (*Anat*) calf.

Waffe ['vafə] *f* (*pl* **-n**) weapon.

Waffel ['vafəl] *f* (*pl* **-n**) waffle; (*Eis*) wafer.

waffenlos ['vafənloɪs] *adj* unarmed. **waffnen** *v* arm. **Waffenstillstand** *m* armistice.

wagehalsig ['vaɪgəhalsɪç] *adj* reckless, daring. **Wagemut** *m* daring. **wagen** *v* dare, risk, venture. **sich wagen** venture.

Wagen ['vaɪgən] *m* (*pl* **-**) (*Mot*) car; (*Kutsche*) coach; (*Karren*) wagon, cart; (*Eisenbahn*) carriage.

*wägen ['vɛɪgən] *v* weigh.

Wagen‖führer *m* driver. **-heber** *m* (*Mot*) jack.

Waggon [va'gɔ] *m* (*pl* **-s**) (railway) wagon.

Wagnis ['vaɪknis] *neut* (*pl* **-se**) (*Mut*) daring; (*Unternehmen*) venture; (*Risiko*) risk.

wahl [vaɪl] *f* (*pl* **-en**) choice; (*Pol*) election. **wahlberechtigt** *adj* enfranchised, entitled to vote. **Wahl‖bezirk** *m* constituency, electoral district. **-bude** *f* polling booth.

wählen ['vɛɪlən] *v* choose; (*Pol*) elect; (*Telef*) dial.

wählerisch ['vɛɪlərɪʃ] *adj* particular, fussy, choosy. **Wählerschaft** *f* electorate, voters *pl*.

Wahl‖feldzug *m* (election) campaign.

-gang *m* ballot. **wahllos** *adj* indiscriminate. **Wahlrecht** *neut* franchise, suffrage.

Wählscheibe ['vɛɪlʃaibə] *f* (telephone) dial.

Wahl‖tag *m* election day. **-zettel** *m* ballot (paper).

Wahn [vaɪn] *m* (*unz*.) delusion; madness. **-sinn** *m* insanity, madness. **wahnsinnig** *adj* insane, mad. **Wahnsinnige(r)** madman, madwoman.

wahr [vaɪr] *adj* true; (*wirklich*) real; (*echt*) genuine.

wahren ['vaɪrən] *v* take care of; (*schützen*) protect; (*erhalten*) maintain.

währen ['vɛɪrən] *v* last.

während ['vɛɪrənt] *prep* during. *conj* while.

wahrhaft ['vaɪrhaft] *adj* true, genuine. *adv* really, truly. **-ig** *adj* sincere, truthful. *adv* really, indeed. **Wahr‖haftigkeit** *f* truthfulness. **-heit** *f* (*pl* **-en**) truth. **wahr‖nehmen** *v* perceive; (*Interessen*) protect; (*Gelegenheit*) seize, take. **-sagen** *v* foretell (the future). **-scheinlich** *adj* likely, probable. **Wahrscheinlichkeit** *f* probability.

Wahrung ['vaɪruŋ] *f* preservation, maintenance.

Währung ['vɛɪruŋ] *f* (*pl* **-en**) currency.

Waise ['vaizə] (*pl* **-n**) orphan. **-nknabe** *m* orphan boy.

Wal [vaɪl] *m* (*pl* **-e**) whale.

Wald [valt] *m* (*pl* **Wälder**) wood, forest. **-beere** *f* cranberry. **-brand** *m* forest fire. **waldig** *adj* wooded. **Wald‖ung** *f* (*pl* **-en**) woodland. **-wirtschaft** *f* forestry.

Walfang ['vaɪlfaŋ] *m* whaling.

Wall [val] *m* (*pl* **Wälle**) earthworks *pl*, embankment.

wallen ['valən] *v* boil.

*wallfahren ['valfaɪrən] *v* go on a pilgrimage. **Wall‖fahrer** *m* pilgrim. **-fahrt** *f* pilgrimage.

Walnuß ['valnus] *f* walnut.

Wal‖öl *neut* whale-oil. **-roß** *neut* walrus.

Walze ['valtsə] *f* (*pl* **-n**) roller. **walzen** *v* roll; (*tanzen*) waltz.

wälzen ['vɛltsən] *v* roll.

Walzer ['valtsər] *m* (*pl* **-**) waltz.

Wand [vant] *f* (*pl* **Wände**) wall.

Wandel ['vandəl] *m* change. **wandelbar** *adj* variable; (*Person*) changeable, fickle. **wandeln** *v* change. **sich wandeln in** change *or* turn into.

Wanderer ['vandərər] *m* (*pl* -) wanderer; (*auf dem Lande*) hiker, rambler. **Wanderlust** *f* wanderlust. **wandern** *v* wander; ramble, hike. **-d** *adj* wandering; (*Volk, Tiere*) migratory. **Wanderung** *f* (*pl* -en) (*zu Fuß*) walking-tour, hike; (*Volk, Tiere*) migration.

Wandgemälde ['vantgəmɛldə] *neut* mural.

Wandlung ['vandluŋ] *f* (*pl* -en) change; (*total*) transformation; (*Rel*) transubstantiation.

Wange ['vaŋə] *f* (*pl* -n) cheek.

Wankelmut ['vaŋkəlmuːt] *m* fickleness, inconstancy. **wankelmütig** *adj* fickle, inconstant.

wanken ['vaŋkən] *v* rock, sway; (*Person*) totter, reel; (*fig*) waver, vacillate. **-d** *adj* wavering.

wann [van] *adv* when.

Wanne ['vanə] *f* (*pl* -n) tub; (*Badewanne*) bath(tub). **-bad** *neut* bath.

Wanze ['vantsə] *f* (*pl* -n) bug.

Wappen ['vapən] *neut* (*pl* -) (coat of) arms. **-kunde** *f* heraldry.

Ware ['vaːrə] *f* (*pl* -n) article, commodity. **Waren** *pl* goods, wares, merchandise *sing*. **Waren∥haus** *neut* department store. **-markt** *m* commodity market.

warm [varm] *adj* warm; (*Getränk, Essen*) hot. **warmer Bruder** (*umg.*) homosexual. **Wärme** ['vɛrmə] *f* warmth; temperature; (*Physik*) heat. **wärmen** *v* warm (up), heat. **Wärmflasche** *f* hot-water bottle.

warnen ['varnən] *v* warn. **Warnung** *f* (*pl* -en) warning.

Warschau ['varʃau] *neut* Warsaw.

warten ['vartən] *v* wait; (*pflegen*) care for; (*Maschine*) service, maintain. **warten auf** wait for.

Wärter ['vɛrtər] *m* (*pl* -), **Wärterin** *f* (*pl* -nen) attendant; (*Kranken*) nurse; (*Gefängnis*) warder.

Warte∥saal *m* waiting room. **-zimmer** *neut* waiting room. **Wartung** *f* maintenance, upkeep.

warum [va'rum] *adv* why.

Warze ['vartsə] *f* (*pl* -n) wart; (*Brust*) nipple.

was [vas] *pron* what; (*umg.*) something. **ach was!** nonsense! **was ist mit ...** how about .... **was für ...** what sort of .. *alles was ich sehe* everything that I see.

Waschbecken ['vaʃbekən] *neut* wash basin.

Wäsche ['vɛʃə] *f* (*pl* -n) washing, laundry.

waschecht [vaʃɛçt] *adj* (*Farbe*) (colour-) fast; (*fig*) thorough, dyed-in-the-wool.

Wäsche∥klammer *f* clothes-peg. (*US*) clothes-pin. **-korb** *m* laundry basket. **-leine** *f* clothes-line.

***waschen** [vaʃən] *v* wash.

Wäscherei ['vɛʃa'rai] *f* (*pl* -en) laundry.

Wasch∥lappen *m* facecloth. **-maschine** *f* washing machine. **-mittel** *neut* detergent, washing powder. **-tag** *m* wash(ing) day.

Wasser ['vasər] *neut* (*pl* -) water. **-abfluß** *m* drain. **-abfuhr** *f* drainage. **-behälter** *m* tank, reservoir. **-dampf** *m* steam, water vapour.

wasser∥dicht *adj* waterproof; (*Gefäß*) watertight. **-fest** *adj* waterproof.

wässerig ['vɛsəriç] *adj* watery.

Wasser∥kraftwerk *neut* hydroelectric plant. **-leitung** *f* water mains *pl*. **-mann** *m* (*Astrol*) Aquarius.

wässern ['vɛsərn] *v* water; (*bewässern*) irrigate; (*Erbsen, usw.*) soak.

Wasser∥pflanze *f* aquatic plant. **-rad** *neut* water wheel. **-stoff** *m* hydrogen. **-tier** *neut* aquatic animal.

Wässerung ['vɛsəruŋ] *f* watering; (*Bewässern*) irrigation.

Wasser∥versorgung *f* water supply. **-weg** *m* waterway. **-werk** *neut* waterworks *pl*.

Watte ['vatə] *f* (*pl* -n) wadding, cotton wool. **-bausch** *m* swab.

weben ['veːbən] *v* weave. **Web∥er** *m* (*pl* -), **Weberin** *f* (*pl* -nen) weaver. **-stoff** *m* textile. **-stuhl** *m* loom.

Wechsel ['vɛksəl] *m* (*pl* -) change; (*Austausch*) exchange; (*Komm*) bill (of exchange). **-folge** *f* alternation. **-geld** *neut* change. **-jahre** *pl* menopause *sing*, change of life *sing*. **wechseln** *v* (ex)change; (*variieren*) vary. **wechselseitig** *adj* alternating; (*gegenseitig*) mutual, reciprocal. **Wechsel∥strom** *m* alternating current. **-zahn** *f* milk tooth.

wecken ['vɛkən] *v* awaken, wake up. **Wecker** *m* (*pl* -) alarm clock.

wedeln ['veːdəln] *v* (*Schwanz*) wag.

weder ['veːdər] *conj* neither. **weder ... noch ...**, neither ... nor ... ,

weg [vɛk] *adv* away, off, gone. *Hände weg!* hands off! *er ist schon weg* he has already left. *meine Uhr ist weg* my watch has gone. **weit weg** far off. **Weg** *m* (*pl* -e) way; (*Straße*) road; (*Pfad*) path.

weg‖bleiben *v* stay away. –blicken *v* look away. –bringen *v* take away, remove.

wegen ['veɪgən] *prep* because of, on account of.

weg‖fahren *v* drive away; (*abfahren*) leave. –fallen *v* fall away; (*aufhören*) stop; (*ausgelassen werden*) be omitted. –führen *v* lead away. –gehen *v* go away. –kommen *v* get away. –lassen *v* omit. –müssen *v* must go, have to leave.

Wegnahme [vɛknaːmə] *f* (*pl* -n) confiscation, seizure. wegnehmen *v* take away; (*beschlagnahmen*) confiscate, seize; (*Zeit, Raum*) occupy.

weg‖räumen *v* clear away. –schaffen *v* get rid of. –schikken *v* send away. –schließen *v* lock away. –treiben *v* drive off.

Wegweiser [veɪkvaizər] *m* (*pl* -) signpost; (*Buch, Mensch*) guide.

weg‖wenden *v* turn aside. –werfen *v* throw away, discard. –werfend *adj* disdainful. –ziehen *v* pull aside; (*Wohnsitz wechseln*) move away.

weh [veɪ] *adj* sore, painful; (*seelisch*) sad. *interj* alas. mein Hals tut mir weh my throat hurts. sich weh tun hurt oneself. jemandem weh tun hurt someone, cause someone pain. Weh *neut* (*pl* -e) pain; sorrow.

Wehe ['veɪə] *f* (*pl* -n) drift (of snow or sand). wehen *v* blow; (*Fahne*) flutter.

Wehr[1] [veɪr] *f* (*pl* -en) (*Waffe*) weapon; (*Schutz*) defence; (*Rüstung*) armament; (*Widerstand*) resistance.

Wehr[2] *neut* (*pl* -e) weir, dam.

Wehrdienst ['veɪrdiːnst] *m* military service. –verweigerer *m* conscientious objector. wehren *v* restrain. sich wehren gegen defend oneself against. wehrlos *adj* (*waffenlos*) unarmed; (*schutzlos*) defenceless. Wehr‖macht *f* armed forces *pl*. –pflicht *f* compulsory military service. –pflichtige(r) person liable for military service.

Weib [vaip] *neut* (*pl* -er) woman; (*Gattin*) wife. –chen *neut* (*Tier*) female. weiblich *adj* female; (*Gramm*) feminine.

weich [vaiç] *adj* soft; (*sanft*) gentle.

Weiche ['vaiçə] *f* (*pl* -n) (*Anat*) side, flank.

weichen[1] ['vaiçən] *v* soften; (*einweichen*) soak.

weichen[2] *v* give way; (*nachgeben*) yield; (*Preise*) fall.

Weichheit ['vaiçhait] *f* softness. weichherzig *adj* tender-hearted, gentle. Weichkäse *m* soft cheese. weichlich *adj* soft, weak, effeminate.

Weide[1] ['vaidə] *f* (*pl* -n) (*Baum*) willow.

Weide[2] *f* (*pl* -n) (*Wiese*) pasture.

*weiden ['vaidən] *v* graze. sich weiden an feast one's eyes on.

weigern ['vaigərn] *v* sich weigern refuse. Weigerung *f* (*pl* -en) refusal.

Weihe ['vaiə] *f* (*pl* -n) consecration; (*Einweihung*) initiation. weihen *v* consecrate.

Weihnachten ['vainaxtən] *neut* (*pl* -) Christmas. Weihnachts‖abend *m* Christmas Eve. –baum *m* Christmas tree. –geschenk *neut* Christmas present. –lied *neut* Christmas carol. –mann *m* Father Christmas, (*US*) Santa Claus.

weil [vail] *conj* because, since.

Weile ['vailə] *f* while, short time.

Wein [vain] *m* (*pl* -e) wine; (*Pflanze*) vine. –berg *m* vineyard. –brand *m* brandy.

weinen ['vainən] *v* cry, weep. Weinen *neut* crying, weeping, tears *pl*.

Wein‖lese *f* (*pl* -n) vintage. –stock *m* vine. –stube *f* wine bar. –traube *f* bunch of grapes.

weise ['vaizə] *adj* wise.

Weise ['vaizə] *f* (*pl* -n) manner, way; (*Melodie*) melody. Art und Weise manner, way. auf diese/jede/kleine Weise in this way/in any case/by no means.

weisen ['vaizən] *v* show; (*Finger, Zeiger*) point. weisen auf point to. weisen nach direct to.

Weisheit ['vaishait] *f* (*pl* -en) wisdom. –szahn *m* wisdom tooth.

weiß [vais] *adj* white. Weißbrot *neut* white bread. Weiße *f* whiteness. Weiße(r) White (man/woman). weiß‖en *v* whitewash. –glühend *adj* white-hot. Weiß‖kohl *m* (white) cabbage. –waren *pl* linens. –wein *m* white wine.

weit [vait] *adj* wide; (*breit*) broad; (*geräumig*) vast, spacious; (*lang*) long; (*entfernt*) far (off). bei weitem by far. von weitem from a distance. weit entfernt (von) far away (from). weit‖ab *adv* far away. –aus *adv* by far. Weite *f* (*pl* -n) width; (*Ausdehnung*) extent; (*Größe*) size. weiten *v* widen; (*vergrößern*) enlarge.

weiter ['vaitər] adj wider; (*Entfernung*) farther; (*zusätlich*) further. adv (*Entfernung*) farther; (*fig*) further; (*sonst*) else; (*weiterhin*) furthermore. **ohne weiteres** directly, immediately. **bis auf weiteres** for the present. **weiter nichts?** nothing else? **und so weiter** and so forth. **es geht weiter** it goes on. **weiter‖bringen** v harp on. **−geben** v pass (to). **−gehen** v move on. **−hin** adv moreover, furthermore. **−kommen** v make progress, get on. **−machen** v carry on.
weit‖gehend adj far-reaching. **−her** adv from afar. **−hergeholt** adj far-fetched. **−herzig** adj broad-minded. **−reichend** adj far-reaching. **−sichtig** adj far-sighted. **−verbreitet** adj widespread.
Weizen ['vaitsən] m wheat. **−brot** neut white bread. **−kleie** f bran.
welch [vɛlç] adj, pron which, what, who. **welche** pl some, any. *welch ein Glück!* what luck! *welches Kind?* which child? *welche schöne Blumen* what beautiful flowers. *möchtest du welche?* would you like some?
welk [vɛlk] adj withered, wilting v wither.
Welle ['vɛlə] f (pl -n) wave; (*Tech*) shaft, axle v wave; (*rollen*) roll. **Wellen‖länge** f wavelength. **−sittich** m budgerigar.
Welt [vɛlt] f (pl -en) world. **−all** neut universe. **−anschauung** f (pl -en) philosophical outlook. **welt‖berühmt** adj world-famous. **−bürgerlich** adj cosmopolitan. **−erschütternd** adj world-shaking. **−lich** adj worldly, mundane. **Welt‖macht** f world power. **−raum** m (outer) space. **−rekord** m world record.
wem [veːm] pron to whom.
wen [veːn] pron whom.
Wende ['vɛndə] f (pl -n) turn; (*Änderung*) change. **−I** f (pl -n) coil, spiral. **wenden** v turn. **Wendepunkt** m turning point. **wendig** adj manoeuvrable; (*Person*) agile. **Wendung** f (pl -en) turn; (*Änderung*) change.
wenig ['veːniç] adj little. adv not much, slightly. **ein wenig** a little. **wenige** pl a few. **−er** adj less, fewer. **wenigst** adj least. **am wenigsten** adv least (of all). **wenigstens** adv at least.
wenn [vɛn] conj (*falls*) if; (*sobald*) when. **auch wenn** even if. **wenn nicht** unless. **wenn nur** if only.

wer [veːr] pron who; (*derjenige, der*) whoever.
Werbe‖büro neut advertising agency. **−feldzug** m advertising campaign.
werben ['vɛrbən] v advertise, publicize; (*Rekruten*) enlist. **Werb‖esendung** f commercial. **−ung** f advertising.
***werden** ['verdən] v become; (*allmählich*) grow; (*Futurum*) will, shall; (*Passiv*) be. *es wird dunkel* it is growing or getting dark. *er wird kommen* he will come. *er will Arzt werden* he wants to be a doctor. *der Baum wurde gefällt* the tree was felled. *würden Sie so freundlich sein?* would you be so kind? **Werden** neut development, growth. **werdend** adj developing, growing; (*Mutter*) expectant.
***werfen** ['vɛrfən] v throw.
Werft [vɛrft] f (pl -en) shipyard, dockyard.
Werk [vɛrk] neut (pl -e) work; (*Fabrik*) factory, works pl; (*Getriebe*) mechanism. **−statt** or **stelle** f workshop. **−tag** m working day. **−zeug** neut tool.
Wermut ['veːrmuːt] m wormwood; (*Wein*) vermouth.
wert [veːrt] adj worth; (*würdig*) worthy; (*lieb*) dear. **für wert halten** consider worthwhile. **nicht der Mühe wert** not worth the bother. **fünf Mark wert** worth five Marks. **Wert** m value, worth. **wert‖en** v value. **−los** adj worthless. **Wert‖sachen** pl valuables. **−ung** f (pl -en) (e)valuation.
Wesen ['veːzən] neut (pl -) being; (*Kern*) essence; (*Natur*) nature; (*Benehmen*) conduct. **−sart** f nature, character. **wesentlich** adj essential.
weshalb [vɛs'halp] adv, conj why.
Wespe ['vɛspə] f (pl -n) wasp.
wessen ['vɛsən] pron (*Person*) whose; (*Sache*) of which.
West [vɛst] m west.
Weste ['vɛstə] f (pl -n) waistcoat.
Westen ['vɛstən] m west. **West‖europa** f western Europe. **−falen** neut Westphalia. **−indien** neut West Indies pl. **westlich** adj western; (*Wind, Richtung*) westerly. **Westmark** f West German mark.
wett [vɛt] adj equal, even.
Wettbewerb ['vɛtbəverp] m competition. **−er** m competitor. **wettbewerbsfähig** adj competitive.
Wette ['vɛtə] f (pl -n) bet. **Wettefer** m

rivalry. **wetteifern mit** vie with, compete with. **wetten** v bet.
Wetter ['vɛtər] neut (pl -) weather. —**bericht** m weather report. —**kunde** f meteorology. —**vorhersage** f weather forecast.
Wett‖kampf m contest, match. —**kämpfer** m contestant. —**lauf** m race. —**streit** m contest.
wichtig ['viçtiç] adj important. **Wichtig‖keit** f importance. —**tuer** m busybody; pompous person.
Widder ['vidər] m (pl -) ram; (Astrol) Aries.
wider ['vi:dər] prep against, contrary to. —**fahren** v happen to, befall.
Wider‖haken m barbed hook. —**hall** m response; (Echo) echo. **widerhallen** v echo.
wider‖legen v refute. —**lich** adj repulsive; (ekelhaft) disgusting. —**natürlich** adj unnatural. —**rechtlich** adj unlawful, illegal.
Widerruf ['vi:dəru:f] m (Befehl) revocation, countermand; (Nachricht) denial. **widerrufen** v revoke, countermand; deny.
widersetzen [vi:dər'zɛtsən] v **sich widersetzen** oppose. **widersetzlich** adj obstructive.
wider‖spenstig adj contrary, difficult, stubborn. —**spiegeln** v reflect. —**sprechen** v contradict. **Widerspruch** m contradiction.
Widerstand ['vi:dərʃtant] m resistance, opposition.
*widerstehen [vi:dər'ʃte:ən] v resist.
Widerstreit ['vi:dərʃtrait] m (Kampf) conflict; (Widersprüche) opposition.
widerwärtig ['vi:dərvɛrtiç] adj disgusting, repulsive.
Widerwille ['vi:dərvilə] m aversion, intense dislike. **widerwillig** adj reluctant, unwilling.
widmen ['vitmən] v devote, dedicate; (Buch) dedicate. **Widmung** f (pl -en) dedication.
widrig ['vi:driç] adj adverse, unfavourable.
wie [vi:] adv how. conj as.
wieder ['vi:dər] adv again; (zurück) back. **immer wieder** again and again.
Wiederaufbau ['vi:dəraufbau] m reconstruction, rebuilding. **wiederaufbauen** v reconstruct, rebuild. **Wiederauf‖erstehung** f resurrection. —**nahme** f resumption. **wiederauf‖nehmen** v resume.

—**tauchen** v come to light again, resurface.
*wieder‖bringen v bring back, return. —erkennen v recognize.
Wiedergabe ['vi:dərgaibə] f reproduction. **wiedergeben** v give back, return; (darbieten) render.
wiedergeboren ['vi:dərgəbɔirən] adj reborn, regenerated. **Wiedergeburt** f rebirth, regeneration.
*wieder‖gewinnen v recover, retrieve. —gutmachen v make up for, compensate for.
wiederholen [vi:dər'ho:lən] v repeat. **wiederholt** adj repeated. **Wiederholung** f (pl -en) repetition.
Wiederhören ['vi:dərhœirən] n **auf Wiederhören!** (Telef) goodbye!
wieder‖kehren v return. —kommen v come back, return.
*wiedersehen ['vi:dərze:ən] v see or meet again. **Wiedersehen** neut reunion. **auf Widersehen!** goodbye!
wiederum ['vi:dərum] adv (nochmals) again, afresh; (andererseits) on the other hand.
wieder‖vereinigen v reunite; (versöhnen) reconcile. —verheiraten v remarry.
Wiege ['vi:gə] f (pl -n) cradle.
wiegen¹ ['vi:gən] v (Gewicht) weigh.
wiegen² v (sanft schaukeln) rock.
Wiegenlied ['vi:gənli:t] neut lullaby.
wiehern ['vi:ərn] v neigh; (Mensch) guffaw.
Wien [vi:n] neut Vienna.
Wiese ['vi:zə] f (pl -n) meadow.
Wiesel ['vi:zəl] neut (pl -) weasel.
wieso [vi'zo:] adv why.
wieviel [vi'fi:l] adj, adv how much. **wieviele** pl how many.
wild [vilt] adj wild; (unzivilisiert, ungestüm) savage. **Wild** neut game. —**dieb** m poacher. —**heit** f wildness; savageness. —**leder** neut deerskin. —**nis** f wilderness.
Wille ['vilə] m (pl -n) or **Willen** m (pl -) will. **um ... willen** for the sake of. **willens‖schwach** adj weak-willed. —**stark** adj strong-willed. **willig** adj willing.
willkommen ['vilkɔmən] adj welcome. **willkommen heißen** v welcome, greet. **Willkommen** neut welcome.
Willkür ['vilky:r] f arbitrariness, whim. **willkürlich** adj arbitrary.
wimmeln ['vimɛln] v **wimmeln von** swarm or teem with.

Wimper ['vimpər] f (pl -n) eyelash. **ohne mit der Wimper zu zucken** without batting an eyelid.

Wind [vint] m (pl -e) wind.

Winde ['vində] f (pl -n) windlass; (Bot) bindweed.

Windel ['vindəl] f (pl -n) nappy, (US) diaper.

***winden** ['vindən] v wind, twist. **sich winden** wind.

Wind||hund m greyhound. **-mühle** f windmill. **-pokken** pl chickenpox sing. **-schutzscheibe** f windscreen, (US) windshield. **-stoß** m gust, blast of wind.

Windung ['vindun] f (pl -en) winding, turn.

Wink [vink] m (pl -e) sign; (Hand) wave; (Kopf) nod; (Augen) wink; (fig) hint.

Winkel ['vinkəl] m (pl -) (Ecke) corner; (Math) angle. **winkelig** adj angular. **winkelrecht** adj rectangular.

Winter ['vintər] m (pl -) winter. **winterlich** adj wintry. **Winter||schlaf** m hibernation. **-sport** m winter sports pl.

winzig ['vintsiç] adj tiny.

Wipfel ['vipfəl] m (pl -) treetop.

Wippe ['vipə] f (pl -n) seesaw, balance.

wir [viːr] pron we.

Wirbel ['virbəl] m (pl -) whirl; (Wasser) whirlpool; (Luft) whirlwind; (Trommeln) roll; (Rücken) vertebra; (Scheitel) crown (of head). **wirbel||los** adj spineless; (Tiere) invertebrate. **-n** v whirl, swirl; (Trommeln) roll. **Wirbel||säule** f spine. **-tier** neut vertebrate. **-wind** m whirlwind.

wirken ['virkən] v work (on), act (on). **-d** adj active; (erfolgreich) effective. **wirklich** adj real, actual; (echt) genuine. **Wirklichkeit** f reality. **wirksam** adj effective. **Wirkung** f (pl -en) effect.

wirr [viːr] adj tangled, disorderly; (Haare) dishevelled. **Wirrwarr** m chaos, jumble, disorder.

Wirt [virt] m (pl -e) innkeeper, landlord; (Gastgeber) host; (Zimmervermieter) landlord. **-in** f (pl -nen) innkeeper, landlady; hostess; landlady. **wirtlich** adj hospitable.

Wirtschaft ['virtʃaft] f (pl -en) economy; (Haushaltung) housekeeping; (Gaststätte) inn, public house. **wirtschaft||en** v manage; (Haushalt) keep house. **-lich** adj economic; (sparsam) economical. **Wirtschafts||krise** f economic crisis. **-politik** f economic policy. **-wunder** neut economic miracle.

Wirtshaus ['virtshaus] neut inn, public house.

wischen ['viʃən] v wipe. **Wischlappen** m cloth, duster.

wispeln ['vispəln] or **wispern** v whisper.

Wißbegier(de) ['visbəgiːr(də)] f intellectual curiosity, thirst for learning. **wißbegierig** adj inquisitive, eager to learn.

***wissen** ['visən] v know. **etwas tun wissen** know how to do something. **Wissen** neut knowledge.

Wissenschaft ['visənʃaft] f (pl -en) science, knowledge. **-ler** m (pl -), **-lerin** f (pl -nen) scientist. **wissenschaftlich** adj scientific.

wissentlich ['visəntliç] adj conscious, deliberate. adv knowingly, wittingly.

Witterung ['vitərun] f (pl -en) weather (conditions).

Witwe ['vitvə] f (pl -n) widow. **Witwer** m (pl -) widower.

Witz [vits] m (pl -e) (Gabe) wit; (Spaß) joke. **-bold** m witty fellow, clown. **-blatt** neut comic (paper). **witzig** adj witty; (spaßhaft) humorous, funny. **witzeln über** v joke about.

wo [voː] adv where. conj when. **ach wo!** what nonsense! **wo||anders** adv elsewhere. **-bei** adv whereby, by which.

Woche ['vɔxə] f (pl -n) week. **Wochen||blatt** neut weekly (paper). **-ende** neut weekend.

wöchentlich ['vœçtliç] adj weekly.

Wodka ['vɔdkə] m (pl -s) vodka.

wo||durch adv whereby, by which; (Frage) how? by what means? **-für** adv for which; (Frage) for what? what ... for? **-gegen** adv against which. conj whereas. **-her** adv from where, whence. **-hin** adv (to) where, whither.

wohl [voːl] adv well; (vermutend) probably, I suppose. **Wohl** neut well-being, welfare.

wohlauf [voːlauf] adv well. interj come on! cheer up!

Wohl||befinden neut well-being, (good) health. **-behagen** neut comfort.

wohl||bekannt adj well-known. **-erzogen** adj well brought up.

Wohlfahrt ['voːlfaːrt] f welfare. **-sstaat** m welfare state.

wohl‖gemeint *adj* well-intentioned. −geraten *adj* well done; (*Kind*) well-behaved.

Wohl‖geruch *m* perfume, fragrance. −geschmack *m* pleasant *or* agreeable taste.

wohlhabend ['voːlhaɪbənt] *adj* well-to-do, well-off.

Wohlklang ['voːlklaŋ] *m* harmony.

Wohlstand ['voːlʃtant] *m* prosperity, affluence. −sgesellschaft *f* affluent society.

Wohl‖tat *f* kindness, kind deed; (*Annehmlichkeit*) boon, benefit. −täter *m* benefactor. −täterin *f* benefactress. wohltätig *adj* charitable. Wohltätigkeit *f* charity. −sverein *m* charitable association.

*wohltun ['voːltuːn] *v* do good.

Wohlwollen ['voːlvɔlən] *neut* good will, benevolence. wohlwollend *adj* benevolent.

wohnen ['voːnən] *v* live, dwell, reside. wohnhaft *adj* resident. Wohn‖ort *m* place of residence. −-Schlafzimmer *neut* bed-sitting room, (*umg.*) bedsit. −ung *f* (*pl* -en) flat, (*US*) apartment. −wagen *m* caravan, (*US*) trailer. −zimmer *neut* living-room, sitting-room.

Wölbung ['vœlbuŋ] *f* (*pl* -en) vault, arch, dome.

Wolf [vɔlf] *m* (*pl* Wölfe) wolf.

Wölfin ['vœlfin] *f* (*pl* -nen) she-wolf.

Wolke ['vɔlkə] *f* (*pl* -n) cloud. −nkratzer *m* skyscraper.

Wolle ['vɔlə] *f* (*pl* -n) wool.

*wollen[1] ['vɔlən] *v* want, wish. *ich will gehen* I want to go, I intend to go. *ich will nicht gehen* I don't want to go, I will not go. *wollen Sie bitte ...* would you please .... *tun Sie, was Sie wollen* do as you please.

wollen[2] *adj* woollen, (*US*) woolen.

wollig ['vɔliç] *adj* woolly.

Wollust ['vɔlust] *f* lust, voluptuousness. wollüstig *adj* lustful, voluptuous, sensual.

wo‖mit *adv* with which; (*Frage*) with what? −nach *adv* after which, whereupon.

Wonne ['vɔnə] *f* (*pl* -n) bliss; (*Freude*) joy; (*Entzücken*) rapture.

woran [voˈran] *adv* on which. woran denkst du? what are you thinking about? woran liegt es, daß ... ? how is it that ... ? wo‖rauf *adv* upon which, whereupon. −raus *adv* from which, whence. −rin *adv* in(to) which.

Wort [vɔrt] 1 *neut* (*pl* Wörter) word. 2 *neut* (*pl* Worte) (spoken) word. Wörterbuch ['vœrtərbux] *neut* dictionary. wörtlich *adj* literal. Wort‖schatz *m* vocabulary. −spiel *neut* pun.

wovon [voˈfɔn] of *or* from which; (*Frage*) from what? *wovon lebt er?* what does he live on? *wovon spricht er?* what is he talking about? wozu *adv* to which; (*warum*) what ... for, why.

Wrack [vrak] *neut* (*pl* -s) wreck.

*wringen ['vriŋən] *v* wring.

Wucher ['vuːxər] *m* profiteering. wuchern *v* profiteer; (*Pflanze*) proliferate, be rampant. Wucherpreis *m* exorbitant price.

Wuchs [*m* (*pl* Wüchse) growth; (*Körperbau*) physique, build.

Wucht [vuxt] *f* (*pl* -en) weight, impetus, force. wuchtig *adj* heavy, weighty.

wülen ['vyːlən] *v* root, dig; (*durchstöbern*) rummage; (*Gefühle*) well up. sich wühlen in burrow into. wühlerisch *adj* subversive.

Wulst [vulst] *m* (*pl* Wülste) swelling, bulge. wulstig *adj* swollen.

wund [vunt] *adj* sore. Wunde *f* (*pl* -n) wound.

Wunder ['vundər] *neut* (*pl* -) miracle, wonder. wunderbar *adj* wonderful, marvellous. Wunder‖kind *neut* child prodigy. −land *neut* fairy-land. wunder‖lich *adj* odd, strange, peculiar. −n *v* surprise, astonish. sich wundern über be astonished by, wonder at. wunderschön *adj* (very) beautiful. Wundertat *f* miracle, miraculous feat.

Wunsch [vunʃ] *m* (*pl* Wünsche) wish, desire.

wünschen ['vynʃən] *v* wish, desire. −swert *adj* desirable.

Würde ['vyrdə] *f* (*pl* -n) dignity; (*Ehre*) honour. würde‖los *adj* undignified. −voll *adj* dignified. würdig *adj* worthy. −en *v* appreciate. Würdigung *f* (*pl* -en) appreciation.

Wurf [vurf] *m* (*pl* Würfe) throw, cast; (*Tiere*) litter, brood.

Würfel ['vyrfəl] *m* (*pl* -) cube; (*Spielstein*) die.

würgen ['vyrgən] *v* choke; (*erwürgen*) strangle, throttle.

Wurm [vurm] *m* (*pl* **Würmer**) worm.
wurmig *adj* worm-eaten.
Wurst [vurst] *f* (*pl* **Würste**) sausage.
Würstchen ['vyrstçən] *neut* (*pl* -) (small) sausage; (*Mensch*) little man, insignificant person.
Würze ['vyrtsə] *f* (*pl* -n) seasoning, spice.
Wurzel ['vyrtsəl] *f* (*pl* -n) root. **wurzeln** *v* take root; (*fig*) be rooted in.
würzen ['vyrtsən] *v* season, spice. **würzig** *adj* seasoned, spiced.
wüst [vyst] *adj* desert, desolate; (*wirr*) disorderly; (*Person*) coarse, vile. **Würste** *f* (*pl* -n) desert, waste.
wut [vuːt] *f* rage, fury.
wüten ['vyːtən] *v* rage, be furious. **-d** *adj* furious.

X

X-Beine ['iksbainə] *pl* knock-knees. **X-beinig** *adj* knock-kneed.
x-mal ['iksmaːl] *adj* (*umg.*) many times, *n* times.
X-Strahlen ['iksʃtraːlən] *pl* x-rays.

Z

Zacke ['tsakə] *f* (*pl* -n) *or* **Zacken** *m* (*pl* -) point, jag; (*Gabel*) prong; (*Kamm*) tooth. **zackig** *adj* pointed, jagged; pronged; toothed.
zaghaft ['tsaːkhaft] *adj* timid.
zäh [tseː] *adj* tough; (*Flüssigkeit*) thick; (*Person*) stubborn.
Zahl [tsaːl] *f* (*pl* -en) number; (*Ziffer*) figure, numeral. **zahlbar** *adj* payable.
zahlen *v* pay.
zählbar ['tseːlbaːr] *adj* countable. **zählen** *v* count; (*Sport*) keep the score. **zählen auf** count *or* rely on.
Zahler ['tsaːlər] *m* (*pl* -) payer.
Zähler ['tseːlər] *m* (*pl* -) counter; (*Bank*) teller; (*Gerät*) meter, recorder.
zahl|||los *adj* countless. **-reich** *adj* numerous. **Zahl|||tag** *m* payday. **-ung** *f* (*pl* -en) payment.
Zählung ['tseːluŋ] *f* (*pl* -en) counting; (*Volkszählung*) census.
zahlungs|||fähig [*adj* (*Komm*) solvent. **-unfähig** *adj* insolvent.

zahm [tsaːm] *adj* tame.
zähmen ['tseːmən] *v* tame.
Zahn [tsaːn] *m* (*pl* **Zähne**) tooth. **-arzt** *m* dentist. **-bürste** *f* toothbrush. **-fleisch** *neut* gum, gums *pl*. **-paste** *f* toothpaste. **-rad** *neut* cogwheel, gearwheel. **-schmerz** *m* toothache.
Zange ['tsaŋə] *f* (*pl* -n) pliers *pl*, tongs *pl*; (*Pinzette*) tweezers *pl*.
Zank [tsaŋk] *m* (*pl* **Zänke**) quarrel. **zanken** *v* scold. **sich zanken** quarrel.
Zapfen ['tsapfən] *m* (*pl* -) plug, bung; (*Bot*) cone.
zappelig ['tsapəliç] *adj* fidgety. **zappeln** *v* fidget.
Zar [tsaːr] *m* (*pl* -en) tsar, czar. **-in** *f* (*pl* -nen) tsarina.
zart [tsaːrt] *adj* (*Fleisch*, *Gemüt*) tender; (*sanft*) gentle, soft; (*zerbrechlich*) delicate. **-heit** *f* tenderness; gentleness.
zärtlich ['tseːrtliç] *adj* tender, loving, affectionate. **Zärtlichkeit** *f* tenderness, affection.
Zauber ['tsaubər] *m* (*pl* -) magic. **-bann** *m* spell, charm. **-ei** *f* magic, sorcery. **-er** *m* (*pl* -) magician, sorcerer. **-erin** *f* (*pl* -nen) magician, sorceress. **zauberhaft** *adj* magical. **Zauber|||kunst** *f* sorcery; (*Sinnestäuschung*) conjuring. **-künstler** *m* conjurer. **-kunststück** *neut* conjuring tricks *pl*. **zaubern** *v* practise magic; (*Zauberkunst*) conjure. **Zauberspruch** *m* magic spell.
zaudern ['tsaudərn] *v* hesitate, waver.
Zaum [tsaum] *m* (*pl* **Zäume**) rein, bridle. **zäumen** ['tsɔymən] *v* (*Pferd*) bridle; (*fig*) curb, restrain.
Zaun [tsaun] *m* (*pl* **Zäune**) fence; (*Hecke*) hedge.
Zebra ['tseːbra] *neut* (*pl* -s) zebra.
Zeche ['tseçə] *f* (*pl* -n) (*Gasthaus*) bill; (*Bergwerk*) mine, pit.
Zehe ['tseːə] *f* (*pl* -n) toe. **-nspitze** *f* tip of the toe.
zehn [tseːn] *pron*, *adj* ten. **zehnte** *adj* tenth. **Zehntel** *neut* tenth (part).
zehren ['tseːrən] *v* **zehren an** (*fig*) gnaw at. **zehren von** live *or* feed on.
Zeichen ['tsaiçən] *neut* (*pl* -) sign; (*Merkmal*) mark; (*Signal*) signal; (*Hinweis*) indication. **-brett** *neut* drawing board. **-(trick)film** *m* animated cartoon. **zeichnen** *v* draw; (*kennzeichnen*) mark; (*unterschreiben*) sign; (*Muster*)

design. **Zeichnung** *f* drawing; marking; (*Muster*) design.

Zeigefinger ['tsaigəfiŋər] *m* forefinger, index finger. **zeigen** *v* point out, show; (*zur Schau stellen*) show, display; (*beweisen*) demonstrate, show. **Zeiger** *m* pointer, indicator; (*Uhr*) hand.

Zeile ['tsailə] *f* (*pl* -n) line.

Zeit [tsait] *f* (*pl* -en) time. **auf Zeit** on credit. **freie Zeit** spare *or* free time. **für alle Zeiten** for all time. **in kurzer Zeit** shortly, soon. **Zeit‖alter** *neut* age, era. —**folge** *f* chronological order. —**geist** *m* spirit of the age.

Zeitgenosse ['tsaitgənəsə] *m* (*pl* -n), **Zeitgenossin** *f* (*pl* -nen) contemporary. **zeitgenössisch** *adj* contemporary.

zeitig ['tsaitiç] *adj* early.

Zeit‖karte *f* season ticket. —**lang** *f* while. **ein Zeitlang** for some time, for a while. **Zeitlauf** *m* course of time.

zeitlich ['tsaitliç] *adj* temporal.

Zeit‖punkt *m* (point in) time, moment. —**raum** *m* period. —**schrift** *f* magazine, periodical.

Zeitung ['tsaituŋ] *f* (*pl* -en) newspaper. **Zeitungs‖anzeigt** *f* newspaper advertisement. —**ausschnitt** *m* press cutting. —**händler** *m* newsagent. —**stand** *m* newsstand, kiosk. —**wesen** *neut* the press, journalism.

Zeit‖verschwendung *f* waste of time. —**vertreib** *m* pastime, diversion. **zeitweilig** *adj* temporary.

Zeitwort ['tsaitvərt] *neut* verb.

Zelle ['tsɛlə] *f* (*pl* -n) cell.

Zelt [tsɛlt] *neut* (*pl* -e) tent. —**decke** *f* awning, canopy. **zelten** *v* camp. **Zeltplatz** *m* camp.

Zement [tse'mɛnt] *m* (*pl* -e) cement.

Zensur [tsɛn'zuːr] *f* (*pl* -en) censorship; (*Schule*) mark.

Zentimeter [tsɛnti'meːtər] *m or neut* centimetre.

Zentner ['tsɛntnər] *m* (*pl* -) hundredweight, 50 kilos.

zentral [tsɛn'traːl] *adj* central. **Zentrale** *f* (*pl* -n) central office; (*Telef*) telephone exchange. **Zentral‖heizung** *f* central heating. —**isierung** *f* centralization. **Zentrum** *neut* (*pl* Zentren) centre.

zerbrechen [tsɛr'brɛçən] *v* break (in pieces), shatter. **zerbrechlich** *adj* fragile, breakable.

zerdrücken [tsɛr'drykən] *v* crush; (*Kleider*) crumple, crease.

Zeremonie [tseremo'niː] *f* (*pl* -n) ceremony. **zeremoniell** *adj* ceremonial.

Zerfall [tsɛr'fal] *m* decay, disintegration; (*Chem*) decomposition. **zerfallen** *v* disintegrate, fall to pieces; (*auflösen*) dissolve. **zer fallen mit** fall out with.

zerfetzen [tsɛr'fɛtsən] *v* shred, tear up.

*****zerfressen** [tsɛr'frɛsən] *v* gnaw; (*Chem*) corrode.

*****zergehen** [tsɛr'geːən] *v* melt.

zergliedern [tsɛr'gliːdərn] *v* dismember; (*fig*) analyse.

zerhacken [tsɛr'hakən] *v* chop up, chop into pieces.

zerkleinern [tsɛr'klainərn] *v* cut up, chop up.

zerlegen [tsɛr'leːgən] *v* take apart, separate; (*Fleisch*) carve; (*fig*) analyse. **Zerlegung** *f* (*pl* -en) taking apart; carving; analysis.

zerlumpt [tsɛr'lumpt] *adj* ragged.

zermahlen [tsɛr'maːlən] *v* grind.

zermürben [tsɛr'myrbən] *v* wear down. **Zermürbung** *f* attrition. —**skrieg** *m* war of attrition.

zerplatzen [tsɛr'platsən] *v* explode, burst.

zerquetschen [tsɛr'kvɛtʃən] *v* squash, crush.

Zerrbild ['tsɛrbilt] *neut* distortion, caricature.

*****zerreißen** [tsɛr'raißən] *v* tear up/to pieces; (*entzweigehen*) rip, tear, break.

zerren ['tsɛrən] *v* tug, pull; (*Med*) strain, pull. **Zerrung** *f* (*pl* -en) (*Med*) strain.

zerschellen [tsɛr'ʃɛlən] *v* be dashed to pieces.

*****zerschlagen** [tsɛr'ʃlaːgən] *v* knock *or* smash to pieces.

zerschlissen [tsɛr'ʃlisən] *adj* tattered, shredded.

*****zerschneiden** [tsɛr'ʃnaidən] *v* cut up.

zersetzen [tsɛr'zɛtsən] *v* disintegrate; (*untergraben*) undermine, demoralize. **sich zersetzen** disintegrate; (*Chem*) decompose. **Zersetzung** *f* disintegration.

zersplittern [tsɛr'ʃplitərn] *v* splinter, shatter; (*fig*) split up. **Zersplitterung** *f* splintering; splitting-up.

zersprengen [tsɛr'ʃprɛŋən] *v* blow up, burst (open).

zerstäuben *v* pulverize; (*Flüssigkeit*) spray, atomize. **Zerstäuber** *m* spray atomizer.

zerstören [tsɛr'ʃtœːrən] *v* destroy. **–d** *adj* destructive. **Zerstör‖er** *m* destroyer. **–ung** *f* destruction.

zerstreuen [tsɛr'ʃtrɔyən] *v* disperse, scatter; (*unterhalten*) amuse, entertain. **zerstreut** *adj* scattered; (*geistig*) distracted, absent-minded. **Zerstreuung** *f* dispersion; distraction; (*Unterhaltung*) amusement.

zerteilen [tsɛr'tailən] *v* divide, separate; (*zerstückeln*) cut up.

*zertreten [tsɛr'treːtən] *v* tread on, trample on.

zertrümmern [tsɛr'trymərn] *v* smash, wreck; (*vernichten*) destroy.

zerzausen [tsɛr'tsauzən] *v* rumple, tousle. **zerzaust** *adj* tousled, dishevelled.

zetern ['tseːtərn] *v* cry out, shout (for help).

Zettel ['tsɛtəl] *m* (*pl* -) slip (of paper); (*Merkzettel*) note; (*Preis*) ticket.

Zeug [tsɔyk] *neut* (*pl* -e) material, stuff; (*Arbeitsgeräte*) tools *pl*; (*allerlei Dinge*) stuff, things *pl*.

Zeuge ['tsɔygə] *m* (*pl* -n) witness.

zeugen[1] ['tsɔygən] *v* testify, give evidence. **von etwas zeugen** be evidence of something.

zeugen[2] *v* (*Kind*) procreate, beget; (*fig*) generate, produce.

Zeugen‖bank *f* witness box. **–beweis** *m* evidence. **Zeugin** (*pl* -nen) *f* (female) witness. **Zeugnis** *neut* evidence, testimony; (*Bescheinigung*) certificate; (*Schule*) report.

Zeugung ['tsɔyguŋ] *f* (*pl* -en) generation, procreation.

Zickzack ['tsiktsak] *m* (*pl* -e) zigzag.

Ziege ['tsiːgə] *f* (*pl* -n) goat.

Ziegel ['tsiːgəl] *m* (*pl* -) (*Backstein*) brick; (*Dachziegel*) (roof-)tile. **–stein** *m* brick.

Ziegen‖bock *m* billy goat. **–leder** *neut* kid (leather), goatskin. **–milch** *f* goat's milk.

*ziehen ['tsiːən] *v* pull, draw; (*Zeichnen*) draw; (*strecken*) stretch; (*wandern*) wander; (*marschieren*) march; (*Tee*) infuse; (*Zigarre*) draw *or* pull (on); (*umziehen*) move. **es zieht** (*Luft*) there is a draught. **sich in die Länge ziehen** drag on.

Ziel [tsiːl] *neut* (*pl* -e) aim, goal; (*Geschoß*) target; (*Wettlauf*) finish. **ziel‖en** *v* aim (at). **–los** *adj* aimless. **Zielscheibe** *f* target.

ziemlich ['tsiːmliç] *adj* considerable. *adv* rather, moderately.

Zier [tsiːr] *f* (*pl* -en) decoration. **zier‖en** *v* decorate. **sich zieren** be affected, behave with affectation. **–lich** *adj* dainty; (*elegant*) elegant.

Ziffer ['tsifər] *f* (*pl* -n) cipher, numeral. **–blatt** *neut* clock-face.

Zigarette [tsiga'rɛtə] *f* (*pl* -n) cigarette. **Zigaretten‖etui** *neut* cigarette case. **–stümmel** *m* cigarette end. **Zigarre** *f* (*pl* -n) cigar.

Zigeuner [tsi'gɔynər] *m* (*pl* -), **Zigeunerin** *f* (*pl* -nen) Gipsy.

Zimmer ['tsimər] *neut* (*pl* -) room. **–arbeit** *f* carpentry. **–mann** *m* carpenter. **–spiel** *neut* (parlour) game.

zimperlich ['tsimpərliç] *adj* prim.

Zimt [tsimt] *m* (*pl* -e) cinnamon.

Zink [tsiŋk] *neut* zinc.

Zinke ['tsiŋkə] *f* (*pl* -n) prong; (*Kamm*) tooth.

Zinn [tsin] *neut* tin. **zinnern** *adj* tin. **Zinnfolie** *f* tinfoil.

Zins [tsins] *m* (*pl* -en) (*Miete*) rent; (*Abgabe*) tax, duty. **Zinsen** *pl* interest. **Zinsfuß** *m* rate of interest.

Zipfel ['tsipfəl] *m* (*pl* -) tip; (*Ecke*) corner.

Zirkel ['tsiːrkəl] *m* (*pl* -) (*Kreis*) circle; (*Gerät*) (pair of) compasses *pl*.

Zirkus ['tsirkus] *m* (*pl* -se) circus.

zirpen ['tsirpən] *v* chirp.

zischen ['tsiʃən] *v* kiss.

Zitat [tsi'taːt] *neut* (*pl* -e) quotation, quote. **zitieren** *v* quote, cite; (*vorladen*) summon.

Zitrone [tsi'troːnə] *f* (*pl* -n) lemon.

zittern ['tsitərn] *v* tremble, shake.

Zitze ['tsitsə] *f* (*pl* -n) nipple, teat.

zivil [tsi'viːl] *adj* civil. **Zivilisation** *f* (*unz.*) civilization. **zivil‖isieren** *v* civilize. **–isiert** *adj* civilized, cultured. **Zivil‖ist** *m* (*pl* -en) civilian. **–kleidung** *f* civilian clothes *pl*.

zögern ['tsœːgərn] *v* hesitate.

Zoll[1] [tsɔl] *m* (*pl* -e) (*Längenmaß*) inch. **Zoll**[2] *m* (*pl* **Zölle**) (customs) duty; (*umg.*: *Zollabfertigungsstelle*) customs *pl*. **Zoll‖abfertigung** *f* customs clearance. **–beamte(r)** *m* customs official.

Zone ['tsoːnə] *f* (*pl* -n) zone.

Zoo [tsoː] *m* (*pl* -s) zoo. **–loge** *m* (*pl* -n) zoologist. **–logie** *f* zoology. **zoologisch** *adj* zoological.

Zopf [tsɔpf] *m* (*pl* **Zöpfe**) plait, pigtail.

Zorn [tsɔrn] *m* anger. **zornig** *adj* angry.

zu [tsuː] *prep* (*Richtung*) to, toward(s); (*Ziet, Ort*) at, in; (*neben*) beside. *adv* too; (*geschlossen*) closed, shut. **zu Hause** at home. **zu verkaufen** for sale. **zu Mittag** at noon. **zu Fuß** on foot. **ab und zu** now and then. **um zu** in order to.

Zubehör ['tsuːbəhœːr] *neut* (*pl* **-e**) fittings *pl*; (*Tech*) accessories *pl*. **-teil** *neut* attachment, accessory.

zubereiten ['tsuːbəraitən] *v* prepare.

*zubringen ['tsuːbriŋən] *v* bring *or* take (to); (*Zeit*) spend.

Zucht [tsuxt] **1** *f* (*unz.*) discipline; (*Pflanzen*) cultivation, breeding; (*Vieh*) rearing, breeding. **2** *f* (*pl* **-en**) breed.

züchten ['tsyçtən] *v* breed. **Züchter** *m* breeder; (*Bienen*) beekeeper; (*Pflanzen*) grower.

züchtigen ['tsyçtigən] *v* punish, discipline. **Züchtigung** *f* (*pl* **-en**) punishment.

zuchtlos ['tsuxtloɪs] *adj* undisciplined.

Zuck [tsuk] *m* (*pl* **-e**) jerk. **zucken** *v* start, jerk.

Zucker ['tsukər] *m* sugar. **zuckerkrank** *adj* diabetic. **Zucker‖kranke(r)** *m* diabetic. **-krankheit** *f* diabetes. **-rohr** *m* sugarcane.

zudecken ['tsuːdɛkən] *v* cover (up).

zudem [tsuˈdeɪm] *adv* moreover, besides.

zudrehen ['tsuːdreɪən] *v* turn off.

zudringlich ['tsuːdriŋliç] *adj* importunate, pushing.

zueinander [tsuainˈandər] *adv* to each other.

zuerst [tsuˈeɪrst] *adv* (at) first.

Zufahrt ['tsuːfaːrt] *f* approach, driving in. **-straße** *f* access road; (*Haus*) driveway.

Zufall ['tsuːfal] *m* chance, accident. **glücklicher Zufall** happy coincidence. **zufällig** *adj* accidental, chance; *adv* by chance, accidentally.

Zuflucht ['tsuːfluxt] *f* refuge, shelter.

Zufluß ['tsuːflus] *m* influx; (*Fluß*) tributary; (*Waren*) supply.

zufolge [tsuˈfɔlgə] *prep* owing to, in consequence of.

zufrieden [tsuˈfriːdən] *adj* contented. **Zufriedenheit** *f* content(ment). **zufriedenstellen** *v* satisfy.

zufügen ['tsuːfyɡən] *v* add (to); (*Böses*) inflict (on).

Zufuhr ['tsuːfuːr] *f* (*pl* **-en**) supply. **zuführen** *v* supply; (*zuleiten*) lead to.

Zug [tsuːk] *m* (*pl* **Züge**) pull; (*Eisenbahn*) train; (*Charakter*) trait; (*Gesicht*) feature; (*Luft*) draught; (*Schub*) thrust; (*Brettspiel*) move; (*Einatmen*) inhalation; (*Rauchen*) puff, pull; (*Festzug*) procession; (*Zeichnen*) stroke, dash; (*Umriß*) outline; (*Vögel*) migration.

Zugabe ['tsuːɡaɪbə] *f* addition; (*Zuschlag*) extra.

Zugang ['tsuːɡaŋ] *m* entry, access; (*Eingang*) entrance; accession. **zugänglich** *adj* accessible; (*Mensch*) approachable.

Zugbrücke ['tsuːɡbrykə] *f* drawbridge.

*zugeben ['tsuːɡeɪbən] *v* add; (*einräumen*) admit; (*gestatten*) permit.

zugegen [tsuˈɡeɪɡən] *adj* present.

*zugehen ['tsuːɡeɪən] *v* close, be closed; (*weitergehen*) go on; (*geschehen*) happen. **zugehören** ['tsuːɡəhœːrən] *v* belong (to).

Zügel ['tsyːɡəl] *m* (*pl* **-**) rein(s); (*fig*) curb. **zügel‖los** *adj* unrestrained, unbridled. **-n** *v* rein; (*beherrschen*) control, curb.

Zugeständnis ['tsuːɡəʃtɛntnis] *neut* concession.

*zugestehen ['tsuːɡəʃteɪən] *v* admit, concede.

Zugführer ['tsuːkfyːrər] *m* (*Eisenbahn*) guard, (*US*) conductor.

*zugießen ['tsuːɡiːsən] *v* pour (in).

zugig ['tsuːɡiç] *adj* draughty.

Zugluft ['tsuːɡluft] *f* draught.

*zugreifen ['tsuːɡraifən] *v* grasp, grab; (*helfen*) lend a hand; (*bei Tisch*) help oneself.

zugrunde [tsuˈɡrundə] *adv* **zugrunde gehen** *v* perish, be ruined.

zugunsten [tsuˈɡunstən] *prep* in favour of.

zugute [tsuˈɡuːtə] *adv* to one's advantage. **zugute halten** *v* take into consideration, allow for.

*zuhalten ['tsuːhaltən] *v* keep shut. **zuhalten auf** head for. **Zuhälter** *m* pimp.

zuhanden [tsuˈhandən] *adj* (ready) at hand, ready.

Zuhause [tsuˈhauzə] *f* (*unz.*) home.

zuhören ['tsuːhœːrən] *v* listen. **Zuhörer** *m* (*pl* **-**), **Zuhörerin** *f* (*pl* **-nen**) listener. **Zuhörer** *pl* audience *sing*; (*Radio*) listeners.

zuklappen ['tsuːklapən] *v* slam, clap shut.

zuknöpfen ['tsuːknœpfən] *v* button up.

*zukommen ['tsuːkɔmən] *v* (*gebühren*) befit. **zukommen lassen** send, supply. **zukommen auf** come up to.

Zukunft ['tsuːkunft] f future. **zukünftig** adj future; adv in (the) future.

Zulage ['tsuːlaːgə] f extra pay, bonus.

zulänglich ['tsuːlɛŋlɪç] adj sufficient.

***zulassen** ['tsuːlasən] v permit, admit; (hereinlassen) let in, admit. **zulässig** adj permissible. **Zulassung** f permission; admission; (Mot) registration. **–sschein** m permit, licence.

zuleiten ['tsuːlaɪtən] v lead to.

zuletzt [tsuˈlɛtst] adv finally, last.

zuliebe [tsuˈliːbə] adv **jemandem zuliebe** to please someone.

Zulieferer ['tsuːliːfərər] m (pl -) subcontractor.

zum [tsum] prep+art **zu dem**.

zumachen ['tsuːmaxən] v shut, close.

zumeist [tsuˈmaɪst] adv mostly.

zumindest [tsuˈmɪndəst] adv at least.

zumute [tsuˈmuːtə] adv **gut/schlecht zumute sein** be in high/low spirits.

zumuten ['tsuːmuːtən] v expect, demand. **Zumutung** f presumption, unreasonable expectation.

zunächst [tsuˈnɛːçst] adv first (of all). prep near, close to.

Zunahme ['tsuːnaːmə] f (pl -n) increase.

Zuname ['tsuːnaːmə] m surname.

zünden ['tsyndən] v catch fire, light; (Mot, Tech) ignite.

Zunder ['tsundər] m (pl -) tinder.

Zünder ['tsyndər] m (pl -) fuse, detonator. **Zünd‖kerze** f sparking plug. **–schlüssel** m ignition key. **–ung** f ignition; (Sprengladung) detonation.

***zunehmen** ['tsuːneːmən] v increase; (wachsen) grow; (dicker werden) put on weight. **–d** adj increasing, accelerating.

zuneigen ['tsuːnaɪgən] v incline, lean; (fig) incline, tend. **Zuneigung** f inclination; (Sympathie) affection.

Zunft [tsunft] f (pl Zünfte) guild.

Zunge ['tsuŋə] f (pl -n) tongue. **zungenfertig** adj glib, fluent.

zunichte [tsuˈnɪçtə] adv **zunichte machen** (Hoffnungen) destroy, shatter; (Pläne) frustrate.

zunicken ['tsuːnɪkən] v nod to.

zunutze [tsuˈnutsə] adv **sich etwas zunutze machen** utilize something, put something to use.

zuoberst [tsuˈoːbərst] adv at the top.

zupfen ['tsupfən] v pluck; (Fasern) pick.

zur [tsuːr] prep+art **zu der**.

zurechnen ['tsuːrɛçnən] v (zuschreiben) ascribe, attribute. **Zurechnung** f attribution.

zurecht [tsuˈrɛçt] adv right, correctly, in order. **sich zurechtfinden** v find one's way. **zurechtkommen** v arrive in time. **zurechtkommen mit** get along with. **zurecht‖machen** v prepare. **–weisen** v reprimand.

zureden ['tsuːreːdən] v urge, coax.

zureichen ['tsuːraɪçən] v (ausreichen) do, be enough; (hinreichen) hand, pass. **–d** adj sufficient.

zurichten ['tsuːrɪçtən] v prepare, get ready; (umg.) mess up, make a mess of.

zürnen ['tsyrnən] v be angry.

zurück [tsuˈryk] adv back(wards); (hinten) behind. **–behalten** v keep back, detain. **–bekommen** v get back, recover. **–bezahlen** v refund, pay back. **–bleiben** v remain behind. **–blicken** v look back. **–bringen** v bring back. **–datieren** v backdate; (stammen aus) date back. **–erstatten** v return, restore; (ausgelegtes Geld) reimburse. **–fahren** v drive back; (vor Schreck) recoil, start.

Zurückgabe [tsuˈrykgaːbə] f restitution, restoration. **zurückgeben** v give back, restore.

zurück‖gehen v go back, return; (nachlassen) decrease, fall off. **zurückgehen auf** originate in, go back to. **–gezogen** adj retiring, withdrawn.

zurückhalten [tsuˈrykhaltən] v (Person) keep, detain; (Sache) retain, withhold. **–d** adj reserved; (vorsichtig) cautious. **Zurückhaltung** f reserve.

zurück‖kehren v return. **–kommen** v come back; (wieder aufgreifen) revert (to). **–legen** v put aside; (Geld) put by. **–melden** v report back.

Zurücknahme [tsuˈryknaːmə] f (pl -n) withdrawal, taking back. **zurücknehmen** v take back; (Worte) withdraw; (Anordnung, Auftrag) cancel.

zurück‖scheuen v shrink back (from), shy (at). **–schicken** v send back. **–setzen** v put or place back; (herabsetzen) reduce; (Person) neglect, slight. **–strahlen** v reflect. **–reten** v step back; (vom Posten) resign, retire. **–weisen** v refuse, reject. **–zahlen** v pay back, repay. **–ziehen** v draw back, withdraw. **sich zurückziehen** withdraw, retire.

Zuruf ['tsuːruːf] *m* shout. **zurufen** *v* shout, call.

Zusage ['tsuːzaɪɡə] *f* promise; (*Bejahung*) assent, consent. **zusagen** *v* (*versprechen*) promise; (*Einladung*) accept, agree to come; (*gefallen*) suit, please.

zusammen [tsuˈzamən] *adv* together; (*insgesamt*) all told, all together.

Zusammenarbeit *f* cooperation. **zusammenarbeiten** *v* cooperate.

zusammenballen *v* roll up; (*Faust*) clench. **sich zusammenballen** gather.

***zusammenbrechen** *v* collapse, break down. **Zusammenbruch** *m* collapse.

zusammendrängen *v* **sich zusammendrängen** crowd together.

***zusammen‖fahren** *v* travel together; (*aufeinanderstoßen*) collide; (*zusammenschrecken*) wince, start. **–fallen** *v* fall down, collapse; coincide.

zusammenfassen *v* summarize. **–d** *adj* comprehensive. **Zusammenfassung** *f* summary.

zusammengesetzt *adj* composed, compounded.

Zusammenhang *m* (*verbindung*) connection; (*Text*) context. **zusammenhängen** *v* (*verbunden sein*) be connected. **–d** *adj* coherent.

zusammenklappen *v* fold up.

Zusammenkunft *f* (*pl* **Zusammenkünfte**) meeting.

zusammen‖legen *v* put together; (*falten*) fold (up); (*vereinigen*) combine; (*Geld*) pool. **–passen** *v* go (well) together, match; (*Menschen*) get on well.

Zusammenprall *m* collision. **zusammenprallen** *v* collide.

***zusammenschließen** *v* join together. **sich zusammenschließen** unite. **Zusammenschluß** *m* union, merger.

zusammensetzen *v* put together, construct. **sich zusammensetzen** sit down with one another; (*bestehen*) consist (of). **Zusammensetz‖spiel** *neut* jigsaw puzzle. **–ung** *f* composition.

zusammenstellen *v* (*vereinigen*) join; (*vergleichen*) compare.

Zusammenstoß *m* collision; (*Streit*) clash, conflict. **zusammenstoßen** *v* collide; clash, conflict.

Zusammentreffen *neut* coincidence; (*Begegnung*) encounter, meeting.

***zusammenziehen** *v* close, draw together; (*verkürzen*) shorten, contract;

(*verbinden*) join together; (*sammeln*) gather. **sich zusammenziehen** (*Stoff*) shrink. **Zusammenziehung** *f* shrinking; contraction.

Zusatz ['tsuːzats] *m* addition; (*Ergänzung*) supplement; (*Anhang*) appendix. **zusätzlich** *adj* additional, extra.

zuschauen ['tsuːʃauən] *v* watch, look on, observe. **Zuschauer** *m* (*pl* -), **Zuschauerin** *f* (*pl* -nen) spectator, onlooker.

Zuschlag ['tsuːʃlaɪk] *m* surcharge, extra charge. **zuschlagen** *v* hit (out); (*Tür*) slam (shut).

***zuschließen** ['tsuːʃliːsən] *v* lock (up).

***zuschneiden** ['tsuːʃnaɪdən] *v* cut out. **Zuschnitt** *m* cut, style.

***zuschreiben** ['tsuːʃraɪbən] *v* attribute, ascribe; (*übertragen*) transfer to. *das hast du dir selbst zuzuschreiben* you have yourself to blame for that.

Zuschuß ['tsuːʃus] *m* subsidy, allowance.

***zusehen** ['tsuːzeːən] *v* look on, watch. **zusehen, daß** see to it that.

***zusenden** ['tsuːzɛndən] *v* send on, forward.

zusetzen ['tsuːzɛtsən] *v* (*hinzufügen*) add; (*verlieren*) lose; (*bedrängen*) press, importune.

Zuspruch ['tsuːʃprux] *m* encouragement, approval.

Zustand ['tsuːʃtant] *m* condition, state.

zustande [tsuˈʃtandə] *adv* **zustande bringen** achieve, bring about. **zustande kommen** come about, materialize.

zuständig ['tsuːʃtɛndiç] *adj* appropriate; competent; responsible.

zustellen ['tsuːʃtɛlən] *v* deliver; (*Klage*) serve on. **Zustellung** *f* (*pl* -en) delivery.

zustimmen ['tsuːʃtimən] *v* consent, agree. **Zustimmung** *f* consent, agreement.

zustopfen ['tsuːʃtɔpfən] *v* plug (up), stop (up); (*flicken*) darn.

***zustoßen** ['tsuːʃtoːsən] *v* (*Tür*) push to; (*geschehen*) happen (to), befall.

zutage [tsuˈtaɪɡə] *adv* **zutage bringen** bring to light.

Zutaten ['tsuːtaːtən] *f pl* ingredients; (*Beiwerk*) trimmings.

zuteilen ['tsuːtaɪlən] *v* assign, allocate, issue. **Zuteilung** *f* allocation.

zutiefst [tsuˈtiːfst] *adv* deeply.

***zutragen** ['tsuːtraɪɡən] *v* carry to. **sich zutragen** happen, take place. **zuträglich** *adj* beneficial.

zutrauen ['tsuːtrauən] v credit (with), believe (of). **Zutrauen** neut confidence, trust, faith.

***zutreffen** ['tsuːtrɛfən] v be right, be or hold true. **–d** adj right, accurate.

Zutritt ['tsuːtrɪt] m access. **Zutritt verboten!** keep out! no admission!

***zutun** ['tsuːtuːn] v (hinzutun) add; (schließen) shut.

zuverlässig ['tsuːfɛrlɛsiç] adj reliable. **Zuverlässigkeit** f reliability.

Zuversicht ['tsuːfɛrzɪçt] f confidence, trust. **zuversichtlich** adj confident.

zuviel [tsuˈfiːl] adv too much.

zuvor [tsuˈfoːr] adv before, previously. **–kommen** v anticipate.

Zuwachs ['tsuːvaks] m growth; (Vermehrung) increase.

zuwege [tsuˈveːgə] adv **zuwege bringen** bring about, cause.

zuweilen [tsuˈvailən] adv sometimes, at times.

***zuweisen** ['tsuːvaizən] v assign, allot.

***zuwenden** ['tsuːvɛndən] v turn (towards); (geben) present, let have. **sich zuwenden** apply oneself (to).

zuwider [tsuˈviːdər] prep (entgegen) contrary to. adj (widerwärtig) repugnant.

zuwinken ['tsuːvɪŋkən] v wave (to).

***zuziehen** ['tsuːtsiːən] v draw together; (Vorhänge) draw; (Wohnung) move in. **sich zuziehen** incur; (Med) contract. catch.

Zwang [tsvaŋ] m (pl Zwänge) compulsion; (Gewalt) force; (Hemmung) restraint.

zwängen ['tsvɛŋən] v force, press.

zwanglos ['tsvaŋloːs] adj unconstrained; (ohne Förmlichkeit) informal. **Zwangs‖arbeit** f hard labour. **–kauf** m compulsory purchase. **zwangsläufig** adj inevitable.

zwanzig ['tsvantsiç] pron, adj twenty. **zwanzigst** adj twentieth.

zwar [tsvaːr] adv indeed, certainly. **und zwar** namely, in fact.

Zweck [tsvɛk] m (pl -e) purpose, object; (Ziel) goal. **es hat keinen Zweck** it's pointless, it is of no use.

Zwecke ['tsvɛkə] m (pl -n) tack; (Reißnagel) drawing pin, (US) thumbtack.

zweck‖los adj pointless. **–mäßig** adj expedient, appropriate. **–s** prep for the purpose of.

zwei [tsvai] pron, adj two. **zwei‖deutig** adj ambiguous. **–erlei** adj of two kinds or sorts.

Zweifel ['tsvaifəl] m (pl -) doubt. **zweifel‖haft** adj doubtful. **–los** adj doubtless. **–n** v doubt.

Zweig [tsvaik] m (pl -e) branch, twig; (fig) branch. **–stelle** f branch (office).

zwei‖jährig adj two-year-old; (Bot) biennial. **–jährlich** adj biennial. **–mal** adv twice. **–seitig** adj two-sided; (fig) bilateral. **–sprachig** adj bilingual.

zweit [tsvait] adj second. **–ens** adv secondly. **–klassig** adj second-rate.

zweiwöchentlich ['tsvaivœçəntliç] adj fortnightly.

Zwerchfell ['tsvɛrçfɛl] neut diaphragm.

Zwerg [tsvɛrk] m (pl -e) dwarf. **zwergenhaft** adj dwarf.

Zwetsche ['tsvɛtʃə] or **Zwetschge** f (pl -n) plum.

Zwick [tsvik] m (pl -e) pinch. **zwicken** v pinch; (Fahrschein) punch, clip.

Zwieback ['tsviːbak] m (pl -e) rusk, biscuit.

Zwiebel ['tsviːbəl] f (pl -n) onion; (Blumen) bulb.

Zwiegespräch ['tsviːgərʃprɛç] neut dialogue.

Zwielicht ['tsviːliçt] neut twilight.

Zwiespalt ['tsviːʃpalt] m (inner) conflict; (Uneinigkeit) dissension, discord.

Zwietracht ['tsviːtraxt] f conflict, dissension.

Zwilling ['tsvilɪŋ] m (pl -e) twin. **Zwillinge** pl (Astrol) Gemini. **Zwillings‖bruder** m twin brother. **–schwester** f twin sister.

Zwinge ['tsviŋə] f (pl -n) vice.

***zwingen** ['tsviŋən] force, compel; (leisten können) manage, cope with.

zwischen ['tsviʃən] prep between; (mitten unter) among. **Zwischen‖bemerkung** f remark, aside. **–händler** m middleman. **–raum** m (intervening) space, interval. **–satz** m insertion. **–stunde** f free period, break, interval. **–zeit** f interim, interval. **in der Zwischenzeit** (in the) meantime.

zwitschern ['tsvitʃərn] v chirp, twitter.

zwo [tsvoː] V zwei.

zwölf [tsvœlf] pron, adj twelve. **zwölft** adj twelfth.

zyklisch ['tsyːkliʃ] adj cyclic.

Zyklone [tsyˈkloːnə] f (pl -n) low-pressure area, depression.

Zyklus ['tsyːklus] *m* (*pl* **Zyklen**) cycle.
Zylinder [tsi'lindər] *m* (*pl* -) cylinder;
(*Hut*) top hat. **-kopf** *m* cylinder head.
Zyniker ['tsyːnikər] *m* (*pl* -) cynic. **zynisch**
adj cynical.
Zypern ['tsyːpərn] *neut* Cyprus. **Zyprer** *m*
(*pl* -), **Zyprerin** *f* (*pl* **-nen**) Cypriot.
zyprisch *adj* Cypriot.